SPIRIT LAKE

BOOKS BY MacKINLAY KANTOR

Fiction

DIVERSEY • EL GOES SOUTH • THE JAYBIRD

LONG REMEMBER • THE VOICE OF BUGLE ANN

AROUSE AND BEWARE • THE ROMANCE OF ROSY RIDGE

THE NOISE OF THEIR WINGS • HERE LIES HOLLY SPRINGS

VALEDICTORY • CUBA LIBRE • GENTLE ANNIE

HAPPY LAND • AUTHOR'S CHOICE • GLORY FOR ME

MIDNIGHT LACE • WICKED WATER • THE GOOD FAMILY

ONE WILD OAT • SIGNAL THIRTY-TWO • DON'T TOUCH ME

WARWHOOP • THE DAUGHTER OF BUGLE ANN

GOD AND MY COUNTRY • ANDERSONVILLE

THE WORK OF ST. FRANCIS

IF THE SOUTH HAD WON THE CIVIL WAR

Juvenile

ANGLEWORMS ON TOAST

LEE AND GRANT AT APPOMATTOX

GETTYSBURG

Personalia

BUT LOOK, THE MORN

LOBO

Verse

TURKEY IN THE STRAW

SPIRIT LAKE

by

MacKINLAY KANTOR

THE WORLD PUBLISHING COMPANY

CLEVELAND AND NEW YORK

Published by The World Publishing Company
2231 West 110th Street, Cleveland 2, Ohio

Published simultaneously in Canada by
Nelson, Foster & Scott Ltd.

Library of Congress Catalog Card Number: 61-8164

FIRST EDITION

WP761

TO DONALD FRIEDE

SPIRIT LAKE

I

Abbie's father called from a distance, urging her to hasten, but the girl kept hovering above the hen and chicks she loved. Her pale lips trembled wordlessly; her frightened eyes were sticky, yet the message of mingled apprehension and reassurance could not be spoken aloud. Stay here, oh hold fast, oh do guard the little ones . . . crooning prevailed within her, sporadic, intense. Her frame and sapling spirit were anguished. Abbie's worry and disordered prayers seemed spraying out to soak the warped poles and dry sod of which this sagging stable was composed. (It was a stable earlier—now only a leftover chicken shack to be abandoned on the prairie behind the Gardner family as they made their way to the Shell Rock River.) Dear baby chickens, please stay well hid. Belovèd mother hen, take them into grass if the Indans come nigh.

All the while she wailed without voice, her hard nimble hands were at their frantic chore, snapping kernels loose from the cob. Abbie Gardner's fear was the natural alarm of an impressionable female faced with danger; but also it had found an illusive mate, and so had procreated with that white thin Terror of Imaginings which flits as constant companion beside every nervous young girl. . . . Their progeny became a litter, a horde—shapeless Frights hid in the roof, among mats of moldy prairie hay. They crawled Abbie's fair flesh beneath her skirts, prickled like ants on her arms, lodged in her hair—horned and blubbering Terrors made up of Indians and spooks and spiders. They spread fairly into the nest with the croaking hen.

Her father roared, Abbie Gardner, you come here!

Dear things, I have no other dear things but you. I have not even a kitten.

She had shelled the last pebbles of corn into the lap of her faded frock as she huddled. The bare cob fell from her hands and (scarcely could she see through thickening tears) she shook her gown frantically over the concave surface of a boulder on which one corner of the crazy stable depended. Many shiny grayish bits went scattering over the earth itself, but more stayed upon the rock; the girl caught up a stone with which to mash them. *Pound, crunch, pound* . . . suddenly Abbie was aware that her father's remote halloos had faded into a more ominous silence. For the first time her mouth could make a sound.

Some dinner for you . . . she tried to comfort the chickens, but in quiver and blindness she made a jam of the words. There sounded only the *r* and *n* sounds, a snarl like a cat's; then Abbie was on her bare feet again.

The tall shape of her father expanded outside the entrance.

What in tunket you a-doing, girl?

Twas her. The chicks. . . .

You get a hustle on! I been yelling my heart out for you. Want the wild men should get you?

Nnno—

Want they should get the whole family of us?

Nnno—

Everybody's in the wagons. Come *along!*

As Rowland Gardner took the girl by the hand and drew her out of the shack, he added, I feel like giving you a lick! Abbie was so deep in distress that the threat went unheard and unevaluated—a hollow threat at best. Seldom had Rowland Gardner slapped one of his children. It was a forbearance not commonly observed by fathers of his class in the year of 1855.

Before they reached the wagon Abbie remembered vividly that a chicken had been the cause of this disaster, so in cruel and appropriate extension of Old Testamental justices the baby chicks must suffer. Her tears came like an explosion. Rowland Gardner thought that she was weeping out of terror (but in fear for her own safety, not for the chicks' and the hen's). His ineffectual misshapen brown hand came against her back and shoulders several times in light pushing blows intended to be a reassurance, a reiteration of the fact: Father's here, you got nothing to fret about, Nobody's going to hurt you, I'll take care of you, Twill be all right. But Abbie squalled so intently that she was not even aware of the comfort offered. Ahead now was the family wagon, she saw it through mist and ginger . . . two wagons, and a third coming up the road, and all those broad cow-faces turning to look at her, and sun hot on her shoulders, sun hot on the grained wooden hub. She put her bare foot lightly on it (take care, Thou Unshod Child, to miss the hotter iron band that binds it!) and ascended with her mother dragging from above, her father pushing from behind, and tears still squirting. . . .

There wandered sometimes through this region a grinning young man, sixteen years old, whose name was My-Soldier. In the same moment when Abbie scrambled aloft into the wagon, the fellow named Mitaakichita, or My-Soldier, was a safe forty-six miles away; he was trying to spear a pike in a lake of Minnesota Territory. But the fancy of several frightened families placed My-Soldier and a thousand outrageous companions in every nearby ambush from which it would be possible for armed enemies to leap yelling. My-Soldier had a well-realized propensity for finding or inventing trouble wherever he moved.

Earlier in this month of June he had come traipsing with a few cronies to a four-year-old cabin near Willow Creek. They'd been there several times, or at least others of their kind had been there; and young Jim Dickirson knew what to do when he saw them coming. Jim went and hid his gun. Doubtless the Indians were aware that he owned a gun—you couldn't live in a new country without guns—but at least if they didn't see the weapon they wouldn't think much about guns; and if they said to Jim Dickirson, You jot jun? he'd just say, No, No, and shake his head; and then probably most of the Indians would laugh, and they would gabble together and say what a tall liar the white man was; then Jim would give them something to eat, and they'd all go away until next time.

When Jim saw them filing solemnly around the slough which drained into Willow Creek, he stopped turning the crank of his grindstone and hurried into the house. His gun was only a musket, and the Indians usually craved rifles most of all; but you could kill turkey or deer with this weapon with equal facility, depending on what you loaded with—if you could stalk close enough to your game, naturally. Jim removed the cap from the tumbler and slid his musket into a disordered bed in the corner. His wife was up, she'd got up to entertain company, and she stood trembling with both hands on the back of the chair Jim had fashioned out of green planks when first they came to the Clear Lake region. The chair was warped completely out of shape, but for a wonder the legs were still solid; Mrs. Dickirson could lean there safely. She'd gowned herself for the company. She stood with bare feet planted on rough puncheons, turning pained hollow eyes on her husband as hastily he tousled bedclothing over the gun.

Oh, Jim. Indans? Again?

Yup.

Wondered why you stopped a-grinding, said Mrs. Luttrell. Reckoned twould take Indans to make you stop!—and actually she laughed.

The rest of the company consisted of Abbie Gardner and her mother Frances.

Abigail, directed the mother in her clipped York State accent, stand close to me.

Jim. Where be they?

Coming south past the slough.

Be there many?

Dickirson stood well within the door, squinting out into the prairie glare, counting. I make it six. No . . . seven. . . .

Husband, I feel so puny like. But— Save some of the sugar, do! Put it in bed—

I can do that, Mrs., cried Abbie suddenly. Her mother threw out a hand to restrain her (the first Indians they'd ever met in Iowa had tried to buy the youngest Gardner daughter because of her yellow hair; and Frances Gardner was terrified accordingly) but Abbie had already flown toward the sugar bucket which was balanced atop the flour barrel. She hoisted the wooden pail, dragged it down, meanwhile pressing the wooden cover tight against the top. Mr. Dickirson had gone trading to the store at Masonic Grove only a week before; the sugar bucket was almost filled. The skinny girl lugged the bucket over to the bed—*Mind: don't dump it on the musket, child!*—and poured out a mound of brown chunks and gravel into a nest between blankets where Mrs. Dickirson had been lying until the others arrived. Hain't a quart left, she vowed, but tis enough for *them.*

Better leave more'n that, called Dickirson without turning from his vigil at the doorway. They get a handful apiece, and maybe they're satisfied. They get too little and then they want other stuff—

Put two-three handfuls back in that bucket! ordered Mrs. Luttrell quickly.

Abbie despised Indians—first, because they were always wanting to buy her, and, second, because sometimes they made bold to put their dirty hands upon her hair. The Indian women were apt to do this especially; often when they came to beg they would fetch along some friend who had never seen a blonde girl before, so more hair rubbing would ensue; and Abbie hated lice more than she hated bedbugs (unfortunately both species figured prominently in her life). She obeyed Mrs. Dickirson's imploring look more than she obeyed Mrs. Luttrell's bidding; resentfully she dug her hands into the sugar and put back several handfuls.

Hain't that enough, Mrs.?

Reckon twill do, sighed Mrs. Dickirson. . . . The two elder women descended on her with outstretched hands. Now, Frances Gardner cried, you get yourself back in bed—

Twill help keep the gun and sugar safer, too, Mrs. Luttrell declared. Indans don't like sick people—womenfolks least of all!

Abbie replaced the bucket on top of the flour barrel. Her mother and Mrs. Luttrell held their arms around the sick woman and their hands beneath her elbows; they walked her the few steps to the bed. Ager's coming back, oh dear—! she gasped, and her teeth were chattering before her friends had drawn the covers over her. This was not the season when ague was most prevalent, but Mrs. Dickirson's shaking and fever knew no season or limit. The Gardners had half a box of Doctor Sappington's pills, and Abbie had volunteered to carry this medicine to the sufferer; but her mother refused to permit her to make the journey alone, so long as rumors of Indians persisted. As for Mrs. Marcus Luttrell, she had fetched a bottle containing a very common remedy: it was rhubarb wine, bottled originally at the East. In a glass of this wine a live crawfish had been placed the night before, and in the morning Mrs. Luttrell poured the wine into a small bottle and hastened with it to the Dickirson house. She was much disappointed on arrival to find that Mrs. Dickirson had breakfasted already.

Sakes a mercy, twon't do no good now! Crawdaddy wine has got to be took on an empty stomach.

Well . . . I am sorry that I et something already . . . but with the ager you got to eat and drink when you can. Even if your teeth are rattling on the cup . . . and mine was! But . . . when you got the fever you don't feel like eating a-tall . . . so . . . like now, you see . . . I got the fever again for awhile, and I feel so drowsy like. . . .

Well, sakes! But you drink this crawdaddy wine tomorrow morning, bright and early, before you've et. Course, I ain't had a touch of shakes since two years agone, and I do firmly believe that it was because I et three hard-boiled eggs on Good Friday last year, and again this year. Course, too– Is your husband a-listening? Ah, no, there he goes with that plaguèd grindstone again. *Well–!*

Even under the harsh keening of the grindstone sound her voice went lower in modesty.

–They do say that if a body can get hold of a pound of beef–raw beef it's got to be, naturally, what ain't cooked or put down in a beef barrel– And I don't know where that could be had now, for nobody's a-butchering in June, and there's precious few cattle to be spared in these parts– Well, if we was to take a pound of that beef, and then you could pee in a pan, and we could save the pee– You'd have to go two-three times, maybe, unless you passed a lot of water all to once– And then, we was to boil that pound of beef in your own pee, and feed it to a black dog, and he was to eat the whole pound up– Well, there ain't any folks around the lake with a black dog, to the best of my notion, but maybe some movers might come through–

While these suggestions for the relief of the patient were being made, and while Mrs. Gardner and her daughter were appearing on the scene to offer their tin box of Doctor Sappington's licorice, myrrh, quinine, and oil of sassafras, the party of Indians headed by My-Soldier stepped steadily across the prairie. They had heard recently that there was a settler at the north end of Clear Lake who owned a barrel of whiskey, so the young men were come begging since they had nothing to offer in trade. They ranged in age from fifteen to twenty-two or thereabouts, though the fifteen-year-old was a man in fact since he had killed two Winnebago. Of these one was a woman, but that made no difference. Mitaakichita led this party, however, since he was the man to first catch upon the rumor about whiskey (actually it was baseless gossip; no one at the lake had any whiskey, except old Mr. Hewitt who used to be a trader, and he had one bottle of whiskey kept as snake-bite remedy, and would not part with an ounce of this unless he saw the fang marks with his own eyes). My-Soldier strode ahead of his friends, rehearsing what he would say to the whites. He was looked upon as a linguist by his companions, since he could speak a number of English words, and had also learned several French words when once he'd gone gathering wild rice on the Upper Mississippi with his grandfather. Ordinarily the Dakota did not approve of speaking any language spoken by whites; and those who actually became proficient in English or in any other white man's tongue stood disapproved; but My-Soldier often adopted the role of a rollicking clown, so his deviations were regarded with tolerance or amusement. You–man–jiv–whiss–kee, he would repeat from time to time. At first the others ignored him, then one or two began to grunt in response each time My-Soldier chanted the words. Soon, as they walked, they were replying in affirmative unison. *Ho! . . . ho!*

You–man–jib–whiss–kee!

Ho! . . . Ho!

You–man–jib–jiv– (He was not sure how to pronounce *give.*)

Ho! . . .

Whiss–kee!

Hokshidanwakpa, or River-Boy (the youth who had killed two Winnebago), started an extension, another version of the *Ho! Ho!* response. He began: *Ho! Ha! He! Che!*–but promptly was hushed up by the others. He had started to sing a war song, and this was by no means a war party. The young men were not equipped or painted for war, had no intention of fighting, did not have anyone to fight against. This was no time to be singing about the Upstanding Rough Straight Penis or anything similar. After that the group plodded in silence until they came in sight of the first cabin at the east of the tiny Clear Lake settlement; this was the home of James Dickirson.

Before the Indians rounded the bend of the nearest slough, Dickirson went out into his yard. Calmly he put his back to the approaching young men and stood for a moment, giving every impression of ease and idleness (his heart was beating at a gallop; it always did in such instances). But he felt like a veteran, he had been here for some four years, he thought that he knew how to handle Indians if anybody did–no matter whether they turned out to be Winnebago, Sauk, Fox, stray Pottawatomi (once a group had trailed that way), or the more dreaded Sioux. The wanderers now approaching were of course the latter–Dakota, as they preferred to call themselves–and he had known that when first he could make out their feathers and braids and general attire. Several wore feathers, several didn't, several had bound braids, several didn't have them; but their stature and the dirty blue blouses of trade calico would have proclaimed them as Dakota to any observant person. Sensibly Jim Dickirson had not mentioned this to the women in the house. The mere thought of Dakota put most women into hysteria. A Winnebago had been murdered by his Western enemies near the lake—was it a year before, or two years?—and unfortunately some of the womenfolks had seen the dead body after it lay swollen.

Jim Dickirson made a face at the recollection. Then, in the most leisurely manner he might contrive, he picked up his axe and turned toward the grindstone. Nearby the little tribe of family chickens pecked and croaked contentedly.

That stone was his link with life back home in Missouri: it had belonged to Jim's father, and before that to a favorite great-uncle. It was an awkward thing to pack along to Iowa, but Dickirson tied it on the back of his wagon just the same. Now he had it braced up beside a niggerhead boulder; and his wife had urged him to make a small charge for sharpening tools there. Jim refused to accept money for such services. It was just that he would let no one else turn this treasured stone. It was an heirloom—practically his only heirloom, except for a brassy turnip watch which wouldn't run—and when he gripped the crank and when he heard the whine of the great solid wheel against a tilted blade, and when he saw sparks come skittering out— Well, he thought he was a boy again, thought he was back home again. Not that he really wanted to be either. . . .

The Indians were close. He could hear not only their muttered conversation, he could hear them brushing through grass which came up tall beside the dooryard. It was time to turn and recognize them, time to forget that the prairie was so broad and the white people so few, and that the bright bluejoint hay of June had belonged to Indians before any other people put down a claim. Jim Dickirson gave two or three turns to the wheel of the stone, a cry went up from his axe blade; then he took the blade away and let the gray solid wheel revolve to its lurching stop. He stood sedately, axe in hand, turning to look at the sweaty brown faces which loomed nearer.

My-Soldier said, Hay—wo.

Dickirson said, *Anpetu-washte.* A hunter had told him that this was *good day* in Dakota, and he had learned the word painstakingly; but no Indian ever seemed to know what he meant.

Hay-wo! cried My-Soldier again. All the Indians stopped.

Hello to you.

They were halted by the indefinite edge of the trampled area which might have been called the cabin's dooryard. They had crossed a dark band of encircling plowed sod, had pressed through nearer weeds, and were grouped at the corner of the garden patch. The young man behind the plump grinning leader was sniffing noisily with wide nostrils. He bent down, still sniffing, he pulled up an onion, smelled at the onion, then threw it far over his head and behind him. There sounded a rumble of laughter from the crowd of them. Dickirson was pleased momentarily to hear them laugh like that.

You—man—jib—whiss—kee! called My-Soldier, and he flattened his hand and waggled the fingers.

Dickirson shook his head. No got whiskey, he told them clearly. He heard a scurry behind him—one of the women must have come to the cabin door and then jumped back—

No—jot—whiss—kee? No—no—no?

No, repeated Jim Dickirson firmly. No got! Whiskey make sick. Whiskey bad!

. . . Well, it wasn't this white man who had the whiskey; maybe it was another one; they'd try farther on. . . . They pressed into a knot and discussed the matter. Jim Dickirson showed sublime indifference to the whole problem of whiskey by lifting his axe to the stone once more. The visitors seemed friendly enough; and Dickirson signaled them to come closer. Five stayed where they were, but My-Soldier and River-Boy walked warily forward, stared at the whirling stone for awhile; then they turned and directed the rest to approach. The Dickirson chickens shrieked and scuttled in all directions. Indians were a close crowd around Dickirson now; he thought he'd choke at the smell of them.

When the edge was turned perfectly, he held up the axe to exhibit the sharpness.

My-Soldier put out a finger.

Take care, Jim warned. Tis razor-sharp—

My-Soldier cut his finger slightly, the blood came. He waved the bloody finger foolishly in front of Dickirson's face while the others gave out their rumble of amusement. My-Soldier whipped forth his knife, and passed the blade back and forth several times close in front of Dickirson's eyes. Jim held steady, did not pull back, knew that he dared not pull back.

My-Soldier lowered his knife—just a regular trade knife, Jim saw promptly, very coarse steel—and taking Dickirson's hand, he clamped the white man's fingers around the hilt.

You—man—

Make sharp?

Ho!

In all Jim sharpened nine knives. Two of these big fellows were carrying two knives apiece, a big knife and a little one—he couldn't imagine why. One of the little knives was a Barlow pocketknife with the blade rusted open, and that took the very finest edge of all because the steel was better tempered to begin with. The Dakota talked together in what seemed to be increasing excitement and interest as the chore progressed. They kept pointing to the stone; perhaps they wanted to trade for it, but that had happened before, and Jim held a ready answer to any such proposition: the stone had to be properly taken care of, had to be oiled and dressed, it took years to learn how, that was the reason no other white man in the region had a grindstone, it would be useless to any new owner . . . furthermore, it was worth at least the price of two horses. Maybe they wouldn't understand his words precisely, but they could receive a communication of the general idea.

His mind ran away into the cabin while he worked; he could picture his wife shaking in bed with that condemned ague. And honestly she was just turning into skin and bone nowadays, and how he prayed that she'd be shut of the ailment!– And the neighbor folks huddled back in shadows, staring out of the open door, and wishing that there were more menfolks about the place, wishing that the Indians would go away–

There, said Jim Dickirson, handing back the last knife. That's the whole caboodle.

My-Soldier made a rather pleading gesture toward the cabin. You–jib–whiss–kee?

No! snapped Dickirson. He was coming rapidly to the end of his sufferance, and he fought to keep his voice down, fought to keep his fist from forming . . . fought for patience . . . he could feel sweat oozing from under his hat. I–ain't–got–no–whiskey! Whiskey–bad!

There was a long silence. Jot shug? inquired some other beggar who hadn't spoken before.

Yes. Got shug. I–go–fetch.

He didn't want any of those women bringing out the sugar bucket, least of all the young girl. She was only eleven or twelve but– He'd heard– Dakota–

I go fetch sugar, he repeated as he turned toward the house. He hadn't stepped onto the split log in front of the door when there was a concerted yell and a tumbled squawking behind him. Dickirson whirled. The Indians were weaving in a quick transport of amusement. My-Soldier had seen the Dickirson rooster, and was plunging about trying to seize the creature. It was an active White Brahma with feathered shanks and a great bluff about it– That cock had even driven a couple of dogs away from the house! But now the rooster was terrified at the menace which sprang its way, and dashed in circles, vivid comb shining. The burly shape of My-Soldier went flashing after it, jerking almost as rapidly as the rooster, changing pace with lightning speed, soiled blue calico streaking out behind, soiled bare brown legs dancing, arm extended for the encounter. The rest of the Dakota clapped and waved, jigging up and down in appreciation of the spectacle. *Ho–ho–ho!* My-Soldier gabbled over and over, *Anpaohotonna chinchadan mawanon kta!,* which would have seemed to Dickirson an absurd way of saying, I will steal the chicken! —even if Dickirson could have understood My-Soldier, which he couldn't. Jim stood momentarily irresolute, though he heard alarmed protestation and queries bursting from the house behind. A cock was not too great a price to pay for the departure of these dangerous visitors; still, it was the only rooster he had; and when might he be able to trade for another, when some mover had a rooster to spare?— He hoped desperately that the fool critter would solve the problem by darting straight out into safety of the grass, and then the fool Dakota would have to give up the chase. But no—there was that blame chicken speeding in ever smaller circles, dodging away from other Indians, whirling back fairly between its pursuer's legs, and— Oh, that did the trick! The big Indian tripped and blundered, staggered out of balance to the left, crashed sprawling across the grindstone. You could hear the snap of the trestle's legs as the thing went to destruction—hear the solid splintering smash of that treasured disk as it dumped its brittle weight upon the wide boulder, and dissolved instantly into pieces— Just pieces, that was all: just chunks of grindstone.

Pink was all Jim Dickirson could see for a moment—just pink, pink, pink—and there was a smell of pepper in his nose. In rosy haze the arising figure of the young Dakota seemed to jerk and jest. Just as if he was a-thumbing his nose and—

—My grindstone. *My grindstone!* Brought it all the way from—

—This heathen Dakota got to chasing my rooster, and he knocked it over, and tis smashed beyond repair—

Somewhere in the pleading world behind him Jim's wife had been helped to the doorway. She was crying: Jim— Oh, don't— You've got the axe. Don't hit him with the axe, Jim! Don't, don't! They'll kill us all—

His own voice spoke out abruptly. He couldn't control it, hadn't thought of the words, wouldn't have used such words in front of womenfolks . . . just as if it were another man's voice. Why, you crazy son of a bitch!—Jim Dickirson exclaimed. His feet swam over the ground, he hauled back his fist and knocked My-Soldier flat.

Silence hardened around them. Only the burnished cock, the lunatic incitement of the whole business, went caroling out into weedy thickets beyond the dooryard; and everyone stood stock still as if they strove to preserve attention in order to hear the diminishing protests of the White Brahma.

So the fall over the grindstone had put this blame Indian on the ground for a first time, and Jim Dickirson's blow had put him there a second time; and now he was on his feet again, with hand gliding to his knife sheath. But the sheath was empty: he'd lost that knife during the hurly-burly, and it lay somewhere around.

(Abbie Gardner, clutched against her mother at the cabin door, would hear Mrs. Dickirson's voice often in nights to come. The woman would recite her doleful litany in a manner to end sleep, not to bring it on. *Jim, put down your axe— Jim, put down—your axe—*)

Why, they stand there like clothed and feathered posts!—was the thought which crawled in the white man's mind. He could not have translated the thought into words, poetic or no; but the notion prevailed . . . just posts, that's all. Pillars of salt, like Lot's wife. Six Lot's wives, never stirring. But male Lot's wives, and not made of salt at all—made of skin and hide and clamshell ornaments and filthy calico—and that one has his rifle gripped in two hands, and he's raising it slightly, and his thumb is sliding back toward the hammer—

Jim addressed him directly. He waved to make the man understand. Don't—cock—gun. I got—gun—too.

Slowly the barrel tilted back toward high sky, and a thankfulness burned in Dickirson's throat: the thankfulness choked him. He belched as he stepped toward the quarrelsome My-Soldier—

Get—out, Jim whispered. All—go. . . . His mind hunted for a word, he thought he'd found it. *Ya,* he said. He dropped his axe and waved toward empty grass from which these interlopers had risen. *Ya!* You—go—

My-Soldier squatted. Jim thought in astonishment that the critter was deliberately getting down on the ground again; and that was peculiar, for Jim Dickirson had a sneaky recollection that no Indian liked to be seen upon the ground (he thought he'd heard that somewhere) because being seen lying upon the ground made the Indian seem childish or undignified. They crawled the ground only in hunting pursuits or in warfare; and this man had been sprawled twice—twas his own clumsiness and deviltry—

My-Soldier squatted quickly, he came up quickly. Jim saw the brownish-reddish-blackish hand coiling around a chunk of grindstone. So that was it, was it? The fellow couldn't find his knife, so now he was going to come hellbent with a piece of rock. And—*my grindstone*— There was another fragment, maybe a larger one, lying beside Jim's foot—the toe of his boot touched it. So he too had dropped and had come up again, and he too held his weapon, and it belonged to him. It was appropriate. Great-uncle Zechariah's stone—

Then they were collided, slammed together, embraced unlovingly. Stench of smoke and grease and sweat (and, God knew: snake oil, beaver musk, skunk tallow?) was in Jim Dickirson's nose. He saw the riven edge of the grindstone relic cleaving toward him; he pushed his head down against My-Soldier's chest and felt the slice creasing across his hair; but the aimed blow did not find him, there was no shock, no blackening. With a growl of relief he butted the Indian away, and struck outward and across as the man reeled. He heard a thud, that was what he wanted to hear. *By God, I heard it pop against his head, and I hope I've killed him, I do, I do!— And I've never hoped to kill a fellow human being before—!*

—But he ain't human.

—Or ain't he?

—Laying all quiet, laying on his side, with fresh chicken droppings squeezed like sorghum from under his cheek, and a wet place in his hair already.

—And— By gum. I feel sorry for him now. I do!

The womenfolks were fussing as if already they felt scalping knives on their heads. Jim stood breathing fast, looking at the six motionless Dakota, six pillars of—

The chunk of grindstone fell from his hand. Without turning his head, he spoke into the hullabaloo at the house door. Mrs. Luttrell, please to fetch my musket. Put a cap on it first. Caps in a box on the high shelf. Y'understand? Y'hear me, Mrs. Luttrell? Please to fetch—

At that moment the willing Mrs. Luttrell was unable to stir. She and Mrs. Gardner were supporting the sick woman who had come reeling out of bed at the first confusion. They were trying to wrap the quivering body in a comforter, trying to hold her upright, trying perhaps to still her frantic babbling; and neither could be spared from this task, or at least thought she could not be spared. . . . There came a light scurry over the path . . . Jim closed his grip on the full-stocked musket. He flashed his glance briefly toward the lock; yes, the cap was in place. Mr. Dickirson, breathed the little Gardner girl beside him, be you going to shoot them? She spoke eagerly, as if applauding such intent. . . . The Indians had not stirred from their position, but a mumble spread among them as the child appeared. *Hinzi* . . . Jim caught the two syllables, and thought that the Dakota referred to the girl's blonde tresses; he was right in this.

(And then, Abbie told her elder sister Eliza and her popeyed little brother Rowly a few hours later— And then, one of tother Indans come over and got down besides the Indan that Mr. Dickirson had hit. First off he looked up and says, Make die! and then Mr. Dickirson says, Huh-uh, no make die! and then the Indan looked down at the hurt Indan again, and he says, *Ho!* No make die! and then the hurt Indan tried to get up, and his hair was all bloody, and then he kind of fell back on the ground, and he twisted clear around and used his hands—like we do when we're playing at being frogs in the grass—and he pushed himself up from the ground, and finally he set up and rubbed his head real slow. And then they all started to jabber, and they kept looking at us. Ma was yelling at me to haste back to the cabin, but I just couldn't move. And Mr. Dickirson stood there with his gun; I guess he didn't Take Aim but he kind of made like he was ready to shoot. Next thing we knew, the hurt Indan was standing up, and he was scowling terrible, and jabbering too—and then he'd look at us and pretend like he was cutting his own throat with his finger.)

Mrs. Dickirson supplicated with her jellied mouth: Jjjjjim. You cccccan't shoot but wuwuwuwuonce. They'll kkkkkill ever'body. Dddddo you cccccome here—

Won't stir a foot, said Dickirson. I'll go down a-fighting.

They'll kkkkkill ever'body—!

Dickirson did not budge. My-Soldier leveled a bloody finger at him as if pointing a pistol. He said thickly: You—man—try—make—die! *Kakish, waun!* Now—you—man—jiv—*horse!*

The other Dakota were arrayed beside him—seven men, four of them very tall—facing the one man and the girl and the three women in the doorway. They had their knives, some had rifles, two had bows—

No—got—horse, Jim told them. Both of his horses had been lent to Joseph Hewitt, and at that moment were hauling a load in timber near the Clear Lake outlet.

You—jot—horse. My-Soldier indicated the sod stable, but Dickirson stood impassive. Two of the Dakota walked over to the stable and peered inside; of these two, one was River-Boy. They came back to rejoin My-Soldier.

River-Boy said, Here is one white man speaks the truth. No horse in his stable. Would you know what This One would do? This One would kill now, in the same manner in which This One kill the two Winnebago.

Yes, said My-Soldier, That One would kill. And how many white men are there in these new villages, and over on the river at the east, in the other new villages? Many men have horses—many. We have no horses, our fathers killed our horses and we all ate them in the winter when we starved; and we have been unable to steal any from the Winnebago, because the Winnebago have fewer and fewer horses, and they are growing poor as we are poor. So we kill now, kill all, take scalps—

Ho! cried River-Boy, bright-eyed and quick-breathing. One of the others spoke in agreement with him; but the rest were listening to My-Soldier. The offense had been committed against him, so they listened.

—And then white men come, many, and follow us very fast because they have horses and we do not have horses. And all of us they kill.

—So I say, he must give me money. Give me many gifts!

Ho, ho, ho, ho! and the eldest even made a gesture of contempt at the annoyed outvoted River-Boy. My-Soldier shook his aching head, turned around, and glowered long at Jim Dickirson in the pathway. The little girl had retreated to the house, but the Indians could see her behind the women, peeping out amid a cluster of faces and gowns and comforter in the doorway. (Ah, said young River-Boy that night. You know what I do, had I money and horses, were I rich? I buy that Yellow Hair—if only she was a little bigger—and I fuck her until she yell for mercy. And I show no mercy.)

You—man—no—jot—horse! You—man—jiv—money. *Money!*

You'll get no money from me! Not whilst I can stand on my feet—

Mrs. Dickirson shrilled, Jim! Give them *anything*— Oh, Heav'nly Father, she sobbed as she fell back into Mrs. Gardner's arms, I can't stand this. Can't *stand* this . . . !

Another Indian, who had not spoken before, said clearly: Jiv, jiv hun-dred doddar.

Dickirson compressed the hysterical laugh which tried to shake loose from his throat. If I had a hundred dollars I'd move to the White House!

Jiv—jib—jiv—mon—money—hun—dred— Jiv hun-dred dodd-ar— Now they were singing it like a song, the pack of them, and prowling toward him at a shuffling pace. The tallest youngest man (River-Boy again; but what could his name matter to Jim Dickirson, then or any other time?) lifted his legs as if he were trying to dance. My-Soldier, with the blackest look of all and with drying blood like paint on his face, was stalking ahead with a hand out, still snapping his fingers back against his palm. Jiv—hun—dred—mon—*ee!*

Mrs. Dickirson sobbed as the two friends sought to guide her back to shelter: No, no! They'll get him—they'll get us all— She screamed at Abbie, though the girl was only a yard away from her: Abbie, child—in the clock—in the Seth Thomas— Right over there'n the shelf! There's five dollars and eighty cents in silver!

. . . It might have been ten minutes later—it seemed ten hours later—when the Indians were all gone. They had taken the five dollars and eighty cents, the quilt from Mrs. Dickirson's shoulders, another quilt and two blankets, the sugar bucket (but they threw this away within half a mile, after they had gobbled up the sugar; so the bucket was recovered promptly but with the lid broken; and the Indians did not find the rest of the sugar in bed). They carried off also a big pewter ladle, several goose-feather pillows, a bullet mold, and a copy of *German Popular Stories* belonging to a child of the Dickirsons. Fortunately the child was spending the day with Captain Joe Hewitt and the team, and could not see this treasured book being borne away across the prairie, the Indians ripping out pages in their excitement at examining the Cruikshank etchings reproduced therein.

. . . Well, neighbors said they wouldn't stand for such banditry, not for one minute; and folks went to Masonic Grove for help, and the next day there were a good twenty-five men riding on an Indian hunt. They caught up with the robbers at Brush Point, about seven miles north on Lime Creek. John Long, who was named as captain of the company, gave the young Indians a lecture which he hoped they wouldn't forget. They got back the money and most of the other stuff, though quilts were dirtied, pillows torn, and the picture book defaced.

But that was just the beginning. All week there bristled new reports of more Indians being seen; and on one occasion the womenfolks were sufficiently alarmed to run out and hide in grass, so that they might not be burned up in their homes. All the women fled to the grass except Mary Luce, Abigail Gardner's big sister, who was married to Harvey Luce and had come along with the Gardners from the East. Mary just sat by the table, calm as you please, with Baby Amanda nursing avidly, and with a tin bowl of johnnycake soaked in milk before her. She kept on eating johnnycake with a spoon while everybody else ran to hide. Mary said: If I'm to be scalped, I'll not be scalped hungry. Baby's getting her dinner, and I reckon I'm going to get mine! Because I *am* hungry. Nursing mothers get that way. I mind when I was a-nursing Bertie, I used to get plain starved in the middle of the night. And when I was *carrying* this baby– Why, I'd make Husband get up out of bed and fetch me bread and 'lasses! . . . But no one remained to hear Mary Luce finish this speech, because the safety of the weeds was beckoning. The womenfolks hid there for all of two hours.

Then, right around three o'clock of the night, there was a banging on their door, and a lot of whispering. Abbie raised up in bed, sleepy and fearful and wondering. She saw her father and brother-in-law shoving the flour barrel against the door after they had fastened the bar. Soon she could hear her father talking to her mother, though he tried to keep his voice low. Looks like the real thing this time, Mrs. We got to pack up and get out of here. Wayland Ashton just come by, and he says it's a fact: there's a tribe of Dakota camped on the prairie over west of the lake. Two men were out hunting for strayed oxen, and they seen the fires. They conclude there's maybe one-two thousand of the enemy. Far too many for us men around here to handle, so we've got to scoot.

Mr. Gardner, where we going to scoot to?

Way Ashton says he's heading for the Shell Rock, and most everybody else will go there. Tis a good road–not too many sloughs, less you get south of Nora Springs. Mrs.–

And his pitying voice went lower until his youngest daughter could barely hear the affliction in his tone.

—Tain't as if we hadn't ever lived on the Shell Rock before. We've been there, we know folks—

Yes! We've been there, and put in an awful winter, just last winter—

But you've *got* to rise! Look over there in the corner— Harvey's already got Mary up. Don't wake the children if you can help it, for awhile. Rowly would just get in the way—

Rowland, came her soft demanding whisper. It was a matter of moment when she addressed him by his Christian name.

Mrs.?

Do you repeat the Lord's Prayer with me. Then I'll have strength—to get up—

I will lift up mine eyes unto the hills, from whence cometh my help, he quoted immediately.

Not that. The Lord's Prayer—

Rowland Gardner pulled off his nightcap, his shaggy black graying hair stood out in all directions. He knelt beside the bed; and Eliza, sleeping next to her mother, never stirred; nor did the five-year-old Rowly; but Abbie was awake and all ears. Again a fruitless speculation provoked her: why did not her mother and father sleep together as other married folks slept, why did Ma and the girls sleep together, why did Pa sleep on a pallet on the floor? . . . She wondered if she were committing a sin in listening to a prayer in which she was not joining. Then—oh, he would, he *would*— Her brother-in-law, Harvey Luce, realized what was going on; and he bustled across the room to kneel beside Rowland Gardner and put his hand on his shoulder. Harvey seemed to think that a prayer was never—well, official—unless he conducted it. His voice rasped out, a queer boyish voice, breaking and apologetic, yet somehow stronger and easier to hear than the older man's; and so Harvey Luce awakened all the children, including Baby Amanda.

. . . On earth, as it is in Heaven. Give us this day our daily bread, and forgive us our trespasses, as we forgive those who. . . . There were nine people in that cabin for trespassers to trespass against. Rowland Gardner, his wife Frances, and their daughters Eliza and Abigail and son Rowland; and their eldest daughter, Mary, with her husband, Harvey Luce, and their two infants, Albert and Amanda.

This was the morning when Abbie pounded the corn kernels for her baby chicks. Late that night their party of fugitives camped in a grove, still west of the Shell Rock River, nearly fifty strong. As always the Gardner wagon was drawn to one side of the encampment —off by itself in the woods, so to speak. This was because Rowland Gardner was happier when he was by himself, away from other people. He was a bony man with grizzled beard and deep-set imploring eyes. Always he was requesting of Providence a hope and a promise, yet seldom was the promise fulfilled. Only the hope might lure him, because he was still young enough and fanciful enough to find perpetual hope in a novelty.

II

Gardner was only forty years old, he was still lusty. Sometimes in the most tired hours of the night a carnal spirit overcame him, carnal flesh turned to iron hot off a forge.

He lay in his mended blanket a little to one side of the fire—not between wagon and fire—so, when wakeful, he could watch the wagon in the low light and see that all was well. He slept with shotgun loaded and capped beside him. He kept the hammer down; he did not have it at cock; someone might be hurt. The unfamiliar and little-used rifle lay on the other side of him.

Once there was a quickening of flesh. He thought of Frances and her femaleness, of the many times he'd known her. He craved to know her again; but there was fear in engaging in such acts close to the children. The children were grown too tall; it wasn't as it was in the nights when Mary slept, blind and silent as a rosy little bat, from dusk till dawn—the nights when Abbie and Rowly were not, when Eliza hibernated in her cradle. It was safe then; you could Do Things whenever you wanted to, or whenever your wife would let you.

Less than a year previously in their westward journeyings, an incident occurred which frightened both parents out of iniquitous desire. It was several days after they crossed the Mississippi at Davenport and headed toward the northwest settlements. Gardner had traded off a box of bolts; he had been trading bolts all the way from the East. He'd sold some more bolts—or rather, traded them—to a mover who was headed for Council Bluffs. That night the family fared on saltpetered beef, stewed beans, saleratus biscuits, even a jar of quince pickles which the mover's wife had thrown in to make the trade.

The Luces, with a faster team, were a full day's journey ahead, so the Gardners encamped alone. The children were sound asleep. It was nigh on to midnight, and then Frances arose. She had to Go Out. She didn't even whisper to him, she just went. Rowland Gardner waited a few minutes, then arose suddenly in the grip of rapacious decision. He followed his wife's trail into the bushes; she was coming back. He put his arms around her; she said her usual

No, no, don't now, Mr. Gardner. Don't. You might put me in the family way, spite of my age.

He kept nuzzling up against her, stroking the nervous body apparent through the stained gown, pressing his hairy face against the mouth usually kept so strictly tense, so thinly disciplined. He worked this seduction with face and mouth and hands. She yielded . . . they went down together in a little glade amid the hazelbrush. . . . They were working hard, gasping (copulating with that kind of shamed concentration displayed only by those to whom the act is a thing to be frowned upon in their belief, and who feel that they must get it over quickly before they are struck dead; so they pour out their violence . . . it comes spurting, forced by the compression of law and custom and religious dictum).

They were so: there was a faint drift of firelight in their direction, a portion of moon showing above, just a faint light, not too much. But, oh, her eyes, close to his own: eyes nearly closed at times, then opening, pushing out with hypnotic purpose, captivating him, swelling at him; her tight wide mouth grown loose, open so slightly . . . her tongue was showing . . . they pumped and struggled; she was gasping, her bare heels strumming. . . .

Then he heard a sound, he lifted his head in fright. He saw his daughter Abbie. She walked steadily toward them in the narrow section of grass which led to the camp site through hazelbrush. Rowland jumped up; but his pants were down around his feet. He could not move: he was hobbled by his trousers—and all in that condition, erect, enraged by the interruption, ready to murder an interloper—

Frances came up off the ground as a bird might have flown, and her skirts were down around her bare feet in a twinkling. He heard her cry with a little choking sound: Abbie, child! But Gardner brayed behind her—embarrassed madness forced the words from his mouth—

Abigail Gardner, you get out of here!

(It was never known whether the girl was walking in her sleep or not. Neither mother nor father dared mutually to discuss the incident again. They kept it from each other, a secret shaved into two pieces and buried deep.)

. . . The mother went toward the girl . . . Frances was crooning now, although just as frightened and filled with guilt as was her husband. But she knew how to cope with the situation. Blind instinct taught her. She murmured: Child, were you scairt? Abbie— Why, you were walking in your sleep, weren't you? Come now, Sissy, tis all right!

By that time the girl blubbered wildly, she was wailing her boohoos. Her infant brother stirred in the wagon, and wondered what was happening, and cried out about it. (He had forgotten, when morning came.) The mother led the child back and put her to bed again in the wagon. Later they spoke of the incident as Abbie's Bad Dream, and Abbie believed that she had one. . . . She mumbled shyly to her mother, once when she suffered fever: I think I had another bad dream. Bout you and Pa. I dreamt you was on the ground, and then he got up and bellered at me.

Hush, hush, don't talk about such things, child! Course twas just a bad dream. Why, your Pa scarce ever bellers at you! Now just forget that dream. Let it go from you.

There must be no repetition of such an experience. Therefore Rowland dared not lie beside his wife now. He might not lie with her again, or even near her (because in lying near her, soon he would be lying with her), until once more a situation prevailed wherein the children were housed away, snug and safe; but still separated by the distinct boundary which lies between children and adults, the immature and the mature: the barricade of their own virginity. Like traditional fathers of all times and climes, Gardner had normal apprehension concerning his children. He was too honest to believe or even pretend that he had been a hand-servant of creation, deeded spiritually to the task. In selfish exemplification of his masculinity he had sought a female, had found her, had cohabited with her on many occasions. And their four children (and the two other younguns dead back East) were conceived in the rich dripping sin described so glowingly by Doctor Jonathan Edwards and others!

But they were Rowland's flesh and his responsibility. They had not asked to breathe in the first place, and certainly were not now asking to starve or to be butchered by savages. Gardner had done the best he could for them; but his best, at least until this time, was not good enough. According to his own father's testimony, he had been a failure at work in a store which had been conducted by Gardners into the third generation. In a New Haven comb factory he had seen others—people come fresher than he to the job—rewarded and promoted, while he toiled meagerly and under disapproving regard of his superiors. As a book salesman he had not been able to secure enough orders to keep the bodies and souls of his infants together. (He was tormented by the idea that the two dead babies had actually starved to death, that they would not have succumbed had the larder been better stocked. This was not true; but sometimes Rowland Gardner almost enjoyed torturing himself with the notion.)

He guessed that he had been more able as a sawyer than at any other pursuit he'd attempted. Store boy, combmaker, book salesman, sawmill hand, sawmill owner, boardinghouse keeper, railroad-grader . . . Connecticut village; Connecticut city; Twin Lakes, New York; Steuben County, New York; Ohio; Indiana; Shell Rock, Iowa; now Clear Lake, Iowa; now fleeing from Clear Lake, Iowa; and would the wild men get them, here in a streamside grove or on the open prairie?– Would the wild men burn their place at Clear Lake, or would they never appear (so often rumors sped aggressively, and yet Indians had never whooped in their hearing) and thus let Gardners and Hewitts and Luces and Dickirsons and all the rest of the folks return safely to their farms?

And what if he couldn't get ahead on the Clear Lake farm? What other farm was waiting for him? Where? Out yonder?

Another sawmill, one of these days? Oh, he'd been popular with his customers; and he liked the sound of the saw, liked the moist mealy heaps of sawdust, the planks stacked for drying. But creditors walked off with the mill at Greenwood and creditors seized the mill at Rexville . . . twasn't his fault that a new blade snapped on the second using, twasn't his fault that he had a bad fire, twasn't his fault that unprecedented ice packs took out the dam; no, twas just hard luck.

. . . That railroad-grading job in northwest Ohio. He'd signed the contract in good faith, was doing fairly well until the gang crossed the line into Indiana. But Gardner guessed that he wasn't much of an executive, maybe not even a very good foreman. Those drunken Irish always caroused and got into fights on Saturday nights, and half of them wouldn't show up for work Monday morning. There was that wet spell: the Indiana countryside turned into a mire, teams lost their footing, scrapers bogged down. Then a rival outfit hired some of his best men away from him, by offering wages which Gardner couldn't afford to match (not by the terms of that danged contract, he couldn't! –and he'd thought he had it all ciphered out neatly, with even what they called a Cushion for Exigencies). . . . And so there were those eight free niggers who came along and applied for work. Rowland Gardner engaged them thankfully. But the rest of the white men said they wouldn't work alongside niggers, nor sleep nor mess with them; and Rowland had all sorts of ideas on that very subject– He wasn't any ranting Abolitionist; really he despised extremists of all sorts, and especially folks who went around advocating violence and slave rebellions– But he saw the principle of the thing; saw it clearly. He made a speech to his gang. He said that in the eyes of this great Nation, and by interpretation of the Constitution and the Declaration of Independence, those free niggers were just as free as any white men, and just as good citizens– Good land, how dared the Irish to disagree with him on this! They didn't scarcely know about the Declaration, and some of them were only ten months away from places like Cork and Antrim and–and– And what they called the Old Sod. Gardner felt it was his bounden duty to put them right on this problem, so indeed they could go on and become good Americans in their own good time, when they'd forgotten some of their heathenish and sinful drunken Irish ways. . . . So that one big fellow with orange-colored stubble on his face (some of the gang called him Ginger and some of them called him Paddy Whack or something like that)—well, he hollered out in interruption, and said that the high-sounding words of the boss were far and away over his head; but all he knew was that he would nayther sleep nor eat nor scrape nor shovel alongside those wooly-haired Naygers! And he was cheered for this. Gardner told him curtly to get down off that wagon—that *he* was the employer and the wage payer, if they *were* the wage earners, and he'd do all the speechmaking that was to be done around there. About that time somebody struck him on the ear, and he turned around and saw a lot of fists flying, and he thought that he knocked one man down (or maybe two; he told his wife that he had managed to dispose of two or three before he was overwhelmed), and then he saw the handle of a pick whizzing down. That was the last he remembered until he came to, along toward evening . . . he felt the split and pressure of his throbbing head, and found the eldest Negro bathing him with wet rags and trying to pour gin into his mouth. The Irish were gone, all gone. They had taken a lot of shovels and picks and other tools with them when they decamped. . . .

There was said to be a fine railroad-grading opportunity awaiting him out in the Iowa country. But when he got to Davenport he couldn't find a trace of that Mr. Cecil Barkes Pomeroy with whom he'd exchanged some letters; and it seemed that no one had ever heard of the Davenport, Cedar Valley & Northern Railroad. All the way up to Shell Rock, twas about the same story: yes, some folks had heard of that railway company (two irate individuals had even bought some of the subscription stock, paying thirty per cent cash down; thus they looked with intense suspicion on Gardner when he mentioned the D.C.V. & N.). But now there seemed to be no office, no headquarters, no officers, no managers, no railroad, no job. Gardners and Luces made a straitened winter of it in Shell Rock; but Clear Lake had sounded better. So—

Heavy as so many parcels of pig iron or not, those boxes of bolts saved the day. They were a small if solid treasure rescued from the sawmill disaster. Gardner had bought an extra-fine saw, but it wasn't yet installed at the mill when the mortgage-holder swooped upon him, so it couldn't be claimed along with the rest of the property . . . he guessed that there must be a suit pending about this, back in York State. But a man offered to trade him a stock of bolts for the saw. Gardner couldn't take the new saw west to Ohio with him, because he swore he'd never engage in a sawmill again; but beautiful hand-reamed bolts and nuts could be peddled along the way—people needed things like that, away out in the country far from machine shops, when wagon tongues or wheels or yokes or furniture came apart . . . bolts could be peddled, Rowland Gardner peddled them.

Ah, was his touch the touch of disaster to any enterprise? It must not be longer, here in Iowa. If only the Indians faded back into those smoky distances from which always they seemed threatening— If only the family could return to the Clear Lake farm— And little Abbie return to her hen and the chicks—

In his gloom, Rowland smiled tenderly at thought of his sleeping children and grandchildren. Mary, camped over at the other side of this grove next to the Hewitts— Mary, with her quite-too-pious husband (but Harvey was a steady man; willing to work hard; never had a smoke or a chew or a drink in all his young life; mustn't forget that, even if he did pray out loud a mite too frequently)— And the grinning grandson Bertie, and the tiny new granddaughter Amanda—

Adversity . . . starvation? Never again, never! It must not be. Regardless of everyone else, he, Rowland Gardner, must chop, plow, dig, cut, grab, save, retain. He should slave through every waking moment and set great tasks for himself while asleep. His very dreams must be a task worthy of accomplishment, his dreams must not become repeated misadventures.

The fire was down. He got up to pile on a chunk of stump which he had lugged earlier, and on which Mrs. Gardner had sat for a time. He looked at the stump stewing on the coals, small flames beginning to dress it. He thought of Frances pressing her body upon it, thought of her body, and then made himself forget her body and look only at the flames, and note how soon they would consume this fresh trophy just as eventually he and his family would be consumed by ravages of time or disease or accident or attack.

. . . My dear ones . . . oh, my dear ones!

. . . And who am I to stand mooning and unmanly, crooning to myself about my dear ones, when I brought them to this pretty pass?

But it was senseless and unprofitable to upbraid his own spirit by derision. He must think instead of individuals like Doc Horsham, in his native Connecticut. Rowland Gardner was designated as middle-aged, but still he was a biological generation younger than Doc Horsham had been when Horsham achieved success. The old fellow had tried to make a living at painting miniatures, running a cider mill, teaching school, serving as a policeman, water witching, stuffing pigeons and woodpeckers and squirrels, peddling broadcloth among shopkeepers . . . he had tried so many things. And then at fifty-eight or thereabouts he had come up with a series of squat brown bottles with labels on them. The labels said: *Dr. Horsham's Nerve Tincture,* and bore the likeness of a bearded Kris Kringle who looked nothing at all like Doc Horsham (who was doctor only by self-applied courtesy). But actually the tincture was of value: it soothed you when you were lame and sore. Rowland Gardner's father swore by the stuff, and so—soon—did thousands of other people. . . .

Doc Horsham was rich; he grew progressively richer; he rode in a green paneled coach with yellow wheels—his pale puffy eyes bulging quizzically behind the half-moons of his spectacles, his powdered face growing more tumid year by year, the lines draping thicker around the pursy mouth . . . that mouth which bore always a slight smile, as if Doc Horsham recognized himself as a fraud.

And yet he was not a fraud! He had become a success; clergymen and bankers went out of their way to greet him in public.

Might not something like this befall Rowland Gardner?

Perhaps . . . who knew?

Certainly he could not make a nerve tincture. He would not know where to begin, or what to mix. And there were so few people to sell medicine to, in this reedy wilderness.

Perhaps something else would happen. He might find gold or diamonds in the very soil he turned up, on the shores of Clear Lake. If only the Indians didn't burn the house down, if only this panic was another false alarm, if only he could take his family back home.

(In Gardner's brain lurked the suspicion which he had feared to voice to Clear Lake neighbors, because men resent being robbed of their most dire beliefs: that this mass consternation was unfounded and idiotic—that Wayland Ashton's friends had seen nothing except an out-of-season prairie fire crawling in pieces on higher ground between the sloughs—that tipis and poised armed warriors were all a myth. He would not know how right he was, not until three weeks had been passed at a silly uncomfortable camp near Nora Springs, and they were all back in their cabins, with not so much as a teacup stolen or a roof broken in . . . the mother hen would be missing—maybe a hawk took her—but Abbie's chicks would be grown and gangling, housing themselves still in the sod stable . . . and he would not dare speak a word about the notion he'd held all along, and which he hadn't been bold enough to utter to family or friends.)

This night he guessed wearily that his fault was not in idleness, he had never been an idle man. He had dreamed, dreamed long filmy thoughts; yet it seemed that he worked as hard when he was dreaming as when he was bending his back or using his fingers. At school, Master Willard used to say, That lad dreams too much!—and point at him with his ferule, and sometimes give him a stroke across the knuckles with that same ferule in order to snap him into energy. Rowland was never able, as a boy, to split as many kindlings as his brother Rollo; nor were the kindlings as straight and true, as much of a size as Rollo's. It seemed that he spent longer at the woodpile than Rollo, too; it took him longer to fill the box beside the stove. Rollo was never cautioned and criticized and blamed, as was Rowland, for standing like a graven image with hatchet in hand, seeming to regard the chopping block with loathing when actually his thoughts were a thousand miles away.

He had dreamed too consistently for the good of his family; but it was difficult to tell where dreams ended and studies began. For Gardner had studied hard (with that exalted addiction peculiar to men who might have been scholarly in pursuit but were denied the opportunity afforded by universities or even by an academy). He read almanacs, bound copies of old English magazines, capsulized nature lore and geographical works, verse; he read philosophers whom he could not understand—it gave him an excitement to see unfamiliar words spread before him on the page—yet he was not enough of the exploring scientist to ferret out their meanings. He did not polish his own speech with the good oil gained from books; but continued to dwell persistently in a colloquial world. He talked the talk of mill hands and carters and haymakers.

An individual with less humility might have blamed the world at large for his failure to prosper in it; but Gardner felt that the fault was mainly in himself. Still he could not identify it nor prescribe for it.

Was Clear Lake the limit of his tether—or Nora Springs, over here on the Shell Rock River? Or, weathers and bodies and wagons and marshes and fires and Indians willing, should he convey his family in another season to another place? The diamonds, the bursting granaries, the Doc-Horsham-kind-of-fortunes, might be waiting ahead . . . not far . . . just another few dippings of the sun, another few star flashes ahead, another few bird songs. The country was crawling with movers, and he talked with almost every mover who came along; it took him away from the plow, of course; but he liked to stand with one foot hoisted up on a wheel, liked to hear talk about the Fort Dodge country, the upper Des Moines country, the Okoboji country. And one of those places might be better for the Gardners than Clear Lake was proving to be; so again they might become movers themselves (well, now, to be sure: at one time he had accumulated some little money from his combmaking trade, but successive ventures had done away with that. Still, if he and Harvey sold their Clear Lake claims to some newcomers, why then they'd be free to travel further west!).

If Indians were hereabouts, and ready to fall on them, surely they would have fallen ere now. . . .

He touched the two guns in turn for reassurance. Though he was only a middling shot, the weapons themselves were comforting in their walnut and metal. He watched the crinkling flames, took satisfaction in the presence of neighbors' fires sprinkled through the grove, heard a neighbor's baby asking for the breast and falling greedily silent when it was given him. He heard straying birds who acted only in blackness, heard owls go hunting; and he was certain that, mourning on remote ridges beyond the woodland and the wagons of all these fleeing people, wolves howled.

He slept at last, he dreamed of villainies which the unexplored months and years ahead might offer. Diphtheria: he saw it, smelt it, heard the harsh gargling, the choke and throat grabbing, saw fever in the face.

(And that fire is nigh down to a bed of coals! Yet, so tired, so much pushing and lifting and loading and driving . . . ah, let me lie motionless, give me the fortune of lassitude . . . make me fetch . . . no . . . more . . . wood . . . oh, wolves . . .)

Summer complaint: it was there, waiting in swamp holes, in new-dug wells. And all the ague: Frances and the young girls and the babies might fall prey to it and feel their spleens turn hard as flint, and then go to shaking with remittent chills as that poor Dickirson woman must lie shaking in her wagon now.

And—how did it say, in that old fairy tale he used to read as a child?— *Nothing to bite or break.* Starvation clawed in a winter to come, and Frances Gardner looked at the shelves, and there was nothing on them, nothing. She lifted up the meal sack, and it was a loose thing, with powder in it, not enough powder to bake a single pone. Rowland went out to hunt, he expended ammunition, he shot nothing, the ammunition was all gone. The children screamed at first, and then their cries grew weaker, and finally there was barely a whimper from any of them; then the pervading silence. . . . He went far from home to seek food, he waded in drifts, fell through the ice, was drowned; the family did not know where he had gone! They died again (left sole alone, with not even this incompetent to provide for them)!

He heard prayers holding out a suggestion of life and of resurrection; but those priestly voices faded.

It was night again, Indians were coming. They were dressed not as local Indians; Rowland Gardner imagined them dressed as the Indians he had seen in old prints and woodcuts, when he was younger: hair shaved off except for a single lock, their faces patterned in bright paint. Not a man of them was under eight feet tall; and of course they were wide in proportion, brawnier than any blacksmith or lumberman.

Gardner cowered with his family in a frail cabin which he had erected; but it was not well built, it was weak and tottery, a kind of lattice. With each clawing of Indian fingers outside, the whole meshed structure shook, and the children—all very small, even Mary—screamed afresh.

Get out, he tried to cry. Go way! Be off with ye!

They laughed as maniacs laugh, and every now and again a wide grinning crimson-and-chalk-smeared face came up to the window (for there was a window somehow) and the creature looked in, grimaced, withdrew, and then was supplanted by another who also was laughing.

Be off! he shrieked again, as if mere words would do it. And soon not even the words could be wrenched from his throat. He burbled, made indefinite small sounds. . . .

Why did I bring them here? came in one agonized flash.

Who was outside? *Indians!*

Sweat came thicker and colder.

Then the sight of a great reddish arm, knocking with its elbow against the six-paned window. Around the arm was clamped a broad bracelet of solid gold. Little Rowly shrieked. The cry came like spread scissors from his throat: two sharp points of cry. Then glass splintered out of the window frame, and big red bodies were crawling through. They crept down the latticework, they snaked across the floor, they took Mary first. Some were hauling on one leg, some on the other, they split her up the middle, they flung the two raw fragments, boiling with blood—flung them to the ends of the universe.

Eliza was next; her father did not see what happened to her, nor what happened to Abigail. Then they had Mrs. Gardner. One after another they pounced upon her . . . and one was sitting on her head, more were holding down her arms, more were holding her limbs apart and tearing the petticoats away from them. Then other Indians were gliding between, pumping spasmodically as he had pumped—he, Rowland, when he lay with her in the forest and was discovered by Abbie. . . .

They split her apart finally as they had split the daughter. They stamped little Rowly into puncheons of the floor with their broad bare feet, stamping so heavily, so many feet, that soon they made a pancake of the child. . . . Then they were all looking at him—at Rowland Gardner—and beaming with delight, and coming closer. . . .

Gardner was on his feet. He must have made some urgent sound, for he had awakened Frances; the blotch of her head was thrust out from the wagon cover.

Mr. Gardner. She spoke barely above a whisper so that she might not awaken the rest. I heard a kind of yell or something. Thought I did. It woke me!

He was dressed in cold sweat.

Ain't nothing round here. He tried to smile through the darkness but his lips were a blubbering stew. Never heard a thing. Must have been a bird, or a critter or a child yonder in the grove. I'm going to fetch some wood.

III

Reared in and living in walled hilly places through most of her life, Abbie had never been fully conscious of clouds before she came to the Iowa country. Out here clouds supported the very sky or rolled restlessly beneath it. They cavorted like colts, they were a structure, they were witches, they were a population around you. Back East you looked out of a window at the world; here you went to the door, if you were a woman or a girl, and grown tired, tired to death from backbreaking work and the smells inside— You went outside the door and stood and of course you looked at the clouds, for they were all there was to see.

The baby cried; if you were Sister Mary you went back inside to tend to the baby or to attend to a thousand other things. But clouds walked with you, they came rolling in at the door, they occupied your mind. You could not forget that they were pillars, that they were a stockade, they were ponies running loose.

If someone had asked Abbie before she came to the prairie, and she had been able to reply articulately— If someone had asked her as to the color of clouds, she would have replied: Yes. Two colors, I think. There are white clouds—great big soft ones—and then there are storm clouds; they're dark, and they kind of frighten you.

But here there was no color she did not find in the clouds. She had seen them turn to a venomous red when a prairie fire came too close. Cloud people and cloud animals walked and rode; no wonder that Indians saw people and animals in them, saw people and animals in everything! There was no shape which the clouds did not assume, and there was no height to which they might not pile. They were soap, soapsuds: you thought you might wash your hands in them. They were not clouds but clods for the violent hands of storms to fling in your face. Clouds were spooks which came walking by day or by night; they were toys for children to play with; they had force, they secreted whole cargoes of water, they romped and rolled, they were sheep in a field. Clouds were a kiss or might be a danger. At times she thought they were kin to the few wild men who went past on their sorry horses, or who walked in sorrier state.

(Her father called them wild men. He didn't call them Indians or

Injuns or Indans as other people did. He just called them wild men; and so they were.)

Clouds embraced the sun, some days they hid it, other days they ran away from it. Wild men and clouds alike, they were tossing all over the place, they walked in your dreams. Many's the time when Abbie saw a weak little cloud, an infant cloud, picked up and carried away, kidnaped by larger fiercer gypsy clouds, and thus eaten up because they were cannibals. . . .

It wasn't that there were always clouds in the sky; of course there weren't. Days came when the region was arched over from tip to tip —the whole great upside-down washtub of sky—by a hard compelling blazing white-blue; with the sun leering, leering, hurting, hurting, baking you up, small house and family of you, as victims were gobbled in fairy tales.

Secretly the girl recognized the clouds' capacity for cruelty, and dreaded them accordingly; yet she had the feeling that there were priests and teachers and prophets among them.

They were horses. . . .

Horses, she said in her heart, but not too frequently to her mother and sisters; because her mother and sisters were practical females. Sometimes they laughed at Abbie. . . . Horses, and ain't they just a-running wild! . . . So they were, a whole stableful turned loose, and loping off in the south and west, loping to get themselves burnt by the sun.

Reckon wild men are riding them.

Reckon they are *not!*

Look, you can see their feathers.

Ain't no feathers on the ones I see go past here! Just all lousy. One of the women had on a sunbonnet— Ma said she believed she'd stole it somewhere.

. . . And that one riding ahead must be his wife—must be his squaw —and look at the baby she's got, the baby she's holding.

. . . There they all go, into the sun and down behind it.

. . . And not just horses tonight. Some of them are children, running and playing games.

Here we come.

Where from?

New York.

What's your trade?

Ice cream and lemonade.

Playing games and running toward the sun, ending up immersed in it.

Some people saw these same things, saw only clouds. Abbie witnessed the walls of a dungeon, and bars of Paradise glinting down—slanting ladderlike bars; and Saints huddled below in their chains, but looking up to accept the promise of God above. Long light of the few colored Biblical pictures she had observed . . . glorious bars of light coming between, motes dancing through their fissures . . . when they were cracked apart you saw beams of Holy light, Holy ladders . . . birds became motes flying amid a golden stream.

A child might see shapes which others did not see; yet the constantly changing procession of bundles and towers and runaway cattle affected each individual to the extent of his capability for imagination.

Men looked at the clouds and said, There's rain up there. They said, It's going to hail. They had known the weather back in Herkimer County and Bucks County; now they must come to know it here. Twas a different weather . . . the clouds were different, there were more of them.

Clouds did not make the weather, but they indicated it, they helped it along. It was wise to keep on good terms with the clouds. They were so far away, they had so much strength, they were aloof. Oh, they were gaunt or they were fat, they were running like mad or they were standing still and thus implacable. They were of the community but not in it. They had more secrets than a wild gooseberry had spines. Some may have been lined with silver, many were a solid pulp; but whatever their texture and substance, from whatever materials they were made, they lived, they abounded in this region as it seemed clouds had never abounded elsewhere. It was as if the mottled inhabitants of a far kingdom had been turned loose to come and haunt you; if they weren't doing it one day, they were doing it the next. Sometimes there existed a week of solid sky with no clouds to taint it, no clouds to nurse you away from the sun; but soon there was bound to be a week in which you never saw the sun. Sixteen days one time . . . Abbie had counted. . . .

Flat clouds, cloth without shape: they were the dull ones. But usually some little herds came wandering in front of them, blown by different winds, and soon they shadowed a glossy water where wild men said that Spirits lived. . . .

Better not start today, looks too cloudy.

Oh, Ma, we going to get a cyclone? Ma, what'll we do if a cyclone comes?

Now you just keep still! Ain't no cyclone going to get you. But if one *does* come– Well, if I ain't to home, if you're alone with the other kids, you just scrooch down in that hole Pa dug to put the potatoes in.

And then when you come back, Ma, you might find the whole cabin blowed away. Wouldn't that be funny?

Your Pa wouldn't think so–not as hard as he and Harvey worked to put it up! Then where'd you sleep, anyway? Out under the stars?

Out under the clouds, Ma.

IV

The little Hidatsa Indian girl was scarred the day she was born, scarred within minutes after her birth. Neighbors were attending her mother, and one of them jostled a shelf hung above her mother's bed. There fell a shower of colored stones which an elder sister had found near a little stream, months before, and had saved carefully as treasures, as a kind of medicine; everyone knew certain rocks were *hopadi;* they were by way of being sacred.

Several of the stones were large enough to have killed the baby then and there, if they had struck fairly upon her head. But the tumbling chunks gave her a glancing blow only: they tore cheek and lip, the whole side of that infant's face still soaked with the juices of birth.

A great outcry ensued. People in nearby lodges rushed to the scene of disaster, and all talked about it, and children and dogs surrounded the door in plenty. It was yelled that the baby might die, and some people advised that when her naming-day came, she be named Woman-Dies-Almost-As-Soon-As-She-Is-Born. Other suggestions were made, while the poor wailing mite was washed and treated, and people were wondering how she would ever suck with that bruised bloody mouth. It was thought to call her Rocks-Fall-Upon-Woman, or Bleeding-Face, or Hurt-Badly-When-Small.

Also hullabaloo occurred in trying to identify the culprit who had jostled the shelf, knocking loose one of the rawhide strings by which it was held, and thus precipitating the accident. A general accusation was made against a young neighbor named Willow-Whip, and Willow-Whip's husband declared that he would take a stick and beat his wife to teach her a lesson. Amid shrieks which could be heard far, Willow-Whip refused to admit that she was culpable; and her mother-in-law intervened, and took her away to lament in her own lodge.

All this excitement was unperceived at the time by the father of the baby, Man-Walking-On-Mussel-Shells, who did a woman's work cheerfully in the family cornfield because one of his wives was down sick, one was incompetent as a gardener, and the third was in the process of childbirth. He pulled up green sucker shoots which were forming around the main stems of corn, and found satisfaction in tearing them loose and hearing them pop as he broke them. He said to himself,

Oh, this is a sign. Why are my fingers wet with corn-water? It is because I have been pulling up corn-suckers; and by this sign should come the name of the child. Boy or girl, the child shall be named Corn-Sucker.

He did not mind doing a woman's work at this time. First, there was no one else to do it, and the suckers would take the strong life from central stems if they were not eradicated. And, second, most of his friends could not twit him about what he was doing (as assuredly they would have done had they seen him). The friends were gone to the river, which ran lower, hour by hour, following a drought in the country far up the river but not here. It was rumored that several large fish had been seen in the shallows, and could be penned and captured if everyone worked together. Thus most of the men and many boys of the village were wading in brown Missouri shallows, except a half-dozen young men who had gone two days before to try to steal horses from the Dakota, and Willow-Whip's husband, to whom a fish was not good medicine.

In the cornfields it was hot for early summer, and Man-Walking-On-Mussel-Shells had told his eldest daughter, Green-Night-Butterfly, to fetch him water when the sun reached its extreme height. She was late in coming: a small, round-shouldered, dirty-fringed creature, treading painstakingly so as not to hurt the young corn, and bearing a swollen bladder of water in a small basket. Her father had full intent to scold her for tardiness, to point at the sun, to show her how high the sun was gone, and now it was starting down again. But her first words frightened him so, that he would have forgiven her anything in order to be assured—as soon she assured him—that the baby would not die.

He drank deeply, slowly, and prepared to leave the cornfield at once.

Will the child be able to feed? he demanded.

Not yet. The women say it is too young.

You tell me that it is a girl?

A girl. They are saying that she should be named Woman-Hurt-When-Rocks-Fall-Down, or names like that.

Nay, she will not be named that, cried the father. I have named the child already, even before I knew that she was hurt, even before I knew that she was born. She shall be called Corn-Sucker.

This was the way the story was recited to poor Corn-Sucker, after she grew old enough to understand. It was told often in the family. . . . The father died when Corn-Sucker had not yet grown past her mother's middle. He wasted miserably in pain for nearly a full moon after he was shot. He was shot when walking by the margin of the river. He fell there, and dragged himself part way to the village, crawling along, pulling himself by his hands before some boys found him and carried him the rest of the way. He was very weak by that time and could tell but little. He told more before the night, after medicine songs had been sung, and after he had been given several concoctions to drink. He said that he did not even see the men who fired at him before the bullets struck. He had blunt arrows with him, he was hunting for birds, when suddenly a boat must have come round the bend, and the men in it fired almost as soon as they saw him. It was thought that the men were French; there were said to be Frenchmen on the river. But no one in the village had seen a white man, except at a distance, for a long time.

After hearing these tidings, a number of friends of Man-Walking-On-Mussel-Shells decided to make war against those whites in the boat. They painted, danced, sang, and went off with their weapons in the night, traveling the rest of the night, not feeling any weariness after their dance, but nerved by the thought of war. They followed down the river for another day and a night, meeting some hunters who said, Yes, the boat had gone on ahead. The current was not running stoutly; but the white men were working with oars, and also they had a small sail. Whenever the river bent in a direction where the wind was right it would help them. The Hidatsa men never caught up with the French whites; they almost did so, but then they came to the land of the Dakota, and saw signs of a large war party, so they turned back. They arrived home in ignominy, with the women coming out and calling them Women.

Meanwhile, Corn-Sucker's father suffered, and evil spirits took possession of him. He talked in other tongues, he made speeches no one could understand as he writhed. One ball had gone through one hip and lodged in the other thigh, another ball had struck him in the belly. So he died.

After that there was not much meat in the lodge; Man-Walking-On-Mussel-Shells had left no sons. He had given up expecting or even hoping to have a son before Corn-Sucker was born. However, corn was medicine in that household. Always they did well with their corn, even in the worst seasons when the sun, the corn's fierce enemy, beat down week after week, and other people's fields dried up. But these women carried water from the river; they worked long and hard, early and late; they made their corn bear, often a great deal better than their neighbors' fields and always somewhat better.

The dead father had left nine kernels of corn, of different tints, in his medicine parfleche. In a way these kernels were now medicine for Corn-Sucker. Also there was her name to be taken into consideration, and also the growth of that name, which came because her father had his hands wet with corn-water at the very moment of her birth and the moment of her disfigurement. Sometimes the women were able to trade corn and squash for bits of meat from other neighbors, when the hunters had had success; thus in a way they ran a kind of boarding-house, cooking *dopatsa-makihike*—Four-Vegetables-Mixed—for visiting bachelors or men whose wives were sick.

Two winters after the winter following the death of Man-Walking-On-Mussel-Shells, an uncle of his became a widower, when bad spirits got into the chest and throat of his wife, and strangled her. By spring-time this man, Gray-Other-Goose, was so lonely that he moved in with Corn-Sucker's mother and the other two wives (whom sometimes the girl called her aunts, and sometimes her big sisters) and made them all his wives. He was an old man, but very keen in matters of the hunt. He was adept at constructing traps and snares, even though his eyes were sick and he could not see to shoot well any more. Often now there was enough meat in the lodge for the whole family, sometimes more than they needed; then they dried it and put it away.

Corn-Sucker's dread by this time was not that she would starve, but that no one would ever wish to marry her. It seemed that she was justified in this fear. The sight of her left eye had not been injured in the calamity of her infancy; but still the eye looked far out to the left, and gave her a peculiar appearance even if one did not stop to consider the rest of her face. Her left cheek was a twisted wad, the mouth had been sliced, the little corner of upper and lower lip did not move while the main lips talked.

For weeks after the birth, Corn-Sucker's mother had been compelled to milk her own breast by hand and, following this operation, drip the milk painstakingly into the mouth of the baby. The torn lips never grew together properly, although an attempt was made at sewing them; then the lips puffed up alarmingly, the child was hot, again the family feared that she would die. They removed the stitches; after some days the puffing was gone, the child was cool once more.

It was pitiful, because the right side of her face was handsome. If you stood only on her right side and looked at her, you would have thought that she was beautiful; then she turned her head and you saw.

A bad boy of the village was cruel to her when she grew able to toddle about and understand things which were said. He was a bigger boy; he called the infant Half-Face, and yipped that she was the embodiment of an evil spirit. . . . A sudden snow-tempest occurred entirely out of season, late the next autumn, and this bad boy had gone to a remote riverside thicket, trying to kill prairie hens; so he was trapped in whiteness by the storm, and was never found until after wolves had reduced him to bones with tooth marks on them. It was considered by some philosophers that this constituted a punishment for his taunting the little girl. No one ever teased her openly again—not because all the people in the village were noble; but those who were ignoble were afraid to tease her.

Corn-Sucker was so tractable and (in enforced loneliness of her maidenhood) so willing to work at helping her other relatives, including the nitwit aunt, that she found favor in the eyes of all. They praised her openly—praised her to disparagement of other relatives small and large. Most of the young villagers did not react badly to this. Continued praise of Corn-Sucker and the example of diligence she set, and the great power, almost a medicine, which she seemed to exert over things in the garden—these won respect and not a little envy from other girls. By the time Corn-Sucker was a woman in fact, and could remain proudly aloof from the world whenever the moon made her do so, she had more than one *ikupa*—she had three or four. One was her favorite. The girl's name was Mouse-Sits-Up-Tomorrow but mostly she was called Mouse. There was no word quite so nice as the word *ikupa.* It meant that there was a girl who was not your sister, but whom you loved as a sister, perhaps even more than any girl might love her sister. Unhappy was the girl who had no *ikupa.* The others felt more sorry for her, or scornful of her, as their natures suggested, than they might have felt were she older and no young men came about.

The fields of Corn-Sucker's family and fields of the family of Mouse-Sits-Up-Tomorrow lay side by side. Thus the corn-watchers' stage was built by mutual activity of women of the two families, though Gray-Other-Goose himself cut the green cottonwood limb which was to serve as ladder, and carved out the three steps on it. It was not labor which Mouse and Corn-Sucker faced when they went out before dawn to begin their watch, taking along food and their materials for the day's work (usually embroidery): it was a joy. Sometimes the mother of one of them came along or joined them later, sometimes other relatives; but mostly through the corn-watching season it was just the two of them, visited frequently by another *ikupa* or two.

There was little worry about the attacks of birds at the late season; but boys and ponies were a constant menace. Boys were harder to see than the ponies. You could see ponies easily when they came to try to steal the green corn; but the boys were great little sneaks, and would creep low; even from the high platform of the watchers' stage it was difficult to see them, though the girls shaded their eyes and kept a constant watch while they sang to the corn. The corn was as their babies, because they had been present and had participated during the implanting of seeds. And, as in the case of children conceived and nourished in their bodies and ejected from those same bodies, they would find pride in the power of the mature corn, later on.

They sang: *You green ears of corn, you are very young. You are our babies, for you have no hair upon your faces. The horse came to take you, and we drove him away with sticks. The bad boy came to take you, and we drove him away with insults; he fled in fear.*

They sang not only to the corn, but shyly and coquettishly to one another. They bent low over their work with dressed skins and tinted porcupine quills which constituted their materials for embroidery—ever and again letting their little sharp hawks' gaze come up to sweep the field and pry into heat mists which danced and writhed beyond the farther boundaries. One girl would sing, barely looking at her chum, or perhaps not looking at all, because she felt impact of the knowledge that her words dealt with the possibility of love; and love was too strong a matter to be treated lightly. *My* ikupa, *what do you wish to see? you said to me. . . . What I wish to see is corn silk coming out on the growing ear. But what you wish to see is that naughty young man coming by!*

Before their eyes . . . the scattered brake of long bent polished leaves, twitching and talking when hot breeze found them . . . ranks of sunflowers beyond, sunflowers not yet come to their completion; squash vines and bean vines crawling . . . planted sticks or piles of rock or mere well-shaped pointed mounds of earth dried there: sign-posts for the boundaries of family farms. The hobbled ponies out beyond . . . some were always working their bonds loose, and thus constituting a renewed threat to the fields. High-piled clouds, none of them showing on the horizon through the first hours of day, and then coming up slowly, repiling their fluff, building higher and puffier, seeming to grow from nothingness, yet spreading and thickening until late in the day a storm threatened; but seldom did it come, even though the sun was hid. Then magically the old gray-white Men of the Clouds went ambling off into space, off perhaps to make a new acquaintance with Thunder-Birds and to return on another angry date, bringing Thunder-Birds with them. The hot dry raw tan banks which marked the Missouri's margin . . . often there came an indistinct wild cry from those shores. Was it a bird? Was it a fish talking, or was it merely the yelling of a dog who went there with boys? Or was it the boys themselves? Perhaps enemies were appearing. . . . The girls arose, shading their eyes, examining distances, watching for any menace which might attack their precious corn; and then settling down again.

They sipped water in between times when they grew hot; they brought plenty of water, always. Watchers would dry on the stages without water, dry as the corn itself would be made to dry later. . . . Before the sun had reached its height they would have fires going in little booths along the edges of the field; perhaps two or three fires would suffice to cook lunch for watchers from the whole village. They would boil squash or beans, sometimes cook more complicated dishes. Not always did they wait until noon to cook, not always did they terminate their cooking and eating then. If one happened to grow hungry when the morning was only half spent, she started to make a fire. Should there be meat, she cooked that: a bit of fresh buffalo meat was laid on the coals; dried meat was impaled on a leaning stick and left to char itself.

Booths were made of willow switches bearing all their leaves, tied together at the top, and sometimes interwoven with other willow withes; there was no other covering. A great sight and a great smell, to see blue smoke coming up from these booths, and to smell the faint toasting of willow leaves which cooked along with burning wood in the process.

Should relatives wander near—a few men coming back from a hunt, possibly—you offered them food, unless they were boys of near your own age (perhaps the love-boys of other girls). Then even though they were relatives, you offered them only water, you did not cook for them. You felt a trepidation in their male presence; and felt, rather than understood, why some elder mother or grandmother often came along with the watchers, and watched the watchers even while they watched the corn.

. . . You ate squash boiled alone, you were very fond of squash. Later in the season, during the Harvest Moon, you ate green corn boiled with the squash. You ate it out of a spoon made from the thorny stem of the squash: the green stem, bent and split, with a small stick wedged to keep it open, and thus make a spoon out of it. But you were careful, the thorns did not hurt your mouth, you knew how to use such a spoon. You dipped it into the old pot; and one was a very old pot, it had belonged to your grandmother, it was of copper lined with tin, and it was traded from the French long ago, or so people said. It was important to have a pot like that in the family. Your grandmother and your mother were proud of it; now you were proud of it too.

Most of the girls had many brothers and sisters, more than Corn-Sucker had; she had few. Because it was not only the children of your father and mother who were your brothers and sisters; the children of your father's brothers were also your brothers and sisters, though the children of your father's sisters were only your cousins. And, on the mother's side, the children of your mother's sisters—they too were your own brothers and sisters; but the children of your mother's brothers were only cousins. This made for many brothers and sisters, as anyone could see. Corn-Sucker wished sometimes sadly that she had more.

There was a boy named Yesterday-Ate-Beaver, and another named Meadowlark-Calls-His-Name. The two were inseparable companions; but were related neither to Corn-Sucker nor to her *ikupa* nor to any other girls nearby. These boys the girls liked especially to tease: they came so often, standing close, staring; they were very bad, very impertinent; they stared constantly, and the girls had to keep looking down at their quills until their eyes hurt with the close attention they gave their work, in order to avoid looking at Yesterday-Ate-Beaver and his friend. The steady, evaluating, yet somehow cynical stare of the youths went through them like a hot ramrod pushed into soft meat. Almost they felt scorched by the boys' look, as the soft tongue of a buffalo would have been scorched by a glowing rod which impaled it in preparation for cookery. . . .

They could not offer these boys even water, because they were not relatives. The girls told themselves that they would not have offered water anyway, relatives or no—the boys offended them so with this persistent peering and swaggering.

Mouse-Sits-Up-Tomorrow had a sharp tongue, and used it like a lash on these youths.

She said, You had better not try to steal corn.

They said, Ah, we stole corn yesterday, and you did not see us! Your eyes are no better than those of an old woman.

That is what you say, to make us sad because our corn was stolen! But we know that it was not stolen. You were not in the field.

Oh, we stole corn, and from you!

You have stolen none of our corn, you bad boys; but if you try we shall beat you with sticks!

Mouse taught the other girls a song to sing to the boys. It was inferred that she had made it up herself, but perhaps she had got it from her aunt. Mouse could make up many songs, but it is likely she had not made up this one. This was not a Love Song, but a Song To Tease. There was a symbolism about it which did not escape the discerning wits of the girls who chanted it after Mouse taught them. Many of the old stories recited in the lodges had that same kind of symbolism. There were many frank references also to dung, to the begetting and bearing of children, to the act of mating alleged to take place sometimes between men and animals.

This was the song: *You bad boys, you are all alike! Your bow is like a bent basket hoop; you poor boys, you have to run on the prairie barefoot; your arrows are fit for nothing but to shoot up into the sky!*

The girls felt delighted with their situation in existence as females, when they chanted thus. They knew that an average man might have twice the strength of an average woman. They knew that they were not shaped for the hunt or for war, and also that when men demonstrated that they were weak in war, they were called Women. Yet this was but a sexual insult applied by one sex to the other. They themselves were gratified at being female; they felt wiser than any male, wholly superior to any boy alive. They were conscious of that far-reaching inverted power of She who is sought, or will be sought when She is older. They felt that with their softer hands they could wield the very wand of life, that it flew farther than any arrow.

Yesterday-Ate-Beaver and Meadowlark-Calls-His-Name were so indignant at the singing of Mouse's song that they went away with dark faces, and did not seem to speak to each other while they were yet within sight of the girls. . . . Still, the pair were drawn to return again and again to the cornfields and the watchers' stages.

Once they essayed to wrench off some fat ears from stalks directly in front of the stage, thus showing their contempt for the girls policing the area. Yesterday-Ate-Beaver made an actual sign of contempt, holding out his palm flat, and snapping his thumb and second finger, and then extending all his fingers toward the little figures on the platform.

But the thieves had not noticed Mouse's grandmother, who was boiling beans in one of the booths directly behind them. She emerged suddenly to throw brands at them—surprising, intimidating, and mildly burning them all at once, so that they dropped the stolen ears and fled howling.

Mouse, Corn-Sucker, and two friends who happened to be with them were delighted at this. Together they made a song about it. *You bad boys, you are young and green; but you can be burned more easily than the green corn. It was only a lame old woman who put coals of fire on you; but the very hawks in the sky heard you yell with pain. We do not think you are boys, we think you are little owls crying.*

Nevertheless before long the villains had returned (not to steal corn again, for their lesson had been taught them). They came to brag and stare as before; sometimes other boys were with them. They talked boldly, telling of their prowess at hunting buffalo. True, usually they did have their bows when they happened by; but the girls did not believe that any of their arrows had ever been blooded in buffalo. The boys told great stories, not directly to the girls, but in their hearing. They talked to each other, they were smug in lying.

Yesterday-Ate-Beaver said, It was a very large bull. . . . Aye, quite the largest we have killed in weeks. It did not take us long to cut him open.

Nay, nay, said Meadowlark-Calls-His-Name. My knife was sharp!

Mine too. It was quite the largest buffalo tripe I have ever seen, when we cut it out. Ah, we scraped it a little bit but not too much, said Yesterday-Ate-Beaver. We left the good taste in the raw tripe. We did not scrape it off.

Meadowlark-Calls-His-Name said, It was a great red puddle of blood which formed in the bull's belly after we had opened him up That is good sauce; it is the best sauce.

True, brother.

So we dipped the raw tripe in the sauce of blood, and so we ate.

Aye, we ate long and well.

Then they were patting their bellies, and trying to manage to belch, in order to show how much blood and raw tripe of the buffalo they had eaten.

In answer to this, the girls soon had another song. *The big bull buffalo said, I am mighty, my hide is thick. I cannot be killed by weak arrows of talkative boys. I must be killed by a man. I think that maybe those boys killed a frog!*

So they went rivaling and squabbling through all the moons, beginning perhaps in the Sunflower-Planting Moon. . . . When the Drying Moon had come, the stages were long since deserted; and rivalries that existed between the sexes must be exerted within the village itself, or around pits wherein corn and vegetables were put away, and where girls worked with the women, helping to store against winter. Then on, through the cold moon of the Shedding Horns, into the Hand Moon—usually the coldest of all—and into the Raccoon Moon which followed.

Even in the winters when there was no smallpox walking on scaly itching feet among the lodges, the winter seemed many years long. The girls felt that they were years older when another Planting Moon had come.

. . . Once more the first pale frail shoots would rise spearing up out of the earth; once more crows would dig and steal, so innumerable replantings must occur. This hill and that would be replanted, until corn grew too tall for the crows to steal its seed. . . . Once more the damp spreading rustle would ensue. You could hear corn growing, even off in the village; you could hear it swelling, unlacing itself, bursting free. Older folks talked knowingly of how the baby corn spirits would extend their hands, asking for water of the night. Surely they received it; for were not those pearls of moisture gathered in the deep pockets between leaves and stalks when morning came?

As surely as the fields rose up with their growth, so persisted the long war between boys and girls; though it changed in character as the individuals changed; and new little girls came to take the place of elder watchers who had sat on those perches during the few previous years, but now were busy with more intimate domestic tasks—with the business of bearing children . . . and yielding to their husbands in dawn before they went to bathe in the Missouri.

Still Corn-Sucker did her long stint on the stages . . . year after year she sat there.

Once she had a dream wherein a beautiful cow calf buffalo, all gleaming white, came up to her on the prairie and said:

Come with me, sister. My own face is beautiful. I will give it all to you, for I have been told that I will sicken and die, and will need my face no longer.

Many times Corn-Sucker had dreams wherein she thought both sides of her face were but blankness. Again, she had another dream, so vivid that she got up determined to do the thing suggested. This was to make a small mask or curtain of fine-dressed skin, tenderly embroidered with quills, which would hang from a headband and cover the left side of her face, and be gathered up under her chin below the slope of her jaw. It would be tied around her neck loosely, with gay red strands. Almost did she make this thing in fact (she begged a bit of fine pliable doeskin from the store of her mother). But there was never the opportunity to do anything about it: she would have had to work in secret, she felt that other people would have jeered at her when they discovered what she was doing. It was better to go on as she had gone . . . that cut twisted mass of tissue, the peculiar separated lips apparent to the village and to any strangers passing.

Only a stranger, she felt, would ever want her for a wife, and he would be likely a man blind in one eye, so he could see only the right side of her face . . . perhaps his blind eye would not let him witness the ugliness.

Corn-Sucker lived into the drudging maidenhood of the unwanted, the cast-aside.

There was only one other distorted person in the village, and she hobbled severely when she walked; her legs were bent like the wings of some birds. This woman, whose name was Cow-Buffalo-Makes-Strings, was years older than Corn-Sucker, and had found refuge in a practiced merriment. She made other people laugh. She would do things which no woman was supposed to do, but people laughed just the same. And if someone became enraged at her antics and gave her a whipping, Cow-Buffalo-Makes-Strings laughed as she was being whipped. The cripple's family had been wiped out by a smallpox epidemic but she went on jesting. Only the very light-brained might find refuge from congenital sorrow such as this cripple found. The honest Corn-Sucker attempted no such nonsense to make herself into the second professional clown of the village. It was not likely that such a course would have brought her a man anyway. Cow-Buffalo-Makes-Strings had no man, and jokes were made about that, too, by villagers. She was at once a buffoon and a butt. There was nothing to be gained in emulating her; but it did not even occur to the little woman with the scarred face to do just that.

Had she been sly and calculating, Corn-Sucker might have found another road which led to a more active and exerting life. She might have become a kind of seeress or medicine woman. Often this was the refuge of those with wry bodies: they became witches, and won repute, respect, not a little fear, and hatred. But docile Corn-Sucker could never have shaped herself as a grim and pompous harridan. In fact she pitied the sick so much that she was almost terrified by them, and could never have danced or groveled in their presence, shaking rattles and pretending to have intercourse with spirits.

She loved the simple fact of seed and a green thing growing from it.

She was painstaking and devoted in any household task. Everyone knew she made the best corncob-ash cake, for flavoring, in the entire village—better than men had ever eaten before—and they came and begged this substance, and gave her meat in exchange.

Long since, her sisters were married and gone to other lodges. The older women dropped away. There were left only herself and the later father, Gray-Other-Goose, and by this time he was of advanced age and almost completely blind. He liked to sit at his door and give advice to younger men on war and hunting activities.

The pattern of existence repeated itself regularly for Corn-Sucker, punctuated by a few struggles and tragedies. There was always the threat of smallpox, which had struck so cruelly at these Hidatsa and their close neighbors and friends, the Mandan. There was now much intermarriage because of the worse-than-decimation which had occurred. Children of a Hidatsa mother learned first her language; but Mandan words kept poking into the conversation. . . . It was always so: the fate of the good solid tribe, weakened by conquest which had overwhelmed it. In this case disease had been the conqueror; but still men like Gray-Other-Goose shook their heads on hearing Mandan words, and knowing of marriages which came about between the two portions of this vast northwestern family. They said it was not like this in the old days.

And they said that there were not many white men on the river in the old days, and in the very old days there were no white men at all. But now the *Mashi* came up or down in their keelboats with increasing frequency.

When word of such approach flashed through the village, cautious women and children and even men ran to hide. Folk possessed of more curiosity or recklessness crept to stations where they might watch the mighty craft and hear faintly the cries of men who worked them. It needed many white men to force one of those great keelboats upstream! They passed to the rear of the boat in a long row, bending their weight against the poles they lugged, fairly forcing the boat out from under their feet, marching and bending and shoving in slavery; and then they passed back to the front on the opposite running board, and had to do it all over again, in never-ending file. When they reached ripples and shallower water, almost directly opposite the Hidatsa gardens, it was then that the whites must produce a thick rope, and struggle along the bank, putting aside their poles and heaving on the mighty cordelle burdening their shoulders. Oh, it was not wise to let yourself be seen by white men!—they might shoot, as those French whites had shot Man-Walking-On-Mussel-Shells. It was well to remain concealed until they'd struggled out of sight, and the river was unthreatened by them and lay in muddy peace once more.

A few times amid freshets following the summer storms, Corn-Sucker had heard a blast of steam, and she had seen black smoke. In common with most of the rest of humanity, she had fled far. Flecking sparks, the coarse torn smoke, a banging paddle wheel— *Tsakak!*— A steamboat was a dangerous and horrid thing! Old men said that there were never steamboats in the very old days.

It was now many winters since Corn-Sucker had become wholly a woman. Still she went to the watchers' stations regularly with young girls; but Mouse no longer sat beside her; Mouse's daughter did instead, and the daughter had her own *ikupa* now.

Songs of the watchers went drifting out toward that dreamy rim of cottonwoods beside the river; heat waves twitched as always they had twitched; young men came by, they heard themselves taunted by the virgins as their fathers had been taunted.

You young man of the Dog Society, you said to me, When I go to the East on a war party, you will hear news of me, how brave I am.

The girls concentrated in docility, observing the work of their hands, passing quills back and forth, giggling when one of them lost a bit of sinew used for sewing; but their beady eyes were bright with naughtiness. They knew every movement and frown of the boys whom they scouted, even though they appeared never to watch. . . .

I have heard news of you. When the fight was on, you ran and hid! And you think you are a brave young man! Behold, you have joined the Dog Society. Therefore I call you just plain dog!

One of the boys whom they thus provoked was a clan cousin of Mouse's daughter. He turned beside cut bundles of brush which fenced the little field, and shouted with an attempt at good humor, Sing louder, cousin! That was all he could say. The other youths strolled on with faces averted. They twisted in their course, went past another watchers' platform in the second field beyond; and again they were told indirectly how ignominious they were.

No longer did Corn-Sucker join in such songs. It was better that young girls should sing them. She sat, body motionless, but eyes seeing all. She sat with the weight of her plump muscular toil-tried body resting on her bottom and her haunch—knees bent, legs drawn back, feet turned in on her right side, as all the women sat. Men might sit with their limbs crossed; not the women. The feet were drawn back on the right side, always.

Years had relegated Corn-Sucker to the position of a kind of aunt or chaperone. She might no longer exhibit herself as a female eventually in need of a man; but she was still in need of a man, desperately so. However, older men seldom approached the fields; and when they did it was on an errand legitimate—pertaining to the fields themselves, or to family instruction or discipline. They all knew Corn-Sucker, had known her long, and would not have looked at her anyway.

She had done every little thing which she knew or which was storied to her. One morning, some years before, a meadowlark had told her to eat flowers. Over and over again he said it. He rose and sped and descended before her and rose again. Eat flowers, he said. Ah, truly. Eat flowers. Eat flowers, Corn-Sucker! So she had eaten them. Everyone ate sunflower seed; but she ate the flowers themselves—ate the petals when they were soft, and munched them, and did not like them; but it might be that these were the ones. She gathered other posies in prairie grass: little blue and violet flowers, pink ones also. And these she dried, and pounded them to a pulp, and baked them into cakes and ate them, to no avail.

For a time she chewed no meat with her white even teeth, and actually neglected the Four-Vegetables-Mixed which was the delight of women when they went to the fields. Of course she was bound to find an evil flower; so she found it. Bad spirits got into her mouth: they corrugated her tongue and made it sore, they puffed her misshapen lips. She was a good while doctoring herself; so she ate no more flowers.

Perhaps a wicked prairie wolf (they were always up to tricks) had put himself into the shape of a meadowlark and had captured the meadowlark's voice and song, and had given this false advice—a prairie wolf, or even one of the great wolves from the North, the fierce kind which came down only in winter.

Later she turned to the notion of a holy stone. She went hunting for one, and found a rock which she might call her own in a gully near the river: a flat, lone, dry gully where no one went, where the pellets of a few animals were to be seen on the rock itself. This stone Corn-Sucker painted in three colors. She sketched a variety of symbols, working secretly of course, with no one to observe her, and dully admiring her handiwork under the thin staring sun. She painted appropriate symbols, painted a symbol for herself. She painted several men, all of them mounted. If a man were sent to her, which seemed unlikely, she hoped that he would be rich, with many horses.

There she put out food, morning and night. The food was always eaten; spirits must have approved. Yet no man came her way.

One busy bright day Corn-Sucker entered the village to find that her stepfather, Gray-Other-Goose, was gone away.

She had come in laden with heavy ropes of corn ears, for this was the moon in which corn was husked and dried. Twas a weary task for one woman working by herself! But Corn-Sucker had no meat, and she might not manage a husking feast without meat.

It had been far different when she was a little girl: then with her father living—or even later, after the advent of Gray-Other-Goose—there was meat. Thus the crier of some society (perhaps the Fox Society or Dog Society, or even the proud Black Mouth Society) might be notified. High on the roof of the society's lodge he would stand, and he would call loudly: All you of this Society, come hither! You have been asked to husk corn! When you all get here, then we will go to That One's garden and husk corn! . . . Ah, a fine sight to see the men of the Black Mouth Society marching out to the fields! And in old years they always carried their guns, dreading a sudden attack by the Dakota. But as they neared the fields they would sing, hoping that girls might hear them. If a man had a sweetheart, or a girl whom he wished to make his sweetheart, among those women, he would yell shrilly when he saw her, and be sure that she should recognize his voice. The young men were willing to husk corn, because it was then that they could see the girls close to them! . . . But no young man ever tried to make himself into an object of attention for poor Corn-Sucker. She worked, she carried braided corn ears to hang across the back of her family's pony; shyly she helped to serve out the buffalo side when it was cooked, and saw the busy huskers eat with joyful appetites; and each man had with him a small sharp stick with which he skewered such portions of the gift meat as he could not then eat, and he carried these bits home to eat later.

But all this had happened in the Long Ago. Now there was no meat in the lodge of Corn-Sucker, and thus no society might be invited to husk; and Gray-Other-Goose was old and he was blind.

On this day people had seen him wandering but no one knew his destination. It must have been difficult for him, in sightlessness, to find his medicine bag and secure his weapons, but he had taken them: the club, the knife, and the old bow and long-unused arrows—these were gone from the lodge. Only antique things, as used in the Long Ago—he did not carry off his gun. The neighbors were busy; but several had seen him go tottering with blanket over his head and shoulders. They had questioned him but he would not reply. They'd gossiped idly about it, and said, Gray-Other-Goose thinks he is young again. *Hao.* He thinks perhaps he is going to make war, or to hunt buffalo! Then they said no more, since their minds and hands were occupied mainly with other things.

How far could a sickly blind ancient go stumbling, what course would he follow? Corn-Sucker inquired of some children at play beyond the lodges. The children were running in circles, playing with their whistles, wheeling the whistles at the end of limber sticks, flapping them about as the taut gut threw them this way and that with their feathers, and running hard, so that the whistles would make a shrill piping. It was the sound of play, the sound of mystery and childhood.

. . . They said only, The old man goes alone, and long ago. We have seen him go. Then they went back to their scuffling and galloping, and to the delightful keening of the little toys.

Corn-Sucker tried to track her stepfather, but the marks of the children's scuffling, as they cavorted in circles, had long since wiped out the trail, and also there were ponies wandering about. Perhaps a person more skilled than she could have found the trail, but she could not find it. She went wandering, hit or miss, prowling along ridges west of the village. At last she found Gray-Other-Goose. It was near the place where the dead were put. A badger had dug a great hole at one time and then had abandoned it. Corn-Sucker remembered seeing that hole before: other smaller animals perhaps went therein, or snakes. At any rate there was a large depression scooped at the entrance to the badger's den, and in this aperture the old man was doubled up in a foetal position. His knees were drawn against his tattooed chest, his dirty almost transparent claws locked around his knees. The pulp of his chin pressed tight against his knees—the near-to-toothless mouth set in a line, waxy hair tufted out of his ears. He would not or could not speak, his body was cold. Yet Corn-Sucker doubted that he was actually dead—he had lived so long, seemed eternal. His skin was dry as if tanned to a permanency, and tanned also must be the spirits living inside. Of these spirits there were four: and one would remain here at the hole (or perhaps linger for four days near the family lodge; people argued about this, and it was a matter of doubt); one would ascend directly into the air; the third spirit was destined to walk the Way of the Souls; and the fourth must necessarily accompany that desiccated body when the body was tied atop its scaffold.

The figures of two tired hunters emerged presently from dimness, and Corn-Sucker knew them and hailed them. They came to bend beside her and look. They examined the old man and assured her that, yes, he was dead, but very newly dead. He might have died while she was hovering by.

She sent word to the village that she would watch; so watch she did, a little distance away. She covered the body of Gray-Other-Goose with its blanket, and huddled in her own blanket by a bit of a fire sprung from coals which a kindly neighbor brought out from the village. He fetched also the battered French musket which had been a pride of the elderly man. Gripping this loaded but uncertain gun, Corn-Sucker maintained her vigil through the night in case any wolves should appear. . . . A few of them howled remotely, and she thought that she heard strange treadings and turnings in the darkness; then she put more chips upon the blaze. Once she threw a burning stick at something—it could not have been a wolf, it was too small.

The next day, in ceremonial observance, Corn-Sucker cut short her hair and smeared her face with white-yellow clay. Women helped her to prepare the corpse for its rest, and they met with difficulty in pulling out the stiffened legs; but they did straighten them after a fashion. They bound Gray-Other-Goose tight in shabby robes; so the warped limbs were straightened even more by pressure of the thongs. A scaffold was built, he was hoisted there. Eventually when only bones were left, the bones would be buried carefully to save them from animals . . . he went armed and equipped on his journey. Corn-Sucker lugged bowls of meat, cooked squash, and sunflower seeds for his rationing, and then she applied herself to that perfunctory mourning awarded to those who were antiquated and frail. She hoped that the old man might make intercession for her, since all other departed relatives had failed her in this. She composed her lonely song and tried to wail it, but did better at whispering. *You who were my father, and have gone far, tell them in That Place that I think the meadowlark lied to me. Perhaps it was a prairie wolf who took the shape of a lark; but no man has come. When in the other life I was corn, I think I had a husband, because always there is young corn, and the corn was my baby. I could have no baby had I no husband!*

She meditated about her age, and wondered if she could still have a child if she lay with a man. She had been a woman for a very long time. *I think that I should like to be a cow elk next time, for there is always rutting among elks in the Rutting Moon.* This fancy appealed to her strongly, for she saw herself as a handsome cow elk surrounded by even more handsome males, and some of them were fighting over her.

Through her mourning (which was more a demonstration for personal advantage than a lament) Corn-Sucker hypnotized herself into a state where the rest of existence left her, and where she was concerned only with subjects relating to the dead man, his spirit and his body, his relations with the world beyond, and relating to the state of her own future and own identity. Her self-concern was not materialistic, she did not fret and lament about her neglected corn. Trudging alone, she had managed to strip all the ears from stalks in her field. These ears were heaped in a great pile, and she hoped that the pile was still dry. Friends might have covered it for her; she did not know. Once the corn had been gathered in baskets and dumped down, it was proper to cut off all outer husks and braid thin inner husks together, thus making a rope of the braided ears. More than five tens of ears in a single string, and these were heavy to carry! Corn-Sucker had transported but two of them to the lodge when she discovered the absence of Gray-Other-Goose. Those two big strands consisted of seed corn, carefully selected. Always she chose her seed corn first, before husking and flailing off the common ears for winter use.

But now she was not worrying about the neglected crop, she was thinking only of a pole. No pole had been erected beside the corpse, and she must dig a hole and erect a post; otherwise how could the spirit which remained with the body climb up and down? He would need to climb down to partake of food she had put out for him, and for other reasons as well; then he would need to climb back again.

Her blanket was a shabby one: a trade blanket (bartered from some

Dakota for tobacco when they had come peacefully to trade in a long-ago autumn) originally green and red, but now the red had faded and was dirtied to a somber brown, the green was gray. Still the worn fabric felt thick, and held out the wind of night surrounding her. She sat motionless on the ridge, a hummock barely to be discerned against the sky. Wind blew away the last clouds after sundown, there were many stars. Remnants of the previous moon had been eaten up, and no new moon was yet set in the sky. Corn-Sucker could remember being worried and appalled when a little child, when first she heard about the mice eating the moon; and now, since she knew that it was a regular phenomenon, and the mice could not be restrained, she accepted this matter philosophically. Sometimes in distant years with other children she had sat watching the moon. . . . It is smaller, they said. See, the mice have eaten in at the side; they have eaten off a great deal more since last night. . . . Sometimes it seemed that the children could see the mice: a populous horde of them, all chewing, chewing. They were voracious. It was suggested that Spirit Dogs which roam in upper space should fall upon the mice and eat them; but actually you could not blame the tiny creatures for gnawing as they did: the moon was so soft, golden in some lights, greenish in others, silver sometimes, the color of snow or ice.

On this ridge, doing her duty by her stepfather, she heard distant wolves again; but she would not need the musket on this night. Wolves could not reach Gray-Other-Goose where he was tied. Personally she had no fear of these small wolves; she called them brothers when she was in the mood. There was much to be learned from them, men said, if you watched closely.

No clouds, no new moon appearing bit by bit, uneaten by mystic rodents, undisturbed—and then in final days a great round wafer to present a meal for the mice. No moon of any kind, no shred of cloud, no haunting yellow and hollow blue above and beyond her. Pathways of the spirits appeared on high. . . .

A crusted gleaming road with its long branch and its short; there the spirits traveled, there Gray-Other-Goose was trudging now; at least one of his four spirits was journeying. Corn-Sucker pushed back her blanket and stared long at the sky, at its crowded slivers and specks, and especially at that fat trail ornate with milky particles. Could she see him there—old man bowed and blind, traveling by the sense of his nose as a blind dog might have gone? It seemed that she could see him.

She made a new song.

The Way of the Souls is very bright this night. My father, they said that you could not see; but now you walk alone, and no one is leading you. It is the long path which you go, for there walk the good. They go to the Village of the Dead. The bad go on the short path, and then they fall over the edge. Hukahe! *I can see them falling: they go deep into space, and there they are tortured always. I cannot hear their yells this night, but I have heard them yell.*

Before sunrise she sang another song, a heartfelt plea that Gray-Other-Goose continue intercession for her. When she returned in her next form, she asked that she might be allowed to return in the shape of a pony, a mare. She said she would be a very good pony and would not steal corn. But persistent in her imagination she saw a mare and heard her whinny eagerly, and saw the full-maned male buffeting at her with his slender legs, and rising up with his body against hers, as she had seen horses do. One portion of her heart was glad, that such a thing could be; the other part was unhappy, because she had never been such a mare.

When Corn-Sucker terminated her initial mourning, it was a dry sunny day. She went to the village for tools, she fetched digging stick and a hoe. The stick was merely one of convenient size, pointed on the end, and hardened by being toasted in the fire. The hoe was formed of the shoulder bone of a buffalo, fastened to its handle by tight strands of rawhide which had dried and tightened until they held the thing as firmly as if it were set in rock.

With these implements she dug a deep pit, a post hole of little width, in hard soil beside that scaffold where lay the body of Gray-Other-Goose with its bound robes lifting and falling in a breeze. When the hole was deep enough she put down her tools and went to a creek below the ridge, where cottonwoods and aspens were growing. There she cut her pole. It did not take her long, for her knife was very sharp; always she kept her knives sharp, honed on the best fragments of boulders for her purpose; and of course these rocks were *hopa* also.

Corn-Sucker set her pole deeply into the pit, weighting stones around the base, planting it solidly so that storms might not twist it loose. At last she had done all that she could do to assist her departed relative. One of his several spirits would travel easily up and down this post, leaving the scaffold or regaining it as required. And if another spirit had not heard her prayer as it walked that white road in the sky, it could not be the fault of Corn-Sucker.

She had produced the family ghost-bag and made a rack to hang it on, early that morning, before she brought the tools. The ghost-bag lay on its frame near the door of the lodge, with fringe whipping gaily. Into this elderly stitched pouch, decorated by embroidery of her own hands and her mother's, the woman stuffed several articles personal to Gray-Other-Goose: things which he had treasured, yet things which had never been made part of the contents of his own medicine bag. There was the dried ear of a grizzly bear; he had fought that bear in his youth, killed it, cut off its ear during the fight before he killed it. It would have been part of the contents of his medicine bag, except for the fact that bears were bad medicine for the father of Gray-Other-Goose. . . . There was a bent silver coin which a British fur trader had given him in payment for something or other, many years before; the coin had the face of a woman clearly discernible on one side. The man had cherished this coin, and believed sincerely that it was worth the value of several horses. Also there was a scraggly lock of the old man's own hair, which Corn-Sucker had worried off his head when he lay dead at the entrance of the badger hole.

The single soul of the four possessed by Gray-Other-Goose which was identified mainly with the lodge where he had dwelt, would now take up its housing in the ghost-bag; it would be comfortable there, it was hoped, until the time of transition was passed, and another of the quadruple spirits had traversed safely the Way of the Souls.

With rites concluded, the shorn Corn-Sucker washed mourning clay from her face, and went to the fields by the river. She found her pile of corn intact: yes, considerate people had spread a portion of an old tipi cover into place above the heap, fastening it with pegs against the ground so that no ponies might come robbing. Here was rich accumulation of the five varieties which Corn-Sucker reared: soft white, soft yellow, hard white, hard yellow, the gummy. And two big braided strings already carried to the lodge for seed!

Now she must procure a pot of water, and blow water from her mouth upon the husks because they had dried too long in abandonment: inner husks would not braid well unless they were dampened. And when she had prepared the weighty ropes and gathered up all loose ears, she must bear these burdens to the drying stage beside her lodge. There the flailing would ensue.

She worked in loneliness but with the dedication of necessity. Soon a swelling would affect even her hard tireless fingers as she abused them with task piled upon task. Winter was long, there must be food in the lodge. And. if neighbors had success in their hunting that fall, she would need corn to trade for meat.

She made a new song. Part of it was a song she had heard years before, and learned then; some of the words and thoughts were new; yet it was her song, and related to the death of the corn: its drying, its unresponsive quality, the life-giving uses to which it would be put. A tender thought lived amid the rude words. Still Corn-Sucker could not bring herself actually to chant the song aloud—it droned only in her heart as she worked.

Denuded dun-colored stalks, robbed of their treasure, made a fuzz beyond her consciousness, wind talked amid the fields' rags and tatters. High above the Missouri there was only one bird flying. Two wandering ponies had pushed down the light barricade which rimmed a farther field, and were moving leisurely at hobbled pace, seeking nubbins which might have eluded the observation of workers when the area was last gone over. A distant mumble and crying of the village itself, thinned with shrieks of playing children and nervous outcry of puppies, rose vaguely behind her.

. . . She was alone; she had no one now to live with her in her lodge, no one to share the dry repetitious life she led. It appeared that there was nothing but a toil-worn dream ahead . . . then her turn would come to stretch silent upon a windy scaffold and have the ragged robes whipped about her frame.

She was alone . . . there must be no one else in the fields . . . yet why did one of those ponies blow occasionally through nostrils and lips, and make a sound as of horse-talk to a man? Now the other pony was talking too. . . .

Some time later she stiffened with an unfamiliar sense of peril, as she recognized that a man was watching her.

Simultaneously she became aware of him through an unnamed sense and also saw him and smelled him, as he sat motionless, cross-legged against a middle-sized cottonwood tree which for years had shaded the watchers' platform of Corn-Sucker's family.

Until the wind fetched her an odor of rancid grease which thickened his braids, he might have been a dusky large lump of the earth itself —so dusty was he, so much a part of the caked autumn soil. Those portions of his attire which moved in the breeze seemed as indigenous as the tags of corn leaves fringing and blowing loose. How or when he had crept upon her, the woman did not know. His must have been the disturbance and presence observed by the ponies.

She looked again, fearfully turning up eyes which seemed not even to wander in his direction. She saw that he was a Dakota. He had the jutting triangular face of those people, with pushed spreading nostrils, deep-set lines above the jaws, the implacable protruding chin. He might have appeared like a wild potato or a wild onion, dug laboriously from the soil, except that he was not dug up laboriously: he merely appeared, there he was.

He had fought . . . there was indication of war in two flat black-and-white eagle feathers which lay across his head—one thrust out toward the rear, stiff as the tail of a jay, one lying down like a cow-lick, and both twisted with yarn into his hair where the braids joined. He was not a young man; he had many more years than Corn-Sucker herself, that was obvious. And his face was pitted; smallpox had walked in his lodge, wherever his lodge was set.

There he existed, flexed in menace. The woman saw a shine of weapons. There was metal apparent in the hilt of a knife, the longer grimmer darker metal of the gun that lay within his arm. She saw the wide curve of leather marking a revolver's pouch: this man wore a six-shooter, she had never seen a six-shooter, she had heard of them. (And one time great laughter in the village greeted the tale of men who'd encountered white soldiers armed with cannon and revolvers. They had said that the white men were not content with bringing around a wagon and shooting wagon tongue at them; they must also shoot butcher knife at them. . . .)

Corn-Sucker said nothing to the man for all her fear; it was not suitable that she should speak to him. She was a lone woman working with stony cobs. But slyly she looked again. . . . The man had a hat, but was not wearing it upon his head. It was a black hat, felt, of the slouched variety; it was fastened around his neck by thongs, it hung down upon his neck and upon his back, but he had it crushed against the tree. His eyes were reddened but unmoving, they watched her, they were filmed; and his face was so much the face of a Dakota that it terrified her even more in this knowledge.

He must have come alone to make war.

It was long since a lone Dakota had ventured into their region to make war. It was long since there had been a pitched battle; yet the woman could remember parties of Hidatsa who went out in desultory fashion to steal horses from their neighbors at the south. Neighbors and enemies they were, not the affectionate relatives which Mandan had become.

Now the man spoke to Corn-Sucker in Mandan, to her surprise. He said, You work corn.

Aye.

He said, I watch you alone. In most times women work corn together.

She did not answer, she kept toiling. Her reason told her to be less fearful. The man could not be engaged in making war unless certain Dakota went thus, with no paint on their faces; she had never heard that they did. She did not know that her Hidatsa populace also were Dakota; yet they never called themselves Dakota, they thought that the quarrelsome people to the south were of a different nation. She knew more than a few words of Dakota, because there had been prisoners of that blood in the village when she was young, and one of them was a little boy; she had played with him; she remembered how he used to stand and stare at her mutilated face, and then laugh and run away.

Yes, the man spoke in the Mandan tongue; but it cost him effort to choose the words; they were halting and disarranged as if an idiot spoke. Yet, however fearsome to look upon, he was no idiot. He still sat utterly without motion, watching her.

Presently he asked if she spoke Dakota.

She said, I am Hidatsa.

I know I am in land of Hidatsa and Mandan. Once I live with Mandan.

The stranger added almost comfortably, I kill one of my own people, and so go to live near Mandan or Hidatsa. . . . Why cut short your hair?

My father dies.

A palpitation disturbed the workaday pose of Corn-Sucker's body as she sat beside the heap with face turned down. She felt horror, also fascination . . . she had never seen a man like this . . . she had talked to very few strangers. Twice in her life she had spoken to strangers after she was grown.

Perhaps my people kill you when they find you here.

He spat. I kill them easily when they approach. I have this gun. It has two barrels. I have a pistol-shoots-six, I can kill eight men, before they come to me—before I use knife or bow or club! I am very strong even though I have grown sons!

She went on dutifully with her work, quite unable to rise or stir even if she had been ordered to.

I am the father of twins!

Then he said no more, so that this remarkable fact might lay its egg of thought in her mind, and the thought could hatch and burst forth, and she would appreciate the quality of him who sat near her.

He seemed proud rather than reluctant to state that he was the father of twins. No father of twins whom she had heard discussed was other than perplexed. Everyone knew that twins were mere transitory visitors upon this Earth, that they had lived here before—perhaps had chosen to return (perhaps had returned to Earth for some reason other than choice, but it was a good and important reason) and might decide to leave this mundane existence at any time. Two sets of twins had been born in that village within the memory of Corn-Sucker; but one pair died within a few days after birth (that was understandable: they had gone away, for compelling purpose). Well she remembered the others. They were of repute from the start; everything they said or did was commented upon at length. Perhaps the things they said and did were not much different from the utterances and acts of other children; yet in the case of twins there was simultaneously an urgency, a mystery, and an inscrutable power about their breathing, their running, their talk, their gesticulations. . . . The father of the surviving Hidatsa twins had perished when his pony stepped into a hole while going fast on a hunt; he died before his children were born. Thus it stood that Corn-Sucker had never to her knowledge conversed with the father of living twins, and something in her breast kept fluttering at the mere reflected importance which this conveyed.

One did not know how many times twins had been on Earth before, nor when they would leave, or how; one did not know whether they would come back again, ever. Their sayings and doings were matters of wonder.

Here was the father of twins, before her eyes!

He went into Eastern Dakota speech with excitement when he spoke of his twins. Corn-Sucker was hard-pressed to follow him in this strange tongue. She understood words now and then; she thought that one of the man's twins was named Roaring-Cloud, she could not understand the name of the other. She told the man once again, told him twice, that she was *Hewaktokto* (as the Dakota called her kind) and did not well understand his talk. He continued in a low coarse tone near to a grumble; he spoke as if his lips were frozen. It was a very male tone as well . . . strangely she thought of the rutting elk. She shivered inside, did not move, kept on with her work.

At last the stranger left his squat of concealment, rifle and all, and stood close to her, importunate. He initiated an awkward more intimate conversation. Queries and expressions passed between them in Hidatsa, in Mandan, in Isantie Dakota; even signs were used in some degree. . . . That night, when she was returned to the earthen lodge where she had lived for so long and now dwelt so alone, Corn-Sucker had her recollections of flowers mingled with the picture and sound of sexual savagery among the elk. She did not question this situation. Perhaps it seemed unusual, but also it was unusual to find an armed Dakota squatting beside the community cornfield.

This man remarked on several obvious things, and then went peaceably toward the river. . . .

Naturally although shyly she had inquired of the stranger where he dwelt and what he ate. He had grunted scornfully before he vanished. Corn-Sucker knew that sometimes men did not eat for days when they were on the hunt or making war. This she had heard from Gray-Other-Goose, and many others. As a girl, during the few occasions when war parties went out, she had helped to pack the little balls of sunflower seeds which many of the men wished to carry for provender. . . . Others said that they would not eat until they held enemy scalps in their hands. Others swore that they would not eat until they returned home. Some fanatics declared that they would never eat again; but few people believed this; of course none of the older people believed it. (They had seen too many war parties go off, trotting into night or haze beside the Missouri. People prayed strange prayers and made strange assertions at such times; so also was there weirdness and absurdity in war experience, as in Corn-Sucker's meeting with a slant-faced man in the single patch of the cottonwood shade.)

This notion of cottonwoods recurred to confound her during the night. Cottonwoods were of mystic importance to Hidatsa; it was a profanation for a Dakota to sit in the dark patch made by the tree trunk; would he be punished now, or only if he repeated the offense?

With weary mind and sore fingers the woman lay alone in her bed (not that always she had not been alone in a bed; but now no one else slept in the huge lodge). A smell of burning moccasins from across the way came to strike through her nostrils and fright her senses. In that opposite lodge lived an old man named Saw-Hawk-Carry-Off-Lizard, and he and Gray-Other-Goose had quarreled on several occasions. They had been rivals. Saw-Hawk-Carry-Off-Lizard remained in the debt of the deceased Gray-Other-Goose—a gambling debt. Probably he had harbored that resentment and even fear which debtors so often award to their creditors. At any rate he must have dreaded that a ghost of Gray-Other-Goose would return sometime before the fourth night and penetrate to his bed. There was an efficacious method of protecting oneself from a *nohidahi* under such circumstances. The old neighbor employed this method. He took a pair of discarded moccasins and forced hot coals against them until they stank and smoldered. These reeking smoking things he fastened on a stick outside his door, and they polluted the night. Never would a baleful ghost approach through their stink.

But no longer was Corn-Sucker concerned vitally with memories of her relative gone high and long in the spotted sky, or lurking around the lodge of his youth, or crawling down a pole to feed. Nor did she countenance, by more than merest recognition, any awareness of the surly disgruntled neighbor who scorched old moccasins to protect himself. Her black eyes stared roundly into the empty air of the home. She thought of a big ugly man with hat and braids and rifle, heard the grunting intonation of his talk, heard him scorn her.

He said, You have only half a face.

It was when I was a baby: rocks fell.

He said, I think an enemy does this to you long ago. You are not young.

She bowed, said nothing.

He kept taunting her. No bird ever bite you, no lightning ever strike you. If you are put in water, no fish eat you!

She sat with lowered gaze, tried to keep weaving the tough strands. On any other occasion she would have been aware of the increased pain she was wearing into her raw hand; this day she felt nothing, nothing.

At night, remembering, she had the memory intermingled with illusion of a furious buffalo bull, or a stallion standing on hind legs and striking wildly at the mare with his forefeet as he strove to enter. During a portion of the night Corn-Sucker trotted in a circle of nightmare and agony. Again she offered sacrifices on lonely stones, again she heard the birds say, Eat flowers, Corn-Sucker, and she ate them . . . thus evil spirits came, she felt her mouth swollen.

There could have been release from this fright and confusion had she roused the village when first she came home. She could have gone to the police, the soldiers. She could have said, By the river beyond the cornfield I saw him go. He is a stranger, a Dakota. Armed! Perhaps he comes to make war; he is not painted for war; still I think he is alone!

The men might have gone out and followed him and run him down and killed him. But she was a woman, and lonely and aching and dry; no stallion or bull had ever struck her with his hoofs.

Before the sun came smoking above cold ridges toward the east, she was off to the fields. Of course the stranger returned to her. Once again she became aware of him without seeing his approach. He came when the sun was high; she had begun to fear that he would not reappear at all. Two other women went past soon after Corn-Sucker began her work, seated on the ground. They hovered for a while to gossip, but the scarred maiden did not encourage them to linger. One was a girl who long before had sat with Corn-Sucker on the watchers' stage at that same field; but Corn-Sucker, for all friendly affection of the past, did not wish her to stand there now.

She did not know that the grim Dakota was lying close, weak eyes watching, face pushed through corn stubble, muscles and weapons ready for any approach. Rather did she imagine that he was there, in such position and mood. Finally the women drifted on toward the river, talking as they went. They searched for a lost pony. If they found the pony, Corn-Sucker hoped that they would not fetch it back through the cornfield, and so they did not.

Presently the newcomer emerged as if from earth in the holy cottonwood shade, saying, My name is—

He told the name. He uttered it first in the manner of those Isantie Dakota to which his Wahpekute group belonged. Then, when Corn-Sucker did not understand, could not understand, he grew impatient near to violence. He jeered at her, spoke in Yanktonai, translating at last into Mandan. He said that his name was End-Red, or Red-End; but the name had reference to his maleness, to that male thing which the Dakota called a *che*. When he was a baby a bad spirit had crawled into the tip of his *che* and puffed it hurtfully. He, in baby fashion, screamed constantly; and when a mystery man brought no benefit it was decided to amputate—not the entire end of his *che*—ah, no!—but that fold of skin covering the end. This was done, and blood appeared, bathing the tip of his tiny instrument for some time. *Inkpaduta?* Red-End? It was reasonable for the name to be applied.

The experience of this recital was unique for the busy Corn-Sucker —to hear of that ancient swelling and surgery, and of the unfortunate stranger child who endured the pain. Ordinarily this would have been the talk of men—man speaking to man—not because esssential delicacy prevailed, but because few men would have bothered to speak intimately and lengthily to a woman. It was preferable to speak to men only. . . . Still she could not think of him as End-Red or Red-End; she thought of him as designated by a queer piling up of soft Dakota syllables. She thought of him only as Inkpaduta (and would thereafter, to the limit of the time she spent with him). Had he been Hidatsa and declared that his name was His-Shield, she would have considered him to be His-Shield, for that was what *Itamidaki* meant. Had he termed himself as Sprinkle-Pussy-Willows, she would have thought of him as being so named—*Mashuakazadutoti*. It was the translation of Dakota terminology which built a chore for her; he was not an understandable *Icpuhishi* or Red-End; he was Inkpaduta.

Before noon he said, I need a woman.

She held her eyes fastened against her knees and against the corn, watching her fingers work.

Aye, I have many winters; still I am not an old man, still I need a woman.

Corn-Sucker murmured weakly, in at least pretended humble fright: You say you are the father of twins. Where is the mother of the twins?

She dies, frozen to death long ago. Beside a river, many sleeps from here.

You have other wives.

Sometimes I have many wives. No woman with me now.

He paused as if brooding on misfortunes, and then made her understand that he might call her Half-Face, but still he wished her to come with him. Because she was a woman.

She inquired falteringly, Why think you I would leave my people and go with you?

You come; or I take the butt of this gun, I smash your head. Later carrion birds assemble. Then your people find you here!

Corn-Sucker was dizzy with terrified wonder at these two remarkable meetings in these two most remarkable days of her life. . . . She feared to be struck upon the head. She knew that this man was capable of killing her; she did not wish to be killed; she would rather go with him and take what was offered.

She did not lift her head. She said, I come.

It occurred to her that in fact his face was uglier than hers. At least one half of her countenance was a beauty, or so she had been told when young, so she had always believed. This Dakota evinced unpleasantness not only of pockmarks but of character. There was nothing in his disposition or manner which a woman might worship except his stressed masculinity. Eyes were cruel, mouth cruel, the entire attitude pompous and overbearing. He would have seemed besotted had it not been for his extreme height—well over six feet when he stood. (Corn-Sucker did not measure in feet or inches, but she knew that he stood taller than the watchers' platform set above the tattered broken cornstalks. He could have stood at one side of a powerful buffalo and his head would have been apparent above the hump.) He bragged of strength and murders, uttered threats. There was no doubt that he would beat her; but he would do more than that because he said that he needed a woman. She tried to tell herself that she had no choice. Yet concealed voices of custom were crying, Ah, Corn-Sucker, yes, there is a choice. You should go back to the village now; he'd not dare to kill you. If he shot, twould bring the men and they'd pursue him. If he did not shoot, but struggled with you, you might yell; resultingly the men would rush with their bows and knives. Some Hidatsa he might kill, the others would kill him soon!

. . . She had eaten flowers as instructed by the meadowlark. The meadowlark had said nothing whatsoever about time; she realized that now. Many many snows had come since that day. It was so long ago: even Gray-Other-Goose had not been dried to a husk then. He had sat outside the lodge with his chest bare, proud of the broad straight pattern of his tattooing; he had more tattoo marks than his neighbor across the way—his rival. He had sat in sun in those days, speaking advice and anecdote to all . . . so long ago . . . the meadowlark said, Eat flowers, Corn-Sucker. And she had eaten them.

Now a man arose as from the soil—even a man of middle age, and dangerous—but he was the father of twins. Corn-Sucker considered the bull animals. . . . He had ordered her to go with him, she had said that she would go. Her heart told her that no other mate would ever grow from dust to sit in the sacred cottonwood shadow, and brag and threaten and tempt and bluster at her. She waited as she had sat the day before, as she had sat long ago when a girl, on the stage—sat with legs bent along the right side of her body, feet turned out in their worn moccasins, sat with thin soft blackened hide of her garment gracing a body which had never fattened and distended as did the bodies of most older women . . . perhaps that was because she had had no children, had no man.

No longer were her pinkened hands busy with the sere husks.

If the *maku*, the cottonwood, let him lounge in region of its trunk (unnecessary now for protecting coolness because the weather was not hot, but necessary for concealment from the eyes of the village)—if the cottonwood let him, an outlander, remain without blemish or blight or a furious twitch of its motionless branches—then indeed that must be a sign. Cottonwoods did not belong to Dakota; they belonged to Hidatsa, as in turn Hidatsa belonged to the cottonwoods. Everyone knew that. Corn-Sucker herself had heard many small entities in a great cottonwood, crying. It would happen when rough tearing froth of the brown Missouri came gnawing against soft banks; and sent a great trunk leaning, tilting farther, until finally it lurched wallowing with a roar, a snapping of branches, a last futile tossing of green-dressed limbs. But still it would be retained by roots to anchorage in the bank, until the river had its way with the thing; that was when you could hear babies wailing. Corn-Sucker had stood near with other young people and listened to the crying, she had it identified to her by elders. Frail voices would squeal as long as the thing lay tethered to an original area where it had grown. Then one by one the ropes of roots would snap; at each snap there ensued a nodding and bowing of the hulk, and finally with a last ripping the thing would go churning off, putting its gray head down, lifting again, twirled and twisted by the flood. Then the cottonwood spirits would fall silent; they might mourn no longer, not when roots were broken. But their tremulous tiny lamentation, identified to all above the Missouri's mumble, was something to make you start and shudder as you heard it, something to haunt your dreams.

Corn-Sucker did not believe that a cottonwood wished to speak to a Dakota. No more had she believed earlier that a sacred Hidatsa *maku* dared permit a foreigner (often they were avowed enemies, these Dakota; at best they were traders who came to buy corn in the autumn; and even then they were watched with suspicion) to lounge and shelter without protest.

There must be a promise in the unique rupture of a belief . . . she feared to reckon further at the moment.

Inkpaduta was speaking to her impatiently.

Go to village.

I go, she said abjectly.

You bring to me a robe—nay, two robes. Have you two robes?

I bring them.

You make packs of them, for you to carry. But you must not come while sun is still here— People see you! I find you here at night. Fetch food for journey. You have meat?

There has been no one in our lodge to kill meat. I have dried squash.

He gave a growl of discontent.

I have *mapasipisa*. Or *mapi*.

What is that?

It is the seed of sunflowers. They are good. I make them into balls. Men take them on the hunt and to war.

Inkpaduta was silent, but he appeared to accept this offering before it was given actually.

I have corn.

Is corn ground?

I can grind it. I will grind it.

He said in that frequent colloquial present tense of the Dakota: Tonight I am here. All your people in village go to their beds, and I am here. I am two coyotes. I call to you as two coyotes call. It is when all dogs bark . . . I am dog-coyote calling, she-coyote answering, dog-coyote calling. Then you come.

In this way coyotes and their breeding mingled with other assemblages of lustful animals in Corn-Sucker's mind. When she lifted her frightened but entranced gaze, Inkpaduta was gone. She did not know where he had faded—into the corn perhaps, or into brown dirt itself.

V

After he could honestly put the title of Doctor in front of his name (when he was nearly twenty-one years of age) Isaac Harriott considered that a crucial week of his student career occurred during the fifth month after he began his apprenticeship under Doctor Maws. Illinois was especially glum and raw through that November; and the chill would have been bearable and not depressing were skies clean and winds fresh. But despondent clouds lay like a weight on village and on heart. Isaac Harriott had never dwelt away from home before. He loved his home, and tormented himself with visions which included everything from the dog Scud (who was not permitted to accompany his young master to Doctor Maws' residence) to his mother's apple pickles; and back again to Father's ardent hymns, a favorite patchwork cushion across which Isaac used to sprawl while reading, and the cat Bounty with her four kittens in a box.

Isaac Harriott, called commonly Harry, was sixteen years and two months old. His own home was at the other end of the village of Pekin, and it might just as well have been in Pekin, China.

. . . But can't he live at home, Doctor, and go back and forth?

. . . Not the right thing to do, Mr. Harriott: an apprentice should be with his preceptor, waking or sleeping. That's the way of it.

. . . But Harry says he'd come, early mornings, whatever hour you require him, and stay as late as you have need.

. . . Suppose I need him in the middle of the night? Part of a prentice's chore is to take care of the horse, so who's going to hitch up for me? You've got to remember this, too: I like your Harry, and he appears intelligent and eager, and I'm willing to take him on. But if he went to read medicine elsewhere—say in Springfield with Doctor Haygood or up at Peoria with Doctor Cantwell—they'd tax him possibly fifty or a hundred dollars per year to read with them; and I'm not charging Harry one red cent!

(Once poor Scud had seen or heard or smelt Harry riding past with Doctor Maws, and he ran after the equipage, barking and leaping and hollering until the fat horse reared, and Doctor Maws made Harry get out and send the dog home—and Harry actually had to threaten Scud with the whip to make him go!)

In excess of this grief was the fact that Harry's bosom friend Sylvester Tracy marched off to California with parents and uncles, with every chance of meeting wild Indians, wild horses, gold, Mexicans, grizzly bears, or maybe the whole lot of them. And the meek-eyed girl Harry'd liked so well at merrymakings in St. Louis the year before was now rumored to be affianced to a steamboat pilot: she was going to be grown up—a wife, a married lady in a home of her own—and here he was in peonage, still held to be a boy. An errand boy, a mere stable groom— A stableboy—

Harry, lad, you seem upset, you're just looking at your book, never turning a page; do you find Hahnemann that dull indeed?

Oh, no, sir!

Harry, lad! I would never say that homeopathy has every answer, any more than I would say that every answer will be found in time; but Hahnemann is an important figure in the medical profession, and should bear attentive reading for that reason if for no other, and look at what's happening back in Ohio! They have in all truth summoned a homeopathic teacher to a chair in the Cincinnati Eclectic Institute!—

Have they—really?—

Lad, you're fretting, fretting silently: speak up!—

Well, it's— It's just that— I was thinking, whilst I was getting down Brownie's bedding straw a while ago— If I *had* gone to medical college, instead of—

Very well, Harry, which college?—

I—I hadn't thought, sir. But—

Suppose for a starter we take some place not too far distant such as Illinois College, down at Jacksonville? That'll do, they opened their medical school there five or six years ago, I recall that they gave free tuition to any students who promised to become missionaries: a most praiseworthy and Christian enterprise, you see! And where's the medical school now, even if they did graduate forty students or so? Tis closed down, tight; and why?— Because Doctor Prince became too flagrant in his activities of *resurrection!*

But, sir, I'd not thought of Jacksonville. I'd heard about Franklin, up to St. Charles. They've a very fine faculty, I'm told—

Harry, lad, for one they've had Delamater; and some of his worst detractors suggested that he should have been one of the first patients in his own new madhouse! Not that I agree totally in that opinion; but, for your information; the Franklin Medical College is no more—

No more?—

Maybe you haven't heard, but I have; tis closed down, shut up, closed tight as the one in Jacksonville. And why, again? More *resurrection!* They had a famous brawl over that, I assure you: tis rumored that several students were shot dead when a mob of people attacked the school; and tis a positive fact that Doctor George Richards got a bullet through his lung!—

Oh, Doctor Maws, please— I don't mean to seem ungrateful for this —this opportunity. You're most patient, sir, and— And Mrs. Maws is good to me and— I like old Brownie; I don't mind currying him, and cleaning out his stall— It's only that— Well, I thought that a certificate from a bona fide medical school might—

To begin with, Harry, you're too young. Take Rush, in Chicago: you can't graduate unless you're twenty-one; then—you've got to have three years of study with a respectable physician—that's their very word for it: respectable—do you consider me to be respectable? . . . And what of the finances? You've got to take two courses of lectures; and do you know the price?— Sixty dollars for a sixteen weeks' course!— Don't gape, lad—you heard me correctly— Yes, sixty dollars, to say nothing of a five-dollar charge for dissecting, and a graduation fee of twenty dollars in the end; and think you that your father could undertake that financial burden?— And what of your found, your living, all your expense while dwelling in Chicago? Hundreds of dollars, Harry; that's what twould cost!

. . . Doctor Maws was no figure to inspire immediate trust or affection in strangers. When new residents summoned him for help and then saw the face and bearing of the man on whom they'd need to depend, they were apt to feel an alarm and a sinking. They had not expected a pouter pigeon to come to them in their affliction, and he was a pouter pigeon who had come. Doctor Maws was only boy-sized as to stature (the sixteen-year-old apprentice Harriott fairly towered above him) and though his shoulders were broad his broken chest pushed forward like a bird's breast. His neck was bent sharply backward, and then sharply forward again; roosting on this forward projection was the thick head, dressed in curly white hair—narrow eyes, deep-set eyes, broad flattened nose, and a broad mouth from which issued a continuous high-pitched jet of loquacity. Doctor Maws (he was fond of reporting it, himself) had been run over by a herd of frightened cattle when he was a boy; and he was pounded and dragged until people thought that the resultant bloody pulp would never rise again. It was his childhood of wretched invalidism, and eventual recovery into this aggressive distortion, which named him to be a physician. During his career he had encountered savants and charlatans, and seemed to have learned something from both camps. He had known and worked beside every notorious or noteworthy practitioner from Richard Carter to Daniel Drake, if his stories could be believed. There was very little reason for not believing them; the perpetual flow of anecdote had the bite and ring of actuality. . . . People complained that Doctor Maws' fees were too high; but he shrilled that such was his scale, and he was bound to stick to it and to raise his prices proportionately as the buying power of a shilling decreased. Down in Springfield, for instance, Doctor Haygood and the others were charging one dollar for a daytime visit in town; but Doctor Maws was charging a dollar and a quarter; and for travel up to four miles they were charging two dollars whereas Maws charged two-fifty. The fact that the bulk of these fees defied collection did not enter into the picture: it was the principle of the thing. Springfield doctors charged one dollar for verbal advice, and Doctor Maws charged nothing at all; but he reserved the right to give any weird verbal advice which struck his fancy; and if he did not like the applicant, or considered him deleterious to community decency, he was apt to suggest the bloodcurdling recipes and routines of witchcraft. . . . In time most families came to appreciate Maws' courage, directness, and persistency; it was a relief to see him swaggering up the path, his bent arms swinging as if flexed for a fight, the thick jaw lifting from its seat against the pushed-out chest to spew forth a jargon of anecdote, reminiscence, history, quackery, direction, general reassurance. Children especially were devoted to him, and some of the smaller and simpler-minded of these considered him one with themselves: he seemed so like a waddling little boy dressed up in grandfather's clothing. A tiny ailing girl was told by her mother that Doctor Maws was coming to see her; whereat the invalid chirped, Oh, isn't that nice!— And if I get better we can go coasting together in my little wagon! . . . He exuded that greatest comfort of all: the comfort and sustaining fiber which rise from a source totally unexpected, and mingle a humor and a bantering, and suggest that both life and death are jests to tickle the fancy.

That was Isaac Harriott's low ebb: the night when in inexcusable infantile homesickness he whined that he should have gone to medical school instead. By the first of the year it would have taken a keg of gunpowder to blow him away from Doctor Maws' side.

Maws found in the stripling a courtesy and an easy masculine charm which he himself had never owned—would never have owned in nature, even if the mooing herd had not slammed his body into gargoyle shape. He looked up Harry's birth date, and saw that he was barely over the line from Virgo into Libra (the same mind which clung secretly to certain incantations and simples might still embrace an application of astrology). He saw in this bony young face an embodiment of Librans' talents and virtues, saw the boy eventually measuring human justice as well as healing drugs in the traditional scales of his own Sign. He liked Harry's patience, his love of animals and affection for the queerer cattle of the human race, his native fairness, his quick admission of private weakness, his drollery—the social shyness which verily would make him sought after socially the older he grew. Physically he admired the crisp short-cut hair, the solemn wide gaze, the ranginess of a body which appeared next door to frailty and actually was tough as braided string. All the doctor's own children had died in infancy or in early childhood (Physician, heal thyself!) and perhaps for this reason as well as for his devotion to eccentricity, the doctor had been unwilling to take any youth to read medicine with him until Harry came his way.

It was not unlikely that Doctor Thomas Maws was the first medical practitioner in the State of Illinois to carry a stethoscope in his saddlebag.

Isaac Harriott thought that it would be impossible to set down the doctor's monologue honestly as the stream pattered forth. Maws reminded the boy of only one other person he had ever met: a gardener who sold produce from door to door in St. Louis, and would ripple out the list of edibles, as he stood with baskets on the step, and cart waiting behind him, as if there were no such things as punctuation or diction or a squandering of human breath in all existence . . . I got lettuce radishes onions beets carrots peas beans corn potatoes what you want today lady?— Isaac Harriott thought that he should like to capture at least some portions of Doctor Maws' eternal discourse; and—weary in late night, with eyes falling shut—Harry tried to scribble it from memory in an old copybook. But the effect was not there, it was all too elusive. The prattling narrative, the wisdoms, tomfooleries, stupidities—the crusading holinesses—they were commingled like shreds of cabbage in a salad bowl. There was no separating one crimped piece from another. The man rambled and damned and admired and lamented and praised and prophesied and scouted in one protracted exhalation; you could lift the true from the false, the godly thing from the iniquitous, only if you sat at Doctor Maws' feet or rinsed the pewter bedpan beside him. No one might perform such office whose flesh had never been touched by Maws' flesh, who had never shared the same air.

(Harry was engaged with a dream one night. He owned a machine, a bright buzzing chunk of mechanism with sparkles of electricity winking out of it; and attached to this machine was a tube with a horn on the end. He held the horn before Doctor Maws' blurring mouth and said, Talk, please. . . . What for, Harry, lad? . . . For posterity, sir! Your own voice will be recorded permanently by this strange means. . . . And— Oh, more wonder of wonders in the dream! The doctor's mouth opened obediently, but all was silence which came forth, the doctor could not speak a word while confronted with this intrusive invention! . . . Isaac Harriott awakened laughing; and later counseled himself earnestly to refuse such vain dreams in the future, and to concentrate his waking and sleeping energies upon anatomy and *materia medica* and the proper way to hold a pulsimeter or to squeeze a syringe.)

. . . Then this fellow had ridden with me possibly three miles when next thing I knew he pulled out a pocket pistol, put it tight against my side; says, Your money or your life. I says, I got to hold the horse; tis dark and stormy and he's fractious and I daren't let the reins slip, young man. There's a silver dollar next that old snuffbox in my small pocket and maybe six or eight coppers in the big pocket, so take my money, but if you don't spare my life there's Mrs. Arabella Beecher's you'll be fetching along with you too, for they say she's bad took and it may be a case for the knife; least I've got to bleed her. He looked at me for a long time, then lowered his weapon and asked, Be you a doctor? I says, Be I anything else? Says he, I got a misery all the while in my gut. Feel here!—and I felt and twas a tumor big as a goose egg or nigh so. Says I, Can't do a thing for you now, but if you promise to take shelter in them pines I'll pick you up on the way back. Twas twilight when I returned but he was still there; and to shorten a long tale I drove him back to the village, put him on my sofa, got my niece to hold the pan; and I took out that tumor—twas hard as putty and covered with hair, and the patient bled less than a pint. Kept the tumor in a jar for years but twas lost when we had the fire in Kentucky; and every Christmastide that robber wrote me a letter of blessing and thanks; but last one was from a jail in New Orleans, so I reckon he was hanged in the end. . . . Unhealthy place, they say, though I've never visited it. But well do I recall also what was written of Michigan, how when citizens first plowed the land they thus set free the malarial gases, and how the people did sicken and quake. *Don't go to Michigan,* the poet wrote, *that land of ills; the word means ague, fever and chills.* But when the epidemic erysipelas struck the country some six-eight years agone, twas infinitely worse in Indiana than in Michigan! As a boy I was instructed that birch catkins should be collected on a Friday morning, without your speaking to a soul first, and then they should be rubbed upon the affected parts. Never tried it, though, for Granny had a better treatment than that; and Doctor Hathaway taught me more. Hathaway, by the by, had been acquainted with Elisha Perkins—he was the tractor man—invented and manufactured and peddled the Perkinese Tractors for extracting disease from the body—little rods of metal they were, and sold for a handsome sum, and they do say that George Washington himself bought a set of them, and they do say that Perkins and his son Ben made a colossal fortune out of the tractors; and I've known of people still peddling very similar contraptions from house to house, right under our noses.

. . . Man like Daniel Drake would go hog-wild momentarily if you but mentioned the fakes like Perkins. You'd think he'd seen enough stupidity in mankind to rob the matter of its shock; but Drake's a highly hearty man with an awful fire burning. He's still professor at the Louisville Med Institute and I received a letter from this great man only a month agone. How I wish everybody could hear him at his lecturing!—when he was speaking in Cincinnati twas a thing to hear, and people not even in his classes would slip into the room and stand there rooted just to catch the majesty of the man. He was like a preacher when he really felt the power a-working, and he'd sway and bend and his voice would rise like a wind, like a hurricane wind. He was just a human cyclone a-lecturing; and I've seen carpenters and masons at work on the place put down their tools and come with a scamper to hear Doctor Drake, although when he spoke of humoral pathology they'd never know what he meant, and when he talked of reading Quincy's dispensatory and grinding quicksilver into *unguentum mercuriale* he could have been speaking Shawnee for all they got out of it. But it was just the eloquence and passion of the man that charmed their souls, and maybe they went away as better men for merely being there before him. Ah, how he loves to quote the masters of the past and quote himself into the bargain. Ah, Harry, lad, am I a fit preceptor? *It is not necessary,* says old Daniel Drake, *that a preceptor should be a man of genius, but it is indispensable that he should possess a sound and discriminating judgment, otherwise he will be a blind guide. . . . A man of sound morals and chastened habits* . . . and I've forever been too busy to play with fleeting lecheries. Put a man's nose to the grindstone and keep it there, and where's the gaming and where's the wining and where's the looseness? And in medical pursuit I've had my principles: away with the disgust, away with the horrors, keep them for the root doctors and the Indian men and the grannyizing! I can make a good eyewash from March snow with the next man; and you've seen the buckeye that I carry in my pocket, and I've never suffered recurrence of the rheumatiz since I started to carry it. But I've never recommended scrubbing out your mouth with your own piss in order to clean your breath and cure the malady of your gums; and I've never counseled a woman with a goiter to approach a corpse and have the cold dead hand lifted and placed upon the swelling. Never told a soul to evacuate his corns by rubbing them with a cotton rag and then hiding the rag in a coffin with a body soon to be put away; never told a man suffering with the galloping consump to suck the teat of a healthy woman! Tis done and tis preached and tis believed by silly folk and maybe by some who aren't so silly; but tis not in my pursuit or habit. No more than I'll plug a hollow tooth with tinfoil, for the bad humors are still there in its roots and they're bound to exude, foil or not; and if the pullikin can't reach the rotten tooth, no matter how tight you fasten the grip, then I'd much prefer to call in some strong men to hold the patient fast whilst I sliced the gum open and yanked the root loose from his jaw.

. . . Yes, yes—I've done it so, more times than I can count—and I have met with hemorrhage I couldn't stem with any power I knew, and so I've seen the patient pass away, and heard myself called Butcher. And I have been greeted with suppuration and usually could cope with that if I was fortunate. But never did I bring about intended or prolonged suppuration with a seton or by any other means of irritation. There's that Jew down in Kentucky—we've got him on the shelf, and I recommend him to you, Harry, lad, most wholeheartedly. Rosenstein's the name and you should read his *Theory and Practice of Homeopathy* even if you never plan to embrace the practice. *The time is passed,* says Rosenstein, *when a judicious practitioner can ever think of such a thing as doing any good by a prolonged suppuration.* Does that make sense to you? Go think on it—but remember too that a fistula not artificially induced but resulting from the original traumatic injury to the patient has served its purpose heretofore. How else would Beaumont have achieved his digestive studies? Tis a good fifteen years since he published his *Experiments and Observations on the Gastric Juice and the Physiology of Digestion* but nobody's been able to add much to it since. And all because a half-breed French Indian up on the Lakes got himself plugged in the belly with a load of coarse shot, and the fistulous opening in his stomach never healed! There was Beaumont, taking the patient into his own home when the authorities said that they could pay for the patient's keep no longer, and watching the half-breed's digestive apparatus through the fistula, year after year. Drake says a good doctor should be *devoted to his profession, jealous of its character, ambitious of its honors,* so that young Doctor Beaumont measured up, or who's to say he didn't? . . .

So it continued in all hours and seasons—the sharp voice cracking away, the fund pouring out, the recollective lancet slicing a fresh fat vein when the old one had flattened. Here was drama and philosophy to mark a young man's hours; and it was not remarkable that Isaac Harriott still heard Doctor Maws' voice in his sleep, long after that voice had fallen silent, long after snores were arising from the old people's chamber, after their midnight village was spread cold and leafless to the stare of the moon.

It was as if Mrs. Maws had given up talking years before, because of her obvious inability to get a word in edgewise: she was grown into a placid chunky creature with oily silver ringlets of the same brightness as her husband's. Seldom did she speak a word (except when testifying at prayer meeting) beyond necessity. Breakfast's ready; cat wants out; Harry, tell Doctor to fetch me some salt from the store; need another scuttle of coal; Harry, here's a pan of gingersnaps for you to take to your Ma; give this note from Mrs. Farnsworth to Doctor; the youngest Martin was by—they need some calomel; supper's ready; time for prayers. This was all she ever said or needed to say. Winter or summer, except for the interruption of prayer meeting on Wednesday and evening services on Sunday, Mrs. Maws went to bed at nine o'clock and rose at five. Her husband, like all harried physicians, could maintain no schedule. Since he was considerably older than his wife and since the taxing demands on time and energy were unpredictable, he grew fond of setting a task for Harry, and then going promptly blissfully to sleep, fully clothed even to his boots, on that same sofa where often he performed surgery. An apprentice reading medicine in a doctor's home was expected commonly to assist with household tasks of varying natures, as if he were a son of the family. Isaac Harriott found himself torn between an established domestic routine, on the one hand, and the dangerous—sometimes ludicrous, sometimes dismal—requirements of medical uncertainty, on the other.

Of a Sunday night he would draw water from the cistern by hand, filling three big wooden tubs in readiness for Mrs. Maws' Monday morning washing; then he would get into bed, draw the candle close on its rickety little stand, and prop the *Cyclopaedia of Practical Medicine* before his eyes. He fought a losing battle against the microscopic enemies of dedicated intent which began swarming sleepily into his body through its extremities.

It would be eleven or twelve o'clock, and he would jerk from slumber like a squirrel torn out of its nest by shot . . . the bell!

This was a diabolical invention of Harry's, arranged so that the doctor might not be disturbed by too-foolishly apprehensive young fathers, as happened now and again; or by some seedy and stumbling individual who had lingered too late at Johnny Clark's Tavern House, and who was certain that Doctor Maws alone might protect him from shakes, snakes, and alligators. A card tacked at the front door read, *Night Bell,* and a loop of hempen cord dangled beside it. This cord led aloft through a series of screw eyes set in the front clapboards; it passed through an aperture to operate a cowbell suspended directly above Harry's garret bed.

Stairs crunching under his own tread, tree toads or icy branches weaving mysterious night sounds in their respective seasons; and always a dog barking somewhere up the road, be it winter or July . . . the repeated challenging disapproving *rowff! rowff! rowff!* of a fierce unknown watchdog (no, not his own Scud in the lane on the other side of town!—that was never Scud's honest jolly voice)—a dog who had been disturbed by the passing of hoofs, and who told all of Pekin and attempted to tell all of Illinois that there were trouble and pain and peril riding the wind.

Latch unfastened, the solid wooden door creaking, the white face and nervous eyes glaring back into his candle beam.

Be *you* the doctor?

Nope. He's here, though. What's ado, Mr.?

S'my wife. I'm scairt about her. I rode clean over here from tother side the crick.

What's your name, Mr.?

George Giverby. Maybe you've heard—

(So he had, so had all the community, so did Doctor Maws know: a slatternly cabin where other slatternly tribes had dwelt before this slatternly tribe moved in; family fights, family thrashings; the starved dogs prowling, the unwashed children; the brother said to have been beaten to death by an angry mob in Kentucky; tools alleged to have been stolen from a local wagonmaker and sold, twas said, in order to buy drink; the trial before Justice Souder, the acquittal, the warning, the threat—)

What seems to be the trouble, Mr. Giverby?

She just lays there. But breathing kind of fast, and she don't seem to know me or the younguns. Awhile ago she was kind of groaning. And she—she passed a lot of blood when she did her business, right there in bed. I think—maybe she et something—

Let's see—that's about four miles—

Reckon between three and four—

All right, Mr. Giverby. You head right back home. I'll wake the doctor, hitch up, and we'll be right along! . . .

Always there was such a pride in saying that *we*.

The knocking on the wall beside Doctor's door, the stirring in the bed, the sharp rousing, Yep? which came singing from the gloom. Whispered description and confabulation; then a lamp burning in the doctor's office room as he selected medicines (ah, *that* was the thing! To be able to know chalk from cheese and acetate of lime from sugar of milk, and strychnine from opium . . . to know, to know, to know!) as Harry prodded out a sniffing burbling old Brownie, and hoisted the collar over his head, and felt for tug-slots in darkness. And Harry being well aware, and Doctor Maws being acutely well aware, that whether the patient wakened or not, whether the patient lived or died, whether knife was employed or the lancet, whether there were sweats induced or cold packs wrapped around the pale smelly body, whether rum or rhubarb was forced into the pale smelly mouth— Whether a baby wailed or no, whether a cat jumped up on the bed while Harry was holding the lantern and the doctor working— Whether the husband was drunk or sober when they got there, or when they left— There would be nothing out of it. Not a dime, not a dollar, not a torn scrap of wildcat currency, not a greasy wad of paper with *The Tunis & Harbert Stage Company Agrees to pay to Bearer, on July the First, 1846, or at any date thereafter, the sum of TWO DOLLARS SPECIE* in fancy half-defaced italics, and a picture of a brand-new stagecoach crammed with passengers and drawn by six mettlesome horses— There would be nothing. Just the first angry streak of pink sunrise running like a lash above eastern groves, just lonely breezes twitching the roadside grass . . . and behind them the remembrance of a mumble, the fumbling shake of a knotty clammy hand, the words: Doc, we're kind of hard pressed right now. But I got a young pig penned up—kind of a wild pig that was running in the woods, side the crick. I'll butcher him, come right weather, and bring him by.

(Oh, yes, once in a long while the pig was brought—or a bag of hickory nuts, or a small sack of oats, or a basket of stolen apples. Once in a long while.)

. . . Like I say, Harry, lad, Hippocrates ran up against the same kind of trouble we run up against today—I mean *resurrection* trouble. For the opportunities of dissection were denied to him, the Greeks wouldn't tolerate it, Greeks had what they called too much respect for the human body. But think you I could have handled a case like this one back yonder up the creek, if I hadn't done my share of dissection in my student days—and after? Wouldn't have known where to start, wouldn't have known where to end. So a night like this and a case like this convinces me all the more that as soon as you've absorbed sufficient anatomy and physiology—by the by, you got to remind me to dig out two old ones—Innes on muscles, and Cheselden on bones—and set those two before you— Well, we'll just have to do some cautious *resurrecting* of our own. Does that offend and frighten you, Harry, lad? Needn't bother you too sorely. No, no—you look willing and brisk for the fray; tis light enough now for me to see the glint in your eye, and it makes me chuckle! But we'll have to be cautious and tight-lipped; oh, almighty cautious and tight-lipped!—if we're to have another Old Jupe around. That's what I always call them—cadavers male or female. Old Jupe. Well, Doctor Hathaway used to term them so his own self, so I picked it up from him when I was young. Though land knows where we'll get one; maybe have to make one ourselves . . . now wouldn't that be the ticket? Take that worthless scut back there, her husband, not worth the pinch of powder in the pan to light the charge to shoot him; just a hog wallower and a bully and a bruiser; and I bet a round hundred dollars gold that *he* was the party of the first part who kicked the party of the second part— Kicked her out of bed, like enough. Well, he'd make a rattling fine Old Jupe, he would; but then how'd the children fare? No, Harry, lad, murder's not in my line, though I've been tempted cruelly many's the time—twould be so easy; but then you're setting yourself up to be God Almighty, and He don't like that. Though I have— Oh, well, any doctor'll tell the same story if he's got a grain of honesty and several grains of pity in his nature. Your hand can get heavy with the dose at times, especially when there's a cancer that defiles the very air, and when the eyes look up at you and seem to be a-saying, *Doctor, it hurts so bad— Oh, please to let me rest a while!* Yes, yes— But that's not fitting for student ears to hear nor for student mind to consider. . . . Take care: better give Brownie his head, you like to upset us in the ditch! . . . Well, well. We'll have another Old Jupe in mercy's good time, though I don't fancy getting ourselves shot a-doing it like Doctor Richards did, nor hailed up before the trustees, like those young fellows at Ohio Med some years agone, who were using the hospital patients as fast as they succumbed. But we're in a later time than Hippocrates, so we've got to employ the most modern methods. And that reminds me that his is not the only oath worth recollecting, for any man in our profession. Ever hear of King Louis, ever hear of King Charles? So? They took an oath at Strasbourg about a thousand years ago: *By God's love and the Christian people and our common salvation, as God shall give me knowledge and power*— That's it, you see, well fit to remember. *As God shall give me knowledge and power*— Harry, lad! I told you—look out—the ditch again— Why, there you are, fast asleep whilst you drive!—

Wwwhat? Oh, no, sir— No, sir. I'm not asleep—

Now, don't get wherrited. Brownie knows the way. You just set back easy on the seat, and give old Brownie his head. We'll both take forty winks. Many's the time, before you came to read with me, when I never wakened up until we'd pulled right into the carriage shed and stopped; and then Brownie'd tell me about it, and whicker to be unhitched. . . .

It was not until the following year, the early winter of 1850, that they came into possession of an Old Jupe; though Isaac Harriott had dwelt on the possibility a hundred times, achieving a variety of thrills and horrors in contemplation. (Later he recalled distinctly how he threw down a peeling thick volume on his bed one night, dusted the powder of rubbed calfskin off his hands, and thought in anger: I'm sick of reading about ossicles! I want to *see* an ossicle! . . . sick of reading about *musculi* . . . I want to *see* a muscle.)

It happened in God's own time, as reckoned by Doctor Maws and Harry—or in the Devil's own time, as surely would have been reckoned by the citizenry at large—that a party of movers made camp in a clump of trees a mile or two southwest of town. They were a disheartened group, such as often drifted eastward, shuttling through much more populous packs driving determinedly toward the west. In this case, as was told to a coterie of local residents who gathered sympathetically in an hour of trial, there had figured already a drowning, a claim-jumping, cows struck by lightning, a disastrous fire, and the miseries of endemic fever. Whatever their tribulations, these people were headed for Ohio, nor had grief come to an end now. A man suffered savage pain and shortness of breath, moaned, fell in a coma. . . . Doctor Maws and Isaac Harriott, driving at noon from a lengthy professional tussle in southern regions where the doctor had served successfully as hand-servant at the advent of a fat baby girl, were brought to a stop on the edge of town by Justice Souder. The judge descended from his gig and stood waiting in the road. . . .

Guess you couldn't have done much good, anyway, Doctor. From the way they spoke, he was a goner the moment of the first seizure.

Well, well, sorry I wasn't to hand, Justice. Sounds like an infirm heart from your description. Doubtless a clot in the ventricles—

I drove out there, soon as I heard they couldn't reach you. But twas all over by that time.

Where'd you say they were encamped?

Beside those trees halfway to the Garrett place.

You're confident that the patient was dead?

Certain. I took a look at him myself before I'd permit burial. I've seen many dead ones, you may be aware, in my previous capacity as High Sheriff!—and Justice Souder twisted up a thick satanic eyebrow with the pardonable pride of a man who had served in many official positions including the Legislature.

You say they buried him on the spot?

Actually, there didn't seem any reason for them not to. They were shy on funds, hoped to make their victuals last until they reached Ohio; so I felt twould be cruelty to protract the formalities. That land there has been entailed—you know, the big fuss between McCullough and a Swede named Hanson?—and neither one of them's in these parts any longer. Twould take Millard Fillmore himself to figure out just who that grove does belong to. So I said, Proceed with your interment. I saw to it that they piled on some rocks afterward. Twouldn't do, to have dogs or hogs digging around there.

No indeed!—agreed Doctor Maws wholeheartedly. He fell into a rare and complete silence for the rest of the journey. Harry was thankful for that, since he was occupied with his own thoughts; they were akin to the visions of a youngster who dreams about squibs and Catherine wheels on the eve of the Glorious Fourth.

When they turned in at the driveway beside the Maws house, the doctor shook himself and snapped his thumb against his finger.

Harry, lad.

Yes, sir.

Stead of your measuring out salts and papering them, after we've fed, do you get the light wagon into a state of readiness. This buggy—

He thrust his head close to Harry's, and made severe faces, winking both eyes, wrinkling his mashed nose.

—This buggy's got the fantods. Did you hear how twas squeaking a moment ago? I'm afraid that axle's going to give way again, and we dare not be bereft of transportation. So best to prepare the wagon. The wagon wheels need grease, too, or they'll scream like all possessed. Think you can turn the trick single-handed? Best for me to catch a nap.

Yes, sir! I can shove a couple of sawbucks underneath, and take off each wheel in turn. They're light in weight—

Axle grease in that old bucket just inside the door, and it has a paddle in it! In addition, we wish to take no chance of getting mired down, case we get a call out beyond those marshes somewhere; so you'd better put a shovel and a spade—maybe the old pickaxe—in the wagon. Oh, yes—there's also a coil of half-inch rope hanging next the grain chest. Better put that in the wagôn too. And— And what about Brownie's blanket? The old one that the rats got to?—

Tis bundled up, tied and hanging in a loop of wire, just as you bid me to do it, replied Harry, with sharp-footed delicious chills marching up and down his spine.

Well, that should be stowed in as well. Can't ever tell about these sloughs in early winter: we might need the rope, case we had to be hauled out. Might need the blanket, case we had to spend the night on the prairie. Course, the surface is froze solid just now, but I don't think frost has yet penetrated too deep. But you can't ever be sure, can't ever be sure!— Harry, lad, do you look after Brownie. I'll have the Mrs. keep your meat and potatoes hot on the back of the stove.

Sir—

Yes, lad? and Maws went through the recurrent hurting discipline of swinging his bent short-legged shape to the ground.

What—what about—Mrs. Maws?—

Oh, yes, indeed! There was another matter—

Doctor Maws interrupted Harry with a cackle of surprise at his own omission.

It's just this, Harry: for some time now I've been planning to have a laboratory. Twould be more convenient for both of us whilst you're reading with me; wonder that I never mentioned it before! Course, tis very dark, and we'll need to illuminate with coal oil— I refer, of course, to the old buttery next the woodshed. See—right over there—under the big elm? Even got a stove in it; I guess the Daggs' hired man used to sleep there before I purchased this place from them. Nice thing about a laboratory, you know—and I haven't had one in years—But tis the privacy of the thing— No intrusions, none *whatsoever.* I always place a small sign on the door telling the nature of the place, and mentioning poisonous drugs and acids should some prowler grow inquisitive. And then, you realize, a big strong hasp and a good padlock— There's a bar on the inside of the door, too. That hired man must have been scairt of burglars!

He went at his strutting limp away from the buggy, then turned suddenly and came back. He leaned, Harry had to bend down to hear the words.

One thing a medical man should prize above all else, lad: the companionship and understanding of a sympathetic helpmate! So I do hope you're fortunate enough to acquire one when the time is ripe and intended. A woman who doesn't come messing around your life with silly female nosiness—who doesn't come prying inquisitively into your medicine bag *or* your laboratory. Yes, indeed—that's the sort of woman to be gifted with!

And above all, Harry, lad, above all: a religious woman—one who has undying faith in the power and beneficence of Jehovah—a clear and firm belief in the Hereafter— And in the Resurrection, Harry. The glory and necessity of *resurrection!* . . .

Late that night a note was placed on the house door, a note declaring: *Doctor gone on case. Back at daylight.* Sometime after two o'clock in the morning, Harry guided Brownie to a safe halt behind cottonwoods. He and Doctor Maws got down from the wagon and investigated in different directions through the trampled whiskers of grass until Harry nearly stumbled over a long-shaped pile of assembled stones. In dull red light of their masked lantern, Maws read aloud the inscription printed laboriously in blunt lead-penciled capitals on a broken piece of board. HEER LIES JOS. HATCHAW BRN WESTFIELD N.J. 1803 DIDE ILLNOY DEC 5 1850. Isaac Harriott found himself praying very hard for the soul of a lonely obscure poverty-stricken individual who had endured his last pangs in a cold wind without either doctor or preacher at hand. He held the thought (yet in an immediate instant refused to admit or countenance it) that if Doctor Maws had said, Well, lad, let's not disturb him after all, he came far, let him sleep unprovoked— If Maws had scattered but a crumb of this thought in Harry's direction, the youth would have led a rapid retreat and with high and thankful heart.

But the doctor only whispered: Yep, here tis. Don't scatter the rocks far and wide. We've got to set them back in place.

Yes, sir, came a curdled whisper. . . . And then, while shifting little boulders away from the tomb. . . .

Dddoctor—

Don't talk so loud, lad! Road's just over there a piece. What is it?

He's from—New Jersey. Same as me. Westfield. That's not far from Bound Brook where I was born.

You two traveled a long piece to meet, didn't you? . . . Guess these clods aren't froze too tight together yet. Bust them loose with the pick, Harry, when you're rid of the rocks. I'll help you shovel. Difficult for me to use a pick; had these adhesions ever since the cattle trampled me when I was small.

. . . *Who shall roll us away the stone from the door of the sepulchre?*

. . . *And came and rolled back the stone from the door.*

. . . *And they found the stone rolled away from the sepulchre.*

. . . *And seeth the stone taken away from the sepulchre.*

. . . *By this time he stinketh.*

Joseph Hatchaw was not buried too deeply. His survivors—his relatives or friends, whatever they were—had possessed apparently neither strength nor time nor will to excavate an orthodox grave.

In hotter weather, whispered Doctor Maws, I reckon dogs would have been attracted to this spot. Or wolves, in the old days. . . . The

Gospels repeated themselves in Isaac Harriott's mind no further—at least with meaning or accuracy—for there was no stench: just a dank chilly smell of gravelly soil, and later the taint of dirty garments which Joseph Hatchaw had impregnated with his own sad dirtiness in life, and which he wore in death. The ghouls slid strands of rope beneath the body and hoisted it out. Maws moved like a gnome of legendry, bending above the corpse and slitting efficiently the bag of rotten canvas wagon cover which served as outer shroud. When the gaunt stubbled countenance had been exposed he knelt down to examine it.

Might or might not be a case of heart stoppage—could have been a stroke. Color of the corpse means nothing after all these hours. Well, we'll see, once we get on the inside of this customer!

He sniffed disapprovingly. And help me, Harry, lad, to rip off these terrible duds of his! We'll put them back in the grave.

More terrified at thought of demonstrating weakness now than he had been terrified by initial revelation, Harry moved willing unpracticed hands about the chore. Coat, shirt, pants, socks worn through, the mockery of underdrawers— Oh, live insects were still creeping sluggishly in underclothing and beard, for all their hours of entombment!— The doctor directed that only the canvas should be retained. This was done, then the whole was covered tightly with Brownie's rat-nibbled blanket. How flat he seems, lying there, Harry kept thinking. How very flat—

Fill her up!

With gratitude the youth shoveled at this task; he worked without cessation, gasping for breath between shovel-loads, making cloddy earth fly in an intermittent stream.

Now we'll rock her up again. And don't forget the marker.

. . . Think that's about the way it was, sir?

Pretty close. Course, the entire mound is slightly lower; I suppose we should have thought of that. When I participated in a resurrection once, back in Ohio, we even put a heavy post into the original coffin—we didn't quite know why, but it seemed that we were fooling somebody. . . . There, that's better now. . . . Oh, move those two whitish rocks up nearer the head. . . . Yes, so. That's how they were. We don't need to worry about these bits of gravel and soil strewn around —they didn't make a very neat task of it, those movers. . . .

The suspicious Brownie spoke critically when they approached lugging the swathed body. Brownie tried to move away with the wagon; but Harry had the horse tied. Maws went to the animal's head to mutter reassurance, once they'd dragged the burden across the tailboard. Harry worked proper concealment with some pieces of old sacking. The tools he placed under this material beside the stolen corpse. Then, blowing out the lantern, they drove toward town.

Brownie tried to break into a nervous trot at first but calmed down before long, accepting a peculiar cargo which he had sensed as being undesirable. To their fright, however, the grave robbers encountered another lantern in the first roadway within the edge of town. It was borne by Justice Souder, and Harry heard the doctor mutter some of his infrequent swearwords while a vague light floated toward them, revolving its design against the ground.

Who's there? demanded Doctor Maws. Harry's hands were shaking so badly that he could scarcely hold the ribbons.

Souder. Who's that? Sounded like Doc Maws—

Tis me, all right. Been on a case—

Oh.

The lantern was beside them now, Justice Souder holding it higher to illuminate their faces and his own.

Didn't recognize your rig, Doctor!

Oh, I thought I'd have to ford a stream or two, and the buggy's getting weak.

Who's sick?

Another plaguèd wagonful of movers. They sent a boy on horseback. They'd seen my sign when they came through town today.

(That was safe enough. Any season, cold or hot, except during worst storms, there were always strangers driving through Pekin—and through every other town in Illinois, it was supposed.)

Anything serious?

Oh, a fat old man concluded he was snakebit in his blankets; but tis just a pure and simple case of gout. My land, how he did howl when I examined him! Didn't he, Harry, lad? Really howl?

He—surely did—sir—

Trouble in a situation like this is that gout requires steady and conscientious treatment, so there wasn't much I could do for him beyond administering sulphate of morphia. A respectable outfit: they paid without a murmur. Bound only as far as Louisa County, Ioway—just beyond the Mississippi—so the patient can accept protracted treatment very soon. What are you doing out at this unearthly hour, Justice?

Souder laughed. That nuisance of a cat—the one we call Cinnamon. He's the pride of the Mrs., though I'd be just as happy if Cinny never showed up again. He wasn't home to supper—hadn't been home all day—and the Mrs. is in a state. She was fretting and grieving, couldn't lay quiet. So I says, Tarnation, woman, I'll go and *look for* the blame critter! Probably got in a fight or a courting spree somewhere; he's big enough and old enough for such jinks now, though the Mrs. thinks not, thinks he's still a kitten—

Neither of the grave robbers spoke until they were safe in the Maws barn. Then the dry-lipped boy said: Close call, sir, wasn't it?

Not so close. Wait'll you hear a dose of buckshot singing nigh as I've heard it—then twill be close! . . . Harry, lad, we daren't leave Old Jupe in the wagon, count of the rats. We'll carry him into the *laboratory*, lock him safe, and if we can catch an interval during the day we'll wash him clean and pickle him.

How—how's that, sir?

Oh, I'll mix a splendid alcoholic pickle, I assure you. Ever notice that long flat box up here on the rafters? There—throw the light—Just past the old hayrakes? That's the one. Lined with thin zinc, watertight, and has been employed before this.

Yes, sir. Want me to get her down now?

Safer in daylight, said the doctor succinctly; and soon Old Jupe, formerly Joseph Hatchaw, was ensconced in his shed, and soon the sinners were in bed.

It was because he felt so severely like a sinner, in fact, that Isaac Harriott tossed and rolled. He thought of Mrs. Souder, twitching sleeplessly in her worry about an errant cat, and he sought to find amusement in the notion; but he could not even smile to himself. He had scrubbed long above the big kitchen basin, but still he imagined that oil of death stained his entire being obscenely. From the narrow stairway he heard a steady pulsation of Doctor Maws' snores resounding; the doctor slept proudly and sanely as if he were fresh come from a delivery, an amputation, a noble administering of generous skills.

Harry considered prison, ostracism, community hatred; yet these possibilities did not itch him so severely as the realization that he had done a thing which not even Hippocrates dared do . . . were the Greeks correct in their belief? Was the consecration of burial a rite so pure that the man who rifled a resting place must walk forever condemned by his own knowledge of the fact, even though the world was none the wiser?

In distressed seeking for excuse, for shriving, he could feel the grim process of maturity overpowering. Some became men earlier, some later; and this passion which swept Isaac Harriott had descended early in his eighteenth year. Would he ever dare to pursue the investigation of flesh on which, only a few hours earlier, he had been so keenly determined? Would—would he dare to hold the knife?—

An answer to perplexity came and whispered over his wrinkled pillow shortly before sunrise. He got up and stood on half-frozen naked feet beside the tiny window, watched the dawn; it was not intrinsically a beautiful dawn; but quickly the youth found heart as he stared into gray soft smokiness. Night, long hardening the world with its black, had lifted once more. There was indeed a thing called resurrection, and not solely the Holy re-emergence of another age. There was a process called eternal life, it should be recognized by all. For a vermin-ridden beast of a human could, when approached by dedicated soul and hands, contribute to enrichment of the life he had left.

Here was the shed, down yonder, here roosted Old Jupe. His life was nothing of account, he went out in doleful futility, had not stored up a dime or an acorn; it seemed unlikely that he had ever sung a song or viewed a beauty. His people broke the clods, tumbled them over him, fled away. He was a fruitless and pathetic botch of the humanity to which he might have attained, were Fate more kind, had God not been too busy, had winds blown differently.

But whereas his soul was in certainty as emasculated by starvation as his body, that wizened body might now become a treasure. Oh, dear Lord, prayed Harry, let me be an instrument in Thy hands, as I hold the tempered sharp instrument in my own! Let a child lie docile instead of wailing, let a mother cough no more, let a strong man—smitten by wheels and lightnings and bullets—regain power, let him flex his brave muscles again. All because I know, I know, because I *shall know!* Thy Old Jupe shall aid in teaching me, the evil thing shall become an honor again.

VI

Corn-Sucker reasoned that Inkpaduta had been spawned by the soil, and was now for the moment returned to it. So it was fitting that Corn-Sucker should be surrounded by earthen walls of her family lodge as she lay staring through early hours of night. The lodge was much larger a home than Corn-Sucker and Gray-Other-Goose had needed for the two of them; but once there had been many beds. A family of buffalo could have found housing there. Ponies long gone into bones had been stabled in that lodge, to the right of the door as one entered; some of the posts which walled them off from the family still had pony hair in cracks between portions worn to the smoothness of petals by their rubbing. Powder of old manure was a faint yellow spice in dust beyond the barricade.

A year or two before, as Gray-Other-Goose grew frailer and felt the cold more keenly, Corn-Sucker had moved her bed and his closer to the fire. They made in this way a little island of humanity, old male and young middle-aged female, in hollow darkness and chill.

Now she was solitary on this island for the last time.

The four posts supporting the lodge's main burden of rafters, stringers, withes, grass, and sods were alive. They had their separate entity, spirit-like and spirit-named, as indeed the entire house was alive and had its general entity and spirit along with its components. Offerings had been made to the four posts, a girlhood generation earlier, when Corn-Sucker was barely old enough to be concerned with corn and watchers' stages and her *ikupa.* The offerings were bound high on the posts; they had shrunken and hardened there—the three which were the hides of buffalo calves. They had tightened like metal, were rigid and rich with dust in corrugated folds. One was the hide of a spotted calf; two had been the color of wet garden soil beside the river—nearly the color of the flooding river itself when the tan silt thickened it; but now they were faded, and displayed wounds put into them by activity of grubs and the wee teeth of mice. The fourth post was ornamented with a length of calico, once stamped with red and blue but now a patterned kind of gray. The mother of Corn-Sucker had bartered that rare calico away from a Mandan woman who, in earlier turn, had bargained it from a Canadian trader.

It was a sleek and wonderful piece of goods to begin with; any woman in the village would have been proud to fashion a garment from it. Corn-Sucker's mother thought it more valuable than the hide of any buffalo calf, even the spotted one; but Man-Walking-On-Mussel-Shells had no such keen sense of value. He was even reluctant to admit the calico as a gift fit for the spirit who lived in that particular post. In time the woman persuaded him to her opinion, however; so the calico was knotted tightly and accepted by the spirit—quite obviously, since it did not fall down. The knot did not come apart; insects and animals did not destroy the calico. It was there, though gray with a hint of pink still showing if you pulled the rotten folds apart. How strange that it should fade, for not much light came into that lodge....

These objects of devotion, and the unseen household wraiths who provoked them— These the woman would be leaving forever if she went away with the pockmarked Inkpaduta, and surely she was going.

These, and the medicine bag with its treasures; and the old gun; the other weapons; the bullboat hanging aloft in the pony stable—its hide split deeply on one margin—no longer river-worthy, but still a bullboat in which the family had traveled when they went upriver to follow the hunt . . . robes—the many, many robes; the squash knives; the dried-up paints . . . the very stones which had torn Corn-Sucker's face on the day of her birth; they were still there somewhere . . . tinder and kindling, the fires which would never be made. And there was a generous cache-pit beneath its secret dressing of wood ashes and tight-drawn hides and protecting grass: corn piled evenly, squash in the middle of it all, the coiled circlets of hard-dried squash sliced by bone knives; beans of many colors . . . but someone would find the food in time and use it. Corn-Sucker was certain of that. Hunger might come to the village before winter was done; hunger had come before.

She would be abandoning graves and home and bones and parched food and old toys and wrappings and spirits alike. It was not customary for people to abandon these things. Yet there was no threat in Corn-Sucker's training or human experience to prevent her from strangely departing into informal vagabond matrimony.

The barking of the dogs, mentioned by Inkpaduta, was a rite protracted each midnight no matter what the season or weather. Did they have a signal, and who was the leader, and what was the purpose —what inner demand exerted itself under scabrous hide, beneath the pricked foxy ears? Why sang thus the Old Wolf squeezed into a shapeless ghost, pulped into the bony chamber of each flat skull? No one knew, and the dogs themselves would never tell, no matter how often you asked them with speech or in silence. One dog would begin, aiming his nose at stars or unseen clouds— His *yap-yap-yowww* would go bounding, pebbles of sound tossed against the hard cold sky; and so the other dogs of the village would rise from tight-wound sleep, or come slinking out of scavenging forays among the lodges; and they too would point noses aloft and push the sound upward out of their bodies. It had its beginnings (the cry) perhaps in their bellies where chewed-up bones and scraps of stolen gristle lay simmering amid sharp secreted bile; and the cry went on, crawling through gullets, past pointed evil teeth, distorted amid the slobber of quivering tongues and lips scrolled back along the jaws; and it would come into the midnight smoky world and be discernible, to affect the ears of all who waked or slept. How many dogs were in this village no one knew, no one had ever counted or would count. But they were many: some few were pets; more would be beaten or slain for thievery; fat ones would be tied and starved for days, and then given platters of buffalo fat and entrails with which to gorge themselves before they were slammed on their heads and carried triumphantly to be cooked for honored guests—cooked whole, like four-legged partridges stuffed with the sleek fruit of their own voracity. If their hides were white they would be served only to most honored dignitaries. Their white coats would be displayed, with the bonded fresh bloodstains upon them as proof of the rarity of these roasted puddings.

In the loose circle of coyotes who drifted ceaselessly at night beyond sprawling hummocks which made the village, would quiver an awakening and response. The dogs feared the coyotes, the coyotes hated the dogs, and killed them impetuously when in sufficient numbers to outbrave a native cowardice. But coyotes did not always hate a dog-bitch when she was eager and dripping, and snarling in her heat, but ready for mounting and the pointed insertion offered boldly by a male coyote when he slunk up to the lonely prairie post where she had been tied. Thus wolf blood boiled constantly through bodies of these curs; and it sounded in the barking which was a dog-barking to begin with, but thinned into a bay and wailing . . . it broke and sank again to become a nettled discussion of animals who long since had deserted their dusty dens to become the companions, however unfavored, of men.

So the coyotes would hear, and would shake their evil heads, perhaps trembling to discomfit the very bugs infesting their ragged hair. Their howl would lift to mingle with that earlier outpouring: a true wolf-tune, fluted high and rounded, sagging at last into a spasmodic chortling where each coyote talked with the voices of ten. There might have been twenty coyotes near the village, but they sounded like a tribe, and outnumbered the dogs with their echoes.

Out of the long wide twisted receptacle of the Missouri River valley this screaming symphony blended in ugliness and power—a thousand fleshy fanged instruments a-playing; and their chorus struck the high sky, and might have affrighted the very Souls who trudged above that blaze of white lights, or might have been greeted with indignation or philosophy by the stark clouds themselves; until the whole vocal trickery sank to become a gossip and a mutter, and finally a silence to offend the ears of listeners by its very emptiness.

On this night the silence was broken out of tradition by the determined talking of two coyotes—a dog and a she—who spoke belatedly. Corn-Sucker arose shaking, and for a few minutes was half crouched in the gloom with her misshapen face bent down as if in prayer (although she was not praying, she was only fearing to leave the lodge where she had spent her life, and to which she knew she should never return if she went now).

She went.

All burdened with implements, robes and food and the family kettle and her precious personal nine kernels of corn (bundles long since prepared, tied tightly, ready for the journey), her squat figure swam slow and soundless from lodge shadow to lodge shadow, and avoided the few uneven patches of fire reflection—avoided travois or upended bullboat or the skeletal forests of drying racks. Dogs came to learn who this person might be, and what she was doing; she spoke in muted whisper to those dogs she knew, ignored the rest; they fell back and let her pass without challenge, for she was Hidatsa and familiar in her smell.

From one lodge door the fire blaze stroked out high and sharp; a girl was sick there (Corn-Sucker knew of this) and voices were discussing the child's illness. This was the home of friends: the lodge of Mouse-Sits-Up-Tomorrow, who had been Corn-Sucker's *ikupa* when they were young, and her husband Spotted-Horn.

I will go and fetch Dances-With-All-People. I have a good calfskin to give him.

Nay, do not go now. We wait for morning; I am giving her water to drink. See, she drinks with thirst, she would not drink before.

Dances-With-All-People makes medicine, and I have the skin tanned. He will make a very good medicine for our daughter, if I give him that skin.

Nay, wait! She will not sleep if Dances-With-All-People shakes his rattle and sings, and rolls before her on the ground. It is good to wait.

We should not wait.

We wait!

And Corn-Sucker, listening and hardened into a thick black wad in the dimness, a wad with luggage on her back— She would never know whether the young girl lived or died, she would never hear again the voice of Mouse, never see the scaffold where Gray-Other-Goose was tied, never hear these same village children running as they waved their feathered bone whistles, never feast with her people, never stand beside her parents' bones, never observe youngest corn starting from its brown bed while watchers chased the birds away, never perhaps hear the Missouri ripping at cottonwoods in flood, never hear cottonwood voices stilled as the brittle ridged trunks went bobbing away....

She did make some sort of sound; it came from her before she could choke it back, and two dogs rose up to sniff and wonder and then subside once more. Corn-Sucker continued on her course, tripping over an old sled of buffalo ribs which some boy had left carelessly to beset any midnight wanderer; she got her foot tangled in the thong by which the sled was dragged in play (why now a sled? There would be no snow for another Moon or two; it could be even longer. O Little Boy, put back your sled, store it in the lodge beside the ponies' place, it might be broken apart before snow comes, and then you could not slide on the nearest hill!) and soon the woman had left all lodges behind her, and she could hear the river, and wind shaking dry cornstalks of the fields, and making a steady cool music through bark and twigs of the watchers' stages.

The man was waiting beside the tree where she had seen him first.

Is it you? He muttered the question as a jeer.

Aye.

You are long in coming. I beat you.

Corn-Sucker stood with head bowed.

You have robes? Food?

Aye.

I beat you now. . . . Nay, I do not beat you, because you cry out, and awaken village. But sometime I beat you because you are so slow!

Aye, she whispered.

But I need a woman! Woman, we go.

She followed him to the river; even on short acquaintance he knew where wide shallows were, where riffles would rise little higher than your thighs in this dry season and at this crossing. He went ahead, carrying weapons and ammunition pouch held above his head. Both Inkpaduta and Corn-Sucker were hoping in desperation that they would not stumble—he, because of his need for dry powder and guns—she, because she wished not to soak the food and robes (then food would have to be dried in sunlight, and if there were no sunlight, next day?— And robes, once soaked, would make her bundles so heavy that she would be unable to carry such equipment, whipping or no whipping).

Neither of them fell while wading the river, but the man as leader turned abruptly before they had come out of soft unseen silt on the farther shore, and went pressing upstream, seeming heedless of quicksand dangers. He did not know this river or this region well . . . was he plodding astray? . . . he'd said he was an eastern Dakota, and this upstream road was taking him away from his own people at every step. Corn-Sucker followed him with wonder and doubt, but followed without spoken question and showing no reluctance. This was a matter for him to decide. No wise or obedient woman questioned her man's plan when it came to war or the hunt; and this was all on the verge of war, and somewhat like a hunt as well.

. . . Her man? Now she had a man, was having him, would have him, he would have her. For whole minutes the dim nighttime fence of cottonwoods along the shore swayed as if wind had struck; but the thin breeze was not powerful enough to manage such mischief; actually the trees did not move their stripped boughs. It was only a hysteria, an unreality brought about by Corn-Sucker's eyes and wits when she let her thought dwell upon this situation. Overhead the sky was an unblemished robe such as the woman carried in her two packs. Clouds stretched tautly as if held in place by bands of fresh rawhide which tightened and stiffened as they dried and pulled the darkness higher and harsher. Inkpaduta was an armed giant, plashing steadily, circling mounds of driftwood and half-buried logs in water and muck.

They traveled in this way around a bend of the river. They were a long journey above the village and west of it before the man halted and grunted at Corn-Sucker, telling her to stand and wait. He went off exploring, and the woman's back was breaking before he burst silently from parent darkness again, and came to beckon and chide her . . . monster he was, a tall piece of night more intense and dangerous than the darkness which produced him, but walking weaponless.

We go here. Soon ground is hard, we leave no tracks.

She followed him through various difficulties of pools and brushwood (but water still stirred and rippled, their footprints would be filled and would vanish).

This place.

He helped her up on the bank, not in manner of kindness or courtesy, but because, so weighted with freight, she would have fallen backward into the river without assistance.

Inkpaduta picked up his rifle and other weapons.

I would rest, breathed the woman weakly.

He hesitated, then replied: I smoke for journey.

There had been no clamor from the village—would have been no noises, even had a neighbor gone to Corn-Sucker's lodge without any understandable reason and found her missing. People would have thought quite likely that she might have gone to the hill where Gray-Other-Goose lay stiff and changing. . . . It was safe for Inkpaduta to light his pipe; the air would disperse the odor of tobacco before it blew toward the Hidatsa. . . . He smashed out some sparks with a trader's flint, fired a wad of tinder, held the fire nakedly between thick calloused fingers, and lighted the tobacco he had pressed into his pipe bowl. She sat at a respectful distance, leaning against packs, her legs drawn back and to the right (as she had sat through those endless seasons above the cornfields; and she remembered vaguely her girlhood now, and thought of her *ikupa,* and thought again of bulls or stallions, and was amazed to find her own sweat flowing). She watched the intense small glow from the pipe—saw it turned in turn to each of the winds; the man must be observing some fashion of prayer for their journey as he smoked. He was stout with evil, yet it seemed that he prayed. . . .

He emptied out his ashes, and scratched a pit for them, and she could hear him making the surface of the clay innocent once more.

We go.

He started ahead, and left her to struggle to her feet and adjust the vast weight of packs.

Now they traveled west across the prairie. It was as if they had gone a great portion of a day's journey, or a night's, before the man halted again. If the moon had been riding clear, it would have descended two palm lengths before they stopped (thus you could reckon time by the moon: you held your arm toward the moon, flattened your hand against the moon, and in this way you counted time). But at least now the buffalo robe of the sky was thinning and ripping where it was tied in the west; there winked a star where darkness was shredded, then another star, then a herd of small stars gathered dancing around one great bold star.

River, said Inkpaduta.

Corn-Sucker followed him into a valley. This was no river she had visited ever before, it was not the Missouri, but must be one of the Little Mother Rivers who helped to give life to the Missouri. . . . They went down the margin of this stream for a long time, bending slowly into the dusk-before-dawn until spirits of the Missouri began to trill ahead of them. At every step the woman could feel her moccasins go down into sand, but there was no water—her moccasins actually were drying as she walked; and why and how dared Inkpaduta leave such open record of their journey, if he was wary of pursuit?

At full dawn he showed to her the reason. *Hohe,* he said, and came near to shredding his nicked face in a grin as he held up one foot and indicated his own moccasin.

I wear the shoes of Assiniboin. Your men follow us, they think I take you to Assiniboin country.

It was true: his were not the shoes of Dakota, she had observed

Dakota moccasins before this—knew the form and stitching and angles of decoration, and had seen how their shape was different from the footgear of Hidatsa.

Inkpaduta had led her once more, wading for tortured and tortuous distances in Missouri water; but at last, in the grim sunrise, and with infinite care, he assisted Corn-Sucker to crawl upon a tumbled tree trunk, ordered her to wash her feet well, that no muddy traces might be left to read; then Inkpaduta commanded her to follow him inshore until they stepped upon hard beaten land; and he even returned with caution to dust the surfaces of clay until all trace of scuffling footsteps was eradicated.

They cannot follow, his deep voice said with pride.

They would not follow! I have no man to trail us and wish to claim me. No husband, no father, no brother, no son. I have no man.

Your people like not for you to go off with Dakota! In quick anger he brandished his hand. She thought that he meant to strike her, and stood meekly waiting the blow. . . . He grunted, growled something in a dialect she could not understand; but he did not strike. He was unready to beat her as yet.

Half-Face! he said.

That is not my name. My name is Corn-Sucker.

I call you Half-Face, d'ye hear? Half-Face, you walk before me. South. Go to that hill!

He pointed out which hill he meant. It was the second highest in a chain which bordered against the pinkish southern sky, and seemed to have had a gaunt crest at one time, but now the crest was scraped away. . . . Corn-Sucker tramped sore-footed, never daring to look back; but she knew that he must be lingering behind to blot out whatever trail the two of them had left. Since he was to implant the notion of an Assiniboin kidnaper in the minds of any Hidatsa who might pursue, it was essential that the trail should be lost where the two of them had last entered Missouri waters, heading upstream. . . . So Inkpaduta haunted along on her path, dusting the earth now and again, straightening a bent tuft of weed, disposing carefully of a broken tuft, leaving the prairie unspoiled and untarnished by their combined tread.

Sun was above the eastern hill rims, its light splintering weakly among brown and reddish menaces of cloud, when Inkpaduta joined Corn-Sucker in an old buffalo wallow on top of the indicated hill. Here they were safe from scrutiny. While Corn-Sucker sat aching, and drifted very nearly asleep (she would have slept, except for the Weary Spirits who dwelt within her legs and arms, and kept jerking and strumming against her tired flesh) the man spread himself down inside the saucer of the wallow, and with his head behind a clump of wind-twitched grass and with his nearsighted blinking gaze striking steadily against the great plain, he watched for pursuit. There came no pursuit. Corn-Sucker thought idly that no one had even missed her in that distant village as yet.

We sleep, said Inkpaduta. Woman, make my bed.

She unbound the packs. They prepared their first home in this saucer where buffalo had scratched and rolled. Inkpaduta, rifle under his hand, seemed asleep almost as soon as he turned within the robe. It took Corn-Sucker much longer to go to sleep. Sometimes the sun melted through clouds as it danced higher, and found the two furry wads—a little way apart in the open depression—and was kind to them with warmth . . . it was good, for the wind blew chillier this day.

Corn-Sucker awakened when the sun was high, and thought long of a wedding feast, and gifts which would be no part of her experience. (The man had awakened many times, aroused by an alarm of training and habit which sent him creeping to the wallow's rim, compelled him to examine the region with strained and watering eyes, and sent him back in security to slumber again.)

Corn-Sucker thought hopelessly, I wish that this might be *uahe.*

Certainly it was no formal marriage! It would be *kidahe;* though she was not the first Hidatsa to make an informal union nor would she be the last. A girl friend of Corn-Sucker's had made *kidahe* with an *Adakadaho*—an Arickaree. He had come to trade in friendly fashion with his upstream neighbors, had remained to go on a hunt, had been charmed by the appearance and voice and skills of Bird-Flower, a girl who sat often on the stages with Corn-Sucker and other friends. He asked to marry her, and said that he had two ponies at home among the Ree—he would go to the Ree village and fetch the ponies, and give them to the father of Bird-Flower. But the girl's father wished her to marry Yesterday-Ate-Beaver, who had already offered himself, and who could offer also a sixteen-skin tipi for hunting trips up the river, a new bullboat, two silver British coins, and four ponies (but one was lame and fit only for hauling a travois). Covetous of this wealth, the father refused the young Ree, even though he saw his pretty daughter turned to sulking. Soon Bird-Flower eloped with the Ree, to the indignation of the prospective father-in-law and to the amusement of villagers. The girl's father wished to pursue the truants, and even restrung his bow and selected certain arrows; but elders in the family soon dissuaded him from taking any severe measures. The young pair remained out on the prairie for ten days or so—just where they went no one was certain, but they must indeed have visited the Arickaree tribe, for when they returned in the triumph of newlyweds they were riding two ponies and leading a third. Two of these ponies were duly presented to the now-somewhat-mollified father, and he in turn gave the Ree a wolf-fang necklace, a trade blanket, and several baskets of pemmican. It was a clear case of *kidahe,* or informal marriage, and so no feast was held; but no one cared very much; and people were amused at seeing the Ree living with docility in the lodge of Bird-Flower's family. Yesterday-Ate-Beaver was teased insufferably by the village girls until finally he married someone else.

. . . Your face is dark, cried Inkpaduta in annoyance, after he had awakened again.

My heart is dark also.

You stay sad at coming with me, and I take this old bow—it is not good for much, it is cracked, so I must have a new bow—and I beat you with it, all the way back to Missouri River!

I cannot help being sad, because this is not *uahe*.

What is that, woman?

Haltingly she explained until at last he understood the Hidatsa terms employed. Inkpaduta gave no appearance of rage—in fact the dented skin of his face expanded in a weird smile (but often, as the woman was to learn, he smiled when devils of fury were ruling him). By this time he was standing above Corn-Sucker who sat lugubriously on her robe. Suddenly Inkpaduta swung back his left leg and kicked. The toe of his moccasin caught her on the side of her mouth where the scar tissue puffed out; and this portion of her face had always been more sensitive than the rest. The weight and force of the kick flung Corn-Sucker clear of the blanket, and strange stars and suns and moons exploded like gunshots inside her head. She lay with her bruised mouth dribbling blood, while the man kicked her repeatedly. Some of the blood went down to mark the clay, some oozed back into Corn-Sucker's mouth and let her taste salt as she grunted audibly at each successive blow of Inkpaduta's foot. These kicks, however, were lighter in force—more a repeated gesture of contempt and discipline than a punishment—and were strong enough only to move her body each time they landed on her thighs and back and buttocks.

We have no more talk of *uahe* or whatever you fool earth-lodge-dwellers call it!

Nay, she agreed, mumbling with freshly sore mouth, and trying to spit out blood at the same time.

D'ye hear?

I hear.

No more!

Nay. . . .

Or I kick the fool head from your shoulders!

Aye!

With face like yours, you talk of marriage gifts! And who give I them to, and who gives them to me? You say your father is dead—you say you have no one. I give you a kick for a marriage gift! If you have not the *shan* between your legs I care not whether you are here or in the village! Half-Face—ha! What of your *shan*? Is that scarred and split too? Soon we see!

Corn-Sucker sat up at last and drew her robe over her head. Inkpaduta stamped dangerously around her for a while—she could hear the pounding of his wicked feet (although he kicked no more . . . probably he was afraid of injuring her too severely for her to be used for his pleasure . . . dully she considered this, and it gave her some hope for the future) but at last his fit of anger wore itself out, and he withdrew to examine the empty chilly plain to the north and east.

No one comes, he reported at last almost pleasantly.

Corn-Sucker feared to speak in reply, and her mouth was puffing out badly; but she released herself from folds of the robe, and stood up shakily, licking at the drying blood and running damp fingers across her chin to remove the stains.

Woman, we eat.

We have squash.

But no meat! What of that stuff you say—? What you call it? Balls of sunflower seed?

Mapasipisa. Or *mapi* we say too. Here, in this pot.

Shyly she offered him two of the balls, and Inkpaduta took them without a word, but with suspicion, and began to munch. Promptly he wore a look of surprise. Good! he said.

Aye, the woman whispered. She selected a ball for herself.

He said rudely, Where are your manners? Do *Hewaktokto* women have bad manners to eat with the men? Now you are Wahpekute Dakota—you wait until I finish!

I wait. She bowed humbly.

In fact she was more than pleased at this first real deference or appreciation which he had displayed, in enjoying the *mapi*. With pride her hurt recollection took her back to the task of manufacture. First seeds were parched and then pounded in her mortar until oil was expressed. (Baby sunflower seeds were an especial pleasure in this recipe, although it was twice the work to harvest and thresh them. It was better, too, that they be touched by frost; they seemed to exude more oil when frosted, and tasted sweeter. Corn-Sucker recalled with satisfaction that all the seeds used in this collection of balls were from baby sunflowers; she had carried the tiny flakes out of doors after threshing, and spread them to await the frost, and next morning they were silvered.) So the oil had been beaten free, and then the pulp was squeezed to roundness between fingers and palm of the hand (as boys made mud balls to use for missiles in their wars). And then each firm-packed wad was cupped within Corn-Sucker's two hands and shaken with care, to draw out even more oil by gentle vibration; thus the little rations grew firm enough to pack and handle. . . . Ah, she had heard Gray-Other-Goose say many times,

I would go to war with only a *mapi* ball wrapped in the thin membrane of a buffalo's heart! I would carry it in my soft-skin bag, hanging at my left side, along with my awl and moccasin patches! I would nibble the ball when I grew weary, when I was worn down by need for sleep! I would taste and swallow this good medicine! If weary, I would become strengthened—if sleepy, my eyes would open again! I would feel young, and could bound like a calf, and could travel all night, and have the wish and energy for combat! . . .

Inkpaduta ate three of the sunflower balls, but turned up his nose at dried squash. Carelessly he signaled to Corn-Sucker that now she might eat. It was difficult for her to eat because of her sore jaws; she tried to munch a corn ball, but gave up in pain; she chewed dried squash instead, for the stuff softened readily in the moisture of her mouth; and she ate also some various loose bits which had been rubbed loose from *mapi* balls in the pot.

Why bring you that big pot? No wonder you cannot travel fast!

It was the pot of my mother, and before her the pot of my grandmother, and before that it came from the white French.

It is too heavy for fast travel. We bury here.

Forgetting his kicks and threats, Corn-Sucker was the defiant woman all of a sudden. She said, so sternly that she was amazed at herself: You are a man, and cooking pots are no concern of yours! You concern yourself with your gun and other things which are heavy enough. I tell you now—I take this pot wherever we go!

Inkpaduta stared for a moment—at first astonished, then infuriated, then appearing to be somewhat baffled. At once it was apparent to Corn-Sucker that Dakota must share with Hidatsa the definition of men's tasks and responsibilities, and women's.

Finally he went off to the brink of the torn hill, grumbling: We trade the pot when we go among Yanktonai! I need it to trade for caps and cartridges!

Both Inkpaduta and Corn-Sucker were very thirsty, but they had no water. He gave no sign of his thirst; the woman sighed audibly, thinking of water. She was grateful when he signed to her that she should make up the packs again. This time he led the way, striding down the south slope of the hill, and striking off directly into the south where another low chain of rounded ridges blocked the view. Corn-Sucker saw no life on the dry cool land except for a dying coyote whom they encountered—a coyote too weak to snarl, and perishing of a putridity which could be smelled many fathoms down the wind. Also there were several ravens hanging close, but they went flapping away. They had managed to peck out the coyote's eyes, and had begun on his ears, mouth, nose, and anus. Inkpaduta, seemingly reluctant to dirty his club with this stinking flesh, found a stone and performed one of the few kindnesses of his life in braining the beast.

Corn-Sucker stood safely upwind, watching with disgust, pity, relief.

The man bent down and worked a broken arrow loose from the festering ribs. He looked at the relic curiously, then put it out of sight down an old gopher hole. My arrow, he said.

Your arrow?

One day I shoot this coyote, before I come to your village. But my aim is bad, or there comes wind. (He refused to mention his bad eyesight.) So I do not kill. He runs.

Why shoot coyote?

Woman, he is meat. But now rotten meat, so we eat him not.

You eat coyote? she marveled, shuddering.

All people eat dog!

Aye. But—coyote—

You are now like Wahpekute, and Wahpekute eat all. Eat coyote, eat snake, eat skunk. All good meat for Wahpekute!

Aye, muttered Corn-Sucker reluctantly; but promising herself that she would not eat coyote—no, not even if the man kicked her into insensibility.

This afternoon he was walking ahead, his pace nearly twice as long as Corn-Sucker's, so in each segment of their journey he progressed far beyond her; and then he would stand in a mocking attitude, waiting for her to approach. It was as if he said to himself continually: Here she comes at last—a woman with her burdens. This is half a hunt and half a war. Why am I still driven by my need of the woman-thing; that I should be crazy enough to adopt this creature? Make haste, there, weak but necessary slave!

Then she reached his position . . . he would be paying no attention to her by the time she arrived, he would be scanning the region for signs of smoke or other suggestions of war parties or young men gone a-hunting. Frequently he moved forward before she came up to the place where he had been standing.

Inkpaduta made no longer the slightest effort to disguise their trail; he was confident that his preliminary tactics of concealment had been successful. The aching and thirst-provoked Corn-Sucker was just as confident that no person in the Hidatsa village might ever follow, even had anyone known just where and why she had gone, and with whom. More likely in the slight ripple of emotional excitement caused by the death of Gray-Other-Goose, many villagers might believe that Corn-Sucker had been lured or carried off by a *mahopamiis*. Such creatures were evil witches who dwelt in the nearest timbered regions, and came round only to make mischief. Corn-Sucker had heard from her mother many tales of the wickedness effected by one *mahopamiis* or more; and personally (in a life already quite lengthy, and crowded with observation and legend) she knew of a child who had been strangled in its bed by such a demon. The baby was discovered at dawn, dead, with no mark upon its body, but with a heavy robe lying across its little face and wound under the body in peculiar fashion. The infant had been healthy and crowing before it went to sleep. Clearly this was the work of the *mahopamiis*. . . .

While the sun was hiding under shabby clouds halfway down the sky, the pair found water. They had observed some relic cottonwoods and willows along an empty creek-bed; Inkpaduta grunted, and pointed out these trees after he had searched for enemies from the nearest northerly ridge. Down they went, Corn-Sucker stumbling unsteadily beneath the crushing weight she bore. No water could be seen at first, but Inkpaduta told the woman to dig. She had no implements, and there was no wood of sufficient width to be whittled into a spade. The man offered his knife, but Corn-Sucker shook her head; she had a knife of her own, and doubtless it was sharper than his. She cut a stub of willow, pointed it, and set to work—loosening the sandy soil with her sharp stick and tossing out the accumulation rapidly with her hands, as a dog might have gone seeking a gopher. She made a wide basin in the sand, and dug it deeper steadily at the center. Soon the sand was displaying moisture. The delighted Corn-Sucker signed to Inkpaduta that water would be found at half a fathom's depth. (She extended only one arm: a fathom was the width of a woman's two arms extended wide.) Eagerly the pair squatted, when the pit was completed to the proper depth, and watched water draining in with maddening slowness. The man lay on his belly and plunged his face into the hole, and drank first. He drank through three fillings; then he had enough, and waved Corn-Sucker to her own drinking.

In the end, she remembered to explore her packs and produce an empty bladder.

Inkpaduta stared. You have bladder. You do not fill bladder at that last river this morning! *De shicha!* This is bad!

She murmured guiltily: I do not remember. I have these packs to carry. . . .

I kick you again! he roared. He plunged toward her. Corn-Sucker wailed, and dodged away. She tripped and fell across the packs, and flung her arm over her face and shut her eyes tightly, awaiting assault. The man stood over her, breathing heavily; but some mercy ruled, and he did not kick. She heard him belch, from all the water he had consumed; then she squinted one eye from under her arm to see him turn away. He said, This time you fill the bladder, d'ye hear?

Aye, she whispered, and got up shakily.

A bladder could not be carried successfully for any distance unless borne in a basket. Corn-Sucker had brought no woven basket (the packs were bound with strips of hide) but in the treasured cooking pot contained there she had a scrotum basket or pail. The scrotum of a bull buffalo was the toughest hide of all. She herself had made this receptacle as she'd made many before: she'd spread the mouth of the thing with a small hoop of pliable chokecherry, filling the bag with sand, letting it dry until it was rigid as metal. Always it had seemed odd to Corn-Sucker when she observed hair still clinging to this iron-hard substance . . . the resulting basket was larger than the crown of a white man's hat, much larger than the scrotum ever appeared in life as it swung between the buffalo's hind legs. Keenly aware of the origin of the utensil, Corn-Sucker felt a tremor again and again as she worked methodically—filling the bladder with precious water, squeezing it into the scrotum basket, tying the whole atop the uppermost bundle. The sexual force and deviltry of a huge bull had once been contained within that object; now it held water. Inkpaduta would drink that water later—

And later, he—

And later—

They had traveled over one swell of ground beyond the water hole and part way up a second, when Inkpaduta—the length of a cornfield ahead of the woman—became a statue. Corn-Sucker stopped and waited; she knew not why he was halting in this way, but she perceived urgency in his attitude. The man went down slowly to his knees, remained motionless for another period of time, and then with gestures invited the woman to creep forward. She reckoned that he might have heard or smelled some human disturbance ahead (could it be a war party of Ree? And against whom were they going to war?) and needed no further advice to crawl as painstakingly and quietly as if she were a hunter approaching a herd.

She was puzzled as the man licked his finger and put it up to detect direction of the wind. Could there be a hostile village beyond the summit of this wide hill? Then, as a faint quacking chorus reached her hearing, the woman understood. They were approaching a colony of prairie dogs; and this would require cautious stalking.

Inkpaduta crawled to the top of the slope. He had tested the wind, it blew toward them from the crest, and only sound or motion would betray their presence to the animals. It was difficult for Corn-Sucker to slither up, pressed beneath the weight of baggage on her back, but she was curious to see this man at his hunting. She made her way in complete silence, progressing perhaps a finger's length with each forward exertion. By the time she gained the summit Inkpaduta had abandoned all his weapons except his bow and two arrows, and was gone down toward the hummocks of the prairie-dog town. Corn-Sucker lay on her belly behind weeds anchored toughly to the soil. It was impossble for her to find Inkpaduta, even knowing that he was there. She saw him only when he seemed to erupt noiselessly from the pocked disturbed gravel and braced himself on one knee, to shoot. His first arrow caught a dog through the body: the creature twisted in the air, diving for its den in last reflexive purpose before it flopped inert. The air was crowded with piping whistles of alarm. The whine of Inkpaduta's second shot rose while echoes of the first were still thrumming. This second arrow, launched so hastily, did not fly with complete accuracy (the Dakota's bad eyes seemed plaguing him but sporadically; he shot well now). The arrow caught a dog at the base of its head, and the brain must have been injured, for the creature went bouncing erratically—not toward its hole, but first in one direction, then another. The surviving throng of little beasts were well into their burrows. The man sprang after his quarry and caught up with the animal as it tumbled in a demented circle. Sunlight drove out between low buff clouds in the west, and played a torch over this single area of the ridge even while the surrounding plain lay somber. Sunlight caught Inkpaduta's leering face, sunlight painted it with rare yellow. The watching woman caught her breath at utter ferocity revealed: never had she seen a countenance so ardently scrolled in the laughter of making death. Inkpaduta's hand snapped out, caught the squeaking varmint by the hind legs, then bashed the creature with an audible thud to the baked ground at his feet. The Dakota's big moccasin came down on the prairie dog's head once —again—again—again. When gleefully he held up the fat corpse the head was a lolling wafer of bright pink fur, wet, smashed flat.

Now he snatched the other animal, worked to withdraw both arrows, and came back to his guns and his new woman with red arrows in his red right hand, and the two bodies dangling from the clutch of his left.

Corn-Sucker looked at him, bright-eyed with a commingling of admiration for his stalking and shooting, and terror at the fierce happiness in which his wide slabbed face was dressed.

Ah, you love to kill! The words were garbled, in recognition of her own fear of him.

He showed gaps in his stubbly stained teeth as he screamed: I kill, I kill, I kill! My foot smells good with blood!

In ludicrous gesture he went into a little dance on that hilltop, hopping up and down on his left foot, raising his right moccasin to show Corn-Sucker the colored grease on the sole. He kept yelling, as in a chant: I kill Tasagi! I kill Wamdisapa my own father! I kill Atkukukinma, and he also is Wahpekute!

The individual names Corn-Sucker had never heard before, and she could but hear them now, never retain them. But the word Wahpekute he had spoken frequently.

She faltered: You say you are Wahpekute. Yet you say you kill Wahpekute. . . .

Because I kill!

You kill own people?

I kill man who takes my treasure! . . . This is what Corn-Sucker thought that he said; but even the trivial bloodletting of the rodents slain at their colony had so excited Inkpaduta that he was gone into a torrent of revelation, in racing dialect which she could not understand. He calmed his body but not his speech. Corn-Sucker sat to rest against the bundles, agitated at memory of the spectacle she had witnessed. For a few minutes indeed Inkpaduta had seemed like a mystery man, talking ferociously of traffic with all manner of devils and spirits, and posturing in a jig made the more frightening by his own great stature.

She saw that his eyes were streaming as if with the exudation of tears—and why should he cry, when his face had been convulsed with gobbling pleasure only a short time before?

He stood in one spot, having dropped the prairie dogs to the ground in front of Corn-Sucker. He stood gesturing as he harangued, waving first his bow, then the soiled arrows, then waving both together. He spoke as if relating some sort of personal account—spoke of tipis on a river to the east, spoke of murder, spoke of some penance or restitution which he was making or must still make. He talked of ponies, of Yanktonai friends, of white people who refused to pay him a share of riches which they had paid to other less-deserving Dakota. But the fluency of his screed, together with the many proper names of people wholly unfamiliar (and the piling of horror on horror, death on death, murder on murder) served only to befuddle Corn-Sucker—and thus diminish her dread.

Above all it was a strange rudeness which she witnessed in him, in that so often he spoke of people by their actual names. He did not utter the roundabout references to which Corn-Sucker was accustomed. He did not say, I went to the lodge of That One. Nor did he say, I went to the lodge of The Old One. He said instead: I went to the lodge of He-Shot-Four, or, I went to the lodge of Man-Catches-Horses!

Naturally it was difficult sometimes to recognize identity of the individual referred to, when one said merely: That One has asked me to talk to thee.

But it was the polite way to speak nevertheless.

Did all Dakota speak like Inkpaduta? She was almost certain that they did not. But did all Wahpekute Dakota speak like this? She did not know. Deep within Corn-Sucker there began to distend the slow fear that this man was more of a permanent outcast from his own people than she had first believed.

Again he brushed his knuckles against his eyes. She saw rheumy fluid oily on his knuckle-skin.

Water, he said.

She twisted the bladder out of the scrotum basket and offered it to Inkpaduta. He drank, handed back the bladder, and said quietly and almost politely: Drink.

Corn-Sucker shook her head. She was not suffering from thirst, and there was no telling when they would come to more water.

You bring prairie dogs.

Aye. She added the two bodies to her staggering load. Inkpaduta gathered up his weapons and ammunition pouch, adjusted straps and belts, and then started down the hill past the silent prairie-dog town. Corn-Sucker wondered, as she followed lurching and sore-footed, what had brought those animals into such vocal activity. Perhaps a rattlesnake crawled among the dens. . . . Sun was hiding, the brown clouds rotted apart to let it fall, rays came up sharp and briefly like porcupine quills in a design; then the design was gone, and there existed only the old tough hide of the clouded sky, the hard rolling plain, the sadness of it, bushy weeds revolving in thin chill wind of autumn like shapeless orphans who had no home.

The Dakota had roved this land as he made his wild way north to the Hidatsa country; with his sore wet eyes he recognized landmarks and identified them to his companion, halting in advance to point out now and then a pile of boulders or an eroded slash in a ridge. Without deviation he led the way to their camping place for the night. When he made the fire sign to Corn-Sucker she was glad. She had feared that he might compel her to eat raw prairie dog and always she quailed at the thought of raw meat. A natural gentility did not subscribe to such atavistic joy (doubtless the boasting of boys, heard long ago in her girlhood when they talked loudly of dripping buffalo tripe, had influenced her. And often she had seen Man-Walking-On-Mussel-Shells and his cronies enjoying bloody hearts and other innards; but she cringed just the same). The place selected was an empty watercourse between two eroded hills. The nature of sand and brush suggested that water could be found here; so Corn-Sucker found it, but only by digging long, and the hole was much slower to fill than the preceding one. Dead cottonwood twigs and some old roots provided fuel. In the scanty light of this blaze Corn-Sucker prepared the two plump carcasses to bake, making a mud pie of each. Inkpaduta had deigned to slit the prairie dogs while the woman was toiling at the water hole; but he was driven by an immediately selfish desire rather than a wish to aid her in what was palpably woman's work. With his fingers he tore out the wads of entrails, and wolfed down both hearts and one of the livers, together with other selected tidbits. The second liver he tossed to Corn-Sucker, but she refused it, and the man laughed aloud.

You not be good Wahpekute, he teased, without noticeable ill-humor. He picked up the tiny liver where she had let it lie and ate it willingly, spitting out bits of bark and gravel which had adhered, and licking his chin and upper lip.

In comfort of the flickering light, Corn-Sucker fed the fire steadily, working the glowing wood around each mud pie. Again she was glad in her heart, and almost felt a song coming up within her; but she feared still to make a song in the bitter domination of Inkpaduta's company. Had she been able to sing she might have chanted: *You were two sly prairie dogs, but the hunter found you with his arrows. You wished to flee but the arrows would not let you, so now you shall be hot fresh meat when you are cooked. And your hides will come off in the baked mud when the pies are opened, so we shall not need to choke on your hair. Oh, prairie-dog women weep tonight in the village of prairie dogs! But other babies will be born.*

. . . They ate thankfully, according to turn, and the man had the decency to accord Corn-Sucker almost one entire animal to herself, though the meat was nearly cool by that time. She chewed some dried squash as well, though Inkpaduta scorned the vegetable; he demanded more *mapi*, and now only a few balls were left of the supply she'd brought.

At thought of night, and that experience which might befall, her hands shook so aimlessly that she could scarcely manage her tasks.

She was surprised when the man directed her to fetch their packs farther up the ravine into darkness.

You say this is where we camp, she expostulated wearily.

I sleep not by cooking-fire. Never sleep by fire in strange land! . . . He explained grudgingly that young men of some tribe or other, eager to take their first scalps in order to prove themselves as men, might prowl to the scene, drawn by firelight.

Camp was made in a cleft higher on the incline—a secret place shielded from night breezes, and where they could observe the *mitskapa*, the rosy fruit of the dying fire, fathoms below them. Working nervously in the dark, Corn-Sucker managed to unpack and spread out the robes. She had a gift for Inkpaduta, she did not know whether to offer it now or later. He was ruffianly in treatment of her, but she had prophesied that to herself all along, and still she had come. He did not merit a present because of any nobility of affection which he awarded, because he had awarded none; but he was now her husband (even in *kidahe!*) and as such she must pay him tribute.

When he growled, I smoke, after settling himself on his robe, Corn-Sucker was decided instantly. Clouds were blown away, the stars were shining. With eyes accustomed readily to the pale light which came down from the Way of the Souls, the woman could see that Inkpaduta was fumbling for pipe, tobacco, tinder, flint, and steel. She knew the nature of his tobacco—it was not true tobacco, but made chiefly of the inner bark of the dogwood or perhaps red willow. She had smelled that acrid smell when Dakota came to trade, and smoked with Hidatsa before the trade was made, and after, and on parting. Women did not smoke (except often the very old women, and sometimes medicine women: the pathetic Cow-Buffalo-Makes-Strings smoked, though only to draw attention to herself) but Corn-Sucker had long known the difference between good tobacco and bad.

She found her treasured packet, wrapped in an old membrane, and she crept to Inkpaduta's side. I give you, she said.

He seemed glowering through starlight; then his fingers closed on the offering. What give you?

I give this to smoke. It is of my own making.

What make you, woman?

Good tobacco.

My tobacco is good tobacco!

She told him tremulously, My own tobacco is best tobacco.

He sniffed at the tiny package. *Pananitachani*, he said.

Nay. That is what Dakota call tobacco of the Arickaree; it is made from leaves and stems. But my tobacco is made from flowers! Only the green part of the blossoms; the white part is thrown away.

Why make you this tobacco, woman? Why give?

Her voice trailed off abjectly. In the late summer, I make it. . . .

In that ruling stillness of night and hill and wind above them, the stillness of stars coming down, stillness following the wail and jabber of coyotes on distant eminences who regarded these wayfarers with puzzled hostility, and screamed about it— In this silence fairly could she hear the man's fingers working with her gift, unflapping the membrane pouch, feeling the dainty store all richly moistened with buffalo fat; she could hear his sniffing.

I smoke, he said at last. With flogged satisfaction Corn-Sucker knew that the present was accepted.

She felt the necessity to make no song about the tobacco, but she could have told much in a song. She might have constructed poesy about the tidy rows of blooming plants, and how their acid would get into your eyes when you picked; and Inkpaduta, if a woman, might never have come to such picking because his eyes were often sore already.

. . . Her thumbnail pinching off the white portion of the bloom (it had no worth as a scrap to smoke) and ah! how many trips to the field, every fourth day and no oftener, so that new flowers might come in some profusion; and only perhaps one-fourth of the scrotum basket filled at each picking; and how the quantity would diminish in bulk when it was cured!

Her own father—and later her new father, Gray-Other-Goose—always made a sacred matter of the drying, with two skulls and a holy pipe arrayed upon a hide within the lodge, and tender tiny blossoms spread before them as if the picked flowers themselves were at worship. A shaft of sunlight penetrated through the smoke hole, and the hide was moved bit by bit to follow this sunbeam as it traced its way across the floor. No one ever strolled between the fire and blossoms spread upon this liturgical hide. It would have been a disrespect to do so, for the entire pattern was now become sacred—it was *hopa.*

Corn-Sucker would have sung also of the buffalo fat, roasted on the point of a stick over coals until it was dripping . . . the suet-laden stick moved like a wand over the dried blossoms, touching here, touching there; and then the blossoms were transported even closer to the fire, and tilted so that globules of fat might be cooked into them . . . stirring all the while. . . .

Inkpaduta seemed ready to stuff his pipe bowl with tobacco. The woman had the temerity to whisper a warning: Chop first with your knife. Chop very fine; then you smoke better.

He grumbled, but she felt and saw him take his knife from the sheath. At last sparks flew, tinder caught, the coal was stuffed, the delicate tobacco glowed. If her body had not been so belabored by exhaustion and mistreatment, Corn-Sucker would have sung. She did make an inarticulate sound, but not enough to bring forth any sullen query from the man.

She lay upon her own robe, waiting, fearing. Her body yelled for its sleep; she could not sleep. Not long after Inkpaduta finished smoking, she knew to her wonderment that he too had lain down and wrapped himself; soon he was snoring. Corn-Sucker posed many questions about this before she fell asleep. . . . Why did he say he needed a woman? What of those twins, what of his other boasting in the day or two before? She knew, as surely all people must know, that the advent of twins was evidence of remarkable sexual prowess on the part of the male parent, together with the other mysteries attending twins. This man had demanded her, stormed at her, abused her in the assertion of vicious masculine force; yet he did not order her to lie with him.

That event might befall in the dawn. Plenty of women's gossip had reached Corn-Sucker's spinsterish ears. The act was said to occur frequently at dawn, when men awakened.

So she was not too surprised, but only quivering in anticipation, when gruffly Inkpaduta ordered her to join him on his robe in the next day's grayness . . . shape of ridges could be seen, coyotes were silent, not even a bird cried. Corn-Sucker had roused at the man's rousing, she saw him go to make water, saw him return; but he did not lie down again, he only sat brooding. Perhaps he was thinking gloomily of youth and energy which had sloughed from him through the years. She hoped that his disconsolation would not engender some fresh enactment of savagery.

But desire was in his heart, even though the initial ability eluded him. As light increased, Corn-Sucker heard strange sounds and saw strange motions, and realized in confusion that the man was working with himself as sometimes naughty boys were seen handling their own bodies. Perhaps he was aware of her scrutiny all along, but he did not turn enraged; he only gasped when he was ready: Woman, you come!

She crawled in servility to his robe, going on hands and knees and settling there. Impelled by sudden ruling fright and modesty, Corn-Sucker closed her eyes and covered them. She felt her ragged fringed gown being lifted, felt her limbs being spread apart. When Inkpaduta tried to force his way inside her, her maidenhood restrained him. He grew panting and furious, pushed ferociously, wrenched her arm from her eyes, seized her wrists, pressed her arms wide, buckled his grasp on her wrists until she lamented aloud.

You cry! he mumbled accusingly.

Nnnay.

When the resisting membrane broke belatedly she may have been keening again. She knew that a blow caught her on her broken mouth, the man's poisonous hot breath seemed taking her own breath away. Ah, was this it? and why had the cows and mares shuddered as if in longing? . . . But, responding to the man's ferocity in motion, Corn-Sucker began once more to entertain those visions of stallions which had provoked and befuddled her since girlhood. In accompaniment she heard a remote voice squeaking and saying little encouraging Hidatsa words (her voice? Not Inkpaduta's—it had to be her voice, crying these incitements to frenzy) and in the end that madness of all mating women, of all time and of whatever tribes, overwhelmed her. She clasped her legs around the man's back, drummed him with her swollen naked heels, whooped until the sunrise heard her.

Oh, that sun gazed like an owl with one red eye! Inkpaduta lay flat upon the robe, not even bothering to cover his shrunken maleness, and he sighed now and then. Singularly these murmurings acted upon Corn-Sucker's mother heart, as if the grotesque Dakota had become now a very small boy indeed; so she crept back to him, caressing his hard dinted face with her hand, touching him no more heavily than a butterfly might have touched a flower. He snarled, spat, hit blindly at her, even though he kept his eyes closed as if concentrating upon a recovery of power.

When the sun was one hand above the untenanted ridges, the pair had eaten a few scraps of corn ball (this time the man chewed squash; there was no more meat) and had eaten the last of the *mapi*, and were on their way again, but heading this day toward the southeast. The only words Inkpaduta spoke after he had lain with her, were: I take you to land of the Dakota. . . . They went pacing down the slope, circled the gash of southern ravines, and then were journeying once more upon the plain. The daylight scrutinized them and identified them by shape, but with the chilliness of autumn which moved out of the north as tempests of migrant birds might fly—a piece of autumn here, a piece over yonder, but autumn winging south and winter threatening behind it. Had eyes looked down on the travelers with the vision of those same fleeing geese and trumpeter swans, they would have seen two fragment shadows extended from the easterly sun, going ant-wise around obstacles; and always one a little way ahead and one a little way behind. Later the obscurity of the dun plain claimed them and wiped them out, as if they had gone to earth as some insects go.

VII

Once, during the last winter Isaac Harriott spent in Illinois, ice and snow dressed the recently designated Atlanta area for weeks Doctor Francis Taney empowered Harry to go to an auction sale and bid on a cutter. It was one of two cutters in the immediate region; people generally regarded this contraption as an impractical novelty; if folks had to travel abroad in winter they should put a wagon box on runners, twas said, that they might transport their produce and their families in straw-packed comfort. Cutters were probably all right for fops at the East, they were ridiculous in the Illinois country. This being the ruling opinion of the neighborhood, there were few rival bidders. Harry made his acquisition at a low price, and reported home in triumph.

Body's banged up a mite, and the forged strip on one runner is bent like a fishhook. But I got it for six dollars in currency. And Blacksmith Bales said he'd fix the runner for the price of an all-around shoeing job.

How'll you get it to the forge?

It's already *at* the forge, said the proud young man. I hauled it over there my own self.

Didn't think you were hefty enough.

Well, I did fall down a time or two on the ice–

Hurt yourself?

Superficial contusions, sir.

. . . The next Friday night they returned in the cutter from a fracture case. Contrary to the habit of Doctor Maws, Doctor Taney much preferred to do the driving on any occasion when he was not too tired. In spicy shivering moonlight, Harry drew down comfortably within coarse buffalo robes, and reviewed the bone-setting job he had just performed almost single-handed. He himself thought his work excellent; but in all self-awarded approval he recognized nervously that Doctor Taney had not spoken a word since they started back from the isolated farmhouse where the patient lay.

Harry was overcoming gradually his awe of this second preceptor, though he had been afraid of the doctor to begin with. Acutely he missed life in the Maws household at Pekin; he had grown to love

Thomas Maws as he might have loved a grandfather. Here in Atlanta (formerly called Xenia, and booming rapidly because of the new railroad) Harry's existence was parceled out between the apprentice medical and surgical practice which he performed under F. X. Taney's stern gaze, and the demands of apothecary pursuit at a drugstore. The drugstore owner was a sallow petulant invalid who could barely creep behind counters, and sometimes could not even rise from his bed. No one had been able to diagnose this man's ailment, so he was forever dosing himself from his own stock. . . . Harry suspected that his employer was addicted to concoctions more deplorable than Cephalic Snuff or Preston's Salts.

The situation might not make for the same strange mingling of spiritual excitement and relaxed spiritual peace which Isaac Harriott had enjoyed in Doctor Maws' society, from the days before he could tell the pharynx from the epiglottis, the larynx from the esophagus. But he had been counseled that he was weak in his pharmacopoeia; his future life would never consist of a series of dramatic surgeries.

. . . Better ten persistent bellyaches cured, Maws preached, than one fancy ovariotomy. That's the way twill be, Harry, lad. Take my old friend Ben Dudley—I've told you what he says and you've seen it oft enough in print. You were thrilled to the quick to read how he ligated the subclavian artery with favorable results, a whole twenty-five years agone— Remember? Twas for axillary aneurysm— But what says good Ben Dudley to the young today? Lay by the lancet! he declares; and by that he means the knife as well. . . . Ah, no—one can't discard the knife completely, and you never shall; indeed the world will need the knife for long to come. But proper preparatory treatment will win more wars than all the lithotomies that good Ben Dudley has ever performed. Tis better to keep the patients from building stones within their bladders, than to take up the knife to cut those same stones loose. . . . I'll warrant that you're often more confused than you'll admit, when it comes to diagnosis and prescription. . . .

His priest was talking now and the honest Harry listened. He was courageous enough to send himself into a final year's exile at the busy village of Atlanta, where he could concentrate on correcting his weakness in a drugstore. (There was no place for him in the drugstore at home.) He dreaded the tincture press, the mighty iron mortar, the Swift's drug mill; with set jaw he put himself to these slaveries. At least, if he was not finding immediate happiness in his perpetual attack upon a cob of sugar of milk, he was discovering a hardy virtue.

But out of his association with Doctor Taney had risen a new and uncomfortable complication which did not vanish readily. To begin with, Taney was as imposing in appearance as Maws was bizarre. Spare, terse, stony-eyed, grim-lined, he had a saturnine austerity of speech to rival Maws' loquacity. And at sixty-two he was still supple;

he walked as Harry imagined that panthers walked. Harry held the belief that Taney was consciously disapproving of all society in general and himself in particular. Also Doctor Taney had been reared in Roman Catholicism (which the Protestant elder Harriotts held to be a Faith best not talked about, and which to the simple Isaac became both fright and confusion). Also he was a relative, however distant, of the eminent Roger B. Taney. It might make any stripling, no matter how sincerely dedicated, somewhat nervous to sit in the same buggy with kin of the most noted American jurist, no less—the Chief Justice of the United States Supreme Court, the husband of the sister of Francis Scott Key! At first it seemed to the student that rockets were glaring redly whenever Doctor Taney looked his way, bombs bursting in air whenever Doctor Taney spoke. As a matter of fact, the tall thin-lipped man spoke seldom enough. That became another reason for trembling.

Harry.

Yes, sir—

The moon found groves on the prairie's rim and named them to be menacing; and one frigid light shone from a house hidden in blackness of the nearest grove, and struck like a cry for assistance across the snow.

That fracture back yonder—

Yes, sir?

. . . The cutter's runners ripped keenly among icy ruts, they were slicing like knives . . . the speedy bay horse blew out his breath against the freeze. Isaac Harriott sat tense and stiff, knew that his hands were hard-clenched.

What if it hadn't been simple?

Sir?

Compound, say. Complications. Same member, same bone, same region. But primary lacerations, copious hemorrhage. Ah—hemorrhage controlled— Now, then?

Harry drew a long breath, he seemed to be drawing in frozen buffalo fur as he breathed. He strangled (and was telling himself, as he counseled so frequently: Don't be asinine! He's a man, he's a human being even if he is a mackerel-snapper, even if he is connected to The Great. He'd look the same as me or Pa or Doctor Maws himself, if he ever got to be an Old Jupe!).

Extension, sir. I'd have put on extension.

What manner of apparatus?

Harry explained in detail about lines and weights.

Anything else?

Ahhh . . . yes, sir! Fracture box. I'd have had to employ it.

Filled with—?

Sawdust, sir.

Or anything else?

Well— Bran, if sawdust wasn't available.

I'll be damned! cried Taney. Twas exactly what I used!

Sir? asked Harry weakly, and in enormous relief.

Said twas exactly what I employed.

What—what case, Doctor Taney?

This one.

I—I don't quite—

I'm not talking about that lady. One who fell on the stoop. Nay. I'm referring to this cutter.

But—

Doctor Taney slowed his horse deliberately, so that the act of driving would not require immediate attention; and when he turned to address Harry the icy moonlight made witches' eyes out of his icy spectacles.

Where'd you buy this cutter?

At the auction, as you—

Yes. What auction?

Harry began to understand that Doctor Taney was playing some peculiar game which afforded him grim enjoyment.

At the auction of a Mr. Lyall's effects, sir.

A man I knew. Patient of mine. Also knew him when we were young. Back in Maryland. Man named Judson Lyall.

Yes, sir. But—this cutter?—

Twas this cutter killed him.

Isaac Harriott remembered the twisted runner, and splinters torn from the little sleigh's body.

An accident, Doctor Taney?

I said the cutter killed him. Twasn't that. Twas his own avarice and blindness and cruelty.

Now was the time for the youth to wait in wondering respectful silence, and let the elder man's story emerge. Doctor Maws would have given hours to the recital, Doctor Taney took possibly twenty minutes. For more than one reason Harry remembered this night as he might have recalled a great gift or award. It was again (as on the acquisition of the first Old Jupe) a door opening, a finger pointing, a voice behind the voice which was speaking— This other voice behind the voice uttering the words, telling one: Walk this way. I cannot offer you all wisdom or indeed any wisdom, for wisdom is self-acquired only. But I can point the way; so come through this door, and follow the path, and do not deviate!

Runners of the cutter were slitting very slowly now, the hard far cold moon was growing benevolent. . . .

This man Lyall. Knew him slightly in Maryland before the war. I don't mean that ornery little Mexican War—I mean our fight with the

British. Second fight with the British. Forty years agone. Not a runt, but there was something small and grafting in his manner. Eyes always seemed to be thinking thoughts other than the ones he spoke. And he didn't talk much. Not much more than I do.

(This would be the longest single sermon ever offered by Taney.)

Just before Bladensburg, that rout the redcoats made of us. Nevertheless we captured a prisoner. I was serving in the militia under Winder. Lyall's in the same regiment. He was a corporal, I was a captain. Prisoner was a British officer. Young fellow, seemed rich, had a heavy purse. Our troops weren't all of 'em thieves, so he was allowed to keep his purse. Might buy him extra food in prison. Bivouacked for the night. Lyall set to guard the prisoner. Morning comes, prisoner's gone. Lyall said the lad jumped on him with a bludgeon; had taken French leave before he could fire. Or his own piece flashed in the pan. Or something. Some kind of silly tale. Lyall's commander was suspicious. Searched him. Jud Lyall had a lot of English gold on him. Hadn't had any money before. Was nigh a pauper. They tried him. Articles Fifty-two, Fifty-six, and Eighty-one. Court debated, couldn't agree, said evidence insufficient. Circumstantial. Finally discharged, but under a cloud.

He came West. First Indiana, then here. Was dwelling here—New Castle—when I came on the scene, years later. British money apparently gave him a start in life. Had purchased a stock of goods. Peddled; then ran a store. Bought land, saved, bought more land. Loaned money at interest. High interest rates. Regular miser. But selfish, took good things for himself, made everybody else eat second table. People said Lyall ate all the breasts of the birds, gave his wife and children the neck. Not the Pope's nose!

Harry shivered to hear a Roman Catholic use this expression, and dared to glance swiftly at his companion; but the doctor was staring straight ahead, his face unyielding in the moonlight. . . .

Wife was pale, pretty, sad, frightened. People said Lyall bought her from her father for the price of a note. Maybe so. Had two children, boy and a girl. Girl grew up. Wanted to marry a missionary. Father said Nay. Missionary was poor, missionaries had no money. Wouldn't let her marry. She slunk around, dried up. Embittered, sickly, unhappy spinster. Finally took consumption. I couldn't help her much. Recommended rest, rich diet, eggs, cream, such victuals. Don't believe she got much of that. Eggs could be sold, so could the cream. Girl coughed, not enough covers on her bed. Father had plenty of covers on his. I cursed him out, recall doing it. Took covers off her father's bed. Bundled Florinda up, took her home to my house. My housekeeper cared for her till she passed on. Had severe hemorrhage at the end. . . .

The doctor was silent through the distance past an extensive cornfield. Harry ventured to prod him.

The son, sir?

He was long grown up, of course. Eldest of the two. Operated a general store over in Beardstown. Didn't have his father's knack. Made unsound investments. Financial trouble. Father wouldn't lend him money. Owed seven hundred on one mortgage. Store stock pledged. Man began pressing him. All varieties of trouble. Wife had milk sickness– You know–?

Doctor Taney turned quickly to offer a challenge.

Morbo lacteo, said Harry.

The doctor grunted approvingly, and drove in silence for a time; but soon resumed.

Boy couldn't pay. Came here to his father's farm. Begged and pleaded with his father, desiring to borrow seven hundred. Judson Lyall wouldn't let him have it. Said he was a bad risk. No security. Son went back to Beardstown. Took his shotgun, went in the barn, put the muzzle in his mouth, pushed the trigger with his toe. . . .

Lyall drove a horse, bad disposition. Skittish, always plunging. A biter, too. People couldn't understand why he wouldn't bite Jud Lyall. Wished he would. Rather wished so, myself. Except I'd have had to treat him. He was very slow pay. Ha–Jud Lyall–slow pay–redundant! Anyway Lyall was driving. Going to a foreclosure sale, doubtless. This cutter. Winter, icy weather like this. Some boys throwing snowballs–iceballs, maybe– One of them hit the horse. He ran away. Upset the cutter. Well, you saw. . . .

Threw Lyall out. Compound fracture. Left femur just above the knee. Did my best for him–extension, fracture box, way you described. . . . Bad suppuration. Protracted. Sequestra kept emerging. . . .

Wife was sick, same time. Took to her bed following son's suicide. I was certain twas a stone. Wished to perform a lithotomy. Jud Lyall said Nay. Wanted to know how much twould cost. I said a hundred. In Springfield might have cost double that. He still said Nay. Too expensive, doctors no good, bloodsuckers. I said I'd do it gratis. Couldn't win his permission. He was still suspicious; guess he thought I'd sue him later. While he was making up his mind, wife died.

Then came Lyall's own turn. Suppuration increased in affected region. Refused to be localized, broke out elsewhere. Think it traveled in the blood. Strange thing, such cases, know more about them some day. . . . Traveled for months and months. Came out on top of his head. Wretched man. We were having an epidemic. Hard to get tenderers for the sick. Nobody wished to wait on Lyall. Mean man. Earlier I'd suggested amputation. If he'd listened to me he might have lived. He said, How much? I said, We'll make it reasonable. Say fifty. . . . Nay, nay, nay—just like that. Once again I said gratis. He wouldn't consider it. So. . . .

And he was alone when he died. Sole alone! Got abusive to the old woman I'd persuaded to nurse him. Christian duty, I told her. She was Irish. Son had been drowned in Lake Michigan. I said I'd pay for special Requiem Mass for her son if she'd take care of Lyall. Persuaded her to go. He was so cantankerous that she walked out. Yes. About a month before you came to Atlanta. He died alone. . . .

Doctor Taney said nothing more until the cutter began to slither and drag sidewise at the first lonely street intersection in Atlanta, where snow and ice were worn from the frozen ground.

Then he asked Harry abruptly, Bother you, son? Riding in this cutter? Lyall's cutter?

Not in the slightest, sir. I'm glad you've got it.

Ha. What think you of a hellion like that? Wicked?

Wholly so! agreed the young man with fervor.

But more than that. Know what else?

What, Doctor?

He was a fool! Plain undeniable condemned unadulterated fool. Had every opportunity. Threw everything away, for money. Military honor, patriotic decency. Abandoned them to begin with. Money, money, money! People can't realize it: money means nothing. Oh, twill keep you warm, keep you fed, sometimes keep you from pain—not always. Buy knickknacks with it. About all it's good for. Not worth selling your soul for. Lyall sold his. Scorned by the Army, hated by his neighbors. Killed his daughter, killed his son, killed his wife. Finally killed himself. Too belatedly to suit most people! What did his money buy for him? Not even a comfortable respected death. Because he was a damn fool!

The doctor guided the cutter skillfully into the carriageway beside his white house; and when the horse had stopped Taney handed the lines to Harry and turned back the heavy robe, preparing to swing to the ground. But he hesitated; then, seeming to come to a decision, drew the robe over himself again although he did not take back the reins. To Harry's bewilderment Doctor Taney began to recite verses which sounded as if they'd come from the Scriptures. In the young man's hearing Doctor Taney had never quoted anything before, except a few medical opinions; and seldom were these quoted verbatim. In speaking ordinarily he scarcely moved his lips, nor did he move them more than ordinarily now; yet his lean flat voice made the words even more memorable than they were in essence.

Give unto him who is of kin to thee his reasonable due; and also to the poor and the stranger: this is better for those who seek the face of God; and they shall prosper. What's that, son?

Harry was puzzled, but in pride and energy (and in gratitude for

Doctor Taney's newly demonstrated humanity) he spoke with assurance. Why, it must be from the Bible, Doctor.

Ah? Who do you think said it?

Why, I think—Jesus. Or maybe—the Apostle Paul?—

The doctor continued: *Whatever ye shall give in usury, to be an increase of men's substance, shall not be increased by the blessing of God; but whatever ye shall give in alms, for God's sake, they shall receive a twofold reward.* Good advice, ah?

Tis indeed, sir. But maybe— Is it from something in the Old Testament?

Far more recent than that. Know what the Koran is?

The Bible of the Jews?

Nay. Thinking of the Talmud. Verses which I just gave are from the Koran. Maybe you've heard it called the Alkoran of Mohammed. Same thing. He founded the Moslem religion.

But you, sir?— A—a Catholic—

Sense is sense, charity's charity, no matter who makes it. I'm not the first Catholic to read that great book. Trust I shan't be the last. Priest named Father Marracci translated the Koran. Into Latin. Over a hundred and fifty years ago. Time of Pope Innocent the Eleventh. Man named Sale translated it into English, not long afterward. Old copy in my father's library. . . . But I can't recommend it to you. You've too much else to do. Young. Much to learn. Much. . . .

Now the doctor did descend from the buggy. He stood flexing his hands in their shabby fur mittens, beating his hands against his shabby fur-clad breast. He turned, the high moon sharpened his face, sculptured his face into bone and shadow.

Something you ought to remember, son. Lyall wasn't the only fool. All people are damn fools. Maybe not all. But most. Almost everybody's damn fools! Remember that.

Doctor Taney went into his house; Isaac Harriott drove on to unhitch, attend the horse, close the barn door, and go up to the kitchen along a sooty shrunken path he had shoveled before the freeze set in. The doctor had lunched and vanished already; but the coffeepot was still on the stove, and a platter of bread and butter and cold sausages and pickles on the table. It was the established task of Doctor Taney's housekeeper to set out some such fare whenever her employer had a night call; and Harry helped himself liberally. He sat munching and drinking for a time, with Catholics and Moslems and greed and suppuration jumbled together in his tired addled head. He wished that he might read noble books as Doctor Taney had done, and memorize the most cogent quotations, as he'd been taught to memorize Scriptural texts in Sabbath school years before. But how might one read for enrichment of the soul when he had to grind away at learning this complicated profession of his choice—when he had to grind, literally and figuratively, with pestle in hand; and meanwhile trying to absorb the qualities and effects of opium, sulphur, wormwood, ipecac, magnesia, ginseng, calamine, calomel, cantharides, calumba, camphor, cloves, cassia, creta preparata, and castor oil?

Harry went up to his room (far finer as to furnishings and proportions than his quarters had been at the Maws', but never loved so well). He felt very much abused. . . . He had disrobed down to his drawers when there sounded Doctor Taney's now familiar two sharp taps on the door panel. Promptly Harry opened the door. The doctor was in his long flannel nightgown and crumpled cap, candle in hand. The young man blinked as he saw the old man's toughened features cracking into a slight smile.

Came to beg pardon, son.

Sssir?

Granted?

Of—of course, sir! But—what—

Gave advice, willy-nilly. Unsolicited. Wrong kind of advice. Told you to understand that all people are damn fools. Wrong advice, because you're young. Nothing worse in the world than that. Young person who believes that all people are damn fools! And shows it. Nothing worse! Forget I ever said it. Something for old codgers to recognize and believe. Not for the young. Nay.

. . . The doctor went down the narrow hall, walking with head bent forward meditatively, walking lithely in his strange easy glide. Harry closed the door, blew out his candle, and dove into the big high bed. He explored with bare feet cautiously, then relaxed in joy. Yes—it was there—old Mrs. Sawyer seldom forgot it, on a cold night: the brick, tightly pinned in its flannel cover. And the brick was still warm, even though it had been there for a long time. The foot of the bed was all warm.

Suddenly he wondered what it would be like to have a beautiful young wife beside him, a beautiful young wife who kept the bed warm while he was gone on a call; and welcomed him back, and—

She might have merciful pale eyes with the shine of laughter dwelling in them— And raven locks— Ah, that should be it: hair so black as to look blue, hair black as a crow's wing—

He tried to concentrate his attention on such a vision, but the mortar and pestle kept intruding . . . and then the leg which he had just set . . . Doctor Taney must approve. Else he would not have broken these months of silence with a tale and a philosophy. Harry might never love Taney as he loved Maws and would always love him. But from that night forward he had an affection for this room which he'd never held before; and anyone might always claim his entire attention by mentioning the Koran. Unfortunately few people ever did so.

In all his young life Harry never saw a copy of the Koran; so this book was not among his few effects boxed and roped to accompany him when he traveled to Minnesota Territory in 1854 to set up practice there. He had not a large store of books, but was very proud of the ones he owned. They were old favorites, the same books if not the same copies over which he had pored (and often so paining to the eyes in candle-flame!) through his five years of concentrated study and apprenticeship: Innes, Hahnemann, Cheselden, Rush on fevers, Hamilton on obstetrics, Gross's *Elements of Pathological Anatomy,* Cullen's *Materia Medica and Practice,* Graham's *Lectures on the Science of Human Health;* and above all a late acquisition—the redoubtable Daniel Drake's *A Systematic, Historical, Etiological and Practical Treatise, on the Principal Diseases of the Interior Valley of North America as They Appear in the Caucasian, African, Indian, and Esquimaux Varieties of Its Population.*

In Pekin his father said in jolly humor: Harry, you expect to do much doctoring amongst the Esquimaux in Minnesota?

Tisn't complete yet—Doctor Drake's work. This is but the first volume—

But— Esquimaux? Stuff!

No siree! I really sacrificed, in order to buy this one. You know how I've always liked candies—spent liberally in order to buy them, whenever I had the money—

And stole, when you didn't have any money!

Oh, Pa!

From Tiffendahl's shop, when you were six or so. I was looking over his stock of chisels, and you slipped behindst the counter whilst Tiffendahl and I were busy with the chisels, and you helped yourself to peppermints, horehound, and whatnot. Filt your pockets. I had to give you the licking of your life. And take all that truck back to the shop.

I was little! said Harry in self-extenuation. And unregenerate, and shouldn't be blamed. What I meant to emphasize, Pa, was that I didn't want to be a leech on poor old sickly Mr. Emil Portman there in Atlanta. He did keep a stock of wintergreens and gumdrops and such—especially licorice caramels—but when I first went into his store, part days, I'd weigh out the candies whenever I took any, and put the money in the till. Then I thought, Oh: how I'd like to be the possessor of Doctor Drake's new book!—but it didn't fit into my budget somehow. So: I just quit eating candies. Each time I felt myself getting candy-hungry, I'd decide how much I *would* have eaten *if* I'd eaten candy; and then charge myself accordingly, demand payment of myself, collect from myself, and put the currency in my old blue sock that mother knitted for me—the one I'd lost the mate to. The day after Doctor Taney said, Why'n't you start practicing, Harry?— I counted out my currency, and ordered Doctor Drake. Course, the first volume is just General Etiology. There's more to come. . . . A vigorous exercise in self-denial, sir! Ain't you proud of me?

Certain, said the elder Harriott. And, I might add, it's better for your teeth, Doctor.

Now, odd that you should say that! Doctor Maws held to the theory that unrestrained consumption of sugar—

Hoist up your corner of this case, Doc! Else we'll never get the hemp around it tight!

Harry cut a magnificent stencil for use in marking his baggage: *Del. to Dr. Isaac Harriott Hotel Meadows St. Paul Minn. Terr.* The Hotel Meadows had been recommended to him by a patient, a crippled man who hobbled through Atlanta and had but recently come down from the upper river; Harry wrote to the landlord of the Meadows, requesting a response, and received a more or less illiterate reply assuring him of accommodations when he arrived. There were many tales about travelers losing their belongings on river boats—tales about theft, about baggage being put ashore and left at a lonely landing in order to make room for some higher-paying perishable load. It was well to have one's boxes marked legibly and indelibly. Also the abbreviated *Dr.* looked very fine, and might serve as a variety of advertisement in a new country. There were already over a thousand inhabitants of St. Paul, some people said over two thousand; but that figure might or might not include the nearby settlement of Canadians, known as Little Canada. . . . Harry was stepping forth into the world with most of his drugstore wages intact, and with some residue of professional fees still left to him, once he'd clothed himself properly. Doctor Taney had insisted that Harry accept a fair proportion (estimated generously by the doctor himself) of the income accruing from treatment and surgery in which Harry participated during his year at Atlanta. When the young man felt his hand enveloped in Doctor Taney's obdurate clutch during the final handshake, and felt himself choking with emotion as he stood before the old man's chill metallic gaze, he found also that his last preceptor was presenting him with a letter of recommendation. At least that was how Taney described the sealed and folded paper.

Don't read it now. Not to open till you're on the boat! Bound for Minnesota.

. . . *A large business has already been done by the steamboats that sail regularly between Galena and St. Paul and Stillwater.* So declared one of the popular tourists' and emigrants' Guides. *The products of the chase, and the fruits of the field are exported in considerable quantities . . . the real prosperity of the territory seems to be ensured. . . . Farmers, laborers, and professional men, are daily ascending the rivers in search of a new home. The day indeed is not distant, when the for-*

ests will be laid low, and the flowery prairies be converted into fields and gardens, producing every necessary to the use and enjoyment of man. Earth, air, and water abound in the prerequisites of man's happiness and enjoyment, and are only awaiting his advent to yield up their now unused abundance.

Isaac Harriott's boxes were lifted from a levee at Galena, and their proprietor walked across the gangplank of the steamboat *Nominee* carrying his carpetbag in one hand and a leather satchel (title and name printed clearly upon it, by use of his homemade stencil) in the other. In that satchel, besides cautious selection of pills, powders, and liquids, were Harry's stethoscope, lancet, surgical scissors, knives, a small saw, tooth forceps, a compact bundle of scraped lint, syringes, and a pulsimeter. One of the boxes to be shipped contained his books; another the bulk of his drugs; another his mortar and pestle, a set of balances, two pewter hot-water bottles, and a pewter bedpan. All the clothing he wore was paid for except for his new fawn-colored jacket (Tailor Beck was gone out of town when Harry left Pekin; but Harry had deposited nine dollars with his father to pay the balance of his tailor's bill; so one could count the jacket as paid for). His mother had worked him three new shirts out of goods he'd bought after critical consideration; she'd presented him also with three new pairs of socks, and two beautiful stocks—one of black silk, one of a rosy-greenish-blackish material which their neighbor Mr. Angus MacOuan declared to be the Lindsay tartan. Isaac Harriott's sturdy boots might also be designated as new, since they were but four weeks away from the cobbler. After paying for passage and freight, he had thirty-one dollars and seventy-six cents in his purse; but two twenty-dollar gold pieces were sewed into the lining of his pantaloons at the waist. Doubtless he would need to buy a horse on arrival in Minnesota Territory, but hoped to cover part of this expenditure with a note. He was in a state of purpose, artistic glory, anticipation, and spiritual dedication which might have been deeded him from the combined reservoirs of General George Washington, Miss Jenny Lind, Christopher Columbus, and Peter the Hermit. . . . This was August; and Harry would observe his twenty-first birthday on September the twenty-fourth. Neither Doctor Maws nor Doctor Taney owned a beard, but Isaac Harriott hoped desperately to own one. He shaved his face every day in a resolution to promote the growth of hair, yet little beard-stubble peppered the foam on his razor blade. He was not daunted; he'd tried every mixture suggested in his pharmacopoeia, without success; had eventually found himself reduced to secret experiments with everything from mare's milk to bear's tallow . . . no visible results, but he kept trying.

Harry was the first passenger to board the steamer, and his was the first freight to be lugged. He gave an old Negro two bits to insure this.

But after other passengers had trooped aboard there came an almost unendurable wait while barrels were rolled on and off—the Galena freight to be delivered, the upriver cargo to be stowed.

What on earth is in all those barrels? the exasperated voyager asked of an unkempt brown-faced man lounging beside him.

Whiskey, pork, and flour, the passenger replied promptly. I name them in the order of their considered importance!

To underline this opinion the man shoved a green-glass flask under Harry's nose, but the young doctor mumbled thanks and shook his head. The stranger shrugged, swallowed heavily from the bottle, replaced it on his hip.

No whiskey being made up yonder, he said. Not yet anyways. Not many hogs being raised. Practically no flour being ground. So—

He gestured toward the confusion of turning barrels and bent backs.

He gave Isaac Harriott his name—Barnabas Lock, called Barn Lock by all and sundry, he insisted; he was a Minnesota resident. Harry was smitten by the notion that Barn Lock might be his first patient in the new territory (the whiskey smell around him was a solid brown fog) but he learned that this gentleman lived far up the St. Croix River.

Where you camping in St. Paul? The Meadows? Hell, they won't have room for you.

Harry told him rather loftily that he carried a letter of confirmation in his pocket.

Doesn't mean a thing. Raff Meadows is the biggest liar up the big river, if that's possible; good-humored as a cone of sugar, but he drinks more'n I do, if that's possible. Better come up the St. Croix with me'n *mitawin*.

What's that, sir?

Tis the Dakota word for *my wife*, and she is mine. Woman-Says-No is her name; I made a good trade for her, five years agone, and never regretted it. That's my business: trader. But mostly Winnebagoes up my way, some Chippeways. Dakotas come round, they all fight, rip off everybody's hair. Two Chippeways tried to scalp *mitawin* four-five years ago. I kilt them both. Shot one, knocked the other's head off with my butt. Butt of my gun, I mean.

The man laughed loudly, and other people looked at him curiously. Isaac Harriott was embarrassed. He wished to leave this noisy companion, but did not know quite how to withdraw without appearing either pompous or scornful.

You come up the St. Croix with me, boy, and you'll savor sport such as you never met before. Fishing, deer-shooting, birds—

Harry told the man he was a physician, bound to take up practice in St. Paul.

I never! You hain't dry behind the ears, and you go to pouring out physics! Don't you come my way with your dratted pills and potions, young Doc. I doctor Indian fashion when I need to—nature's way, you see. Sweating and snakeroot for fevers, you see; and then purge myself with a soup of walnut bark—peeled upwards, naturally. My wife got the dysentery last year whilst I was away a-trading, and when I got home I cured her quick as scat. Used bloodroot to do it. Indian way, nature's way. I even cured my wife's brother of the smallpox, one time! Yes, I did. Used pokeberry leaves.

Been buying my trade stock, down the big river here. Also it cost me twenty-nine dollars and forty-five cents just for a few personal supplies. And then think of the freight!

Harry coughed. Excuse me, Mr. Lock.

He lowered his voice discreetly. But I must go to the privy—

Got to go myself, boomed Barn Lock. I'll go along and shake the dew with you. No—you're heading wrong—it's back this way—

They stood side by side above the tin trough; Barn Lock was finished long before Harry could begin, but still he stood discoursing. Harry belonged to that uncomfortable race of young men who are easily constricted by emotion, or by having a crowd around them when they prefer privacy; and Barn Lock made several coarse jests about this fact, and even suggested an Indian remedy, which did not help matters in the slightest. His face looked like harness with bristles on it, the bent strands of reddish hair clung oily and thick, matting his greasy coat collar. He bore with him other bad odors besides the stench of liquor.

Barnabas Lock took to following Harry everywhere he went about the decks. . . . Got a good new stock—small stock, but well selected. Would have purchased more, but I got drunk and lost half my capital in a game of euchre. Guess that was in Beardstown. Nope, I wasn't down that far. More likely twas up here in Dubuque, opposite. I've got ammunition: powder, lead, shot, caps, flints—everything. Tobacco of course, and beads and mirrors. The usual items: plenty of paint, vermilion, ocher, everything. Few bolts of calico. I sell plenty red calico to the Chips, but the Dakotas prefer the blue—

Isaac Harriott cried in desperation: I can't understand you, sir! You —baffle me—

How so? and Barn Lock backed away in some distrust; then brought out his flask and emptied it down his throat.

A man like you, sir. You employ words like *prefer* and *savor* and *purchase* and *considered importance*. Yet you're content to dwell far up in the forest—lead a lonely life—with—with— Your pardon, sir: I mean no insult. But with an Indian squaw for a wife—

It was difficult for Barn Lock to focus his gaze on Harry, though he tried with stubborn dignity. He had a severe cast in one eye, and that eye looked out across the rail at a levee, and the other eye looked through the doctor and beyond him.

There was a shock in realizing that the man could speak so softly.

Shit, boy. The woods are full of them. Full of us.

I don't understand—

Course you don't. Hain't been up there. But men like myself— Well, we're West. Northwest, if you will. We're in the woods. Spend our lives out here. We've got our reasons. What d'ye want to call us? Exiles? That's what we are. Exiles.

He added in complete *non sequitur:* If that's possible.

Lock moved away from Harry; the youth was confused but relieved. But when the puffing creaking *Nominee* turned out of the Fever River into the Mississippi, Harry smelled and felt the trader close again. By this time Barn Lock was lurching, leaning hard against the rail, then pitching away from it. The trader managed to get his arm across the young man's shoulder, and Harry stood weaving with him, tightening his muscles, stiffening strong legs to keep the heavier body from pulling him to the deck.

Woods along the St. Croix are full of us! And up beyond, towards Red River and over towards the lake. Oh, yes—I started to read for the law when I was young, back in Pennsylvania. And I know a man up St. Croix way, lives on a dirt floor— Well, at least I got *flooring* in my place! And that man can spout, if you'll pay heed—

He held up his hand and extended one shaking finger after another, to count the languages.

Latin. French. Greek. German. English, of course. That's five white folks' languages. And—pay heed—

Barn Lock contracted his trembling hand into a large soiled fist, then released the fingers again, one by one.

Winnebago. Chippeway. Dakota. I've heard him rattle them all. And—he *says*—Pottawatomi. Four Indian languages. Nine lllanguages in all. He lives on a dirt floor, without ary woman to his name. Don't know what he does about that. Maybe goes out in the woods and fffinds a she-bear. Though I'd hate to—to do that. Wouldn't you, now, hey? Hate to? Wouldn't you?

Yes, indeed, said Isaac Harriott with heartiness. No she-bears for me, either! Come over here, Mr. Lock. Good place to sit down. . . .

There were crates nearby with canvas lashed over them, and on this seat Harry installed the trader, keeping him company until Mr. Lock lay back across the canvas, groaned, and flung his arm over his eyes; then the new doctor tiptoed away.

He was free from demand or annoyance now for the first time since he'd boarded the *Nominee;* and he wished to be free of all people. This was a state difficult to achieve, for the boat was crowded, every boat on the river was crowded. At last on a lower deck Harry squeezed between stacks of barrels and found a place against the rail where there were no other passengers shoving or gossiping, no immediate sound except the mutter of machinery and a swishing heave of the wheel. Then, not until then, was he able to open the sealed letter which Doctor Taney had given him nearly three weeks before.

. . . Doctor Isaac Harriott. Respected Sir: . . .

Harry blinked rapidly, he watched the thrashing wake on the river until his vision cleared. It was as if he could hear Doctor Taney speaking; yet that must be a false illusion, for seldom did Doctor Taney construct complete sentences when speaking; this might occur only when he took pen in hand.

. . . Pray to permit me, as a friend and fellow practitioner, to welcome you into the ranks of a profession which, though notable for the arduous demands which it places upon the individual, is equally embellished with the names of those whose devotion, sincerity & high courage have long been an inspiring example to mankind.

. . . Not to say that also there exists not an abominable tribe of monsters & charlatans who keep them company; both in the past and present; and I fear well into the future!

. . . My dear Harry, I presumed to offer you candid philosophical advice on but one occasion, and was then impelled promptly to rescind it. Therefore I shall remain mute on the subject; and consign you (but wholly devoid of personal misgiving or reservation) to the perils, aggravations & the few wholly rewarding moments, of your career.

. . . I remain, sir, your obedient servant & affectionate friend, Francis X. Taney.

Isaac Harriott squeezed the letter in his hand; he squeezed with it the two banknotes, each for twenty dollars, which were enclosed. He welcomed the shudder of the boat, thudding of piston arms, crush of blades flailing; then he could not hear his own weeping, could only feel it, only mop the tears with his calico handkerchief.

Steamboat travel was a novelty, but known to his experience. With his parents he had journeyed down the Illinois River and the Mississippi to St. Louis, then back up again. In other circumstances Harry would have welcomed the churning and soot (he'd thought idly that silent bees or some sort of day moths were lodging in his hair, touching his ears; it turned out that these were flakes of damp black soot which swept to roost on him) but he was so lost in reverie and ambitious yearning that he stood in an unperceiving daze. He did have wit enough to seek shelter from the clinging soot-feathers; but never responded to the furious clanging of the dinner bell—was appreciative only of the fact that he had more room when hungrier passengers went stampeding away.

Isaac Harriott was aroused from meditation only when he heard someone say that a man had died in public, two decks above. Then he became all doctor. He held an inkling of what he might find, as he swarmed up with an assembling throng: Barn Lock, sprawled on the deck in front of the crates, a wide strip of vomit glistening from his open jaws. No one moved to aid or lift him; the trader was deadly motionless, but he lived. His rough breathing was half a snore, it seemed to keep time and pace with the boat's engines.

Now, listen, bub—don't go to pushing me—

Let me pass! snapped Harry. I'm a doctor!

The path opened, he was kneeling, the magic satchel beside him, it had not left Harry's clutch, now he knew that he must never let loose of it. Jabber and hum of the crowd muted appropriately as Harry went about his examination. Barn Lock's face had become of a pumpkin color, but the pulse was stouter and steadier than Harry'd thought to find it.

If a vein had not already burst within that abused skull—

Needs to be bled, said Harriott clearly. He discarded the handkerchief with which he'd been wiping spume from the sagging mouth. He looked up, and promptly designated two faces in the circle rimming around.

You— And you. Gentlemen, help me to get him up on that cargo pile.

Hands were slid beneath, other people got out of the way, Harry shepherded them, the big body was hoisted and stretched.

I'm an Army man, said one of the faces, the one with the fierce black mustaches. You give the orders, Doctor. We'll help.

Thanks, sir. We need a basin. Pitcher of water. Clean cloths—

. . . Hell, let's take him inside! Put him on a settee—

. . . Enos, ain't you folks got a stateroom? What I thought! Bub—Doctor, you call yourself— This ain't a fit place for treating—

Isaac Harriott told them sharply: This man is my patient. He's not to be moved. Might expire on the way—

He felt the big soldier appraising him in an instant, then heard the welcome agreement of a sustaining voice: I'm with the doctor on this. He's but a youngster, but I think he knows his business. Just let him handle the job!

Harry was conscious of no further disagreement or interruption, was conscious of nothing except a hairy arm exposed beneath his sight, the condition of puffed blood vessels . . . keen path of the lancet, the induced hemorrhage, sound and smell of blood in the washpan . . . patient's snoring respiration . . . there was a flurry in that crowd over yonder, it didn't matter, the Army man was keeping them at bay, some inquisitive young girls had approached, one of them had seen and fainted . . . fool girl to come peeking around!—served her right. People carried her away; now she was crying hysterically somewhere back on the deck . . . Gross said sixteen to twenty-four ounces at a single bloodletting; but this case suggested apoplexy or next thing to it

. . . The *Cyclopaedia of Practical Medicine* counseled you to study the action of pulse and heart, proceeding accordingly . . .. in some cases you might safely take as much as forty ounces.

Isaac Harriott wiped his hands on a ragged tea-towel and took up his stethoscope again. . . .

Barnabas Lock moaned, Where'my?

Lie still, Mr. Lock. You've been sick.

Wanna go take a piss.

Lie still!

Who's a-bossing me . . . ?

You idiot, lie still. You've lost a great deal of blood.

Oh . . . ?

You had a very close shave! Fortunate not to be paralyzed—or dead. Now behave yourself.

Where's *mitawin*?

She's not here, she's home, up on the St. Croix. You're not to talk any more.

I—wanna go take—

Shut up!

Doctor, said Captain Royal Bagnell, wish we'd had you at Fort Crawford. Our surgeon would have killed him.

Thank you, sir, said Doctor Isaac Harriott with serenity. But beneath his calm, his little boy's soul pleaded: Was that well done, Doctor Taney? Was that well done, Doctor Maws? Oh, I pray that it was, I pray that it was!

VIII

As Inkpaduta and Corn-Sucker progressed southeastward toward Snake Creek and the James River, and after they had recrossed the Missouri, the woman experienced the menses. Her husband made her sleep far apart from him at night. Corn-Sucker had been hopeful that soon she might bear Inkpaduta a son—if not indeed twins!—and was chagrined to find herself in a long-familiar condition (perhaps this man was too old to give her a son, far too old to repeat the phenomenon of twins; but she herself was not too old; it was proved). He invoked a strange word, *ishnati;* that was her situation, he said; and even if they were in a village she should be compelled to dwell apart from him, from an entire family, and from all men, living in a tiny lodge of her own until the influence of the moon was departed. But in this time at least there came the satisfaction of better fare. Inkpaduta shot a huge goose—it was flapping lamely about the edge of a cold drying marsh, it might have been injured by an eagle, and could not fly; yet its flesh was fit even for Hidatsa to eat (and by this time she'd learned that Wahpekute would eat almost anything; or at least this Wahpekute would do so!). Whether Corn-Sucker was now *ishnati* or no, the husband permitted her to pluck and prepare the goose. He seized upon the entrails when she scooped them out of the carcass; threatened her with a blow for presuming to dispose of them; said, You are now Wahpekute Dakota, you eat Wahpekute way! . . . Therefore entrails were placed above the coals, even before chunks of goose began to steam in the cooking pot; they toasted and blackened fatly there, and did smell very good indeed. Never had Corn-Sucker eaten entrails before, but she knew that men often did, especially when hunting or with a war party. She ate them now. She found them to her taste, though she was allowed but a fraction of the whole; since the charred intestines were a great delicacy in the eyes and to the stomach of her master, and he gobbled the bulk. Corn-Sucker made a song, and sang it patiently to herself after being banished to her lonely robe-camp away from the fire. *O great gray mida!— O goose with white and black upon your neck! Fast and high did you fly one time, as also does fly a soul when it goes to the Way of the Souls. Now you have walked the Way of the Flame. Your tender colored insides have sat upon the flame. Squeak, squeak, sputter, sputter!—go the Spirits of the Fat Goose. They are good within my mouth; so one day I shall fly as you have flown.*

No longer need Corn-Sucker break her back to carry a load. This was especially a benefit when the crooked - spirits - which - dance - and - hurt - within - the - bellies - of - women - and - especially - women - who - have - borne - no - children were assailing her. . . . Inkpaduta was mounted, so was she. He rode a spotted pony, she rode a white. There was mystery about these horses; but when timidly she asked Inkpaduta for some explanation of their coming, he only grunted at her. Later he laughed shortly as if a very amusing notion had occurred to him, and said that the ponies were *wakan.* This meant the same as *hopa* in Corn-Sucker's own language, or almost the same, and the innocent bride actually believed that the ponies were supernatural at first. However, after deliberation on the sorcery of their appearance, she was inclined to discard this belief.

They had had no horses, there were none to be seen on the prairie, the smoke of no villages might be seen, there were no signs of war parties or other mounted journeyings. So there were no horses. . . .

And at night Inkpaduta had been about to signal for a camp at one spot, then he had signed that she must wait. He went ahead to a ridge and poked and examined for a time, then he came back and said, Woman, we go! So they had gone on, but not too far (and her heart was glad, for she was weary). Again Inkpaduta halted, and this time a fire was made. They had with them two gophers and a hawk. Corn-Sucker began to prepare the food for cooking, and when she looked up from her task Inkpaduta was vanished. . . . The woman waited long, first in perplexity, then in sorrow, then in fear. Air was thin and clear and cool, and a moon had been given back, and had been growing larger for two nights, and promised to grow large and round again so that the mice might begin eating it once more. But this new moon went lower and lower in its plump short bow-shape, and still Inkpaduta did not return. Had he been slain, however silently? Had he fallen dead beneath the stroke of some bad Spirit? Perhaps he had been stifled or strangled in utter silence by a *mahopamiis;* yet he was so stout and fierce—even though old—that it seemed his strength might surpass even that of a *mahopamiis;* unless of course Inkpaduta were sleeping and an easy prey to the witch. But he had not been sleeping. He had been standing, walking, prowling about, dangerous and awake. . . . Could Inkpaduta have been assailed by a serpent? He had spoken of traveling toward the headwaters of Snake Creek; and ever since girlhood Corn-Sucker had heard of this creek (she did not know that there were in the wide wild plains many Snake Creeks, and this was not the one which was meant) where lay the Snake House. It was spoken of as *Mapokshaati,* and was said to be reeking with serpents great and small, but only at certain seasons. Well, then. Might not this be the season of the serpents? And if the travelers had reached the Snake Creek proximity, might not a serpent have come forth to crawl in their direction, seeking some quarry, and finding it in the tall old man with the pocked face? Well, then!

The gophers were boiled, the hawk roasted; where was the man who'd eat them? Corn-Sucker dared not eat before Inkpaduta ate; and she had been very hungry before; now she had no hunger; she felt much alone and bereft; she would have welcomed even his slap or his kick if only the man might return, and return strong and sound. The curved moon slanted down to touch a western ridge, darkness rose higher and thicker, the night chill stiffened . . . dared the woman go forth to seek more fuel? . . . there were stunted willows nearby and a starveling leafless cottonwood; there she could find fuel, she might build up the fire . . . now wolves were talking of the lone woman who huddled defenseless beneath their gaze and scent. Ah, where has he gone, what has become of him? I do not know, I am ignorant. *Madahishe!* . . .

She had her knife, no other weapon; this was a land unfamiliar to Corn-Sucker; if Inkpaduta did not return it would be the end of her. She was in or near the land of the Dakota, and if any Dakota found her—even were they Wahpekute—they would not believe that she was the wife of a Dakota, and so they would kill her and dry her scalp upon a hoop, and dance with it.

Or, alone, she would starve slowly.

. . . Where has he gone?

At long last, when the moon was sunk, Corn-Sucker became aware that the fierce starved silence held disturbance . . . it was silence, but there ran an uneven current more felt than heard. She'd huddled under her robe, lamenting silently, never daring to wail as she wished; but now she drew the robe aside tremulously and exposed first her face and finally her entire head. With unprotected ears she could hear some sort of footfalls. She feared that one of the horrid Old-Women-Who-Live-in-Woodlands-Far-Away-and-Unnamed was coming to smother her or to lead her into abject slavery where she would exist forever as a ghost. . . . Or was it a crawling serpent of gigantic size, slithering all the way from its cavern near Snake Creek? . . . There came the hollow echo of a hoof upon a stone, but still the woman was unable to take heart, and remained in dread. Ah, that was the step of a pony —perhaps more than one pony's steps—and it must mean that some Dakota were riding her way.

. . . I know not where he is gone. I am alone. Will he return before the enemy have killed me and taken my scalp? Ah, I am ignorant!

. . . *Madahishe!*

The Dakota came closer and closer to the fire. Corn-Sucker pulled her robe across her face and cowered, waiting the arrow to impale her, the bullet to blast her, the club to crush her skull. But they were not a ravening war party, they were Inkpaduta and two ponies; he rode one pony, the other came behind.

Woman, where is meat?

In firelight he made a hunger sign after he had dismounted, rubbing the edges of his hands back and forth across his middle; then he turned and herded the ponies to hobble them.

Food was not burnt or spoilt completely; meat was fried black on one side of the dressed hawk, the slender gopher flesh had boiled and steamed from tiny bones. . . . When Corn-Sucker asked timidly about the ponies, the man gave his grunt; and later his statement about the miracle, the *wakan* ponies.

In time, wrapped in her exile from the fire on this night, she concluded that these horses were not a product of enchantment.

No Mystery Man was present. Who had prayed, who had danced, who had effected medicine? No one.

Thunder-Birds had said nothing, there were no Thunder-Birds on this night; no shooting of the Thunder-Birds' arrows, with bright splintered shafts to smite a tree or a lodge or the very ground itself. The weather was growing cold; it was late in the season for Thunder-Birds.

No. . . .

Inkpaduta was old and knowledgeable and stalwart and cruel, but he had uttered no claim to being a conjurer. Indeed he was the father of twins, but— That must have been long before. And— No!

Furthermore, with her own eyes Corn-Sucker had observed Inkpaduta producing two sets of hobbles in order to secure the ponies for the night; and if he'd carried hobbles with him before, she'd not seen them, so where might they have been secreted all through this journeying?

No.

Corn-Sucker began to tell herself that she must have been unduly influenced by the confusion of the Dakota language. Whereas her people spoke of a horse as a strong dog (or used syllables very close to this meaning) Inkpaduta had sometimes spoken of a horse as a great dog and sometimes as a sacred or holy dog. Might he not have spoken so on this evening, and thus have conveyed the impression that the horses were not in fact awarded to him by spirits, but were merely horses?

Ah!

She hunted seriously in fragmentary thought for the answer to these riddles, as once she had searched for relief from her spinsterhood. Now she was no longer an enforced virgin; she had been with a man, even though immediately she was to bear him no child. It seemed that forever she encountered some perplexity. What might she paint or dream or sacrifice, in securing an answer?—what might she offer, and to whom?

But it was a relief to be confident that these ponies were not *hopa* or *wakan,* but merely ponies.

Inkpaduta might have stolen them from some village or from travelers. Yet she had seen no village . . . there had been no smoke, no marks of people on the march . . . all was emptiness or desolation. For many days of stubborn walking she and the man had encountered only birds or animals, and not many of those.

The woman's body stiffened, grew hot, a fresh idea came ruling. These ponies belonged to her husband! They had been his, all along, and were left in this region to be reclaimed as he passed this way again. Why? Because of the hobbles, primarily; but more than that—Inkpaduta carried a horn-handled quirt when he came riding. Were the horses stolen, cut loose and sneaked from the proximity of a camp or village, they would have had no quirts attached to them. Nor would they have borne saddles or saddle-skins or pads. . . . But had Inkpaduta been using a saddle? She'd never observed, in thankfulness at his safe return, and in fright about fancied enemies coming upon her. . . .

Yes, yes—his own horses!

In venturing out of the land of Dakota and into a region of other peoples, he would have been too conspicuous on horseback, unable to conceal his trail. So, exploring north and west, he must needs travel on foot. The ponies would have been left behind.

She'd heard Gray-Other-Goose repeating with satisfaction a tale of his exploit against the Crow. As a young man Gray-Other-Goose decided to achieve fame by proceeding alone into an enemy village which lay at a great distance. He rode as far as he dared ride, then hobbled his pony, and left it in a valley. The pony could not stray afield disastrously when its legs were tied together—when it could move only in the awkward hopping of a hobbled steed. It might fall and hurt itself, but could not leave the valley readily; and if it left the valley it might move only slowly. Following the pony's trail would be a quick simple matter. Gray-Other-Goose related that there was water—*hao!* Water!—but very little grass at that season. . . . The pony was in good condition to begin with, and might not suffer severely. It could be killed or stolen by some other wanderer; but he did not expect anyone else to come wandering; indeed no one did come. The pony was safe beside the same rivulet where he'd left it when Gray-Other-Goose returned after many sleeps. He had killed no *Kihatsa* but he had stolen a handsome shield from the tipi of a rich and bold and famous leader of the *Kihatsa.* The shield was hanging on the outside of the lodge, close beside the door, to proclaim how rich and bold and famous was the owner; and now Gray-Other-Goose had carried it away! Also he struck with his hand two Crow who sought to stop him as he fled with this trophy (but he thought honestly that they were confused by darkness and surprise; this he admitted). For years he bore his captured shield to feasts and dances and to meetings of the Black Mouth Society of which he was once a respected member. Then he carried it to war against a remote tribe, the Shoshonee in the mountains. There he had his shield taken from him, and was badly hurt into the bargain. . . .

Like this Hidatsa second father of Corn-Sucker, the big Dakota must have left ponies hobbled when he came north. Perhaps they strayed far, even constricted by their thongs. That was why Inkpaduta took so long about the business of finding them. Then he would have lingered to reclaim saddles or pads . . . and bridles . . . and his quirt . . . wherever he'd secreted his horse furniture. . . .

This situation demanded a song.

Corn-Sucker sang softly, she made her voice weak and small, she did not wish to be beaten again. Inkpaduta would bruise her if she disturbed his slumber. *My husband, you left your ponies in a valley, while you explored. Now you return, not with a war shield of the Crow, but with a woman of the Hidatsa. Surely ponies are glad for this reason; I heard one of them laugh as horses laugh! It may be that you, my husband, have other ponies in a secret land to which we go. Them will I hear laugh as well.*

Next morning it turned out that Inkpaduta had but one horse pad; on this he rode because he was a man, and he was Inkpaduta, and must have the best. Corn-Sucker exhibited shrewdness at improvising proper packs. She shaved off part of her skirt to make strings for lashing. The man growled that she was too slow. With docility she explained that it was because she was still in the *ishnati* condition, but did not expect to be so after one more sleep. He only growled, kicked carelessly at her, missed with the kick (she was growing adept at dodging his abuse, and seldom did he attempt to follow it up unless truly enraged). They rode past two more sleeps, and once more Corn-Sucker was allowed to lie with the man. On the third day after securing the ponies, the travelers began to encounter signs of men and tribal activity: old fires, horse dung, buffalo dung, old and new buffalo carcasses, travois marks, hoofprints. They observed smokes in the south and east. Corn-Sucker thought she saw a throng of mounted men on the distant skyline, then the troop disappeared . . . Inkpaduta's sore eyes would not let him see these people; and when the woman insisted that they were there he said only: We come soon to the Ihanktonwanna.

Corn-Sucker felt alarm but also anticipation at the thought of meeting these wild people on their own ground. Besides the Hidatsa folk and their distinct but still allied Mandan associates, she had seen very few strangers, ever, except for remote fearful glimpses of white men traveling the river. Rare parties of Dakota come to buy corn; the Ree who married Bird-Flower; the very few prisoners taken in war; French traders (were there three of these whom she had met, or four?) who were declared to be French, yet they looked like the *Hidushidi*—the Assiniboin—and furthermore they spoke with the tongues of Assiniboin.

Almost did she forget the ache in her thighs and bottom from unaccustomed riding. Dakota—an entire nation of them—she would be seeing them soon! They lived in tipis the whole year round, they had no settled town of earth lodges like civilized people, like Hidatsa. It was well enough to dwell in a tipi while you were gone hunting (this meant more work for the women, naturally, for putting up tipis and taking them down was the work of women exclusively; and still it was a novelty, and younger girls especially were excited about the tipi season, and talked rapidly about the hunt, and prayed that many buffalo would be killed) yet how would it seem if one had no home to return to? No beams, no posts, no firm roof, no drying racks interlaced outside the door, no storage pits beneath the floor. How would it seem to be a wild person? And she had walked into informal marriage with a wild person, had left all civilization behind. Now she too might turn wild. . . .

Rain fell late in the afternoon, thinned into a drizzle, then a mist. Low wide ridges over which Inkpaduta set the course were touched with a grayness like doves' feathers; and presently in this grayness appeared two shapes speeding. They were men on horses, they circled rapidly to the west, then behind Inkpaduta and Corn-Sucker into the north, then swung again along a swell of prairie on the left flank. These were young men on red-and-white ponies, and they said no word or made no other sound as curiously they circled the two strangers. Both were armed, but neither made a threatening gesture; only did they gallop and gallop, lying low along their horses at first; and the tough rapid sound of the ponies' feet could be heard as gradually the riders swung in, closer, closer. For a time Inkpaduta gave them no heed; he must have known they were present from the first, but he seemed staring rigidly ahead as he rode. At last when the fleet spotted ponies were so close that their rolling eyes could be seen, and when all four ponies were talking constantly and inquisitively back and forth, the tall old man halted, held up his hand, sat motionless as warily the two young men approached. Corn-Sucker also pulled up her pony and sat waiting; and she too did not speak, but her eyes were wide, and she could feel nervous spirits breathing against her back. The young men wore long fringed leggings and fluttering shirts of dressed doeskin. They wore their hair strangely: each had a loose forelock hanging over his forehead. The woman had never seen men who wore their hair dressed in such fashion. They did not dismount, nor did Inkpaduta dismount. The talk exchanged was so rapid and flowing that Corn-Sucker could understand very few words. She heard something about a man named apparently Iyotankashunktokecha, or Wolf-Sits-Down; but they did not speak the Dakota language of Inkpaduta—all their *h*'s were become *k*'s, and there were other alterations; Corn-Sucker could not well follow what was said. They did not seem about to strike or shoot; they only stared steadily throughout the conversation, rarely flicking their glances toward the woman. At last they wheeled their ponies away, swung in a tight circle, and once more raced close to Corn-Sucker, gazing so intently at her scarred face that almost instinctively she put up her hand to cover the mutilation. Then both of the young men laughed aloud. They danced away into the east, disappearing over the nearest fold of earth, but they seemed to be bending back southward as they went.

Woman, we ride.

They traveled on, and when they had forded a stream scarcely wider than a pony's length, they climbed another ridge and saw the encampment of the Yanktonai below them. These people were in the act of setting up their tipis. They had been hunting buffalo, and successfully: led horses were all over the place, some still bearing heaps of fresh meat upon their backs, roped and covered with green hides. Corn-Sucker saw this great quantity of meat with appreciation; she had been half-starved, sometimes wholly starved when they camped supperless. Much she preferred the squash and corn and *mapi* of accustomed diet, but roasted buffalo meat would taste Oh! so very good! . . . Water formed thickly in her mouth, and ran out of her split lip, and she wiped it away with a tired hand.

Now Wolf-Sits-Down rode to meet them. He came with the same two young men on spotted ponies accompanying him, although this time they did not approach so closely as before; they remained behind, sitting their horses as Corn-Sucker sat hers, and at a polite distance; while Inkpaduta and Wolf-Sits-Down dismounted and prepared to smoke. The woman could hear much of the talk now; there was something about the way in which this Yanktonai spoke which made it simpler for her to follow him. Wolf-Sits-Down was taller even than Inkpaduta, much thinner, much younger. He had an enormous bent nose and a bright pink scar across that nose and into the right cheek. Like the two boys who'd come out to spy upon them he wore a great tuft of hair blowing down across his forehead. The upper part of his body was clad in a garment such as Corn-Sucker had never seen before. Later she learned that this was the vest of white men, and greatly fancied as apparel by people who had contact with the whites. The vest was of black cloth, ornamented with quillwork in regular designs (but the woman thought that she could do better embroidery than that!—had done so, when she was a mere girl). Wolf-Sits-Down wore also a wolf-tooth necklace to which was fastened a piece of bright metal cut into the shape of a house built of logs. The small tin cabin had peculiar indentations upon it, stamped deeply into the surface, and men believed them odd but decorative, seeming to convey additional importance to the wearer. . . . The marks read *Tippecanoe and Tyler Too.* But no one knew this. . . .

Inkpaduta said, You kill much meat.

Aye, it is good. We kill at least ten tens of buffalo.

You have much meat.

Aye. Good. We want much meat. We pray and give red cloth to the spirits of the buffalo. It is the last red cloth This One owns, but This One gives it to the buffalo when This One prays. So we have meat.

Inkpaduta said, I have no meat.

This One gives you meat.

From where she waited on her pony Corn-Sucker could hear and understand all that was said, thus far; but a wind lifted from the hill and came down against them, and dry short weeds rattled and tussled in the wind; it became so that she could not hear too clearly, and could not get the sense of all she heard because of cryptic references to people and matters unknown.

. . . Little-Crow . . . comes . . .

. . . Now in your village? *Eze!*

. . . Two sleeps agone, perhaps three sleeps . . . says you kill. . . .

. . . All . . . kill . . .

. . . Kill too much.

. . . When I go . . . Unpashota . . . white soldiers. . . .

. . . But all your people do. . . .

. . . The Mdewakantonwanna and. . . .

. . . You have been cast out of. . . .

. . . To the land of the Hidatsa, go very far. This is now . . . Hidatsa wife I have with me.

. . . Give you meat, but that is all! This One leads the hunt today, but That One has more power than This One!

They had smoked but a few puffs to begin with. Tobacco ceased to burn while they crouched in this discussion. When Wolf-Sits-Down went suddenly to his horse, Inkpaduta turned grinning toward Corn-Sucker and she caught her breath— She was terrified by the smile of his face— Oh, now he will beat me again, he may slay me!—was the limp thought which rose sluggishly in the woman's terrified mind. But the husband's rage was not directed at her, though she would have suffered had they been alone, had she got in his way. Promptly on cessation of this conference the two young men whirled their ponies while Wolf-Sits-Down mounted his own horse; then he led the way down toward the busy encampment. Corn-Sucker thought that the young men on the spotted ponies were soldiers (in this she was correct; they were leading members of the Angry Dogs Society, and thus they served as policemen or soldiers).

Sullenly the old Wahpekute directed her to follow him. They rode to the edge of the camping activity, but only to the edge. Likely enough Inkpaduta, meeting with such chilly reception from his distant Dakota cousins, did not wish to tarry even for a night. But he was held by the lure of buffalo meat; and, however maddened and resentful he might be, he knew that meat would be given him. For this Corn-Sucker was dully grateful.

He signed for her to build a fire. Already they were surrounded (but at a safe distance) by a great many wholly impudent children. Some of the children were stark naked, even though wind blew increasingly colder, and the Hidatsa woman was scandalized anew. Ah, yes, she was come among wild people, and she did not like to be among these wild ones! As she went toward the river's cottonwoods to seek fuel she saw groups of women occupied with putting up their tipis. Why, why, what was this? These Yanktonai did not even know how to erect a tipi properly; yet they were said to live in tents all the time. They were erecting first, in every instance, a tripod of poles, and then leaning other poles against them. The veriest dullard among Hidatsa women knew that you must have four poles—never three!—fastened together for the beginning of the tipi frame. Corn-Sucker was saddened increasingly by the ignorance and primitive attitudes manifest. Were all other Dakota like this? Were Wahpekute like this, or even worse? . . . She felt far from her people, far from her home, far from her own life. This was a new and dreadful career in which she roved.

But she had a man . . . she tried once more to think of stallions and buffalo bulls as she gathered dry wood, but could no longer see these creatures rearing and amatory.

It occurred to Corn-Sucker that in justice she was now being tortured for running away from home; all because a man asked her to go.

Pakapi. To be torn, as she had walked through briers!

Pakade. A skewer of wood forced through her heart. . . .

When she returned, stepping wide and erratically beneath the weight of wood, she found the horses hobbled. Inkpaduta sat upon his robe, sulkily regarding a pile of buffalo meat which had been sent by Wolf-Sits-Down according to promise. See, he said, spitting toward the heap. Do we receive shoulders or hams? No! Only the tough leg pieces!

Children were gone from their vicinity, Inkpaduta had snarled at them and they fled in fright. Now other families' tipi covers were in place; and fires burned, a smell of cooking began to drift. It might have been cozy and domestic, if one could close one's eyes and forget the queer forelocks hanging down from the heads of these savage folk; but Corn-Sucker did not dare to shut her eyes.

She prepared kindling. She had flint and steel of her own, she did not need to ask the man for his, and he made no move to offer the pouch—just sat glaring at the meat. But where was the good in toiling with flint, nursing tinder, blowing and waving above the scant coals, when fires blazed all around? Wild people or not, she should ask them for fire. Timidly she turned and started toward the closest tipi; and it was not too near, perhaps as far away as a little boy could shoot an arrow. Corn-Sucker believed that she heard Inkpaduta speaking to her, muttering something. Perhaps he was ordering her to come back, but she pretended not to hear (already she'd learned that this was a refuge and expedient, and she must have avoided certain thrashings by feigning deafness).

Fire crackled within the neighbors' tipi—smoke was already drawing out past ears which directed the vent—but also another blaze burned on the earth in front of the door. Two old women and three young girls worked in the dusk, building a stage for drying meat above this fire. Some tiny children went shrieking, scooting into the lodge as Corn-Sucker aproached; it seemed that they fled from her as little ones at home might have been demoralized by mention of a ghost, a *nohidahi*.

The women stopped working, the young girls moved closer to their elders.

Corn-Sucker was trying valiantly to form proper Dakota words as she crossed the open ground. It could be that these people would not understand her . . . at least she must try.

She begged plaintively: You—give—fire?

The eldest woman, a crone with tufts of gray whiskers scattered on her hard wrinkled face, gave a thin shout which was probably a laugh but sounded more like a bleat of pain.

Fire? Thou, woman, wish a brand?

This One wishes fire.

The old woman hauled a shaft of dry willow from the blaze. Pennons of flame were wrapping and snapping on the upper half. Here, the old woman said, and offered the stick not unkindly. Behind her the girls giggled and whispered together; Corn-Sucker knew that they were talking about her face, as strangers must.

Here, the ancient said again, as the younger woman's hands closed on the stick. Do thou—take this brand—to—bad man—thy husband—Do thou—burn out—his eyes! . . . Again she let loose her shrill squawk of mirth, but already Corn-Sucker was in retreat with the sparking smoking torch, and feeling that her heart was like a cold dead frog which could jump no more.

Inkpaduta slept or pretended to sleep on his robe while Corn-Sucker tended the fire, let larger chunks of wood burn down into coals, worried off slices of the leg-meat (they were tough, as identified) and broiled these slices on the coals. Delicacies such as liver, heart, or tripe the greedy Inkpaduta would have devoured raw with a sauce of blood; but these sinewy portions might defy even his sturdy jaws unless they were cooked.

. . . Here is meat, she said softly.

The man sat up glowering afresh. Despite preoccupation and resentment he ate with such avidity that Corn-Sucker was compelled to hack off some fresh slices and burn new coals in order to prepare a modest supply for herself. She measured and estimated: at this rate there would be only enough meat to last the pair through two more sleeps—possibly through three sleeps, if they were sparing. And Inkpaduta would never spare. Might not the Ihanktonwanna give them additional meat, in satisfaction at ridding themselves of unwelcome visitors? Perhaps?

These people, she said while eating gloomily.

What say you, Half-Face?

She was saddened further by his rude application of the epithet but continued as boldly as she might. . . . The Yanktonai. They are not kind. They have no hospitality—

What say you in your vile Hidatsa tongue?

Corn-Sucker tried to explain what was meant by hospitality, but did not know the appropriate Dakota terminology. Still she fumbled persistently, attempting to express her awareness of the stern treatment presented.

He jeered. *Ohanpi!* This band—the band of Yanktonai led by Three-Men, by Wolf-Sits-Down—are not *ohanpi.* If you mean *ohanpi,* speak the word!

I know not the word.

Now you know the word! Speak it, speak it, speak it! he ordered idiotically.

Damp darkness had closed round them while they cooked and ate . . . night ruled, a clouded night pierced and reddened by fifty fires; but there was no comfort in the blazes, they were baleful . . . wilderness fiends and witches seemed mending and busy around each glow, the Yanktonai were become *mahopamiis.*

Corn-Sucker could chew buffalo meat no longer, she could not swallow the last wad which remained in her mouth. She spat it into the fire.

Ohanpi, she whispered. Hospitable. These people are not hospitable.

And why not? They hate me! They hate me because I kill!

Need you kill forever?

I kill forever!

He began a long recital of the many deaths he had made, including that of his own father. Corn-Sucker listened sickishly; she could not avoid listening, his voice was there, awful words were there. Fuss and mumble and barking of the tented village were too remote to drown Inkpaduta's monologue.

—And thus the Yanktonai wish me not! One time I hunt with Wolf-Sits-Down. Not now—I hunt not with him now. He does fear me!

Corn-Sucker knew that she must respond, else his rage would rise to destroy her.

Had we been strangers, she suggested mournfully. Had we been strangers come to my village, coming in peace even if we had no gifts to bring— Had we been cousins, as you a Wahpekute are cousin to these people— Had my village hunted, and killed much meat— They would say, Come live in my lodge. We have beds for you! Ah, they would give you dainties, not meat of the legs! They would give you *ahoka.*

What mean you, what mean you? Vile Hidatsa word—

I mean—ah—*pakshin*—

Kidney, eh? You know Dakota word, you use it not. Half-Face!—he screamed.

. . . Once Corn-Sucker had nearly scalded herself when she broke an earthenware pot in which water had grown hot. She recalled the combined amazement and anguish with which, in one scant instant, the passion of the steaming stuff exploded against her . . . one moment it was all safe, contained in brittleness . . . the next moment the shell was gone, water free in the world, it was all over her as if she'd crushed a swan's egg, her world was boiling water in which she writhed. . . .

So it happened now: Inkpaduta's spite had been checked within him, jetting out only in angry childish complaint— Then the shell was dissolved, vanished, nonexistent.

His entire fury of body and soul came flailing from every direction. He was standing above her as she sat abject—

Kidney! she heard him shriek. How like you this in your kidney?

She saw the kick coming, was in no position to twist away from that thudding moccasin. The powerful foot, driving force of the leg behind it . . . the blow went deep below her ribs, she sprawled across the fire, coals hissed against her flesh where it was bare and unprotected, coals stung and sank in and clung to her hide and ragged gown of deer's hide, coals were in her hair. The next kick batted her away from the fire, but still coals kept sticking and searing.

Her long scream went up like a rising lark, but never with the beauty of a lark's song or flight; her scream was a harsh wounded bird soaring, on, on, higher, until it seemed that it was snapped short off because of its own speed and attenuated rising.

Aiiiiii—

Repeated thud and pound, repeated thud and pound, repeated—

Ah, a wolf in camp, a small prairie wolf trying to voice its grief; she heard that voice; it was her own voice!— Ah, that bad boy, when she was but a toddler— Ampaapaka was his name—Mosquito-Neck— The same boy who'd twitted Corn-Sucker about her torn face, the boy who was lost in the blizzard— His bones were found— And before he died in the storm he did a thing one day— A friend had dug out a baby coyote, and tried to rear it as a pet; but as it was growing larger it bit Mosquito-Neck upon the hand— So Mosquito-Neck bided his time; and when the friend was not about, Mosquito-Neck dropped a robe over the baby coyote so that it could not bite or scratch him further, and he carried it to a hill above the village; and it was related that he kept the robe tied about the creature's head, so still the coyote could not bite him. But Mosquito-Neck could reach the baby coyote, reach it with his knife— First he cut off the baby's tail, then he cut out its tiny privates, then he cut— And all the while, even with its head muffled in the heavy robe, the coyote cried— It cried— People said, What is that? It is very strange! It is a coyote, or is it, or is it not? It seems to howl with a very small voice, and far away— And in the daytime; coyotes should not howl in daytime— But still it complains! And thus people ran about, this way and that, seeking for the cause of the sound; and at last some women mounted to the hill, and there they found Mosquito-Neck with what was now left of the small creature, but enough was left that still it cried— And some of the girls chased Mosquito-Neck, and threw stones at him, and one stone hit him; and now he cried. But he did not die; he lived! He lived to mock at Corn-Sucker. And then came his hunt for the prairie hens, and the great storm took his life, and later the tooth marks were on his bones. But wailing of the baby prairie wolf stayed long in the ears of those who heard it; and Corn-Sucker was one who heard it . . . so she heard it now, or thought she heard it . . . twas her own voice shrieking faintly because so little breath was left in her body; and she could not draw breath; the kicks kept coming—

Then other voices were heard, and the sound of feet not kicking but striking the earth softly strongly as the feet ran. There lived a great growling and fuming in the night—a sound as of dogs or horses fighting (not the hatred and protest which they uttered, but the sound of their bodies tumbling) and at first Corn-Sucker could not lift her head and blink out the tears in order to see what befell—she might only roll and toss and groan, and put her hands against her body, take her hands away with fresh moanings, shake her head against the dry soil, try to make moisture in her mouth, enough moisture to drain the dirt out of her mouth—

And when at last she could hear and could see, she sat up weakly and saw that big figures of men had emerged from the night; they had seized Inkpaduta and kept him from kicking Corn-Sucker further—

For already she had traveled to some little distance from the fire, driven there painfully by the kick, kick, kick as he shoved her across the hard ground—

By this time there were many people at hand. The wild flocks with the hanging forelocks had assembled in families and multitudes; and children were there in plenty, some of the children crying in fright, and some chattering and pointing; and a great many dogs barked also. And wood was put upon the nearest fires, strong brightness pushed the night away—

Three young men had their arms around Inkpaduta; but it was no embrace of affection they gave, they were making him docile for the moment. They held his arms and they held his neck; and they were very strong young men, they needed to be strong, for he was stronger than many or most.

Someone said to Corn-Sucker, *Tanke*. My elder sister. You walk?

Ah, she said.

Hands were on her. She yelped once, then bit her ugly lip in order to remain silent; for these were strangers, she should not cry out before them. . . . Ahhh. She was compelled to make a sound.

You walk?

Echahe! she gasped. I walk.

The Yanktonai were ferocious tent dwellers, but kind to a victim in pain; or at least kind to this victim of her husband. Two talkative women touched Corn-Sucker gently with the tips of the fingers. They sent a young girl scurrying off to their lodge; and when that girl returned she carried a parfleche. This when opened was found to contain tallow which smelled very strong; certain leaves had been cooked with the tallow and were still mixed through it, but the Yanktonai women did not explain what sort of leaves these were. Gently they spread the strange tallow upon the head and face and legs and arms of Corn-Sucker where coals had left their mark.

Those were soldiers who restrained Inkpaduta; they were members of the Angry Dogs Society; so she heard people saying, and the wild folk described them with admiration and awe, as if the Angry Dogs were a very great society indeed; and Corn-Sucker thought they must be as great among the Yanktonai as were the Black Mouths among the Hidatsa; and feebly she wondered what society among the Wahpekute was Inkpaduta's; but probably he would not be allowed to join such a society, because he hated so completely, and was hated.

Do not kill my husband, the woman pleaded, still gasping. Her sides ached, her back ached, she ached inside, her entire body was a-throb. . . . Do not kill. . . .

Someone laughed. We do not kill!

Inkpaduta said, You give to me my club. Then I kill many!

. . . Have you his club, O Thou One called One-Who-Causes-Storm?

. . . I have his club.

. . . His rifle?

. . . Oh, yes. That One named Hungry-Orphan has also his bow and pistol-shoots-six. His knife is taken from him!

So they spoke, and Corn-Sucker could understand much of what they said; but still the voices seemed to come from far away, and there were flies and bees within her ears because she was weak and hurt (one day unwittingly she had trod upon a lizard, and it popped and squeaked all at once as it burst beneath the pressure of her moccasin; and her body felt now as the lizard's body must have felt when it was squashed).

Corn-Sucker vomited a little, wiped her mouth with her lame arm; but the tallow was sweet upon her burns.

Wolf-Sits-Down was there, his scar looking white across his face in the red light. He said accusingly to Inkpaduta: This One gives you meat, and you do this!

She is my wife. I beat my own wife. A man beats his wife!

Aye. But it is a great noise.

Because she howls!

A woman howls when she is beaten; but it is too great a noise for our people when they hunt, and are tired.

I beat my own wife. D'ye hear?

But why do you also try to burn her? My child awakes screaming, my smallest son, my favorite little one, said Wolf-Sits-Down. We like not this *owodutaton,* this disturbance among us. If you would kill your wife, take her among your Wahpekute. There you kill her.

Another man said clearly but in a hoarse voice: The Wahpekute will not have him. That is why he wanders.

Corn-Sucker judged that the speaker was Three-Men, of whom she had heard; and she had heard Wolf-Sits-Down say that Three-Men had more power than he; he must be a great person among the barbaric Ihanktonwanna, offering wisdom and justice in council, luck when hunting, owning many feathers of the eagle's tail won in war. He seemed impressive as a bull buffalo at this moment, for his thick body was draped in the robe of a spotted calf, his thick graying hair braided up with weasel tails; obviously he had come from important discussion or from an assembling of his society. He had not approved of this undignified and—to him—ludicrous interruption. Nor had anyone else approved.

Three-Men's solid face was a slab of leather which had been blackened by smoke. His lips moved barely as he talked; yet a hush fell when he began to speak, and even the noisy children listened, though they might not know the meaning of his words (yet it was possible that when they were grown old they could tell their own grandchildren: *Eyakesh!* Even I! When I am young, it is many years ago, and yet I remember; though now I must pull out my own gray hairs by the roots as you see me do. The great man, Three-Men! He stands before me as you stand, as close before my eyes as now you stand. I hear him speak, and he is very great. *Eyakesh!* Him I see and hear!).

He said to all: I know this man, this Red-End, Inkpaduta. He is a bad man. He has slain his own father, Black-Eagle, and still our cousins the Wahpekute and our other cousins the Village of Spirit Lake, and our other cousins the Village in the Leaves, and our other cousins the Village of the Marsh—they speak of this. He has slain also Tasagi—His-Cane—and all our cousins speak of this. He has slain many more. The Wahpekute want him not, and he makes his lodge alone.

All this is true, that now I speak!

Three-Men paused briefly. There sounded a gruff *Hoah!* from the listeners.

They sell their lands, said Three-Men. All these cousins I name sell their lands to the Eastern Two-Legged-Ones with the long knives. First sell the Village of the Marsh and the Village in the Leaves. Then the Village of Spirit Lake and the Leaf-Shooters meet in council with the Eastern Two-Legged-Ones; and they agree to this thing. But That One called Inkpaduta is not with his brothers, the Leaf-Shooters. Why is he not with them? It is because they do not let him be with them. He is sent away because of his sins, and makes his lodge alone, as I speak.

Hoah!

(All the words of Three-Men were heard by Corn-Sucker, although she could not understand some of the words, again because Three-Men used a *k* instead of an *h* in many of his words. . . . She was very sad, and she did long to cut off her hair once more and to paint her sore body pale with clay, that she might mourn.)

But he comes each year when the *wawichakichupi* is to be paid in the land of the *Minisota,* the place of the Slightly Clouded Water. He asks each season for his *wawichakichupi*—his annuity. The agent of the Eastern Two-Legged-Ones does not pay Inkpaduta his annuity, for he owns no annuity—he is not one of those who make the treaty, he has no share. He asks for that which is not his own. He is a dishonest man. *Owotanna shni!*

Again the men approved the words of Three-Men; and all said, Aye! During one of his pauses of affirmation, Three-Men signed for the soldiers to release Inkpaduta; he must show that he had no fear of this fellow, armed or unarmed, and he himself held no weapon. Inkpaduta's pipe had been broken into two pieces during the struggle, one piece lay before him; he bent deliberately, picked up the bit of pipe; and a moment later a woman of the throng reached out a reluctant hand and offered the other fragment to him. He stood now as if oblivious to all that was said in accusal, impervious to disgrace. One of his big hands twisted against the other; he would fit the two portions of pipe together, take them apart again, fit them together again.

He said grumpily but clearly: My pipe is broken. I cannot smoke, and it is many sleeps to my lodge. I ask for pipe.

This One gives to you a pipe, said Wolf-Sits-Down. When the sun rises. Then you receive back your weapons, and you go.

Inkpaduta responded churlishly. I go!

It is an old pipe I give you, Wolf-Sits-Down told him. I do not want it more. It tastes bad when I smoke. This I give to you, when comes the sun. Never will I hunt with you again.

I go!

Let him ride beyond that river which men call Inyaniake, said Three-Men. Let him ride to the land of the *Minisota*. We like not some of our cousins there; but we do not make war against them because they are our cousins. Myself, I should rather fight Pawnee!

Every man agreed to this with relish, and all said, *Ho. Ho!*

I kill two Pawnee, boasted Inkpaduta as if in self-extenuation. *Idatahn!* I boast! It is winter, and they sleep by their fire. One I kill with my best arrow. The other rises to fight. . . . I boast! . . . We fight, I cut him with my knife, then I burst the brains from his head with a big stick. It is good to see his brains loose and scattered and very fresh and wet! But so his scalp is hurt, it does not make a good scalp when I take off his hair. And of the other one I take the scalp; I have two scalps of Pawnee, and I take them to my people, and we dance long, and my people say, Inkpaduta is a great man in war. He slays two Pawnee. *Idatahn!*

So say you?

So I say. I boast! This is true. *Wichaka!*

This I believe, Three-Men said. It is good that you kill two *Padani*. Is that not so?

There was a shout of agreement.

But other things you do are not good! The other things are bad that you do, and we want you not, and the Village of the Leaf-Shooters, your own Wahpekute, want you not. We send you not in darkness. We say only that you shall not return to us, *toketu kashta*. We send you from us when comes the sun. We give you meat, we give back to you your rifle, your pistol-shoots-six, your bow, we give all. That One gives to you a pipe to replace your broken pipe, but he says that it is an old pipe and tastes bad!

Inkpaduta did not look at him. He stood looking at the ground, but his face was scrolled in ferocity, and he breathed heavily. Without doubt he was thinking now of the two Pawnee he had killed, and wishing to make more deaths.

He said, I go!

Does your woman go with you? She may remain here. We have once a Hidatsa woman, long ago we have her with our people, and she marries a man named Thunder-Sounds-Steadily and gives him three sons. But Thunder-Sounds-Steadily is long dead, also is the woman long dead. So I say, this wife of yours may remain in our village does she wish to remain. And then you shall not kill her. Is this not true?

And now many eyes were turned on Corn-Sucker; and it was not proper that she speak when men were talking, and when it was much like a council; but indeed people seemed waiting for her to speak.

She could not make her voice loud, yet all seemed to hear her. . . . Nay, Inkpaduta is my husband. I go when he goes! He is *mihihna*.

Three-Men and Wolf-Sits-Down looked at each other, and seemed disapproving of her decision; yet there was nothing more for them to say.

To our lodges! called Three-Men. All go!—and soon the crowd dispersed, even to the last children leering back at them. Inkpaduta and Corn-Sucker slept apart in their robes spread on the ground, and did not speak to each other; though it was long before Corn-Sucker could sleep because of her hurting body. When the sun was a hand's breadth above the horizon on the next day, they were gone riding silently into the east; and for more than three sleeps Inkpaduta did not speak to the woman; then slowly (gruffly and coarsely, as always) he began to speak to her. Her heart was lightened at once when he spoke.

IX

(If a man who dwells in solitude has a mind, he will learn to use his mind despite any absence of schoolmasters, any paucity of books. If there is water of emotion in his heart, the lonely richness—trees themselves and creatures living among them—will tempt it out and send it circulating.)

Some folks in that Ohio region might have deemed Morris Markham as next to illiterate, though he could read and add and subtract, and write with misspellings, but legibly.

No more than any other boy did he like to be thwacked when he was small. Master Everett Dowsing taught by means of hickory switches, slaps, concentrated derision. Because the stone-faced boy with long black hair was silent, and never volunteered a recitation, the old man thought him a dunce and treated him accordingly.

Unfortunately Morris had a tendency toward constructing numerals and letters backward; this to Master Dowsing seemed a deliberate flouting of everything that he set for the pupil. Morris would make a B with the two horizontal loops to the left instead of to the right, he would make a 10 with the zero in front of the digit.

Now mark ye. I have set it on the slate: copy as you're bid!

It looked to Morris as if he had done the job perfectly. Next thing he knew, an angry finger snapped against the top of his skull.

Go set ye on the stool! . . . So he would be pilloried.

Mr. Dowsing bloomed fair in the schoolroom acclamation of other scholars who feared to refrain from applauding his wit. Never did he attain to that community importance held by some few wise and kindly schoolmasters: he was looked down upon by adults, he knew that he was scorned. The only place he could shine was in the schoolroom where frightened boys and girls (he was allowed to teach girls also, there being no other master available) smirked as he tortured the less adept.

He was that worst despot of all: the weak and unaccomplished tyrant.

Gradually submitting to fiendish discipline, Morris Markham managed to leave off reversing his B's and D's. He put the zero behind the numeral instead of ahead of it; but it was a pain to him, and he would knit his soft brows, and glower at the slate; a sweat would come out on him. Still the manipulation of numerals baffled him; he could never learn to divide.

Mr. Dowsing had a shiny head with bumps on it, and across these bumps longitudinal lines of thin hair were oiled and brushed flat. Almost it looked like strands of hair painted on the head of an old corpse (except in those days Morris had never seen an old corpse or indeed a new one). Mr. Dowsing spoke in treacly tones when he addressed adults of the community, encountering them at the store or along a road. But when he spoke to children his voice was ringing and had a finality.

When he addressed the minister, or even farmers, and said, Good morning, he emphasized the *Good;* his voice lifted.

He met Morris's uncle, trudging with shotgun caught in the crook of his arm, a string of fresh-killed pigeons hung over the uncle's shoulder. The schoolmaster cried, *Good* morning, Mr. Markham! *Good* morning, indeed. *What* a Nimrod you are!

But he was jailer talking to jailbird when he addressed the nephew in school. . . . Mr. Dowsing never paid any attention to children outside of school. He accepted the fact that they were gone for the moment from his grasp. He walked as if lost in concentration of noble thought, as if planning a noble deed or two. He swallowed frequently while he walked in silence, twisting his mouth each time he swallowed. His teeth were bad, and he ran his tongue around them, feeling for bits of food still stuck there. His eyes were weak, his spectacles not of the best. He had one pair with gilt bows which he wore especially for walking out, when it was not necessary for him to see objects close at hand. These would be clamped across the bridge of his narrow peakèd nose, and he would turn his face down, watching the toes of his boots, as if he indulged himself in ponderous considerations. He wore pantaloons of an old-fashioned variety with straps passing under and buckled against his boots. The pantaloons were tight on his thin calves, bunching out at the knee, mended on the seat, mended badly by Mr. Dowsing himself. You looked at his utter poverty, and you did not pity him for it, you hated him the more. In school his breath was the reek of neglected backhouse when he bent close to chide you —or, rarely, to fawn upon one of the prettier girls; and the poor girl would grow pale and turn her face away.

(Samantha Perry was taken out of school—her mother said solely because of the master's bad breath, not because of his inefficiency and cruelty. Inefficiency was common among schoolmasters of the region and the period; cruelty was a habit, even a sport.)

Master Dowsing taught by rhyme whenever he could find a rhyme to fit the lesson. From time to time he brought forth a nasty little book called *Marmaduke Multiply's Merry Method of Making Minor*

Mathematicians and strove to have his scholars learn letter-perfect the doggerel contained therein. (Morris was more fascinated by the title page than by the content of this volume. It was published in London and was identified as having been printed for J. Harris, Corner of St. Paul's Church-yard, in 1816. How ever might a book be printed in the corner of a churchyard? The boy meditated so profoundly upon this that he had no acceptance, no retention of the peculiar couplets.)

6 times 6 *are* 36
This pretty bird is Cousin Dick's.

6 times 7 *are* 42
This is the road which leads to Looe.

6 times 8 *are* 48
Dear Aunt! your dress is out of date.

6 times 9 *are* 54
Dear Ma'am I'll ne'er deceive you more.

6 times 10 *are* 60
This pretty cap will fix me.

6 times 11 *are* 66
We're four by Honors, and three by tricks.

6 times 12 *are* 72
Methinks I hear the loud Curfew.

One day when Morris Markham was ten (it was during Second Term: that was in the early winter of the year, and the children's labor was not required at home) Master Dowsing called upon Morris to recite the mysteries of 6 times 11 and 6 times 12. For this quaking student Honors or tricks or a Curfew held no significance, and he made a botch of his recitation. I'll learn ye, said Dowsing, and reached up his coarse brittle hands, fumbling among switches he kept on the shelf above his desk. He took out a big switch and crooked his crusty finger at Morris.

There was no thought of running away; when the master summoned you, you must go. Urine boiled the boy's leg inside his jeans; but he went up to the master and felt the cruel hand go round his collar. Morris pulled, he waltzed suspended like a dummy at the end of the old man's arm. The switch basted him and soon broke under the impact, because it was a switch antique.

Mr. Dowsing grew increasingly angry when the switch snapped. He reached for a fresh one, and assaulted the boy anew. . . . Now, he said, set ye on that stool! (There used to be a dunce cap, but some of the scholars had destroyed it, no new one had been made.)

The boy's legs and buttocks were so sore that he could not sit upon the stool. He slid down; the master screamed, and motioned him back. Morris was desperate. He thought if this were to be the school which he must attend until man-grown, he would die now instead. Mr. Dowsing made a dive, the boy glided away, the children watched with open mouths, they were gasping for breath; and some of the girls would have nightmares because they thought that surely now Mr. Dowsing would beat the life out of Morris, as often he had threatened to do. The boy melted behind the tall desk. The master waved his ferule; he struck wildly, he missed, struck again. The ferule had a metal edge, and it snapped on the desk, breaking into fragments, and one of the fragments cut the master's hand.

This flowing of Mr. Dowsing's own blood washed from him any rags of probity in which he might have claimed to be dressed before. He exploded into a screaming monster who would have cowered in a corner and flung up his useless arms in defense against the attack of a peer; but whose whole purpose became the subjugation—nay, the destruction—of a slighter creature who danced beyond his reach. Each corner of the desk got in his way progressively. His old thighs were bruised by the contact; he whirled and stamped giddily, clawing with outstretched hands, seizing nothing, giving forth an extended screech punctuated by identifiable curses—oaths such as none of the children had heard him use ere now.

The children themselves were making an accompanying sound: partly the intake of breath, partly the exhalation of terror and amazement, a babble as might have cackled from a pen of mixed poultry. The girls wailed Oh and Ah with fragile squeaking, the boys muttered a more deliberate encouragement to the rebel (though Morris had never achieved great popularity among his mates because of his native shyness). Switches were useless things. Mr. Dowsing began to throw books: one of them hit the child. Mr. Dowsing hurled his stool: it missed. He plunged quaking through the doorway which led to a woodshed at the rear. (A round stove of sheet iron was set up adjacent to the master's platform, and here children could come for their recitations, and to warm themselves in severest weather; of course the master basked in a constant glow.) There boomed a scramble and tumbling in the woodshed, as if the master had fallen against the pile. . . . Some of the girls and smaller boys ran squawking toward the rear of the room, which was in fact the end where the front door was closed against cold. The demon Dowsing reappeared in the woodshed doorway with a length of blue beech in his hand. It was chopped jagged at the ends; twould serve as a bludgeon; thus surely he intended to use it.

The hand of ten-year-old Morris Markham sought a weapon and found it. A grenade: the master's inkwell.

It flashed—a bulbous comet with a thin black tail. The man staggered but did not fall as the missile popped against his forehead. His shriek pierced the roof while the stuff burned into his eyes. The master jigged, striking at his own wet black face in excruciating blindness.

Morris did not linger to watch him skip. He burrowed away through the other scholars, snatched his tippet and fur cap from a hook, shook the mittens out of his cap, put them on, slammed the outer door behind him. He was winding himself in the big knitted scarf as he ran. For the first time he began to cry. He knew that his battle of defense was immoral and illegal: no boy might defend himself against a schoolmaster with the approval of the world any more than he might have defended himself against the dictates of Almighty God.

Morris had no thought of returning to the raw-sided house where he lived with his uncle and aunt. . . . His mother had died of something called stomach inflammation when he was very small . . . his father went through the river ice during midwinter fishing several years before—at least that was where they always thought the father went; they found nothing but tracks and a fish spear. . . . Morris was positive that he would be beaten for what he had done. His uncle was a calm little man whom many neighbors called lazy because he was no good at farming. (Actually he worked harder in the woods than they worked on their cleared acres.) Morris had never been beaten by his uncle; he had been threatened a time or two when he sinned, that was all. It was impossible to think that one might throw an inkwell in the master's face, and escape intact or approved. First he would be beaten by his uncle; then he would be taken away in chains by the sheriff and tied to a post in the town square and flogged again, publicly, with a cattle whip. After that he would be put into a dungeon for life. Morris did not know where a dungeon might be, he had never seen one here in western Ohio; yet a dungeon seemed appropriate and merited.

A few sections of this area still lay in swampland; they would lie that way for a long time. Morris knew that Mr. Dowsing could not follow him into the woods even if he were able to make out the trail; and it might take a long time for his uncle to find him, and for the sheriff who would fume in his wake. The boy had flint and steel in his pocket, because it had been a designated chore this week to go early to the schoolhouse in order to kindle the fire each morning.

He ran for nearly two miles through the nearest rough patch of swamp, going on high ground where he knew a way already. Then he skulked past the cornfield of a neighbor, and plunged into deeper forest beyond. When he halted at last—exhausted by flight but with sobs worn out—he realized that he was in a region which he had visited two or three times, but still did not know well.

He found the split ruins of a great poplar, torn out by lightning and tumbled into a windfall on the ground. Here he made his camp. The bark was peeling, dry on top of the limbs. His fingers went in between the bark and wood, and found little films like frailest paper, which might be pulverized into tinder. So Morris worked . . . there was slow agony in awaiting the spark, the longer agony . . . sparking again and again . . . finally a flame crept. He blew and blew. Almost he had forgotten the dreadful scene in the schoolhouse. He had a fire.

The boy made his bed of leaves still clinging to the low branches of scrub oaks; such leaves always clung for a season before they weathered away. He shaped a nest of them, and wormed his way into the nest. He shook as a stray starving dog might have trembled. There was fever in him by this time. His face felt hot, his hands quivered; when he dreamed, he dreamed that his mother was being carried off in a box. That was the way he always dreamed of her, he never saw her walking.

He awoke in earliest dusk, healed to some degree by the remoteness of the woods. He thrust his small wild face from hiding, and listened and sniffed. He was desperately hungry. He did not know what to eat, unless he might find some nuts on higher ground and crack them between stones. It was too late in the year for frogs. In warmer weather he might have been able to club some frogs and, with his Barlow knife, remove their saddles and cook them over his fire. He did go afield, seeking squirrels or birds, not knowing how he might take them. He saw no game; the birds and critters already were gone to bed, and the light grew dimmer.

Snow had fallen a time or two. Old and new snow shone here in the swamp, though gone from open fields beyond; the recent sun had done away with it. But here in lone shadowed places there was a crust remaining: it cemented ancient brown leaves together, made crystal on the undersides of the leaves. Small pools held their thin margins of bright knives of glass, thin fairy knives of ice. It was an easy way to get a drink: you could reach into the edge of a pool, break off handfuls of splinters, eat them.

Returning to his camp site from dusky fruitless wanderings, Morris circled a thicket on one of the higher islands of the swamp, and then stopped short. Rabbits: they were here, apparently they were many. In and out among weeds and water sprouts, their little paths were traced in profusion. He could not remember when he had not known rabbit tracks. So familiar they were: interlacing, mixed together in main avenues, the preliminary slash of the hind paws into thin sprinkled snow which had dried there . . . front paws coming down . . . the single-double track of rabbits. Anyone should recognize that, he thought. He saw no rabbits, however. Doubtless all were in their sets: gray mounds of fur, ears laid back, motionless, dozing.

The memory of a story leaped full-bodied into his mind (as recollection comes to a child because of the limited knowledge, the limited fund of recollection which he possesses). The story concerned an elderly Indian of the long ago in that region, who crushed both his feet in some solitary accident, and could not stir from the covert where the mishap occurred. He was many miles from camp; it was cold; he dared not try to crawl all the way; he must remain where he was until someone found him. . . . No one found him for many weeks. He was not dead, he was in good condition. There had been many rabbits living or assembling in that scrap of timber tenanted by the crippled Indian. Though he had no weapons except a knife he waxed happy there. He snared rabbits: he fixed little nooses, took them thus. . . . Morris heard his uncle's voice telling the tale. He rather thought that it was told before his father died, he seemed to remember his father sitting by the fireplace.

He thought it not impossible for him to construct a noose of sorts. He was resourceful, he had to be, he had been taught to be. Morris could not have been more than five years old when he was set to the task of scaling fish. He had helped to dress out game which was shot, when he was very little older than that; although he was not allowed to shoot a rifle until he was eight, and then he had to rest the barrel in the crotch of a sapling, and he didn't hit a thing.

He examined his clothing. True, he could unravel one of the thick knitted cuffs of his yarn mittens; but he was afraid that the yarn would not be stout enough to hold a rabbit, to choke the life from it, and certainly a noose of yarn would not slide easily. His galluses also were knitted. No help there; and he wore no belt. He sat down and investigated his boots. They were cobbled in a nearby town, and Morris's uncle had traded off fox pelts in order to get them, and had home-cobbled them himself, in mending, later on. The tops were gashed down on the outer side of each leg for greater ease in pulling the boots on and taking them off, and this slit was secured by laced rawhide. The boots would stay on without the rawhide lacing; it was merely that the laces made them more snug. Morris had his laces out in no time at all, and spliced them. He knew how to make a slipknot. . . . It was difficult to secure the rawhide properly above a rabbit path, and he did not know whether rabbits were as sensitive to the odor of man as were other animals trapped by his uncle. He rather imagined not: how else could the Indian have managed when he was crippled? Twas worth a try.

Morris broke branches of dry dead thorn. He built little barricades on either side, at right angles to what seemed to be the main traveled path, where tracks were so numerous as to make nearly a ditch in the light snow. Unless they wished to go around the entire structure (and he made it wide) rabbits would have to travel on that path. Finally there was nothing more to do, which was well, since it was almost dead dark. He left the noose arranged, praying as he left it: Oh, Lord, our Heavenly Father, oh do send me a rabbit, for I am starving! Dear Lord, please hear my prayer! Amen. He crept to the nest of leaves and mined deep, reaching out his stiff mittened hands again and again to pull more leaves over himself. He shivered long; but gradually the heat of his own body, contained in his clothing, warmed him. His feet ached, encased in boots, unaccustomed as he was to go to bed while wearing his boots.

The many blows of the switches wielded by Mr. Dowsing had ridged his backside. Moving his mittened hand, even through the thickness of trousers he could feel how the flesh had risen in protest. He would be a mass of interlaced red there, could he but see the marks.

Rats, weasels, wild things of the swamp . . . foxes, bobcats . . . they traveled near, he thought he heard the light pressure of their feet. There were whispers of twigs falling. There was a distant howl: owl or wolf, what was it? He went off wandering aloof through darkness, emancipated from imprisonment of his own body. He went into space, saw the long black box in which his mother lay, heard one of the men, as leader, mutter, One, two, *hup;* and they hoisted his mother in the box, and bore her into evenings which grew steadily darker until you could not even see the procession disappearing.

Somewhere, trailing among phantasmagoria of true sounds and fancied sights, he lost himself . . . night . . . awake momentarily . . . alone . . . oh, where was he? The woods . . . yes, swamps round about. He was on a higher island, a small island, he was in his nest; but the cold was attacking again. . . . He slept more.

Then he awoke quickly, fiercely, and there was grayness around. The night was finishing, perhaps Morris Markham's life was finishing. How long did it take for one to starve? Always he had been well fed before; there had been lean periods in the lives of the Markhams, but they did not hunger long. Now his stomach felt as if it were a dried apple, twisted, rubbery. It was dry and it was empty; so why should those bubbles come up in his throat?—they hurt him, and tasted sour when they exploded. He thought that a knife was sticking his middle. He pushed blindly out of the leaves. Not once had he risen during the night to replenish the fire. There were four small ends of smoldering logs—little nubbins trailing their windrows of soft white ash to mark the path along which the logs had burned. Morris shoved these fragments together, and brought dry leaves. Flames came up to comfort heart and body.

He paused only long enough to relieve his aching bladder, and to eat a few slivers of ice from the nearest water hole; then he brought more wood until his fire was not a campfire, it was a bonfire. But his knotted stomach hurt him still. He lay prone to bury his face in the pool, he drank greedily. Water seemed splashing coldly through his insides.

Then a thought struck him more sharply than the lash of Master Dowsing's switch.

He bounced up off the mat of half-frozen leaves and vines, and struggled through underbrush toward the thicket of the rabbits. He had forgotten his snare! Truly he did not expect to find that he had caught anything (he had baited his first trotline when he was perhaps six, he had studied the lesson set before any wise fisherman to learn, and had committed it well . . . there is nothing on the line, you know that, you have affirmed it before you begin to draw in the line . . . and when there is a big catfish sawing back and forth, fighting the pressures of the cord in front and the boulder behind . . . then that is a special gift, newly awarded, pristine, shaped and polished by a smiling Fate)! Limber leafless twigs lashed back at him as he struck them aside. He received fresh scratches, did not care; he rushed on through.

At first he thought that a trained rabbit was standing on its hind legs, like a bear or a dog in the traveling menagerie he had heard about but never seen. It was a large bunny, stiff with death and cold, its head lolled coyly to one side. The strip of rawhide went taut to the bending small sapling above. There were traces in the snow where the animal's poor feet had touched and torn in the struggle; and the creature's eyes were closed, because this was a slow death by strangulation. The eyes were not open as sometimes were the eyes of rabbits you shot.

This was a precious thing. It was his, his, his! Not only would sustenance soon be creeping through the channels of his body; but a greater glory lived in the pink transparent ears, the tenderness of gray fur, the paws so pathetic. This trophy he had rived away from nature without the aid of gunpowder. Had he just concluded the choking of a healthy young bear with naked hands, Morris could have felt no prouder.

He went to his camp in deliberate dignity, rawhide coiled in his pocket against future need, the soft stiff shape in his arms. Vaguely it seemed to him that his own face felt fatter than it had felt before. He was wearing the mask of the gloating . . . his eyes felt as if they shone like newly run rifle balls. . . .

His uncle Melancthon watched from a willow brake as the boy squatted down to begin butchering. Uncle Melly had prowled the edge of the swamp before daybreak, feeling confident that he would pick up his nephew's trace there. He found tracks easily in the first light; Morris had fled with no attempt to conceal his trail, he had not thought that Master Dowsing would pursue him. If the sheriff took out after him, it would probably be with dogs; and he knew of no way to avoid leaving a scent for them to follow. . . . Uncle Melly watched critically until his nephew had shaped a crude mud pie and put the rabbit into the fire to bake. Then he frightened the boy by breaking his way through the willows with a crackle like gunfire. He leaned his old Pennsylvania rifle in a safe place, and sat down on Morris's bed.

Ought to tied his legs together and hung him up, the uncle said. Twould be easier to get the guts out that way, easier than flat. You didn't have no stump to work on.

Morris kept sticking the blade of his knife into the hard ground to clean off blood and fur.

Now, said Uncle Melly, them ashes is bound to cool quick. You ought to put some firebrands atop whilst you've got your game in. . . . Nother thing: ought to turn it over at least twice. Bakes evener. But it's ticklish to do, cause you're apt to bust it open with the stick, and twill be too hot for you to use your hands. Ought to have a paddle or something. Whyn't you go whittle one?

Uncle Melly, how'd you know where I was?

Left a trail wide enough for the preacher and principal deacons.

Is—is?— Morris tried to say the word *sheriff,* and could not get it out. Finally he mumbled something that sounded like *sheriff,* and Uncle Melly responded properly.

Don't know nothing bout no sheriff. When you didn't appear to home, I went over and talked to the Perry younguns. They tolt me bout you and the master, and how you flung the inkwell. Well, some of the scholars had to lead him home. He couldn't see, not for hours. You like to blinded him.

Don't care.

Reckon you don't.

Figured they'd put me in jail.

Oh, he's mean as sin, and no great shakes of a schoolmaster! Times I hear things like this, I'm glad I can barely write my own name. And I did have to make my mark until I was thirty or so; then the preacher's wife, she taught me. But I don't believe no good ever come of education pounded in with a maul.

Twasn't no maul. Twas hickory switches.

Whatever twas. What you aim to do now?

I think I got enough schooling, Uncle Melly. I can say some of the multiplication table. Though I do hate to cipher. Don't cipher as well as some. But I can read the Holy Writ. You've heard me.

Yes, though you read mighty labored like. But twas hard for you, starting off on the Begats. At Sabbath school they should have started you on something easy like Psalms.

Psalms ain't easy, said Morris. Just you try to read them sometime.

I never will. . . . I wasted time a-hunting you, added Uncle Melly suddenly. I should have been going clean round my trap line.

Didn't know you had any set yet.

Got a few nigh to the ponds. Liable to get a thaw and the fur'd spoil; so I've only set the ones I can visit quick. First good dead freeze I'll lay out the whole line. Want to learn to trap? Twill be hard work.

Yes, sir, said Morris Markham. I want to trap.

. . . Thus he came to the end of formal schooling. For his purposes a more significant curriculum awaited: the science of beaver castor, the mathematics of the stars themselves, economy of peltries and flesh, the liberal arts which lie in the shape and texture and pattern of dry froth blown from a cattail's head, the philosophies inherent in quiet grass and quiet trees when the earth lies sleeping.

In such a mode the quasi-illiterate Morris Markham became well educated in time, and fully in command of himself because of the discipline exacted by rigors. When he grew older he felt the need for women . . . never did he feel the need for books, or the copybooks of the past which he had not opened and which would never be forced into his hands.

The vicious mathematical enigma assumed the form of a mosquito; thus it lived to fly in front, to bite him on nose or wrist, to plague him.

The chemical formula was sheerest mystery . . . what roots had decayed to make it, and in what muck?

Animal problems were substituted for the human.

(In time the sensitive and intelligent woodsman will become a savant, however devoid of formalities and degrees, if he but accept the puzzles put to him by lizards and aspen leaves, and try rationally to solve them; and, if unable to solve them, accept their puzzle in all its complication.)

X

The next year, in 1841, Uncle Melly decided to dispose of his land and go west into the Big Miami Reserve. Trapping had become unproductive in that Ohio neighborhood, and Uncle Melly did not wish to resume the farming activity he'd always loathed: no longer did he own sufficient draft animals—his very wagon was decayed out of disuse and neglect. Accordingly he found a westbound freighter with room enough to carry the family's few effects; and Melancthon Markham and his nephew walked all the way to Indiana woods where the Miamis were now moving out. Aunt Eunice rode on the one wheezing mare still left to the Markhams. They pre-empted a location in the forest some miles east of Lafountain's Reserve at Wildcat Rapids. Soon the town of Kokomo began to grow in that same county (nursed into being, folks declared, by a liberal application of Uncle Dave Foster's forty-rod whiskey). Richardville County became Howard County in a later season, but that made little difference to the Markhams—they were interested in marten skins and deadfalls, not in the organization of bailiwicks.

Morris Markham spent his youth in contentedly reducing the fish, bird, and animal population of north central Indiana. He did not confine himself to his own locality as he grew tall and experienced; he ranged to the Wabash, and down that stream through Carroll County into swamps and dark thickets of Tippecanoe County, and north again along the Tippecanoe River. In 1849 he heard that the hills of Brown County afforded some foxes; there were said to be black foxes down in Brown County or at least one fabulous black fox. Morris drifted to Brown County, wandering down in the late autumn as warmer weather drained away into the south. He spent a calm and satisfying solitary winter in a cat-faced shed which he erected at the head of a ravine. He did take a black fox. He went to Indianapolis with this trophy, where two dealers bid against each other for the prize as Morris wandered serenely back and forth between them. Finally he disposed of the pelt for two hundred and thirty dollars, and was trailed out of Indianapolis (he despised that town, all a-bustle with its new railroad, and was only too happy to leave it) by several toughs who sought to deprive the woodsman of his fortune. One man Morris left for dead in a gully. He was never certain whether the man was actually dead or not; but doubtless he succumbed later. Two more crept to the nearest village with buckshot in their legs, and one fled back to Indianapolis intact but badly frightened. Morris Markham continued with content up the White River and Cicero Creek, then strolled down Turkey Creek toward Howard County and home. He chipped a certain stone out of the chimney, removed the stone, put in his long brown hand, and drew forth a pewter teapot with the handle and spout broken off. With his current season's windfall he now had over seven hundred dollars in the pot. It was likely that none of the neighbors would have thought he had more than seven dollars, if that. Morris fell in love, in this same year of 1850, however. His infatuation carried him to New York City where he squandered the bulk of his savings in pursuing a hopeless and ridiculous devotion. Then—wiser, but not particularly sadder; in fact uplifted in soul because of a mystic and maturing emotional experience—he came back to Indiana and was looked upon with bewilderment by the neighbors, many of whom adored him.

Morris, where on earth you been?

Oh, wandering, like usual.

But—in the summer? Couldn't do no trapping in August—

No. I been fishing some. (Indeed this was a fact; one day on a Hudson River pier, weary of taverns and traffic and importuning crowds, he had given a dime to a youngster to let him hold his improvised fishing pole; but Morris caught nothing at all.)

Fishing, hey. Whereabouts?

Oh, here and there.

. . . His old aunt had broken her hip when Morris was twelve. She remained sick abed for nearly a year, cared for tenderly by Morris and Uncle Melancthon. Then she died. Morris and Uncle Melly trapped and hunted together or singly for another few years. They had thought the bears long since cleaned out of their region; but when Morris Markham was sixteen it was rumored that bears lurked in a wooded region up in Wabash County. These creatures were believed to have strayed down from thick Michigan forests; Morris scouted the whole notion, but Uncle Melly believed that it was worth a try. They had a serious and indeed acrimonious disagreement on this subject, and Uncle Melly said that he would go after bears single-handed. He did have a bear trap up on the stringers of the shed adjoining the little house; the trap was duly cleaned and greased, and this cumbersome instrument Uncle Melly toted in his barrow all the way to Wabash County, old as he was. There he prowled the woods, actually did discover large bear tracks, and in a propitious place he attempted to set the trap. Apparently one of the heavy tension screws was rusted through . . . it was broken short off when people stumbled upon Uncle Melly. Whatever had happened, however the disaster befell, those mighty toothed jaws had snapped shut and caught Uncle Melly by both wrists; and there he was, alone and chained and agonizing in the cold, and how he must have cried for help!—until his screams grew weaker and trailed away into nothingness, and long icy slumber claimed him. . . . Sometimes, for years afterward, Morris Markham would start up at night, imagining that he heard his uncle pleading; and it was not pleasant to consider that they had separated at least in a pet if not in anger just before this tragedy—when they'd loved and trusted each other always before. But the youth learned his philosophies aptly. There was nothing to be done about the situation now, except to bring the poor body back to Howard County so the old man might lie beside his wife. This chore was managed during that same winter; and young Morris had stones cut for both graves. Whenever he thought of Uncle Melly, Morris would smile with affection, and wink the tears out of his eyes as he whispered (lone men do talk to themselves, and often): To think, Uncle Melly, that you was right all along! There was a bear! Man named Henry Landon shot it, only two days after your body was found! And—and— I'll never set a bear trap, myself. Not ever! Too blame cruel!

The former Big Miami Reserve was still a frontier in those years, though towns were prospering in other portions of Indiana, though ambitious towns were swelling, hundreds of miles to the west. Thus the practicality of pioneer mores ruled: no one tried to appoint a guardian for the Markham lad—to bind him out, to subdue or civilize him. He went an aloof respected way as he had always gone. Doubtless there were men in the vicinity who looked with covetous eyes upon Uncle Melly's property; but they knew that Morris would kill anyone who tampered with him—anyone wearing the trappings of legality or unadorned with them: it was as simple as that. Morris was regarded generally as a free agent, in hardy command of his own life and fortunes; no preachers or constables came pussyfooting on his trail.

His favorite clan of human beings was the tribe of Howes. You could count twelve of them, tall or small (and also there existed four mounds beneath a cedar tree in Jefferson County, far to the south, to show where the first four Howe children ended up during the epidemic of '32). A certain clergyman deemed this unhappiness An Afflicting Dispensation of Providence, but other people called it simply The Cholery. Fourteen children in all were borne by the sweet-tempered Millicent Howe, though nowadays she told women friends in confidence that she believed her childbearing days were done—she hadn't endured the Monthlies in over three years— The tight knob of hard-wound hair on the back of her head no longer looked like a piece of shiny polished coal—it looked like a piece of shiny polished glass. Millie Howe's voice was forever lenient and apologetic; but she had so little to apologize for, except for poverty!—and she could always find time to doctor a boy's hurt foot or finger, always find time to bake huge tins of hermits (when indeed they owned the flour and sugar and molasses and soda essential). The orphan Markham lad first appeared at the Howe place at the age of fourteen, and shyly requested permission to trap muskrats in the back slough of their land. He went away with his nose wiped, some comforting oil poured into a sore ear, the seat of his pants newly patched, and his mouth full of hermits. Also he had been given permission to trap. When Morris came across haws or hazelnuts in proper season, these delicacies were conveyed promptly to the Howes; and they never lacked for savory pigeons when flocks broke down the beech limbs in squatting there for mast. The Howes were essentially farmers, not woodsmen, but not successful farmers; the elder children shone better at a play-party than in the oatfields. Only one bumper crop was ever reared by the Howes; that crop was children. The gaunt gray house, never painted since the day it was raised, seemed bursting at seams and doors and windows and cornices with frantic young people who laughed, tussled, sang, early and late . . . they were always chasing each other round and round across the filthy littered dooryard; always somebody was running; if you merely halted in that back road and looked up at the soiled house you were bound to see some figure, bulky or tiny, on the run, and usually another figure chasing after the first one. . . . People wondered how on earth the Howes kept their souls and bodies together; and indeed that was about all they managed to do—keep soul and body together. The only time they ever sat quietly was during the Bible reading which followed their morning meal. Wouldn't be much of a meal, either—eggs could be traded, so they seldom ate eggs; and sometimes there was milk, and sometimes not; and sometimes butter, and sometimes not. There was always mush, and if they had no milk they ate the mush fried in pork fat; and if they had no sugar they put sorghum on the cornmeal mush. Sometimes Morris Markham would bring a bounty of fish from lines which he kept set in the deep active creek . . . once he remembered fishing through the ice at a place called Little Willer Bend, and taking one red horse after another with his spear. Red horse were commonly looked upon as a trash fish because they had so many bones through their flesh, but the meat itself was sweeter than trout—you just had to go slow about the eating, and not gag yourself on a bone. Anyway, Morris soon had enough red horse for an army to eat, even an army of Howes; he bundled the freezing orangish mass together and lugged it Howe-wards into the frosty rising sun. He was welcomed with boyish roars and girlish squeals as always. Big frying pans smoked and spat on the range for a time, and then thirteen people sat down to a banquet . . . no second table at the Howes'! They had two long wide planks put up on sawhorses to make a table, and usually they sat several on each side and Pa and Ma at the ends (in earlier years, Millie Howe always had the baby on her lap) and some of the urchins sat on big blocks of wood instead of chairs. Joel Howe kept a long leafless wand of stiff dried willow on the floor beside his place, and if any child grew too obstreperous or noisily petulant, Joel Howe would reach down the long table with his willow and give that child a swat on the hand, warning him to mind his manners. . . . Folks used to laugh and say that Joel Howe had a face for the top of his head, and the top of his head for his face. This was because his head was completely devoid of hair, and it was always peeling off, and the places where it peeled made an odd expression, something like eyes and nose and mouth. His face was so thick with reddish whiskers—you never knew whether it was a widespread beard which the man kept pruned to extreme shortness, or merely that he hadn't shaved for a week or so. . . . Joel, like his wife, spoke in a mild soft manner; and his voice rose at the end of each utterance he made as if he were asking a question. When he read the Scriptures it seemed always that he was asking questions even when obviously there was none to be asked. Morris Markham remembered the day when he brought that especially large catch of red horse: when it came time to eat, Morris was squeezed in at the table between Jonathan and Liddy. Everyone talked at once, and no one except Sardis got out of hand; then this small girl received a swat on the wrist for misbehaving; but Sardis didn't cry—she just glowered at her father, and then yelled in her tiny-girl accent: Oh, you bad man! You try to sassinate me!—and how the roar burst up; and Joel Howe sat with his scrubby face clasped in both hands, rocking to and fro as he laughed.

They were good people to be with, those Howes. It made you feel good inside, just to hear them and see them. Morris did not quite know why this was so, for they attained so little in the world; and really were lazy and improvident (judged by prevailing standards of Howard County); but he'd learned early, as one valued crumb in his colossal loaf of woodland education, that if a thing is true it is true, and need not be explained or even commented upon, unless it be for an additional benefit inherent in the repetition.

Always after breakfast old Joel Howe read the Scriptures.

Thy word is a lamp unto my feet?—and a light unto my path?

I have sworn?—and I will perform it?—that I will keep thy righteous judgments?

I am afflicted very much?—quicken me, O Lord?—according unto thy word?

Lydia Howe, called more frequently Liddy, was Morris Markham's favorite of all the family. He might have fallen in love with her except for discrepancy in their ages—when he was sixteen, say, and dreaming secretly and secretively about matters female, why, Liddy was a little thing half his age! And in the year when honestly Morris was consumed with passion for a woman he had never met in his life—that was in his twenty-first year—Liddy was only twelve and just beginning to wear her skirts longer in order to conceal her changing legs. She welcomed longer gowns even more than most girls might, because of a slight deformity. After Morris came back from his journey to New York in fact (from his vague summer's fishing expedition, according to the belief of Howes and others) he found that Alvin Noble was always making excuses to go to the Howe farm, and Alvin had never done that before.

Alvin looked to be a preacher or teacher or poet but was in fact a young carpenter and joiner. Fairly did he resemble his name (Morris Markham remembered mention of knights and nobles and such, in schoolbooks; he did not know whether a noble might also be a knight, but suspected that he could, if he were a very special and brave noble) and Noble was a sound respected name in that State: there was a Noblesville, a memory of Governor Noah Noble, a Noble County, and so on.

Morris encountered Alvin Noble first when they were in their middle teens; Morris was shooting squirrels for the pot, squirrels to be taken to Kokomo and peddled there; and Alvin and his father drove into a strip of hardwood timber in order to select a tree which might yield burled lumber for their cabinetmaking. They hungered for fat squirrels, so Morris gave them a generous bag because the elder Noble owned that timberland (but it was not posted with *No Trespassing* signs—commonly most of the forest was open cheerfully to all comers; and some portions seemed to belong to the world at large, for no one might secure a clear title to them). Alvin Noble seemed drawn to the quiet tanned young hunter, asked him questions about his rifle, was allowed to shoot it—did in fact wound one squirrel—Morris had to throw sticks at the suffering furry thing in order to knock it out of the tree where it had lodged, and dispatch it with a blow. Alvin Noble looked sadly at the death he'd made, and said that he thought he would never enjoy hunting. Fairly did he look his name—long-limbed, long-faced, with huge gray eyes which peered out in patient wonderment from under delicately arched brows. But already his big hands were the hands of an artisan—he had started to learn his trade when he was twelve, and his hands were gnarled, scarred, calloused in odd places; his arms and back were heavily muscled.

This was the man who grew to love Liddy Howe almost before she was ready for love.

Lydia was the sworn chum of Alvin Noble's cousin, Elizabeth Burtch, who lived in a neat farmhouse less than a mile from the down-at-the-heels hive of the Howes. The two girls had held loyal passion, each for the other, almost since they were toddlers; they exchanged hair bracelets and finger rings, gave nosegays back and forth, they knitted nubias and mittens for mutual gifting at Christmastide. What was more natural, in such case, than that Alvin should fetch along his young friend Joe Thatcher when he came courting Liddy (when she was fourteen, and Lizzie the same age) and that Joe should make sheep's eyes at Lizzie Burtch and keep her out of the way, while Alvin courted Liddy Howe? . . . Morris Markham, aloof, grown perhaps a little cynical because of certain unrecorded passages in his life, smiled tolerantly at the antics of younger folk. . . . A double wedding was held when the girls were fifteen years of age. Old Joel Howe had to sell off some cattle in order to pay for his share of the festivities, but he did not complain; and the younger Howes chortled in glee when one of them suddenly decided that Big Sister was marrying a Noble man!

(Her voice was not musical, but it was soft, often it had the quality of a question, she seemed to be asking something, seemed to be expecting a reply which might please or amuse her and others. It was not that she was seeking comfort; she gave comfort, did not ask for it; she found it in all people and all nature as needed. Lydia was a little taller in height than most girls; she had been ungainly as a child; but now it was a blossoming in every true sense of the word. . . . Once when she was small she suffered severely from fever. She lay hot, staring or muttering on the cot where they placed her, and giving incoherent cries. She did not recognize her mother for a time; and when she could speak intelligibly, it was to complain of an ache in leg and hip. . . . My limb, she kept saying, Oh, Ma, my limb! It hurts so. I can't stretch it. . . . Fever departed, and in time she could stretch her leg. But there was always a weakness; and Lydia was shy of the fact, when with females in the intimacy of a bedchamber, when what she called *her hurt limb* seemed to be slightly smaller than the other. She could not hippety-hop as deftly as other girls, but the lameness did not interfere with her walking. At fifteen Lydia Howe was accounted to be one of the prettiest young women in Howard County and certainly the very prettiest in her own neighborhood. . . . When Alvin Noble looked at her hair and saw the way it took the color out of the sunlight and held it, he thought of the inner core of red cedar. Alvin had built many chests and wardrobes lined with cedar; he enjoyed touching this wood with his hands . . . Lydia's hair! When moonlight found it it was filmy. . . . Alvin considered often in his virginal years—wondered secretly, and of course in shame, but wondered still—how it would be if he were in bed with Lydia. . . . In a bed together, they were near the window, her face turned away from him, he saw only her hair. At last moonlight drilled through the panes and came down and touched her hair. . . . He wondered what it would be like to be with her in bed, be able to reach out cautiously, wrapping his hands tenderly in that hair until she awoke; then he would lower his face and smell the hair. . . . Her mild drawling voice was unlike voices of her sisters or mother. Her tiny eyes had red lights in them. Red shone in some people's eyes; Alvin had seen red fire come into black eyes, for instance, when people were enraged. But if Lydia were ever enraged no one saw her in such condition. If a thing was too ignoble, too preposterous, it served only to amuse her . . . as if her warm pulpy little mouth smiled in concert with the crinkling blaze in her dark eyes . . . as if she said, What fools these mortals be! or, How grotesque! or, Great heavens to Betsy, what a mistake! . . . A cruel thing forced her to close her eyes. . . . Her eyelids were soft, thick; they came down, squeezed shut, there were little crimps on their surface; then at last, when Lydia had mastered emotion, the lids went up and you could see her eyes again, and for a moment there was no crimson light in them at all. . . . Her mother said, I never had a spat with Liddy in my life. . . . Her brothers tried to fuss with her sometimes; but she only laughed or ran away. It was seldom that any emotion caused her to burst into tears. But she was not phlegmatic, she could feel. . . . The disability of her right leg caused her to droop her head toward the left. She pulled with her head as if compensating for the strain and tilt of it; and thus, when she threw her head back to laugh, it went always to one side, turning on her long graceful neck. . . . Her breasts must be things of beauty—her bosom was so round, her waist so slim. Alvin Noble would find out, and did . . . yea, things of great beauty, objects of excitement and incitement, they became his toys! He had thought she would be horrified; she was not horrified at all. She only smiled lazily as he fondled her. Sometimes, in the heat of their final encounter, her eyes would close—perhaps the only time they closed except in sleep, or when she sought escape from a fell reminder. . . . Her lips would fall open; she would breathe an ecstasy, but quietly, quietly, until all was done. . . . Joel Howe wished eagerly to give Lydia a silk dress when she was married—she'd prayed for a silk for years—but of course it couldn't be managed. Joel and Millie had to settle for calico; but the goods was of a new pattern, and very pretty—tiny pink apple blossoms on a gray background. . . . A bright thing for a young woman; and she was a bright young thing.)

One evening in late July, 1855, when he himself was twenty-five, Morris Markham walked up the narrow back road to the Howe place, carrying by its tail a large turtle which he was bringing as a gift to Old Mrs. Millie Howe. (That is what he and everyone else called her. She was forty-seven years of age.) Morris glanced at the sun and reckoned that it was about a quarter after six by the clock; that was all right: the Howes sat down to eat before six o'clock usually, or even earlier when they couldn't hold off the voracious four smaller children—all boys—any longer. Morris didn't want these warm-spirited people to think that they had to feed him every time he showed up. But he'd taken this fine snapper on a single line which he kept set in a lonely swamp hole unvisited by other people—he'd warred with that turtle, tried to shoot it, missed; he blamed the turtle for killing a puppy which foolishly had followed Morris to this tarn; he'd seen the turtle drag water birds beneath the surface like some subterranean ogre. A lot of folks thought snappers unfit for food— How wrong they were! Morris Markham felt a keen sense of triumph at ridding the swamps of a demon, in one breath; and in the next breath he was conscious of the slow affection and satisfaction in his relationship to a dear woman who served as the symbol of Motherhood. She'd mentioned wistfully that she hadn't tasted turtle soup in years . . . oh, she did love that broth! Her aunt, back in Massachusetts, used to pour a noggin of dandelion wine into the simmering pot when they had turtle soup. . . .

Morris wished that he might be fetching some dandelion wine to Old Mrs. Millie Howe as well, but he had no wine or spirits of any kind. He had not tasted an alcoholic drink for almost five years—not since the last night he spent in New York City— Ah! Best not to dwell on that.

But as if to remind him, he heard a mourning dove—the muted evening call, notes seemed rolling out richer thicker slower than in the daytime song—it was a melody more comforting or more mournful than the daytime song, depending upon how a man felt at the moment, Morris supposed. Through his parted lips came as a single whisper, a woman's name. Then he went on, changing the turtle from hand to hand every few rods because of its weight.

There clung a light mist—the traditional smoky blue mist of a midsummer evening in Howard County coming up, gray and indefinite, close at hand, falling into opulent blue-green as you gazed among groves toward the approaching sunset, thickening to purplish in farther reaches. Trees were motionless except where they stood exposed to the most trifling touch of breeze; and then the lighter-hung walnut leaves twitched slightly at the top, while heavier maple leaves and even the gum leaves hung uninspired, unwavering. Corn was man-high and ragged, tassled out, ears depending away from the stalks; and every ear bannered with its white-pale-green silk . . . not too long before twould be big enough to roast!—and then watch the raccoons come a-stealing!

Morris came round the bend approaching the farmstead, and saw ugly toppling unpainted sheds dignified by the approach of night. They were like a group of misshapen old men, pretending to or even possessing a false importance they'd never really earned . . . he'd often seen outbuildings undergoing such transformation as dusk came staining them . . . to say nothing of moonlight . . . blame that turtle!—Twas heavy . . . hollyhocks. He smiled to see them raising china faces. Mrs. Howe's dozen stalks of hollyhock—she never had a chance to raise more—clustered tall in the corner by the house ell, not yet knocked and twisted by summer storms. They were very proud of their first high blossoms, proud of the fat and weighty buds below . . . they look, thought Morris Markham, like girls in their teens dressed up for Sabbath school. Kind of simpering . . . but they'll make good mothers by and by. . . .

He was welcomed vociferously by four full-grown dogs and a committee of assorted puppies before he'd walked into the house yard. This pack tussled and tumbled about the man's legs, all trying to pay their respects to the headless turtle at once. Morris was interested to note that Noble and Thatcher dogs were here; the young folks must have come a-visiting. He progressed around the corner of the house to the rear, going slowly, trying not to step on puppies. I swear, Morris, you look like that Pie Piper fellow we used to read about, cried the ruddy young Jonathan Howe. Been a-piping dogs, have you? . . . Everyone was there—five daughters, five sons, Alvin Noble, the Thatchers—everyone laughing and welcoming Morris; and the lonely hunter's heart rose and swelled. He preferred to spend most of his hours away from other men, but also he liked to be loved—to have some sort of busy plaguing noisy warm boiling frying laughing home into which he could step, when and if he wanted to step there. They'd brought out the greasy planks and sawbucks and had erected their long table under the old grapevine arbor where chickens wandered at will and creamed their droppings between kegs and chair legs and stool legs. The people were still at table, just finishing. . . . Blame heifer tried to get away from the rain? said Old Joel Howe. Took shelter under that lone oak down in the pasture?—and the lightning struck her dead as scat? So we butchered out of season a-yesterday?—now, Morris, you come and set down to some nice lightning-struck beef?—land knows we got enough and to spare?

No, he had fed already—ate a whole big durn catfish.

But— What was *that?*

That was a jutting boat-shaped wagon of a type he'd often seen driven and occupied by movers traveling through the country. After Morris had duly presented his turtle to Millie Howe, and had duly admired and snapped his fingers at and whistled at young John Noble, who sat, aged one year, owl-eyed and looking very much like his father, on his father's knee– After these amenities, Markham went to examine the big wagon which was drawn up just past the well and the dilapidated dairy shed, its tongue dropped and team tied out (but still wearing their harness, feeding at the edge of the weedy orchard). Noble and Thatcher and Jonathan Howe, followed by a sprinkling of young male Howes, came along to show off the wagon.

Whose?

Ourn, said Joe Thatcher; and in the same instant– His, said Alvin Noble. The two friends looked at each other and grinned. Like this, Joe explained. Fellow comes into my father's smithy–you know, I'm just a *helper* there– (He emphasized the word *helper* sarcastically. Joe Thatcher felt keenly his father's unwillingness to take him into full partnership. This had been hinted as a rite which might occur upon Joe Thatcher's marriage, but if a promise was implied it was never kept.) –And he says: Know where I can sell a good wagon? He'd come from Connecticut or somewheres; first they lost one child, then they lost another, and finally his wife she sickened, and cried, and wished to go back home. So their journey to the West halted right here in this county. And I talked to Alvin, and we agreed to go in cahoots; so I made the swap. Alvin he won't admit tis half his yet, not till he pays me his share.

I'm trying to raise the cash, said Alvin Noble solemnly, his wide brows scrolling higher. Hard to do so with family cares, and now the little one.

Liz and me hain't got no little one yet, declared Thatcher. But tain't from lack of effort, or not knowing how to shoe the little critter if we get it!–and everybody laughed; the small Howe boys especially snorting through their noses at being allowed to overhear the elders' intimacy in Matters Ordinarily Not Discussed.

Morris asked, What in tunket you want with a rig like this?

Well, said Joe, and looked at Alvin; then they both looked away, and then back at Morris Markham, shyly but affirmatively.

You got Western fever?

Yep.

Why in heck?

We discussed it substantially; and it looks good to us. Our women-folks specially cotton to the idea!

But where'll you go?

Ioway, we figure.

But why in heck?

Philetus and Levi and Alfred and Jacob! Noble commanded (with that unique power of importance which rises from a direct order issued in a soft voice)– You kids skin out of here, now!

Aw, the small boys moaned; but they respected and loved their brother-in-law, so they went away.

The three friends might now discuss the situation in more detail.

Joe Thatcher was grown increasingly resentful of his father. Old man's shop, old man's forge, old man's bellows! You'd think I hadn't done nothing there since I was a little shaver and used to gather up the spilt nails, and blow the fire! Why, Saturdays I shoe two to his one! . . . Alvin Noble's plaint was not the same; his relations with his own parent were more equable; but there just wasn't much chance for a carpenter or cabinetmaker around there. Not enough building going on. Either people didn't need any new houses or chests or cupboards, or else they were too poor to have them built. You'd need to move to Kokomo or Marion in order to really get ahead. And Kokomo had only about six hundred inhabitants; it might not grow much larger, ever. And the price of land was awful high; if a man wanted to rise in the world by buying a chunk of ground so that his wife and kids might have a home of their own, case something bad befell, why– How many men could afford to pay these prices? Swampland was cheap, rough wooded land cheap enough; but twas only good to run hogs in, or a few scrawny head of woods cattle; all the improved drained cleared areas were out of sight in price– For a young man, anyway, still starting in life! And out there in that Ioway country you could get all you wanted for a dollar and a quarter per acre. Well, maybe not all you wanted; but what was wrong with three hundred and twenty acres? Legally you were allowed to claim that much from the Government; you just went out and stepped it off. Then, if you only broke five acres of sod, twas recognized as the beginning of your claim of ownership–that mere act of plowing would hold the place for six months–case you didn't have the cash all at once– Or a cabin. Eight logs high, with a roof on top: that was good for six months also. Just as good as if you had a Government patent in your pocket!

I ain't apt at ciphering, said Morris. But still you got to pay Uncle Sam. Let's see: three hundred and twenty acres, at a dollar and a quarter an acre–

Four hundred dollars, the friends said in unison. Thatcher added quickly: But what with my blacksmithing and Alvin's carpentry, and both raising a crop together–and the womenfolks can help with the crop–we figure to get together eight hundred dollars the first year; and thus pay for our land. By combined efforts–

Alvin Noble said slowly: Don't forget the old man, and his land.

That's right! Twelve hundred dollars, if you must, for the three places. But if the old man sells out, here, he'll have plenty of cash to pay for his new land, and plenty to spare.

You mean—Old Joel Howe's going too?

Talking that way.

Morris pointed to the wagon. Everybody—in that?

Now all laughed at the notion. Father Howe'll have wagons, said Alvin. He'll need plenty of wagon space for that flock.

Thatcher suggested easily, Oh, some of them girls are bound to get married off from time to time, along the way. Morris, I commend to you the Ioway country. Come along with us!

Not me, Jody. I hain't no shakes as a farmer.

What about all them wild animals and birds, in woodlands and prairies, hey?

Morris merely smiled and shook his head. He'd seen plenty of movers going West, especially these last five or six years; he didn't think much of them; why, the Iowa country must be already fairly crawling with people, reeking with new towns! . . .

But Old Joel Howe said No, and had an up-to-date map to prove it. He spread out his map in the fierce glow of the descending sun, and all the men gathered round to crowd their faces above the map and poke their fingers at it. The map was attached to a little red book; Morris spelled out the title slowly to himself: *Colton's Western Tourist and Emigrant's Guide.* The map offered official proof that here were whole counties which hadn't even been surveyed. Watered, but not too wet; just an occasional little river flowing south through them. They looked like very nice counties, attractively tinted in yellow, blue, green, pink— There was even a Howard County out there, too! They all bore attractive names, those pretty colored squares and oblongs which beckoned from the map, unmarred by section lines of the older more populous counties . . . Franklin, Wright, Humboldt, Pocahontas, Clay, Dickinson. . . . Look at that, Morris, said Joe Thatcher. They got lakes up in Dickinson. Plenty of fish. Bound to be!

Liddy cried, What? Oh, Jody, you ain't trying to give Morris a dose of Ioway fever too?—and the women shrilled with their light high-pitched excited laughter, until Joel Howe held up his finger to claim attention.

He had another book, written by a man named Plumbe; and he dipped alternately into both volumes, holding one book in his right hand, one in his left, trying to hold his loose bent specs on his nose at the same time; and all crowded close to hear every word. They felt, somewhat guiltily, that this was more exciting reading than the Chronicles and Kings and Proverbs which Old Joel served up to them as regular fare.

Listen to this, now? *The large white corn of the south?* . . . it says fifty or one hundred bushels per acre? And the yellow flint corn'll grow anywhere, it says: forty to seventy-five bushels per acre? . . . and . . .

where is it? . . . oh, yes . . . *prairies are easily converted to cultivation? —and its natural pastures afford peculiar facilities for the rearing of cattle, and sheep farming?* . . . *The sheep and hog are here raised with little or no trouble?—the natural productions of the forest and prairie affording a plentiful subsistence?* . . . and . . . oh, here . . . *free from many of the dangers incident to newly settled countries?— it offers the greatest inducements to immigrants and others to make it their homes?*

That means no Indians will come a-bothering, Millie Howe explained to her youngest sons.

Aw! sounded the combined disappointment.

Well, course there might be some. But they'd be friendly.

Jacob and Alfred began to circulate off across the yard, playing that they were Indians; Philetus and Levi caroused after them, dancing about, clapping their hands against their mouths in contrived war whoops. Their big brother Jonathan yelled: You all go over there past them currant bushes, you're going to make such a racket! . . . The boys obeyed, they caught up sticks and began to make threatening gestures at one another.

It says right here? said Old Joel Howe. *There is not a hostile tribe of Indians within a thousand miles of the Territory?*

. . . What's that author mean—Territory?

. . . Guess he wrote the book fore Ioway was a State.

. . . Oh.

These Sioux have always been on the best and most friendly terms with the whites?—and make it their boast?—that they have never shed a white man's blood?

And then . . . climate-wise? . . . right here on this page? *Very erroneous ideas are entertained abroad?—in relation to the winters in Iowa? They are supposed to be very long, dreary, and intensely cold? —with great quantities of snow? The very reverse is the fact? Pleasanter winters I have never experienced?—from New York to North Carolina? I have never seen snow a foot deep since I have been in the Territory?*

So says the man. Joseph Thatcher spoke doubtfully.

Well, Jody—tis right here in black and white! said his wife Elizabeth, who'd been looking over Old Joel's shoulder.

I speck we'll go, Old Joel murmured in a far-away voice. He put down the book for a moment. . . . I can sell at the drop of a hat? Mr. Powell from the bank has been hectoring me to buy the place away from me? Course, the mortgage'll have to be satisfied first off? . . . but then we could get our supplies and stuff together . . . ?

He looked speechlessly at his wife. Millie stood wrapping her hands in her ragged brown-checked apron; her eyes were very bright.

Twould be a relief, Mr. Howe, she said, addressing her husband but seeming to utter a formal verdict to the group. Then she whispered: Only thing I don't like is leaving the sod of Indiana and them four poor little graves.

Everyone followed her glance toward the trees in the south (as if you could see all the way down to Jefferson County, but you couldn't). Then everyone looked just as hastily in other directions.

We ain't got ahead here at home, very fast. . . . Millie Howe gave a dry chuckle; but somehow it seemed like a girl's light laugh—it might have been her daughter Lydia a-chuckling. . . . And what a relief to have a pleasant winter! I vow we had two foot of icy slush all froze last year, from January till the first of March. And then that one big freeze that come late—I lost half my baby chicks—

Old Joel picked up a book again and squinted desperately at the page through the strong light reflected from the west; he began to read aloud once more, but already the women were gathering up the supper things. Morris Markham listened to the reading for a few minutes longer, then took his leave. He was ambushed by four active Indians at the head of the lane; but ran fast away from their shrieks and made a good escape.

He walked slowly when he came to the back road, staring out and up at the active fruitful sky, feeling the display hot upon his face. He had spent nearly an hour at the Howes' . . . familiar clouds had had their chance to lift from the horizon. There lay a solid bank of ripened peach, marred with a few loose-strewn clouds blown free by the sudden exercise of winds. Morris Markham felt that all the clouds were going to erupt into freedom before long; there was going to be some kind of pink celebration over yonder . . . yet more clouds formed behind them.

Here were animals on his left. Not wild ones; these were Howe critters—never bred in sufficient numbers to fill the pastures—because of mismanagement (and definitely because of a weak bull, too old to go about his business properly). But these few spring calves were the size of deer by now, feeling a strong and active independence . . only the late-dropped urchins were still slopping after their mothers. The others were out tossing their tails and switching around and butting each other with their heads. . . .

Let's see. He was about two years older than Alvin Noble, four years older than Johnny Howe, seven years older than big Jody Thatcher— Yes, they were really young folks, the lot of them. And the womenfolks were just girls . . . motherhood or no motherhood, Liddy was a beaming girl and would always remain so. . . .

So maybe they had a right to rare around, like the calves, and do a lot of butting against Fate!

Oh, yes, twas natural.

(Now at twenty-five he felt inexpressibly agèd and wise and tolerant.)

This had been a year of extremely heavy foliage; weeds and grasses gave forth a heady almost noxious smell. Out of dark fallen underbrush, briars, green growths difficult to penetrate, there rose an ancient hint of moths, of night-flying creatures of all sorts, to come sporting and feeding and scooting and tasting and making mystery— Later, later, after dark— Oh, twas the whole character of the region— Pervading deep solemnity of approaching darkness and lonely dankness, in which trees and undergrowth knew a great deal more than the humans who pierced and traveled them. Thickets were silent . . . such secrets as they owned were even more sinister secrets a hundred years ago . . . long hundred years ago, before the world ever heard of Harrison or Tecumseh or Tippecanoe . . . they would keep those secrets to themselves.

Morris Markham stood appraising the region as if he'd just seen it for the first time.

No, by gum!

This was not a friendly or beckoning or welcoming kind of country. Long ago it could have been a challenge to the energetic young (because of its mystery, because all mystery is challenging). But somehow now he knew the wet and dry places all too well, knew everything which swam or crawled.

O feeling of dampness, feeling of stubbiness, of dwarfing . . . groves so forlorn, waiting without hope . . . over that way was the Burtch place, over that way the Mast place, over that other way the Skidd place. Out ahead dwelt the Greens and the Radleys and the Middletons. And now Morris realized that he had walked or waded every inch of this territory, one time or another.

Nigh onto fourteen years of it.

Maybe too long?

And he listened to mountebank crows in their eternal infernal tiring chorus, all saying the same thing over and over, making an identical repeated squawking scream as if they were led in unison by some crow chorister with a pitch pipe clasped in his claw, wings waving to direct. . . . Probably they've found an owl, thought Morris. They're always chasing owls.

Fierce and torn the sunset! . . . clouds broken and scattered like stock in a field being chased by dogs. There lurked thunder and electricity, conflicts in the upper strata . . . a muttering and hullabaloo going on up there. . . . Clouds torn, fragmented thinly, mixed up . . . it was a hodgepodge. Somebody had dumped out a rag bag of clouds (Aunt Eunice's old rag bag? Well, she had one; it was still hanging in a corner; had hung there untouched for a dozen years. Maybe mice had a home in it now. It smelled sort of mousy; and Morris Markham was just a hunter and fisherman and trapper, a-batching it; he wasn't any great shakes as a housekeeper).

Rag bag of clouds, insolent final glare of the witching hidden sun, spilled up behind the encumbrance of a rising storm.

Color stares at you. . . . Says, Who are you? Says, What you want? Says, What you think you're going to do about it? . . .

Why, certainly, surely! That was why so many young people went in the direction of the sun, plunging as if they wanted to smite it.

And down underneath, on the flat framework of Howard County itself, there was a kind of old widow feeling about the whole business. Looked like the country had a lot one time, maybe. Maybe it loved one time, maybe, and was loved in turn.

But now?

Old widow country.

(And he'd never felt that way about the region before.)

Go home in the gathering dark, now, and go to bed.

And still suggestion of a fiery carnival out ahead, and storms to come.

. . . Obeying his self-applied injunction, Morris strode promptly home, promptly went to bed, sternly and promptly went to sleep. But in the middle of a persistent hammering rainfall, in the middle of the night, in the middle of some dream of wandering an unfamiliar wood —he started up out of sleep, left his bed, stood barelegged in his shirt in the middle of the floor.

Well, by gol! That wasn't Uncle Melly's voice which had awakened him, not this time. It was Old Joel Howe's voice, and Old Joel was reading again—reading the last sentences he'd recited from the page of that little red-and-gold Colton's Western Tourist thing—just as he, Morris, was saying good night to them all.

Though the buffalo, once the denizen of this beautiful country, is now almost extinct?—and though the elk is only found in the wild recesses not yet occupied by civilization?—a great variety of wild animals remain?—and afford pleasure to the sportsman and profit to the hunter?

Well, gol damn you, Old Joel Howe! Why you come a-waking people up at this time of night?

. . . But twould be a sad day when the Howes were gone. Just imagine: walking the back road on one fine morning, and going up the lane, and seeing the house all cobbled up and painted, and new faces looking out at you, and a new dog coming—one that growled, maybe— You'd say: Hi. Don't mean to bother you. But— Lady, where's the Howes?

. . . Gone, Mr.

. . . Gone? Gone where?

. . . Gone away out West somewheres. Oh, land yes, I recall now: they've gone to the Ioway country! They sold out, lock-stock-and-barrel, and they've gone.

. . . Gone, gone, gone to smite the sun!

. . . And you won't never see them again.

. . . And you can come round here a hundred times, but the dog will still growl at you; and I can't be bothered with asking you in to have a plate of supper; and I ain't going to sew no buttons on your coat; and I ain't going to knit you no pair of socks, no matter how forlorn you look at me!

. . Bring all the prime dark mink pelts you want—bring two of those pretty pelts to Liddy, to make a tippet to wrap around her pretty slanted neck—to fetch out the jumping red fire from her eyes—Bring 'em, then! But Liddy won't be here at all, for she's gone, gone, gone in truth.

. . . And so's Alvin Noble, with his quiet slow decent talk, and his big solemn gray gaze.

. . . And all them young boys skirmishing around, making wild Indian noises. Gone West, they are! To the Ioway country.

. . Departed, departed, beyond redemption. And Jody Thatcher too, with his oaken arms and his hands like hams, and the hoarse chuckle and young male sweat-smell of him. And that pretty Lizzie Thatcher. Departed for keeps!

. . . And extensive riot and chasing and outcry of the numerous Howes—their improvidence and amiability—and making you always welcome, making you always feel to home; telling you always to pull up a chair, and have some popcorn, and put your soggy boots in front of the careless blaze. Gone! For good! Permanently! Departed! Vanished!

. . . Might as well all be dead. Gad!

The wolf, panther, and wildcat are still numerous?—and in the wooded districts the black bear is found? Foxes, raccoons, opossums, gophers, porcupines, squirrels, and the otter?—inhabit almost the whole unsettled country?

Once he'd owned a fair illusion, had gone East following it, had been sweltered by crowds, elbowed and sneered at and wheedled at and approached by low characters—all in seeking the shape and voice of a certain beauty— And then, beauty-less, he'd fled away (however uplifted and ripened by having been deeply in love) and he'd sworn that he'd have no truck with cities, ever, ever, ever.

But this midnight was neither hour nor season in which to review the charm and heartbreak and rapture of a younger year. He'd mull it over again sometime, when he was far gone and a soul detached—he'd savor each detail, wrap them in the end, all the details, as he'd make a pack of his dried hides. He would tie the pieces up securely, swing them over his shoulder, walk off with them again all roped and put away.

But not now. For the kindly neighbor read on.

Deer are also quite numerous?—and the muskrat and common rabbit are incredibly prolific? Among the bird tribes are wild turkeys, prairie hens, grouse, partridges, woodcocks?

By mighty! Why'm I standing here?

Tis all so simple, all so plain. I can't understand why I didn't realize it first off.

That's my place!

Course! I got to go long with them.

Geese, ducks, loons, pelicans, plovers, snipes? . . . are among the aquatic birds that visit the rivers, lakes and sluices? Bees swarm in the forests?—the rivers and creeks abound with excellent fish?—and the insect tribes, varied and beautiful, add gaudiness to the scene?

Why'm I standing here?

(Morris Markham did not stand for long. This revelation occurred early in the morning, before dawn on the twenty-sixth of July. He sold his house and small patch of ground a week before Joel Howe parted from his own acres; Morris carted his own stuff over to the Howe place, and these articles were auctioned at the same time his friends' goods were auctioned. . . . One Howe girl, three years older than Lydia, married a neighboring farmer and stayed behind. The others—Howes, Nobles, Thatchers, Morris Markham, and all—went along to Iowa, late in August. Two more girls were wedded within a few months of their arrival in Franklin County, Iowa. . . . It was too late to make a crop when they arrived in Franklin County, and the throng of Hoosiers lived up an appreciable share of their substance in getting through the winter. A renewed descent of frigid weather came to plague them in April— You could walk across the West Fork of the Iowa River on the ice! Thus planting was delayed until June; they'd never make a fit crop now!—and what of food and critter feed for the winter to come? Neither did cattle nor sheep nor hogs seem rearing themselves on these uplands with the placid facility suggested in guidebooks. . . . Morris Markham disliked Franklin County because of the rarity of forests, though he trapped muskrats with fair success in prairie sloughs during the cold weather. While scrawny oats and corn shoots were pushing belatedly reluctantly from new-turned soil, during the summer of '56, he trudged off across swales into the far northwest. He returned to his loved ones within the month, and his thin bearded face wore a delighted glare. Lakes, he said. Prettiest lakes you ever see! Plenty timber too. Prairie land rolling away on all sides, if you don't want to clear. Not a soul living there! Just plain stuffed with game and birds—you could stand easy on your own doorstep, if you had one, and shoot a meal of venison any time you wanted to. Tis called the Spirit Lake country. Folks, I'm a-going! . . . They all sold out and went, little bugs crawling the wide westerly reaches where a million other bugs were on the move.)

XI

Something seems to be way over there.

What?

Don't know. Something. Animals way out there somewhere, you can see their heads and backs, see them at a distance, far distance. Know they have heads and backs.

What be they?

Don't know. There's so much green between, so much blue fuzz beyond.

(Nothing fuzzy about the sky: tis hollow, fragile, hard. . . . As if a substance can be fragile and hard all to once't? . . . You know it's so, and the sky knows; and heat comes blindly. . . . There are times when you want to sing to the prairie. You think you've a song ready in throat and in heart, ready to issue from your lips. That is usually in early morning when there's excitement waiting back yonder behind the eastern horizon, sun coming up in its variety of colors which change and fade . . . fade as hope and promise fade . . . the sky fades too, goes brittle and hot.)

Something waiting, way out there.

None of us knows what it is.

Maybe something we forgot, maybe something we're still remembering (and ran away and tried to forget, and couldn't; like a woman, or a foundry, or a chicken-pickery; or maybe stealing a mite box from Sunday school when you were young; and still you couldn't forget it, and always carried a lean memory of your own wickedness).

Something out there.

Maybe a new courthouse better than the courthouse you knew.

Maybe a shanty not as good as the one the pigs lived in at Uncle Nineveh's.

Something waiting. . . .

Oh, what's those, what's those? They're feeding, they got their heads down!

Buffalo! you yell in your soul, and reach for the gun, and then they go scampering . . . bounding away, high through high grass, they've got strange shine and shape to their heads.

Maybe deer? Big deer?

Don't know. They're far and going fast.

Cloud shadow; we are in a pool of it. We are dark, the world is lighter round about, we are dark and shaded. Thank you, Mr. Cloud, thank you kindly.

Birds? Plenty, a-wading, a-feeding there. One of them's down in the water as if he's going swimming; the others stand sedately on long legs just beyond. Now they march, they have their beaks thrust out as if spying something; soon they will go down, the sharp beak hunting, feeding . . . *what's that?* cries their sentinel, and he senses you and your kind, and they all go screaming.

Polish the sky, Unseen Enemies. You got it in for us.

Go ahead and rub it up, Unseen Enemies, burnish it still more than tis burnished already. You got the polish for copper and for brass. Get to work on the sun, else you cannot fry us as you believe we should be cooked.

Edna whimpers, she puts her head in her mother's lap; in the sickening-rocking wagon she tries to sleep, she can't, she is too hot and breathless and lifeless.

Not much tepid water left in the buckets; and a long way to the next slough. And some people say you shouldn't drink this slough water on the prairie—say it gives you chills, say it will give you the intermittents. But you've got to drink, so you drink recklessly, you bury your face, you drink long, keep gulping until you have no more strength left to gulp. Then you fill the buckets, and they splash in the wagon, and half the water comes out and wastes. The critters have drunk their fill, they go reluctantly under the glare with heads hung low. They seem meditating about cool rocky pastures they left long ago.

Back where?

Back somewhere.

A vague half-forgotten Somewhere Behind.

And the Somewhere Ahead, Someplace Ahead you can't even identify. You know not what it is, you may only hope.

. . . Uncle Nineveh was a regular Tartar, and how I did loathe a-working for him! He was so tight! Everything about him was tight: skin on his skull was tight, and his jaws were tight, and his clothes were too tight, and the little house had a tight look about it. He was the tightest tightwad in the tight little church. Oh, Mr., he'd squeeze me, and act so snide, and skin me down! Always showing in the accounts where he was taking out this-or-that, for what Rachel and I had bought at the store. I know he set down larger amounts than actually we purchased. But what could we say or do? Cause he'd come up with something from two months agone; and Rachel, she couldn't remember whether twas half a pound, like he said, or only a quarter pound like she believed. Well, Mr.! Man couldn't get ahead fast in a situation like that. And where else was there to turn to? Couldn't scarcely get a crop out of the old farm no longer: soil too wore out. And the barn needed refurbishing. And I tried to put a new roof on our house; but Uncle Nineveh, he got the shingles for me, said he'd get them cheap. They was half full of holes when they come. Twas that shingle job that done it. I said, Rachel, let's get.

So we got.

Oh, look in summer, summer nights. . . .

Just see them lightning bugs—

Pale glow, so soft and kind of silver-green and clever—

Some calls them fireflies— A hundred million little lights a-blinking—

. . . Ah, they knew I had deserted—the whole village knew full well. They knew I'd run away from the Army; knew I was scairt; looked at me with contempt in their faces. I couldn't scarcely blame them, for I *was* scairt, and that's the honest truth. And I *had* run away. Reckon the Army might have caught me and fetched me back, only they didn't know where I'd gone to. Twasn't to my village, twas to my sister's; she lived a pretty piece. But word was bound to get around. One day I figured maybe they'd send soldiers, or maybe a couple of selectmen in a wagon, and one of them carrying a horse pistol, say.

So I lit out.

. . . Don't know where I'm going, don't know where you're going, don't know where we're all going. Some talk of the Fort Dodge country; some say there's good land out along the Little Sioux.

I know a fellow's gone up into Minnesota country, try to make it the forestry way.

Well, I never did like chopping down trees too much.

Me neither.

They say this prairie land is too sour to grow trees, that's the reason it doesn't grow them. But I see a man back there; he had a piece of prairie, twas awful hard for him to plow it; he said he'd broke two plows a-trying. Eventually he got it ripped up. He showed me the prettiest beets you ever see! Had fresh garden peas also. Onions was a-blossoming already, but he had a new crop in. I just looked at him. Said, We can't grow truck like this, back where I come from.

I know blame well you can't, he says. But out here it's different.

Then what's this about the prairie being sour—not fit to grow a thing?

He said, That's bull-shit. I know blame well why the prairie hain't got no trees. It's count of these fires that sweep across, every now and again. When you see one coming, Mr., you want to cut for it, you want to lay back and go! There's many a bunch of bones been found cooked black: horse bones and ox bones and man bones too. There was a whole family burned up, two seasons agone, not five mile north of here. But the prairie results from them fires, and I know they destroyed all the trees long ago; so trees won't grow nowhere, cept next to the rivers.

Got an idea, he says, and puts his face close to mine. Got an idea.

If I could figure out a way to tie a chain onto a big hunk of this soil, then rip it off with oxen!

Twould work, I think. Matted so thick, just like a mesh of wire: thick blanket of wire or grass roots all over the whole place. No wonder I busted those two plowshares. Had to get what they call a breaking plow, finally, to do the deed. But I done it. And now look at my garden. Plumb full of garden sass. Ain't that pretty?

So we all come, so we're a-going.

O wonder. . . !

See them great big dandelions—biggest fluffy heads of dried old dandelion bloom I ever see—

No, little lady, them hain't no dandelions! Folks out this way calls them goatweed.

Goatweed? Now why is that? I don't see ary goat about!

But there's plenty other critters. Enough to make good hunting, had we the time; and if the weather wasn't hot as tis today, and if the meat would keep—

But meat wouldn't keep, meat would spoil. We had to throw out that last keg of pickled pork—it smelt to high heaven—

(Wicked blazing sun, high tight sun of polished brass and copper. All the other hard hot high polished metal things you can name.)

. . . Look out yonder. What is that smoke?

Tain't smoke. I swear it's Indans.

No, tain't no Indans . . . nothing but birds, birds, birds.

Something way out there. . . .

Yes, tis birds! Great big long-legged ones, and look how straight they stick out their legs when they fly, and look at their long necks stretched in front. . . . Oh, see the sun upon them!

Them's what they call whooping cranes.

What say?

Whooping cranes. Whoopers, we call them out here.

Wild birds?

Everything's wild out here.

. . . No, no timber where you're going. Ain't wood enough to build a chicken house. What you got to do is this: bust the sod in low land, where the sod's real heavy, and make your furrow maybe sixteen inches or a foot and a half wide. Then you cut the sod into chunks. Follow me?

I follow you!

And pile up them chunks like brick. Like you was building a red brick house, cept you use sod.

. . . What's that funny smell?

Tis flowers, smelling that way.

But they don't smell like flowers.

Tis called hound's-tongue.

They're all over everywhere. They stink!

Well, Willis, you just hold your nose. . . .

Aye, they're bad flowers. But take a look at all the good ones, little boy and little girl. The stars-of-Bethlehem, and puss-bloomies making hills pale purple in the early spring, and then the darker purple of crowfoot violets following, and the wild pink sweet Williams following later still; and all puccoons; and shooting stars to follow them; and sweet flags and the tiger lilies; and draw your breath, and suck that sweetness in. The bluejoint smell . . . tis like a drug.

. . . How much to cross?

One dollar for your wagon and your team.

Why, that's highway robbery!

Now, listen, Mr.! Want to build a scow, the way I did? And sweep it back and forth on this here river like I got to do? I said One Dollar.

How much for my two sons here? They hain't got no team. They're just a-walking, side the wagon.

Them's foot passengers. Thirteen cents a head.

Thirteen *cents?*

That's what I said. And thirteen cents for every head of loose cattle they're a-driving.

And for them sheep and hogs?

Six cents apiece.

Now, look here, Mr. Ferryman! You'll break my pocketbook in two.

Ain't that just too bad? You want to ford? You try to swim your stock across, you'll drown them all!

. . . Drowning too—the peril of the brown twisting tide. And blazes running out ahead, and creditors behind, and ague makes that ague cake inside your gut (and can you sleep at night? Oh, no! Them skeeters never let you sleep . . . the kids was fussing half the night. We used up all our oil of pennyroyal, first night we camped beside a slough. We nigh to cooked with smudges all around us, our eyes was red and raw from smoke when morning come—we couldn't scarcely see— And then another night to follow, with that bite and hum and whine of skeeters in our ears and in our eyes—and biting, stabbing on our arms and ankles—and sweat—and hitting them—and lumps all over— Granny's face was just one mass of lumps, and—gad!—you ought to seen the baby—it was pitiful—).

And the insect tribes, varied and beautiful, add gaudiness to the scene.

That was before the baby died?

A week or so, a week or so.

(And little board stuck up, or little rare white prairie stone, with red keel markings on it. *Solomon McCoy. B 1855 D 1856. Rest Darling.)*

Oh, Ma, we got to leave him? Leave Baby Sol away out here? . . .

Jessie . . . wipe . . . your eyes. . . .

Something waiting, way ahead.

Oh, what's a-waiting?

Don't know. Something. . . .

Ugh. What's this stuff in the water?

Only–wiggletails–

Why, Pa–it's little bugs.

Sarah, where's the rag? You got to strain them out. You'll take the fever if you don't. Now, strain real careful. . . .

Know what that fellow tolt me, back there? Said he counted careful; thirty days he counted. Know how many he counted in that month–went past his place, and every one headed for the Ioway country, or so he says–? Know how many wagons went by? *One thousand seven hundred and forty-three!* He swears tis Heaven's truth! Seventeen-hundred forty-three wagons, just in one month–

Hell, there won't be no land left for nobody!

Oh, yes there will.

I bet not! . . . Nother man I talked to, down in Burlington. He said they counted immigrants down there, not wagons. And in a single month at Burlington, they counted twenty thousand folks. All going West–

No land left for me, no land left for thee, no land left for Cousin Peter or Brother Ben or Sister Susie!

Oh, yes, there will be. . . .

God Almighty!

Hush. Parson's standing, just over yonder–

Well, I mean– *Gosh* Almighty! But what kind of land is it? Swamp-land, awful great big swamps and marshes, and out on the high prairie too. Man says: Why, that's Little Hell Slough you're a-coming to. Might lose an ox in there, and maybe a child or two. But then, just beyond, you'll come to *Big* Hell Slough; and if you try to cross *that*, you'll lose your teams and all your wagons and all your womenfolks and the whole parcel of children, and you'll have to swim out and come back and start all over again.

Bad land, wet land, mean land, muddy land, poison land, sour land, hot land, drowned land, skeeter land, ague land–

Oh, no–good land! Rich and bountiful land! . . .

Aw-haw-haw-haw–

Leonidas Tucker, you stop that bellering or I'm going to smack you!

But– *Aw-haw-haw-haw-haw*– Ma, I'm thirsty!

Well, we hain't got no more water, and this ain't fit to drink. Twill give you chills and fever, maybe *kill* you *dead*, drinking this stuff! You heard your Pa—he said tis full of wiggletails— You got to wait till we get to a good clean crick—

Aw-haw-haw-haw-haw— I wan a drink-a-*water*—

Leonidas, you listen to me! Look at Sissy. Is she bellering? No, she ain't. And I bet she's just as thirsty as you are! Look at Pa, out there side that team, and having to walk, and the sun hot as tis. Is *he* bellering? No, he ain't—and I bet he's just as—

But—I—wan—a—drink—a—

Slap!

Aw-haw-haw-haw-haw—

. . . What you call that little pistol?

Tain't a pistol, really. They term this a revolver.

Yes, I know. But what make?

Maynard's Patent, they call this one.

How many rounds she shoot?

Five. Just a regular load. Black powder and round balls.

Can you hit much with her?

Why, Mr., I hain't never tried!

. . . What's that sound, like horns a-blowing?

Prairie hens.

Hear them rumble, hear them rustle, see them strutting, see them fly? See the old cocks seek the hens? Every time a fire comes, I guess it burns a million nests; and if you fancy roasted eggs, you'll walk out here in all the hot and smoking dusty blackness, and find ten million eggs of prairie hens—

Good to eat?

Surely. If the old hens hain't been setting too long.

Just listen to them prairie chickens!

Oh, yes, I hear.

See them?

Oh, yes, I see them. Prairie hens. . . .

Torn from a world of tyrants,
Beneath this western sky
We formed a new dominion,
A land of libertye.
The world shall own we're masters here!
Then hasten on the day:
Huzza, huzza, huzza, huzza
For free Americay!

Now, you kids come away from that fire; stop that there singing; hush your noise; you got to go to bed; you're disturbing the neighbors.

Can't call them *neighbors*—

I mean them folks camped over next them cottonwoods.

King Alcohol has many forms
By which he catches men;
He is a beast of many horns,
And ever thus has been.
There is rum and gin, and beer and wine,
And brandy of logwood hue;
And these, with other fiends combined,
Will make any man look blue.

Phineas!

Yes, Ma—

Pa's going to come over there and lay on gad, less you quit that singing!

Ma, can we sing a hymn?

I'll ask Pa. . . . Yes, your Pa says you can sing just one hymn; then you got to quit singing; everybody's bone tired; and you woke your Pa up twice already! But take heed—don't sing no more secular songs.

Sweet fields, beyond the swelling flood,
Stand dressed in living green;
So to the Jews old Canaan stood
While Jordan rolled between. . . .

Like always: something waiting out ahead.

Keep a-going.

Going to—? Where—?

Going somewhere. You don't quite know where. Maybe up past Fort Atkinson way. Maybe out to the Fort Dodge country. Maybe out towards Boyer Lake. Maybe to the Little Sioux country. Or up towards Spirit Lake.

Pale pink county, pale green county, peach-colored county, pretty pale yellow county on the pale torn map.

Going somewhere.

Wish you could see just where.

Could we but climb where Moses stood,
And view the landscape o'er—
Not Jordan's stream, nor death's cold flood,
Should fright us from the shore!

XII

Mr. Barnabas Lock had been correct in prophecy about the Hotel Meadows in St. Paul. There was no room at the inn—not for Isaac Harriott. When he appeared at the hotel (arriving by night, in a pouring rain, and with a sullen half-breed hauling his boxes in a handcart) he was greeted only with apologies from the mealy-mouthed proprietor. His display of the letter of confirmation brought Mr. Raff Meadows to the verge of tears. . . . Doctor, I never done a thing like this before in all my life! But just put yourself in my position. Got a big influx last week—party of land-hunters going up the St. Peter's, and they swore they'd be gone a-Friday, and they're still here, sleeping three in a bed mostly. Well, man alive, I can't throw them out bodily, now can I? Or maybe you'd care to try? Oh, please don't think too harshly of me; but what am I to do? I had the best of intentions in your case; and now I can't even offer you a table to sleep on. Just take a look in the dining room! . . . Isaac Harriott looked and saw the long tables occupied by an unkempt slumbering multitude.

I trust you shan't turn me out in this rainstorm, he said witheringly.

Well, I can offer you a corner of the public room to pile your baggage in.

Mightn't there be room elsewhere? I mean—another inn—?

They're chockablock, Doctor. The whole town's chockablock!

Harry had never heard the expression before but its meaning was unmistakable. His boxes were fetched from the cart and heaped in a corner of a low-ceiled smoky room where rough men (and several even rougher-looking women) crowded together—arguing, laughing, telling tales, and paying no heed to the newcomer. Most of them were drinking whiskey out of tin cups, which made the tipplers appear somehow more lewd and debased than if they'd been drinking from glasses. Harry prepared to award his dirty little porter a generous fifty cents, and was outraged when the fellow angrily demanded a dollar. Henry stood confident that he was being victimized for youth and greenness, and took a very stubborn attitude; at last the half-breed agreed to accept sixty-five cents, but he spoke a curse even while he pocketed the money. Had the stripling doctor needed further evidence of the general bestiality of his surroundings, it came his way amply before morning. Harry lingered near the stove until his clothing was dry, and then folded his jacket for a pillow and tried to sleep upon the boxes, with a yellow bandana handkerchief over his eyes. In his life there were three homes of which he might think with wistfulness, and he lay stiffly while mingling Doctor Maws and Doctor Taney and his parents in illusion. Harry was abjectly homesick in every sense of the word, and wished that he could find relief in tears; he did emit a shaking dry sob; then the lunacy of the sound frightened him into better control. Near him a drunken man mumbled repeatedly the familiar obscene doggerel beginning: *Oh, she ripped and she tore—* until finally another man (who sounded bigger and heartier and generally more decent) ordered him away.

After perhaps an hour, Harry hovered on the verge of slumber when quickly he was sharpened into angry consciousness. He found himself standing erect, swinging his fist into empty space.

Hey, what's the matter with you?

Someone was trying to pick my pocket!

Don't say? Don't know who it could of been—

A little old feller just skun out of the door—

I seen him run, just as this young feller jumped up—

Isaac Harriott hoped only that someone would not cut his throat if indeed he did sleep, later on. He lay down again, but found it impossible to rest with pounding pulse and clenched fist. He got up wearily, and asked to be directed to the privy. In seeking this relief, he walked down a dark smelly passage and opened the wrong door. Instead of a toilet chamber, Harry found himself looking into a lamplit room where three young men were standing around a bed. On the bed was crouched an Indian girl with short-cut hair and with her skirts drawn up around her fat waist. A fourth young man, stark naked, was with her on the bed, engaged in violent performance of a bizarre sexual act; and it seemed that the others must be waiting their turns —one was starting to unfasten his trousers. Appalled, outraged, Harry fled away; but the wicked scene was stamped into his brain with clarity; he was long in ridding himself of the picture, long in forgetting that the horrid revelers had not been annoyed at his intrusion—they had only turned and laughed, and one of them sang out something about: Twill cost you two bits! . . . Ah, these river towns! He'd been but a boy when living in St. Louis but he'd heard stories to raise the hair. And now he had seen.

Before daybreak a fight took place in the roadway outside the Meadows, and the loser lay wailing until a group of hotel guests went out and lugged him inside. Isaac Harriott welcomed this occurrence callously; if he could work at his doctoring he'd be happy again, whether he'd rested or not. He ordered the man to be placed on the bar, and lamps to be set close. Actually the victim (a cousin of Raff

Meadows, and one of the late imbibers in the public room) turned out to be more terrified than hurt. His face was bruised, his clothing muddied and torn, he had a shallow knife slash across his shoulder; but the artery was untouched. They poured more whiskey into the man, and Harry washed the shoulder and took several stitches to draw the rent flesh together. The world seemed mending also . . . rain had stopped, the sky grayed and pinkened . . . Raff Meadows helped the wounded inebriate up to his own room. Less than an hour later platters of fried catfish and fried prairie hen were being served to early risers, along with crackers and scalding tea. Doctor Isaac Harriott acquitted himself amply at this meal; and was gratified to find that Mr. Meadows would accept no money for his breakfast.

What you charging for your services rendered, Doc?

Well. Twas only minor surgery. But at night—

Harry thought rapidly. He did not wish to achieve a reputation for high prices, not in this new location of his choice. He should have liked very much to receive five dollars; but preferred to err on the low side rather than the high.

Would three dollars be reasonable, Mr. Meadows? Or say—two-fifty?

Now, I'll tell you! Cousin Singleton hasn't got a cent left on him; appears to have spent the last portion of the night down at Auntie Judy's place—she's got girls there, you know—and he appears to be cleaned out. Now, you've et a good breakfast; so let us say *one* dollar, and I'll give it to you right now, on behalf of Cousin Singleton. Oh, yes!—and you can leave your baggage here, rent free, until you find quarters for yourself. I'll watch it real careful. . . .

Harry did not wish to leave his satchel under any circumstances (it might be opened, and his stethoscope or some other valuable item removed) so he carried the badge of his profession with him wherever he strode that morning. He tried two hotels; one had no space available; at the other it was suggested that he might wish to share a room, and a bed, with a missionary who had lately come down from the Red River country. His possible bedfellow was pointed out to him where he sat at breakfast—a man with execrable table manners, soiled linen, unpleasant bulging eyes. Isaac Harriott declined politely, and continued a hopeless survey. . . . He had never felt of such little account before, not in his nearly-twenty-one years. In his father's house, in whatever town they happened to dwell, he enjoyed security of loves and humors. In Pekin and in Atlanta he had been a youth of importance because he was reading medicine with respected men. But here no one seemed to care whether he lived or died or—in general—whether anyone else lived or died. Harry saw Indians, he saw soldiers, he saw rivermen, lumbermen in herds; they shivered without reality, it was as if he witnessed them through a frosted windowpane. How could he set up practice if he had no office, how ever could he live without a place to lodge? He was exhausted from tenseness of the three-hundred-and-twenty-seven-mile steamboat journey, wearied further by the sleepless night he'd passed. Attempted theft . . . obscenities and smells of the Meadows' public room . . . that uncouth evil of which he'd had a brief glimpse in a midnight chamber . . . the fight and stabbing: these swam and stank and writhed in recollection. Not even the thought of surgery performed could erase them, or cause him joy in having chosen St. Paul.

St. Paul, indeed!

> *Wherefore God also gave them up to uncleanness through the lusts of their own hearts, to dishonour their own bodies between themselves.*

Harry thought of his father reading the Epistle to the Romans. Again a weight of loneliness and frustration lay upon him.

. . . What had happened to pride, purpose, soaring ambition?

How ever did one recover a faith in himself, if faith had drained away?

He stood on the high cliff between two landing slopes, he gazed out over the glinting river and curving valleys which dreamed in their late summer haze. The *Nominee* lay just below, and there were two other steamboats tied—Harry had heard people discussing their arrival that morning—the *Greek Slave* and the *Minnesota Belle*. Urgently he longed to get back aboard the *Nominee* or one of the others, have his boxes stowed along with him; and not set foot upon the shore again until Fever River was behind him and Galena beckoning—the portal to Illinois, to establish sanity.

. . . But what would Rosenstein have done? Or good Ben Dudley?

. . . Or Daniel Drake?

. . . And Beaumont? *Devoted to his profession, jealous of its character, ambitious of its honors.*

His private saints and— (How miraculous the year of 1785! For Dudley, Drake, and Beaumont were all born in it.) Now Drake and Beaumont were recently gone; he'd read in the newspapers of their passing, and mourned accordingly. Dudley lived on but he was old. There should be rising earnest younger men to occupy the vacant places, to take up satchels which the elders were putting down. Why not . . . himself? . . .

The steamboat which bore Isaac Harriott up the river had made its usual halt at Prairie du Chien, and there was time for the new doctor to wander ashore and walk the same slope which William Beaumont had trod. Harry gaped at the dull buildings which comprised Fort Crawford. Oh, a man must dare and a man must seek! . . . Suspended homeless and heartless as he was now, here on the bluff above the river at St. Paul, Harry felt a quickening of shame. Were Beaumont standing in his boots, and lithe and young as he was lithe and young, would he flee ignominiously away down the river, or even consider such flight? Never!

In imagination the youth heard the voices of doubters and detractors scolding away at William Beaumont. . . . Never bring that patient down here! Tis absurd! You're assigned to Fort Crawford: what will happen to your military duties? And also the civilian populace is dependent upon you! Why, you've already performed experiments on that wounded Alexis Saint-Martin. Or observations—years ago, at Mackinac! What did you say?—the charge carried away part of the sixth rib, a portion of the lower lung, the left end of the stomach? And there's still an opening? Why, doctor, the man'll die on your hands! And you can't *observe* gastric action and the physiology of digestion. No one can. It's never been done! . . .

Harry addressed his cowering self keenly: You were inspired when you stopped at Fort Crawford the other day. Why can't you be inspired now? Fifty separate experiments in two years—think of that! And only with such equipment as was available a quarter century ago. Had he the benefit of *modern* equipment—

Calling himself *coward, coward, coward* under his breath, the fledgling physician hastened away. Before he had traveled a hundred yards, he was stricken with an excellent idea. There was no possibility of a hasty advertisement in either of the two newspapers; already he'd found that neither paper would be issued again until the following week. But he should go canvassing, literally from door to door! Certainly he could not afford to build a house for himself; but there must not be more than a few hundred houses—or buildings of any kind—in the town; and making inquiry at each of these was a task not insurmountable. If worst came to worst, and nothing had turned up by nightfall, he might still be able to share a bed with the Red River missionary. (Definitely he found even a soiled and ugly missionary preferable to the perils of the Meadows.)

Regaling himself with an inspired plan for action, and feeling quick hunger, Harriott walked smartly to the nearest store, bought pork and crackers and a stone bottle of Campbell's Edinburgh Ale, and enjoyed solitary picnic under a big tree near the bluff. Then, swinging his satchel, he visited in turn a crowded log cabin, a new brick house, a new stone house, and a white-painted cottage with a steep sloped roof, shadowed by lazy thick-trunked basswoods. . . . To this haven Harry conveyed promptly his boxes of goods in three wheelbarrow trips, employing a barrow lent to him by a neighbor. Once again the world was mending.

His landlady was Mrs. Atta Rusk, widow of Sergeant Samuel Rusk. She had lived in the region since 1837 when her husband was stationed (for the second time) at Fort Snelling. . . . Folks used to say that my Sammy was the tallest man in the Fifth Infantry! . She treasured now a portrait of her departed mate. . . . Twas painted by Corporal Dubose. He was a great one for painting pictures, and my Sammy paid him eleven dollars for this; though he didn't confess to me until after years! . . . The picture represented the late blue-clad Sergeant Rusk as brandishing a bayoneted musket, while indulging in altercation with a bald eagle hovering just above his tall cap.

Sergeant Rusk had been dead for only nine months but the widow said that her loneliness seemed of nine years' duration. Her children were scattered, most of them married; one was a pilot, but now working chiefly on the lower Mississippi; another was himself a sergeant in the Army, serving in Washington Territory; two of the girls lived in Illinois, and one of them near Peoria—Harry was certain that he'd heard of her husband, a farmer named Swanson!—and what a small world it was, with Pekin and Peoria only a few miles apart, and Harry's own parents dwelling in Pekin, and Mrs. Rusk's own daughter Ruth dwelling just north of Peoria; and here he was, moving cozily in under Mrs. Rusk's roof!

She grew to call Isaac Harriott sonny, and he did not mind in the least.

Oh, sonny, I was just a-thinking this afternoon, how I used to feel I was rattling around this little house! Didn't want no boarders; such a hard lot as most of them are nowadays; and one of them boarders stole Mrs. Gertie Wilcox's silver mug that come from her mother's side!

Long before his death the retired sergeant had acquired land near the Falls of St. Anthony; income from this property served to keep the widow from penury. But she welcomed Harry's advent for social as well as financial reasons. . . . I do like to see folks coming and going! And I do hope that lots of them seek you for doctoring! . . . Loose skin of her sagging face was puckered into so many small folds that it looked like an empty sack; out of this toughened tangle her brown eyes, concentrated and intent, peeked engagingly like wrens peering from a box.

The advent of Mrs. Atta Rusk in Harry's life, and the months he spent living in her house, taught the youth many things about himself and thus about all people (he learned that only in the knowing of a man's self may he be equipped to understand others). He found that he was utterly dependent on humanity in personal as well as professional life—he must never let himself be divorced from love—he could no more live alone than he could practice medicine and surgery alone. (If only he might earn enough money to support a wife, he should marry; but where was Miss Raven Tresses? He saw her nowhere about.) And there were people who took quick advantage of an affection offered readily . . . they sinned against you, distorted your deeded tenderness as a weapon to be turned against your own body and heart. Yet twas better to be wounded in this way than to offer no opportunity for a wounding! Much as he respected and admired the man, Isaac Harriott had no desire to be a Francis X. Taney; severity would not be his way in the world. People might criticize Harry as overly enthusiastic, overly ebullient; they could never call him cold. He had much rather be chuckled at, or even scorned, than feared. . . . He found that he was overcoming the awkwardness of the very young adult in dealing with children, found that he could have a way with them (he remembered Doctor Maws, and the little girl who wished for Maws to go coasting with her in her wagon). When he could make a mite forget or at least ignore his misery, by giving the little sufferer a laugh to chew on, Harry was happier than if he had dealt surgically and successfully with a far more ticklish case. When he healed the children, he wondered how Christ had felt, and soon supposed that He had felt very much the same way—clean and ringing, full of vibrations as a well-cast bell. When the children died, Harry kept his dignity before the bereaved—offered whatever condolence he could reach to them—then went home hard-faced and cried into his pillow. He supposed that his heart was congenitally an open one, yet now the door swung even wider and more freely; and what matter if a few sneaks or vagabonds crept through the portal and abused him?—the precious people came too. . . . He learned that a benevolent doctor must be a keen military commander—his knowledge and his skill equip the battalions, employ them and deploy them against forces of Disintegration. Sometimes even the best commander may be guilty of a tactical blunder or a fault in his over-all strategy; then needlessly (but never carelessly, never as a sloven) he sends men to their death. And then he must not let the memory lie snuggled hideously within his shirt to bite him, to weaken and unfit him for further war. Or else he shall command no longer! . . . Nay, Doctor Taney; Nay, Doctor Maws—Nay, good Doctor Drake and all ye others whom I've never met but whom I swear and reckon by! I will not let the recollection of an error take the stars from my shoulders— I will hold the recollection into the flame of my purpose, soften it, take up the hammer, with strong tongs I will grip the glowing recollection upon the short anvil of my experience and my book larnin'!— Beat it, beat it flat, reheat it, shape it, make a new weapon out of the fault; and when it cools I shall sharpen it and go into battle again—better armed, wiser than before! . . .

There was a carpenter's son who mashed his foot and ankle beneath a hurtling pile of timbers, mashed them beyond any improvement or relief by surgery. Harry amputated, hovered daily and nightly by the bed, saw the sufferer grow strong and a sufferer no longer (except for that low-burning cripple's flame forever in his eyes). He saw the young Swede bounding energetically on his crutch, then on a wooden peg; so Harry's voice was buoyant when he cried, Good day to you,

Hjalmer! But the father, an immigrant who had much difficulty in learning even a few words of English, was hard put to plane out a living for himself—and while there was much building in progress at St. Paul, there were many carpenters about. Neither poor Mr. Thorson nor his son could pay as much as a quarter dollar toward the debt incurred. But they had their rough artisans' ability, they had their tools. Harry owned enough money to buy boards and shingles; though he did not acquire a horse until the next spring. . . . The young doctor and Mrs. Rusk held lengthy conferences, and finally an agreement was reached to their mutual satisfaction. Arvid and Hjalmer Thorson constructed a one-room addition to the Rusk house, attached to the south ell, and there was built a separate entrance opposite the edge of the vegetable garden. Isaac Harriott himself made the sidewalk (a rather unsteady one) of stone slabs hauled to the site by another impecunious but grateful patient. This structure would revert to Mrs. Rusk's possession if ever and when ever Harry departed for other regions; then she might rent it to a new tenant; but meanwhile—eager though she'd grown for visitors—she no longer had to endure frightened or bloated or coughing customers seated on her sofa while they waited to consult Harry in the back bedroom. A tall post grew outside the picket fence with a sign (again, patient-painted!—barter was so often the order of the day) which announced to the world that Isaac Harriott, Physician & Surgeon, stood ready to succor the needy By Appointment. Of course no one ever made an appointment; people merely came, or sent children to summon him; or sadly enough, for days on end, nobody came. Other doctors had established themselves in the neighborhood long before Harriott appeared; and the Minnesota climate was salubrious for mankind if not for hopeful young medical practitioners.

But as the river closed solid in ice, the long northern winter set in with its increase of sore throats, rheumatism, quinsy, pleurisy, more serious afflictions. There were also traumatic injuries peculiar to the season—the frostbites, the fractures. Harry did not starve, nor was Atta Rusk ever out of pocket in cooking his dinners. Like many another lonely kindly widow she was careless at kitchencraft, inclined to be untidy—she slopped things on her little wood range, and the place smelled always of scorched food. Yet loaves and stews which she produced were invariably tasty, welcome to the palate, nourishing to a stringy young frame. Mrs. Rusk's recipes for dumplings, ham and beans, pork and hominy, and baking powder biscuits were sent to Mrs. Harriott in Illinois; and Mrs. Rusk's daughter and her husband took Sunday dinner with the Harriotts when they came to Pekin from the Peoria neighborhood at Christmastime. Thus flourished homely trust and harmony. . . . Again Harry had found comfort. He savored it, he looked forward to reaching home on a blasting night when a solitary lamp burned to welcome him. Now he owned a short bearskin coat stitched by a Chippeway woman—it kept him happy even in twenty-five-below-zero nights—but it was flung aside the moment he returned to his quarters and built up the fire. Then, tiptoeing on chill-stockinged feet to guard against disturbing his friend, he would open the door which led into the main house, and go exploring the shed kitchen, candle in hand. Here were delight, wealth, succulence, spread to his selection. Mrs. Rusk was a born saver, she never threw food away, unless twas spoiled by summer heat. Under the slanted roof of the summer kitchen stood two wide tables: these were larder and refrigerator; last Sunday's prairie hen would be stored in frost along with last Thursday's boiled potatoes. Wild rice, fried pork, the haunch of baked moose-meat, minced pie, the turkey carcass, the remains of sweet pickerel taken through the ice and hawked by a copper-faced urchin . . . all the treasure of pickles and jellies kept in the main kitchen, so that they might not freeze solid and split their jars . . . *what'll ye have, Doctor?—what'll ye have?* . . . he would make his eager selection: a bit of this, a dab of that, slice of moose, wedge of pie, measure of corn pudding, mound of gooseberry jam; and the platter would be set beside his stove to thaw and tempt him, while he correlated professional records for the past twenty-four hours, made the few pathetic entries in his cashbook, or scratched out letters to Maws, to Taney, to his parents.

The wrinkled landlady gave Harry a better recipe than could be cooked in an oven. She mentioned casually that two of her offspring were quilled babies. Harry had heard the term, but regarded it as something from the lore of granny-izing and not to be tolerated seriously—any more than one would feed chicken droppings to a colicky infant, or insert wart blood in a split willow stem in order to cure warts. In fact Harry had never come across a satisfactory cure for warts; he had two big rough warts on his right hand; and it was the bane of his life to have weird prescriptions offered. . . .

But tis true, sonny!

Mrs. Rusk, I don't doubt—

Guess you're kind of laughing up your sleeve, she said knowingly. Well, you just laugh if it suits you! But each time I'd been long in labor, getting nowhere; and once twas a doctor that blew on the quill, and once twas a kind of Injun granny-woman; and both times the babies come right prompt.

But weren't many of the doctors more or less old granny-women in those days, ma'am?

Some was, tis true. But twasn't as long ago as you make it sound—Less see, maybe thirty year or so? And, sonny, I'd swear by a goose quill and a smidgin of snuff, if I was young today and belated in bringing forth my child! . . .

This conversation recurred to Harry's mind one night less than a week later when he stood above the bed of a perspiring unmarried girl who'd yelped with each pang as long as she had the breath for yelling, and then relapsed into a series of groans which grew alarmingly weaker as the hours dragged. The girl's mother roosted close, a croaking hen who reiterated nonsensical gabble, blaming the girl for looseness and lying, until with savagery Harry expelled the woman from the room. He was desperate. He felt as well as saw the patient's strength paling away. Oh, if only there were some sort of forceps which it might be safe to use without danger of injuring either mother or child! Doctor Taney had spoken of such instruments, but condemned their employment; and Doctor Maws had never even mentioned them—it was doubtful if he'd heard of any such modern appliances—only primitive types which had been found sadly wanting.

The patient's skin was clammy under sweat, her eyes puffed out, she saw nothing, her pulse flagged.

Then—

By gravy! Twas worth a try—

At the door. . . . Mr. Huldworth?

Huh? The unamiable response from a pallet beyond.

I saw you taking snuff—

Well, what's that got to do with it?

Listen carefully to me, sir! Your daughter's very low—

Serve her right if she—

How dare you speak that way? Listen to me, man! Bring me your snuff. I said, *Bring me your snuff!* And a goose quill. That's what I said—a goose quill! You've a bundle of them, up above the fireplace—

The materials were fetched. Harry quickly cut a quill, made his tiny pipe of the thing, loaded it with the fine yellow snuff, and blew the charge into the girl's damp nostril. She went into a paroxysm of sneezing. Two minutes later Harry was dangling the red small monster and slapping breath of life into its glistening body.

. . . He rapped at his landlady's door and woke her up to offer a prayer of thanks . . . it seemed indicated . . . he could not have slept if he'd tried to wait until morning.

Sonny, I *am* so glad I tolt you! What mother was it?

Name's Samantha Huldworth. In that old shebang due west of Gratiot's warehouse. She's—got no husband—

I know! And no decent upbringing, which is how she come to this pretty pass. I seen her go past here a-Saturday, big as a barn. Folks have reckoned twas that mean Kadsey boy, one who got drownded a couple of months past. . . . Poor little thing! And poor little baby. Might be better for all, had you let them go out quiet-like.

No, ma'am! Not if I'm to call myself a doctor! cried Harry with passion.

Pshaw, no! Course you couldn't. . . . Sonny, know what I'm fixing to do? Gift you with a present for your satchel. Snuff— I got it on the pantry shelf. Twas my Sammy's, and twill be nice and dry in its box. And I'll fix you some special goose quills, for memory's sake. . . .

An operation for lacrymal fistula; chills, bilious fevers, scarlatina; amputation of a riverman's crushed hand; asthma, diphtheria, whooping cough, scrofula; successful operation for inguinal hernia; treatment of gunshot wounds; hopeless consumption, hopeless cancer, hopeless melancholia; teeth, teeth, teeth (and twice a case of lockjaw following); an attempted Caesarean section (it was all he could do—try—the patient succumbed); always the parturitions; always the pills, always the grinding and rolling and powdering and mixing and papering; always the erysipelas, always the mumps.

Mrs. Rusk had two cartilaginous tumors on the bones of her right foot, which had annoyed her for years. Isaac Harriott removed these without the slightest difficulty or postoperative complication; and he knew now how Cheselden felt when he performed his first iridectomy; or Hunter, when he tied the femoral artery in the canal of the triceps, in operating for popliteal aneurism!

. . . I'd like to speak with you alone, Mr. Hawkins. Please to close the door. Thank you. . . . Mr. Hawkins, I'm sorry to tell you that I think your wife is suffering from a malignant tumor of the parotid gland. A cancer, in other words. . . . No, sir—I'm terribly sorry—I can't promise a thing.

. . . How far did the little fellow fall, Mrs. Renard? From that second limb of the tree? Ah-huh. . . . And when did he first complain that—that his head hurt? Ah-huh. . . . And how long was he in this stupor before you summoned me? Ah-huh.

. . . Now, I'm going to give you some powder, Mrs. Horsley. Tis in six small papers, all held together in this larger packet. Now, please to pay close heed. You will need to draw and heat water, just as hot as you can bear it— You have a tin tub? Good. You must fill that tub with sufficient hot water so that the—uh—mid-section— In other words, the thighs and lower abdomen— Will be *completely covered* with water when you take your position in the tub. Mix *one* of these small papers of powder in the water immediately before getting into the tub; and remain there at least ten minutes, each time. Do you understand the instructions? Good. . . . Yes, tonight just before retiring. Again, tomorrow morning immediately after rising, as soon as you've—uh—used the pot. Again, tomorrow midday.

. . . What's this I hear of you, Abijah? You knocked the spoon from your mother's hand? Well, well, well! Trouble was, I suppose, it wasn't a *magic* spoon. But this spoon, you see—the one I've got—*is* a magic spoon! Indeed it is. And this is Magic Elixir, in this bottle. See how pretty it is when I pour it—pretty as strawberry jam, and just about the same color! . . . What say, Abijah? Where'd I get it? Why, from the fairies. . . . Oh, yes, indeed there are—plenty of fairies, in that ravine just behind your well. I saw two a while ago, when I rode past. Big Master Fairy, he had a green jacket, red hat, purple feather in his hat. And he held his mouth open. In amazement! *Real* wide. Just the way I'm doing now. I'll wager you can't hold your mouth open that wide. Not as wide as I can. Well, suppose we try. . . . One, two, three: *open*—wider— And this Big Master Fairy said, *In we go!* Just—like—*that!* . . . Now, that didn't taste dreadful, did it? And you can have another drink of nice cold water.

. . . Well, sir! You may be a deacon, just as you say. But that's not the Michigan Rash you've got. To state it very frankly, sir, you've got a bad case of the Venus' Curse. . . . Very well, sir, you say that I've insulted you. And *try* another doctor, as you choose! Very well. And *don't* pay me a cent. But I know a case of the clap when I see it!

. . . I'm sorry, Mr. Cravere. I came as fast as I could, the moment you sent for me. But your mother's—gone.

One evening in the late spring of 1855, at dusk, Harry was summoned to the Hotel Meadows to see a Mr. Snyder. Raff Meadows, who'd entertained a high opinion of Harry's skills ever since that first morning when Doctor Harriott sewed up the knife slash for Cousin Singleton, frequently sent for the young doctor when some guest at the hotel was in need of medical or surgical attention. (This was flattering, but not too often rewarding in the financial field; many such patients were careless in payment—they Didn't Have the Cash on Them at the Moment, or They'd Leave It With the Landlord—and then forgot. However, a call was a call, and always Harry responded promptly unless otherwise engaged.) He was out in the garden helping Mrs. Rusk to plant the last of her potatoes. This was still the Dark of the Moon, and urgency demanded that potatoes—growing beneath the ground—should be planted in such season. . . . Harry went into the house, washed his hands, gathered up his satchel, and set off for the Meadows, with the boy who'd brought the message rolling a hoop ahead of him. Barely could he see that dancing dodging figure in the roadway, for darkness gathered swiftly and a light cold rain began to fall. Harry turned up the collar of his woolen jacket and wished as always that he owned a mackintosh or an oilcloth cape; but he'd bought a horse for travel to distant houses, was still in debt on this account, did not think it wise to afford the luxury of rainy-weather clothing until he became more solvent.

As he walked briskly he held no inkling of the immediate hour, did not know that he was soon to meet the dear friend of his young life.

Where is the patient, Mr. Meadows?

He's up in Number Five. Billy'll show you—

I remember Number Five, sir. Tis the big corner room.

Raff Meadows bent confidentially close, which was an unpleasant habit of his because of his sweetish-sour whiskey breath. Don't need to fret, this trip, Doc. This Snyder's got plenty of cash! You can charge him a nice fat fee—

I'll request my regular fee, said Harry with dignity. What seems to be the trouble with your Mr. Snyder?

Got a sore leg. He was limping bad when he come in last night, and could scarcely walk around the premises today. A kind of Canuck, he is. First come down here three-four years ago from the Red River country. Lives down Red Wing way now, I guess. You know—about sixty miles down the Mississip—

Snyder did not sound much like a French-Canadian name; but already in his short Minnesota experience Harry had learned that there were all types and conditions of Canucks. The boatmen, raftsmen, hunters, and the like— They were generally a gay if imprudent lot; often they wore a colorful mixture of Indian and citizens' dress which seemed to delight their souls: stocking caps, Capuchin hoods, sashes, scarves with feathers and quillwork. There was a flare and dash and swagger about them; but they were heavy drinkers, forever kissing Black Betty; and when they fought (usually among themselves) the knife wounds were woeful. Making some mental reservation as to the financial condition of M. Snyder, Harry felt his way along the dark corridor—someone had carried off the lighted candle at the stairhead—and rapped briskly at the door of Number Five. This was the best and most expensive room in the house—the only one with a fireplace of its own. It had been reserved originally as personal quarters of the proprietor, but after his wife died Meadows preferred to profit by charging an extra heavy tariff for this chamber.

Enter, said a pleasant voice.

Harry went inside and closed the door. Mr. Snyder—apparently it was he—sat before the fire with his right leg propped up on another chair and pillow in front of him. I do not rise, *Monsieur le Docteur,* he said, and laughed easily.

No need, sir. I'd prefer that you didn't, if you're troubled with your limb!

It came as something of a shock to observe the patient's costume. Here he was in the most expensive room at the Meadows, yet he wore garments as worn by the roughest *voyageurs* who brawled and guzzled and ripped at each other, and slept among kegs stacked along the river front. He wore, under the soiled striped coat thrown carelessly over his calico shirt, an Indian breechclout of deerskin, and there were moccasins on his feet. He had removed the legging from his right leg, but wore the other legging, gartered and fringed, on his left. Mr. Snyder was young, perhaps but little older than Isaac Harriott himself. Bones of his cheeks and jaw cragged out under a mousy beard, and his ears were very large and round, his nose freckled, and his hair long—almost lengthy enough to be braided like an Indian's. He sat in the round-shouldered rakish slouch of the lofty angular one who is accustomed to bend toward shorter people. Could he be six feet three or four inches in height? At least that. And thin as a beanpole.

Your leg, Mr. Snyder? Tis troubling you?

The man said nothing, he only smiled, and pointed toward an inflamed swelling above his right shin. Harry put down his satchel, and went around to kneel beside Snyder. He frowned, reached back, drew the candle closer. I wish you had summoned me while twas still daylight, he said frankly.

I believed that it might open of its own accord. It has done so, many other times. *Monsieur le Docteur,* there is on the table in the corner a lamp. . . . The man spoke mildly, softly but distinctly; he made the *s* sounds long in his words, slighted the *h*'s.

Harry lighted the lamp, arranged it on another stool drawn up. The hairy leg was scarred and misshapen under its swelling. Harry said, This will hurt!—and ran his fingers lightly around the area in exploration. Snyder drew in a long steady breath, but did not move his leg in the slightest.

You've had a fracture, some time or other.

A fracture. But yes.

I said—a broken leg—

Yes. I know. It was broken.

How long ago? Harry looked up at him keenly.

Snyder frowned in thought. I think it is— Ah. Possibly six or seven years.

Could have been a bullet wound, sir?

The patient said with calm: It was an injury. I do not speak of it so much.

That is your own business. But how long has it been troubling you, on this occasion? Now?

Snyder explained. This injury came to him under odd circumstances, and proper medical care was not available at the moment; so the break in the leg was improperly set. One of the bones had been splintered, and bits of the bone tried to emerge above the old wound, now and then. . . . Yes, yes—it was a good leg—he could walk, exercise, climb, run—he was not severely handicapped generally! But at times like this, when inflammation set in, he knew that another crumb of old bone waited beneath the skin, trying to appear.

I believe there may be more than one fragment, Mr. Snyder.

Ah. Perhaps many?

A great deal of fluid has collected, and this should drain easily. I'll be glad to open it for you. Your skin is very tough, and it might take days for it to break open and let the seropurulent matter—or whatever fluid *is* there—emerge. But twill be painful. Shouldn't you like—ah—some whiskey?

Snyder smiled. I never drink whiskey. Sometimes a little rum, or wine when it is possible.

Why, you're not a true Canadian, sir!

No, said Mr. Snyder seriously, I am French.

But—aren't most of these Canucks—?

Of French ancestry? *Mais oui.* But I was born in France.

Harry opened his satchel and took out his packet of smaller instruments, wrapped in a clean white cloth. He seldom observed or handled that little package without hearing Doctor Maws' voice. . . . Ah, some might say that twas an affectation. But, Harry, lad, if good Ben Dudley is affected in his brain, then let us all admit the same insanity! Boiling water—this he stresses. Now, who'd rather eat off a dirty trencher than a clean one? Not I, not you, not any proper sort. So I say, let's keep our instruments immaculate, affectation or no. And not since I was thirty have I stropped a knife upon my boot!

Harry began to examine his knives. Always he thought it best to keep up a casual conversation; he felt it put a patient more at his ease. . . . You'll excuse me. But isn't Snyder a name unusual for a Frenchman?

The patient was silent for so long that Harriott feared he must have offended him. He looked up in query, but the young man was lying back serenely in his chair, long hair pushed into a nest against the crushed hood of the old blanket coat, and his mouth turned up under his whiskers in that same wise steady smile.

Actually the name is Schneider. But so many people, for so long a time—they say Snyder. So—I say Snyder too. It is easier that way.

But even Schneider—

It is a name from Alsace. There are many Germans there. Are you ready to cut me, *Monsieur le Docteur?*

Quite ready, sir.

Then pray proceed.

Harry sliced deeply. Pale liquid stood out momentarily like a slender straw, spurting from the first incision, then falling back into a thick ripple as the knife plowed the length of the soft area. Snyder clicked his tongue rapidly against his teeth, the only sound he made. Harry sopped juices with a swab of muslin, then sniffed at it cautiously. Merely a watery serum, smelling rather like bran. . . . I feared we'd find pus, he said. No pus here.

The bone—it is there?

Harry left a fresh swab upon the wound, and held the other bundle near the lamp for examination. Here's a spiculum . . . here's another . . . very tiny. . . . He turned back to the leg, dabbed deftly with a corner of the swab, and in triumph presented Snyder with the fruit of his search.

The term for these is *sequestra*, Mr. Snyder. Tis a piece of shattered bone; likely it has roved in the region of the injury for years.

The thing was like a crushed jagged bean, honeycombed, nearly as black as coal. Snyder plucked it off the cloth and rolled it between his fingers. . . . You do not wish to squeeze? Maybe you find more.

Isaac Harriott shook his head. I may be wrong, but I have a notion that squeezing actually bruises the tissues; it delays healing. How long will you be in St. Paul, sir?

I can be here as long as I like, replied the young man, as if surprised that everyone should not know this.

Then I'll put in a scrap of rag, that the drainage may continue. So. . . . Now, for a bandage. . . . Should you need a stitch or two, we can effect that later. Meanwhile stay off your limb as much as you can; use a pot here in the room until tomorrow—don't walk to the privy. Have them send your victuals up to you, and give your limb a good rest. May I add—you are a model patient. Never let out a squawk!

Squawk? What is—? Ah, yes! I did not scream? But it serves nothing to scream.

I wish that more people might realize that!

When Harry had finished wrapping the bandage, Snyder lay back with a sigh and stretched his long arms above his head. Soon he said (speaking aloud, but also as if it were a personal observation voiced from himself as speaker to himself as auditor, and not directed to Doctor Harriott's attention): I like a good doctor! I am very much at home with a good doctor.

Harry, at the washstand in the corner, was so surprised that he almost dropped the knife he was drying on a towel.

You say you like doctors?

A good doctor. In my life was such a one.

I take it he didn't attend you in this fracture of yours!

Mais non! Snyder chuckled gently. I was far away from him! But now he is dead.

The Frenchman rested his head easily on the chair back, turning away to watch the small crawl of flames around a single log in the fireplace. Firelight gilded the hair on his face, seemed to twitch at his nostrils, seemed to make his nostrils open and close; yet that was nonsense, it could be only shadows. Then the face turned back toward Harriott, the smile shone.

Monsieur. Will you join me in wine?

To his amazement, Harry heard himself uttering no outright refusal. I'm not accustomed to strong drink, Mr. Snyder. But—

Wine is never strong drink.

Harry quoted lightheartedly: Wine is a mocker, strong drink is raging!

Is that poetry?

Not exactly. Tis from the Bible. Proverbs. Are you a Catholic?

Yes and no! It was a godless home from which I came, Doctor. My father was truly godless, my grandfather godless. *Monsieur le Curé* did not come so often to our house! He added, after a moment: It was just as well. . . . The wine is on the shelf yonder. You say I must not walk, so you must wait upon me! And bring also the glass for yourself. Please?

Harry fetched bottle and glasses, he felt devilish about the whole matter. Tis just that—I shouldn't wish to unfit myself to give proper attention to a patient—

This wine, it will not make you to be unfit!

Snyder filled their glasses, they lifted them, saluted each other in silence. . . . Harry's own people were teetotalers, Maws never drank a drop, Doctor Taney sometimes took a glass or two late at night. Harry had tasted spirits rarely, wine only occasionally (when offered to him in a fashion of ceremony, as now). He enjoyed beer, but it was an expensive import; he did not often regale himself with such luxury, could not afford to do so.

This was shipped up from Galena?

From New Orleans.

It is very good.

You have no other patient now? No other bad limb? Then pray sit down, my new friend.

Snyder began to speak of himself. His English vocabulary was adequate, it was only that his accent became a slight hindrance at times. He said that when he went to the university in Paris, years before, he made the acquaintance of an English youth who soon became his close friend. He began to learn English so that he might grow closer to Eric and eventually to Eric's people—so that he might visit them in England as an accepted and articulate intimate; for Eric had little linguistic facility and could not possibly bridge the gulf into French; it remained for Snyder to build his own bridge to the other nationality.

Here was an experience novel in Isaac Harriott's life. He had held contact with numerous Canucks and picturesque frontier wanderers of other breeds; you could number the Barn Locks of this region by the dozen; but never before had he encountered that specimen (peculiar to the American backwoods, he surmised) who might be designated as the erudite sophisticate in buckskins. It would be a matter for later speculation and wonderment.

Snyder did cause Harry to feel ignorant, limited, impoverished; and truly (outside earnest accomplishment in his dedicated profession)

Harry was all of those things. But also the mere being-in-the-room with Snyder brought a combination of contentment, diversion, appreciation of humankind; strangely too it fetched a rekindling of that eager personal ambition which had barely smoldered during recent months. This phenomenon Harry could not well understand. If a man made you feel limited, how also could he tweak the ears of your ambition and make the animal spring from its doze?

It was the young doctor's first and only experience of the kind. He thought it a rarity, would never have believed that this had occurred often in the experience of many other men living and dead; never did think so, to his dying day. . . . His instantaneous harmony with Snyder was baffling, it was captivating; and also, in a way, shattering. But since he was a simple-minded healthy male, he felt no erotic flutter in the presence of a man whom he'd loved almost on sight, and who seemed to love him as quickly; and since he realized so little of the enormous complexity in human relationship, he could entertain no doubt or repugnance in yielding to a new affection. He had not known before that it was possible for a man to encounter a man, and suddenly cry to himself: This is the man for me! Why should we not work in the world together? We must! . . . Without military experience, he was unaware of the incident occurring repeatedly among soldiers: a routine order, a subsequent reporting, the coming together for the first time; the mutual appreciation and perception extending, intertwining, given, and accepted without its being recognized by a word; the gay or sullen—but forever persistent—devotion which makes a soldier lame and helpless when serving alongside or under the command of any man except his worshiped one, his trusted one . . . harsh tight straps binding the two souls, drawn up a belt-buckle-notch tighter with each battle ensuing . . . the burnt-powdery love which it takes a shell to blast, a squealing bullet to penetrate and kill; and which may never be battle-killed at all, if the soldiers are lucky—but dwells on through retirement, evoked always by a song, a tobacco smell, a raucous anecdote, a whiskey taste—the tears inside when guns crackle in a distant firing squad, when boots slam in marching cadence, when the Colors go by.

One evening during late winter, when leaving thankfully the bedside of a chronic complainer whose selfish imagination bedeviled doctors and relatives alike, Harry had been halted in a street near the river front by a sound of gunfire. With others he ran to the scene of the shooting. They found a dead man lying on top of two single-barreled pistols, while his antagonist was sprawled a few yards distant, Colt's revolver still gripped in his hand. This man was not yet dead; he would die soon; he had one ball in his chest, another in his bowels, and bloody bubbles blew from his mouth and from the hole between his ribs with each respiration. According to witnesses the fight had started in a saloon. The dead man, one Sampson, had threatened a Mr. Garland with his pistols; and Garland rushed to his lodgings next door and returned armed. Now he was conveyed to a sofa in the quarters of the saloon proprietor, where he died some twenty minutes later . . . no use in probing for the bullets, no use in doing anything besides putting compresses on the wounds, and giving the victim brandy and water which he demanded with weak profanity.

. . . Son of a bitch. Son of a bitch!

A minister had been summoned but was not yet arrived. Some of the more godly in the throng counseled the wounded man that he should not go to meet his Maker while reeking with oaths.

. . . Son of a bitch. Glad I shot him. He said—he said—

What indeed had Mr. Sampson said?

. . . Said bout Major Mills. Fifteenth. Fifteenth Infantry.

Yup. I heard them.

They were arguing bout the Mexican War.

Old soldiers, I guess.

. . . Said Mills wasn't no soldier. Christ! Mills'd been worth—hundred of him. Better'n anybody in *his* God damn—

A man whispered to Isaac Harriott. Young doc, can't you get him to stop talking?

Harry murmured, What difference does it make? He has no chance. . . . Harry was big-eyed. This was the closest he had ever come to witnessing a duel.

. . . Twas at Churubusco. I mean—

. . . Mills says, You're hit. Just a scratch, I says.

. . . Give me a drink from his own flask.

. . . Bound to join dragoons in pursuit.

. . . Said he wasn't no soldier!

. . . And vicious horse threw him. Right amongst—

. . . Always looking after his men!

. . . On the march. If we had time—boil coffee—he'd tell us. Precious few commanders—do—that.

. . . Said Mills was just a lawyer from Yale! Why, by God—

. . . Unhorsed. Grabbed musket from some damn Greaser. Laid—all about him—

. . . Old Freddy Mills! Best—

. . . Why's a-getting so dark?

. . . That son a bitch Sampson!

. . . Aghhhh.

There had been something holy which Isaac Harriott sensed in this seemingly sordid death. The name Mills hung in his mind for days. He asked Mrs. Rusk if she had ever known a Major Mills. . . . Was he Fifth Infantry, she wanted to know? No, Fifteenth. . . . Course she never knew him. Knew just about everybody in the Fifth, specially after they came up to Snelling. . . . But that's the way of it, sonny, in the Army. Man loves his comrade or his commander, and you daren't say boo bout him. My Sammy was just the same way where Major J. H. Vose was concerned. Big recruit, man nigh as big as my Sammy, got to criticizing the major, and Sammy marched him out behind the barracks and took off his own stripes. He didn't care if the man *had* been a pugilist! Thank the good Lord I never seen that fight; I couldn't of stood it; the boys said they fair drug up the ground. I guess you might say my Sammy was whipped, in the end; but he give that recruit a cracked jaw and a mighty sore kidney to think about. And he didn't go to criticizing Major Vose no more! That's how tis in the Army. Man gets to love another man. Full well! . . .

This was no war, no army; it was only patient and surgeon, on the face of it—a peculiar meeting with an enigmatical foreigner in careless savage attire. Yet Snyder was the first man of his own generation whom Harry had ever greeted with immediate fondness; and Harry knew also that Snyder found joy in him. They anticipated each other in thought, sometimes almost in spoken word; they laughed at everything and at nothing. Each was possessed of an ardent wish to tell all, tell much, tell of past disappointment, early confusion, pain, desire, conflict, hope—to build a fancy of future delights and struggles in which they might participate.

Was it the wine? Harry had a sudden fear.

He made bold to ask Snyder: Is it the wine? I've had two or three glasses—and I'm not—accustomed—

But I am accustomed, said Snyder. Here we sit, and talk for hours. I tell you things I tell to no one else! It cannot be the wine, my friend. No. It is so much more than that. It is the beginning of a friendship.

Can't call you Mr.—or Snyder—any longer. What is your name?

My Christian name is Bertell. Some time—not now, it is far too long—I tell you how I am given that name. And much more I have to tell you. But that can wait. We see each other much more. And so we talk! And I am to call you Isaac, Isaac? Or what you say in America: Ike?

Folks do, sometimes. But when I was a little shaver the other youngers took to calling me Harry, because my name was Harriott. So I will be Harry to you, Bertell.

Bert. That is how you say it here. Bert Snyder.

God bless you, Bert! I must go. People may have been needing me.

But your Madame Rusk, she knew you were here! She would have sent the word, no? Had you been needed?—

I guess she would. But—I must be fit. For the fray!

Good night. And may the dear God bless also you, Harry.

Mind, now. Stay off that leg—

Oh, yes, that I shall do. I do what the good doctor tells me I must do. And you are a good doctor, my friend Harry.

They shook hands. Bert Snyder said, when Harry was at the door: There was another doctor, as I have told. He was the father I never had. Sometime, when there is long in which to talk, I tell you of him. And more—oh, so much more. Good night, Harry.

Good night, Bert.

Isaac Harriott went home exulting. He felt quickened in every fiber—keen and alert and able, almost to the point of violence. He was tasting more than that wine which had made its labored two-thousand-mile journey from New Orleans. He was tasting the heady power of human stimulation, rising only from a shared faith, a shared humor, a shared and willing understanding.

Mrs. Rusk had been in her bed since dark. He moved quietly in his own room, not wanting to disturb her; yet actually he wished that he might rouse her and tell of Bert Snyder; he knew, after the many recitals concerning Sergeant Samuel Rusk and his military friends, that she would understand. . . . His own parents might not understand. But for the first time he realized the admiration inherent in Doctor Thomas Maws' chirping tales of the man he always called good Ben Dudley.

Harry might write no letters on this night, might tote up no accounts. He scorned to enter in his cashbook the one dollar and thirty-five cents he'd taken in. . . . And Bert? Grief! He could take no money from Bert, no more than he might have charged Mrs. Rusk for removing tumors—no more than he could have charged his own mother for yanking that loose molar, two days before he left Pekin. . . . It seemed so long before. Illinois was far, it was a mist. Father and mother were shrouded in mist, as he reckoned them now. But the Northwest was bright, pungent, invigorating. He knew now why he had left the familiar towns. It was to feel this trenchant novelty.

Why, yes, yes! This was inspiration.

He'd heard much of inspiration—a word too commonly bandied and misused. But this was it.

The girl with the jet-black hair? Ah. She'd appear.

She was somewhere. . . .

He'd told Bert that he owned such hopeful illusion. Bert smiled, and nodded sympathetically. He said: I know. I too have the dream of the young lady, the perfect one. But I have not found her. Mine does not have the black hair. She is blonde. But I see her so clearly in some times! Maybe she is under the bed now? . . . He'd gestured gaily, his eyebrows went on high. Both men laughed; their laughter seemed to fit together like a good tenor and a good bass, singing.

Bert had been in the French revolution. And Harry'd heard that the French Revolution took place before his own father was born;

but Bert explained that this was another one. It came about in 1848; the students rioted and fought ardently. Then later, apparently after a change in government (much of the detail could not be followed by Isaac Harriott, for Bert's descriptions and digressions poured in an unchecked flow, studded with names like Pujol and Cavaignac, and with references to the June Massacres) a group of young men—Bert and his English friend Eric Pakington included—were slated for death or for deportation to North Africa. They elected to flee across the English Channel in a small sailboat instead. Eric and one other fugitive were shot dead, and Bertell Snyder and some of the rest wounded, when a foolish but well-aimed volley was fired into the boat off jetties at Boulogne.

From England the young Frenchman traveled on to Canada, then down into the Red River country, and eventually to the upper Mississippi region. . . . It seemed that he had inherited a fortune; he spoke of visits to banking houses both in Montreal and New York. . . . He must have so much money that he was totally uninterested in money; he spoke casually of losing seventeen thousand dollars in the lumber business. He was more concerned with relating the story of a mistress he acquired one time in the city of Quebec—a lithe girl with flaming red hair who was so badly tongue-tied that she could barely speak, in any language!—and who stole Bertell's watch and ran away to the United States with a middle-aged Hungarian juggler!— Bert Snyder lay quaking in his chair, tears running into his beard, as he described the false-hearted Josephine. He laughed himself into the same delighted speechlessness when Harry described resurrectionist activities in Illinois; or when Harry told about the plump peddler's wife whom he delivered of a baby in the new railroad station at Atlanta, with the excited peddler swarming up a closed door on the outside, clinging to the transom, shrieking at the top of his lungs: Pray to God, Momma —pray to God! . . .

Both Bert and Harry loved dogs and cats; and neither could understand why commonly folks were supposed to prefer only dogs, or only cats.

They both believed in God; but by this time neither was exactly certain what form of worship should endure; and both thought it better to practice a supreme tolerance toward all manner of religious professions—Catholic, Protestant, pagan, Quakers, or whatnot—so long as they were an evidence of sincerity.

They both loved apple pie.

They both loved guns; but Harry declared that he never had time to go gunning, and had never been able to afford a beautiful gun; still he had shot a chicken hawk on the wing—killed it dead, first shot, with Doctor Taney's rifle; and Bert Snyder had experienced a fight with a wildcat which he firmly believed to have been rabid, and he had a badly scarred left shoulder to show for it; and still he could not understand why he had never come down with the rabies. Oh, perhaps the wildcat was not rabid after all! But it had acted so strangely—

Bert Snyder thought women's breasts were the most attractive portion of the creatures' anatomy; but Harry preferred the ankles and rounded calves; and both admitted to being acutely excited in watching a woman brush her hair.

Both men had suffered dreadful nightmares when they were small, but not after they grew up.

Bert Snyder said that he could read English and French with almost equal facility. . . . They both admired Dickens, but with reservations; and both thought that Dickens had been extremely unfair to America, and were solidly indignant about it; and both had found the first half, say, of the *Pickwick Papers* amusing, but thought that the tale became rather boring and repetitious in the end; and both considered *A Christmas Carol* the most delightful work in the world, with especial emphasis on the Cratchits.

Bert's first sexual encounter was with the daughter of a housekeeper in Paris, and had been consummated in a linen room; and her name was Yvette; and he was fifteen years old at the time. Harry's first such encounter was with the daughter of his Sunday school teacher in St. Louis, and was consummated on a lawn behind some lilac bushes while Edna's parents were at prayer meeting; and she was very fat and very stupid, if exceedingly sensual; and he was fifteen years old at the time, but Edna was seventeen, and should have known better!

Ah, they laughed! . . .

They both loved lilacs, were spiritually enriched by the smell and sight of the blossoms. Bert Snyder said that there were many lilacs surrounding his boyhood home in southern France.

They both loved horses, loved the good oily horse-smell, but both confessed to cutting sorry figures on horseback.

Bert was afraid of rats, and Harry was actually afraid of mice. Neither feared snakes, neither even minded handling a harmless snake. Both had killed many rattlesnakes, and Bert had killed two copperheads and—in Europe—an adder; and Harry was almost certain that one time he had killed a cottonmouth moccasin, although it might have been only a nonvenomous water snake.

They both liked mustard pickles.

Bert had never read the Koran. Harry quoted to him the gem of charitable philosophy which he had learned letter perfect from Doctor Taney.

Neither of them believed consciously in Hell; though both admitted to a certain disquietude in regarding the possibility thereof.

Bert had come to America because he wished energetically to dwell in a new country—he thought he would be happier in a new country than in Europe. Isaac Harriott had come to Minnesota because he thought he would find better professional prospects in a new State.

Both confessed to some disappointment in the sprawling commercially minded place which St. Paul was rapidly becoming.

Harry said that he detested mathematics; and Bertell Snyder abhorred the whole idea of archaeology. He said that it was a pathetic waste of mankind's energy to pour it into a study of the Past, when an exciting Present was all about, and when the even more exciting Future ran toward you in mystery and challenge.

Both deplored the premise of Know-Nothingism. Bert admitted lugubriously to being a foreigner and a quondam Catholic, but was confident that if born in the United States he could never have cried for nativism in the political structure of his Country. Harry believed cynically that the Know-Nothings would find themselves just as powerless against Democrats in the South as had been the earlier Whigs at the North.

Some might scorn wild rice as a fare fit only for dirty Indians, but Bertell Snyder and Isaac Harriott loved wild rice.

Neither man could countenance for one moment a person who was careless with firearms!

Both stood enthralled before good music, but neither could play an instrument of any kind. Both enjoyed singing. Both admitted that they could sing rather well!

Harry said that he had never experienced luxury—he had, in fact, been on rather short commons throughout his years; but his childhood and youth were flavored contentedly with the devotion of affectionate parents. And Bert said that he had never experienced true poverty; but his mother was dead, his father had never loved him (nor had his father been capable of love); and when Bert was a little boy he often cried himself to sleep, wishing that someone in his family might love him.

Each trusted that someday he would be the father of numerous children. Neither had been a member of a large family, but both thought that large families must be jolly.

Bert admitted that commonly he wore the costume of a *voyageur* (as worn by most men in the Red River country, for instance) because it made people turn and look at him, and he rather liked to be looked at—it compensated somehow for lonely miseries endured when young. Harry admitted that one of the dreams of his life was to be pointed out wherever he went—to have people say: Why, there goes Doctor Harriott! Yes, that man is none other than Doctor Harriott!

They laughed. . . .

Each loved to smoke a good pipe; but Harry had precious little opportunity for smoking; he did not think that it looked well for a doctor to go about puffing a pipe, and perhaps spilling ashes all over his patients (as one of the other St. Paul doctors did)!

Both felt that it would be a wonderful thing to aid in founding a brand-new town somewhere in the wilderness, and then to watch that first village grow into an ideal young city; but, again, neither felt truly that St. Paul was the answer. They were rather inclined to shake their heads over the place.

Both deplored coarseness, and so much crudity and coarseness and embattled ignorance was demonstrated in a river town. They agreed in this opinion solemnly.

Bert said that the most delicious thing he had ever tasted in his life was a wild French mushroom known as the *chanterelle;* and Harry said that the most delicious thing he'd ever tasted in his life was a wild mushroom called the morel, which grew in open oak woods in Illinois, in May. Bert doubted that there were any *chanterelles* in Minnesota—he'd never seen any, but they might be somewhere about in the proper season; and Harry had never been in Minnesota in May before, and thought it might be too far north for morels to grow. Furthermore he had no time for mushroom hunting. . . .

Both men admitted to a selfish joy in performing charitable acts. Yes, twas supposedly a lovely thing to do—but, after all, wasn't it serving selfishness in the last analysis? Ha, ha! Then let us all be more selfish, progressively as we go through life!

Harry had thrashed a man larger than himself, for whipping an old horse, in Pekin; and Bert had thrashed a riverman—a veritable giant—because the man kicked an Indian child. But both had, one time or another, been beaten by bullies. . . .

They both loved baked potatoes, especially with salt and butter and plenty of black pepper.

Neither could bear to hear a woman curse.

Both really hated to write letters—they felt that it was a regular chore. But Bertell Snyder sighed, and said that nowadays he had no one to write letters to, except for the Pakingtons—the parents of his dead friend Eric. And an old man in Paris named Fardeau. And he had not written to the Pakingtons or to Colonel Fardeau in a very long time. He was ashamed about this. But—

The most exciting erotic union of Bert's life had come when he met up with a quiet little bespectacled governess in England. The most exciting and surprising erotic moment in Harry's limited experience had come when the somewhat eccentric wife of a visiting clergyman —it was during his final month in Atlanta, Illinois—maneuvered all her relatives away from the house for a night, feigned illness, sent for Harry, and then hauled him into bed with her when he appeared.

They both thought that the nether limbs of women were more

captivating when clad in stockings than when bare. Also they were of the unanimous opinion that most men felt that way.

Both esteemed the singing of grosbeaks, both deplored the screeching of loons.

A good rare porterhouse steak was, next to a beautiful girl, without question the most beautiful thing in the world!

. . . Next time you come, said Bert, we have the porterhouse!

The next time that Harry came, they had exactly nothing. He came at eleven o'clock Sunday evening in order to look at the wound on Bert's leg, remove the wick, and refresh the bandage. For nearly forty hours previously Harry had been struggling with the Death Angel in a filthy shack near the old slaughterhouses, southwest of St. Paul and across the river, not far from Fort Snelling. The entire personnel of a destitute family who had squatted there lay vomiting and writhing, clutching their stomachs. Putrid pork, perhaps?—winter pork improperly cured, and thawed and frozen and thawed again with the coming of spring? Certainly Harry did not know, nor did the neighbors who had taken pity on these quarter-Dakota paupers, and summoned a doctor.

Thought the two littlest ones were goners when I got there, Isaac Harriott told his friend. You said I was a good doctor. Damn it, I had to be one yesterday! And all night, and today.

On this occasion it was Harry who slumped in the deep chair. Bertell Snyder, happy to have a clean bandage, lay across the bed in breechclout and calico shirt, a clay pipe jammed between his teeth. He had grown restless; the leg really bothered him no longer, except for a soreness around the incision; and he confessed that he had used the privy instead of the chamber pot since Saturday noon, and had gone downstairs to supper both evenings.

Doesn't matter, really. I'd just hoped to keep you quiet for a time. From now on tis a question of suiting your own convenience.

I need the sewing, Harry? No?

Reckon not. She's drawing in nicely. If granulated tissue starts to form, I'll burn it off with caustic.

Zut!

Twon't be bad. Silver nitrate. Just stings for a while. . . .

Harry!

Yes?

In my chair, you were going to sleep. Your head was falling forward. You go home! . . . You have a drink of rum before you go?

No, sir*ee!*

Then go!

By gum, I'm *gone.*

He had about three quarters of an hour of heavy slumber after he fell into bed at Mrs. Rusk's; then he was dressed and hastening toward the river front through a soapy fog. This was the night when the *War Eagle* landed twelve hours late, and a rich Easterner fell all the way down a staircase as the steamboat groaned up to the shore. It was Captain Harris's opinion that if the man hadn't been drunk he would have been killed; and Isaac Harriott's opinion that if the man hadn't been drunk he wouldn't have fallen in the first place. Doctor Shaffer was out of town, gone up the St. Croix; Doctor Evans was attending on a parturition which he dared not leave; and Doctor Droege was bending over a very small patient who combined the problems of croup and severe swellings within both ears. The steamboat captains knew all the doctors of earlier residence in St. Paul, and called upon them when a doctor was needed; but now a deckhand was sent in search of Harry. . . . The rich Easterner, who had thought to seek out lumbering opportunities in the region (since he'd learned that Government control of stumpage was a mere gesture, and forests could be raided with impunity) was found to have sustained four broken ribs and a fracture of the left humerus, together with a slight brain concussion. Once again Harry learned that he had been crossed—and by a well-to-do patient, at that!—when the *War Eagle* steamed back down the river on the second day following, bearing chastened freight in the shape of a bruised Easterner who had had quite enough of the Northwest. No money, and no address of the patient, was put into Harry's hands.

He felt rather bitterly on the subject, as he complained to Bert Snyder; but still it was an old story.

I suppose they did that to Hippocrates, too!

It is entirely possible, Bert agreed. This modern nineteenth century, it has not the only mean ones!

And down-river he'll probably get drunk again, and break the other arm!

I wish he might break his neck as well!

So do I! agreed Harry; who was quickly horrified at having said such a thing, and didn't mean a word of it.

He was compelled later to exonerate the bibulous traveler and apologize to him *in absentia*. At the end of Monday afternoon, when Mrs. Rusk had barely gone into the house to start slicing ham, and when Harry was raking a seedbed for her, he looked up to see a lean picturesque figure capering down the road outside the pickets, waving violently as he came. It was Bert, limping but slightly, and in a rapture.

You must think not the evil thoughts of that man Monsieur Pelligrew! He has left something for you, after all!

You rascal! You shouldn't have walked all this way—

Oh, my limb, she is feeling fine. But only see what is here—

It was a soiled white envelope with a dab of wax on the back, and it seemed to contain coins wrapped in paper. In crooked capitals: *Dr. I. Harriet. By Hand* was printed as an address.

Where'd this thing come from, Bert?

From Monsieur Meadows. It was left for you at the bar, and in care of Meadows; he has asked if you would be back to see me soon; I said I do not think so; so now I fetch it to you!

On examination the envelope proved to contain a ten-dollar gold piece and two twenty-dollar gold pieces. The Liberty Heads on the obverse looked especially seraphic, with eagles especially courageous on the reverse. Isaac Harriott sat down on the wellcurb. . . . Fifty dollars gold!

And now we must both deny the bad thing we are saying, about how we wish he would fall and break his neck!

Oh, I do, sir—I do. Most earnestly. Dear Mr. Pelligrew!

Dear Mr. Pelligrew! repeated Bert Snyder with feeling.

. . . Mrs. Rusk said to him, when supper dishes were being dried and when Isaac Harriott had gone across the way to look after his horse—and to dose a neighbor's baby: What's Mr. Meadows going to say when Harry asks him bout that envelope that was left, and Mr. Meadows don't know nothing bout no envelope?

. . . *Madame!*

. . . Well, you just *Madame* me all you please, young Mr. Frenchy; but I wasn't born yesterday, if Harry was!

. . . *Madame!* You—you would not reveal to him—your suspicion—?

. . . Silly critter. Course I wouldn't.

. . . Because he is so dedicated, so generous, and he does work so hard; and has such a little to show for it—

. . . Think I don't know that? Mrs. Rusk lifted her apron to her eyes.

. . . Then I tell you! Monsieur Meadows will say nothing, exactly nothing, except that indeed the envelope was left for our Harry by a man from the steamboat—he did not know exactly who he was! That is what he will tell Harry when he is asked and if he is asked, because I have given to him a five-dollar gold piece for his own, to say this thing. And Meadows is a man who knows— How you say it?—ah. Which side of his bread is having the butter?

. . . Guess Harry'd just about die, if he knew.

. . . *Et alors?* He will never know!

. . . Course not. Not from me!

They stared at each other for a moment, then formally shook hands. Bertell Snyder kissed the hand of Mrs. Rusk before he released it, and old Mrs. Rusk colored pink. She cried: Now, you— Be*have!*

From the town of Red Wing, Bertell wrote a letter in the spring of 1856. Doctor Isaac Harriott. My Very Dear Friend: I take my pen in hand most enthusiastically to tell you of an excitement. I know you have thought nothing so much of Red Wing, since when you passed by the place on your journey to St. Paul in 1854 there was not so much to see. Not so very much, it is possible, except a few Indians; and that old Indian farmer with the name of John Bush; and was it that the missionary, the Reverend Mr. Hancock, also was here? I know you did set your foot at Wacouta, but that is on the eastern shore of this beautiful Lake Pepin. In any event, it is of no matter. What I now describe to you is an ambitious undertaking. It is that we are manufacturing a company of men, to be known possibly as the Red Wing Townsite Company; and in the manufacture of this company the Honorable William Freeborn takes a most forward part. Also may I say that my humble self also face the plan with what in my native language we term *une exaltation spiritueuse!* That is a jest that I make to you, Harry, for of a certainty the word *spiritueux* refers to the ardent spirit that is drunken from a glass. But never could my own spirit be more ardent than now! Do you recall how it was that we sat within a room at the Hotel Meadows and spoke of what a great thing it might become, if we should engage in organization of a new town—a town to be contrived in the wilderness, thus manufactured there, all of the new? This now is our plan! Also I shall mention that there are two brothers of England; the name is Granger, and their home was in the County of Kent, where I have set my foot also. The two brothers, of the names Carl and William Granger, are also of the utmost excitement to this plan. It is proposed that they, with my humble self, shall proceed with all despatch to the *reconnaissance* of this wilderness to the west—I employ that word, it is French, but also I think you have the same word in the English language. We will in truth be explorers of a new land. On our efforts will the hope and fortunes of others stand or fall. What an excitable possibility! Now I proceed with the most important part of the suggestion, which is that you, Doctor Isaac Harriott, shall become one with us as a member of our elected company! Surely in a new village, not to say later a city, will be the need for a courageous doctor of vitality and great skills. In such a new place you will be *the only one of doctors,* and that is both honor and opportunity, is it not? How much to be preferred to the City of St. Paul! Oh, dear friend Harry, come to be with us in this our expedition! We plan to depart as soon as equipment *et cetera* is planned and forthcoming. We go to the west and the south. Great is the conversation thereof. I hear talk of both Rice County and Blue Earth County, and there is a lake called by the name Omanhu which some would have explored to this view; also a river of the name Watonwan; and then a party of other lakes beneath the line of Iowa State (where never have I been) which are called the Spirit Lakes, or as some do call them by the Indian language of Okoboji. This most recent consideration has interested the brothers Granger excessively, since the Iowa soil is said to be black and procreative in the extreme, so unlike the light brown soil of the garden of your dear Madame Rusk, and with fertility of a great nature. But wherever we do go, I request that you join our little army. Now you will say, What does it cost?—I do not possess the money. Ah! But little money is the requirement; no one is entering large sums into the treasury thereof (excepting possibly the Honorable M. Freeborn and myself) for most people do not have available the money—like unto yourself, dear Harry. So what will be the cost? You have told me that your debt for your horse is by this time paid, and even you have a few dollars put beside you, and you have incurred no more debts than that. Your savings of the year, which proudly you did describe in your most recent letter, should prove sufficient, and more than so, to supply your share of victuals, condiments, powder, shot, *équipage,* and all else needed for the expedition. What of your horse? Is it that he is capable for a wilderness journey? You might ride him to this place—but sixty or seventy miles distance—or fetch upon a steamboat, and make a trade in Red Wing; or possibly you should wish to sell him at St. Paul more favorably, and purchase a new mount upon arrival. I have seen a perfect pony to suffice for you—a wiry spotted pony of the Indians; his name is Lazarus, for one time he was thought to die, yet did recover! And can be had most cheaply because his owner returns soon to Chicago. Once again I cry to you, New, new, new!—a village of our own to be constructed in the wilds, where Mankind has not held the opportunity for defacement and ugliness—or all the brawling and disgust—But this shall be built on high for the purpose of civilization; and so when we have found a perfection of spot, so will the plan be erected for a perfection of a future life. Ah, my friend, I wax excited at the prospect! So now, you must give up your life there, and journey at once to Red Wing, to join three hardy adventurers and faithful believers in the most glorious future of the Red Wing Townsite Company. Offer to Madame my most affectionate wishes; and I know she should be sorry to see you go; but rooms are so hard to come by in St. Paul that she might let out your quarters handsomely. And tell her to forgive us for berefting her of your kindly young self, but a better opportunity now waits than ever before for you; for soon many settlers will come! Of this I am convinced. When once we have found the spot most ideal, then shall the armies of the new citizens advance! My dear Harry, send down by the next steamboat a letter saying that you hasten to do this thing; or better than that still, be on board that steamboat? But in any event you must come soon. You too are a dreamer, but better still you are practical. A practical dreamer—ha! So must we all be. *Vive la* Red Wing Townsite Company! *Vive la compagnie!* I remain, sir, your obedient servant and affectionate friend. . . .

Sonny.

Yes'm. . . .

You're just standing there, and you must of read Bert's letter a score of times already. . . . So you're a-going? My, how I'll miss you! But tis for the best—

I didn't say I was going, Mrs. Rusk.

Oh, land, sonny—your face says so! . . . Minds me a mite of how I first felt when my Sammy left me to go down Georgia-Florida way, and fight them dratted Indians.

Why, ma'am, I'm not going anywhere to fight any Indians. I'm a doctor! And we want to build a new town—all our own and—

See? You're going to do it, just like I said.

I—I haven't made up my mind—

Oh, twaddle! You'll go.

XIII

When not yet nine years old, Harvey Luce was made to swear upon the Bible that he would never be a minister of the Gospel. (If he had possessed sufficient riotous imagination, he might have conjectured during adult life that certain other boys had been made to swear upon the Bible—one time or another—that they *would* be ministers. But he owned little imagination and practically no store of humor.) This oath was squeezed out of Harvey because his Uncle Johnson Lowder's wife had one time fallen prey both to a weakness of the flesh and to the design of an archfiend. The anticlerical promise did no one any good at all, and served only to cause Harvey untold frustration up to and including the hour of his death. He might have bloomed serene as a minister of whatever ilk; but he was stupidly if delightedly miserable, most of the time, in his role of layman. Thus he found felicity only when neglected, criticized, pointedly ignored, professionally put upon, or when actually enduring physical pain. In those moments he was smugly conscious of a vague resemblance between himself and a Being who suffered upbraiding, betrayal, reviling, scourging, and finally Crucifixion.

Harvey Luce had a mother who died of puerperal fever when he was fourteen months old. His father died of sunstroke (they begged him to come in from the field, he said the hay had to be cut, they begged in vain) when Harvey was five. Thereupon the boy was conveyed to the home of one Mr. Lowder, a distant connection by marriage, who'd practiced in his time both the tanner's trade and the tailor's art, and in the 1830s enjoyed favorable reputation there in Huron County, Ohio, as a master dyer. Uncle Johnson, as Mr. Lowder taught the child to call him, possessed a snug if tiny house and had a neat untalkative housekeeper, almost a generation older than himself, whom he ravished once or twice each week. He frequented her room only in latest darkest hours of the night. No one in all Norwalk ever dreamed of this liaison; Johnson Lowder himself might have engendered suspicion; but Mrs. Angers' hair was cotton-white, she was born during the Revolutionary War, she had a grandson who was a devout Methodist blacksmith over six feet two inches in height, and she herself taught a Sabbath school bevy of innocent junior femininity known as the Dewdrops. When, at the age of seven, Harvey Luce first heard sounds of smothered revelry which traveled up to his hearing in a chamber above the sitting room, he believed that the house was haunted; he prayed to be delivered from ghosts. Only in preadolescent curiosity did he muster the slim courage to go exploring in his bare feet, listen outside a latched door, learn the frantic truth. Then, when he was thirteen or so, Harvey wandered crazedly about on one occasion, entertaining the savagery of an ulcerated tooth. He came face to face with Uncle Johnson Lowder as that worthy stepped nightshirted out of Mrs. Angers' room. They stared, silently and mutually for a long moment, and then went in opposite directions without exchanging a word. Johnson Lowder may not have slept much the rest of the night, but he was his usual tight-spoken self at breakfast; and when he addressed the swollen-faced youth it was only to say: Haste with your porridge, Harvey. I got to measure out those mordants for you, soon as we get to the shop! . . . Neither boy nor man ever mentioned the midnight encounter. Mr. Lowder may have thought that toothache was deranging Harvey Luce to an extent wherein he did not recognize the significance of the incident. As for Harvey, he prayed nightly for the souls of both Uncle Johnson Lowder and Mrs. Tabitha Angers, whom he typified as adulterers. A few years later he listened to some knowledgeable men, whose conversation suggested that neither a man nor a woman was guilty of adultery when neither of them possessed a spouse. Thereafter Harvey designated the pair to himself as mere fornicators, and felt more relieved about their future. They were hypocrites however . . . and one night, still in his teens but increasingly pious, when again he detected sounds of a riotous indescribable lechery savored by old age and middle age, he slept only to dream that an Apostle stood before him and damned these two as Scribes and Pharisees!

Harvey had been compelled to affirm in sacred promise that he would never don the Cloth, as a result of the following happenstance:

At the age of eight he was so moved by exhortations of a visiting Methodist that he rushed home from church glassy-eyed, stood upright upon the settle, and began to preach a lengthy sermon to the cat and her kittens. When Mrs. Angers returned less precipitately she heard the treble voice attempting to build its sonorous utterances in the sitting room. She slipped in from the kitchen and stood behind an open door, impressed enormously by the repetitive oratory. She touched her eyes with her apron, left smudges of flour on her face, thought: *A little child shall lead them.* She thought also of her own sins (they were merely carnal, and had nothing to do with cruelty, selfishness, or blasphemy), she forgave herself for those sins as well as she was able; and since she had a youthfully elastic conscience under her sober mien, this was not too difficult and did not take too long.

When Johnson Lowder appeared, ready to partake of Sunday dinner (Mr. Lowder contributed financially to the support of Methodism, but never attended church services; and he was happier on the Sabbath when he skulked into his shop by the rear door and occupied himself with pouring acetate of lead into a solution of alum) Mrs. Angers made signs of silence and secrecy and led him within earshot of the young evangelist.

An I say unto you, Brethren . . . that . . . an this is the Holy Writ of the great Jehovah . . . ye have offended gainst the Lord an . . . an lie down an your cup runneth over . . . an . . . your trespass against the Lord is great . . . an surely the fierce wrath of the Lord Almighty is upon you . . . an goodness an mercy. . . .

What in time's going on in there, Mrs.?

Tis the boy. Just hearken to that! He's preaching.

He's *what?*

Only hearken, like I said! Mr. Lowder, that child's possessed by a Holy Spirit. I warrant you he's one to carry the Word!

Carry fiddlesticks! grunted the uncomfortable Johnson Lowder. He retreated to the woodshed where he lingered through delicious smell and smoke and sizzled harmony of chicken frying near at hand. Ordinarily he would have been ravenous, for he was a sturdy man and loved fried chicken, and had been astir since dawn. But now his face was stony, his lips moved soundlessly; repeatedly he mopped his face. The image of that boy stayed before him—a chunky figure with spiny black hair stiffened as if in fright, eyes blank and shiny as agates, thick lip pouting while the vacuous utterances were mouthed. Mr. Lowder gasped, muttered an undeniable curse, and went out to jam a fork desperately into garden soil. He was impervious to the censure of spying neighbors; but the disturbance of his spirit was great.

He ate almost nothing at dinner. He sat staring at the child for whose welfare he had accepted the responsibility more than three years before. He felt that he could not stand by idly and see this stocky infant march toward a beckoning doom. Mr. Lowder may have been a bit warped; but at least he was well intentioned according to his lights, and his sincerity was marred only by abiding hysterical prejudice. An hour after the conclusion of dinner, he appeared unto Master Harvey where the latter sprawled before that same settle, Bible open before him, and trying to spell out the reproof which Samuel visited upon Saul.

Want you to come take a walk, Harvey.

Yes, sir, Uncle, mumbled the boy with reluctance.

Fetch that Bible, too, was the unexpected command.

They tramped far past scattered houses at the edge of the village, climbed over Farmer Crowley's wooden gate, crossed his sheep pasture, smelled the banks of wild crab-apple blossoms, entered a thin woodland which dreamed of May all the way up the lazy little creek. They would have been a strange pair to observe, but few people observed them even before they'd left the town . . . the spare angular dyer with stained hands and wrists which were testimony to his profession, digging his home-cut hickory cane against spring soil as he strode . . . the squat little boy with broad visored cap, the boy with baby face and marble eyes, scampering to keep up with the tall man, hugging a battered Bible against his chest as he trotted.

Lowder led the way to a quiet place beneath curved outcroppings of rotten stone, where new moss grew thick with miniature reddish blossoms blowing on its green felt surface. There were scattered slabs here and there (like pews?) and corroded shelves threw back and muted the voices. A shadow of Worship fell here (as in a church?) and Johnson Lowder's face looked grim as the face of a deacon.

The boy Harvey wondered: Why was Uncle Johnson never addressed as Deacon Lowder? Why did he not go to church, along with Mrs. Angers and Harvey Luce?

Lowder took the Bible from the lad, placed it upon a stone; he sat himself down upon a lower stone (wasn't he something like a minister behind his pulpit?) and motioned for Harvey to move close.

Harvey, take off your cap.

Harvey took it off.

You got to swear.

Sir?

Swear on the Bible.

Swear . . . ?

I guess maybe you don't understand about an oath; but an oath sworn upon the Scriptures is Holy to them that believe, and has got to be observed. Same way in court. Witness takes his oath upon the Bible. Now, boy, I'm responsible for you, responsible *to* you when you get bigger. You must do as I bid you.

Harvey Luce blinked his round eyes, and bobbed his head because this seemed to be expected of him.

—Bible's all right, Christianity's all right. Maybe we can't live without them. Folks think I try to, but I do my own share of praying. In private. I hain't prayed in public since—

—But the Bible nor Christianity ain't what's wrong! Tis the practitioners of Christianity— No, I don't refer to folks who just *believe,* and go to church. I mean the preachers themselves. Saints named only as such to themselves, *by* themselves! They get together and they say: Brother, we welcome you into our fold. Come join our saintliness. We're all preachers; you come and be a preacher along with us! Agreed? Very good—we now pronounce you a saint and a preacher!

Go ye into all the lands, and preach the Gospel to all the people. That's what they say. But that isn't what they do.

—Maybe some does. I just met the dullard kind. And also—

—Because religion is solely a cloak to hide the wickedness! Man can dress himself up till you'd think he was one of the Twelve! And stand up there mouthing about Love Thy Neighbor and Praise the Lord on High, till an honest man would puke! Why, boy, I tell you I've heard—!

Johnson Lowder's low terse voice cracked apart suddenly, and Harvey's eyes bulged still more as he saw tears upon the dyer's cheeks.

Swear! the man said thickly.

Yyyes sir! Yyyes, Uncle Johnson!

That hain't no way to do it. Put your right hand on this Bible . . . that's right. And remember always that you took an oath on the Writ you affirm to be Holy, so you can't never go back on it. Agreed?

The frightened boy mumbled a response.

Say like this: I, Harvey Luce—

I, Hhharvey Luce—

Do solemnly swear upon this Bible—

Do sssolemnly swear upon this Bbbible—

That I shall never become—

That I ssshall nnnever become—

A minister of the Gospel!

A—mmminister—of the Gospel. . . .

There. That's done!

There—that's—

No, no, twas just what I was saying aloud, boy! You finished, you done it, you've given your sacred promise!

After a few minutes during which time he sat humped, lost in his own thoughts, the man inquired not unkindly: Feel better?

Yes, sir, the boy whispered again—not knowing why he was agreeing, not yet agonized by any realization of a foolish commitment which would be an inevitable burden to him. Thereupon Johnson Lowder arose and stalked homeward, with the short-legged Harvey running again to keep up with him. Horrifyingly they forgot the Bible, left it lying on moss, and Harvey had to go back all the way from Crowley's gate in order to retrieve the neglected Book.

Lowder never confessed the enormity which he had visited upon a hapless orphan—not for some years, not until this question rose sharply in conversation with Mrs. Angers. As for Harvey, he did not mention the business of Bible and oath, not to a soul, until he was grown and married; this was not odd, for he lived as a child aloof, had no boyish confidences with anyone, owned no chums; and did not suffer much in such deprivation because innately he lacked the poesy and sensitivity and vibrancy which make an individual to be ridden by hags. Uncle Johnson in no way objected to his attendance at church nor to his Bible-reading. Thus the memory of the dramatic oath and all mysteries surrounding it assumed the form of a single engraving in Harvey's recollection—but an engraving without color or life, and with no explanatory text printed underneath. It was like an uninterpreted picture which a child witnesses in a book or framed upon a wall; there are sheep or knights or dogs or a riot there—but where, and why? He stares at the picture, does not understand it, asks no one to explain; the memory of the picture remains with him but as no portion of his active life; it hangs forever with a veil across it. . . .

Had there existed any explanatory text (for the eventual adult, never for the original child) it might have read in this way:

Johnson Lowder, dominated through childhood by a vigorous hard-working widow who was his mother, exhibited rebellion previously unsuspected by kin and neighbors when he married a young lady Methodist who had recently come with her people to that Ohio community. Alice made of Johnson a convert to Methodism, to the rage of the Widow Lowder who'd reared him as a Baptist.

Johnson Lowder, not having an especially doctrinal mind, knew little of the fundamental differences between the two sects, and cared less.

Johnson Lowder took his bride into the only home he possessed, which was the one ruled by his mother. The Widow Lowder, although no longer in abounding health, cooked all the meals, told Alice what to buy off the butcher's cart, told Alice how to make the beds, told Alice how much bluing to put in the wash, planned the spring garden, told Alice when to feed the cat, named the kittens, laid out the sewing and knitting for Alice, criticized Alice's ironing, criticized Alice's sweeping, instructed Alice when and how to prepare rags for a new rug, planned where the rug should be placed, complained about Alice's way of doing her hair, addressed everything she said at table to Johnson and ignored Alice; and never for a single week neglected to explain to Alice that the Baptist Faith and the Baptist Faith alone might be the staff on which mankind could rely during the tortuous journey to the grave.

Johnson Lowder took no note of these developments; or, if indeed he did note them, found them of importance inferior to the compound colors which he contrived in his vats with increasing skill, and as a result of which he received orders and contracts from as far away as Cincinnati.

A peripatetic exhorter rode into town and occupied the Methodist pulpit for a fortnight of soul saving. This worthy was high of forehead, gleaming of eye, unctuous of voice, and most persuasive of manner. He bought a new chaise while in Norwalk, and rolled about the community by day, calling on the female contingent and having in every case, as he expressed it, a word of prayer with them. He persisted in appearing daily at the Lowder gate; but the widow, who had no time for Methodists be they itinerant or no, flounced off into her kitchen and read the Third Chapter of St. Matthew until she was black in the face. Behind the closed door of the sitting room, Alice Lowder knelt in prayer with the Reverend Mr. Silas Underhill Steep, or listened entranced to his recital of missionary days in Darkest Burma, when he had labored alongside no less a personage than Adoniram Judson. (So he said. Nor did he explain how he happened to be missionarying along with a proselytized Baptist.)

The last public service conducted by the Reverend Steep took place appropriately on a Sunday evening, and Johnson Lowder did not escort his wife thither, as he was much more eager to spend the evening in the shop where he could create a lucrative and necessary sky blue by mixing six parts of bran, six parts of indigo, six parts of potash, and one part of madder, and boiling them long and critically. At a late hour he went to his home and found the connubial bed unoccupied. In a high state of alarm he roused his mother, who was ailing increasingly and had retired immediately after supper (while Alice rushed the dishes through their suds so that she might not be late at meeting). Until informed, the widow was not aware that her daughter-in-law had not come home; but the invalid now had a good many things to say about fly-by-night evangelists, especially those of alleged Wesleyan persuasion. Johnson Lowder raced to the home of the local pastor and to residences of various family friends, but no one knew Alice's whereabouts: she had been at meeting, that was all they knew, they supposed that she'd returned home at an appropriate hour. Johnson Lowder and several other concerned individuals spent some time in wandering with lanterns, calling aloud the name of the vanished bride; but no response was forthcoming, and no trace could be found.

The Reverend Mr. Silas Underhill Steep was departed from his lodgings, having driven that night professedly toward Huron, where he'd declared his intention of conducting further devotions and performing further conversions.

Old Mr. Haberlein, a local carriage maker, was one of those aroused; and promptly he fell into a condition which for a time robbed him of his acquired English. The Reverend Steep had given only a token deposit on the new chaise, and had promised that payment in full would be made on Monday. . . .

No historian of Huron County or of the Lowders might reproduce with ease a chronology of subsequent events, since gossip was rife and the situation confusing. The truants were reported successively as having been observed in Sandusky, Bucyrus, or in a dozen towns farther east, throughout the Western Reserve. Common belief held that

Johnson Lowder and Carriage Maker Haberlein were not the only citizens to suffer from depredations of the self-styled missionary, since he was accused of having made off with many other pieces of portable property, including an heirloom watch belonging to the blind Miss Minerva Wadsworth, and a china-pig bank owned by the youngest Crowley child, said to have contained not less than seven dollars in coins and fractional currency. Nerved by a kind of delighted wrath, sustained by the choice tonicity of I-told-you-so, even the hoarse-voiced Widow Clementine Lowder could rise from her bed and go trembling to the front fence in order to discuss latest advices with passers-by.

Her son remained barricaded behind dye kettles, cooking his persistent grief, chagrin, and embarrassment along with carbonate of potash and sulphuric acid. He specialized in out-of-town orders for several months—at least until his mother died, and genuine pity might slake the bitterness of community scandal.

Johnson was convinced that disgrace, and not cancer of the throat, had brought about his mother's demise. Thus he charged the Reverend Mr. Steep with being a murderer as well as an adulterer, thief, swindler, seducer, and kidnaper. . . . At least a portion of these crimes must have been expiated by the itinerant during the following March, however. A newspaper item from Kentucky reported an episode in which horsewhips, tar, feathers, a rail, and the Reverend Silas Underhill Steep figured in grotesque if entirely merited commingling.

Alice herself had been abandoned in Wheeling, Virginia, but apparently entertained no notion of returning to Ohio. Mr. Jethro Higel, who served as Norwalk postmaster, violated the ethics of his profession by describing certain folded sheets, daubed with wax, which came in the usual manner of Collect on Delivery and were addressed to Alice's father, Timothy Barron. The humiliated Barrons were believed to have sent money to Alice, but no one knew for a certainty; and the Barrons would say nothing about it, and moved on to Illinois that same year. Rumor next ascribed to Alice Lowder a bigamous marriage in Virginia. When a fresh siege of cholera struck the upper Ohio Valley it carried off the erring as well as the redeemed, for sweet Alice was listed among the victims. . . . The song *Ben Bolt* became immensely popular, some years later, but Johnson Lowder always held a pardonable aversion to it.

Since the tragedy occurred when Harvey Luce was an infant it is not remarkable that he remained unenlightened as to the reasons for Uncle Johnson's vagary until he himself was approaching manhood. A word here, a nod there, a cryptic statement let fall by Mrs. Angers . . . these built together and made sense eventually . . . although a youth possessed of more human curiosity would have spied out the essentials for himself long before. As a matter of fact, Harvey was not really interested enough to do so. He cared nothing for puzzles or mysteries. He blinked emptily at the pageant of mankind, trying to fit the populations always into a Biblical design where they would not fit, trying always to dress them in Hebraic robes which they refused to wear. This was his eternal and only flight from actuality, and exhibited the sole imagination which he might employ; and that, again, was not truly imagination, since to Harvey Luce the Old and New Testaments were both actuality, to be invoked literally as often as possible.

Because he never got into any sort of trouble in boyhood, he won a great reputation for reliability; when basically his only reliability consisted in performing a given task with ordinary credit, if it were thoroughly lined out to him in advance. If he had no distinct pattern by which to proceed, he was apt to make a botch of anything attempted; but these failures were few, since almost invariably the pattern was indeed set before him, the dyeing formula was tacked upon the wall, the watch ticked precisely, the pot was taken off the fire. When his lack of initiative betrayed him into ludicrous inadequacy no one could really believe that he had failed—least of all, Uncle Johnson Lowder. Every other reason in the world was ascribed, from unprecedented hot weather or unprecedented cold weather, to an adulteration of chemicals by the drug manufacturers. Harvey *looked* so very good. His fat eyes were so brown and round, his solid earnest face pink as the pinks tended in Mrs. Angers' flower beds, and soft as the fuzzy belly of one of the perennial kittens.

Never in his life did he skulk behind sheds to smoke grapevine or cornsilk (none of the other boys would have had him for a moment); never did he get into fights (there was good reason for that: he was built like a little black ox and had the same sort of thews apparent, so even the most turbulent bullies avoided him); he did not snicker in a bench-corner huddle and drive his Sabbath school teacher to distraction by snorting over fancied obscene allusions discovered in hymnbook or in Testament (he was too sedentary to indulge in fancies fairylike or lewd). He had the pathetic hoarse squawking tone of adolescence in his voice by the time he was twelve, and never lost it, so that in consequence all strangers promptly believed him as sincere and guileless as children are supposed (falsely) to be. But they were right in this: Harvey Luce was sincere, because he owned a feeble one-track brain unvexed by switches, sidetracks, or other confusions—and he was guileless, not through noble choice, but principally because he was stupid.

Simpering people (and there are many in each community, with all the basic intelligence of katydids and all the accumulated wisdom of road-walking hens) looked at Harvey, smirked, nodded back and forth at one another . . . the men compressed their stern bearded lips, nodded again, and said: There is a young fellow who is going to make his mark in the world! (He would, too: habitually on the debit side of the Ledger of Accomplishment.) Ladies rolled up their soulful eyes and murmured: Still waters run deep! (Which was an abomination unto fact, since the rushing waters of the not-too-distant Huron River had drowned more than one unfortunate when roaring springtime floods descended; and the quietest pool in the region was Mr. Allen Crowley's cow pond, all of two feet deep above the mud.)

Harvey was but fifteen when Mr. Spartacus Wilson died and left the church sexton-less and janitor-less. With unanimous approval of elders and deacons alike, for the first time in local history the responsibility of these combined offices was awarded to a lad of tender years. Harvey sighed, and declared only that he hoped he might prove himself worthy of the stewardship. (Those were his exact words.) The fact that such functions were traditionally unpaid did not enter into the situation. Harvey Luce was so universally regarded as a plump bundle of chaste virtues, honesties, and sobrieties, that even Johnson Lowder could not view the appointment with too much suspicion.

Lowder said only—once, as if worried: Harvey. Now, you ain't going to let this go to your head?

I'll try not to, sir. With God helping me!

I mean—it's kind of a step up the vestry ladder. You remember what you swore—swore upon the Bible? That still holds. Twill hold forever!

Oh, I know it, Uncle Johnson. I know I can't never be a preacher, I've sworn *not* to be. But I don't ask it. All I ask is the opportunity to kneel before the Lord my God as an humble servitor!

It was a touching thing to see Harvey sweeping out the little church in a Sunday dawn, to see him carrying ashes from two stoves in a Monday dawn after the stoves had cooled . . . to see an emergency obtrude, such as the advent of an extremely female coon-dog, pursued by a panting file of miscellaneous suitors: this aggregation wallowed down the aisle in the middle of services whilst the Reverend Mr. Moulton was intoning from First Corinthians: *Know ye not that they which run in a race run all, but one receiveth the prize?* . . . to see the red-faced Harvey arise, tiptoe to the left rear door beside the platform, open the door, deftly expel the slathering tribe (this was almost easier done than said. Everyone knew Betsy Cole, who belonged to Mr. Fred Cole the butcher, and her loose affections embraced the world at large; but all you had to do to her was to say, *Betsy, go home!*—and she would tuck her bent tail between her legs and light out for home, heat or no heat)—

To see Harvey in a January Friday dawn, sternly assaulting icy iron of the churchyard soil with a pick, long before other gravediggers arrived on the scene (Grandpa Hubbard would be laid to rest on this day. He had been dead since Monday—but of course it was winter—and his daughters had finally arrived from eastern Pennsylvania)—

Had any irreverent soul ventured to suggest that this lad did not represent all rectitude—past, present, and dreamed of—the statement would have been dismissed as calumniation.

The very first month after he assumed these honored tasks, Harvey forgot and left two windows open, of an evening following prayer meeting. A torrential rain blew fiercely at three o'clock the next morning and drenched the new carpeting along the north side of the church and utterly ruined the finish of three new pews presented recently by Mr. Seth Tollyman, a local banker (these pews had been tacitly reserved for the use of the Tollyman family, nephews, cousins, and in-laws). Not one soul in that congregation ever cherished the slanderous notion that Harvey Luce had left the windows open, nor did Harvey himself think so; he thought he remembered closing them tightly, and said so. It was believed faithfully that roisterers from a vile den at the crossroads, Tuck's Tavern, had forced the windows, climbed in, and deliberately defiled the sanctuary with revelries best hinted at than discussed; they left the windows open following their retreat. Minerva Wadsworth herself, who dwelt next door, had heard the sounds of this invasion (or thought she had) and, since she was almost bat-blind, her hearing was considered to be proportionately acute and her testimony thus reliable. The niece who dwelt in luckless serfdom as Miss Wadsworth's companion was influenced sufficiently to believe that she had seen shadowy vagabond forms flitting about the premises. People pitied Harvey beyond estimation, for he had to work extra long at taking up the carpeting, drying it, putting down fresh straw beneath, putting down the carpet again. Mr. Seth Tollyman was moved sufficiently to pay a cabinetmaker for refinishing the pews. Consummate indignation ruled against Tuck's Tavern and its habitués. Old Bill Bernatzki, a foreigner who traipsed weaving but cocky about the streets through his nonslumbering hours, was suspected to be one of the malefactors; and Methodists and even Baptists alike, with not a few Presbyterians, spoke more harshly of Bill Bernatzki than ever before.

When Harvey Luce was twenty-one he journeyed eastward. The late Widow Lowder's younger brother, a man named Pitcairn, had lived to what was considered a great age—seventy-nine—in western York State. Johnson Lowder was the only relative and thus the only heir to survive him. A letter arrived from an attorney-at-law in Steuben County (this letter had black wax sealing the folds) and after some hours of reflection Uncle Johnson called Harvey into session with him.

Tis my old Uncle Clovis. The last of my mother's side. He's passed away, back in Steuben County, New York.

How joyful will be your meeting—! said Harvey Luce. As you join immortal hands on the Heavenly Shore!

Maybe so. Though I never saw him but once, and that was fifty years agone. Anyway, he's left it to me.

Left—?

Whatever properties he had. Wan't anybody else for him to leave them to, he added truthfully.

Don't grieve, Uncle Johnson! We may hope that he died in the blessed assurance of Eternal Life!

Maybe so. Though Ma used to tell that he was called Old Clove by the villagers, and could swear the hide right off a horse; and once he was believed to have put rum in the feedbox oats of a racing filly, and— But we oughtn't to speak ill of the dead.

At least, said Harvey, he has reached a Land where sinners are found not, and sermons are needed not.

We trust! Well, the situation is so: some of the property has got a mortgage on it, some hasn't; there's cash in the savings bank, but some debts to be paid; and a man wants to buy Uncle Clovis's cottage, right off, and— The whole matter to be settled up, you see. . . . Harvey, you've but come to man's estate. But I just can't go. Would have to make that long journey now in hot weather, and I'm not as young as I was: past sixty. And here's the order from Hibbs and Son: that same yellow again, and tis a tricky shade. You've got those first bolts of goods already in the alumine bath, hain't you?

Just as you bade me do, sir.

Good; but there's more following within the week. And that wine-red order for Lucas Brothers in Cincinnati; and the last freight they sent was I-don't-know-how-late. With business pressing me like this, I just daren't leave!

Three days later Harvey Luce, limp carpetbag stuffed beneath his seat and pie-hat jammed upon his round head, was enjoying a first venture from Huron into the outer world, and he thought Lake Erie to be a veritable ocean. When he considered the sober excursion before him, it was to name it in the parlance of talents, stewards, vineyards. . . . He read his Bible much of the time when he wasn't munching out of a lunch basket which had been crammed with eggs, sandwiches, and pie by old Mrs. Angers; and he felt a guilty shudder of delight when he heard a small boy cry out, Ma, I wish we had some big fat pickles like that one the preacher's eating over there acrost! For this summary identification—if a false one—the child became endowed with all that remained in the jar of Mrs. Angers' locally famous cinnamon gherkins.

In York State the emissary was greeted with trepidation by Lawyer Boylston, who considered him a trifle young for the trust reposed; but in short order the attorney came under the simple spell of Harvey's clear-eyed probity, as indeed did everyone whom he met in the villages of Greenwood and Rexville. (Two tough-principled businessmen also evaluated him keenly for what he was. Shortly the estate accruing to Johnson Lowder was some eight hundred dollars leaner, in consequence.) Powers of attorney were produced, collections were made, debts paid, property peddled. Uncle Clovis Pitcairn's handmade invalid chair was presented gratis to a crippled woman instead of being sold for the seven dollars it might have fetched; Harvey believed sincerely that Johnson Lowder did not wish to lay up treasures on earth, where moth and rust doth corrupt, and where thieves break through and steal; and he repeated this to a number of people (and was promptly taken advantage of again by a grim-faced Congregationalist carpenter who padded his bill undetected).

There was the matter of the Pitcairn house. Three offers had been posted for this property, but Lawyer Boylston suggested that the sales value of the place might be enhanced considerably by the effecting of minor repairs, including a renovated back porch.

It was to secure lumber for this undertaking that Harvey Luce walked to the sawmill operated by one Rowland Gardner, and there he met his fate in the winsome shape of Miss Mary, the eldest daughter. (Abbie was barely eight at the time, Eliza a little older, and Rowly but an infant.) Harvey Luce stood at the door of the mill, with the family cottage only a few rods distant, while he dickered with tall Rowland Gardner for joists and planks. (Neither man was a good dickerer; and, if this might be believed possible, each cheated himself roundly on one item or another before the deal was executed.) Harvey heard a warm good-natured youthful female voice singing while its owner struggled with languishing embers beneath the soap kettle: *There is a land of pure delight where saints immortal reign.* Mary Gardner was of that age when she had first discovered tremendous emotional power inherent in a hopeful hymn or in an honestly shouted sermon (the age at which sloe-eyed girls in convents clutch their rosaries more tightly than before, and consider the possibility of taking Church Orders; and one sees herself perhaps entertaining an apparition of the Virgin on some laborious mountain path or other). In more secular moments of her fancy, Mary was wont to discuss secretly with herself the possibility of marriage with various bachelors —mostly young farmers—whom she'd met at church or at the mill. She would embroider stray scraps of paper with her excellent copperplate script; writing, Mrs. Osbert F. Marvel, Mrs. Mary Gardner Marvel, Mrs. Pliny Grinstaff, Mrs. Mary G. Grinstaff, Mr. & Mrs. Pliny Grinstaff, Miss Mary Gardner and Mr. Walter Claxton, Mr. and Mrs. Walter W. Claxton, and similar vague and ill-assorted dreams, and crushing the papers into little balls and tossing them hastily into the fireplace if her mother or one of her sisters came nigh. She was fourteen, and inordinately ripe for the plucking.

Manufacture of soft soap was a smelly and burdensome task not too far removed in process from certain dyeing activities; furthermore a fire was a fire, and if one knew how to keep a steady fire under a kettle of orchil or cochineal one might also know how to feed the blaze beneath a kettle of lye, mutton tallow, and chicken guts. Harvey Luce became an eager fire tender on this morning, and joined in Mary's hymns. He received expressions of sympathy on his recent bereavement, as most people thereabouts considered him to be a bona fide nephew of Uncle Clovis Pitcairn's nephew; and he mumbled hoarsely but winningly to Mary Gardner: A few more revolving years, and we shall all transfer our camping ground to the Groves of Bliss!

He was invited to stay to dinner, held Rowly on his lap while Mrs. Gardner and the girls hastened about with biscuits, peas, and a fresh-slaughtered guinea fowl, got his lap nicely wetted, and blurted out humble reference to his labors for the Methodists in Norwalk, Ohio. Since the Gardners embraced the tenets of Methodism with heart and soul, this was a most salubrious coming-together. Mary Gardner and Harvey Luce knelt side by side at prayer meeting the next Wednesday night, and they both testified courageously; neighbors were moved by their earnest revelation. . . . Neighbors came to shake hands, smother with embraces, slap upon the back (Harvey's back), pester with advice, dab away polite tears, and eat poor worried Mrs. Rowland Gardner down to her last few brown hens, when the marriage was celebrated after an unsullied but whirlwind courtship of three mortal weeks.

Being wholly without guile, Harvey had never attempted to give the impression to his new father-in-law that he was anything but a drawer of water and a hewer of wood insofar as Uncle Johnson Lowder's inheritance of the Clovis Pitcairn estate (in the end a rather meager one) was concerned. Nevertheless Rowland Gardner, hopeful of fortune as always, could not separate himself from the notion that Harvey might partake of vague generosities and emoluments. He felt that he should much rather see Daughter Mary wedded safely to a God-fearing United States citizen than becoming a kind of missionarying Margaret Fuller to Chinese heathen, which she had frequently expressed a fever to be. . . . Huron County, Ohio, seemed half a world away to the damp-eyed Frances Gardner, who had never been out of New York State; but Rowland wasn't laying by any fortune there in Rexville, and often he took a dream of California or some other portion of the Golden West to his couch, these nights . . . might even try Ohio himself. He wondered what opportunity could offer in Norwalk to an experienced combmaker, book agent, and sawyer.

Norwalk was prepared for the arrival of the bridal pair. Harvey had written of his meeting with Miss Mary, and the matrimonial prospects. His missive was comprehensible but misspelled; the rearing managed by Uncle Johnson Lowder had included more hours with dye sticks than with school slates in hand. Harvey's chief reading had always been Scriptural in content, and the King James Version was not necessarily a handbook on orthography.

I prey for your blessing on this union. The yung lady to whom I have offered my hart and hand seems to possess no vanity nor common weeknesses of girlish flibber-jibbets as often we have observed among yung ladies at home. She is meek and filled with virtue, and her family is of steady habbits. I prey you, dear uncle, do not critisize me for taking such a step without due consiltation on the matter; but I feel it necessary that I should cleave unto her. I reelize you are standing the fare and other expenses of this jurney undertaken in your behalf, but I will reumburse you for expenses incurt by my wife on the return jurney. As you may know, I am of saving habbits and have put by a tidy sum out of the wages paid me by you: better than three hundred dollars as of now, which sum should be sifficient for a starter. Could we not stop at Mrs. Vollmers boarding house till I find more perminent quarters within our means?—it is a Temperance house. But I must heed the Sermon in Matthew Sixth Chapter: *For your heavenly Father knoweth that ye have need of all these things. But seek ye first the kingdom of God.*

Johnson Lowder had been ordinarily conversant with the Sermon on the Mount, in years before he was compelled to witness a swine trampling his pearl; but he felt providently that in this case he should do more than behold the fowls of the air, and that the necessity for both meat and raiment did enter into Harvey's picture. Johnson was not noted as a man freehanded or even comparably generous . . . the majority of his mother's family had been parsimonious hard-bitten New Englanders who gripped their pence tightly. But he wished to demonstrate affection to Harvey, and he realized that now an extra mouth (and probably later some little mouths) needed to be fed.

Few women but must be moved by romantic aspects of a honeymoon and the founding of a new household. Mrs. Angers was no exception. She whisked lamely with bright eyes and gnarled busy hands, making the sitting room ready for a young couple's tenancy. Johnson fetched down from the attic a walnut bedstead which had been his parents', and set it up anew. By this time he had acquired three residential properties in the village, besides his own. He gulped as he foresaw a decrease in future income from rentals . . . nevertheless he gave notice to the tenant of the smallest of these cottages, directing the man to find other quarters by the first of the following month. Harvey Luce would receive free occupancy of this dwelling, in addition to his wage as assistant dyer. (Uncle Johnson saw no necessity for making an outright gift and transferring the house to Harvey's ownership.)

The bride fitted acceptably into local circles after her arrival. Her few gowns were scrutinized by the ladies and won favorable report for their modesty, her bonnet was regarded as a trifle too beribboned (but after all, she was a mere child and came from the East!) and her clear willing voice added power to hymns. In due course her pregnancy was observed, whispered about by the jealous, advised upon by the more practical and doting; and when little Albert was delivered successfully by Granny Coyne the next year, people declared him a paragon. A star was cut out of gold paper and pasted upon the Sunday school cradle roll, with his name inscribed upon it.

Mary Luce had not yet reached her sixteenth birthday when the baby arrived, and separation from her family was telling on her. Whatever Rowland Gardner's shortcomings as provider, the Gardner home had offered fervency and often a merriment not met with here. Mary missed her mother's uncomplaining strength and occasional bursts of almost girlish confidence, missed her father's awed or amused voice as he savored his favorite household relaxation in the evenings (reading aloud: he read everything he could get his hands on—a Scott novel lent to him by Judge John Justice or Lawyer William Boylston, a torn copy of *Harper's New Monthly Magazine,* or a newspaper left at the sawmill by some forgetful customer). Mary considered with nostalgia the shrill wranglings, noisy imaginings, and occasional hair-pullings indulged in by her younger sisters. Little Rowly was but a baby when she left; she had a baby of her own now, with all the cuddlesome raptures and downright drudgery attendant. Still, she missed her tiny brother, learned in letters what he had said or what he had upset or how his trottings kept the family on the alert . . . she envisioned the colored hills of York State as opposed to a gray raw village in the Ohio flatlands. Harvey wondered why so often he awakened groggily to find her crying in bed beside him; but if her lonely grief was transmitted to him he accepted it only as a cross to be borne, a burden to be hoisted, and dearly did he welcome crosses and all manner of burdens. Mary never visited the shop or dye works if she could avoid it, not even after her solemn spouse, in response to nagging, contrived a wagon for her to pull the baby in, that little Albert might take the air. Two mismated pairs of wheels sustained a wooden box, and Harvey pointed out with his usual contented melancholy that the thing might be placed upon runners, come winter; but the equipage squeaked hideously and no amount of greasing seemed to suffice. Mary Luce knew that her approach was heralded along the street by mechanical outcry, and became embarrassed proportionately, though the baby seemed to enjoy the noise. . . . Harsh odors of bubbling mordants and raw indigo or fustic offended her nostrils and her eyes. Also she grew waspish at welcoming a man who was forever tinted to the elbows with whatever shade had last been mixed. She never knew, as evening approached, whether he would appear red-handed or green-handed or black-handed. Other people were accustomed to this occupational peculiarity of Harvey and Uncle Johnson, but Mary might never welcome it or fail to cringe. Furthermore, consecutive baths of chemicals brought about rashes and peelings of the skin, the more so when certain technical tasks were protracted. Mary fought stiffly to keep from shuddering away at her husband's touch.

Harvey became aware of scorn or pettishness on Mary's part only rarely. Most of the time he was occupied in performing his designated chores, and preoccupied with the necessity to serve his Master, to glean, to muzzle not the ox, to put away childish things, to seek not his own glory, to render unto Caesar, and to refuse defilement by thefts, covetousness, wickedness, deceit, lasciviousness, an evil eye, blasphemy, pride, and foolishness (St. Mark 7:22). Often the task seemed insurmountable; but he only shook his spiritual head blindly, and welcomed anew an overpowering sense of inadequacy.

He was engaged at this season in reading the Bible through for the third time (he had begun his initial studies in that far-off year when Uncle Johnson swore him to a secular existence). The reading went faster than before—he could read much more rapidly and accurately, in proportion, than he could write—but still he must break the long words with implied hyphens in order to voice them at all. The youthful wife and mother might not welcome his reading aloud as she had her father's. When he returned to the little house at night Harvey Luce regarded himself as a husbandman come from the fields or as a shepherd who had folded his sheep; he was willing to embrace the extravagance of Heaven knew how many candles in a given month, in order to proceed with his delicious perusal.

Pa used to read *Harper's,* times.

But, wife, we got no other books than this. We need none.

Tain't a book—*Harper's.* Tis a magazine. And he read novels and things, too.

Novels!—replied Harvey in alarm.

Not the saucy silly kind, he didn't have truck with those. But Walter Scott. I mind *Ivanhoe.* Twas all about knights and Normans, and an old Jew, and a great big man named Front de Buff— And, oh—Rebecca and Rowena! They were just real beauties, both of them—

The husbandman shook his head, and smiled with distrust. But your Pa's a good churchman; I know he must have read the Scriptures. Fact, I heard him do so when I was at your place in Rexville—

Course he did, and I love the Book as well as any person might!

But I love the Psalms, and Gospels and Acts, and even Jeremiah— Just makes the shivers run up and down my spine—

Bible, said Harvey reprovingly, is not sposed to give you the shivers.

Maybe not, husband. But—but when *I* read!—she added with sudden rebellious fire— I just skip to them parts!

He said sadly, grinning in the lugubrious acceptance of criticism: Guess we're not sposed to skip.

Well, who says so?

There goes the baby, he muttered.

She jumped up, listened, then bounced back into the rocker with her yarn and needles. No, tain't the baby. It's just that old tomcat of Mrs. Poynter's hollering around after the Quackenbushes' girl cat—

Mary! he gasped, shocked anew at mention of feline depravity.

Well, that's what he's a-doing! And Bertie's sound asleep—when *he* squawls he just raises the roof! . . . All right, husband, if you must, you must. Pray read ahead.

He began willingly where he had left off at the interruption.

And they gave unto them, of the cities of ref-fuge, She-chem in Mount Eph-ra-im with her sub-burbs; they gave also Ge-zer with her sub-burbs,

And Jok-me-am with her sub-burbs, and Beth-ho-ron with her sub-burbs,

And Aij-a-lon with her sub-burbs, and Gath-rim-mon with her sub-burbs:

And out of the half tribe of Man-ass-eh; A-ner with her sub-burbs, and Bil-e-am with her sub-burbs, for the family of the rem-nant of the sons of Ko-hath.

. . . Knitting soon tumbled into the calico lap, the gray ball rolled across the floor. Mary's pale-lidded eyes were closed, her set face had fallen back against the plaid cushion as she dozed. Harvey sighed, felt rewardingly left alone and misunderstood, knew that there was One Above Who Understood. He continued reading, but silently, until his gaze could no longer fasten itself against the filming page.

Joy came to the irked young wife one day in the summer following, when she was called aside at the Sunday school picnic and informed, Your Pa's looking for you.

Mary's mouth opened wide; she gasped, gaped, strangled. My *Pa*?

Says he is. He's in a wagon, over't the edge of the grove.

Mary caught up her skirts, began to run, then whirled and came shrieking for Bertie. (The child was big enough now to scamper unsteadily about, and to point his finger at a horse and say, Washy, and to point his finger at a pig, and grunt; but Bertie made exactly that same sound when he wished to visit the privy or to sit upon his little pot. Thus disaster befell frequently because of an understandable confusion in interpreting a plea for toilet assistance, and the identification of swine.)

Harvey Luce, exchanging on this bright summer's day the labors of quercitron bark and steaming kettles for the labors of hammock, hamper, and lemonade tub— Harvey gazed from the huddle where he was trying to tie three clamoring members of his Willing Workers class into burlap shroudings for a sack race, and cried out in alarm to his wife. What had happened. . . ?

Tis my father! Folks say he's here! Bertie, come with Ma!—

Harvey soon joined his relatives in pleasant cottonwood shade, where the womenfolks laughed and cried in the same breath, and Bertie tugged gleefully at his grandfather's sparse beard with both hands. . . . What had befallen, what brought the Gardners all the way to Huron County in a sudden historic leap? Rowland Gardner explained briefly about the unexpected offer of a grading contract in northwestern Ohio (he did not say that his sawmill had been seized by creditors, he said that he had *disposed* of sawmill and cottage). Mr. and Mrs. Gardner, with Eliza, Abbie, and Rowly, were welcomed into the bosom of festivity, with Harvey Luce being summoned hastily in advance to deal with two of his Willing Workers who evinced an un-Christianlike tendency to settle differences arising out of the sack race with profanity and fists.

This was a summer of flux, the currents were twisting Harvey. He thought it all God's will, and beamed piteously. Mrs. Angers had recently been summoned, as Harvey put it, to that pure Country where no farewell would ever be heard, nor tear of regret ever flow. Uncle Johnson, uncertain and bereft in the old house, was considering an offer which had been made for his little dye works by a rival dyer from Sandusky. This man had a son who assisted him, and if the sale were made there might be no further livelihood for Harvey in Norwalk, at least not in his established trade. The ensuing devastating change was so much a product of implacability manifest by outside powers, that Harvey could do little more than blink at its rapid progression. In fact, a day less than two weeks after the Gardners' coming saw the Luces stowed into a wagon of their own, and driving ahead of Rowland Gardner toward the unfamiliar vastness of Williams County and Fulton County—ahead, because they drove the younger and better team. Harvey had never heaved against the handles of a scraper before, but he was sturdy, and proposed to operate a scraper in the employ of his father-in-law.

(Fate was kind to him in this venture. Fate allowed him to bruise his knees and lame his back almost as much as he desired while earning, as he was pleased to say, his daily bread by the sweat of his brow. Fate was unkind only in that it sent Harvey on an errand of repairs, in that hour when the Irish gang visited their thrashing upon

Gardner. Harvey was six miles away at the time, else he might have attempted to rebuke a storm and temper a sea; and the waters of such ignorant rage formed a surface upon which most definitely it would have been unwise for him to walk. Thus Mary still could boast of a live husband instead of a dead martyr, when these modern Israelites began scouting for manna in the wilderness of Sin, or rather, Okoboji.)

As for Mary, she soon displayed the affable spirit of yore, for now the two families were one. According to pattern set by other amiable and courageous young women before her, she did not mind slim pickings from a kettle so long as the fire beneath it was kindled by rubbing a song against a hope. Furthermore her father acquired—by barter, purchase, or gift, during the three years before A Pillar of Cloud by Day guided the little band to their final residence— He had acquired a one-volume encyclopedia, three books by Sir Walter Scott, three by Charles Dickens, two by Elizabeth Wetherell, a red-bound volume called *Western Scenes and Reminiscences* (which seemed singularly appropriate to people already dwelling at the West) a copy of *The Song of Hiawatha,* and eleven soiled copies of *Gleason's Pictorial.* Most of these works had been chewed on their margins, and a trifle into the text in some cases, by mice or rats with a literary proclivity. But even the most rodent-gnawed reading matter available was a delight to the ears of Mrs. Luce, compared to those portions of Ezekiel into which her husband's enchantment had progressed during that long-ago month when they departed from Norwalk. *And by the border of Ju-dah, from the east side unto the west side, shall be the off-er-ing which ye shall offer of five and twenty thousand reeds in breadth, and in length as one of the other parts, from the east side unto the west side.* Mary now listened nightly with bated breath to the most heart-rending persecutions which ever beset an Elizabeth Wetherell heroine, just as she had tried to listen, but with extremely unbated breath, to the arrangement of the Restored Tribes.

The Spirit Lake country or the Okoboji country (these terms seemed to be used interchangeably) had won the Gardner-Luce contingent away from rival considerations of the Fort Dodge country, the Woodbury County country, and all the rest of them. Once the properties at Clear Lake had been turned over to a troop of eager Norwegians, Rowland Gardner and Harvey Luce counted what seemed an amazing profit. They prepared to enrich themselves anew by establishing a home farther west. It would be too late in the year to put in a crop when they reached unpopulated regions, but they had enough money to carry them through the winter; they'd not had that long a pocket in Shell Rock! Long since they'd traded off their horses for oxen, as better suited to prairie plowing and hauling; but now Gardner insisted on buying an additional wagon and stocking it generously with flour, pork, meal, and a hundred other necessities.

Think we need all this truck? asked Harvey Luce with a lugubrious smile. *The Lord shall give you in the evening flesh to eat, and in the morning bread to the full!*

Now, look here, Harvey. Do you recall how twas a year ago last winter, when we blame near starved?

We didn't have so much money then—

That's what I mean. We got the cash, and I aim to stock up.

But we're headed for a *wilderness,* Mr. Gardner! Flowing with milk and honey—

Well, you go out and look for a good bee tree when we get there! And maybe find a she-buffalo coming fresh, he added under his breath. Gardner considered himself as good a Christian as the next Methodist, nor was he given to vulgar allusions in his speech; but sometimes his son-in-law tried his patience to extremity.

Frances Gardner and her eldest daughter shared identical if unvoiced opinion about the wisdom of this hegira. They looked upon the move with unqualified favor. Small towns and villages in which she had dwelt sporadically and without profit, for a toilsome generation, bore for Frances only a connotation of neglected rooms which needed to be scrubbed and made habitable, garden soil filled with broken teacups and rotting shoes, neighbors who might display a welcoming kindness but who were positive to join in general criticism of and withdrawal from the Gardners when final disaster ensued. Twin Lakes, Greenwood, Rexville, Ohio, Indiana, Shell Rock: this assemblage of regions designated for Frances a robbing of Peter and a paying of Paul, the repetition of which had worn her resiliency to the thinness of ragged abandoned calico—no longer fit for a patch, or a strand to be sewed for a rug—good for a mop rag, good for nothing else. Clear Lake was growing into a village, the nearby Masonic Grove showed signs of developing into a town. Profit realized from the sale of their land would assuredly be dissipated if they remained; and if the land had *not* been sold there would indeed have been no profit. An untenanted goal such as the Lake Okoboji toward which they now advanced might spell harder work than ever before, and might pose certain unfamiliar perils; but at least no women would whisper in church that Frances Gardner was wearing that same broken-rimmed bonnet again this year, with only the ribbons turned on it; and no Mr. Apgar would come to the door grim-jawed, with Rowland Gardner's overdue note in his pocket; no Mr. and Mrs. Cameron would say at the store, We're sorry to send you home with an empty basket, Abbie. But you tell your Ma we can't let her have nothing more on credit, till the old account's squared up! There would be no store, no Camerons, no church, no unpaid doctors, no Mr. Apgar, no notes, no mortgages. Rowland

Gardner had the money to pay for his land and the Luces', all strapped into his scuffed black wallet. The plowing of not more than five acres of ground would hold a new claim for six months; the building of a cabin at least eight logs high, with a roof, would serve in lieu of breaking an additional five acres; and would hold the claim intact against possible land-hungry newcomers for an additional six months. There was at least the lapse of a year before any money would have to be paid across the board to the Government; and right now Mr. Gardner *had* the money, or rather he and Harvey Luce had it, though Rowland Gardner was banker.

Probably this was fitting since he was of elder years. But—

Frances had made the common mistake of believing that Harvey, with his impression of steady uncomplaining dependability, was better fitted to assume charge of the mutual treasury. With reluctance she managed to convey this suggestion to her husband in a series of hints, and was surprised to be met with a flat refusal.

(By this time Rowland was able to observe that nothing of Uncle Johnson Lowder's strict acumen had rubbed off on Harvey. Mary's father had rather supposed her to be living in well-ordered bliss, and was astonished to reach Norwalk and find her a drudge in one of the village's smallest and most illy located cottages. Furthermore, Gardner had the monetary incompetent's occasional ability to smell out a fellow incompetent when given only the faintest scent of evidence. . . . But an incompetent may not so readily recognize the keen-nerved skinflint, and therein he meets recurrent doom!)

Rain or shine, Mary Luce was delighted to be voyaging with her fair young children into a fair young land; she sang whole-souled appreciation of Jordan, Canaan, Galilee, and Sharon while she jounced little Mandy in the wagon and managed to turn the heel of a sock at the same time. There would be no dye works in the Spirit Lake country! Harvey's hands and forearms would be unblemished, no longer parti-colored and scabrous; he would carry no longer the reek of lead acetate and carthamin in his clothes. . . . Mary cringed at the thought of a diet of locusts, but she liked honey. And prairie hens thrummed away from them in flocks beyond counting. She sang, *Let all our songs abound, and all our tears be dry. We're marching thro' Immanuel's ground to fairer worlds on high. . . .*

Abbie Gardner had to be warned a dozen times a day: Keep your bunnit on your head, Miss. Not hanging down your back like that. Know what, young lady?—if you don't wear your bunnit constant you'll get all freckled and *tanned!* On the other hand, her sister Eliza did not have to be warned: one could not have pried Eliza's bonnet off her head with a crowbar; she hid in the depths of the great black slatted thing like a novice taking refuge in her cell. But there was nothing nun-like in her intimate reflections. She had no wish to be disfigured by freckles or tan. Eliza was now wearing her skirts down and her hair up; and recently she'd met a youth named Henry Tretz, who paused with his party of movers to lay in a supply of salted fish at Clear Lake. This beaming powerful young German had a plume of shining blond hair; he resembled the storied Vikings or heroic North Sea sailors whom Eliza'd heard her father read about. In halting but quite understandable English he looked down at Eliza Gardner and said, Such a beautiful white skin have you on your face! . . . *Nein.* He did not know exactly where his party was bound. But his uncle, it was often he was speaking of a place named Spirit Lake. . . . *Ja, Fraulein?* So also goes your family to Spirit Lake? *Das ist gut!* And maybe it is you I see again?

Abbie inquired, with sly curiosity, What's that tune, Liza?

What tune?

You was humming it in the wagon, a while back; and just now, whilst we was lugging these things past the slough.

Don't know what you mean! said the snappish Eliza with a toss of her head.

Twas a *dance tune!* Abbie cried in consternation.

Twas not!

Spose I tolt Ma? Spose I tolt–?

Twas not a dance tune. Twas a play-party tune!

Ahhh, the one that old Mr. Whiskers Wiggett used to play on his fiddle; and they danced all night over't that awful Widder Holman's place, and they had liquor by the *jug!* And folks said some of the girls went out in the *oatfield* with some of the *menfolks!* And Reverent Cowden he preached a whole sermon bout it! And that tune–I know!–tis called *Hell on the Wabash!* No decent Christian girl ought to–

Aw, you tend to your own knitting, Miss!

Abbie herself, whatever her concern over moral decline in her unpredictable nigh-grown-up sister, was pleased to be headed for Okoboji. The Gardners and Luces had been informed on what was considered to be good authority that there were no Indians resident in that place. Thus wheedling grunting surly dirty groups would no longer be offending the landscape and trying to put their hands on Abbie's yellow hair. And suggesting that they *buy* her. Ugh. Abbie was not certain which she detested the most–sulphur and molasses, or garter snakes–but she was quite certain that she hated Indians more than either of these pests in her life. A quiet blue tree-rimmed lake, a pristine oil-painted lake . . . vaguely she thought of it as being decorated with windmills, water lilies, delightful rustic bridges. She should fetch quantities of water lilies home in her apron. . . .

Little Rowly Gardner wished for his family to begin dwelling at Okoboji or Spirit Lake–which he called Spurt Lake–because an older boy had told him there were many bears out there. During the previous spring a stubbly man (with a peculiar smell about him) had strolled into their community, leading a black bear secured by thick leather collar and greasy chain. If you gave the man a penny, the bear would dance for you; and Rowly and his playmates had begged no less than six pennies from hard-taxed relatives. Thus the bear stood upon his hind legs and danced six times. He danced waltzes, a reel, a jig, and a cotillion, or so the man said. . . . Was it difficult to train a bear to dance? . . . Not in the laste! cried the proprietor. Now, ye take old Broo there—that's his name, I call him Broo, sometimes I spake to him as Brian Broo!— He's gentle as a lamb getting milk from its mother, now isn't he? I had only to sprinkle a bit of salt on his tail, and from then on he followed me like a shadow. He slapes by me side at night, and would rather dance than ate! Now, like a dear lad, be after asking your good mother for another penny; for whiskey's dear in these parts, and Broo likes his dram, indade he does! . . . Rowly and his nephew Bertie, two years his junior, had well-laid plans for the capture, training, and instruction of Spirit Lake bears; and both had stolen salt and carried a supply in their shirt pockets, in case any Spirit Lake bears should come straying out in advance of their arrival.

Rowland Gardner presented Harvey Luce with a gift more precious than rubies. This was a chunky little book, almost a cube in size, which Gardner had fetched back to Clear Lake from the town of Waterloo, when once he made a trip there for supplies. This book, together with the bundle of *Gleason's* and the new poem written by Mr. Longfellow, had been acquired from a craftsman who needed a dozen of Rowland Gardner's smallest bolts but who had little use for printed word or words, since he could not read. No one might know how this agate-type book had found its way into possession of an illiterate saddler and harness mender. The loose cover was inscribed in faded stamping, *Wissett Church. Not To Be Taken Away,* and prayers contained therein were studded with references to Queen Victoria; nor might an intoxicated reader disregard Her Majesty's Declaration on a snuff-stained page: *Being by God's Ordinance, according to Our just Title, Defender of the Faith . . . within these Our Dominions. We hold it most agreeable to this Our Queenly Office, and Our own religious Zeal, to conserve and maintain the Church committed to Our Charge, in Unity of true Religion, and in the Bond of Peace.* Neither Harvey's comprehension nor his discernment were quite fit to cope with this verbiage; but he became fascinated progressively, as he spelled his way through the fine print, with the importance of liturgies implied.

Wife.

What say?

This book goes clear back.

Clear back to where?

Clear back to olden times!

Well, lots of things that Pa reads, they go clear back to olden times too. You don't think that Roderick Vick Alpine was just happening a-Friday, do you?

Yes, but hark unto this. *Ar-tic-les Agreed Upon by the Arch-bish-ops and Bish-ops of Both Prov-in-ces and the Whole Cler-gy in the Con-vo-ca-tion hol-den at Lon-don in the Year Fifteen Sixty-two—*

You know, Mr. Luce, that sounds mighty Catholic to me!

Oh, Mary, tain't really Catholic. Tis talk from the Church of England; and the fathers of Methodism come from the Church of England —that's what the Reverent Moulton always preached.

Harvey Luce, you showed me tother day yourself where there was a whole chapter called The Ordering of Priests! If *that* ain't Catholic, I don't know what is. Anytime anybody wants to go to—to— To ordering *priests!* Well, you can just bet he's a Roman Catholic at heart, and maybe wants the old Pope to be setting in the White House stead of President Pierce and— And everything! . . . Albert Johnson *Luce,* you and Rowly get right *out* of that pork tub and go clean yourselves up!

Harvey sought to argue no further with his spouse. Dumbly he was almost grateful to her for deriding or at least disapproving of his new religious studies. Such antagonism, however mildly suggested, gave him the comfortable feeling that he went unappreciated and unencouraged. A severely cut toe or a burned finger might not have pleased him more.

When we, our wearied limbs to rest,
Sat down by proud Euphrates' stream,
We wept, with doleful thoughts oppressed,
And Zion was our mournful theme.

With this invigorating gem, as he strode beside his team or as he rode and drove, Harvey Luce sent the birds racketing up from sloughs ahead.

He thought often of Uncle Johnson Lowder, he thought of Mrs. Angers, whom he now considered to be standing on Zion's walls, proclaiming a risen and exalted Saviour, and redeemed utterly from carnal pursuits which had occupied a portion of her nights when Harvey was a boy. He thought of the fact that he, Harvey, had known of sin shared by those two people, and had never breathed a word of their lechery to a soul. Did not such knowledge, with resultant forbearance, then, place him almost in the role of Confessor? . . . Vaguely somehow or other he had heard of Edward the Confessor, and he wondered just who Edward the Confessor was; perhaps he should find out something about him in this weighty eye-punishing little mystery which he carried through the day snuggled like a brick inside his shirt. . . . He thought of his Oath upon the Bible. Nay, he might never be a preacher by profession. Ordination would not be his (lest he be Damned; and often in secret pondering he thought of Damnation with a pardonable thrill, as had other martyrs who came before). But there was nothing in that Oath to prevent him from voicing songs of praise or abnegation, nothing to prevent his realization to the fullest of whatever powers he might possess as a future janitor-sexton-chorister-deacon-Sunday-school-teacher in a populous community which would someday extend itself along Okoboji shores. He marched with psalmody enrapturing him, with stubby sunburnt nose turned aloft. He was not the first man to enter a wilderness more violent than his own conception of it, nor the first man to fill his soul with baggage which would only clutter it almost beyond endurance, nor the first man to believe that that same endurance was inspired and sustained by Almighty God instead of by his own brutish tomfoolery.

XIV

Inkpaduta's horse died after he and Corn-Sucker reached the land of the Slightly Clouded Water. There was no knowing why the horse died, but it was easy to see how he died. (It did occur to Corn-Sucker that evil medicine might have been contrived, and deliberately. Inkpaduta was known to many people who could not be called his friends . . . he might just as surely be plagued by spirits who effected unpleasant revenges upon him.) One day the pony was sure-footed and traveling well, the next day the pony would not or could not travel. Inkpaduta, exasperated into frenzy, broke off a willow club and beat the beast as Corn-Sucker had never seen a pony beaten before. She turned away from the sight, and sat her own uneasy horse with face bent down inside her blanket; but hearing each blow that was struck—hearing the pony utter no scream but only a bubbling gasp each time the flail came down upon its flanks. When at last the tall old Dakota wore himself out and tossed away the splintered club, Corn-Sucker was nerved into observation. She saw that the spotted horse—oozing blood from its scourged hide—stood trembling with head hung low. From time to time a gluey liquid dripped from the horse's muzzle.

He is sick, she said with shaking voice.

Aye! I make him more sick!—but Inkpaduta did not go to seek another bludgeon. He beat the pony no more, but stood to one side and regarded the animal in an attitude of alarm. Corn-Sucker dismounted (there was no point in her remaining on her own pony, she could ride nowhere alone) and for the better part of an hour the two stood near, staring at ugly mystery. The horse grunted, released several streams of manure, but this was all like bloody yellow water. At last, wounded flanks heaving spasmodically, the pony stumbled a few paces forward; first its hind legs dissolved and spread, then the forelegs bent . . . it was on the ground . . . it gave a despairing snort and tumbled over on its side. The off eye rolled back in the skull, rolled out again, and remained fixed and puffed, the white seeming to turn to yellow, the brown turning slowly to blue.

When after a long while Inkpaduta was certain that the beast was dead, he said only: Someone does this to me.

Corn-Sucker inquired timidly: A *mahopamiis?*

Nay, Half-Face! No more of your fool Hidatsa gods or words, d'ye hear? My horse dies. Now you walk!

He stood looking at the dead pony, and walked around the body slowly, as if measuring the amount of meat represented, and discarding reluctantly the notion of any butchering to be done. With relief the woman heard him growling: *Taku shicha.* This is evil. We take not the meat!

He removed the twisted bridle (he had wrenched off girth and saddle pad at the first, before he started beating). He added these articles to the packs, gathered up his weapons, then threw himself astride the pony which Corn-Sucker had ridden from that first time when he reclaimed his horses. In appearance it was the meanest and sorriest of the two, and so of course had been awarded to her; but in constant association she had grown fond of the tattered creature, and called him My-Good-White-Pony-Does-Not-Steal-Corn, in her own fancy.

These packs, Inkpaduta said accusingly. I cannot ride a pony with packs. I look like a woman! Half-Face, you take packs!—and so this thing she must do.

Off they went, Inkpaduta riding, Corn-Sucker shambling behind him under the now-unfamiliar burdens; until, as afternoon sun fell behind a fringe of trees on a ridge, the man had ridden out of her sight completely, there was only the track of hoofmarks to guide her. It was not too difficult to see the way, for in this *Minisota* country into which they had penetrated at last, there was herbage in more profusion than Corn-Sucker had ever dreamed that it might grow. Quiet groves, studdings of thin forest round the many small bodies of water, and rich but drying grasses to cover most of the earth between, even on long sloping uplands where no trees could be seen . . . the woman might not understand why it was called the Land of Slightly Clouded Water—the Land of Milky Water—for on those days when the sun shone, she saw ponds blue past all imagining . . . she wondered at scraps of blue beauty dazzling far ahead, far behind, far on either side.

This night she came laboring up at last, when Inkpaduta had selected a spot to camp for the night, and had hobbled the sad pale pony, and sat smoking.

Where are rabbits I kill this day?— (For he had fairly smelled them out in their hidden sets, had slain them with arrows, bad eyes or not.)

They are here, she gasped. Under your horse pad.

Make fire, cook rabbits! But when you make fire, you fetch it to me, d'ye hear? I use all my tinder, I have no more tinder for my pipe.

While she was performing the preliminary tasks she heard him grunting as if to himself: *Aowakpagi!*—or something similar, which she assumed betrayed the man's impatience to resume his smoking. . . . She furnished the desired coals. Two times more Inkpaduta smoked before the meat was cooked. Exhausted as she was from the grueling journey on foot and under packs, Corn-Sucker might still speculate on this nervousness which ruled her husband. It had increased since first they rode among these sprawling lakes. . . .

Into fire-touched darkness he pointed later, with a leg of rabbit in his hand, and said: One sleep more. Perhaps two sleeps? Nay, one sleep!—enough. We come to my people.

Corn-Sucker's heart bounded inside her ribs like a gopher, in the thought that at last they might cease wandering. It was some moments before she dared to speak.

Husband. We come to your village?

He muttered something about it's not being exactly a village. My people travel, he said. We stay in one place for hunting. Then we go. Soon I find my sons! They go with me to the Agency. . . .

She did not know what an Agency was, nor an Agent. She had never heard of such things among the Hidatsa. For a wonder, Inkpaduta seemed willing to talk of these matters, willing to explain. He told her that many Dakota—Wahpekute among them—formerly had owned this entire region. It was their land. Then a thing had been done: the land had been sold to the Two-Legged-Ones-With-Long-Knives from the East. Each year goods and money were to be paid, and they would be paid by an Agent; but it seemed that Inkpaduta had not been among those Dakota who made agreement with whites to sell the land to them. Land was taken from him; still he had not sold it.

(Corn-Sucker did not understand these details; and now she remembered that the Yanktonai had talked in a similar vein. Her tired brain sought to leap from point to point, trailing his recital as she had trailed his pony through late afternoon . . . still she could not quite come up with it.)

. . . They sell their lands, said Three-Men. All these cousins I name sell their lands . . . but Inkpaduta is not with his brothers, the Leaf-Shooters. Why is he not with them? It is because they do not let him be with them . . . makes his lodge alone. . . .

She asked cautiously, when he had fallen silent: The others sell land, why you not sell land?

I am not there!

But why are you not there?

Because again I kill!

Must you always kill?

I kill!

Her feeble questions sent him into truculence. Soon he was standing instead of sitting, soon she feared that she would be the post erected as a symbol of enmity, a ceremonial post for him to mutilate—or, if not to mutilate, to strike repeatedly— Corn-Sucker regretted that she had ever voiced a query. She made herself as small and unresisting as possible, staring steadily at the ground and at some glistening insect which, warmed by the adjacent fire, had poked its head from an earthen den and remained half in and half out of the ground, twitching its antennae as if scenting globules of grease spattered about—

Inkpaduta strode and stamped.

Aye, I kill!

He named them, victim after victim, beginning with Tasagi and continuing with Wamdisapa his father, and on to the rest.

I kill Atkukukinma! He is the last I kill. Thus I go to land of the Ihanktonwanna, even unto land of the Hidatsa. I tell you this, I tell you when first we meet beside the cornfield. That is why I go! Because I kill Atkukukinma!

It seemed that this last death which Inkpaduta had made—the death of the man named He-Resembles-His-Father—came about because of an argument over a previous annuity payment. The white agent had refused to pay money or goods to Inkpaduta, or any person of his— His gens? His family? His clan? His band? It was so difficult to know what had occurred . . . now she was past caring, for his breath steamed overhead, his voice went on high, he swung his arms dangerously, lifted his feet, slammed his moccasins back against the ground as if once more stamping a prairie dog into paste.

He'd gone to He-Resembles-His-Father, he'd said: My cousin! You take goods from the agent of the Eastern Two-Legged-Ones. He tells me that this is the portion of payment for the Wahpekute. But you are not all the Wahpekute. For I too am Wahpekute. Now you give to me my share!

And this thing He-Resembles-His-Father would not do. When Inkpaduta grew more insistent, he was pushed out of the village.

—I wait one sleep. He comes not!

—Two more sleeps I wait, I wait in the willows. For past those willows he must go if he goes to hunt, or goes to his horses; that is the way he goes!

—And on this last day, after three sleeps, He-Resembles-His-Father comes. Thus I kill him. I boast! I do take his scalp, for it can be his people think that Chippeway do come.

—But his people know that Chippeway do not come. They trail me, and I hide. They are good trailers. All Wahpekute trail well; and these are my brothers the Wahpekute; and it is my brother, a Wahpekute, whom I kill!

—Soon they kill me, if I go not! My own people speak with me. My twin sons come to me. First comes my son Roaring-Cloud. And That One does say to me: You go. Go far! The Wahpekute people come, and they are many. We are few. For we are *akantanhan wichashta*. We are outlaws!

—Then comes my son Fire-Cloud. And he does say to me: Go now!

You kill He-Resembles-His-Father, and now his people kill you, do you not go far. For we are not enough to fight the other Wahpekute in war. For we are few, and we are outlaws!

—I go. I go to the land of the Yanktonai, and beyond that land. I go!

—But now I do return!

He did not strike Corn-Sucker, did not demand a response from her. Possibly it was a recognition of his proximity to his own people, and a meeting to be attained in one or two more sleeps, which dulled the wrath into which (habitually, and dwelling with horrid love upon his murders, as a kinder man might meditate above sacred treasures in a medicine parfleche) he'd whipped himself in this recounting. Before he stepped aside to make his water, however, Inkpaduta spoke of some compensation required of his people . . . had that been paid? He did not know. It was a matter of their stealing horses from the whites, or from the Chippeway at the North, and in turn offering these horses to the band of Wahpekute Dakota in which He-Resembles-His-Father had been an influence—perhaps even the most influential man—a man with as much power among his own kind as Three-Men and Wolf-Sits-Down exerted among the buffalo hunters at the West.

Thoughout the night Inkpaduta's nervousness increased rather than abated. The woman awakened several times to find him seated before a freshly fed blaze, or wandering about, seeming to listen for the approach of other persons, baleful or welcoming as they might be. In weeks of traveling Corn-Sucker had never witnessed her husband in such a state of protracted wakefulness. He muttered constantly to himself, and to her when he saw her awake—he grumbled about spirit water—if he had spirit water he would drink much; but he had no flask, they'd seen no whiskey traders on their course, though he'd watched for signs of them ever since leaving the James River.

Once he came to her robe, rolled the woman over on her back, labored to perform an act which he could not perform. He gave up in petulance. He kicked her resentfully in contempt (contempt of himself surely, though an expressed contempt of her) and went back to the fire to smoke. He growled that his stock of tobacco was almost exhausted. . . . A small owl perched on a dead limb near them. Inkpaduta took up bow and blunt arrow, missed, the owl flew away, the man cried that bad spirits were tormenting him. He went to search for the arrow, failed to find it. When Corn-Sucker awakened finally in a clammy dawn, it was to see her husband squatted close to the impoverished gray fire, his fierce old face drooped down against his chest. He was snoring heavily.

To her amazement and relief he asserted that she, instead of he, should ride the pony on this day. Ah, he said, you walk slow. You go no faster than a wounded turtle crawling! We never find my people in one sleep or two sleeps or three sleeps, do you not ride. Fasten the packs upon the pony, Half-Face. You ride!

. . . Did he have other wives in the straying village which he sought? Did he beat them also, as so often he attacked her? Would the other wife or wives be antagonistic in turn to Corn-Sucker, because she was Hidatsa and a stranger? These speculations occupied the woman much of the time as she rode forward this day, with an unpleasant breeze beating after her from the northwest. It seemed that the journey had lasted for a lifetime; now they were deep into that frosting period which Inkpaduta called *wiwazupi,* but which in Corn-Sucker's mind was the *mida-paxidiwidic,* the Leaf-Turn-Yellow Moon. Dull sky smoked with last flocks of birds trailing out their patterns, weaving long and high toward the south. Were she in her own village, Corn-Sucker would have been working as all neighbors worked, preparing to remove to winter lodges. . . . There was a community excitement, an adventure always in this annual undertaking! She thought of cache-pits prepared snug and deep beneath each earthen lodge, with corn and beans and squashes packed neatly, almost with ritualistic propriety, awaiting their use on the return in spring. Corn-Sucker felt a dreary disquietude increasing throughout the somber day. She feared that there were no cache-pits among the Wahpekute—there could not be, if those people wandered so consistently. So when snow came thick, and no hunting might be performed, what would they eat? She feared that the poor white pony would be killed for meat. . . . She dropped her hand gently to the pony's neck, reaching over past the pack which bulked before her; and found a comfort in warmth and strength of the animal's tough hairy hide.

She looked ahead. Inkpaduta was tramping steadily there, he'd ordered her to stay behind him. Old as he was, he walked with ease as fast as or faster than the horse might move. Aye, he was strong . . . still he had not been able to maintain a male hardihood in the night when he struggled fervently to do so.

U! *Who was the woman who departed from her village, from her people living, from her people dead and drying on their scaffolds?*

U! *I am she.*

Who was the woman who was tempted away from her village, and left her lodge and corn and many treasures?

U! *Because of thought of the buffalo bulls, and the male elk, and the stallions.*

I am she.

And now I know, I know all that a woman may know, I suffer all that a woman may suffer, except the pain of childbirth; that I may never do; it would seem that never shall I bear a child.

I am she!

Now comes a wide fresh moon, and again the mice nibble it to nothingness. But in winter we may not eat, for these Itahatski *may have no cache-pits, and may not have hunted successfully, to have the meat dried in strips, to have the fat boiled from bones and pressed into bladders for storage.*

U! *We starve.*

They were not yet starving but indeed they were foodless this day. They had eaten every scrap of the rabbits in the previous evening, had seen no game along the way except once Corn-Sucker'd seen two deer bounding off at a tremendous distance, barely to be discerned by her. Inkpaduta had not seen them at all.

But the sharpness of his hearing persisted. Suddenly—when the sun was beginning to slide lower under its robe of clouds—he turned into a statue ahead of her, and signed for Corn-Sucker to remain motionless. . . . He said a little later: *Mazakan!* Gun! I hear a shot; again I hear a shot. So that is two hunters together, for there is not time for one hunter to reload!

They were halted on a ridge above a narrow bending lake, a lake more like a river than a lake. Inkpaduta examined the landscape ahead.

Perhaps a shoots-six? she asked, timid at making any suggestion.

Nay, Half-Face! You know nothing of guns, d'ye hear? For a pistol-shoots-six makes a noise unlike a gun. These are hunters. Two!

Perhaps—? She made another fearful suggestion. A war party of Chippeway?

Never here now, for we are below the Agency, they dare not come below the Agency. No longer dare they come here! . . . He speculated in silence, then added: It can be that I hear guns of white people. But I think I hear guns of Wahpekute. Now follow me, woman! We go to the lake shore.

He hastened carelessly, he feared no enemies ahead of him, there was no war with the whites. Almost he was running when he came to the reed-grown shore. Corn-Sucker observed that the nearer surface was dotted with weedy lodges— Were they the lodges of beaver? No, no—the lodges of muskrats— Several bulging chunky animals went plashing under the surface as they approached, but Inkpaduta was not thinking of a hunt (oh, now Corn-Sucker told herself that she would even eat muskrat—if well-cooked— Gladly would she eat muskrat!)—his mind was on distant reports of rifles which he'd heard.

He had declared that all the Wahpekute could trail well, but Corn-Sucker was astonished anew at seeing her husband exemplify this skill. It was as if his rheumy eyes had a hidden charge and tolerance unsummoned at ordinary times—a fiery ammunition of capability lying stored, unused until occasion snapped the cap and exploded this load into temporary keenness. As when he had hunted prairie dogs . . . he prowled the margin of the reeds, studied gravel lying wet where blown water had touched it—gravel heaped flatly above the watermark, ending precipitately where gnawed sod arched over and turf began. He went down the shore line to the south, until he was only a fading bending squatting rising creature half lost in cold mist, unidentifiable as a man— Then he came back, looming larger coarser, more definite as the mist let him through—savage and unspeaking when he passed in his light peering dancing manner, the crushed black hat swinging between his shoulders, bent dirty broken eagle feathers swaying, the weapons nudging against him or clamped tight beneath his great bent arms—

She sat upon a boulder. The pony crunched frost-dried grasses behind her; she sat without moving, watching her man gliding and peeking into the north along the shore; and it was good suddenly to know that they were in land of those Dakota from which he had sprung; and they need not hold the fear of young men from other nations creeping to slay them, merely for possession of their hair. A crow called among spectral trees, was answered by another crow; raw black voices of these raucous birds set up a rebounding echo, a stirring in the heart. Corn-Sucker forgot her hunger, she relaxed in safety of this watery region.

She spoke Dakota words aloud, though softly, murmuring the appellation . . . *Mini-sota* . . . water in the narrow twisted lake shimmered dully. A muskrat rose and swam far, with long divided ripples of his passage streaking slowly behind him.

Winter, you ride from the north and west, whence we come.

Madaduk! *Next winter! You come riding, and the crow hears you in your icy hoof-falls, coming nearer; and one day you will rage with snow and wind, or in the night you will rage so.*

So indeed also the muskrat has heard your approach, your riding and the blowing sound of your horses' hoofs; and so he has built himself a lodge where the very ice of this lake may keep him warm, and where he may sleep; and all his family of muskrats may sleep as well.

But I should not like to sleep in the lodge of the muskrats!

Tsakak! *Nay.*

Had I muskrats now, I would build a fire and cook them; and say to the spirits of the muskrats: We thank you for the good hot meat, the dripping of fat, the warm fat in our mouths.

Presently, as clouds shrouded the waning sun more heavily and as mist diminished, she heard Inkpaduta utter a low but summoning cry. It was the sound of a crow, yet again not a crow sound—there lived a deliberate human quality in the hail (as if noticeably the voice of a human called in crow language, saying: I am a man who now speaks with the tongue of a crow—not a crow who calls as a man! This was the first time Inkpaduta had ever cried such a signal to her). The squawk lifted her off the rock where she sat, as if she'd been prodded by a stick. Looking up along the shore she could see that the man beckoned imperatively for her to advance. She began to lead the pony northward in response; she watched Inkpaduta; he signed for her to leave the pony where it was; she obeyed. Progressing steadily over smooth slanting turf which spread above the pebbly margin, she joined the man where he stood beneath a poplar tree. His dark slabbed pocked face was emotionless, but the eyes burned under their scabrous pink lids.

Here, scorched down into sod, existed garbage and the residue of recent fires. Embers were cold, and deposits of thin surface ash had blown out to the east beyond each fire, but Inkpaduta picked up a bone, and showed her: grease and flesh still clung to the little bone. An ant crawled from the bone onto the man's finger.

My people, he said. Here! They feast on the *sinkpe!*

How say you?

Sinkpe, you fool Hidatsa!—he snarled in annoyance. He did not know her word for muskrat, but pointed to the lodges in the lake, and so she understood. Still he did not proceed with a wrath characteristically increased, he was too pleased at having found traces of the Wahpekute.

He indicated a series of four stones: three were placed upon one another, the largest stone at the bottom, the middle-sized stone next, a small stone on top; and at one side another stone was set against the pile. He said: You see? They go to the south, but I think they go round this water to the north, then they go south—they show no trail south upon this shore!

He said: They go to the water we call *Hoganmna,* the Smelling-Like-Fish water. D'ye see?

(A strange awareness touched Corn-Sucker in this moment, a knowledge not related to the present speech or fact, but one coming to her only because she was a woman. She realized that Inkpaduta needed her not so much for that thing he called indelicately her *shan*—needed her not for a woman-to-lie-with-constantly—but she knew that he needed her for companionship. He was not happy when alone. He wished someone to speak to, to point things out to, as much as he desired a fire builder or a cook or a female entity to overpower upon a robe. This quick knowledge did not bereave her of a woman's consciousness or a woman's physical response. In this moment she was glad to be with him, to be summoned and shown the former camp of his wandering villagers . . . aye, he beat her and kicked her because he was consumed by violence; he was a killer, also a beater and a kicker, and so needed someone to beat and to kick; as truly he must kill when the time came for him to kill!)

It is my twin son Fire-Cloud who writes thus.

Now he stood close beside the lone leafless tree, showing her where bark had been hacked away—a rough square had been chopped from the bark.

You see? This is water, this is fish; and smell goes up from water!

She would never have known the intelligence conveyed—(nor, she suspected, would anyone else not of that gens have known) were it not explained. There loomed a few symbols marked upon the smooth scarred poplar flesh; they were unlike sacred symbols of the Hidatsa. Fire-Cloud had worked heedlessly with sharpened charcoal; still his father understood the written language readily. There were pointed shapes—aye!—lodges— Water showed in a waving brown line. And, as Inkpaduta'd explained, that thing at the side was a fish . . . another shaking line of smell arose from it. . . .

Is this place far, my husband? The place where they go?

It is one sleep. But perhaps they make camp, do they find many *sinkpe* more. Or other meat! We find my people! We find meat! We go!—

He hastened back down the shore to where she'd left the pony, and by the time Corn-Sucker came puffing up to the spot he was mounted on the horse and going away from her. Nor did he complain about packs bulging against him, nor did he say that they made a woman out of him, made him appear ridiculous . . . he rode purposefully toward the south, and left her to stumble following; but she was grateful that the packs were on the horse instead of upon her own back.

Sun had coasted halfway to a southwestern fuzz of trees and melting grass, the sun was a vagabond hiding its shamed face under weak clouds, when Corn-Sucker saw the first of her husband's Wahpekute band. She followed the horse track into a flat creek valley where a few cedar trees poked up like lean dark sentinels against shaggier woodland beyond. When still at a great distance she saw the pony halted riderless. A few human figures crouched against a mat of tan rippling reeds which bordered a slough. These figures assumed identity as Corn-Sucker came shyly nearer. She averted her face as much as possible while she trudged, saying in her attitude that she was a woman, they were men, she would not presume to intrude. The figures were Inkpaduta and two strangers . . . the strangers must have carried tobacco, for Inkpaduta's tobacco was finished, and all three smoked as they sat. Inkpaduta must have explained that he had taken a Hidatsa wife. They turned to look at the woman from time to time during her approach, then resumed their conversation; then they would turn again to look at her—not her husband, but the strangers, would turn and look. When she was still politely removed from them she halted, stood motionless but unsummoned, and at last slid down to sit upon the dry chilly grass. Wind chewed persistently at her back. Corn-Sucker drew up the robe to shield herself from wind, and remained mute. She watched muddy breeze-streaked water of the slough into which this creek came emptying. If other women had been with her they might all have stared saucily at the men, and speculated among themselves as to what was being said; but Corn-Sucker was alone, these were men unknown to her even if known to her husband; she pretended that there were no men anywhere about, acted as if they did not exist, acted as if she were a solitary individual sitting, she knew not why, in an untenanted landscape.

That night she came to know the identity of these two, and of a number of others—all so harsh and sullen and vindictive and generally inhuman that they paraded across her consciousness as a trail of evil spirits might have danced in illness—a collection of *mahopamiis* to baffle the most devoted mystery man and send him delving into his medicine bag for new charms, into his lore for new songs.

The two men who sat smoking with Inkpaduta were one of his twin sons—Mahpiyapeta, or Fire-Cloud, who had written that message on the skinned tree—and a man named Itoyetonka—He-Wears-Anything-That-Makes-Him-Look-Frightful. As it might have been with the Hidatsa, this name was abbreviated in common reference; just as her *ikupa* of long ago, Mouse-Sits-Up-Tomorrow, was ordinarily spoken of or addressed as Mouse. The other twin, Roaring-Cloud (and soon to be recognized as Inkpaduta's favorite) was absent from the encampment along with two cronies. It was hoped by wives of the band that they were gone hunting deer; but a more cynical notion prevailed among the men that this little party drifted about the fringe of white settlements, trying to beg or steal some whiskey; or else that they had gone to the Lower Agency, waiting there for Inkpaduta to appear on his annual pilgrimage in search of an annuity share.

Fire-Cloud was even taller than Inkpaduta, but did not resemble the father much in countenance; except that he too had a face badly tattooed by smallpox. Like Inkpaduta he wore his hair in solid greasy braids—the braids were encased in membranous wrappings, tied with old yarn which still showed a tint of red. Above his breechclout and leggings he wore a brown jacket, a white man's jacket of material unknown to Corn-Sucker until now: she had never seen denim before. Fire-Cloud carried with him a handsome rifle, so new that only a small quantity of rust dimmed the steely glint of the barrel. It was of this rifle that he talked and boasted, on meeting his father. The woman heard a few intelligible words now and then, when wind slackened and did not blow all the rapid mumble of Dakota speech away from her.

Fire-Cloud had stolen the rifle out of a wagon during one recent night. Corn-Sucker had heard of wagons, but had never seen one. Soon she would see many wagons.

. . . White man with hair white.

. . . Fire . . . but do not see me.
. . . *Idatahn!* . . . could kill all if . . . make war!
. . . Dogs bark but they . . .
. . . And trade for ammunition from . . . I boast!

He-Wears-Anything wore nothing particularly frightful—it was merely a name awarded for some earlier cause. He was a squat man with a face so dark as to be almost black. (There were said to be black men in the world. Long ago Corn-Sucker's second father, Gray-Other-Goose, had seen a black man who traveled trading with a party of French.) The woman wondered whether in fact He-Wears-Anything might be one of the black men of legend. This fellow was slightly lame; he had very long arms, and waved them when he talked. His voice was coarse, hurtful to the ears as the nearby talking of a disturbed jay. At first Corn-Sucker thought that he had donned a robe composed of bumpy furs; later she realized that these were dead muskrats hanging around his shoulders. She told herself that she should be glad to see meat; surely Inkpaduta would receive promptly a portion of the kill; these were his people, and had he not declared that he was their head man? Aye, he had so declared!—he used a Dakota word, but she believed that this word meant Head Man, or Man of Most Influence, Man of Most Power, Man To Be Consulted.

She was the wife of a Head Man! And here was meat—fresh-killed—immediately before her eyes. But her heart did not rejoice, her heart was dull and unresponding. The song she made as she waited was a lamentation.

Within me is a small wounded animal. It cries.

I know not the name of this animal. It lies tight under my breast within the cage of my ribs. And now in daylight it makes its sadness. In night it will make a mightier sadness.

Oh, my sister! the small wounded animal does say, I cry!
Little One, have they cut off thy toes?
Aye. They have cut off my legs!
Little One, have they cut off the tip of thy tail?
Aye. They have cut off my entire tail!

It cries, the small wounded animal cries in sadness, partly because it is wounded; but mostly because I may not name its name.

The camp of the band, reached just before the sun went into its burrow on a fold of prairie, consisted of five lodges set in a shallow creek valley where sentinel willows squatted and bent along the trailing watercourse. Inkpaduta's people had halted here because of profusion of muskrat hummocks in a marsh shortly to the west. (Prevailing winds would blow sounds and smells of the temporary village away from the *sinkpe* and not alarm them into retreat.) The Smelling-Like-Fish water lay, undisturbed by these wanderers, a half-day's journey to the south. But in a grassy slough dwelt unkilled quantities of meat. The Wahpekute had come upon the new muskrat colony unexpectedly, and accordingly altered their plan to suit convenience.

With Roaring-Cloud and his two companions still absent, there were, including Inkpaduta, nine men now present at the encampment: nine men, seven women including Corn-Sucker, and seven children. Corn-Sucker was made to understand later by the women that in fact there were two more lodges owned by the band; but they had not been set up; families of the absent ones had moved in with relatives or close friends. (Could it indeed be termed a friendship—the virtuous relationship of loved and respected companions—which these gross paupers held for each other?) Inkpaduta himself stalked into the lodge of his son Fire-Cloud, and seemed claiming it as his own; he began to issue commands. He was followed by the dazed Corn-Sucker who stood with head bowed, appalled by stench and chatter, and by the savage assault which one boy was visiting upon a smaller brother or cousin. The aggressor had perhaps six winters in age, the victim perhaps three or four . . . the larger child was sitting astride the smaller, whom he'd thrown to the ground in the center of the lodge, and he had the littler boy's head pressed between his knees. Spasmodically his black fingernails raked down the cheeks of the miserable grimy mite held suffering by his larger weight. The smaller child emitted a new slithering shriek each time his skin was tormented, but for a while no one of the adults gave any heed. A strand of yellow mucus blew from the nostril of the tortured. The torturer snarled with delight, and with his thumb forced the mucus into the dirty blubbering mouth which pouted up at him, and threw back his own head with a triumphant cry. Corn-Sucker, driven to desperation, picked up a strip of kindling which might do duty as a punitive switch; she saw Fire-Cloud staring steadily and enigmatically at her from beyond the smoke and leer of the sparking fire; haltingly she dropped her switch, and turned away from the bestial sight. At last another woman (this was Inkpaduta's daughter, whom he'd never mentioned before, but who was married to a man named Kahdahda, or Rattle-Strike, now gone prowling with Roaring-Cloud) was infuriated beyond endurance by the noise. She turned, struck the elder child a powerful blow with the flat of her hand, and thus knocked him against the edge of the fire. He was burned enough to scream in pain, pick himself up, run from the lodge. After a moment the smaller boy, still mourning, arose and unaccountably went staggering out into dusk instead of seeking safety among sprawling piles of robes. Once outside his howls went up anew. There was no sanity in the entire episode, no reason or decency seeming to rule among inmates of the tipi.

In sickening contrast of recollection Corn-Sucker thought of her own childhood, her own family's lodge.

—Why weeps the child, Green-Night-Butterfly?

(And that weeping child was Corn-Sucker.)

—My father, she weeps because she was punished by our mother.

—My wife, why punish you the child?

—Oh, she did a bad thing, a very bad thing! An evil sprite took possession of her, and caused her to put ashes into the jar of cold water which I had fetched, ready to use in cooking and for us to drink. Great masses of ashes did she put into the pot, with her little hands, before I could seize her! Then did I pour water over her head, and the water was very cold. So she cries aloud!

—My wife, do you think that the cold water has washed the imps from out the head of our youngest daughter?

—She's been very naughty of late! I think perhaps one dose of ice-cold water would never serve. Perhaps she should have another such washing?

—Or else an owl might come and take her away!

—True, true. Owls have been known to carry off children who do bad deeds. This I have always heard.

—Aye. An owl might come!

(Far in the back of the lodge, that soft hoot arising suddenly: *Hooooo . . . hooooo.* There might be smothered giggles from the women . . . Corn-Sucker herself was certain—or almost certain—that an owl could not fly away with her in his claws; an owl was too small, she was grown too large for an owl to carry. And yet . . . yet . . . an especially robust owl, a sacred owl, an Owl of Mysteries? Could it lift her into dangerous night air, and bear her to a distant tree, and rip her flesh from her bones, all the time hooting in awful glee? Perhaps it was possible. So she must hide! . . . Where should she hide? Close to her grandmother—that was the safest place, except for the usual desire to be near her mother; and she was angry with her mother because of the icy punishing bath. Thus she went trotting across the hard-packed lodge floor, through cavorting shadows of firelight now turned increasingly mischievous each instant; and purposefully she sought a smell and warmth of her grandmother—heard the yielding laugh, felt a robe drawn around to cover her naughty head, to shield her from possible attack of a patrolling owl. . . . Another *hooooo* might be heard, another vague warning or two—but drawn out and fading, as if the Owl of Mysteries were willing to retire without his prey. And there was the friendly bony characteristic feel of those stiff thin knees, the old hand coming down to lie contented across her little shoulders . . . good smell of cooked corn, boiled squash in the air which stole to greet her wee nose; and smell of the grandmother too . . . ah, no one else had the scent of Grandmother—a cozy musky meaty tobaccoish smell! For Grandmother was old, and she was a woman; but was old enough to smoke a pipe; no one seemed to think it outlandish for her to do so; she had many winters, many tales to tell. . . . No more hooting now, only the genial conversation of elders, sound of a bubbling pot, the odor and sputter of meat a-roasting, the good hum, the village dogs barking beyond. The little girl slept, promising herself vaguely that she would put no more ashes into a waterpot . . . loving to snuggle against Grandmother. She slept.)

Corn-Sucker recognized a terrible truth. Her perception was whetted by dire experience; disgust and misery brought keen awareness.

Clemency, respectability, forbearance– These could not form the excellence of Hidatsa alone!

She'd seen the Ihanktonwanna, even briefly, wild as they were with their green buffalo hides and skittish ponies, and forelocks whipping as they loped. They'd given birth and training to men as dignified and capable as Three-Men and Wolf-Sits-Down. Some of their children might scamper naked, but what nastiness did they offer? They offered none.

And of the other Dakota, there must be villages where probity could rule; there must be villagers who let it rule them.

Why had the Wahpekute exiled this tall Inkpaduta with his dented face, and all the storms which ruled him?

He himself had told.

He recited what his sons had said.

We are few. For we are akantanhan wichashta. *We are outlaws!*

Here stood five lodges, not one with new clean hides to form it. The texture of the tipis was abomination–stained and greasy, tattered, carelessly mended. Piles of robes where people slept were stinking. Lice crawled in the hair of women, children–Corn-Sucker watched dully from her forlorn crouch. A woman held a baby, she saw and heard the woman jabbering shrilly in her dialect; and even while she spoke, the woman's hands were busy with the baby's hair . . . she found a louse, withdrew it, cracked the thing between her teeth.

I grieve! . . .

There must be Wahpekute gentes, off to the north, where folk were as prideful and as cleanly as Hidatsa, in their own manner.

Corn-Sucker thought of women she had known, going to wash in the Missouri in that hour when a summer sun appeared. Beyond the cold darkness of this region and this season, there must be lakes or beaver ponds where women went to wash; but they would not be like these cackling cursing inhabitants of patched-up hovels.

Tsakak! Nay, they would not be.

Any woman could scrape and tan a robe, could sew it fresh and neatly. These people of Inkpaduta's had among them many guns . . . why did the men not go to hunt, and bring back proper hides, to let the women build a proper lodge in every case? And did they never warm and dry the tangles which did duty as their couches?

Stink was thick, stink was bad. Someone had been sick within this lodge—a child, perhaps—and nobody had cleaned the mess away. This Corn-Sucker could tell. It was the stink of sickness.

We are outlaws. So he'd said, repeating more than once. She'd not realized what was meant when her husband spoke those words—or rather, when he quoted what his twin sons had said to him.

Other men came to this lodge, came and went. Corn-Sucker heard them identified by their names, her soul was poisoned by their names.

She heard them discussing the pecuniary adjustment achieved with the other Wahpekute following the death of He-Resembles-His-Father, and Inkpaduta's subsequent flight. Ten horses had been stolen, either from Indian enemies or white movers and settlements. Duly these horses were turned over to the offended family. Now the others could not slay Inkpaduta on sight: they had accepted compensation, as established by custom. . . .

Her soul was poisoned by their names!

Her heart had been stamped flat by her husband's moccasins.

Dazedly she listened . . . she heard, she did not understand all, did not wish to understand. *Tsakak!* She wished that she might not even hear.

Once in a while a child peeped into the tipi and ran away again. Inkpaduta paid no attention to his new-fetched bride, he spoke of her but not to her; he laughed, said that her name was Half-Face; rudely people came close, bent or squatted to look at her face, rose and gossiped about it.

She is ugly. Are all Hidatsa so?

But I need a woman. Her I find working corn. I say, Woman, we go, we go together!

One time someone cuts her face and makes it ugly?

It is in a war that this is done?

Nay, no war. She says that stones fall down upon her.

Ah, her Hidatsa husband does this— Cuts her, strikes her with a club!

No husband does she have! Her *shan* is tight, her *shan* is tougher than a young girl's, when first I climb upon her!

Grunting, laughter . . . giddy laughter. . . .

Oh, that I had spirit water! Is there no spirit water here? I am weary after the long journey. I drink spirit water, d'ye hear?

Say to That One: we have no spirit water. But if the others return soon, they bring spirit water. . . .

They drink it all! I know my son! He drinks it all!

Ho! agreed the rest.

Their mumbling laughter. . . .

From trance Corn-Sucker was drawn by the hand of Woman-Shakes-With-Cold, the wife of Rattle-Strike.

Rise, Hidatsa woman! You seek more wood. I cannot leave the rats—children knock them into the fire, or steal them when ready to eat! . . . Hand closed on her shoulder, fingers digging deep and shaking Corn-Sucker's shoulder . . . the lined dirty face bending close to hers was not intrinsically an evil face, it was only bloated and sagging, the youth gone early from it.

Corn-Sucker arose sluggishly and gazed at the *sinkpe* cooking round the blaze. There were eight or ten of the skinned muskrats roosting in a circle, each impaled on a tilted wand thrust into the earth floor of the lodge. Their hides had been stripped off, but portions of hide or ears still adhered to bloody skulls which were blackening against flame and smoke; the smell of burnt hair mixed thickly with the smell of scorched bodies. This meat had been set to cooking while Corn-Sucker was lost in lugubrious thought, she had not even been aware of the preparation.

Aye, she whispered. I bring wood. Where find I wood?

Woman-Shakes explained in detail, and Corn-Sucker was wearily surprised to find how much she understood. Turn toward the stream, before you pass next lodge. You'll see willow trees, but the dry branches are gone from nearest ones; we've been here for two sleeps. Farther willow trees still have dead wood. There is one dead willow, fallen across the stream. Knife I give you—

Nay, I have knife.

Axe I give you, said Woman-Shakes-With-Cold, and pressed the handle of a small steel hatchet toward her. It was a curious axe (stolen from whites, but Corn-Sucker did not know this) and when in natural explorative gesture she ran her finger lightly down the blade she felt how nicked and dull it was. Even in this earliness of late autumn night already it was too dark for her to seek a stone with which the axe might be whetted. Even if she had a whetstone, it would take too long.

She had been told to bring wood, she must bring wood.

The woman called after her sharply: Much wood! We have none for the night. You bring one load, you return, you bring more!

Was this now her own lodge, Corn-Sucker's lodge; or was Woman-Shakes the mistress of the tipi? Inkpaduta had shouldered his way into the place as if it belonged to him. Had his son or sons—and their wives—been dwelling in that tipi while the older man was gone on his journey? Or was it theirs to begin with?—and did Inkpaduta have no lodge of his own, even as he'd had no wife until he badgered the Hidatsa woman into distressing elopement?

A few scrawny dogs circled like wolves in the thickening dusk, they greeted the stranger woman with warning snarls, trotted away—but circling still—and then one and then another made a threatening jump in her direction, exploding with a snap and louder snarl in the instant of his leap. Corn-Sucker felt that surely she would be bitten, she had never been afraid of dogs before, now she was afraid. Blindly she swung the blunt side of her hatchet when a fresh slinking form seemed about to maltreat her. The blow caught the beast on the side of his long nose, spun him around in the air, he tumbled howling and fled away with louder outcry, increasing his shrieks of pain with mounting fear as he ran. The other dogs piled away, not toward Corn-Sucker, but after the runaway wretch whom now they seemed bent on tearing apart. Two or three of the firelit lodge doors were darkened by figures; people came out to see what had happened. Voices of women speared up, scolding the dogs, promising retribution if this hullabaloo continued. . . . Corn-Sucker trudged on down the tight-twisted course of the stream, confused dog-noises and noises-made-by-people abating slowly behind her. With eyes grown accustomed to gloom, she found the fallen willow, waded the creek to reach more slender branches, began breaking or pounding them off. Beyond her other rooted willows tilted like vagrant spooks, writhed stiffly against darkening clouds, stabbed the night with leafless fingers. The moon was choked and gone, mice chewed it unwitnessed . . . who could see them now?

Corn-Sucker secured enough wood to make two bundles as big as she could manage; she would have contrived larger bundles had it been daylight, could she have seen better where to place her uncertain feet on the homeward trip. Woman-Shakes had stated the necessity of other loads, however; so Corn-Sucker left the hatchet—it would be needed, she'd return immediately. The camp dogs would not venture to stage an assault again. They'd been chastened, she knew their kind. (True wolves might have attacked again and again; but these were only half-wolves, eighth-wolves; they did not retain the full vindictiveness of the wild ones; now they would fear her, and retire hastily if growling when she came.) Her trained hands moved knowingly in dull light, twisting frostbitten weeds into a rope for binding the mounds of faggots. Then she hoisted these knobby awkward bulks and waded into the chuckling creek. At the farther bank her foot slipped on a round stone—she tripped off-balance, pitched forward and to one side. In desperation the woman whirled her bundles out and ahead as she fell. Both landed on the turf beyond . . . they'd burn, they were not soaked. But she herself sprawled almost at full length, landing with an enormous splash which forced cold muddy creek water into her eyes and mouth, up her nose, into her ears. Corn-Sucker crawled up over the bank, and in that moment she was sobbing without tears. Convulsions shook her drenched body . . . unholy lodges and faces of the outcast Wahpekute reeked in her vision, blending and quacking like figures of people at a dance.

The names . . . oh, horror! Those men . . . their very names were evil. . . .

Within me is a small wounded animal. It cries!
I know not the name of this animal.
Little One, have they cut off thy toes?

She knew that often people—men especially—were given new names, later names—not the names awarded them on their naming-days when they lay infinitesimal, swaddled in the down of cattail weeds to keep them warm, to serve as their blankets and their diapers. . . .

A man might be named Laughs-Like-Small-Bird in infancy; but during his first hunt he would have the agility to cut a spotted buffalo calf from the runaway herd and kill it with a single arrow (a great thing indeed it was, to possess the robe of a spotted calf!) and thus almost formally he would be offered a new name; and that name should be Kills-Fast-Spotted-Calf, or perhaps merely Spotted-Calf. But then later, if the youth went to war, a thing could take place in the grand stampede of fighting: Spotted-Calf might be unhorsed, and the enemy Crow seek to ride him down. Suppose two Crow tried to do this thing. The first Crow might be shot dead by Spotted-Calf as his horse came plunging forward; then Spotted-Calf would stand unarmed except for the knife at his belt; the single charge within his gun was expended when he killed the first Crow, and his bow was broken when he fell from his own horse. This second Crow might seek to stab him with a lance, or to lean out and strike down Spotted-Calf with his club; and Spotted-Calf would bound in strong desperation, grasp the weapon, tumble the enemy upon the ground, and there they would roll and fight, and in the end Spotted-Calf would kill also this second Crow. And he would take the hair of both Crow whom he'd killed. All this deed would be witnessed from a distance by the friends of Spotted-Calf. They'd shake their heads in wonder, and cry: He fights best when he is walking! In the celebration which ensued when once victorious warriors returned to their village, a new name might be conferred upon Spotted-Calf. No longer would they call him Spotted-Calf, but forever men would say: Aye, Fights-Best-Walking is a leading member of the Black Mouth Society!—or they might gossip: Do you know? The daughter of White-Fire-He-Holds has been desired by Fights-Best-Walking, and he will marry her!

They would use now the new name given him because of what he did in war.

Some people believed that these new names were as nicknames—they were second and third names, not to be trusted for use as well as the first name. Somewhere there might lurk a stubborn aunt or grandsire who'd say, I know his name! It is not Fights-Best-Walking. I was there when he was born, I ate a slice of buffalo tongue in gladness on that day. And this is his name; his name is Laughs-Like-Small-Bird. This I know, and this I tell!

But others might use the new name.

There were names of reprobate Dakota which Corn-Sucker had heard, and which she recalled as now she lay collapsed beside her faggot bundles. They were not the bold or comforting or appealing names of men who had honor in their faces; they were names constructed out of lust and out of degrading activity—contrived from offal, rape, from thievery and gas of bowel. They'd been applied to disgusting individuals by disgusting tongues and throats. They stuck as excrement of dogs might make a glue upon a moccasin.

She knew impolite words of the Dakota tongue as one always gathers in profanity—the designation of the private parts, obscenities —when learning a new language. Ah, Inkpaduta spat these words all too often. She had learned!

Hushan. He was a man, or passed for one; his wife had come with him, they sat within the lodge. But *hu* meant to-have-sexual-intercourse-with— And *shan*. Inkpaduta had sneered or threatened, employing the Dakota word for her woman-thing. Hushan! Has-Intercourse-With-Vagina . . . this was his name, he was called by this!

A very tall youth, greeted as Tawachehawakan . . . the men had twitted him in her hearing; one called him by his former name which was River-Boy. And others said: Nay, you do forget. No longer is he known as River-Boy! You remember the new name he wins before the winter, when we hunt far in Minisota, and we find that lone young woman of the Winnebago blood, who gathers rice? Tawachehawakan . . . we call him by this name! His-Curly-Sacred-Penis. . . . For *tawa* meant his, and *che* was the man-thing, and *ha* meant curled or curly, and *wakan* meant the same to Dakota that *hopa* meant to Hidatsa.

They continued like a list of damned and fallen—like persons who walked the Way of the Souls, but marched on the shorter path, and so had toppled off and screamed their dying course down through the skies. Ugly words, brutal names, brutal faces wearing the names, gaping mouths to jeer and curse and make a nastiness.

Rattle-Strike . . . there was sound of war and hitting in the very thought. Though the twins still retained a notion of humanity in their appellations: Roaring-Cloud and Fire-Cloud . . . and He-Has-Done-Walking seemed a quiet ordinary name. But what of He-Wears-Anything-That-Makes-Him-Look-Frightful? And the burly young man with jagged cicatrice across his forehead—the one called Nashkakamdaskiya, or Bursts-Frog-Open? When had he crushed a wet green Frog Brother so wantonly, and why? And the other ragamuffins she'd considered with cringing and hopelessness? . . . The man whose face was worse scarred than her own face; he'd had his nose bitten off in a fight, there was a wadded pulp of scar tissue in the middle of his face from which the exposed nostrils drained. Yet he'd dared to squat for minutes, peering at Corn-Sucker, and he it was who asked if all

Hidatsa women were as ill-favored as she! The name of this man was Tachanachekahota . . . One-Staggering-Big-Brown-Testicle. . . . Worst of all was the Titonwan from far across western wilderness, the squat oldish man who had no wife, and rolled *l*-sounds on his tongue, the sounds which others could not utter. Tatelezashinshichamna . . . so he spoke of himself in lewdest pompous utterance, while the starveling outlaws called him Tatedezashinshichamna. Those syllables strung together referred to a person who emitted noisome gas from the bottom of his body . . . Makes-Fat-Bad-Smelling-Wind: that was the monster's name. And so he made it constantly, she'd heard and smelled him in the lodge!

There was another person, who was referred to as On-Oldish-Man. What did such a name mean? This Corn-Sucker could not perceive readily; yet the Wahpekute seemed savoring a contemptible delight in uttering the name—Bahata—and it must be redolent of something libidinous beyond her reckoning.

By their own admission members of the band were but newly come to this spot to make their camp, to continue feasting on muskrats; yet already the space outside their tipis was plastered with filth of every description. Even in coolness the reek of decaying muskrat entrails rose on high.

Corn-Sucker could recollect a loose profligate family of her native village, who were censured often for the disgraceful condition of their lodge and the area around it. No one liked to live beside them; and at length it was ordered by the soldiers that they must remove to a point apart from the rest, and build a new lodge if they chose; and it was agreed that their old lodge should be burned; and so it was. The women of this family wailed loudly; but there was no help for it—flames shafted with laughter as if glad for a purifying destruction. Days later, when smoke no longer lifted from the smolder, the rest of the wreckage was pulled down.

But no police, or soldiers, seemed to exist here—there was no discipline except the unpredictable rages of Inkpaduta himself—and just when and where they might strike no one could say.

Oh. One tipi was made not of skins, it was made of cotton cloth, and the cloth was torn and rotten.

Oh. One child she had seen, was sick! It whined, its eyes were dull, its mouth hung open, its belly was distended. Yet no measures were taken for the curing of this child, the women did not seem to care about it, no mystery man was summoned. Oh.

Oh. The names! So suggestive of wormy evil which festered in every heart.

Oh. All had been expelled from their original homes! They were made to withdraw and wander, because of vices they'd exhibited, the murders and other iniquities they'd perpetrated. They clung with greasy affection to hateful new names they'd slapped upon each other, just as they wallowed in excrement of a Village of the Damned, an encampment of vagabonds more to be feared than the gaunt *mahop-amiis* whom she'd dreaded always.

These were the people of her husband. Now with these, forevermore, Corn-Sucker's life must be spent.

But one day she should sicken and die.

Shivering with the drenching she'd received, empty in stomach and in heart, the woman bent herself beneath bundles of wood and went reeling back toward coarse voices and the fires.

The axe she'd left across the creek; and she would return repeatedly for wood until she was told that no more was needed.

Because of thought of the buffalo bulls, and the male elk. . . .

Who was the woman. . . ?

I am she!

Little One, have they cut off thy toes?

The small wounded animal cries . . . but mostly because I may not name its name.

XV

Something out ahead, something in the wind.

Turning to face the east wind keenly and letting the force of it come against the naked chest (having a vision of masses of pale forceful air and sunlight bracing against that bared chest, tanning it to the flavor of honey).

Oh, blow away bison, brush away brant. . . .

What's a-doing at the East, Mr. Wind? You're heading at us from that direction.

From Cincinnati. The despatches give but a confused report of progress there. Buchanan, however, would seem to be the leading idea thus far.

So if it's Old Buck, why, tis Old Buck. And what's the difference who's President, when all is said and done? Franklin Pierce never done me no good. He ever do you any good?

Not so's I could notice it. Fillmore do you any good?

Not so's I could notice it. Did Taylor?— Or Polk?—

What really counted was my situation at home. And at the store—

My situation with Uncle Nineveh—

With Pa. With Ma. With folks who came to the mill.

With the preacher.

With the folks who came, or didn't come, to the shop—

My situation with the Squire.

With Mr. Gordell who owned the quarry.

And big Bossy Lanahan who bossed the section gang—

My situation with that squint-eyed little Evalina McCortney, that I got in the family way; and her old man said we'd got to marry—and I didn't wish to marry her at all, nor marry no one—so I skun out—

No President of the United States could do a thing about such matters, nor concern himself with them. What's the grain-in-a-peck of difference about the convention at Cincinnati? . . . Buchanan? Old Buck, we call him? Let it be.

Let it pass, as the wind passeth.

He restoreth my soul.

God? God Almighty? Or just that long-calling Mr. Wind?

Blow wild in the roses, blue winds of the West. . . .

But still coming from the East; so turn around, and rest, and face up to the pursuing persistent breeze, and open the shirt of your soul, and let your soul tan and harden and be colored by the vastness, as your body is tanned.

What'd you say was in the daily prints, back yonder, Old Rare East Wind?

Brooklyn Sympathy for Sumner. The Brooklynites held a meeting on Saturday night, at the City Hotel, to express their indignation at the assault on Mr. Sumner. . . . Strong resolutions were adopted and speeches made by Mayor Hall, Gen. Duryea, Gen. Nye, John C. Winslow, Rev. Mr. Hatfield, Rev. H. W. Beecher, Hon. Charles Allen. . . .

That's what I heard them fellows talking about, back at that there tavern where the lady charged us fifty cents— Yep. You heard me! *Fifty cents apiece* for dinner, children half price; and you couldn't down half of it for the grease!— So we've not got that long a pocket; tis campfire cookery from now on; and, Sairy, take care you don't burn them beans black like you done last time—

They were talking of Mr. Sumner. Forty-five— Too old for a man to get cane-whipped, I'll be bound! And that Congressman from the South—man named Brooks, wasn't it?—was younger and stouter by far; and some younger man ought to teach him a lesson—

Slave territory? Free territory? Who cares? We ain't headed for Kansas. We're headed for the Northwest Ioway country. Ain't no slaves there, nor worry and fret concerning such matters; and there warn't no worry and fret about slaves, back in Allegheny County where I come from.

We're walking the raw independent prairie now, feeling the wind.

That Sumner business. . . . Say, Mr.! Just where in hell *is* Brooklyn? Ain't it around Boston somewheres?

Doesn't matter in this jungly grass, doesn't matter amongst these deep black sloughs. Doesn't matter when the wind is racing past your ears.

Wagons bog down everywhere except on highest ground. You got to keep the teams toiling, toiling protracted to keep the wagons in motion; and lots of places we got to push.

Everybody get down from the wagons, now! Get rid of that extry weight. You get down, Gideon. Get down, Jackie, get down Nance, get down Wiletta, get down Sairy, get down Ma— Granny can stay in, with the baby (don't neither of them weigh much). And all push, push . . . push . . . else we'll be mired, and have to slough down again!

(But usually we feel the mean powerful wind shoving against us, shoving square in our faces to hinder, stead of shoving behind us, to help. For the west wind prevails!)

. . . I thought they was good enough wagons to begin with, when Absalom and I put our savings together to have them built; course we helped with the building too, much as we were able, much as the wagonmaker would let us, to cut down on the cost. And will you believe me now? Wagonmaker was a man named Shoemaker. Yes siree, that's right. Man named Shoemaker, making wagons! . . . Well, he said twas not what he'd call a Cones*to*ga sort; but more like some wagons he learnt to build in the Old Country, back in Merry England when he was a prentice there. Said twas mainly a Cornish wagon or a Devon wagon—sort of that type, one of them queer foreign names; he talked of many, so I don't remember *preezactly*—

You can see how sound this here one's built, as to wheels and frame. But all too heavy! Twelve big spokes in them high rear wheels, fourteen smaller spokes in the smaller lower front ones. And iron-tired by the best smith in Allegheny County! And that boat-shaped idee has saved our bacon more than once't. For the box is caulked just as a boat would be caulked; and so we'd fix our ropes, and hitch the critters on, and here she comes, a-coasting cross the slithery mud, inch at a time, sliding like a boat at sea— But only inching, coming slow and—oh, so slow.

But sometimes she's away too heavy, and the slough is way too deep—she wouldn't float on that thin water, not with all such freight aboard— (And the wind ruffling from all directions, to turn the surface of the slough to little waves—oh, down she'd go, with everything aboard! So we'd got to unload—)

Many hands make a light task, younguns, so all to work! Slough's too mean, hill's too steep, gulley's too narrow; get stuck for good, lost for good—we'd end up setting here useless, stead of going on to a spandy-new home in the Okoboji country— Take it all out, and we'll wade and carry, and come back to wade and fetch and carry once again and once again . . . we'll draw the empty boats of the boxes acrost, and get the wheels back on again. So all to work—even the littlest, next to the baby in size— Well, yes you can, Gracie child. You carry that dipper and that rolling pin, whilst Uncle Absalom he carries *you*—

Unload the plow, we'll drag it through, water'n mud won't hurt the plow, by Gad! . . . Unload the warp beams for the loom, the reels and shuttles, swifts and winding blades—take out that bag of turnips, take out the Bible, sacks of seed, take out the chairs we've got tied up on top. Take out that crate of chickens. Gideon and Jackie can lug it over—

Oh, Ma! Regret to say we've got a dead one. Yep—just look-a-here. Your fine Dominicker. Here she is, on the bottom. Thought she was croaking kind of funny this morning; and she wouldn't eat, and— But you still got the Leghorns left—

Unload the doctor book, take out the quilts, take out the keg of sugar, the saleratus, take out the sack of salt, the little album that our Nancy fetched along, with all the neighbors' names and poetry inscribed therein— *Friendship's Treasury*—

Unload the tender memories of Allegheny County! I guess you won't be seeing Scriggs's store nor the cooperage nor the churchyard nor the apple trees again—not for a while you won't—

To my valued friend, Nancy Norman. With the best wishes and fervent blessing of her pastor. Rev. D. L. Thomason. April the 26th, 1856.

Now you might think it Odd o' Me, to try to write a Poetry. But I do take my pen in hand, to wish you success in the "Ioway Land." Sincerely your respectful friend & former schoolmate, Aretus B. Blaine. 4/26/56.

In your woodpile of memory place a stick for me. With a hug, Mary Lu Kuhl, Mon. Apr. 28 1856.

Friend Nancy. We hope you find Fame & Fortune in a new home of your selection. May the Heav'nly Father attend thee. Sincerely, Geo. C. Kuhl, 28 April 1856.

May you enjoy a long life of willing service to others. Your schoolmistress, (Miss) Bessie L. Lyon. April the 30th, 1856. N.B.—The day of Our Nancy's departure from our midst.

Take out the shotgun, take out the meal, unpack the meager linen, unload the crated wool wheel, flax wheel—unload the shovel and the saw and maul and hammers and the auger and the axes. We got to carry again! If we hired a freighter to lug all this stuff, he'd charge us three cents per pound to haul anything from the Mississip; and you could buy a farm for that!

Worry the oxen through, worry the cows, lead and goad them through the wide rich mire with its muddy smells and snakes and bugs, and all the birds to rise a-screaming out ahead; for we're invaders, birds think that we got no business here. Come along Benjy, come along Bright, come along Ahab, come along Annie, lead old Barney, lead old Pilate, lead old Pest, get the critters to the other side, tug old Clover through the mud, soothe her with a *Sooooo Boss, Sooooo Clover*, come along, old lady— Don't let her flounder and sink; she's coming fresh, we'll need milk for the youngers when we get there, when we get where we're a-going—

Where we going, Pa?

Going to have a fine new home some day. All our own. Can't no Squire Sifert come around and say, Your time's up, you hain't paid your interest as was stipulated, you got to get off the place! No, no, young folks—twill be all ours.

But where?

Call it the Okoboji country.

Can't say the name, Pa. Call it the Okay— What?

Shoot! Call it the Spirit Lake country. Tis all the same.

Nancy, you got that bundle of feather pillows? Don't let them get wet.

Once more, my soul, the rising day
Salutes my waking eyes;
Once more, my voice, the tribute pay
To Him that rolls the skies.

Three-four yoke of oxen to draw the breaking plow? Well, we got them. And I'll walk to the side and forward, driving the teams; and on the beam of the plow will be a toolbox, and Uncle Absalom will be holding the plow– And, yes, Gracie–it's you I'm speaking to now, and ain't your eyes the widest! Cause Uncle Absalom will *let you set up on that toolbox,* just as big as if you was growed–and was a man, say, helping to break prairie–and you can ride up there all day, a-clinging sound and sharp, and you will hear the slithering snapping sound of all them tough grassy roots sliced loose, and watch that roll of sod curving up and over, with the greasy shine of the wide plowshare showing fat in the sun– Twenty inches wide, that sod will be folding off the blade: that's nigh to two foot wide! And you can see all the small colored flowers–the pinks and violets and gold and sky and apple colors in the tiny mass of blossoms–see them rise so gently and so willingly, and nod their small fresh faces as if to say, Hi, Gracie– And then they'll nod so tremulous in a lasting turning and recognition–

(Oh, this is the end, the last delicate sporting, the dainty colored beckoning and farewell!)

And then they'll curtsy ere they sink and double under, with the vast damp oily weight of fresh wrapped sod above–

And you'll want to shed a tear at seeing them vanish; but you'll never shed that tear, for more florets are a-waiting in advance to speak to you, to dance mildly and turn and bow in their tinted lace– And tain't only flowers to haunt you; but you'll feel the pull and force of all those tons of oxen bulging on ahead, and feel the weight of mighty plow and quite resistless plowshare–

Feel the prairie cut apart to suit our purpose.

That's you, small Gracie. Twill be so. A-riding on the plow, a-slicing up the sod.

Up to the fields where angels lie,
And living waters gently roll,
Fain would my thoughts ascend on high. . . .

Well, I read it. Read it in a big city paper; and the man who wrote the letter said that Ioway had more first-class arable land, in a healthy climate, than any other State in the United States. . . . A million and one ways to make a living out ahead, and only one way back home; and that way poison-mean and small.

. . . Blow us ahead of you, Mr. East Wind. Tell your cousin in the West not to rise up to plague us.

. . . Now, take cut timber. They say as how you can sell it. There's thirty-six sections of land in every township; but old Uncle Sam still owns a lot of the timberland, and *he won't sell.* But— Newcomers cut and haul a mite of timber, just the same. And where do they cut it? Just ask them, and they'll tell you: Why, I cut my timber off *Section Thirty-Seven!* That's where I cut it! . . . See? Section Thirty-Seven! Who's sold now? I ask you, and you tell me. Who's *sold?*

But who we going to sell it to, out there? If there ain't any other *folks,* how we going to sell timber?—

Oh, we'll cut and trim and pile and stack and cord— We'll be the first on hand. For more are coming. Every ferry fetches them, heaving them across the Mississip. A dozen here, two families there, a colony coming over yonder, we got to hurry. . . . Get up, get up! Huddup, huddup! Never say Whoa, never say Die.

Dollar and a quarter per acre. Say you only got eighty acres, and that would cost you a hundred dollars. Costs two dollars per acre to break it, roughly, so you'd break it for a hundred and sixty; and then if you needed to fence twould cost maybe seventy cents per rod; and that would boost the bill by three hundred and thirty-six dollars. (I'm taking this estimate from a man named Eldridge; he wrote in a paper back East; I got the clipping right here in my wallet.) Well, that's a farm purchased and broke and opened and fenced for an outlay of five hundred and ninety-six dollars. But then, look at your income! First year you ought to raise forty acres of wheat, and at seventy cents per bushel that'd bring in the neat little sum of eight hundred and forty dollars; and thirty acres of corn, say thirty cents per bushel, would fetch another five hundred and forty; and ten acres of potatoes, say fifty cents a bushel, would fetch another thousand dollars. That leaves a balance of exactly seventeen hundred and eighty-four dollars after taking out your original expenditure. Eldridge's figures! Plain and simple. There's your year's work and your farm clear, he says. If you can beat that in the State of New York, just let me know! . . .

Or Pennsylvania either. Or the backside of Ohio. Or back Down East.

—How's that?

—Eighty acres used up, in them figures? And where you going to live, you say?

—And where you going to pasture your stock, and who you going to sell all that wheat and corn, and them potatoes, to?

—Why—we'd live. We'd—

And pasture all the critters on the open prairie, that ain't yet been sold or broken!

—And— And—

—And you say: how's there going to be other folks around, to sell grain and garden truck to, if the prairie surrounding you is unsold and unbroken? Where's your market, you say?

—Why—

We'd live, by gravy, I tell you, we'd get along! We *will* get along. There'll be markets, there'll be towns, there'll be plenty, there'll be enough and plenty.

Who tolt me? Well, you may not believe it, but the wind tolt me! Strong wind from back East, whopping us ahead of it. The wind tolt us, we heard it in the breeze a-creasing past our ears.

Indyuns? Who cares bout Indyuns? We seen a parcel of them back here at the last timber, they come around wanting something to eat. They ain't nothing to wherrit yourself about—didn't have a gun or a spear or a stripe of war paint in the lot. And they already sold their land—it belongs to the Government, fair and square, all signed over by a treaty. So they got to bide by it, or soldiers'll come and settle their bacon right quick! And a settler he tolt me how to stay on the right side of an Indyun, anyways. No trouble at all, he says. Just raise watermillions. That was it: watermillions or water*melons* or whatever you want to call them. He said years ago when he dwelt down near the Agency—when Ioway was but a Territory— He said the Indyuns would come for miles around, just to get them millions! They growed them on a little farm at the Agency there; and them Brown-Boys got so cussed million-hungry they would have et the place bare in no time at all. So the Agent, he said, You Indyuns from This Village can come this week and get some millions. You Indyuns from That Village can come next week and get *your* millions. . . . And did they come? My, Mr.! By the tribe! . . . Liked watermillions next best to whiskey. So you can always stay on the good side of any Indyun in the world, granted you got the millions to feed them on.

So we'll put in a big patch. That we will!

(O lean insistent wind coming steady behind us, and blowing the critters' longer hairs, blowing them northwest in the direction we're bound, blowing the thick banks of reeds, carving into them like plows to come!)

What bear you, Mr. Following Wind, in the shape of news? Do I care? Not I!

You care, Absalom? .... Not you.

In the House a bill was passed authorizing the purchase of fifteen thousand copies of Dr. Kane's Arctic Expedition.

Want to go Arctic-wards? Not I! We're headed Spirit Lake-wards. And the winters are said to be sweet as sorghum up that way. Balmy even in January, so they say. In March the first puss-bloomies start to come. All puffed out delicate and purplish, like gold-eyed baby kittens on the hills. So they say. . . . No Arctic in mine! No North Pole for us!

The Committee on Foreign Affairs were instructed to inquire into the expediency of forbidding the engagement of American vessels in the Chinese Coolie trade.

Want to go amongst the heathen Chinees? Ho-ho! Ruther go amongst the heathen Indyuns!

The Emperor of France has signalized the birth of his son by offering an amnesty to all political exiles who would return and take the oath of allegiance. . . . Of the eleven thousand persons transported to Africa in 1848, only three hundred and six remained in exile. . . .

Want to go to France? And get drunk drinking wine, like all those Frenchmen, and– And dancing in the streets light-mindedly? Ho-ho!

Want to head Africa-wards, and get et up by the black cannibals, or maybe a lion or an elephant or some such critter? Not by a dang sight! I'd ruther shoot me a mess of prairie hens.

And deer out ahead. Everybody knows that. All the deermeat you can eat, and all the pigeons; and you don't got to poach on neighbors' land; tis all free for the asking, free for the shooting. Oh, Mr.!—just let me at them pigeons—nice fat-breasted ones. Reckon I'll fetch home a wagonload, first time they come to roost. Man told me they come down so thick in the Ioway timber they're fit to break the branches.

The new Cunard steamer Persia . . . *made the shortest passage ever performed across the Atlantic, accomplishing the voyage from Liverpool to New York in nine days twelve hours and seventeen minutes.*

Who's bound for Liverpool (wherever that might be)? Not us!

You want to go to Persia, now? What a plaguèd foolish idee! We're headed for the Okoboji country.

Pa. How you say that, please– Oaky–?

Fiddlesticks! Say Spirit Lake. I tolt you. Tis easier.

Wait for the wagon, wait for the wagon,
Wait for the wagon, and we'll all take a ride.

*

Then I looked to the North, and I looked to the East,
And I hollered for the ox-cart to come on,
With four gray horses a-driven on the lead,
To take us to the other side of Jordan.

*

There is a land mine eye hath seen
In visions of enraptured thought–
So bright that all which spreads between
Is with its radiant glory fraught.

*

Wait for the wagon, wait for the wagon. . . .

I see timber ahead. Long low bank of it, roosting like a ship hanging on her anchor at sea. Must be timber long a river . . . now what would that be? The upper Ioway River? Naw, we've passed that. Boone River timber? It could be. Des Moines River timber—the east fork? It could be.

. . . Timber says (all the trees conversing together): We been here a long time. But before we was here, there dwelt space and the grasses; and us trees are just as serene in our own good time—just as pleased and cool, just as serene, as were the low blowing plants before a one of us trees was sprouted . . . frogs'll be sounding thick at night. . . . The prairie comes a-answering. Lone, lone . . . says the prairie without any trees on it . . . far, far . . . and plum-colored mist at dusk when bugs and frogs are peeping in the sloughs . . . and when you leave the timber, and it goes down behind you like that same ship a-sinking . . . whisper comes up from timber banks . . . you mount the last long swell where you can see them . . . oh, we're waiting, we are here; and yet there's something out beyond. . . . Oh, go and find it! We won't tell you what it is, but there's something on ahead. . . .

And now we've got an eventide when hearts are heavy; and we all feel remote and so uncommon weak, because tis Death that trots behind us like a wolf (trots each day, he does, but seldom being seen; and now he's squatted close, as if behind the nearest lonely bank of weeds, and watching us).

Them tiny funny deaths at first: the two pet mice that Gideon yelped to fetch along, and said he'd have a circus one fine day, he said he'd teach them tricks; and so the little lad, he clung to that small homemade cage like all possessed. He tried to feed and water proper, changed their nest of grass each day, and it was kind of pitiful to see the care that youngun languished on those mice . . . but still they died.

And then that hen of Ma's, and then another hen—we had to fling them out—not fit for eating, for we didn't know just what complaint they died of—so we had to fling them out, and leave them there for carrion.

And then old Santa Anna—how we all did love that dog! But, sakes alive, we couldn't stay to hunt him, stay forever when we couldn't find him! And maybe he was drownded, but we never knew. We called him Santa Anna cause he'd lost one leg in puppyhood—twas caught in a steel trap, and had to be cut off— And course I would have whopped him on the head and thus cut short his misery, but how them children all did bawl! So then I says, Do tell! Well, if you want to let him try it on three legs . . . and so they did, and what a dog he was! He couldn't win no races, but he was an A-One watchdog, Mr., and the best all-round ratter that we ever had upon the place. For once old

Sant got hold of anything, he never would let go. Now, Absalom will swear that old Sant saved his life, the time that Durham bull had knocked Ab down; and Sant he grabbed that big bull's nose, and he just clung there, no matter how that bull did stamp and rave! Well, anyway. We'd sloughed down—that was a-Tuesday—and done another job of unloading, and wading and carrying, and hoisting here and hoisting there; and there we were, all mud, and tired, and loaded up again . . . and where was Sant? Just nowhere to be seen. He'd been acrost the slough, upon the other side, when we were starting; and now he was no place at all. Old Sant, Old Sant— Here, Sant!—Come, Sant!—*pheeeet, pheeeet*—and shrill and lonely whistles sounding; but never bark or holler did we hear. The boys went back, and tried to track him; course they couldn't—too much mud— He'd just completely disappeared, and all out there alone and unperceived. He hadn't run on any trail, we hadn't heard him giving voice as he went limping, trying to pursue— Oh, no—he hadn't run *off* anything; but surely something had made *way* with him! And Ab he fired off his gun, a-hoping that would fetch him; but the swales they just give back the echo, and the sun shone wan and mystic underneath its hot gray clouds . . . so far, so far, so lone, so lone . . . well, you see how twas. We had to leave him, even if he lived. And if he'd died: same way. We had to leave him where he was. Oh, Sant . . . *please,* Sant . . . the younguns calling till each voice wore raw, but no glad bark or yelp to answer them. I guess we could of stayed till Doomsday or till Judgment, and it would have been the same. And bigger boys a-snuffling, and little Gracie with her face hid deep within her mother's lap. Well, on we went, we had to go! It might have been a death, we didn't know. Maybe an eagle— But we didn't see none flying near. Maybe a rattlesnake— But we didn't hear Sant crying—and he'd been sure to cry, had he been snake-struck. And so we never knew and never will. Twas a sorry fire which we made that night.

And no one saying anything (the younger children whimpering, the elder kind of mumbling to one another) and we old folks so grim and businesslike, and trying to talk of more important matters like the feed around the place, and was that Pest ox lame, and what about the feed out yonder? But in the back of every brain there roved the picture of an old white dog with brown spots on him, and all his snorting and his wagging, and the pie he stole one time and tried to gulp it whole, and so it burnt him, and he hollered out like all possessed. And times Ma cooked molasses taffy for the little ones to pull, and Sant would beg— Oh, caution, yes, he wanted some! Indeed he did!—and then the boys would give him just a little bit; and course twould latch his jaws together just like they was glued; and first he'd put up one paw, shake his head, and then he'd lift the other paw, and try to dig that candy out; and all of us a-laughing fit to bust; and old Sant not recriminating at us— Just swabbing at that juicy sticky taffy with his paw, as much to say: Now, don't mind me, good people— I'm awkward eating it, but I do like the taste!—

This was the dog we'd think of, way out there someplace. We prayed that he was dead—sucked down inside the slough by all them mire-muds and quicksands—and now I reckon that he was— But there was that chill haunting feeling that he roamed, alone and maybe hurt, or maybe blinded somehow— Maybe got his mouth hurt, so's he couldn't plead for help— Or maybe laying wounded somewheres, saying to himself: I wish my folks would come and find me. Sure they will! I'd come to them, were they in need. And so I know they'll come to me! . . . Away out there, in grass and emptiness bereft, and left behind; without a morsel for to feed, without a hand to touch . . . just lone, and maybe hearing us when last and sad we drove and strode away. . . .

But still that's dog's death, trivial beside a man's or woman's.

And here she lies, so mute and frail and stiff: by far the eldest of the lot, but bound to come along.

We said: Now, Granny, you can live with Cousin Hep. She wants to have you. . . . No, says Gran, I'm coming long.

Or over with the Appersons? There's two of them your nieces, and they both got nice big houses—they have lots of room. And Lon, he come up to the fence a-Friday—left his planting, and he come and said: Tell Granny that we'd like to have her here with us, if all you folks are going West! . . . Oh, no, says Granny. I'm a-going too. And so she came.

She liked to hold the baby in the wagon. That tiny thing, it fairly lived in Granny's arms, and squawled like all possessed when taken from her.

I'm coming long. I'll always hear them words of her'n.

So it was flies and skeeters, maybe; and the wettings that we got in rains; and jarring, jarring of the wagon; and that fright when we upset, down there by Monticello, though it didn't seem to more than shake her at the time; and then the water in the sloughs (at first we drunk it, didn't know no better); then a little chill, and then the shaking fever, and another chill.

At last we stopped and camped, we had to.

That's why we're halted on this rise of ground; we're here to part with Granny, for twas here she left us.

And there's timber back behind, like drifting froth, a smudge above the grass (again, the sinking of a ship . . . ?) And nothing, nothing out ahead . . . I mean, there's naught that we can see.

But something waiting . . . ?

Ab. You read the Prayer Book. I can't see to read.

. . . For when thou art angry, all our days are gone: we bring our years to an end, as it were a tale that is told.

The days of our age are threescore years and ten; and though men be so strong, that they come to fourscore years—

Or womenfolks, our Nancy whispers soft.

—Yet is their strength then but labour and sorrow; so soon passeth it away, and we are gone. . . .

O teach us to number our days, that we may apply our hearts unto wisdom.

Turn thee again, O Lord, at the last: and be gracious unto thy servants.

And Grandpa gone for twenty years, and back in Allegheny County —he's buried there, a whole nineteen years and seven months agone. We had to bust the frosty clods, we had to chop and pry in frozen ground to dig that grave.

But here the prairie soil is soft, and kind of warming. May it be a comforter to shroud her neat.

What say you, children, to the eighty years? For she was eighty in the month of May. That's eighty years agone: you knit your brows and figure it. Now, Gideon, lad—you're good at ciphering. Can you whisper of that year?

Ah-ha! You got it!

God bless us all, God bless our loved United States, and most of all . . . dear Lord, bless Granny. . . .

Can't you hear that martial music in the wind of night?

Father'n I went down to camp
Along with Captain Goodin,
And there we see the men and boys
As thick as hasty puddin.

That was it, the year! And you can hear the fifes a-squealing, and you can smell the burnt bear's fat within the hearthside ash, and you can smell the hoecakes roasting brown, and you can hear a fiddle tune and hear a prayer; and hear the heavy wheels a-turning (oh, cart wheels heavier than ours, I will be bound!) and hear Virginia deer a-running in the woods, and see the ships a-flapping out their sails; and hear the grumble of the cannon; and see them tricorn hats a-waving, hear the cheering of the people, and the sorrow of the widows, feel the shudder of the orphans when their fathers never come . . . and most of all a bell, *a bell,* a great round tone to stroke like thunder and like softer music, and like fire-warning—

Ring, oh ring!—for Liberty!

That was it, the year in which our Granny saw the light; Gid had it quite correct.

Seventeen-Hundred-Seventy-six!

Here she lies, away out here. New land, fresh unsoiled soil to put her in. . . .

We'll bed her deep and soft. Ain't got no rocks to put on top; but if we put her deep . . . oh, deep . . . then she'll be snug enough. Too deep for—anything—to dig. They'd never know about her laying here.

. . . Assemble close in early darkness near her couch, and brood a moment on the wealth which we inter. All the old hand-wove and village-forged, the pewter mug that come across the Water with nothing but a scratch upon its bottom; and then that softer silver mug with little crowns and things, and letters dented into it; the things from Far Back Yonder, the Colonial Things. Folks still talked about the Boston Tea Party, and they glowered still about the Boston Massacre, when she was born! Why, Paul Revere had scarce put back his horse into the stable— Only thirteen months, he'd stabled up that horse, before Gran Norman saw the light of day— And then her baby name was Leah Tanner.

Ben Franklin . . . warming pans . . . and old gold boxes full of snuff (those were things that rich folks had, along with tiny miniatures with pearls around the edge). And those weren't Gran's inheritance—ah, no! For she growed up amongst the ash-leach and the twisting of the yarn. She growed up in days when little folks was bound; when lunatics was farmed to anyone who'd care for them—they claimed!—and keep them chained and safe from wreaking harm. . . .

The Tories, and the Declaration; and old John Hancock writing out his name so big and bold, and saying: There—King George won't need to use his specs to see *my* name!— And you mind Molly Pitcher, and the tales of John Paul Jones? Well, that was Granny's time, her baby time.

No modern methods then! Not one big steamship on the seas, not one! And nary railroad builded, nor an engine tooting on the rails! The telegraph . . . who'd ever heard or dreamt? The cotton gin . . . well, I ain't sure, Wiletta: tis something that they use down South; and it ain't *gin*—you never *drink* it— But it hadn't been invented anyway. Nor spinning mills. This calico and factory we buy nowadays—tweren't even dreamt of. Everything was wove by hand, by slow machines, in people's houses—just the way we'll have to do out here, when we run out of duds, until the railroad comes. And Jackie, that revolver—that little Colt's revolver that you got— It hadn't been invented neither. Single-barreled, all the pistols was! And modern men a-planning for a trans-Atlantic cable, bringing news of all the world— It didn't dwell in wild imagination! Percussion caps, and ether—all the modern things we hear about— Nobody knew. Them Colonies was primitive!

. . . And now we leave her solitary in the wrapping of a soil that wasn't even English in the hour of her birth. Honest, children—so you've heard me— They called this here *Louisiana.* This whole country out here past the Mississip. Belonged to Frenchmen, or to Spain, or somebody— Twas foreign; and one day our Government they bought it outright, paying millions, I've been told. I mind how Pa remembered when twas bought, and folks said What Extravagance— But then old Uncle Sam, he had to buy it once again, from all them Indyuns—

We'll read another prayer. And, womenfolks—do cease your weeping.

For this ain't defeat; tis triumph and tis proof. They're something noble for to think about. Full eighty years! The thirteen children, live and dead; the bullets run at night, the Mohawks in the barley field, the Mohawks up the valley . . . maple sugar . . . and the wealth of work, the hands shrunk into claws from toil, the joints growed out lopsided on her hands . . . and always silent courage in her soul . . . and little crinkly curtains on her eyes (most folks would call them eyelids; but they weren't—no longer—just the littlest crinkly curtains. Then they'd lift, and you'd see deep black fire burning bright in each old eye)—

Oh, Absalom, you read again. For I can't even hold the Book of Common Prayer! . . . Lift up that torch of twisted weeds, young Jackie, so's your Unk can see.

Thou knowest, Lord, the secrets of our hearts; shut not thy merciful ears to our prayer; but spare us, Lord most holy, O God most mighty, O holy and merciful Saviour, thou most worthy Judge eternal, suffer us not, at our last hour, for any pains of death, to fall from thee.

(Dream world, dream place, dream bait for minds a-hunting as they go ahead. They all delude themselves; perhaps aware that they are suffering from self-delusion, but never minding it at all . . . and camps of timber sleep and wait in their damp smoke, the prairie waits as well when groves are gone.)

We parted from the East the way we parted from the dead, there's no more East left in us when new sunrise comes; we eat the colors of the sunrise, wave goodbye to old and settled regions underneath the big bright coin of rising sun. We swing around to meet the new-come western wind. Gid-*dap!* we cry, and slouch advancing through the grass, and soon we feel the sun upon our shoulder blades. A feathery western wind will burn our faces as we go.

It's got the fuzz of gophers in it, oil of skunks, the foam blown from an Indyun pony's mouth; tis thorny as a rose . . . the larks rise up . . . ten million yellow-headed blackbirds in a swale . . . the western wind does clang like forks a-ringing on a frying pan, it rumbles like the wheels which bear our load. Twill kill or cure (and in our case pray solemn to the Lord that it may cure)!

Hello there, stanch West Wind! You'll purify the blood, I'll warrant you—and better still than Moffat's Vegetable Life Pills and Phoenix Bitters—oh, yes, we know of those. The advertisers say: *They are known by their fruits; their good works testify for them.* Well, take a big dose of this wind, and feel it driving out the bad complaints: the asthma stops its stifling, acute and chronic rheumatism fade away, the gout and giddiness are gone, the jaundice, leprosy, and palpitation of the heart . . . they fall away, we feel them not . . . the ulcers and the worms are gone. We stride like burnished skeletons, our bones are clean again, the western wind has picked them clean.

We hunger like the young, a goodly way to hunger.

What'll ye take, O Stranger? You'll join us in corn bread and common doins?

Or if you hanker after chicken fixins, load your gun and fare afield.

They're all around, you'll hear their wings a-beating, see the glint upon their wings. . . .

Wait for the wagon, wait for the wagon,
Wait for the wagon, and we'll all take a ride!

(Why is it Man holds notion of a perfect life? He knows far better, if his head is hard. There's no perfection anywhere, not in that filmy haze beyond the slough ahead, no more than you could find it in the wheel marks filling up with water past that slough behind. Man takes his own confusion and his weakness, lugs them with him, carries them in bushel or in bag; he totes along his own disease. Was he a trickster at the East? He'll be a trickster out ahead. . . . Did he cheat his neighbor and his wife, did he put sand in sugar where he came from —lard in butter, water in the vinegar? He'll do that all again. And if he ran from bulls in Jersey, he'll flee from monsters out at Okoboji; and if he wouldn't stand and fight in Massachusetts, he'll never fight on his new doorstep, even when the wolves come snapping. . . . Tis like a-hustling into battle: the weak grow weaker in the powder smoke, the liar never learns to tell a truth. Tis like Religion, practiced hard: the soul that's decent in the first essential becomes then thrice-ennobled by his little glimpse of God—the thief and torturer but use Religion as a tent to put above them, and let them swindle, whip within its shade. . . . You nod, agree to all of this; and yet you've got that splinter in your eye. Tis sharp as needles . . . little gleaming splinter like the sun a-finding mica in a rock. One tiny glint which says: True, true! . . . And yet, and yet . . . I got a notion, Mr.! I didn't do too well back in Connecticut—or there in Plainfield, there in old Scioto— But I tell you: if we take up land out here—and nobody's a-pressing us— If Kathy keeps her health— And if the boys don't all get snake-bit, or don't get the mumps– If we can only soften up the ager cake within the belly of our life, why then– I tell you: twill be *diff-er-ent!*)

The prairie is a sea without a limit, and so it makes you think of seas you may have known way off the coast of Maine . . . same feel of emptiness: and yet you know that neither prairie nor the seas are empty. There is a life beneath its slumbered surface as beneath the surface of the sea, a life both beautiful and threatening . . . could kill you, or could offer food and benefit and lovely weed. Above each wilderness the flocks lift zealous with their cries; for birds know all about the menaces and wonder which disport within the waves. They talk their languages, and tell. . . : But these aren't gulls, they're prairie hens, and hawks which hang suspended, and giant eagles over all. On this sea prairie there lie mist and memory. But yet its very vastness, as the vastness of the ocean, is a threat we can't ignore. From every pond the birds arise with chunks of red upon their wings, and blackness turned to silver by the sun; they speak and squabble, bicker, haunted. Their snipping wiry voices cry: Ah, we were hatched in this wild waste, we know its ways, we love it, feed of it– Yet one day it will slay us, rot the polish from our wings!

O Ahab, Eli, Simeon– One time you went by boat, and now you put your legs around a horse, or plod beside an ox! You're not embarked in dory or in catboat or in schooner which you knew off Kennebunkport, Boothbay, or off Ragged Isle! But still you're lonely voyagers pursued by salty distances, and bound to be destroyed if you stay out at sea too long.

And are there elements to satisfy ambition, is there treasure in the surges out ahead? A doll for every Angeline?–stout and grinning prideful husbands for our Kate and our Sophronia?–stars to make the striplings beat their breasts and toss their manes, and yell: The light and sparkle, power of the skies . . . endow me, dearest Lord on High!– Oh, will we find them when the sun comes up again behind us–when a thousand suns have come?

You could go hunting them forever, as the first strange-shapen boats went out to seek their saffron and their pearls and arrows . . . could come back with riches in the hold . . . or never come again.

The waves break on black shelves of the Iberian coast, and . . . what is that? . . . a wooden pin, a scrap of net? Tis something lifting in the foam, and falling back again. A shred of sail, a flake of rudder wood, long varnished by the medicine of waters, with the barnacles like blackened jewels, and weeds a-growing? And far far up by Greenland, maybe, is another piece . . . with cousin wreckages already soaked, and gone below, and gone below to hide from all the blowing and the rime.

Once more, my voice, the tribute pay
To Him that rolls the skies. . . .

*

Wait for the wagon, wait for the wagon. . . .

*

Says Gran, I'm coming long.

*

Thou knowest, Lord, the secrets of our hearts.

XVI

From his matchless companion, Bertell Snyder, Isaac Harriott learned the story of a boy named Robert Didier.

This tale was told in compelling sessions as the two pushed on together up the course of the Cannon River and past a wide-strewn maze of lakes which lay beyond. Titanka, Tanninan, Okaman . . . it was as if soft Indian syllables had sprouted loose from the map and spread glimmering in easy wetness throughout the summer days.

Two other active members of the Company—the Granger brothers, William and Carl—took charge of carts and oxen. (They traveled as Northerners traveled—four of the capacious Red River carts hitched in tandem fashion like cars of a railway train.) They had managed oxen at home in England, they exuded good-natured but cynical Kentish smiles whenever they witnessed Harry or Bert endeavoring to direct or even yoke up the teams of critters. The youthful doctor and the Frenchman were happier, too, when left to their own devices. Eagerly they assumed the task of providing game for the table (preliminary accomplishment did not support a mutually stated opinion as to their excellent marksmanship . . . William Granger said to Carl: Aye, they burn a tidy bit of powder, they do!) and also of preparing meals. Their ponies carried them well in advance of the slow-grinding carts, even when they ranged off past sloughs or into timber. They would establish a camp site; the smoke of their new fire served as guide to the Grangers, who came trailing up contentedly about the time when prairie hens were turning plumply brown, or when perch were curling in a skillet which Bert carried through the day, tied and padded with unspeakable dish towels, beside his saddle.

For the first time in life, Harry had a protracted sense of being lifted beyond study, beyond toil or striving. He was aware of this in cumulative experience when he lay at night with eyes closed against the fire flicker. He explored the sensation and wondered about it in those precious secret moments of consciousness left to him between a last exchange of conversation with the other men, and the blissful void of slumber opening ahead. He knew that the tale which he had heard (and still was hearing for days on end) became not a mere narration of human bleeding and longing, and merciless but exalting experience. It was a chant which might have been sung in the skies . . . only up Above, beyond the stain of Man and his fussings, could there tinkle the harps fit to accompany this legend. Time and distance collapsed, grew unimportant while the singing continued.

Increasingly during the fourteen months of their friendship Harry had wondered as to the qualities which set Bert Snyder apart from other folk— Which portion of his strange fey difference was native to him? And which portion had been instilled by what befell?

At last Harry knew the answer. He bowed before it, he felt a prayer sounding in his spirit while he bowed.

Isaac Harriott might not know the entire story any more than Bert Snyder himself might know it. A single voice was powerless to speak it all. Yet the song went ringing off into space and mystery, accompanied by the footfalls, the whispering, the trampling antics of all those who contribute to an epic—who speak and dance ahead, behind, in the middle of an epic—and declare it to be both a record and a dream.

Once upon a time there was a boy named Robert Didier.

Robert spent his boyhood near the village of Gigouzac, France, not far from the River Lot. He was wiry and round-shouldered both as a child and as a youth. His eyes were hazel-colored and intent. In moments of excitement (which rose frequently as a brew in his soul but seldom were stimulated by the outside world) Robert's eyes seemed to protrude from their tender casings. The boy's ears were large though delicate, and stuck out noticeably on either side of his head. Sometimes he saw in books the pictures of tropical monkeys who had ears like his own. His hair was clay-colored—very soft, and falling into bangs across his forehead.

The family's sullen asthmatic housekeeper set great store by her abilities as a seamstress, and she kept Robert in more than a sufficiency of dotted-pink cambric shirts. The woman liked to feel that she had made a good bargain for herself, and one time purchased an entire bolt of this material. Pink spots appeared everywhere in the household, especially in her aprons and in Robert's shirts. These shirts he regarded as a badge of indignity, something to be worn only by tiny boys; also there were too many frills and pleats. He much preferred the simple overalls of peasant boys roundabout, and wore such garments whenever he could manage to elude Madame Paquet.

Any passers-by strolling in the park where stood the big castellated house of the Didiers would have seen Robert running shyly—a child with a face eager, a child desiring love as many children seek affection who win it not. . . . Robert had a cat face, not a kitten face. His wide thin mouth was compressed as if he'd tightened it into immobility in self-discipline (he had). Freckles spread across his cheeks, more thickly on his nose, and brought a brightness to his countenance. He seemed to be saying always: Do you like me? I could like you, if you would let me. Oh, please to like me. . . . When he was in the woods he seemed sprung from the woods, native to moss and beeches. The forest was an odd place to look for love, unless one sought the love of hares and hummingbirds.

Robert Didier's father had written two books, his grandfather seven. The two men looked nothing alike, for one was fluttering and nervous, the other pulpy and torpid. Yet each Didier wore an identical scrap of red ribbon in his moldy lapel, and each could talk interminably on the subject of megalithic remains. Each looked a little like a megalithic remain himself.

Robert remained withdrawn from sire and grandsire, fleeing their petulance and suffocation. Antiquity was represented first in the left wing of the house itself, where round towers, wearing the dignified patina of silvered and brownish lichens, had survived since the twelfth century. Portions of the structure had been remodeled as late as during the childhood of Robert's own father, but seemed stained already by the slow smoke of time. The boy considered that the very frogs who lived in low areas where once there had been a moat— That these frogs, too, wore moss on their backs—the identical creatures who'd uttered evening grumblings when Robert's grandfather was young enough to be frightened by them.

. . . Slates were old, so were conical pinnacles above each tower. Robert craved the sleek, the brittle, the unmarred, unweathered appurtenances of modernity; but modernity was not tolerated here: it would interfere with proper exploration and veneration of the past.

Cases of artifacts built along an upper corridor gave forth their own odor of camphor, and it was old camphor.

The grandfather, Laurent Didier, sat below a lamp suspended by a corroded brass chain. The magnifying glass in his cracked fingers was old; there were a million minute scars upon the table surface; the torn sheet of foolscap on which Grandfather placed a potsherd was old; so was the dust of the sherd, and so, forgotten, was the maker of that sherd. . . . Lynette the cook was old; so, it seemed, was the food she prepared, and Robert did not relish it; nor could he generously and willingly endure the other smells that moved as ghosts might have moved through high cold doorways. . . . Oh, give me greenness and freshness! he prayed in a youth so young that he could scarcely identify the wish which lived within him. Give me verdure; let me, myself, be as verdant as fresh chestnut leaves and their candelabra blossoms. . . . But the chestnut trees themselves are old!

Physically he ran away from the mustiness, and often was lambasted cruelly for such truancy.

. . . A newness of my own—something new for me? Robert could not identify the thing he sought; yet he believed that he tasted it when chewing gum from the pine trees.

Moments of high emotional excitement occurred when the pretty Countess de Lacapelle, a near neighbor, was driven past. Her carriage was a new one with a shine to it—not the rattly cracked-leather split-cushioned relic in which Robert's father and grandfather rode to take the air.

. . . In an earlier time, from the moment the boy could first remember, there was a companion for Robert—a dog named Captain. Captain too was elderly; he went blind, and one day he was missing, and no one would talk about him.

. . . Maybe, Robert thought, this new thing I seek will have the shape of a flower.

He wondered what texture the flower would bear, wondered as to the color of its petals.

His father and grandfather went walking on field trips, with a servant to carry baskets, mattocks, other tools. They went far, walked long, dug long. They came home speaking of sherds and projectile points. They talked of incising and spalls, spoke of skeletal remains. Robert's grandfather had no teeth left to him, and his false teeth were a pain. He grew to leaving those false teeth out altogether; and subsisted mostly on frumenty, puréed potatoes, creamed pigeon, other soft substances which he could mash with his gums. When he was ill, the local doctor who came to attend Grandfather also was bearded and gray; there was even an awful age to the battered gold knob tipping his cane. His gray horse wore a hat, and dozed under the green plush of the oak trees; his carriage squeaked in elder litany when the doctor climbed into it again.

Was there a newness anywhere amid the region? Robert doubted, but still he hoped; and he implored in dreams. . . . Crows or rooks which walked the wide shelving lawn were tattered; some of their tail feathers had come out; when André the gardener was ordered to reduce their numbers, he did it with a very *old* shotgun.

As Robert fled periodically from the decrepitude surrounding his life, he felt that he was running almost as frenziedly from regional names as from mildew. Crayssac, Parnac, Goujounac, Nadillac, Thedirac, Cessac, and their own adjacent village of Gigouzac. . . . He understood competently the ancient origin, the vulgarization of *Acum,* but liked the names no better for that understanding. Robert could recall another existence: it was filmy, and he was much smaller, and thus the adults in that earlier life were of giant size in proportion; yet it was in Paris, not in the Lot. A harsh terminal syllable did not leap to offend your ears, whenever a name was mentioned in Paris.

The boy sped along roadways, hunting for something lively and bright and personal, giving small fear to dark coverts . . . dragons might have lurked in the Bois de Boulogne of his infancy (a ruthless nurse had peopled the park with them) but he was tall now, he was a young man of ten, twelve, fourteen. His tutor with shiny pink face, the tutor with bad breath and mincing gait and butterfly gestures—this tyrant made him sweat at Greek, Latin, mathematics, astronomy; the tutor taught his pupil a Vedic effusion, and kept calling on Robert to recite it again and again, though he forgot the chant from one week to the next, and always had to bone up on it. . . . M. Amboise Lambert had no grounding in archaeology, so this subject, with related historical studies, was ignored by him. It might well be! Robert had heard nothing but paleontology and archaeology, at table or in family conclave, from the hour of awakening intelligence. (He dressed his relatives in the hooded garb of Inquisitors, and recollected them as having strapped him to a table, opening up the crust of his head with a gimlet and siphoning into his brain a mixed sauce of dinosaurs, apes, copper, bronze, dolmens, Pharaohs, saber-toothed tigers, and Tartessians.) At fifteen Robert would be packed off to the university—kept on short commons in a garret, no doubt; for the Didiers were miserly and never indulgent—and directed to bury his natural life amid scarabs, stone awls, tomb dust, parchment, bones.

Then Robert found his cave. *Un petit écureuil* led him to it. He reckoned the squirrel as very new; he supposed that it was only a few months old, it was such a baby; its breast was snowy and its tiny jowls like silk, and they puffed and quivered as the creature chewed beech mast and looked at Robert impertinently.

At home in The Fortress there was a cased-up population of animals and fowl. . . .

(Naturally the inhabitants of the countryside spoke of the Didier house as The Château. But Robert had grown to think of their home as The Fortress; for very early it seemed to him that forces of antipathy and selfishness had been walled up there, waiting with a sneer to defend themselves against any benevolent invasion.)

The Fortress's zoo consisted of various magpies, starlings, hawks, larks, and a hoopoe bird, all poised on wires and maintaining attitudes of extreme belligerency. They seemed consigned to combat against a troop of weasels, a civet cat, foxes, a wolf, a hedgehog, and two bats; the whole dusty snarly fluttering debacle was about to ensue within a vast glass arena. (Robert envisioned himself, his father, his grandfather, and various professors and secretaries who came to their board at times, as dining within a similar sealed enclosure, eating off potsherds.) The fresh clean squirrel, brushed and scrubbed and polished as to claws and teeth, was alive and dancing, squirting with energy. Robert had no wish to kill the *petit écureuil;* he was not a hunter by instinct; the slaughter of the rooks had affected him deeply, even though they were old, and in his hatred of the elderly it was logical to wish them expunged also. But he rather pitied those musty creatures in the putrid glass cabinet, and he wondered often about the trigger finger and forgotten pearls of shot which had brought them to this solidified doom.

(That stuffed hoopoe bird fascinated Robert, particularly because of its outstanding ruff and crest, much like the pictured war bonnet of a Red Indian in the American wilds—even though its spice-colored feathers were gnawed noticeably by unseen insects, camphor or no camphor. . . . His grandfather said: What is that? You admire the hoopoe? You have made a most absurd choice! . . . Grandfather Laurent Didier tugged at his spiny beard, as if wishing to expel other insects which might have penetrated there also. He asserted that the hoopoe was filthy in its habits, and frankly he did not know how or why this particular specimen had been included in the collection. Then Grandfather went waddling away down the dark third-story passage, affronted by recollection of some ugly trick he must have seen a hoopoe bird play upon itself. Grandfather ambled slowly but purposefully, his hairy hands spread across the crooks of two supporting canes, the eternal magnifying glass dangling on a ribbon around his thick neck, his linen somewhat soiled, a fringe of hair shaggy above his ears, and on the back of his neck a curtain of hair curling over the shabby broadcloth collar. Robert could have been excused for thinking of his grandfather as some sort of hoopoe bird.)

Robert met the squirrel on the river road which accompanied the pure little stream of the Vert as it giggled over waving beds of cress on its way to a rendezvous with the Lot at Castelfranc. This was a Sunday in May, shortly before Pentecost. There was love among the peasants; girls had dressed in their favorite petticoats and kerchiefs, sturdy young men came beaming after them. There was wine of joy in the air, and the joy of wine circulating in picnic groups. The lonely boy looked with longing eyes: these people were all so gay, there was so little gaiety for him at The Fortress.

Then the squirrel scampered and he went chasing it. It postured over tumbled stones, luring him. He delved through thickets, hid behind a silvery beech trunk, peered out and saw the wee squirrel peeping at him. Robert carried a net in which he had thought to capture some toads and bring them home for pets. He might keep them in a box filled with moss in his room, and feed them on flies or scraps from his own dinners. Now he engaged to snare the squirrel with his net—not to slay it, but he did have a wooden cage in which pet white rats had lived and died. No creature occupied the cage now; perhaps the squirrel would enjoy living there . . . Robert should fetch nuts and acorns for it, teach it little pranks. How amazed M. Lambert might be, if Robert were to let the squirrel emerge slyly from his pocket and dart across the school table, just as the tutor was in the act of laying out one of those poisonous Catilinarian orations or another hoary Vedic psalm! . . .

Net at the ready, Robert preyed forward, but the sly wisp of fur was gone scooting to shelter in a loose cairn of stones before the boy could get within five meters of it. He was chagrined, but set to work stoically moving the slabs, trusting as each stone was removed that he might see a beady eye winking at him. These rocks, all gardened with beds of moss and infinitesimal flowers, represented the dissolution of a boundary wall, or perhaps were the product of a hillside avalanche: there were larger boulders looming on a wooded slope above. Robert worked consistently, patiently, as any youth might do when dedicated to some trivial pursuit of his own, not prescribed by decree of parent or master. Before he reached the bottom of the pile the little squirrel must have escaped through opposite interstices, for he saw no evidence of occupancy beyond a few scraps of acorn and sodden nut hulls. There did seem to be, however, a beckoning blackness in the side of the hill itself. Robert got down on his knees, and then lay on his belly, straining to excavate some wafers of limestone rotted half away from parent ledges. When this was done, the boy had achieved an opening large enough for him to thrust his head and shoulders inside the hill. He pushed his body forward until the light of day was blocked off by his own elongated bulk, and he stretched his arms into dank emptiness; he twisted his fingers about, waved hands loosely at the wrists. He could touch nothing, nothing. Perhaps this was a den once inhabited by bears or boars, and the thought rather disturbed Robert, and he backed out precipitately. Still it seemed that he had heard the slender voices of water fairies speaking musically down there within the treasury of the hill . . . perhaps a secret spring? If so, it would be his own spring—a new one—and unsullied by the drinking of other people before he came! This notion tickled his fancy very much; and he squatted for half an hour, fascinated by the irregular mysterious hole, deliberating on the possibilities of enlarging the aperture so that he might achieve entry. But equipment would be needed—tools, to pry loose the shelving platters and chop the roots which bound them—and he would need a lamp also. Ha!—his father owned an oil lantern of a type which Louis Didier, the father, had declared was used by miners; and M. Didier had actually carried that lantern into an Egyptian tomb, and loved to tell about it at length over his after-dinner glass until Grandfather fell to nodding. Robert knew where the lamp was kept, and also the implements which the archaeologists used in their eternal explorative digging. (They did not go out to dig so often nowadays; Grandfather was growing fatter and less energetic; and Robert's father was at his desk afternoon and evening, inditing the manuscript of a new book with his pointed calligraphy. Its title was: *Evidences of*

Primitive Domestic Culture in the Haute Dordogne and Region of the Lot. There were to be included illustrations of various artifacts and ornaments; a graduate student from Paris was even now in residence at The Fortress, being bedeviled incessantly by both of the elder Didiers as he toiled at preliminary sketches.) Robert concluded that his search for the virgin spring must wait for at least two days; a family expedition was planned for the next day; but he might be able to pre-empt the things he needed, and steal away on Tuesday after lessons, when *Monsieur le Précepteur* had gone poking off about his trout fishing (usually unrewarded).

Monday's excursion was accomplished amid the patched upholstery of the family carriage—grandfather, father, son; with André the gardener in role of coachman, and wearing his brass-buttoned green velvet jacket—insufferably proud André became whenever he donned this coat, though nap of the velvet was long since worn off on skirts and elbows. Their destination was the château at Mercuès, perhaps fifteen kilometers distant, and there they arrived for luncheon. Robert was always emancipated from his studies for these trips to Mercuès, and considered them to be unadulterated holidays; and he was nearly as pleased when the genial Doctor Pelacoy made returning social visits to the Didier home (the cuisine at home was sadly inferior to the delicious pigeon pies and *truite meunière* served up on the Pelacoy table). The Pelacoys had known the Didiers for a century at least, and Doctor Pelacoy's daughter and Robert's mother had become chums when they were at the convent. Doctor Pelacoy said that Robert resembled his mother; and he had let Robert play with his snuffbox and wind his watch—it was almost the first thing Robert could remember.

Be it said that the learnèd Messieurs Laurent and Louis Didier respected the doctor chiefly because he had served as a military surgeon in Africa Minor and had visited ruins there.

The château at Mercuès was as old as or older than the Didier château near Gigouzac, but the boy never felt the stagnation or fustiness at Mercuès which he suffered in his own home. The Mercuès château was infinitely larger, but in better repair, and it did not contain stiff aggregations of moldering birds and beasts. It was instead thronged by good-natured ecclesiastical ghosts, for it had housed a succession of bishops until the passing of the Bishop Cousin de Grainville in 1828. Then the Pelacoys, whose own house had been destroyed by fire, bought the château from the Church, and settled easily among relics of an antiquity which seemed as liberal as the Didiers' was discomfiting.

As if it were yesterday, Robert could recall an incident of an earlier age—perhaps when he was seven or eight years old. Father and Grandfather were speculating over some Roman coins which had been unearthed by the Pelacoy gardeners, and the bald burly Doctor Pelacoy strolled into a high-ceiled sitting room which gave on the east terrace of the château at Mercuès. There he found the small Robert much at home in a high-backed damask-covered chair with slender wooden gryphons for arms. He was neither fretting nor wriggling, but sitting in contentment with folded hands, absorbed in savoring a sweetness which crept from plastered walls, from the flaked painting above the fireplace (a nearly life-sized young man with wings and armor was engaged in stabbing to death a prostrate antagonist; but the antagonist represented veriest Evil, it had been explained to Robert, and hence the slaughter should be approved). A good warmth, winter or summer, dwelt in that room, though this was summer at its best. Through tall opened doors could be seen the clipped lawn of the terrace—that terrace constructed by Bishop Habert when plague offended the land, and the resourceful bishop provided this enterprise, so that workmen might have food, and might be removed from slums where pestilence was creeping. Doctor Pelacoy himself had explained all this to Robert while the boy sat on his lap one rainy day; and assured him that walls nearly ten meters high had first been built, and then filled in with earth carried by donkey-back and man-back from far and wide. . . .

This afternoon the child jumped to proper attention, and bowed.

Oh, sit down, my son, sit down! cried Pelacoy. This is no dancing school! He laughed. Were you becoming wearied at our long absence? Should you not like to see the Roman coins?

No, thank you, *Monsieur le Docteur,* came the polite voice. And then: We have many Roman coins at home. . . .

No doubt, no doubt! Well, should you like to go and see the *pigeonnier* again? You'll recall where it is: just below the southwest corner of the château, on the steep cliff. That little path out beyond the balustrade—

Thank you, no, *Monsieur le Docteur.*

As a matter of fact, Robert detested pigeons, perhaps because his grandfather was forever chewing an *émincé* of their flesh with his shrunken old gums. The pigeon tower itself was an antique—it might have been originally a Roman turret; and the dung of the doves was a stench from the past, and their yodeling an annoyance. No!

Then: May I just sit in this room?

You like to sit here, hey? The doctor's blue eyes were pale but discerning under their bushy gray brows.

Very much, sir.

Why is that, now? Why sit here in this room?

Robert thought for a time. Then he answered haltingly: Because the room has a kindness, sir. Perhaps—like a mother— Though I cannot remember my mother—

Doctor Pelacoy stood gazing out across the terrace, past an ivied tower, over the gentle valley of the Lot, far to that pink-roofed sprawl where the town of Cahors lay in pleasant disorder on its hills. He turned at last from the open door. He said: Most peculiar that you should say that, my son! I mean, saying that the room has a kindness. You know, of course, that the bishops of this diocese dwelt here for a very long time—whole generations of bishops, so to speak!

He laughed, then grew sober and even more tender again.

They were a good lot, on the whole, and during the Revolution, when most of the Church properties in France were razed or pillaged by mobs who had grown to hate the clergy, the Church properties and advocates of Catholicism in this region escaped the worst indignity. . . . Do you understand what I am saying, Robert? Oh, of course you do, of course you do!

Robert slid back into that enjoyable chair, and Doctor Pelacoy came over and presided beside him, with that hand (which had carved so much flesh and tied so many ligatures) stroking Robert's head. He said: The people of the Lot, people of the Haute Dordogne and Vézère valleys, had reason to remember the generosities given them by open hands and open hearts. So these bishops were spared. . . . But that was not what I set out to tell you, my sensitive and imaginative child! I meant to tell you of the venerable Bishop Alain de Solminihac. This was his favorite room in the château. He must have sat here often, planning the good deeds he would perform for poor folk. He was traditionally respected for his charities. And here, Robert—

He lowered his voice (when emotionally touched he was inclined to bellow like an old bull).

—In this room, in Sixteen Fifty-nine, the good Bishop Alain died! I am sure that it is his presence which you feel.

The doctor went away, and shortly Robert heard the shriller, more inquiring, more petulant tones of his parent and grandparent as they joined Pelacoy on the terrace outside. But for a long while the little boy sat there, legs extending straight out across the damask, wondering at the tale he'd heard. He held a fancy of Bishop Alain—imagined that he could see a smiling seated figure in its habit and miter, with an aura of rose and gold. There was antiquity in this vision, but it was not the same antiquity which (frightening and offending Robert in that museum which was his home) would provoke him to rebellion as he grew older. It was instead the sum of human compassion and comfort, offered freely by a sturdy soul which seemed, in emerging emanation, as young as the chestnut blooms with their pink hearts and silken stamens. I wish we had this room at home, thought Robert; and so always he wished it, but that miracle could not be.

More than the magic room was permeated by presence of Alain de Solminihac: iris and bridal wreath were charmed by his memory, that dark cedar of Lebanon rising above the northern battlements reflected a strength of vanished greatness. Surrounding walls traced over the hilltop—some spilled and tousled, some remaining in defensive solidity—were testimony to the wisdom and courage of a great man (perhaps of many other fine spirits as well as this particular prelate's; but Robert did not know who they were, he could remember only the one name; therefore he endowed his own very personal Bishop Alain with the virtues worn by a multitude).

. . . On the May Monday before Pentecost, when Robert Didier again visited Mercuès as a stripling of fourteen, he anticipated the descent of the Holy Spirit upon the Apostles by a matter of days. The Holy Spirit fell over him in charm before the crazy carriage had rocked its protesting way up that circuitous road approaching the château. All was as he remembered it: the moat choked with ivy roots, Judas trees, a few lilacs—dark blankets of ivy swarming on towers, spicy smells from the vaulted kitchen belowstairs—even the prolific setter bitch who came sporting to welcome them, her burred tail flourishing like a bell rope; and again she had a herd of bastard spotted puppies squeaking ravenously after her. This dog—Rougette was her name—enjoyed conceiving puppies very much, but did not enjoy nursing them. Her opulent dugs were always oozing milk, and the offspring tumbled after her, squeaking and sniffing with indignant hunger. It was Doctor Pelacoy's frequent chore to arrest Rougette and lift her into the nursing pen he'd had a gardener contrive beside the east outer stairway, and then he'd lift the puppies in after her, one by one; and Rougette would stand hopelessly with the most hangdog expression in the world while her children tugged at her teats. Robert rejoiced at seeing this comedy repeated, but Laurent and Louis Didier had hustled straightway into the library, to evaluate the latest dug-up bit of junk: a rusted scrap of dagger sheath. Was it Roman, was it Gothic? Robert cared nothing for their verdict nor for the relic itself; so he stood with his tough old friend beside the latticed pen, discussing the pups. He heard his latest growth praised (he was tall for fourteen, but of course he was nearly fifteen); and he agreed that Superflu would be an ideal name for the runt of the litter.

The bluff heartiness of Doctor Pelacoy worked its usual warmth in Robert's spirit. Vaguely the boy wondered how the doctor might ever consider Father and Grandfather as friends to be welcomed. He did not understand that a sentimental association relating to earlier generations was observed consistently by Pelacoy as a manner of ritual. Then too there was the friendship of the doctor's adored daughter, now the wife of an official in Martinique, with Robert's own mother. (It was unlikely that the doctor would have tolerated those limited archaeologists for five minutes, had it not been for the family bond and for his sincere appreciation of Robert as a person from the start. The doctor had never owned a son; this was his deepest regret.)

. . . And what have you been doing of late, besides studying? Any sports, hey?

No, *Monsieur le Docteur*. Sometimes I accompany my tutor on a fishing trip; but really I do not enjoy fishing, and prefer much more to roam the forests.

But no decayed bones and pottery debris for you? Not to your taste, I suspect!

Robert grinned, and rejoiced when Doctor Pelacoy beamed back at him in complete understanding. The essential joviality of the man possessed the boy's spirit, and he had a strong inclination to confide . . . but what might he confide, what happy secret might he reveal? Ah!

His big eyes began to puff, stimulated by recollection of shelving rocks, the dark mystery of the suspected cavern, the possibility of an unsampled spring. Yesterday, sir, Robert began in dramatic solemnity— On a hillside not far from Gigouzac, I discovered—

Louis Didier came flying out across the upper terrace and down the wide steps. He brandished a scuffed calfskin-bound book in his delicate hand, and had a finger thrust into it to mark a place. His spectacles were clamped loosely on his high-bridged nose, his black ribbon was a-flutter; he tried to pat his mop of coarse gray hair into place as he flurried toward them. . . . Military complex, Celtic type! he was crying. Definitely Celtic! My dear Henri, allow me to read you a paragraph written by the late Abbé de Moustier—

In inevitable pattern he ignored the very existence of his son, had eyes and attention only for the older man.

Robert heard Doctor Pelacoy give a brief sigh. Robert might never understand through intuition, reasoning, or through being directly informed (Doctor Pelacoy would die of apoplexy before long, and thus Robert would lose the one old friend he possessed) that honestly Pelacoy believed the Didiers to be mere parasites feeding off the skin of existence, whatever their historical erudition or accomplishment. Neither did Doctor Pelacoy care a fig for Celtic scabbards, Roman coins, a barrow, or a megalithic trace. He loved to see warm bodies and warm spirits exerting themselves among lively tribes. He loved hard work, appreciated tears and lewd jests alike—had actually enjoyed being under enemy fire, now that he could look back on such incidents from civilian sanctuary. He was a good old soldier as well as a generous, honest, and attentive surgeon. He had had many mistresses: one and all remembered him with enthusiasm.

When he thought of the Didiers at all (which was infrequently, except for thinking of his dear little friend Robert) he considered them as specimens fit to inhabit their own necropolis. Those birds and beasts had been collected by Louis Didier's much elder brother, a mean and effeminate consumptive who had been dead for years. Did Robert identify his own grandfather as a hoopoe bird? Then Pelacoy ticketed both Laurent and Louis Didier as a couple of vultures—one fat and one scrawny, but looking much alike nevertheless—who had hacked out their careers by pecking into the past and ignoring completely the charm of the present which was all around them—and never in God's world thinking of the future at all! How very unfortunate that the all-too-worldly parents of that charming Thérèse Berganty had married her off to Louis Didier, chiefly because he and his father had more rents coming in than they could well employ for any purpose beyond that of archaeology! They knew not how to live, love, wine, dine, laugh! . . . Still, Robert would not now be in existence if— Oh, well, why not shrug, and shake one's head, and chuckle about the whole dull matter?

Doctor Pelacoy held up an agile finger at Louis Didier, to warn him that he was interrupting. Then he turned and bent deliberately toward Robert.

And what was it you discovered yesterday, not far from Gigouzac?

Robert mumbled (conscious of his father's exasperation, which would be directed against him in no small way): I discovered a small squirrel, *Monsieur le Docteur*.

. . . No, no—he could not tell of his ideas about the concealed spring . . . and already he was calling it, to himself, the Mysterious Fresh Spring of the Jolly Young Elves . . . he could not venture a word of revelation, not with his father standing close: an alien presence, unsolicitous, uncomprehending.

Doctor Pelacoy let loose a guffaw. Hey! Was that all? Why, they're thick as cabbage butterflies along these walls! Well, what about your little squirrel? A very special one, no doubt. Pity you didn't have a pistol with you, now, wasn't it?

I—I shouldn't have wished to kill him, sir.

Not kill him? Ridiculous! How else could a *petit écureuil* be welcomed into that remarkable menagerie which was assembled by poor Emilion, your late uncle? Why, a live squirrel would play the very mischief in the Didier mansion! Pull out the magpies' tail feathers, carry off your father's potsherds, make musses under the bed—

I had planned to make a pet of him if I could catch him, sir, said Robert faintly, standing stooped and gaunt, with his Adam's apple showing.

The father took a cue from Pelacoy's bantering address. We'll have no squirrels in our house, Louis Didier declared shortly. Nuisance enough to have you, my dear son!

His chattering humorless laughter sounded stridently.

And now, Henri, if you will permit me to interject a few words unrelated to *more important matters, such as squirrels,* I have found, in this collection of folios written by the Abbé de Moustier, a lucid description of a similar specimen unearthed near Tarbes in Seventeen Hundred and Thirty-four—

Robert's face flamed in pain akin to hatred when his father spoke those words about, *Nuisance enough to have you;* although the remark verified his own constant opinion of his father's attitude toward him. The bitter blaze continued rankling inside, long after his face had cooled, and it was extinguished only by waters and wines and crisp cress salad of a generous luncheon. There were omelettes, sweetbreads with truffles, roast chicken. Robert was a healthy and voracious youngster if a thin one; Doctor Pelacoy rumbled on gleefully about his wolfish appetite, but all Louis Didier said was that the boy didn't eat like that at home, and must be showing off; and Grandfather could say nothing intelligible because he had his teeth out while eating.

Replete to the point of momentary stupidity, the youth was permitted to leave the table while his elders indulged in lengthy reminiscence over their coffee (rather, the doctor did the reminiscing, while the Didiers waited in impatience to resume their favorite and almost only topic of conversation). Robert stole as usual to his favorite room—now he designated it to himself as the Beloved Bishop Alain Room—and watched gardeners bending their backs across the wide lawn as they set out summer plants. . . . Why must some people always toil while others lazed for hours? . . . Gold must be the answer. . . . Yes, yes, to be sure: it was certainly a matter of the lack or the possession of gold. Doctor Pelacoy was well endowed, else he could never maintain this handsome well-kept château. And while Robert's own people lived in decrepitude, they must do that out of preference: they had gold. Each kept his own strongbox, and Robert had heard the solid jangle of coins thrust into little bags when rents were paid; and sometimes a lawyer and a banker both visited The Fortress simultaneously, and then there was talk of drafts, investments, Paris and London exchange.

Robert rose from the sainted chair abruptly, letting the cordial spell of the room fall from him like a discarded dressing gown. He could hear no longer a fancied encouraging murmur of ancient and generous voices, he could hear only his own hot ambitious breath. Gold came from the ground—from mines, from holes in the ground! Suppose he entered the cave, large or small, which lay beyond the cleft into which he had extended his pioneering arms on Sunday, and found a mine of gold! Would it not spell freedom and security, could he not with quickness take a man's place in the world instead of a child's? Assuredly!

It was as if he could hear his father sneering, feel his grandfather molesting him with astonished gaze.

—How was that, again, young fellow? You say you're off to new lands, fresh frontiers—that you now stand no longer enslaved to us—to Madame Paquet's pink shirts—to Latin, to Monsieur Lambert, to the recitation of Sanskrit—to Lynette's cold vegetables, and the hoopoe bird, and Uncle Emilion's entire collection, and—?

—I'm sorry, Father, but I must be gone!

—Outrageous! What do you mean? I'll take a cane to you! Just where, my ambitious young wanderer, do you think you're bound?

—Actually I hadn't yet decided. But I'm departing this very morning. Thank you very much—I shan't need André—I've engaged old Pierre Livernon to drive me to Cahors. There I shall take the express coach to Toulouse. From there— Actually, as I say, I haven't decided! Either Bordeaux or Marseille. I can't make up my mind whether it shall be North or South America. Some new place, I assure you. Whatever strikes my fancy!

—Sheer madness, do you hear me? Where's my stick—? I'll—

—I warn you, Papa, do not attempt to strike me again. Should you do so, I shall secure damages from you in a Court of Law.

—Ha-ha, listen to the infant! He talks of hiring lawyers when actually he hasn't a *sou!* Ha-ha—not a *sou—!*

The hand thrust behind him to lift negligently the bag which he had kept concealed all along.

—Is that the truth? Mockingly. . . . Not a *sou,* eh? Well, what do you call this? And this?

More bags. . . .

—And this? And this? . . . Actually, Father, I'm very well off. I have a great deal of gold in these bags, and I know where to obtain more whenever I wish. Where did I get it? Never mind! I didn't steal it—not out of your chest, nor Grandfather's, nor from any other place. If the truth must be known, I found a gold mine.

—*Au revoir,* Papa. I'll arrange to have appropriate New Year's gifts sent to you from—oh, Brazil, the war-torn Republic of Mexico— New York, New Orleans, Quebec—some such place—

—But, my dear son—

Tears now—false and undainty weeping— What, oh, what have we lost? they would be sobbing. It is the truth: he means it, he is going! Only look at the set of his jaw!

—But, our dear child—

—Farewell, Messieurs, farewell!

Regularly the boy hoped that some minor disaster would keep them overnight at Mercuès, as had occurred once when an axle cracked on the carriage. (André backed it into a wall just as they began the homeward journey.) This time Robert begged of Fate that they be not delayed for even an extra hour. He remained aloof, white-faced, and intent, perspiring even in this easy Maytime; and when summoned to the ceremony of leave-taking he was so mute and abstracted that the doctor insisted on taking his pulse, looking at his tongue and throat—and, finally, pinching Robert's nose. . . . Clouds tumbled from the west, grew leathery and cumbersome, began to leak rain. André struggled to put up the bent top of the carriage, with Robert trying to help, and getting his finger squashed, and being criticized. His grandfather lectured him as if he had sustained the injury purposely. It was raining with determination before they passed the village of Boissières, and horses and carriage had a slippery squeaking time of it as they labored along gullies to the northeast. But Robert might have been in the remote Mexico or Quebec of his imaginings as he sat with knotted muscles on the seat beside André. Even the stench of André's pipe, usually a gas to be avoided like a privy smell, was comfort and promise . . . Robert thought of a pick, a mattock, a narrow spade; he thought of the miner's lamp, and where was the oil kept? . . . Yes—Lynette filled household lamps in that passageway leading to the basement store-chamber; and Madame Paquet always unlocked the store-chambers as soon as she came ringing with keys from her room each morning. No chance of filling the lantern during a sly midnight sortie; but at least he could obtain the tools and have them ready.

Once at home, Robert made a gesture toward the sour soup and burned soufflé which followed it, then retreated to his own quarters. The Didiers were scarcely aware of his departure; they were deep in an argument concerning some Thracian lake dwellings described by Herodotus. The fire was dying on his hearth, mortally hurt by rain driving down the chimney, but the boy made no effort to dump dry fuel over the weak glow. He removed his shoes, flung himself upon the bed, lay twisted and alert beneath the covers until sounds had ceased belowstairs, and the elders were retired to lamplit drudgery in their respective studies. Then Robert scouted in stocking feet, found the coast clear; and within ten minutes had secured the essential tools and hidden them among drenched lilac bushes at a far corner of the lawn.

Robert did not yield in dread to the sepulchral atmosphere of the place; it was a balefulness long since grown familiar and so to be scorned. But even after he was safely returned to bed, and night-gowned for the vigil until next day, his mind went scooting up and down dark passageways like a rat.

Gold, now: that was the stuff for him, the solution to all puzzled miseries, the rope to lift him from this dungeon of existence. A good man might remain serene in comfort, as the admired Doctor Pelacoy did, or a bad man might repeat his vices with assurance. Take the wicked Sir Simon de Digue, for instance. He was a knight who stalked in legend wearing greasy armor and the countenance of a pig—reputedly he had built The Fortress, centuries before, as a retreat wherein he might give himself over to debaucheries. A pale little housemaid filled Robert's ears and his recollection with woeful stories concerning the evil once wrought within those walls. At first the boy had himself taken on paleness, and nightmares were a successive torment; but after the unfortunate maid was removed to her own home, and thence to a lunatic asylum, Robert had sense enough to conclude that her tales were the embroideries of a deranged fancy; and stanchly he no longer permitted the grotesque nobleman to inhabit his dreams.

. . . But, yes, Monsieur Robert, it is true! Far and wide he would range with his men-at-arms, gathering luckless boys and girls wherever he came across them. Then they would be chained, and carried back to this very château with their shirts stuffed into their mouths!

. . . Well, why didn't their parents call for— For soldiers?

The young woman crossed herself repeatedly, and was baffled for a moment, but only for a moment.

. . . Because, young Monsieur Robert, all the soldiers were in the pay of the evil Sir Simon de Digue! Then, once he had his victims within these very walls, they would never be seen again. Only their shrieks might be heard! No peasant could be found who dared to walk the road from Gigouzac to Ussel at night. The screams of those unfortunate prisoners would have driven any listener to madness!

. . . But—Cécile—what— What would he *do* to them?

. . . Ah, that you may well ask! It was so terrible that I cannot bring myself to tell you. I cannot! . . . Ah, very well then, if you must indeed listen to the horrifying story. . . . You see, Monsieur Robert, he fancied young girls the most! Young boys he would take—boys such as yourself—but only when he could find no girls. But when he had taken captive the girls— Ah, good God! He would remove all their clothing. I blush to tell it, but that is what Sir Simon de Digue would do. So, stripping off their petticoats, their very chemises and underpinning, he would chain them in a long row. In that dungeon at the base of the tower behind the kitchens, Monsieur—the one now used for a coalroom— That was the scene of his worst villainies! My God, what yells they would give— Often I have thought, since I came to service here, that I heard them wailing in the night! From one end of that row to the other he would stride, whip in hand. First a very thin small switch, as one might use, say, for a puppy. But he had a great store of whips—larger and larger—and these he would use in turn. First very small, the whips, you see. But steadily larger; until at last he would hold a huge lash made from— Made from— The hide of an elephant! Yes, that is logical, you see, for Sir Simon had been to the Holy Wars!

. . . But, Cécile, my father says that Sir Simon was thought so poorly of— Drunk most of the time, my father declares. He was thought so poorly of, by the Duke, that he was not permitted to join in the Crusades and thus never in fact did go to Palestine.

. . . Now, my dear young man, it is not proper for one like myself to question the knowledge of your good father, Monsieur Louis Didier, who has not only read but written books, and has been honored by the King! Nevertheless, the bloodstains are in that room *to this day*. I have seen them myself, before the coal was removed from baskets, before the stones were covered with coal dust. Blood, blood, everywhere— Great dried pools of it! And what, pray, except a whip of the elephant's hide, could draw so much blood from those poor soft white bodies? A young girl, after all, does not have too much blood within her. She needs take much care, therefore, each month when— But such subjects are not fit for your ears! You may be assured, however, that the huge whip was employed. And amid frightful screams and groans! . . . Are you certain that you have not heard their spirits hallooing in the night, even now? Are you *certain?* . . .

Robert's initial illusions on this May night (after finally he found slumber, for all his concentration on the marvelous exploit of the next day) were in fact concerned with Sir Simon de Digue again; but the monster became in Robert's version more of a buffoon than an ogre, and the boy laughed to see Sir Simon riding an elephant through the front gate of The Fortress, up the broad stone stairway, and into the hall where Uncle Emilion's exhibit wilted under the destruction of mites. Father and Grandfather retreated resentfully before Sir Simon, objecting with vehemence to the elephant's ever becoming a part of that collection. It is too big! they kept crying. It cannot possibly leave room for the hoopoe bird! . . . Oh, very well, retorted Sir Simon de Digue, I'll pay you in gold. Handsomely. . . . A great change ensued in their demeanor, and they exchanged sly glances. Ah, gold! Well, yes, that would put a different light on the matter. . . .

Robert chortled in his sleep with sufficient volume to awaken himself. He lay looking out into the night beyond his narrow bow-slit windows. He thought he heard a nightingale, rain or no rain, and lay remembering how he had listened to nightingales on that one occasion when he slept at the dear Château de Mercuès. . . . Did nightingales spout their music in South America, in Canada? He must look in a book. But this bird sounded like an extremely young nightingale; perhaps she was a friend of the frisking squirrel above the road to St. Denis, who had cleverly tricked Robert into the first phase of his adventure.

He lay aware of slumber coming back to wrap him; with each realization of its approach he was ready to spring into taut consciousness again. The war against sleep went on, finally the boy succumbed; but when aroused by a distant clatter and motion in the kitchen he was charged with wide-awake scheming. Shivering in anticipation he washed in icy water, dressed himself, and lay without boots under the blanket again, waiting through an elapsing year until Madame Paquet came fussily into her domestic world. There should be no more sleep for Robert, not this day (until he lay down once more to consider a mystery more profound than any ghost stories gushed by an ailing servant girl).

Restlessly he hung against the window or alternately listened at his corridor door until beyond mistake he heard Madame upbraiding the slovenly Lynette below. Then came the first grand hazard: spying from behind archways and out of closets, having the unperceiving Madame Paquet come so close that he could name the separate music of keys clustered at her belt, savoring an observation of the kitchen maid as she selected potatoes from a bin . . . her wide short skirts lifted, in her bending, sufficiently for flesh to be revealed above her knitted hose. . . .

Robert filched the lantern from its dusty cupboard shelf, filled it, wiped accumulated charcoal off the wick. He stole a slice of Viennese phosphorus matches; they were ready to split into convenient sections when you tore them from their wafer. He regained his room only a few jumps ahead of the maid who managed his tray. The youth leaped into bed, lantern and all, and drew the bedclothes up to his chin before she appeared in the doorway. He was short of breath with all this haste, but produced a fit of strangled coughing for the girl's benefit.

Are you ill, Monsieur Robert?

A trifle, he murmured languidly.

Yes, your face is red! Then you will not wish coffee, perhaps? . . . Melicent's sallow face brightened perceptibly as she planned to drink Robert's coffee on the way down, preferring it to the toasted grain coffee furnished to servants.

Oh, leave it, leave it, together with milk and bread. I may have the strength to take some breakfast before long. But my stomach is badly upset! Will you be so good as to request *Monsieur le Précepteur* to come to my room, when he is ready for the day?

The disappointed Melicent withdrew, and M. Amboise Lambert came to the room a half-hour later. Robert made good the time by disposing of both lantern and breakfast; he massaged his face into renewed redness, and practiced a sickroom whisper.

You are indeed ill, Robert? queried Monsieur Lambert with satisfaction. He hoped that the boy was suffering.

Robert loathed everything about his tutor: the irritable girlish voice, the deerlike eyes, the fat lips, the way Lambert's long hair hung in pasty separate strands. The hair was of that empty color somewhere between native blondness and the encroaching dead hue of a premature whitening. The tutor reciprocated cordially his pupil's hostility; although he had tried to fawn over him, when first Lambert came to the home several years before. M. Lambert had not been in his new post five days when he sought to fondle Robert indecently. The boy happened to be holding an iron stove-shaker at the time, and he dropped this implement upon M. Lambert's carpet-slippered toes. . . . Robert never even considered reporting the incident to his father. He regarded his father neither as a source of encouragement nor protection. A weaker child might have shriveled beneath the neglect which Robert Didier endured stoically all the way up from infancy; as for Robert, he only shrugged in his green soul, and accepted with fatalism the knowledge that he must fight his own battles—whether against vipers in the shrubbery, bad dreams, nettles, bullies encountered in the village, or lecherously inclined tutors. . . . M. Lambert limped for weeks; he was compelled to soak his swollen foot in hot water at odd hours. Likely the boy had succeeded in fracturing a bone or two in his adroit defense.

Amboise Lambert was afraid to flog him, dreading the eventual retaliation not of a parent but of the pupil himself. Since Lambert had been dismissed summarily from several posts in the recent past, he was compelled to regard his present situation as a sinecure, and did not wish to be separated from it (he was poor as a grasshopper). He revenged himself through season after season by laying out inordinate schedules of Greek and Latin, and introducing the Vedic demands partly as a deliberate act of mayhem against the boy's spirit, and partly to make himself appear more erudite, and favored resultingly in the eyes of his employer. . . .

Thank you, sir, whispered Robert, although there was no reason why the tutor should be thanked. I'm afraid that my stomach is severely upset. The luncheon was rich, at the Château de Mercuès—

And you overindulged. How perfectly dreadful of you! I heard your grandfather mentioning it on his return last evening!

Robert tried to look both humble and ashamed.

One holiday on Monday, and now in your sick condition you will claim another today! This is no way in which to achieve culture!

I am seldom ill, Monsieur.

Well, I'll admit *that!* But also you are very seldom willing to apply yourself as a good student should! When the time comes for you to enter the university, just how do you think you'll fare, my good fellow?

I'll make up for this by working doubly hard tomorrow, replied Robert, who had no intention of doing anything of the kind.

—What? I can't believe it. You've found gold, in a mine? Oh, Robert, please to share your good fortune with me!

—Not one scrap, Monsieur Lambert! Not one nugget, not one flake of the precious metal will I give you. That is final!

—Oh, my admired Robert, please to reconsider! Just a wee sack of the leftover gold dust, perhaps? A tiny sackful, which you won't really need—?

Tears and spasms—spouting, disgusting, stomach-turning, womanish tears.

—Oh, please, Robert! Only a crumb— The veriest fragment?

—Never!

No reason why you can't study while you lie abed, you know!

My head is aching. . . . I suppose, Monsieur, that you'll be off to the waters of the Vert? How I wish that I were well enough to accompany you! lied Robert.

Well, you're forever twitting me about my lack of success with the trout; but I'll have you know that I took four fish yesterday! Lambert tossed his head, the stringy locks flew, he smoothed them down with a pudgy hand.

They were small trout, of course. But they made a lovely supper for Hilaire, the artist who is drawing for your father, and myself. We dined, long before your late return from Mercuès—

Hilaire seems such a dear fellow, said Robert's weak voice.

Lambert whirled and gave him a look of pained fury, suspecting mockery. But Robert tried to appear only debilitated, and thus tolerant of all human frailty. . . . The tutor adjured him to study; Robert countered by pleading that he might take a walk—a very limited walk, later, in open air, if his condition improved. The tutor marked out a section in *Cicero's Orations* which he had brought with him, and ordered Robert to have it translated correctly as a stint which he might well perform in bed. It was not a day's work, not by any means, but this act served to emphasize authority. Then Lambert tossed his head, gave all the glare which his lustrous eyes would permit, and went flouncing off to examine his fishing tackle and to mend the lid of his old creel. . . . Robert had the Latin translated within twenty minutes of his departure; it seemed that he had never worked so rapidly or with such skill. Ponderous phrases fairly sang and scintillated, brightening into life, bedizening the French in which they were now dressed.

Again the youth clung at the slot of the south window, waiting for Lambert to go about his fishing. Finally he saw the tutor trotting down the driveway and turning left in the direction of Ussel. That meant that he would be fishing in upstream waters of the Vert—not farther down, where the shallow river ran only a meadow's breadth away from the Hillside of the Guiding Squirrel and its urgent cavern.

There was no peril of encountering Father and Grandfather: neither of the elders ever rose before ten. All their lives they had burned midnight candles, midnight oil; the bulk of their historic labors was achieved in bat-haunted gloom. . . . There was little reason for the servants to get about their business as early as they did in this slovenly ménage; but Madame Paquet was country-born and country-bred, and to her daylight was a sacred thing: she had everybody up and doing by six o'clock in this season. Now Lynette and the maids wrangled about some missing dish towels, Madame was counting linen religiously before stowing it in cupboards, André was busy at the stable with a fork. Within bare minutes after Lambert's departure, Robert stood in the lilac brake, lantern dangling from his belt, as he tried to decide about the purloined tools. In the end he took but two—a crowbar, and a short-handled hoe with a thick wide blade, to serve as combination pick and shovel. Any heavier load than this would have him staggering when he climbed that wooded hill. And he must reserve a sufficient allotment of his strength for the homeward trip. Gold was said to be very heavy.

(By this time Robert Didier did not reasonably doubt that he would discover gold this day.)

Rain had stopped before dawn, but its lingering chill was condensed into mist which still touched the face as one walked abroad. The sky was a gray rag—it looked like the rags with which Lynette wiped out the cooking pots. A cleaner fairer fog fastened itself in layers above each hollow of the hills, and traced in a separate cold leisurely ribbon to mark the course of the Vert. Through this mystic curling milk of wild vapors the forests studded out in strength as one came close to the trees, then fell into dripping anonymity behind, as their greenness was submerged. Robert trod on paths within the confines of the château park until he had reached the last long-breached wall; he made his way carefully through the gap, avoiding wiry spurs of blackberry which reached out farther each springtime week; and he came to a shrine poised at the bottom of the cart road.

It was not a pretentious shrine—only a cross of ragged brown rust thrusting up from graduated stone blocks where the moss was padded with coral fruit and flowers. Once there had been Virgin and Child appliquéd against the ironwork, but these figures were eaten away by corrosion. A portion of the Virgin's robe was still extant, and one foot of the Child. Robert paused in sincerity, put down his crowbar and hoe, and said a prayer. He was aware that his lips barely moved, and that the muttered syllables tumbled within mouth and throat; he was praying just the same, in heart and spirit.

. . . I have lied, and will confess freely when I am with *Monsieur le Curé* again. Please, dear Holy Mother, forgive me for my lies; they were most necessary. Help me to find the Mysterious Fresh Spring of the Jolly Young Elves. I wish it for my own! But most of all, help me to find gold, for gold means manhood and freedom. Should I find it, I swear to give a generous portion to the Church. I might— I might even erect a new shrine. Here, on this spot! The rusty iron is a humiliation, and I shall replace it—and you, dear Holy Mother and Infant—with marble.

Silently the youth wiped his sweating forehead with his cap, put on his cap, picked up his tools, and went down the road to Gigouzac, and through that scattered village of stone houses, tavern, church, and mill. He met only Grandmother Durban, and later two peasants driving oxen to the fields. Grandmother Durban was reputed by the vanished Cécile to be a witch, because she had a crinkled face and black mustache; but Robert felt that this was nonsense. If Grandmother Durban's cherry trees bore their fruit earlier than any other trees in the vicinity, it was because they were of an early-bearing variety; and even the jealous André (whose cherries were forever falling prey to flies and mildew) said the same thing. Grandmother carried a basket of cherries now, bound to sell them to the tavern-keeper, but her dark face rippled and her fangs showed when she recognized Robert.

A holiday, young sir? But why the hoe? Is the youngest Didier to become a tiller of the soil?

Just a bit of digging for—for my father, *Grandmère*. He digs—you know, frequently—for scientific purposes.

Ah, yes, I know. The science of history and bones! . . . Let me offer you a *cerise*, young sir. They are so sweet!

Oh, thank you, *Grandmère*, but— Well, then, just a couple—

Take this handful.

Oh, but— Please—

You see how very good they are? The best! But take care; do not swallow too fast; do not swallow the *noyau de cerise*, or you'll wake up to find a cherry tree growing inside you! . . .

Robert thanked the woman, and hurried past her. He was acutely conscious of having not a *sou* to his name, just as his father twitted him in imagined encounter. But at New Year's he had been awarded gifts of coin from his kin and from Doctor Pelacoy (the latter gave most generously), and in that week Robert had presented Grandmother Durban a silver franc. So—

Gigouzac flowed tenderly into fog behind him. As he passed the last blank-walled barn he was almost running. An absurd notion lurked to taunt him: a fear that the discovery of the hole had been but an illusion—something imagined two days previously, but ready to blast him, once he arrived at the spot, by its nonexistence.

All Robert's life he had been twitted about daydreaming. He admitted to himself that he daydreamed more than he should have done: undoubtedly his path would have been smoother through recent years, where elders were concerned, if he had curbed this propensity for vain imagination. Had he made a great noise of industry instead (whether truly industrious or not) he might have tricked his tutor into withholding spiteful criticism, and his father into less frequent application of the rod. Actually Robert was grown too tall now to accept corporal punishment with grace; it had been a full year since the cane bruised him, though sometimes Louis Didier still made threatening gestures. . . . The boy remembered with clarity an earlier incident; it occurred three summers before, when he was only eleven. He'd come past a corner of the estate—on the edge of a copse opposite the shrine, it was—and found a party of gypsies preparing to settle down. Covered carts seemed bursting with these nomads: they were an abusive menace with their matted hair and snot-nosed children and peevish dogs. When Robert ventured the assertion that they must not squat there, the women flocked toward him with curses, and he was positive that one of the men brandished a knife. Robert dashed for the château as fast he as could leg it. Was it not a common assertion that gypsies kidnaped children and drained their blood to drink?— Old folks in the village swore to the fact. The boy blundered into a conference in the library where his father and grandfather were closeted with their estate agent from Dijon, and mouthed out his story of alarm and pursuit (by this time he was certain that he had heard male gypsies thundering after him all the way up to The Fortress's gate).

Your story is absurd! Monsieur Marnay came up the road only an hour ago, and he has reported no gypsies. Did you observe any such rascals, Monsieur?

Not a gypsy, said M. Marnay, rolling up his eyes.

You see? By my soul, Robert, I'll beat you for this!

But they're *there,* Father! Just now! I saw them! They had knives— You come—bring André with his gun— You'll soon see them encamped—

Encamped? Of course, Monsieur, they could have moved in immediately after you passed by—

That is possible, agreed Marnay; and even Grandfather nodded his head, and chirped an excoriation. Gypsies were abominated by the Didiers. Once the archaeologists had lost all the tools which they left at a tumulus they were excavating—gypsies carried off the implements during lunchtime. And chickens had been stolen, berry bushes stripped— Linen from the grass, harness from the stable—

Robert declared on his soul that he had seen tents and kettles and at least fifty armed ruffians. (By this time he believed honestly that he had witnessed such an assemblage.) Soon his father left off doubting—such was the vivid force of Robert's bloodcurdling tale—and a punitive expedition was formed. Pistols were fetched and primed, André loaded his shotgun, and even M. Marnay armed himself with the sword cane which Louis Didier had carried when he visited Egypt. They all went babbling down the lane, with M. Lambert and the household staff drifting well to the rear, although Lynette did carry along a pitcher of hot water to throw at the despised *gitanes.* The white-faced Robert was a willing guide; he led them to the exact spot and they found— Exactly nothing. Gypsies were fled—dogs, caravan, filthy babies, knives, and all. In vain Robert pointed out some stray wheel-crushings in the grass and a heap of wet mule manure; no one believed his story. Snarlingly his farther demanded that he produce the abandoned campfires (his naughty imagination, again: he'd been so carried away by the encounter that actually he'd sworn to fires and smoke) but by this time Robert dared only hang his head, and sniffle. Louis Didier lost his temper and reason along with it. Ordinarily he might have had the decency to punish Robert in private; now he had no control whatsoever, could not speak a coherent word, could only mouth and drool in fury. He broke a limb from a thorny hedgerow, and some of the thorns were still on the branch as he applied it to his son. Servants fled from the scene; but Lambert remained to watch. Robert could remember seeing the tutor (he was fairly new in the household then) staring with his doe's eyes, with fat lips apart— He could see the tutor glutting himself with a sensual joy at the obscene thrashing. It was the little ferret-faced M. Marnay (an utter stranger to Robert, but bless his soul!) who finally prevailed upon Louis Didier to desist.

So the unholy overactive imagination of Robert had stimulated him into miseries before, and might have done so again in a new fashion. Rocks, narrow rotten ledges, alluring emptiness of space inside the hole: were these to be trusted, even in hardy recollection? Sweating mildly at the outset, the boy was hot and drenched—his shirt stuck to his ribs as he labored up that solitary tilted grove above the St. Denis road.

Ah, now—it couldn't be this far— No squirrel had ever shepherded him on such endless mountain climbing—

Just as despair collapsed his limbs, the boy's heart swelled and shook. There it was, there it was—barely beyond those young fig trees and blackberry tangles!—the disparted cairn, scattered whitish stones—lichens scabrous where they'd been scraped— And the hole, the precious small aperture, as black as if the air inside it was a tar.

Rain had washed loose dirt around the cranny, but Robert plunged glorifying hands into this mud and flung the stuff about exultantly until he'd scooped out the same clearance as of two days before. He lay on his belly for a gratifying scrutiny, rolled over with a wriggle; then arose, and stubbornly controlled himself to the task. But he felt like dancing!

His swollen finger, pinched between the carriage stays, bothered him not at all. It took him only fifteen minutes to hack out enough crumbling limestone to assure an easy entry. Layers were decayed, weakened by roots and erosion (the youth learned, after truly he stood inside the hill, that portions of the exterior facing had caved in of their own accord. The place might have attracted attention of hunters or woodcutters long before this, had it not been for the protecting heap of looser debris above). He regretted that he'd neglected to provide himself with a knife, but the blade of the hoe was made to serve. He worried a straight young sapling from its base, cleaned off the twigs, and bent the stick through the hole in order to measure the distance. There existed a floor at a depth of only a couple of meters or less—a floor wide and solid enough for him to stand upon. He banged around the whole area with the sapling's tip. Surely he might drop into the cave with confidence.

Robert started to slide backward through the hole, then snaked promptly out again. His lantern . . . there in the green misty gloom of early morning he lit the wick with his very first match: this in itself seemed a good omen. It occurred to Robert also that he might need some sort of tool or weapon, and wisely he set crowbar, hoe, and lamp in positions where he could reach them with his long arm from within. He said a brief prayer. Tears afflicted his eyes, he winked the tears away; and his heart was a vociferous companion inside his chest.

The boy shoved himself backward into the opening. He felt power of an immense secrecy reaching up—a drapery of darkness and secrecy—and he was sliding into it with petition and weeping and a bursting soul. His shoes found solid anchorage upon the earth and rocks already accumulated. He thanked God; he reached a shaking hand through the crevice to drag in the lighted lantern.

He turned, and a wet voice trilled to meet him in welcome. The Mysterious Fresh Spring of the Jolly Young Elves: here it was, a reality; and seldom ever had Robert's longings become realities.

But the spring dwelt here amid several drooping stalactites, on the farther limit of this narrow kennel, and its droplets sputtered in irregular music—a very faint melody, even as one moved closer. But it was wet talk, cavern talk. Robert's dream stood achieved. He would be the first to drink here. Not even the wildest serf-collared woodsmen of rustic centuries had ever stood where he was standing! The youth knew beyond question that he was in a holy place; it whispered and trickled of purity.

With light held high, he took several cautious steps across the area.

Nearer the moisture and stalactites and misshapen deposits which grew up to meet them, he learned that the surface was uncluttered: there were no more platters of stone, no accumulation of drifted clay underfoot. He stood as on a flagged floor. With devotion Robert bent his head and twisted his neck beneath the fitful spatter, to observe the rite of his first drinking. Some drops came down to touch his face, one globule raced into his eye and stung it momentarily; but he did accept a bit of water in his mouth. He swallowed, and could feel the cool few drops mingling with fluids already in his body—vanishing, dissolving there—and he gave gratitude.

O spring, O my own spring, I thank you. . . .

Now for the gold. Hurrah!

A cleft ran past the stalactites and curved upward between two shouldering masses of pale porous stone. Robert marched onward with the lantern guiding. He could hear no sound, as the rare musical note of the spring fell away, but the slam of his excited heart. He thought of hiding . . . he had hidden in the dark when a child, shut himself into a great cupboard among hanging clothes, listened to voices calling in search of him . . . but here there were no clothes, no tread of other feet along the ramp which led up and out and far into unplumbed wilderness space.

. . . He stood at the mouth or doorway of a distorted room. No other water trickled to spread its salts. The place seemed arid as a piece of toast, the swollen walls were of the tint and texture of toast, beaded with calcite.

Robert shifted his lantern, its glow wavered toward the wall farthest from him. He saw—

He gasped, stumbled closer. The thing he saw was a head, an embellishment of a deer's head and neck. Antlers and—

And what was this, of another color, streaming off over a rounded cornice beyond the deer? Another drawing or painting blended with the first. A buffalo. Or—

Rabidly he flourished the lantern. They were crowding him, up and down and all around, a galaxy of animals, all sizes, shapes, varieties.

Agony, agony—!

Boys from the village must have been here, gaining entrance doubtless through some connected hole elsewhere on the hill; and they had come equipped with paints and brushes.

They had chosen to deface these pocked surfaces in the same riotous version of spite which caused people to carve *Raoul et Marie 1838* on a pillar outside a cathedral . . . *J. LeBon 8 août 1827* scratched with a diamond ring on the leaded window of a palace chamber . . . the horde of petty Charleses and Célestes and Jeans and Marcels and Blanches who had nothing to offer to the past but a jeer, nothing to offer to unprovoked nature but a defacement. They were undistinguished, insensitive, contemptible; but they were assertive in spite of their triviality (or maybe because of it) and so chose to cut and pick and smear wherever they went on their Sunday strolling; and they wished not to honor a dignity or a purity, wished only to mar these beauties in the disgraceful present; and had nothing to award the disgraced future but their own worthless names!

Robert swung the lantern shaft back and forth, faced it up and down, found always the same: more deer, more bears, more oxen, wearing colors of tan, rufous, mustard, grays, and jets of charcoal. Hadn't those village children any blues or greens or crimsons in their nasty little paintboxes?

. . . And I'd supposed I was the first person to step within these channels, the very first!

Robert lamented . . . O silly boys! Go swabbing at the wall behind the *église* if you must, and just let the priest catch you at it!— Or let *Monsieur le Maire* observe you in the act of daubing on the stones of the community well; and you'll be thrashed appropriately for your trouble!

But why didn't you stay out of here; why was it necessary for you to defile my cave?

Solemnly the water dripped at the lower spring, but Robert was too far removed to hear it. Solemnly this darkness of the vault awaited the cessation of his lantern light. There was no dampness—only a moderate coolness, and an austere quiet which exaggerated the weight of the hill overhead—made it into lead, lead, lead—a mountainous chunk of impervious metal, cast in a volcanic crucible larger than the whole of France or the European continent; poured out to congeal and then to cool, and then to remain rigid—cast permanently like shapeless armor which disliked the sun, welcomed only darkness.

And the darkness said: I too am Silence.

And the silence said: I too am Darkness. I wait, I wait, I stand waiting, sit waiting, lie waiting. I am waiting whether awake or asleep.

Both the silence and the darkness said: We are A Thing Called Waiting.

. . . *No, no. Oh, no!*

. . . Let me out, let me emerge from here—rise like a swallow from its hole—let me shoot up and out, never come back.

. . . Who is present? I'll call the roll. Answer, please, when your name is called. Say: Here! Say only that.

. . . Village boys, with ornate boxes put together by Swiss toymakers, German toymakers—bought by a doting aunt at a price she could ill afford, perhaps, and sent by coach-express from Dijon. Red, yellow, blue, black, and white: stir them tenderly, little Francois, little René. You'll contrive a rufous and a mustard and the charcoal tints as well; only those, only those; mix your primary hues skillfully, and now you can make a bison!

. . . Ah, let me gibber at my own stupidity! Village boys, indeed!

. . . No one has been here! No one, no one, no one. Only myself. I am here now, and here alone.

. . . My God, it's all around me! Do you know what I just saw, you unyielding Thing Called Waiting? Do you know, did you feel, did you see it too? A Chinese horse!

. . . And bison, whole brigades of bison, sprawling and dancing and galloping, superimposed upon the backs and horns of other spirited ruminants— Ho, ho! That's what Father would call them: ruminants. They are free scampering herds, with arrows or spears or lances being hurled at them, and dodging the projectile points— Ho, ho, Grandfather! Projectile points—I know your lingo all too well! I've seen you and Papa, scraping and checking and weighing and measuring and conjuring and conjecturing with your damnable fragments of bone— I've seen you do it, my whole life long.

. . . Yes, I said it, I mean it. My whole life long! How long is my life? Not yet fifteen years! And I know what I've been told, and what I've heard.

. . . I just saw a woolly rhinoceros. Do you realize what I'm saying? No village boy ever heard of a woolly rhinoceros, much less saw a picture of one. But I've seen them until I couldn't wish to consider them more—seen them with their two horns and their wall-divided nostrils and their short legs and their coated chunky bodies, seen them in your wretched old books and folios, O revered Sire and Grandsire—

. . . And there hasn't been a woolly rhinoceros in France for the past twenty thousand years.

. . . *Twenty thousand years.*

Robert lunged forward. He lived in fear not of the monsters, but truly of himself. He feared himself: because there must be some remarkable horror in his nature which had caused the gods (judging that they were just, as gods must inevitably be) to condemn him to such discovery.

I, of all people! he sought to scream. And he did make some squirrel-like chatter which went off into magnifying and repetition through laden canyons until his ears received the final blast as a stuttering whoop.

He thought that a dozen tribes of squat men were spying on him from suspended platforms. They ran along, barefoot or in hide sandals, to keep him company; and then he knew that the march of all their feet was merely the march of his own feet, echoing along a fissure of the world where no other footsteps had sounded since the last cave artist extinguished his torches, wrapped up his ochers in a skin, and carried them into Paleolithic dawn. . . .

A sloe-eyed black bull extended as a bull in life, its hoofs lifted to paw you, its horns curved to make a vicious welcome . . . what was that leggèd fragment in its path, now being trampled to bits? . . . A man who'd sought to combat the bull? And half a yellow cow, a good four meters in length, with her forefeet buried in a horse's flank, her tail traced across a bison's jaw. The stags were lumbering as mastodons or tiny as rats; they circled with bears and rabbit-sized steeds along each jutting precipice, around each scroll of grainy rock. They pirouetted on the ceiling, said Farewell with a devilish twist of their antler tips as they went herding out of sight into some blacker chancel where the miner's lamp could never follow.

Goat, calf, lion, boar, and one sad bird to watch them at their slaughter. . . .

Robert Didier tripped over a stony seam and fell forward with arms thrown out instinctively to break his fall. The lantern flew, its light swept muddled across walls and roof before the boy's startled stare, and as he sprawled he waited for the burst of glass which did not come. He heard a clink, rattle and rolling; then, surrounded by pitchy nothingness, he smelled spilled oil. No longer did he bear a light.

The lantern might still be in repair, could he but find it.

He lay nearly motionless. He did not know how long he was wadded on the cavern's floor—could never guess at what passage of time might have ensued, when later he summoned this moment into memory.

. . . I too am Darkness.

. . . Yea, and Waiting.

. . . Don't forget dear Silence! (That was what Silence said to this mingled entity which was Itself and the Others.)

. . . Oh, please to tell me where do I come in? A mere mortal like myself, wearing flesh, and feeling a burn on my sore knee when I wet my finger with saliva and touch it to the skin beneath my torn clothing— Where do I come in? I am Robert Didier—

. . . We don't care who you are. Nobody asked you to come in!

. . . But— The *petit écureuil?* I meant only to take him as a friend, as a pet; I meant no harm to him nor to any animal. Oh, you nations of buffalo and great fierce pigs, and bulls with feet upraised to strike— Don't gore or trample me, I beg you! I did not attempt to slay the squirrel, had no intention of doing such a thing! Why, why— Animals are my friends. I love them dearly. Rougette and the puppies and— And Prince and Marguerite, our team of horses. There was Captain, of course, but he is long dead. . . . Oh, my *God.* Is he *here?*— Is Captain *here,* with the rest of you?

. . . Robert. You were selfish?

. . . Yes.

. . . Avaricious?

. . . But yes.

. . . You lied?

. . . I stand guilty.

. . . Gold, gold, gold! That's all you wanted, like any cheap robber in a ballad. Already you have become morally contaminated by your cupidity. No more morals than that precious Sir Simon de Digue! . . .

Whisper it . . . their stark laughter . . . let it not come too loud, for twill start an echo; and echoes are conversations to be avoided in this place of all places.

. . . The Satanic Trinity, our Trinity— Darkness and Silence and Waiting—we are old. Much older than Laurent Didier, for instance: why, he's but an unblemished raindrop fresh-formed by clouds, and coasting down the cheek of a cherry in Grandmère Durban's garden! . . . You think the Revolution is an Old Thing, a good half century in the past, and more? Twas an hour ago! No, no—fifteen minutes ago—a scant tick of Doctor Pelacoy's great watch. And that time when the dear doctor let you wind it, when you wore dresses still— That was but half a tick ago. . . . And Sissy Lambert and his infernal Latin and Greek! Why, the Romans and Pericles and Herodotus and Alcibiades and all that crowd— They're worthless acolytes milling around our altar, mere stableboys to our herds! We might let 'em scrape out the fresh manure of a morning, should you feel that they're tall enough to accept the responsibility! A challenging responsibility, you understand: to clean up after a rhinoceros who pushed his way through the weeds hereabouts when these cracks and precipices were fresh off the geological shelves—when the hills had still their price marks chalked on 'em, so to speak!

. . . Who was Catherine, who was Richelieu, who were the Louis'? Upstarts, the whole lot—pretenders to antiquity, the *nouveau riche* of historical record, with scandals as fresh as a newly hatched wren's appetite!

. . . Go beyond Moors and Goths. Discard Hun and Vandal, Phoenician and Carthaginian . . . Scipio is a *garçon* just ready to meet his schoolmaster for the first time, and Hannibal is an apprentice before the turning-lathe! Go beyond those talayots of the Mediterranean isles that Laurent and Louis Didier are always prattling about— Why, we were lame and gray-bearded, lurching under impact of our years, before those hollow beehives were heaped together!

. . . We are Waiting.

By all that is holy, by all that is timeless, by all that is a force of God or devil, I must find my lamp!

Robert assorted his thought, piled it together, made a strong bundle of thought as one would tie faggots together. Nights of the cavern (twenty thousand years of nights) were bundled also, swathed around one another in the same fashion; and these nights swaddled Robert until it was not a simple struggle of eyes endeavoring to pierce and shape the howling dark: it was blindness.

Quite blind, forever and irredeemably blind, he let hand go seeking pocket, let fingers find the mischievous matches (same kind of modern matches, wicked Austrian things: he'd calmly set fire to his own house, when he was three or four or so, and saw matches employed for the first time—and he stole matches, and managed to kindle a blaze in the library . . . how Madame came shrieking, and Babette the nurse! There was a great brown-edged hole in the rug to this day). He let his fingers stray also amid crushed folds of cloth until they closed on the scrap of striking paper.

Once more he was armed against the impress of Eternity.

A first match showed nothing except hollowness and shadows distorted, shadows writhing to assault the gaze; and the fierce illumination was a stab through the boy's eyes and into his skull. But he persisted, struck another light, another. Each time he went floundering ahead. The lantern had tumbled somewhere beyond that bundled-up ridge which tripped his feet. In spicy stink of the fourth popping he saw a faint gleam of glass and tin.

He found the lantern. Through intermittent darkness again, Robert fondled the instrument, felt it all over, smelled it, shook it. Much oil had run out; there was still a splashing in the tank however. Robert loosened his shirt, extended the sleeve, wiped the lantern thoroughly to guard against explosion. With care he placed the thing on a flat table of rock, opened the little door, and ripped another match against the card (only a slender morsel of the phosphorous sticks left to him now). A sparkling, an oily reek; then an infant coal crawling the soaked wick . . . coal lengthened, erected suddenly a sprout of gold . . . it burst, hissed, widened. The boy caught his breath. But he needed to worry no longer: flame had gripped the wick, it lived. He might carry Blessed Light with him now, if he did not linger in this insane stock pen until the fuel was exhausted.

He stood, venturing no further, but turning the beam on a circuit to make a final reckoning before his retreat.

The main duct of the higher cave—the second story, so to speak—was in some places nearly as wide as the carriage lane which led from boundary gates at the Didier château; in some places much narrower. Floor, swelling or receding walls, ceiling with rippled hollows and bulges—all were a compress of the same pale crystalline-cheeked stone; and the few stalactitic formations did not disturb or alter that mural riot . . . stalactites had dripped and dried before ever artists appeared on the scene. . . .

Once a great moth swept at night into the Didier house. The men had laughed with scoffing at what they called the hunter's frenzy of young Robert, who groped and galloped to catch this pulsating creature (but again it was not because he desired to slay the thing; he only wanted to make intimate contact with such beauty—wanted to make a jewelry and a pet of beauty). And that moth displayed on its patterned wings the very colors which Robert now saw repeated in layered confusion, loping off into vistas where his feeble lantern could not go spearing after them. The same russet, the same grays, the same areas of palest mustard or lemon; and always that pronounced edging of charcoal black, the blot of charcoal black.

Did this constitute a worship, a necromancy, or an incitement to the chase?

No matter!

Robert spoke the two words in a low voice. The echoes of his words built up into a quick chatter of conversation, then fell and died. But no longer did he stand fearful before busy echoes. His temporary immurement in dark, frightening as it might have been, had given him a kinship, an identity with buck and doe and capering buffalo and extinct horse and flat-headed bear—a cousinship with their creators, so long unspeaking in the oldest dust of all.

The artesian force of youth came bursting through body and soul. With rapture Robert fought to stifle an unintelligible halloo which tussled in his throat . . . if uttered, that shriek of ecstasy would go striking off into the labyrinth beyond, and return bellowing like a mob, to claim his last wit and sense of hearing.

He'd thought he hated the past, he had sought to wrestle loose from its dead vines!

And all the time he'd hated only his father and grandfather—their magpie activity, their conceit, their utter oblivion to the ringing fascination of today's existence. They found Robert's presence in their life a bore, an annoyance, a thing unpalatable; he was a spider scuttling over their dingy counterpane, so they put their thumbs upon him; he was a mouse, and so they called *Minet! Minet!* to the cat; he was an imp, they sought to exorcise him.

But the past was not that desiccated cadaver which the Didiers declared it to be by act and attitude. It was A Thing Called Waiting; here in this tinted channel Robert had learned the truth. It was A Thing Called Waiting, which halted stoically until you stood ready to summon it; and then it emerged with grumble of bison and baying of wild mules, and the bawling of hunters who went down to death before them.

. . . Robert had one bad moment when painstakingly he had retreated down into the Room of the Mysterious Fresh Spring. He thought that someone must have crept on the outside of the hill and entombed him—someone (in dreadful inversion of an Easter lesson) had repiled the stones above his sepulcher. But it was only that fog thickened over the whole area; the aperture of the entrance showed brown instead of bright. The boy mounted his heap of fallen slabs—the inside stairway, so to speak—and put his face into the young outer world. He was familiar with this blank phenomenon which occurred often in this part of France, especially when seasons were changing: a quick alteration of temperature; condensation; all moisture becoming a cool solid steam—the trees who'd known each other for ten years or a hundred, appearing as strangers now, and drawing apart and barely speaking—the few birds who spoke sounding like musical little alarmists, in a tizzy about the whole business.

He wished that he might know the time of day; then rejected the thought as rapidly as it appeared to him. What was a given hour or a given day, when one had stood stricken with the awareness of twenty millennia? And when one (an obscure weakling, a scrawny Infant in the Eyes of the Law, a Nobody even to tutor and kin) understood that he had been set apart, favored, knighted, crowned—? Endowed with an experience, and its resulting perception, which had befallen no other human of his age or planet?

He knew things they didn't know in the *Académie*, had seen things which no *Académicien* might ever see, were it not for the will and graciousness of Robert Didier. He was so young that the memory of his first sexual gratification (managed at night in his bed, with an illusion of a short-skirted maidservant before his panting face) still haunted him as a recent and cardinal sin. Yet he owned no impulse to caper across the face of his nation or across all nations, boasting ruthlessly as he went.

Robert was awed into a humility of holiness.

Not for the fraction of an instant did he consider keeping his secret from Louis and Laurent Didier. They were his people. Petulant, selfishly critical, downright vicious as the one might be—and selfishly oblivious as the other might be—they were his parent and grandparent; it was right and righteous that they should be the first to know. After all, Robert himself could not go posting northward to claim an audience at the Tuileries, nor could he hustle off to Rome and the Pope's chamber. It would remain for the elder Didiers to perform these rewarding chores.

Their names would be spread—not only in scientific journals and privately printed folios—but throughout the active press of all continents. In England, Germany, America, intelligent men would knot together and say, The Didiers? Ah, yes, those Frenchmen who discovered the cavern filled with ancient paintings! Or rather it was the boy who discovered the cavern—but of course he was young, and only through the teaching of his people did he know the truth when he saw it graven before his eyes! Ah, yes—I hear that there's quite a mob at Gigouzac these days. The roads are choked with carriages, and they've got a new coach line set up, direct through Bergerac from Bordeaux. We ourselves intend to go, next summer, sailing to Bordeaux. We're getting up a party, here at the University. Should you care to accompany us? It must be arranged well in advance, you see— Each party of foreign pilgrims has to wait its turn—

As this elaboration extended in heaving talkative pageant, Robert entertained suddenly another thought; entertained was scarcely the word, the notion spat flashing into his brain. He wrenched out of the opening, stood trembling aimlessly, then blew out the lantern he'd shoved ahead of him. He dropped the lantern and sprang away past the gouged rocks, and made precipitous haste down the slope through fog. He was conscious of his knee's soreness, where he'd fallen in the cave; the knee slowed his speed, he could not travel as rapidly as he wished. Robert was looking wildly about him through the mist, peering this way and that, turning completely around every now and then; and then striking off in a loose pained gallop once more. Any stranger, seeing him, would have thought him grown unaccountably crazed, but he was in serious purpose. He was searching for a boundary marker.

At last he discovered the gladdening little turret, half hidden by a growth of furze outside an elongated moss-wrapped mound which was all that remained of an old wall. Robert knelt beside the heap, examined it, rubbed his fingers over the top white-washed stone in thankful intimacy. He looked back up the hill, and gulped with thanksgiving. Yes, yes, he knew this marker—had seen it many times; and unless he was gravely mistaken there were two others like it farther along the road toward St. Denis. The cavern was situated in land owned by Robert's grandfather; so there could be no question of rival claimants, once the news poured out. All land bordering this juncture with the narrow road which wound up toward the village of Uzech—it was all Laurent Didier's, and so eventually should become the property of Louis Didier, and so eventually should become the property of—

Whether he knew it now or not, Grandfather was sole proprietor of the ravening panorama, the refutation of what had hitherto been believed about Paleolithic man.

Slowly, head bent in more than a gangling habitual stoop, Robert made his way back to the cave's entrance and stood irresolute for a time. . . . Herdsmen, farm boys a-wandering on some woodland business? Seldom did such people come this way; yet it was not safe to leave the place carelessly torn and opened. Rough black darkness of the little doorway was an invitation which no one might now disregard. Laboriously, feeling a weariness he'd never felt earlier, bowed by anxiety and responsibility of his unexpected stewardship, Robert heaped loose stones to build a barricade across the entrance. He hacked some furze, brought old rotten boughs, grubbed up some armloads of decayed leaves. . . . There, that would do for a time. You'd have to stand within five meters of the cavern's mouth to realize that this was not merely another tangle of forest refuse. . . . Sliding the hoe and crowbar among sprouts of nearby elderberries, Robert was about to leave the lantern also; then he remembered: it must be filled, it must be examined for possible damage before he carried it as a torch to light the elder Didiers on their sacred pilgrimage.

He secured the empty lantern at his belt once more, faded away through the mists, and was soon moving east toward Gigouzac. Almost he limped in a trance, but enough consciousness remained with Robert to make him appreciate the oddity of fog, thickening to celebrate a fantastic rite which the cave adventure had become. He reached ahead of his years to recognize a symbolism: this vapor was the vapor of Ignorance, in which scholars of the buried centuries might grope perpetually unless they stumbled across the solid guideposts which, by veriest chance, could emerge to confront and direct them.

. . . Now great bulk ahead, the wide weapons of horns spreading; and how and why might the limned herds have extracted themselves from that cavern and come out to tread the St. Denis road? Here they formed, pushing fairly in front of him; and Robert Didier staggered to the grassy verge, imploring dumbly that they should not swerve to trample him.

A man was shaped: Jacques Labastide, a farmer, accompanying his oxen out to the plow.

Good day.

Who's there? Peering. Why, the young Didier, indeed! Well, it's not such a good day, with this annoying fog—

It will lift soon.

It had *better* lift! Step along there, Maréchal! and the man vanished, waving his goad with a great show of authority over the mammoth Limousin oxen who would do their amiable tan-clad best in sun or fog—it was all one to them—

O thronging black-and-buff-and-ruddy herds, O straying rhinoceros, O miniature stallions frisking motionless! And Labastide the farmer could have walked this road until the week they carry him to this cemetery beyond the wall, and he would never know what's hiding yonder past the beeches. If it hadn't been for me! Ha—if it hadn't been for the squirrel—

. . . And why did I want the tiny squirrel?

. . . My own loneliness tells the answer. Now I shall never be lonely any longer! I'll be listened to, welcomed, respected. I'll be—

. . . Oh, dear God. I'll be *loved!*

. . . And what others progressed along this road, as Labastide now goes to his field, and I go to the upheaval of my own making—? What others? There were people, now dead, such as my mother—people of the modern world. And Doctor Pelacoy, of course; and— Oh, other doctors, and soldiers, and all the dukes, the princes of the Church, serfs, Crusaders, the Romans in their armored kilts, the Goths whose hands they chopped—

. . . And more and more, before them, before this was a road, when it was only a path beneath the lumpy shadow of boulders—before it was a path, when it was only a tangle of riven trees the early sharp lightnings had toppled here. And the uncouth warriors whose ears had never yet been terrorized by a blast of Roman trumpets— Oho, long before a Roman trumpet had been cast or hammered or ornamented—

. . . No one of them knew, no one of them knew!

. . . And I am swimming through this fog today; but the fog thickens into layers like bedclothing, and is wrapped or rolled away in strips, and one can very nearly see the sun fighting to burn its way through.

. . . And I know!

. . . Only I: Robert the inept, Robert the hooted, Robert the ingrate, Robert the dawdler, Robert the scorned!

. . . Only I!

It was less than one kilometer from the cavern to the village, less than two kilometers from the village to The Fortress . . . along this distance Robert stalked the lifting whiteness on feet which barely grazed the road. He knew that his jaw was sagging, he did not care; he felt saliva running on his dirty chin, did not care, smudged it off with a dirtier sleeve. His spirit would lie dormant for minutes at a time, silent and ungrowing as a seed in winter, surrounded by frozen earth of a conscious humility. Then it would bound and burst, it would be a chestnut in a pan, cracking, splitting; and in that same breath Robert would be the gourmet tasting the roasted chestnut, knowing its meat for a good ration to make the whole well-fed future into a banquet he'd never even considered as being his, through all the pallid childhood. . . .

His feet pushed wet grass, he found the shrine in lichens and rustiness. Robert wished to compose and utter a prayer of gratitude (ah, gold I requested; and how ever could I have been so debased!) but words would not shape firmly enough for him to seize upon them. Virgin and Child, all the Holy Multitude associated with them: they became another fancied mural, blotting on the face of the fog.

He found only one word—or rather one formed thought, for speech was not a power Robert owned as he halted here.

The thought was: Wonder.

Wonder. . . .

And A Thing Called Waiting.

The boy made the sign of the cross. He blinked a last mist out of his eyes. His gaze was now more capable: it could penetrate the fog of actuality or fogs of ignorance and superstition. He went up the woodland path toward The Fortress, walking with head bowed even further, more of a penitent than a conqueror. By the time he trod gravel at the front entrance, sun had pressed through the evaporating clamminess; and sun stood high in the south beyond the valley of the Vert. Midday.

Robert Didier had not expected to greet an audience newly fledged and gathered together (so he believed, in his trance) for the sole purpose of receiving the news he carried. Yet he did find such an assemblage after he had put down the lantern on a bench and moved like a sleepwalker up the wide concavity of stone stairs. A table was prepared for luncheon—if one might dignify by that term the ill-flavored soup, greasy *pâté,* dry cutlets, wan stringy asparagus—all about to be dished up by Lynette. *Couverts* were laid . . . Robert counted mechanically: no place for himself.

Well, then, he commiserated— Well, then. They think I'm still confined to my bed. Has no one visited my room? I might have died, might have vomited and strangled, for all of them!

He grinned weakly, and climbed a shorter circular stairway leading to the next wide hall above. Voices drew him on—dry chattering voices, yapping together in a wrangled chorus not commonly heard here at the noon hour, seldom heard at any other time. Could it be weasels and hawks within the glass case—did starling argue against pronouncements of the hoopoe bird? Oh, you moth-eaten mob, you dusty-eared and dusty-feathered crew!—Robert exclaimed to the horrid *mélange,* as he paused to deride them. One baby bison, done in ocher on a serene wall, is worth all the meddling taxidermy which has been stitched and stuffed!

He turned toward his father's room (illusion of Louis Didier incited him more than the thought of *Grandpère*) but the noise of confabulation fell behind him. He turned back, went gliding over gritty flagstones to Laurent Didier's library at the rear. A little chamber which had been set aside for the artist's activity was adjacent, actually connecting with the old man's study. There was no little chamber in proximity to the den of Louis Didier, so this rear room had been made to serve.

It was a conference of great minds. Drawings had been spread on the oak table near a casemented window, opposite Grandfather's own table and desk. Louis Didier brandished a sketch in his hand as he sought to override the voiced opinion of others. Grandfather, squat as a black-skullcapped frog in his wide low chair, was quacking just as earnestly; and M. Lambert, no longer in fishing dress, attempted to utter a verdict which had been solicited of him—but he was ignored in the issuing of it. Hilaire Bonnet, the illustrator, threw his wet wounded gaze from one to another, dabbed at raw nostrils with a tattered wad of silk handkerchief, sniffled the residue of mucus back into his head (he was always suffering from catarrhal complaints; drafts in this château had not improved his situation) and prated hopelessly: You *said* you wished foregrounds indicated in these illustrations of the dolmens! You did, indeed you did!

. . . But rabbits in the grass! I requested no rabbits!

. . . Pardon, but possibly the artist has only overemphasized—

. . . A hare—or rabbit, if you will—detracts! The eye goes to—

. . . I thought an animal, a bird, or a bit of gorse, would afford a dramatic contrast—

. . . But they're all over the place—everywhere! You've even put in picknickers and a peasant's cart in this larger view of—

. . . The eye of the beholder is not first concerned with—

. . . Too much foreground, or background, causes conflict and disturbance. The chief message of such an illustration—

. . . *Mon Dieu,* now he's put wildflowers beside this skull exposed *in situ* at our digging on the isle of Minorca—!

. . . But, Monsieur Louis Didier, you said Bright and Gay! To brighten them up a trifle— Not make them dull like the illustrations in Feller's *Dictionnaire Historique*—

. . . There are no illustrations in Feller's *Dictionnaire Historique*—not in any of the seventeen volumes! Except in the first volume: a woodcut of Abbé François Xavier de Feller himself. Furthermore, it's a mere compendium of names and biographies, and not to be compared to a highly specialized work such as my own. Don't talk like an ass, my dear young Monsieur Hilaire! Dickinson, Dicquemare, Dictynne, Dictys, Diderot, *Didier!*— A dictionary, I tell you—

. . . Some other book, then, which you showed me. It too was stamped in gilt, and had a red patch on the backbone!—almost wept the unhappy Hilaire Bonnet.

Someone discovered Robert, discovering at first only his face, and not taking in the torn and muddied garments, the smudges, the spectral detachment. Someone said, Well, Robert, what do you desire? Someone else said, Why, he's up and— And not in his bed— Look at your costume, young man! Did you topple out of the window?

Robert! Speak up— This was his father, advancing pompous and puzzled, yet giving forth the sneer he always conferred.

You thought I was ill, Papa. Yet you did not even visit me.

Why, what ungracious words are these! A youth, speaking to his father! What do you think I am, my dear young man—a nursemaid?

Send for Madame Paquet, if you've got the megrims, and she'll give you a physic—

Robert said, But I wasn't ill, you see.

I thought as much! exclaimed M. Lambert. You see how he vexes me, sir, with this malingering? I've complained and complained—actually, I do *hate* to be complaining about Robert all the time— But if a professor is not to receive co-operation from his student—

Grandfather said: Look at his clothing. Been tumbling in the byre, have you? A nice pair of pantaloons—ruined, gone! He thinks pantaloons grow on trees, no doubt—

Robert said, I've been in a cave.

A cave? One repeated the exclamation, others clucked and complained; Robert thought there were a dozen people instead of four. But ill-favored as they were, and perniciously as they had used him, they were still the convocation he must address.

I've been in a cavern.

The boy's out of his mind. Sick boys don't go in caverns—

But he's not sick. He just admitted it!

A cavern? What do you mean? Where?

One you know nothing of.

Are you being impudent deliberately, my son?

No, Papa. I've been in a cavern. Look at my clothes— You mentioned the state they're in. Well—a cavern. I discovered it.

Discovered. . . ?

Papa, do you remember my speaking of *le petit écureuil* yesterday at the Château de Mercuès? It was that squirrel, you see, which led me to this cave of which I speak—

Laurent Didier turned away with a snort, and pounded his scabby hands against the arms of his chair. Are we to sit here listening to the nonsense of this child, Messieurs, or are we to get about our business? You asked me for my opinion of these preliminary drawings, Louis: well, I've given it. And the tutor knows little of this subject matter, but you asked him as well. Come, come, Louis—let's get on with it! The luncheon bell is about to ring, and I've not half finished with my morning's cataloguing—

Robert said, not caring if he interrupted, but knowing that the eyes of the other three were still on him: While you were out hoping to catch trout, Monsieur Lambert—

I did catch two, I'll have you know! cried the irate M. Lambert.

While you were catching trout, I was finding bigger game.

Ah, you always pretend that you wouldn't hurt a fly! You're forever taking the attitude that you have a special understanding with all wild creatures. I just know that you were the one who let my lark out of his cage— And he sang absolutely beautifully, Hilaire, indeed he did!

Louis Didier shouted rudely, Get out, *garçon!* You're disrupting a discussion of the utmost importance—

Robert did not stir . . . there was a patronizing twist of his mouth under its mask of dried clay. Papa, can you envision a group of illustrations in which the animals did not detract from the prehistoric remains, but in fact—*were* the prehistoric remains?

I told you, *get out!* I'll take a stick—

You'll take no stick, Father—and Robert's barefaced defiance brought a concerted gasp from all four.

You must hear what I have to say! This morning I entered the cavern which I discovered on Sunday. Before my eyes appeared a treasure which no man has ever seen: drawings, paintings—all over the walls, abutments, ceilings, ledges. Some are life-size, some exaggerated, some distorted—many are even deliberately representational. They are more beautiful than anything in the Musée National at the Palace of the Louvre!

Hilaire the illustrator burst the angry tension resulting from (in their consideration) Robert's absurd statement. Hilaire Bonnet had been a whipping boy and butt for long enough; he was shy, envenomed with inferiority before the clamoring world, and extremely uncertain of even his own slender talents. Criticism piled on criticism had been more than his sagging shoulders could bear. He'd longed only to regain his own bedchamber and wait for Amboise Lambert, his old friend (Lambert had recommended Hilaire enthusiastically for this assignment, and suggested that the artist be summoned from Paris for even the small fee which Louis Didier was willing to pay . . . the chambers of M. Lambert and M. Bonnet were connecting chambers) to comfort him. It was priceless, now that the son of the family should appear and substitute himself as an object for castigation.

Hilaire Bonnet opened his wide mouth and let loose a wail of laughter. Certainly such mirth would not offend the elder Didiers; they'd approve instead—find in it a sanction of their own disdain. . . .

O dear young Robert! We're delighted to learn that you've discovered a second *Mona Lisa.* What about a second *Aphrodite of Melos?*

The squeal of Amboise Lambert arose to mingle with Hilaire Bonnet's, but the Didiers did not join in this frolic; they were too incensed. Laurent Didier tried to grope up out of his chair in dudgeon, and cried, Eh, eh! and flapped his swollen hands as he always did when he wished someone to help him arise. Louis Didier thrust out a long arm and grasped Robert by his shirt collar. Robert twisted away from him, to the ripping of cloth.

A *Venus de Milo?* the boy crowed in the sardonic humor of his enforced maturity. Ah, she's there—and she's a woolly rhinoceros!

Or shall we say: a cow bison? They're all apparent, all to be observed, these beasts that you people have only guessed at while you tried to reconstruct them from their bones!

Grandfather was gasping something about, Jackanapes—! Louis Didier floundered bug-eyed toward the assault.

Don't try to shake me, Father! It'll do no good— You can't shake away a fact. And these drawings are a fact! I've just seen them—every one the product of some artist of that time. Wasn't it you yourself who taught me that the woolly rhinoceros became extinct at least twenty thousand years ago? But he's parading on my cavern wall this very minute. Now, who could have seen him—to paint him in this way?—and along with him the extinct hyena and the extinct elk and the extinct boar? It's the whole Paleolithic Age come to life, good people—that's what it is! No man ever witnessed such a pageant before. How should you like to astonish the Academy with this bit of gossip?

Robert turned toward Amboise Lambert, and bowed. A trifle more antique, Monsieur, than a Vedic psalm? Don't you agree?

Louis Didier's face trembled as he stared at his son. The rigidity of unspeakable affront occupied his entire being . . . and Bonnet's gushing laughter was long since shorn off, and Lambert (remembering the fierce delight of that flogging with the thorn branch) slipped delicately behind M. Bonnet's chair and stood breathing in gulps, waiting.

Laurent Didier had finally hoisted himself to his feet and was searching fretfully for his canes. Why should this child seek to ridicule us? the thick voice demanded. Don't spare the rod, Louis. Teach him a lesson he'll not forget!

The father whispered dryly: I don't know his motives—not I. But this is derision of an unforgivable sort! Why should he come bursting in here, clamoring in contempt? Why, why, *why?*

The man's voice rose higher in power.

He knows well enough that Paleolithic man was a primitive of the lowest order; and now he comes babbling about a *salon des arts!* Oh, he's grown too big for his breeches—or so he thinks. . . . So we know nothing, do we, son? We've spent our lives in this field, and in adjacent enterprises; and now you, in your superior infantile erudition, would tell us that you've discovered a cavern where those same troglodytes discoursed the fauna of their time?— A private showing, as it were, arranged only for the eyes of Robert Didier, eluding the scrutiny of all others? What did you think I'd give you for this trashy fabrication?

A franc to buy sweetmeats, mumbled Grandfather.

I'll sweeten your meat, my dear Robert! shrieked Louis. His hand waved out, open and flopping. He flagged desperate fingers in the direction of Laurent Didier, and all without turning from his vengeful scrutiny of Robert. . . . Father! Give me thy cane! Give—me—thy—*cane!*

Robert stood pilloried where he'd hoped to be applauded. They were all against him, all opposed—they would be the worst enemies any soul might encounter, the most implacable torturers ever consigned to a crime.

Perhaps he saw some gypsies too, said the scornful grandfather. Complete with cooking pots and fires!

You mean— You don't believe me? Don't believe I've found a cavern—? With—with the woolly rhinoceros depicted—? With—bison—?

I'll bison *you!*—and Louis' hand closed on the stout black cane which was offered. Come here, Robert! I say— I command you, as my child— Come *here!*

The boy did not move. He held a confused awareness that he was grown to manhood—owned fierce active cream in his testicles— He was a man, however skinny. He had pried rocks, could break up mountainsides if he wanted to! He'd gone against accumulated dangers of twenty millennia, and had come off victor. He'd not go down to defeat again.

With an inarticulate wail Louis Didier rushed upon him, flailing the black knotty cane. Robert caught the cane with his hands before the blow reached his body. The two figures writhed into a sculpted mass. The hour of Louis Didier's ignominy was here. Robert thought, even as he threw the force of his arms against his father's mediocre weight, and twisted to one side and down— He thought, It's remarkably easy —I should have tried it when I was young—

He had too that unexpected and inexplicable burst of pity which nobility can feel for an antagonist, even in a moment of keen conflict. He possessed a last lingering wish to love his father as he strove against him. . . . You tall thin Being with musty clothes and rancid breath, you never had a chance to be a sweetness or an elegance! You were not so strong as I, you were a parchment to begin with, you let your parent put his blots and scribbles on you. But I have my mother's blood, the dash of the Berganty tribe about me; and one of them had a cannon ball strike off his leg in Prussia, and he wrapped the stump with his sash, and lay on a hayrick directing his battalions until he had no more voice, no more Berganty blood! And one went to the guillotine laughing uproariously at his own sallies; and one ran through two footpads with his rapier when he was upwards of seventy! . . . You've not got my foment or my virtues. Poor long-legged opinionated beetle, I pity you!

Why, oh why did you not . . . (His heart cried it while his stringy muscles contended).

. . . Why did you not offer me a light-blown nonsense, a white-headed dandelion to puff upon, a tale of huntsmen and heroes, a kiss? You might have given me the truffle-flavored omelette of family fare, the dear food my mother never lived to serve me; but you didn't, you nearsighted wraith, you male witch, you scarecrow! And Grandfather is the dropsical crow to be scared off— Clatter your rags and streamers; say, Away with him!

The cane, with which Louis Didier might have killed his son or rendered him an idiot (had the intended blow ever come down upon the boy's head) spun free in Robert's thin iron fists. He whirled from the gobbling specter which his father had become. He swung the black stick high in the air and brought it down against the oak table where illustrations were arrayed. The sting leaped through Robert's hands, through his arms, up into his shoulders, but the crash of shivering brittle wood was music.

He stood gasping, one end of the cane still clutched; dazzled dark splinters were bent in all directions; and the broken end of the weapon had flown through space to strike M. Amboise Lambert fairly on the jaw. Lambert clapped his hand against his face, he began to jig. His first yell went whistling off down halls and stairways, came echoing back in a clamor (so like the echoes in my cavern! thought Robert).

Cochon! cried Louis Didier, hating his gangling son as he'd never owned the force to hate another human being. He took one shaky step toward Robert, then stopped. His wild eye was on that shattered remnant of the old walking stick which the boy still held.

Robert did not know whether he might have attacked his father with this object or not. Thinking about it through years which remained to him, thinking about it many times, he could never estimate. Might he have struck or stabbed Louis Didier, could he have brought himself to an assault, when he'd been asserting only in defense? He could not say, did not know, never knew.

Now he heard himself crying: Unworthy, unworthy! . . . How many times did he repeat the word? . . . *Indigne, indigne, indigne!* All of you! . . .

His grandfather was declaring, in unsteady but sanctimonious accents, that a youth who attacked his parent could and should and would be sent to prison.

Prison? shrilled the boy. My God, I've lived in prison all my life. And you're the jailers! He threw the butt of cane through the opened mullioned window; all five people heard a squall from Lynette as the missile struck close to her in the courtyard.

You wouldn't believe! Robert cried. I came hurrying to tell you, and you wouldn't believe— You had only derision, only cruelty to offer! As always, as always! Well, I'll tell you this— Tell all of you! You'll never know! I'll see that you *never know!*

He burst into tears and, turning away, ran blindly through the door, hurt his shoulder against the stone archway outside, bounced off, and went running. He galloped down two flights of stairs, unaware as to pursuit or clamor . . . perhaps there rose no further sounds for a time except the howling of the injured tutor; but possibly his father did follow him a little way, at least with excoriation and threats, and demands that he return to face punishment. . . . Robert sped out into the rear courtyard, passed the open cistern where two red amazed faces were staring above their water buckets, and he raced across the plank bridge spanning a mudhole where once lay a moat. He did not witness lilac bushes, André in the garden, birds flying away from him, the sacred shrine at the foot of the hill. (Later he had one recollection of Gigouzac. It was nailed on his memory as he went hammering through the village: a young girl with her arms full of puppies, sitting on a low wall, and then sliding off the wall in fright while Robert hustled toward her, demented.)

Never let them find it now. Never, never!

. . . Robert stood panting in front of the entrance he'd concealed. He'd filled it up under fog, the light was glaring savagely against him now; sun was so high and intense that it blobbed his long shadow into a toad's shape against the barricade of stones. . . . Oho, you stampeding beauties, you with the antlers and the tusks and charcoal hair, I'm here to make certain that profane eyes may never wound you, the trowels and mattocks of Unbelievers never seek you out! . . . The boy clawed into the wet hillside until his fingernails were distended by pebbled scrapings jammed beneath them— One rock loose— By God, a big one, all I can heft! . . . and he went grunting bowlegged with his burden and dumped it on the pile of trash.

But, oh, at that rate, twould take a year and more—

Robert remembered the crowbar then, and went sprawling to secure it. He looked up at the steepening hillside. It bent and twisted above stunted trees, outcroppings grew thicker and bolder the higher the hill went, the more it straightened into semblance of a cliff. Boulders up there, and plenty—a myriad of rain-washed rocks, big and little; and some were large as ovens, some small as oranges, but all flung heedlessly into melon heaps where Time and floods and earthquakes and giants had carelessly disposed them. *Now we'll see!* Robert scrambled up the nearest cleft where he could find foothold; he went whipped by berry vines, gashed by their thorns, waving his crowbar to balance himself as a wild Indian might have come posturing with a lance. He reached a shelf, paused, and looked down. No, not here; the face was solid. But farther up, *farther up*, amid those blossomed weeds where miniature blue butterflies were prancing— Ah, *here!*—and the acrid juice oozed from his scratches; but he did not feel the scratches, felt nothing save his demon's drive. *Now, we'll see— Ha!* For the heap had slid not too long since from some higher spilling; and some of the boulders spread flat as warming pans, some tapering as the *comportes* in which a season's grapes were lugged on carts, and all messed round with grainy storage of silt and gravel.

Let us go free, the pile was saying to Robert. Let us go free, and we'll do the trick. Handsomely!

One tall lopsided chunk of granite held the whole; it had come heaving and slipping—out of clouds perhaps—but never had it gathered force enough to smash the bent tough oak which balked it from a further toppling. The gnarly tree had life, it was trying to bind knotted branches over and behind the stone, it was imploring, Stay with me always. I'll grow around you and keep you for my own! . . . A smaller rock squeezed beneath—cracked fairly into the oaken roots— And others, babies, and clay and gravel in their drifted paste. . . .

Robert's crowbar sank, a narrow stream of silt began to run into lower weeds. Robert forced the rod savagely, dug and drilled, strained his body to make a leverage. His hands slipped, he landed in the blackberries, cried out in pain, arose and fought and sagged once more. One yellowed plate of stone crunched off and went banging down into the greenery; there was a ponderous tilt, a sound of indecision from the tipped tonnage of the biggest boulder, the oak tree whined and crunched and bent. Then it seemed as if the great stone was walking toward Robert, nodding its bearded face as it came. Once more the boy fell into torture of the vines, and closed his eyes. He heard the entire caravan of littered stones give a sigh and acquiescence, as if they were awkward Bedouins who'd camped there for a little space; and then a bell had jingled or a horn had spoken— Some sort of admonishment, some order to the journey; and now they were rising to travel again—

The largest boulder fell forward past Robert so close that it brushed a wind across his face. Leaping in this gayest sport of all, little brothers followed, then a landslide of shale and earth with weight of rain behind. Bushes, pygmy branches waved a protest as the hard cascade came mauling over them; then they were abraded, scraped loose, and let their tattered members go streaking out like banners to join the bounding torrent. Down in the road which led to St. Denis two peasants, brothers, walked beside their oxcart, but stopped in alarm at hearing a mumble and welter from the hill.

Mon Dieu, Lucien, what's happening up there?

It sounds like thunder. . . . No, it's stopped . . . a few stones still rolling through the woodland. A great slide of rock, surely!

Ah, that's what they call an avalanche.

—Is it, indeed?

But yes. When I was in the Pyrenees—

Oh, always boasting about your travels; just because I'm lame, and had to stay at home!

Not at all, not at all! But when I was in the Pyrenees with our Uncle Martin, helping to construct that bridge in the hills south of Lourdes, there came a great avalanche. It swept two houses and a mill along with it—and they say that at least five or six people were carried to their death! They never did manage to dig them all out. Too deep, you understand—too many thousandweight of earth and rubbish—

They strolled toward St. Denis with their mended plow in the cart, they went on talking about avalanches and—soon—other disasters. Robert Didier did not hear them, did not see them, did not recognize that they were on the road. He got up at last, when only a few streams of pebbles still trickled warily among the barked trees which had managed to remain erect. The youth climbed slowly down the slide, starting a fresh tumbling of fragments now and then when his feet teetered amid the rubble. . . . Where was his cavern, the treasure chest of horned bewitching beauty? Gone, locked away, blotted into anonymity and submissiveness. Where there had been greenery was now only a slanted windrow of raw pale stones.

Never find you now! Never, never! . . . Robert went stepping aimlessly into a lower forest where no disturbance had come crushing, where no rocks rolled.

(His familiar world was bounded only by Paris on the north, Pau on the south—Switzerland on the east, Bordeaux on the west. Within this area, and throughout continents overseas where now he felt that he should turn, there lived but one hearth where he dared sit.)

When Robert broke through bushes into the indolent roadway of early afternoon, he turned toward Gigouzac instead of away from it. Through miracle and strife of the day, he had eaten not one bite of food since he munched bread in the early morning; yet he was not conscious of hunger, was aware only of weakness . . . a sore persistent melody, like spring insects in grass, trilled within his ears. At Gigouzac he half expected to see relatives and tutor and illustrator braced beside the village well, armed as they'd been weaponed when they went against the gypsies—motioning him toward The Fortress, and saying: This way! We've the chains ready, and shall put you in the coal pit where once Sir Simon lined his victims!

Four? he queried dully. I withstood my father, but could I withstand all four of them at once—? Even Sissy Lambert, and that sickly artist—?

They were not there, no one was there except two children romping, and Grandpère Durban traveling shakily with his cane. Robert heard his own mumbled greeting; Grandpère looked at him severely because of his ragged bloody apparel, but the old man said not a word: he was dumb, deprived of speech, had never spoken since a mine exploded beside him in the Wars . . . he stared his perplexity and disapproval, then went bending toward his hillside house. . . . Robert bore to the right, crossing the merry water, glancing down and seeing cresses, seeing one small fish wriggling cozily in the cool current. Then the knowledge of placid beauties fell away from him and he traveled dark and lonely under the sun, forcing his uneven stride past the church, across another branch of the Vert, up through tortuous windings toward ridges sprawling across the south. . . . When the afternoon was much farther gone, and Robert had neared the tiny town of Boissières, his strength left him, he thought it gone forever. He piled into a couch of bent weighted grass beneath a wall, lay pursing his lips and swallowing dryly, sensing a few bright poppies close to his eyes. He slept solidly, drunkenly.

A woman's voice awakened him. . . . Can't you rise, I say? Are you dead or only sleeping?

Robert sat up groggily; then squinted in alarm, gazing back up the road to the northeast. He saw no one coming after him, he turned to look at the woman. She had a face like a mottled peach, a face with peach fuzz on it; she was smiling, there was a mixed aroma of dairies and perspiration about her. She leaned over her gate— He'd not known that there was a gate so close, a bare three meters away—

I said, Are you a gypsy?

No, Madame. I'm from—Gigouzac—

Does that mean that Gigouzac people are now going to make a habit of snoring before my door? Dear, dear! I thought you were a gypsy—you're dirty enough. Do you come from a very poor family, you poor boy?

No, Madame, he said without considering.

Then I don't know what your people are thinking of, letting you travel about in such attire. Muddy, torn, bloody, and all scratched, too! Were you in a fight with some other lad? My brother Estève was always fighting! Poor Estève—he stepped upon a rake, and his leg swelled to the size of a tree—believe it or not, as you please— But he died. Yes, the year of the cold winter. You appear to be hungry. Are you hungry?

Oh, Madame—

Very well, I'll feed you something. But I shan't take you into my house, you're too filthy. Here—

She opened the gate.

Here on this bench; you shall sit here. Let's see, what shall I bring you?

I—I have no money, Madame—

Then there's all the more reason that I should feed you! What do you think I conduct—a wayside inn? Not if I can help it!— She was extremely fat, he saw now, bulging out of her black apron. She waddled up the stair which led into her stone house, and disappeared.

Robert slumped upon the bench with his eyes closed. Presently he felt a cat rubbing against his leg, but he was too tired to look at the cat.

The woman returned with a wooden tray. Upon this she had spread several slices of bread, a round of cheese, a bowl of crisp radishes, and a blue pitcher filled with milk. There, she said, please my heart! I swear, you must have run away from a cruel father!

Yes, Madame, answered Robert softly.

And you admit it too. What a lad! Very much like my poor brother Estève, before he stepped upon the sharpened rake. What is your name, boy?

He munched bread and cheese, trying to decide what his name should be at this moment. André Paquet, he told her finally, thinking of gardener and wheezing housekeeper without zest.

An odd name indeed! Well, there used to be Paquets over here to the west, at Nuzejouls, but I heard that they were a wild lot; and the old man drank *eau de vie* until he was fairly pickled in it. Not any cousins of yours, I hope. No? Ah, that's good!

. . . She did not mention her own name. He ate every scrap of the bread, every grain of cheese except for one lump which he fed to the begging cat. He emptied the pitcher of milk, and ate all the radishes except two. When he had thanked the fat woman and turned out on his way, he looked back to see her pushing her plump mottled face across the solid gate again, and calling: Good luck now, wherever you may go! But wash your face in the first stream! . . . So he would never know her name, he would never see the village of Boissières again. But the memory of this woman, the taste of her cheese and radishes, would stay with him perpetually; and he would save it as a precious charm—as a lady keeps scraps of favorite dress goods in a bag, as a man hoards the moldy dog collar and the belt plate. Sometimes (grown older and sometimes even wearier, and faced with all variety of dangers) Robert would think of the fat woman as he lay trying to sleep, and he would smile.

This evening it was long after dark when he reached the Château de Mercuès. Wind was beginning to whine, Robert wore no jacket. He stood shivering before the high closed gates, hugging himself, clanging at the bell repeatedly before a squat bearded figure emerged from the keep at the left-hand side.

What's all this clatter? . . . A lantern was held up inside the metal bars. . . . Give an account of yourself, before I turn the dog loose—

Shredded raw as he was, Robert could giggle. It's only Rougette; she'll only try to jump on me.

Good Lord, here's the young Didier! But— Where's your father's carriage? And your grandfather? Has the carriage upset? Are you hurt?

. . . He heard voices, felt the guiding hand under his elbow, knew that they were progressing uphill past the black cedar; yet this was not reality. The woman at Boissières had represented reality, with her loose chatter and simple charity. In recollection he limped back to her bench, and felt the cat rubbing. . . .

Doctor Pelacoy cried, Robert! What's happened—?— And he too thought that there had been a wreck.

Oh, nothing.

But it's past nine at night, and you're here alone. Where's the carriage? And—

Robert waited until the old woodman who kept the gate had retreated across the courtyard. Then he whispered: I've run away from home.

The doctor stood making faces under the cobwebbed lantern which hung above the east doorway of the court. . . . I felt confident that you would have to do that in time! But—so young—

I found a cavern. With Paleolithic drawings. And they wouldn't believe it, wouldn't believe a word! All they did was to—insult. Then Father tried to beat me. I broke Grandfather's cane—

Robert, are you starving?

The boy broke down and sobbed, A woman gave me some luncheon. But I'm so tired! I walked all the way—after—

Without another word, the doctor escorted Robert to (of all places) the room of Bishop Alain de Solminihac. Doctor Pelacoy had been lounging there with copies of old journals piled on a table beside his chair, nudging the decanter on its tray. For all the absurdity of a knitted pink nightcap pulled over his bald head, Doctor Pelacoy might have been wearing the regimentals of his youth, thought the boy. His shabby robe was of a military blue with red facings, and was bound around his thick figure by a cord with a brassy tinge. He hauled on the bell rope in the corner, had to haul several times. When a sleepy and surprised-looking servant appeared, Doctor Pelacoy ordered that more glasses be fetched, along with a flask of spirits. . . . He filled their glasses with a man-sized dose, each, and peremptorily gestured for Robert to drink.

Monsieur le Docteur, I'm— I'm but a boy! Robert managed a weak titter.

You're chilled through, and worn to the point of exhaustion. This is armagnac, and has a wildcat in every bottle. A tame wildcat. . . . The doctor chuckled at his own trivial jest, but he was watching appraisingly and with compassion. . . . Drink it slowly—a sip at a time—and it will be a benefit. . . .

The Didiers did not drink spirits habitually. In his life Robert had managed to sample only a few dregs of *crème de noix.* This stuff was infinitely stronger, and had a snap to it. Robert coughed, tears flew from his eyes, he strangled. Doctor Pelacoy laughed, and gave him a tumbler of water; but when equilibrium was restored he motioned toward the brandy again. The next few sips went down more easily.

Now, then, said Pelacoy. Tell all.

Robert began haltingly, but soon was stumbling over himself, and backtracking and duplicating in narration, as emotion shook his adolescent voice. The man listened patiently, interrupting every now and then with a guiding question; and at last Robert was back with the squirrel, where he should have been in the first place. From there on the tale proceeded lucidly, though it was replete with extraneous detail concerning Madame Paquet and Monsieur Lambert and even Grandmother Durban with her cherries. Robert Didier, influenced by fury, pain, the screaming of his brutalized body, and the final crash of the avalanche he'd produced— He felt that all of history's martyrdom had been his. He was a boil, his entire soul was a boil and swelling . . . then the doctor had thrust in the sharp probe of his mere presence, and rank hot liquid came spurting in a stream, needle-thin, but giving blessed relief to every tissue by the cessation of heat and pressure.

The room itself was a benevolence, the hearth fire a gem, the brandy a worthy medicine. One of those vagabond winds which sprawl at night out of the Lot valley had assailed the château on its pinnacle, and there were bangings and creakings of shutters and vanes and loose doors. But the fire was a core of kindness not to be disturbed by such trivial resoundings . . . light twirled up to polish the marbled mantel-edge, the spotted rug became a pavement of Heaven (O freedom to voice one's woes, O salve of mortal sympathy!)— The chair with stained cushion was a cloud within Heaven's own precinct; the vigorous doctor was become an Apostle in one breath and a shrewd commander in the next—a colonel fresh come from triumphant old wars and even ready for new ones.

Nor was it necessary to prompt or direct Robert any longer. His sad fierce story marched impressively. When he reached a description of the paintings in the cavern, Doctor Pelacoy uttered a sharp exclamation. He leaned forward, glowered, slapped both his knees. . . . He arose presently and began to pace the room, signifying by a wave of his hand that the boy should continue, should take no notice of the slow stride and hoarse breathing. . . . Sometime or other he returned to his chair, but Robert (with cavern and Father and fog and antique stags dissolving in his recollection—with voice crusty and splintering —with muscles aching and feet puffed and throat protesting against the armagnac) did not even see the man sit down.

He knew only that his chronicle had worn itself out at last, as the ballads of troubadours must have come to their own end in this château one time.

He slouched, ears ringing, the fireplace retreating and coming back; and Doctor Pelacoy, sitting with face bent against his hand, also diffused and receded and then formed again stancher than before.

Is that the whole story, my boy?

Yes. I walked—all the way—

And when they come to take you home—?

They do not know where I am.

They'll soon learn, they're bound to learn!

I won't return. I'll die first.

Or die if they do succeed in returning you to Gigouzac! The doctor muttered these last words as if to himself. Or perhaps commit a justifiable patricide—

He came over to Robert's chair and knelt down slowly on one plump knee. His hand crushed the boy's.

Robert.

Monsieur? whispered the dry split voice.

I have, put away where one puts the true and dear trivial things, a little book. I saw it only a few hours ago, when I was getting those journals out of the same chest.

He indicated the stack of thumbed, blotted folders on the center table. . . . My diaries. Notes, journals, half-written records— I jotted them down, whenever I could— It was difficult, sometimes. Sometimes I had exhausted all the ink in my portable inkwell, and there was no other ink to be had— When I was young, Robert, and fresh from my studies, and fresh come to serve under Bonaparte! Ah, yes: where was I? I've told you: Albeck, Austerlitz, Jena, Hanau. In the end, a place called Waterloo. That's where I was no longer a youth, and didn't have the boots off my feet for four days and four nights! Ah, well, no matter now—

(And using the tone of one who thought that it did matter, very much indeed!)

. . . I was examining these diaries, and recalling sights and sounds and names and old laughter and old curses. A lone man—an old man—must have something to look at, of an evening—

And in that same chest is the little book I mentioned. It is a prayer book; it belonged to your mother. My dear Geneviève admired it greatly; so it became a present from your own mother to my daughter, when they were girls together. I fancy Geneviève would have it with her now in far-off Martinique; but the little prayer book was lost to sight for a long time, and only turned up a year or two ago, caught behind a loose shelf in Geneviève's bedchamber. Should I send it to her? Well, I haven't sent it; I'm selfish, you see.

Robert. Were I to go now, and fetch that little prayer book— A thing doubly sacred, remember, especially to you— For not only is it a prayer book, but it was once your mother's. Ah, if she'd lived, perhaps your life might have been—

Robert. If I brought the book—

Doctor Pelacoy smiled, his ragged eyebrows went up. Robert, staring hypnotized into the doctor's eyes, saw the oil of tears seeming to reflect back his own weeping.

My boy, you have been given to romances in the past. Tut-tut, I'm not defending Louis for beating you when the gypsies lurked about your yard gates! But I do remember that, when you were very small, you saw peacocks out here in the shrubbery; and we hadn't had a peacock on the place in five years.

Robert whispered, Roosters, sir. I remember.

Very well, then—roosters. And the ghost of a Roman centurion—in the *pigeonnier,* wasn't it?

Merely a fluttering of white wings, I now think, *Monsieur.* It was dusk, and I was badly disturbed by the thought of Romans. Grandfather had talked of catacombs, all the way over here in the carriage.

Robert. You've had your romances—

I have, sir.

Is this one?

No, sir.

Would you put your hand upon your mother's prayer book, and swear that every word you've told me is the truth?

. . . He could not catch his breath for a moment; his lungs were empty, there was no air to feed them; and his ears were twin anvils with sledges of heart and armagnac going against them. Robert writhed back in his chair, then twisted forward and embraced Doctor Pelacoy convulsively.

He screamed: Oh, please, the *book!* Fetch it, my dear doctor, Fetch it! I'll swear from now until my dying day! *Fetch the book!*

. . . A hundred years later, Robert felt the man patting his hand. Now he could draw breath again, could know this reassurance and accept it in the same charity in which it was given.

I shan't bring the book, Robert. Unnecessary!

The boy said, his lame voice low in that graceful echoing room with its collapsing fire: If you were to engage some men, *Monsieur le Docteur.* Men with picks and other tools—windlasses, perhaps— I doubt that it would take more than a week to remove the stones; perhaps not even that long. And then—you could see—

You've sealed it, said Pelacoy abruptly. Now he was standing by the cold rattling window with his back to Robert. He repeated: You've sealed the cavern. By God, we'll leave it sealed.

Soon (without abandoning his position by the mirrored ebony panes; and surely he could see nothing out there except chipped balustrades and the wet dust of ripened acacia blossoms blowing by) he seemed addressing a phantom congregation. He was aware of Robert, and appealed directly to the boy when he wished to; but it was as if whole nations long dead or now alert, or those to be manufactured in the future, were affected by Doctor Pelacoy's words. So he in turn was impressed by their suggested presence.

. . . You're very young, of course. But thoughtful, and with the native heart your mother gave you. You got no heart from those pitiful dust-disturbers! So you'll bear with me when I tell you that we may live only in our own hours. Some people are bound to crowd every hour and every minute with activity and feeling; the most of mankind offer but a wastage and an emptiness. It makes you wonder why they were given those hours in the first place!

. . . You haven't asked me for advice, except in the manner of your coming to me in acute distress; and I'm proud and happy that you came. You see, Robert, you've been the son I never had; may you long continue to be that son! Again I say: you're young, but you've suffered much in your short life; and only suffering can bring any maturity worth owning.

. . . So I say: let the beasts stay put. They've kept—very well, according to your description—through most of humanity's important endeavors. Let them keep a little while longer. You can't shoulder the responsibility of their emergence now; and your father and grandfather (forgive me this slander, but it is justified) have shown themselves to be suspicious petty ingrates. It's a treasure they don't deserve to share in; but if you did indeed allow them the opportunity, they'd snatch the whole treasure. All of it, mark my words, all of it! They'd not leave you so much as a crust. And they'd be eternally jealous, in their meager little souls, because this thing was dumped into your lap by the good God— Perhaps in recompense for a childhood of affliction: who shall say?— And all the Didiers were ever able to find, through endless barrow-diggings and siftings of tomb dust, were miscellaneous rubbishes sufficient to get them a publisher and a decoration. Honors awarded only by their own kind, you see! It's a mutual back-scratching and belly-warming that these *Académiciens* go through!

. . . So I hear that the woolly rhinoceros hasn't champed our grasses for some twenty thousand years? I wouldn't know, you see: I can cut off your leg or your arm, slit your carcass and extract a handsome tumor— I can bleed you dry, but I can't extract the special knowledge which you hold in your busy little brain! Well, then. People haven't known, most of them, of the very existence of such a horse or such a stag or such a buffalo; people have not known that Paleolithic man was capable of artistic expression and ever sought to practice it; only you, Robert Didier, are in possession of that special knowledge. But how much good will it do for you to disseminate such abstruse information? Will it get the abused pauper off the streets, the whore out of her bedroom, the lunatic out of his cage? Not at all. Men will remark: woolly rhinoceros? Here in France, and they had their miniatures painted? Who painted them—our own Ingres, from Montauban? You don't say! Very interesting, to be sure; but we must to the business at hand. I'll lend you the thousand francs; but you must have the interest ready in hand, each quarter of the year, or I'll take your shop and everything that's in it. And in the meantime I'll go home —browbeat my daughter, mock at my son, insult my grandmother, neglect my wife, seduce the laundress's daughter, lie to the priest, testify falsely in court— Of course I shall do those things, because I'm a human being, am I not? And I fear that the bulk of men have been doing these things all along, since Robert Didier's herd of prehistoric bulls chased the first sanctimonious *bourgeois* out of his cave and into a house! *Et alors?* I'll feed ground glass to the neighbor's dog, I'll refuse to fix the crooked flagstones in front of my door—because it would take money from my wallet to do the trick—and thus the half-blind old scissors-mender will find his broken hip and his doom, when he comes by again. I'll tell my mistress I didn't touch a woman all the time I was in Brussels, and make her believe that I had thoughts only of her, and couldn't wait to get back to her couch— And then I'll give her the *maladie* which I picked up in Brussels the night before I left, and make her an outcast and a walking suppuration in the end. . . . Surely, surely! Remember, by the way, that the first interest payment is due on the fifteenth of March! . . . And I'll go to war, too (but only if they make me) and I'll say: Georges, it's your turn to fetch the water!—and all the time I'll know that the enemy are watching that spring—they have their muskets trained on it— But I'm not fond of Georges, you see, because the captain clapped him on the shoulder and said that he wished he had an entire company like him, and no captain ever said such a thing about me. . . . And I'll find the dry place in the barn, and let the thin little recruit sleep under the water leak; and I'll hide the last loaf under straw, and swear to my comrades that it was blown up when powder exploded; and they'll go supperless; and in the middle of the night I'll sneak to the bread and feed myself, and no one will be the wiser; so I'll maintain my strength for an arduous campaign to come.

. . . How many painted bison does it take to make a foreclosed mortgage, a cuckolded husband, or a traduced Christ?

. . . Robert. Let them maintain their infernal bounding and loping. But there in the cave, Robert—*there in the cave!* Why drive them out into the light of day?

. . . It's not the epoch-making event that you thought it to be. A flurry in the Academy? For a certainty. Attention from artists and journalists? Of course! A revision of historic attitudes, as practiced by those scholars active in the field? Quite likely. But— An installation of pity and generosity and dedication within the brain and spirit of humanity? Ah, Robert, you faultless dreamer! . . . Will one appreciate a poppy's blood who never appreciated it before? Will the teamster stop beating his horse if he is a horsewhipper to begin with? Will the termagant think charitable thoughts about the lass who lives across the way, if she has breathed only jealousy and spleen theretofore? Will the surgeon (forgive me for this also; but I've seen it)—Will the surgeon put by the bottle to which he is a secret slave, and go—clean and dry, without a tremor—to slit his patient's head?—Or will he shrug, in the end, and say: It is a pity. I did everything I could. But, unfortunately, the man died. There was a severe hemorrhage, his blood refused to coagulate. Unfortunate, I repeat! His blood should have coagulated properly!

. . . It's impractical, you'll now understand, to lead those creatures out of the hillside and let them pasture along the Vert. Not only impractical—it's downright unpalatable and unacceptable to most of us. I can assure you that I have behaved myself— Well, let me say, better than *some* men, at least. There are a *few* sins which I have not committed! And so my conscience is clearer than some other consciences (but honestly I've wondered often if a clouded conscience *does* keep a villain from his slumbers. I'll bet he snores like the newest noisiest locomotive engine)! But no more do I want your painted tribes of extinct bovines and porcines and ovines and cervines— No more do I want them romping over my awareness, and trampling my carefully nurtured lilies. Because they'd be a rebuke to every century which has followed them; and I hear from that noted excavator, Robert Didier, that there have been some two hundred such centuries.

. . . They would be a rebuke and a castigation however merited. They would tell us that the appreciation of beauty and the art of worship are not recent accomplishments. They were present in those crooked fastnesses; but we, the race, never took them to our hearts or found in them any proper rule for living. We were perverse and greedy, and wallowed in our own brutality and ignorance, as a pig rolls in his own fresh turds! The gazelle was dancing on the wall, as you have discovered for us, long before Homer ever rolled up his blank eyes and cried, I have a story to tell you! And neither the gazelle nor Homer did us a particle of good, Robert—*not one iota.*

Doctor Pelacoy stood in a silence which seemed as long as his impassioned harangue, and Robert thought that he must have gone to sleep, standing up— Must have been mesmerized into silence by the bitterness and futility of his conclusions. But he sighed at last, emerged from rigidity of speechlessness, went to poke the fire. Flames came up for a minute or two; again the doctor's seamed face could be discerned clearly in candlelight and firelight.

Wonder of wonders, thought the exhausted boy, he does not seem at all lugubrious!

. . . But there is something else, Robert, something excitingly persistent. Remember—when you were small—you felt it, in this room? And so we may feel it now, together. And, if the nations don't blow themselves up on their own powder wagons, more people may come to know that beneficence, and to exert it. Twill be a very long time in coming, I fancy. I'm old now, and I grow cross and savage in thinking of the infernal stupidity of most people, and their degrading trivialities and ferocities and feebleness. But, my God—give them time! Thus far, you and I, we've given them only twenty thousand years.

. . . There was that young Englishman, not long ago. . . . I'm well aware, as a good Frenchman, that one should never genuflect to the English—with their stiffness, their costive emotions. Often I've opened up their bodies. And the first time—forgive me!—I very nearly expected to find cold mutton and biscuits instead of guts. But there were guts, and damned good guts too. . . . Well, a young Englishman with the phthisis (but I think he may have been half Gaul or Latin in his heart)— He wrote of some old pot dug up in Greece, and of the graceful figures chasing on its surface. He quoted to us: *Beauty is truth, truth beauty*, and declared still further that such awareness is all we need to know in this our life.

. . . I can't agree! The man who'll recognize a beauty can't be taught; he's got to have the love of beauty in his first young heart, put there by the fairies at his cradle. Have love of beauty; but let it be the lump of sugar which you give the horse for joy—and make certain that he's had his grass and grain before he takes the sugar.

. . . Have patience, Robert—patience. Have courage, and resiliency.

The doctor laughed.

. . . And I'd add humor to that dose; but it so happens that I never met a man with strong resiliency who didn't have a mighty humor also. And bawdy humor—oh, so often— Bawdy!

. . . Resiliency. Just like a willow in the wind. The beech tree snaps and dies, the willow's still a-bending.

. . . No more armagnac, now? Oho, you shake your head. You'll never be a toper.

. . . And so let me conduct you to your bed. You shall sleep this night in the room of my dear Geneviève. And have no further problems concerning Didiers or historical treasures gone begging; but only good thoughts and dreams of your mother, Thérèse Berganty. She was a sweet one, Robert—a perfect little darling! It's a pity you never got to know her.

It was a matter of tradition among surgeons who had worked with Pelacoy that he made up his mind about a case very promptly and then stuck to his guns—or rather, to his knives. When Doctor Pelacoy said, Amputate!—the member came off, that's all there was to it. A number of his patients may have been buried beneath the solid little tombstones of his quick decisions, but doubtless many more were saved for whatever life might award them. In the case of Robert Didier, the doctor performed his amputation with lightning speed. Long before noon the next day, Robert had ridden to Cahors on the docile saddle pony, Subalterne, a family pensioner and once the favorite of Geneviève Pelacoy. Daglan the woodman-stableman rode along to lead Subalterne home again; he had many amusing things to say (amusing, at least to Daglan) about the way Robert was dressed. His costume had come out of a chest in Daglan's cottage, and it may have fitted Daglan's son before he went to sea, but assuredly did not fit Robert Didier. People on the post coach, bound up the north road toward Brive and Limoges, smiled to see a clean-scrubbed peasant boy in jacket and pantaloons too roomy for him. But actually, of course, he was no longer Robert Didier.

Doctor Pelacoy brought to the completion of this episode all the verve he might have given to a fete-time masque or a game of pirates played with five-year-olds. Let us see, he mused. Didier won't do at all; because you must enter the university as intended; and if you were Robert Didier you'd soon be discovered by some colleague of Louis'—once he emerged from his papyrus and his bone-bins!—and packed off to Gigouzac for the flogging of your life!

Doctor Pelacoy turned to the color of the fresh strawberries he was eating, thinking of such a thing.

Schneider, he said. That's the name for us, the name for you! He was the kindly one, the gay one, the loyal one—an Alsatian, Gustave Schneider, may the saints bless his memory and keep it golden! Oh, what a way to die: a handful of horseshoe nails spilled into his chest, in Sicily—the enemy was low on ammunition, you see. May such a fate never befall you, Robert! . . . But while we're proceeding with the planning of this little opera, I'd just as soon we dispensed with the Robert, too. Again, one of those dodos in Paris might put two and two together, if ever a search were conducted. God knows why it should be; personally, I should think they'd be glad to get rid of you; perhaps your tutor especially! Now, we need something similar to Robert—so you'll respond when you hear it mentioned, hey? Bertrand, perhaps? . . . Ah, I've a much better one: Bertell. That shall be it: Bertell Schneider! For when Schneider and little Paul Chotard and myself were enjoying our student days together, a big male cat moved in with us from the alleys; perhaps we needed a cheap companion, for we were not allowed luxurious funds, and often could have no girls around, ha-ha! We named our cat Bertell; and if you can say why, at this moment, it's more than I can say. Bertell Schneider! Oh, what a name to employ as the hero of our opera!

. . . Can you sing well, Robert? Not in this year, I fancy, with your voice squawking with youth. And neither can I—although I love to roar, but people won't put up with my singing, and slam their hands over their ears! Come—have more strawberries—

In Limoges the new and excited young M. Bertell Schneider spent a week in the home of Pelacoy's cousin, while being fitted with a simple wardrobe. He continued on to Paris, and the shelter afforded by the house of one Colonel Fardeau—like Doctor Pelacoy a veteran of storied campaigns. Nothing whatsoever could shake the immediate and protracted belief of this good-natured little turkey cock that Bertell Schneider was an autumnal and natural son of Doctor Pelacoy. Why else, then, all these hints that the name might be an assumed one? Why else, then, the doctor's concern and devotion—the frequent letters exchanged, the adequate funds provided—the impassioned statement of the lad himself that he must *prove himself worthy* to Doctor Pelacoy? There was no riddle about this at all, in Colonel Fardeau's opinion; he found satisfaction in discharging his sentimental obligation to his old friend, and he hoped only that Bertell's mother had been very pretty, very abandoned in bed, and had met with no untimely end.

. . . I demand that you reveal his whereabouts! cried Louis Didier.

. . . I regret very much that it is impossible for me to do so, Louis.

. . . Henri! You'd come between a father and his son—

. . . Certainly, whenever I consider it necessary.

. . . I demand—!

. . . Cease your demands. This is a professional case: I'm the doctor, and must observe professional reticence. If you hadn't acted the combined roles of ignorant brute and sublime idiot, I might feel differently about the matter. All I can say is that Robert is far away, in good hands, not too restricted but intelligently observed— Chaperoned? Ha, not such a good word—better for a girl. But he's doing well at his studies; and he's been ill only once—from overeating on stuffed goose, I hear. As a matter of fact, Louis, I had thought to ask you to reimburse me for the outlay on Robert, but have decided that I shall not. It's a privilege, and I'm enjoying it. And of course, with your father ailing increasingly, it may not be long before you inherit everything; and then, of course, when you're gone—

. . . I shall disinherit Robert! the father screamed.

. . . In that case, I'll probably leave him a generous portion of my own estate. By the way, have you encountered any references to Paleolithic art in your recent researches? . . .

Within two years Bertell Schneider went from crowd to crowd, from harangue to harangue, and finally found himself frantically digging up stones as he had done at Gigouzac, but this time it was to make a barricade. The Revolution of 1848 swept him along in its noisy trough, and bullets made their cat snarls. . . . He was saved for another life and another death, very far away.

(Three times after he died the Germans would come bursting into his country; and in the year of the third invasion, boys would go seeking their dog in a woodland hole at Lascaux, near the village of Montignac; but the horses and hinds of Gigouzac would still be poised unobserved amid their secrecy, along with A Thing Called Waiting.)

XVII

Eery—Irey—Ickery—Ann,
Fillsom—fallsom—Nicholas—John,
Queevey—quavey—English—navy—
Gee—haw—buck!

Oho, Rowly's It!

Naw I ain't neither. She was pointing right at Bertie! Bertie's It. Ain't you, Bertie?

You didn't say One-two-three, Liza—

Didn't I? Very well.

One—two—three,
Out—goes—she!
With—a—dish—pan
On—her—knee!

Abbie's It! Run, you kids—run hide! *Hide!*

The three others fled screaming as Abbie leaped against the bur-oak tree, cushioned her face on folded arms, and began to count with yelling inarticulate speed: Five—ten—fifteen—twenty—twenty-five—thirty—thirty-five—forty—

In certain moods of infantile reversion which often perplex a young girl, Eliza Gardner would find herself willing, even eager, to play with the children. Her presence made four of them in a game. As four in number, they could manage group sports in which two or three little people might not find joy.

Eliza's father and brother-in-law toiled enthusiastically at house-building (they owned only their experience in the construction of a cabin at Clear Lake; but Rowland Gardner had learned much about lumber when he was in the sawmill business, and that helped) while Mrs. Gardner and Mary prepared the meals, did the washing, and spoiled little Amanda between times. The families slept in their wagons. They had soap and pork and candles and meal and dried fruits in sufficiency—supplies fetched for winter use seemed like a store inexhaustible. Life was genial, undemanding, mainly undisciplined. Eliza and Abbie might be of little aid at this season, except in fetching water from the lake, fetching firewood, helping to wash clothes and to scrub out the pots and skillets. Also it was their task to air the bedclothing, draping comforters and blankets in sunlight over the hazelbrush. But mainly they dwelt in an extended picnic except during rainy weather. Then they were all cooped up in the wagons, and the little boys abraded everybody's nerves including their own. Rowly bullied Bertie, Bertie scratched back, Rowly roared and slapped, the boys were shaken or spanked, Baby Mandy howled in sympathy. But it did not rain often during July and August.

Earlier in summertime the girls had picked strawberries until their hands were as pink as were the hands of Harvey Luce when he worked at the dyeing trade. Tiny wild strawberries colored up through swales along the edge of every woodland; at the height of their profusion you could see from distance a ruddy blush underlying the soft basket-woven fabric of the grass. You could pick a big bucketful in half an hour, even keeping your mouth crammed while you picked. But now in a later season appeared larger coarser berries, often guarded with spines and thorns; these grew on bushes and vines tangled heedlessly around the damp insect-haunted clearings where oaks and lindens thinned apart. Raspberries, dewberries, gooseberries, currants, wild grapes: they had ripened or would ripen progressively in laggard easygoing relays . . . some Master Horticulturist arranged a benefit for gentle hungry folks who asked only to munch sun, drink the dew, fatten on fairy juices. Birds found the berries, the Gardners and Luces found them. Abbie discovered also a rattlesnake sunning itself, when she was following after a yellow-winged grasshopper to catch him for fish bait. She pried out a big stone, tossed it with both hands (though with eyes squeezed tightly shut), the snake buzzed and adjusted its fat wounded coils, Abbie found stone after stone, lugged the stones, heaved them between squeals, she nearly buried the mashed reptile beneath the pile. Her father, drawn by this outcry, arrived to finish off the rattler with a club, and he amputated the string of nine rattles with a button at the tip. Abbie was enough of a tomboy to wear this savage gaud on an old blue ribbon after it had been cured. Eliza shivered forth maidenly injunctions for Abbie to keep her distance.

Twon't hurt you, Liza. It's *dead.*

Ooh, *how can* you wear that dang thing round your *neck?* Ma, make her take it off—

Pa said that Mr. Jim Dickirson told him at Clear Lake that if you wore a rattlesnake's rattles twould make you brave!

Ooh, who wants to be *brave?* Ma, make her— Abigail Gardner, you quit shaking that thing at me!

Liza's-mad, cried Abbie. And-I-am-glad!-And-I-know-what'll-please-her:-a-bottle-of-wine-to-make-her-shine,-and-*Henry-Tretz*-to-squeeze-her!

Abigail Gardner, you stop that this minute or I'll *pull your hair—!*

Yah, can't catch me—

Oh, Abbie, for conscience' sake, said Frances. Stop pestering your sister. Sometimes you don't act like two well-brought-up young ladies, you act like a couple hoydens and that's all there is to it. Liza, you leave off coloring and simpering, Miss; now I want you to hang out this wash, and then you put that bucket of— She lowered her voice to the politely ominous whisper used in speaking of female matters. *Cloths*—to soak. Abbie, do you take the old neck yoke and carrying buckets, and fill this tub I've just turned out. And you ain't to plague Eliza by shaking them rattles at her. I still got a ready hand with a switch, if you *are* thirteen!

William—Trimmitty—is—a—good—water—man,
Catches—hens—puts—them—in—pens.
Some—lay—eggs—and—some—lay—none:
White—Foot—Speckle—Foot—
Trip—trap—and—be—gone—
O—U—T—spells—Out!

Why, Abbie, you here too?

Shhh. I snuck in from under these grapevines—

Goodness, I thought I was the only one knew this place—

Shhh. Here comes Bertie—

Oh, he's looking every which way!

Liza, he's awful little. Hope he don't start a-crying if he can't find nobody— Where's Rowly hid?

Tother side that great big log.

The big hollow one? Oh, yes, I see him—

Abbie, I think Bertie's getting ready to bawl!

He's an awful bawl-baby. Sister Mary humors him too much—

Shhh. Yes. But I guess we ought to give him a clue. Let's both yell *Cooop!*—but kind of short.

All ready?

Yes.

Now!

Cooop!

He's coming.

Better let him catch us, this time. Cause he's little.

Member when we used to play I-Spy and Toss-the-Wicket with the Starkwethers and Crockers and Danas, back in York State?

Oh, yes. And the Armstrongs— I just couldn't *abide* Elsie Starkwether! She always had a snotty nose and she was always a-whining—

Eee! Here's Bertie! *Eee!* He's peeking in, he sees us—! Run, run, Sis! Run, Bertie—

Eeee!

Abbie—don't run—*too* fast—

No. . . .

Here we come.

Where from?

New York.

What's your trade?

Ice cream and lemonade.

Show us some!

Eliza and Rowly pretended to act, as they were actors on the stage, they pretended to be churning, Abbie and Bertie screamed together (Abbie being just a bit the earliest to interpret the charade): *Churning!* The others fled, Liza catching up her long loose skirts as she scuttled; but Abbie did not tag her before she was safe at Base. Bertie very nearly caught Rowly. . . . Rowly and Bertie whispered long with giggling explosive whispers, they advanced, recited the litany somewhat haltingly, they made wild motions with their arms, they swung violently, bent and postured.

Rowly's sisters and Bertie's aunts guessed vociferously.

Scything grass?

No!

Gardening!

No. . . .

Chopping down trees!

The two small boys whirled and sprinted toward Base, the two nearly woman-grown girls rushing after them with ragged calico bundles of their gowns held up, bare legs flashing with speed, the right hands extended to try to grasp, to seize, to capture. Both shrieking boys reached Base safely.

(To grasp, to seize, to capture a bright green moment which ran as the ground squirrels run, as fly the truant sulphur-colored butterflies which blink in tinted yellow snowstorm where glade flowers are the thickest . . . there will never be a moment like this. This is it!—ah, this very second!—yet now the second has fled, we felt the dust of its wings fleet and delicate upon our fingers. . . . Was that a raindrop on my cheek? Nay, only the pure cream let fly by a bird which arched its pinions and spread its fluid dung into the smiling air around, and said, The offering of my nervous airborne body is needed by lushness far beneath, if lushness may continue. . . . *Ugh*, I yelled. Oh, nasty! Lookit my face, lookit my finger, see what the blame hawk went and did! . . . Well, don't take on so, Little One. Wipe it clean with a leaf, spit on the leaf, wipe it clean, don't fuss. Everything is wilderness, and so tis clean. . . . Excrement? What indeed is excrement? Never in a wilderness. . . . Seize and capture storied bison . . . ah, those bones we found . . . and that wide-spreading skull, and Pa guessed twas a buffalo, because of a smooth-rotting stick with arrowhead still fastened on it. . . . Acquire the melodious tiny lavender-colored bird—

What a pipe he plays!—and keep him within your gown and within your heart, and bring him forth in quiet rapture as a comfort, should there come tormenting.)

Green gravel, green gravel,
The grass is so green. . . .

*

London Bridge is falling down,
Falling down, falling down.
London Bridge is falling down,
My fair lady. . . .

*

A bushel of wheat and a bushel of clover.
All 'at ain't ready
Can't hide over!

*

My—father—bought—me—
A—new—red—trunk—
How—many—nails—were—in—it?

Well, am I It?

No, Rowly. Tain't over yet: see, you got to say how many nails are in it—

But I don't know!

Oh, Abbie, quit your laughing. He's little, he don't understand. Now I'll splain to you—you pay close heed— You pay heed too, Bertie, whilst Aunt Liza splains to you—

Well, we don't like this new Counting Out. Whyn't you say Eery-Irey or Eeny-Meeny or something?

Now, listen. Liza'll splain. Tis because you don't *know* how many nails are in the trunk. That makes the difference. You can say any number you want to—

Did Pa honest buy you a new red trunk, one time?

No, no, *no!* Tis just another Counting *Out*. Oh, land of Goshen, how'll I make you understand? . . . Now, *listen.* If you say a number —any number—Sister'll *count* to that number, poking with my finger like, each time. Just like any Counting Out. See?

No. Let Bertie say the number.

He don't know his numbers, he's only four years old.

Do *too* know my numbers!

All right, you can say the number, Bertie. Now, I'll start afresh:

My—father—bought—me—
A—new—red—trunk—
Now—many—nails—were—in—it?

Now, *say,* Bertie. Speak up!

Four?

Four. One–two–three–four.
One–two–three–out–goes–he–
With–a–dish–pan–on–his–knee!

Bertie's It, Bertie's It! . . . hide . . . *hide!*

. . . Liza.

. . . What?

. . . He can't *really* count to a hundred by fives, or to fifty by ones, or anything.

. . . Course not. But he likes to pretend. He just stands up gainst that tree, and makes a lot of mumbles, and then he yells *Coming!* See . . . here he comes now. Scrooch down! . . .

(And be young, be extremely tender, be babyish and trivial, let the light wind ripple you as it ripples water, let it sway you as it curls the tiniest fuzz of tanager's feather caught upon shredding bark of the wild grapevine. Flee barefooted, your feet harder than sole leather, your small dirty feet actually turned to leather and feeling only the sharpest of pebbles, feeling never common thorns.)

I know! Let's play Statue.

Gee–Statue–

I wanna play Statue–

Course you can. You come play, Bertie–

Hoo-hoo! You kids come in now. Getting late. Come now, get you to bed in the wagon–

Aw, *no!* All nice shiny moonlight–

Liza? Abbie?

Yes, Ma.

If you girls want to stay out and play awhile, you watch the boys careful. Don't let them get nigh the house–

Wife, I think tis time for Bertie to come say his prayers.

I know, Mr. Luce. But he can say them pretty soon–they're having so much fun out there in the moon, and the girls have been setting on the stumps, watching that new-risen moon, and they'll look after him and Rowly for a while–

Well, all right. But don't let him forget to say his prayers. You did, tother night.

Now, Abbie, let's play Statue!

All right. Liza, you want to come, help the boys play Statue?

Huh-uh. Tis nice just watching that moon. . . .

Bet you're mooning about Henry Tretz! All right, boys, I'm coming, Abbie'll play with you. . . . Albert Johnson *Luce,* you come away from over by that house! Your Pa says there's some big loose logs that ain't pinned fast yet, and they're liable to fall down on you–

Let us whirl you first, Abbie.

All right. You both catch hold of my hand. Here . . . *whirl* me!

(And be three figures in the vast kindliness of untarnished light, posturing in your turns, standing with shadowy arms flung out, shadowy necks bent, shadowy heads twisted back, poised inelegantly on shadowy limbs, each a statue in your turn. Imagine yourself as stone or marble . . . but you'll never be a statue: you're too lively and too fluid, your flesh is full of springs, your little minds are full of frog-talkings and fish-skitterings, you have the wires of the berry-vines for your skeletons, the musk of summer's early night is in your nostrils, and so it drives you mad. . . . Go hopping on your course and send your chuckle up against the stars . . . the moon is washing them to paleness, soon there'll be few stars . . . only pervading delicacy of paint that's spread from Heaven, only the clear and shrinking moon to make you think of God amid your revels. You'll stand aloof, poised until your muscles ache and let you down; and eyes which watched you might grow quickly wet with sympathy, and an earnest voice might say: Why, these are only children, and they're having fun. Oh, *ain't* they having fun! . . . And never knowing that, for a moment, you stand encompassed by a vision—that you stand with silly hand all taloned like a claw—and yet in that same formless vagrant moment you have reached into the moon and touched the robe of One to whom you'll later offer doleful prayers.)

Perforce, a child exists subservient to rules of fact and nature, but his dreams do not, his dreams go flying. So might each of these young have been hauled whirling aloft, to chuckle at their divorcement from Earth and the admonishment of elders. A kindly bird with vast wings could have drawn them high into moonlight, together or singly, and let them see their region carpeted. Taller or smaller, they'd all dreamt of such exalted gyrations . . . the child is a dullard who's never ridden on clouds. But no clouds creamed the space upon this evening. There ruled only gentle warmth, a night shining in the quality of a mysterious polished mirror, alive with moths and skeeters, sacred to whizzings of the furry brindled mustached birds whose legend had them sucking for the milk of goats. You could call them nightjars, bullbats, call them pisks or will-o'-the-wisps, call them whippoorwills; twas all the same: they skated fast a-feeding, tingled the forests with their cry.

And so the child, with fancies unblunted by encroachment of maturity, might beguile himself into a notion wherein he was scooped up by a safe and generous wingèd thing as big as a new log house, and borne far far into the pungent glowing reaches . . . I'll take ye for a ride, says the enormous beaming bird. I'll show ye the world, show ye the night.

Thus he carried one young girl or one shockheaded tiny boy, or carried the whole clan swaying snugly in a napkin woven of the moonbeams themselves, as a stork hefts its babies in caricature. The oaks became as grass, falling fast away, the nearer lake turned into a twisting silver puddle, the other lakes were seen adjoining it. There were the Okoboji lakes and Spirit Lake spread out as an adornment, misshapen bangles to decorate the world's surface. (One mile ascended against the pale majesty of the moon? Five miles in the air—a hundred? No one knew. No one could reckon a measurement of upper space, there was not even a common myth to aid in estimation. So few balloonists had ever swung within the sky that their accomplishment went undescribed.) No mundane father or schoolmarm was bossing this reverie, whether indulged in singly or collectively. There could be no limit, no end or beginning or border to it; the night bird in the dream was their host and guard and conveyance. . . . I'll take ye up, he said. And fetch ye back to earth quite safe again.

Far to the north below them was tacked the solid silver of Spirit Lake, nearly five miles long and nigh as wide at its widest. South and east, and swinging westerly again, bent the bow-shape of East Okoboji, sometimes half a mile across, mostly narrower, the forests blackening its edges. And pointed out to west and north, the serrated spearhead of West Okoboji let moonlight polish it, lying docile in its own sheath of oaken groves. Were they fastened together, these glinting mystic bodies? Scarcely did you know or care: the tiny straits were so shadowed and tenuous, the guarding ridges of land so slim. Spilled out and spangled into paler prairies on all sides were the baby lakes, the fishponds—wet glacial pockets with room for a flock of ducks to swim on each, or room perhaps for a dozen flocks, or scarcely room for a dozen birds.

Chicken guts, whispered a child in its instant infant recognition of the macabre and the stickily ridiculous. Ah, yes, tis so! Like when I seen Ma emptying out the carcass of a fowl. There's big old Spirit Lake above, and that's the heart, and maybe the Okoboji lakes are the liver and gizzard and things attached; and there's all that long stringy stuff . . . soft lumps, and growing whiter the larger they get, and Ma said those were eggs that hadn't yet been laid by the hen, and she'd put them in the stuffing!

Some thirty miles of wandering wet brightness, glued against the world's forgotten surface . . . waters spread, curling, compressed, tightened, places where you could nearly throw a stone across, places where you'd have to swim if you could swim, places where your Pa would have to take you in a canoe if so you owned a canoe, but you didn't own one.

Miniwakan, the voices of long dead Dakota said to you in the air, because you were still very young, and thus a creature of magic, and thus able to embrace all languages, grasp all beauties with only the most casual turn of the wrist or of the mind. Miniwakan . . . Spirit Lake. Minitanka . . . the Big Water, that's West Okoboji. And there's

East Okoboji so far below the tips of our tired dirty toes; and Okoboji means a Place of Rest; that's what that old hunter said who come by a-Sunday.

Mr. Harshman was his name, and he said he wasn't settled no place, said he was just a rover; and sometimes he sold his meat or his pelts way down in Fort Dodge, wherever that may be, and sometimes he sold them way up St. Peter's way, wherever that may be. Old Mr. Harshman could talk some Indan talk, and he tolt us what the names of these lakes might mean; but just about everybody off yonder calls the whole caboodle Spirit Lake and lets it go at that.

He said that right now there wasn't no Indans around, and not to wherrit ourselves about them. But he warned of rattlesnakes.

And he said the lakes was very deep. Said no one alive, Indan or white, knew the depth of some of them holes.

Said that it was told how no Indan would even paddle his canoe on the waters of Spirit Lake, cause twas haunted. Not our own West Okoboji, here at this southeastern point; not East Okoboji, over past the Narrows; they wasn't sposed to be the dwelling place of spirits (though some Indans did think so—not the most, just some—and they said one time all their old grandfather Indans and grandmother Indans lived *actually down under the water,* and some of them still dwelt there. But that couldn't be so. Pshaw! Cause they'd be drownded).

And he liked Abbie's snake rattles, and said if she sewed them fast to her bunnet, she'd never catch a headache.

And he said that if Baby Mandy was to have a red yarn string tied round her neck or round her toe, she'd never be bothered by hobgoblins.

But he kind of winked at Ma and Mary when he said it.

And on that greasy string he pulled from underneath his shirt, he had two teeth and a bone: and one was a wolf's tooth, and that would make him brave if he met the most ferocious animals; and one was a squirrel's tooth, and that would make him wise to tell a million things that ordinary folks could never understand; and that small bone was just a knuckle from a black hog's foot (a wild black hog he said he'd shot one time with his Kentucky rifle, and he let us children stroke the shiny maple stock of that same gun) and long as Mr. Harshman wore that bone beneath his clothing he would never suffer from the rheumatiz.

. . . No Mr. Harshman a-trudging now, he wouldn't be wandering at night, cause he couldn't see to stalk or shoot, he'd be on his blanket. Maybe somewhere below, in dark contours of the wilderness, we can see the single speckle of his fire?

Never. Not a spark or smidgin. If fire's there tis hidden—it has the lid of matted woodlands squeezed above it.

. . . So onward, out, and higher still the considerate bird went planing with his passenger or passengers; and only when the young dreamer or dreamers grew tired of reckless soaring fantasy would the bushy wings be leadened by a weariness as well; and thus the bird felt need to chirp, I'll take ye home. Then the land would whirl to meet them, contrasting ceramics of prairie and timberland and lake waters rising from barest tints into a thick paint, then into a stippling . . . faster, faster, take the earth-bound strangers down! . . . oh, are we falling? Let us scream! . . . but nay, nay, tis only that the will-o'-the-wisp is diving with us, he's still strong and living, so are we . . . and now prairie-woodland patches are a hasty fabric, now they are embossed and puffed like quilting, now trees begin to thrust their tips and branches, the lakes recede to be observed no more. And on elastic grass once more I am deposited, or all of us are gently dumped. The bird has croaked its last, has said, Indeed I took ye for a jaunt, I carried ye so high and far. Now utter thanks to me and God.

The evening's late, the moon's gone higher, grass is damp, the wild sweet clearing grass is cool and silvered. Mother calls; and here the snorers snore, the tired elder folk. We join them in their slumber, but with a recollection of vistas and of flight, a notion which the grown-ups never own, because they're young no longer.

Sometimes the caravan of children paraded away through open woods for a considerable distance, wearing always that peculiar hint of a beggar troupe, mendicants or gypsies, which such bevies suggest when they are assorted as to age and sex and stature; and more especially when their clothing is shabby, as all clothing of these people was well-worn and fringed. Bertie's loose breeches were of faded calico, and patched upon the seat, stained at the knees. Abbie's coarse gown had a rim of brighter brown around the bottom of the skirt where the hem had been let out to conceal her changing *limbs.* Rowly's face and shirt were painted with dried berry juices, Eliza's slat bonnet had bird droppings on the top, of which she was happily unaware . . . they traveled with squeal and chatter, all were scratched and brown-legged and hard-footed. They'd said that they were going to pick the fat gooseberries with spines all over them (but spines cooked to softness in a pie or jam, they didn't stick you when you ate). Abbie carried a tin pail, Eliza a basket, birds gushed away from them, the squirrels fussed off in alarm, Eliza wore her tight ragged sleeves buttoned down to the wrist in order to protect her fair skin.

(Sure, Harshman the hunter had said. There's new folks moved in at Springfield . . . oh, maybe twenty mile, or maybe less. That's top of the Des Moines River, over northeast. Family named Thomas. One named Stewart. The Wood brothers got a store—they was there first. And cousins of mine, both of the same name: Harshman. Also a young German boy named Henry Tretz . . . Henry *Tretz?* . . . So

I said: a young Dutchy. The folks he was traveling with struck on farther north, up towards the Agency, but he wanted to stay. . . . *Henry Tretz!* Oh, maiden, peer within the unrippled bucket of lake water, on a bench in shadow of the wagon, and let its mirror tell you that your face is fair.)

Less go look at the punkin field!

Less!

A patch of pumpkin vines had been discovered during the earliest exploration the troop made toward the vicinity of the Narrows, a slender reach of water connecting East and West Okoboji lakes. This was on the third day following the Gardner-Luce arrival, the day after Abbie attacked her rattlesnake. On the edge of a glade which dissolved into oaks and hickories along a low bluff rising from East Okoboji, the little band found themselves entangled in ropes of vines, with familiar big orange-colored flowers and wide flapping leaves. They stumbled over squat green pumpkins in profusion. Wild punkins, the children yelled. Won't Ma and Mary be tickled! Plenty of pie-timber! And we can make punkin-heads, come chill weather, and maybe Ma'll leave us have some candle stubs to fix inside!

What's punkin-heads?

Don't you mind, Bertie? We had them at Clear Lake.

I forget. . . .

Some calls them jack-lights or jack-lanterns. You cut all the punkin out, with a real sharp knife, and carve it up like a *skull.* They're just scairy!

Want to make one now. . . .

No, they're far too little and green.

Want to make a little one, and scare Mandy.

Albert Johnson *Luce,* don't you dast go frighting your baby sister! No! We ain't going to make none now. Abbie, less hasten home and tell the folks we found a whole field of wild punkins.

Hain't no such thing, said Rowland Gardner positively when he'd heard the news.

He held an important puzzle in his mind. He and Harvey had walked the northern and eastern shore of West Okoboji, to ascertain whether there might be a site for their claims more favorable than the spot where first they'd encamped; and suddenly they had heard several gunshots. Preliminary cautious examination of the area revealed no strangers, Indian or white, yet both men felt disquietude. The sounds of shotguns and rifles were unmistakable . . . they planned to investigate more thoroughly on the next day. Women and children had not heard the shooting; neither man wished to alarm his family by mentioning the worry.

Pa, we *seen* the punkins.

But I don't think there are any wild punkins. Gourds, yes. Mayhap these was gourds?

No, siree. We girls seen them, and the little boys too. Real honest-to-goodness *punkins.*

How fur off?

Maybe as fur as from our place to Clear Lake, around to the outlet, said Eliza.

Oh, no, Liza, not that fur!

Well, pretty nigh.

Gardner glanced at the sun. We got time. We'll go now. . . . No, you boys stay to home, you got short legs, can't go fast. Girls'll show me where tis.

Gardner took his loaded rifle with him, but fortunately the girls saw nothing alarming in this: they supposed merely that their father had some thought of hunting along the way. Back at the wagon, Harvey Luce guarded the remaining members of the flock with shotgun and mumbled prayer.

In that scraggly clearing with sunset light staining the tree trunks at the east, Rowland received his second shock of the day as he turned copious green leaves aside with his boot. Someone's planted these, he said gloomily. They are punkins, sure as you're born. A host of them.

But, Pa. Who—?

Don't know.

Wild men?

Don't consider it likely.

But there ain't no *folks* around—

Well. I can't figure just who or why.

Gardner said no more until, shepherding the girls along with him, and watching musky dusky thickets with trepidation, they were once more approaching the wagon camp. He did not wish to alarm his daughters, to upset Frances, to keep tiny boys restricted to a single slope and clearing, when free beauty shimmered on every side. . . . For this was why they'd come here: to grub and axe a living from undirtied unexploited unconfused regions, until in easy course the woodlands were indeed populated, spoiled, and thus grown valuable . . . a purse could be fattened again.

The shots which he and Harvey Luce had heard that day still rang in his ears. But maybe they'd been fired only by wild men . . . tractable good-tempered wild men unlike the scurvy galoots who'd frightened them at Clear Lake—simple lakeside dwellers who might pace smiling to greet them, bearing gifts of venison and popcorn (ah, pretty Pilgrim illusion!) and saying, like Samoset in a long-mossed Massachusetts legend: Welcome, English!

Gardner said, Tis just that you young folks ought to stay within beck and call. Could be bogs or quicksands about; we don't know the neighborhood as yet. Mind, you hold close.

Yes, Pa, the girls murmured. Despite his intentions they were alarmed vaguely at the moment (and quite ready to forget the injunction in another day).

The mystery of the pumpkin-planting was not solved for a fortnight, and in the meantime the Gardners had discovered new neighbors.

But Harvey Luce marked an elm tree with his axe, to blaze the location of a sweet copious spring discovered beyond the pumpkins and near the Narrows (quoting in his adolescent whine: Behold, I will stand before thee there upon the rock in Ho-reb; and thou shalt smite the rock, and there shall come water out of it, that the people may drink! Rowland Gardner felt that same queasiness which affected him increasingly whenever Harvey gathered up the Scriptures and lugged them in by the ears). The girls and little boys, trailing once more in that direction, examined fresh fibers around the blade-scar and discovered that this was indeed slippery elm. Abbie was the first to chew the inner bark and delight at such confection, and pronounce it edible.

Member, Liza? We used to have it at Shell Rock. Goody, goody!

Ma says it makes medicine, too.

I don't care bout medicine. But tis *scrump*tuous to chew!—and Abbie's soft chin was all a-drip.

Rowly asked, through full and oozing mouth, How'd we know it ain't plain piss elm?

Rowland Smith *Gard*ner, don't you dare say that word again, or—I'll—tell—*Pa!* Eliza sought to shake her brother, but he dodged away.

So'll I tell! cried the shocked Abigail. You call an elm that ain't a slippery elm a *water* elm, Mr. Smart!

It was for the slippery elm tree that the excursionists were bound, one hot forenoon at the first of August, when they heard an outlandish creaking, shouting, and squealing ahead of them. It was the combined protestation of wheels, human voices, animal uproar. They did not well know whether diversion or threat was suggested in the sounds. For a few moments the children jigged and darted, exclaiming that they should run back to the wagons— No, they should wait and see what on earth— Was someone being tortured? Did wild men approach? At last Eliza stood shuddering, little boys drawn close to her skirts, while Abbie scouted fearfully through a low bank of hazelbrush. At the edge of the pumpkin-planting she crouched in disbelief, then beckoned for the others to come on. . . .

There wrangled a fierce noisy invasion: two long wagons drawn by oxen, a burly youth on horseback, a small herd of cows, shouts, hand-wavings, two boys and a little girl running after the cattle with sticks and hooting. Out of this flapping progressive assemblage rose the squeals first heard, now shriller and more protracted with each lurching of a wheel across a hummock or log. Waddling on the nigh side of those three yokes of oxen which drew the first big wagon walked a man whose corpulence might match that of the beasts he drove.

It was learned later that Mr. James Mattock did not know his exact weight, but he had tipped the beam at three hundred and fifty-six pounds the last time he stood upon a scale, and that was when the tribe boarded an Ohio river ark. His clothes were smeared and greasy beyond description (Just hog-shit, he was to announce cheerfully. Can't handle hogs thout getting them all over you). He wore a wide leather belt with bosses of shining brass. His beard was the color of old straw, and built his chin into a square slab; a torn black hat was pushed to the back of his huge bald head. Rowly and Bertie thought that he was ready to eat them up, ready to eat anyone up.

There's the God damn punkin patch! Keep them bastards out of it!

Squeeeee–

Are we there, Pa? Are we there?

Sure you're here! Agnes, that brindle cow's in the damn grapevines! Get herself strangulated–

Squeeeee–

I think the boar's got loose in the wagon–

No he hain't. Just ornery–

Quaaaaaah–

Where we going to build our house? Pa–where–?

Mooooo–

Hey, Danny! Over here–follow the wagons–

Due ahead! See them big basswoods? Right above there–

Squeeeee–

Git over there, you fat-assed–

Gee, boy, *gee–!*

Rooooo–

Ag-nass! That brindle's heading for the punkins–

> *Oh, the beggar-man he grabbed her,*
> *And he rolled her on the floor,*
> *With a toora-loora-loora–*

Pa, when we going to start building our house? Pa, when–?

Start cutting trees tomorrow if the God damn weather holds–

Jim Mattock, you mind your speech!

Squeeeee–

Rowly and Bertie had seen many movers that season, they had never seen any movers like these, they had never heard of any such movers. Profanity was uncountenanced in the Gardner household, undreamed-of in the Luce family. Obscene phrases uttered by other small fry had penetrated the private lore of both small boys during their short seasons of awareness, and they had seen and heard two fierce teamsters cursing savagely as they fought (Harvey Luce prayed for the embattled sinners when offering Grace within the hour). Not all denizens of Iowa communities had been Saved or even purified by the example and habit of more enlightened families around them. But a howling crew such as this was not commonly to be observed on any reach of prairie, in any timberland.

Bertie Luce especially held a swift terrifying notion of the Pharaoh's horsemen and pursuing Egyptian charioteers who had poisoned his dreams necessarily since babyhood. His claw-fingers closed tighter on his aunt's gown, his tiny tough arms stiffened and jerked until the goods tore; but the popeyed Eliza was unaware of injury to her attire as she stood gaping in disbelief. Wild men, wild white men, wild white children, ogres, witches, circus procession, Antiques and Horribles, herd of buffalo, cannibals, heathen, Goliath, jailbirds, Herod's soldiers, infidels, lunatics, Daniel's lions . . . the jouncing screaming aggregation was so commingled and identified by innocent minds, until an even more piercing yell from sharp-eyed little Agnes Mattock brought the whole parade to a halt. Agnes had seen the cluster of young strangers. She advanced boldly, supported by two brothers.

The Gardners did not flee, though they entertained the impulse to do so. Abbie and Eliza had secured a glimpse of sunbonnets beneath the puckered wagon covers, and had taken additional reassurance from the aplomb of the scrawny maiden who slapped cows with her switch. In a few moments all were exchanging identities and information.

Especially were the Gardner girls relieved to hear that this pumpkin patch was not the work of Indians—it had been planted by Mr. Jim Mattock when he and Robby Matheson, the young man on horseback, visited Okoboji during the previous spring.

Hain't you folks found my claim-marks? roared Mattock.

Pa didn't say. We only got here sixteenth of July.

What's the name—Garner?

Gardner, sir. Our sister Mary Luce, and her husband, they live with us. This here's their little boy—

James Mattock bellowed, caught up Bertie, whirled him head over heels above his head, roared like a bull, and set the child back upon the ground in a dazed condition. You tell your Pa and tother man to come see us! You say you're nigh a mile over yonder, so our claims won't conflict. We got it all stepped off and papered proper, cording to the God damn law! One claim for us, one for Robby's folks, case they come out from Delaware County next spring. Got to step them off careful, count these sons-a-bitching claim jumpers—

Jim, you mind your speech, front of these young ladies!

Mary Mattock was nearly as tall as her husband but nothing like so weighty. Her burden of dark hair was roped into a mound atop her head . . . she was pleasured beyond description, she told the girls, to find that there were other womenfolks now living in the area, where she'd thought to have but her own two daughters for company. It was obvious that she saw jolly female times ahead; but the discomfited Gardners were not at all certain that their own mother would share the ruddy-faced Mrs. Mattock's enthusiasm for such encounter, nor for any social intercourse beyond barest necessity.

(Honest, Ma, cried Abbie in a stiff voice. They had one wagon with nothing in it cept *pigs;* one awful old boar, and some brood sows! And all the time whilst we talked to Mrs. Mattock, and her girls and— That great fat Mr. Mattock was wandering around looking at his punkin patch and saying things like: This'll be good feed, Robby boy. For hogs and cattle too. I hope to *shit,* it will! . . . Abbie! Don't —don't *say* such— Spose your Pa would hear you! . . . Well, Pa, ought to heard *him,* that's all! That's what he *said.* And he was singing a song about a beggar man and—and—the man in the song, *he grabbed her and he rolled her on the floor!* . . . Abigail Gardner, don't sully your lips with such awful words! . . . Cross my heart and hope to die, Ma, that's what he *sang.*)

Despite their shuddering before the ruffianly newcomers, Eliza and Abbie were disappointed to find that the eldest Mattock daughter, Alice, was all of eighteen. To their notion she might as well have been thirty. Cattle-Driver Agnes was only ten: she fell into the trough of age between Abbie and Rowly. There were three Mattock boys. The youngest was the size of Albert Luce; but Harvey Luce forbade his son to journey Mattock-wards, once his horrified ears had been assaulted by a girlish version of the beggarman song.

Nevertheless there lived gentility in the soul and manner of Alice Mattock. Frances Gardner and Mary Luce warmed easily to Alice when she walked the mile to their camp, and later to their house, to borrow this or that . . . to bring a huge toothsome pike from the lake (Ain't he a handsome fellow, though? Pap and I took three this morning early. Far more than all of us can eat; and we didn't want this fine fish to spoil). Alice had a long low-bridged nose, a long upper lip, an expanse of forehead; her cool gray-blue eyes gazed calmly from under thick brows, and were lashed softly and luxuriantly. The voices of her parents were uncouth voices, heavy or shrill by turns, the yap of her little sister and brothers was generally a high-pitched offense which made the hearer coil and tighten inside. The voice of Alice was low, serene . . . Abbie, an avid collector of wraith and imagery, thought of a mild woodland stream when she heard Alice Mattock speaking . . . the brook was unpebbled, unhurried, deep, and substantial—leaves floated half-submerged, deer came to drink in approved secrecy. It was as if the long-faced young woman with the wide forehead and coal-black berger curl had rejected all the lewd rudeness of her father and clacking chatter of her mother—rejecting them not critically or with contempt, but only with a poised tolerance which might have been hers as an inherited gift and did not need to be acquired through will or discipline. It was as if she said to all (speaking without words, only with graciousness of her big pale eyes): I'm of better stock, truly. Tain't my fault, tain't my doing or conceit; tis just that I'm a throwback to some quieter blood, and they can't help it if they ain't, poor things. But they're my folks, and so I'll serve and honor them, well as I am able.

Mrs. Gardner and her eldest daughter talked of Alice and Robby Matheson.

Reckon she's promised to him, Mary. That's the reason he's come with them.

Ma, she couldn't be. Cause—

Cause why?

Cause he's so kind of unspeaking. All that Robby does is just grunt and grin. He can't scarcely utter a responsive word. Just nods and giggles. And he *sweats* so bad—

Mary!

Well, he does! He fair stinks of it, every time he's stood near! When he come over, driving back our Satan ox that strayed clean to the Narrows, twas real hot and I got a real strong whiff of him—

*Ma*ry!

I wouldn't say it in hearing of the girls. But you and I are both married ladies, and I tell you frankly that—

Don't you keep unsettling my innards, Miss!

I ain't no Miss, Ma, I'm a Mrs. And that *presperation* of his—

For mercy's sake, Mary, change the subject!

Well, I don't see how a nice girl like Alice Mattock—and she is nice, Ma, no matter how that outfit curses and rips and carries on—I don't see how she could consider Robby. Reckon he just came along to help Old Man Mattock—kind of like a hired man. And they say his folks may settle out this way next year— I don't think she'd consider wedding such a bumpkin for one single moment.

Mary added shrewdly, I'd like to see her marry a man like Bert Snyder or Doctor Harriott.

XVIII

The two of them loved to hang suspended in their canoe, pasted on a transparent layer of green-brown veiling. This was the surface of West Okoboji. When wind did not come touching or troubling, the voyagers could look down into shadowed clarity and count colored stones which seemed to lie four feet beneath them and actually lay twelve or twenty.

None of the Red Wing Company owned much experience in handling canoes, though Bertell Snyder had traveled on rafts and in river barges, and had been a passenger and assistant paddler in Canadian *bateaux* on occasion. Neither he nor Isaac Harriott had learned to swim until grown; when forced by necessity to swim, they flailed clumsily with much violence and splashing. They thought they were lucky to be alive after the first three or four upsets. They stayed close to the shore line through future journeyings, and kept their guns tied to their belts by long cords.

Bert's beautiful Purdey rifle went down into fifteen feet of water within a half-hour after he'd first glided upon West Okoboji, and he could not reach that depth in any floundering dive, though he kept trying until he was half drowned. Finally Harry said, Hi, Mr.! I have a notion; and don't forget that I weigh the least of any of us. . . . Struggling, with much discussion, they hoisted a huge boulder into the canoe, and propelled it to the region of the vanished rifle. The canoe was tipped over, while Harry wrapped his arms around the stone. He plummeted to the bottom, striking less than a fathom away from Mr. Purdey's walnut-stocked marvel. The young doctor struggled back to the surface with aching lungs, and lights bursting inside his skull, but with the gun clutched in a death grip. Bert, clinging to the canoe, grabbed Harry by his blond hair which fortunately had grown long during the western trip. On shore, and watching critically, Bill Granger said, Bean't no gun would tempt me so to play the fool!—but Harry was hero of the day nevertheless.

The canoe had been acquired at Loon Lake, a few miles to the north of Spirit Lake, whither the Red Wing quartet traveled after a brief visit at the new settlement of Springfield. A boat of some sort would be necessary for proper examination and enjoyment of the fabled waters which lay to the south; and here was a lone English-speaking half-breed who said that his name was Renville. Camped on Loon Lake, he fished quietly for perch. His canoe was of Chippeway manufacture and had been bought at Fort Ridgely by a party of home-seeking Irish, and carried along in a wagon. Some accident or other opened up the bow of the craft; the travelers, ignorant of primitive handicraft, abandoned the canoe as worthless on the shore. Here Renville found it and promptly managed repairs. . . . Aye, he was willing to sell, he was strapped, he needed money. He needed six dollars badly, and would they pay six dollars? Harry remained at Loon Lake while the others took the Red River carts on to Spirit Lake, unloaded baggage; and Carl Granger and Bert Snyder drove back with one cart to take up the canoe.

Harry preened himself on his acquisition of the Dakota tongue, as taught by young Renville, boring the others with this erudition.

Ateunyanpi mahpiya ekta nanke chin. How's that?

Come, now. Tis jargon, lad.

No jargon about it, Carl. *Ateunyanpi mahpiya ekta nanke chin!*

Harry. Should you like to have a lesson in French?

Ah, hush. You're jealous, the two of you, because neither of you can speak Dakota, and I can! *Ateunyanpi*—

Aye, lad, aye. And what does it mean?

Means, Our Father which art in Heaven. You ought to have heard that Renville chap rip off the whole prayer.

Harry, did he teach you more?

Well . . . I was standing up next to a willow, making water, and he laughed, and pointed, and told me the Dakota word for my Thing. *Che.* Like it was spelled C-H-A-Y. He said that the un-Christianized Indians set great store by privates—always talking about them. He said that they had the act of copulation mingled up with the act of war; and that's the reason that womenfolks were so fearful of the Dakota. With mighty good excuse! And his mother was a full-blooded Dakota, so he should know! But over in Illinois everybody always talked of them as Sioux—

Bert said, You may blame us for that.

Blame who?

The French. This I learn when first I come to the United States. The French have taken an Indian word and—how you say?—corrupted it. *Nadouessioux*. The meaning is Enemies.

Such experiences and discussion were boyish trivia, but enjoyable trivia. Snyder and Harriott confided mutually a score of times during their first week at Okoboji: they had never felt so young in their lives. Bert said that their normal youth must have been put away for them by gods, as one might deposit money. It had now been returned severalfold, as might accrue to a wise investor making wise investment. And, cried Harry in response, they did not really deserve the experience at all, because the deposit was not of their own making: Bert's was the fruit of spiritual starvation, parental selfishness, the bleak cruelties he'd endured. Harry's own disacquaintance with jovialities accruing to other boys was compounded of his addiction to a chosen calling, the years of slavery and concentration, cold lonely years of midnight candles. Now the two men scouted blissfully on their ponies—they swam, fished, yelled, tussled. They tried to run down a wildcat (with no success, since the dog had little nose, only vast unruly eagerness for a scrimmage). Bert had developed proficiency as a rough-and-tumble fighter despite his wounded shin; Harry'd learned a few scientific wrestling locks from a skilled young neighbor when he was only thirteen or so. He'd never had much opportunity to employ them since; but now his wiry shape and the much taller lankiness of his friend were welded in frequent straining exertion. Thus they settled many small matters of camp duty or protocol. The brothers Granger dodged out of the way to avoid the grinning gasping combatants—the Grangers knocked out their pipes, shook their heads in amused tolerance, warned the wrestlers not to tackle *them,* said: Ah, they be a pair, those two! . . . Lee, the dog, snuffled damply; he tried to aid first one, then the other; he had to be restrained, with Carl Granger, his master, sitting on the thick grunting body.

A comparison of notes indicated that the Red Wing Company and the Gardner-Luce contingent reached the lakes within a day or two of each other. Only twenty-four hours after Bert lost his Purdey rifle, and had it recovered by Harry, the Red Wing Company were enjoying a luncheon of fish and biscuit when Lee went into a spasm. They leaped up to find two armed men regarding them somewhat fearfully from the edge of a thicket. This was their introduction to Rowland Gardner and Harvey Luce. Late that afternoon the Red Wingers went calling on womenfolks and children at the wagon camp, and a riotous picnic supper ensued. The younger children followed Bert about as if he were a Pied Piper. Rowland Gardner was overjoyed at the prospect of male companionship other than that afforded by his fanatic son-in-law; in imagination he foresaw long evenings when fires spat snugly and books passed from hand to hand. Also not a little of his apprehension about taking his flock into an unpopulated region was dissipated in the knowledge that a doctor was at hand, to be relied upon in case of emergency. Gardner slept more soundly than he had slept in many years, he worked daily at the cabin until he was ready to drop. So did Harvey, but Harvey could be sustained by blind doddering faith and an identification of himself with Disciples, Apostles, patriarchs, and prophets. He was too insensate to contemplate those nightmarish specters which had beset the elder man. Rowland Gardner suffered no more bad dreams—not until new and insoluble problems arose to perplex him (this came about only in clutch of a season to follow).

Gardner said to himself, on learning that the Red Wing Company had decided on an area just north of the Narrows: Their town'll rise nearby, but not too close. We'll not be in the swim of things. And—no mortgages. I'll never sign another mortgage, not on anything! I won't need to. Got our land and the money to pay for it. And then—If the town does rise beside us, our land'll be worth more, and I can sell profitably. If I *need* to sell.

Less than a mile away from him (as any hard-voiced crow might fly, and as dozens of them went winging every hour) the young men envisioned their town.

The Grangers saw a village very like their own Aldington in Kent—but larger and somehow finer—and an Aldington in which the Grangers were well-to-do, as assuredly they were not well-to-do in the Aldington left behind.

Now, William, who'll be lord of the manor?

That I will.

You'll not let me be?

Na. I'll be like old Deedes, I will!

I've been thinking a bit. Remember, William, at the Church of St. Martin, how the charitable bequests were listed on the wall?

Aye. Signed by the churchwardens in Seventeen Sixty-six—

That's right. And the grandest bequest of the lot was the two hundred and forty pounds left by the old Rector White. Were it not?

Aye. To be laid out in good security.

William, twould be fine to leave more than that. Think on't. Us poor ones!

Might be able to leave five hundred, we might.

If I prosper as I hope to prosper, I'll leave more!

Much as a thousand pounds, Carl?

Aye. Tis good to think on't.

Bertell Snyder declared that there might arise not only a town but soon a city. Twould be the Paris of the future, the Paris of the New World! The lakes would serve as the Seine, the Narrows would be bridged by a Pont Neuf! Isaac Harriott argued a good deal with Bert about this. Harry wished that the place might somehow preserve its rusticity but still adhere to a classical design. Both of them, however, saw their future town as a place well-ordered and sweet-smelling, in which the majority of the citizens held college degrees. (There was some pathos in this ideal on the part of the young man who had never been able to attend medical school, and the other young man who had been belabored out of his university by the whip of revolution. Each observed that pathetic quality in the other's illusion, neither recognized it in his own.)

Naturally the excited Harry saw himself as the most influential physician, presiding over all matters of health. He dressed Bert Snyder in robes of mayoralty, although not at all certain by what means this political elevation might be achieved. Beyond their own eminence, he generously set up the Grangers as moneyed merchants or mill-owners. Outside the specific fortunes of these Red Wing enthusiasts, he erected academies, Courts of Law, white-spired churches.

Only the most freshly clad women strolled the streets, bright-bonneted, carrying pretty colored parasols. . . .

Children of the town did not transgress when they romped, they muted their voices. (This idyl was cherished by Isaac Harriott only before the Mattocks appeared on the scene.) If children needed his professional attention at all it was but for minor and polite illnesses. The children never muddied themselves. Their worst fractures were only greenstick, there was no thrusting of raw splintered bones through their civilized skins.

No sewers emitted a stink . . . why, why—he had not considered sewers until the Grangers prosaically mentioned the possibility of such installations! Somehow Harry had assumed that a pristine population would have no need of sewers.

Of this he chuckled to Bert Snyder.

Ah. Harry, what do we call our town?

Well. Red Wing?

But already there is one Red Wing in Minnesota.

I know. But don't forget we're now in the State of Iowa. This could be the town of Red Wing, Dickinson County, Iowa.

Mais oui. But two Red Wings make for much confusion. One time I sent a letter to Paris, in France. Long afterward I learn that it is delivered instead to a town called Paris, Kentucky.

Very well. Shall you agree to Okobojiopolis?

That is an amalgamation of the Indian and the Greek which does not run so well off the tongue!

Spirit Lake City?

Perhaps.

Frankly, Bert, I prefer Okobojiopolis—

Et alors? Now I shall wrestle you for honor of the name!

None of them bothered to seek economic justification for the founding and growth of their imagined city. Vaguely all four men held fancies concerning a productive rural region from which herds and raw products of the farms would flow, centralizing in their sweep on Okoboji City or whatever the place was called, until mills hummed day and night—until there were packing houses replete with hams, and presses which oozed cider and vinegar in pungent streams—Iron horses came champing across rolling prairies, came steaming from the East to have their cars loaded with produce, to turn in miraculous circle and bear these trains of victuals back to a needy world.

Harry stocked the widespread farms with clean spotted cattle. Horses which drew the wagons were ample firm-flanked beasts, as seen in oil paintings of some paradise in Devonshire or Normandy, and each had fluffy hair growing on his hocks. Farmers (almost Isaac Harriott called them husbandmen) were immaculate, clad often in smocks. They were fecund, God-fearing, each a Samson in his own right, and none of them indulged in strong drink, nor rented land on shares: each *owned* his own farm. Trees of their orchards fairly split the limbs under a burden of scarlet golden-peppered apples, each weighing an even pound apiece. Twas always early autumn, the sun came down affectionately and was not too hot. Twas always harvest-time. Cows offered their milk copiously and fed entirely upon clover . . . yes, clover, not prairie grass. Harry didn't know how the clover got there, he supposed that it would be a simple matter to sow it. He saw sowers going forth—clean, well-set-up men again, like sowers pictured in stained glass (he remembered a church window in St. Louis), each with a bag slung at his side, each reaching in his sturdy hand for fat seeds to be tossed, to sprout and grow and ripen easily, without care.

Harry envisioned not a weevil, not an insidious worm.

Twas always sunny in daytime, the rains fell only at night.

The dogs bit no one, and they never went mad.

All of the cats had kittens; the kittens played with balls of yarn on piazzas, beside the rocking chairs of beaming grandmothers who sat knitting.

Each evening debating societies met in some public place, and the judges of the debates were actual judges from the Courts he'd founded in his fancy. Every judge was bearded, incorruptible, and bound for the United States Senate.

Resolved: That the Negro has suffered more at the hands of the white man than has the Indian.

Isaac Harriott was on the team presenting the case for the negative. (He thought of that slim tan half-breed Renville who'd sold the canoe, he thought of the few other Indians he had met, or the many he'd seen pacing along roadways in St. Paul. Ah, veritable children of Nature . . . although he rather felt like greeting them with a scrubbing brush in one hand and a wad of soft soap in the other. But that was because they'd been debased through contact with the whites!)

Resolved: That the Negro—

There was even a theater of sorts. Chaste excerpts from the works of William Shakespeare were presented by thespian societies; even ministers might attend these doings. A young lady with masses of soft black hair— Miss Raven Tresses, in fact! She arose in statuesque power to assume the role of Portia. Her voice was melodious, it vibrated softly with emotion. Her eyes were clear, cool, all-seeing. She had a magnificent body, she was gowned magnificently, she held her head erect with pride, she was very pure.

The quality of mercy is not strained,
It droppeth as the gentle rain from heaven
. . . Consider this,
That, in the course of justice, none of us
Should see salvation . . .
They also serve who only stand and wait.

No, no, something wrong about that! Not Shakespeare. . . . Goldsmith? Cowper? Ben Jonson? He did not know, he feared he'd never know. Too much Innes, too much Cheselden, Rosenstein, Daniel Drake, good Ben Dudley, *Cyclopaedia of Practical Medicine.*

Anyway, the young woman who spoke the lines spoke them with queenly grace, queenly intonation. Yes, her father was one of those same judges.

Harry was not certain, but sometimes it seemed that her name actually was Portia.

In time he married her. Promptly they had ten or twelve children, all of a size and about equally divided as to sex. Isaac Harriott himself did not attend Mrs. Raven Tresses in childbirth, he could not have made himself do so. There were limits! But he owned trustworthy colleagues—men of sense and courage and scientific erudition—though Isaac Harriott himself was the senior in community confidence.

When he went his rounds to visit innumerable patients, he rolled in a black chaise with red wheels, and his dappled horse was a pacer. You could look far down the green-shaded tunnel of the avenue, and see Doctor Harriott approaching—you'd know him by the way that fine gray whirled out his feet in the pacing. (Harry thought tenderly of his own family as he visited other homes less substantial, less fortunate in all ways than his. Several of his daughters seemed to be named Victoria, but really there was nothing odd in that. All had very curly hair done up with blue ribbons, and they were excellent little needlewomen; and also could bake thimble-cookies which would melt in your mouth; and on being presented to adults they performed the most captivating curtsies. Also his sons minded their manners nicely; but they were manly little fellows withal, could throw a straight ball, could wrestle and box, could handle bows and arrows with a dexterity to confound any Lincolnshire bowman of legend.)

. . . Harry, man, thou'rt dreaming again?

. . . Guess I was, Carl. Forgive me.

. . . Oh, Harry. You occupy your thoughts with the new town of Spirit Lake City?

. . . Bert, you couldn't be more mistook. Okobojiopolis!

. . . Ah. You wish to wrestle for the name again? Last time it was I who threw you!

. . . No, I won't wrestle you, you frog-eating Frenchy! You wish to incapacitate me for the proper practice of my profession? And it's my turn to fetch firewood. . . .

Squire Witherspoon, the richest man in Okobojiopolis, had weakened during the night, and was thought to be on the verge of passing away. Relatives were weeping when Doctor Harriott arrived (ah, often had he heard and seen them weeping so; but in most times the tears were the tears of the poor . . . he felt such tears to be brinier than those of the rich) and Isaac Harriott entered the sickroom.

The squire's voice was but a whisper. Doctor. Before I—go to my Reward—I wish to tell you of my gratitude for your attentive care—

The old voice grew weaker.

—Let me tell you now, Doctor Harriott, that I have remembered you in my will. Substantially—

That is very kind of you, sir, Harry could hear himself saying. But I trust that I shall not be awarded the fruits of your benevolence for many years yet. Here, I have prepared a dose for you.

And the powder went into the tumbler, and water was stirred, and a faithful nurse in immaculate white propped the old man up so that he might drink as Harry held the glass to his shriveled lips. Squire Witherspoon lay back with a sigh—

There, sir! You'll soon be feeling better. I hope to find you chipper as a colt when next I return. And I am confident, Squire, that I will! Good morning—

He went on to the bedroom of the Honorable Mr. Phineas Scriggs.

Dash it all, Harriott, cried Scriggs testily. Those pills which you left did me no good at all. Only ill. D'ye hear me? Ill!

Then, said Harry soothingly, we must needs try another dosage. Here, I've contrived some new pills. They do indeed contain strychnine; but only a mite, sir, only a mite. Now, then: a sip of water and—*down* they go! You'll feel better in a trice. Two now, two before you have your supper—

Isaac Harriott rolled on his way. Pace, pace, pace flew the swinging legs of his powerful horse, hummmmm went the wheels of the chaise.

The learned Professor Van Wezel was down with the gout, and fuming terribly about it. It iss now to my botany I vish to return!

And return you shall, my dear fellow!—cried the doctor gaily. But not until you have obeyed my dictates, and remained in the snug harbor of your bed until Friday. I cannot be responsible for your condition, Professor, if you do not obey me in all things. All things! Ha, ha—

Pace, pace, hummmmm. . . . Sometimes the street was named Broad

Street, sometimes Broadway, sometimes Washington Avenue, sometimes Capitol Boulevard. Elms along it were as tall as storied New England elms, perhaps even taller.

Whose resplendent white-pillared house was this, upon the right, with a new picket fence over which red roses clambered? That was none other than the domicile of Judge Darius Alexander Wellington, and he was Isaac Harriott's father-in-law, sire of the handsome Portia. Isaac saluted with his whip as he flashed by, then put down his whip in order to reach up and stroke the beard which was growing more and more luxuriant these days . . . just as his bank account swelled to enhanced proportions . . . just as white turnips grew plumper in his garden, just as potatoes grew mealier, and his hens laid an increasing number of eggs.

He used the knife, and removed a wen from the forehead of Colonel MacTavish—working speedily, deftly, without causing the colonel a quiver of pain. He requested a basin in which he might wash his hands, and the basin was fetched on a plated tray, and there was a snowy linen towel to go with it. . . . Almost merrily, yet with a dignity and religious reassurance about him, Harry presided at the bearing-bed of Colonel MacTavish's daughter-in-law; and he was the first to announce to the colonel that he was the possessor of a new grandson.

The old man curled up his fierce mustachios. The child shall be named for you, Doctor. Isaac Harriott MacTavish! What think you of that, sir?

I am more than honored, sir. And I shall take the utmost pride in presenting my namesake—your grandson, sir—with a *silver mug.*

Whirring on his way again . . . rolling from Capitol Boulevard over to Franklin Street, on to Temple, across Main, past the square, past the common. . . .

Once he stopped at a humble cottage to examine the pretty but pale little daughter of an honest shirt-stitcher who dwelt there. The good woman was in tears. She offered her all, a few copper coins, but Harry smiled gently and waved the money away.

I shall send a servant, ma'am, with a basket containing wine jelly, beef broth, and wheaten bread for your ailing daughter. Think not to offer payment, I would not touch a stiver! But in order to lighten the burden now resting on your shoulders, pray allow me . . . tut, tut! I *insist!* . . . the woman's grateful hand closed on the gold pieces, she burst into renewed sobbing, but this time her tears were tears of thankfulness and of hope.

After he had examined the wife of the Reverend Doctor John Alden Standish, president of the University (for by this time there was indeed a university) and pronounced her on the mend, Harry was invited to join the Reverend Doctor in port and English biscuits.

. . . Then we be all agreed?

. . . Aye, William. Here where these two lakes are joining.

. . . Twill call for a surveyor.

. . . Ah, most certainly. Perhaps, Grangers, one of us should return to Red Wing immediately and bring back a surveyor for the purpose now? Harry, what is your opinion?

. . . Ah, he don't answer, not he.

. . . Harry!

. . . Huh? Oh, gentlemen—Carl, William, Bert—I *am* sorry. I was off somewhere, lost in thought.

. . . Ah, he's forever lost in thought these days, he is! I should hate to have a broken leg. He'd prescribe castor oil, he would.

Doctor Isaac Harriott traveled homeward in his chaise. Suddenly there was a running and screaming ahead. A tiny child had fallen into the lake, while trying to capture fat yellow ducklings; and when brought up to the surface seemed more dead than alive. A terrified procession of people hastened forward, bearing among them the inert dripping body. Doctor Harriott leaped from his carriage (sometimes the chaise became a four-wheeler) in a flash. He was rolling up his sleeves . . . the Grim Reaper stood close at this moment. Harry must fend the creature off . . . and did.

Within an hour he was able to stand quietly in the presence of Mr. Paul Revere Witherspoon, the town's leading banker, and murmur, After all, sir, I only did my duty.

But, Doctor—do you realize what you've done? You've saved my youngest child, the pride of my heart, my little golden-haired Priscilla! Everything I have, Doctor, is yours—if you will but take it. Everything! And I am worth no mean sum in property, Doctor, no mean sum!

For myself, sir, I can accept nothing.

But I insist—

No, sir, quite impossible. However, there is a crying need—

Need, Doctor? Please state it.

There are children hungry in the wintertime. There are medicines to be purchased for the sick, blankets and coal for the needy!

(Where, where indeed? In Okobojiopolis? Impossible . . . not in this Athenian-Parisian-Washingtonian Arcady! But . . . somewhere. . . .)

The best of surgical skill should be available at all times, Mr. Witherspoon, to serve the needs of all, irrespective of race, color, creed, or financial status.

Doctor Harriott, I agree sincerely.

Beds, warmth, shelter, cleanliness—the wisest of surgeons, the most exalted of nurses, the acme of perfection in modern drugs and equipment! And readily available to all, sir, completely free of charge!

Doctor Harriott, you are a man of character! No one could assay you better than I, who am compelled daily to judge the faces of men in the marts of trade. . . . Actually, I had not expected you to accept a fortune from me in reward for saving the life of my child! On the other hand, twas the least I could do, to offer it. But now I shall follow your wise and generous counsel, and shall summon my lawyers and—and—and financial advisors—to an immediate conference. A vast charitable institution shall be erected promptly—a combined hospital, orphanage, and old people's shelter, of the most excellent planning and construction. I promise that ground shall be broken within the fortnight . . . and may I request, Doctor, that you yourself wield the golden spade to lift the first soil? And one more request: please, oh please, permit the institution to bear your name? Surely it is not too much to ask that you grant me this boon?

Thus the name of Isaac Harriott would be calcified as a benefactor of that Mankind which he adored with whole-souled acceptance.

. . . When blasted finally from his musings, Harry recognized himself as prig and infant. He confessed as much, to Bertell Snyder.

Prig? The meaning escapes me. I know the word but—

Oh, the devil! It means that I'm affected, pretending to all sorts of successes and— Nobilities which I don't possess! Tis this damn gorgeous paradise we're in. Whole blame place has affected my reason. I should be called down to the Meadows in the middle of the night, and have to attend a diarrhoeaic consumptive with a knife stuck in his guts!

Very well, Harry. I do understand. But show me the man who never becomes either child or prig, and I will show you only half a man.

As more newcomers began to assemble in the region through last days of summer (and strained at hoisting up their cabins while katydids rasped of frost to come) both Harriott and Snyder suffered compounding impatience. They were shamed and not a little perplexed at their own attitude; they muttered in confession to each other, even while the brothers Granger beamed upon one covey of arrivals after another. The Grangers carried with them a solitary peasant purpose: they observed that they had found success in battening down the whole area north of the straits for the Red Wing Company's future townsite, and were grateful proportionately. Hopeful Red Wingers they'd left behind on the Mississippi had no illusions about a tenantless town to be built, a serene settlement properly civilized and yet unapproachable (there were no plank roads or railways coursing among the stars)! But Harry and Bert were so active in imagination—and therefore so draped in dreams—that they had difficulty in separating a holy ambition from the necessity at hand. This despite all Bertell Snyder's prating about a practical approach. . . . They wanted people, knew that future success depended upon people, yet they cringed or even glowered as the cattle began to bawl and the axes to slice.

Gardners and Luces were all right; they were a mile away or thereabouts; their children formed an amusing ragged little procession; Rowland Gardner's hopeful explorations into literature and even into realms of history, science, and philosophy deserved attention; the doleful sanctimonious Harvey Luce would instill a kind of cruel taunting merriment in any sophisticated spirit. But it seemed initially that the Mattocks were an infliction. Successively the young men encountered Jim Mattock, Robby Matheson, Mrs. Mattock, some of the children. Big Jim's profanity and obscenities re-echoed wearyingly, Robby was bovine, Mary Mattock reminded both Bert and Harry of tiresome housewives they'd known in towns at the East. (Yea, Illinois and St. Paul and Canada were now become the East.) The naughty Daniel and Agnes stood down by the inlet and threw stones at Carl Granger's bulldog when Lee went mouthing after waterfowl amid the rushes.

Harry. Is it that we could have done better with our nearest neighbors?

Gad, yes!

But those bad children—actually a stone did strike Lee, and made him yell— They say they have an elder sister, quite the young lady.

I vow she probably cusses as bad as the old man—

But if she *is* a young lady, maybe we should go to call?

—And doubtless is as corpulent as the old man. With an intellect like that unfortunate Robby; and she squeals like one of their dratted hogs—

You must wait until she has an attack of the vapors, Harry, or some common disease of the young ladies. Then will you be called upon to attend her.

Thank you, nay.

But you are a doctor, and if summoned you must go.

Doubtless she's as durable as a battle-axe, and looks like one!

I think that I will go to call, then, alone. The mischievous Bert added: Who knows? She may be the blonde one I seek!

You ain't going nowhere today, Mr. We're housebuilding. The first house in Okobojiopolis—

Pardon, Monsieur. In Spirit Lake City—

Eventually it was a blow to the jaunty smugness of both Snyder and Harriott when they learned that Jim Mattock had looked upon them with equal scorn in the first meeting or two or three. Mattock possessed a congenital hill-bred suspicion of all foreigners; hence Bert Snyder, with his accent and the bright shreds of *voyageur's* attire still remaining to him, was an object to be ignored or at least one to shy away from. Harry had the misfortune to be a youthful doctor, and all youthful doctors were worse than worthless in Mr. James Mattock's estimation. Years before, while still living in Indiana, Mattock had suffered from a persistent sore throat which afflicted him for weeks and unfitted him for his ardent endeavors in field and hog lot. Finally it was decided to call in a doctor. The patient had never before experienced professional medical attention. Old Doctor Galloway was laid in his grave but a fortnight earlier; and the young man who took over the community burden was inexperienced in general practice, and possessed solely an apothecary's background. He compounded gum camphor, castile soap, turpentine, opium, oil of origanum, and alcohol, and saw to it that Mr. Mattock was introduced to this mixture two or three times daily. Inflammation did not subside, the thwarted doctor talked lugubriously of cancer. Terrified, Mattock managed to have himself conveyed by stage all the way to New Albany, where he took refuge in the house of his wife's sister, and became a subject for experimentation at the hands of an even younger, more stupid, less experienced, more opinionated Man of Healing. This gawk laid forth a program of emetics. He submitted his victim to such treatment twice each day, tapering reluctantly to a once-a-day plan, and he talked of a thrice-a-week system to be followed as the disease gave ground. Jim Mattock rebelled, threw Doctor Elbridge bodily out of the house, and he then sought the attention of one Granny Flums, an elderly Switzeress who kept eleven cats in her cottage and specialized in the treatment of piles. Promptly the crone achieved a miraculous cure by employing tea composed of sage, honey, salt, vinegar, and cayenne. Jim Mattock had never consulted a doctor since. He swore that he would never again consult a doctor, especially a young one, unless carried to him unconscious and upon a stretcher.

The aloofness manifested by the Gardner-Luce clan, to begin with, was ascribed to an overly Christian ardor—one which had been shown by countless other people in the past—whether in Indiana or in Delaware County, Iowa. Mattock was fiercely unpopularly atheistic. His blatant cursing and crudity were delayed revolt against a self-consciously Godly grandsire—inheritance, in turn, from a father whose eighteenth-century childhood was one long torture of Psalms, imprisonment, catechisms, lashings, prayers, enforced starvation, and other Worthy Works.

The Mattocks would have been both puzzled and wounded by the attitude of their neighbors, except that no Mattock might ever nurse a puzzle or a wound for long (when they died it would be in amazement that anything so grimly terminating as Death could be met up with). The nature of Jim and all his tribe was to exhibit a coarse slovenly gaiety in the face of disappointment or privation (refuting happily the shopworn notion of somber taciturn mountaineers). Jim Mattock had been reared on a hillside near the Kentucky-Tennessee line—the youngest in a rowdy throng of brothers who feuded consistently with a clan named Skene living two ridges away. One Christmas week, when Jim was twenty and when whiskey bubbled throughout the valleys in traditional revelry, and rifle shots snapped and whirred, Jim Mattock's father encountered a throng of Skenes at the creek ford. Later he staggered home without his ears—just holes and torn bloody patches on the sides of his head. The Mattock boys took their flintlocks and powder horns into Skene territory, they distributed themselves behind fences and outbuildings. All the Skenes tall enough to bear arms or inflict mayhem were obliterated during the following night and day, taking two of the Mattocks along with them. Rumor had it that manacles or hangmen's nooses were awaiting the survivors; so Jim Mattock thought it politic to withdraw into quieter more level regions toward the north. His mother sewed up a slit in his scalp with linen thread, and he walked off in darkness, tramping all the way to Harrodsburg the first week. He was fond of relating to his children that he never missed a meal on this trip, though often his diet was roasted rabbit without salt—he had neglected, in haste, to fetch any salt along with him! The strapping hill boy could turn his hand to anything requiring the application of thick muscles and a strong back: he chopped wood, loaded logs, worked in a quarry for two days . . . worked in a slope coal mine, mashed his foot when a roof fell in . . . he limped always afterward, never seeming to mind that he limped. At home his favorite tasks had been concerned with the critters on the place, especially hogs; he had a way with those beasts, hogs seemed to understand him and he them; Jim's brothers had always declared that it was because Jim so resembled a hog himself, though he weighed perhaps only fifteen stone at that time in his life. Luck carried him into an encounter with a speculator who was attempting to persuade more than four hundred reluctant swine to visit the Louisville market. Several of the drivers, wearied of a clamorous exasperating five-miles-per-day pace, had decamped; the drover was desperate; he offered Jim Mattock fantastic wages. Jim stowed his rifle and bundle in the ox-drawn wagon, and taught the amazed speculator how to sew hogs' eyelids together. He had heard this trick related by a maternal grandfather who'd practiced it in Virginia in Colonial times. Now the smelly grunting drove made record time toward the Ohio, and Jim Mattock met the love of his life when she waited on table in an eating house near Shelbyville. Her name was Mary Callaway. Winningly she claimed kinship with the famous Colonel Callaway of Daniel Boone days. . . . Jim Mattock accompanied Mr. Mackaleer, the speculator, together with his four hundred squealers, on to market at Louisville. There Mr. Mackaleer proved himself the biggest swine of the lot, after the herd was driven into pens beside the river. A man claiming to be the speculator's agent presented to James Mattock a cotton tobacco-sack containing Jim's alleged wages for the drive: a sum reckoned at one dollar per day instead of the princely three dollars per day which the desperate speculator had mentioned in the first place. Other drivers withdrew, grumbling, to a rumshop; but Jim Mattock spent a pleasant afternoon at the farthest hogpen, admiring the conformation of various individual pigs, decrying weak points in others, and discoursing learnedly on hogs in general to the edification of river-front loafers. When Mr. Mackaleer came skulking to rejoin his agent at dusk, Jim Mattock carried Mr. Mackaleer among tilted ice-cakes in the Ohio River where, doused beneath the surface for an interval, Mr. Mackaleer decided that three dollars per day was indeed an equable and not at all exorbitant wage. The money being paid directly by the shivering speculator, James Mattock journeyed to the fateful tavern on the Shelbyville road, where he spent an entire evening and an entire jug of cider in persuading Miss Callaway to become his bride. The couple were blissfully happy from then on (Mary gave birth to eight children, three of whom died in infancy and thus brought the only blackness which might besmirch their lives until their lives were ended). The Mattocks withdrew into southern Indiana, avoiding Louisville en route, since it was gossiped that constables in that city were searching for a heartless giant who went about habitually trying to drown innocent hog speculators.

Seldom did the Mattock family roll in plenty, but never did they even approach starvation. Always there were hogs turning over the sod, hogs snorting through the woods in search of acorns and mast and roots, hogs streaming toward the pole feeding-lot in converging swarms when Jim Mattock heaved himself up on the fence and sent his mighty *Sooooeeee!* ripping across the landscape. Never did this hard-working colossus encounter a season in which hogs could not be sold for cash on the hoof, or at least traded for meal, salt, sugar, seed corn, linsey-woolsey, and other necessities. Also he held a mighty ambition which, if realized, might make him the Swine King of southern Indiana. In this complex plan there figured the crossing of Berkshires with Tamworths and even the increased development of new Poland Chinas from Butler County, Ohio, to be mixed into Byfield or Irish Grazier stock. Jim Mattock had no book learning in animal husbandry but he had a gift for doing the right thing at the right time where hog-flesh was concerned. He experimented with feeding formulas, using selected specimens from his herd, while the rest ranged destructively through summer forests; he made agreements with the proprietors of two nearby slaughterhouses to exchange a generous quantity of winter-killed pork for the annual crop of offal and bones from these abattoirs. His sows farrowed out more pigs than any of his neighbors', his herd put on more meat and more rapidly. He invented a mechanical feeder for an orphaned litter by boring holes in a hollowed log and providing wet-rag teats, and (he roared gleefully to Mary Mattock) the God damn thing worked, and you just ought to come out and see those little sons-a-bitches sucking!

. . . Jim, you mind your language.

. . . Jesus Christ, you ought to see them little bastards!

. . . Jim Mattock, you mind—

One day a number of his favorites refused to respond to bellowed summons which had always fetched them in chortling columns; they failed to come up and feed. Jim found them feverish or chilled in disordered nests among the ravines. Swine fever had come smiting. In desperation Jim cut open the carcasses of the first to die, and found evidences of a plague which, up until this time, had been purely legendary but still terrifying to contemplate. Skin was blotched with purple, there were bloody spots on the lungs, on the surface of the hearts; there were ulcers of the intestines. He fought sternly, trying to isolate individuals which did not as yet show any symptoms, scattering lime over the feeding lot; but was defeated in the end. He did not know—perhaps field mice and birds triumphed, serving the plague as devilish little handmaidens, carrying an unseen commodity from the dying to the hale. Buzzards appeared in swarms before Jim and Mary Mattock, together with such assistants as they were able to engage, could put the sad swollen population out of sight and smell. Mattock felt that he had had enough of Indiana. There was a place to the West where twas said that swine fever had never yet found a foothold! He sold his land and, using funds thus secured together with his small savings, bought a farm in Delaware County, Iowa. Here he raised up new herds through successive breeding seasons, and made an annual drive to a Dubuque packing plant. 1855 marked the last time he undertook such a feat—it was too risky, too burdensome; too many head were swept away in a sudden freshet on the North Fork of the Maquoketa River. But big Jim was only in his fortieth year; abounding scheme and excitement were milling still within his baldish skull. Farms not as desirable as his were going for twenty dollars an acre, right there in Delaware County; land in the northwestern areas of Iowa could be had for a dollar and a quarter. . . . Where would he find his market? Ha—he'd forget all about drives in another year or two. Take up good high-and-dry woodland (but with plenty of fresh water alongside), farrow out in the spring months when most of the litters could survive, wean at eight weeks or so, feed odds and ends—grain, potatoes, pumpkins—until the pigs were ready to feed in the woods. Confine maybe in September, feed cooked pumpkins and other vegetables with maybe a couple of bushels of corn to the barrel! *Slaughter* in the cold weather—right there on the place!—and *haul dressed pork* to the settlements: Fort Dodge, Webster City, Waterloo, and the rest. Trade pork for grain, as he'd done back in Indiana. By God, maybe he'd be the boss of a full-fledged packing plant, one of these times. *Somebody* had to start the business on the frontier; might as well be he!

And a good big herd of cattle in another year or so, so's the hogs could hog down the droppings, way they'd done back in Indiana!

Sleds wouldn't have to come back empty from the settlements. Trade for salt and charcoal and whatever else was needed, lug it home, butcher again—cold weather—freight out some fresh loads of dressed hogs on the sleds, freight back some loads of grain for sow-feed in the spring!

. . . God damn it, Mary. You and Alice are fine help, and that little Agnes and Danny are getting tall enough to do some good. Way I figure it we can make a mint, less'n that fucking swine fever follers us to the Okoboji country!

. . . Jim, you hush your vileness.

. . . Son of a bitch if I don't build a God damn slaughterhouse right on the spot! Mary, I'm heading that way soon as the weather breaks. Talked to those Mathesons over yonder, and the old man'd maybe like to try it too. I'll take young Robby long with me—take up land for both damn families, soon as we pick a place. Put in a big planting of punkins; prairie's too God damn wet to freight in our plunder in the spring anyways, and to drive our stock. Punkins'll yield well in new earth thout no care—we'll be up to our ass in punkins by the time the prairie dries out in late summer, time we can all get there. You keeps your legs tied together till I get back!

. . . No, Alice and me can open a *whorehouse*. How'd you like that, sir?

. . . By God, you hain't no fit wife *nor* mother. Come here, woman, and I'll paddle your butt! . . . Mary, we work hard, we can make a God damn fortune this way, with any luck.

. . . With any luck, Jim!

. . . Dad burn me if I don't feel lucky right now. And kind of horny too! Where's all the small fry?

. . . Alice footed it through the snow over to the Parsons' place to get a clutch of eggs for that old Cackle-top hen: she's trying to set. Took little Aggie with her. Boys all hill-sliding over in the gully—hear 'em?

. . . Hey, woman, how about it?

. . . How about it yourself, Mr. Tickle-breeches? But don't get clean disrobed—we hain't got time!

These people were not savage but in charity they might have been called warty, hard-skinned. They were scarred and calloused by straps of toil, the harness of primitive dangers and adversities. Individually or together, Jim and Mary Mattock exemplified a host of virtues which were mouthed about by exhorters—virtues praised universally by churchgoers, Temperance addicts, Abolitionists. Neither Jim nor Mary was ever willfully cruel to a child, or to an animal either, except in yielding to considered demands (the hogs' sewn-together eyelids was an example of ruthlessness which Jim held necessary). A certain gigantic Elder Corbin in Indiana was known to beat his teams and his family; but Jim Mattock's discipline was inflicted by a slap on the rump (when the child was small, only); and he did not often whip a horse or a mule—he bullied the critter with curses. Hounds and kittens alike tried to swarm over Mattock's lap when he sat down, if that vast swollen roundness of belly and thighs might be called a lap. He jollied his infants with vulgar rhymes even before the children were old enough to understand the words; their lullabies were murderous ballads concerning patricide, matricide, infanticide. Some children might hear a parental voice chanting *Old Hundred* or a Lowell Mason hymn amid first filmy recollection, but in the sweet-flavored mind of Alice Mattock, the eldest (twas those three offspring following her who occupied weed-grown graves) there rang always a remembered recitation of Lord Thomas's pique: *He led her in the hall . . . and there with his sword he cut off her head, and dashed it against the wall!* Elder Corinthian Corbin would not have approved of this tender ditty, but then Elder Corbin never sang to his own children. Jim Mattock sang to his. He sang: *She took a knife both long and sharp, and stabbed those babes unto the heart.* Elder Corbin puffed out his bulbous eyes, stood with huge hands clasped meekly in front of him, his hard wide jaw sagged and rose, he was a veritable mountain of self-conscious humility, his shadow fell across three benches filled with frightened worshipers. He sang: *Life is the time to serve the Lord, the time t'insure the great reward; and, while the lamp holds out to burn, the vilest sinner may return.* Elder Corinthian Corbin regarded Jim Mattock as a vilest sinner, but he did not wish him to return (as if he had ever been there in the first place!) nor did he wish Jim Mattock to enter the church, or even waft his hog scent toward that structure. Each Christmas season (but on the date which Mr. Mattock called Old Christmas) Mr. Mattock got roaring drunk, and, in a year when pork fetched a good price, he would go waddling up and down the roadway with a jug in his hand, insisting that each passer-by join him in—as he described it—guzzling down a few slops. In the end he would weave a staggering path to his home, and be helped to bed by his wife; her speech would be accusing, her touch kindly. For the benefit of wife and children, Jim Mattock might be roaring: *Oh, Naples Joan would make them groan, who ardently did succor! But Jane Shore, Jane Shore, King Edward he would fuck her!*

Living a life of damnation in the clutch of Elder Corinthian Corbin was an orphan, the illegitimate son of a deceased Jeffersonville slavey; this round-shouldered blobber-lipped child had been put into the Corbin guardianship by a benevolent court, and he was known throughout the community as Slow Solomon. One spring morning Elder Corinthian Corbin observed some boys snapping marbles, gathered in a hunched voluble mob around a ring drawn in the dust; and—sure enough—one of the marble-gamblers was Slow Solly. The bound-boy had been drawn from productive garden toil by the fascination of shiny agates; though where Slow Solly had ever acquired a taw might not be determined, since pocket-pennies were a luxury unknown to him. Plying a limp braided whip, Elder Corbin began to entice Slow Solly all the way back to his neglected spading fork, while other marble players scattered to the winds, and women came out on their porches and held aprons against their frightened mouths. Slow Solly's screams very nearly drowned out the indignant asseverations of a brood sow recently purchased by Mr. James Mattock and now being transported to her new domicile in a cart. Mr. Mattock descended from the cart and removed the whip from Elder Corbin's grasp. Elder Corbin sought to kick Mr. Mattock in the groin, but managed to deliver only a glancing blow with his big boot. Mr. Mattock felled Elder Corbin to the earth. Elder Corbin, after an unsuccessful attempt to gouge out Mr. Mattock's eye, sought to depart houseward or at least to some place of comparative safety. Mr. Mattock accelerated the Elder on his course by use of the whip which had formerly been applied to Slow Solly, until the whip fell apart; then he used his fists once more. Before rendering the Elder unconscious, James Mattock adjured him to abstain from punitive programs directed against Slow Solly in the future, or the Elder's long nose would be ripped out of his face. Elder Corinthian Corbin was unable to appear at church the next Sunday. . . . Mr. Mattock spent two days in the calaboose during which time he amused himself with renditions of *The Bonny Earl of Murray, Barbara Allen's Cruelty,* and *The Whore of Babel,* to further detriment of the community peace. After payment of a small cash fine, plus costs, he halted only long enough to repeat his admonition to Elder Corbin through a smashed window at the latter's residence, and then rolled home, sending news of his liberation on ahead up the lane by booming a familiar chorus: *Whose head be that, upon the bed, where my head ought to be?* Chicken and dumplings were served at a celebration dinner.

Mary Mattock had experienced some schooling and was passably literate. She it was who taught Jim basic arithmetic, which permitted him to add and subtract (although he could not learn to divide or multiply: in his task of reckoning hog feed, for instance, he multiplied six times fifteen by scratching down six fifteens in a column, and adding them up); and he learned also to write his name, and hers, and the children's names; and she taught him to read a few words in coarse print. Jim Mattock gave that false impression of stupidity which bellowing, fat, rough-spoken, rough-featured individuals give. He was unlettered, unread, uninformed on any subject except swine and rudimentary farming; but definitely he was not stupid. He recognized, and so did his wife, that the Elder Corbins of this world were not fairly representative of the body of affirmed Christians. He had met brawlers, drunkards, roisterers, swaggering heathens who were even less to be loved than parsimonious and post-thrashing deacons. He had native sense enough to know that there were as many hypocrites hurling stones at church structures from the outside as there were mealy-mouthed skinflints who sipped at Communion. He'd known a publican who treated a bound-boy in more dastardly fashion than Elder Corinthian Corbin had treated his; and in Kentucky he had stood in awe and watched one frail young priest enter a plague-ridden shack to nurse a tribe of outcast Negroes whom no one else would touch. When cholera swept along the Ohio River, people witnessed deeds of saintly devotion performed by Catholics and Protestants alike. The most generous-hearted and heroic man in Clarke County might have been the little Jewish tailor who still wore the beard and cap and garb of Hebrew fathers—who sat, dreaming of rabbinical robes which he had never been able to put on, reading his Talmud to the wonder or scorn of townspeople. Tailor Mose it was, the first to volunteer, who was lowered into a well-shaft where two diggers had been overcome by damps, and who attached ropes by which the victims were drawn up to be resuscitated; he himself was unconscious when at last pulled into the air, and so he died, for he was not a sturdy man—only his heart was sturdy, his soul stout in sacrifice. Folks buried him, an enlightened minister read from the Psalms. A stone was erected bearing only the legend: *Here Lies a Brave Jew Named Mose*—for no one could spell or even pronounce Tailor Mose's last name . . . but then floods came, next April, and the stone was taken away, and other stones and many graves as well. Only the Ohio River knew to what far fields the Brave Jew might have been transported.

Sometimes when Jim Mattock looked up at cool lonely stars he wondered vaguely about these things . . . but not for long, not for long! There were chores to be done, a living to make—there was a farrowing sow to be tended, a bawdy song to be yelled, Jim's own litter was a-needing him.

Jim Mattock never Bore False Witness in his life, nor did Mary. Jim Mattock never Committed Adultery, nor did his spouse (if questioned, they would have insisted that they didn't have time). No hungry beggar was turned away unfed from the Mattock door; Mary served such drifters, always, with whatever was at hand; if Jim were about, he enlivened the repast with insistence that he couldn't afford to feed every lazy bastard in Creation. . . . Small children climbed into bed with him and jumped on his chest. . . . The Mattocks Did Not Covet. They Did Not Make Graven Images; had they constructed the likeness of anything to worship, probably it would have been the likeness of a healthy hog—say, a shoat putting on weight in his early winter feeding. The Mattocks Did Not Steal. Even the despised Corbin could have dropped his purse on their doorstep: it would have been returned to him none the lighter. Big Jim would have declared: I don't want nobody's God damn money but my own! . . . They had faith in each other; they found hope in each other, and in Nature; they offered a robust ruffianly charity to any portion of humanity in need of it, or willing to accept what they could give.

(At Okoboji, as Rowland Gardner's acquaintanceship with Jim Mattock extended—out of immediacy and necessity, despite any degree of family disapproval—Gardner found himself fretted by a quotation from the Apostle Paul which faintly he could recall. He did not consult Harvey Luce on this, but searched it out in his own Bible privately. *Therefore if I know not the meaning of the voice, I shall be unto him that speaketh a barbarian, and he that speaketh shall be a barbarian unto me.* He would not have admitted it to a soul, but sometimes it seemed to Rowland Gardner that the Bible was couched in gratuitously puzzling terms. He wished that he might have found The Word as unvexing and boldly apparent as his son-in-law seemed to find it.)

As soon as the new house was able to receive his family, Mattock set out with Robby Matheson, to secure the balance of their breeding stock, together with shoats destined to carry the Mattocks through the winter. They had shuttled these animals all the way from Delaware County after attempting unsuccessfully to make the journey in a single emigration—wagons, children, cattle, hogs, and all. They'd found it impossible to slough down the loaded wagons while herding hogs at the same time. Every mile of the distance was traversed by Jim and Robby five successive times: twice in the spring, thrice in the summer. Jim said that he had a speaking acquaintance with every God damn frog and blackbird in every God damn pond along the way. His little fortune in crossbred Poland Chinas had been left in trust at the southern tip of Middle Lake, guarded and fed by one Emmet Bryan. Bryan would be paid in shoats. Half a dozen Irish families were removed to this site from Kane County, Illinois; folks called their settlement the Irish colony; it was located in the center of Palo Alto County, between thirty and forty miles from the Okoboji straits even if you traveled in a beeline.

Two mornings after her father's departure, Alice Mattock went down to the shore and began timidly to hoo-hoo at the Minnesotans across the way. They were busy with belated construction of their cabin, and for a time did not hear Alice calling. At length the bulldog began to snuffle and bark, so Carl Granger put down his saw and followed Lee to the straits. He returned promptly, he told Isaac Harriott to come down off the roof where Harry had been securing shakes.

You've more than roofs to think about now, Doctor.

What?

Tis the young lady from that new house yonder. She wants to see you, she does.

Ah, Harry! The vapors! cried Bert Snyder from the chimney scaffold.

Harry fetched his satchel from the tent, and walked along a new-trodden path which led through bushes to a point near the water's edge. When he looked across the shimmering shallows and saw Alice, he could not well believe his own eyes. He'd never seen her before . . . on the two occasions when he'd strolled to the Mattock site (gingerly, he admitted) the eldest daughter was absent—gone to the Gardners' once, off fishing with her little brothers the other time. Sardonically he had expected to encounter some sort of pig-woman or pig-girl. He had not thought to meet a lady . . . shining hair. . . .

Yes, Miss? I'm Doctor Harriott.

I'm sorry . . . bother you . . . brother Daniel. . . .

Cool wind destroyed some of her words, he could not catch them. Wind ruffled the straits, and a fish threw itself out of the water to bite the breeze and fall back with a tempting splash. Coloring sumac shone red-orange behind the girl. She wore a full gown of faded gray-blue calico; her curl lay like a soft jet rope against her neck.

Miss, I can't hear you. You'll need to yell louder!

My brother Daniel. Tis the ager, but it gets worse and worse, poor child. We've . . . no remedy at hand . . . if you. . . .

I'll come, but first shall need to select some drugs. Is it the dumb or the shaking ague, or chill fever?

Mam thinks . . . intermittents. . . .

Ah. How old is he?

Bout twelve.

Do the spasms occur regularly?

Reckon you couldn't set your watch by them. Mam wanted . . . try soot coffee but not . . . soot in new chimney. . . .

I'll be right along.

Harry returned to the tent, ignoring queries and humorously intended remarks by the others. His very silence chided them into silence. They settled down to concentrated work on the cabin, realizing that they stood rebuked. Week after week this slender man had been their fellow hunter, planner, camper. (He was junior in contribution to the Red Wing Townsite Company, and the one least concerned with its aims. In Red Wing dwelt Bill Granger's wife and babies. Carl Granger had no wife, but the tiny settlement on the Mississippi had been the first home he knew in America, and thus Red Wingers' aims were his own. Even Bertell Snyder owned property there and knew all the inhabitants.) Harry had joined in every jollity, had lived a rough-and-tumble life along with other young males, had submitted to criticism and teasing because much of the time he was dreaming—as Bert put it, very nearly out loud. The barrier between physician and laymen had not been apparent before. Quickly in these few minutes it reared itself between Harriott and his companions.

A doctor held the power of life, the ability to grapple against destruction, he held this power in knuckles and muscles and nerves of his hands. He had knowledge pressed into his brain which other men might not even pretend to own—there was no use in their pretending, had they wished to do so—they might not own it. A capable doctor was on intimate terms with spirits of niter, Glauber's salts, zinc sulphate, dyanthos, spigelia, and a thousand other mysteries incomprehensible to the man with the sickle, the man with the loom, the man with the parade of oxen in yoke. If the man with the satchel in his hand spoke of aorta, duodenum, clavicles, or the *bronchus principalis*, he knew what he was talking about. He knew that anatomical names were usually Latin, that the names of diseases were usually Greek; he spoke of this without ostentation, as if he thought that everybody should know it; yet everybody did not know it, and you were amazed at this sudden casual intelligence he had given you, and wondered what use you could make of it, and of course you could make none. He might sniff at a tiny unlabeled flask and say, Oh, yes, potassium bitartrate, or he might say, Oh, yes—balsam copaiba!—and this you could not say for all your sniffing. The capable surgeon examined the silent bloodstained dummy under his hands, and whispered (communing with gods and witches alike): Ah-huh. Parietal fracture, beyond a doubt. Might be occipital as well! . . . The surgeon knew where to cut, and when; he opened the skin, spread it with his instruments, he opened the vein when it needed to be opened, he sewed the slit which needed to be sewed; he looked at the man you hadn't thought to be killed, and he said, This man is dead. And there was the blank solid fact, the cold solid termination, and it had happened, and you'd thought it not so, but there it was, the doctor said so. You might be able to outshoot the doctor, outwrestle him, outlift him, perhaps outwalk him; ah, you could do a variety of things much better than could the doctor!— If you were of a religious bent you might outpray him, outworship him; and if you were a mystic you might outbrood him, outwonder him, outponder him; and if you were interested in making money and storing it up, very easily could you jingle and count and secrete more money than the doctor— Why, almost any fool could! If you were a charlatan (never possessed of facts and skills, but feigning, in order to seduce the credulous) you hid away from him; he knew, you did not know; he'd felt whole acres of dead pickled human tissues with his searching fingers, and you hadn't; he'd put his hands into the earliest and liveliest life of all, those juices surrounding that stubborn loose-shaped skull which came butting its way into the world—and, Oh! so many times he'd done it; and wet his fingers with umbilical blood afterward; he'd manipulated the freshest living, and tended the woman from whom this new wet thing was now separated; and you hadn't, you hadn't, you didn't know, you weren't a doctor. The word was spoken, the request given, the voice said, Please let me speak with the doctor!—and the doctor went, and he knew what to say and do, because he was a man of medicine and surgery; and you did not go or know, because you were not such a man; and there was a wall between Him Who Was a Doctor and Him Who Was Not —a complex elastic unseen wall—but twas there, twould be there.

Harry removed the tight-fitting lid from his case of drugs and took out a set of scales. Already he had quinine, sulphuric acid, and brandy in his satchel; but treatment of this case would require a febrifuge, and thus he needed Epsom salts; also a child was the patient, which suggested materials for coloring. Also among the drugs was a bottle of a certain tonic wine tincture which Harry had made up before leaving Minnesota. He took that along. He kept thinking of a distant figure (not the patient as yet unseen; the patient was a formless faceless lump in fancy ahead). He thought of the girl with luminous hair—

The Red Wing Company's canoe was drawn up among thick rushes on the north side of the strait. The men kept it at that point to use as a ferry: no sense in wetting feet and clothing by wading across, though often Harry and Bert went splashing through on horseback. A few shoves of the paddle, and Harry was on the south side. He gazed up seriously at the woman who came to meet him. He climbed from the canoe, drew the craft up on shore, then he and Miss Mattock were moving away together. His own scuffed boots seemed to build a clumsy tramping and crunching sound, he hadn't realized that he made so much noise when he walked. The tall Mattock girl floated almost silently beside him—her feet were bare—strong, long, well-proportioned. Already there was a path of sorts leading up to the grove of oaks and hickories. Harry indicated that the girl should precede him . . . she inclined her head, bowed and laughed in the same instant, laughed at nothing at all, the doctor chuckled too . . . neither of them could have told why they laughed, neither of them needed to tell or explain. But Harriott could watch those handsome firm feet leading on . . . Alice's gown was a bit shorter than most women commonly wore theirs: Harry presumed that this was to serve convenience and not through deliberate immodesty . . . her ankles were slender, beautifully formed . . . Harry thought of them as swelling abruptly into round full voluptuous calves. His face turned hot. *Come, come, sir—you're bound on a professional call.*

Your young brother—

Alice Mattock halted and swung round to face him with her wide clear gaze.

About twelve, you say?

Less see. His birthday was last June and— Yes, Doctor. Twelve.

I'm afraid he was the one who was throwing rocks at our bulldog!

Him and Agnes, most likely. They get so naughty, times. But now they like the dog, and the dog likes them. Comes over frequent, to beg at table.

Hope you don't feed him, he's fat enough now.

Oh, the younguns like to give him a little snack. They miss Ranger that we used to have. Ranger was kilt by a boar down in Delaware.

*Del*aware?

Delaware County, Ioway, sir. That's where we come from, most recent. But— Hadn't we best go on to the house?

Just one moment. Twas my fault—strayed from the subject. Tell me your brother's name.

Daniel McElroy Mattock.

It helps, you see, if a doctor knows young folks' names. Then he can greet them by name—they're not so frightened of a stranger—

She nodded gravely, she agreed, she understood.

And—Your name?

I'm Alice.

Just Alice—? He added, as they started on again, Not Alice McElroy Mattock?

No, I'm Alice Anderson. See— And she did not turn her head again, but picked her way up the slope with full attention to the trail. Yet her easy voice drifted back with clarity and (this was a kinship of imagery unknown to either the doctor or the young Gardner girl—neither would ever know that the other had followed the same fancy) Isaac Harriott thought of unhurried water in a woodland where leaves floated, where deer came to drink . . . he thought of a pure dark stream, could find strength and honesty in the cool taste of it.

See, Mam had Granny Anderson tending her when I was born. Twas back in Indi*an*. So I'm Alice Anderson. And Danny— Granny McElroy was tending Mam when Danny was born. So—

They went on to the Mattock house. Agnes, Jacob, and Jackson were playing at Store in front of the split log step. Agnes had a stock of mullein leaves, green walnuts, sumac berries, and acorns, all arranged in neat piles; and the two little boys were customers, paying for goods they bought in currency of pebbles. The children backed off and stood giggling at the newcomer . . . he was a doctor, and there was mystery and excitement in that . . . they could not recall having seen a doctor come to their house before.

Alice said: You kids hain't to come bothering whilst Doctor Harriott's here.

The children broke into fresh snorts. They fled, scuttling off among wide-spaced oaks toward the pumpkin patch.

Alice called after them: And don't you run too fur away, neither. Member there was a bear come around last night!

Harry turned quickly. There was?

I guess likely he was interested in Pap's hogs. They got to squealing something awful, and I run out with Pap's gun—

Alice gave a light furry chuckle . . . why, what a lovely sound!

—The cap had slipped off; I didn't have no other. Anyways, I was scairt I'd just maybe wound the bear and then he'd eat me up. I waved the gun at him and told him, Scat—go way!

Did he go?

Yes, sir. Just walked off, unconcerned.

I think you're a very brave young lady, Miss Alice.

Oh, I reckon he wasn't too fierce an old bear. Seemed friendly like.

The door opened, Harry was ushered into the single room, Mary Mattock bustled forward. A redheaded boy was huddled in bed at the far corner of the room.

Harry mumbled something about not having been inside the house before. The mother and the daughter let an expressive glance fly between them when he said it.

(The Gardner-Luce cabin was long since completed. Harry had been there. Now Rowland Gardner and his son-in-law were building stables. Once the stables were completed they'd set to work on a cabin to accommodate the Luces alone. If winter weather held off long enough, Harvey and Mary with their children would enjoy their own home for the first time since leaving Ohio. Only a common house was built at Clear Lake, only a common house rented at Shell Rock. If the season didn't stay fit for more housebuilding, all the Luces and the Gardners must needs den up together. Gardner confessed frankly to Harry and to Bert Snyder that he didn't relish such a prospect, not with three tots underfoot; so the Red Wing people talked sporadically of going to the neighbors' assistance, but it only amounted to talk. Not one of the four was skillful at carpentry: they possessed a variety of other skills, but it happened that not a man of them had ever engaged in building a log house before. Also Bill Granger fretted—he wished to be rid of an onerous job, and return to Red Wing and his little family as soon as possible.)

The hurried looks exchanged by Alice and Mary Mattock stemmed from the fact that James Mattock had suggested a housewarming, a week before.

. . . I got two whole jugs of rum, by God! We could raise hell half the night. We hain't got no damn fiddle, but Robby can rattle bones, and you got your jew's-harp—

. . . Jim Mattock, every time you get in liquor you fall mighty sick the next day! Member last Old Christmas, back in Delaware? You—

. . . God damn it to hell, woman. I didn't say I was going to drink the whole blame two jugs my own self—

. . . Got sick all over the stoop, middle of the night! You couldn't get out in the yard in time. You was a-staggering like—

. . . All right, all right. And I upset the God damn piss-pot, too! But a house ain't a house thout a housewarming—

. . . Jim. Wouldn't nobody come.

. . . What you mean, wouldn't nobody come? Why, we'd vite them Gardners, and their daughter and her—

. . . Surely: the parson-kind-of-man. Think he'd shine at a play-party, you silly old slob? I rather think not. He'd start a-preaching right off—

. . . And them young fellers over cross the water here? I bet that young Frenchy knows how to kick up his heels and dance. And them Englishmen, they like a dram or so. Why, I run into an Englishman one time in Louisville—man nigh as big as myself—fact, I think his belly and ass *was* bigger'n mine—and he could take a whole nipper-kin of brandy and down it, neat, just like he was drinking God damn spring water—

. . . Jim. I tolt you. Wouldn't nobody come to our housewarming. You just chase the notion out of your big fat head. Cause—

. . . Why not, hey? Christ in the Mountains, and Him Crucified! Why wouldn't they come if we vited them? God damn it, *why?*

. . . Cause they don't seem friendly.

. . . Bet they— Would come— Bet—

. . . Stand-offish, that's what they be! The whole parcel of our neighbors. Stand-offish! You just forget about the whole matter.

. . . Why, I bet—

. . . Alice. You tell your father.

. . . Pap. Mam's right. They wouldn't come.

But at least one had come now, the youngest of the Red Wing folks; and he happened to be a Man of Healing, and was so to be respected, so to be regarded with awe. Danny Mattock, shivering under a mound of covers in the wide corner-bed, regarded him so. Daniel

Mattock's eyes were very large in his sallow drawn face. His mouth trembled also, the open lips shook and drooled, but not with an approach of tears. Never before in his dozen years had he been attended by a doctor; and when he got well (oh, dear *if* ever he felt better!) he would boast extensively to Agnes and his younger brothers, and make himself insufferable.

Danny had expected to see an exceptionally tall gentleman with a gray beard, like old Doctor Kamphoefner in Delaware County; and this man was not especially tall, and he had no beard whatsoever. He advanced good-naturedly toward the bed—he said, Why, here's my new friend, Daniel McElroy Mattock! What happened to you, Daniel? Did a bear bite you?— Then his fingers were pressing not too hurtfully on Danny's wrist, and then his fingers (they seemed strong fingers, yet they were gentle too, gentler than Danny's mother's fingers) were turning back Danny's eyelids, and he was saying: Golly, I heard someone say you had black eyes, and you haven't at all: yours are gray. Just fancy that! Well, people are always telling fibs. Or maybe they said that you had a *black eye*? Acquired in a fight, is that so? But who on earth were you fighting? A robber, or a pugilist? Actually, you haven't *got* a black eye, have you . . . ?

When a man—even a doctor, even a stranger—took as much notice of you as this, and talked with such runaway jollity, somehow the ague cake didn't press so hurtfully on your insides. You could even grin up at him and whisper, Nope. . . .

Ah. Regular paroxysms, I think your daughter said, ma'am?

Sir?

The shakes come at regular intervals, almost exactly the same time each day?

Oh, yes, Doctor. He's just been miserable. Won't eat nothing—

You have a watch or a clock, Mrs. Mattock? Have you noticed the time when they occur?

Oh, yes, Doctor. Just a touch later each morning. See—there's our old clock over there on the shelf— It don't always work—kind of busted and jingly inside—when you wind it, specially. But tis working at present. And I'd say that the misery strikes him a smidge tardier each morning—maybe fifteen minutes or so— Ain't that right, Alice?

The Voice of the Brown Cool Stream said: Yes, Mam.

Well, I'm glad to hear you say that, Mrs. Mattock.

(He could see Doctor Dailey as if in print, looming from a page. *Favorable when the paroxysms are* postponed; *unfavorable when* anticipated . . . he could see Daniel Drake as if in print, forever the words of Drake sprang into his brain from the treasury which was Drake . . . *intermittent fever, simple, and inflammatory; malignant inter-*

mittent fever; remittent fever; malignant remittent fever; protracted, relapsing, and vernal intermittent fevers. . . .)

Ma'am, have you been administering medicine to Danny?

No, we hain't got nothing to give him. No quinine, nothing. Did have some Doc Sappington pills, but we run out when I got the ager myself, while back.

Do you stand cured?

Mainly, Doctor. Get a few shakes once in a while, not frequent. All the younguns have had a touch, like most folks when fall's coming on. Poor Danny's the worst off. I wanted to make him some soot coffee, but the soot's got to be scraped from a chimley; and we're so recent moved into this new house that I couldn't get much soot off'n the inside and—

Harry tasted the tonic wine tincture which he had fetched. It didn't pass muster—too long made up, too much warm weather; the stuff had gone foul even in fermentation.

What you got there, Doctor?

Tonic wine tincture, but I fear it's past its usefulness. A lad of discrimination, such as Daniel here, wouldn't tolerate it! And you are that, of course, aren't you, Dan? A lad of discrimination?

What's tonic wine tincture? demanded Mary suspiciously.

Ma'am, it doesn't really matter, since I'm throwing out this batch anyway. But one of the most important ingredients is Peruvian bark. . . .

Harry set to work at the rough table, preparing to mix a new potion for the young sufferer. He had decided on a medicament known as febrifuge wine. There were stained greasy plates and forks all over the place, left from breakfast, and Alice Mattock hastened across the room to clear these away. She brought a wet rag, she wiped the boards vigorously. Working at such close quarters, she brushed back against the doctor unwittingly. Harry sprang away with a mumbled apology. . . . But even in that second he had felt warmth and power of her thigh through the concealing layers of thin cloth, had known the rich roundness of her buttock. In quick reaction his face was flushing, he felt the flooding hotness of his face, was annoyed with himself for blushing like a callow youth. (Actually he didn't know what the word *callow* meant; he'd heard it applied to youths; he thought that perhaps it meant *pale,* like a tallow candle.) He strove to master his embarrassment. He kept declaiming a formula for tonic wine tincture, even while he opened his satchel and brought out drugs and scales to fabricate an entirely different remedy. . . . Two quarts of port wine to begin with, if you were to make a good-sized batch. That couldn't be done here at the lakes, could it? Ha-ha—who had any port wine, indeed? Sulphur, capsicum, cinnamon, and the bark of the wild cherry tree, as well as Peruvian bark. But when employing the latter he always pulverized it himself! That was the trouble with big drug houses—you couldn't trust them around a corner—you purchased pulverized Peruvian bark and you got an article vastly adulterated. . . .

Pshaw, there seemed no end to the blushing and quailing! For he'd used the word *adulterated*, and now it was Alice Mattock who was coloring and withdrawing, and turning her head away. Obviously she was not familiar with the term as applied to a product alloyed and made impure; she must be thinking of *adultery*. Oh, pshaw . . . damn it all, anyway! And, placing such construction on the term, she might think that deliberately he had inserted those syllables in casual conversation in order to hint . . . to make her think of subjects unfit for maidens to consider . . . because her father was in the habit of roaring imprecations and obscenities? Then she must suffer as a victim, and one whom men might assume to be sportive and unchaste, merely because her father . . . oh, the devil!

Harry had the lame feeling that the keen and assured Doctor Harriott, forever in command of himself when professionally engaged at St. Paul, was cutting a sorry figure here in this frontier shack.

Forget all about the girl, damn it! Good Lord, he knew females, didn't he? He was a physician and surgeon: he'd dosed youngish females, cauterized their dog bites and cat scratches, treated their internals, delivered their babies legitimate and illegitimate alike. He knew women's flesh and pelvic structure, was familiar with menstrual difficulties and debilities, knew how to use a vaginal syringe, had used one many times.

Well, pshaw. . . .

That is . . . damn it!

God damn it!

Forget her!

Or, at least— Ignore her!

Certainly.

Who was she? Just another female. Daughter of a pioneer hog-breeder. Inelegant. Barefoot. Spoke colloquially. Untutored, shabby, probably illiterate!

. . . What say, Daniel? Why, tis a scale.

. . . Yes, certainly, I know. Fish have scales. You're entirely correct. But this is a balance scale. Or, shall we say, a set of balances. You weigh things with them.

. . . Oh, yes, any tiny thing. But this is what a druggist or a doctor uses in order to weigh medicines properly. Now, watch carefully. Two ounces of sugar . . . yes, that is correct. It's for *you*. You're going to have *white* sugar—just think of that. When was the last time you had white sugar? Ah-huh.

. . . And this? Why, it's mystery medicine! . . . What's that? Now, look here, sir—if I gave away all my secrets to you, how ever could I make a living as a doctor? You'd have all the knowledge, and where would I be? I doubt not that you'd go around practicing yourself. Folks would say, We shan't call Doctor Harriott. He doesn't know so much! No. They'd say, Why not summon Doctor Daniel McElroy Mattock? He knows as much as Doctor Harriott knows!

Quinine was weighed, Epsom salts— Fifteen drops of sulphuric acid were duly dripped in, a gill of brandy poured. Harry stirred the mixture into a measured pint of spring water and, elucidating gaily to Danny on the therapeutic benefits of color, bedizened the compound with tincture of red sanders. Harry consigned this febrifuge wine to storage in an old B. & O. whiskey flask. He warned that Daniel McElroy Mattock should not be permitted more than three wineglasses of the fluid in a single day— One in the morning, one at noon, one at night. Yes, indeed, that was all he could have, even though he might beg for more—

Since it was approaching noon now, Danny would be allowed to swallow one glass immediately.

He gulped it down with eagerness, gasped, coughed, made a wretched face.

I—dddon't—lllike it!

Goodness sakes. Tis delicious! Think of all that brandy and sugar— Why, you saw me putting in the white sugar—with your own eyes you saw me! And that pretty red stuff—

No! I won't tttake no mmmore—

Daniel McElroy Mattock, you'll do just what the doctor says! I don't want to hear no—

Just a moment, ma'am. Dan, you like licorice? Hey? Do you?

I dddunno—

I mean lickrish.

Yyyes. I like *that.*

Then you shall have some. Very next dose of medicine you take—tonight, twill be—you get lickrish. How's that? No more red stuff which you don't like to swallow. No, sir. Lickrish. Will that suit?

Yyyes.

Dan, said Alice quietly. Sickly or no, please to mend your manners.

Yyyes, *sir. . . .*

Harry had a thick solution of licorice in his drug chest, back at the tent. He had never added the stuff to febrifuge wine before, but knew that there could be no harmful result. Sometimes, when treating very tiny patients, he had mixed five or six grains of quinine in a two-ounce vial, along with a tablespoonful of white sugar, and filled the flask with water. A teaspoonful of this compound, given with licorice to conceal the taste, was accepted readily by most children.

Mrs. Mattock said, One time, back East, when I was bad took with the ager, they give me what they called Doctor Krieder's pills. Guess I took maybe twenty. They brung a cure.

Yes, I know, ma'am. But I dislike to prescribe opium, especially where little folks are concerned.

Opium? I didn't say—

Harry was repacking his satchel. . . . Doctor Krieder's pills contain a substance known as Dover's powders. Dover's powders contain opium. Not a sovereign remedy of mine, not by any means. But the formula for the febrifuge wine which I am prescribing for my friend Daniel McElroy Mattock, comes from one of the most successful physicians in Saginaw; and Saginaw was notorious for its ague before this gentleman arrived on the scene. May I quote my first preceptor, Doctor Thomas Maws: *Don't go to Michigan, that land of ills; the word means ague, fever and chills.*

Well, we hain't a-going there!

Nor are we. The Red Wing Company stays put!

I thought one of them Englishmen tolt my husband he was going back to Minnesota?

That's William Granger—he has a wife and babies in Red Wing, and he'll return to them soon. But his brother Carl, together with Bertell Snyder and myself, will winter here: that's why we're building our house. And I must get back to it now. Daniel, lad, are you still shaking?

Yyyes . . . sssir. . . .

Poor feller! Well, I'm also leaving for you a delightful gift in the shape of a physic. Tis here, ma'am, in this cup. Please administer it as soon as his current fit has worn off. Daniel, I shan't humbug you—tis nasty stuff. But a couple of quick swallows and it's down. And twill help you so that you'll soon be out of bed and gathering nuts, like any other squirrel.

Dddon't . . . wwwant no. . . .

Promise to swallow it down with no ruckus, and I've a present for you. Is that agreeable? Yes? Good!

Harry awarded to Danny a flint arrowhead which he had picked up that morning. He told Mary Mattock that she might now admit the younger children, who had been beating periodically upon the door and then scampering off with shrieks.

Doctor Harriott . . . we're short of cash. I hain't got none. Husband took the purse with him.

Harry's original impulse had been to wave away airily all offers of payment—to declare that his first visit was made invariably on a gratuitous basis. But this place had become his community, his future home; new settlers jolted into the region; strangers named Howe and Noble and Thatcher were housebuilding on the farther shore of East

Okoboji; rumors spread about someone's settling on the west shore of Spirit Lake—

Ma'am, you've all these hogs. I take it you'll be doing some butchering when the weather cools off? . . . Ah, so. Then may I accept payment in pork, later on? Say a-dollar-and-a-quarter's worth? Thank you. . . . Good day, ma'am. Good day, Daniel McElroy. Miss Alice, will you be kind enough to accompany me, in order to fetch back this bottle, after I've redeemed the febrifuge with delicious lickrish?

As he walked with Alice among the trees Harry was smitten by a blinding impressive flash of recollection. He was a little boy again, he didn't wish to go to school, he hated school. He had hidden beneath the covers as long as possible, then his father ordered him out. Ah, school . . dismal grayish slates, squeaking pencils, master's tiresome voice, drafty room with its winter smells of drying wool, smells of many little bodies long unwashed. The columns of sums set out by the master . . . but there was *breakfast* to come first. Oh, lovely, lovely breakfast! The coffee, a platter of hot golden mush slices with crisp varying patterns of brown scorched into each slice . . . richness of the lean-streaked pork . . . plum preserves. And even while he ate, he was dreading school. But he thought: There's the *walk to school,* first. I can enjoy *that,* first. . . . And then he traveled amid snowbanks, stamping along in a deep rut between blue-shadowed drifts, his feet warm and dancing inside their thick knitted stockings, inside the brand-new boots with shiny copper plates . . . body alive and muscular within patched coarse clothing—but who cared about patches?—the body was bounding with energy! . . . He thought: Oh, dang! School to come—that gol danged old school—I can't avoid it, and my walk's half done—I'm here in front of the Striebel place already. But, hold on!—I've still got to turn here, and go down the lane to the left— And that black dog Nicky will come out from the next house—he almost always does come out—and I like that dog, and I'll get to pet him, just a second or two—and then he'll grin, rolling up his lip and showing his teeth in that funny way he has— I've still got *that* to look forward to!

The entire remembrance leaped into being, its chronology compressed. Harry saw everything at once extended and yet superimposed; he could taste the hot fried mush, see diamonds on the snow's crust, feel the dog's nose thrust against his welcoming mitten, and all in an instant. So dwelt he now, in current frenzy of excitement, with a mingled dread of deprivation to follow.

I do not wish to leave her, I find such pleasure in being with her, ah, I do not wish to leave her, nay, nay, nay! But there is the walk down to the strait . . . *that's* still to come . . . I mean tis half over now. But wait, wait— Should she come over in the canoe, or wait until I come back, after I've added licorice to this dratted febrifuge? Oh, I must not be taken away from her—I wish to stand near her— By Gad, she might accidentally press against my body again! Once more I'd feel the fierce power of that curving living limb, under the cloth, under her skirts— And hear her voice, and see those thick soft brows draw back from her eyes when she smiles—

So I'll ask her to come in the canoe—

No, no! Bert and the Grangers standing around! Why, they'd stop working promptly, and come down off the roof and— Yes, yes, I can fairly see them a-doing it! Both Grangers a-grinning like— What is that they say? A Cheshy cat? And Bert speaking jaunty gallantries, and— No! I shan't take her over!

Here we are beside the water, and . . .

Why, what ails you, man? You're not a schoolboy, not a bumpkin. You're a physician and surgeon, making your way in the world—going to help found the Athens of the West, the Paris of the Prairies— *Helping* to found it, right now. Okobojiopolis! What of the fine chaise with red wheels, what of your father-in-law, Judge Darius Alexander Wellington? What of Colonel MacTavish, and the Reverend Doctor John Alden Standish, president of the University? And Mr. Paul Revere Witherspoon, and the hospital? Set your mind to your business! Consider Doctor William Dailey and his summation of the ague!

The form *which fevers assume in this respect is called their type. There are, therefore, three principal types: i.e., the quotidian, the tertian, and the quartan types. Quotidians generally come on in the morning; tertians about noon; and quartans in the afternoon.*

Miss Alice—

Yes, sir?

Would you mind waiting here for me? I mean— Of course, I can take you over if— But that canoe's a trickster— Sometimes it upsets— I mean, with two in it— Shouldn't wish you to get a wetting—

Alice looked about her, and spied a smooth boulder nesting amid a tangle of tree roots near the pebbly margin. She went to the boulder, seated herself, folded the bluish calico gown around her legs. She looked up at Harry, and smiled. I'll wait here, the gentle voice was saying. Tis so nice and quiet and kind of peaceful. I'll wait.

Harry sped across the water and stepped out of the canoe. Before he started through the reeds, he turned toward Alice Mattock, seated so demurely in the shade yonder. He waved his free hand, she waved back at him. Something beautiful flew between them in the simple salutes exchanged. Harry went breathlessly up the path; he tried to compel himself to remember— In which row and layer of bottles had the licorice solution been packed? Discipline and compulsion were weak. He still saw the girl with the polished curl, saw only her, did not see woods or weather about him.

. . . But what of your family, sir? Your daughters, all named Victoria, and your queenly wife, Portia?

. . . My God, my God! The daughter of that profane bellowing hog-breeder, daughter of that shrill-spoken biddy I just left— Rustic lass with tough bare feet— Sister of those yelping children— She, she, she! *She* is Portia, *she* is Miss Raven Tresses! Bert Snyder'll never let me hear the end of this! Miss Raven Tresses! Merciful God in Heaven!

XIX

Charley Flandrau enjoyed being called Major. He was called Major these days because he'd newly come to be an Indian agent, and traditionally Indian agents were so designated. Charley Flandrau was twenty-eight years old, and possessed a muscular pair of striding legs which could take him, and had taken him on many occasions, the distance of fifty miles in a day. His profession was that of a lawyer, although he had little practice; there were few people in his new world to serve as clients, and of these few even fewer had any money. But several times he'd walked from his home near Traverse des Sioux all the way to the land office at Winona, to look after his neighbors' property rights—had walked the hundred and fifty miles in three days, attended to the land-office business (that term was coming into popular usage as a suggestion of abundant dealings; but scarcely were these dealings so!) and then Mr. Flandrau marched the hundred and fifty miles back to a green-golden-hazy-brown Minnesota River valley again. Charley had also a striding sort of mind which went out and explored eternally, and came back to him and reported. He felt himself to be a person of enormous capabilities, but knew that he should appear modest about it all; and so he did. Charley looked in his jagged scrap of mirror and did not like the shape of his mouth and chin: they held character but they were not handsome. He saw that his nose was handsome, his gaze clear and penetrating. So promptly he grew a thick beard and mustache, and was pleased by the change. Now he appeared to be older than twenty-eight. His eyes were challenging but able to scintillate in varieties of humor. He liked to tell of his early youth—it was crammed with experiences which he recalled as delightful or, at the worst, fraught with excitement and peril. Charley's father had set the boy to his books at Georgetown, District of Columbia; twas a good school of its kind, quite eligible to receive the son of one who had been a quondam partner of Aaron Burr; but Charley found the life dully decorous and the curriculum exasperating. At the age of thirteen he fled aboard a revenue cutter which was ready to sail away down the Potomac, and promptly found himself far up an icy waving mast, in a storm off

Cape Charles. His eyes would fire darkly as he told of this. . . . Later he shipped on several merchant vessels.

. . . The first mate was a Mr. Harbison, and often he was drunk! This was one of the times. He came on deck, picked up that coil, said, Who spliced this line? The way he said it really enraged me. I cried, I did!—and didn't add the *Sir.* Next moment I was picking myself up out of the scuppers, and blood was rushing from my smashed nostrils, and my wrist was broken. Here, feel the lumps on the bones! A permanent souvenir, awarded me by one Mr. Harbison. I was advised later that he died during an attack of delirium at Savannah, and I was appropriately delighted to hear of it! . . .

Settlers along the upper Minnesota River placed reliance upon Charley Flandrau, and sent him to represent them in the Territorial Council. He made his frequent journeys to St. Paul by that means of travel best suited to his body and his nature: he walked. He would walk the seventy-five miles from Traverse des Sioux by a direct route, with only a few hours stopover in Shakopee. In such activity a man could have his feet bitten by frost during the colder months, and so did Charley Flandrau often suffer freezings. His face had been frozen frequently, sometimes his hands went numb and gray inside his furry mittens, sometimes there was no feeling in his feet. In the spring of 1856 he'd limped to find his doctor, on arrival at St. Paul, but learned that Doctor Droege was attending on an emergency miles away; folks sent him on to another man, a man even younger than Charley Flandrau. The patient walked gingerly into the doctor's presence, told his story, pulled off boots and socks, had his feet examined, and sat waiting while the practitioner prepared a mysterious mixture.

Now, what is that base, Doctor? Alcohol?

No, sir. Rain water.

Why rain water? Why not water from the well?

Rain water's better.

In every case?

No. In this case.

Ah. What's that you're measuring now?

Hydrochloric acid.

Good lord!

Excuse me, Mr. Flandrau. Should you like to treat your own case?

No, no, no, Doctor! Pray proceed. Tis just that I'm possessed of a great bump of curiosity, phrenologically speaking!

You see, sir, you've come to me complaining about itching feet. You have a history of frostbite; and the itching feet become downright painful and interfere with your walking. It so happens that I regard hydrochloric acid and rain water as a specific in such cases—proper proportions, of course. Furthermore, since your home is at some distance, I shall provide you with the formula *and* a phial of acid. But only *rain* water, y'understand. . . .

Now, I've sponged your feet with the solution. Feel better?

Doctor Harriott, you're a wizard! *In*finitely better already!

The proportion is one to seven: one ounce acid, seven ounces rain water. Tis perfectly safe—won't burn—you can wet your socks with the preparation. I don't warrant that it will cure your condition, but it has cured others.

I'm very much in your debt.

Not at all, sir, should you have any hard money on you!

After he had put on his socks and boots, Flandrau fetched out the blackened little doeskin pouch which served as his purse. The bill, Doctor?

Harry added up. Fifty cents for the office visit (twould be a dollar if it had to go on the books)— Fifty cents for medication. And here's your bottle of hydrochloric acid—mind, you keep it well-packed— That's very expensive; you know how dear freight is.

Indeed I do! Constantly we're urged to do something about that in the Council. But the steamboat owners have us by the throat—

Say two dollars, entire.

Charley Flandrau extracted a quarter-eagle from his purse, and received five dimes in change. But Harry's eye was on the pouch.

Just observing the designs. That beadwork—tis neither Chip nor Winnebago, is it?

Dakota. They're my neighbors. And—I say this in some confidence, Doctor, since it's not yet confirmed— Rumor informs me that I'll soon be named as agent for the Dakotas.

Harry extended his hand in congratulation. So we may meet again before long!

Splendid! You're coming up the Minnesota River?

Harry discussed eagerly the Red Wing Company and their ambitions; he displayed wooden cases in which he was stowing books. Flandrau slapped his hands together in approval. . . . Why, I'm well acquainted with Mr. Freeborn, naturally. And I met Bert Snyder when I first came up the river, in 'Fifty-three. I'd count him as one of the most intelligent men in the Territory. Do halt to visit me at either Agency if you come nigh.

We shall. Gladly—

And come along now, to luncheon at the Fuller House!

I'd like nothing better. But you see my situation: I must continue packing. And a man's coming to see about buying my horse. I've hopes of taking the old *War Eagle* down to Red Wing, a-Friday.

. . . Charles Flandrau was not tormented by superstition; but he was willing to entertain various superstitions if he found their content amusing or even suggestive of drama. When he was small someone had told him that the name of Charles was unlucky in the extreme. Look at all those miserable Charleses! Charles the First, Charles the Second, the Young Pretender. All of them lost their heads or their hopes. And what of our own American history? Take General Charles Lee in the Revolution: tried, found guilty, looked upon with contempt by Washington, dismissed from the Service. And the British commander at Yorktown— Unhappy man, Lord Charles Cornwallis! He had to surrender. And even that wretched wrist-breaking mate on the *Bonnie Barb* was named Charles Harbison!

All through his young life Charley Flandrau had collected unfortunate Charleses. His latest acquisition was Charles Sumner, feared to be crippled for life after a cruel beating (though already it had been hinted in the press that Senator Sumner did not tend to minimize the severity of his condition). So should he, Charles Flandrau, find only a beheading, a rejection, a wounding in the end? The chief portion of his spirit screamed Nonsense at the idea; he felt so strong (even with itching burning aching feet, the winter frostbite's residue). He felt so omniscient, so keen, so ready to be active and to be entertained rather than depressed by follies of humanity. He stood ready, twenty-four hours a day, to right a wrong wherever he might be able to do so; to identify the worm in the apple, and expunge it without further ceremony; he felt a resource within himself in matters great and small. Minnesota was his place, he'd been here less than three years, already he felt as much a part of the wide pretty lake-drenched soil as its native pipestone. Penury? Twas a bagatelle. Starvation? One need never starve—you dwelt in comfort if you had a wit about you. Ha: that first winter in the Traverse region. He'd found himself sheltered with a Scotsman; they had no money, few supplies, the Scot said they'd have to hunt for a living; but the weather'd turned very cold. No game around, nothing to hunt except a plethora of wolves. Then a Dakota lad rode his exhausted pony into the lee of their cabin; they took the *hokshidan* inside for a night, to keep the poor little fellow from freezing to death; but, lo and behold, with morning they found the pony dead outside. Well, they fed the unhappy little Indian, saw him headed on foot toward his family's lodge—twas only about four miles up the river—and then Charley Flandrau declared, Here's our bait.

Bait? Whit wey?

Wolves, man! Must be a thousand of them, lurking all around here in the brush. They made the night hideous, didn't they?

Aye. But we can no stand oot here with our guns. Havers!—we'd die as the poor pony did.

We needn't. Lay hold of his tail—I'll drag the head—

But we can no eat *wolves*.

Yes, yes, we'll eat them—indirectly. Come on, we'll manage.

Well, they dragged and pried and bullied that pony's carcass through the snow until they had it hauled to a spot about two rods directly beyond the cabin's window. Twas simple. They removed one of the six windowlights and trained their guns, stuffed with buckshot, on the frozen body. Stiff in ice or no, that pony smelt like sirloin to those wolves. They came round by night, relay after relay. Charley Flandrau and his friend could lie warmly in bed, and then one of them might be snoring while the other listened; and then the other would shake the one who was snoring, and whisper, *Wolves.* So then they'd both arch up out of the blankets (so black outside that no individual villain could be observed, but those sights were set squarely on the carcass) and they'd say, One, two, three, *bam*— Or maybe there'd be a sort of double roar of the guns, a *bam-bam* when they didn't fire quite simultaneously. And then what yells would rise outside! . . . Out of bed, through the door, round two corners of the cabin the men would go rushing, one with the axe, one with the hatchet. Chop, crunch, thud: dispatching the wounded wolves, of course. They'd drag them inside, to skin the next day. No trick to it: plenty of horsemeat, plenty of wolves. In all they slew forty-two, and the pelts brought seventy-five cents apiece from nearby traders. What could you buy with thirty-one dollars and fifty cents? Everything, practically everything. Meal, bacon, tobacco, salt fish, whiskey, powder at fifty cents per pound, shot at four dollars for a large sack, tobacco at fifty cents per pound, dried apples, sugar, coffee, flour . . . ha. Twas demonstrating resource, that's what it was. Charley Flandrau's deep bright eyes snapped with the sense of it all. He felt very resourceful, very stout—most alert and promising and benevolently crafty—very fortunate, completely un-Charley-ish.

He was growing speedily these days into that most happily anointed of men: the one who has a good skill and the energy to apply it, who feels he owns the answers, who is confident that the exercise of his particular profession may achieve a widespread elevation of human conduct and human content. (So feels the consecrated parson, so feel the good Ben Dudleys and burgeoning Isaac Harriotts, so feel the high-minded military, the professors warm with sympathy and eager to disseminate truths.) Charley had thought that he hated the law, but he was a child then: tomes frightened him, and he was irked by the deceit of certain people who merely pretended to interpret—who were sodden taskmasters instead of guides. How delighted was Charles Flandrau, now that he'd turned his back on the sea and its damp adventures, now that he'd given up the mahogany-cutter's trade— How pleased was Flandrau that he'd buried himself—at long last and with sternness—in his father's law library, in New York State! For he'd gained something to fetch along into the West, something more profound than those vague hopes carried by most who came.

He'd gained the law! He had it with him in soul and intellect. Law could be spread across the riverside hills, could lace the prairies, new communities might rise tranquil but fervid within a fabric of the law. (Surely a lone hawk rose up and cried for *justice* from the skies!) There must be equability, cleanliness, the newcomers themselves must yield to discipline and fact of the law; dedicated fresh legislators must be bound by it. But not too forcibly; you couldn't bind humanity with the iron tautness of shrinking rawhide, then they'd all be crippled. You must widen the law, enlarge it, exert it decently, tailor or extend it into a tent to cover new demands.

Charley Flandrau's fine gaze sparkled with the notion of subsidies of esteem to be awarded to all who deserved them; and he thought that the deserving were many.

He did not venture beyond this clear scheme of merits and responsibilities. Most people were good at heart: see that they be treated so. Wickedness was demonstrated in an unholy minority; thus the wicked must be restrained; build a jail!—but make it not a pit of horrors, else men might be shamed. Like the hearty physician and teacher and parson and colonel, he was certain that he knew credible solutions for most problems, would folks but listen to him. The doctor was expected to cure—so he *should*, he *must* cure! The pedagogue was commissioned to conduct and explain, the minister had the obligation of cleansing the spirit (or at least of using soap and water supplied by the Almighty). And he who carried sword or truncheon, by desire and by choice and through competent training, should erect a security for all; twas his bounden duty, he was sworn to it.

And the lawyer would be a counselor and a judge. He'd say: We'll exert in this fashion or that fashion, because that is the law; and without our good law there would be no tolerance, no safety, no confidence, no eventual fulfillment.

. . . The Minnesota Territory has been acquired.

. . . *Quo Warranto?*

. . . By right of purchase.

. . . Did the manner of purchase constitute a malfeasance?

. . . In my opinion, most assuredly!

. . . Do you indeed refer to an hereditament or freehold, in the conveyance of which a certain abatement was intrinsic? Think you that the Indians might secure a writ of replevin? Why, we shall invoke the law of Eminent Domain! You have expressed a unilateral attitude. Indeed we whites have paid for the Minnesota Territory, *quantum valebat.*

. . . Ah, so say you.

But Mr. Flandrau was pliant enough to manage a shrug; he was no longer a stripling, he'd learned that it was impossible to reform the past. You could bring order to the present, and thus pray for a fairer year to come.

Truly he felt very sorry for the Indians. Most of them did not as yet know what had happened to them: they were confused and resentful; still they did not understand. Future generations might know the truth. Twould not be his appointed task to explain to them . . . Naturally he believed that before too long he would be on the Bench. Once on the Bench, twould become his enterprise to administer justice, to do the right thing rather than the wrong thing; and it remained for the law itself to tell him which was right and which was wrong.

His proficient strong young mind found no disharmony between the schemes laid on for the management of men, and the nature of men themselves. . . . Not consciously, at least. Oh, there were a few puzzles, there were moments (he'd experienced them already, with a trifle of wriggling) when nothing seemed to fit and nothing seemed to suffice. But seriously Charley Flandrau ascribed such temporary bewilderment to his own inexperience. With accumulation of observation, and thus an accumulation of proof, he would be able to find the answers. Of this he was heartily confident. Why, how efficacious could be the advice and preachings of a priest who doubted? Of what effect might be the lecture of a mentor insecure in his knowledge? (Knowledge was a definite commodity: you went and searched for it, quarried it, picked it, plucked it, shot it down, packed it up, took it home with you, kept it safe; you had knowledge stored, no one could steal it from you, knowledge could not be robbed away.) Would you feel trust beneath fingers and instruments of a surgeon who confessed: Frankly, I'm not sure whether I should ligate or suture? And if a soldier were insecure in his estimate of a situation, and hesitated about whether to press his attack on the morrow, or to order immediate withdrawal from an untenable position?— What then? How now?

Charles Flandrau was charmed to feel that he could separate the chalk from the cheese, the shoddy from the substantial, the true from the untrue, most of the time. He did not wish to wade through unsolved riddles. He pitied those flounderers who were compelled to do so, solely through ineptitude or lack of decision. Ha—how fortunate that almost always the world was vivid instead of vague!

But he did pity the Indians. Sometimes his heart made a weeping in their behalf, because his heart was open and cordial.

In the late autumn of 1856, when Flandrau had served as United States agent for the Sioux for three months, he entertained a visitor in the person of his friend the Scotsman. One sunlit day the new agent arrived at the Lower Agency—named by the Dakota as *Chan-*

duta, or Redwood. It was situated near that point where the Redwood River ran purposeful and dark out of a gulley fenced by narrow shelving cliffs, and lost itself in steady flow of the Minnesota. Scarcely had Charley stepped ashore when he was greeted by a Christianized youth who admired him and who wished to be the first to utter good tidings.

Major, *koda kin hi!*

Come, come, Simeon. I'm still struggling hopelessly with Dakota. Speak to me in English.

Simeon He-Gets-Up-And-Stands translated: Major, friend comes.

What friend is that?

Friend of you. Hair of him is *gitkatka*—hair is pink. On his face many *hdeshkashka gitkatka* also!—and Simeon began to jab his own face with rapid strokes of his finger.

By cracky. Stuart Garvie!

The young agent sent a halloo toward the cabins, and was soon pleased to see a wide-shouldered freckled-faced Garvie moving down the path.

Charley, lad, I thought you were no to hame.

Well, I've got two homes these days, if you can call 'em that. Here, at the Lower Agency; and the Upper Agency at *Pezihutazizi.*

Garvie blinked his blue eyes. Aye, the Yellow Medicine River.

Correct, sir. How'm I progressing linguistically?

You've made a wee bit progress, said Garvie with caution. Give us a report. Did you shoot any wolves the nicht?

Garvie was tasting better fare in Minnesota Territory than he'd enjoyed in his native Kilmarnock. There he began as a bobbin boy and progressed drearily through apprenticeship until he'd learned to weave. He owned a mildly horrifying storybook fairy-tale background which included grim attic lodgings, a cholera epidemic, scourgings inflicted by a fanatically religious stepfather, and later the witnessing of drunken murder committed by a fellow craftsman in Paisley. He'd emigrated in 1851. (Once, when a boy, Stuart Garvie had run away from Kilmarnock and made himself a secret den under a stone wall beside the ruins of Dean castle, north of town. There he subsisted for a fortnight, feeding mainly on blackbirds which he killed with a slingshot, until stormy weather drove him back to thralldom among the tenements and looms. But such independent venture had given him desire to lead sometime a hunter's life in a more salubrious region; and at the age of twenty-two he'd found serene if not too remunerative freedom among the frontier uplands of America.) He was an easy-moving bullock of a man whose freckles plastered like orange scars over face, neck, and shoulders. Besides his Bible he possessed but one book—Burns, naturally—and most of the poems he had learned verbatim. He'd put Charley Flandrau to sleep on more than one stormy penned-up afternoon with, *But now the supper crowns their simple board, the halesome parritch, chief o' Scotia's food; the soupe their only hawkie does afford, that 'yont the hallan snugly chows her cood; the dame brings forth, in complimental mood, to grace the lad, her well-hained kebbuck fell.* Flandrau could be excused for coming to the firm conviction that there was nothing in this world more boring to the non-Scot than Robert Burns. But, putting *The Cotter* aside, he was very fond of Garvie; partly because they had shared short commons and rough dangers, and partly because he found in Stuart Garvie an excellent listener, who was gifted in giving him, by word or hint or mere silent attitude, the exact stimulation which Flandrau needed to send him into a powerful summation and reassortment of his—Flandrau's—own ideas, and even into very passable oratory.

Stuart lounged about while the agent worked (bristling with responsibilities, and consciously aware that a white man watched—and more than that, a friend, but a friend perhaps critical and shrewdly evaluating). It seemed that some of the Indians above the Yellow Medicine were late in coming in for their payments; goods had been distributed accordingly, and money paid out; Flandrau had notations of all such transactions, but these items must now be incorporated in master ledgers here at Redwood. Also there were bales, boxes, and barrels to be housed at the Lower Agency; it was difficult to maintain two points of distribution, but that was the way of it: always goods were being juggled back and forth between the depots. Missionaries up yonder at Lac-qui-Parle and Yellow Medicine had sent two packets of letters to be mailed back East; these must be dispatched downriver to Traverse des Sioux without delay, and thence they would be carried to St. Paul and the steamboats. Charley kept up a running fire of comment and explanation while supervising these details. . . . He had a bag of gold coins to be locked in the strongbox under his bed. There were two fresh-killed deer sent down as a gift to Missionary John P. Williamson and his flock— Get some boys, Simeon— And you, Titus, and you, John— Deliver the deer to Doctor Williamson promptly—

Garvie knew something of the Dakota, he had hunted among and with them for some years now.

Who was it was late for the payments, Charley?

Sisitonwanna. The Dryers-on-the-Shoulder crowd. You must realize that the bulk of them have moved northwest now, up around Lake Traverse and the Coteau des Prairies.

But yon Indians have aye been greedy for their gifts.

Not gifts, Mr. Garvie. Payments!

Aw richt, payments. Why—?

Ah, they were hunting. Rumors of buffalo to the west. But the buffalo had moved on down between the Big Sioux and the James before the Isanties ever caught up with them. Likely the Yanktonais killed the buffalo instead.

Are the Wahpetonwanna now dwelling far in the northwest as well?

No, they're closer to hand—Lac-qui-Parle and Big Stone. Many Christians among them.

And the Wahpekute?

Flandrau gestured toward the south. They come here for the payments, those bands which were signatory to the treaties five years ago. But not all are entitled to participate in any distribution.

Charley, ye ken the big Wahpekute? The bad one? Does he appear?

. . . In the winter of their first meeting—that winter of Flandrau's arrival in the Territory—the two had traveled almost to headwaters of the Blue Earth, the Le Sueur, the Watonwan. Charley, flat of pocketbook and also appalled by slim legal pickings in St. Paul, was engaged for a modest free to go tramping on a tour of exploration. Several well-to-do men were interested in the project: they wished to have the region surveyed with a view to accessibility, agricultural possibilities, potential townsites. Garvie went with Flandrau, he knew the country better than most. Far up the Watonwan, in a grove beside the lake, the young men made a comfortable snow-camp; they spent two nights there, snug beneath a lean-to, and sleeping pleasantly on mounds of balsam; they returned on the third evening to find the place plundered—fir burned, blankets and venison stolen, windbreak destroyed. Furiously they began to follow tracks which unknown marauders had left behind them, but a storm came up. The explorers were compelled to return and build a new shelter and one nothing like so comfortable. At dawn, with winds lessened and snow no longer descending, they traveled south once more and walked into the camp of Inkpaduta's people. Vigorously Inkpaduta and his companions denied that they had been the despoilers; but Garvie held a cocked shotgun upon them while Charley Flandrau roved on a tour of inspection. Promptly he discovered the missing blankets and a few other articles which had been borne to this place by the thieves. Actually the Indians seemed more amused than discomfited at being caught red-handed in their naughtiness. Garvie made signs about soldiers coming down from Fort Snelling; and Flandrau gave a demonstration of marksmanship by fastening a stray playing card against a cottonwood and shooting out the single big spot with his pistol (ace of diamonds: half the pack had blown away in a high wind—he didn't know how or why he happened to have three cards still carried in his pocket)! The Wahpekute pretended to be little stirred by this demonstration, though actually they were much impressed, according to Garvie. But they were interested in examining the playing card; perhaps they had never seen one before. The two white men went away, leaving Indians still gathered together, passing the card from hand to hand, mumbling about it. Flandrau and Garvie did not think that the robbers attempted to follow them, but they made hasty tracks out of the country for all that. . . .

The bad one? I wish there were but one.

I refer to Inkpaduta.

Gad, Garvie, I feared I'd miss that ace of diamonds! Father and I used to hold pistol competitions, in camera as it were, when I was reading law at Whitesboro; and I learned not to miss—he was somewhat sensitive about the notion of poor marksmanship—the Burr-Hamilton business, you see—he'd been Burr's law partner, as I've told you. But I was nervous when faced by Inkpaduta and his rapscallions—

Did he have aught to say of yon incident, when he came this year to the payments?

Ah, he didn't come, praise be. The superintendent informs me that he did appear in 'Fifty-four and made a grand nuisance of himself—threats and attempted bullying—demanded an annuity which was in no way his. . Speaking of the superintendent, let me tell you that alteration in the manner of distribution is now in the offing. This is projected by some wiseacre in Washington, for reasons best known to himself. I will receive, from the Superintendent of Indian Affairs at St. Paul, the money— Mint boxes, of course. In silver and gold, twill probably amount to a full wagonload! This I must convey up here to the agencies. In the meantime, appropriate stocks of goods will be delivered by the contractors, by boat. A new census of the Indians will be taken and—

With Charley Flandrau still talking spiritedly, final chores were performed, and the two young men sought Charley's private room behind the office. One of the first things which Flandrau had learned in this pursuit was that he must not be seen drinking, either at Redwood or at Yellow Medicine. No liquors were included in supplies furnished as a portion of the annual installments, although many Indians always asked for whiskey or rum, and expressed disappointment when none was forthcoming. Also the missionaries, now active at both agencies as well as at Lac-qui-Parle, would have been deeply disturbed—they would have considered the slightest bibulous demonstration as an offense against their teachings, against all churchly deportment.

This situation Charley Flandrau explained to Garvie as he fastened the chamber door, drew a demijohn from its hiding place, and poured out fresh spring water from a jar.

And an overt act against their safety as well, man! We must have no liquor flowing in these parts—officially. Williamson and Riggs and all the rest are dwelling on top of a powder keg, and they know it! Here's to ye, Garvie.

To ye. Pity we've no a carcass of a wee pony. We'd slay more wolves the nicht.

They chuckled, recalling a lone cabin against the woods near Traverse—slinking shapes, the howls and snarling, boom of guns, the tedious job of skinning at which they toiled—the feel of coarse wolf-hair, stench of blood— These sips of whiskey and water made the men feel slightly ceremonious, drawn apart from others by affection and the ropes of common experience.

Tin cups in hand, they drifted to the small window and stood looking down the valley as it shimmered in sun of afternoon.

A bonnie day ootbye, Charley.

Beautiful! The warmest November, on the whole, that I've witnessed since coming to the Territory. Only a few brief intervals of rain or chill—

Still, we ken what winter can be like.

Remember the day you went through the ice on Okaman Lake?

Aye! Shall we tilt the joog once more?

Quantum meruit.

(Haze was smoke and smoke was haze, you could not tell where the one mingled its existence with the other. The river ran brown-silver and beckoning, hiding away into southeasterly regions where each bold hill dreamed of the feathered people who had dwelt upon it. Scrapped amid rolling bare forests were surviving dabs of color—a brilliance of conifers jutting up, the wisp of clinging painted vine; and always dust which rose in blue blush from fires real or fancied; always the notion of sweet-kerneled nuts, of small wild apples bitten by frost, of furry beasts asleep in the brush, waiting to rise and prowl by night.)

Simeon Nazinhannazin trotted pad-pad through the office and tried the latch of Flandrau's bedroom door. Finding that the door was bolted he began to beat rapidly with his flat hands.

Yes, yes, what's ado? yelled Flandrau. He hid the whiskey behind his strongbox under the bed.

Major, comes That One!

Flandrau unbolted the door and flung it open. Comes who?

Simeon He-Gets-Up-And-Stands breathed heavily and glowered into space. He was a thick-bodied youth with a face like a fresh-cured flitch of bacon; he had allowed the missionaries to cut his hair, had been called a woman by old friends because he wore hand-me-downs of the whites; he had been soldier-killed (suffered the loss of his blankets: his family cut them into ribbons); he used to own a pet field mouse which lived in his pocket, but the mouse was stamped to death by Simeon's own father. This young man had suffered rebuke and ostracism because of his affiliation with the whites; he was in this season a minor Christian martyr. (He would revert in a later

year, he had not yet reverted.) He spewed forth a flat toneless run-together stream of syllables, he spoke in Dakota. *Ka taku shicha entanhan eunhdaku-po.*

What's that you're yammering, Simeon? asked the mystified Flandrau.

Stuart Garvie translated tardily, after consideration. And what ugly-bad from us-deliver—

Ah, the Lord's Prayer. Deliver us from evil. Is that it, Sim?

Echahe, Major. Comes That One of bad death!

Simeon edged past the two white men and, with care, and standing well aside from the window itself, he peered out at an angle toward the gate.

Shi! he whispered, and signaled for Flandrau to join him. *Shi!* That Old One of smallpox, and loving not Heavenly Father, and love many evil— Comes for noo-it-tee. Comes for *wawichakichupi.* Same unto Prodal Son. Prodal Son say: Father, goods mine will-be the that me-mine-give!

Garvie muttered, For sic reason I left Killie. Fash the Prodigal Son! *Father, give me the portion of goods that falleth to me.* Twas the entire Fifteenth Chapter of Saint Luke that I was compelled to commit to memory, and all because I'd dared squander—

Charles Flandrau crowded past Simeon up to the little window. Come here and speak of the devil, Garvie!

Whit—?

Inkpaduta, said Flandrau.

The huge hard-faced outlaw stood pompously near a well which was curbed up about thirty yards beyond the office door. An Indian child had fallen into that well during the first week when the new agent appeared at Redwood, in August; and Flandrau himself had sprung down in order to make the rescue. (He found the boy treading water fiercely, and hauled *Chashke* up into the light of day, apparently little the worse for his experience.) Charles Flandrau decreed that a fence be built in order to minimize future dangers. It was beside this fence that Inkpaduta waited now, although his twin sons had stepped over the low barrier; one was peering into the depths, the other examined the rope. Flandrau did not know that these men were Roaring-Cloud and Fire-Cloud; he would learn their identity a few minutes later. The twins had accompanied their father on his angry quest, but no others of the band were here. Roaring-Cloud looked especially barbarous and menacing. He was not as tall as his father or brother but possessed his sire's wide thick mouth, with the same deep creases slanting alongside it. When you stood close to him you could see that his eyes were slightly crossed, and thus his expression was perhaps more intently baleful than either of the others'. His father and brother wore their hair in braids, and so did he; but

Roaring-Cloud's braids were firmest, they swung like solid clubs; and oily black hair on top of his head was parted so tightly that it seemed painted into place. From shoulders to patched moccasins his solid body was wound in a dark blue blanket on which old dried blood (blood of animals, thought the white men? Blood of humans, perchance?) had settled its stains.

Now, Sim, said Flandrau. They've got guns, all three of them. Any Indian knows blame well that he's not to approach this Agency office whilst carrying weapons. That's the rule, and I insist on keeping it.

Aye, Major!

There's shelves under that shed roof out beyond the gate, high up, out of reach of children. Tell them to leave their weapons there. Nobody'll take them. *Wakan!*

Aye, Major. But Simeon threw a nervous glance over his shoulder. Maybe That One say he leave guns not—

Then That One can precious well go flouncing off where he came from!

Aye, Major.

When I ring Agent's Bell, they come in. Not until. You understand?

Aye. God made us all, he added piously. With some reluctance he went to relay the instructions.

Charley Flandrau opened a flat oilcloth-covered trunk which he had brought down the river, and which accompanied him in the boat each time he moved. He took out a bandsman's tunic, of United States Army blue, replete with bars of worsted lace in artillery red; there were tarnished gilt epaulets sewn incongruously onto the shoulders. As he removed his buckskin shirt and buttoned himself into this gaudy coat he saw a look of amazement on Stuart Garvie's face, and began to laugh.

My friend Captain Sherman, up at Snelling, has provided me with this adornment. Handsome, eh?

Tis daft, Charley!

Not so crazy as you might believe. A wise soldier told me that no officer of the Government, civil or military, should ever appear among savages in less than a major general's uniform. Ha—I can't literally follow his advice, but my toggery will be as imposing as glittering colors can make it!

Do they no give soldiers for guard duty?

Certainly, at the payments. We had them at Yellow Medicine, but they've all returned to the fort now. This is no regular payment. In any event, I can't give these vagabonds as much as a quarter dollar. They've got no business appearing here; and that I must tell them!

A picket barrier with a wide counter on top was lined squarely across the log-walled office. Behind this fence stood two tables and a big walnut secretaire. There were fireplaces at both ends of the room

—wide-mouthed edifices, built of hill stone—but they yawned sooty and cobwebbed. No fires had burned therein since the fantastic unseasonable chill of Friday, June thirteenth: the coldest summer's day which most folks ever witnessed. Everything seemed topsy-turvy this year insofar as weather was concerned. Here it was, late November, and almost as warm as August! One of the missionaries' little girls had picked a nosegay of violets for Flandrau when he was at Yellow Medicine, three days before. . . .

The agent settled himself between secretaire and table in a big chair with panther-skin cushions on seat and back. He opened two ledgers and drew an inkwell close; he thought it best that he should be discovered while performing impressive mysteries with his pen. On the opposite side of the table Stuart Garvie sat in a smaller chair. He turned partially away from his host, and slid a hand within loose skirts of his greasy jacket. With no enthusiasm did he contemplate the advent of Inkpaduta and others of that scrofulous gang—not when soldiers were absent. Charley Flandrau seemed dismayingly casual about this intrusion; there wasn't a rifle in sight; who knew what knives or tomahawks the Indians might tote beneath their blankets, whether they'd put by their guns or not? Garvie's hairy hand found the small round butt of his Allen and Thurber pepperbox (it had a double-action mechanism).

I'll call them in—and Charley lifted a battered bronze bell and rang it vigorously. Faintly from the yard outside the open door sounded an immediate answering jingle. The Dakota were coming.

Inkpaduta blocked the doorway first, followed closely by Fire-Cloud and Roaring-Cloud. They seemed a stagnant but still moving mass of faded blankets, fringes contrived as decoration or fringes gashed by wear and tear, thudding blackened moccasins, sweat, oils, stained bent feathers, twisted cords and straps from which their pouches swung . . . yes, yes, all were wearing knives!—the two younger men had clubs or hatchets lumping beneath their robes. That jingle rose from a skunk-skin bag slung over the tallest Indian's shoulder: twas made from the whole hide of the animal, legs and head and dried paws and all . . . the white stripe was marred with old blood, old ash. Attached to feet and nose and tail of the dried critter were six tiny sleigh bells, and these gave forth a mild disarming melody with each movement of the man who wore them. Inkpaduta had his revolver holster belted on, but as he halted before the counter he lifted the wide curling flap to show that the holster was empty.

Flandrau stood up, conscious of his own bright trappings, feeling that he was in masquerade. (He could not accustom himself to the wearing of that jacket, much as he vindicated the act; he had a lurking notion that a sergeant and a file of soldiers should arrest him for getting himself up falsely in such rig.) Garvie remained seated, he clutched the concealed revolver more tightly. The Christian boy, Simeon, paused immediately inside the doorway. His eyes snapped from Flandrau to the big dangerous figures in front, and back again.

Good day, said Charles Flandrau. Why–come–you?

The ugly mouth of the pocked-faced Wahpekute worked and twisted but no sound came forth. He lifted his right hand and brought it well out in front of his body, neck-high. His fingers pointed upward. He drew in the huge scarred hand toward himself, at the same time lowering it slightly. The gaze of the scornful rheumy eyes was held steadily on the agent's face; in manner Inkpaduta was oblivious to the existence of the two men who accompanied him.

Again and again he repeated the gesture.

Give–me, Flandrau said in a low voice. That's the sign. Give–me.

Garvie whispered, Should you no send for yon missionary, to interpret for you?

I think we'll make out, twixt the three of us. But do you rise, Garvie, and stand near me. Simeon, please to come closer. . . Flandrau was returning Inkpaduta's steady stare as he spoke. He indicated the two younger Indians, and made a quick question sign, holding his right hand forth, palm outward, fingers separated, moving the hand back and forth slightly as he twisted his wrist. What–men? he demanded in English. Who? Who–men?

Simeon He-Gets-Up-And-Stands felt that since signs were being employed he too would use them. Giving the Wahpekute a wide berth, he came up to the slatted gate; thus the agent might see his signs, some of which would have been hidden by the counter. Simeon put the palmar surface of his left hand in front of his abdomen, with index and second fingers extended, separated, and other fingers and thumb closed. With his right hand he described parturition, flapping the back of the hand away from his body, down past his crotch. Flandrau was confused, he knew a few signs, he knew not many.

Oh, said Garvie, behind him. Twins! I ken that one.

Hokshichekpapi! Simeon cried. Two, two, son two! Inkpaduta son two, Major. Two son of he. Tall one name Cloud-Fire, Fire-Cloud. Blanket Blue man name Cloud-Roar, Mahpiyahoton, Roar-Cloud.

No heavenly twins, not by a damned sight! But we're making little progress this way. Stay where you be, Sim. And, Garvie, will you move over alongside of me. We'll employ English, Dakota, signs, whatever we can: beat the thing to pieces, hang it up to dry! I've a lead pencil here, and shall keep a complete record of the exchange, for practicality's sake. I don't wish to have this big thief hanging about the premises, here *or* at Yellow Medicine. My manifold record book?– Here. We'll start from scratch.

Flandrau squared his shoulders, and held the notebook ready with pencil poised. Pray proceed, Garvie, Simeon. You've both more signs and more Dakota than I. Sim's English is rudimentary but he can pronounce *l* and *g*—

He fixed his vivid gaze upon the face of Inkpaduta. O Inkpaduta, he asked clearly. Why come?

As each question was received, as each reply was made understandable, Flandrau wrote it down. (He studied the pages that night by candlelight before he slept, he thought about this meeting from time to time during the winter, would think of it even more poignantly in later months.)

. . . Why do you come?

. . . Get annuity. To collect money and goods.

. . . But you have no annuity due you! You and your people have none. You did not sign the treaty when other Wahpekute sign treaty.

. . . I was not there.

. . . You go many places.

. . . I go many places.

. . . Do you remember me?

. . . One time here is Man-With-White-Whiskers.

. . . Do you remember me, on the prairie?

No answer.

. . . And this man with hair red. Do you remember?

No answer.

. . . One time, in winter, you steal our blankets. One time you steal our deermeat. One time you burn our camp. Do you remember?

. . . *Ho.* You, man, shoot pistol! You shoot *wakan* thing.

(Simeon had some difficulty with this, and for the moment Garvie and Flandrau were amused. Inkpaduta did remember the playing card. There sounded a grunt from Fire-Cloud and he fumbled deep in his skunk-skin pouch while all watched curiously. He slid out a miniature parfleche, slid it back; he produced two membrane-wrapped pouches, put them back. Finally he drew forth a crumpled mildewed wad, and held it up to exhibit to all. It was the playing card which Flandrau had drilled, or at least the remains of it. Quite evidently the outcast Wahpekute had awarded an opinion of significance to the thing; at least it had been kept. . Fire-Cloud put the scrap back into the bag, then folded his arms and stood impassive. This was the only evidence of interest displayed by either twin throughout the interview.)

. . . You ask for annuity. There is none for you. These words have been spoken before.

. . . Aye. These words spoken before.

. . . Two seasons ago, you came, asking for annuity. The other agent, the man-with-the-white-whiskers, tells me this.

. . . Aye. Man-With-White-Whiskers. I come. Two winters since. You receive no annuity.

. . . That is true. Man-With-White-Whiskers does not give. My people starve.

. . . Other Wahpekute do not starve.

. . . That is true. Other Wahpekute do not starve.

. . . Many months ago, you kill He-Resembles-His-Father.

No answer.

. . . Is this not true?

No answer.

. . . Do you not talk, we cannot talk.

No answer.

. . . You kill He-Resembles-His-Father! All people know of this. You kill him because he does not give to you part of his annuity. You fight with He-Resembles-His-Father. And it is his annuity which you ask for, it is not yours, you have no annuity. This man you kill.

. . . My people give to his people ten ponies. Now his people cannot kill me.

. . . Your people steal many ponies from the white settlers, to give to the family of He-Resembles-His-Father and to the good Wahpekute.

No answer.

. . . You are bad Wahpekute, because you steal and kill.

(Sim translated this last into Dakota very fearfully indeed. Inkpaduta gave him a ferocious look, and cried an insult; he said that Simeon was a woman. Garvie heard this, he understood it. Garvie cuddled his concealed revolver, and was cheered at the thought of the loaded capped barrels and the double-action mechanism.)

. . . I come for annuity. Give me!

. . . You did not sign a treaty. Your father did not sign a treaty. Some Wahpekute signed treaty. But they say you have been cast away from your people, many winters since. I have no goods, no money for you. The Government has no blankets, no food, no powder, no calico for you, no money for you.

. . . Next year?

. . . Not next year, no year, never!

. . . My people starve.

. . . You must hunt. Why do you not hunt?

No answer.

. . . In this world are many Indians who do not receive annuities. They fish, they grow corn, they hunt, they eat, they do not starve. These things you too must do.

. . . Give to me my annuity.

. . . Go away!

. . . Then I will steal.

. . . Go!

. . . I will kill again.

. . . Then you shall be punished. Go away!

Flandrau and Garvie stood inside the wide doorway of the office and watched Inkpaduta and his sons crossing the open ground, watched children fleeing in all directions in front of them, saw women catching up their children and scuttling to shelter. Dakota men withdrew, they looked the other way. Perhaps a third of the local Dakota (mixed bands, drifters, some would-be agriculturalists—all were Isantie, and a handful were of Wahpekute stock) professed to be Christians. But the rest, whether or not they deplored the introduction of white men's attire and white men's hymns and prayers, maintained at least a surface cordiality with agent and nearby traders. They had no desire to consort with these notorious visitors; they feared even to be seen looking at them.

Inkpaduta and the twins retrieved their weapons from under the shed roof, and went tramping into the south without once looking back. Thick brush grew along a trail which curved up the rising ground. Soon the outlaws were beyond view, hidden by hazel bushes and a stockade of trees; they came into sight once more in an open area—three distinct figures at first, then a crawling disordered blot of dull color softened by haze, softened eventually into vanishment.

Sim?—called Flandrau sharply, seeing him nowhere about.

Aye, Major. Simeon had withdrawn into the farthest corner of office space outside the little fence, and was kneeling in front of a bench. Flandrau realized that he had interrupted a session of prayer.

I'm sorry, Sim—

Finish pray now, Major. God bless—you!

Very well, God bless you as well. Simeon, that last sign Inkpaduta made, when he turned before going out through this door— Did you see it?

Aye. See.

He held his hands—like this—index fingers pointing up? Then he made a fast twisting of his wrists—like this. Right finger pointing at left finger, left finger pointing at right finger, back and forth—fast—like this. What means it?

I've ne'er witnessed it before, said Garvie.

Mean bad, Major. Bad talk, bad thing. Mean *quarrel!*

Ah. Very well, Sim. You were of excellent assistance at the translating. We should have been whipped without you.

The puzzled boy asked, Whip?

Never mind. I have a gift for you. A present.

Good!

Here tis—a half dollar—

Thank, Major, thank! I give to Lord?

I shouldn't if I were you. Just a fair tithe—ten per cent. Possibly that's all the Lord's entitled to, in this instance. You give Lord five cents on Sunday, spend forty-five cents in trade store.

Lo, heart! mumbled Simeon, still considering the Prodigal Son. We-good and we-rejoice. Fare-well.

Farewell, Simeon.

With the departure of the young Dakota, Flandrau ripped at fastenings of the ornate tunic and went to toss the garment upon his bed. He reappeared, pulling on the stitched hide shirt which was more to his taste.

Were you to give me the lend of a rod, said Garvie, I'd seek to tempt a pickerel.

Rods up under the eaves yonder; and I've hooks and lines in plenty. Do you wish to try a spear, as our brown friends do?

Muckle fortune have I with a spear! I'll take the rod. Will you accompany me, Charley?

You tempt me. But I've all my ledger work. Neglected to take my master ledger along to the Upper Agency, drat it; and all transactions must be entered from my notes.

He dropped into the chair beside the table, and thumbed at pages for a moment. But not for long: he twisted impatiently, slammed the covers of the book together. He sat frowning, biting on the tip of his black wooden penholder, wiggling the pen point up and down by pressure of his strong even teeth.

He removed the penholder from his mouth. They should fish. Or hunt. But they'll never do it.

Who?

Inkpaduta and his sons and all the rest of their miserable herd.

Indians are a lazy lot.

Flandrau cried as if suffering personal affront: No they're *not!* Hunting is hard work, as you know full well—why, you're a hunter by trade!—and tis but one of their difficult chores. In order to exist, you see. Ah, I'm not speaking now of Inkpaduta and his kind. They *are* worthless; but their own tribes deemed them as worthless ere the whites did. No, sir, I refer to the bulk of the Dakota. Sometimes I venture to believe that a better race of aboriginal men never inhabited the earth!

These remarks were typical of Charles Flandrau's passion and enthusiasm. Stuart Garvie nodded in tolerance. He could imagine that he had known the impetuous boy long before he skipped away from school at Georgetown and went to sea. He imagined his rebelling once more at being forced back to his studies, pictured his attempt at mahogany-cutting, saw him recoiling from an artisan's life, and quickly embracing the legal profession with fanatic zeal; and wearying once more of the hidebound, the absolute; and plunging restlessly off to the frontier.

Garvie inquired: But are yon Indians no deceitful?

By gum, sir, they're human! Like all savages, they'll deceive *when they expect to be deceived.* In their relationships with the whites, they expect to be overreached.

Flandrau added wryly, And generally they're not disappointed.

His friend felt uncomfortable at the implied accusation against the white race. Oh, Charley, Charley— If you're to be Indian agent, your duty must lie in representing the Government, not the Indian!

By gum, I don't see why I can't represent them both!

I'm glad I'm no an agent. I couldna thole it.

The Indian *had* to sell his land, sir! He knew as well as anyone that he had to retire before the advance of a superior force. Twasn't a case of inducement, twas compulsion. All the Indian could hope for was to make the best bargain he could!

If the Indian didna wish to sign a treaty, he should no hae signed it.

Aw, damn it, Garvie!

By this time Flandrau had come through the gate and was planted before the open door, knotting the hands clasped behind his back. He stood for long impolite moments, presenting his back to his friend —stood with strong legs set firmly apart, as if glaring after the vanished Inkpaduta and sending a message which might reach the monster and draw him back . . . a message which might be in effect an apology—not to the stubborn grasping murderous Wahpekute, but to those people who had given him birth, and had offered a decency and discipline which he had not the grace to accept.

Charley Flandrau turned, smiled, held out his hand to the other man.

Forgive my bridling, sir.

Ah, you're an old blether, Charley. And aye a tawpy.

What's that?

It means you're— Soft-hearted, lad. An innocent.

I'm nothing of the kind! Let's return to this matter of treaties for the moment. These transactions are *called* treaties, but they are treaties in name only. The superior power demands the land and offers compensation; the inferior power knows perfectly well that, if it does not accept the terms, it will be forced out of its domains ultimately. So it accepts. This comprises the elements of all Indian treaties.

He stood in silence, reviewing the significance of his own words. Despite the gravity inherent in this summation of an offense against morals and human dignity, Flandrau was young enough to revel in the awareness of a thing well said. He felt a glow of childish self-esteem. This was correct, this was honest, he had said it, he was proud to have said it! He would say more (he wished that his audience was not limited to a lone Garvie).

He said: It is natural, under these conditions, that there should be discontented Indians. Assuredly I could not justify their rising in bloody rebellion, and would resist them if they tried. Nevertheless, were I a Dakota, I should feel very rebellious! There are some seventy-five hundred of them, by the best estimate, who come under the administration of this Agency. I doubt that one hundred of them will ever become satisfactory farmers.

Weel, lad, as you said to that wicked one, they can always take a wheen prairie hens. Or—

Ah, Garvie, for how long, how long? Tis the result of a superior race colliding with an inferior one. New settlements are being erected each month, new farms parceled. One day the deer and the turkeys and doves will be frazzled out. These lands are wanted by the whites, and *will be had.* And, in the majority of cases, you might as well attempt to put a hoe into the hands of a deposed monarch of France, as to make a husbandman of a Sioux warrior! . . .

Garvie trudged away to the river with his fishing gear (oh, go upstream, above the mouth of the Redwood if you can wade it—there's that big rock near the south bank, and a fine quiet pool just below; with any luck you'll take a splendid mess!) and one side of Charles Flandrau's brain became devoted to the mechanical task of copying the annuity entries; but the other portion went speeding off above leafless hills, and visited in scattered cabins and lodges. He'd spoken of an Indian uprising, and so that might occur. The onrush of whites was suddenly grown too speedy, too thick, there was too rapid a dislocation of tribes and bands; Indians moved to Lake Traverse and beyond, but to what length might they find refuge there? A single Messiah towering among them, when the time was right . . . Flandrau sat motionless, appalled by a vision of crackling haystacks, bellowing cattle, limp bodies dragged out; and over all he thought he heard the screaming of women. (Indian children they were, they made those screams, they were playing at war near the well-fence.) Oho—Simeon He-Gets-Up-And-Stands had prayed this afternoon, but how long would he keep praying?

Flandrau turned Page Forty-seven of his ledger.

When Stuart Garvie came back, just before sunset, he met a sticky Simeon who walked proudly with a tube of red cinnamon candy protruding from his mouth. Garvie nodded amiably, and Simeon Nazinhannazin said again, We-good and we-rejoice. There was nothing fey in Garvie's nature, he was not born with a veil across his face, had no second sight. This was just as well. Less than six years ahead waited the rudeness of his death: one made without warning, and at this same Lower Agency, by quick gunshot and slicing knife, and effected by this same Simeon, with all God Blesses and Prodal Sons thoroughly forgotten or at least put aside.

XX

William and Margaret Ann Marble had reached Spirit Lake on a bright windy forenoon in the middle of September. The first thing William did on his arrival was to go down and examine rocks along the shore. Peggy Ann would have been surprised had he not gone for such purpose.

He was a brown-red rock of a man. With her shoes on, she stood slightly taller than he.

They met in a church in Michigan, he was with his cousins as she was with hers. His thick neck seemed ready to split the blue stock tightened around it for Sunday; the Collingwood tribe sat small beside this bulk of a stranger cousin. Margaret Ann Phipps's own Cousin Lettie sensed a question from the quiet widow sitting beside her. Although Peggy Ann still wore her weeds for the deceased Phipps, she would put them off in another week or so.

Everyone was singing *That day of wrath, that dreadful day, when heav'n and earth shall pass away,* and thus Cousin Lettie was able to whisper behind her mutilated hymnbook, with pages falling out of it even as her words had fallen from the singing.

He's Dorcas Collingwood's cousin. Name of Marble.

Where from?

Don't know. He's come to visit, folks say. She added later: They say by trade he's a stonecutter.

Peggy Ann went home thinking it appropriate that there could be a stonecutter named Marble.

Lettie's spouse, Abner Dale, invited the stonecutter to take supper with them, come Saturday. Abner must have been instigated in this by Lettie herself, since Abner seldom displayed social acumen or initiative. But William Marble did come, looking more like a rock than ever, and ate largely of the salt fish and baked beans which sustained the Dales as former New Englanders each Saturday evening. When they were done with their meal, Abner said that he had to go to the shop. Lettie said that she had to put the small fry to bed, and Aunt Precious announced that she had to do up the dishes; thus they left Peggy to the task of entertaining the guest.

There was a book bound in black with a gold-stamped cover which

Cousin Lettie was talked into buying by a subscription agent, much against her husband's wishes. Now it had been delivered, and lay importantly upon the parlor table. *The Lives of the Sachems. Together with Descriptive Accounts of Their Personalities, Tribal Histories, and Manner of Waging Warfare, with Added Reminiscences by Travelers at the West.* It boasted a hand-painted frontispiece, together with several hand-painted illustrations scattered throughout the text, illustrations in which reds flowed easily into blues and greens. The young people studied this work meticulously. William Marble announced that he had long intended to go to the West and soon meant to do so. Of course the West to which the book had reference was actually and mainly Michigan, Ohio, and such local regions. Marble talked of a West which lay farther on.

Whereabouts do you intend to settle, Mr. Marble?

Thinking of the Ioway country. Tis a new State, and ought to afford a chance to one of my trade.

He seemed about to say more, but clamped his jaws shut. His jaws were beardless, wide, building into a solidly protruding chin. His nose sloped back against a low broad forehead. His eyes were hazel, small amiable eyes; they disappeared in his head on those rare occasions when he laughed.

Abner Dale, who had wrestled throughout several counties before he was married—but now was permitted by Cousin Lettie to wrestle no longer—announced later that he should hate to wrestle with William Marble.

Not much neck. Couldn't get a lock around it. And did you notice them arms? And I warrant you also them thighs.

Cousin Lettie cried, Mr. Dale! and Aunt Precious cried Ab*ner*! in a shocked chorus which sounded as one word.

Well, I warrant you, just the same, he could take a fall out of any man in this region! He's quick as a cat. I seen him yesterday in Mr. Maltby's yard next the shop, when he come to chat with the masons there. One of the prentices let go a hammer and it sailed square at Marble. He ducked, easy as could be. I swear he caught the thing in his hand! First he gives the prentice such a tongue-lashing that I thought the younger would weep. And then he was kindly—he come over and showed him how to hold the handle proper. . . .

Soon there was a berry social given by ladies of the church, and following that there were several walks home together from prayer meeting. On the fourth of these occasions, William Marble lingered with wide hands fastened around the tops of the fence pickets. He lingered until Aunt Precious, a much slower walker, had come along with neighbor friends, and had left them and gone into the house, after talking brightly about what a fine night it was, when of course the sky was soaked with clouds.

Marble bulked dark beside the Widow Phipps.

She thought that she must soon go into the house, or neighbors might be scandalized.

You going to the Sons of Temperance picnic a-Tuesday?

I hadn't thought to, Mr. Marble.

Wish to go? I'd be pleased to scort you. I calculate to set forth from here a-Thursday.

There was emptiness around them in that moment.

Mr. Marble, you intend to set forth for the West, the Ioway country?

That I do! I've stayed here long enough. . . . Then massively, stolidly, he told her more: he had saved *over nine hundred dollars.* Then he stopped talking again, and stood regarding her silently through the gloom.

Mr. Marble, she said with trembling voice, would you choose to come in and set awhile?

Without another word he opened the gate for her, and they went in where the lamp was lighted but all the people were gone to bed. He placed himself on the edge of the settee brought from Massachusetts; he was not comfortable on a chair of ordinary width, he was built so massively. In chiseled phrases and sentences he gave her the story of his life.

Poor boy, he said, born in Monroe County. Never had much schooling. Apprenticed to a stonecutter at the age of ten. Thought maybe he'd like to be a doctor some time—the cutting kind—but there was no chance for him to work for any doctor and learn the doctor business. It didn't pay to start, and he had to earn money. His folks died when The Cholery struck, and there were three younger sisters to look after. Well, they were married now—two of them well-married. He had them off his hands, and he had been working hard this past year or so. But then came a quarrel with his former employer—later his partner—in Detroit. The man was always busy with the bottle, so William Marble pulled up stakes and left. Hadn't known just where he would go, but now had settled definitely on the Ioway country.

He sat regarding Peggy Ann mutely; and finally he arose, rubbed his prematurely thinned hair, and smiled. He reached for his hat and said that he must go.

I'll be around at ten a-Tuesday, to scort you to the picnic. Hope it doesn't rain.

He went tramping out. Peggy lay long awake that night with Aunt Precious snoring beside her. She wondered whether she should regard Mr. Marble's autobiographical sketch in the manner of a pointless declaration of fact, or as a proposal. When the late Mr. Phipps proposed marriage he quoted poetry, but that was his way. Phipps was sad, confused, nervous, forever quoting poetry. Consumption carried him off. She feared at first that the consumption might be catching (people argued about that) but she had never felt in better health in her life than now. Here was a strength flowing from William Marble; but that strength moved heavily, solidly, like a quarried slab swaying in chains.

They attended the Temperance picnic. It did rain right in the middle of things, and part of the assemblage sought shelter in Mr. Windhorn's barn, and part beneath his implement and vehicle shed. Mr. Windhorn was a wagonmaker by trade and there were many vehicles to sit upon or in. Peggy Ann found herself with Mr. Marble on the high seat of a spring wagon. The wagon smelled cleanly and aromatically of fresh paint, and she hoped that the paint was not too fresh, and kept sliding her fingers beneath her skirts to see if she were sticking.

Marble said, At the West they travel in these things. Only way to go. No railroads yet in most spots.

Yes, I've heard tell.

Care to try? he asked. That was his proposal.

No wonder that the first thing he did after arriving at Spirit Lake was to go and examine rocks on the shore, to be one with boulders for a time. . . .

The Marbles' initial Iowa experience in Linn County had been the merest incident. William said that he was by no means a rolling stone, and certainly he didn't look it. When he got settled he wanted to stay settled; but this could not be in Linn County. He had made an error: the community held no need of his services; other craftsmen of his trade were already ensconced. Of these, one was elderly and also addicted to the bottle (this might have been an occupational failing among stonecutters and masons). Peggy argued mildly with her husband—hesitantly, as befitted a bride. She said that the community might soon reshape itself and offer them an opportunity not available just now.

You mean set here and wait for that man to die? Not my way! I made a mistake, and'll be the first to say so. Waited a little too long to come to this place. Got to get to a newer place. Got to start from scratch with a place growing up around us. Only way to do!

Once again Peggy Ann lay awake, but for a different reason. There was no snoring beside her in this life, William Marble did not snore like Aunt Precious (nor did he wear a lace cap!). Reflected light from the dying fire touched the boulder of his fuzzy head which would so soon grow bald. She wanted to smile and reach over and touch that fuzz, and take strength from solidity underneath, although she never felt that his brain was frozen—only his manner and his habits. He did not have a stone for a brain or a stone for a heart—he just appeared to have them. She should accept courage from his solemnity, from the quiet force of him, and never dread a move to a new location. But she shivered, thinking of bears and Indians. Still, on consideration, she felt that William Marble, chisel or mallet or hammer in hand, would be a fair match for any panther or any Indian, any live creature offering threat.

We're moving, he told her one day. Our money is going fast, I don't like to see it go. Ruther store it up. We're moving to Spirit Lake.

Where's Spirit Lake, husband?

Clear to yonder and gone, in Dickinson County. That's mainly just on paper. But I've talked twice this week with some folks who've been there—yes, actually *been* there—kind of hunting and exploring about. They say that land is being taken up in the next county; settlements are growing. Just the way it was not too long ago, right here in Linn County.

We'd have to buy a team, husband.

Oxen would do.

Yes, but—

Secondhand wagon, good and substantial! Bought it already. Fellow stops by; he's leaving for the East; got enough of this country; his folks perished in a prairie fire. He was selling off his goods. Said he didn't need the wagon no longer; planned to go East a-horseback. I'm to cut stones for his family graves, so we made a trade.

She had hoped to find a niche in some such small community as those they saw on the way: first, little towns with piles of yellow planks sawed for siding, and the musketry of hammers . . . poundings all about, the grate of saws . . . they left the sawmills behind them. They found fresher places where people were chopping at logs, and then came sod houses with flowers not yet growing on their new-cut roofs. But no (William affirmed to her time and again, not in the manner of a repeated confession, but as something understood all along) there was no one—no other family—no one at Spirit Lake, not yet. There would be.

Marble wore a belt of gold around his waist. It was heavy, but he wore the gold for safety's sake (outlaws on the frontier? They'd heard stories). At least in the wagon; he might not wear it when he set to work. Five hundred dollars in the belt; William had the rest in a pouch —what was left after their ill-fated venture in Linn County. He said that they could buy supplies enough to last until people started to move in; then folks would need him to build their chimneys, to shape the stones for their doorsteps. He regarded scornfully those log houses going up along the way. William said that stone houses would be superior, and he'd show these people a thing or two. He pointed out great glacial boulders bulging from the prairie, and he left the wagon often to examine them, to see how they would split.

William wished to hunt game for their larder. He had never hunted in his life, but now he would learn. He had bought a rifle, he practiced with it assiduously as they journeyed. Soon he became an excellent shot. A stonecutter's eyes and a stonecutter's nerveless hands turned the trick—he had thought so all along, now he proved it. At first William would shoot only at a mark until he felt that he had learned. He said that he didn't want to cripple any animal and have it creep away to die. The first creature which he killed was a prairie cock, strutting boldly and making queer sounds, thrusting out its feathers; the bird marched perhaps fifty yards away. William Marble took steady aim and shot the head off the bird. Peggy Ann saw the head fly in a bloody spray . she squealed, she shut her eyes and beat her hands together. All William said was, Got him! Want to pick him up whilst I'm busy with the team? You can pluck him when we make camp.

Spirit Lake seemed an excessively lonely region as the Marbles gazed at torn brown waters spangling before them.

West side'll be better. Cause we won't get prevailing wind cross solid ice when the lake freezes...

Coming thus to an unpopulated shore and facing winter, Peggy Ann shivered in her soul, and feared that face and body would show it. She wondered if other women at the West felt the same way.

Not more than four hours later her husband had selected the site for their dwelling, and was down by the shore eagerly appraising boulders. They lay massed where pushing ice of centuries placed them—installed at the base of a bank some twenty feet in height . . higher or lower at other places. The stones' children had been carved off, long since, from the bodies of mother boulders. Slammed or caressed by ceaseless water, they were now smooth; they lay head-sized and bean-sized along the shore, they made the shore.

Here scrambled the broad man, his scratched peeling boots busy and slipping as he sought to evaluate the treasure he would claim.

Build a house! he crowed. Woman, I could build a tabernacle out of these!

He wanted to go to no other distance; here he would stay, and take up the land in legality. A city was bound to erect itself within these precincts. One mile, two miles, five miles away? It didn't matter. He was here first.

But later, when Peggy Ann had a fire going, and the inevitable chunks of prairie hen were browning in her spider (she had learned a crude camp cookery while on the road from Linn County) William's bounding enthusiasm seemed to have drained itself into the torn waters below them. He sat morosely upon a keg.

Husband, she pleaded, what's ado? Cat got your tongue?

No, not a cat.

He said presently: But I was a-studying. Tis mighty late in the year. First off I'd have to seek out limestone and make a kiln and burn the stone, order to get sufficient lime for my mortar. So that's a mortar problem of the very first sort. And then: labor of dressing the stone, cause I shouldn't want to build unless I built right. Likely we'd be deep in snow fore we had a roof on. Much as I hate it, I can't see us in nothing but a log shack.

Peggy Ann grew to share his depression. She had entertained the vision of an ample stone house where wind and sleet screamed at the outside while a gossiping fire burned within. There were such houses in Darke County, Ohio, where she was born.

William had no training as an axeman. His first assault against the timber was an overwhelming chore. He learned soberly from experience, however, as indeed he could learn any task wherein a combination of visual and manual skills was essential. Soon the work went faster. He selected a size of log which he hoped might not be beyond his strength to manage, and stubbornly sought and felled only trees which would adhere to this pattern.

There were frantic beauty and terror at Spirit Lake, a terror dwelling also in the beauty. Most of the days were warm, but light frail frost spoke uncompromisingly of winter when it came down at night to glisten the trodden green around their wagon. The oxen licked at that same silver melting down their rumps. Peggy Ann spoke brightly of Jack Frost when they crept out from under the dirty wagon cover in each dawn; but William knit his russet brows, shook his head, made a smacking sound with his lips

It behooved them, he announced by word and example, to step lively. He must cut, rain or shine, wet or dry. He must cut when rain blew in persistence and soaked him through, and even extinguished the fire on several occasions. Sometimes the couple had to wring out their wet duds and hang them at the other end of the wagon to avoid a melancholy dripping on the comforters. They learned to build a very small cooking fire under the wagon between the wheels, with blaze at a feeble minimum; but smoke filled Peggy Ann's eyes whenever she tended the fire or dumped potatoes into the ashes. For four solid days of blowing rain, the Marbles lived upon burned potatoes and scorched raw pork; and both of them sniffled and rubbed their raw wet noses. On the fifth day their store of potatoes was finished, they ate nothing but pork. Come Sunday, the young wife had a resourceful notion. She improvised an oven with spider and skillet, and baked corncakes while the rain still blew. Come Monday, clouds lifted and scudded across the lake and carried the polluting rain with them. It had brought down many bright leaves, but autumn began to gleam again. There ensued a rewarding dryness; their clothing was no longer moist, their colds dried up.

The only direct skill which the woman might contribute to the building of the house was in peeling bark from logs to hasten their bleaching. Her husband kept well ahead of her with his chopping and toting of timber.

Peggy Ann could hit nothing with the rifle. William tried to teach her, but she insisted on squeezing her eyes shut when she pulled the trigger, purely because this gun was a rifle, and had been designed to kill Mexicans and Indians in battle, or white people in feuds. A shotgun was something else, and seemed somehow more domestic and neighborly; she had fired a shotgun at birds a few times when she was younger; one of her brothers owned such a gun. William fetched along an old shotgun from Michigan: the stock was bound with wire, split halfway up, but it still hung together. The gun was very dangerous to use, but neither of them realized this. William loaded it for Peggy Ann and she fared forth. She shot a fat squirrel, blowing it half to pieces. She made a small stew of the remains, but shot lodged in the Marbles' teeth. Peggy Ann felt that she was a lamentable failure as a huntress.

She looked at the vast spread piles of logs upended and drying—seasoning, was what William called it. He said that he shouldn't put green timber into a house; but still most of this would be partly green, he feared. Her heart sank. How would he ever roll up one log upon another, how would he be able to get them as high as the rooftree? . . . What about the roof? One man . . . and she dared not strain herself trying to help. She had had female troubles frequently ever since she was a girl; perhaps that was the reason that she conceived no children—had conceived none with Phipps, seemed unable to conceive now.

Husband, she said timidly, I wouldn't want you to get a—what they call it? A—a ruction—

He was embarrassed and laughed shortly. A rupture? Don't you wherrit yourself. I won't get none.

She imagined William straining with tautness, pushing the log high, higher . . . he held it balanced in a crotch-pole, muscles stood out on his neck and shoulders, he gasped . . . the log slipped and came down and smote him on the head, and oh, dear good Lord, where was he now, where was she? . . .

You was a-grunting, he said kindly in the night, shaking her.

Guess I just had a bad dream. . . . She turned over and put her face against his smelly shirt, put her nose there, smelled the smell of him, found relief and reassurance. Please, no more such dreams. . . .

Around them beauty flared though rains had brought part of it down and painted the earth. These linden leaves were coined by God, yellow as golden money. Wild ivy turned blazing scarlet or blushed with lavender in deeper woods. Red oak leaves mixed their crimson and green in eccentric patterns determined by shape and by veins in the leaves. A blue haze dwelt in that encircling endless grove across the lake—a grove which lay otherwise untenanted. It was so close that, with a spyglass, if you had one, you could have seen people walking there, were there people to walk.

When first William said Spirit Lake, his wife considered the new location in terms of Lake Huron; once she had lived a while near that shore. Lake Huron was apt to become a turbulent ocean where ships careened in distress and men were drowned, where waves tore harshly down from Mackinac in certain weathers and made the tossing horizon as keen and sharp as if it had been drawn with a steel pen. Without conscious thought on the subject Peggy Ann had supposed that perhaps Spirit Lake would be like that, and so a place to be dreaded.

She considered it now as cozy—almost cozy—and it would bear the serene innocence of babyhood if you lived here a while and understood more about it. Oh, yes—perhaps people had been drowned (perhaps Indians had, perhaps lonely scouting white men wandering out in canoes). Where were the spirits in the lake, and who were they the spirits of? These yearning worries and wonders remained with the young woman only briefly, for there was too much else demanding her attention: the treading to and fro, and bending, and gathering of firewood, and walking in weeds. Her skirts grew ragged as an old hen's feathers. Her shoes, uncobbled for such work, burst at the seams. She toiled long by the fire trying to sew them up, while William was dozing even before he climbed into the wagon.

Several times during those brief weeks of wagon-dwelling existence they heard guns being fired; once a shot sounded quite close at hand. William Marble was concerned about the possible approach of hostile Indians. He carried his rifle with him when he went out to chop, because now he had to go a considerable distance away from the shore in order to find young trees of proper dimension. He bade Peggy Ann keep the old shotgun loaded and capped, but uncocked, leaning against a stump while she worked at her bark-stripping. She carried the shotgun with her whenever she went down for water, an awkward thing to do. She wondered whether she might be able to shoot an Indian if required. At least she had shot a squirrel!

Three times during the last days before they reached Spirit Lake they'd encountered groups of Indians. Peggy could not have found it in her heart to shoot any one of these: they were such pitiful offscourings. Their moccasins were worn to shreds, sometimes they had their feet tied up in rags, but many were barefoot. They trod like wilderness tramps in faded stained remnants of blue goods called trade calico which was kept by storekeepers especially for sale to Indians. Some had scraps of blanket around their shoulders. Beneath the crusted dirt their faces were graven by poverty, illness, every discouragement, every privation, every disappointment and bereavement. Never again would they find a joy; their eyes told the story. Children were shockheaded and sickly; Peggy Ann beheld babies who whined consistently and gave out their own pitiful cough. Indian men remained at a distance, holding guns (but not in manner of threat), keeping their skeletal-ribbed dogs close. They were staring not at, but past, the movers; they let the women do the begging. Peggy Ann pressed a handful of sugar into one filthy palm after another. But the palms kept flapping back at her, more and more, the children were reaching too. At last William said, Enough of this, and touched the lead ox with his goad; off the Marbles went. Indian women moved after them, still begging, and of course the children came along.

They all keep saying the same thing, husband! Whisk, whisk, whisk —what do they mean?

Whiskey, that's what they want. We've none to give them, and never will have! Have you forgot? He smiled back across the flank of a nigh ox, in one of his rare humors. I'm a Temperance man. Have you forgot the Temperance picnic?

She wondered what manner of Indians these might be. As a girl she had read tales of Pontiac's War . . . of Catherine, the beautiful Ojibway girl, who warned the handsome English commander . . . of how warriors sawed off their rifles and hid them beneath blankets. She felt that such Indians must have been made of sterner cleaner stuff than these. Probably they took good care of their feathers, washed them when necessary, kept their knives properly sharpened; probably they smelled no worse than honest cattle; perhaps they even bathed a-Saturday night. She wondered what sort of tubs they might have in their wigwams, and how ever did they heat the water? But a stench of these tousled scabrous modern paupers came up across the tailboard of the wagon, and smote her nostrils, and fairly made her sick while they trotted there.

She kept calling back severely: No, no more! No, go away! Finally the women stopped, stood irresolute, turned back. Children scampered for a time, trailing still; then they too halted and made derisive gestures. Some were thumbing their noses. It was the rankest ingratitude.

Husband, what are they? (She had heard of Sioux Indians, and knew that there were some in the Iowa country, and she believed that Sioux was a name to fear). Are these Sioux?

Don't know what they might be. Maybe Mesquakies. Member tother night when we stopped near that inn after we forded the river, and the lady sold you some bacon? Well, I was talking with a feller inside, and he spoke of Mesquakies. Said that was the name for a certain tribe of them hereabouts somewhere, who wouldn't join the other Indians in a war. So they called them that, and it means deserters. Don't know what these are. They stink bad enough to be anything bad!

On the Marbles went, swaying, grinding through interlacing wet ruts where other people had gone. Peggy craned her neck and looked back: the little cluster of beggars was vanished. There existed nothing but grass, pale sky above, loose wild clouds.

Now, at Spirit Lake, Indians were not her principal worry. She grew to hold increasing concern with the problem of William and his log-pile: how would the logs be put up? How ever might the cabin be raised, especially in its uppermost portions? Again, though not in midnight delusion, but in actual consideration during the daytime, she shuddered at her notion of the forked stick slipping (no matter how William's struggling muscles sought to hold it aloft) and the log pounding down.

In torment she asked him again and again, until he grew annoyed with repeated questions, and cried: Well, I'll manage!—I tolt you so afore, didn't I?

She dared not ask again.

It was on the forty-seventh day of their static residence in the wagon at their new homesite (according to the stubby-penciled check marks in William Marble's almanac) that they heard an outcry rising through woods behind them in the evening. It seemed to be a human voice—high, nasal, not unpleasant—calling: *Oh . . . arr . . . oh . . . ar . . . oh.* Soon the voice grew more distinct A man was calling, Hello the fire! Hello! William had grasped his rifle. Peggy could not have reached the shotgun or any other weapon—she was so mystified and yet delighted at hearing the voice of one who was undeniably a white man.

She gasped, Hain't no Indian, husband!

They say there's gangs of robbers out here!

He kept gripping his gun, and looking toward woods away from the lake; firelight prevented his seeing anything beyond. Belatedly he whirled and whispered, Best get away from the fire! They both crept from the blaze and stood in half-light amid the underbrush, straining their ears and eyes.

Presently there came the thrust of feet moving through drifted dryness. And in that sound of approach rose all the recollection of other autumns and other feet walking in Michigan leaves, or in fallen pungent scraps from Ohio oaks and elms. The odor of a childhood unformed but quite unvexed came smoking into Peggy's mind as if drawn through her nostrils with the powder of crushed leaves, and an image of little folks building bonfires.

Firelight shone intently, they saw a face and eyes, here was a man ducking toward them. He carried a gun, he appeared to have a dead animal hanging over his shoulder, maybe two.

Hello to you, newcomers, sounded that same easy vibrant voice.

My name's Morris Markham. Set down your gun, Mr. I ain't a-going to shoot.

Slowly William obeyed.

What's the name, stranger?

Marble. William Marble.

Been here long? The man smiled; he was young, his eyes glittered like eyes of a snake or a bird. He was an uncaught thing before them, elusive yet somehow friendly.

Peggy Ann thought: What was that critter Aunt Precious had in a picture? She said twas a heathen god, not to be admired. A faun!

He threw down two chunks of raw meat with hide and hair still on them. There existed a tan smell about this man which spoke of kinship profound but exasperating: the relationship to horns and tails and hoofs, not belonging to any variety of devils, but particular to a woolly four-footed population. Peggy Ann thought of untamed sheep and goats she had heard mentioned; they did not dwell, she believed, in Iowa, but farther west somewhere. Yet here the man Markham stood goatlike.

(Also he seemed to have the twist of a mink's body within his own.)

His scanty beard bore a dust of leaves gleaned from some thicket where he had pushed his way through, watching. His hair was stiffened down with grease like an Indian's, and his eyes, as later he sat by the Marbles' sober domestic blaze, seemed to say in their glitter: Ah-ha, I might arise stealthily and run away amid the oaks, and you should try to catch me . . . try oh try, but you can't! No one can ever catch me or shoot a hole in my hide. . . .

There was comfort in having him come to them—a fellow white, but one patently invulnerable to arrows of the wild.

Peggy offered shyly a crumbling wedge of journeycake. She put the warm skillet back upon the coals and fried a little more pork—all the newcomer wanted—he sopped his chunks of cornbread in the grease.

He said, appreciatively yet lightly— He said that he had eaten a bird at noon.

He talked in brief phrases as William Marble talked, but there was a difference. Whereas Marble's truncated statements seemed to have been lopped and sawed off, this man Markham went like an insect from topic to topic, poised lightly.

Lean-to, he said. That was where he dwelt when he was to home. Lean-to smack up against the new cabin of his friends Noble and Thatcher. All from Howard County, Indiana.

He thought he had smelled smoke two-three times when he passed near the western shore of Spirit Lake, but he hadn't seen no smoke. Reckoned twas only Indians cooking fish; sometimes they did cook fish. So he hadn't troubled to come nigh before. Oh, yes, lots of folks there—not on their lake, no other settler that he knew of—but on the two lakes below. . . . He called himself a hunter and trapper by trade. Course he couldn't do no real trapping till snow flew. Pelts would spoil.

Nobles, Thatchers . . . yep, each couple had a little tyke. Then there was the Howes, not much more than a mile distant. Whole raft of youngers they had. . . . Over yonder, near the straits, betwixt East and West Okoboji, there was the Mattocks; they had a raft of youngers as well. Then four men from Red Wing, Minnesota (the Red Wing Company, neighbors called them). And the Gardners and Luces. Oh, twas quite a settlement. Though kind of thun out.

I shoot for the pot, he said. Strictly kill to eat. Then trapping later on—that'll be my business. Lining up trap lines now. Seeking good sites, looking for beaver sign. First real snowfall, out go the traps!

How could he determine what was a real snowfall?

Oh, he said. My uncle in Ohio and Indiana: he come from the hills in Vermont long ago, where there was more snow. He said the first snow was a snow you could track a cat through. . . . But here (his eyes grew brighter with a fancied deviltry)—we've got no cats. So a bobcat will have to do. First snow I can track a bobcat through, out go the traps!

His shrewd gaze had made out the shape of a neatly finished stone chimney built up with loving labor by William . . . peeled logs roosting in their thick V's alongside, unpeeled logs beyond.

How do you calculate to raise your house single-handed? He glanced briefly at Peggy Ann, saw that she was neither horse nor peasant. He repeated firmly: Single-handed?

Well, said William, slightly nettled. Figured I could do it if I so elected.

Many hands make a milder task. I'll fetch some folks.

William rattled fingers against his tired knee in what was, for him, excessive nervousness. Can't pay much.

Markham regarded him with surprise. Nobody pays in these parts! We just help out. Like I hunt for the pot; then maybe some of the womenfolk can stitch me a new jacket, when I need one and have got the hides.

He wore jeans and buckskin, he wore moccasins of an Indian. He went to sleep by their fire with the ease of a limber-legged puppy, even before they had climbed into the wagon.

When they looked out in the first grayness of morning, he was gone.

He had left them a gift: a quarter of venison, one of the two small quarters he was carrying tied with rawhide strings when he came, and which had looked like two separate animals. All raw and bloody-looking as they were, Peggy Ann appreciated the fact that the stranger hung the chunks of meat over the lowest limb of a small bur oak before he came to the fireside. Beefsteak was weeks and weeks behind them . . . in quiet glee the Marbles stood regarding the slowly swaying gift, with a few ants crawling on it . . . later there would come flies, even in this chilly weather there would be a few flies: great polished greenish-goldish things, to dart and buzz like bees in any warming of the day.

Morris Markham returned the next week to warn them in advance of neighborly invasion. Hard-working men would need to eat a lot; Markham knew a pair of greenhorns when he saw them. Calmly he spoke those very words to Peggy Ann, winking one eye and raising his eyebrow lightly as he laughed. The Marbles had only a keg and a half of pork left, and there was the winter coming on.

Markham motioned with his thumb. You got a pretty good larder. Spirit Lake. Show you.

He ran down the steep bank along a path worn visibly by Peggy Ann's feet. In a few moments he had taken line and hook from his pouch, and had cut a young poplar for a pole. He removed his moccasins, rolled up his breeches, waded out into the jouncing water. Markham snapped up some minnows with his hat (or were they minnows?—small fish of some sort, driven into shallows by enemies, where waves were torn beyond the weeds). Markham split a shot with his knife, bit it tight upon the line, and tossed the hook far out. When it was struck and when the bait was gorged down, he battled a large pike, by use of pole in his left hand, and right hand clutching the line. He lost the first fish, it ran like a thin wolf in the water and tore loose against a tangle of weed. But the man merely shrugged, bent the hook again between his fingers, looked at it critically, whetted it with a pebble and spittle; then on went another minnow, out went the bait again. This time he worked the fish home. Twas a walleye, he said.

Notice how those eyes bug out?

He caught a second, smaller, and then a third fish, an enormous creature. It champed wide tooth-laden jaws, and flopped and twisted after Markham had swung it in past the boulders. Oh, that must go nine or ten! Reckon we've got enough fish.

Peggy Ann was wondering how she'd ever clean them; she had cleaned only small trout, in all her life before.

Same way, said Morris Markham. They're easier, if anything, big like this. Club them on the head. Scale them fore they're gutted. Easier to hold; then just slit the meat off outside the ribs.

He put away his hook and line, and again laughed at the lake and said it was a larder which never would fail (except when the cross-grained fish grew ornery and wouldn't bite at all). Kindly he scaled one fish and left Peggy Ann to do the others. Perspiring and trembling happily at the serious task, she sought to follow instructions.

William Marble called down a Thank-You from his scaffold of saplings built against the chimney top. He said that he would have gone out to hunt—yes, he could shoot, a little—but he thought it wiser to dress off the chimney first.

Said Markham, We'll just see what's skittering around.

He shook his head at the old shotgun which was offered, and patted his own rifle. He faded deftly away through the brush, making much less noise now than he had made when he walked toward their fire the first time. Twice they heard the sound of his rifle, then he was back. He had two turkeys, both with the heads shot off cleanly.

They just set up and begged!

Encouraged by Peggy Ann's praise and by Marble's terse appreciation, Morris Markham now reckoned that he would kill a deer. He went to the woods again and prowled until dusk, but was forced to return empty-handed. He said he reckoned the two shots of his rifle, which disposed of the turkeys, had frightened any deer away from the vicinity.

Again he slept by the Marble fire, and what a reassurance it was to have him there. And what a reassurance it must be to the Nobles and Thatchers, to be aware of him in his lean-to built against their cabin wall—whatever sort of people they were, whatever fears they might have entertained if Markham had not been there.

It turned cooler in the middle of the night, it drizzled for hours, the fire almost went out. Markham awakened, brought to his feet by drifting wetness. He found nearby a great claw-bottom stump which Marble had shunned for fuel because it was half rotten, and also infested with ants. The ants did not seem to bite Markham as he carried the thing . . . he knew how fire would eat into the punk inside the stump's shell and hold and glow in the face of almost any downpour. He staggered up with the weight of the thing clamped against his chest by the grip of bent steely arms, and, keeping his moccasined feet close together, lowered the stump fairly atop the fire. Flames were smothered for a time, and smoke poured out all around; but soon there was a sly jet of color from one internal hollow, then from another; so the fire caught and held, the fire was saved, rain still fell and hissed.

All this Peggy Ann witnessed because she had Gone Out; she had to Go Out; she could not use the vessel in the wagon for fear the stranger lying so close would hear the gush. So, with great effort to proceed in silence, she made her way past her husband's feet and under lines of hanging clothes, to the front of the wagon; she slipped out over the wheel, stepped down to the hub, withdrew into bushes. Then she returned, saw the hunter rising, and she watched, wound in her shawl, while he worked at keeping a comfort for them. . . . Oh, mercy! —now, stained blanket and all, he was going to bed right under their wagon, fairly in the scatter of embers where the storm-time cooking fire had burned! Of course there were nothing but scattered bits of charcoal left; they had not had a fire there for some time; but Peggy quailed to think of any individual bedding himself with such aplomb amid ashes and charcoal. At last, shivering in petticoat and shawl, she had to return to the wagon willy-nilly. She prayed that Markham would not stir, and that, if not asleep, he would pretend to be asleep. He did not move, his bundle did not twitch. The young woman soared up over the wheel like a flicker going to her home in a stub, and quickly was safe beside William. . . . She did not know it, but under the wagon Morris Markham smiled compassionately before he returned to sleep.

Next forenoon the sound of a wagon came banging. Markham heard it first and went to guide the neighbors. It was thought that perhaps five neighbors would come, and now appeared only two, accompanied however by another man named Emory Skelton who with his wife had camped near the Noble-Thatcher house to rest his teams for a few days. Skelton was bound from Minnesota to the Woodbury County country where friends of his were planning to take up land. He claimed to be a joiner by trade, and was not averse to lending his services for a day or so (this he kept saying in firm tones, as if calling attention to his own generosity). Joseph Thatcher could not come. His wife was lying sick again—it seemed that she was often ill since the birth of her child; nor could Doctor Harriott come, he was attending her. But here was Alvin Noble (and, as a youth in Indiana years before had held the same opinion, Peggy Ann thought that Noble was appropriately named). Bertell Snyder and the Grangers were far behind in the accumulation of a winter's wood supply, so they did not appear; and Bill Granger must return to Red Wing soon. Harvey Luce came . . . he had been designated by Markham as the God-fearing son-in-law of Mr. Rowland Gardner. (Well, Markham amended cautiously, I guess instead it's God-*dreading*.)

The narrow wagon was piled with tools which the helpers thought they might need. Peggy Ann Marble observed that these people had neglected to fetch any blankets. . . . And that dreadful Skelton man . . . she was glad to learn that he was not a neighbor, would not be settled nearby. He reminded her of a blacksmith she had known back in Michigan. (The smith was a garrulous monster possessed of many misinformations concerning judges, Members of Congress, the President himself. He always Had It On Good Authority, or, Somebody Told Him But He wasn't At Liberty To Give The Name.) Emory Skelton displayed the same loose smile, the same pendulous lower lip turning out to reveal large yellow teeth. Young Mrs. Marble suspected that he might be filled with gossip and opinions no more substantial than those of Blacksmith Rath. He kept telling William Marble, for instance, that Marble had the posts for his house laid out mistakenly: the house should face the south, not the east.

. . . . Mr. Harvey Luce grew silent and appeared to show a hurt whenever one of the others chanted any fragment of a secular song while working that day. Mr. Luce sang, but his songs were all Hymns of Praise. Instead of cursing, as any ordinary human would have done when his finger was pinched between two logs, Harvey only shook the wounded member, blinked with humility, let his hymn arise again. It was apparent that he enjoyed being a beast of burden, enjoyed being put upon by others, if they would only be willing to take advantage of him. He accepted severe bumps and squeezes (he suffered three that first day) as a Saint might have welcomed stigmata.

. . . Twas confusing to have so many people about, and all at once and all together. They seemed like a herd. Twas odd, and a little aggravating, and a little frightening as well. Peggy Ann wished that the distance from their homes was not so great: then some of the womenfolks might have come. But even three women would have seemed like a throng, and now five men stood here together, and four of them were strangers—that is, Morris Markham was still a stranger, although not a complete one. The settlers were all big—two tall, and two thick—and all were hairy, or at least stubbly. They sounded like men, they ate like men, they talked like men, they smelled like men. Oh, dear! . . . They had been polite enough on arrival. They said, Howdy Ma'am, Howdy Mrs., Good day to you, or at least mumbled something. But soon they paid not as much attention to her as they might have paid to a squaw, and Mrs. Marble was indignant proportionately.

She had first risen that morning when the sky above the eastern shore of Spirit Lake was a fading hollow strip of cherry and purple. But there was not enough light; she went back under the covers again; her husband only grunted and turned, because he knew that it was too dark for him to see his work. Then she was up again when the cherry had paled to color of the mild cosmos in a garden, when the purple had paled to warmhearted blue. Then she could see. She had been busy with fire and turkeys and cornbread ever since. She took several small onions from their precious soggy store and sacrificed them into a queer stuffing she made of corn meal and pork fat. One of the turkeys was overcooked and almost fell apart before it was pulled apart, and some of the stuffing did land in the fire. The other bird was scorched seemingly on all sides, but actually one side was almost raw underneath the charring; and on the other side the bird had burned clear through until the bones blackened. At home, and when younger, Peggy Ann might have been in tears. But this wild lakeside, she thought, was no place for tears. She clamped her jaws together until a loose tooth throbbed at the pressure. She reset the precious brass pins which hiked up her overskirt (not too immodestly, she prayed) and went on serving food. She had no platter; both of her platters had been broken between Linn County and Spirit Lake, as had many other dishes, because of improper packing. She had not known how to pack things in a wagon for prairie travel where there were no roads. She did not realize the extent of the jolting and jouncing—enough to bump a body's teeth from her head!—and she was positive that was how she had loosened one tooth of her lower jaw—by biting down savagely, when they almost upset in that ford on the Boone River. She served out food on an oblong tin tray, and it did look too distressing; what would her cousins have thought? The tray had been advertised as a genuine japanned article, but most of the japanning was gone by now; and so of course were the figments of daisies which adorned it. The Marbles owned two three-tined forks and two two-tined forks; those were all the forks they had, except the big one Peggy used for cooking; but these men preferred to eat with their hands. They sucked loose flesh from the fowl, licked their lips, licked their fingers. . . . She strove to forget that Mr. Markham had, early that morning, inquired so innocently about her stuffing preparations for the turkeys that it seemed he was twitting her. He said that the Indians were reputed to roast birds, guts and all, whenever they had a mind to. And when Peggy Ann expressed horror, he said that the Indians actually *ate the guts*. She was almost sick on the spot—and how could she cook?—but cook she did.

And how might five men ever consume the bulk of two turkeys at a single meal? But they did. She saw them do it, she shuddered in the seeing. They stood in dirty flannels, dirty jeans, dirty coats, with dirty hats on the backs of their tousled heads (Morris Markham looked out of place among them in shine and wrinkle of grimed deerskins). It seemed that they were tainting her own William with their coarseness, making him into some kind of frontier vagabond along with themselves. They stood waving scorched drumsticks or chunks of corn pone as they talked. They talked of logs, and of a settlement which was building up near at hand. They called it Springfield. There were said to be six or seven families at Springfield already. No, Mr. Skelton insisted, there were nine families; and they had a store too. . . . It was only eighteen miles across the prairie.

The Wood brothers, said Markham. I been there afore this. There's some brothers, name of Wood, have got that store. Traded some traps off to them. Shot a young bear near at hand, backed the meat over there; we made the trade.

William Marble inquired enviously: Sell them the pelt too? (He would have liked very much to shoot a bear.)

Alvin Noble said with appreciation: No, Mr. He gave the pelt to my wife. It's real nice for our little one to lie on and sleep. . . . His sober eyes smiled across at Morris Markham. Peggy Ann sensed a sympathy and indulgence between the two men, and felt better because of it.

Still it seemed that for a good hour and a half after their arrival, the neighbors did much talking, much eating, and no building whatsoever. Then, while she was sorting the greasy remnants of turkey, and saving what she could from the wreckage, she looked up; and all in a minute they had fallen to work. They knew just how they were going to proceed, and where. William had marked the area in front of the chimney with stakes. Emory Skelton insisted volubly that a puncheon floor should be laid first, but Marble explained that he had no puncheons split for the purpose; he didn't want that sort of wood floor—to trip and fall upon, to have things go down between the cracks. He was going to build a stone floor. And next season (time allowing, he added cautiously) he'd be glad to do the same thing for his neighbors, if they had plenty of rocks to hand, the way he did.

Logs were laid out encompassing the rectangular barren patch of earth which Marble had leveled, between a large oak and a larger basswood, near the brink of the lakeside precipice. It was Mr. Noble's task to stand with sharp axe ready, notching the logs evenly and cleanly as fast as they were set down, and in between times smoothing off the ends—dovetailing, he called it—while the other men strained, lifted, carried.

Mind me tomorrow, said Noble to William. Before we start home, I'll show you how to split shakes.

With these willing people actually beginning to produce the house before her eyes, Peggy felt a lessening of annoyance with them. . . . Soon she was almost abject in a secret but emphatic shame. The neighbors were to collect no wage for this chore; Markham had been very definite about that. Here they were, chopping and pinching and grunting, and saying, Hold on a second whilst I get my end; and then, Up we go! *Ahhh . . . . uhhh!* They performed the task of slaves or of friends; but they were not actuated by dread of a penalty which shirking slaves must hold, nor spurred by love of her and her husband (for three of them had never seen the Marbles before). There was something more than that. She tried to decide what it might be, she could not decide. By this time Peggy Ann was disgusted thoroughly with her own earlier prim aversions. She must try to make it up to the men somehow. She smiled upon them shyly when she went to the lake and came from it. They were so busy that they did not even look at her.

She had a broad red burn across three fingers, and little smarting peppery burns scattered all over her nose and cheeks, and on her lips, where the grease had come spattering. She thought it a light price to pay for benefits awarded. No longer need she be plagued by the notion of William Marble in lonely struggle, smashed by a toppling log. Bone and muscle and solid wits of generous strangers had spared him such suffering, and she should be grateful forever. Peggy took a glowing sacrificial pride in her domestic ordeal. With a chip and handfuls of leaves she had scrubbed out most of the slime adhering to the inside of the pork keg, and—with top pressed down firmly, and weighted by a heavy stone—she'd used the thing for safekeeping the fish which Markham caught the day before. He had shown her how to make a little cairn of stones, and set the keg firmly in the shallows.

. . Course, some large animal might come along and steal your fish! But there's small animals could come a-thieving too, if you kept the fish on land. So take your choice.

No bear or other creature had raided during the night; naturally they expected none to come during the day. The pike were firm, cool, in fine condition.

Some day, she thought, they would have a springhouse. There bubbled two springs close at hand.

The men were of a will to work as long as daylight sustained them. Sweet colors of sunset reminded Peggy of nothing so much as petunias grown in her mother's garden, far back at the East. There was an associated comfort in recognizing that her mother had had a house; and now she too would have a house of her own—even in this lonely reckless place. In time (she looked through smoke of cooking at the wall of mortised logs, and men climbing there) she too would have petunias. Her husband could saw an old keg in half, and thus they would have a petunia bucket on each side of the front door; and the mystery of other sunsets long to come would rise from behind the cabin and find their tints reflected; dawns would discover the flowers.

She thought benignly of the growing house and all that it might hold. But at this moment it bulked harsh, a stranger thing, and was an actual encumbrance to the woodland, and did not belong.

She must cook fish as she had never cooked fish before, as no woman had ever cooked fish before. She longed to see stars of pleasure quickening in the eyes of her assorted heroes, she longed to listen to their delighted exclamations. She soaked fragments of turkey stuffing left from noon, made a paste of the mixture, got the paste too thin, poured in more meal. She had no eggs to form her batter—she longed for eggs—considered that perhaps Mr. Markham could find eggs for her somewhere amid prairie grass, or hidden in thickets—wild birds' eggs. Yet winter was not far away. Twas likely that even untamed undomesticated uneducated hens knew better than to build nests and start laying in such a season. . . . She sifted in a little more meal, prayed that the stuff would stick. . . .Vinegar, that's what Aunt Precious had used the year before. Peggy Ann remembered: a peddler came by, pushing a two-wheeled cart, crying that he had taken fish from the river, and proclaiming the cheapness of his wares; though Aunt Precious considered that the price was dear, and told the man so, as she stood counting coins out of her purse. But Aunt put the little speckled fish to bake, and now her niece recalled with joy a spicy odor—vinegar, twas—each slab of fish anointed lightly as it lay steaming. Aunt Precious sprinkled black peppercorns into the pan, added two leaves of bay . . Oh, joy!—in the little basket tied high in the wagon, the basket which held her few papers of spices, Peggy Ann had both peppercorns and bay leaves!

William stood above her as she knelt in the dusk. He asked tersely: Bout ready to feed us again, woman?

Her hot face turned with indignation; but his eyes had disappeared in their deep sockets, he was grinning under his new beard. This was a joke designed to show the other men who trooped behind him that commonly he did not address his wife as a slave or as an inferior, but only when teasing.

She lifted the skillet which lay inverted as a lid for the deep spider, and found steam and aroma, and the usual volley of grease specks trying to maim her.

First batch is done, husband. Please to fetch the tray off the wagon's tail.

He brought the tray. With care she ladled out a cargo of juicy chunks. The other men sniffed appreciatively.

There's journeycake; here tis, hot in this tin.

Alvin Noble cleared his throat politely. His mild dreamy voice asked: You're not a-going to set and eat with us, Mrs. Marble?

She laughed. This spider's only so big; got to put in a fresh batch of fish, and watch it. Twill be done in a jiffy.

The men were very tired. They had worked without ceasing since the sun was high; now the sun was gone. Last metal of its reflection sparkled amid tree trunks on the slope toward the west. The workers did not stand to eat their night meal as they had stood to eat at noon. They squatted heavily, looking with hope at the tray and a large pie tin which William placed on a log among them.

The broken whining voice of Harvey Luce spoke: If no man raises objection, might you be so good as to let me ask a Blessing on this food? We didn't ask none at noon!—he added accusingly.

Go ahead, Mr. Luce, said Markham agreeably. But don't take too long.

Luce stood with eyes squeezed shut. Already it was dark enough under the trees for firelight to wash unevenly across his broad childish face.

Dear Lord, we ask Thy indulgence upon this provender, and those of us who would eat of it. Grant that it may nourish us to do Thy will, and serve Thee eternally, and sing Thy praises—

All the men had their heads bowed, and Peggy Ann bowed also beside the fire. But she stole a glance at Morris Markham—he seemed restive, stirring on his haunches as he crouched, but twisting his head from side to side even while his face was turned down. She thought of a small boy condemned to a dreary session of church: ritual, prayers, sermons which he did not understand. She could not help smiling at the notion.

—Grant that he who is without sin among us shall cast the first stone—

(At whom, it was not clear.)

—And thus no stones shall forever be cast. Let us feed forever only in the Garden of Mercy, and only on the fruits which Thou hast put before us—

There was coughing, swaying. Reluctantly Harvey Luce clenched his fists, then opened his hands—defeated and thwarted almost as much as he longed to be. He was the sort of man, thought Peggy (and with a consciousness far removed from Holiness), for whom one felt contempt and affection in the same moment. You longed to do something to help him. If you were wise you knew that you never could.

—We ask this indulgence and we petition Thy loving-kindness in the name of Christ Jesus. Amen.

Never did hear a kettle of pike so blest, said Markham. Luce turned away from him. The others drew close to the log; then impelled by starvation, Harvey Luce swung lamely round to join them. . . . There was a gesturing, a reaching forth, a pulling back.

Go ahead, Mr.

No, after you, Brother.

Let Marble go ahead, he's boss.

No, I—

Markham cried in amusement: Tarnation!—and grabbed with both hands.

Dog-tired from bending, lifting, kneeling, stirring, trudging—feeling more witch than woman, her face and fingers smeared with goose grease against the soreness of burns—Margaret Ann Marble felt a joy as she observed the diners' voracity even in their silence. She was aware that man after man turned to look at her curiously while he ate. They lifted tiny pike bones from between their lips—they did not throw them carelessly on the ground, as some of them had tossed turkey bones. They put their bones in the corner of the japanned tray.

The new batch, husband, said Peggy with authority. Tis done now! Please to fetch the platter again!

She scraped jackstraw bones into the fire before she heaped more pike from the spider.

Man alive . . . she heard Noble saying it, heard him with glee. . . . I do wish Mrs. Noble could learn to cook fish like this!

That night there were four wrapped sausages beside the fire instead of one. In the wagon, against her inert husband, Peggy Ann slept the sleep of the weary, the burnt, the satisfied.

Steel of late autumn entered into invisible framework of night air. The more talkative wild population had gone away into the South, or had had their voices stilled by maturity. A weasel slew a careless young owl in the basswood beside the newborn cabin. An hour later that same weasel was slain by an older wiser owl of another species. A wolf, not gaunt by any means, came padding from the prairie, smelled distrustfully the smells of man and man's cookery, withdrew as daintily and hauntingly as he had come.

No, none of the neighbors had thought to fetch a blanket—except Markham, of course, who always carried his; he never knew just when he would sleep in the woods, or probably where. But Peggy had produced comforters and home-woven woolen blankets from their small supply. She quailed at the thought of her precious bedclothing being mixed with boots and embers and fresh clay upon the trodden ground, but there was no help for it. These people had given much—she must give as well, no matter how much sousing she would have to manage in the tub which had been tied on the back of their wagon all the way from Linn County.

With morning she forgot such small woes. Morris Markham came to offer a fresh string of fish before ever she had the tea a-boiling. A new kind—he called these silver bass—and said they were very good for the pan; and he went down to the shore and cleaned and scaled the whole catch himself when he saw that she had so much to do. The other men sniffed like dogs when once more the spider was hot, and they asked however did she do such things with fish, and what was the magic she worked.

Just a mite of vinegar and some peppercorns and bay leaves. I'd be glad to spare you some, she said eagerly.

We got plenty vinegar in our wagon, said Skelton. But what did you say?— Corns?

Peggy Ann felt rich and courtly, like the storied benevolent lady of a brick mansion, as she prepared tiny packets of spices for all three men—quite ignoring Morris Markham, who preferred to be ignored where the exigencies of civilized households were concerned. Noble admitted also to owning vinegar at home; but Harvey Luce only shook his head and smiled sadly when he was asked the same question. Peggy Ann insisted on escorting this persecuted saint to the wagon and getting out her brown jug. She poured vinegar into the old wooden canteen which he carried, until the canteen was quite full. It was for his wife, she kept saying—and for his mother-in-law, Mrs. Gardner.

. . . Prides himself on being a lay preacher!—Markham came to whisper to her, in late afternoon when the cabin's final rafter had been fastened in place. Reckon he'd like it, if you asked him to say a prayer on this new house ere we leave.

Course I shall; we'd be humbly grateful! Peggy Ann looked with awe at the pile of peeled ugliness which had not been there a day and a night and a day before. Houses don't just grow, she thought. Takes men to make them. She would not care how endlessly Harvey Luce prayed, nor how fulsomely.

Alvin Noble was long in teaching William Marble to split shakes. They worked at some distance in the woods where proper lumber was at hand; the others trailed to their side to listen and observe. Then the builders tramped back from the grove, and stood looking at the house, in some ways admiring their handiwork, but already critical of it, finding things which were wrong. Skelton kept insisting that Marble had planned too big—there was no need for a cabin of such size, just for the two of them. Twould be mean to heat; the chinking would take a long time; take a nine-by-twelve—that should be ample for any couple. Emory Skelton knew loads of folks in Minnesota who had no larger. Some with big families—

The woman and I, said Marble slowly. We don't want to be bumping into each other. Twelve-by-fourteen hain't none too big.

. . . Yes, he would get the roof on promptly. He was deeply appreciative of the lesson he'd had in splitting the long thin shingles. Roof first, then chinking. Chips first, driven in by a mallet, then plaster to fill and cover. Floor could wait for the last.

You got your windies to think about, cried Skelton. Now, some uses greased paper, some uses buckskin. Paper lets in more light but twon't last. I did know some folks up Mendota way who had their windies et by varmints—

Marble looked soberly at the rooftree and guessed that he would manage. Peggy Ann, listening as belatedly she scrubbed the noonday skillets, knew that already he was considering the stone floor—imagining how his chisel would feel, going into the solid rock—delighting in the clever shaping, the tessellating—

Brothers, warned Harvey Luce.

He bared his dark-quilled head to the clear windy sky and closed his eyes against distractions of this world. The men all looked at their boots or at the ground. Peggy Ann left the fireside to come and stand devoutly downcast behind them. This time no one made sounds or writhings. There was no food waiting to be eaten.

For all the plaintive slavishness with which he faced existence, Harvey Luce had an illusion . . . it was not necessarily original; probably he had borrowed it from someone else whom he admired; but the illusion prevailed, he could voice it. He spoke of Hebrew children in the wilderness, he mentioned Biblical rivers and deserts, and in effect likened them to this pretty little series of lakes beside which the settlers stood. He mixed Testaments in a manner to alarm any theologian; but sincerity was ruling. He implored that they be spared from Philistines, roaring lions, adders, the snare of the fowler. He practically demanded manna, and in that strange confusion of the zealous layman he seemed to threaten God Himself with the wrath of Christ, if no manna were forthcoming. He kept referring to the new cabin as a hearthside—which Peggy Ann thought must please her husband well enough, since William considered that the stone hearth was the most important thing about the structure.

There came a round of solemn handshaking. Peggy Ann offered her hand and her thanks to each of the men. Morris Markham gave his foxy grin, and went gliding along the lake toward Minnesota, while the other three yoked up and turned on their southward trail. Before they left, Peggy Ann Marble presented to Harvey Luce the two turkey wishbones which she had saved and cleaned. The Noble child was an infant; but Luce was said to have a boy of four or so, and a young brother-in-law but slightly older. It was to these children that Peggy Ann sent the wishbones, adorned with tufts of pink and blue yarn to make them festive, and wrapped in a scrap of an old copy of the *Burlington Hawkeye*.

Day after day tight-clinging oaken foliage shriveled and curled beneath the sun. Squirrels gargled a staccato chorus, and straying winds whirled loose leaves with a smell like cinnamon. Peggy trudged with a basket, picking up black walnuts. She mashed off their tarry hulls upon a rock which was soon painted to the same rich umber of seeming permanency as were her hands. The nuts were placed in the new loft to dry. William said that they would have decent planks up there if anyone ever started a sawmill in the vicinity; meanwhile he regretted that he could not build a loft of stone. The new house took every second of Marble's waking time. It did not take all his strength, it could not take all his strength, he had power enough and to spare. But days grew shorter—there was so much to do, so little daylight to do it in. Shakes for the roof and the anchoring thereof —the longer split pieces, not much longer or wider or thicker than shakes, for the loft floor—the ladder to be built against the wall—the one-legged bedstead in a corner (Morris Markham came by, and he called the one-legged bed a Prairie Rascal—he said that's what they were called)— Windows—

Grinning and enthused, William took down three milled window frames, each patterned to admit six separate panes of glass. He took these down from where they had been tied beneath the wagon bows. Peggy Ann had seen them all along and had not realized what they were; she thought that they were swinging racks to put things on; they had served so during the journey. But now he lifted out also a small solid box which had been at the back end of the wagon, alongside his stonecutter's tools. What was that? Oh, lead, he'd said carelessly. Lead for running bullets, woman. This was his joke and his great surprise for her; in innocence she believed him. Now he unpacked the box with a devotion like fear.

Windowpanes, two dozens of them. Eighteen for the three windows —six for spares, or perhaps for another window if William ever decided to cut one and could build the sash and frame.

Peggy Ann got down on her knees to watch.

Not one broken thus far!—he kept crying. No . . . intact! . . . no . intact!

When he lifted delighted gaze she saw sweat on his forehead. . . . Every one survived. That glazier in Linn knew how to pack!

Better'n me, said the wife sadly. With my dishes.

Well, you ain't no glazier. Ain't supposed to be.

Have we putty, too, husband?

He give me a man-sized daub of it; I can work it up with oil if it's too dried out; he tolt me how.

When one considered the perils and complications of this enterprise, the stone floor was quite the easiest part of it all, even after William had to construct a primitive furnace and burn some lime in order to make the proper mortar. He did not need much mortar, for the cracks were not wide. He had put his stones together as a jeweler might have arranged gems. But all stones were precious to this man, they were as sacred to him as they were rumored to be to some Indians.

In a November daybreak, with the lake as gray as the sky, the sky as wind-torn and threatening as the lake, William Marble climbed into the wagon and awakened his wife.

Thought I'd tell you. Want to come see? She's dry and set!

He had been up for the better part of an hour, and Peggy Ann had never heard him dress and go. She arose on one elbow, reaching the other hand to push back wisps of hair which had strayed from nightcap confinement.

William, she said. (Sometimes she addressed him thus, especially when awakened suddenly from sleep, or perhaps in passion.) What's ado? What's dry and set?

The floor. I just tried it. I couldn't rest no longer but had to get up and see. This is the day she should be set, mortar and all. And she is. I couldn't even hammer her loose with a billet.

. Weather threats were a jest—the fakery of dawn which prevailed often in this region. Clouds flew away, the pure windy sky shone clear as a knife blade.

Peggy could not understand why the first thing she wanted to do in their house was to make the bed. With some sense of shame she tried to explore this impulse and the motive prompting it. Inner delicacy, if not wisdom, prevented her from suggesting to her husband that she entertained what he would have called queer notions.

She supposed in a way that it was because all people were born in beds; and their initial remembrance, usually, was of snuggling up to a warm body. While busy through the hours, planning with conscious brain, and directing swiftly her limbs and hands throughout their homemaking activity, she grasped at the skirts of a wispy idea which she feared was born in shame and nourished on lustful juices. This was the thought that there was more to beds than the mere fact of children being born in them. The children had to be made first. Father and mother had to get together, and they did that in bed. Peggy Ann's cheeks grew hot as she considered the deviltry of such a thought; yet stubbornly she persisted in countenancing it.

Husband, you know we talked: we've got only the two feather beds, and no pad nor mattress to go underneath. I member when I was maybe ten or twelve: twas at Aunt Precious's house, when I was little. Pa lay failing at home, and I had to stay there with her, count of the sickness. Well, she kept nothing beneath her feather beds. She held that it wasn't healthy to do so. And no matter how I plumped them up when I made my bed, before morning those ropes of the bedstead would be fair sawing into my back—little as I was, light as a feather—

I planned on straw, replied William, but there ain't no straw hereabouts. I could go cut some more prairie hay. But that would leave you sole alone; and there's all the heavy lifting, and you couldn't get chests and boxes and kegs out of that wagon thout hurting yourself.

We did talk of leaves, husband. I think leaves would serve. They're just so thick under all the trees, and I could get big armloads in a jiffy. And they'd pack down solid but not too solid.

You try it. But I aim to cut some extra prairie hay later. And delay your leaf-gathering till the sun has dried the leaves sufficient. Twouldn't do to put them in the bed trough while they're damp.

All morning the two of them hauled and trotted. Peggy Ann kept looking up at the sky, numbering new-formed clouds, hoping that none would cover the sun. None did. Before noon the mat of fallen foliage throughout the grove seemed warm, springy. Then she filled the trough of the one-legged bed with a pungent harvest. She guessed that before long the leaves would crumble to dust; yet she thought their veins and stems would still provide a degree of cushioning. In nervous ritual she placed her feather beds atop the heap, plumping them repeatedly until it seemed that every goose feather must stand alive and quivering. She tucked in smoothly the yellowish linen sheets which her Cousin Lettie had stitched for her as a matrimonial gift, and which she had never used before. Then came light woolen blankets, then comforters.

Hain't dead of winter yet. Woman, we'll roast.

I just want us comfy. . . . She puffed up the pillows.

Earlier she had held hope of a mystic fire lighted by her own hands for the first time upon that hearth, but this could never be; already paler stones showed their scorching. William had lighted fire after fire while he was completing the chimney, in order to be sure of the draft. After all, she reasoned, perhaps it was better that way. What could be more sacred than fires built, actually, during the long birth of the structure?

Before nightfall they were installed. The wagon was drawn up beside a rough pole pen wherein the oxen stood chewing, and soon lay chewing. At first the Marbles had let their critters roam but they strayed far. Either William or Peggy had to waste time searching them out and driving them back. Yet the animals must be turned loose to graze, and had to wander to some distance in order to feed well. No form of tethering or hobbling was practicable because of the profusion of bushes and trees and resulting entanglements. Already the heaviest ox had been brought to his knees violently, with strain and injury resulting. . . . The Marbles had brought no bells. But with resource William sacrificed a portion of a tin spout which he kept tied under the wagon, and which had suffered various squeezings and bendings on the journey. This spout, hammered into workable condition again, was intended to conserve rain water. Rain would drain into a barrel from the eaves, as in Michigan. But of course they had not been able to fetch along a barrel big enough to do any good; there was no cooper's shop in the neighborhood as yet; and just how might anyone construct eaves spouts beneath a shake roof? Maybe William could devise a series of wooden troughs later on, if he found time. (He had dreams of a stone cistern to receive water.) At Spirit Lake he held little compunction about cutting off the end of the tin spout and hammering out four crude bells for the oxen to wear. The clappers were made of bullets: the oxen gave forth a jolly tinny muting as they moved soberly among trees. They always stayed together because they were friends. Come late afternoon, they were herded leisurely homeward. By the time snow fell thick, Marble proposed to have finished an adequate stable, made roughly of poles insulated with grass and leaves, with a sod roof above the poles. Again and again he would yoke up, drive beyond the grove and cut prairie hay until the wagon was piled high. That hay was a joy: brilliant little flowers of autumn tangled amidst the grasses when first the Marbles arrived, and now were dessicated like spices by the frosts.

Was it often in time, Peggy Ann wondered, that men fed their cattle on flowers?

In the first coming of dusk there was no sound save the crackling of a new fire at a new hearthside (almost lovingly the woman remembered Harvey Luce and his prayer; it would have affected Luce to know of her thought) and the occasional crinkling melody of oxen bells which William had forgotten to remove for the night. Also steam forced from the iron pot with a sound. Peggy Ann took her hooked poker and lifted the heavy lid to see whether beans were done. They had bubbled there for hours after soaking through the night; and she had put in the pork and sorghum and vinegar an hour earlier.

Ready yet? asked the hungry man.

What you think? She offered a spoon with beans and liquid hot in the bowl of it.

Cautiously he sucked and tasted. Seems first-rate to me!

Let us give the corncake another few minutes; then I'll serve us.

At last they sat on their stools at the little puncheon table, two surviving plates of rose-and-cream ironware before them, the one surviving dish of blue-and-white ironware in the middle, corncake hot upon the japanned tray. William was professedly a religious man (true—he and Peggy Ann had first seen each other in church, and had courted in religious shadow) but always he was reluctant to voice prayers or graces. Nevertheless tonight he ducked his head hastily over his plate.

Dear God, he blurted, for this we thank Thee!

He took his wife by such surprise that barely did she have time to turn her face down, and realize that he was asking a Blessing; then he was reaching for the beans.

When they finished eating, William went to see after the critters, to remove their bells belatedly, and to fetch more wood for morning in his return.

Got to build a mighty tall woodpile right up against this door, he said. Snow might fall deep.

Twas printed in Mr. Plumbe's book, cried Peggy Ann accusingly, that this country never has more than a foot of snow.

Indians say different.

Well, what Indians do you know, husband?

That Morris Markham, he's met up with them. He says that sometimes there's awful snows. I mean to have a mountain of wood where we can put our hands on it.

. . . In firelight the Marbles prepared themselves for the night. They were disconcerted by unfamiliar brightness: flames fell lower and lower, but still there was more light than they were accustomed to in the wagon.

I smell something, said William, in bed.

Must be the sheets.

Why would they smell queer?

Count of the lavender. They were old sheets first, and in the family, but when she made us the gift of them Cousin Lettie had cut them down more to modern size, and she sewed new hems. They had lavender sprinkled in to keep them sweet; and that's the way I left them folded in the little chest. Course, I just took them out today. Do you think—?

Her whisper fell lower. But his question had burnt a new whimsy into her brain.

—Think they smell bad?

No, just queer. But kind of—

Sweet?

Yes, he replied decisively. Sweet.

Peggy lay staring up at unfamiliar designs of stiff light and shadow where spread the loft floor, their ceiling. Later she thought that William must be sleeping; yet there rose no sound of heavy breathing. Then he began to wriggle around in bed, he turned and put his back against her. He was the first one into bed that night . . . and she did not know . . . in the wagon box which had been their bed ever since leaving Linn County, usually William had worn his shirt, the heavy shirt of daytime occupation. So it smelt of him, of his days, of his sweat. He was a man, a good man. Of the two men whose smells she had known she liked his the better. . . . It was distressingly indelicate even to consider a comparison of smells of men. She wondered if any other woman had ever done so. Probably only wicked women had. . . . Sometimes . . . yes . . . sometimes she felt very wicked.

Could be the leaves, she said softly, not as if to disturb him.

What say?

I thought maybe you was asleep. I meant that smell: could be leaves, too, as well as lavender.

Soon his broad hard hand came to slide across her bosom, to explore and blend with the breast farthest away from him, her right breast. She began to stiffen and thrill to his touch. How wonderful! —she thought with the first little lights flashing before her closed eyes. How remarkable! His hand, forever so tough and firm with rocks and tools, so gentle with me.

She murmured, Can't stand it—

He breathed his question close to her ear—a single sound, shapeless, no word, just a question.

I mean—tis the feather bed, I guess. She giggled nervously. . . . William, she whispered, using the rare name. We're not customed to a bed. Seems so soft, and sinking way down, kind of. We been in that wagon so long, just on comforters. Well— I mean— We did have these feather beds. But they went so hard, gainst the floor of the wagon–

Yep, they did. His durable voice had grown tender in this beginning of intimacy, along with the smoothness, the provocative touch of his fingers.

William, she gasped. Could we–? Do you spose twould be all right –could we get out of bed, and–? I mean–down on the floor–?

He was silent for so long, considering the notion–and even withdrawing his hand–that she feared he was disgusted or offended. You mean on the stones? he asked doubtfully.

I could pull down some of these comforters, and twould be soft enough. Tis just– Oh, this going way deep into the leaves! She giggled wildly again.

Agreeable to me.

He started to push himself into a position to climb across her, if necessary, from the corner where the bed was built.

William . . . again . . . so tiny and furry she made the word, it became only a kitten's sound. Would you humor me?

He was resting half upright, his arm extended down, his hand braced in bedclothing.

Words tumbled furiously from her mouth, tumbled out of heart and soul . . . because of guilt she contemplated, a sensual deed she would perform.

Would you mind going outside whilst I got things ready?

He chuckled. You're a funny one. We've always took off our clothes together in the wagon, hain't we? And when we had our cottage down in Linn.

I know. But now–this night–the fire's still giving off so much light– We're in the new house! she gasped, as if that explained everything.

Whatever you say.

So she pushed her feet and legs out of bed, and drew the long nightgown to cover them. William crept around past her and stepped down to the stones. She saw that he was wearing a nightshirt; she hadn't observed this before, yet of course the material had felt different, different from his shirt.

He jammed his bare feet into boots, threw an old gray shawl around his shoulders (only of late, or in chilly rains, had it been cold enough for him to use that shawl when he walked forth). He withdrew the stout iron pipe he had brought from Linn County to bar the door; and so it had been barred on this first night. But he lifted it from flanges, stood it in the doorside corner, and went calmly into a frosty world without looking back. Moonlight was admitted for a moment–Peggy Ann had forgotten about that wide new-risen moon, she had been watching the fire—and then the door closed solidly, substantially. Oh, the whole house was built solidly, substantially.

The young woman leaped from bed and scooted to her round-lidded trunk in the corner; she called it her chest, although it was scarce big enough for a chest. Her fingers flew, seeking and doing (this was in preparation for an act of erotic intensity. She held that quivering pathetic fear of the erotic worn by those who have experienced little such fulfillment, but who have dreamed long and in fierce fascination; and whose souls are perpetual secret fugitives from the dictum of the ordinary, the accepted, the proper, the prim). Then she remembered that she must prepare their couch first; and so she did, growing more excited in the task, tearing fiercely at the bed. She folded two comforters to make a thickness . . . it was at one side of the fireplace, half in shadow, half in ruddiness . . . there she built the little pallet, and spread blankets atop for smoothness—light soft blankets; often she'd thought them soft as silk, they had a crinkly feeling when she stroked them, she loved to stroke them.

. . . She was prepared at last . . . ah, no: a pillow or two, those would be necessary, the lovers might fall asleep eventually close to pleasant watching coals, the first night fire to burn upon that hearth. She fetched pillows, and put herself upon the pallet, and turned half a loose flimsy blanket across her body. She tried to assemble her voice and send it out to summon her lover, but it was a weak cry at first, embarrassed and fretful; she had to call several times before William heard her and came and brought the moonlight for another moment. She turned her face toward the fire, she watched only the fire now, dared watch only the fire. She heard portentous metallic settling of the bar within flanges (set as firmly into wood beside the door as if they had grown there) and she smothered her face against the tossed border of the blanket, feeling abandoned in the looseness of her hair. What if he should disapprove? She had always feared that he might disapprove fundamentally of licentious antics. William Marble was not like Phipps, yet she loved William more than ever she had loved Phipps. But Phipps was given to madness: a madness she had learned to share with untrammeled delight (as if gone dementedly a-whoring) in the short time before his advancing illness kept them apart. No, she'd not caught the consumption, it seemed strange, doctors and grannies seemed to think it might be catching, but she had not come down with it, she must be very strongly constituted . . . no frail and anaemic young thing, a victim of palpitations and wanness; just violent cramps every twenty-six days.

She felt and heard her man coming closer through involved shadows, heard the snap of his knees as he knelt in preparation to lie beside her.

William . . . mumble from extremity of space, it seemed to come from outside the tight walls of this large new-smelling house, all one-hundred-and-sixty-eight square feet of it.

William, she spoke again, but it was in a mumble composed of the *w* sound and the *m*; she seemed to say Wim. Do something else, husband, please do!

He waited, halted in motions of kneeling and sliding close to her. He was saying nothing, waiting for her adjuration.

Please, Wim, to take off your–*nightshirt.*

The last word ripped forth with an explosion of her breath, she lay glad that her face was hidden.

His answering voice grated flatly. You mean–?

(This night he called her Margaret before they were entwined; seldom did he command her name. It was not the custom, not among people who had reared him or among others whom they knew. But now he spoke of her as Margaret. . . . There was, or should be, no great problem at hand! They were married folks, they had a right– They had– She did not even lie within his arms as yet; still he spoke her name.)

Margaret. You mean–be naked?

You *have.* (She cried it, she was so frantic.) You have, William, you have! Times, you most got mad. I–I was most scared of you once. You–you used a cuss word. You said– You said, This damn nightshirt gets in my way! And you took it off. And–and a couple of other times–

Margaret! He spoke with the tone of minister, the tone of judge. You said Damn.

Well, *you* did. You said it too. Now I'm no better than you are. We both said it.

Perhaps it was only half a minute that he remained motionless; it seemed much longer. She thought that she could hear wooden machinery of his mind at work like a mill's machinery. She had never heard of machinery fashioned from stone . . . well, partly from stone: the burr of a mill . . . yes, millstones grinding together. That was what was going on within him. Suddenly, with confused joy in victory, she heard the sliding of the shirt's fabric across his skin and hair . . . he was rolling close. She waited, congealed, as he lifted the edge of the blankets, pushed under, pushed himself against her. Then quickly he too was stiff–not stiff with ardor but with astonishment.

Margaret. . . . Twas not a reprimand, twas a statement. . . . You hain't got any nightgown on, either. But what–?

Ah, William, put your arms around me, my William, put your arms around me!

He succumbed dutifully–dutifully, yea!–too overwhelmed, too shocked to remain austere.

Ah, she loved his smell: twas a better smell than her other man had worn.

What is it? he asked again and again. What—?

Not yet could she build the four syllables to answer him, to tell the story of her descent into carnality.

What is it, Margaret? Tain't lavender.

No, she chirped. Per-fume-er-y! Almost she spelled out the word, broke it into its four parts. As if saying: Now you can see for a fact, you can see what a vile woman I am at heart. And all along you had thought me decent.

Wim . . . words pouring, the smooth intent touch of his great hand had done it. And so she could not restrain her explanation, tossed out like long broken waves reaching against the lake shore when pike were dancing, when Morris Markham was pulling out the pike. (Oh, never think of Markham now.)

Wim. Tis perfumery, French perfumery, I had a bottle, a little bottle, I had it all along, twas given to me long ago!

His right arm lived beneath her, it had slid all the way and come around, his mighty hand was cupping gently above her breast.

I reckon you're just a strumpet at heart, said William Marble.

Yes, yes, I am! Blindly she swung her head up from the pillow, twisted her neck, felt his beard brushing her disordered un-night-capped hair (that must be another lewdness, she thought, in fresh consuming flood of anguish); then she shut her eyes, her nose and cheeks were crushed against the man's hairy breast. Her tongue came out, seeking through contact the very mixture of her body and his. Little wet words were mumbled, a mumble made purely of the flesh, the flesh of both.

William. . . .

Love me. . . .

William. . . .

Oh, dear William, *love me*. . . .

A moment more and he was beginning to love her; in later moments he was loving her hard, and harder than ever, oh, dear God, than ever before, oh, so hard, and all the warmth of it, and oh, the toughness, and the iron and buckskin of the male, and the perfume and silk of femininity, even the most rampant outrageous portion and type of femininity. She was all woman and all women, oh utterly a woman at last, at last, she had waited, there was nothing to conceal, now he knew everything, he knew all, and oh, and oh, and oh, and oh, and William, William, William, and long she'd thought to scream, she had forced the scream back from her lips and into her throat before, when first they slept together after their marriage, and then later, when they were in Linn, and then all the time in the wagon, and when they did it in the wagon she wanted to scream, she wanted sometimes to let forth her exhausted and exulting passion in a single cry, but now she was crying almost as loudly as she wished to cry, and he was demanding fiercely boyishly amidst the spasmodic twitching and striving of their encounter, he was saying, Margaret, we got to have a child!—Margaret, you hear me, a child, a *child!*—and Yes, and Yes, and Oh, and Oh, and William, give me a child, give me a child, give me a child! and then the scream shot out in that final driven second, she screamed to the new house in its glory, she screamed to walls and ceilings, stones beneath them, the comforters underneath them and atop the stones, she screamed to shameless scent with which she'd bathed her skin and hair, screamed to all the desperate wilderness where they were installed, screamed to moon out yonder, the sheer mild tawny moon awaiting and a-watching upon that roof and o'er that designated hearthside, and so it was a hearthside, and so they were in it, they were making a hearthside now. *Ah!* she screamed. *Ahhh!* and in the same almighty instant his breath burst in a roar.

There was only the once this night, could be only the once.

Long she lay watching the fire color, smelling chemical fragrance of logs which dissolved in their last ripeness close at hand. Any wise wife, she considered, would have slipped from the arms of the sleeping man who loved her, and who had awarded her this joy and this supremacy . . . would have slipped out, gone to the outdoor heap of wood so carefully placed (and oh, he was dependable in every way, was William) and would have taken sticks and fetched them in and put them on the fire and built it up again. But she did not move, could only watch the toughening coals . . . be female in the knowledge that when it was necessary, William would build a fire again. The night was not so cold.

Later, far later (remote on prairies beyond their woods the wolves must be howling again . . . some few wolves talking of colder weather to follow, and maybe famine; but Peggy Ann could not hear them. Only if she were to go outside would she hear them, and thank goodness she wouldn't have to go outside for any purpose any more: there was the vessel beneath the bed) she was wraith and giantess. She slipped easily, soft as soot, from the loose sleeping clutch of William's arms, and rose and dutifully donned her nightdress.

Chill began to find her but it was a clean chill. Never the chill of sickness, nor chill of frightening future. Ah, maybe . . . she did believe it sincerely, and prayed a million prayers simultaneously, that this might be true. . . . She felt it . . . had never felt this way before . . . even at this moment there might be the beginnings of a child deep within that sacred snuggled place where children grew?

Majestic as a goddess . . . there were pictures, she had seen them, goddesses so strong, and they carried shields, and wore flowing draperies, and had crowns or helmets to suggest their might, and some of them bore swords or tridents or other weapons of authority. So that was the sort of goddess she was, but weaponless. The only weapon she bore was her own self, the self she'd upheld and used as she wished to use it. Wound up in the shawl at last (the shawl which William had worn) she put down her nose and smelled the sweat and wood-ash smell in those folds, and loved all odors which she found.

There was new light coming to her now, coming through shiny sparkling panes of the windows—the first time she'd seen moonlight through those panes installed last week. It had shone in nights before, but she had not been there to see the silver and neither had William. This new-risen moonlight was a part of them and their abode. (She did not think consciously: My house, my husband, my child to come, perhaps; yet mingling of the thought was all around her, awarded by Holy God within the moon.) She stood up by the window and put her cheek against the pane; it was chill enough outside for mist to form there, and so she moved her cheek against a fresh pane, and held her breath that she might see.

Tallow, she considered, the tallow of white tallow dips . . . and so it looked like tallow dips a-slanting loosely, twisted . . . oh, bent dips, they were . . . and coming through the trees. The moon was sliding upward farther past the largest basswood trunk, and so more of its light came down, slanting on the window, and she could see the little pools of tallow . . . no, no, she must not so designate it, for tallow was a dead and clammy thing. She'd thought of tallow as the texture of the Dead, perhaps . . . but this was something else . . . had more of metal in it, more of frost. There was a limp and kindly treasure in the moon.

Our house, she thought. Our place, our lake. Down through trees she saw a lakeside ripple break, and so the moonlight made its spattering . . . twas over all, a hush throughout the trees. It said, I'm lingering, lingering, here as always, lingering.

She thought: And moonlight lay upon this place when there were only Indians, and it will spread and melt eternally . . . and people come, and others yet unborn. Unborn within the unborn . . . so they roll unfolding forth. For always there's a fold within the folded humankind which has not yet been turned; and so in time that fold untwists itself . . . and so you find—another fold.

She thought she felt a microscopic morsel squirming delicately among those secret glossy drops which hid within her.

Who and what are we, she wondered, to accomplish such nobility?

. . . How strange!—nobility arises from a sinful act!

. . . Not for one moment do I now believe that we are doomed to torment!

. . . Yes, yes, we are still young, so very young (as years are reckoned).

. . . We've built our house.

. . . The love of living, love of husband, sudden new love of a place and time and gracious walls encompassing.

Peggy Ann wiped off her tears with fringe of the old shawl. Once more she witnessed only moonlight, pacifying under and among the great tree trunks, and coming loose to blend upon the ground. Thickness, mat of leaves loose scattered there, and ah, the frost upon them!

Now what was that? A twitching? There was naught to fear. It could not be a beast or villain stalking down upon them; none would be allowed on such a night.

A poem of the past . . . a little book, and they were reading it aloud. The master said, Miss Margaret Ann, will you please to read the next? She read it dutifully . . . it came in fragment form to haunt her, and to blend with age and place and night. *By midnight moons, o'er moistening dews* . . . it was that poet, and she'd loved the reading of his poetry. What was his name? Freneau? It chanted, stayed with her, amid the wonder of this Spirit Lake, the new life that was theirs. *By midnight moons, o'er moistening dews, the hunter still the deer pursues, the hunter and the deer, a shade.* Now she could witness Indians fairly, they were there. *And long shall timorous Fancy see the painted chief, and pointed spear.* They seemed gliding and waiting but she could not call them a menace. She watched the phantasms, considered them with affection.

XXI

Through the autumn days which marched in spicy procession there was excitement in hearing a wheel creak, a neigh, the sound of voices rising. Strangers might be coming! Abbie Gardner was jubilant at the advent of strangers; she would rush heedlessly, hoping to be the first to greet anyone who rode in that direction. She prayed to find a new girl, one of her own age, journeying in; but none appeared.

There came instead the Messrs. Wheelock, Parmenter, Wiltfong, and Howe. Wiltfong was guiding the other three. He was a trapper whom Morris Markham had encountered on a trip to the south; the three young men whom he conducted were all brothers-in-law, and made jolly sport of the fact.

Sissy, we'd expected to find only Indians; but instead, here's a pretty miss like you. . . .

We got a Mr. Howe up here, too.

Possibly a long-lost cousin of ours? Possibly a wealthy one?

Abbie reckoned that few in the Okoboji region were very wealthy. . . . His name is Old Joel Howe, and he comes from Indiana, and he's got a whole scad of boys, and the Mrs., and he's got Sardis too. But she's already growed into young ladyhood.

Ah, said Lawyer Howe, the years are fleeting, my dear damsel. *Tempus fugit!*—and in almost no time at all you yourself will be in young ladyhood—and kneeling at the altar!

Us Methodists don't do much kneeling. Sister Mary says it's acting like Catholics to do so.

Good heavens, lass! Then I shall be very chary about kneeling!—and Mr. Howe tweaked Abbie's sun-bleached hair lightly, and she colored to have him do it. She led the men on to the house, where Rowland Gardner walked to meet them.

They had taken up land at the foot of Spirit Lake, not too far below the Marble place. They were bound for their homes in Jasper County, but planned to return in the spring; and later, when they had houses prepared, would fetch their families. They congratulated the Red Wing Company on their choice of a town site. Isaac Harriott withdrew a deep-driven splinter which had lodged under Mr. Wiltfong's fingernail, and the three brothers-in-law discoursed learnedly on England with Carl Granger, and on France with Bertell Snyder. Successively they called on Mattocks, Howes, and the Noble and Thatcher families. Then they galloped off, and everyone at the lakes was brighter for their visit, and felt a breath of prosperity in the breeze.

Rowland Gardner had met one Doctor Strong when he traveled down the Des Moines River to purchase a last load of supplies for winter. At Fort Dodge he was bearing a sack of meal out of the mill, when he was confronted by an individual who affected a pointed beard, a staccato manner of speech, a nervous handshake.

Permit me to introduce myself. The name is Strong—E. B. N. Strong —and I am a physician and surgeon. I am told that you have taken up property in the Okoboji country. . . .

The doctor went on to fire many questions about land and living conditions at the lakes, about current denizens of the region, and prospects of a town. Gardner felt somewhat confounded because he could not answer every question put to him. Strong said that he had visited Springfield, across the Minnesota line, and halfway intended to settle there; a house was already available for his family. However, favorable descriptions of Okoboji reached his ears. He thought he might have a look at the place. . . . Doctor Strong was in his late thirties, growing a little paunchy around the middle. His pale eyes held forever an intense stare, and yet the stare was not directed at you when he spoke to you: it was turned in some odd way past your head. His mouth was full and firm, uncompromising, the staring eyes were more protuberant than most. . . .

Halfway home on his solitary journey, Rowland Gardner was smitten suddenly with the notion that he would much rather have Isaac Harriott attend him in illness than Doctor Strong. He could not quite understand his feeling in the matter, for obviously Strong was Harry's senior in years, experience, and no doubt in education as well.

Actually Gardner never expected to see Strong again, and was much surprised when the doctor appeared at Okoboji, driving in a heavily laden Concord wagon with his wife and a tiny daughter.

The doctor's wife was in poor health—her complexion pasty, her nostrils thin, a plaintive quality in her voice. She confessed to Frances Gardner and Mary Luce that she had never known a well day since little Prudence was born. And here she was, in the family way again.

Why, you poor thing! whispered Frances Gardner warmly. Can't the doctor offer nothing to give you strength?

Actually, droned the weary voice, female complaints aren't in his line. He's good at using the knife, and he's specially skilled at amputations. But something happened to my internals when I had the first baby, and Husband says that a cure is beyond his powers. I only pray I won't miscarry now.

Why, you poor thing! No—you're not to stir a hand. You set right down here and *rest.* Mary and the girls and me—we'll do all the supper fixings that's to be done. You poor thing! . . .

Mary Luce and Harvey gave up their bed to the Strongs that night. Mary slept with her sisters, Harvey slept on the floor beside his father-in-law. There was not much bedclothing available. Abbie and Eliza had been set to the task of washing comforters and blankets, only a few hours before the Strongs' arrival; everything was wet.

(Frances Gardner said that there was no help for it: they had to start the winter with clean things. The weather was so bright now: things would dry in no time! The system called for use of the large iron kettle and two wooden tubs. Rowland Gardner swung the kettle from its tripod in the yard, and the girls fetched water and tended the fire. Tubs were filled with batches of quilts, hot water and soft soap were put in, the trampling ensued. . . . I always did like to tromp quilts! . . . But it makes your feet and limbs all *pink!* . . . The little boys demanded their turn, they climbed into one tub and danced furiously about; inevitably they became engaged in a fight. Bertie cried that his uncle had splashed soap into his eyes deliberately, Rowly cried that he hadn't . . . shrieks and swatting . . . the boys were banished. Eliza and Abbie proceeded with the work.)

Next noon, at dinner, people seemed looking at Eliza Gardner searchingly, and she could not imagine what was wrong. When the meal was done there ensued a family council.

Liza, child. You've got an invite.

What—?

Doctor and Mrs. Strong—they desire you to go on to Springfield. Spend a while with them.

Eliza was bewildered.

You don't have to go less you want to, Rowland Gardner put in quickly.

*Spring*field! gasped Eliza.

Mrs. Strong explained weakly: See, child, I feel poorly so much of the time. If you choose to come up and live with us awhile, twould help out. With little Prudence and all. There's a fine house we're going to be living in, there—house half again as big as this—

*Spring*field!

I know what, said Abbie suddenly.

Her sister turned with cold menace. Abbie Gardner, if you dast—

But I know—

Abigail *Gard*ner! I'll pull your *hair!*

Abbie, said the mother, this hain't no concern of yourn. It's Liza's got the invite—not you.

I know why she wants to go!—and Abbie skipped delightedly out of the house. From a safe distance she began caroling: *Liza's mad, and I am glad, and I know what will please her.*

In dusk that evening, Rowland Gardner was coming away from the oxen when he encountered his wife near the colossal woodpile which heightened and extended each day as Gardner and Luce fed it. (They were determined not to be cold in the winter; the work on Harvey's house must wait until an adequate supply of wood was effected. What indeed was an adequate supply? Nobody seemed to know. It wouldn't take too much wood in winter if the weather continued like this.)

Husband.

He stopped and surveyed Frances mutely.

You think it's all right?

Well, she seems to want to go.

Course she does. But its account of that young Tretz she got acquainted with, back at Clear Lake.

Oh, yes, there was that party of Germans come through—

He's up there to Springfield, Mr. Harshman told of it. And Doctor Strong says he knows him: lives with another family there, working on the place.

Rowland said guardedly: Our Liza's a good Christian girl. She wouldn't be up to no tricks—

That young man: *he* might be up to tricks.

The parents looked at each other.

Frances, she'll get paid?

Just a dab. Dime a day, they said.

And twill help us, not having so many to feed here.

Oh, it's so far away: a whole day's trip! We wouldn't be like to see her often, specially if the weather turned bad.

But she wants to go.

Yes, I know she does—

So I say, let her go.

Husband—Rowland—she's a young girl, and— That man—the doctor. Do you spose he means well by her?

Pears like a gentleman to me: well-spoken, educated—

I know, but— Oh, I want to be *sure.*

Frances. We can't be sure about anything in this life.

No. . . .

Actually there was no reason to fear for Eliza. Doctor Strong would have been properly offended at any doubt pertaining to his conduct toward a young girl domiciled with him. He had never sinned in such respect, and was heartless in his condemnation of people who did demonstrate such vices, or indeed any sexual vices. Neither did he drink, use what he called The Weed, or allow profanity to soil his lips. He had been accepted early into the Congregationalist faith. But he was one of those inherent weaklings who, from the cradle, stand embittered against stronger gayer humans. His own faith in himself was meager although he made sanctimonious pretense of dedication to his profession. He had performed any number of irrational amputations and other excisions. When he held the knife he felt a gratifying sense of might. When a patient wailed or snarled under Strong's ministration he experienced momentary enchantment at knowing that he possessed such power. In most other categories of conduct he was cowering, resentful, disappointed.

He measured everyone by the inaccurate tape of his own shoddy personality. For example, when at school at the East, he had consorted frequently with a youth named Willie Wastrom who, before he reached the age of thirty, was said to have piled up at least twenty thousand dollars profit from the business of manufacturing iron for railroads. Edwin Benjamin Nodworth Strong could not believe that Willie had earned so much money—or, if he did believe it, pretended not to. He never missed an opportunity to say something slighting about Mr. William Wastrom, the alleged genius of the rails; and he hinted often that chicanery was involved in Mr. Wastrom's supposed success. This was partially because Noddy Strong had not saved twenty thousand dollars, or even twenty thousand cents. But the tree of his contempt did not have its roots in a soil of jealousy alone. He was actuated also by the fact that he and Willie Wastrom had once evaded classes together and gone to a puppet show; and Doctor Strong felt that no one who had shared such boyhood intimacy with himself could really amount to much. . . . Besides Willie and many other lads, there was, at the Albany Classical School which Noddy Strong attended before he went to medical college, a student named Herman. Herman published a sensationally successful book, his very first book, while he was still in his twenties; and a number of other distinguished works followed. E. B. N. Strong, reading often of these accomplishments on the part of Herman, greeted each favorable comment with snorts. Flatly did he refuse to read a line which the man had written: Herman had had a wooden locker immediately next to his own, in the Albany school, and anyone who had had a locker next to that of E. B. N. Strong could be no acceptable author, because E. B. N. Strong could scarcely write a coherent note to aunt or creditor, could entertain or affect or influence no one— No one would have paid a cent for anything which *he* set down on paper!—this he recognized, secretly but soundly. If he were to write doggerel (and he could not write even doggerel) a village newspaper would have refused to print it; and recognition of this fact caused him to scout the merest mention of Herman's name. Herman's name was Melville. . . . When Noddy Strong was very young he spent two summers at a farm owned by his uncle. Across the orchard stood another farmhouse occupied by a sturdy dairyman and his wife and their freckled son. Noddy and Freck used to go fishing together in a nearby creek, and Freck was not the most successful fisherman in York State but neither was Noddy Strong. Nearly twenty years later Noddy became much annoyed at learning that Freck, a graduate West Pointer, had been brevetted captain for gallantry displayed during the attack on Chapultepec. Doctor Strong thought it ludicrous to be asked to believe that anyone with whom he had fished unrewardingly for trout, with whom he had crushed caterpillars, with whom he had munched bread-and-butter-and-brown-sugar, could perform a bold deed in battle or even attend the United States Military Academy, let alone graduate from it. Doctor Strong would not have lasted out two days at West Point, and he knew it; he would have fled Mexico at the first cannon-blast or bullet-whine, and he knew it—with a mixture of self-pity, self-loathing, self-excuse.

Therefore he smiled wisely and wryly when the brave young soldier was mentioned. He said: The Army may think him to be a hero, but—

Eh, what say? Do you know the man personally, Doctor?

Yes indeed. But—

You mean that it may have been a matter of deception? That—perhaps someone else—? And this man received credit to which he was not actually entitled? Why, that's dreadful, Doctor Strong, dreadful!

Ah, well, let's not discuss it!—but Doctor Strong would look very knowing, and he would compress his lips, raise his eyebrows, and shrug once more.

(He was that most unhappy and persistent detractor of all: the starveling who scents hot gravy-laden meats, but cries that the feast is inedible for the reason that he has not been invited to partake of it, and knows that he will never be allowed to do so.)

. . . Eliza Gardner's few duds were packed and she prepared to drive happily into slavey-hood with the Strongs.

Her father's beard filled her face as he put his farewell kiss upon her shiny pink forehead.

Goodbye, Pa.

Now, you be a good girl, Liza.

Yes, Pa, I will be. Goodbye, Pa.

(Say it again, Eliza Gardner.)

She accepted a moist kiss from Harvey Luce.

I trust, dear sister, that you will sing forever the glad tidings of Salvation!

Oh, yes, Brother Harvey, I will.

When the Master calls, may the shock of corn be fully ripe.

Yes, yes! I mean—

(Goodbye to him. You will not whisper it another time.)

Abbie had no longer the heart to twit Eliza about her lovelorn condition, to chant gibing references to Henry Tretz. She feared vaguely that when she saw Eliza again, her sister would be already wedded to Henry Tretz. In the paleness of dawn Abbie had realized the gravity of this departure. Quickly she wrapped her arms around the slumbering Eliza and dripped tears against her neck. She would lose, as of this day, the companion nearest her—would lose playmate, fellow gossip, sparring partner, rival, fellow giggler and whisperer, fellow teaser and squealer, enemy and friend.

See . . . Liza. I took Pa's little sharp knife and . . . cut . . . *ah-huh, ah-huh, ah-huh* . . . this nnnnnut. I carved . . . *ah-huh* . . . this heart on't. See? . . . Tis in . . . two halves. One for you and one . . . for me. You gggggot to keep your . . . half-a-nut . . . always. Won't you . . . Liza?

Yes . . . I wwwwwill . . . Abbie. . . .

The farewell clutch of Sister Mary.

Now, dear little Sis, you always be ladylike.

Yes, I wwwwwill . . . Mary.

And we'll hope to come see you up there in Springfield *real soon.* And maybe . . . and. . . .

Oh, goodbye, Mary. . . .

(For always, Eliza Gardner. Say it, tis the truth. For always.)

Hugs from the boys, their grins turned up to her. The squeezing of Baby Mandy. *Who's going to look after my little Rowly and my little Bertie and my dear little Baby* Mandy *whilst I'm gone?*

(Ah, who indeed? Wild men? Yes, dear girl. Wild men.)

The clutch of mother, the feeling and smell of mother—the mother scent, mother warmth, mother sound, mother pressure.

Heaven bless you, dear daughter Eliza—

Heaven bbbbbless you, Ma.

Goodbye.

(Tis such a long time, such a long long time. Forever takes so long to happen.)

Voices calling back and forth along a track between the solemn trees.

Goodbye.

Bye. . . .

Bye. . . .

Until faintly the last remembrance dies out, and only unseen birds seem echoing it.

There came the last warm day and night of the year, the year's final thunder. Thunder talked down to Abbie through the roof. It said in a mutter of many low voices that a storm was distant, but strolling closer. Thunder had not one voice but a chorus, all deep-chested and (she thought suddenly) feminine. . . . Why not a chorus of men? No, those were women's voices, however deep. She thought of a sewing circle of swarthy women gossiping, passing judgment, nodding their heads more or less in unison; one of them would laugh with heavy cynicism; then another would say something unkind; then another of the thick-chested fat-breasted women would voice a direct threat; again they would all nod . . . thunder . . . she saw them. They wore their hair in braids; their skins were dark and oily. She thought of a neighbor her family had known in actuality, a neighbor woman with a black mustache (and when the woman perspired how the little globules of oil would hang around each hair of that defacement)! It was of women like Mrs. Croan that the convocation was made. Or were they squaws—the consorts of wild men—squat brick-faced women in Agency calico, women with old grease on their frayed gowns?

The thunder. Was it Indian talk, or English?

Abbie had feared storms when she was small. Now she feared them even more acutely because she had been in so many tempests—had been exposed in a wagon when lightning seemed to pierce the ground all around, when lightning was not a shaft but actual exploding balls of fire to bounce. Once again on hearing ugly sullen voices of storm, she imagined that she was a mere urchin, she was screaming.

. . . Frances Gardner said, Children. Hush that silly noise. Eliza, hush!

. . . Tain't me that's crying—tis Abbie. She's just yelling her head off!

. . . Abigail Gardner, you stop it!

. . . I can't, I can't, it gets right in my eyes!

. . . Her mother came and brought a dark yarn stocking and put it across her eyes, and gave her a little spank; Abbie burrowed deeper into the feather bed. Her sister complained that Abbie's foot was sticking her; Abbie shoved with both feet, and Eliza inched away, snarling, then fell asleep again. Thunder thudded and rolled, still the flash came cursing, but Abbie could not see it through that blessèd stocking. Blessèd, blessèd stocking. . . .

Thunder bumped to extinction across empty low ridges beyond the woods; no longer lived there a panic, or images concerning it. But the young girl's thoughts kept waking and straying. She loved this lakeside grove in which the new home had been made, she touched and handled a memory of summer as she lay among the crowded sleepers. Summer and the colored autumn so long prevailing . . . she'd found steady confidence, idyllic benevolence among these Iowa forests even when it was hard work or a doleful errand which took her into them. Rhododendrons and laurel grew back East, a thick stand of bushes through which fierce beasts might be believed to wander. Here it seemed that there should be only sheep. In Iowa the tough dry wires of blackberry and raspberry vines appeared curving from a tangle reserved especially for their propagation; the very gooseberry bushes were rounded, ornate; surely they had been set out. Picturesque mats of lawn wore short grass between the bushes as if grazed over by contented domestic animals.

When the Gardners dwelt in Greenwood there stood, two doors away from them, a small brown house. A sign swung out from the porch: *Mrs. A. T. A. Hubbard. Seamstress. Aprons a Specialty.* Abbie learned her first letters from that sign (*a, b, c, d, e.* Mary taught them to her; but Abbie did not learn the letter *f* because there was no *f* on the sign). Old Mrs. Hubbard was a kindly woman in a cap with a pink frill; Abbie liked nothing so well as to go a-calling on her, for Mrs. Hubbard could and did make gumdrops—whenever she had the wherewithal, and could purchase gum arabic. But even sweets did not afford the same sensuous delight which arose when Abbie stood before a certain picture which hung in its dust directly beneath the high shelf where Mrs. Hubbard kept her spools. It was an oil painting, brought from England when Mrs. Hubbard herself was young. Doubtless it was not even a moderately expensive painting, or poor Mrs. Hubbard would have sold the picture long before. (Many times she had to live on skim milk and porridge when customers were few.) The painting depicted oak trees, and there were creatures under them which the child thought must be sheep, spotted ones; but old Mrs Hubbard told her that they were fawns.

Calm oaks which held up the sky in these groves about Okoboji were very like the English oaks in that remote oil painting. They were as substantial uncles and grandfathers, trustworthy preachers and schoolmasters. Some were shaggy, serenely bold as the trapper who strolled past the Gardner cabin . . . they recognized their own age, but bore it beautifully. Abbie did not pretend that her new woodland was an English one, yet she heard solemn winds conversing in the picturesque branches. She'd seen, in summer heat, leaves turning their pale sides outward and upward, as they had been painted in her memory . . . the gentle wind and the leaves said that everything had happened centuries before; there was nothing left to happen now.

Abigail walked dreaming when she should have been gathering nuts. Nuts were thought to have little value as food; they were looked upon as a confection, yet her father doted on them. Times when he was not too sleepy, when the family sat sharing a comfort near the fire before bedtime, he would say, Couldn't somebody crack me a nut? So she should have been seeking the fruit of hickories, not acorns; she should have been counting the nuts, surveying and prospecting against frost, learning which nuts were nearer at hand, easier to get at. She had been told to do this whenever she went searching for the ox which strayed, whenever she went picking up kindling. She loved to fade off down cozy aisles because in doing so she was walking into the painting she had admired (and in a way she was smelling the clean smell of the dimity on which Mrs. Hubbard sewed, hearing the snip of her shears, tasting once more a gumdrop softening slowly, homemade, melting upon the tongue). Oh, sheep never came, and she did not see the fawns, though she was confident that there must be some about—there were so many deer. (Twice her father shot deer from their very doorstep, without budging off of it.) Yet the fawns Abbie did not witness; and if she had come upon them lying in some secret covert, she would have noted at once that they were wild American fawns, kin of the wild men. She would have feared that they were not placid, there'd be no comfort in them, they'd not be docile and ordered in their habits.

She looked at the gooseberry bushes, the seemingly clipped glades between them, and thought of small fabrics which she had seen worked there, very early in the morning, when first she walked that way.

Fairy tablecloths, she told her little brother. They must of been having folks to tea.

They wasn't there yesterday!

No, they come during the night.

What's folks a-doing, having tea in the night? . . . Rowly could not share the contentment she found in viewing these fragile things, so quickly vanished by sun and wind, stricken away by their own treading feet. The fairy tablecloths were all a joy to Abbie and they suggested simple civilized pleasures to be realized sometime under these very oaks.

Grass so green, so thick, yet not long enough to be twisted and beaten down into bunches. Grass for a shepherd to walk across, a shepherd as in Mrs. Hubbard's painting, a man carrying a crook in his hand. There was another man, a huntsman (but of a mild sort). And far beyond lifted some chimneys, and Mrs. Hubbard said that they marked the manor house. She couldn't think of the name of the family, but she was sure that that picture had been painted near the village of her childhood, a place named Boughton Aluph. A park, she called it: something-or-other park. So here was this Iowa park, strung along the lakeside as if ruled and surveyed for young lovers to walk over, for children to frolic in, or for old men to roam idly with their canes. . . .

You thought of homely matters like sun-warmed wooden benches and rocking chairs with cross-stitched cushions; you thought of pale butter gleaming freshly made in a big applewood bowl; you thought of puppies tumbling, and cows mooing peacefully to say that they were ready to be milked. And you thought of a milkmaid, and maybe that was you, yourself, in one of Mrs. Hubbard's blue aprons, going out to pail a cow. Abbie sang in her heart if not with her lips . . . *oh! Lilly, sweet Lilly, dear Lilly Dale* . . . she felt that sadness which might hasten when aprons could no longer be worn, or butter tasted; when flails could no longer beat, or shepherds go hunting lambs; when there was naught but the wild rose that blossomed on the little green grave.

She never saw that grave as her own. It was always Lilly Dale's grave or someone else's. Abbie lingered beside it, wept tenderly, and then went home, filling her bonnet with marigolds on the way. . . .

These were the woods she saw and loved, and lived among, and cherished in recollection as cold weather drew near. Sometimes secretly she guessed that far in advance of wagons one lone artist came walking. He had halted to paint these woods, then had discarded them.

Less illusory were factual recollections of the Gardners' meanderings across summertime prairies. With flowers now fallen prey to evening frosts it was delicious to consider the profusion of an earlier June. . . . Where were they traveling? Abbie couldn't remember, but twas a day when the flowers were a riot all around them. Abbie and Eliza kept climbing down from the wagon, saying, Here's a new one, oh, see, oh, look, oh, sister, I want that, oh, sis, look *there!* So their mother cautioned them, she said that they would disturb their oxen while the animals were drinking. Rowland Gardner sat and smiled; once he laughed out loud with some strange joy, sharing their excitement.

Abbie brought a bundle of fresh flowers in her ragged frock. Please, Pa, what's this?

He took up a wisp between his fingers and rolled the stem gently, and peered into the face of the flower as if the wee blueness might answer—give answer to a question he was asking, yet which he dared not voice.

Reckon this is a lupine.

Oh, Pa, didn't you say that about the pinkish one?

Well, it might have been.

Eliza giggled and whispered to her sister that their father called every strange flower a lupine.

Now see here, daughters.

He cleared his throat.

Once I read a little botany, and I do remember some things. Now, here—this petal part—this is called the corolla—

And what's them three green things underneath, on the back side?

That, he said importantly, is the calyx.

And them pretty little fuzzy things right smack in the middle, Pa? They got yellow on the tips, and they're all fuzz.

I reckon them are pistils.

Pistols? the girls echoed in disbelief. Little Rowly pricked up his ears at the delightful mention of firearms.

This here is a flower kind of pistil; tain't even spelt the same way. It's what makes the flower grow, I guess—got the little seeds in it to start a new one. No— His forehead wrinkled as he thought about it.

No. Them ain't pistils a-tall. Them are stamens. I think the pistil is this green thing in the middle. Well, one or the other of them has *got* to be! And that's why we'll have new flowers again. . . .

Pa, look at these luscious ones *I've* got. I found 'em, Abbie didn't get any! Look, they're kind of pinkish and red. Could these be sort of phlox, like we had in the garden back East?

Could be, he said judiciously. He lifted this new flower to examine it. Could be. Reckon it's a kind of wild phlox. Yes, that's just what it is!

Flocks, flocks, flocks, chanted Rowly. Flocks-of-sheep, flocks-of-sheep—

Bubby, you hush up whilst I try to splain this to the girls. . . . Again his face scrolled sadly. . . . Only I guess there isn't much more I can say. That's about the sum total of my botany knowledge! Well, let's get the critters out of here and get back on the road.

The prairie was all width, all warmth, all pleasure. Larks went crazy around them, crying about the gifts of June, they came down again, came close to show their gold, the black upon their chests, the little dab of white.

Abbie thought, Just one big flower garden!

. . . Mystery of thunder, illusion of ordered park and English oil painting, recollection of flowers. Why should you lie dormant and unheeding, when the active mind could take you roving amid wonders? Eliza was long since gone to Springfield (some folks spoke of the place as Des Moines City or *the* Des Moines City, since this settlement was rising on upper reaches of the river of that name) and Abbie slept now with Ma. Rowland Gardner groaned or whistled in exhausted slumber on his pallet, the Luces were in their own bed, Mandy in her cradle, the two small boys—uncle and nephew—squeezed into a trundle bed. Seven other folks, all lost, gone, unresponsive, drugged—

Not one of them ever wakened to share with Abigail a marvel which befell. Twas on one of the rare chilly nights . . . in the uncertainty of adolescence, an odd experience called her.

Rowland Gardner had left a fire lapping, spitting on the hearth. Abbie did not know what time it was, she was not accustomed to telling time except by the sun. (There was only one watch in the family, and that would not work. Her father kept it in a cigar box with other keepsakes. The family clock had been stolen out of their wagon during the flight to the Shell Rock.) So Abigail awoke, not knowing hour or night or century, floating in space, conscious of the nudge of her mother in the bed, yet lifted somehow beyond, suspended above shabby covers. She lay warm, shrouded; she looked toward the fire.

There sat a little girl.

This was no child of the family nor child of any neighbor. Twas not Agnes Mattock. Abbie had never seen the girl before; she remembered, would remember long, a sheen of firelight on the child's smooth-brushed hair. The visitor leaned forward, never turning her head, regarding intently the blaze. Ever and anon she lifted her hands from her aproned lap and held them out as if they needed momentary warmth, and then drew her hands into her lap again.

The child might have been a real child who wandered from God knows where; she might have been no child at all, might have been a ghost. But she was there, Abbie saw her clearly. She saw frail pale arms go out, watched the palms extend and lift and spread their fingers. This stranger was nothing fierce or misshapen from the woods, no specter equipped with malformations; she had a normal complement of fingers, she warmed her hands.

It was as if she sensed the waking girl nearby, yet was stubborn and would not turn her head, but leaned closer to the fire with each fearful breath that Abbie drew. It was as if she said, I am here, you see me in my calico, my clean gown. I have wandered from somewhere, have come out of space, I sit by your fire. Do you mind? If you mind, twill do you no good. I *shall* sit by your fire!

Abbie boosted herself upright but Frances Gardner did not stir. Never before had Abbie seen anything to tempt her into an expression of mortal disbelief.

The stranger child . . . light danced with charm and caution upon delicate wood-grained hair which cased her head.

Abbie thought: I am so afraid of her, I dare not speak, where does she come from? Is she human, or a fairy from the plain, or a captive of one of the Indians we hear storied about, far beneath the texture of the lake? Someone hidden down there and kept tied? Maybe she has loosed her bonds and run away? No longer does she need to listen to a thudding drum beneath the water. She has come free.

Illusion (if it were illusion) persisted long, and with such striking force that finally, under impact of the repeated blows of realization, Abbie lay back and covered her face. She stared within the comforters, fearing to look out again to prove whether or not she was bereft of wits.

She counseled herself weakly: Now you are a big girl, you are almost a young lady. You have Made the Change, which Ma spoke about in whispers. Yes, you are grown—not to be frighted! You are bold; you killed a snake; you plucked Rowly from the mire when he fell in; you gave warning of the fire which approached—a whole prairie was seething, and even the critters were scairt. But you weren't scairt, or, if you were, you pretended not to be. You were stout enough to cope with such things! Pray rise, stare at the little girl. Challenge her. . . .

She managed to get her claws on the edge of the covers. Wriggling slyly, she rose aloft once more.

She sat up in bed.

Lo and behold!—no child was to be seen—only the empty stool—a chunk of oak which Rowland Gardner had axed, and into which he had inserted three whittled legs. It was there by the fire, but the child was gone, the caging door was shut.

How had the little girl got in or gone out?

This was something Abbie would never dare to relate to her parents, or to Eliza or Mary.

Long did she wonder, later that same night and on subsequent nights, about the advent of the little girl. Where did she come from, why had she come, why were only Abbie's eyes open to see her? In imagining she endowed the other child with a weird past . . . she wondered how old she was. The girl did not appear to be above ten or twelve—not as old as Abbie. Yet there were serenity and fortitude about her. Abbie saw her so clearly in recollection—she could have drawn a picture, had she been sufficiently talented with her pencil.

Before dawn she found courage to sneak up and try the door. No, twas not barred; no one had remembered to slide the bar into place, it didn't slide well. It was held by a crotch at one end and by an awkward notch, cut into thick wood, at the other. Twas not a good bar; and often enough her parents neglected completely to put it in place, when they were very tired. So the door had not been barred, and that might have been the way in which a stranger could have crept inside. But why did the Gardners and Luces not hear the creak of hinges?

Was the child a demon in pinafore? Was she a sprite sent by some malevolence in the outside world, to lure Abbie or other children, to guide them into treachery?

Was she but a family wraith, stealing from past or future?

(Ah, the hidden, the inscrutable, the never-to-be-told!)

. . . Where did you come from, Other Little Girl? Were you real? Were you merely a trick of my mind, because we are in a lonely place, and lead a lonely existence? Did a mover's wagon stop nearby, and did you wander from it? Were you walking in your sleep, and did you return to your wagon again? Did wheels revolve, come morning, and did you and all the other people go wrenching off into western space? . . .

Lonely child, lonely fire, lonely souls asleep and awake. . . . An unidentified poet's voice lived within Abbie and reiterated these things. There was nothing in her surroundings to stimulate the psalm, the truant verses she made. Yet worship lived on. A secret fragrance stayed with her until she was grown taller by a few months, and brutalities came, with horror enough to wipe from recollection any truant perfume of a dream, any calico figure who danced therein or sat motionless by the fire, warming her hands.

Rowland Gardner owned his private consideration of wraiths, his private love of them. If Abbie's fancies had been reported to him (by process unknown) he would have been too shy and restrained to question her further, to discuss or speculate. Had he perceived that his neighbor Mrs. Marble—miles away on the Spirit Lake margin—witnessed that spectacle recorded by the poet Freneau, he might even have greeted the idea with humor. Like most primitive visionaries, he thought that his spooks were the only ones. He became acquainted with them during one morning of the previous summer when he walked on a solitary ramble—to prospect for log-trees of the proper size, he'd announced; but actually he went to rid himself temporarily of his son-in-law's company.

There was constant light rain. Mist lay afflictive on the lakes, wind walked with a slight chill. You could hear wind speaking amid old oaks high above; young oaks gave their own reply, they mingled in conversation, waved downturned branches restlessly. Gardner strolled the woods for perhaps fifty rods, and then turned toward the shore line, climbing as he went. There was a shapeless mound running along much of the shore, formed he did not know how: perhaps by erosion, perhaps by original retreat of the glacier which had left these wide wet pockets on the landscape; or possibly it resulted from the extended pushing of ice cakes, with rocks washed up by storms through the centuries. The mound spread higher and became a hill. When Gardner reached the summit he was standing twenty or thirty feet above the water. Here again were young trees; their leaves were different, their sleek green acorns different, many of them, from the few he had seen and remembered back East. He thought of the names of trees which he had read in one of the emigrants' guidebooks: white oak, red oak, bur oak, black oak; there were many, he didn't know them all. And all would be hard to cut. He stood in the low drift of sumac which spilled up over thicketed cliffsides, and saw that some sumac leaves were already coloring.

Best get about it, wind said above his ears. Twill be different in December.

He tried to dramatize his own position to himself and thus take a courage he might not have possessed otherwise. He tried to tell himself that he was standing on his native heath (but he had done that before, and always he left that native heath to find another).

The opposite shores did not mock him, they remained placid under touch of thickening rain, and under light breezes which must be melting among those distant mist-drenched trees. He could not see them tossing, the wind was not strong enough for that; but surely breezes moved there, as they moved about the tall sad lonely man here—where they walked with the cool importance of breezes untamed, not subservient to any agency.

Rain increased, it was pelting him now. He turned out the brim of his old hat so that water would drip free from his body and not run down his neck. The lake itself was made of zinc, soft zinc, the mere thought of zinc. Coves were many and mysterious, and which of them harbored an enemy? Rowland Gardner felt his hands empty of any gun, and shook his head: it was unwise to wander thus unarmed. He thought of wicked forms stealing up through the brush, those same mad shapes he had glimpsed in his dream, and whom he had seen do ill to his family and to himself. He shook his head again.

Might have been better off back in Rexville? . . . No, no, this was right! This was the place! Everything must be here; richness fought its way, tangling up the steep hillside; there were a few reeds in the lake, a few willows at the edge, and then began the tangle. Sumac, of course, and five-leaved ivy. Bits of red showing there, like Indian feathers . . . and this seemed to be some kind of light young cherry. It had bark like a cherry tree, although so small and slender. And here was one of the cherries, dangling before his eyes. Gardner picked it off, bit into the small orb, and instantly the portion of his mouth and tongue which touched it felt puckered. Ah, no good, no black cherry.

The choke variety, he said aloud.

Now the lake seemed truly to mock him, it grew glassy when the wind slowed. Then it rifted and puckered, like tissue of his own mouth on nibbling the cherry. And what was behind all that mist, and where were the wild people whom he dreaded?

There had been a story about Spirit Lake: the wandering trapper Jo Harshman told it— Yes, Spirit Lake, but might it not apply to the Okobojis as well, since all were part of the same pattern? Indians said that these waters were haunted; the Indians must know. They said that half of their people were dwelling underneath the surface still. In a faraway age all the tribes had dwelt down there; and then one young man, more explorative than the rest, had approached the edge of this underwater paradise and seen a great root hanging down. He grasped the root as he might grasp a rope. He climbed and climbed, and burst forth into the day, the sunshine above. He shook the water off his body, and stood drying in the sun, and then called his excitement back to his mates. So the rest of the folks started climbing, one after another—man and squaw and little child—they ascended, until a goodly portion of the nation had progressed into dry daylight, all shaking the water off them, and laughing because they stood in the sun. And then another woman tried to climb up the root. She was a pregnant woman; her weight was too much, the root snapped in two, and back she fell, and there was a cry. . . . The lake lay motionless, unblemished by emerging figures; and underneath the tribes remained, the others left there. So they were there today; this the Indians said. The root had broken, there was no other link, no way for them to emerge.

But, said the Indians, if you went back, if you dared to go back and abide by the water at night and in certain seasons, you could hear the others underneath. Sometimes they were calling up, sometimes blaming their freed brethren for leaving; sometimes they were saying, Come back! Sometimes they were saying, We are dancing, but you cannot dance with us because you do not dwell beneath the waves.

Oh, yes, and the sound of their drums could be heard when there was a storm, they were drumming and yelling.

And who was the better off?—Gardner wondered, perusing this legendry. The ones who had emerged?—or those or were soaked and sodden, far down in the depths, actually making fires where fires could not be built, putting up tipis? What did they fashion them out of—the skins of fish? And dancing, always dancing when the time was right. . . .

Gardner declared that he heard the percussive thud of a distant drum, a submerged and wet one. He turned away from the shore.

He thought, Ah, no drum! What this country needs is the sound of axes going into wood. Leave us make that sound!

As he returned to the wagons his imagination was haunted by a notion of those aborigines beneath the water. Only from gleanings in picture books could he imagine how they might dance. He knew that they shuffled in a circle . . . he had seen the pictures, he had heard stories. He knew so little about Indians. He knew so little, yet he felt so much. And the very dampness of the lake had reached out and infected him, and made him different from the Gardner who came driving hither two weeks before.

He concocted a mixed-up confusion of all the Indians he had ever seen or heard about or seen pictured, or who had populated his nightmares. He saw them with shaven heads, long braids, long black unrestrained hair hanging loose. He saw them with shells around their necks, and bear claws. He saw them barefoot, or wearing many types of moccasins, and fringed leggings with scalp-hair on the seams. He saw them stark naked, or dressed in white men's breeches, or wrapped in blankets . . . still dancing, far underneath . . . and the fish sped away from them, the frogs were numbed and humbled.

Deep tone of their throbbing tom-toms was like a chorus of monster bullfrogs, and when the whitecaps blew free, as they must in more violent storms– Well, that would be the feathers a-blowing!

Now they had buffalo horns fashioned in some way so that they might adorn their heads; they had their weapons in their hands: stone axes, sharp metallic axes bought from traders. They waved arrows and guns and spears, and lances with decorations, they circled and yelled. If you stood there in nighttime, could you see the gleam of their fire coming up—a dull redness? Could you make out shapes passing the blaze, and hear the screams of captives they tortured? Was it a war dance, or was it an imploring for some benefit to be given by the gods? He did not know. But all the way back to the wagon he heard them pounding and jumping in the lake alongside him.

XXII

In desperation Inkpaduta had announced to Charles Flandrau that he would steal and he would kill again. It was bluster on his part; at this time actually he had no intention of making war or even effecting a sneaky murder. He could recall vividly his brief captivity of a few years before, when he had been a prisoner of the white soldiers, held as a hostage in order to accelerate the return of some property stolen from settlers in the Boyer River country. The sight of an ornate blue jacket worn by Flandrau had awakened unpleasant recollections of the Fort Dodge outhouse in which Inkpaduta was locked with one companion. Sometimes their jailer neglected to feed the captives for two or three days on end, and even then there was very little meat offered: they were given scraps from the common mess, which seemed to include cooked grass and other things which the captives did not relish. There was a guard who often amused himself by spitting tobacco between the crude bars of the window. Soldiers laughed and talked to each other about this as they gathered outside. Inkpaduta did not understand what they said, but he felt the sting of the juice in his eye. He remembered how voices had sounded.

. . . What you up to, Casey?

. . . Trying to hit that smaller one in there. Already hit the big one.

. . . Hell, you ain't half the ex-pec-tor-*at*-or that I am!

. . . I'll lay you two bits.

. . . Hell, you ain't got two bits.

. . . Lay you a glass at the sutler's.

. . . Done!

Splah!

. . . Ah ha, you missed, Lew.

. . . Son-of-a-bitch dodged, that's what's the matter. But I ought to get three tries. Don't I get two more tries?

. . . You take two more tries, then I'll take my three.

Splah!

. . . Missed the little one, by God. You hit the big one again!

Inkpaduta planned to steal at the first opportunity, however. He should not steal while he was anywhere near the Lower Agency: Fort

Ridgely lay too close, and those soldiers traveled rapidly, on good horses or on long-legged mules. When he and his sons reached an area less occupied by bands of law-abiding Wahpekute (these he wished to avoid, because they despised him so roundly) they planned to steal—steal anything—chickens, beeves, food of any kind—or more especially, horses. The outlaws had journeyed up to the Minnesota on foot for it was essential that they leave their horses behind. There were but a handful of ponies now owned by Inkpaduta's people, and most of those ponies were in poor condition; still they would be needed for hauling. The Little-Stream-of-the-Hot-Water: (they were moving to this Minikata) lay a short distance south and west of the Okobojis; a warm spring gave the place its name. It had long been a favorite camping ground during late autumn and early winter if the season were a mild one, as this was being mild. Rattle-Strike and the others were directed to remove there. And few good lodgepoles could be found in the Little-Stream-of-the-Hot-Water region—*Echahe!*—ponies were essential to make the move.

Inkpaduta and his sons tramped long and hard, as recently the father had tramped those plains west of the Missouri River. Anyone observing them might have thought that they traveled tirelessly, but in fact they grew very weary. It was the weariness of frustration. The fact that long-sought annuities had again been refused them lay like soggy rags around Inkpaduta's heart. His sons were slightly more philosophical about the matter: almost they had no recollection of any life except that of outlawry and privation. Their father might entertain a memory of beaded elk-skin shirts, many horses, droves of fat buffalo rounded up and driven gleefully over riverside precipices, decorated pipe bags, feathered lances with obsidian points— *Hehehe!*—it was difficult to believe now, but once Inkpaduta had carried a shield of buffalo hide garnished with eagle feathers; once he possessed three wives, all young; one time he gave feasts, and wore an otter-skin robe for fine dress; in gambling he staked two or even three ponies on the single lifting of a moccasin!— None of these glories could be remembered by the twins. They had grown up in mendicancy, they had inherited little except the scorn of adjacent tribesmen and an addiction to violence. Somehow a terror of the elder gods was still theirs (as such terror was embraced stubbornly by their father) but they had been trained in none of the ancient courtesies. If they were aware of traditional deportment it was but to flout all custom. Their wives showed no reluctance to speak coarsely and directly to Inkpaduta, never hesitated to look him in the face, except perhaps when he threatened them overtly. Boldly their wives used the names of Roaring-Cloud and Fire-Cloud when speaking of their husbands; the wives did not say, This child's father, as other Wahpekute would have done. And in his turn Inkpaduta addressed his daughters-in-law directly, heedlessly, and did not hesitate to use their names. Rattle-Strike, his son-in-law, talked crudely to Inkpaduta, looking on his face as he did so. No one in the band hesitated at using the names of others, or in revealing their own names. Ceremonial feasts went uncelebrated as a rule. The twins had never known the discipline of a soldier society. Their women stole from each other; so did other women of their dirty herd; children died of neglect, or went undisciplined and uninstructed if they managed to survive.

The night after leaving the Redwood region the three disgruntled travelers slept supperless. At least they could know the comfort of a fire, for in this country it was safe for them to sleep beside the flames. With empty stomachs sour and protesting, they renewed their march at the scratch of dawn. They tried to kill birds, missed killing the birds, the brothers railed at each other; Inkpaduta stalked silently, hating his sons, jealous of their youth, wishing to find horses he might steal. In a belated glaring sunrise two smokes were discerned to the southeast, smokes which they had not seen on their upward journey. They studied those faint low streamers and decided that they came from houses built recently by white settlers: clearly they were not a sign of Wahpekute camps, there was not enough smoke, the wisps arose singly and seemed shaped by chimneys. Accordingly the men altered the direction of their tramping, and soon were rewarded by encountering a yellow dog, lop-eared and whining, which had strayed away from house or wagon. This dog was hungry, and desperately seeking human companionship. It ran straightway into their hands, and was brained in an instant. Inkpaduta munched raw heart and liver while his sons built a weed fire and roasted, more or less, the rest of the carcass. . . . They went on toward the nearest smoke.

Here was a spanking sod house filled with newly settled Germans. These people were stricken by the advent of three armed Indians; the only Indians whom they'd met previously were of the Christianized variety and did not at all resemble Inkpaduta and Fire-Cloud and Roaring-Cloud. Responsive to the growling of their visitors, the trembling Germans fetched out fried cakes and pork which they'd just prepared for their own meal. Five pairs of round blue eyes (eyes of a young man and woman, eyes of their two little girls, eyes of the baby boy) watched as the precious food was swallowed down. . . . *Ach!* was it now that all of them would be tortured to death? Otto Rager clenched his big fists; but his gun was unloaded, and the Indians had thrown his axe out into the grass, and his shovel lay up on the sod roof. Would now he be able to fight with his bare hands? Sweat pearled out on Otto's peeling forehead– And Uncle Klaus and his brothers and sisters had warned of just such dangers, before Otto brought his family away from impoverished safety of that beautiful cottage near Plauen, in Saxony–

Ate, said Roaring-Cloud, sniffing happily as he glared at the terrified young Mrs. Rager. *Ate!* We take woman?

Nay. It is too near. Soldiers come.

You say you kill!—sneered Roaring-Cloud. You do not kill. You do not even take woman!

It is too near Agency, too near Fort. You are Head Man?

Nay, father. I am not Head Man. . . . We kill oxen?

Inkpaduta debated the question with himself briefly. Cattle-killing, this close to Fort Ridgely, might bring a summary penalty. Nay! Break gun, he said.

Accordingly they ruined Mr. Rager's musket by pounding off the hammer, and then performed a mild plundering of the shanty. There was not much for them to take; they took a bag of coffee and a box of gun caps and whatever sugar they could find; they did not wish to load themselves heavily. Inkpaduta, past master at this sort of freebooting, knew that he and his sons would be pursued across dry easily traveled prairies if their depredations were considered too relentless. Soldiers would not deign to follow them, prompted merely by the theft of food from these poor settlers, the mere spoiling of a gun. If they shot oxen, soldiers might come. If they took woman, soldiers might come. If they killed whites, most surely soldiers would come.

He said *Witkotkoka!* Fool! In winter we steal more, we take women in winter. It is hard for soldiers to follow us in winter! Never now! We are not one full sleep away from the Agency!

He said, We go.

They left this petrified family and went on toward the second smoke. It was very close; you could even see the sod cabin, a wad against a ridge, when you looked south from the breaking which had been plowed around the house-of-white-people-with-all-blue-eyes. As they bore steadily down, prepared for a fresh victimizing, they received a disconcerting surprise. Two tall men moved out from the tunnel-like doorway and stood waiting with rifles in their hands. The approach had been witnessed; and these men would fight, they might even shoot while the Dakota were approaching.

We go, ordered Inkpaduta again.

They changed their course, bearing to the west. They could feel the white men gazing after them. The three Indians did not once turn their heads, they ignored the place as if they had not seen it, did not care to see it (they had killed and eaten the lost puppy of these white men, but they did not know that. Nor did the white men know, nor would they ever learn of the summary butchering and breakfast. They would wonder what on earth had happened to Bowser, they would not know that Bowser passed his own dooryard with no farewell salute, lurching half digested within fierce brown bellies).

. . . Just hunters, I guess, Elmo.

. . . Maybe so. I didn't like their looks.

. . . Aw, most of these dusty-noses won't bother no one. They even got a preacher for them, up Redwood way!

. . . Maybe so. But let's hustle over to the Dutchman's, see if everything's all right.

. . . Naw, hell. I'm holler. Less finish eating first.

Many hours' journey to the south, somewhere between headwaters of the Watonwan and the big bend of the upper Des Moines River, the Indians observed a bundle of insect shapes progressing sluggishly across a ridge before them. *Shuktanka!* they whispered, and that would have been enough to bring them out of doze and monotony of weary pacing in any season, but especially now. Aye, horses!—three horses! The Wahpekute went down into a prairie hollow to mumble about it . . . horses and a wagon, two horses drawing the wagon, a led horse behind. And they moved slowly, slowly—it would be a simple matter to overtake them. But Inkpaduta, whose wars or raids were plotted to incur the least possible risk to himself, ruled that the wagon's occupants must be scrutinized with care. Accordingly he and his sons sped down a watercourse which twisted before them, and gave opportunity for them to take up a station further along the route which it seemed was being traversed. From time to time he sent one of the others up to higher prairie, to crouch concealed amid the grass, and observe. *Inyun!* Truly!—still the wagon poked along toward the east. It seemed that two people rode on the seat; no one else accompanied the wagon either mounted or afoot. At last, from a brake of dry willows, the Dakota heard a plaint of ungreased wheels, the snorting, the clank and harness-song approaching. The wagon came up over a lip of prairie, halted, turned left, went on at a lurch, halted again, and nearly upset as it turned back to the right. Now there appeared to be but one person on the seat, a woman; and she was baffled as to how to proceed. The bandits trotted downhill and caught up with the wagon before it reached the creek. Awareness of their presence came to the woman only when the twins seized the team's bridles, and Inkpaduta himself climbed up to peer into the box and glower at her. She screamed long and loud. But even her shrieks could not awaken a man who lay amid kegs and bundles of blankets, with one boot still caught up on the leather-cushioned board from which he had fallen over backward.

Witko! Inkpaduta cried with delight. He is drunk.

Good, good. Then there is spirit water in this wagon?

Aye, if he drinks not all of it!

The woman yells much. You hit her on the head?

Nay. We will not. We do not need to kill. . . .

She yells, she yells loudly!

No one hears.

The wagon belonged to the sot who lay in it, one Payton Lorimer, who was known on the frontier as Honest Pay, because he had been run out of at least a half-dozen communities for forgery, larceny, wife-beating, sodomy, and other demonstrations of solid virtue. Honest Pay's latest venture had been an expedition to the Pipestone region, where he intended to sell whiskey to those tribes who, he'd learned, visited this sacred but popular quarry frequently. Physical anguish overwhelmed Mr. Lorimer before he reached his goal. These days he had a gnawing nagging fiery sensation in his middle which he feared to be cancer, and it was assuaged only by copious draughts of vinegar. Two jugs of vinegar had been smashed to smithereens in an upsetting of the wagon; thus he ran short in supply. Bereft of vinegar, he began on his own stock of whiskey. This was unfortunate, since the kegs had been filled according to a common formula which included not only cheap trade whiskey but spring water, tobacco plugs, and cayenne pepper as well. Honest Pay had heard that the Indians preferred strong liquor and had been determined to gratify their taste. His consort, a woebegone trull named Lulu (they'd met some years earlier when he became her visitor in a bawdyhouse on the edge of Galena) was not actually his wife by bell-and-book; but she suffered as acutely as any sedately wedded Mrs. Lorimer might have suffered. She'd wailed at Lorimer to return to the settlements; Honest Pay didn't wish to go back, he was sure he'd make a fortune out of selling his horrid concoction to unsophisticated Indians of the plains; but internal agonies compelled him finally to yield. The Lorimers were in the second day of their eastbound about-face journey when the Wahpekute spied them. Honest Pay had been drunk since noon, and unable to drive; but he was able to roost on the seat until the past few minutes, then he toppled back upon the load.

Inkpaduta ignored the woman. In exhaustion she ceased her wails, and shrank away, chewing her hand, as the old Indian peered into her husband's face and even gave him a tentative shake or two.

Witko! he affirmed to the others. This is true! He drinks much.

He hauled around at the man's clothing until he found a pocket containing the wallet which most white men carried. Inkpaduta ripped open the pocket and extracted a pouch. It proved to contain three gold coins and some silver and pennies.

Mon-ee, he growled. *Mazaska!* He rebuttoned the wallet and jammed it under his belt.

His sons were unfastening harness from the team. These horses are old, they reported to their father. But they are strong. We take?

Aye, we take. Is old also other horse behind?

He is younger. Nay, it is *shuktanka wiye,* it is a mare. She is mine? asked Roaring-Cloud, although knowing very well what the answer would be.

I take mare. I am Head Man.

Roaring-Cloud and Fire-Cloud were not too familiar with the harness of white men, so with their knives they cut most of it away; they tied the team to the sides of the wagon, and crawled up to rummage along with their father. Whiskey they found in two barrels; and now the twins regretted that they had cut the harness; were this team still hitched to the wagon, they would be able to carry off the entire cargo. Such a hope was expunged promptly by their father. Inkpaduta had no wish to be so burdened. Who knew who these people were? They might have friends among the soldiers! They might have companions who traveled behind and were even now drawing close. Unimpeded by the wagon, the robbers could travel hastily, freely, toward their new camp below West Okoboji.

None of them wished to possess this woman. . . .

She is old!

Aye, old. She is ugly!

Aye, ugly. *Shicha!*

They found seven Army canteens which Honest Pay had procured from a corrupt sergeant at Fort Snelling. They filled these canteens from a barrel in which the bung had already been loosed. A rusty tin cup was handy. They began to drink, grunting and gasping with stimulation as the stuff burned them. There was a stone jug from which the inert Lorimer dosed himself; they filled that up again. Fire-Cloud labored seriously to tie this jug snugly on one of the horses with scraps of harness. No second jug could be discovered, nor any other small receptacle in which whiskey might be lugged away. Some raw bacon was found, they consumed that; they found brown sugar, and ate it all; there was nothing else in the meager store of eatables to tempt them, although the twins achieved a sport in flinging handfuls of cornmeal about.

Roaring-Cloud lifted his hatchet, preparing to burst open the whiskey barrels and thus destroy what they might not carry off, but Inkpaduta roared at him to desist.

We take horses! Who pulls wagon? This woman?

Nay, woman cannot pull wagon. . . .

She walks! When the man awakens, he walks also. They cannot carry barrels of spirit water with them! They must leave it behind, it is here, we know where it lies, no other person knows!

And one day we come again, for more spirit water! cried the enchanted sons. *Ate,* thou knowest much!

Okiksamya waun, said Inkpaduta modestly. I am acting wisely.

They had not harmed the woman to any serious extent, they had but cuffed her when she tottered in their way. They knew a little about bits, had seen bits on other occasions when they stole horses from white people; thus they left bits in the horses' mouths as they lashed the demoralized creatures away from that pillaged wagon. All but Inkpaduta's mare; she wore a simple halter, he would handle her so. A slightly battered Lulu huddled on the wagon seat, wringing her hands and attempting to pray. The Wahpekute had no pity for her (though her appearance might have extracted at least a few squirts of pity from almost any other dry hearts: her torn dirty frock, hard wings of shoulder blades squeezing out against colorless fabric, the graying hair like cords, yellowish eyes in pale pink sockets, the blubbering lip and reedy voice). They spat in her general direction as they left.

Owanyah shicha! Roaring-Cloud sneered in parting. How ugly you are!

No one fucks you! cried his brother.

No one fucks her, no one wishes to, she is a bone, she is an old bone that the dogs chew and cast aside! Ugly!

Aye, agreed their father, riding ahead. *Shicha!*

This was the only charity befalling poor Lulu on this day: the fact that she could not know what was said. Their abuse and condemnation, mouthed thus unintelligibly, might in no way affect the hopeless drab, might in no way increase her destitution. She retained memories still, though they squatted unexamined and unsavored in the back of her brain. But there had been a time when a man gave her a gold locket, a time when another man gave her real pearl earrings, a time when she had a stuffed reticule hidden under her mound of sweaty feather beds . . . there'd been seasons of her first youth in New Orleans when she knew the taste of oysters, and pigeon breasts poached in wine . . . in St. Louis she was the veritable queen of Paul Essart's Pleasure Parlors, and had four silk dresses and God knew how many satin petticoats, and a chemise edged in pink lace, and a jet marabou tippet, and was famed among the steamboat men as Leaping Lulu. Now she was sickly, bruised, foodless, horseless, moneyless. Her papery hands ached from the reins, they were wounded from adjusting those buckles which Honest Pay had been too incompetent to fasten. She did not know how to rouse her husband, she did not know when he would awaken, did not know *if* he would awaken. Where was the nearest house, the nearest white people? She did not know. She kept crying.

Mocking voices floated back to her. *Shicha! Shicha!*

(You are old, said the vast impervious November sky. You are old, and you are not well, and you are bereft of sustenance and opportunity, and you are out here, and you are alone. And winter will descend. And you have nothing. Nothing, said the silent sky.)

The Wahpekute hustled away toward the Iowa border, drinking as they rode. When they reached the Des Moines River it was considered sensible to push their horses along through the shallows for a time, to break their trail. Then over hills and on down prairies, with spirit water speaking in wet voices within the canteens, spirit water hot inside them and knifing their gullets each time they swallowed. They halted before dusk, made a fire; drank more spirit water, were not hungry because they drank; they bragged and squawked and sang, they drank again. Roaring-Cloud fell across the edge of the fire and burnt his left arm; next morning his forearm was huge with blisters. That day they found the new abode of their people on the Little-Stream-of-the-Hot-Water, and rode into camp in a mutually poisonous mood. Corn-Sucker came timidly to greet Inkpaduta and received a kick in the face before he'd dismounted.

Every man of the group and one woman also lay drunk when winter struck, on the day which followed. The cross-grained wife of He-Has-Done-Walking, who was always tormenting and twitting Corn-Sucker, and trying to steal from her— This harridan had tumbled in a posture of abandon (skirt pulled up and legs open) on bare ground opposite the door of her own lodge. The Hidatsa woman saved the harpy's life soon after snow howled over them all. She caught the big body by its shoulders and dragged the monster into her own tipi; but still this woman had lain outside long enough to be half-frozen, and when she roused it was to mourn about her throbbing hands and feet, and to condemn Corn-Sucker for leaving her exposed for so long. Three other wives were not completely drunk, but might be considered tipsy, and were not good for much when it came to making a belated defense against disaster. The brunt fell upon Corn-Sucker and upon Cloud-Woman, the wife of He-Wears-Anything; and upon Woman-Shakes-With-Cold, Inkpaduta's daughter. This unfortunate had seen her father stupefied on scores of other occasions, had seen her husband and her twin brothers in the same condition, as they were fallen now. She bore a corrugated scar extending from her left eye socket up into her hair—a souvenir of Inkpaduta's tenderness when, at the age of twelve, she had sought to minister to his need.

Children ran berserk, or were heaped whining for food among lice-ridden robes, in the lodges.

Hay! We must cut hay, more and more! cried Corn-Sucker. Have thee knife, my sister?

Aye, Cloud-Woman gasped, I have knife.

Hasten, hasten, we must cut! O daughter of That Old One, do thou bring logs and branches to cover hay— Else we die!

Unkinyankapi! shrieked the unhappy and aptly named Woman-Shakes-With-Cold. We run!

They toiled savagely in screaming wind on the prairie above their narrow creek valley, chopping hay. They crammed it into sacks fashioned quickly of trade blankets. Howling air tried to dash and swirl the cut grasses away from them, the bent toiling women tussled against fine snow which struck with the velocity of bullets, they stumbled back down to the six lodges and dumped their loads against pegged tipi covers. Woman-Shakes piled brush, stones, broken logs over the hay to hold it down; fierce bitter sleet helped to cement this banked insulation. There was time to attend to but three lodges. Quite naturally they served the lodge of Corn-Sucker and Woman-Shakes the first of all, for that was where Inkpaduta dwelt nowadays. Next the lodge of Cloud-Woman; next, the lodge of the twins' wives . . . they were scarcely able to circle this with torn grass and debris before snow was gashing too thickly, violently; twas too deep up on the prairie, they could cut no more hay.

Three and four and five miles away, in homes protected for the moment by lakeside timber, white people were cowed by this ice and screech, and some of them marked it down in their almanacs: Monday, the very first day of December. That was when it began, that was not when it ended.

The snow was a pale woman whom you might have loved one time, but now she was dead. Still she came haunting and walking and licking, so you identified her as a vampire. She was all around you; you had little strength to avoid her murderous caresses, scarcely did you have the will and wish. Once she'd owned charms and pleasantries; she'd danced before you in her bangles, she'd rippled frosty skirts in the wind to provoke you, exhibited her white satin flounces; and had made you feel vigorous and capable as you witnessed. But now her hollow teeth went into you. Maybe you suffered fever but she drained you of it promptly. With serene clammy confidence she sought to make you one with the frigidity of her own teats and talons. This she knew she would do, and she sang about it in your ears . . . steel wind humming far across the prairies, and wiring around your head and going into your ears and coming bitterly out of your nose. Your blood pulsed, chilling away and freezing and vanishing under drainage established by the snow's white fangs, the snow's white syringes.

There had been states in which you had admired snow, felt snow to be a benefit. You could remember those conditions now. . . .

First off there were watery cracked windowpanes; on these the fairies made their paintings; you breathed to dispel them. You put up a tiny finger and made messes of the ferns, and then a hole appeared—a porthole in frost. Through this aperture you saw the snow beyond. It was cake and icing, a wide-extended comfit, arching smooth and rounded and sugary, with pines black-green beyond the border. It was cut into delightful candy drifts . . . the wan candles gleamed in Mr. Mansfield's distant house. You could see them yellow over the paleness when it was only midafternoon and the sky clung dark above.

A wild small bird flew, hunting shelter from storms; and another came to join him, and they teetered and danced amid the pines, and twitched their little crests as they peeped at you and at the window. You heard your mother talk about putting out crumbs for the birds. She put them out; fugitive birds descended whirling to fetch the crumbs away. A jay came too (you thought he was a bluebird), you heard the rasp of jays' voices bickering, snow seeming to swallow the sound, and you longed to go and roll in it.

In a later winter you were wound in flannel scarves. Barely could you remember that box sled: a cubical green box, fastened atop Big Brother's sled. Granther was dragging you, and turning around to leer delightedly at the swaddled child he hauled along, his faded wet eyes throwing out a joyous flame from beneath the ragged fur of his cap. You rode and rode with a heavy knitted cap of your own shoved down around your ears, breath freezing on the flannel in front of your face, your nose running; but forever you were loving the snow.

When you were older you tried to make a sliding sleigh of your own; but Granther helped you with the runners because you could not get them right. Twas done at last: a low sleek thing, scarce more than six inches high from bottom of the runners to top of the sled. Wooden runners they were, with holes bored out to make them lighter, and thus make the sled fleeter.

And Uncle Mephib (his name was really Mephibosheth, because he was the son of Granther Jonathan, and was lame in both his feet, as related in Second Samuel) was sparking one of the Kimball spinsters, when a new storm came, a heavy one. Uncle Mephib couldn't get home on his clubfeet, and had to sleep on the floor for two nights in front of the Kimball fire, and how he was teased about it later!

So you did Uncle Mephib's chores—his morning chores and his evening chores in addition to your own. Very wearying tasks they were: so much feed to be got down, so much milking, so much feeding of the pigs; all in addition to your own wood-splitting and chopping and lugging of wood, and cutting of the ice, and fetching in of water.

So Uncle Mephib appeared limping, two days late, sheepish and full of explanations and apologies. When he saw the way you had done his work, he said, By cracky, boy, I'll reward you.

That week he took your sled away with him in the pung, and carried it down to Mr. Dill the blacksmith. Both Mr. Dill and Uncle Mephib had been in battle one time, fighting the British from behind barricades at a place called Sackett's Harbor. Mr. Dill would do just about anything that Uncle Mephib wanted him to do. So when Unk brought back your sled it had been freshly painted: a pale red, almost pink, and the letters across the top of the sled said *Fly Away,* and had little wiggly lines, intended to be wings, arching out from them. Best of all, Mr. Dill had put iron runners on the bottom of the wooden ones, and honed them up until they were sharp. How you could tear, if the hills were the least bit icy!

You flew away, away, snow loving you, you loving it. Down you bounded; you whipped round the curve in the old steep lane, not the tortuous shallow lane . . . woods were fuzzy on both sides, coming up dark out of snow so pure . . . you throwing your weight to one side of the sled, curving your legs around, kicking your boots in the air as you went, to balance and turn and guide. There were two deer, stark in the middle of the lane, cast in metal like images of deer watching you; you gave a yell which was only a sigh to warn them; they went bounding away through and over the deadfalls; you didn't hit the deer, you merely frightened them. On you went, on you soared, on you glided more tractably when you came to a level place, then speeded on the next slope. Your *Fly Away* could flee farther than any other sled on the mountain.

Over the sharp edge of the road you went—bounced down into the Clarks' garden and plunged into a snowdrift. You like to broke your neck! Mr. Clark came out, pulling at his beard, and asked did you drop from Mars. You felt very silly, with old hollyhock stalks sticking up out of the snow all around you, and the numb tingle of your chin . . . you put up your hand. Blood was beginning to come, because it was a scrape as well as a bruise; you rubbed blood on the back of your hand and looked at the back of your hand. Blood seemed freezing into splintery bits; and your bare hand might have frozen, too, had it not been for the Clarks: you'd lost a mitten on the way.

In you went, with a handful of snow to rub across your chin, though Mrs. Clark insisted on dousing it with arnica. What a face you made! And how you gritted your teeth, and the whistle went through them when the arnica stung! But you couldn't make much of a yell, because Reba Clark was watching from the kitchen door . . . long brown braids hanging Indian fashion down the sides of her round cheeks, down along her smooth neck (again, you thought of snow).

Inside that neat house was the glow of fire, the acrid smell of washing with soft soap, the smell of pease porridge—the pungency of a frosted cheese nubbin from the shanty and the half-frozen slab of minced pie which Mrs. Clark gave you for a snack. Then you were going up the mountain again, touching your chin with tentative fingers in the unfamiliar mitten with which they had provided you . . . dragging the *Fly Away* sled, and thinking a little of Reba Clark, because you were thirteen now and could think of girls. And remembering wilder and wilder that long soaring seeking flight down the mountain . . . deer rigid, watching you, then spilling away through the snow. Oh, pure the snow, and decent and good, and promising to the taste even when it hurt you.

But those were light-minded joys, savored by a childish soul as round and pink as a stripèd winter apple put away in a barrel.

She came like a witch, this snow, now in your maturity; she would not let you have maturity for long, she intended to stifle and terminate your struggle, and expunge all elder years before they began. She had every fang, every claw, every weapon for her freezing hideous program; she laughed in your teeth and in her own. O termagant storm, with knives for grinning, and light salty rustle for her laughing! —she had her own joke and would never share it; and the dead leaves and birds went blowing down without your seeing them and without her caring—there was no remorse or explanation left—only the storm and bitter cold, only thickening persistent snow.

The tempest drove against a once tender world for three days, three nights, into the fourth day. It stunned the Wahpekute in their tiny village. No one of them, not even the eldest (when at last all the spirit water was consumed, Inkpaduta emerged into frantic consciousness . . . he tried to remember . . .) could recall readily a winter storm of such intensity. As it ceased the world lay gagged, there was no whisper in woodlands, only a groan of dying wind from low hills which humped away beyond. On level ground the starchy deposit reached nearly to Corn-Sucker's shoulders. She and the other women fought stubbornly, mauling and bucking to reach a sparse island of willows with sentinel cottonwoods above. Wood must be fetched, no matter what the price, no matter if they perished as they floundered. Every scrap of wood in the camp was used up—the fingered limbs of brush which had been dragged to hold the banking of prairie grass —the talons of stump-roots— These had been clawed out long since and fed to the fires. The outcasts pressed together under their robes, suffering drearily in mutual stench as children mourned, as last morsels of muskrat disappeared.

. . . Why come you to this lodge? We have no food.

. . . *Unkiye unchuwitapi.* We are cold.

. . . Our fire is small!

. . . We have no fire, we have no wood. Our fire dies! We are cold . . . we come. . . .

Plated over the landscape was a crust of white iron; it could slice into your skin like a knife if you were careless. The contour of slopes was altered, the creek had disappeared, a low valley glared hard and lifeless up against a taunting sun. Fathom by fathom the women hacked their path to the willows, they ripped and whittled to gather precious fragments. In wood there was life. You could not eat wood, but the lean flames ate it. Spirits in the flames cried for wood, spirits reached out their shredded hands. More fuel, more fuel! said spirits-living-in-flames. Feed us or we die!

(Leagues away into the north, the decent Wahpekute reposed snugly in their homes . . . you held a vague thought of such comfort. Ice had bound them tight as it bound all the world; but they had wood because they worked for it, they had meat because they worked at hunting; their lodge covers were tightly banked, the decorated dew-cloths made second canopies inside to retain the heat. Pots would be bubbling, no matter how winds raved outside. No matter how deep the whiteness, corn was ready to be munched. Children played little games among themselves or—tiring of trivial gaieties—they listened owlishly as the elders talked of once-upon-a-time elk hunting, once-upon-a-time wars against Chippeway or Sauk. At night the stars flashed in a hard sky, the Way of the Souls seemed snapping with life, you could hear those spangled points of light singing. Solid coldness bit against a face pushed out from a tipi, coldness smote the face, slapped it, sent it into hasty withdrawal. Back into warmth of the lodge . . . forget the spite outside, think only of corn to crack between your teeth, the good hot broth to be sucked up if you did hunger. Tobacco smoke hung like cobwebs; it matted in shadows and breathed back the powdery cedar of its flavor. A Very Old One recited a myth. Each child held his breath, for they had heard the story before, and loved it, as children love the fancied terrors. *Now, in night, Sharp-Grass does take his knife, and finding Boy-Beloved sleeping with the two women, he cuts off his head!* The sharp intake of breath . . . all are listening. *When people know that Boy-Beloved lies without his head, there is tumult! So to the house of the Teal they go, but his grandmother places him on top of tipi. They enter, but only a little brown heron comes flying out. Hence the fowl that is called* hokagi-chana, *the Little-Brown-Heron, is the grandmother of the Teal-Duck! It flies away, it alights in the corner of a marsh.* The ancient voice goes on, cold seems whirring outside. It is good to be in a cozy lodge, it is good to have food, good to smell tobacco, look long upon the fire, feel the kindness and family blessing.)

Inkpaduta influenced his people but only into destruction. He would not hunt for a living any longer, or cause others to hunt; he said that it was better to steal, or to send women begging; and if begging was to be accomplished, they must take up tenancy near houses of the whites. The first day after they moved to the *Minikata,* other women led the way to a lodge-of-whites, and Corn-Sucker followed along. She had seen so few whites. She had never begged from them, did not know how to proceed. They reached the Gardner cabin and stood in the dooryard. The Dakota women gestured and uttered strange words. Peeeeez . . . eeeeet? They made these sounds and were rewarded with salt, potatoes, a piece of venison. Corn-Sucker was frightened, her heart beat rapidly as she looked upon the whites. She was glad when at last they were departed and shambling back home again between the sloughs.

She asked, Do all white people give?

Nay, Hidatsa woman. All do not give!

Some give? Only some? When you speak strange words—

Some give. One does not know, one never knows. This One never knows!

Inkpaduta could hunt and hunt well—this was known by Corn-Sucker, she had seen. And when faced with a multitude of opportunities to secure food which they favored especially, every man of the straying village could hunt and hunt well. Witness the constant feasting on the *sinkpe*, the muskrats, until all which the Wahpekute could find had been killed. But the edge of hunters' husbandry was dulled—not by borrowing, but by sheer laziness and reprobation. As boys they had learned many skills of the hunt. It took effort to employ such skills. Now they felt it easier to steal a horse, and later sell it for food if necessary; easier to pilfer from an unguarded wagon; easier (and giving more pleasure) to pillage an unguarded camp. Had they hunted through the long mild autumn when weather was fair, they might have had much food stored. Corn-Sucker was appalled by their improvidence. She'd even heard the men referring to the fact that fur of the muskrats was especially heavy this season!—yet they had disregarded such obvious warning, had failed to demand that firewood should be gathered and hoarded against any sudden need. To demand that food be secured and stored.

Now what could they eat?

They could eat a pony.

Twas the white pony which appeared magically with that other spotted horse, when Inkpaduta returned to Corn-Sucker by night in bare ridged wildernesses far beyond the village of the Ihanktonwanna. *Hao!*—she had grown fond of the little horse. But after the storm it lay dead. Its eyeballs were not bulged out as had been the eyeballs of the sick-other-pony-beaten-by-Inkpaduta; its eyes were shut, and the mane was frozen stiff, and snow was blown away from the wan blankness of its broad head, and a portion of the pony's tail was frozen up through ice crust like a clump of weeds. The animal had been stabled in a sheltering thicket with the other horses, where they might put their butts to the wind, and hold their heads down; might squeeze close for whatever warmth each yielded to the others; and munch twigs, chew bark off the few sad saplings. No wolves had crept in to assault the carcass— There were no wolves about. They were gone into woods below the southern folds of prairie. They had followed retreating deer into denser timberland along watercourses; deer and wolves, bait and predators alike, both were departed. That should have been additional sign and warning of furious whirls, cruel temperatures to come; but the idle and the unworthy declined to pay heed.

(There would be not a wolf in the Okoboji region until spring. They'd prowl the settlements of Woodbury County instead, linger hungrily along the Little Sioux and the Raccoon, tear throats out of house dogs on the Soldier River and the Boyer and the Boone, gobble up stray travelers or wood choppers now and then, follow children who trod their path toward a slab-sided school. The wolves knew that starvation was pressing from empty spaces north and west. They knew that the Spirit Lake country would become as bald as pottery, devoid of meat as a cold licked platter. Miles to the south, now, they talked of these matters by night. Their scream went up in frost in Webster County; but here was only a suspended dome of silence.)

My-Good-White-Pony-Does-Not-Steal-Corn, you carried me upon your back when I was weary. Now your bones are ice.

My-Good-White-Pony, one time you chewed grasses. Now your teeth are ice.

My-Pony, had you been of the Hidatsa, you would have been sheltered in an earthen lodge. These people have no room for ponies in their lodges! But we did have room, we did make room for our ponies. When I was a child we heard our ponies breathing and stamping in lodges, and it was good to hear our ponies.

They said: We are with you, and our breath is your breath, and we keep you warm.

Then was I warm, now am I cold.

Pony, mutimiha! *We will eat you.*

And this thing came to be: the pony was eaten. Women chopped down through the tough whitish hide, and there was no fat beneath this hide, but the exploring blades went on and on. They used their squaw axes, they cut under the ribs, they smashed the ribs one by one, and bent them upward to break them as small limbs of trees are bent into unnatural positions so that they may be broken off. And later these broken bones could be stewed into soup, and then the cooked bones would be gnawed to nothingness. All was eaten. Inkpaduta ate the tongue of this white pony. Rattle-Strike and his wife ate liver and kidney and stringy horseflesh; and also Corn-Sucker did eat of this flesh, and Woman-Shakes did eat, and children were given some of this same horse-beef, this *tado.* The twin sons did eat of the heart, and also their wives and their children, for all were hungry. Hams of the pony were eaten, and its long-strung muscles were boiled and chewed, boiled and chewed again. Hushan ate of the *chonicha,* the fresh thawed meat, and his wife ate; and thus also did Kechonmani and the ugly wife of him; and He-Wears-Anything and his wife Cloud-Woman ate this pony meat. And all children in the village ate.

Sometimes at night and sometimes in fierce staring sunlight the winds tore at loose snow, and whirled it up like whirling trees of snow, fat twisting whirlwinds of snow which fell away and died and rose up again. By morning shone the dogs-of-the-sun, the *pechuza,* blurred glaring marks of yellow in the hazy sky. Only when it is very cold do the *pechuza* come to sit beside the sun, their master.

It was not a large pony; it had been large enough for Corn-Sucker and her packs, or for Inkpaduta to ride upon; that was all the larger it was. It was large when you'd looked at it, alive and walking; but dead and shaved and torn into food, it did not seem large. There were twenty-more-six people in these lodges and all were hungry. It is not good to starve.

Everyone did wish that the pony might have been taller and might have carried more fat.

Men were compelled to go and do the work of women, for snow was too deep, and the women were not as strong as men; and it was necessary that women cut up the pony's body, and melt ice from meat and bones, and cook that food. So wood was brought by the men; all of them were taller and stronger than the women, and there were twelve men and only seven women, and twelve men can fetch more wood than seven women (though bringing wood is the work of women). But it is not good to freeze.

When new winds came they caught all the loose snow and tossed it into small mountains; thus in some places the snow was as high as a tipi, and in some places higher; for more snow fell each time the skies went dark. In some places the wind scoured snow away from the earth until reeds and fuzz of grass and other dead dried plants showed through, and the snow was not as deep as is high a moccasin, and one walked without wading in snow. Then suddenly the drifts began once more, and they were deep and tall, and men might not surmount them; but men could go around.

It had been summer before, it was a dread winter now; it was all winters which people had ever seen, piling on top of each other, one winter above the other, and all crushing down at once.

The bowels of the pony were chewed, and all the bones were cooked; the brain was long since eaten; the eyes had been boiled. The teeth alone were left; you cannot make a soup out of pony's teeth, out of any teeth. The skull was split and chopped; all the pieces were boiled.

Men brought wood, and thus the boiling went on and on; for there was the skin of the pony to be boiled as well. It is a soup which is made from skin and chopped-up-skull-of-a-horse; and if you starve you think that it is a good soup; but you cannot chew the skin because it is tough. You try to chew the skin. It is too tough. . . .

And all the men who were unmarried did also eat of the pony and all its parts which could be chewed or gnawed: Bahata ate, and

One-Staggering ate, and the dark-faced Titonwan whose name was Makes-Fat-Bad-Smelling-Wind—he did eat; but he said that this was not the good meat of the buffalo on which he had been nourished in his own country many sleeps to the west, and it was not the meat of a cow. Makes-Fat-Bad said that horse meat was too sweet, and so did all; but they were hungry and they ate.

His-Curly-Sacred-Penis fed on the remains of the white pony. And once his name had been River-Boy, and he was tall and young; and he was a Wahpekute from far to the east. Bursts-Frog-Open ate, along with him; and one time the name of this young man was My-Soldier, and he was the youth whom Jim Dickirson had struck with his piece of grindstone, he carried the scar. He did not like white men. Truly he did not like many men.

Of this band of people with Inkpaduta, few did like anyone.

Bursts-Frog-Open was a thief even when others were not thieves. One time, when all were cold and all were hungry again, it was that Corn-Sucker dropped from her robe the small membrane which contained those precious nine kernels of corn which she had carried with her all the way from her Hidatsa home (corn was her medicine; and each of these kernels was of a color different from the others). The young man Bursts-Frog-Open knew that corn was precious to Corn-Sucker. But he hid those kernels away. Later he ate them all. Corn-Sucker did not know what had happened to the hoarded seeds. She mourned, she thought that a *mahopamiis* might have taken them.

The bitter cold continued. It was thought to kill another horse; but how could they travel later if they had no horses?

A dog was killed. When there are twenty-more-six people, tall and small, to be fed— A dog is not much meat.

Another dog was killed, and another dog.

Many deeds done by the young My-Soldier were crimes in the reckoning of other people. But in his own mind he never found himself guilty of a wickedness: these were things which he felt impelled to do, and why should custom or practiced belief interfere in any way? He thought of himself as above regulation. His admiration of himself was immeasurable, he was braggart as well as sneak. When very young, and thinking first of lying with a girl, he told the comrades of his own group that he had indeed lain with a girl. They asked him which girl, and he named a certain girl; but it was not true, he had never lain with her. Rumor soon conveyed the story to the little girl's parents; and her father went to the father of My-Soldier and said, Should I not punish thy son? Do you not punish him? Should I not slay thy son? . . . But the women of the family said, Nay, it was untrue, no one had lain with this girl. Thus the youth was apprehended in a barefaced lie. He was said to have spoken loosely on both sides of his mouth, he was said to have spoken like a white man (although at this time he had heard few white men speak; but they were said to speak loosely). All the village remarked on this, and fingers were snapped at My-Soldier, and other gestures of contempt were made in his direction wherever he walked. Had he been older he might have been soldier-killed—his blanket and his coat would then have been cut to pieces! But men said that he was *hokshika,* not grown tall enough for a soldier-killing, he had no status as hunter or warrior. While people discussed the matter of his punishment, and while he moved unpunished, My-Soldier took matters into his own hands by running away. He went to the east until he found himself in a village of the whites, near the Wakpatanka, the great river. There he hung about, begging and stealing by turns, and he had enough, he did not starve. A family of Winnebago trooped into the settlement. My-Soldier watched them with curiosity and a studied hatred, for he had been taught that the Winnebago were the enemies of all Dakota. There was one daughter of the Winnebago who had eight or nine winters, but not as many winters as were had by My-Soldier, who had ten-again-three winters. These people were poor and sad, for they had no tipi and no ponies and no gun, and they lived in a lodge made of leaves-and-branches-of-trees-fastened-together. With other families of the Winnebago, they had been removed from this country which they knew and where always they had lived, and they were taken under guard to a new place; but they did not like the place to which they were removed. So toilsomely they made their way back into the country which they knew and loved, but now they found that a village of whites had been built. My-Soldier lay motionless in thick willows and wet grasses; he watched the family of squatters. Most of all he watched the little girl. He watched for hours. Finally he saw the child sent forth with a basket and a knife; it was evident that she had been ordered to dig the long-root-under-yellow-flower-which-grows-in-mud. These roots could be eaten, and the Winnebago were hungry. My-Soldier trailed the child silently until she was gone far from her lodge, and was engaged in solitary splashings and diggings. She had a few of the long porous roots gathered when the youth caught up with her. He leaped upon the child, once she emerged from the water and stood upon solid earth, and he kept her from screaming by stuffing a portion of those same glutinous roots into her thin little mouth. He did not wish her to scream, for then the cries might be heard by her father and her grown brother, and they might come and kill My-Soldier. He did what he pleased with the girl, in damp quivering grass (at the time he did not know well how to do the thing he sought most to do; but he tried to do the thing; and he was emboldened in protracting the attempt by sight of blood upon the little girl's thighs, and all the resistance which she made against him with her writhing body). Then, when desire burst loose from him, he left the child gargling and moaning, and traveled away. He traveled toward the north. He thought later that he should have struck the girl upon the head with a stone or a club, but he had no stone or club, and anyway did not think of doing such a thing at the time when it might have been done. But she was *Hotanke,* she was Winnebago. So he should have killed her. (Later he told other Wahpekute that he had indeed killed a Winnebago.) The girl's father and brother did not pursue My-Soldier long. He was a good hour ahead of them, and he decided also to walk in a stream; they were not exceptional at tracking, so eventually they turned back. The next day the fugitive encountered white families journeying with wagons, and he trotted after the wagons for miles, wearing the people down with his reiterated plea of, Eeeeet? and his constant reapplication of a hunger sign. They gave him hard crackers and sugar, hoping to be rid of him. But he slipped up to their camp when all were asleep, and the men snoring loudly; and no one was on watch because these whites were newly come to the prairies and did not suspect that any threat would be poised against them. They owned no dog, My-Soldier had quickly observed that they owned no dog. In the middle of the night My-Soldier crept on his raid. It was as often he had played at warring and pilfering and hunting and horse-stealing with other boys. But this was no play, this was a raid. He was soon richer by a short-handled axe and a brass-mounted pistol (the flint came loose from the pistol's hammer, and was lost, and the pistol would not shoot; but later My-Soldier stole flints from his father, and made the weapon to shoot). He stole also a black pony although it was a lame pony and traveled slowly . . . perhaps the whites might have caught up with him had they awakened suddenly, but they did not awaken. Thus, filled with vainglory which found ready expression from his quick-running mouth, did My-Soldier return to his village very soon; and he expected to be recognized as a man. Because had he not stolen a horse and weapons from the whites, had he not taken a Winnebago girl, had he not also (he said) slain her?

Instead of being feted he was punished. Adjacent families of the Wahpekute said that My-Soldier had fled away to escape whatever penalty was to be meted out in recognition of his previous fault. They said that if his father did not punish him the soldiers would be called upon to do so. The Head Man of their village was a grim-faced elder warrior named Matotanzani or Healthy-Gray-Bear, who had long distinguished himself in wars against the Sauk (also his brother was the father of the girl about whom My-Soldier had lied, and Healthy-Gray-Bear had little patience with My-Soldier's behavior). My-Soldier had not done penance for his misdeed, had given no gifts to the father of the girl, had observed no tribal ceremonies pursuant to his establishing himself as a man. He was thought to be too young to be accepted into manhood. Yet My-Soldier had tried to act the part of a man, and was thus guilty of flouting holy custom! Healthy-Gray-Bear expressed an opinion that the youth should be treated as a bad boy, he should be ducked in cold water as sometimes bad boys were punished. So he was thrown into cold water five times. Each time he scrambled out, asking for mercy; he was flung back again; but five times were enough. Also the pony which My-Soldier had stolen from whites was given to the family of the girl whose name was scandalized. The black pony was lame, it was decided to kill the black pony. . . . The injured family ate the pony, and they gave no part of the meat to My-Soldier's family, but gave some of the meat to other families. My-Soldier thought it wrong that they should do this.

He was oversized, taller and stronger than most boys his age, and he bullied the other boys incessantly; they loathed him.

The next year several boys whom he knew were permitted to go into solitary retreat on the prairie, that they might pray and dream, and receive signs and know mysteries. It was stated frankly that those who qualified might be allowed to dance the Sun Dance on their return, and thus be received into a society of full-grown men and warriors.

The father of My-Soldier said to his son: You do not go. It is said that you are too young; you do not go in this summer; perhaps in the next summer.

My-Soldier said to his father: I know a boy named Three-Good-Sticks, and Three-Good-Sticks is to go; and I have as many winters as he!

But the Head Man does say that you shall not go! All are agreed on this. All men of the Little-Fox Society say this same thing.

So other boys went, and My-Soldier did not go. His heart turned dark.

In that same summer the youth seduced or overpowered (no one ever quite knew how the thing was accomplished) his female cousin, a girl named Little-Fire-Woman. He did this thing not once but many times. He did it first when Little-Fire-Woman went into a thicket to gather juneberries and My-Soldier followed her there. Once having been taught the act of intimacy, it may have been that the girl desired very much to repeat it; and it may have been that My-Soldier did not necessarily employ force to cause her to submit again. She was a stupid creature, a willing but incompetent worker. She was of an age to marry, but no man offered presents to her father. Little-Fire-Woman was excessively fat . . . also she had a habit of indulging in meaningless titterings which most people considered ridiculous. When witnesses came upon My-Soldier and Little-Fire-Woman lying together, and told later of what they had seen, no one knew quite what to do about it. The pair could not be made to marry, because this cousin was *hanka-shi* and thus forbidden to My-Soldier . . . no man might marry his female cousin! But still, My-Soldier was not yet a man. What should be done?

While deliberations were being held, the burly boy solved the problem, for the moment at least, by running away again. This time he did not travel east, but went north across high wide prairies until he found the village of the Makatooze Wahpekute, those who dwelt on the River of the Blue Earth. This was the occasion of his first meeting with River-Boy, whose name became His-Curly-Sacred-Penis later on. Their lives were mingled after that, they shared an almost studious deviltry. When they stole, they stole not only from whites who happened to be moving through the region, but they stole from people of their own Wahpekute gentes. My-Soldier stole from his own lodge, from his own father. He stole gun flints and later a rifle. He stole from his father's medicine bundle; so beyond doubt he was mad. No sane person, be he ever so debased, might think to withstand the force exerted by four species of medicine: fowls, quadrupeds, medicinal herbs, medicinal trees. The demented My-Soldier had failed of admittance into true manhood and into the Order of the Sacred Dance. He was too dronish to contrive medicine of his own: thus he stole. Truly he raped and looted a mystic skin-wrapped treasure (and the *wakan* sack must consist necessarily of either weasel-hide, raccoon-hide, squirrel-hide, otter-hide, loon-skin . . . some men said that one variety of fishskin might be permitted; and of course the skin of serpents. This was as ordained in a remote past by the great *Unktehi*, whose bones were found rarely, washed out of gravel; and one of the noble monster's bones might be taller than a tall man). The *wakan* sack of My-Soldier's father was made cunningly of the hide of a red squirrel. From this holy pouch the evil youth stole the down of a female swan, a kinky mass of buffalo hair, some boneset roots, slivers chipped from roots of a walnut tree. (*Toko!* He would not enjoy a long life. His life would be very short. There was no hope for him. He should be killed. He would be killed if ever he came within sight of his own kin or villagers again. And My-Soldier would have no red dish and spoon with which to eat in the Life to Come; for red dishes and spoons were a fine thing to have, and would be awarded only to the brave, the honorable, the circumspect. He deserved none and would receive none!) He robbed the bundle also of a dried human ear which had wonderful properties, and of a corroded medal given to his grandfather by the English king of long ago. He thought that it would make him greater than his father, greater even than Healthy-Gray-Bear, to have these trophies in his possession. He had no scruples, he much preferred to do the thing that other folk held it wrong to do. Thus he was ruled away from respect or consideration, and at seventeen he drifted into the little legion of the hated and scorned and feared. River-Boy came along with him.

Now the name of My-Soldier was become Bursts-Frog-Open.

Why was this?

Because his hand was strong.

. . . He said, My hand is strongest!

Others of the outlaws denied that his hand was strongest. The twins said that their hands were very strong. So said He-Wears-Anything. So said One-Staggering, the man without a nose.

But the former River-Boy, who had lately been given the name of His-Curly-Sacred-Penis, declared that it was true: the hand of his friend must be the strongest. He urged that his friend demonstrate the power of his hand. This was done by My-Soldier.

He went down to a marsh near which the few lodges were established at this time, and he lay amid summery reeds beside a pool where green flowers lay like flecks of green ice upon the blackness of the water. When the moment was right and ripe, the hand of My-Soldier went forward quickly, and closed. When he arose he held, caught tightly by the legs, the *tontontanka,* the fat heavy bullfrog with the deep voice. When he returned to the Wahpekute there were those who laughed, and said, What means this? It means nothing! Anyone—a mere boy, for instance—can catch a frog! This does not mean that the hand of this young man is strongest. Nay! It means only that his hand is swift; and many hands are swift.

But His-Curly-Sacred, knowing the strength of his friend's hand, said only, Watch. All stood watching.

The hand of My-Soldier began to close around the body of the frog, and the frog was very large, and its skin was tough. Tighter, tighter closed the hand of My-Soldier as he stood with arm extended, holding the frog far out in front of him. The mouth of the frog was wide open, and bright bulging eyes were thrusting out of its head. First one eye popped loose from the head with a small sound, and then the other eye popped loose with a small sound, and the two eyes swung by their attached strings as crab apples swing when a breeze rushes hard against them. The mouth of the frog was very wide now, its sticky tongue hung free, the colored portions of its inner body began to appear within those distended jaws. Then appeared the stomach of the frog, and also appeared the wet feathery body of a small swallow which the frog had eaten not long before it was caught. Then appeared other entrails of the frog; and people exclaimed aloud, for it was a strange thing to see the mere squeezing of a single hand doing all this to the body of a frog, and a *tontontanka* at that, and not a mere *nashka,* an ordinary frog.

(Yet when they gave the youth his new name they did not name him Tontontankakamdaskiya but they named him Nashkakamdaskiya which means Bursts-Frog-Open; because it was easier to say this than to say Bursts-Bullfrog-Open. The young man did not mind, he was glad to have a new name.)

And when he had finished squeezing, all the entrails of the frog had come out of its body, and the tough warty skin was empty and flat as a parfleche from which pemmican has been taken out, to eat, in time of famine; and then the dry worn hide of the parfleche itself must be boiled, to make a soup; but it is not a good soup which is made in this way (it is not good to starve).

XXIII

When that thing come screeching, and I listened to the howl of it, I thought: I'm better off in here than out there, or my name ain't Sil Waggoner. Old Bill Dog he thought the same. He didn't have much tail—somebody'd whacked it off when he was a pup, fore I acquired him or he acquired me, or whatever— Didn't have much tail, but what he did have he'd plant right tight over his bunghole, and try to press it between his hind legs, every time I opened the door. Like to say, Gracious, Mr.! Don't put me out in that plaguèd wind and snow—don't make me go! And I'd say to him, Hain't you lucky? How'd you like to be out there, hey? And twas like he said he didn't want to be, no way.

So I stretched front the fire and congratulated myself. I was setting neat and I knew it. Kept laughing as I thought of my logrolling. There hain't a white neighbor within thirty mile, not that I know of; but mine's a timber claim in part, and twas easy to cut enough to make a Ten-by-Twelve, eight foot high on the walls. (Slim logs, naturally, for a double wall to be banked solid with sod in between. Snugness was what I craved.) Had them logs stacked for drying in no time at all. Been a fur man and even mountain man in my time, and timber man as well. In such pursuits you learn to use an axe, or else you ain't going to be no kind of man for long. But, working sole alone, I couldn't get them twelve-foot logs up to the top, even slender as they was. So I figured like this: I'd got the logs cut, I'd let them weather—even choose some good chunks of long-grain which would split for shingles, and thus rive out my shakes— Have all the pieces, so to speak, to be put together. If folks come round that might help with the raising of the house, fine enough. If they didn't come, I'd just set tight until they *did.* Built myself a neat little soddy in two three days, and Bill Dog and I was cozy in that. Dug her in, deep enough and high enough so's I could use her for a stable if I was ever fortunate to get that cabin up. Well. Chance come along in the shape of a three-striper and four army privates. They'd rode down from Ridgely looking for some Indin horse thieves, but the Indins had skun out; though I guess the soldiers did recover three stolen horses and deliver them back to the rightful owners. They was on their way returning to the fort when they seen my smoke and come to learn what was what. When I seen who was nearing, I went to meet them with a bottle. We had a nip or two, and then I says: Gentlemen, I got a jug as well. (Didn't tell them that I had more'n one jug buried, to last me through the winter if twas bad, and sure as shooting she looked like she was going to be.) Gentlemen, I tell you: let's raise up my house, and when it's up I'll then produce my jug and a quarter-eagle apiece. You can't earn money that fast in the Army. Or leastways I couldn't when I was youthful and served under Colonel Henry Dodge in the old First Dragoons! We had this house up so fast twould make your head spin; and then our heads really did spin a little, count of the jug. They took their sore heads on to Ridgely next morning, and here I was a-chuckling beside my new mansion, with only the fireplace to go.

Time of the storm, though, in December: you've heard folks say twas cold as a witch's teat, but that cold would of froze the teats clean off any witch *I* ever see. How the wind did blow and the snow did pile! Clean to my ridgepole at that there side the cabin! Man congratulates himself if he's snug amid such matters, and Bill Dog and I was snug enough. Had pemmican, jerked venison in plenty; smoked fish by the quintal, or so it seemed; two kegs fat salt pork I'd freighted in behind my critters and hadn't even touched; barrel of flour, nother of meal; plenty salt, sorghum, vinegar, sugar, and such fixings. Didn't need no candles—Bill Dog and I went to bed with the prairie birds and rose in the same good company. Pine knots around if we had to make a glim.

For recreation I owned a Bible that belonged to my dead mother. I'd treasured that little Book my whole life through, though strayed from many of its teachings. I'd lain with many's the woman, but I stayed away from bats and cows, and didn't go around breaking the legs of any pure young girls. I'd had two wives within my time, but both of them was tawny—one Arapaho and one Pawnee—and both was long since departed. . . . Still I liked to read my mother's Book, times. Reading mighty slow, howsomever—we didn't catch much schooling down in the Femme Osage where I was born. I'd busted the Third, Fourth, Sixth, and Seventh Commandments wide open. Kind of preened myself that I'd been able to keep the First, Second, Eighth, Ninth, and Tenth. Fifth always bewildered me. Man I knew up the Missouri had committed what he called the Shorter Catechism when he was a younger— Oh, I don't know how much he'd committed but he'd committed a great share. And he said it like this: *Fifth Commandment requireth the preserving the honor of, and performing the duties belonging to, every one in their several places and relations, as superiors, inferiors, or equals.* Again and again I'd wheedle him into saying it out loud, and all I earned was bewilderment. How was a man to know whether he'd broke the Fifth or not? Wasn't no way I could savvy it, so I just give up.

Well. Bible was all I had for reading matter, cept a raggy *New-York Daily Times,* date of September first. Some mover give it to me, passing in October. I could trick my eyesight any time I figured twas worth it, and that was seldom. *Kansas is realizing all the horrors of anarchy and civil war. . . . Murder of eight pro-Slavery men on Pottowatomie Creek, by a party of Free State men. The victims were most horribly mutilated. In some instances, after their throats had been cut, their legs and arms had been chopped off and their eyes gouged out. All the pro-Slavery families at Hickory Point were driven off at the point of the bayonet, and their horses and provisions stolen by the Free State men.* Says I to Bill Dog, Hain't you glad that you and me's settled down to spend a comfortable old age in Minnesota Territory where there ain't things like that a-happening? And Bill he lowed he was glad. And don't, he says, read me no more of them ass-in-*ine* bulletins bout such doings, or bout Newport that also it tolt in the same paper. *The Great Ball At Newport. . . . It has given to the Bellevue an* éclat *which no other house in Newport can boast of, and will be closely followed up by a series of hops, charades, concerts, masquerades, tableaux, and other social amusements, that will end the season in a most brilliant manner.* Says I to Bill Dog, And hain't you pleasured that you got no necessity for putting on white tar-le-ton and crimson bro-cade and flounces of black lace, and going peer-oh-etting like Mrs. Woodville from Baltimore or Miss Schaumberg from Philadelphia or Mrs. Morgan Livingston from New-York, with a white lace man-till-a and blue feathers in your hair? And Bill he lowed he didn't want no part of it.

He who runs may read, like the fellow says. But truly I didn't need to read no way. Just set happied with a notion of our blessings: everything from saleratus to dried peaches and back again. Potatoes down in the potato hole to keep them far below frost; turnips also; onions; name it, Mr., and we'll feed! Whole big keg of prairie hens that I put down in salt, out in the solid lean-to that I tacked against the cabin's end, to say nothing of four fresh deer a-hanging inside there, and now they'd be froze solid for the season, and thus preserved.

Lean-to chinked and rocked right tight: couldn't ary a rat get inside, let alone a larger varmint. Bear might come, try to rip off the door, but I've met bears afore this—and bigger ones than they got here, and grayer, by gad. That's how come these pink wads on the side of my head, and my left ear tore half off. Grizzly. But he's laying out, up past Fort Benton somewheres, and *he* ain't hearing nothing out of *either* ear. Long ago, that was. . . .

One kind of varmints was around here, howsomever, but they made tracks and I reckon are still making them. Twas maybe a fortnight fore the storm began. I'd seen elk sign; went to some distance to follow it up, but fortune didn't smile. Bill Dog was minding the manse, and minding it loudly as I thought, for I could hear him when I topped that rise of prairie out yonder. Two varmints they were, both bent on making solution of the big brass padlock and heavy chain I'd tinkered to the slab door of that lean-to. I've learnt, the mean way, that twas wise to lock up when there was movers going through the country, and every once in awhile some movers did come through. But these varmints wasn't movers—not for the moment, anyways. I had my double-barreled Kaintuck, and put the first ball into the logs smack betwixt their heads. No, no, I had no call to kill!—didn't want to have a bunch of yellowbellies waiting for me in the weeds every time I stepped outside to make my water. Tis kind of like a boys' game with Indins: they like to steal, but if you tag an ordinary Indin at it, he just thinks he's tagged, and then he laughs, and maybe starts right in to beg instead. They wasn't none from hereabouts. I hadn't seen their like afore; and all the local Wapakoots had left me strictly minding my own business, for I wouldn't even yield a nipperkin of whiskey; they knew it well. . . . I turned up the second barrel, and locked it, and let drive again; but by this time the bastards was halfway to the crick and going hard. I creased that ball acrost, maybe two foot or so above them; oh, yes, Mr.—they heard it make its music, and it was like putting a fresh charge in a can of powder tied behind a cat (if folks are mean enough). They fairly soared! I was loaded up again, by the time they stopped to make a few insulting signs. They didn't know my old Kaintuck would take six fingers in a load—thought that they was well beyond my range. So I put another ball above their heads—twas right down by that little draw, behint that single cottonwood. You ought to seen the tracks they made, with one more ball a-singing on its way, and me a-whooping and a-hollering like I was gone demented, and Bill Dog a-trying to tear down the house door to join in. . . . No, no, they hain't been here again, and I don't reckon that they'll come. I figure there's one old white-shock-headed turkey cock that they ain't going to wherrit any more, whether I affix that padlock or I don't.

So here come some of the poisonest weather that a man could meet. I wouldn't have give a mouse-pelt for ary soul that was caught in it. Twas blue cold. That's the worst: the air truly turns to blue, and there is a kind of whining sound like a gang of fiddlers was standing back yonder somewheres, all drawing their long bows acrost their strings, keeping steady, drawing on and on, but always playing that same note. And if you try to face it, you think it's bees or yellow jackets that have got around you in a mass; but actually tis only pebbles of the snow, driving like salt-and-pepper from a shotgun that's fired square in your face, and stinging all the while. You can't breathe, you can't see, the air's solid with it, you can't hear nothing but that screech of mighty unseen fiddlers and the wild strings that they're a-playing on; and it all pours like angry needle tips a-jabbing at your hide, and itching up your nose until the snot flows out and freezes so you got twin icicles a-hanging . . . and forcing through your lids against your eyeballs, till you think your eyes are bloodied and the blood is freezing there as well; but still it all looks dark and blue!

I'd planned my wood and thought I planned it well. Two stacks on either side the door, starting in as high as I could reach, and stretching out a couple rods on either side. No matter now which quarter marked the storm, I'd have the shelter of one pile or tother. Thus I made it my business to see that I started taking wood from off *the furthest end away;* and thus there'd always be some fuel for evil days, right next the door. But, pshaw! The going to the stable—that was something else. I had my critters there in the old soddy; two yoke was all I had—I'd sold the rest—but they was all I'd need for any future hauling. . . . Pshaw!—when I stepped out from shelter of that woodpile I liked to choke to death. Worse than that, I couldn't see a blame thing. Well, shit and soap and sulphur!—they'd abide right where they was, those oxen. They'd had plenty hay the last time I seen to 'em, and the snow was bound to blow inside, and they'd eat that— You couldn't teach an ox that he should build a fire, melt the snow, boil the water, and then drink *that,* rather than munch snow firsthand. They'd suffer slightly if the snow kept up, but only slightly; and I never seen an ox that wasn't built for suffering.

So now my problem was to find my house again. Would you believe it? I hadn't gone a rod beyond the woodpiles' end—I'd swear to that—and yet my house was *gone*. Yes, sir, clean gone. I ducked my head against my chest, and lifted up my fists to half protect my face, and started back through all that rush of sand and fleas and pepper, salt, and emptiness, and lack of breath— Why, certainly, my house *was there*. But *twasn't*.

Now, this will be a caution (what I says) if I fall down to die right here in my front yard!

But Bill Dog saved the day. He didn't like to be alone, and so he made protest gainst the whole idee. I heard him bark, just faint, but I heard him; and twas quite the other way around; seemed like my gol damn house had moved around the compass; but there he was, a-barking in the wrong direction, so I started working toward him. Next thing I knew I stumbled fair against my woodpile; and I fought my way along that jagged pile. But I was on the wrong side—had to climb back to the other end, and round the corner of it—and there I was, quite sheltered, but my mouth was open wide and I was crying tears of ice. Hadn't been for that blame dog, I'd ended up down by the crick somewheres; and someone *might* have found me when it thawed again, if ever it *did* thaw. . . . We had a little nip on that; leastways I did.

And then a-setting through those hours, with one window darkened steady as the snow went mounting, until finally it blotted out; there wasn't even paleness in the window any more. But Bill and I were contented as two ticks in a fox's ear, pleased and fat. I had corn biscuits with a splash of sorghum; fried a plate of pork and onions; my Bill Dog he had a piece of venison complete with bone, and he licked the last fried onion off my tin. Spread myself on robes before the fire, old Bill a-laying close. I tried to read my mother's Bible, but I couldn't spell it out to suit—the print is mighty small, the flames and light was jumpy, and I went to sleep on *Better is a dinner of herbs where love is* . . . and so I dreamt about it. Dreamt about another fire in the Femme Osage of Old Mizzoo, some forty years agone. Dreamt about an old man talking, telling tales; and that old man he wasn't me, his name was Daniel Boone. We called him Colonel. And he'd let the neighbor kids come in and listen whilst he yarned. He set there with white-braided locks, and he told of being took by Indins years before, when he was hunting on the Green (that's in Kentucky). *The women,* Colonel Boone was saying in his quiet elder voice, *they fell a-searching of my hunting-shirt, to see what I was toting.* . . .

Then I waked again—not Daniel Boone, but me, Silvanus Waggoner—and there I was alone in Minnesota Territory; and I was getting long in years. Once in awhile I couldn't help but brood. Now, take Bill Dog: I reckoned him as five or six, in age, and how much longer would he be with me? Five year, if I was lucky. And then I'd be alone (tis sad that dogs are always older, faster, than the men they're wedded to). And Little-Woman-Never-Cries was buried under rocks so long before (she died in trying to bear the only son I ever might have had) and Pretty-Gopher-Running, she was gone nigh onto fifteen years, of the consump. Oh, after that I batched it strictly, seeking females only when I felt the need. But there was more to lonesomeness than seeking females, or forgetting them. There was the times I'd look down at that brindled dog and want to scream at him: Gol damn it, *talk!* Why can't you *talk?* . . . For I'd gone talking to myself, and answering as well; twas quite a habit, growing steadily; and that's the way a lone man gets a name for lunacy so frequent. And more than that: the wish to have another form within those walls; the times when you were weary, wearier than any slave that ever worked, because you'd drove yourself so hard; and all you wished to do was rid yourself of boots, extend your feet, just set and stare into that fire . . . wouldn't it be a wonder if you dozed, and then awakened smart, with smells of cooking all around?—and heard a kindly light-formed laugh, a woman's laugh, with pride and all appreciation flowing in her tone— And heard her say: Pull up now, Sil. I got the meat well-cooked; and here's the hot-bread fresh . . . I want that you should taste this wild grape jam I made whilst you was hunting!

Well. Nothing in the Bible matches that for lonesomeness (the feel within you, worse than any words). And then you'd mutter: Aw, tarnation . . . and pick up them softened fuzzy scraps of *New-York Daily Times* again, and try to fix your smoky eyes upon the lines of print, and try to spell it out again.

The disease was undoubtedly introduced on Yellow Hook and along that shore from infected vessels anchored for awhile in the Channel between Fort Hamilton and Staten Island.

Disease, disease. You didn't care how many people died of it.

And reach around and twist the banjo from the peg where it was hung, push back the rawhide loop to get it clear, and feel the fingers tightening and loosening, and hear the strings make little clinks and jinks; then start a-whacking soft and slow . . . not knowing what to sing, trying to sing something lately popular that I'd heard sung on a steamboat when I come up the Mississip some months before.

I'm dreaming of sweet Hallie . . . listen to that mockingbird, listen to that mockingbird . . . but twas a new song, and I didn't know the words, and wasn't certain of the tune.

Home to me his trumpets peal, and at my side he'll softly kneel, with a gold distaff and a golden reel. Ko-mell-a-lolla-boo, shy-doo-rah.

. . . Now, Bill Dog, why you fretting?

. . . Don't you like my music?

Frog went a-wooing, he did ride! Kemo, kimo, kay-ro! Sword and a pistol by his side! Kemo, kimo, kay-ro!

. . . By gol, you don't pay me grace nor heed.

. . . Naw, you don't want to go out. Listen to that wind!

Kemo, kimo, kay-ay-row! Strim, stram, flom-a-diddle, lolly-bolly-rig-dam! Mule met a kimo!

. . . Now, look here, sir! When I was last out for wood, you went along. Stood about two foot from the door, and sprayed them logs; and then you hiked it for the fireside. You sure don't need to go again.

So he led us down to cypress swamp; the ground was low and mucky. There stood John Bull in martial pomp, and here was old Kentucky! O Kentucky . . . ye hunters of Kentucky! O Kentucky. . . .

. . . Howling, are you? By dad, that's adding insult! Don't need to howl because it's coming night, and storming still—twon't do no good to howl. This crazy wind and sleet and God alone knows what depth of snow by now— It ain't a-going to stop just cause you whine and moan.

. . . By dad, I'll give you one to howl about!

What become of your bloodhounds, Lord Ronald, my son? What become of your bloodhounds, my pretty one? Oh, they puffed and they died . . . mother, make my bed soon, for I'm wearied of hunting, and fain would lie doon.

By God. That damn dog.

Couldn't be anyone out there.

He's plumb crazy!

Just scairt of the storm, I reckon. Can't blame him.

Oh, I fear you are poisoned, Lord Ronald, my son! Oh, I fear you are poisoned, my pretty one! . . . Oh, yes, I am poisoned—

Well, that's enough for me! *Couldn't* be anybody out there. But—

After I'd carried her inside she kept mumbling: *Light . . . light . . .* through her frozen lips; which I took to mean that she'd glimpsed a little bit of firelight that kind of skittered crost the drifts. Oh, yes, that's what she must of seen, although she couldn't see it fur.

This looked like quite a chore, and right at first I never thought to save her. But I had one tub and one big bucket, so I started in. Tried to prop her on a mound of robes, propped high on her side, with both arms hanging off into the bucket of icy water, and both limbs pushed down into the tub. I pulped up a bunch of onions and spread the wet sauce over her face and ears—she hadn't looked like much to start with, poor old thing, and didn't look like nothing human or female now, with all that onion mess a-pasted over her and fairly in her hair. But still she owned gumption, and she'd try to talk. Kept saying weakly: *Light* . . . and after while she says, *My man . . . went down in it . . . back there somewheres. Drunk* . . . and I says, Lady, if your man's out there, and drunk, he *ain't,* that's all, he *ain't!* He's down in hell this minute, and will be the drunkest that he's ever been fore he gets out of hell! I says, part way to answer all her mumblings, and part way to give me comfort whilst I toiled, a-rubbing them poor limbs of her'n with ice, one at a time— I says: If he's out there somewheres behint where you was laying, there couldn't *fifty* Bill Dogs locate him. I'll dig him out sometime next spring. Just get yourself all customed up to widowhood! . . . I might have added also: And customed up to life without two hands and without any feet!—but couldn't bring myself to even say the words, and hated much to think them. But in another hour I could take a little heart; I watched the solid ice a-coming out, and forming on her limbs. If you had ever see the like, you'd ne'er forget. Just solid casings, solid ice, a-rising through the raw skin where I'd rubbed and worn it red with rubbing —solid blocks of ice around both feet— And solid gloves—ice, you know —around both hands—

She'd moan like a sick cat at times, and other hours she would be so silent that I thought her dead. And helpless as a baby wren; I had to tend her every way. I stowed her in the bed, she got it wet right off; and finally I had sense enough to employ a wide flat pan I'd bought when I was fitting out: twas meant for cooking maple sap, but it would serve. I'd put my hands within her armpits, hoist her up in bed, and set her on the pan—

She wasn't conscious much until the second day that followed. And now I turn away from recollecting all the agonizing that she had, when blood was flowing once again into them blackened swolled-up members of her body. But still I nursed and tussled, whilst she raved or whilst she mumbled . . . Indins . . . ah, they'd took the team her husband drove . . . took a led horse that her husband bought from movers that he met . . . vinegar, she talked about, and whiskey too . . . and gut-aches that her husband sobbed of . . . and just the way I'd thought her dead, she thought that she was dead herself. And who was I, if that befell? If she was dead— Who was I? Angel, devil, spook? She didn't know.

And for some reason Bill Dog liked to lay beside her bed. He wouldn't move for hours: just lay quiet, beating tail against puncheons of the floor, like he was saying she belonged to him. He was the one who'd sensed that she was in the snow.

Feel better, lady?

Yes.

Limbs still a-hurting pretty bad, I reckon.

Yes . . . it hurts so much.

Now, don't you cry again, lady. Twon't do no good.

I'm . . . crying . . . cause my limbs . . . they'll have to cut them off . . . now, won't they?

Nope.

You mean— I won't be crippled?

Oh, kind of, for awhile. But I've seen frosted limbs as bad or worse than your'n, and seen the people get the use of them again. Your hands and feet are better by the hour.

Where is this?

What say?

I mean—where am I? Is this—in a town?

Hell no, madam. Hain't another shack in thirty mile. We're nigh the South Fork of the Watonwan. But not too nigh.

What's—your name?

Sil Waggoner. Silvanus, if I want to sound important.

Is—there—anybody else—?

Nobody else. I'm wifeless, childless. But I ain't Bill Dog-less. That's him, laying there beside you.

I can't—see—

Don't you bother. Your face is all swolled up. Just try and catch a snooze. . . .

. . . *Oh!*

There, there, sister. Everything's all right.

I guess I was . . . asleep again.

Three hours, more or less. Now, how'd you like a little broth?

Oh, yes . . . please . . .

That taste right good?

Oh, yes. What is it?

Well, if I was one kind of Indin, I'd say *hupa.* If I was another kind I'd say *wahanpi.* And thus twould go. But I ain't any kind of Indin, so we'll just call it any kind of soup you want to say. . . . What's that? Oh, it's got deermeat, bones, and onions, prairie hen, a smidge of turnip and potato— Right good, ain't it? Bill Dog likes it too.

Where is he?

Bill Dog? Right beside you. See?

Oh, yes. I think . . . I'm seeing better now.

So you are. Ain't so fat-faced as before. You know, twas Bill that found you.

Yes. I member when you tolt me . . . seems so long ago. But he couldn't find Pay, could he? Could he? Pay Lorimer . . . my husband?

No, I tolt you that as well. Reckon your man Pay is gone to the Good Place in a chariot of snow!

No, no, he couldn't— Couldn't go! Not there. Just to—the Bad Place. Cause he's . . . bad . . . like me. That's where I'll go.

Where?

The Bad Place.

I don't think you're going nowhere right away. But why the Bad Place?

Cause I was bad. My whole life long. I guess . . . times when you're at death's door . . . a body thinks about such things. My whole life long, I said! My *whole life*— Mr., you know what I was, through all my younger years? A whore. That's what I was. You heard me. Just a whore.

Gol damn it, lady, who's to judge? And what's the difference? Who's the worst—the whores, or men who use 'em? I've used plenty in my time. And I don't feel so *bad,* right now!

That's cause you're good.

Well, some would laugh at that! Now, I want—

Mr.?

My name is Sil.

Mr. Sil. What you been—your whole life long?

Oh, this and that and tother. I was in the Army one time—First Dragoons. Went way up the Muddy, worked for the American Fur, worked for the Choteaus, beat around some mean country along of

Jim Bridger and such. Been a sutler too. Hunted hides. Farmer, storekeep, factor, lumberman. This and that and tother, like I said. But this is my place now. I'm getting old, I aim to set. Also, old lady, I aim to put you back to sleep again, if I have to whop you on the head! Ahh—you want to use your fancy pot again, afore you go to sleep?

No . . . I don't . . . need to.

. . . Oh.

Well, that sounds better! First time you hain't woke a-yelling.

What day is—today?

Tis Thursday.

Is it storming still?

Kind of quitting now. But mighty deep—the drifts. And all-plumb-festered *cold.*

Why, Mr. Sil, my eyes is *so* much better! I can really see.

Oh, your whole face is better. And your feet's much better, too. I took a good look at them, while ago. Flesh is lightening. But they're still all swolled up terrible.

And they do hurt awful. But—I kind of hate to say it—I'm right hungry—

Well, we'll tend to *that,* immediate.

. . . Mr. Sil.

You was quiet, for so long, I thought you'd drapped asleep again.

I was watching, whilst you cooked. Mr. Sil—your ear. I—I was watching—

My left ear? Gol damn grizzly. Long ago. Me and Jim Bridger—

Yes. But— You—ever been in New Orleans? Long ago, I mean?—

Nope.

You ever been—in St. Louis? Long ago?—

Was in St. Louis just eight months agone. Fore I come up to St. Paul and—

But— In St. Louis, many years since?

A hundred times, I reckon.

Did you ever go to Essart's Pleasure Parlors?

Ha, ha! Did I? When I was younger. Don't mind telling you—since—ah—you tolt me how you spent *your* years— I used to rip it off five times a night!

With me.

What say? What say? How's *that?*

You member Lulu?

Why—I— *Lulu!* She was—

I'm her.

I—I don't know what to say—

Course, I don't look the same no more. I'm old, and all used up.

You hain't *storying?*

Course not. I knew I'd seen that ear before. And heard—about the grizzly bear—

Lulu. . . . I'm. . . . Gol damn, my hands are shaking!
Hain't it queer?
If anybody'd . . . tolt me. . . .
Hain't it queer?

XXIV

Old Joel Howe's father was known so commonly as Uncle Benny throughout his Kentucky community that even most of his own children also called him Uncle Benny. He was a big-boned man with a bald head, white whiskers rimming his broad face, and he had prematurely white hair at the age of thirty-nine (when Joel was born to Uncle Benny's third wife. Little Joel had many half brothers and half sisters, some of them old enough to be his aunts and uncles. That fierce country, folks said, was hard on wives. Uncle Benny took even a fourth wife before he died). A huge goiter adorned his neck. It hung in a seamed brown pouch which might have been prepared by a harness maker; maybe it was this goiter, or some ailment associated with it, which caused Uncle Benny's eyes to protrude so that they became like distended pale marbles with shiny black spots on them. Later on, Joel found himself both disgusted and pitying, at viewing this infirmity of his father's; but when he was very small, and proportionately insensitive, Joel had thought of taking the eyes out of his father's head—complete with tiny red veins and faint tinted discolorations—and playing marble with them. (In his neighborhood the boys never said, Let's play at marbles. They said, Let's play at marble.)

Uncle Benny Howe was concerned chiefly, when he talked or reminisced, with two matters: he was concerned with Indians, and with beans. His frequent references to, and regard for, beans suggested that the man must have been impoverished both as to vocabulary and ideas. To begin with, he liked beans very much; and his youngest son detested them—perhaps because they were associated with Uncle Benny and with grotesque eyes and a goiter. At any rate Joel Howe would not eat beans until he was grown; then he made himself do so. Eventually he grew to enjoy them.

The senior Howes had raised beans on their frontier farm: beans, corn, tobacco. The land was just about equally apportioned to those three crops; although there was hay in pastures on the slopes above, where trees had been girdled but never cut down. It was a slovenly way to farm; yet necessary in the early times, when man-strength could not be spared for the constant cutting-down and cutting-up and trimming, essential to the complete clearing away of a forest.

Hence midget axemen were sent among trees to hack through the bark as low down as was practicable, and cut a deep collar, slicing all the way through the bark so that sap could not rise or fall. Soon the tree would die. The foresters felt that, since mutilated trees no longer drew strength from the soil, it was a good place to plant certain crops—crops that would be unimpaired by many shadows of dead trees falling across. Twas uneven work, tilling crops amid this barren grove; twas almost impossible to plow behind an animal; but in those days most everyone hoed anyway.

Uncle Benny Howe raised beans then, and he talked of beans. When he talked of gold money, he spoke of beans. (This was some holdover of city slang awarded by a city-bred comrade on the raw frontier, who always referred to five-dollar gold pieces as beans.) So Uncle Benny would say: I had to pay him two beans for this! . . . He said: I don't care beans about that! . . . He said: A branch fell right in front of me. Like to killed me, had it hit me on the bean! . . .

When little Joel's elder sister acquired a kitten—a whitish thing with dark spots on it, something like a civet cat, but colored differently—and she wished to know what to name her kitten, Uncle Benny said, Whyn't you call him Beans?

Joel heard his father and other men making jokes about beans—something that happened to you when you ate them—and they all stood laughing, when they were passing tobacco plugs from hand to hand, cutting off slices. The parson was there; even he chuckled as they spoke about this mysterious characteristic of beans. Later, after he'd learned exactly what was meant, and when willy-nilly Joel observed that nitrogenous bubbles grew and swelled and burst from the innards of his playmates or workmates—or himself—the others might laugh at such a stenching phenomenon; but Joel was repelled out of all reason; again, it was because this crudity emanated from beans. . . . Beans in the human body, bean vines on the landscape, beans in Uncle Benny Howe's brain!

It was far different (he listened in shuddering rapture) when his father talked about the Shawnee.

Uncle Benny began all stories thus: Twas in the autumn of that year, when a war party of Shawnees come acrost the river. . . .

They were always on the other side of the river to begin with; they always crossed it; forever it was autumn. Thus autumn meant Indians to Joel Howe; thus in drying smoky prairie autumn of 1856, he'd thought of Indians, even though there were none about.

Uncle Benny had been a prisoner of the Shawnee briefly. His elder brother and his sister were killed by them. His father was scalped and left for dead (although old Grandfather recovered, as had some others in such deplorable condition; but he would wear no close-sewn cap to cover his skull. He exhibited the scar to the world. Uncle Benny described it: twas corrugated, drawn, pink, brown; it looked like the top of the head had been burnt off). Grandfather died before Joel was born, in 1805, or at least before Joel Howe could remember him. He died at a great age; he was said to be above eighty in years. In that hard-wrung community a man of eighty was a patriarch to be gaped at. A man of seventy was very very old, to be respected accordingly. A man of sixty was quite an old man . . . he went around saying lugubriously or proudly, as was natural to him: Well, look at me. I've passed my sixtieth milestone! . . . A man of fifty was merely old; a man of forty was rising old; a man of thirty might be called Old Gil Waters, at least if he were married and had a flock of younguns.

Uncle Benny Howe said, Yes, twas autumn when they come. I was out ringing trees. Didn't want to go. I'd heard the elders tell that there was Ingin tracts to be seen; but your grandpa said, Benjamin, there ain't no Ingin stink in these parts or we would have smelt it. Now you go seek the task I set for you.

So I went out, and they snatched me up.

. . . How did they snatch him up?

. . . What was it like?

. . . Wasn't he afeard?

I was ringing the trees as bid. I had a poke of red haws with me. Penny, my sister, and I had picked them haws fore daybreak. Her name was Penelope; she was called Pen, and I was named Ben, and it made kind of trouble round the house when our folks would call one of us and tother one come. But we was friendly-like together, and we both did relish them thorn apples. Our father, he wouldn't have give us no time off for picking such; wasn't enough meat on thorn-apple bones to make jelly or butter. We knew he'd say twas a waste, no matter if we filled our gizzards. We'd made ourselves a compact, fair and square, the evening before; and so we'd skun out together ere daybreak, moving light as mice, and no one knew we was about, scarcely even the dog, and he was no shakes as a watchdog. Penny, she'd constructed a poke out of remnants of an old shift—a cloth poke, but twould do to hold bout anything she chose to put in it. We took that betwixt us and went to where the trees was laden, and they was laden—my!—each looked like a big blossom. We picked and picked in that chilly dawn; picked till our fingers was sore, and we et a share of what we picked; but we put more in the poke until it was a-bulging. Then did we sneak back into the house and lay ourselves down; and scarcely had we settled our bones before the old man was a-stirring.

We'd hid our poke of fruit betwixt sticks of the woodpile, high and dry. Pap persuaded us from our beds; a word or two did it, and we was up and about. I aided him with stable chores whilst our meal was cooking; and then he asked a blessing on it; and we had our meat scraps and porridge, and thus we et, and Pap returned Thanks.

Pen was set to tromping bedclothing in a tub, and I was set to ringing trees. Our father was to hoe nigher to hand; and whilst he was off doing his morning business on the log we used for our privy, I snuck the poke of thorn apples from the woodpile to provision me mongst the forests yonder. I had regrets, for half of them apples belonged to Pen; but I reckoned I would fetch her more, one time or other; and I couldn't leave none behind, else they'd be lost down through the logs of the pile. I run and hid the poke, and then I run back to wait my father, and accept the axe and knife he handed me.

I was plain scairt at all this talk of Shawnees—to which he turnt but a deaf ear, because them scares come frequent: lots of times twas all smoke and no fire. All he said was he didn't care beans about a war party that didn't exist. I scairt easier than he did!

I was working many rods from the house, over a rise of ground, and my heart went down in my bare feet each time I thunk of Ingins, and I needed to eat them pretty red fruits to keep my spirits up.

Well, I chipped and I munched and I chipped and I munched, and seemed like half a day was gone; but maybe twas only an hour or two. Pen and I had et many a thorn apple at daybreak, and then the meal on top of it, and now I'd et half-a-poke of little apples on top of the meal. So the bellyache come, and didn't it ache! Soon I couldn't stand square upright, nor could I bend, my belly hurt so. And tears was flowing, though maybe they wouldn't have flowed had there been other eyes to beholt me.

At last I put my axe into the wood and thrust the knife beside it, and sought to lay down. There was a big log over to the edge of the clearing, with a sunny patch alongside; and a weasel run out one end of the log and away. I didn't even jump, I was so nigh to puking; so finally I did puke, and then I hugged the ground and must have fell asleep.

I woke when being lifted up, and smelling a queer strong smell, and feeling smelly breath against my face. Twas an Ingin which had me, and I mind how he wore big silver bands around both arms—wide silver, beaten out—and didn't they shine! And his grease run over them as he held me. Right off I sought to pray to Merciful Providence to aid and set me free; but I was so scairt and so sickly-like that I could only get the first sound out, and I kept mumbling it, and it made no sense to me nor to the Shawnee who had me, nor maybe to Merciful Providence. . . .

He was streaked heavy with paint: black and white. He had like stripes on his arm and crost his bare chest, where necklaces of claws was hanging, and the chunk of hair on his head stood up like a colt's mane, stiff and brushy; and he had feathers a-braided in it. He'd slapped his great hand crost my mouth first off, so's I couldn't screech; and his other arm was cutting off my wind, squeezing hard upon my neck. So he carried me, lifting me up by head and neck, with my feet a-dangling and kicking for a minute. But not for long, cause he give the awfulest slap I ever felt. And he said, White boy no yell!—and then he kind of laughed, knowing that I wouldn't yell, for I seen the keenest point of a knife afore my eyes. And I didn't yell, neither. Though now I could hear yells back at the house where other Shawnees was a-swarming, and where they took the hair off my father's head, and where they kilt my sister Penny when she started to run away, and where they beat my mother and left her laying. . . .

So the tale would go, and little Joel and others round him gaped. It seemed that their eyes were starting in their heads, protruding as Uncle Benny Howe's eyes protruded. It was not merely one story which he told; there were many stories, but forever about the Shawnee, forever it was autumn. Indians made war in the fall.

Not at Okoboji, not in 1856. Winter came railing instead.

Nobles and Thatchers were disconcerted by the rush and burst of massive snows.

Better tell your Pa to get out his book by that there Mr. Plumbe, said Lizzie Thatcher to Liddy Noble. And let him read it again.

Liz, I just can't believe it! We didn't expect nothing like this!

Neither did anybody else, said Alvin Noble sadly.

Joe Thatcher told the rest: I got his book. When I was by Mr. Howe's a-Tuesday I asked him could I borry it. Couldn't remember how long an ordinary winter was sposed to last. Everybody said our wet cold spring back there in Franklin County was *very unusual* or *un-prec-e-dent-ed* or something like that. . . .

A long shelf had been fastened to the north wall above the beds, and two more above the fireplace—the work of Alvin Noble. Not another household at Okoboji had shelves like these, for not another household at Okoboji included a cabinetmaker (he had found time to put up one shelf for the Howes, but there were demands more pressing than shelves). Thatcher picked his way to the mantel and hunted for the Plumbe book without success; so many things piled there, twas dim above the firelight, twas hard to see. He moved to the long shelf and eventually found the battered little volume.

Beside him, suspended by cords from a shake-paved loft overhead, was a weird receptacle made from an old comforter tied up by its four corners. There came a slight motion in the folds, and Thatcher jumped aside as a trickle of water spattered against his hand.

You naughty John Noble, you! cried the sharp-eyed Liddy in her furry little voice.

What's ado? Alvin asked.

Piddled on me again, said Thatcher.

I guess you let him stay quilted up too long, wife.

I didn't do nothing of the kind. John Q. A. Noble, you listen to me fore I give you an awful belting!—

Elizabeth Thatcher was nursing Baby Dora in bed at the northeast corner of the single room, but she joined in defense of her beloved Lydia. No, Liddy's right, she only put him up there in the quilt ten minutes agone.

A small head with disordered soft brown hair and placid gaze, the head of two-and-a-half-year-old Johnny Noble, peeked over the edge of the strung-up quilt.

John Q. A. Noble, you listen to Ma! If you dast to pee-pee one *single time more,* whilst you're quilted up on high— If you *dast*— I'm going to fetch you down from there, and I'll give you the worst thrashing you *ever* had, and I won't let you sleep up in that quilt *ever again.* You'll have to sleep on the *floor* like a *tramp,* that's what! You need to pee-pee, Ma'll take you down and you can use the pot like—any—other—human—*being.* You hear me?

Yes.

Now, what *ain't* you going to *do,* whilst you're quilted up?

Pee-pee.

I guess *not.*

Elizabeth Thatcher was weary and weak and in constant pain; she'd suffered from phlebitis and other complications almost ever since little Dora was born the previous spring. But she could laugh still. Liddy, you tickle me so. You oughtn't to make me laugh whilst I'm nursing Baby. Must be bad for the milk!

Well, J. Q. A. is entirely too big for such naughtiness!

You find the Plumbe book, Jody? Alvin sighed.

Yep. Let me get nigher the light . . . let's see . . . here tis.

He read aloud mockingly, while an angry new wind escaped into their low valley from prairie madhouses round about, and wrapped coarse snow, and rushed gray flurries past the window.

Pleasanter winters I have never experienced, from New York to North Carolina. I have never seen snow a foot deep, since I have been in the Territory; and the weather is almost a continuous succession of sunshine, far more uninterrupted than I have ever seen in any other part of the world, and no colder than is common, say, in Pennsylvania.

The four young people were silent for several minutes after the reading of this paragraph. Dora slept against the warm thin body of her mother, and even the sinning J. Q. A. Noble lay motionless in his high-swung cradle, as if meditating on those words, and thus preparing for righteous hibernation.

Man ought to be shot.

I don't know, Jody. Man could make a few mistakes.

Yes, yes, I'll warrant you a man could. A few! But this here thing is just one big mistake from start to finish. He's sposed to *know,* by gum! Or he hain't got no business writing a book.

If I could set eyes on Mr. John Plumbe, sounded Lizzie's frail voice, I'd give him a piece of my mind.

You'd have to go all the way to Dubuque to do it. That's where he's a-living.

How'd you know, Alvin?

Old Joel Howe was speaking with a man that knew him, fore we left Franklin County.

Blame it! Man hain't got no business setting down such balderdash, for innocent folks to be persuaded by it.

When'd he write those words, Jody?

Thatcher knelt closer to the flames. . . . Fire's getting low, whispered Liddy. I begin to feel a chill.

Yes, dear wife. We'll build her up in a minute.

Eighteen-hundred-and-thirty-nine, Thatcher reported. That's when it says. *Sketches of Iowa and Wisconsin. Embodying the Experience of a Residence of Three Years in Those Territories. By John Plumbe, Jr. Printed by—*

Eighteen-hundred-and-thirty-nine's quite a spell ago. Seventeen years, night onto eighteen. Climate could have changed. . . .

All looked at one another through the smoky dancing gloom. This was the first time such a thought had been voiced: there was a terrifying suggestion in Alvin Noble's quiet-spoken words. You conjured instantly a picture of glaciers advancing like ponderous oxen out of the north, mountains of ice pushing slowly in to press the hills flat.

Climates do change, said Alvin. We learnt that during school days back in Indi*an*. One time there was great big elephants and pretty tropic flowers, and they all got trapped and froze in the snows. When I was little, I mind Uncle Frank—I used to call him Lunky Lank— I mind him telling about the year of Eighteen-hundred-and-sixteen. He called it Eighteen-hundred-and-froze-to-death. In July, wherever they was a-living then, they had to chop the ice in order to water their stock. Birds were frosted to death in their nests. Nobody could possibly make a crop—

For pity's sake, husband! Do change the subject.

Very well, I will. But it's true.

And fetch some more wood. I'm getting right cold. Going to get under the covers with Lizzie—

You come ahead, honey. I'll move Baby Dory over tother side of me—

Heavens to Betsy, no! I was just a-teasing. I can't very well *knit* in *bed.* And can't see my knitting, neither, less those two lazybones build up a decent fire.

Oh, we'll build it, Lid, we'll build it, cried Joe Thatcher. But I want to say one thing first. I was thinking, as Alvin spoke— Thinking about Pennsylvania. Now, that Mr. Plumbe writes in this book about how Ioway is supposedly no colder than Pennsylvania. But maybe we got no right to censure him for that, or least I hain't got the right. Why? Because my father and grandfather come from there—from the Wyoming valley nigh the upper Susquehanna. Granther was there time of the Wyoming massacre, and he seen horrible happenings: womenfolks tortured and kilt by the Indians and Tories—

Husband, you cease saying such things! Just too scairy—

Hush up, woman. Twas all a long time ago, maybe seventy-five year or so. You scairt of any of these woebegone Indians we seen around *here?* What I meant to say was bout the cold. It gets all-fired cold in Pennsylvania. I heard my people tell the details: drifts and storms, and crusts a man could walk on. So maybe I done an injustice to Mr. Plumbe and his book.

Why so, Jody?

Well, he likens this—the Ioway climate—unto Pennsylvania. But I didn't pay heed to that part of it. Should have thought before we come.

Pshaw. Alvin Noble was chuckling softly.

Why you say Pshaw? demanded Thatcher.

You mean you wouldn't have come out here, if you'd lingered to think about Pennsylvania winters?

The broad-shouldered smith considered the matter, then laughed sheepishly. Alvin, you always get atop me! Course I'd of come. We'd all of come.

Lydia asked, You going to build up our fire, or do you lect to freeze? Come along, Jody.

They bundled up, drew on their mittens, and went to flounder in drifts and to drag a heap of short logs closer to the door. Joseph Thatcher, who loved to sing, and sang often in an unrestrained but somehow tuneful roar— Joe bawled a parody which it seemed he had contrived in honor of his own nickname: *Hi, Jim Along, Jim Along, Jody*— Alvin Noble, who could not carry a tune, and knew it, and was shy about even joining softly in hymns— Alvin sought dutifully to follow his younger friend in the chant. Wind chewed their voices, caught the sound, whirled it away, extinguished it, let it rise again as the wind ran and vanished momentarily, and returned to fret and smother once more. This was the middle of the afternoon. Vague haze of snow and cloud fell lower, stifling, darkening.

The wives took hasty advantage of the men's absence; then Lizzie slid back into bed, examined her sleeping baby, found all serene, and settled under the covers with a sigh. Liddy peeked into the suspended quilt. J. Q. A. also was slumbering.

Drat those men, Lizzie. Wish they'd haste with the firewood! I've gone astray on this row, and can't see to right it. Hate to waste a tallow dip—

Leave it be, her friend told her. What's a dropped stitch or two? I've dropped thousands.

But twill ravel out, if strain is put upon it when worn.

. . . Liddy?

What say, dearie?

Spose I'll ever be better?

Course you will. You heard what Doc Harriott said: milk limb is a weary business. You just got to be patient, and put your trust in the Lord.

Oh, Liddy, I *do* put my trust in the Lord. But seems like He's so plaguèd slow sometimes.

Tut-tut.

I was ailing fore Dory arrived, and I was ailing right after, and then I got better for awhile— Whilst we was traveling out here, praise be. But right off I started ailing again. Liddy, tain't that I *want* to shirk, and place all the burden on your shoulders!

Lizzie burst into tears, as she had done so many times before. Lydia Noble dropped her knitting and flew to comfort the sobbing girl. She sat on the edge of the Thatchers' bed, bending low to put one arm across Elizabeth's chest, squeeze her gently, stroke the coppery kinky hair with her other hand.

You fret about your limb, dearie. But think of me. I've had a weak limb to fret me ever since I was little.

That's why—I'm—crying— You got all this burden of tasks on you, and tain't fair. Tain't *fair*. Oh-ho-ho-ho—

Liddy began gently: Now, now. You just quit your fussing . . . think of your blessings . . . count 'em. You got a fine big man like Jody—

And—it hain't fair—for—him—neither. I can't half fulfill—my—wifely duties—

And you got this little angel of a Dory! And you can nurse her. You got good milk—Doctor says so—spite of all that—what he calls it? —phlebitis. Just think how twould be if you didn't *have* milk. We hain't got a fresh cow, and you'd be sore pressed to feed little Dory. Have to chew up bread and stuff, like in the olden days, and try to put it in her poor little mouth. So you got a real *blessing*.

Yyyess. I know—

Cease your weeping. Now! *Quick!* I'll wipe your face. Hear the menfolks a-coming?

Liddy. You spose Morris Markham is all right? Spose he's safe? Out there somewheres in all this storm—

Course he's safe. You've heard him say, scads of times, that he's more comfortable in the timber than in a house, spite of any weather.

Why, I'll warrant you he's built a cozy wigwam-kind-of-thing, and he's setting in it right this minute, maybe smoking his pipe.

(Outside of the natural joy she found in cherishing her infant—feeding the child, bathing her, fondling her toes and fingers, tracing her eyebrows or tickling in order to make the baby laugh; or only hovering blissfully to watch and worship Dora— Lizzie Thatcher's pleasure during nagging sporadic illnesses was in sharing any aspect of life with the others. So often she was compelled to lie alone. It seemed that infants slept a great deal, and the mother knew that she should not disturb her baby merely to find refuge in a waking human companionship, even companionship of the mute and insignificant. It was that way when the second seizure came on her, immediately after the emigrants reached Okoboji. Then she had to lie in a wagon before the house was built—Liddy would be cooking, or at least preparing food for the pot, Liddy would be hastening from cask to skillet to water bucket—she'd be out of the wagon, with little J. Q. A. trailing alongside or underfoot— Lizzie would lie alone, aware of a fresh and bitter truth: she learned that protracted invalidism casts a blight alike on invalid and the loved ones who are hale. The shadow of sickness builds a barricade as well as a gulf; hearty people grow weary of the frail, much as they may adore them; hearty people have to nerve themselves into attendance, and that is apparent, and the sufferers resent the fact, they grow mumpish or remotely martyred. The strong must consciously put aside their boredom in order to manage thoughtful gesture, engaging question, lighthearted anecdote which may cheer; or else they become dedicated slaves to the sick, not because they truly wish to, but because some involved notions of Christianity and family duty demand such sacrifice; and the invalid—if not too close to doom—will chafe, and burst eventually into tears, curses, upbraidings, depending upon sex or character.)

They were a family of six: two wives, two husbands, two children. The intimacy of youthful fondness was now stretched into a mutual domestic necessity. They'd arrived too late: no crop could be made. The clan had suffered a loss in the absence of Jonathan Howe. He requested permission to remain in Franklin County until spring—no one might blame him; the girl of his choice was healthy, pretty, frontier-bred, agreeable. Jonathan would work for her father through the fall, and help tend his stock during the winter; and thus the young pair were to be endowed with an outfit of their own, come April; then they'd marry, and journey on to the lake country to join the rest. A happiness was ahead for Jonathan; no one wished to oppose him, least of all Old Joel Howe. But it meant that Old Joel, Alvin, Joe, and Morris Markham were faced with the mighty task of erecting three cabins and three sets of stables, aided only by such assistance as the elder Howe boys could render. Alfred and Jacob Howe were of an age where they might have helped a great deal, were they oversized or even normal-sized; but each was small for his age, and Jacob suffered from asthma; neither boy could do heavy lifting. Neighbors came to assist from time to time; but everyone in the region was racing against winter. Adequate supplies of firewood were essential. Morris Markham said that adequate firewood was more than essential, it was imperative. He stroked the fur of animals he had taken, to drive the lesson home—he turned back the hair on raccoon or wildcat, demonstrating how thick it was.

Never seen varmint hair so heavy in Indiana, not ever. She's going to be a cold one.

But the books say—

Don't care what the books say. I was watching a gang of beaver over there nigh the Des Moines. You ought to seen the saplings they were putting away in their larder. She's going to be cold. We got to cut double ordinary wood, and then some.

So they had settled for two cabins and two sets of stables, and there was the distance of nearly a mile between the claims. A lot of time was wasted in hustling back and forth. They put up the Howe house first—partly in deference to the age of Old Joel and Old Mrs. Millie, and partly for practical reasons: after the roof was once on, twould be easier for Mrs. Millie and Sardis and the boys to offer finishing touches, while Old Joel came to aid his son-in-law and friends. The Howe house was built near the south shore of East Okoboji, near a curve where the shore line swung to the north. You could mount to an eminence immediately in back of the cabin, and see smoke of the Red Wing Company's house or the Mattock place, nearly two and a half miles down the widest portion of the lake to the west-southwest. You couldn't see the houses actually—there was a curve of bay and a jutting point between. If you circled the bend of East Okoboji and went north, up hill and down dale through the woods, you reached the valley where the outlet ran. That was the site of the Noble-Thatcher mansion, close on to a mile from the Howes'. Land had been measured off for Jonathan Howe's claim also—they didn't know how legal that was, but they'd marked it just the same; and Jonathan might claim it properly in the spring.

Once snow flies, ain't nobody else going to move in, said Morris Markham.

Affectionately the Howes invited Morris to live with them . . . not that they expected him to do so. Twas a foregone conclusion that he would make his headquarters with the two young couples near the outlet, and so he did. Morris permitted no assistance in the building of his lean-to at the east side of the cabin. You cut firewood, he told Alvin and Joe. Going to need plenty. I'll fix up my own dog kennel.

Morris built this against the chimney end of the cabin: in such a way he would share fireplace-warmth. He made his lean-to of split logs shingled in layers, with clay insulation squeezed between. His floor was fashioned of the same puncheons, smooth side up, raised on rocks above the ground. Solid logs formed the north or head end of the hut; there was no door or window at the south or foot end, but the space was closed by a double thickness of draped deerskins.

Sakes, said Alvin. You'll be snugger than the rest of us.

Snug-as-a-bug-in-a-rug, Morris agreed. But I hain't got no wife.

Guess Jody and I will need to give you the lend.

Now you just do that!

William Marble caused a flurry in the community by tramping down from Spirit Lake, toting his pack of tools. William's conscience provoked him to the visit (he didn't like to think of Peggy Ann alone in nighttime, with door barred and loaded rifle beside her, and the lake reciting wet mournful tales below the bank; but she had told him to go to the Okobojis if he felt that he must). He said shortly that he was ready to build or repair any chimneys of the five cabins, if folks stood willing. He was surprised to find that he could stamp with unqualified approval the chimneys at Red Wing and Mattock cabins: Bill Granger had gathered oasthouse experience in Kent, although his work there had been done in brick, and he knew the fundamentals of flue construction. Big Jim Mattock had built, or assisted in the building of, a dozen cabin chimneys in his time. A few corrections were made at the Gardners' and at the Noble-Thatcher place; but Marble insisted flatly that the cat-and-clay of the Howe house be ripped out.

Else you'll all be scorched from your beds, some fine midnight.

A crude box was fastened to the log lizard; Sardis and the four boys made good sport of gathering hillside stones and dragging them back to the cabin. Joe and Alvin burned lime, and William Marble chipped and dressed. The new chimney soared to completion in a day and a half.

I'm beholden, Mr. Marble? cried Old Joel Howe.

Come next spring, I'll put you in a stone floor.

Marble returned to Spirit Lake, laden also with various edible gifts for Peggy Ann. It was the morning of December first when he walked north. He had not been at home two hours when the great storm struck.

XXV

Sardis Howe demonstrated all the Aquarian's traditional fondness for people and utter dependence on them—all the energy and volubility, the quick depression or rocketing joy. Life would have been easier for her if she had not been a girl. She longed to walk odd byways and collect odd personages; the restraint of specified female conduct was more than she could tolerate with ease. In blissful imaginings she saw herself treading beech-shaded lanes or cowslip-quilted meadows, visiting at pink brick cottages with ornate cornices (did only the most genial witches dwell therein?) and trumpet vines and mossy wellcurbs . . . she considered finding castles and manor houses, tasting entertainment at festal boards. She saw herself whirling in a dance while the liveliest fiddlers creased their strings. (Dancing was not countenanced by the Howes or any of their near neighbors in Indiana, but a girl could dream.) Sardis pictured her own mass of pale hair burst from its fastenings and rippling out in the light of a thousand candelabra, as handsome goateed officers swung her fairly off her feet. She heard herself talkative in half-a-dozen languages; she presided over a *salon* each day; her parlors were crammed with droll or distinguished people . . . generals, noted doctors, diplomats, musicians, authors—they were all about—she managed them, directed them with a gesture, they clung near to feast on the diet of her wit and her philosophy. That was what she did in afternoons and evenings. In mornings she was a charitable priestess . . . she drove to visit those clinics and missions which she supported. She counseled trusting shirtmakers, comforted alike the foundlings and the pathetic unwed mothers of foundlings . . . her largesse and her loyalty were distributed never to gain acclaim or public praise, but because her heart was generous and she found radiance in giving.

(These were some of her dreams, not all. In practice her mother often had a hard time arresting Sardis in order to draft her for dishwashing.)

There had been those trotting figures in the Indiana farmyard, and Sardis was one of the most nervous and fleet. As a very small child she was always running away, and Jonathan would be delegated to the pursuit; it had to be Jonathan—the sisters of Sardis could not catch up with her. She was a nearsighted sprite and often bumped into posts and hurt herself; and if she carried the verve of the Aquarians she labored also under the storied handicap of their ill-fated extremities—forever she was twisting her ankle, bruising her shinbone. (The wail that floated up from a tousled mass of old calico which had just flung itself over a loose fence rail: ahhhhh . . . *Ma!* I've broke my toe *again.*) She was by no means an albino—her eyes were handsome, clear, gray-green, prominent when puffed with emotion. But in babyhood Sardis had been chuckled over as a tow-top; through early childhood people exclaimed, Why, just lookit the hair on that youngun! Almost white!—

It was white.

At school her enemies (she made these readily, as effusive and assertive people do) would insult her. Granny, Snow-top, Whitey, Silver-tip. Her resulting spasms of rage and tears were succeeded by dark sessions of hurt withdrawal. Hence she was never popular; she could have been universally admired, she had beauty and distinction; she needed only to exemplify a bit of patience and tolerance, and her world would have been made—a sound bright ringing world. (Sardises learn patience and tolerance seldom before they grow old.) Sardis toyed with the usual sly certainties which are held by the agonizing young: she didn't belong, she had been adopted by her parents; she was left in a basket on the doorstep—perhaps Father and Mother would confess this fact to her when she was grown, but she knew it now. More fancifully, the devils or elves of those terrifying legends erroneously called fairy tales— These had appeared in aggregation, carried off an infant which actually belonged in the cradle, they'd left their changeling. She—Sardis Howe—was that changeling.

Often she thought of running away from home—not merely scampering over to the Burtches or the Skidds, as a wee fugitive might do and had done— But leaving forever sisters and brothers whom she loved fretfully, leaving the sweet-tempered poverty-beaten parents. Twas not that she scorned or hated a single member of her flock; twas only that she could not fit herself (all knobby and twisted and strangely formed, as she thought her spirit to be) into a box with other candles, and there lie uncomplaining until the hands of Life lifted her out for her burning.

School and church, she'd not yield to them. They breathed the dictum of acquiescence and ritual, immersion in a common pool with dough-faced dullards.

. . . Now, Sardis, child. Teacher must speak to you in private. Hepzibah Berry says she wasn't doing nothing wrong, hadn't hurt you in no way, hadn't plagued nor bothered—hadn't even spoke to you— And there she was, a-setting longside you on the bench— And Teacher just hates to believe it; but little Hep says that you reached over on a sudden and gave her a *pinch.* You pinched her quick-like, and really hurt her bad! And that was why she cried so hard. And it left a *mark.*

Silence.

Sardis, child. Look at me. Look at Teacher. Don't look away. Now, did you do that mean thing? Pinch poor Hep? When she hadn't done nothing to deserve it?

The reluctant whisper. Yes.

But why under the sun? Little Hepzibah Berry hadn't done nothing mean to you!

Silence.

Answer me, Sardis. *Why?*

I dunno.

Well, Teacher'll either have to punish you, or else tell your Pa and see that he punishes you *real hard.* Oh, Sardis, you'll be the death of me! You just set there and– Why did you *do* it? How in conscience could you be so *wicked?*

I dunno.

. . . Justify it not to Teacher, because you may not, you cannot. The thought is occupying you, but words are not ready for your using, they will never be ready. Could you explain that on a sudden you grew to detest the proximity?– There was that goggle-faced little dunce sitting complacent, accepting the patter of words, feeble mind accepting feeble unimaginative explanations– Never reacting, never saying that this was Good or this was Strong or that was Monstrous, or the other was a Palpable Error, and imitative into the bargain– Just sitting, a lump, a pattern of all common droop-witted blobs of flesh which are called people, and never boast a fever or a spice or a fire about them– And you saw her there, and she was next to you, so near, so near, she was trying in her very silence and stupidity to make you one with her– And you could not be one with her, you must not be, you must not let it happen– She was staining you with her ordinariness, exuding a milky smell of her own soul's meagerness– And what would the world think, and all, and all? They would look down at you and say: You must be like *her.* Must be one with Hepzibah Berry and Ruthie Mueller and Leona Skidd and Leota Skidd and Victoria Mast and Naomi Mast and Angelina Currie and all the rest– Your hair–set apart by silver as it may be–your hair is arranged the same as theirs. Your bonnet is much the same, your best calico frock is the same–though poorer and thinner and made over twice from the use of elder sisters– And your face is the same, your thoughts are the same– The song goes: *Sing we now in cheerful measure, hearts and voices filled with pleasure. Swell the chorus; work's before us; loud the strain prolong.* And tis all an utter lie; for they sing in dismal measure, their hearts and voices lie inert, the chorus does not swell, tis sung like a dirge. The voices and spirits are too tractable, they're worth nothing, will get nowhere— And the world, and all, and all, saying: You also, Sardis Howe! You're one with the rest.

Oh, no! Never! I'm not. Shan't be! Never, never, *never!*

So I shall resist, so I shall strike and slay! So I shall—

Shall *pinch Hepzibah Berry.*

Like this.

Deliberately.

Pinch.

Old Joel Howe said sadly the next day: Miss Minnie McCrimmon come by and she tolt me? I didn't think it of you, Sardis? None of the other children—no, not one—ever done a trick like that?

Mute, mute. But tears arising. . . .

Guess there's nothing for it but I must visit the same affliction on you which you put upon that little Hep Berry? You tell your Pa where you pinched the poor critter?

On—the arm.

Do you, Sardis, stick out your arm to me? And pull up the sleeve?

She stood gasping, staring in a quiver as the coarse brown tough finger and thumb (so many years of digging, chopping, pitching, raking, driving) moved steadily nearer. She saw them closing together, saw her own frail flesh ridged between. Then her eyes were closed, and salty moisture stung the darkness. O pressure . . . now twas pain, pain, pain, pain. She wailed, she wanted to squirm away, could not move.

Would he never let go? Was he going to tear the substance out of her arm?

Would it never *stop?*

Oh, *please.* Oh. . . .

There, that's done? As you served that little girl, so did I serve you?

She screamed away from him, ran anguished into the house, hurled herself on a bed, lay sobbing long. After a time her mother came bending beside her, she hugged and petted. Poor daughter. Poor little daughter!

Ma. I won't never do it again. . . .

See that you don't do evil, Sardis. You see how evil hurts the doer thereof.

But tain't just that it hurts. It— It—

Yes, daughter. Lay quiet now. Try to say a prayer.

She tried; she could utter no petitions, could not even shape them. But soon her active rattling mind was up and about, skipping the landscape to a distant Berry farm hidden behind willows. There was the log barn where Mr. Berry had hanged himself (he had a deep cough, he coughed up blood, Jonathan and Liddy and other children had seen him spitting out blood; twas the consump; so he fastened a rope to one of the pole rafters, and jumped off his cart). Mrs. Berry was round-shouldered and hard-faced, and Uncle Pitt who worked their farm nowadays was very cross. Folks said the Berry place yielded well, and the Berry house was newer than the Howe house, and there were not so many mouths to feed. But still. . . . And the two eldest Berry girls—they were almost young ladies—had ribbons on their Sunday bonnets: blue ribbons on Mary's, purple ribbons on Martha's; even Hepzibah Berry owned pink flannel apple blossoms on hers—had been wearing the blossoms even as Sardis reached over and—

Suppose that Hep should die.

Not of the pinching. Nay, she'd never perish of that. Here was the wide welt forming under Sardis's own clear skin, rising from shadow into brownish-black with yellow scattered in it; in a few more hours it would turn to gorgeous plum curdled with pink (as her hand had dyed vividly after she caught it under the down-falling lid of Ma's big wooden chest). You didn't languish into the grave for a thing like that.

But suppose Hepzibah *did* languish. Then how would Sardis feel?

There'd be a dreadful small coffin, Mr. Willie Robarts would make it. Mr. Willie Robarts would come with his friendly smile (but that smile did no good; he was the coffinmaker) and he would have a long peeled stick in his hand; then he would measure the corpse of the deceased, and would cut that stick exactly to the length which the coffin was to be; and with his stub of gray pencil he would mark the fatal figures on the stick as he'd done when Grandma Pringle passed away. *10 23 7½ 13 plenty high 12 will do.* This rigmarole meant that Grandma Pringle's last house was to have a head clearance of ten inches, and would widen out to twenty-three inches at the elbows, and then would taper down to a kind of point—only seven and one-half inches wide, twould be, where the feet were stowed.

But in dread imaginary case the peeled hickory stick would be shorter and marked with a different series of figures, for Hepzibah Berry was infinitely smaller . . . lined with bleached muslin if such material were available. . . . and costing maybe nine whole dollars . . . that was what had been paid, when Grandma Pringle passed away . . . walnut planks planed and fitted. . . .

Oh, Hep, little Hep, poor doughy Hep with the first pinch on your arm, and the crying!

Dear one, don't die. Don't die!

Unveil thy bosom, faithful tomb,
Take this new treasure to thy trust,
And give these sacred relics room
To slumber in the silent dust.

She sought for something to give. Sardis found herself directing a passionate affection toward the distant doltish child with all forces and fibers. Pity her, pity her!—and now comes love like a freshet, drowning all recollection of the cruelty. Ah, unfortunate blank-eyed pendulous-lipped halting-voiced runny-nosed Mutton Head, how I love thee!—how I wish to enfold thee and all thy kind! Gifts of my adoration would I bring—I, the lone unrobed fugitive from other magi—

What might she offer? Ribbons for the hair? Yes, oh, yes—she had six ribbons of varying sizes and coloration, and of condition ranging from smooth to chewed. She would give all of them. All.

And her two dimes, hidden with pressed flowers and bits of quartz and a broken imitation coral necklace, hidden away in her own treasure box— The dimes—press both dimes upon Hepzibah! They'd purchase a joy at Mr. Franklin Horne's crossroads store—something she'd long desired, perhaps. Sardis would stand aloof, watching little Hep at the buying, watching her dimes go across the high counter, observing through proud tears. . . . Dear Hep! She's purchasing peppermint sticks and a picture card and a glass finger ring with the money I provided. I shall find a way to earn more . . . pick berries, sell hickory nuts . . . earn more dimes, give them to this quaint little girl . . . mind, the point of her petticoat is hanging! I must draw her to a secret place and see that it is set right. I must comb her gnarly snarly hair.

And the cup. My own china teacup, with herons and grasses pretty on the sides in two distinct medallions, and the gilt handle but partially broken, and but one crack in the rim. Tis the only cup which I may call my own, and I shall give it to Hepzibah. . . .

Covertly she disappeared from home, and walked through shimmering miles to the Berry place. A merciless sun pasted her shortened shadow against the dust, her tough bare feet stirred the dust, heat waves trembled watery across the fields. Corn was now laid by, there was no one plowing; dry farms stood enchanted, they seemed to house no tenants among their giddy buildings. Only one other person lived on this scorched planet of Howard County, and he was Uncle Billy Burtch who came swimming behind his mules out of shriveling mists, and spoke to the little girl in the shabby black sunbonnet and called her Sissy, and saw that her shadowed face was pale and staring, and smiled from the peak of his age and wisdom as he looked back at the trudging figure and thought how trivial are the troubles of a child.

It was nearing dinnertime when Sardis approached her goal. Figures clustered on the porch, all docile, all at work; and a matted old shepherd dog arose in his swathings of flies and gnat-swarms to say deeply: Who comes? Shall I bark a challenge? It's too hot; I shall make only a menacing mutter, and come sniffing, and keep my lip turned back. . . .

Mary Berry peeled potatoes, and Martha Berry fetched a pan up from the springhouse, and the fat-cheeked Hepzibah sat shelling peas. She stared at Sardis with light green eyes as expressionless as the peas which rolled from under her stubby fingers.

The gifts of Sardis were bound in her one pink cambric handkerchief. Dumbly she poked this little bundle up across an edge of the stoop.

Hep. . . .

Then she could speak no further, could but repeat the syllable until it died in her throat. The *p* sound was lost, Sardis licked her lips, attempted to build the name again, could whisper only, *Heh . . . Heh. . . .*

Go way!

I've—brung you—

Go way. I hate you!

Brung you—some—gifts—

I don't want your nasty old kerchief! Go way!—and her elder sisters were glowering, the big dog growled. Sardis stepped back. She felt her heel squash into a mound of goose manure, the yard was studded with the stuff.

Come to say—I'm sorry— And wish to—love—

Ma! Make her go way!

A humpbacked figure emerged from the house. It was the unhappy mother. She halted in the open doorway, concentrated heat of an old wood range hung around her like a cloak, dots of orange glow danced behind her in the kitchen. She stood glaring, as the embodiment of toil and rural miseries. At worship she had sworn on countless occasions that she loved the Lord; but truly she didn't; she hated the Lord; and hated her own ignorance even as she wallowed her tragic body in that slough of ignorance.

Sardis Howe! You bad girl—get out of here! Don't you never come back. If'n you do— I'll *set old Ned on you!*

As she trotted away over the hazy filthy ground, Sardis could hear that wiry nasal voice piercing behind her. Sardis was dizzy with fever long before she'd reached her own home.

The teacup had fallen out of the pink handkerchief, it flew into many pieces. But she knelt and gathered the fragments, and tied them together along with the dimes and ribbons, and went on under the sun. *Blessed,* she kept whispering.

Blessed are the peacemakers; for they shall be called the children of God. Blessed are they which are persecuted for righteousness' sake.

So am I blessed. Now I . . . shall inherit.

No, tain't right. *For theirs is the kingdom.*

Flavor of dust, smell of dust, the roadside grasses dry and bent in their dressing of dust. Far and hot and lone beyond subservient cornfields rose the rooster cry, the dreary voice of summer's buzz and barrenness, the wail.

Blessed are ye, when men shall revile you, and persecute you, and . . . say all manner of evil.

Sardis stood aloft in whitish glaring sky as she traveled; she stood high and watched herself, said of herself: Ah, that poor girl! She walks far in the brutal summer. But she is trying to be good. She is trying . . . thinnest dust puffed up, seeming to explode between her toes. Again the droning rooster cry.

. . . Her mother said: Why, where you been, you poor hot thing? I do declare, your neck's so hot and dry— Sardis, I been worried clean out of my wits; and Jonathan he went to look for you, all the way down to the crick. Sardis, you ain't got no call to pester me like this! But tell Ma where . . . *the Berry place?* You've walked six whole miles, under this blazing sun? There, there, don't cry, honey. Just lay quiet on the sofy, and Ma'll fetch you a nice drink-a-water.

(Sardis could remember another time when her offering had been rejected. It was when she attended school for her first term . . . long, long ago, for nowadays she was nigh to establishment of her true maidenhood; she was all of ten. But in that other time she had beamed upon a child named John Fell, and finally she approached and murmured that she loved him. He swung his fist and struck her in the eye.)

Sardis found fragmentary but recurrent refuge in the excitement of creation. Once her sister Ethel went to dwell with the elder Mrs. Skidd and serve as companion and hand-servant during an exasperating illness. Ethel's pay was microscopic, but in the end she was awarded a box of water-color paints and brushes, bought from Peddler Peshkin when he came by on his springtime rounds. The box was jet black, so shiny that it might serve as a mirror; and the lid was divided by ridges into separate shallow pots in which paints could be mixed. Ethel toiled sedately at projecting one sunset and one spray of goldenrod; then she washed and dried her brushes and put the bewitching little kit away on a shelf—not in the closet which she shared with the other girls, but in The Folks' closet. Objects stored therein were sacrosanct: that was where Pa kept his gun, where Ma kept the dolls and baby shoes of those four children who had died of The Cholery. Sardis was the first and only Howe to steal anything out of The Folks' closet. She did not call it stealing; if she stole she would go to hell; but she borrowed Ethel's paintbox without Ethel's permission. In secluded sessions behind a rhubarb barricade, she illuminated Crabb's *Family Encyclopaedia; or, An Explanation of Words And Things.* There was a steel-engraved frontispiece which depicted Mercury, guided by Minerva, bearing Science round the World. How rich the daintiness of many tints!— Minerva found herself tricked out in a gown of delicate blue, Mercury's shield and helmet became carmine, spear and armor shone golden. Science was awarded a cinnamon hide and violet draperies around his loins. Many animals, birds, and temples amid the text were illuminated also. Fired with passion of color, Sardis spread herself away from the confinement of engravings and distributed her own interpretations elsewhere. She had no drawing paper, but plain flyleaves of this volume were soft, unsullied, challenging.

She found descriptions of strange peoples scattered through the Encyclopaedia's pages.

> Jews. . . . Although the Jews have lost the distinction of their tribes . . . yet they . . . adhere to the religion of their forefathers. . . . They are the negotiators of money between all nations, and every where distinguished for their successful enterprise, and accumulations of wealth. The lower classes are proverbial for dishonesty.
>
> The Portuguese are friendly and hospitable, but indolent, haughty, ignorant, superstitious, and revengeful. Lisbon is the capital, and contains about 240,000 souls.
>
> Greenlander. A native of Greenland, a cold, desolate region. . . . The coast is usually lined with islands of ice. It is inhabited by Esquimaux, Indians and Norwegians, who are generally diminutive in size, lazy and superstitious. The white bear is the principal animal. . . .
>
> The Russians are hardy and patient, but very ignorant and barbarous; and most of the lower classes are slaves to the nobles. . . .
>
> Frenchman. A native of France, the most beautiful and delightful country in Europe, distinguished for the mildness of its climate and the fertility of its soil. . . . The inhabitants are gay and fickle, but enlightened, active, industrious, and abstemious. . . .

She painted them in pageant. The delight of Sardis ran riot along with her flowing figures, along with cobalts, sea greens, tans, scarlets, lilacs, lemons, charcoals, crimsons. A parade of foreign Natives swept from flyleaf to flyleaf, poured dangerously adjacent to the printed columns when she ran out of space. Fickle, ignorant, active, haughty, hardy—the Hollanders, Highlanders, Russians, Jews, Chinese, and Polanders and the rest went swirling according to her fierce illusion.

Ma, said Ethel Howe, somebody's been at my paints.

Ethel. You mean your paints have been stole? Where—?

No, not taken away, but nigh used up! Ma, I put 'em safe and sound in your closet on the next-to-the-bottom shelf, clean back in the corner. I hadn't looked at 'em for weeks and weeks and weeks—just ain't had time for such fripperies as paints—and I don't care much about artistics anyways, but I thought I'd keep 'em— You know: in the Bottom Drawer, kind of, like folks say—as a hope for the future— You know: if I ever got married, and had a little girl, then maybe she might wish to play at painting with a pretty box of water color—

Well, what do you think, Ma? I was spreading dish towels on the currant bushes, and you gone clean down in the orchard, and Pa nor Jonathan wasn't around—gone to the back pasture— And I looked over and seen an old skunk walking towards the hencoop, just as bold as brass, in broad daylight. I was scairt lest he'd get the last of your fryers, so I just scooted in for Pa's shotgun in your closet, cause I knew he keeps it loaded— But the skunk was fled, when I come out— And, Ma, when I went to put the gun back, I saw my paintbox on the shelf, and I opened the box, and what do you think? All the purple was used up, and most of the blue; and green and yellow and both kinds of reds had been half-used; and there were great big holes in all the other little chunks of paint; and I'd scarcely touched any of 'em before—just teentsie bits off the top— Ma, tis that naughty Sardis: I know it is! She wanted to borry my paints, and I told her No—said I wanted to save 'em— And that was weeks and weeks and weeks agone— Jonathan nor Liddy nor Elvira nor Grace wouldn't take 'em, and the little boys ain't big enough to reach. I know it was that dang Sardis—

Ethel! Don't use such words.

Just the same, I know it was.

*Sar*dis! . . . *Sar*dis *Howe-ow!* You come here. Right this *min*-ute—

The culprit was arraigned and soon pleaded guilty. In vain she sought extenuation by producing Crabb's *Encyclopaedia* which she had hidden in her own drawer beneath a flimsy stock of muslin underwear. She said haughtily that she saw nothing particularly wicked in borrowing a few swabs of paint; paints were intended to be used, not to be hoarded; wasn't the Encyclopaedia much handsomer now?—and look at all those pretty Jews and Greenlanders and Spaniards she had painted, all made up by herself, out of her own mind, and no one had helped her in the least! In vain. By this time Sardis owned thirty-five cents in currency, and she was sentenced to turn this amount over to Ethel. Furthermore, the shiny paintbox with its contents cost eighty-five cents in the first place (Ethel saw Mrs. Skidd making the purchase, and was turned dizzy by the price). So Sardis was sentenced additionally to servitude among Uncle Billy Burtch's apple trees—he'd been needing pickers to get in the crop, and had asked Jonathan's help, but Jonathan was busy hauling corn— Sardis was made to climb a ladder, and she feared ladders and high places; her neck ached; two apples fell on her head; Aunt Sammy Burtch censured her for bruising the apples. And late flies stung her, and a late-crawling caterpillar crept down her neck, and she like to died of fright and disgust— All this she was compelled to suffer until fifty cents had been earned. She stood penniless. But the wounded Ethel planned to buy a new paintbox to save for her purely speculative daughter, when Peddler Peshkin came round again that fall.

Ethel did have the charity to award to Sardis the remains of those first water colors; but by that time Sardis had lost interest in illuminating the Encyclopaedia or any other volume. In her spare time she embraced solitude. She planned to become a poet, if indeed she did not run away to a convent (there was rumored to be such an institution in faraway Vincennes) and become a nun first.

To A Fern
(on pulling one up out of the ground)

O thou little fairy tree,
Plucked from the woodland greensward,
Where butterfly and hunny-bee
Fly with a rythumic motion. . . .

*

Evening

Last night the winds had gone to die,
And God came down to wash the sky. . . .

Sardis devoted herself to verse until she was nearly into her fourteenth year, then she became a musician. This embracing of a fresh art was an outgrowth of poesy. As Christmastide approached she constructed a carol, but the words themselves did not wholly satisfy that longing for expression which ruled her. When carrying stiff cold frozen garments from the clothesline in dusk, hastening and blowing out frost as she shivered in her shawl, she looked through transparent winds toward the blue-green sputtering stars, and saw intervening spaces grown suddenly populous with kneeling shepherds, Heavenly hosts.

A Carol.
by
Sardis Araminta Howe.

There was a star that shone so bright
On that silent holy night.
Out of the sky the angels came
Hoping to bless the tiny babe. . . .

She left off trying to make the correct rhyme which eluded her, she reveled in the obsession of music. Lutes, timbrels, cymbals, harps, and flutes . . . how might they sound, with Celestial fingers manipulating them, Celestial breath activating them? Sardis held a vast vision which made her cry (but only in hiding; often she displayed her weeping in the family circle, but this special emotion was too sacred and overwhelming to exhibit). The vision was a-thrum with the hymning and band-playing of multitudinous seraphim. Actually Sardis could hear the music; yet how might she set it down? Last winter they'd had singing school, and only people in their teens were supposed to attend —and older ones, of course— Thus no other eleven-going-on-twelve-year-older put in an appearance, but Sardis made such a pest of herself at home that a capitulation ensued: she was permitted to accompany the elders. And what happened? Master Gallagher, the singing-school teacher, said that Sardis Howe owned a natural singing voice of great power and clarity—power especially—and he put her in the front row with the very best sopranos. Avidly she refused to miss a single evening session from that time forth; once she and Jonathan waded to the schoolhouse through a snowstorm so thick that often they lost their way and wandered against trees. Another time Sardis had sprained her knee when falling on ice beside the well, and was forced to hobble with a stick, but she insisted on going just the same. *In music with words, the phrasing is to be regulated generally by the words, but sometimes the musical meaning is more important and the words must give way.* She listened well, drew in her breath when it was indicated, exhaled as she was told by the master's nod. *Music now is ringing from our chorus strong. Joining all with cheerful voice, the harmony prolong.* Sardis learned to sing Graceful the Willow, learned to sing O'er Prairie; she learned Leave Me Not, learned Merry May . . . Softly on the Lakelet, Where Sorrows, On Atlantic's Wave, Hope. She learned: *To arms! To arms! Our land to save! The fiend Intemperance pours his cup of woes, and sorrow marks the path in which he goes. To arms, the land to save!* These acquisitions were all very well, and aided in giving her confidence in herself; but still she was too busy singing, and did not acquire any knowledge of the visible score by means of which notes and measures were rendered. Vaguely she became aware of the difference between a staff and a clef, that was about all. It needed only to be pointed out to her that one semibreve was equal to two minims, four crotchets, eight quavers, sixteen semiquavers, or thirty-two demisemiquavers, and she became irked beyond recovery, and her attention was gone admiring the willow, welcoming May, tossing on Atlantic's wave, or merely saving the land from the fiend Intemperance. She wished for the singing to recommence, that was all there was to it. Her lungs should be well filled at every inspiration, her chest should sink in as little as possible, her shoulders should not change position. She had but to hear the master lead with a melody a time or two and she had learned the tune by ear; she did not need to refer to the music, she needed now to learn only the words. Somehow those dreary little fences with objects clinging to the bars never represented a glorious explosion of sound in any event. Therefore the end result of Sardis's initial experience at singing school was that she liked to sing more than ever before; she had impressed a variety of neighbors with her gifts; but could not read a note when it was limned before her on the printed page. So how might she capture and solidify the swells of angelic harmony which worked within her? She felt as strong as a colt, pure as an icicle, holy as the Reverend Chipperfield who guided their local flock . . . tender as her own mother's hands. *There was a star that shone so bright on that silent holy night.* . . . O serene robed choir, garlanded in brightness, your wings fastened among the stars, I know how you should sound! Your music came to me along with the words. It goes up and down, like this, like this . . . *la-la-la-la, la-la-uh, la, la* . . . I hear you singing.

In the end she found that she could retain the melody (her first own tune, home-made, heart-made) by singing it over and over to herself. This she did in bed.

A sleepy protest. Sardis, why you singing?

Just . . . humming.

You woke me up!

I was . . . just singing, Grace. . . .

Well, you quit!

Won't.

Will so!

Girls, what you fussing about in there? Mind you cease, or Ma'll come make you.

Still the angel song clung close, saintly and living to be wrapped around her precious words, when morning brought its cold.

Sardis constructed words and music for the slackening of winter, later on; another song which she entitled *Wake up, Wake-Robin* when the spring actually came; and still another called *Our Glorious Nation* which she sang to the family when they were en route to Gossling's Grove for a Fourth of July celebration. Sardis had meant to reveal none of her compositions until the next winter, when Mr. Gallagher planned to return from Michigan and take up residence in Kokomo again, and go round to various rural neighborhoods in order to conduct singing schools. This time she would learn to write down music, indeed! Until such season, no one must know her enchanting secret. . . . But a miniature brass cannon boomed at intervals in the Gosslings' timber ahead; and they'd just passed the Mast place and caught a glimpse of young Peter Mast in the blue jacket which he'd worn when he served under Zachary Taylor; and Jonathan Howe had half-a-pack of Chinese crackers and two rockets which he intended to set off in the grove. Patriotic exuberance welled stoutly, the heart of Sardis was bursting with it; she could not help herself, she pealed her new song.

We shall chant the wonder of our glorious land.
E'er to give our best support right loyally we stand!
Washington and Adams too,
Tyler and Tippecanoe—
Hand in hand,
Thus forever we shall stand.

—Why, Sardis, that's right pretty—?

—What song is that?

—We didn't have it at school—

—No, nor singing school neither.

—Where'd you learn that song?

—I never heard it afore!

In pride, her face burning, she could not look at her people. The words trembled deliciously: I made it up.

—*You* made it *up*?

—Haw, haw, haw! I bet she never—

—Made it up? Your own self?

—Why, I never heard the—!

—*Girls* don't make up *songs*—

Yes they do! I did. And I've made up others, too.

—Sardis, you ain't trying to *sell* us?

Cross my heart, she said, and crossed it.

Now, that's right pretty? repeated Old Joel Howe. Sardis, you sing it again, and all can learn, and join in the chorus?

Thus she found a preliminary fame. She had not expected to find fame while riding in a squeaky open wagon, sitting with the rest in rows, on old boards laid across from box-edge to box-edge; she had thought to find fame far in a city, in a vast Hall while surrounded by milling admiring strangers. But there was something peculiarly satisfying in family fame, in intimate glory bounded on one side by Ma's approving smile, and on the other by the round wondering faces which her little brothers turned up at her.

Washington and Adams too,
Tyler and Tippecanoe—
Hand in hand,
Thus forever we shall stand.

All were singing as they joined the rest of the community among the trees, and smelled burnt powder, heard dangerous blasts, felt stamping and peril of nervous teams. Less than an hour later old Captain Porter Colburn, presiding chairman of the festivities (what little bird had whispered in his ear?), rose to stroke his beard until the crowd quieted down. And then he said: It has come to the attention of the committee that an original work of patriotic consequence has been composed by a daughter of our noble American community. I make bold at this time to summon to the platform Miss Sardis Howe, daughter of Mr. Joel and Mrs. Millicent Howe, in order that she may regale the assemblage with her most recent offering, entitled, *Our Glorious Nation.* Miss Sardis, will you please to do us the honor? This way, lass, this way! . . . The crowd swayed and receded and came back all around her; she had not thought, oh, she had not thought, thought that she might . . . and shaking feet in the too-tight old shoes (Sister Elvira's outgrown shoes) found the rough log step; and so she was going up, climbing, climbing miserably; oh, what if she should trip and fall? . . . And Captain Port Colburn taking her by the hand, and bowing, and leading her forward, and all those diffused faces, and she blinked, twas like a bad dream, where were the words?—where the music? She thought of Washington, or maybe of Martha Washington, or Molly Pitcher or someone. Or Betsy Ross? And suddenly the strength was in her again; she held her head high; she sang; the handclapping, the hurrahs, shrill whistles of brother Jonathan and his cronies—this approval and recognition struck against the girl like a blast of straw and grit blown off a threshing floor, and made her quiver anew. Yells were arising, coming from every side: *More! More! Again! Sing it again! Sardis, sing. . . .* She saw a misty man, he was standing alone with his back against a big tree, he was clapping more fiercely than anyone else. Sardis thought that he must be Morris Markham; she couldn't see at all well, she needed specs but would not have worn them had she owned them; and was that the Berry girls and their angry mother in the second row of plank seats?—she couldn't tell. Courage returned. She shut her troubled eyes briefly (the fraction of a second, but it seemed longer; and she thought of heroic women she'd learned about from storybooks and from Master Shrallow . . . thought of Betty Zane . . . and Lydia Darrah carrying a message of warning to General Washington at Whitemarsh) and then she was singing the second verse; then the second chorus.

Honor to the memory of those who've gone before,
Honor to the heroes of fierce and ancient war!
Jefferson and Paul Revere,
Yield to them our ardent cheer.
Hand in hand—
Thus forever we shall stand.

Captain Colburn took both her hands in his one big hairy hand, and bent to kiss her on the forehead. The Honorable Mr. Sebastian Wilde (he was in the Legislature!) chucked her under the chin. Somehow she was aided safely down from the platform without stumbling even once, and propelled with pats and kind words and sallies along through the crowd until she found an accolade in the arms of her mother. The oft-disapproving Ethel treated Sardis with new respect, and Sister Liddy actually cried in family triumph.

And the Honorable Mr. Wilde said to somebody: There goes a young lady who will be heard from, I doubt not! That's what he said, Ma! He was right beside me, and I heard him say it!

Sardis, I'm mighty proud of you. So's Pa. But don't you fall *too* proud.

Inevitably as she grew taller, worms of the detractors drilled her.

She suffered a painful siege of quinsy during the following winter, and was compelled to miss most of the singing-school sessions; when she went, she couldn't sing a note, she just had to sit. The good-natured Master Gallagher promised faithfully that he would visit the invalid, and teach her how to write down notes; but he took to courting the tallest prettiest Radley girl; and whatever his kindly intentions, there just wasn't time to spare for the instruction of Sardis Howe. She suffered keenly from this awareness for a week or two; but then she began to write a novel, and rather lost interest in musical composition. *Danger and Devotion: or, Cornelia of the Wilderness. A Tale of Colonial Times. Stirring but Highly Moral.* Sardis took advantage of her winter's wastage to remain in bed frequently, avoiding housework by this means, and pleading that for some reason her fingers were so sore and swollen that she could not mend, piece quilts, sew carpet rags, or perform any other such sedentary chores.

I note that your fingers ain't too hurtful for you to hold a lead pencil, Miss, said her mother shortly.

Pencil's different, Ma.

Oh, yes!

When her novel was published, she planned that it should be illustrated by her own talents. Also it was conceivable that the work might eventually lend itself to operatic purposes; if so, Sardis decided that she should write the music, and perhaps sing the role of Cornelia herself. (She had never heard or seen an opera, she had heard about operas. Her heroine had very pale hair, like her own. In the novel—in all seventeen pages of Chapter the First, Book the First, the color of Cornelia's hair was referred to as ice-blonde.) The work began to lag at the top of Page Eighteen of the manuscript. In lieu of further outline Sardis set down a list of the ten chapter titles allotted to Book the First.

I. *Introducing Our Heroine.*
II. *An Unexpected Visitor.*
III. *Shall We Go?*
IV. *A Secret Warning.*
V. *Cornelia Meets A Rival.*
VI. *Lost In the Forest.*
VII. *Saved!*
VIII. *The Treachery of the Chieftain.*
IX. *Governor Dashcliff's Peril.*
X. *Cornelia's Plan.*

About this time the neighborhood was appalled by tidings concerning the Skidds. Thessalonian Skidd and his brother James had been playing at a variety of Ante-Over, they'd been sailing an old tin plate back and forth across the ridge of their father's barn. The plate lodged on the roof, Thess and James climbed up to rescue it, the roof was slippery with frost, both boys fell, James lit on a shovel and ruptured his internals, and died in an hour; Thess hadn't yet recovered his wits, twas said that his back was broken. Sardis rose from her own bed to join mother and sisters in rendering assistance to the stricken family. She did not return to invalidism—forswore it utterly, in view of greater need facing her. After the white-faced lad regained consciousness it was Sardis who sat long by his bed, Sardis who packed the goose-feather pillows to sustain his bent throbbing body, Sardis who fetched in a bucket of clean snow so that he might dribble hot strings of maple-sugar-syrup off a spoon, and build weird gnarls of maple-sugar-candy in the snow. Daily, often twice daily, she walked the mile and a half to the Skidds and home again. She framed for herself an oath, and uttered it: she would devote herself to the now-trapped, now-misshapen child once so joyous and active; she would be beside him, this should be her missionarying and her service; cat's-cradle, checkers, dominoes, stringing beads, these would be diversions to offer; she'd teach him to knit, if he were willing to learn; she'd read to him, tell him stories, bring to him buttercups and broken flakes of robins' eggs in the spring; she'd never miss a day.

White-haired, white-hot she labored to soothe and amuse the broken Thess. All who saw her were affected by the consecration. A fund of tenderness bubbled within her and was self-renewing, compounding: the more she gave the more she had to offer. This sad boy with a distorted beak of nose smashed flat against his skeletal face (no longer swollen, but only a strip of cartilage and bone, as wrapped in a coating of too-thin skin)— The beady eyes afire with a thought of her arrival: nurse, playmate, entertainer, goddess, the Good One. *Where's Sardis? Hain't Sardis come yet? Ma, look out the windy, see if she's coming up the road.* Such demand became the affirmation of reciprocal trust and dependence, reciprocal passion. She sang to Thess her songs, made new songs from week to week, to sing to him. Her stories were now become his, no longer did she try to scratch them down on paper.

Once upon a time—oh, long ago in the Colony of Massachusetts—there lived a little boy, and his name was— Guess what?

Thess?

Yes, his name was Thess.

Thess Skidd?

Oh, no— This boy was named—Thessalonian Bradford. And one day he was at work in the garden, and he looked up, and there was a great big Indian standing by the gate.

Sardis, was it a—a friendly Indian?

Sure enough, very friendly. And the Indian's name was Chief Massasoit. And Chief Massasoit said: I need a sturdy young white lad to go hunting with me. Would you like to come? And Thess allowed that he would. But just at that moment—

Through the following autumn and winter the pain grew more acute, complaints and crying fits came oftener. By spring there was not nearly so much expressed suffering, there was only the obtundent weakness, the falling away. Thess died in May during a week of storms; the short grave filled up with water as fast as it was dug; twas a sorry burial. In summer days Sardis went often to the mound. In first summer she left sweet Williams—wild lilies in later weeks, brown-eyed susans and sprays of purple mint to follow. She was occupied still with dramatizing her bereavement in that year when the Howes went West. The few young men available in Franklin County came coltish or bumpkinish to lay a kind of suit while the family tarried there; Sardis found no charm in them. Ah, sorely she needed a man, needed love, wished to make a child and to exult in the making and the bearing; but not with any man she'd met. Woods and lakeside and labor became, in trinity, her secret spouse. Yet often she wandered long and lone, drifted away from her brothers, sang softly among the nutmeg smells of autumn. She wished for many things, she dreamed and sang, sometimes spread herself down in the leaves behind sympathetic trees and lay a-sobbing.

XXVI

There had occurred a few hasty erotic adventures, but Isaac Harriott thought that they might as well be forgotten. Never, except in the doctor-patient relationship, had he been lovingly associated with a young woman until he encountered Alice Mattock.

When he was at practice in St. Paul, Atta Rusk was willing, even eager, to welcome him home, to hear every detail which ethics might allow him to relate about the day's events (and also he told her many things which he might have told only to his wife, did he have one). As a widow, mother, grandmother—as the one-time consort of an Army man with all the exposure to roughness and crudities which such a life might entail—Mrs. Rusk made an admirable and responsive confidante. But the great barrier between them was the wall of the generations: it stood in the way, there was no getting around it, they both had to reach over and across. She was old enough to be Harry's grandmother (had Granny Harriott lived, she would have been two years younger than Atta Rusk). When they disagreed in opinion or suggested solution of a problem, she was sure to feel that Harry differed only because of his youth. Oh, he had not lived as long as she; did he own her years he too would see things as she saw them!—and Harry was just as determinedly conscious of the fact that he would *not* see things that way—not ever, not if he lived to be a-hundred-and-ten. Both were lonely; Harry became the elder's sustainer and her pet, she occupied a warm maternal role in his life, she owned the shoulder on which he might weep if he needed to weep; it was a feminine shoulder albeit a bent and angular one. . . . Morris Markham, during one burnished October week, decided that he wanted to take a look at the Minnesota River country; and he was willing to carry north all the mail which people cared to write, for shipment down the river from Fort Ridgely. Isaac Harriott sat in candlelight until past four o'clock in the morning, writing letters. Thus Mrs. Rusk and his parents and two Illinois doctors knew—or would know soon—how he fared. It was heartening to realize that, for them, he had not vanished permanently beneath smoky western horizons.

His love for Alice Mattock, and her love for him, could transcend amatory quiverings of the newly imbued. Alice was ignorant, but her mind was a vibrating essence which learned and remembered effortlessly. In quiet unembarrassed strength she might even correct him on his own misquotations of tales previously related, ambitions previously voiced.

You see, it's like this, Allie: I've long been tinkering with the notion that a new treatment could be successfully applied to compound fractures. . . . Ah. You remember what a compound fracture *is*?

Course I do. Tis when a fractured end of bone breaks right out of the limb—or any other part, I guess— Sticks right out through flesh and skin— Ugh.

That's right. Well, we've got to bear in mind that it's from the vitality of atmospheric particles that all the mischief arises—

You said that's your thee-o-ry. Twasn't yet fully proven.

Yes. But I'm confident that it *can* be proven. Well, now, all that's requisite is to dress the wound with some material substance that's capable of killing those septic germs. Understand?

Course. . . . Just one thing, though. I mind you said that you'd have to hit upon something that was *re*-li-able for such purpose, but still wouldn't be— I mind. *Too potent as a caustic.*

Gol dang, woman! How you fire my own speeches back at me!

She said shyly, Twas what you said.

I'll go on and say more! Allie, you don't mind listening?— For I've no one else to spill it out to. Bert's worn to a frazzle, hearing my theories and the treatments I'd like to apply. He's been long-suffering enough but— And I admit that sometimes *I* get tired of hearing about *France*.

The cool voice, deep and honest. I just love to hear you tell of these things. Course I can't understand all of them, but I try to. Harry—

What, Pretty Thing?

I think that someday you're going to be a truly great doctor.

God willing! Well, listen to this. I believe that a powerful fluid such as phenic acid— Not that we'd wish to excoriate the epidermis, naturally. Say one part of phenic acid to ten or twenty parts of some bland agent such as olive oil. . . . I'm thinking about one case I had, back east in St. Paul. Twas a woman, elderly, about sixty-two years of age. She was riding with her husband in a horse-drawn cart, and the nag took fright at a steamboat whistle. She was thrown violently into the road; and when I first saw her, perhaps two hours after the accident, they'd bandaged up her right forearm. I removed the bandage, and found both the radius and ulna fractured, a little above the wrist— You know—?

Ain't those the two bones of the arm?

Forearm. Now, what's the big bone between elbow and shoulder?

The—the humorist.

You're a most remarkable young lady! But tis pronounced *humerus*.

Well, there was a detached fragment of the radius projecting from the wound—say, about as large as a quarter dollar. I extracted that fragment, of course, and arrested the bleeding by plugging up the orifice with wet lint. But *I swear at this moment* that if I'd overcome my qualms, and had employed a phenolic acid solution as I felt inclined to do—

These two people now walked the world with the assured superiority, even hauteur, worn by those who have come quickly to love with every advantage to themselves and no waste of time in pettifogging. During young Daniel's attack of ague, Harry began a determined and forthright haunting of the Mattock cabin. It was as if he were a wandering ghost previously without tether, who had suddenly discovered his proper abode and was duly grateful in consequence. Alice managed none of the simpering symptoms which the doctor had vaguely supposed must attend all courtship. Invariably she was the first to open the door in response to his soft halloo, though perhaps it was her mother's place to do so. Harry came striding in, tense but talkative and exuberant; he examined his patient, dosed him if the clock indicated such procedure, awarded a few scraps of maple sugar or horehound to all the Mattock young (the Red Wing feres maintained a strict system of share-and-share where their slender stock of luxuries was concerned, and these were Harry's own rations which he doled out)— He racked his brain in search of excuses for escorting Alice Mattock away with him—across the straits, into the woods, over to the neighbors' houses, anywhere—and could find none.

Mary Mattock, recalling the bill which was to be paid later in pork, at first regarded Doctor Harriott's uninvited attentions with alarm.

Doctor, I think the child's just doing fine. His shakes grow fewer and fewer. Hain't no need for you to keep coming, less I send for you.

I just like to keep an eye on things, ma'am. His—uh—immediate responses to the dosage, and—

Honest, Doctor, we're not made of money. I keep thinking that this might cost a pretty penny! And I hope you won't mind my saying it, but Jim my husband's kind of leery of doctors to begin with—

Good heavens, Mrs. Mattock! I wasn't thinking of charging you a cent! I mean—that first visit, naturally— But these other visits are just thrown in. That's the regular system, I assure you. It's commonly done, nowadays— And of course I— We've struck up quite a friendship, haven't we, Daniel McElroy Mattock?

Yes, sir, said the admiring Daniel.

It was during this session that Mary Mattock guessed at the truth of the situation. She was not at all indignant but chiefly amused; she felt a quickening of pride as well. Through childbearing, toil, and coarseness of her life she had never been offended deeply by Big Jim's torrent of obscenity and imprecation. But she hoped that her daughter might find A Nice Man, and Mary stood embattled instantly if she detected aspiration in a swain who was both crude and lewd. Jim Mattock had taken to referring to Alice, or greeting her, as That Old Maid. Here's That Old Maid again! Ain't you ever going to get hitched, lady? Tell That Old Maid to fetch me the big jar of ginger down to the barn. God damn old Cain ox—no, I mean Abel ox—has got the colic, and we got to blow it out of his guts. Where's That Old Maid gone to?—and so on. Neither he nor his wife realized that their own manner of living, their own habit of thought and speech, had placed a definite limitation on the number of presentable young men who might approach their daughter. The parents loved Alice ardently, were more than a little nonplussed by her natural inclination toward personal delicacies and daintiness, considered her to own the beauty which truly she owned (twas no prettiness, only her eyes and hair-gleam gave her beauty), and they were awed by her gentle calm. They lamented, hiddenly and separately, as they saw other fifteen-, sixteen-, and seventeen-year-old girls of Delaware County successfully sparked, standing up with their bridegrooms, and being howlingly charivaried according to custom.

. . . Where's that young fellow works over on the Gurney place, Alice? What's his name?— Kind of Dutchman?—

. . . Luydens.

. . . Oh. Well, he hain't been over lately?

. . . No, Pap.

. . . Looked like you'd got somebody to throw sheep's eyes at you, said Mary Mattock.

. . . Sheep's eyes, hell. Anybody comes to spark *my* daughter's got to throw *hog's* eyes! Ain't that right, Alice? Heh, heh, heh—

. . . Jim Mattock, you quit wherriting her.

. . . Well, God damn it, I ain't hurting her! Am I, Alice? Just wanted to know what had happened to her God damn suitor, that's all. *You* asked her, your own self—

. . . Pap. Mam. If you want to know—

. . . Yes, honey. We're a-listening.

. . . I just sent him off. Tolt him he needn't bother to come no more. That's all.

. . . But why on earth?

. . . Ho, ho, so you handed him the mitten! What's the matter, girl? He try to roll you in the weeds, or—?

. . . No, he didn't do or say nothing ungentleman-like.

. . . Then why—?

. . . I just didn't like him.

Twas the same way where the cooper's son and the blacksmith's son were concerned, the same way with two bachelor farmers who took up abode in the former Gurney house after the Gurneys had sold out and moved to Boone County. Alice Mattock didn't like them, she sent them all on their way, it seemed the thing to do.

. . . Holy Jumping Jesus Christ! Mary, you hear tell of folks being saved for the Fool-killer. Well, what's that girl of ourn a-doing?—saving herself for the Fool-*marrier?* Every young sprig comes around, seems like she tells him to go take a flying fuck at the moon!

. . . Jim Mattock, you mind your speech! And you hain't to say *nothing* to Alice *about* it. Our girl doesn't like a man, she doesn't have to marry him, just to be getting a *man.* Hain't you got a crumb of pride in your nature?

. . . Holy cat's ass, I have so got pride! I just wondered—

. . . Well, you don't got to wonder out loud. Just wonder to your own self, and I'll do the same. Let Alice tend to her own knitting. She's a good girl—far better'n either one of *us*—and she's got a right to some *privacy.*

. . . Course she has. But—

. . . Oh, shut your big mouth.

. . . *Balls!*

Robby Matheson had been the latest to show the girl attention: he thought that it seemed indicated, they were about the same age, he lived and worked with her family, his folks knew her folks. (For some reason never sensibly explainable, girl and boy neighbors were considered to be well-matched solely because they happened to dwell on adjacent farms.) The strong-armed and strong-smelling youth paid his court to Alice mostly by staring at her across the family table, or showing all his front teeth whenever she said anything. Alice compelled herself to smile back at him out of pure charity. Assuming that encouragement was offered, Robby endeavored to display more intimate affection, shortly before the caravan left Delaware County. He lurked in the cob-house until Alice entered with an empty kindling bucket, then Robby threw his arms fiercely around her. He received a stinging blow on the mouth which was as much a scratch as a slap, and actually drew blood.

Well, gosh a-mighty! You don't need to *kill* me.

Let go of me, Robby.

Don't you want to have a little fun? Gosh—

No, not with you.

Not ever?

Not ever!

Well, gosh a-mighty!—

Alice went calmly about her cob-gathering and was not even looking at him any more. Robby slunk away, feeling unjustly maltreated, and for at least an hour he considered informing Mr. Mattock that he was unwilling to make the journey West. However, contemplated attractions of the frontier were a decided lure—as well as contemplated emoluments to be received from a successful hog business—and, since Big Jim had promised him a share in the enterprise, Robby's lowly but persistent financial ambitions overcame any hurt he suffered in rejection. He had no notion that Alice would change her mind. He'd known her now for several years. He was not astute but he recognized that Alice was guided by no mere whim. She didn't want him to kiss her, and that was that, and she never would want him to kiss her. In the end Robby felt relieved, and promised himself that he should not marry until he was twenty-five or so, and had saved at least five hundred dollars. Then he should choose another girl, and would insist on one who wanted him to kiss her (and to do all those other things that boys snickered about, when they were putting a boar in with a sow). So there.

In Delaware County some people named Norris, who'd built a house two miles from the Mattocks, entertained a Rhode Island nephew who was actually a university student. This was the only young man in whom Alice had ever been interested. A play-party was held in the visitor's honor, and he made Alice his favored partner in Skip-to-My-Lou, Ruth-and-Jacob, Kiss-the-Pillow, and other jollities. He fetched her cider, cookies, molasses candy; he recited amusing anecdotes and generally made himself charming. Alice Mattock, only fifteen at the time, regarded this jaunty Easterner, three years her senior, as an accomplished man of the world. She accepted contentedly whatever attentions he was willing to proffer. They might have been many, had he remained in Delaware County, for Benjy Norris was an utterly delightful companion. For the first time in her life Alice imagined herself wedded to a concrete personality and not to an abstract shapeless faceless male of unidentifiable name and body. But there arrived a letter from Pawtucket only eight days after Benjy first came calling at the Mattock home. His mother had met with a serious accident, he was summoned back East, he was rushed to Dubuque and out of Alice's ken, though certainly not out of her recollection. She heard that Benjy was engaged to be married in the spring of 1856; and somehow the news made her more than eager to travel out to a wilderness and hide in it. . . . Isaac Harriott reminded her of the lost Benjy in some ways, when first she met him. Both were blond, both liked to laugh . . . both had short-cropped hair . . . both . . . well . . . and neither man seemed ever to make excuses to touch Alice's body. Perhaps that was the reason that, when in the presence of Doctor Harriott, as when she had been with the other young man, she desired very strongly that he should touch her. This was all very puzzling to Alice, and she decided that it indicated a contrariness peculiar to her own nature and never experienced by any other female. She felt that she should have been ashamed to think these thoughts, but actually was not; and eventually occupied the somewhat peculiar state of being ashamed because she was not ashamed.

When Jim Mattock returned with Robby from the Irish colony, driving an astonishing herd of cattle instead of hogs, his wife interrupted his tempestuous disclosures and explanations with news which, to the feminine soul, was vastly more important.

Alice has got herself a beau.

I'll be dipped in shit! Who?

That nice young doctor acrost the way.

Hell, woman, I hate young doctors!

You better not let our Danny hear you say that, or he'll chew your ear off! He had the meanest case of shakes ever I see, just after you was gone, and Doc Harriott cured him right prompt. Danny's just wild with fondness for him. They've all gone off in the timber this minute—

Who's gone?

Alice and Doctor Harriott and—

Hell's bells, we'll be having a woods colt on our hands!

Won't have nothing of the kind. He's polite and genteel and everything.

Still doesn't mean that the young bastard can't lay a girl down on the grass if he takes the notion to!

Jim, you mind your— Anyways, they couldn't *do it*. Not this time, anyways. The kids are with them, all cept Jackson and Jacob. Agnes swears she seen a bee tree, and she wants to show it to the doctor, so's maybe they can have a mess of honey. And Danny's all well now, and he's gone along—

All right, all right, to hell with the pill-roller! What really matters is that I've made a mo-*ment*-ous change of policy. Just come take a look at these God damn cattle Robby's herding out here! . . . What about the *hogs?* By God, I traded most of them to the Irish! Them people are just crazy for hogs. They claim their country's too wet down there for good grazing—too sloughy—claim they already lost about a dozen head in the son-a-bitching mire. Well, we got plenty high dry prairie here, and if we get a decent open winter they can feed in the open. So I bought—

Indeed the sharp-eyed Agnes had discovered a bee tree, and even observed a second on the way home. She and Daniel soon lost interest when they learned that hours—days, perhaps—might elapse before they could gorge on honey. They took themselves off amid the hazelnuts. Harry and Alice stood examining the tree, a basswood with a conical hollow at the base, watching the blackish workers which drifted in and out, listening to the deep hum inside.

Miss Alice. You can hear them, up in the trunk.

Ain't you fearful of getting stung, Doctor?

Never been stung by a bee in my life, rap-on-wood! An old wives' tale has it that they won't sting some people. Maybe so, maybe not.

I've been stung a few times. Doctor, what's the best treatment for a bee-sting?

Harry laughed. Put mud on it, I guess. Oh, spirits of ammonia will afford some relief and— But I wager you won't be bitten. Come close, and listen . . . tis a strange sound . . . there . . . put your ear tight against the bark . . . listen. . . .

They poised with their heads pressing the dark trunk with its scrolled ridges, hearing the sizzling hymn uttered by a mass of insects in hiding. The buzzing reverberated hollowly through space inside, it was a steady organic sound, there was comfort as it came to you. Harry thought of other substantialities in nature—the roar of flames, the gentility of moonlight, drive of rain, solidity of thunder—he thought of bird-voices, locusts, winds. Alice Mattock's face was very close to his own, only a few inches away, the pale pools of her eyes were his mirror, he could see himself therein. She had her left ear pressed against the tree, he had his right. Idle persistent chant of bees went into his brain, into his nerves and blood, as a drug might have permeated. Here they were, the two of them, drawn close by mystery . . . the dream of Miss Raven Locks! Twas rather absurd to consider it at the moment, when the appealing actuality breathed and was kindly and warm, so near, so near. . . . The drugging fell away, diminishing; no dizzy doping narcosis now, twas a tonic instead! He felt fiercely alert, was conscious of youth and hardiness, knowledges he had gained; he was proud suddenly of experiences, of all experience both rich and embittering.

Miss Alice.

Yes, Doctor?

Must I always say the *Miss?*

I don't quite. . . .

I mean, can't I just say *Alice?*

All right.

And—when we're together, I mean when we're alone—you're not to call me Doctor.

What'll I call you, sir?

And for goodness sakes, no *sir*.

Isaac?

Well, my friends call me Harry.

She considered, still hearing the bees, as he was hearing them. Seems kind of forward, me calling you Harry, when you're so much older, and a real doctor, and everything.

I'm *not* so much older. Was only twenty-three a few weeks past! And you're almost nineteen.

How'd you know?

How'd I know—*what?*

How'd you know, Harry?

There, that's better! Well, Alice— Hi, I know! Can I call you Allie?

Certain, if you want. I kind of like it. The folks never call me Allie, but I like it cause it sounds like— Like a bird or something.

I was thinking that same thought. Well, Allie, I knew how old you were before I ever met you. You know how tis: not many people residing here as yet, and everybody talks about everybody else. I guess possibly that Abbie Gardner told me, she's a bright little gossip.

Here come the kids, she said, and drew away from the tree and from him.

Dang it! I was just about to snatch a kiss, he added, feeling like a very bold rogue as he made the confession.

But she said only, Yes. Here they are— The two children pranced nearer, demanding shrilly to know if any honey had been extracted from the tree as yet.

Harry was filled suddenly with plans. He discoursed on the medicinal properties of honey. Twas believed to be beneficial in treating muscular cramps; twas good for colds or in a cough syrup; actually he'd seen it spread upon burns. Doctor Maws said that milder burns might often yield to a honey poultice—it reduced the hurt, promoted healing—

Now, take this tree. The bees would have to be stupefied before any chopping commenced—

How would you do that?—and, to his joy, Alice whispered the *Harry* which followed, because the youngers were close at hand, but she did employ the name.

I think you smoke them with a fire. Bert Snyder knows, I've heard him talk of it. The smoke puts them to sleep, apparently. A sort of temporary asphyxiation. Well. We could fetch along two axes, and once we got the bees to sleep, Bert and I could fell this tree very quickly. Because of the hollow condition of the trunk, you see.

I ain't sure this is on our land, or on the Matheson claim.

Does it matter, in these wilds?

Back in Delaware, folks were mighty fussy bout other folks cutting their timber.

By gar— That's a Bert-ism, he says that for fun, like some of the Canucks— But, by gar, I think this may be Howe land, at that. Or in between somewhere—

Maybe Mr. Howe would give permission. I hain't never talked with him much, but Sardis is a real nice girl.

I've never met her. I've been called to the Noble-Thatcher place to attend her sister's cousin-by-marriage, Mrs. Thatcher, on several occasions.

Sardis is right jolly and talkative, and she's real pretty, *I* think. Do you reckon your friend Mr. Snyder is acquainted. . . ?

They went away from the bees, but returned some twenty-two hours later. They came as six rather dashing entities: Alice, Harry, Sardis Howe, Bertell Snyder; and Harry's spotted pony Lazarus, and Bert's long-legged chestnut horse Gladiateur. (This beast was called Glad for short, just as the pony was called Laz; a gladiator's name had been given him because when young and not too well broken, he exhibited a nasty habit of striking out with his forefeet. Bert had disciplined Glad out of such bad tricks—he'd learned a great deal about horses from Colonel Fardeau when living in Paris. The colonel was a horseman *par excellence* and kept an almost extravagant stable out at his country place near Marly-le-Roi. Bert reckoned the age of Gladiateur as now being close to five years, and he was constantly pointing out to Harry how the corner nippers in Glad's mouth had been shed and the permanent ones were beginning to appear. Both Laz and Glad were in excellent condition from their diet of grasses unsupplemented by grain: their coats shone, their muzzles were satiny, both animals were gentle but dancing. The young ladies cooed over them, wished to pet them, fed them thorn apples.)

Isaac Harriott had said, as the children foraged ahead on the way home, the previous day: Allie, I've been considering.

What—Harry?

You know I enjoy the small fry, and usually have a jolly time with them. But chopping down trees is something else again. Twould be dangerous to have them along.

I do reckon you're right. No telling—Agnes might take a notion to go kiting right under that tree as you felled it!

Bert and I are no experts. I think we might be rated as pretty good axemen— Heaven knows we've had plenty of practice, of late. But there *could* be an accident—

I'll tell Mam it's best for them to stay to home, Harry. She'll heed me. We don't scarcely ever have arguments. Only Pap—I reckon you've seen how he is—

Ah. Yes.

Mam and Pap rare around, each at tother, mighty frequent. But they don't really mean nothing by it, so we've all grown accustomed. Matter of truth, they're devoted.

Yes. . . . Then, Allie— You wouldn't object to going along with two huge fierce men, Bert and me?

I was kind of considering also. Maybe Sardis Howe'd like to join the company. Then there'd be two of us young ladies and— Twould be better so. If her Ma'll let her. And we spoke of seeking permission from Mr. Howe—

The next morning Bert Snyder became puzzled excessively by the

Christian name of Sardis Howe. This was because of his historical and archaeological background; it had fretted neither Isaac Harriott nor Alice Mattock (the one knew nothing of archaeology, the other had never even heard of it).

Harry. Why would her parents give her that name?

Why not?

But Sardis went— How you say it? Downhill! It decayed, it had scarcely a trace of its one-time magnificence. Oh, *mais oui*—in the days of the Cimmerians and the Persians and also the Athenians, it was well worth fighting for! But that was in the seventh and sixth centuries before the Christian era—

Bert, what on earth are you talking about?

Sardis.

I thought it was a girl's name—

But why? It did not survive importantly of Asia Minor, past the later Byzantine!

Gol dang, Bert. What in time *is* Sardis?

A ruined city. Or rather, of this day, a wasteland with a few ruins. My own grandfather, Laurent Didier, was a visitor to Sardis on one occasion. There were some excellent Ionic columns still visible, but the expense of excavation was obviously so great that the project could not even be contemplated! Harry. Why would they name the poor young lady such a name?

Gad, I don't know.

Harry, is she of beauty?

Alice Mattock tells me that she's real pretty. I don't know. Miss Sardis was gone over to her sister's place when Al— When Miss Alice and I went back to the Howes', to ask about the bee tree.

You are so funny when you endeavor to be sly!

Why so?

You make the great attempt constantly to conceal your rising passion for this most handsome Alice Mattock. It becomes so apparent that you might as well advertise of it in the newspapers! Would, my dear fellow, that I might be so equally fortunate—

Maybe you will be, Bert.

Aha. Let us go and see! Have you looked at your watch? Yes, it is time. No more cutting of our woodpile now, but let us saddle up and be gone. The young ladies await our pleasure. *Vive la, vive la, vive l'amour*—

(They would have been bemused could ever they have learned that Harvey Luce was even more completely addled than Bert by consideration of the name Sardis. When informed casually by Morris Markham that the lone unmarried daughter of the Howes was so designated, Harvey went into earnest perusal of the Scriptures. He was interested neither in Maeonians nor in the Lydian empire itself. But in more than passing familiarity with the Revelation of St. John the Divine he had perused the third chapter thereof. *Thou hast a few names even in Sardis which have not defiled their garments.* Harvey felt happily uncomfortable in rereading the words, and speculating about them . . . *And unto the angel of the church of Sardis write . . . I have not found thy works perfect before God.* He prayed that the christening which Old Joel and Old Mrs. Millie had awarded their daughter might not be suggestive of a predilection on her part toward sins which she would need to repent. However, repentance was a worthy pursuit, and man could hope to reach immortality in adequate and duly affirmed repentance; for his part, Harvey Luce repented hourly of a thousand wickednesses which he did not know how to perpetrate in the first place.)

It turned out, in later discussion achieved by Bert Snyder with Sardis herself, that Sardis's name did have a Scriptural connotation, although it was a corruption of the original.

Ma got it out of the Good Book, back in Indi*an* fore I was born.

My dear young lady, I did not know that many people of the United States read such histories!

Didn't say *a* good book, said *the* Good Book. The Bible! You see, Pa's been a great one for Bible reading, always, specially after breakfast of a morning. All us little ones would sit round and listen to him read, though we couldn't understand the half. Just like at table, too —he'd have a great big long switch, and if any of us tykes were naughty, we'd get a swat. Well, Ma always said she picked it up from Ezekiel, and the first long text I ever learnt for Sabbath school, was this one about my name. Wish to hear it?

By all means.

Thou hast been in Eden the garden of God; every precious stone was thy covering, the sardius, topaz, and the diamond, the beryl, the onyx, and the jasper, the sapphire, the emerald, and the carbuncle, and gold: the workmanship of thy tabrets and of thy pipes was prepared in thee in the day that thou wast created. See?

Indeed I do not see. *Et alors?*—where is Sardis?

Silly thing—Sardius! Very first-named of all the jewels and gems!

Sardius?

Honestly, that's what I was named in the first place, and so it's written in our family Bible. But you know how folks are. Just careless in their talk. Slipshod. At school, and even before I went, seemed like twas easier for everybody and his dog to say Sardis stead of Sardius; so Ma just gave up, and me too, and let them call it that way. Nowadays that's even how I write my signature to anything. Ever hear the beat?

Bert said: Yes, I have. Suppose I were to tell you that my name was not Snyder but Schneider? And that I was christened Bertell in honor of a *tomcat*?

Sardis squawked with laughter. Some of her rich icy hair had blown loose, it went whipping out behind. Her hands were fastened firmly to Bert's wide belt. He pushed Glad ahead, the jouncing couple rode on a separate course among the trees, their voices could be heard (young wiry voices, firm, strung tight) but you could not hear what they were saying. Their laughter came back to Isaac Harriott and Alice.

Alice said: She is a nice girl, ain't she? I think he likes her.

Yes, oh yes, she's charming. I'm sure Bert will enjoy—

And we did get such a fine day for our bee-hunting, didn't we? I was scairt it was going to rain, last evening.

She added simply: Guess I just about prayed that it wouldn't.

(Gentle voice remembered through lead-cold days and weeks to follow. O armored storms, pacing like knights with pennons of wind, the angry mail of hail to blow around your skeletons!—never can you cause me to forget a warmth we observed when bees were still about!)

Allie.

What?

Want to know something?

What?

Today, on our picnic, I'm going to—

And his pulse was hammering, his body hardened and swelling vigorously in the knowledge of her nearness, her clutch on him.

—Kiss you—

All right, she said, as in a dream or prayer.

XXVII

Drifted snow shrank through evaporation, unsteady breezes whipped away the dirty salt, the tails of drifts. Dark porous ice, fruit of meltings, showed up in interlaced patches; and there were areas where the earth was bare with huddles of broken weeds bowing their whipped heads, and nodding and buzzing like children's toys when winds blew from certain directions. The Wahpekute were encouraged to travel farther afield each hour of daylight. Men sought to hunt, the women were heckled, urged to visit lodges of the whites. Four women did set forth one midday in a slow stumbling troop; Corn-Sucker was one of these. The rest turned toward the Gardners', knowing the place, knowing that they had been given food before, and so might expect to receive it again. But Corn-Sucker, as befitted the most docile and willing of the lot, was ordered ahead on a path.

Another lodge of whites lies beyond, said Woman-Shakes-With-Cold. It may be that they give. Go, Hidatsa woman.

Go I alone? asked Corn-Sucker piteously.

Go thee alone, declared the implacable Woman-Shakes.

Aye. I go.

She circled through a blocked forest, crossing and recrossing the obvious trail, until she saw a menacing bulk of grayish logs ahead. Earnestly she desired to flee; but suppose other women returned to the camp bearing contributions of food, and she carried none? Then would she be kicked, kicked hard and frequently. And even now she was weak with hunger. Warily she crept forward, terrified beyond utterance at her solitary proximity to a structure housing whites. (Starvation does not recognize terror, starvation numbs the terror inside, terror is not permitted to command, starvation commands.) There was smell of cooking which emerged from cracks where chinking had fallen out, and that same rich smell seemed to rise from a sooty chimney and fall widely through cold air, and swathe the whole fearful cabin with grease which might nearly be seen. Corn-Sucker's nostrils worked avidly; water dribbled through her slit lip. With shaking hand she dabbed the water away; it would freeze there, would hurt if left.

In spectral fashion she mounted to the step. This step was half a log, you could see adze marks under the dirty trodden glaze. Fierce white voices clattered and fussed within the cabin. A child shrieked —whether in pain or joy the Indian woman did not know—it was a wavering squeal which she heard.

What had those other women, the wives of Inkpaduta's people, said to whites? She tried to remember, tried to build peculiar remembered sounds. Peeeeez . . . jib . . . eeeeet. . . .

Inside the house a dog burst into violence and flung himself against the door. Corn-Sucker could hear the beast, fairly see his teeth snapping. She shrank backward, slipped on ice, fell heavily to the ground in a sitting position. She was still sitting there when men and women—there seemed to be several of them all at once—opened the door and looked out.

Well, prick and the devil, see what we got here!

Why, what you setting there for, you crazy critter?

Guess she fell flat on her ass. Yep, she's a-rubbing it.

Jim Mattock, you mind your speech. Ladies present—

They bulked, the mass of them, some laughing, one bearded, they were noisy about the whole thing. Never had Corn-Sucker seen any man so fat as James Mattock. It must be that he had much meat to eat, much squash! It must be that he was a mighty hunter; no man except a mighty hunter could ever secure so much meat, and wolf it into his mouth, and chew it, and have it go all through his body to puff that body into such size. He was not as tall as Inkpaduta, but in weight he must be heavier than a young buffalo cow. Much meat!

She was standing, trembling, trying to croak, trying to build the sounds she'd heard Dakota women make.

Eeeeet? She drew it out, her scarred mouth trembling as she tried to hold it open, tried to keep her jaws apart to make the word. Eeeeet?

What on earth's she trying to say?

That's *eat* she's a-saying, Robby.

Mary Mattock said decisively: Injan or no, she looks to be a poor starved thing! Fetch her in, Jim, fetch her right inside.

Cat's ass, woman, she'll stink the whole place up!

Can't help it if she does. We ain't going to stand out here and freeze. Nor let her freeze in this cold weather. Tain't Christian.

Jim Mattock's laugh came booming. Well, well, well! If we got to be such professed Christians let's get busy at it!

They made beckoning motions— Corn-Sucker did not well understand their motions, they seemed snapping their hands at her. Behind them a wrinkled-faced dog was growling. . . . Lee, now you hush up! Member you come over here from Red Wing to beg, your own self? Daniel and Agnes, get holt of that dog! Lee, behave yourself, else we'll kick you out and send you home, and how you like that, sir? Their white people's talk poured from the open door like rushing water or like a fast crowded flame spouting from resinous wood; it was all over the place, a hubbub, a mutilation, a complexity of frightening uncouth words.

Corn-Sucker shrank back. Eeeeet? she quavered again.

Mary Mattock exclaimed, Oh, for land's sake! She's scairt right out of her duds! She walked down to Corn-Sucker, took hold of the greasy blanket, gave a tug. Come along, sister. You want to eat, we'll fix you some fixins.

Her husband roared: She may be a sister of yours. Hain't none of mine! Laughter banged and tussled, it struck like stones against the ears.

Then she was inside—she stood in this dangerous place, a white man's lodge. She stood on a wooden floor, she had never stood upon a wooden floor in all her life. She had stood upon the flat roofs of earth lodges; but this did not seem at all the same—it was like standing on a wide rock, as sometimes she had marched upon such shelves in play when young.

Peeeeez . . . ? she wailed. She brought up her arched stiffened hand, bent it toward her mouth, lowered the hand by wrist action, brought it up again; and all the while the confusion, the bellowing strident mirth of this mad place and these mad people was mauling against her ears.

Hell, that's all she knows how to say!

I don't care. Poor old thing. Alice, honey, get that pork over here. There's some in the spider—

Damn it to hell, woman—we hain't got pork to give away to a bunch of damn Injans—

She ain't a bunch of damn Injans! She's just one poor squaw. *An I hungered, an thou did feed me,* or something like that. In the Bible, it says—

Precious lot you know about the Bible!

Mam, she smells awful queer.

That's cause she's an Injan, Daniel. And you do smell kind of prime yourself. You just won't never take a bath.

Water's too blame cold. It froze fore I could try—

Always got some excuse. Daniel, you just fair stink, really and truly! Hain't fitten for you to go complaining bout a poor squaw. Jackson and Jacob, you get out of the way—

Well, *they* stink *too!* Specially Jacob—

That's cause he's scarce growed enough to wipe himself proper when he goes to the privy. Agnes, hand over that big spoon yonder—

A chair had been cleared for Corn-Sucker, she was waved toward it, but she backed away distrustfully. She did not know how to sit in a chair, had never sat in one. A few times in warmer weather she'd seen white people roosting in chairs before their cabin doors; and with the Dakota she had discussed this awkward preference of the whites. Cloud-Woman, the wife of He-Wears-Anything, had told her that she herself had sat in chairs, when begging from the whites, and it was not much different from sitting on a stone or a log, except for that part at the back. And once, while the band was moving south to the Little-Stream-of-the-Hot-Water, white people went by in a wagon. Corn-Sucker had seen an old woman seated on a chair in the rear of the wagon, but she was needing to hold on with both hands.

Corn-Sucker backed as far as she could go, into a corner against a barrel. There she collapsed, sitting down on the floor in her natural posture, ankles to the right. She rolled her eyes to take in the strangeness, she saw what hung above her. The entire upper space of the cabin was filled with drying pumpkin: a grotesque population of pumpkin slices had been impaled on slim rods laid across the sustaining beams. Only half the attic area was a loft (where Robby Matheson and the Mattock boys slept); the rest had become a repository for smoked pork and a forest of pumpkin rings. Festooned among the poles clung strings of odd-sized chunks left over from the slicing—a smoke-darkened tangle where busy mice scampered active and roguish even as Corn-Sucker gazed. . . . What could this material be? It was not *kakui,* was not squash. She had helped to set up ten thousand laden squash rods on the drying stages, she knew squash when she saw it; yet what were these great lopsided rings? She gave a squeak of mingled recognition and bewilderment, then turned to the ordeal of the mendicant.

Eeeeet?

Here tis, you stupid thing. Right in front of you!

Mam, why's she setting on the floor?

She don't know no better. Jacob, I *tolt* you to get out of the way—

Two objects were placed on the floor in front of the visitor (and oh, they did smell so good). One was a tin plate with meat upon it, the other a big tin bowl filled with wads of yellow mush— Why, truly, truly, these people had corn. Yes, this substance was made of corn ground up into meal! It was so like *madakapa* that she felt she must speak of it—tell those noisy fearsome but now-grown-hospitable strangers that she knew their food, or some of it— Her people prepared similar food, centuries distant . . . her village was so far removed from all record . . . perhaps she'd only dreamt that once she dwelt in that village (as one might relate a legend, and at night, and by a fire in an earth lodge with children squeezing close to hear).

Corn-Sucker reached shaking fingers to grasp the tall pewter spoon thrust into the mush. Her eyes sought those of the elder white woman. She murmured with weak contentment: *Amanaki! Amodapi madakapa! Muti madakapa!*

What's she saying, Mam?

Trying to talk. I think she's a-thanking us—

Well, why don't she really *talk?*

Ain't no more talking than a hog makes, I swear!

Pap, can our hogs really talk to each other?

Sure enough. They talk hog Latin. Didn't you ever hear of that?

Laughter rolled and threatened, but even the rough bickering of voices could not deter the little woman from her feast. This was not a squash spoon (how she longed again to hold such a spoon in her hand!—and how carefully she'd made so many of them—the stems cut green before tiny thorns grew hard and sharp, the stems split, and bits of stick inserted to spread them spoon-shaped). But there were several metal spoons in the scrawny lodges of the Wahpekute, and Corn-Sucker had used them before . . . you dug deep into food, heaped a great mass—as much as the spoon would carry— You stuffed your mouth.

Now, meat. There was no need of a spoon for meat. Meat was eaten with the fingers.

. . . Oh, food!

. . . Oh, wonder of food, delight of food, generosity of food!

I'll be dipped— Look at her gobble that stuff—

Mam, she's got the funniest mouth and face.

What makes her look like that?

Mam, ain't that a funny mouth?

Mam, ain't—?

Like enough she got it in a fight. Them Injans is always fighting, the whole blessed time—

Oh, she smells just awful!

Shut your mouth, you don't smell so good yourself.

The cabin was warm; and even though her senses were assailed violently by pungent odors of these people, Corn-Sucker wished that she might lie down upon that floor, and sleep, and sleep long. But perhaps she dared not sleep, even did the men and women and children urge her to do so. For they might kill her while she slept. It had been done; there were many stories about the Chippeway, as told by the Dakota. A Chippeway might let you lie down to sleep, and then kill you. And Inkpaduta had killed enemies while they slept . . . it seemed suddenly that she heard him yelling, I boast! . . . Inkpaduta would say to her: You go beg among the whites. They give you food. Now, where is food from white people? Do you bring some to me? . . . What—what say you? You eat all the food, you bring none to me? Now I beat you!

. . . Not to be beaten on this day! It was too cold, her body had been cold for too long, her body had been without adequate food for too long. Ah, she must ask for more food to eat, and she must not eat it all herself, she must take some food away to the camp—

Eeeeet? she begged as in lamentation. Peeeeez . . . eeeeet?

Well, by God, give the damn old squaw an inch and she'll take—

Jim Mattock, you hush. There hain't no mush left—none cooked—but we got plenty pork, and I'm going to—

Feed all the Injans in the world, till it runs out of their ass?

Jim, you mind your speech.

Must think I'm made of fried pork!

Well, you do look like it, with that big gut of your'n.

The bellowing, the jostling—leering faces pushed close to chuckle and to stare. But the plate was taken up by the tall woman with the tight-wound hair, meat was heaped upon it, the plate came back to the floor, Corn-Sucker raked with frenzied hands. She swallowed down one slab, half-chewed; then she remembered . . . she must save the rest, must take it to the lodge . . . piece by piece she folded greasy chunks inside her blanket, and looked up at the obtruding faces, and offered her piteous smile.

Just look at that!

She's going to carry it off with her!

What I said: trying to feed the whole pissing tribe—

It was Alice who advanced the notion, it was Alice who spoke for the first time since Corn-Sucker had entered the cabin. Mam. Maybe she's got a child at home?

By gad, that could be it!

Hey, sister, what you got to home? What you got in your God damn wigwam? You got papoose? Hey? Papoose?

Corn-Sucker did not know these words. To her a child was a *daka* or a *makadishta* or a *makadishtamatse;* and among the Dakota a child was a *chunkshi* or a *hokshiyokopa* or it was other names; and she did not hear such names spoken; and she had never heard of a wigwam; yet she knew that these whites were demanding to know why she carried the meat away with her instead of eating it then and there . . . and when she had begged for more. . . .

She said: I take it to my husband.

All laughed to hear her say this, because her words were absurd to their ears. Yet she looked up at them with a shy tremulous grin, and in delicacy wiped her deformed mouth with the back of her hand.

She wished that she might give to them a song. A weak song rose within her; yet she would have been too frightened to utter the song, even could she have imagined that whites might understand.

When I was hungry I sought the village of you noisy people, and I told you of my hunger. Then you did put before me meat, and better than meat you gave me madakapa. *It is not the* madakapa *of Hidatsa, but still it was good in my mouth.*

Oh, were I in the village which once I knew, and did you come to me making the hunger sign, then would I feed you on mapi nakapa. *Willingly would I mash squash and beans together when they were boiled, willingly would I parch the hard white corn; with even more willingness would I roast sweet bits of buffalo fat! I grow hungry again in remembering!*

But my village is far.

I shall never see my village again.

I shall be only a cold dark cloud, blowing in cold dark wind.

Ain't she funny? Makes such funny faces, just like she's bout ready to bawl!

Agnes, don't you make sport of the poor thing. How'd you like to be a dirty old Injan squaw—how'd you like that, miss? And never have no house to live in, nor nothing?

Guess I'd have a wigwam.

Christ, Mary, whyn't you get rid of her? Have we got to have her around here all day, stinking up the place, just setting here on her ass?

Again Corn-Sucker whispered for food, but they only laughed uproariously and made peculiar gestures at her with their hands; and the enormous fat man kept jerking his thumb toward the door and saying uncouth words like Go and Out and Wigwam and Papoose, and Go, Go, Go. Soon Corn-Sucker found herself on her feet, being propelled toward the door of the house. No one struck her, no one kicked her, they only pushed against her back and shoulders.

Mam, said Alice. Whyn't you give her the punkin butter?

Why, tis good punkin butter. I hate to waste the whole of it on her.

But none of us'll eat it. We all just plain hate punkin butter.

Jim Mattock yelled, Hell, yes, woman! Get rid of the damn stuff. I mean that big brown crockful. All spoilt, anyway—

No, it hain't neither spoilt. Just got mold on the top, and that mold means that it *hain't* spoiling—

What you kids say about it? Hell, you all hate punkin butter the way I do! And even your Mam won't eat it. . . . Hold a caucus and vote, I say. Now, all in favor signify by saying—

The *Aye!* boomed out in a way to deafen Corn-Sucker and send her staggering against the door.

Mary cried defensively: Well, all right, I give in. Can't get a one of you to eat that nice punkin butter anyway. But I ain't a-going to give her any dried punkin rings—

A mass of mildewed paste was scraped out of the crock and dumped, after some discussion, into a torn scrap of old canvas. This prize they presented to Corn-Sucker; then the door was flung open and she was sent on her way. Carl Granger's dog, which had lain with only an occasional sniffing growl throughout her stay, tore loose from Daniel and plunged toward the Indian woman in her departure;

but a kick from Jim Mattock turned him aside with a howl. Nevertheless Lee's intended assault was enough to unsteady Corn-Sucker on the icy step. Again she lost her balance. She did not fall, this time, but went tottering and skating down the path until equilibrium was recovered. She did not drop the wad of canvas which held the pumpkin butter, but did drop two slices of fried pork, and had to creep back to pick them up. In all this endeavor she failed to see the Red Wing cabin across the straits, or she would have gone there to seek more food.

She had found that begging from the whites was not the perilous and agonizing occupation which she'd feared; they did not, for instance, incite the dog to attack her—they kept the dog from harming her instead. There was a toughness, an actual alarm in the noise and bluster of white people, and they did offer an acrid terrifying smell. But they made much of their noise with laughter, and so they must not all be as cruel or perhaps even as deceitful as she had been led to believe.

Still, there were all manners and conditions of white men and women. For what of those travelers on the Missouri River, who had slain her own father, Man-Walking-On-Mussel-Shells, in the long ago?

Would they have given her food?

No, they would have given her bullets instead.

No food would you have offered me. Oh, you white men in the river boat, who shot my father until at last he died, I say to you now that you were very bad indeed.

Did you give my father meat? Nay, never did you do this thing. Did you give my father corn-meal mush? Nay, never did you do this thing. Did you give my father the other strange strong-odored food which now I hold within this cloth? Desha, desha, desha!

Perhaps now you are as the wicked boy, Mosquito-Neck, of my village. Perhaps wolves have grated their teeth upon your bones.

Corn-Sucker was confident that Inkpaduta would not like the peculiar stuff within the cloth. She tried sadly to decide what to do. Did she fetch only the five odd-sized bits of fried pork to her master, doubtless he would be cruel to her. He would say: What bring you? But only these small pieces? *Eze!* Is there not more? *Hehe!* You eat the rest? . . . His moccasined foot would swing like an axe being swung, the impact would fling her out and down and far.

But did she fetch also a mass of queer-smelling stuff— (No one might ever know what to name it. At first when she saw the white women scraping it from their stone pot, she had thought that it was squash; yet Corn-Sucker had known squash boiled and squash dried and squash mashed—through her life she had known squash—and this was not squash; nay, never did squash have such a smell—) Oh, Inkpaduta spoke evil of Hidatsa words and he spoke evil of Hidatsa foods. What might he not do, if he did not like this food of the whites?

She halted indecisively beside a tree which lay on its side in the snow. Wind had made a drift here, and the drift protected an area in the lee of the trunk. Corn-Sucker huddled to rest and hide from fitful spiteful winds which gushed up from that icebound lake and sent dry snow snapping like sand against her face and eyes. She crouched, her robed back presented to the mean breeze, and squeezed against a limb of the huge tree . . . hard and cold, tiny fruit clinging stubbornly to twigs. It was the sort of tree which the Wahpekute called *utuhu;* it was an oak; oaks did not grow beside the village or in the life Corn-Sucker had known earlier. She had eaten some of the *utuhu* fruit before, soon after they found Inkpaduta's people, and she did not like the fruit. It was so bitter! But in those days she had not starved as now she starved. She gathered a few of these hard frozen berries, burst their rough skins open, splintered their hulls with her nails. But nothing inside, only air, only powder— And see: there were tiny holes in other fruit wadded among the twigs. Bad spirits had crept into the fruit, perhaps when still it grew green.

Corn-Sucker left off exploring the acorns, and got out her sack of pumpkin butter from its warmer hiding inside her robe. It was stiffening, but she ladled off a chunk of it with her thumb, and forced the stuff into her mouth.

Tsakak! This she could not eat! Rather might she break off branches from willows, and gnaw the bark.

Surely Inkpaduta would beat her with his hands, he would maul her with his foot, he would flog her with a stick, if she tried to offer this food as the abundance of her wanderings.

But still someone else might eat the stuff; perhaps one of the children would eat it? It was food. It must not be thrown away.

Even now the tipis were unsettled by urgency. Inkpaduta had been talking of the valley of a river called Inyaniake. It was toward the south, Corn-Sucker'd heard the men in conference. The twins were advising a departure to the west instead, to the land of the Yanktonai. Inkpaduta did not wish to return to the land of the Yanktonai, at least not now. He had his reasons for reluctance (and Corn-Sucker knew what those reasons were) but the others might not understand; nor would Inkpaduta tell them what had occurred when last he was there; nor dared the woman tell, nor would she have told if she had dared.

But even as soon as the next morning he might give an order to the women. Then they would all be taking down the lodges, tying lodgepoles into travois bundles. . . .

Miserable and unequipped and foodless as the camp was, Corn-Sucker felt a benumbed sense of homecoming as she approached.

She smelled smoke, heard the dogs, heard a child of He-Wears-Anything uttering its curling hunger-cry. Ah, she would hide a piece of meat, push it now deeper into a fold of her blanket; and then she would give this bit of food to the child when no one was close to observe!

Inkpaduta sat much as she had left him, staring beyond the fire, gripping the old pipe given him by Wolf-Sits-Down; but the pipe was dead between his fingers.

You find food?

Aye. Her hand went inside the sodden cloth, closed round four curled slabs of pork, fetched them out.

He said in recognition: *Kukushe shin.* Meat of the white men!—and he snatched the offering and downed it, chewing carelessly, swallowing the pieces almost whole. Then he looked up with his sore pink-lidded eyes, and gestured imperatively. You have more? You give!

Nay, Corn-Sucker lied in desperation. She clutched the wad of canvas against herself instead of pushing it out toward the man. . . . It is not good! It is like squash, but it is not squash. You wish not to eat this!

Breathing heavily with immediate anger, he unbent his big joints and rose to tower above her. He jerked the damp bundle from her grasp.

The woman relapsed into a crouch, going down slowly and miserably, coiling herself as Inkpaduta had uncoiled himself; and she slapped a fold of blanket up across her face, hoping to protect her sensitive mouth if his kick caught her there.

At first she heard nothing, she was too apprehensive to hear; there reached her ears only the false frizzling sound of the fire . . . a sound as of cooking, yet there was nothing to cook.

Then it seemed that, unbelievably, she detected the coarse ugly sound of his munching and swallowing. She turned back a corner of her robe and sent a crooked glance upward; and there he stood, forcing the last of the pumpkin butter into his wide mouth—licking his fingers one by one, then licking off those small pasty portions which adhered to the canvas, then licking his own upper lip and chin, and rubbing the back of his hand across his lower face.

Good! he said.

Ki! She would never understand her husband, no one would ever understand him; and she knew that he had no wish to be understood, and preferred to remain a riddle and a menace. But she was thankful not to be beaten.

This Old One remembers. There lies some distance to the west a river which men call by different names; and I name it Chankasnasnata, or River-Where-Limbs-Are-Torn-Off-Trees; and there are other names.

At places along this river, underbrush grows thick and heavy; twisted together are small trees. A man goes slowly among such trees. A man goes as a serpent goes. Many winters agone did my people pass that way when storms came early. Everyone ate! Much meat was killed. For deer had run from drifts in which they would have died. They came to cower among those thickets. The deer munched twigs and willow bark throughout a long winter, the deer did not die of hunger. Nor would anyone die of hunger who came to live near the deer.

Now I do not know where all the deer have gone in a barren season; but they have gone somewhere. Even in this cold they could be treading paths through those same woodlands. . . .

How many sleeps to the place of the deer, Thou Old One?

Many sleeps. We go slowly.

Aye, we go slowly. There is much snow. . . .

Perhaps ten sleeps? I know not. But beyond lie the hunting places of the Ihanktonwanna.

. . . The mind of an Older One is like a wounded rabbit; it seeks the burrow from which it came before. Perhaps a rabbit thinks he may find safety and healing in his burrow; hence he runs in circles, trying always to seek that hole (but he does not find safety or heartiness, he finds death). So the mind of This Old One goes running among burrow entrances of the past, it goes from *ohdoka* to *ohdoka*, hole to hole; it discovers echoes of the past, it listens to them.

Voices tell stories, and as one starves and watches others starve, it is the stories of food that he remembers.

He thinks sometimes that all the myths are myths of food!

I would tell now the story of the Lost Wife. . . . Wolf Chief does lead Young Woman to a great tipi, and into this tipi he invites her. What eat you for food, Young Woman? Buffalo meat, says she. Then he calls two coyotes, and sends them for food, and soon they come bounding in return. In their jaws they bear the shoulder of a fresh-killed buffalo. How make you this for eating? O Wolf Chief, it is boiled, says Young Woman.

See you how this is a story of food?

Now starve we all. We must go to another place, that we may not starve. I care not for spirit water left on the prairie by my sons and by me, when take we horses from ugly-woman and drunken-man-who-sleeps. Snow has smothered spirit water, smothered wagon-which-is-left-on-prairie. So seek we not spirit water.

Seek we food in the Tale of the Fallen Star.

He kills many buffalo; and now the women make racks, and there is much meat to dry on the racks. Old Man and Old Woman are very rich in this meat. The Old Man says, I will tell everyone how rich we are become! In morning he goes to the top of the house and he cries aloud: I, I have abundance laid up! The fat of the big gut I chew! Thus does Old Man make origin of the name meadow lark; for so call we the meadow lark—tashiyakapopopa. *For the word* tashiyaka *is big intestine, the big gut; and the word* popopa *means that it is full of stuff, as some weeds are full of pith, as the young shoots of the elderberry are filled with pith. And the meadow lark has a yellow breast with black in the middle (it is the yellow of morning) and men say that the black stripe is made by a smooth buffalo horn worn for a necklace. . . .*

Old men and old women with active tongues, they sit in lodges of the *tannihan*, the Long Ago (they are among the dead, their bones have fallen from vanished scaffolds) but still the ears of This One may hear their voices in winter wind at night; and they go on with the tale of *Waziya*. This is the northern god who lives at the north, and from his mouth blows the cold.

So this is how he makes the cold, those Old Dead Ones say in telling the tale within my ears.

(It was very long ago when they told this; I was young, I had not yet killed; now I am old and have killed many times.)

He stands with his face to the north, and shakes his blanket, and sudden wind blows from the north. And snow falls all around the camp when Waziya *does this thing, so that the people are snowed in, and they are troubled; for, in being snowed in, they will starve.*

This thing is true! *Ate,* we stay here, we starve!

We do not stay. We go.

Is it that we can beg more food from the whites?

They give us small food.

We have guns. We go to lodges of the whites, take more food?

Then they fight. There are young men among the whites, and they would fight.

We are far away from soldiers now, far from fort. We make war?

We do not make war now. Someday again I kill. *Idatahn!* I have killed many men. I have not killed whites. Someday I kill whites.

And when they scare the buffalo, and all buffalo start to go to their home in one long line, then does Badger shoot his arrow through the long line, and all the buffalo he kills with this single arrow, for each buffalo stands one-behind-the-other, and so all are killed. Which is the fattest one? It is this one! Then does Gray Bear say to Badger: Dress this buffalo quickly! So Badger cuts with his knife, and the blood flows. Oh, there is much meat. . . .

You did speak, Thou Old One, of the river called Inyaniake. You speak not now of this river.

Nay, I speak not of that river. There are new whites dwelling there.

I think they are fewer than these at Okoboji. First seek we deer in the thickets near the western river, the Chankasnasnata. If we find no deer, if once more we starve, we go to lonely lodges of whites on that smaller river to the south. Sometimes there is one house; then one travels for one sleep; then there is another house. It is like lonely lodges in the Minisota country—like unto that lodge of the white-people-with-all-blue-eyes where we take food. What can they do?

They cannot fight.

Nay.

We break guns!

If guns are good, we take guns instead of break guns.

Ate, thou knowest much. . . . Go we on to land of the Ihanktonwanna? They are our cousins.

Nay! Nay! Nay! We go not there.

Thou art Head Man.

Aye. I act wisely. *Okiksamya waun.*

And This Old One loves the story of the Raccoon. For it is a story of deceit and cruelty, and death, and also feasting; and all these things are loved by This Old One.

The crawfish hurries back to crawfish village, and he cries: I find a fat raccoon! But he is dead. I pinch his nose, I pinch his soft paws, I put my fingers in his ribs. He does not move when I do these things, so surely he is dead. . . . Then do all the crawfish people march to where Raccoon is lying, and they dance in a circle around him because they believe that he is dead, and he is very fat, and good to eat, and him will they eat soon. They do sing: We shall have a great feast! On the spotted-face beast with soft smooth paws! He is dead, he is dead! We feast on his flesh! . . . Up leaps Raccoon. Your ugly backs will be broken by me! I break your rough bones! I crunch your ugly claws! And so does Raccoon rush upon them, while women and children run screaming, while men fight bravely but with no success. The crawfish people do not feast on Raccoon. It is Raccoon who feasts on them, on crawfish people!

It is good that Raccoon leaps upon the crawfish people.

It is good that women and children do shriek.

So would I make white women and children run screaming.

So will I do this thing. *Washte.*

One day . . . one night. . . .

They thought him dead, thought him harmless! But it was Raccoon who feasted on the many crawfish.

I would feast!

No man among the Wahpekute now wore his hair braided. Long since the braids had been uncased, unfastened; for loose long hair offered protection against the biting cold. Has-Intercourse and He-

Has-Done-Walking and He-Wears-Anything all owned hoods made for them by their wives; so hoods were made for other men by other wives. Inkpaduta did not order Corn-Sucker to make a hood for him —his thoughts were centered on a faraway series of scraggly thickets where deer might have yarded—he thought of succulent deermeat when he did not think of Raccoon, and how Raccoon deceived the crawfish people and gobbled them in the end. Of her own volition Corn-Sucker sewed up a hood for her husband. It was constructed rudely after the Capuchin pattern brought into an upper Mississippi region by French travelers through two centuries, to be copied later by Indians to the best of their ability. An oblong piece was cut from some scrap of blanket, was then doubled and stitched together along one side. Thus the seam passed from the forehead to the crown of the head; and there were laces for fastening the two corners beneath the chin. Inkpaduta received his gift from the hand which held it toward him shyly—he grunted: This is for a child!—and threw the thing toward the fire. It was loose and flapping, it did not fly as far as the fire, it fell short. Corn-Sucker's heart knew a familiar numbness; but she retrieved the rejected head covering and hung it upon a stick which had been driven to support the tipi-lining above their bed. Grains of sleet began to sting the faces of all, in that painful morning when the women took down their lodges and tied the poles. When Corn-Sucker next saw Inkpaduta, he was wearing the new hood she had sewn! This gave her happiness, even as she scraped her hardened stiff fingers in simultaneous tasks of folding, bundling, dragging, lashing.

I did make for my husband one apoka, *I did make a hat! It is of blue, for the blanket from which it came was blue; and when he wears this hat, his ears will not freeze and fall off, for the fierce ice and wind cannot reach his ears! One day again our sky also may be warm and blue; but it will be a very long time now until summer. Much cold comes first. And many days in which to be hungry!* So she moaned as she worked, but she sang in Hidatsa and the other women did not know what was told in her song. Oh, there were not enough ponies! Many heavy bales were put upon Corn-Sucker's back, and they dragged at the band across her forehead until she feared that her skull would be cracked from its fastenings at her neck, her head would be pulled off backward. She accepted more weight than she could carry. In the first shallow snowbank of their journey she wallowed to a fall, and could not rise again. Inkpaduta called from the back of his mare, bidding her to rise—telling all that Corn-Sucker was grown weak and worthless; he called her Half-Face; he said that there was but one thing to do with the agèd, the weak and worthless, and that was to leave them behind. Corn-Sucker knew that such abandonment had been performed through the years, and often: it came of necessity. If weak people could not travel they must be left behind, though sometimes they were slain before being left. At last Cloud-Woman, the wife of Itoyetonka, came back to her, and lifted the heaviest bundle and strapped it to a travois where children were riding on top of other baggage; Corn-Sucker was helped to her feet, so once more she was ready to attempt the journey. The band straggled out onto the *tinta,* the great-land-without-timber, with sky above an empty western horizon darkening as they inched toward it. The plaint of children too small to know that they must not complain, the reedy sound of journey-song and hunger-song gasped by some of the women as they held their heads low and lurched against the wind— Forbidding silence of all the men struck just as stubbornly upon the ears. In a grove somewhere ahead there might be discovered birds or rabbits; upon the prairie might wait prairie wolves to be shot and eaten. Else these people would need to kill more of their own dogs, need to kill another pony. Perhaps in dry locked forests along the next river to the west could be found hazelnuts still clustered within hard ragged husks, glued to spindly bushes above the snow. The Wahpekute draggled in their thin twisted column, circling slowly to find easier undrifted ways; and sleet grew more intense and needled, the wind hummed in gyrating gusts to harm them. Once a dash of sunlight came through to make shadows flick, and thus revealed the wanderers as more beaten and lonely than before.

XXVIII

In all there were eight Granger children, but two died in infancy, long before William and Carl were born. When William and Carl were grown and gone to America, they used sometimes to discuss the vanished infants, and argue about them. William believed that two baby girls had died, and Carl was just as certain that they were a little brother and a little sister. Dissenting opinion between the Granger brothers was concerned usually with matters out of their past which must necessarily go unproved. If you set out to go from their home to Aldington Corner, and wished to walk entirely on roads instead of crossing through woodland or meadows, was it a shorter distance if you turned left, leaving the Bonnington road and going up past The Elms; or was it shorter if you bore to the right, up the hill as if heading for Lympne, and then at the Lympne road bore directly northwest to Aldington Corner? . . . Take the Slingsby family, the ones at Clap Hill. Was it correct that William Slingsby was five years younger than his wife, or was it (twould be much commoner, indeed) the other way round? And was the wife's name Martha, and was the little daughter named Sarah; or was it the other way round? . . . Take old Butcher, the parish clerk— Was he the proprietor of that huge stripèd cat which actually killed the Matsons' yellow dog; or was it his spotted dog which was killed by the Matsons' yellow cat? . . . If you stood at the wall just south of the pond (a hundred paces south of the Grangers' door) and the day was fine, was it easier to see the Channel glint toward the east, immediately downcoast from Hythe; or could you glimpse the sea more readily if you gazed more to the south, in the direction of Dymchurch?

These genealogical, geographical, and historical facts, and prevailing difference of opinion or interpretation concerning them, beguiled leisure hours of the brothers Granger. They did enjoy some leisure hours in the United States. They had known almost none in Kent.

The Grangers lived in a fire-gutted house overlooking the Romney Marshes. The place was called Monkshurst, and was believed to be haunted, though not by monks. It had carried that Monkshurst name when a family of Tellfords dwelt there in yeoman comfort, back in the time of George the Second. On a night of unspeakable frost (so ran the legend) flames raced through the structures from adjoining stable and granaries to a topmost attic within the gables. Seven Tellfords, old and young, perished in that blaze, along with a maidservant or two. Distant heirs were willing to lease out their lands following the tragedy, but did not exhibit any willingness to rebuild the farmstead itself; nor did they bother to pull down those charred walls. In later years Monkshurst roosted on its eminence above the Royal Military canal, a bewildering tangle of blackened beams, weighty vines, and crumbled tiles; and under the vines existed an eternal crunching puzzle of shattered glass from ancient mullioned windows . . . with age the glass turned to the color of violets, and was prized as gems by neighborhood girls. Out of the wreckage there had survived a small area still sound and reasonably weatherproof, and these three rooms were inhabited briefly by squatters through several decades. Sydney Granger, father of William and Carl, moved there with Meg, his wife, a year after they were married; he won permission to do so because of his sober mien and industry, exemplified daily in fields which the remote surviving Tellfords rented out to Farmer Wilcox and others.

Neither of the Grangers was native to that region. Sydney had been born near the Severn in Gloucestershire, Meg came from a cottage on the banks of the Minsmere in distant Suffolk. Family disasters and economic adversity carried both people to slavery in London when they were still very young; and in each case they craved their original greeneries with passion, and fled down to Kent to pick hops in the first possible season. There they met, amid the drowsy hops; they were promptly betrothed and wedded soon. Sydney's gnarly young hands grew happily around the implements which they had been fastened to in his first boyhood; he did not wish to put them down, nor ever to return to a city. With his wife he became an itinerant, since no permanent situation offered readily. Sometimes in that first year the pair were compelled to sleep under hedgerows like the veriest tinkers; but in time they meandered closer to the Channel, and found their Monkshurst haven. All their children were born in the dilapidated ruin, and promptly (the six survivors) went forth to work in the world, even before they were taught their letters. A small child might earn twopence or threepence per day if set to scaring sparrows out of a new-seeded turnip field, or waving rooks away from the peas. They were serious of face and odd of speech, these infant Grangers; people in the countryside used to laugh at their talk until they grew accustomed; twas such a strange mixture of West Country intonation, East Anglian idiom, with a spray of London slang and local expression over all.

The month before Carl, the baby of the flock, was born, Sydney

Granger rode home unconscious and bloody, carted all the way from Farmer Bromley's cornfield near Bilsington. A careless harvester, jabbing through haze of hot chaff and blown dust, had struck the tine of a metal fork into Sydney Granger's skull. Granger's body recovered in part but his mind was a ringing emptiness, except in those rare moments when he suffered delusions. There was concern throughout the community, and the Squire fetched in an old schoolmate of his who was said to be a noted surgeon. All efforts were in vain. Sydney Granger sat stonily ever after. He liked to stroke kittens, that was almost the only thing he liked to do; and through many days several kittens might be asleep, cuddled in his wide papery hands, or crawling up to his smock-frocked shoulder. Meg and the six children knew increased toil and shorter rations from then on. Even the twin girls were taught to creep among Farmer Wilcox's turnips, pulling out the charlock, before they attained the age of five. Meg Granger worked with steady fury alongside laborers stronger than herself, and they were men at that; and she kept up with them; and she owned but one gown, so she would not wear that; she worked in her shift. Her children fed upon a mash made of turnips and potatoes. Cheese and meat were luxuries undreamed until the children were tall enough to find more remunerative work, and (in the boys' case) to do a little poaching. Then hares and wood pigeons appeared on the family table at Monkshurst; and poor Meg Granger feared that her two elder sons might be seized and transported. But they were not, they got off undetected and scot free. First Staples and then Fratton took the shilling and went tramping away with the Buffs. These lads were so named in honor of early employers to whom their father gave gratitude and devotion; and they were called respectively Stay and Frat; and they cut very fine figures in the uniform of the Royal East Kents. Frat died of fever at Kurnaul, it was learned a long while afterward; and Stay was killed at Punniar. The younger brothers, in their time, turned deaf ears to blandishments of recruiting sergeants, no matter how lean the larder at Monkshurst.

Trudy and Ellie went into service (they wished to be together, with the natural affinity of twins, but such a situation could not be found. Ellie went into Rector Knatchbull's household when she was but thirteen; and Trudy was accepted at the home of the Rector's cousins in Ashford a few months later). Eventually William and Carl became the family mainstays. They grew into jacks-of-all-trades—all the farm trades—and could hire out as competent plowmen when still very young. William preferred working with horses, Carl was the better ox-driver of the two. The Grangers had never been able to acquire any livestock of their own; thus the brothers might serve only those lands where extra labor was needed in season. Sickle, fork, and flail—bramble scythe or chaff cutter—the boys knew the feel and use of these. Also Farmer Wilcox owned a drill, and used to take it round to the neighbors; but often he was busy with his own acres, and he taught the Granger boys the arts of this machine, that they might go planting in his stead. Ten shillings per day for the machine: that was the charge, plus an extra fee for each acre planted; and this per-acre fee was subject to much bargaining and alteration, depending on the terrain involved. Naturally Farmer Wilcox received the lion's share, for he owned the drill; but William and Carl got each a shilling for a day's work, and their board for that day into the bargain. If they fared on the treasures of an especially provident and flavorable kitchen —at the Slingsby home, say, or when working at the Tommy Jameses, or planting for Mr. Tom Dickie—they would save samples of beef pudding and shortcake and dumplings to be sneaked home for the benefit of Mother Meg and the frail staring father whose blank face lighted up when he was awarded these dainties. Father would mumble about it to the kittens, and feed bits to them.

Aye, I see un, he'd say at times.

What did thee see, poor Syd?

See un. . . . Sometimes he pointed.

There's naught past they vines yonder, naught but old broken bricks and ivy. Twas like that when first we came to bide here, Syd.

See un. . . .

She'd tell the boys of this when they came home of an evening, and they'd look at their father with apprehension.

His wits be whacked to the wide, Bill.

Well, don't get in a pucker o'er it. He's always been so.

He thinks it's they Tellfords he's seeing, he does.

No doubt.

Bill, lad. Did ever thee see 'em, thus?

Nah!

Twice in winter I thought I sin 'em, all the one for that.

Nah! There ain't no ghosts. Tis just an old tale.

Trude and El, they sin they Tellfords. Mind their telling on it, now?

Ah, they're girls, they'd fancy brownies and fairies and that.

Bill, take me. I'm no girl. And I sin—

Nah! What?

Tellfords, moving about.

Were they wailing?

Heard nay sound.

Then bean't Tellfords that thee saw. Tellfords is all wailers, fair born to it. When I was cropping taters for Miss Patience Erskine, she told me of their wailing. Well, I said her, I never heard it, and I was born at Monkshurst, like the lot of we Grangers; and how could it be that there's wailing of they Tellfords as was burnt up in they fire, Miss

Patience?—if never I've heard a wail, and I haven't? Nor Brother Carl, neither, I said her.

But I've thought I sin 'em.

Steady, lad, steady. Thee's worked long, thee's done up.

The brothers dwelt in a kind of bitter harmony. Their foreheads were broad, their shoulders broad, their arms long as apes'—the jawbones stuck out of their cheeks. In appearance otherwise they were at variance: William was tighter knit, and paler of eyes and hair; Carl was more stooped in his posture, but he could lift that extra hundredweight which William could not lift for all his straining. And Carl Granger's shock of brown hair was coarse as a horse's tail, and bore a gray streak through the left side of it by the time he was twenty. Both young men owned the fortitude and solemn intensity of those who've had a childhood unembellished with frivolities—people who know little but toil, and who walk remote paths amid old stones and marshes. (There were folk dwelling in the highlands of the Southern United States who might have been their physical doubles; but the Granger boys did not know that; scarcely did they know that there was a nation called the United States.)

They loved Kent without being aware that they loved their county . . . vaguely they felt that they must take pride in being Kentishmen because they were Kentishmen, but would have been stricken dumb—and annoyed at the same time—were they pressed for reasons. They regarded warily the complex mysteries of local hedgerows and birds winking there, and blackberries and cobnuts when they appeared. They said to themselves, These hills are ours. Those elderly Roman-drained fens are Kent. Almost the sea is Kent, shimmering beyond—But no, tis not, tis England, tis called the English Channel. And once upon a time Old Nap was threatening to appear with his vast hordes loaded into fighting ships; so the canal was dug and readied. Aye, they built the Royal Military canal to fog Old Nappy, they did!

The brothers hated their congenital poverty mutely, but steadily and patiently, until at last they found escape from it.

More keenly they had hated the poverty of their parents . . . twas not that they hated their parents: they had first trusted then feared then admired their mother, with all the dire driving of her nature; but they loathed the necessities which darkened her. They looked up and saw a vast sharp curving blade of Need poised above all their heads, like a scythe suspended above haulm, ready to cut. Nevertheless little spatters and crinkles of love stole through the blackthorn forest which tightened its brambles and tried to smother their lives. Aye, some men were hard as flint, and so when love came in like stray light they turned it back, they would not let it penetrate. But underneath their calluses the Grangers were humanly soft as a bed newly spaded. They took whatever beams came in to them amid the bleak thicket, and held them, and whispered to themselves (never to one another): Oh, warm, warm!—or, Sweet, sweet!—and wished hopelessly that more sun was falling through. They pitied their helpless father with all their hearts, and tried roughly to say and do things which would make the frail man smile. He smiled when they fetched him a few green damsons and told him they'd gathered them especially for him, whilst coming home. At such times momentarily a glister came into his eyes, and the sagging lips fell apart, and he seemed about to speak, but he did not speak (except again to gaze limply in detachment toward the ivied shadows, and perhaps murmur, to his family's disquietude: Aye. See un).

They knew the fabled dawn chorus, heard it when waking and even before waking. They singled out the singers, wished lamely that they themselves were but birds, with no necessity to rise and feed (scantily) and go plodding off to a job of ditch-cleaning. . . . Nightingale first, stubborn in intent to render a solitary message ere the lapwings had drowned him out; and later came skylarks calling above the meadows sloping south to where many tough prolific Romney flocks lay like soft pale rocks . . . oh, many rocks and many flocks of sheep in Romney fields.

Always the haste and thought for the farthing, the barest penny, the worn and well-handled shilling so distressingly wanted.

Think on't, lad. How'd thee like it if thee was a ram?

I could nohow abide it.

But a Romney ram, like twere one of they rams us heard Jack Earl a-telling on. Old Pope, he were called. And that sold for five hundred quid.

Thee's dizzied.

Squire he told on't, to Earl himself. Five hundred quid! And there were another—not Old Pope, not he—sold for more'n six hundred!

Like twere some foreigners who paid *that.*

Aye. And they took they ram to America, to father heaven knows how many lambs, and all of they Romney breed. And in far places like New Zealand and that. They've took Romneys there. There's other breeds that get done in with foot rot and liver fluke. But not they Romneys!

Carl, thee sounds like a bloody shepherd.

Glad I bean't.

Nip along. I see old Pinkley waiting at his gate, and then he'll spit and say, Half the morning gone, and it be a tidy bit of fyeing we've got to do.

(Trudge to labor and forget the songs a-following . . . cock pheasant, wood pigeon, and then the wrens and warblers coming in a gush . . . and never waste a turn of the head which shows you that ungainly green woodpecker tugging and heaving at the soil. Well, he must work for his own kind of bread as well, he must!)

They knew the rhymes around them, appreciated all the rhymes but sang them seldom; and then only when they halted to play with a child or two, and thus, in halting so, each paused to be a child once more. Again and again when changes were rung they'd heard the smallest bell in their Saint Martin church saying in clear Sabbath lustiness, as every villager could swear the bell was speaking and had so spoken for a good threescore-and-ten years and more: *I mean to make it understood that though I'm little yet I'm good.* Carl Granger never lifted his spud or sharpened its blade without thinking: *Thistle cut in May, come up again next day. Thistle cut in June, come up again soon. Thistle cut in July will be sure to die.* William Granger used often to wonder if ever he'd marry, if ever he'd have the pence and opportunity for marrying; and if he did, would any children be his? He thought then—and so many times sadly—of words he'd heard his mother repeat, and so he'd learnt them too. *When you've got one you can run. When you've got two you can go. But when you've three—You must bide where you be!* And she, poor soul, with eight (but two dead soon, and young and quickly) and before long a ninny-hammer of a husband to feed as well!

When he was very young Carl Granger stole away to the church to watch the door on St. Mark's Eve. But William would have naught to do with such absurdity; and he teased Carl about his superstition when they trudged to work in the next rainy dawn, and Carl was yawning and weary from his vigil; and William urged Carl to name the other participants, that he might deride them also.

Was it Jem Scott with thee, eh?

Nah.

Or they Londons? Come, lad, come!

Nah.

Or Bob Challock?

Aye.

No wits about him! He fears to walk past Monkshurst by night, count of they Tellfords. And was Will Etching along? He would be.

Aye.

Sorry figures you must have cut, hiding behind they trees! Did you see they shapes a-entering, now?

There was no reply to this query. Carl thought it wrong of William to continue twitting him. He'd gone to the church as one going on a lark; and twas a great night, and he looked forward to it, for there was no larking in his life except at Harvest . . . oh, aye, one time he and William had been allowed to leave home and tramp far past Ashford for a go at the hop-picking (though gypsy swarms who congregated there did not welcome these outsiders, and made them feel that they were interlopers; so the Granger boys never went into that region again. Later William worked at oasthouse construction nearer home). The Challock lad and the Etching lad were bound for the church of St. Martin to prove or disprove the legend surrounding St. Mark's Eve. They would crouch behind tombstones— Nah, they feared not the churchyard itself. If you stared closely at the church door you might witness a parade. Twould be a procession of people known to you, an you saw them at all—villagers, farmers, perhaps even relatives of your own— Twas a sad thing for any apparition to be glimpsed going into the church on that night. For it meant that all who went were to suffer serious sickness or accident during the year to come. And then, if not seen to *re-emerge*, they'd die on't. Twas commonly discussed; but how much of the thing was baseless rumor, and how much was a fact to threaten? Carl Granger, at his then age of ten or thereabouts, felt that his elder brother was most unwise to cry Humbug without investigation. The Widow Thruxted (she was not a witch by any means, but was known far and wide as one of the most able brewers in all the parish) told that she had been passing down the lane past St. Martin (she called the church St. Martin-in-the-Lane, as inspired by a more famous church in London. Who, she asked, had not heard of St. Martin's-in-the-Field?) and twas on St. Mark's Eve; and she glanced toward the church, but not fearfully, for all knew that she had nothing to fear— She witnessed a line of thin shapes moving through the doorway. She recognized Peter Goddard and young Jane Barfrees—she that was a Hougham, and now wedded to Hughey Barfrees the smith— These were all she recognized, for several kept their faces turned away. Then she waited and waited, and when the spectral churchgoers came gliding out again, she observed that neither old Goddard nor the pretty Mrs. Barfrees was among them. But Belinda Fry was, and Widow Thruxted had not seen Belinda going in; but she saw her coming out. And didn't Belinda come within a shade of drowning the very next summer, when she toppled into the canal whilst gathering nosegays with two other girls? And Belinda would have perished then and there, indeed she would, had not shrieks of the children fetched Edward Wilcox on the run, and he it was who dragged Belinda out. So of those unfortunates whom Mrs. Thruxted had *not* seen coming out of the church— Poor Jane Barfrees, dead in childbed on Boxing Day, of all times! And old Peter Goddard, tumbling in the snow whilst tottering down from Clap Hill, and breaking his hip then and there, and no one spying him for an hour at least, and all that frost in his lungs, and then the fever— He was buried before spring.

Carl was pleased that the boys asked him to go with them—ghost-laying, you might say, after a fashion— Just as boys idler than Carl might go bird's-nesting now and then. They crept in the dark, no one saw them. They huddled under beeches, and stared. They waited hour after hour, and saw no march of apparitions, no pacing of unlucky parishioners. Carl would not have admitted it to a soul, but he began to acquire a mighty dread of the very church which he had respected, and which had been so good to him in many ways; and he feared the thought of the sexton— What would happen if the sexton found them there? Might they be dragged off to be confronted by the Rector himself, now? And what would the Rector, that awe-inspiring Mr. Wyndham Knatchbull, say and do? Suddenly there rose a violent shriek from somewhere near the second tower. In a twinkling the three lads were gone out of the churchyard and up the lane to the corner. Etching fled west to his home near The Elms, and Challock and Granger pounded away southeast toward Postling Green. The awful outcry continued, writhing and circling upward like invisible smoke in blackness of night, until the fugitives rushed at last out of hearing. At any other time, sensible boys might have concluded that such yowling rose from the activity of cats—indeed it did sound very like cats, come to think on't— But at that place, and at that hour, and in those circumstances— At least no one might ever compel Carl Granger to tell the whole truth to the brother who derided him. (No one ever did, except for Carl himself; it was years before he told it, and then the two men had their dry chuckling together.)

O gentle church, good generous church of St. Martin! Always the Granger children thought it a wonder that they should be admitted there, ragged as they were, the poorest in the parish; but admitted they were. And some of their first memories were concerned with the little troop as they pressed up the hill past Copperhurst—the troop in which they saw themselves trotting and breathing hard, clambering over the stile, taller ones bending down to aid the smaller, and Mother gasping out, Haste, now, us have no time to dilly dally. Must reach the Aldington road ere bell begins! . . . And gray-trunked pride of mighty beeches, and some churchyard stones the color of chocolate (except that the Grangers never tasted chocolate, not in those times), and the sight of other families coming to worship, as they, the raggle-taggle and unfortunate, were permitted to come— And thought of the woolly-minded father whom they'd left on his bench, wan and staring in the sunlight, with kittens hustling up and down his weak legs, or leaping from the window ledge to his shoulders, and scratching him sometimes when they landed, until the poor man moaned . . . but he never struck at the kittens, not he; he was wounded and lifeless, fading slowly through the years . . . ah, what a figure of a man he were! Hearty and hardy as the best, until that worthless young Frith put the fork in him! Come, William, girls, Carl, haste, there's the ringing now!

. . . *Most heartily we beseech thee with thy favour to behold our most gracious Sovereign Lady, Queen Victoria; and so replenish her with the grace of thy Holy Spirit, that she may always incline to thy will, and walk in thy way: Endue her plenteously with heavenly gifts; grant her in health and wealth long to live; strengthen her that she may vanquish and overcome all her enemies, and finally after this life she may attain everlasting joy and felicity; through Jesus Christ our Lord.*

And underfed overworked Grangers, in their rough patches and darns, whispering Amen along with the rest, and welcome to do so.

The long strain of the Hungry Forties took its toll of the villagers (there were seasons when men had to patrol the fields by night with clubs in their hands, to walk sentry duty against starving folk who crept wisplike from nearby towns to dig taters or turnips, to snatch cabbages and go running away with them). It couldn't be said that Sydney Granger starved, for there were two boys left at home to help with the keeping. But in the spring of 1848 William and Carl returned from a day's planting to find Meg their mother reeling toward them down the overgrown Monkshurst path, waving frantic hands. He don't say nothing, say nothing! He's down aside the bench, and his hands is cruel cold. Oh, he can't be *gone?* But gone he was, with two unfortunate kittens smothered by the fall and pressure of even his frail frame, for they were under the father, poor things—and the old cat mewing about in her search—when the boys lifted Sydney Granger. Carl was twenty then, and his brother twenty-two, but both still remembered the storied march of the apparitions on St. Mark's Eve . . . Carl especially recalled the matter to mind, though he did not then discuss it with anyone else (Bob Challock was long gone to sea, and Will Etching was long in gaol; but he supposed that they remembered the churchyard vigil and the shrieking as well as he). Had he stood there once more, on the previous St. Mark's Eve, would he have seen the fragile shape of his father tottering into the church, and never emerging again, whatever the watch maintained? Might. Aye, he might.

The girls were sent for, and they hurried home and wept with their mother; then came the burial up at St. Martin after the winders had done their task, and the bearers theirs. . . . But three Grangers left at Monkshurst (and no one to peer broodingly off through the ruins and mutter, See un). By autumn Meg had grown so lonely that she yielded to the importunings of her daughter Trudy. This girl was most happy in her situation in far-off Ashford (took one half a day to walk there, it did) and there had risen an opportunity for her mother to join her. One of the staff in that household was marrying and going out to Australia, of all places!—and someone would be needed to replace her. Trudy had spoken to her mistress about it, and the mistress stood willing to interview Meg Granger.

Save for my own home, I've always worked outside. . . . Not after William and Carl were grown to do man's work; then I could bide with your Dad.

Well, he's gone, poor man. . . . And the strange thing about it all is, Mum, that Bessie's the daughter of old Paul, the gardener. And he's used to having her help him with vegetables and ornamentals.

I'd rather like for to do that.

I'm sure old Paul would like to have you, Mum. He says boys are no good—wouldn't have one about the place. He says a clever woman owns a greener thumb than a lad, most of them does. And then I told Mistress how very good you were at both baking and brewing, and how you hired out in Aldington to make cowslip wine, and how very good it was, too. And there's two beds in my room, and you could have one. And they're such kindly folk, Mum, so very kind to all of us. And you'd not be lonely as you are here, with the boys gone all day, and too weary to do more than grunt when they come home of a night—

But who'd *do* for the boys?

Let 'em marry, one or both, cried Trudy flippantly.

They'm saved up a few shillings, this past year or two. With them grown and earning we managed to put a bit by; though your poor father's coffin cost a tidy sum. But neither boy's ever been and spoke of marriage—

Then they can keep bachelor's hall, here at Monkshurst.

Ah, they'd nohow abide that.

But she did go back by coach to Ashford with Trudy; and Mistress was much taken with Meg's substantial qualities; and old Paul (who came suspicious and glowering to the encounter) was edified to find that Meg knew all about Regents—oh, a splendid-cropping tater was those Regents!—and not many folk did. And Paul escorted Meg to his potting shed, and there the sharp-eyed knowledgeable woman immediately picked out a beck—much better for hilling taters than a hoe, she said—and the proud Paul said that the beck was fifty years old at least, and had been hand-forged by his own father-in-law who was by way of being a smith. Aye, they got on.

Meg went off to Ashford permanently about the first of November. Then the boys had a dull and soon a disorderly and frowzy time of it; soon the old pink bricks of the hearth were stained with spillings and drippings; no fire blazed there when they reached home at night. They scratched about and bundled up their own wads of bread and cheese for a later luncheon when they arose before daylight.

Rum life we lead, Carl.

Aye. And getting rummer by the minute.

But she would go. Her heart was set.

I'd nay be one to stay her.

Days grew quickly shorter, the evenings dark and long and long and cold and dark and dark and dark: grim English evenings of November. William and Carl were transplanting trees at Handen Farm over beyond Aldington Corner, and the old public house known as the Walnut Tree gave forth welcoming spears of light as they trudged homeward. Bill Williams, the publican, was an affable host. Welshman though he might be by name, he knew and loved the village and the region round about; and, as the Grangers' brothers had done until they died of it, he'd worn the Queen's uniform in his own time. Carl and William took to lingering long hours in front of the Walnut Tree fireplace, mugs in their hands. They didn't live up their pay; there were just the two of them, and the few coppers that kept their mugs filled they counted as well spent. Saturday nights, now, Mrs. Williams took them into the kitchen, and they had plates of hot sausage and taters. Twas good to sit at a meal in the kitchen, and actually they could afford to. Twas comfortable, companionable, to stroke the Williams' big black dog, and whisper, Good dog, James lad.

One night in that same November, as they lingered in the pub along with various Hookers, Grays, and Coopers, there entered a man named Scott—one of those Scotts whose ancestors had dwelt, proudly and amply, at the village of Smeeth across low ridges to the north. This particular Scott might not be too amply provided with the world's riches, but he was a man of interest in the eyes of all: he had but come back from Canada and, according to his affirmation, could scarcely wait until some family problems were put to rights and he might once more be on the high seas, bound for an enchanting new home beyond the western shores of the Atlantic Ocean.

It was not in Canada that he expected to take up his holding. Twas in a place called I-*o*-wuh, and that was in the United States with the Yanks. There had been formed among Canadians, at some uncertain time in the past, an organization known as the Mississippi Emigration Company; and Mr. Scott bore with him a report printed for benefit of members of that society. Their delegates had visited personally the region called I-*o*-wuh. Now, as Scott sat beside a good light and read aloud, all ordinary conversation was hushed in favor of his reading. He had produced a shabby creased clipping from the Toronto *Mirror* as well, and here was confirmation of the wonders recited.

The Iowa Delegation went on a special mission . . . and have returned after the accomplishment of the design for which they had been sent. They found a country on the west side of the Mississippi, which for beauty and fertility, surpassed all their expectations—a country consisting chiefly of high rolling prairie—which implies an elevated country, with an undulating surface—easily cultivated . . . a country presenting every incitement to sobriety, to industry, and to enterprise, and which affords a much larger reward to the cultivator of the soil, than any of the older States or the Canadas.

Twas Harry, my wife's younger brother. He went out there.

To the I-*o*-wuh place?

Nah, to Canada. And doing right well, he is. But if this new country is better'n that— The speaker shook his head wonderingly, and still doubtfully, and in all appreciation of such bounty.

Be there more to read, Scott?

Aye, the report. What I read was merely from a newspaper. But should you like to hear the report?

There was a murmur of assent. Let me stand you to a glass, said Bill Granger explosively. Twas the first time he'd ever said such a thing in his life, except to Williams the landlord; or to his own brother.

Why, that's very kind of you.

. . . *The soil, is a black, vegetable mould, sometimes mixed with a sandy loam, at others more nearly covered with a stiff sward and heavy coat of natural grass; which soil, after the sod is subdued, is exceedingly easily worked—it stands a drought well, and is not subject to crack, &c. . . . Fall and spring wheat, rye, clover, barley, peas, oats, buckwheat, potatoes, turnips, and all kinds of vegetables, clover, timothy, and also all sorts of tame grass, grow most luxuriantly, and repay well the labor of the husbandman.*

Be there aught about the yield, Scott?

Aye, somewhere. We'll see, now. Ah. *These descriptions of grain scarcely ever fall down, and generally get ripe, and are dry and sound; while it is remarkable that wheat is not troubled with rust or apt to be smutty, nor has such a thing ever been known, in the north of Illinois or Iowa, as its sprouting in the field after cutting, or when in the stack.*

Hard to believe, that.

Aye, very hard to believe.

Like to show un *my* wheat, that I would. They wet year, now?

Same with me. All sprouted and spoilt.

The spring wheat, peas and oats were ripe and nearly all harvested by the end of July.

July? Can't mean that.

So it says. Quite takes my breath away.

Hard to believe.

Aye. Think on't. July!

From what the Delegates observed, they have no doubt but prairie sod, well turned over and planted with corn in season, will produce thirty-five bushels to the acre, without being hoed or touched after planting.

Ah, come, now!

So it says.

Like enough their bushels bean't the same as ourn. What about that, Scott?

Ourn is a bit larger. But still. . . .

Clarence Hooker said, This time I'll stand you to the glass.

Why, that's very kind of you.

When the Granger brothers stepped out of the Walnut Tree that night they were greeted with a fantastic demonstration by the merry dancers. (This was the most vivid display of Northern Lights witnessed in England for many decades.) Shifting, shafting, fanning in arcs across a diffused and ruddy sky, the immense fingers glowed and waggled, and newer fresher crimson stole up like flame between them. Promptly Carl Granger hastened back into the public house and informed the lingerers that Smeeth and Mersham were burning up. There was a hasty exodus to view this catastrophe even at long range; and the voices, the cries of *Fire* aroused those people who lived in nearby cottages, until the entire roadway past Aldington Corner was populated with night-clad watchers bundled up in greatcoats or odd bits of blanket or rug. But in Smeeth and Mersham the folk were convinced that Wye and Hastingleigh were ablaze; in Wye, boys shouted with the excitement of Chilham's flaming; and so it went across the region, with men in Hythe convinced that Canterbury must be a vast blaze, and Canterbury citizens speculating about the horrid red fate of Whitstable and Herne Bay. Eventually a proper identification of the phenomenon was made in most cases, and people watched with admiration and awe instead of alarm.

William and Carl Granger went homeward to the gloomy deserted ruin in a state of confusion. Neither could help but think that the miraculous aurora was a thing of special portent, and directed most decidedly at himself and themselves (as natural violences have been adjusted to personal application, ever since the first advanced simian blinked at an eclipse, and growled because his own private sun was leaving him).

Could be twas the end of the world, Bill!

Nah. Northern Lights, folk calls them.

But who fires them, then?

Thee heard what Bill Williams said. It be summat to do with the North Pole and icebergs and that.

I'm sore afraid of un, and no mistake.

Can't blame thee. We be all afraid.

But their expressed fear was not sufficient to deter them from contemplation of the prevailing mystery. Was it not odd that they had learnt of the miraculous Iowa country in distant America within that same hour when fierce gigantic brushes went swabbing the loose free paint of Almighty God across the high heavens? Angels who contrived those merry dancers, those Northern Lights, possessed complicated wisdom not held by mortals. Twas no secret from the angels that the storied faraway corn could swell into enormous yield *without being hoed or touched after planting.*

So the angels declared: Doubt ye the words of the stranger, as repeated by Mr. Scott so recently come from Canada? Then our sweeping quivering bands and rays shall be a sign!

As a Light shone one time above a stable to point the way. . . .

Mind, then, this other land beyond the seas (and we can see it from our high noble perches, as we look down with ease upon Kent) promises a relief from the bite of poverty which has oppressed thee and thy kind through so many plodding years. . . .

God touches the soil there with a better sun, a richer rain. . . .

Mind the words read forth by Mr. Scott. . . .

The black locust can be raised with the greatest ease imaginable; it has been known to grow from the seed in six years, large enough to be split into four good sized rails, and it is very hardy when young . . . for strength, it surpasses oak . . . grows tall and straight grained, and splits better than the oak, and is excellent for fuel . . . plenty of the seed can be obtained . . . a couple of dollars' worth is sufficient for a farm.

Bill. How many pence in a dollar?

Many as in a shilling, like enough?

Bean't certain. A smartish few.

How'd we get on for dollars?

We'd take our bit of money, they'd give us dollars for un. Scott told on't.

Twould take our all for passage, and then some.

How much did un say must be laid out?

Three to five quid.

Ah, that be a tidy bit!

We could save more, with her gone now.

And separately, not together, but each in knowledge of the other's wakefulness— Each young man stole into the hollow November chill another time or two that same night, and stood looking up at wands and sticks of blaze and quiver in the sky, and considered that a promise was being offered; and a testimonial and urgency was being spelled out for him, one which must be heeded.

Both Grangers worked through the next few months with rare ferocity, and in the spring of 1849 they sailed for America on an emigrant vessel which originated its voyage in London and touched at Dover. They paid three pounds, ten shillings apiece for the cheapest passage obtainable. They were starved, squeezed, tossed about, chilled, wetted, made sick by rotten food. Often they wished gloomily that they had never embarked; but now there was no help for it. (They were a mere two of the two hundred and ninety-nine thousand, four hundred and ninety-eight people from Great Britain who went out to the States or to British colonies in that year.) Only five passengers died on their ship, however, despite a bad crossing and evil fare: three of these were buried at sea, and the bodies of two girls were taken on to New York, in a watertight coffin lined with tin and filled with alcohol; the parents of the dead children had a little money and were willing to pay for this service, that their darlings might rest in the earth near New York, whither they were bound. In the meantime the short casket was placed in a swaying lifeboat. Bill Granger would remember the sound of that shifting grating object in the lifeboat as he went clinging and sliding past it a time or two. Poor younguns, he thought. Oh, poor younguns! —and he'd wonder if ever he'd own any children of his own, now that he was going to the States, and might one day be able to take a woman to wife, and house and feed her. And would his children die as these had done, while still innocent and flaxen-haired; or would they live to grow stout and rich through the mercies of wheat, prairies, peas, corn, and black locust trees? . . . Carl Granger was too ill to walk the decks, most of the time; but he had his own dreams for all that. . . . They were thirty-eight days at sea.

In New York City it happened that Carl was one of the first passengers to line up outside the door of that cabin wherein professional moneychangers functioned. He had two pounds seven shillings and fivepence remaining in his hoard, though the men behind the desk scorned his coppers and would not exchange them for American money. But his brother Bill counted himself fortunate in being conversationally engaged with a good-natured stranger—a native Londoner, no less—who murmured in confidence that he was about to return to England, and needed coin of the realm very much indeed. He offered to pay one dollar more for a guinea than the man inside was paying. Bill turned over his own treasury to this Friend in Need, receiving in return a slim bundle of State Bank notes, which the sophisticate assured him were as good as silver or better. Silver, the Londoner said, was apt to be merely lead in masquerade, produced in quantity by unscrupulous coiners, and victimizing all but the wariest. The Grangers decided that Bill's paper money should be retained as a nest egg against the future. Twould be simpler to hide and transport than heavy coins. . . . The two of them lived on the money obtained by Carl while they prowled river docksides, searching solemnly and in some actual terror for an opportunity to work their way West. (Thus the old State Bank notes were not produced until many weeks later, when the newcomers were in Chicago, and had every bill which they tendered rejected scornfully as counterfeit. William offered the bills again on reaching Iowa, and later in St. Paul

—perhaps the Illinois people had been mistaken?—and promptly found himself awarded a reputation in certain quarters as a counterfeiter or at least a counterfeiter's assistant. Twas hard to live such a thing down, but he did it in time.)

Carl and William had no fortune in finding work the first day along the waterfront. They had various other adventures, in one of which they were set upon by three bullies who sought to rob these unkempt odd-spoken rustics, and who were soon pummeled into flight. The next day, however, they were whistled at by the captain of a small Albany-bound boat, who asked them if they wished to undertake the task of loading and unloading a vast quantity of slippery little casks. The Grangers never knew what was contained in the casks; they speculated about it afterward. Twas some sort of greasy substance—lard or oil—which leaked out and soaked the front of their shirts and pantaloons. It took half the night to get the odoriferous barrels aboard, but in this way the brothers secured passage to Albany. In another three days, by much the same tactics, they found themselves being carried in a canal line boat toward Buffalo.

On lakes and on land, by a variety of means, the Grangers progressed westward. They were not sailors but they worked as sailors, or rather as deckhands. After their murderous Atlantic crossing they had little wish to endure the pitching of a ship; yet the opportunity came their way in Buffalo, and characteristically they accepted it. They were glad that they had done so, although they were nauseated daily all the way to Detroit, Carl especially. The brothers could keep little or nothing on their stomachs, but they worked as they had promised to do. In Detroit they were offered good wages to return to Buffalo and remain with the vessel in a permanent situation, but they refused. They longed for that paradise which the lights in the sky had praised to them. They watched freight drivers loading and outfitting their wagons . . . they went shyly but stubbornly from wharf to wharf, stable to stable, warehouse to warehouse, until they found six wagons prepared to convey cargoes of mill machinery to the West. Then they worked as loaders and wagoners, and reached Chicago, and eventually Muscatine. They stood at last on the soil of Iowa, but not for long. Their most recent employer was one of the early settlers of this new Muscatine (the busy town had been called Bloomington until now) and he gave the Grangers an excellent character when he talked to a certain Mr. Targ. Can you handle cattle? asked Mr. Targ. Aye, that us can. . . . The man had just concluded the purchase of a drove of cows to stock his embryo farm, far up the Mississippi in Minnesota Territory adjacent to Fort Snelling. Two days more, and William and Carl were once more embarked on a steamboat. It was the *Dr. Franklin No. 2*, and with awed ears the young Englishmen heard Mr. Targ concluding his freight arrangements with the master of the boat. Four dollars per head for the cattle!—that was the tariff—a vast sum indeed, since Mr. Targ had paid only seven dollars per head in the first place. . . . The Grangers herded their charges ashore at Fort Snelling after the four-hundred-and-fifty-mile journey: all the cows were sound of wind and limb, and there were two newborn calves to swell the total. In their arms the Grangers carried off the pretty calves whom they'd served as grannies at birth. Later a delighted Mr. Targ paid them their promised wages in St. Paul (a mere five miles distant) and added a substantial and wholly unexpected bonus for good care taken of his herd.

Look thee here, lad. They people gives a good account of this place.

This Minnesota place?

Aye.

You been and changed your mind, William?

We could bide here for a time.

It bean't Iowa, by which we'd set such store. Tis farther north. Come winter twould be right cold. . . .

That were a rare good spot, down below, along of they Indians.

Lake Pepin?

Aye.

A fortnight afterward, cautiously and in some wonderment, the brothers had become two of the earliest settlers in the Red Wing community. (They could not regain the best features of Kent in Minnesota, and did not delude themselves with the hope that they could. But they discovered in sober limited fashion that a substitution for an affinity might be made. Eventually they were happy in accepting it.) They set to work at their first American harvest, and truly it was the only crop they had ever harvested which they had not planted or tended somewhere along the line. Quietly they watched Indians, who had a village here adjacent to the Cannon and the Mississippi, go straining out in canoes to the rice gathering. They saw Indians returning again, triumphant, with their craft filled with wild rice to the gunwales.

And be they wild rice good to eat?

Surely, they were told, there's nothing better. But the Indians started harvesting a-yesterday, and twill all be gathered—or, more likely, blown away by wind—before the week is up.

Their informant was one Friend Biddle. Promptly the Grangers rented a soggy canoe from Friend Biddle for a sixth portion of whatever grain they might fetch in.

They had not thought that ever they would be reaping wild rice, they had never heard of wild rice before. Sight of the purplish-brownish granules heaped up by the Indians fired an agrarian cupidity in their hearts. Cautiously, proceeding as did the friendly Dakota of this nearby village, the brothers poled and paddled their way into a wide reedy forest. They marveled at the persistence and mass of plants, growing out of mud beneath the backwater's surface and rustling up to build a fair jungle above and around the canoemen. Long pretty seeds showered over the men's faces with every twitch of a breeze; they were so loosely attached, now having ripened, that the panicles sprayed grain, wasting it over dark water if you so much as looked at it intently. Carl and William got nowhere, trying to pick rice with their big rough hands.

Want to know summat? We loses the most.

Aye. But they savages gets a tidy bit.

How they does it, I'm sure I don't know.

I thought for to watch un, but oft them stops when we comes close.

Ah, watch now— They two over there—

They'm got curved sticks—

Like a reaper's hook—

And bends the stalks o'er the boat—

Wonderful clever like!

Well, William, let's to shore and cut some hooks.

Delightedly they set to work again, this time toiling with delicacy and patience as did the Indians. It was a mere matter of drawing a bundle of bending stalks over the canoe with their hooked branches, and whipping off the grains. They waded, knelt, squatted, half buried in sliding particles—millions and millions of grains, it seemed. Rice drifted around them in splintery clouds. They worked the heavy canoe back to the riverbank near Friend Biddle's big cabin, and Biddle's daughter fetched Indian baskets for their convenience. There was an old canvas sail or wagon cover: the Grangers used that as a temporary granary, then back they went to pretty rustling forests above the water. All that day, and the next and the next, they worked at filling their crude soggy boat. Soon they were bringing in three loads to the Indians' two; and finally (they observed with straining satisfaction) two loads to the Indians' one. They had disciplined their bodies to a given task almost every moment of their remembered lives. If Nature offered a bounty they would be ready to accept and make use of it. Early on the fourth day came a whirl of black clouds and wind and lashing rains; the Cannon River became a frothing rage, Lake Pepin looked like an enraged Atlantic, the rice harvest was over.

Friend Francis Biddle stood in shelter of his empty stable and appraised the crop. Never did I see such fine rice, and so much; never before, gentlemen. But now it must be dried.

How do us dry un?

Come a fair day tomorrow and I shall show thee. Thee must make a scaffold covered with reeds, and a slow fire is built underneath. . . .

The Grangers' acquaintanceship with that good Quaker, Francis Biddle, had begun aboard the *Dr. Franklin No. 2.* They watched a rawboned man of middle age, a man with wide-brimmed gray hat and wet gray eyes and a steely grayish mouth. He came up the plank, helping along a plump girl whose face was hidden in a huge bonnet. She seemed a very young Young Lady to be the wife of this elder (the brothers considered the matter, but silently and separately). They saw and to some extent overheard the man bargaining with the boat's captain for passage up the river. There had been some sort of calamity in the lives of these people, and now they were hoping to return to their Minnesota home as soon as possible . . . they had no booking . . . they wanted to depart on this very day . . . the *Franklin* was the only steamboat at Muscatine headed upriver. Finally the captain made some adjustment which permitted him to accept two more passengers on an already-crowded boat. The young lady was left in the captain's charge while the tall gray-haired man went ashore for bags and bundles and a barrel or two. The *Franklin* splashed away from its landing with much clanging of bells and blowing of a heavy-throated whistle, and mooing of the cattle (stanchioned on the lower deck: the Grangers had worked all the preceding night at this chore, in flicker of flambeau flames sputtering along the landing). Later that same day Francis Biddle—for he was the gray man—moved to examine the cows. He heard one Granger address the other, employing the *thee* or *thou* of antique English rural speech which they so often used. He approached them at once.

Am I addressing Friends?

In some surprise, the Grangers declared that they were not friends but brothers. In return Mr. Biddle explained his own Quakerhood, although he admitted that he had married out of Meeting (and had been, in certain quarters, disowned because of this act). Nevertheless he still had a fondness for Plain language; he and his daughter spoke Plain to one another, and sometimes to others for whom they had fondness. Biddle and his daughter Ernestine were the victims of recent tragedy. The wife and mother had fallen ill mysteriously, and they had taken her down to St. Louis to consult a doctor cousin. There came a sudden outbreak of cholera, and poor Mrs. Biddle, already ailing, was stricken, though other members of the family escaped. Following her death, the bereaved pair halted in Muscatine to pay a brief visit to relatives, and were now bound for the cabin which they called home. During the trip up the Mississippi, William and Carl grew to realize that they had found a friend to most ably serve their fortunes.

In appearance Francis Biddle gave a false impression of grimness and possible taciturnity. Actually he was one of the sweetest-souled men alive. He did possess a violent temper and fierce physical strength, but had disciplined himself early to keep his temper in solid check. (When a boy, he struck another lad, and put his eye out with the blow; remembrance of this mishap haunted him, and made him generous sometimes to the point of wastefulness.) He was of a roving disposition. He'd left Pennsylvania in first manhood; he'd settled successively in Indiana, Illinois, and finally wandered to the Muscatine (then Bloomington) neighborhood, following in footsteps of another Quaker named Brinton Darlington. For all his scattered charities and inclination to share, Frank Biddle had nevertheless accumulated some small capital. He invested most of this in a sash-and-door factory and then, drawn by notion of a frontier less trammeled, progressed up the big river and finally built a house alongside the Red Wing village. He confessed to a private ambition to serve the Dakota as a missionary, bearing in mind the accomplishments of historic Quakers in Pennsylvania. But he was not a capable linguist, though he made an honest attempt to learn the Dakota tongue. Barely could he understand a name given him by his Indian neighbors: Wichahinchaiha, or Old-Man-Who-Laughs. In the Minnesota country he raised adequate corn and potatoes, took what game and fish his household could use, and did some trading for furs. He did not know the pinch of hunger except perhaps when supplies grew short in an unpredictable winter . . . he had fed more hungry wayfarers than any white man on the river.

Biddle was fascinated by the Grangers, he pressed them for every detail of their hegira from Kent. He had never visited England, but had a brightly tinted love for the English substance and legend. He should have enjoyed living back in the seventeenth century, he was sure; he imagined himself as one of the first Quakers to march zealously forth in Lancashire, spreading magic words to all. *Every believer is a priest unto God.* (He had sought to make the neighboring band of Dakota understand this premise, but met with no success.) He was disappointed to learn that the Grangers had never been in Lancashire and had never heard of Swarthmoor Hall; nor had they heard of George Fox; and he corrected their ignorance throughout the steamboat journey, much to the confusion of William and Carl.

Friend Biddle was delighted when, after their visit to Fort Snelling and St. Paul, the Grangers reappeared at Red Wing. His daughter Ernestine was pleased as well. She had made a modest appraisal of Bill Granger all the way from Muscatine.

I saw that the grace of God which brings salvation had appeared to all men, and that the manifestation of the Spirit was given to every man to profit withal.

(Ernestine Biddle was a simple girl, seeking obviously for maternity and domestic contentment; and willing and able—physically, emotionally—to contribute her share to both successful states. She was not of her father's rangy stature, but stood dumpy and yellow-thatched. She owned large pale eyes fringed with heavy lashes, arched by heavy brows; and her eyes had a latent mesh of wrinkles about them even at this age, sixteen. She belonged to that brave and quiet-spoken race of females who bear a middle-aged appearance in their teens, but who remain long middle-aged; and in eventual old age they look placidly out at the world as if to say: Yes, I saw it. Yes, I did it. It doesn't worry me, and shouldn't worry thee. Tis the same, tis always thus. And adding in the dry quavery voice of ancient fortitude: Be not afraid.)

William and Carl moved into the Biddle barn while they worked at drying rice. Their quarters were commodious, for timber abounded in that region, and a pole stable complete with haymow had been put up easily. They remained there throughout the few sunny weeks which followed; they picked and threshed the Biddle corn, dug the last of the Biddle potatoes. They had great plans for putting in a huge planting of their own potatoes, come spring, if they might obtain a piece of land. The title situation was uncertain in these parts. It appeared that a new treaty must be concluded before honest ownership could be established. Even Friend Biddle was actually still a squatter; and so were the two missionaries who had appeared recently, Aiton and Hancock. And so were the thirty or forty other whites and half-breeds, although all were tolerated by the Indians. . . . For a long time these Dakota had boasted a Head Man named Hupahuduta, hence twas natural for the title of Red Wing to be applied to the place. The Indians themselves called the area by another name, quite lost to Francis Biddle. The active wide-jawed Quaker was balked solidly in his own missionarying efforts by his inability to gain even a foothold on the linguistic ladder . . . he said that he was going to gather *pshincha* and the Indians were amused at this, for the white man meant that he was bound to gather large-leaved tuber roots growing in deep water, the *psincha;* and he had said that he was going to gather flying squirrels! Quiet little Ernestine could understand much of the Dakota language; she picked it up effortlessly; but to William and Carl it always sounded like jargon, and they said so.

During frosty autumn days the Grangers cut the winter's wood while Friend Biddle hunted for the larder. When snow began to whirl through their loosely built mow, the brothers were invited to move into the house, to dwell in a warm tight loft. William Granger and Ernestine Biddle were wedded in the spring of 1850. Both were virginal at the time of their marriage; and he was never to sleep with another woman in his life; nor (although there was less of remark in this) was she ever to sleep with another man. In the next five years she bore him two children and lost two others. When William became a partner in the Red Wing Townsite Company he displayed a determination approaching heroism. It meant that he would have to absent himself from Ernestine for a period of many weeks—perhaps even many months—and by this time he would almost as soon have cut off his own toes as to have cut himself away from her. He did it for the sake of their children.

The advent of Bertell Snyder—or rather Bert's return to Red Wing after numerous earlier visits—solved a domestic problem for Carl. He had not enjoyed living on in the Biddle loft after his brother's departure into wedded life. Carl held an unvoiced yet firm belief that in-laws should not intrude in a purely family circle. He'd observed too much grumpy or splenetic crowding in the cottages of Kent. Here in new America there should be room enough for each individual to have his own house, be he married or a bachelor; or at least room enough for two or three bachelors to have a house of their own.

Friend Francis Biddle was terribly scalded when a connecting rod broke, between two boilers of the steamer *Financier*, and live steam rushed into the cabin; Biddle never recovered his bodily strength, but grew progressively weaker, and died of pneumonia in 1852. This disaster left vacant one of the two bedchambers in the big double cabin, but Carl did not come to occupy it. By that time he was dwelling with a Chicagoan (the same man who later sold the pony Lazarus) and he did not remove from that location until Bert Snyder acquired a cabin and invited Carl to share it. Bert had come to hold a high opinion of the Granger brothers' industry and honesty; he chuckled at the old counterfeiting label which was still pasted upon William from time to time by the ignorant and credulous. Bert arranged with them to farm some of his land on shares, as they had done for Francis Biddle. But sometimes he was absent for months on end, and those were lonely times for Carl. Then the dog Lee came sniffing and snuffling into Carl's life, and awarded him that supreme satisfaction which it seems sometimes that only sniffing and snuffling and utterly worthless dogs may give. (Lee was wet and limping when he appeared; it was as if he had recently emerged from the river. Round the beast's thick neck was fastened a knitted collar with the name *Lee* worked into it in colored yarn. Had he fallen overboard from a steamboat? It seemed likely; and his owners must have believed that Lee was drowned; at any rate they never appeared in Red Wing to claim him. Bert Snyder inquired, the next time he visited St. Paul, but heard no news of a missing pet.) From that time forth Carl and Lee were mainly inseparable; though the dog would snort away on neighborhood rounds to beg, whenever he considered his master too lengthily or dully employed. Lee growled at Indians, and usually gave them a wide berth—with some reason, perhaps, as he was comfortably fat, his brown shiny coat gave him the appearance of a well-cooked sausage. Carl considered that more than one appraising Dakota gaze was turned upon this succulence.

Land sharks infested the region, especially after new treaties were consummated. The Red Wing settlement expanded rapidly. The town was surveyed and platted in 1853. The Grangers had lost their first two claims because of the slyness of speculators; and now they joined fiercely with a vigilance committee in ducking other such gentry in the Mississippi. But they listened to tales of regions farther in the West, where unoccupied land was legally open to settlement at last—waiting merely to be claimed, twas said—and with none of the complication which had attended their Red Wing experience. Thus both William and Carl were happy to join with the Honorable Mr. William Freeborn and others in the formation of an explorative company. Thus they did join, and make the journey to Okoboji, and help to choose a site.

William was more than eager to return to his family, once this task was accomplished. He was ensconced safely for the winter, returned to Ernestine and the children, a good ten days before snows smothered the whole northwest.

Husband, thee didn't tell me how Carl was faring.

Very comfortable they looks—Carl and Bert and the young doctor—in the cabin. They'll all get on well.

And in the spring thee'll take us there.

Aye. Come spring! But now tis murder out.

Writing of the year of Carl Granger's birth, William Cobbett, M.P., described in *The Political Register* those doleful mobs and processions of which the Grangers were a stern pallid part.

. . . In innumerable instances men committed crimes for the purpose of getting into gaol; because the felons in gaol were better fed and better clad than the honest working people. As the working people became poor, the laws relating to them were made more and more severe: and the Poor-Law, that famous law of Elizabeth, which was the greatest glory of England for ages, had by degrees been so mutilated and nullified, that, at last, it was so far from being a protection for the working people, that it had, by its perversions, been made the means of reducing them to a state of wretchedness not to be described. The sole food of the greater part of them had been, for many years, bread, or potatoes, and not half enough of these. They had eaten sheep or cattle that had died from illness; children had been seen stealing food out of hog-troughs; men were found dead . . . lying under a hedge, and when opened by the surgeons nothing but sour sorrel was found in their stomachs. . . .

Besides suffering from want, the working people were made to en-

dure insults and indignities such as even Negroes were never exposed to. They were harnessed like horses or asses and made to draw carts and waggons; they were shut up in pounds made to hold stray cattle; they were made to work with bells round their necks; and they had drivers set over them, just as if they had been galley slaves; they were sold by auction . . . the married men were kept separated from their wives, by force, to prevent them from breeding; and, in short, no human beings were ever before treated so unjustly, with so much insolence, and with such damnable barbarity, as the working people of England had been. Such were the fruits of public debts and funds! Without them, this industrious and moral and brave nation never could have been brought into this degraded state.

True, Carl had not suffered in the most dire situations described with passion by the illustrious Cobbett; nor had the rest of his family. But he had known hunger and drudgery (the worst drudgery of all: that which seems to drag to no reward). In America he could toil just as persistently, and was willing to; and he had toiled in America for six and one-half years; and he regretted stolidly the onrush of winter—there was so little he could do about it.

Come spring. . . .

He mused shyly, he thought of warmer times, of walks he had taken, thought of that first spraying forest of rice above Minnesota waters.

He mused little on a specific future. He wished only for a cessation of snows, and a melting, a wettening, a long sunning. He wanted loose soil, and the feel of his fork sliding into it, and clods smashing apart as he struck them.

Sometimes he remembered the merry dancers above those Kentish ridges—ruddy surges creasing and whispering across the sky—and when he thought of that spectacle the hairs prickled above his shoulder blades, and he breathed deeply.

He was lonely for the brother now long since removed from a daily intimate sharing; he could not give himself warmly to these other two. (Bert Snyder rather thought him a supple honest oaf. Isaac Harriott thought little about Carl Granger one way or the other—Harry was too wrapped in his profession and in his own ambitions and love, to think about much else.) Secretly Carl wondered if he too might find in time an Ernestine, and hoped that he would do so. . . . Should he have married her, instead of William's marrying her? Trouble was, at the time, he'd never thought on't. . . .

Carl Granger was given to quiet misplaced tendernesses. He never happened upon a dead bird (not one slain deliberately for the pot; then it seemed like meat, and not like a wild soft thing dying under mysterious circumstances) without thinking, Ah, so silent, little bird? . . . Possibly there would follow the alarming thought: And in time

I too shall lie mute, unresisting, subject to the whims of every force and chemistry!— Yet he was not within a league of voicing such notions; or even of admitting to himself (consciously, later) that he had possessed them, and they had possessed him.

XXIX

"Give me of your quills, O Hedgehog!
All your quills, O Kagh, the Hedgehog!
I will make a necklace of them,
Make a girdle for my beauty,
And two stars to deck her bosom!"
From a hollow tree the Hedgehog
With his sleepy eyes looked at him,
Shot his shining quills, like arrows,
Saying, with a drowsy murmur,
Through the tangle of his whiskers,
"Take my quills, O Hiawatha!"

Morris Markham interrupted and said flatly, Tain't so.

The hand of Rowland Gardner came down with an open book still gripped. What say, Mr.?

Tain't so. If he's talking about a porcupine—and I guess he is—it just can't happen. Porcupine doesn't shoot his quills.

There were eleven people in the Gardner cabin, not including small children who had been quilted on high for the night. The trundle bed (or truckle bed, as Carl Granger called this article of furniture, to the mystification of others) was an inconvenience on such occasions: it took up too much room on the open floor, there was the risk of someone's tripping and falling upon the occupants. Hence it was shoved away beneath the Prairie Rascal; Rowly, Bertie, and Mandy were swung aloft; folks had to duck their heads when they passed beneath (the boys were older and better-trained than that leaky J. Q. A. Noble; and Baby Mandy was amply diapered).

Readings could be held comfortably only on those few nights open and starlit.

Kind of thought we'd read tonight, Rowland Gardner would say hopefully. You choose to come over at sundown, Doctor?

Gladly. I'll tell Bert, and we'll fetch the ladies if they're willing.

... We hain't had a Reading since the New Year.

... Now, that's right. Been too stormy.

... Looks like twill be clear tonight. Let's have a Reading.

From the ground the quills he gathered,
All the little shining arrows,
Stained them red and blue and yellow,
With the juice of roots and berries.

Couldn't have got them quills like that.

Henry Wadsworth Longfellow, said Gardner, rolling the name out admiringly. He says that the hedgehog shot the quills.

So there! Abbie remarked saucily.

Daughter, you hush. I don't think he'd print it in a book less—

Morris shrugged. Reckon Mr. Longfellow doesn't know much about porcupines.

Once upon a time, Bert Snyder related, I owned a dog which sought to slay a porcupine. *Mon Dieu!*—he returns with his entire face full of quills. It is like he is shot by artillery. Poor dog, his name was Marquette because he is always desiring of the exploration. Poor Marquette!—he does not explore much longer after he is made a pincushion by the porcupine. Soon he is dead.

So you see, Morris.

Don't see a thing. Bert didn't say those quills was fired, nor see them fired. Dog just got a face-full when he tried to tackle the Quill-Pig. They're right poisonous, them spines. Face and mouth swelled up, dog couldn't eat nothing. So he starved.

Paddles none had Hiawatha,
Paddles none he had or needed,
For his thoughts as paddles served him,
And his wishes served to guide him;
Swift or slow at will he glided,
Veered to right or left at pleasure.

Reckon, whispered Morris behind his hand, speaking to Alice Mattock and Harry— Reckon Mr. Longfellow don't know much about a canoe neither.

Tis just a poet's imagination, Morris. Isn't supposed to be real.

I like your book better.

Harry's book was an ample volume, *Historical Collections of the Great West,* which he had acquired while still in Atlanta and first considering a life on the frontier. The work, written by one Henry Howe, offered in turn: *Narratives of the Most Important and Interesting Events in Western History—Remarkable Individual Adventures—Sketches of Frontier Life—Descriptions of Natural Curiosities.* It figured frequently in the Readings. The frontispiece engraving depicted The Aged Pioneer, a goodman who seemed to be engaged in elucidating the events of his life to a collection of small fry. *Some fine summer's evening,* read the quotation below the picture, *he may be seen seated in the porch of his dwelling, his frank, open counte-*

nance beaming with delight as he relates the tale of his early adventures to his little grandchildren, who, clustering about his knees, drink in every word with intense interest.—Page 282.

Harry. You see yourself so.

Guess I do, Bert.

You are the grandsire who explains to the little ones, informing them of his long-ago perils in the new land.

Guess so.

But here we have no perils!

Let's see: what about that first day when our canoe upset, and we both liked to drown?

Ah, you will make much of that, when you have grown old, and wish to impress everyone with danger of the early years. My dear Doctor Pelacoy was forever filling my ears with Austerlitz and Jena. *Wiz, wiz* go the bullets! Observe!—the Prussians advance as if they are on parade! But we are hiding behind the stables and hedgerows, and now we will pick them off! *Wiz! Zut!* I fear you shall be like this, Harry, in the distant future. It is the privilege of elder persons.

It is, said Harry, and I intend to enjoy it.

But no one shoots at us here! We have only the cold weather.

Isn't that bad enough? Men die of weather like this. I know—I've tended them—seen them die.

Other men. Not ourselves.

Course not. We're indestructible.

. . . Harry?

Yep?

I have been fishing through a hole in the ice, and Harvey Luce he came also to fish. He has given us the invitation of Mr. Gardner: do you wish to attend a Reading tonight? No doubt Mr. Luce will open the session by a whining of the Scriptures!

Neighbors observed Bert Snyder thus: gregarious, energetic, alive with jests, almost self-consciously lighthearted. They thought that he was a typical Frenchman, remarked that he was carefree, were awed at learning that he was rich. They had never known many rich people, and not one of the neighbors had known a rich man intimately. They thought that rich men breathed a different sort of air, moved aloof in an elevated world—were not subject to common slaveries of nature—perhaps rich men did not even need to go to the privy, like ordinary mortals! And the Grangers had stated that Mr. Bertell Snyder *was* very rich indeed; and Doctor Harriott did not deny the fact—only he appeared reluctant to discuss the matter. Women tried to counsel themselves repeatedly that there was and should be a gulf between Bert Snyder and common folks; but one and all were captivated by him—a cabin rang with laughter when he entered, children ran to hug his knees. The round-eyed fair-haired Rowly

Gardner planted himself directly in front of the visitor, and stared and grinned; he demanded that Bert repeat those *chansonnettes* with which he enjoyed regaling the little people. Even Bertie Luce announced that he had learned French, could now speak French. He went about his play or the tiny tasks to which he was set, chanting, *Sur leh pong Dah-veeng-yong* in a superior manner.

Bertie asked of the tall jaunty foreigner: Are you really rich?—before Mary Luce could hush him.

For a certainty!

Aw—I bet you ain't.

Albert Johnson *Luce,* you cease your sassiness right this minute or I'll take a switch to you!

Madame Luce, please— No switch. The boy has the right to ask a simple question, and I do not decline to answer him. Little One, You ask me, Am I rich? and now I tell you the entire truth. I am so rich that when I am at home, before I came to Okoboji with the Red Wing Company, I lived in a house made from solid gold. The bed in which I slept has the sheets of gold, and I rested my head on a pillow of solid gold. Even the mice which live also in my house— They are not common mice, like the small gray creatures you have here in your cabin. No. They are silver mice, and they have *gold teeth.*

I bet—they—do not—

And what catches my silver mice with the teeth of gold? My silver cat with the *golden tail!*

Aw—I bet—

And does she have the ordinary eyes of a pussycat? Never. Her eyes are precious stones. Emeralds!

Aw—

So perhaps it is that you do not know what an emerald may be? It is a jewel of a beautiful green color. Let me see—I shall show you now— I must have an emerald or two or maybe more, in my pocket. . . . What? Nothing in this pocket? . . . Only a tobacco pouch in this? . . . Only a penknife in this? What has happened to my emeralds? They have been stolen! No—all I can find is the *noisettes*—Oho, what you call the hazelnuts. One, two, three, four. Come close, I crack them for you, even if you do not believe how very rich I am!

Other people did not witness the haunted lugubrious Bert, but Isaac Harriott was acquainted with him. A few times in St. Paul perhaps he had felt a shadow, a darkening; it was not an intense blackening and sickness, for song or hearty discussion could chase the mood away. But one day on the southwestward journey a fit of depression seized Bertell Snyder (Harry thought that such bitterness might have been invoked by the lengthy exploration, the remembrance and entering once more into that Paleolithic cavern). It had happened also on a few occasions since. He'd be brooding and silent for hours; then the explosion. Harry knew of that earlier life, he could count the Robert Didier years along with Bert; no one else might do so, though doubtless the long-dead Eric Pakington had shared as well. Once indeed Harry practiced a mistaken gaiety in referring to Bert as Robert. Suddenly he thought that his friend was about to strike him.

I am Bertell. Never, never call me by that other name.

The devil. I'm sorry, Bert, if I–

Robert is dead, he died in the château at Mercuès, he died, he was slain by the wise and good Pelacoy! Never taunt me of him!

But I didn't mean to taunt. Twas a mere jest–

A sad jest indeed!

Bert, I apologize humbly–

Oh, *mais oui,* there are documents, there is the legal name. I am a servant of the late Robert Didier, a pensioner of him! I do not like to be retained in this abject condition, but do not possess the courage to do otherwise. Robert has the money, Bertell is a captive. If Bertell were not such a coward, he would have declared his independence long ago. Louis Didier did not disinherit Robert; it is possible that he too was a coward, too considerate of public opinion. But also came first the inheritance from Doctor Pelacoy– Oh, there was too much money, it was baffling and contradictory, it was a burden. If Bertell had desired the life of the boulevards it would have been the end of him. But he did not wish for wine cellars, elaborate carriages, the tables of cards, the wheel of fortune, the many pretty women in rich clothing bought by his means, the idle chatterers hanging about –all the beggars, the thieving butlers and housekeepers, the worthless luxuries: all such things he did not desire, they had no claim on his affection. Ah, the Revolution– It was a shattering experience for a young boy– I suffered much from it, am suffering still– But I wished only for the new green things, wished for honest and affectionate youth to surround me. I wanted the simplicity– So I have gone seeking it, trying the new place– Eternally, eternally, my dear Harry! The new place. So we make here in this happy wilderness a new town? *Une bonne ville, une belle ville!* But then onward will I go to one more new place. I seek for something, something– Eternally! It breaks my heart.

Very well, now let me speak.

Then speak. But do not address me as Robert.

Never again. What I wish to say is this: If you're so badly plagued by possession of money, I know how to relieve you of that misery. By the way, Bert, just where *is* your money?

Oh, everywhere. New York, Montreal, and still also I own many properties in France. I own also a portion of a steamship line, a greater portion of a factory for the manufacture of candles. The men with the starched linen, men with the gold charms *maçonnique,* they sit before me and open their books, and say: Here is the accounting for the past eighteen months!—and maybe they are stealing from me, I do not know. Scarcely do I care; although like all the rich I am annoyed if I have been cheated brazenly.

Well, I tender a suggestion.

Do you wish that I should endow you? You have never asked me, but you have only to speak. I would be so glad!

Now I'm the one who should be insulted.

I mean only that—

Oh, hush! By your own admission you have made the point that money *unearned*—too much money of that kind—is a perplexity and a handicap. I never wish to put my hands on one cent which I haven't acquired by the judicious exercise of my profession. Hope you recognize *that.*

Harry, I stand reproved.

But I've an ambition of another sort. If we do build our town—

Wait until next year. We shall build it!

If we *do* have a town eventually, I wish that you would take some of your money and give us a hospital.

What kind of hospital?

Sometimes I visualize it as a refuge for the old and indigent, sometimes I think of children— A place well-equipped, well-staffed; free beds for anyone who can't pay— The best of sound medical and surgical attention available to every last soul in the community—

And yourself as the head of this fine institution?

Well, *someone* would have to be in charge—

Harry, you are saintly by nature.

I'm nothing of the kind.

You think always of others, how you may help them. I give to you now my most solemn affirmation that if our fine town does arise—and if I have any of my fortune which has not been stolen or lost to me through unwise management— For I am incredibly bad a manager! If this comes to be true, you shall have your community hospital.

Cracky, Bert. What a day that would be!

Can I receive also for free the treatment in my own hospital that I give?

We'll have a special room for you, always waiting. With a fireplace, *and* wine—

Ah, we must not forget the wine— As in St. Paul—

And a special privy built in, adjoining, so you shan't have to walk about on your bad leg!

. . . Mrs. Rusk should be fetched down from St. Paul to take charge of larder and kitchen, Harvey Luce should be engaged as hospital chaplain, Gladiateur and Lazarus must be put into harness to draw the ambulance. Sardis Howe could head the nursing staff. Morris Markham was to emerge as Hospital Huntsman, and bring delicate birds daily from which to make the invalids' stews.

So there skipped a joviality in their hopes; but somber unruliness would rise again in Bert, to be followed by his denunciation of himself for sins of omission—for selfishness, indolence, neglect of opportunity, inability to yield to a primary inspiration. What should he do with himself? He was more futile and worthless than anyone in the settlement (if these few scrawny cabins could be termed a settlement). Let him depart and get himself killed somewhere, fighting for justice! But how should one determine the army of the just? . . . There was that shredded mass of folded crushed newsprint which could barely be identified as the *New York Express*—twas old by months; and James Mattock had brought it back with him when he traded for cattle at the Irish colony. Heaven knew the source of the sheet, barely was it recognizable as the remains of a newspaper. But columns of information could still be deciphered, and thus had been distributed at the last Reading. *By Magnetic Telegraph. Insurrection in Hayti . . . formidable insurrection . . . against the Emperor Soluque . . . a body of from 2000 to 3000 insurgents took possession of a post between this place and Pingrey last night . . . alarm drums were immediately beaten and every male adult in town was ordered to join the troops.* Was not he, Bertell Snyder, wasting his time in dallying on this homely frontier? Ah, he had done little except waste time since the Revolution of '48. But if he went to Hayti to fight for justice, who was there to tell him whether he should enlist with Emperor or insurgents? The bald act of rebellion was not in itself a guaranty of virtue. . . . Yes, yes, yes, when he was a boy he had believed that he should risk extinction by aligning himself with a revolutionary force. But even then the situation was complex, and only by fact and influence of his nativity and youth had he come to a decision, by impulse of heart as well as by reasoning of the intellect. Perhaps the Emperor Soluque represented justice after all, perhaps the insurgents were swayed by evil influences and purposes? So go instead to Spanish America (by instigation of *Harper's New Monthly Magazine* and the voice of Mary Luce taking her turn and mispronouncing therefrom). *Hostilities have opened vigorously between Nicaragua and Costa Rica. Colonel Schlessinger, with about 300 men, was despatched by General Walker to invade the territory of Costa Rica . . . he was surprised at Santa Rosa by a superior force, and totally defeated, with a loss of one third of his men.* Did this magazine inform as to righteousness of the invasion? It did not. How should he, Bert Snyder, determine whether in all decency he should proceed immediately to Spanish America, and enlist— With Walker's army, or with the defending Costa Ricans? Was

William Walker a liberator, as some sought to proclaim him, or was he a bloody-handed professional filibuster, as other angry voices vilified him? Was the newly minted republic of Costa Rica an upright entity, or should it be overthrown as a concession to humanity? Ah, he suspected strongly that the former was true, and that (if he were not a spoiled and baffled young man who no longer possessed the ability for assertion) he should hustle himself to New Orleans and thence by boat to that beleaguered little tropical nation! Other men had died through all history—thousands, probably millions of them—not as hirelings but as idealists. Where was his own idealism, and why did not he state it immediately with a thrust of the sword?

Twas a horrid thing, actually, to have an Henri Pelacoy in one's past. For the old doctor's rough voice came declaiming across a decade, making mockery of the years which his privately christened and privately fabricated Bertell Schneider had lived since he shoved past the jetties at Boulogne. *Some people are bound to crowd every hour and every minute with activity and feeling; the most of mankind offer but a wastage and an emptiness.* And Pelacoy had supposed sublimely that his foster son should scintillate in the former category—a vigorous thing, a shining thing however green—to stimulate himself yearly into fresh and extensive contributions.

So what had the discomposed young man given instead? Wastage, emptiness! . . . Value? He'd offered not a jot.

Profundity of his mighty experience should have given the youth an acceleration beyond the power of most individuals to attain or respond to. How many scourged slaves left their spiritual dungeons to penetrate primitive and archaic dungeons in fact, and to be rewarded with a panorama such as herded before him? These very eyes (shut them, Bert—brandish your fists in front of the closed eyes, drum nervously against the wretched eyelids with your fists) had observed a spectacle glimpsed by no other human being.

Realize that, if you will: no one else!

My eyes alone!

. . . *Only I: Robert the inept, Robert the hooted, Robert the ingrate, Robert the dawdler, Robert the scorned!*

. . . *Only I!*

So now that same mystified and exultant child had grown to be reclassified as a dawdler, and inept into the bargain—exactly as typified in the first place. He might have extolled a philosophy, he might have walked in Franciscan robes and poverty. He might have stood proudly upon a scaffold and uttered an inspiring phrase of farewell which would be force and tonic through centuries ahead. But he'd chosen to squander himself—scattering semen and soul alike throughout a new continent merely because it *was* a new continent! Why hadn't he gone to Australia, say? Or Greenland? Or might he have found reward amid the vines and bog-holes of a wretched Africa? The slave trade was conceded to be an institution fraught with wickedness; no man of nobility might defend it. Why hadn't he gone to Africa and brought along every weapon and cunningness, and devoted himself to slaying rapacious Arabs, and freeing black Afric slaves before they *were* in fact slaves?

In Gigouzac fastnesses a better person might have learned much from contemplation of those painted hyenas and *equidae* and hinds and stags; he'd learned nothing. He chose only to regard them as a pageant to titillate sentiment and dramatic childhood recollection—something to brag about to a beloved friend, but nothing to learn a lesson from! The ocher-traced cave-bear and the fierce bison could have stood in his memory as pedagogues and counselors, and he'd not let them do so. They should have run him down, chopped him to oblivion with their paws and dashing hoofs in the first place; then he would not have emerged from the cavern, and perhaps no one would have found him, and he would have vanished into the misty Vert valley to become a pointless legend, a symbol affrighting peasant children when they misbehaved.

He'd enjoyed educational advantages, and in addition had been nourished amid the whole repository of Western culture: the joy of archways had been his, the magnificence of crumbled turrets and bastions which jutted across ivied slopes; he'd walked on flaggings where princes once stood and fed, had followed thrushes into the still-shaped bedchambers where medieval women conceived and bore their children. And all this he had scorned and shunted aside because he could not abide antiquity, could not rise above the pettiness of his little boy's humiliations, his little boy's resulting hatreds. Scholars saved and scraped, the world over, that they might come to sniff for a moment the invigoration of those lichen scents to which he (Robert or Bertell, as the case might be) had deadened his senses. Every influence believed to contribute to the making of an able powerful man had been his. He was exposed early to extremes and violences of human conduct; he'd possessed a priestly advisor in the shape of Doctor Pelacoy; and early also he had seen young men sacrifice themselves in the heat of belief, had stood among them as they died devoted. Why couldn't he have progressed into a thriving existence? What made him obsolescent, still in his twenties? Ennui? Weakness, cowardice, confusion? Why had he not been able to hold a purpose in his long strong hands, and load it, and aim and fire it, and cry, Hurrah!—Again the bull's-eye! Was it peevishness and selfishness of the Didiers which acted as a corrosion so insidious that even the strong flow of Berganty blood might not resist it?

Mon Dieu. Tell me, my friend, tell me if you can.

Bert. What do you hope to gain by this?

Gain by what?

Self-excoriation. Self-pity, if you will.

But– I am not giving pity to myself. I am blaming myself!

Harry thought for a moment, then managed to state more or less aptly the notion which was in his mind: It occurs to me that in voicing all that blame, you're really appealing for pity. Pity from me, in whom you confide–or–if I'm not handy and there's nobody else to talk to–pity for yourself *from* yourself.

I should know better than to disclose myself to you, to anyone!

In time everyone discloses himself to a doctor, said Harriott rather smugly.

Why am I fascinated by you, a doctor? It is because of that abominable Pelacoy! He made me feel that there was a special knowledge and understanding of the doctors–that he was possessing *la pierre philosophale,* that he was more *moraliste* than *physicien–qu'il avait un entendement et une sympathie universelle–* Ah, my English is lost the more I become *distrait–*!

Bert, you're young still. Not much the elder of myself. There's still a great deal of time left for you to do things.

But I do not know what it is that I wish to do!

In such moods Bert Snyder was scarcely civil when facing Carl Granger, could even come close to picking a quarrel with Harry. Isaac Harriott soothed to the best of his ability, then wisely let the patient be. Bert would emerge shortly from that purgatory of confusion and misdirection which was his, and his alone.

The words of A-gur the son of Ja-keh, even the proph-e-cy: the man spake unto Ith-i-el, even unto Ith-i-el and U-cal.

Mr. Luce was determined to join actively in the Readings, and also Mr. Luce was determined to read from the Scriptures. There fell considerable discussion about this among relatives and neighbors, both in Harvey's presence and out of it. It was not surprising that Harvey's relatives were insistent that Bible reading be not included in any of the evenings' programs. Mary Luce was the most insistent of all.

Husband, you do plenty Bible reading other times.

But it hain't right that we should give so much heed to secular books–and *novels,* too–and not give even a morsel to the Word of God.

Tain't just the Word of God. You want to read every other kind of words too: words of Malachi and Hosea and Joel and Amos, and words of Micah and Habakkuk and Obadiah. A body'd go to sleep just listening to their names.

That's blame near a heathen utterance! declared the shocked Harvey. Never did I expect to hear a wife of mine say–

Mary interrupted tartly: How many other wives you got?

What? Oh, Mary, it's dreadful to hear you make sport of—

Well, husband, I ain't truly making sport. Now, don't you get your dander up, it don't become you. It's just that all the folks won't want to traipse clean over here through snow and woods and everything, and ice and all, and cold as it is—just to hear you a-Bible-reading.

They don't need to listen just to me. Someone else is welcome to—

But this house hain't no *church.*

We'd all be better off, said Harvey happily, miserably, if we had one.

Reckon so, husband. But we got no call to try to turn an innocent friendly gathering of neighbor folks into a season of Worship.

Apostle says, *Let your women keep silence . . . and if they will learn any thing, let them ask their husbands at home: for it is a shame for women to speak.*

Sounds like you've hacked them verses up to suit your own purpose, said Mary shrewdly.

Well, it's what the Apostle Paul *says.* In the Fourteenth Chapter of First Corinthians.

I think the Apostle Paul was a fussy old bachelor, that's what I think.

Mary! You're being downright sack-re*lig*ious!—

No, I ain't. But I want to hear *Hiawatha,* and *Harper's,* and Elizabeth Wetherell— And newspapers and things. And *Little Dorrit.* And *Ballou's Pictorial.* And— And, *The Gipsy's Secret: or, The League of Guilt. A Story of High and Humble Life.*

*Mar*y!

Fortunately for Mr. Luce, the rest were more tolerant of his desires. It was agreed that every Reading be opened with two—not more—chapters of the Bible, to be selected and read by Mr. Luce. Obviously statistical passages—such as those included in the Second Chapter of Ezra, or the Tenth or Twelfth Chapters of Nehemiah, say—were to be ruled out. Also a suggestion was conveyed to Harvey, in manner of diplomacy but firmly, that he should choose chapters of average length; he should not treat the assemblage, for instance, to the Twenty-fourth Chapter of Genesis to be followed immediately by the One Hundred and Nineteenth Psalm. The Twenty-third Psalm was pointed out to him as a model. But it happened that the One Hundred and Nineteenth was one of Harvey Luce's prime favorities, just as it was a favorite of Old Joel Howe. The stubborn Harvey insisted on reading a portion of the One Hundred and Nineteenth at the very first session which followed the issuing of the edict (he felt twas an affliction contrived by the impious and aimed directly at him; and indeed it was; and actually Harvey was more joyful in this martyrdom than he had been for some time). He began with *Daleth;* no one could possibly have put more droning misery into the statement, *My soul cleaveth unto the dust* than Harvey Luce. He read through *He* and *Vau* and *Zain* and *Cheth,* through *Teth* and *Jod* and *Caph.* On the conclusion of the latter section he closed the Bible firmly and sat in contented hopelessness, awaiting those portions of *Hiawatha* which it had been agreed were to follow before *Little Dorrit* (incomplete, unfortunately: Rowland Gardner did not possess the more recent numbers of *Harper's* nor did anyone else) and excerpts from Isaac Harriott's *Historical Collections.* But Harvey had achieved some triumph in a fancied disciplining of Mary, for he put especial emphasis into Verse Fifty-three: *Horror hath taken hold upon me because of the wicked that forsake thy law,* and he had lifted his gaze from the Book and looked ruefully at Mary as he uttered the words. Often he felt rather like the Apostle Paul himself (though sometimes he felt like David), and often like Jeremiah; and forever like Job.

In an earlier session, before being restricted to two chapters or portions thereof, Mr. Luce had done unwitting service to Doctor Harriott when he blundered mournfully through final pages of the Proverbs. As a boy Harry remembered being struck by teachings of Lemuel's mother . . . he'd wondered whether, when in time he became man-grown, he should be fortunate enough to discover a woman whose price was far above rubies. Now he thought that he had found her—untutored, born out of coarseness and stridency, yet as healing to his spirit as the best salve he'd ever mashed and mixed to soothe. Also in her presence he felt emboldened, resourceful; when she was gone from him he found himself in need. He fretted mechanically through workaday activities when she was absent, became ardent in planning when Alice stood restored to him. Even dismal rendition of old wise words by a sanctimonious nit could not rob them of their apt vitality.

She will do him good and not evil all the days of her life . . . indeed, that's Alice in truth!

She riseth also while it is yet night, and giveth meat to her household. That she would do, that she will do!

She girdeth her loins with strength, and strengtheneth her arms. . . . She stretcheth out her hand to the poor.

I think of Alice's loins, grow hard and quickly moist in the mere thinking. But kindliness—aye— And charity— She has them in her nature. I've felt solely fleshly desire for certain young women before; I've never felt such simple good lust intermingled with frantic appreciation of a woman's essential nobility and sweetness, all in the same second.

Might this not be unique? Am I warped, would I descend into ruin if the world were to become aware of such aberration?

But I know that I love Alice; I desire to proclaim the excitement of it to all— I wonder childishly what might befall if I were to interrupt the reader and explode this crowded shanty with a shout: I–love–Alice!

She is not afraid of the snow for her household: for all her household are clothed with scarlet. There's a pretty fancy, and quite absurd, but still I must tell her of it on the homeward trip. . . .

Hist! Bears ahead!

She halted, peering into snow-lightened night. Bears?

Hist! Indians ahead!

I guess them are just shadows and brush.

Practical soul! Can't you scream and faint and melt and quiver, the way young females are supposed to do?

Harry, would you like me better if I was the fainting kind?

Nothing could make me like you better.

Thus they stopped, frozen long together; they wound her blanket around them both; his bearskin coat was thrown open to receive them both; they clung rapt in their bindings, and stars shivered watching.

Alice, I was thinking of those words from the last chapter of Proverbs. *She is not afraid of the snow–*

Honest, I ain't–really. Trouble is, if it got too deep, you couldn't come over to our place.

Next winter we'll have our own place. Think of that!

I do, right constant. I think about it when I'm going to sleep, and I get so breathless–you know, in the thinking–that I just can't get to sleep a-tall.

Will you clothe all our household with scarlet?

You mean–for shame? Like– I'm a scarlet woman?

To me you're pure as this same snow around us! I mean scarlet, as related in the words that Lemuel's mother taught him. *For all her household are clothed with scarlet.*

I'll do it if you say so, Harry. But mightn't it be kind of mon-ot-o-nous? And what would folks think if a doctor come to see them, all dressed up in red? Reckon they'd think he was Satan!

Allie. Know something?

What?

You're more precious than rubies. *Many daughters have done virtuously, but thou excellest them all.*

Oh, Harry dearie–

Say it, Allie dearie.

I do feel so sorry for poor Mr. Harvey Luce! I think he really tries hard to be good, and wants folks to like him; but everybody kind of laughs behind his back; and he knows it too, I reckon, and it makes him feel bad just cause he's *trying* to be good. Oh, I guess I can't state that very well, but– You know what I mean, Harry?

Of course I do. Let me arise up and call you blessèd.

It's the children that's sposed to do that.

Very well, we'll arrange to have forty children. So they can call you blessèd, day and night. You know—when I'm gone on a case.

Harry, kiss me again. Then we got to go; or I speck Pap'll come a-gunning for you.

Allie. Do your folks—know—?

No. Just you and me.

After Harry had left her at the Mattock cabin and had trotted home across snow-muffled ice, he lay listening to the snores of Carl Granger and the dog Lee (it was a question as to which of these two could snore the louder; though there was no doubt whatsoever that Lee could make the worst smells of any member of the company). Harry told himself that he was holding awake because Bert was still abroad. Both Bert and Sardis Howe had attended the Reading, and they were traveling on horseback—Bert had led Lazarus along as a mount for Sardis. Harry and Alice needed to walk but an approximate mile from the Mattocks' to the Gardners' and the same distance in return. But Bert had ridden to the Howes' the previous noon; he and Sardis were faced with a round trip of some nine miles, and the trail was none too clear. Bert would spend the rest of the night at the Howe place, and fetch their horses home next day. Harry attempted to spell out imaginary disasters occurring in prairie snowbanks or woodland hollows, and then he discounted them all: the same trip had been made in the same way on two or three other occasions—once in weather angrier than this night's. Of course there was that time when an unexpected snowstorm came hurtling; then everybody had to remain at the Gardner house. Twas a lark, with folks sleeping all over the floor: barely enough bed space for the womenfolks, with much crowding. He'd insinuated himself into a position next to the bed where Alice snuggled beside Sardis Howe and Mary Luce (Because you are a doctor! Bert chuckled. You are the only one we dare trust to sleep in proximity to the fair sex). Harry was enabled thus to lie with Alice's hand warm in his own. . . . One attempt was made to hold a Reading at the Mattocks' and one at the Red Wing cabin, but such efforts were given up. All four adults of the Gardner-Luce families were enthusiastic devotees—indeed they were instigators of this social activity; to say nothing of Abbie, who read aloud excellently, especially from romances. If sessions were held elsewhere, someone had to stay home to mind the children. Nor did Carl Granger or the senior Mattocks care much for Readings, excepting newspaper accounts; and the old newspapers had long since been bled dry. And Robby Matheson went to sleep during the first ten minutes, and blared forth more reverberating snores than Carl Granger or Lee.

. . . Isaac Harriott did not know whether he waked or slept, but in fancy he returned to the warm woods of late autumn. Again he joined with Bert in chopping down the bee tree. He heard once more a splintering, a ripping loose, the final crash and bounce when the tree lay sprawled. He remembered bright excited faces of Alice and Sardis . . . above all he remembered how Alice looked. A thin spray of dizzy bees—some few more resistant to the numbing effects of smoke than their fellows—came fussing up from the long split trunk . . . the bulk of bees still clung in drugged wads amid powder of dried rotten wood . . . honey dripped and drained. The girls exclaimed over masses of comb woven through basswood hollows. They brought buckets and dippers, began ladling out the honey, it bore a heavy larding of rubbish and dead bees, twould have to be strained. . . Bert was stung twice, the others weren't stung even once. Sardis stated firmly that this wild honey tasted like attar of roses; but no one present had ever tasted attar of roses, let alone Sardis Howe.

And if anybody dies in the family, you got to tell the bees about it or they'll all go way!

Reckon that's just for tame bees, in hives.

Ah, ladies, these are the only bees we have! If I am to die of the great pain of my bee-stings, then you must tell the bees that I am gone!

Doctor'll cure you, said Alice reassuringly.

He will do nothing of the kind. Here I am, suffering so severely, and does he produce cure? *Mais non!*

Put mud on it, Harry told him idly. (And in time he forgot all about Bert and his stings and jollities, forgot Sardis and her gleaming hair and bubbling excited voice; he forgot the horses and the reassuring ripping sound as their coarse teeth crunched against the grass; forgot tastes of cold corncake and cold fried prairie hen, and crab-apple pickles; forgot bees and fire-smell and honey itself. He turned stubbornly away from the knowledge that before the long blue dusk came down they must be all on their homeward way, trailing like a Romany tribe, happily picturesque and amused at themselves, each girl seated precariously on a horse with a bucket of honey juggled on the pad before her, and the men leading on, seeking the levelest route.)

But that afternoon there was only urgency of the present, the concentration of their need.

Allie, let's wander.

I spose we oughtn't to get *too* fur out of sight of Bert and Sardis. Twouldn't be—decent—

Allie, do you care?

No. Not really. . . .

Matter of fact, I suspect they'd be just as glad to have us vanish for a while. They seem to be getting along first-rate.

I'm glad we thought to vite her.

Dear Allie.

She gave back his words. In tone and mood she said the thing he'd hoped that she might say: she said, Dear Harry, in a breathless whisper.

They became a classic. They were figures stepping out of the frieze of all time and all love, they walked traditionally with hands united; but in fastening their hands together they recognized, each in a separate way, what symbolism was involved. This became not the mild affection of casual friendship or even of flirtation; twas instead the promise, mutually given and esteemed, that their entire flesh and spirit and the ardent wholeness of Themselves would be exchanged, and soon. They would fuse as they must be fused; for the melting was a power and exertion intended for people like Themselves; and loose yellow maple leaves blew soft and jagged against their faces, and said Bless You each time they touched.

Harry, we've gone so fur.

Does it matter?

I guess not . . . what was *that?*

A deer! No, two of them. Guess we gave them a start and then some. Just hear them go, tearing away through those thickets.

Pity we left the gun yonder.

But today I don't feel like shooting anything.

No. Tis all so kindly like. Puts me in mind of when I was little. In Indi*an* I used to walk the woods, all alone, by myself. Like this, in the smoky days.

Sounds wonderful, the way you say that.

What?

The smoky days. Sounds like poetry.

Well . . . but I ain't deceived by my ears, Harry. I know I don't speak like you do. I never did have much schooling. There was always so much to do, to help Mam and Pap, and I missed out a lot of terms. And then— You know how *they* talk. Don't it bother you, to listen to me talking just like some old—? Oh, river rat. Or something?

Allie Mattock, I love to hear you speaking. You have the world's loveliest voice, I swear to it.

Shucks.

Well, you do.

Shucks. . . .

Not long after that, they were together in a couch of leaves, their great rustling lovers' bed of basswood beauty, and the flakes from elm and butternut, light limp glory of the ash. Their bed gave forth a savoring of every forest spice, twas a child's plaything as well, and they were children and again elders. The few insects unslain by frosts were harping steadily for them, a few jays and crows gave out distant coarseness; but raw cry of those birds might have been a caroling of young voices far down the thickets of the future, the cry of their own children, Allie's children and Harry's children, putting a claim upon their hearts. Their mouths were long together. He thought that all the ferocity of a startling brawny frontier was in his body; yet he wished also to be tender with her, tender and tense and worshiping. He gasped her name a score of times, cried it until his breath was gone. And all that she could whisper was to tell him, I hain't never done this before.

XXX

The plating remained over the landscape, winds did not take it loose, sun did not melt it. It crushed down, solidified above the roots of veteran weeds. It was not compressed by a pounding of many feet, for there were not many feet to tread it; but weight of wide lonely air squeezed it against the ground. Often enough sun found the snow through thin clouds to make a moisture, then in turn coldness built a new glaze. When sun ruled low in the southwest, an hour or two after midday, the north slopes glinted in mail, ridges in the south wore their hauberk. Winds sneaked in, whispered first, twisted and roiled, tore your hair from under your shawl later. More snow, more coming, colder.

Glad I brought that windy-sash from Clear Lake, said Rowland Gardner. It lets in the sun a mite.

(And they knew that the Mattocks had only oiled paper—no glass; and that Doctor Harriott and Bert Snyder and Carl Granger had but a greased skin tacked across their window frame.)

There had been eight small panes of glass when the Gardner house was built; now there were but seven. Bertie Luce flew into a rage one autumn day: he wanted to go nutting, he wanted his aunts to take him, they said they were too busy to go. Bertie exploded into one of his tantrums, he kicked and roared. Eliza and Abbie (this was shortly before Eliza left for Springfield) sought to restrain the child and drag him toward the cabin. He twisted loose, broke away, found a stone, threw it. The stone whizzed nowhere near the girls, but struck a dishpan on a bench outside the door; it bounced up and shattered a single pane of glass. Now stuffed rags turned frosty on the inside, in early mornings before the fire was up, with breath of inmates congealing.

A peeled log braced upon poles over the privy-hole (it was behind bushes and down the slope to the west a bit)—this log was colder than the air. It nearly scorched the women's thighs when they sat there with skirts drawn up. Some families had two privy-holes—one for men, one for women; but here there were only Gardner and Luce, no other men about, no unmarried ones. In slovenly informal fashion they got along with one privy. It was the custom to *hoo-hoo* when you approached.

Feces in the ditch were solidified. A crude wooden spade, split from the broad face of a halved log, was frozen into earth beside the hole, so the feces could be covered no longer. Combined sewage of the family was dumped morning and night from an old slop jar. Their chamber pots had both been broken when the wagon upset at a river crossing; they owned only a slop jar intended to receive originally the water from washbowls; but it had a flaring top, you could sit upon it, twould serve. (The jar was of tin, painted a dark chocolate color, though much of the paint had chipped off by now . . . there were forget-me-nots decorating the lid. Abbie recalled how once when she was sick and lay abed, the jar was placed nearby in case she puked. She amused herself by counting forget-me-not petals; there were sixty-seven petals, and one chipped and banged place where paint was gone from the lid. How many petals had been expunged? Also there was something on a stem—it seemed half leaf, half caterpillar—pale green—it rather frightened her, she didn't know what it was.)

With winter clutching, the women did not wish to go outdoors at night, and children cried if they were ordered to go. Only the men went, under stars, in storms and in frost. The women stayed inside.

A great black kettle which steamed with water for general purposes (lake water for cooking, warm water to take the chill off the other water in which you washed) stood half in the fireplace and half out, propped up by stones from the shore which cracked and split as heat powdered them.

Hillside stone would be better, said Gardner sagely. I mind once I met a friendly wild man in the Adirondacks, and he spoke good English. He said the Lake Spirits and River Spirits lived in stone brought from the water; they didn't like the fire, and busted up the stone. He said Hill Spirits liked the heat, count of they were customed to the sun. He said hillside rock wouldn't split so much from heat, and Mr. Marble says that's true. I don't know why we ain't got it.

(Neither Gardner nor Harvey Luce had bothered to dig out any hillside stone. Now the ground was like iron.)

If it happened to be Abbie's chore to empty the slop jar of a morning, her mother was always watching sharply. She saw to it that Abbie dipped out hot water from the kettle with a gourd: the tall pot must be rinsed carefully. Steam went high (smelly steam at first) because the receptacle turned cold when it was taken outdoors. Abbie was then cautioned to gather some wood ashes on the edge of the shovel, and dump them into the thing, along with more hot water.

Sweetens the pot, said her mother.

And the girl thought that disgusting; but at least there would be no increased stench in the cabin. . . .

Two sundogs today, said Frances Gardner. If we had some bean porridge hot, we'd turn it into bean porridge cold! Hang it up outside to keep.

The children wanted to know how this might be; so the mother-grandmother told them a story one of her ancestors had recounted. In New England a large pot of bean porridge would be prepared, beans all mashed, pork or bacon to flavor (the children smacked their lips at the thought). And then, after the family had had its fill, the stuff would be put outside to freeze. Twas cut into chunks—yes, with an axe—great big slabs of it chopped out. These icy chunks would be placed in a bag for safekeeping, hung up on a pole extending out from under the eaves, so that critters might not rip it open.

What kind of critters?

Oh, weasels and porkies and such.

There the porridge would hang frozen, ready for future use during a day when men might wish to carry it into the woods for luncheon. When chopping wood in midwinter they might or might not remember to take a pot along with them—some kind of utensil in which to melt the porridge. Often they forgot; so if they had nothing to melt it in, they would eat it cold, gnawing it off.

Her agèd grandfather used to recite this part with a relish, and he would pull back his bearded lips to show his fine teeth, worn down and yellowed, but still strong; and only two of them were gone, and those because they were broken loose in a fight.

Folks don't grow teeth like that nowadays, children!

The Gardner-Luce tribe had eaten all their beans. Rowly and Bertie sought to emulate their fabled grandsire by taking corn-meal mush outside and freezing it. They nibbled at the stuff later, and pretended that they were wild free foresters as their ancestors had been. They played that Iroquois were coming to scalp them. But it was rather a lame play . . . the mush did not taste so good cold as it tasted hot . . . there were no brightly feathered stately Iroquois hereabouts . . . many weeks ago there had been smelly beggars who prayed for meat or sugar and then went their ragged dirty way.

At dawn Isaac Harriott put on his bearskin coat and belted it tightly around his middle, and pulled on his mittens. His fur cap was not at hand, he could not find it without waking Bert and Carl. He wound an old red yarn tippet over his head, and stepped outside; the door gave a reluctant cry as hoarfrost tore from its hinges. He pulled the door into place, the exterior air striking him as if he walked into an icy pool—in depth far over his head, in width stretching past the boundaries of Iowa. During early December he had driven a horseshoe nail into a log outside the window, bent it, and on the nail had hung a case containing thermometer and barometer (these instruments were presented to him by a grateful patient in St. Paul who had no money to pay for an operation). Harry had left the aperture of the case ajar: the instruments should be exposed directly to the atmosphere. Now a stippled silver paint lay over the whole. With thumbnail Harry removed the coating, and felt his being shiver at the squeak.

Twas seventeen degrees below zero.

Harry turned to look at the world. Trees across the lake were umber, a bank of pink lived above them. The lake was a solid shield; the land wore armor in its own shape, roughest bark of the trees was chased with it. Sometime during the night the earth, with all its groves and horny projections, had been turned upside down and dipped into a liquid confection. White, brittle, transparent taffy, hard, clear, the twigs held it. You could eat it, munch long and richly; but the stuff would take the tissue off your insides with its freezing, twould burn your blood away.

Each day the cold, each night the cold. There could be no warm portion of existence left wherein men might find comfort. The world had moved to the position of the moon, and was as cold or colder than the moon was said to be.

O cottontail, deep within your leafy set. O starved wild crow, perched and graven. O imagined catamount walking the branches with great soft feet. . . . All must have been turned into motionless steel, tempered like steel in that dipping. They were no candy, you could not eat them. . . .

Isaac Harriott thought of all the cold he had known or heard storied. He thought of the first true misery of cold which he could remember: in New Jersey he followed a puppy out onto the stoop, trying to catch the puppy. Wind had blown the door shut, and no one had seen little Isaac or heard him go. He could not open the door, he could not reach the high latch to open it. He wailed, beating small hurting hands against the door. He called his mother's name, and his aunt's, he tried to summon others. Soon he was making but a blubbering sound, no words coming forth. (Through nearly twenty years he could hear his own frigid lament.) He huddled in a thin blue jacket with flat gilt buttons, and one of the buttons was gone: he remembered that, he remembered how icy the others were to his touch, as he tried to hug the garment close with one hand, while still scratching the door with the other, and making his cry. Eventually someone heard him. The door was opened, benevolence of warmth dressed him again.

He recalled the chill of his first cadaver (how like an upended corpse he stood now, before ice-locked cabin and motionless glass of oaks!). Doctor Maws kept a fat little wood-stove fire going in that shed where the late Jos. Hatchaw was so meticulously pulled apart upon his wooden table. But fire went down in the night, and there came an exceptionally bad night. Beneath comforters in the attic, Isaac Harriott felt the burglary of pervading chill. It was as if quilts were become comforters in name only: great mounds of cotton and rags holding no heat. Under the quilts he shook and thought of Old Jupe. The corpse must not freeze, the character of tissues would be changed. Doctor Maws had elucidated on that.

Harry put on boots and breeches, and shivered down the two narrow flights of stairs. There was no one to see him, so he made a squaw of himself in one of the ragged comforters. With the bluff of youth he'd pretended that winter was as nothing to him—he was young, he had rampant blood in his body, he was in health, winter and summer were one. In honesty cold weather frightened him to death, and he hated it accordingly (as always he must hate the threatening thing against which we manage little power).

Harry nearly jumped out of his own hide when he opened the door of that low-ceiled room where the cadaver lay, skinless arms and hands stretched and beseeching; for a white swaddled shape turned grinning from the open stove.

Mean weather out, said Doctor Maws in his chirping whisper. Heard a tree snap and explode, while back. You drove far, Harry, lad, and I didn't choose to disturb you. Just thought I'd better build up a little warmth for Old Jupe! . . . So Harry returned to bed, pale bone of candle sputtering in his hand, but the coldness of the cadaver walked on splintery feet behind him.

That was a coldness to recognize now, it seemed returning. Why did he not pry himself out of misery this instant, and retreat into the squalid cabin? At least there was warmth there, whether you breathed other men's breath or your own.

But majesty of the icing held him cemented. There were too many polished talons beginning to show pink in the sunrise, they would not let him stir, they trapped him fast. Every weed was a claw or a bent cluster of slim claws. Myriad claws of the forest: invisibly they penetrated shabby leather, gripped his feet, would not let him budge for a while.

As do all those who are hungry, Abbie entertained visions of food, whether she slept or worked. She'd be fourteen next June, and the lengthening expanding body shrieked for its sustenance, and called louder for more than mere sustenance. It demanded the hard-to-get, the dainty, the passionately hot and flavored dish, the creamy sweetness which should follow. Abbie's fare had been plain most of the time. The Gardners were poor folks, year after year; they'd never boasted more than frugal victuals until after the Clear Lake claim was sold, except in rare festivity. Yet you could not live into your fourteenth year without tasting the delectable (even though such taste ran across your tongue ever so rarely)—not unless you were a waif. The Gardner children were no waifs. They thought of themselves as Ordinary Folks, for few among their acquaintances had more than they. There were stories of waifs in magazines and books, the girls had seen sad little woodcuts or engravings . . . unhappy children were pictured, standing in shredded gowns at street-corner mires in cities, begging hopelessly for coins from amply clad strangers who thronged over the crossings those same waif-girls had been sweeping. There were pathetic anecdotes of match-girls, corn-girls, tiny slaves who picked up coals or chips, starvelings who dwelt in damp cellars and were sent out to beg by fiendish masters, and were beaten savagely if they brought no coppers back to the drunken louts who ruled them. None of those creeping unfortunates might ever know good fare. The Gardners had known pot roast and drumsticks and corndodger and rose-petal jam; they'd tasted marmalade, had spooned up red-flannel hash; the girls remembered old Mrs. Hubbard's gumdrops, they remembered a tang of dandelion greens seasoned with salt and vinegar, the sharp coolness of new pink radishes and tiny frail lettuce leaves still uncrinkled on the edges. Roasting ears, baked apples, partridges swimming in hot brown sauce . . . trout they'd eaten, and catfish, and the cleanest tenderest young cabbages, and the brownest doughnuts. In memory they could smell gnarled tan mushrooms which simmered in beef fat and sent their nutty odor to the nostrils amid salt-smell, pepper-smell, hunger-joy.

Pa. What's this little boy in this here picture?

Ah, less see. It says: *This is poor Tom.*

Who's poor Tom, Pa?

It says: *He is a waif. He has no father and no mother. Poor Tom has no home—*

Pa, what's a wave?

Not wave—*waif.* Means just like it says: he hain't got no folks, nor no place to stay, nor nobody to see after him. He's one of life's unfortunates, this poor Tom in the book here.

Where's he stay? Hain't he got no bed?

Reckon not. It says in this story that goes with the picture: *Poor ragged Tom is fortunate if he can find shelter from the storm, and that he cannot always do. Sometimes he sleeps upon a doorstep, sometimes in an empty barrel. Should you like to be like poor Tom? I should not. For this unhappy child is clad only in rags, and has no wraps to keep him warm in winter. Let every other boy or girl give thanks that he is not like little Tom. See how sad he looks! I fear that he is hungry. Let us fetch him into our nice warm house. Here, little Tom, poor child, do you come here at once! Come into our pleasant home, and let us wash your dirty face, and warm your hands which are blue with cold. Patty, run to Mother at once, and ask her for food for our little guest! Ralph, do you bring sticks to build up the fire! Oh, poor Tom!—you must sob no longer—*

Oh, Pa-hah-hah-hah—

No, no, Abbie—quit crying now, little girl. Here, get up on my knee. It's going to be all right, now, bout poor Tom—

Ah-hah-hahhhhh—

Now, look—look at this other picture. See, they got him set down all comfortable in the chimney corner! See, he's a-smiling already!

Is—he—getting—anything t'eat?

Course he is. It says: *You must sob no longer. See what Patty and Ralph have for you! A great bowl of bread and milk! Oh, children, do see: ragged Tom is glad to have the good bread and milk! And let us never let an unhappy child turn away unfed from our door. But let us remember always the hungry and the needy, as Jesus wishes us to do.*

But—did he get anything more?

Well, I ain't sure about that. . . . Oh, yes, yes, sure—course he did! Soon as he had his bread and milk, they brung him a big plate of stewed pigeon and potatoes! And then—and then— Gingerbread! And applesauce! And—

Where's the picture bout that, Pa?

It hain't here in this book. But I saw it once in *another* book. . . . You can bet your boots, little girl, that Tom got enough! And they took good care of him, too. He didn't have to sleep in a barrel no more!

The ragged Toms of creation, the waifs, the little match-girls— They had not been present among Ohio Methodists on that memorable day when the Gardners came driving in from distant Rexville, and hunted down Sister Mary and Baby Albert and Brother Harvey in the picnic grove. Dinner was spread and served out within an hour after the unexpected visitors arrived. Abbie strayed back in memory across those stretching years . . . ah, long before Clear Lake, long before the filthy Indians made motions about buying her, long before Shell Rock and the Mississippi ferry before that . . . it was far, far. But the recollection struck so keenly that spice and sweetnesses were wet in her mouth, prickling her eager nostrils. There'd been bulging damp baskets, the women whisking cloths off the top, a jangle of tin knives and forks spilled rattling . . . and rising over all, famous odors. Twas a garden of food, those lovely things in kettles and bowls were the blossoms. You might pick and pick. There'd been that nice old German lady—her name was Auntie Olthoff, and she sputtered in broken English to the little strangers of how she was a Lutheran by religion but— Was it that there was no proper Lutheran church in Norwalk, or was it that she'd quarreled with her fellow Lutherans? The Gardner girls could not well make out the fact, but this personal history mattered little: the important thing was that Auntie Olthoff was come to the Methodist picnic, and that the Gardner girls were come also (and none of them expecting, perhaps, that they'd ever be there) and that there were nose-captivating mouth-watering stomach-filling rivalries in progress. . . . You young visitors, you come and eat with us! . . . *Nein,* these girls they eat with me the dinner, *ja!* . . . Why, that's Brother Harvey Luce's little sister-in-laws, them two! You girls like some baked broad beans? . . . No, Mrs. Buxton, I got two places all set for them, right over here on our tablecloth. Now, you come and taste these beet-pickled-eggs, you two nice little things! . . . *Nein,* Mrs. Howell, the girls, I got for them the *Fastnacht Krapfen.* Also the *Kassler Rippchen* I got, *und* to you I give some also for the Mr., *ja.* Auntie Olthoff produced from another basket a large brown crock, and it was covered with a red-checked cloth. Abbie would remember always how a dampness from beneath had soaked through the cloth, and a light sound was made as Mrs. Olthoff turned back the napkin; rich scent went on high. Never before had Abbie and Eliza Gardner eaten potato salad. In their own kitchens, at Rexville and Greenwood and in that earlier home at Twin Lakes, the Gardners had eaten potatoes boiled, fried, mashed, roasted . . . they'd never fared on potato salad, had never heard of it. It lifted its fair onion-studded face; flakes of pickle were there, a scattering of caraway, a smile of sliced eggs. O wonder and bounty, the sour-sweet fragrance. Twas best to eat it, declared Auntie Olthoff, along with slices of the cold pink pork.

Oh, Mrs. This is so *good.* It's just *scrum*-chew-uss! We never had no ham like this before—

Nein, no ham! *Kassler Rippchen,* the loin of pork! In *mein* own smokehouse, as Uncle Otto teach me to do, before he is dead. Come now, you girls, I want also you should eat the cold *Rinderbrust.*

At such a picnic you could wander leisurely from family group to family group, led on by smile and beckoning, proselyted from one cloth to the next by the desire of Norwalk wives to exhibit their triumphs to the strangers. Which might they find the tastier—Mrs. Howell's rummage pickles, or Mrs. Buxton's sour cucumbers? Which scraps fell limper and cooler and sweeter upon the tongue—the slices of cold veal loaf which had come in Mrs. Glendinning's basket, or shavings of cold liver loaf which had traveled from Mrs. Blassingame's kitchen? Might not Mrs. Hayes' green corn pudding offer a cozy rivalry to Mrs. Beattie's maple snaps?—and what of Mrs. Woltman's strawberry turnovers, and what of Mrs. Carmer's cider cake? And Mrs. MacDonald had produced a Shrewsbury cake from her second-largest red willow basket; and the nut cake offered by Mrs. Riesenberg had been fattened with butternut meats exclusively.

Even after these several crowded active young years, you might savor the memory; but memory, in the end, was a lean fare. In dire grasp of unprecedented winter, the Red Wing men were the first to run out of tea, the Gardners and Luces were the first to finish their pork. Nobles and Thatchers exhausted their flour before the Howes did; and suddenly the Mattocks were bereft of both salt and sugar, and they fetched pork and pumpkin slices to the neighbors in exchange for those essentials . . . corn meal was holding up well in the various barrels, except at the Howes'; bacon dwindled, saleratus was vanishing . . . Old Joel Howe waded across to the Red Wing cabin with half a jug of molasses, and received a flask of vinegar and some salted fish in exchange. Everyone was trying to catch fresh fish, on rare occasions when the weather permitted; but few fish could be speared or clubbed, the lake was too deep, fish lay far below where the water was warmest (if any strata of those Okoboji waters might be called warm). Not enough hay had been cut at any cabin save for the Noble-Thatcher place. Here Morris Markham had seen to it that adequate stacks were piled, indeed he'd led the effort with more vigor than was ever exhibited back in Howard County. Twas necessary to reduce the critters' feed; early in the new year they were showing their ribs. People gazed at the solemn gaunt forests north of the lakes, they thought of the Marbles on their distant shore and wondered how it was with them. No one except Morris had set eyes on William and Peggy Ann Marble since the snows came. Morris spent a night at Spirit Lake in late December, and followed his nose home amid fog and new sleet the next day. They'll last through, he said. For a wonder that greenhorn Marble got an elk! Twas weathered in, there amongst them willows long a little lake that's west of their place; and Marble says he knocked him down with his first shot. Then he waded in and finished off Mr. Elk with a sledge hammer. They've two bags of corn, and Marble he shaped a hand mill to grind it—one stone turning top another, with a crank and all. He's great shakes when it comes to stones.

They all thought about Marble's elk, and talked of it. They looked at their oxen, counted the fellows' ribs. Jim Mattock had butchered his last shoat by the middle of January, the last squeal had resounded across icy reaches, last pressure of a sharpened blade scraped the greasy hide. Boiled puddings could be made no longer, anywhere. You needed milk, and no cow in the region was fresh; you needed suet and there was no suet; salt was at a premium, so was sorghum. A tiny ration of salt could be spared for boiled mush; it seemed to award the stuff some dignity if you called it Hasty Pudding; you stirred meal into a pot of boiling water, and added a scanty spray of salt; you could eat the stuff after it had boiled for half an hour; it could be sliced and fried after it was cold; you wished to dress it with more sorghum than was rationed out; the dreary sameness was a trial, and no one came delighted to the board. Faces of the children began to assume that pointed whittled shape worn by the Little People Who Do Without.

Morris Markham came round from house to house, trudging among the crusty hillocks to distribute a prize: red meat, raw meat. No one knew what it might be.

Not the best in the world. But it's meat. I've already et some.

What is it, Morris?

Stubble goose.

What in time is stubble goose?

Call it giant hare, then. Think twould be better boiled.

Giant hare? Like—like a jack rabbit?

Not exactly. Might call it— Oh, call it Okoboji veal! Twon't kill you.

Stews were made, sacred onions and turnips and priceless potatoes were put in; it tasted strong, folks said, and the meat was strangely stringy; but no one wasted this novelty, and happily the dog Lee crushed bones between his broad jaws. Each time thereafter when Morris tramped along, with ice of frozen breath dressed heavily upon his beard, the children in Gardner-Luce or Mattock households came tumbling to see whether he had fetched any more Okoboji veal. Alvin Noble and Joe Thatcher exchanged meaning glances when people laughed about stubble goose, and speculated on its origin. They knew that Morris Markham had some fresh lynx-hides stretched and drying.

There had been so many things to eat in the autumn, there seemed so few now. Everyone wondered what had happened to their stores. There was still a treasury of potatoes under the Gardner floor, buried deep below frost level; in other homes were small stocks of other root vegetables, but these diminished. People had thought that there would be plenty of game in the winter. They'd imagined themselves marching joyously to the hunt and coming back laden with venison. But no one set eyes on a deer after the first storm. Thickets offered their branches like mocking empty hands. Wind howled at night if wolves did not, but there was no comfort in listening to it.

All of the nuts (many bushels had been gathered) were cracked before the end of January.

I swear, wife! I just can't conclude what's happened to our groceries.

We come in July, Mr. Gardner. That's more'n six months, and we've had so many mouths to feed.

But we had so much!

Harvey Luce said: *Send them away, that they may go into the country round about, and into the villages, and buy themselves bread.*

Very well, Son Harvey! How far's Fort Dodge? Or Webster City? Or Waterloo? Just look at them prairies south of here. Snow you could bury this house in, by gad.

Mr. Gardner, we'll have to go, sooner or later.

S'truth. But that big Jim Mattock and Robby—you member how they tried to strike out, week or so ago, and got upset afore they'd gone three mile?

Noble and Thatcher are fashioning some sled runners.

I know, Harvey, I know. Someone will have to fetch a load or so, or we'll just plain starve. And the Red Wingers thought one of them funny carts could get through; but they run into a regular howler in the second hour they was gone, and Bert Snyder said they'd like to go blind in it ere they reached home again. That's how they lost that ox of their'n. He broke a leg and so they shot him. We can count ourselves fortunate that they shared the meat! No, you got to forget about heading for the settlements till the weather holds decent.

The Lord shall preserve thy going out and thy coming in.

But I reckon it taxes His strength to do so, if folks don't wait till the weather is open! No, we just got to wait.

On Monday morning, February second, Noble and Thatcher finished installing their home-steamed home-shaped runners upon the box, thus transforming a long narrow scow-shaped wagon into a sleigh. Morris Markham carried the news throughout the community; thus ten men assembled for a council in the Red Wing cabin. These included, besides the Red Wingers themselves, every adult male then resident at the lakes except William Marble, who was left out of consideration for obvious reasons. Men must be sent to the settlements for supplies. Who should be delegated?

Old Joel Howe and Rowland Gardner were ruled out at once: they were the elders. Harry was excluded from consideration just as promptly; the doctor could not be spared. Bert Snyder was no ox-driver, and oxen alone might penetrate those white fastnesses to the south and east. Robby Matheson's eyes were peculiarly sensitive to whiteness; already he'd been affected by snow-blindness when searching for strayed cattle or doing other errands on the prairie; twas not safe for him to go. Jim Mattock's corpulence was considered calmly; the vote went against him on that account (much to his profanity). Morris Markham had volunteered at once, but the rest said No. If return of the little expedition was long delayed, the men felt that they would rather have Morris at the lakes than wandering somewhere in other counties. He had not been able to fetch in much game, but the only meat taken that winter was brought round by Morris, and almost the only fish. (Just now he was engaged in hunting squirrels. Twas a laborious task, but did pay some small dividend in flesh which was shared by all. He would seek out the high wadded masses of oak leaves which constituted squirrels' winter nests, and would slay the hibernating creatures by shooting through the nests as they slept; then climb up, in some peril, to eject the bodies by poking with a long pole.)

There remained Carl Granger, Harvey Luce, Joe Thatcher, and Alvin Noble. Only one of the latter two might make the trip. They tossed a three-cent piece: heads for Thatcher, tails for Noble—and the obverse shone. Carl Granger had been a willing volunteer (but in fact all had volunteered) and was a unanimous choice because of his tough ranginess of body and his skill at handling oxen. Again Harvey Luce offered himself, but the rest felt that two men only should go—twould cut down on the provisions to be spared for the journey, and also require less consumption of rations on the return trip.

Gentlemen, I guess that does it. Granger and Thatcher go. . . .

This was a decision made by human beings, twas not the decision of Fate. Ten minutes later Carl Granger lay unconscious and was being examined by a deeply concerned Harriott. He'd gone outside along with Joe Thatcher to make water, and lingered one extra unhappy second beneath the eaves. A mass of ice, which had been clinging below the chimney, broke loose and swept down upon him. He took most of the blow upon his unprotected head: lacerations were severe, so was the concussion. (On recovering his senses Carl spent gloomy hours with weird fancies taunting within his bandaged skull . . . my own father twas, and his head be hurt before I was born . . . tine of that fork in Harvest . . . and will I be like him, now, and dwelling stupid as he did? . . . saying only, *See un* . . . like twas the wraiths of they Tellfords he was seeing . . . and I'll be good for naught, as was he?)

Carl, lucky that Nature gave you a good thick skull.

It aches, it does.

No doubt.

And hurts terrible.

Poor fellow! But most of the hurt is from the stitching— I had to sew up your scalp, you know—and twill be better before long.

Bean't I to make the journey?

You can't possibly go. Harvey Luce is to go in your stead. Bert wanted to; but Harvey knows oxen, as Joe Thatcher does. Our horses couldn't budge that big sled through the drifts.

Coo, it hurts.

Just for that I'm going to administer something to ease the pain. Tis bitter, but you'll be glad. . . . Right. Swallow it down.

My Jody. You think to be long on the way?

No longer'n we can help. Don't go to fussing, woman.

I won't.

Alvin and me flipped a three-center, and twas all fair and square.

Yes, I know. Keep your voice down, love. They're still asleep.

Anyways it's better for me to go. Should we get stuck in a drift, I'm a sight stronger'n Alvin.

Oh, Jody, my limb's been so much better of late. Maybe twill be all cured when you get back! Wouldn't that be nice?

Course.

Jody, where you figure to get supplies?

Morris is confident that the Irish ain't got any. And Shippey, down below there, probably won't have none to spare. So we calculate to head for Fort Dodge or Webster City. Fort's a little closer.

Jody, we got so *little* money.

Take a look at this, woman.

Why. . . . All them coins! It's *gold!* Where on earth—?

Bert Snyder. He said if provisions had to be freighted in, to see us all through the winter, there wasn't no man nor woman nor child in this region going hungry through lack of means. So now we got plenty to purchase with.

Husband, he's a true Christian.

Well. He's kind of a Catholic.

Don't care if he *hain't* been baptized by Reverent Moore or anyone else! He's— He's a Good *Samaritan*. . . .

What's the matter with Dory?

Nothing. Don't you mind? That's the way she always fusses when she wakes up wet and hungry.

Gol. I—hate to leave her—

Now, *you're* the one that ain't to fret. Cause Baby Dory'll be here all safe with me, and Alvin and Liddy will look after us. . . .

And do you keep your voices low, voices low, do not disturb the others, they sleep still, the gray cold light is strengthening, the sun is an icy cranberry somewhere below those long mountains and rivers of snow that flow to the south and east.

Harvey Luce will be along soon.

You'll be starting, you'll have the oxen yoked, you'll be boring stubbornly slowly oh so slowly into blank untrodden cold.

Leave me, your crinkle-haired wife.

Leave me, your daughter who cannot yet speak, and who will be muted ere she speaks. Leave me, your child.

Leave us both.

They camped perforce on the open prairie the first night. They said, We won't do this again, but often they did have to do it again. It meant sleeping buried in stiff hay in the sled, or sleeping under the sled between the runners; they tried both methods, but were surprised to find that they rested better in the latter position. Joe Thatcher concluded that in the first instance there was too much cold air and wind passing beneath; snowbanks were warmer than hay, you could wrap yourself in an insulation of snow; and Joe remembered now, Morris Markham had said that was the thing to do.

In either case the two men lay tight as lovers, rough-clad body against rough-clad body, jealous of whatever warmth might be achieved in physical contact, and with their blanket coats and an old buffalo robe wrapped over and under the two of them.

That robe had come all the way from Indiana. Joe remembered using it in winter when he rode sometimes in his father's pung. It might have come from western prairies originally, and perhaps from this very region. Joe was not especially imaginative. He thought that imagination was a kind of careless vice when practiced deliberately; it might be the plaything of giggling girls, mooning boys, poets, and folks like that; but twas wiser and sounder for a man to be forthright, down to earth. Leave imaginings to incompetent dreamers!—imagination was a toy and an indulgence. He did not even entertain the notion that some people—including himself—might not be really able to wield imagination; it could be summoned at will, he supposed, though twas vain or idle to waste time in that way. But he was very young, not too many years away from childhood (and but few children are devoid of imagination, though it may dry up and blow out of them, to be lost in dust as their bodies extend, as their plain dull minds solidify). Thus, while sleeping, Joseph Thatcher was beset with dreams about the skin of that long-forgotten buffalo which now helped in staving off a murderous chill. In life the huge hump-shouldered beast, with its scrubby kinked mane and brooding eyes and its beard— It had fed here, on this same south slope, this same wilderness ridge. An Indian had come creeping, had risen suddenly and sent his arrow through thick flesh and organs between the bones. The beast had gone bounding, it bled its life away and went to its knees at last, it sprawled and died. The Indian approached, proud and pleased; he took his knife and skinned, skinned, skinned. (In Joe's dream Morris Markham had become the Indian. For Thatcher remembered how Markham's knife sounded and looked as it scraped at a raw hide, hauling off the stubborn deposit of fat and slim clinging papery stuff.) Then he bundled up the great gnarled mass of it and carried it off to a trader. The trader said How. The Indian said How. Me got hide. You got firewater? Ugh. How much firewater you give? Me give bottle, said the trader. You give um hide to me, you keep um firewater, take home to wigwam. Ugh. Ugh. Thus the deal was consummated, and the trader had his buffalo robe, and eventually he stowed it away with a thousand others, and all the hides went on a long journey, freighted and boated to the East; and there eventually this hide appeared in Uncle Dave Foster's store in Kokomo, Indiana; and there it was purchased by Grandpa Noah Thatcher to keep him warm in winter; and Grandpa used it only two winters, and then he died; and Joe Thatcher's father used the buffalo robe and used it and used it; and then Joe himself was growing larger and he took to using it; and the weather was cold, very cold indeed. (O Indiana, how could you become so cold? Were you cold all the autumn as well, cold all the spring? Yes, you were cold all summer too.) And twould be nice if I were now beside the forge, Pa's forge back home, and I would watch the hard short yellow blaze creeping harder harder roaring more roaring more paler paler hotter hotter as the bellows forces short hard whirring hot flame through the coals, and as I smell the charred keen nasty strong stench of hot iron shoe burning into hoof as I hold the big bumpy horse-leg bent against my apron . . . cold . . . and buffalo . . . and Harvey Luce murmurs and moves and his breath is like onions, onions. It does not smell like Lizzie's breath. He murmurs, moves, I must move as well to oblige him . . . and buffalo robe . . . and cold . . . and then Joe Thatcher said to Alvin: What you say? Straw-ride? Bobsled ride? All the young folks? That's what I said: Sled-ride. Think the young ladies' folks'll let 'em go? Course they will, cause we're going to be what-you-call-it chaperoned. Well, ain't that nice, I hain't never been chaperoned in all my life, ha-ha! Young Reverent Moore and his wife are going long, and they're right jolly even if he *is* a preacher. And so he was, the Reverent Mr. Moore, all full of fun and tricks, and throwing snowballs till his Mrs. made him quit. And they sang and sang the while they rode, sang minstrel songs—the decent kind, of course—and they sang Auld Lang Syne, sang songs they'd learnt at singing school from Master Gilbert Gallagher, could see him standing up now, shawls falling away from him at the head of the sleigh as he waved his mittened hands, leading them all, and Reverent Moore singing louder than the rest. Sang old Scotch songs. Sang Buy a Broom. *From Teutschland I come mit my light wares all laden, to the land where the blessing of Freedom doth bloom. . . . O, mein lieber Augustin, Augustin, Augustin.* And buffalo robe, all short matted curled brown wads of clinging hair, and somehow burs got caught in there, maybe burs mixed up in the straw, and those Berry girls had brought hot soapstones to keep their feet warm, and everyone teased them bout it. And then they all drew up at the Mast place to be welcomed with a pumpkin pie spread. And later everyone laughing cheering singing as they made their way back across the yard to the bobsled once more, calling Goodbye and Good Night and Thank You to the Masts. But young Peter Mast went along with them just the same, he didn't stay to home, cause he was courting Bella Radley, just as Master Gallagher was still courting Bet Radley, and of course they had to see the Radley girls home. And Master Gallagher and Reverent Moore got in a real tussle in a snowbank, they fell right into it as they were wrastling, cause Reverent Moore was like a boy again, and he tried to stuff some snow down Gallagher's neck; and pretty young Mrs. Moore she laughed, and she said to Joe Thatcher, Sakes, I do declare, he's just full of the old— And then she whispered it, just so you could barely hear her, cause she was the preacher's wife— She said, The *Old Nick!* . . . And singing as the far chill Milky Way kept blinking. And buffalo robe . . . out in the wagon, coming to the Ioway country

. . . and buffalo robe . . . one time, when they were camping in the woods, he and Liz, they snuck away from the camp, just as they had to do at times, just as the Nobles had to do, and course twas long before Liz was in the family way with Baby Dory; but that night, he remembered, he and Liz they Did It on this buffalo robe. Oh Lizzie, you ain't here, tis Harvey Luce instead, and all his heavy breath and snoring; occasionally he jerks and jumps while sleeping . . . and up they come, that same wild Indian, same wild buffalo; but now the poor old buffalo, he ain't got any hide on him, because *I've got his hide.* Stands here in the deep dark drift longside this wagon-box-on-runners-that-we-made, saying, Where's my hide? Where's my hide? Indian says: How. You got um hide, me give you firewater, you give um hide back to my pet buffalo. Well, tarnation, I *won't.* Yes you *will.* No I *won't.* And poor old buffalo standing here, all shivery, just raw white-wrapped flesh like meat a-laying on a butcher's cart back home in Indiana, but it's got a kind of tissue round it, like when you first strip hide from off a beast; and you can even see the arrow sticking out where it went in; and poor old naked hideless buffalo he keeps a-saying, Where's my hide? You got it!—like the ghost story we used to tell when we were kids, bout *Charley, Charley, give me back my golden arm. Charley, Charley, give me back— Who's got my golden arm? Who's got my golden arm? You got it!* Steam arising from that dead patient hide-stripped-off buffalo, great steamy breath a-coming up like jets of smoke from out his nose.

Agh.

Oxen breath.

The critters.

What say?

Didn't say nothing, Harvey. Gad, I'm like to freeze.

Oh, Brother, it is cold!

Streak of dawn showing.

Yes, I see, Brother.

Think your legs and arms is froze?

No, no. The Lord watched over us, the long cold night.

Reckon He did, Harvey. Let's rise, then. See to the critters. Gad, I had some funny dreams.

Making water in the snow, watching steam arise from the hot meager spurts of urine, as steam arose from nostrils of the dreamt-about raw buffalo. And Harvey down on his knees there beside the runner, down in the snow, one mittened hand braced against the tall pin jammed into the socket of the runner; Harvey down on his prayerful knees, mumbling away. Well, let him. Reckon he knows what's good for him.

They reached Lost Island Lake at noon that day, and looked longingly at the first gnarled stunted willows which stood perpetually staggering, perpetually immobile, with the sweep of motionless drifts around them. Here was more timber than they had seen since leaving the last woodland of East Okoboji. Twould be a comfort to linger, assured of adequate fuel, spending the second night between two roaring fires; but their wives and Baby Amanda and Baby Dora spoke across the pale rolling steppes they'd already crossed, and said to them, Go on.

I hain't certain of the road, Harvey. It's all so different from the way it was when we come.

But God Almighty knows, Brother. Just see. He parted them clouds a secont ago, and shone His bright light, and God spake unto me, and tolt me, This way is south, cause the sun hangs here!

You spoke a mouthful. So if *that's* south, *this* is bound to be east. And if we strike due east, we'll hit Des Moines River timber fore nightfall. Just a question of keeping the wind on our left shoulders. Less, of course, the wind changes.

And the wind ceased, and there was a great calm.

I'd ruther it kept blowing from the same direction. Please try and arrange that with the Lord!

Harvey was hurt, Harvey was sure that Joseph Thatcher spoke too lightly of the Lord. He tramped and wallowed in silence for an hour, constantly entreating within himself that Joe be forgiven—he knew not what he said! The oxen breathed their frost, the frost blew against the men and froze over their knitted tippets and ragged blanket drapings. They maintained as steady and direct and easterly a course as it was possible to do; they circled the deeper drifts, swung back to the east stubbornly. They took turns in bursting their way through tails and whorls of loose eddied snow, floundering ahead of the vehicle, lifting their numb legs high, kicking snow aside, making brooms and shovels of their numb clubbed feet, massing snow to right and left by the swing of their boots. This method made a path of sorts for the yokes to follow. Often both young men found themselves at the back of the sled, lending solid weight and muscular force to the advance . . . numb mittened hands braced against runners or wagon box, bitter voices adjuring the oxen to their task. Rarely they came to a slough where all deposits had been spaded away by persistent winds; then they made speed, banging and crunching over hummocks, swaying and Geeing and Hawing to avoid muskrat houses. (These reedy basket-shaped masses were solid as tree stumps, they must be left as they were, you could not drive over them, the improvised sled might be upset, runners broken.) Sometimes Harvey cried that Jehovah had prepared a course for them, for sometimes an entire long stretch of prairie was devoid of drifts. *For thou, Lord, hast made me glad through thy work: I will triumph in the works of thy hands.* Joe Thatcher gave up wondering about Harvey Luce. His first reaction on becoming acquainted with

Harvey had been that Harvey Luce must be a hypocrite, for Joe had never known a man who prated and quoted with such utter persistence who was not a hypocrite, or at least commonly accused of being one; and Joe's general knowledge of preachers was gained from association with likable men like the young Reverend Mr. W. A. Moore—men who were rollickingly human, who faced life with a zest while Harvey faced it with a groan. Joe recognized now that Harvey was no hypocrite. Harvey's demanding sanctimony was an intrinsic structure in his nature; without it he would not have the strength to labor or to starve. Old prattle-mouth, thought Joe in lame chill accusation. But he means what he says . . . says what he means. I'm glad I ain't like that. I guess I won't go to hell, cause I hain't never done many things which was really bad, cept when I was younger. Lord knows I cuss sometimes. And once Alvin and I went to a wedding where the liquor flowed like water—them rough Droutens, it was . . . their girl got married, just fore we left Indiana; and Lizzie nor Liddy wouldn't think of attending, and Old Joel Howe wouldn't go; but Jonathan and Alvin and me we all kind of snuck off and went, and we got so drunk fore we left the Drouten place that we was tottering all over the road, and Jonathan was singing that awful song we learnt out behind the privy at school, bout *Hail Columbia, Happy Land! Baby pissed in Papa's hand. Papa said it didn't hurt, so baby give another squirt.* And finally Jonathan just laid down under a cottonwood, and Alvin nor me couldn't get him to move, so we laid down too, and we all went to sleep; and woke up with fearful headaches—twas past midnight, by the stars—and then we went on home, and didn't we catch Hail Columbia when we got there! But if that's the wrongest sin I ever done, then I ain't going to hell. And I'd ruther go to hell than be like Harvey Luce. But *he* ain't going to hell—the Lord'd never make him go. So it's all . . . puzzling . . . and cold . . . and arms and legs have got the life in them at last, but what a weary throbbing painful life they got and . . . what's that? *What's that?*

Harvey Luce! Looky there!

What is . . . it . . . Brother? I don't see. . . .

Des Moines River timber! Straight ahead. See all that dark gray fuzz? Bound to be it, couldn't be nothing else! *Let's* go, Duke, *let's* go, Spot . . . *gid* dap, Star! *Go* long, Boney!

When I said . . . My foot slippeth . . . thy mercy, O Lord, held me up.

They were sheltered in a hollow before dark, with thick hickories and oaks above, maples down below toward the ice, and hazelbrush walling to the west and north. They wielded shovels, the snow and old crusted leaves flew wide and far. Here was firewood by the ton. They built two huge fires, fairly danced between them, they made foolish small jokes. Harvey even laughed aloud, twice, at the jokes Joe made. Hay was pulled from the sleigh in generous quantity; the critters munched it steadily; they seemed watching the men with canny eyes, seemed saying, You done us a mean turn, but we forgive you for it, cause now we got hay. . . . Here was a warm spring oozing from the hillside, some sort of mineral spring where ice lay curdled in great orangish ripples. The ice was rotten, it gave way like punkwood beneath the smash of an axe, and an open pool of brown water smoked aloft. Twas a boon to oxen and to men, whatever the pungency of its chemicals. Slabs of mush, slices of fresh-soaked pumpkin frizzled in the big frying pan, along with a few chunks of pork which the men doled out to themselves. Sleepily they listened to the munching of the oxen, the rubbing of the oxen, the occasional splash of dung. . . . Time and again either Joe or Harvey awakened (in passing from warmth into chill) and got up quickly to heave another branch against the toppled old elm where their night fire gnawed, and then flew to snuggle against his bedfellow again. Gray pinkness came; they had to leave their coziness, their wild momentary home; they ate more mush, drank hot strong coffee with a precious taste of sugar in it; they yoked up, and went sliding cautiously downhill through the grove. At this point the ice of the Des Moines was sound and clear. Within two hours the first huts of the Irish colony came into view.

Harvey Luce and Joe Thatcher admitted no wish to linger among the Irish. To begin with, the colonists had no food to spare. From child to crone and gaffer they looked surlily at the visitors, they squeezed their shaggy brows down in distrust, seemed fearing that food would be demanded of them, or perhaps some other form of hospitality which they did not choose to offer. Their homes were mainly dugouts, roofed and walled with sod. From these lairs the inhabitants crept forth like shaggy ground squirrels who seemed ready first to bite and then to flee. One dirty-faced girl was wearing a tiny wooden cross suspended from a chain fastened around her neck, and Harvey Luce shivered inwardly at the sight. He awarded these people the almost superstitious awe which limited but staunchly embattled Protestants so often demonstrate in the presence of Roman Catholics (secretly, though not admitting it to himself, Harvey was fascinated by the notion of Catholicism, its liturgy and ornate rites. But the mere sight of a priest frightened him—and he had seen but a few priests in his life. And he would have liked very much to ask many questions of Catholics, but was too shy and baffled to do so). These people were settlers, they had claimed the land, were now proving it up. But they offered the appearance and attitude of fugitive squatters who had drifted to this spot without much intent, and would traipse on across the horizon again, once something occurred to startle them out of apathy and indolence. Thatcher elicited the information that these half-dozen families had already eaten most of the hogs which Jim Mattock traded to them. They had cut a great quantity of hay during the previous year, however, and several snow-roofed stacks still stood in trampled areas between the dugouts, with a few head of lean cattle pulling at them. Joe bargained for sufficient hay to replace the amount already consumed by the travelers' own oxen; it was stuffed upon the sled, and he and Harvey went laboring gladly southeast, driving for a point on the river which neither of them had ever visited but where they hoped to spend the night. A man named Shippey had built a cabin there—the only habitation for miles around—and he was said to welcome all wayfarers with cordiality.

They reached this house in time to join Mr. Shippey and his wife at a hominy supper, but the news they received was distressing.

You mean twouldn't do us any good to go to Fort Dodge?

Not a smidge! Couple of Fort Dodge men only left here a-yesterday. They come up the river a-hunting, but went back empty-handed. No game left in their region. Wild critters was so starved they come right into town—deer and such—and people rushed out and knocked 'em on the heads with hatchets and clubs.

Well, venison ain't bad.

No, but that was early in the winter, right after the first big storm. Since then the supply situation at the Fort has worsened steady, and they say the same is true of Webster City. Whole families run out of provisions or wood—had to move in with other folks—had to buy and borrow and beg in order to keep alive. Ain't enough grists left at any of the mills to feed a bunny rabbit, and the stores are mainly empty of grub. I don't reckon you could purchase enough grub at Fort Dodge *or* Webster City to fill one corner of that big sledge of yourn!

Thatcher and Luce were preoccupied with thought of their trusting families back at the lake. They did not sleep soundly on the floor in front of Shippey's fire. Soon after sunrise they were being braced by a fierce steady wind on the prairie once more.

Franklin County, said Joe. That's the nearest. Where we used to live. Us Indiana folks spent one season there, fore we come out to the Okoboji country.

I hain't never been there, Brother Joseph. Is it fur?

Regret to say that, as the crow flies, it's a good— Joe considered. Well, say seventy-five miles. But we'll have to figure on traveling at least a hundred.

Hold up my goings in thy paths, that my footsteps slip not. Have they got them a town, Brother?

Started one. Little new place named Benjamin. No, let's see— When that party of young men—you member the ones, traveling on horseback?— When they come by last autumn they said the name of the place was being changed—going to call it Hampton or something like that. Jonathan Howe—he's the eldest boy in the tribe—he's there now.

Then there's my brother-in-law, Asa Burtch. And one of the Howe son-in-laws, Enoch Ryan.

Five days later they lurched stiffly, half-starved, into the raw sad village of Hampton. Thatcher's family connections could offer food enough to provide the travelers with good hot meals while the oxen rested; there were beds to be shared; but townspeople shook their heads obstinately when asked to sell the supplies so sorely needed. Cedar Falls or Waterloo, they said. You'll have to go there.

How fur? Oh, how fur?

Maybe sixty mile.

XXXI

Blood-Clot Boy is now gone. Behold, comes an old man with staff in his hand, to meet him. O grandchild, says Old Man, whither do you go? And he replies, I am walking. Then comes flock of the shiyo, *the grouse, and alights beside them. O my grandchild, says Old Man, shoot one* shiyo *for me, for I starve! But Blood-Clot Boy answers, Nay. I go with haste in this direction. And he passes into the south.*

So did the Wahpekute pass into the south, leaving the river of the Chankasnasnata, Where-Limbs-Are-Torn-Off-Trees, when it joined its surface with the dirty freeze of the Missouri. They held unhappy memories of the time they'd spent up the Big Sioux. Very little meat was killed, very few animals were seen. Aye—wood, wood, wood; all the fires burned brightly, cozily, no one was ever cold; but flames snapped in mockery because there had been so little to cook upon them. Abject weeks dragged out as these people crouched in tangled brushland. Ice and floods gave the river its doleful unwieldy name: fierce freshets had undermined most of the taller trees—they toppled and sprawled. And in every March the ice-cakes swung blunt axes to scrape and gouge. Twas a waste, a cruel planet of congealed bayous and drifts, with interlaced dead trunks tangled over all, and stubborn saplings still trying to rear themselves amongst the jackstraws. There should have been many deer yarded along the Big Sioux, as Inkpaduta had known them in other years; but only three deer were shot, and those were sick and starving, they carried little meat.

Another pony had been killed, and another pony; and dogs also had been killed.

The Indians begged their way through the burgeoning town of Sioux City. This was the largest village which most of the band had ever observed. Only Inkpaduta and His-Curly-Sacred and Bursts-Frog-Open had seen so many lodges of whites before. Corn-Sucker was terrified, and did not beg well; she begged less successfully than any other woman, and was beaten accordingly by a smiling spouse. She kept covering her face with her blanket when she stood at the doors of the big lodges. She attempted to remember Eeeet and Peeeez; and Inkpaduta had tried to teach her the word for spirit water. She wished accordingly to ask for Whisk or Wisk or Wis-kee; but it was hard for her to do this, as she had not been reared to speak such sounds, and had acquired a few of them only as gradually she acquired the language of the Dakota. The word *Wisk* made her think of *wishtenkiya* or *wishtenkiyapi* (which had reference to the business of being politely ashamed of one's in-laws; and so you should not look upon them, or speak their names, or have direct communication with them. But these outlaw Wahpekute had little respect for such a custom; they did not observe it except with a kind of sneer, as if to say, Behold how impolite I can be!). Corn-Sucker's dismayed voice was but a whisper, and impatient whites roared at her to begone. But no beggar received much food in this big village, for the whites had few enough victuals for themselves. Even currently, had the Indians but known it, many citizens were gone with their teams, toiling up or down the torturing road which led from Council Bluffs a hundred miles away.

It is not good to starve.

It seemed that no one in the world had much food in this incessant winter. A child of Hushan died, and was left tied up in a lean cottonwood tree near Sioux City. The mother, Wikoshkasapa or Black-Young-Woman— The mother walked wailing. Not even Inkpaduta could object to her outcries, though he hated to hear them, and wished very much to close her mouth for her. But this he dared not do: easily he might have been slain by Hushan or some other offended member of the company. Black-Young-Woman cut off a lock of the child's lice-filled hair and carried it away with her. With that same knife she hacked off her own hair until barely it hung below her ears; her neck was exposed to merciless winds which pressed down from the northwest. With that same knife, again, the mother scratched her legs below the knees until blood ran down into her ragged moccasins, where it curdled and dried and froze; so she wore hosiery of old darkening blood, with spots of fresh red welling through. Black-Young-Woman should have liked to paint her face with charcoal, but only men blackened their faces when mourning for the dead. *Michunkshi*, she would howl, drawing out a quavering second syllable. My daughter! My daughter! . . . She had few personal possessions, but most of these she gave away. She possessed three yards of cotton cloth, which she'd planned to make into a coat or blouse; twas printed cloth, with small red flowers sprinkled on the gray background, and this piece of goods had been stolen slyly by her husband from the Wood brothers' trading store at Springfield early during the previous autumn. It was folded and rolled tightly, and had grown quite dirty and grease-stained from much handling and packing, but it was still a piece of white people's goods and had value. She gave this piece of calico to Corn-Sucker. And to Woman-Shakes she gave an extra pair of blue broadcloth leggings, although one legging was torn. To the generally good-tempered Cloud-Woman she gave a single garter—there had been a pair of these fringed doeskin garters, but one was lost; and also she gave to Cloud-Woman a wide yellow ribbon she'd owned since she was a girl. Sometimes Black-Young-Woman wore this ribbon tied around her neck and sometimes tied around one arm, and now Cloud-Woman might wear it so, and be proud because she had a white people's yellow ribbon. . . . To Female-Cousin-Rabbit the bereaved mother offered nothing at all, because Female-Cousin-Rabbit stood generally as the enemy of Black-Young-Woman, as indeed she was the enemy of others because of her lewd and quarrelsome ways. . . . The lamentation rose persistently . . . *Hunhe, hunhe!* . . . keening long and loud about the dead daughter to whom in fact the mother had awarded little thought or care while the child lived. My daughter, my daughter! . . . But Female-Cousin-Rabbit was not to be put off easily, not to be giftless and ignored; especially when every other woman of the group was given something. Black-Young-Woman had awarded beads to one, a rusty pocketknife to another. A white people's tiny teaspoon (broken in two) and an empty glass flask which once contained vanilla, and had been picked up near a lodge of the whites—these were disposed of. Female-Cousin-Rabbit received nothing, and her fury and acquisitive nature were now displayed. Rudely she lifted from the mourning mother's neck a thin circular plate of silver, an ornament Black-Young-Woman had cherished since girlhood, and which had belonged to her mother before her, and which she wore dangling from a thong. Female-Cousin-Rabbit now slid the string over her own head, and she screeched to all: Consider what this woman gives to me! And, though she had not intended to give away the beloved little silver gaud (scarcely was it as wide as a woman's smallest finger is long) Black-Young-Woman dared offer no objection to this outright barefaced thievery. For had she resisted, or had she taken back the ornament from the thief, it would have been as if she said: I care more for this piece of shining metal than care I for my dead child. . . . The saddest mourning which a woman might make was the mourning for a dead husband. Then, after that in miserable value, was the mourning one made for a dead son; and after that the mourning for a dead daughter. At another time, under other conditions, Black-Young-Woman would have fought off any hands which tried to remove her treasure; she would have screamed and clawed. But now she must accept the affront and the loss meekly, she must admit to the world that the satisfaction of owning any possession was as nothing compared to the loss of her little girl. *Michunkshi! Michunkshi.* My daughter, my daughter! My comfort has departed, my heart is sad. O sad heart, O heart grown sick! My daughter! My joy is turned to sorrow; the light of my eyes is extinguished; all is dark! Never again, O daughter, will I see thee smile. Never again hear the music of thy voice. *Hunhe, hunhe!* Alas! Alas! She trudged at the rear of the tattered parade, her husband rode ahead of her on the pony they owned; he mourned also for the child, he kept his face turned down, and his face was smeared black; but Hushan did not wail, the wailing was left to the woman. When they all went begging again into the village of Sergeant's Bluff, Black-Young-Woman was left with ponies and baggage, along with Inkpaduta, who did not wish to beg at this place (but sometimes in certain moods he might beg or pretend to beg; actually he was looking for an opportunity to steal, or to achieve a quick donation by use of threats or hard looks). She protracted her elegy while the other women were gone, and they could hear her far across implacable snows as they drifted back. Unwashed and uncombed will I mourn for thee, my daughter! (Though this woman did not wash, no one had ever seen her wash; and her child had lived in a repulsive condition.) *Michunkshi,* whose long locks are never again to be braided by me; I give away all my possessions—all, all—for now they mean nothing; my daughter is gone. My daughter! Long she cried, until she could cry no more because she had no voice with which to cry; she tramped at the rear of the procession as before, and sometimes she managed to give a thin little hoot which was heard, but that was all. She had left food in a bowl beside the tree where the emaciated body was lashed; and she was thinking about this food, and imagining how the spirit of her child would come gliding to bend and eat.

Inkpaduta led directly toward the Inyaniake, that river which white men named Little Sioux. Traveling across open prairie for two sleeps (and in one case making a snow camp without fire), he drove himself almost merrily. He was contemplating the sparse settlements along that river. This was the end, there was no choice. As he had said to his sons, he meant now to steal, to kill cattle, to break guns. *Echahe*—twould be joyful to do these things once more, as he had done several months earlier in the lodge of the white-people-with-all-blue-eyes. (He thought of that lonely house so far to the north; he wished that he had been younger; then would he have taken the woman, Fort Ridgely or no Fort Ridgely.)

He thought of Charles Flandrau, and heard his own words spoken doggedly in the agent's presence.

. . . *Give to me my annuity.*

. . . *Go away!*

. . . *Then I will steal!*

. . . *Go!*

. . . *I will kill again.*

He thought that he should not kill again, however, until once more he had reached those same northern prairies. Sioux City was too close at hand, and many white men in that village had guns; also there were plenty of horses. White men of the village would most certainly arm themselves and overtake Inkpaduta's people, were they to kill now.

He would wait until he decided that the time was right to make war.

The time was not right, not now or at this place. But they could steal.

First off they stole corn out of the settlers' fields; for when vast snows smashed down to lock the region, much corn had not been gathered, and it was still fastened to old bent stalks thrusting up out of shallower drifts. (In later years many strange tales would be told by the whites about these incursions; the tales would mount to the stature of myths, and would be repeated and embroidered. One white man would say: It was myself! My dog attacked the Indians while they stole my corn from the field. An Indian did kill my dog, so I did beat that Indian with my fists. Thus all the Indians were very angry, and made much trouble! . . . And later another white person—perhaps a woman—would say: It was my father. He called all the neighbors together, and they went to the Indians' camp and took their guns from them. These guns the white people hid where it was hoped the Indians might not find them; but the Indians did find the guns, and took them away again. So there was more trouble, and later came war! . . . Or a white man would tell the tale: It was my grandfather. He dressed as a soldier, to frighten the Indians; and so did many of his friends, and they blew upon their bugles, and the Indians did think that soldiers came; so then the Indians did flee! . . . Someone else would say: The Indians wished to go down to the camp of the Omaha, but we would not let them go. And someone else said: We told the Indians to go to the Omaha, and shake their hands. We wished to force them to do this thing; but the Dakota feared the Omaha, and they would not go. . . . Many such stories would be told; and no two of the stories would be alike, and almost no two of the white people would tell the same story. And always this is true when tales are told about men who are not known well or understood; and when much snow has fallen during many winters which have passed. It was as if some of the white men cried: *Idatahn!*—I boast! But that could not be true, because no one of these settlers knew how to cry *Idatahn!*)

The Wahpekute stole corn all through a thin ragged settlement called Smithland. Then they made their way north up the Little Sioux. Inkpaduta hoped to find lodges of the whites which were far apart from one another. These he found.

First, the lodge of a man named Hammond. They did not know his name, but this man was alone. And some of the band did go into the lodge of Hammond, and they signed that he must give them food. Mr. Hammond did not wish to do this thing; so him they beat, and left him lying flat; and they shot at his cabin door as they went away. And all which they wanted to take from his cabin, they had taken. It was not wise of Mr. Hammond to refuse to give them what they asked! He was very sorry to be beaten! But even had he given them what the asked, they might have beaten him anyway. No man wishes to be beaten. . . .

Bursts-Frog-Open and Makes-Fat-Bad and His-Curly-Sacred and some others did sing of this matter after they were gone away.

White man, hurry along! White man, hurry along!
White man, get out of the way!
We're coming there again.

Nay, said someone. Do not sing that song.

Why should we not sing?

Do not let Inkpaduta hear thee sing. You sing a war song. All men know this to be a war song. And Inkpuduta does say—

Ah, That Old One! Fie upon him.

You wish to fight That Old One?

Nay. (Hastily.)

He says we are too close to many whites, so we do not kill. So sing thee not a war song!

White man, hello!
Tell your elder brother
You're too slow.

That also is a war song! You sing it not.

Ah, we sing—

Then That Old One may shoot!

Eyakesh. We sing it not.

I make song, said the Titonwan whose name was Makes-Fat-Bad-Smelling-Wind. He did love to sing, to chant, to make announcements and pronouncements, though often men did not pay much heed to him. (That was the reason that he longed to be heard.) But now the hearts of the rest were glad because they had stolen, and now they had more food than they'd owned before, and they chewed up all the sugar which they stole, and they carried off pickled pork which later they would chew. So they gave attention to Makes-Fat-Bad, and heard him, and grunted their affirmation.

O white man! You keep sugar in your lodge.

Ho!

And wet-meat-in-slime, in great-wooden-pot, this you keep.

Ho! Ho!

We ask you for food, but food you do not give. And we have hunger. So it is you whom we strike.

Ho!

Now go we to other lodges, and we take food, and we strike. Who knows? It may be that we find napcho. *Aye, aye, aye!*

Makes-Fat-Bad longed for buffalo, but beef tenderloin would suffice. He thought to kill some cattle, and so did many of the others. Thus he sang of tenderloin. He thought of *napcho,* fresh cut from a warm carcass, with blood dripping.

His-Curly-Sacred-Penis threw in his own contribution to the song, as they went on to join the main body of Wahpekute in shelter of riverside hills.

We did strike a man, and we will strike again. It may be that we take women! I would find a thin young woman with yellow hair. Such a young white woman I see long ago. Her I take!

Ho! Ho!

Of those in the band, each had been compelled to leave his own native circle because of some form of evil which he practiced. There were many kinds of wickedness which they did. Inkpaduta himself had been expelled principally because of flagrant willingness to *tinwichakte,* to murder his fellow tribesmen. Makes-Fat-Bad had done as great a sin: it was his own wife who died of it. But the bad thing done by Bahata, not once but many times, was the act known as *iwichahu.* This is the deed which is done when a man lies not with a woman but with another man. There was no other in this group who would permit Bahata to do that thing with him, though they made jests about it. They gave him the name of On-Oldish-Man.

Bahata had the soft face of a woman (a woman perhaps greasy and slightly hairy) but he was very strong. He trailed well, he was a skilled shot with a gun; and with his bow could send an arrow straighter and farther than even Inkpaduta. Often before the snows set in he had killed more *sinkpe* than most of the men . . . his arrows speared through the muskrats, impaling two or three of them, one after the other, and all before they were alarmed by sound of guns. His arrows gushed fast and almost silently while the puzzled creatures still crouched stupidly on their houses, not knowing whence these rapid deaths came. *Eyakesh*—he was a good hunter, this man Bahata! But he was not liked well. The young men without wives would not let him share any lodge where they dwelt; and he was barely tolerated by He-Wears-Anything, and permitted to sleep in the lodge of Cloud-Woman and He-Wears-Anything and share food with that family, because he was so good a hunter (when there was game to hunt) and thus exceptional at fetching in meat.

Other things were peculiar to Bahata, and one of these was his addiction to feathers. He grew amazingly excited at the sight of down and soft fluff; he enjoyed putting his hands in such loose light substances. When he killed a bird he worked painstakingly, pulling softest shortest fluffiest feathers from its breast; and this down he would compress into a parfleche with other down from other birds, and this down he carried always with him like medicine. When sometimes a chronicle was related pertaining to the *Wakinyan* (those Thunder-Birds whose home was at the far western edge of the earth) then would On-Oldish-Man become rapt in listening to a description of the four sentries who guarded the four doors of the Thunder-Birds' lodge.

Inyun! he would cry, as in a marvel. (Though all knew that he had heard such stories before, and knew each answer to each question which was asked.) What wear they, these sentries?

The down of swans.

Inyun! And of what color?

The down is red.

Red? Red indeed?

Aye. The down of the swans is redder than fresh blood.

Iyanaka! They are completely covered with this down?

All but the heads. Their heads are bare, but otherwise they are covered with such a softness!

And the breathing of Bahata would be quick and strenuous as he listened, as his eyes moved in their deep sockets, as his huge hands trembled and clutched at nothingness. (For he would breathe as breathes a man who has run far without resting, each time he heard talk of swans' down and feathers.) And in the end he might tell of swans which he had shot with his arrows, years ago, when he was but a youth. And his nostrils would seem to grow wider, and sometimes water would drip from his jaw. The eyes of Bahata would be hot and bright when he spoke of these things.

One sleep beyond the plundered house of Mr. Hammond, the Wahpekute approached another cabin which was inhabited by a lone Swede named Axel Anderson. This man had owned a dog, but the creature was lost and frozen earlier in the winter—or perhaps killed by wolves; Axel did not know what had become of Necken the dog, but at least Necken was not present now to give a warning. Axel Anderson had his own way of mourning for Necken: twas by singing an old song of his childhood which always he had fancied, and which without doubt had caused him to so name the dog in the first place. *Necken, han sjunger på bölja blå* . . . this he sang as he sat laboriously mending a rent in his pantaloons. These were his only pants, at least conventional ones. He had sewn two meal sacks together crudely as a substitute; these loose voluminous bloomers, gathered and tied around the waist with a hempen cord, were his attire as he sewed. He was a cherubic round-eyed little man with pink stubble over a shiny face which looked as if it had been boiled. His wife still dwelt in Kalmar, and Axel was preparing a home for her. House and stable had been erected the previous year, with the help of two other emigrants who then went on to Sioux City. On this day Axel counted himself well-used by the world in general and by the Iowa country in particular. The winter had been devilish, fraught with much danger, but he'd survived thus far; his oxen and his cow were in fair condition, as also were the two hogs; his flour and salt and meat would, by careful management, carry him through until spring. Hidden beneath two feather beds brought from the Old Country was a brown wallet containing a hoarded forty-two dollars in gold. In spring he would trade labor with some three-miles-away neighbors for the use of a plow, and he had the money with which to buy all seed required; and if he made a good crop the first year it could be arranged for Freja to come out to America the following spring. Thus he was but perhaps fourteen or fifteen months away from supreme happiness. Nothing lay between himself and such attainment except self-directed slavery; and that was simple since he had known little except labor throughout his life. Axel sang, *Hafvets små elfvor i ringdans ga, och böljorna dansa också.* He anticipated delightedly the last line of that song, for therein mention was made of the goddess Freja; and Axel's wife's name was Freja.

Eight minutes later he had been struck savagely upon the head, his head was bleeding, his hands were tied together, his feet were tied together. He had been dumped upon the floor and in helplessness he watched the looting of his neat cabin and heard distantly the murder of his animals: *mooooo . . . looooo . . .* more shots terminated those throbbing outcries. Poor Necken—had the dog been there he would have been slain also! But Necken was not present to roar an alarm. Thus the assault upon Axel Anderson came unheralded, it began within seconds after the door was pushed open. His gun (an old one, appraised with disdain by these smelly villains) was smashed against the wide rounded hearthstones. The flour barrel was upset, salted beef was being gobbled or shoved into containers for carrying away, all the sugar and coffee were taken. The bed had been pulled apart and the wallet discovered and appropriated. The Indians took also such tools or implements as they fancied: a hand sickle, a pair of antique scissors, spoons and forks, a ladle, tin plates, and of course every knife in the place. Axel wondered achingly whether they would kill him with his own hoe. One Indian kept grinning, and lifting the hoe as if for a quick stroke against Axel's half-bald head; then the Indian would lower the hoe until the blade rested fairly across Axel's eyes; then quickly the Indian would draw back the hoe again as if making ready for a final blow. Freja, never shall I see thee more . . . and the tender lilting song whirled crookedly around his bruised brain. *Ty bland de stjernor, som hander ser. Freja emot honom ler.* The big Bible was hurled through the window, and various dishes followed it, and also Axel Anderson's boots which he had been drying (no, these Indians did not wish to wear boots!—but one of them had already donned Axel's only coat, his dress-up coat with the cloth-covered buttons; and this blue jacket Freja had made with her own hands, as cleverly as a tailor might have done). A vile-looking monster with no nose on his face—only a raw mucus-filled hole for a nose—squatted in the far corner of the room and there, amid grunts and gobblings of the others, proceeded to have a bowel movement upon those clean puncheons which Axel had scrubbed with melted snow and wood ashes, only that morning. Whether the creature did this as a sign of hatred and contempt, or merely because it was warmer here than outside (and there were no privies amid old prairie drifts) might never be known. The Swedish settler thought that it did not matter much, since his possessions were already spoiled away from him, and now he would be slain as he heard his oxen being slain; and then the invaders would ignite the house and cremate Axel's body in the ruins.

Bahata held the hoe and kept tormenting his victim.

Do not kill, warned Inkpaduta gruffly from the doorway. Inkpaduta had been outside, superintending butchery of the cattle; and he had set some women to cutting out the choicer portions.

Nay, I do not kill.

We are near many *Washichun.* They follow soon!

Nay, I do not kill this white man. But I take him! It is long since I have a man.

In a few minutes the rest had tired of committing ruination (in fact there was little more ruination to commit) so they went to dip warm blood from cavities of the oxen, where women had cut out the loins and tongues; and from the body of the cow they had cut also the stomach. Most of the men bent or crouched, thrusting hands into the steaming bodies, and letting cupped palms fill up with blood and other fluids which they then quickly transferred to their mouths. Rattle-Strike and He-Wears-Anything employed spoons they'd stolen, and there was discussion about this: it was believed that at least two of the spoons were of silver, and thus valuable, and should not be used functionally but should be prized as ornaments instead.

In the cabin, Bahata dragged a trussed-up Axel Anderson across the table and rolled him upon his belly and chest. Axel had long since uttered all the curses which he knew in Swedish or English. He could but snarl as the pain of this forcible defilement overwhelmed him.

When at last Bahata was sated, one of Axel Anderson's ankles had broken loose from its bonds; and that wild foot, with the leg bent so that the foot flailed upward, landed a kick which struck On-Oldish-Man's side and hurt him badly enough to make him yell. Then did he pick up a stick from a broken chair, and with this stick he punished the white man severely, thrashing him until his flesh was discolored. Bahata felt avenged, he turned to go. His moccasin caught in a twisted fold: the corner of a loose-filled feather bed. Why, what was this? Bahata picked up the tick and shook it. The mass of material inside was wadded, slithering under pressure of his hands. So on this strange thick blanket did white people sleep, or under it? One small feather blew loose from a seam and gave him the clue. Feathers? Down? Could this be true? In another moment he romped away through the open doorway, waving the thin baggy mattress over his head, ripping the seam open as he ran. Feathers whirled out in a storm. *Toko!*—he cried hoarsely to his fellows. Behold!—and they looked up from their last feeding and butchering to see him surrounded by a cloud. It was as if he had wings, but the wings were coming loose and falling apart and gliding on high and spreading in dissolution. *Toketu he?* people inquired. What is the matter? And then they stood either entranced or musing while Bahata danced amid the falling spray as if he whirled among great snowflakes. There was another such blanket-filled-with-feathers within the cabin: he had seen it, he rushed back to secure it. Desire to possess the treasure of tiny feathers and puffing down excited him so much that he could no longer speak coherently, he could but moan as he hastened; and inside the house his utterance of inane noises mingled strangely with the moaning of Axel Anderson, who was still tied and unable as yet to get loose. Axel groaned in pain and heartbreak and sickness and terror, in the ignominy of this disaster which had swept upon him—so unhinted at, so undeserved. Bahata ignored him. Neither did he strike the captive again or move to release him; he would leave the white man to free himself eventually if he could do so. He himself was ardent for the joy of feathers. He snatched up the second tick from where it lay wadded in a corner, and had torn it open before he reached the door. In this way much of the contents spilled out upon the floor; but Bahata spun round and gathered up these fugitive fluffs in his arms and tried to stuff them back, that he might cavort with them outside in the light wind. And there was blood here, from the house-dweller's wound, and some of the feathers became soggy or at least touched and dampened with it; they became scarlet, oh, scarlet. Like the down of the sentries who stand at the four doors of the lodge of the Thunder-Birds!—Bahata cried within his heart. He wished that he could call such good news aloud, but he could make only mouthings. He stood on a high frozen drift beyond the woodpile, he dipped his hands into the loose sack and gathered many feathers and swung them about until all the air was choked with their flutter. They wheeled and flew. Joy, ah, joy!—the tidings screeched inside him; but silently he jumped and wallowed through new ecstasy, until the contents of the tick were brushed and blown away. Soon he went trudging off toward river timber with others of his clan; but the feathers still rioted, spreading in breeze, hustling and thinning far above lank weeds which poked up through the gray lonely snow. When at last Axel Anderson staggered to close the cabin door he could see a light froth of feathers still blowing like distant autumn milkweed blooms.

Up the course of the Inyaniake the Wahpekute took their twisting way. Now there was food in plenty: rice, beans, chickens, dogs, corn meal, sugar, beef. They lived according to mood, sometimes in bad temper, sometimes roisteringly. It became the custom for little parties to break away from the laggardly advance, and go scouting and pestering through the countryside. There were several tiny settlements; in such areas Inkpaduta warned against violence, he said that the mere threat of violence was sufficient to cause most whites to yield. Twas a joy for a few of the men—sometimes accompanied by women of the band, sometimes not—to go banging on doors of isolated cabins, and stalk inside to make signs of friendship and hunger signs. The wiser rogues timed their visits for noon or dusk, or soon after sunrise of a morning. Thus often they found the *Washichun* sitting down to their meals, and were quickly accepted as guests by terrified householders. After the scamps had received all provender which the whites might give— Then would they go to snatching possessions, to wringing chickens' necks or shooting hogs. Bit by bit they all acquired portions of new wardrobes. . . . Fire-Cloud's two children were clad in plaid dresses. Inkpaduta strutted frequently in a frock coat and beaver hat taken from an abject newcomer to Ida County. . . . This was a way of life which suited the twins to perfection: they went bullying their way north in high spirits. As for their brother-in-law, Kahdahda, he was a lazybones who had always preferred to steal rather than to hunt. Had there been elk up the valley, Bahata and Itoyetonka might have crept after them for pure excitment and profit of the stalk; but Rattle-Strike would have preferred to go pilfering among cabins. Makes-Fat-Bad was happy because he was eating beef these days, though you could not call some of the beef loin-meat in fairness—it might have been cut from the loins of certain sorry winter-wizened beasts, but it tasted like the leg-meat of buffalo bulls which had run hard and long. The others responded to joys of incursion in varying degrees of enthusiasm. One-Staggering and He-Has-Done-Walking spent most of their effort in hunting for spirit water, though the former practiced his own whim of using a cabin as a latrine whenever he could manage. . . . The women whined and grabbed along with the men if they were allowed to come. Sometimes they carried their babies—those who were still lugged on an *iyokopa,* a cradleboard—and let the larger children trot behind. The fathers regarded the presence of these small hangers-on as a nuisance and impediment, however, and cuffed them when they appeared, and sent them back to camp. Corn-Sucker served as warden, guardian, horse-tender, fire-mender, housekeeper. Inkpaduta considered her wholly incompetent as a beggar; and if she were not a good beggar certainly she would be a poor thief; there was no point in fetching her to the pillage. He exhibited his displeasure by awarding his wife more than her usual quota of slaps and kicks; but infinitely she preferred such maltreatment to being flogged along on an expedition aimed at despoilment.

My people stole horses from the Dakota, she sang quietly to a freshly acquired mare which had belonged to a white family in Cherokee County.

It was as in war, it was not like this. For horse-stealing is like war; and so you were stolen, My-Good-Spotted-Pony-Is-Sad.

Tsakak! *We did not steal dishes and robes. No one in my village carried away a pot or blanket which was not his. We did not steal as the Wahpekute steal.*

Tsakak! *They take all, they waste that which they do not take.*

My eyes saw them kill, and leave the meat lying. It was because their hands were full, and they could carry no more.

My eyes saw them pour meal and flour into snow. It is bad to waste, and my heart is sad because I saw them steal and waste. And it is bad to steal. My people did not steal.

They stole only horses.

Do you hear me, My-Good-Spotted-Pony-Is-Sad?

You too were stolen, but you were not wasted.

Now I give thee some crumbs of sugar. But the sugar too was stolen.

I would give back all the things which were stolen, but this I cannot do.

Pony, Pony, within me is a small wounded animal!

The sorrow of Corn-Sucker, even if voiced within hearing of the others, could have had no effect on their activities. It was progressing rapidly to a point where Inkpaduta would be able to exert little restraint. Were they not removed enough now from those big-villages-of-many-lodges-of-whites? Was it not true that they were far from any fort, far from soldiers? The young men remarked on this incessantly. They grew rapidly wealthy in chickens, dog meat, other meat, clothing, horses, guns. Surely they needed new guns.

(Like many of their more tractable relatives among the Dakota, they performed ruination upon weapons through mistreatment and neglect. They left guns exposed, did not dry them when they were soaked, gave no regular attendance with any sort of oil. They let bores choke up with rust, let locks stiffen and freeze. If bound for a hunt, they punched accumulation out of the barrels with a few jabs of the ramrod; they smeared skunk oil, rubbing around triggers and hammers until the tortured mechanism would retract once more; they poked with knife points or bits of wire until a charge could be fired; then they would load and go. . . . Of late they had stolen everything from pepperbox revolvers to old Army musketoons. One man now brandished a Cochran, one a Klein needle gun, one a Sharps of the type known as a Beecher Bible.)

Whatever their accumulation of supplies and armament, they had not yet taken that treasure to be most blissfully regarded by the lustful and unbridled: white women or girls.

They suspected that Inkpaduta's deterrent attitude had its basis in something sadder than a mere reluctance to run risk of pursuit and strife.

. . . *Ateya*, my father, you are old!

. . . I am *baha*. I am oldish, not truly old. . . .

. . . Aye, he's old.

. . . Harken to That Old One!

. . . How know thee that he is old?

. . . It is because he refuses to take women!

They'd pre-empted four sleds of varying types and sizes, together with the horses to draw them; the horses also were of varying types and sizes and conditions of health. Burdened with plunder, the robbers pushed their way into the region of the four corners where Clay, O'Brien, Cherokee, and Buena Vista counties fastened together. Here were scattered families and cabins, as families and cabins were scattered at Okoboji—all of an area, the neighbors knowing one another and valuing one another because neighbors were gems without price; yet with windy miles blowing in snow dust between. On these unfortunates the pack descended like wolves leaping upon exhausted calves.

They tied up a man named Waterman, looted his cabin of clothing, pounded Waterman with a stick of wood. The Bicknells observed their approach, and fled to their neighbors the Kirchners. The Wahpekute gorged on sugar, they flung flour and meal to the winds; they tore down a partition in the deserted Bicknell cabin for no understandable reason. They carried off a teakettle, scraps of carpet, frying pans. They carried off Mrs. Bicknell's spinning wheel; twas interesting to make the wheel buzz and whirl. Roaring-Cloud's wife broke two fingers in trying to stop the wheel by thrusting her hand into it: in a crying fury she took her squaw-axe and smashed the thing to splinters, while her husband stood amused. . . . How many horses taken from the Wilcoxes? All they owned: five. . . . They killed cattle at the Kirchners', cattle at the Frinkes', killed every dog which challenged them, indeed they killed every dog they saw! *Ho,* another sled at the Frinke place? Harness up the horses, load the sled with victuals and clothing, drive it away with chunks of fresh-butchered ox-meat and dead dogs and chickens piled high! Dig into chests for the few banknotes, the small hoards of silver. Take guns, take blankets, pour out molasses on the floor. The *Washichun* know that we are here! . . . Bahata, here lies a whites'-robe-filled-with-feathers. Now tear it open so that the feathers fly, and you may dance among them, and we have mirth at seeing you dance.

. . . Our dog he was a shepherd and he hates Indians so much. They come climbing up the bank from the river, and looking so terrible already. So fierce and dirty! To my husband I say: It is best that to these Indians we act as if nothing is wrong, and we are glad they come.

(I am Mrs. Christian Kirchner, and it is only now a few months that we have been by this new country, before the Indians come.)

But also my two sons come first, and they have taken up claims by this new country. And another son, Augustin—already he has been to California and back; so of Indians he knows something.

And Gust says: *Ja,* it is right to be friendly. That is the best way.

So when come the Indians, it is Gust who goes outside the door; and maybe he talks to them and maybe he gives them some little food, so maybe they do not come inside? But when out goes Gust, goes also the big shepherd dog we call Heine. And Heine— *Ach,* so much he hates the Indians; he makes with his teeth like this, and all a big roar and barking! And— *Bing.* That is what we hear. *Bing.* Somebody shoots. I am so scared I cannot rise from my chair. And my Johnny begins to cry and say, *Mutter,* they have shot Gust!

But it is poor Heine that they shoot. And when they go, also they carry the dead Heine away with them. And why? It is a terrible thing. To eat! *Ja.* Our good shepherd dog they eat.

I'm Mrs. Taylor.

I don't want to talk about what happened after we'd moved in with the Meads, and the Indins come.

My little boy got burnt something terrible when they threw him in the fireplace. Course I wasn't there—afterwards. For awhile. Not till— Morning.

Mrs. Mead was there. She had some dried comfrey roots, a big poke of them, and she put them to soak; then she made poultices out of them roots. I guess it didn't do much good, cause they said Bubby cried all night.

Seemed like I could hear him a-yelling, clear down to the camp. I couldn't really have heard him, but— Kind of seemed like it.

And when I got back, I had some green hyson tea. I guess maybe the Indins didn't know what it was, for they hadn't took it off. I gathered up some of the meal they'd spilt, and with the meal and the green tea I made some new poultices. They helped Bubby.

Guess he'll always be scarred. Real bad. But tain't like he was a girl.

I'm glad he's a boy. I wouldn't want him to be no girl. If he was a girl, and growed tall as Harriet, maybe they'd took him along, too.

Yes, my husband was there, at first. Guess folks are always going to ask that. They'll say, Mrs. Taylor, wasn't your husband to home? And he was there, fore he snuck off to seek aid. But they had guns smack against his head. Any man blames my husband has got to realize that. And then figure out what *he* could of done, if Indins had guns against *his* head.

So I'm not blaming Husband. Not no way.

The rest of it. No, please.

I don't want to talk about it.

Nobody must ask me what happened. *Nobody.*

Oh. . . .

I'm Harriet Mead. I'm seventeen. Mary and me are going over to the Bicknell place today, and show Jane Bicknell how to make wheel collars. Do you know how to make wheel collars? Just lots of folks don't even know how to tat! And I know how to tat. And Pa brung me this little shuttle and a great big hank of thread when last he was to Cedar Falls— I mean— He's in Cedar Falls right *now;* but I mean time afore this.

And being in Cedar Falls now, this winter, is the reason he got Mr. and Mrs. Taylor to move in with us folks. That's so Ma and us girls wouldn't be so lonesome. And he thought that they could kind of look after us whilst he was gone.

I don't blame Mr. Taylor for what happened. I seen a pistol shoved against him on one side, and a shotgun on the other. If he'd so much as moved, they'd have kilt him quick.

. . . Want to see the pattern for a wheel collar? . . . See, this is the one. Twas in an old *Lady Book* that somebody give to Ma. I think it's real pretty; and I'm right sure Jane'll be glad to make one like this, too. Twill look elegant if she wears it with her old red dress.

Case the Indins didn't steal it. The gown, I mean.

So we're going down to the Bicknells' today, and probably we'll stay all night, too.

I don't feel so bad now. Kind of—bruised. My head don't ache no more. But I kind of ache inside. All over.

I hope Jane and her folks won't ask a lot of questions, count of I'd just ruther not talk about— About what happened.

Way off in the background it's like somebody was still shrieking. Not Bubby Taylor—he didn't holler the same way. Like twas a girl screaming.

Maybe that's my own voice I keep hearing, and going on and on. Just wailing continually, but getting weaker, like going off into the distance. . . .

Great big far distance, with the voice kind of wandering in it, like twas a pale sickly child lost and hurt, and keeping crying about it.

Guess nobody'll ever want to marry me now. . . .

Let's see, I forget. Does Jane Bicknell already know how to tat? If not, I got to show her how to thread the shuttle and everything.

She mustn't ask me no questions. She just mustn't.

I'm Emma, and I'm ten; but folks usually take me for older, cause I'm real tall for my size. I mean, for my age.

Yes, Pa was gone way off to Cedar Falls again, and so the Taylors was living in our house. First thing the Indins did when they come in was to start grabbing all sorts of things, and then Ma says, You stop that!—and rushed at 'em, and tried to take back a reticule of her'n they pulled out of the bureau. And a great big tall skinny young Indin, he took hold of Ma's shoulders and slung her clean acrost the room; so she fell down, and she begun to cry. And I thought, Well, you awful old Indins, I guess Mr. Taylor will fix *you!*—and I looked around, and there *he* was, with them Indins holding guns again him. So he just had to stand there and let 'em do things. First chance Mr. Taylor got, he snuck out and started to go for help. Least that's where Ma said he'd gone, later on. He hain't come back yet. Ma says twon't do no good if he does come, for the Indins are already gone. . . . They brung Mrs. Taylor and Harriet back this morning.

I wish Pa had been here. Then maybe it all wouldn't of happened.

Poor Bubby Taylor's a little better now. He was right in front of the fireplace, and one Indin just turned around on a sudden and kicked out with his foot, and Bubby went backwards into the fire. Oh, he screamed so terrible! And his Ma she run and grabbed him out; but by that time his clothes was all afire; and his Ma and my Ma they snatched a quilt and wrapped him in it, and pounded Bubby, to beat out the fire. The Indins was just laughing about it.

Then I didn't see zactly what happened next. Cause that real tall thin young Indin grabbed holt of *me,* and he hauled me right out the door, right in the snow. He kept saying Indin language all the time. I think I know the Indin word for: You come long with me!—or something like that. For he kept saying it over and over. He'd say—It sounded like he said: *Shan!*—and then he'd haul on my arms, and kind of lug me long of him. And then he'd say it like that again: *Shan!*—but I just twisted and kicked as hard as I could, and I kept yelling. Loud as I could!

I guess twas my hollering he didn't like.

Cause he'd took me clean past the dooryard, clean past the chopping block and everything. And then he says something like: *White—woman—bad!* He picked up a stick and give me an awful lick crost the legs. I tried to run back to the house; but that tall Indin he'd grabbed my arm again, and he kept laying on gad. He just kept whipping and whipping, and I kept yelling and yelling! He whipped me all the way, clean back to the house; and then he give me a big shove, right through the doorway, and I went flat on my face and hurt my nose. And then some other Indin reached down, and he pulled up my hair, and I thought: Now he's going to *scalp* me!—but he didn't scalp me a-tall. He just broke the ribbon round my neck and carried off my jewelry. Twas my only jewelry, too. I wish he hadn't took it, for a boy give it to me.

The other Indins had took Mrs. Taylor and my big sister Harriet, and was dragging them off towards the river where the camp was. Mrs. Taylor didn't say much; she kept fighting, or trying to; but two big Indins had her by the arms, and twisted her arms up behind her back, and kept shoving her long of them. And the ones that had Sister Harriet were pulling her, same way; and one held his hand tight over her mouth, so's she couldn't yell the way I'd been doing.

Fore they fetched her down to the camp, though, she got her mouth loose from that hand, and she yelled awful. I could hear her a-pleading even after she'd been drug out of sight. No! No! Oh, no! Please! *No!*

XXXII

Mink, forty to sixty cents.

Coon, prime, thirty-five cents.

Muskrat, six to ten cents.

Red fox, one dollar.

Otter, two-fifty to three-fifty or thereabouts.

Deerskins were fetching maybe ten to twelve cents per pound. . . .

That was about what the wholesalers would be paying in Dubuque, Morris Markham reasoned gloomily.

Marten, maybe two dollars and a half. Beaver? Oh, say fifty to seventy-five cents per pound. And bearskins ranging all the way from one dollar to seven dollars, depending on size and condition. Course he wouldn't have set any bear traps anyway (count of remembering Uncle Melly); but once in awhile, by the laws of luck and averages, he might have been able to shoot a stray bear.

If it weren't for these snows.

What did you call yourself, if you were a trapper who wasn't able to trap? Ex-trapper? Retired trapper?

(Retired by force and solid fury of a winter never seen before!)

Hoped he'd never see such a winter again, by Gad. Everybody hoped so.

Twasn't his fault. He'd looked at it upside down, and back and forth, every which way. Here was weather far too warm: no sense in putting out traps until there fell that long-hoped-for first snow that he could track a bobcat through. And then, in a twinkling, here were frozen drifts which wiped out instantly all thought of running a line.

Later on, if it thawed. . . .

Oh, yes. Later. . . .

In the meantime there was nothing to do but range the woods and lakesides as well as he could, searching for meat. No deer about, no deer whatsoever. No wolves . . . wolves for the pot? Ha. But those lynxes hadn't gone down too bad. And there was always the thought of Marble's elk. If that greenhorn had managed to get himself a snowed-in elk, then Morris would have a better chance than he, should Fortune decide to furnish the elk in some remote thicket.

And there were the nesting squirrels.

Squirrel was mighty small. Furnished less meat than a house cat might have yielded.

Well. He was in this situation, and they were all in it; and there was nothing to do but accept the situation, and try to cope with it. . . .

A man might not move in quiet places as long as Morris had moved in them without becoming a philosopher of more attainment than actually his simple intellect suggested. It was because he absorbed his philosophy through emotion, and so it affected his entire manner of living. It made a difference in the way he regarded birds and animals. (When one looks at animals with a knowledge of their habits and an understanding of how and why they feed upon each other, he is apt to know far more about the two-legged creatures walking around him than he will admit.)

But still Morris hated the bitter ice, because it had robbed him of opportunity to acquit himself. He longed for the green mornings of earlier warmer months. There was a fantastic promise about those dawns. He wondered why mornings held promise: was it only because the day was unspoiled, because new hours were not as yet marred by error? As a boy, back in Howard County, he had recognized the excitement inherent in shadows of groves pinned against a pink rising sun . . . wetness around . . . even when the birds refused to talk of it because they were too busy with their young. Earliest morning quivered almost to the point of alarming you. It was true in winter sometimes; but true always in summer unless storms were near and could be detected in uncertainty of the air. (Somehow it seemed to storm very seldom in early morning. You thought of storms as coming in late afternoon, you thought of storms resounding at night.)

Intrinsic in every moment until the sun was an hour high, was a sense of humanity's awakening. The fiercer mammals had gone back to their lairs already, they were no longer hungry, chewed bones lay behind them. The bronzed little owl sat solemnly on a rafter in his old shed; the larger fiercer paler owl waited on his stub for crows to peck at him; and the crops of both were filled with fur and flesh, they were building their hard little balls and spitting them out.

Things like this Morris Markham knew without even pausing to reckon. They were there, they were the crucial portion of his life. But what was it about morning? The mere fact that grass was still untrodden, unmarked by men who were bound to disturb it? Long shadows beneath the oaks were unwalked upon, the cows had not yet been turned out to spatter their droppings. They would come later to plaster and munch; but now the grass was clean, light metallic moisture hung on every blade of it; catbird or thrasher darted down to wet himself, to wash his face and claws, to flick his tail at the coolness and let the drops go scattering.

Day, what do you offer us all?

Everything, says Day, beaming and comforting, yet somehow already elusive. I will give you all.

Those remembered Indiana mornings grew to be a part of sunrises on the new prairie, but at last the white hands of winter had closed and choked.

(A fair thing about mornings: they merged in your past, and in your appreciation of the moment, and in your anticipation of mornings to come. They were all one, there was timelessness, a feeling that plant and animal voices cried with the lilt of shepherds' instruments played on a hill ahead. . . . We are here, we are here for you. Take us. Make with us your day, your world. Make something good.)

Morris prayed for the weather to become normal, he prayed for a whack at the beaver. Oh, he would drive down his stakes near the dam, the stakes with that slight swelling on their stems for a ring to glide across and then hold hard. The beaver would come, drawn by his lure; traps would snap, victims dive, rings jam, victims drown.

Beaver were thinned to nothing in Indiana. . . .

Well, he thought, just give me a chance to thin them out here! His eyes glittered, the tight grin twisted on his bony face.

Twas not that he hated beaver, or regarded them as pests. Twas not that he was avaricious, loved money for its own sake; twas not even that he loved to kill. Killing was his business; but he loved the dawn perhaps even more than the spot of blood . . . exploded wad of pink tissue, small hole through the fur which told that his single shot had been true, and a critter lay dead. Truly he did feel that he was a wild thing himself, he thought that he had paws as well as feet, and feathers ruffled on his head. He thought of himself as a brown striding fox; but the wolves had better look out! Thus since he was such an active part of wild life, the challenge of wild life was the challenge of himself, and he must meet it, if he were to be a man (as all men must meet first off the challenges they themselves erect).

Long ago he had erected a challenge in front of himself. He loved to play with the recollection, and did so constantly when he was solitary, which was much of the time. The memory was a memory of the only love for a woman which he had held in his life. Persistently he returned to that contemplation. Every detail of Kokomo and every figment of a recalled 1850 summer stood out in colored relief, a fiery illusion above the implacable cold.

Folks had said (he'd heard them)—

Folks had said that there was a nightingale.

Despite his familiarity with the village of Kokomo, Morris did not know many of its citizens by name; he'd spent too much time in the woods, and was shy about speaking to strangers when urgency brought him into town. Even when the local doctor or miller greeted him pleasantly in the road his reply was apt to be a mumble. He smiled only with his eyes.

He asked Uncle Dave Foster at the store.

What say? Nightingale?

Who might know bout nightingales? Who'd I ask?

Uncle Dave stood scowling and considering. We hain't got them around here, have we?

Tis a bird way off in Europe somewheres.

Well, then, I got to think of Europeans. . . . Reckon you could talk to them Judsens or Dahlbergs, but twouldn't do you no good. They're real native Europeans—Scandahoovians—and I can't scarcely understand them when they come in here to trade. They got to point it out to me, whatever they want: starch, coffee, nails, thread, wax.

Mr. Foster reflected longer, then brightened. There's that old Parson Allardice.

Parson?

He hain't preaching no longer—he's too old. He come here recent to live with his daughter, the Widder Campsie: that's the little house under them willers, side the crick. Morning-glory vines on the stoop.

Morris thanked him and turned to go.

They say he went to a university once't. Real smart-spoken old gentleman, but poor as a church mouse. European he may be, but the part of Europe from which he comes is Scotland. You can understand nigh every word he says if you listen close!

Mr. Foster had neglected to mention it, but the Reverend Mr. Hughie Allardice was almost blind, and he groped this way and that for Morris Markham's hand when Morris had screwed up his courage and ventured to present himself on Mrs. Campsie's tiny porch. The woodsman was terrified at his own audacity in approaching a stranger who was both minister and Scotsman. Still he managed to state the purpose of his mission.

A nightingale?

Yes, sir. Ain't none in these parts. Maybe in—Sweden?

Sweden, lad? Ah, I do not know.

Although it was a fairly warm forenoon, the Reverend Mr. Allardice had an old shawl of blue-and-gray plaid bundled around his limbs. He sat in a green-painted Boston rocker, swaying cozily back and forth as he considered Markham's request and tried to place himself, through fancy, once more in proximity to nightingales. He plucked at the shawl fabric while he mused, wrinkled fingers rolling little yarns of fuzz from the wool;. and suddenly he interrupted his reverie by nodding kindly toward his own knee. Yon is Graham, he said. Ye ken?

Morris did not for the life of him understand, but he murmured agreement.

Aye, for we're a sept of the Grahams.

Yes, sir.

Long ago I stood before the Graham of Menteith and preached directly to his proud heart! He'd been sorely cruel to his own child. For this I addressed him.

Yes, sir.

Now, what was it that you—?

Nightingale, mumbled Morris, ready to flee.

Mr. Allardice had a small beautifully shaped head, and the thin silver hair of it had been combed and brushed by his daughter. Films which clouded his eyes were thick and pearly, and when his shrunken eyelids flickered apart Morris had the disquieting illusion that he was held by the stare of the dead. Ah, indeed, came the rustling whisper. Nightingales! We have none in Scotland. But in my youth I was taken by my father down into England, and there hung a birdie in a great wicker cage. Oh, its song was the song of angels!

He was quiet for so long that the visitor thought the ancient parson had fallen asleep, or perhaps had even expired as he hunched, rocking. Papery eyelids were closed, the motion of the chair began to fail. Morris rose in alarm, he thought to summon the old man's daughter—he could hear her at work in the cottage kitchen. But a crunch of his weight on those carelessly constructed floorboards brought the blank eyes open.

Nightingales, Mr. Allardice whispered clearly. And twas long ere I heard the melody again. Twas only about twenty years agone, to be truthful. My son was a sea captain—that was some years before his vessel was lost in a storm off the Cornish coast—and twice he took me on his voyages. I preached sincerely to his crew; and some of them were Papists and some were infidels, and some were Christian men—But I'm glad to say that, with the earnest power of the Lord God, I made good Presbyterians out of several. Ah, well, where were we?

Hunting for nightingales, declared the young man, no longer feeling dread or repugnance, but only human pity for this dreaming little wisp.

Indeed we were, and the minister seemed to laugh lightly under his stained glinting beard. Well, laddie, we'd strained the seams of our water casks in an eastern gale— They blow for days at a time, and such a gale is known as a Levant, for it comes from the east. And we were in merciful need of fresh water, and put into the bay of Alcudia to get some aboard. Twas warm springtime, and with the quieting of the sea the nights were bonny, and the moonlight tender with the providence of God toward man in the estate in which he was created. And, with my son the master of the vessel, I was conveyed into the hills to be entertained by hospitable Mallorcans. Papists they are in truth. You must remember that God in His providence permitted some of the angels, willfully and irrevocably, to fall into sin and damnation!

Of a sudden his frail voice demanded: Are ye Presbyterian?

Disciples of Christ, Morris replied weakly. Kind of.

Mr. Allardice uttered a soft groan. Oh, laddie, I dislike to witness even the mention of Campbellites! Yon Thomas Campbell, and yon Alexander, the son! To say nothing of that miserable Barton Stone with his Last Will and Testament of the Springfield Presbytery! May an all-too-patient and overly charitable God frown not ower justly on their rebellion—

Morris gathered his wits, and interrupted in self-extenuation. But I hain't really been baptized! Not yet. Uncle Melly and Aunt Eunice—They was.

Consider God's sovereignty over us, and propriety in us; consider His fervent zeal for His own worship, and His revengeful indignation against all false worship, as being a spiritual whoredom!

But I hain't really been baptized! cried the desperate Markham.

Ah, I pray that the Spirit will help your infirmities!

Again there dwelt silence, but at last Morris's tongue moved to construct the magic word, Nightingale.

Aye. Twas there that I heard the singing of the angels once more.

There?

In the hills, lad, said the elder impatiently. The mountains of Mallorca.

Did you—see it?

Not I. Only the memory of the cageling in faraway England, seen in my youth.

Are nightingales—beautiful?

To look upon? Not they. Fair enough—rust upon the back and gray upon the breast. But nae gallant and gorgeous as are some birdies, with Joseph's coat of many colors!

Morris felt inexplicable disappointment. He had expected— He did not know. The scarlet of the firebird, the glare of the goldfinch, the lilac-blue jacket of the jay? He'd heard of peacocks, had seen pictures representing peacocks. Something like that. . . .

But the song, sir?

Well, to be sure, the song. They sang through the night, and I've heard it related that in their wild state they sing only in the night, and only in the springtime. They sang with an awful apprehension of the majesty of God, and a deep sense of their own unworthiness, necessities, and sins. They were united to one another in love, they had communion in each other's gifts and graces. They flitted beyond yon moonlight, in yon olive groves, and you couldna see them; but they flew in blackness among the great toosie trees. And those trees, lad, were planted by the pagan Greeks or Romans a thousand years agone!

Morris Markham tried to consider what a thousand years must mean. He could not do so. He had not known that the Romans were pagans, he'd thought that they were Christians. Hadn't the Apostle Paul written a letter. . . ?

They were angels which came down from heaven, having great power; and the earth was lightened with their glory! Twas as recounted in the Eighteenth Chapter of the Revelation! As if they had been in Babylon, ye ken; ah, there they'd been trapped in the habitation of devils, the hold of every foul spirit; they'd been ensnared and imprisoned in the cage of every unclean and hateful bird! But it was out of God's love, to free them perfectly from sin and misery. They were beholding the face of God in light and glory. They were at once pipe and flute and harp, as played by delicate fingers in the shadowed flowery places where they went a-soaring. You never wished to hear another tune when their wee wild throats had fallen still!

After a pause, the old minister whispered as to himself: Muckle need!

Beg pardon?—

You'd never need to hear another song, for you had heard the caroling of saints. Among vineyards and the olive trees. A people that . . . ah, the words elude me the noo, I'm ower old . . . but tis from Isaiah . . . *a people that . . . sacrificeth in gardens.* Twas as if. . . .

The living lips under the dead beard did not move for so long a time that Morris thought: Now I got to take leave. I'm not scairt longer that he's had a spell. Tis just that he's so used up by age that he falls asleep. I'll sneak off.

He was halfway down the path when a faint voice issued again. Laddie?

Yes, sir. Morris came back. I was—taking leave— I thought—

Twas as if the birdies had discovered the estate of Christ's exaltation!

Sir?

Ye ken, I'd forgotten their song, for it played to my ears so long before, when I was but a lad myself. But it came back to me—aye, in shadows and abiding moonlight of the hills in that far land. Mallorca, ye ken. My own son was a sea captain, and we'd sailed into Alcudia to. . . .

Yes, Reverent. You tolt me.

Sunlight swung, the limp cords of morning-glory vines were swung by a light breeze, high sun came through and fell golden over the old man's face, and trembled in other golden patches across the shabby tartan which wrapped his body. Promptly the kindhearted Morris forgot all about Mr. Allardice's blind sectarian savagery. He had a vague thought that God must be recognizing gentle virtues, and lending ceremony to them, lending a visible consecration. What was the word he sought? Anointed!—that was it. He saw that this shrunken relic was gilded by the sun, gilded with affection and respect by a discerning Hand.

Ye ken the Larger Catechism?

Morris did not know what a Catechism might be, so in habitual manner he shook his head without speaking; and then he realized that the Reverend Mr. Allardice could not well see him. He grunted some negative sound.

Ah, well, you yourself told me that you were of the Campbellites' persuasion—tis not to be thought you'd know it! But it tells of Christ exalted in His coming . . . *shall come again at the last day in great power, and in the full manifestation of His own glory, and of His Father's, with all His holy angels, with a shout, with the voice of the archangel, and with the trumpet of God!* Tis the playing of the nightingales, ye ken.

Thank you, Reverent. I'm obliged—

But now— The old man spoke surprisingly. To take up the matter of the pagans. Some of yon Greeks. Have you heard of Philomela?

No, sir.

The Greeks contended in their foolish unenlightened hearts that she was the daughter of an Attican king; and that king gave Philomela's sister Procne to a Thracian king in matrimony. Ah, tis a terrible tale, and you're the better off if you never hear the whole of it! With deceit, and false hearts, and pretense, and mutilation— With incest also, though I hate to utter the foul word—and with cannibalism as well. Does that nae upstand the hackles of a man? Cannibalism! For these two wicked sisters killed the son of that same Thracian monarch, and served him up as meat to his own father! But in the end the pagan gods made birdies of the lot of them. The Thracian king became a hoopoe, and Sister Procne was made into a swallow, and Sister Philomela— A nightingale, laddie! Think of that. For that's the vile contrariness of the unredeemed. She'd lied and she'd slain— Should she no have been punished?

Yes, sir, Morris managed to croak. Punished!

Did this Philomela repent? Na! *Repentance unto life is a saving grace, wrought in the heart of a sinner by the Spirit and word of God.*

Thank you, Reverent Allardice, for telling me bout—

Aye. The nightingale. But to be changed into an angelic birdie is no fit reward for—

No, sir. But— I got to go.

The ancient dominie, bewildered in the slackening of life's force, had communicated his own confusion to Morris; not alone because he discussed strange countries and peoples and stranger myths, but also because he condemned and worshiped in conjoined disarray. One solid truth Morris garnered out of the frail rambling interview, however. This was the fact that a nightingale was indeed a fairy, and that a sensitive spirit would never be the same for having heard a nightingale sing. It was not a desired alteration which the lonely young man sought in himself (yea, he knew that he would be changed if he listened!) but he wished to meet the challenge which had formed because he was a devotee of the voices of birds. He had never heard of this bird until now, and would be haunted and unfulfilled until he opened his ears and snared the secret song out of the air. He thought of walking to New York City, because walking was the sole method of travel with which he was familiar, except on that sad occasion when he had escorted Uncle Melly's body home from Wabash County in a hired wagon. . . .

He hunted among the few papers, pamphlets, and books which had accumulated at home, and discovered a flimsy torn map of the United States, replete with political slogans printed round the edge. The legend showed that it had been designed in 1840; Morris knew through hearsay that several States had entered the Union since then: Florida, Texas, Iowa, Wisconsin. But he had no intention of going to Florida or to the West, so the map was practical for his purposes. By comparing that distance from Howard County to Brown County he was able to achieve an estimate: no use, twould take too long. The nightingale was expected to arrive too soon for Morris to plod across those hundreds of miles. If he went, he must go by stage, vessel, railway train.

His farewell to the Reverend Mr. Allardice still grunted within his ears. *I got to go.* He had meant that he must leave; it was time for him to depart; the swamps and the remote small house were waiting for him. He had been uttering no affirmation of an intent to descend upon a city which he knew he would abhor—there were said to be a good half-a-million people living in that one town. (Morris had hated all idea of population masses since the days when Master Dowsing emphasized with sneer and switch the fact that there were, in the State of Ohio, and according to the most recent census, exactly nine hundred and thirty-seven thousand nine hundred and three living souls.) It was only a few months since Morris had gone from Brown County to Indianapolis to market his winter's fur. The mere recollection of Indianapolis offended him now . . . eight thousand people indeed! Why should there ever be eight thousand individuals gathered together in a single town? For what intent did they crowd?

I got to go.

Morris attempted to dress himself in robes of cynicism or tatters of amusement, but he had no success in any effort to forget the illusion of the nightingale.

Often in summertime, when there could be no hunting or trapping and when fishing grew to be an unenlivened chore, he went to work for neighboring farmers. Sometimes he took his wage in found: a new comforter for his winter bed, crocks of pickles, home-salted meats, and the like. Thus a man didn't necessarily need cash to engage Morris Markham; this was well—cash was hard to come by in that region.

Morris could slave as a farmhand with the best of them; and during the ensuing week he was cutting and stacking oats for Farmer Middleton and Farmer Radley. At the Radleys there was a copy of a Cincinnati newspaper. Young Sally Radley, proud of her scholarship and ability to read aloud with Expression & Articulation, regaled the menfolks with various editorials and despatches while they were eating dinner. She read a long account about the Swedish nightingale. Morris's heart was not in his work that afternoon. His back bent, his arms swung; but it seemed that he stood in a woodland theater and heard a fluting he'd never heard before. Occasionally he gazed across the leagues and saw his workaday self, dusty and straw-prickled above his sweat, submitting to the dignified discipline of field labor.

(He loathed farm work in fact, preferred to be in the woods, thought that sometime he should go into the woods and never more emerge, and remain there forever, and be a wild hunter who sent his peltries down the river but scorned to come himself. He did not own horse, cow, pig, or chicken; the antique barn stood tenantless, rotting and vine-clad on the Markham place. Once Morris had owned a dog, but he felt too tied down and domesticated, so he'd given the dog to the Howes. Oh, he abhorred rake and cradle and sickle and reins; but he could handle them all efficiently, and did so in the summers. His hoard in the pewter teapot told the story. He did not know what he might do with the money, but he found sly pride in accumulating it. He supposed that it made him feel superior to most people in towns and villages, because he had so much more money than they. Then he smiled a light smile at his own cupidity and hypocrisy: if he scorned the activities of labor and traffic and commerce, why should he treasure the emolument?)

I got to go.

Again, a woodland theater, a shapeless hall of greenery. The floor was as a swamp, and quiet waters stood dark and promising around the bulging tree roots, but every frog had hushed himself. At Morris's behest, and for him alone, the nightingale was singing. But in daytime? How dared she? Knew she not the behavior proper to her race? And what were the colors of her down, how shone her wing coverts?

He could not remember the plumage as described by the old Presbyterian minister . . . something about rust and gray, and that sounded dowdy to say the least. Morris decided that, prefer it or not, he must make another trip to Kokomo to have the description repeated. He wished very much to envision the bird correctly; twould not do to make her into an oriole, a redstart, or a waxwing, if she did not wear their rigging. . . . He should have remembered, could not recall the words, he'd been too bamboozled by Mr. Allardice's gratuitous castigation of the Campbellites.

It was eleven days from the time when he strode away from Mrs. Campsie's porch when he stood there again beneath the weight of willows and flower vines. Many morning-glories had gone through their bloom and were fallen to the boards, lying puckered, limp rags of pink and blue, soft abandoned tiny trumpets. Tossed there by . . . a nightingale, perhaps . . . one of those fairies yielding mystic exhortations when the moon was high? The green-painted Boston rocker sat empty—cushions taken away, paint spotted by rains. Morris dwelt some seven miles away from Kokomo in body, and a hundred vistas in spiritual concern—the goings-on of the village were described in his hearing but seldom, and he paid scant attention if indeed he heard. Mrs. Campsie, a shrunken woman with a face like an old soda biscuit, stood peering through a mosquito bar which was nailed to the flimsy doorframe. There were clipped fringes of newspaper fastened at intervals across the frame to discourage houseflies. Mrs. Campsie brought up her apron to red-rimmed eyes when Morris inquired for the Reverend Mr. Hughie Allardice. . . . Didn't Morris know? No, he didn't know. And she said in expressed disapproval that this was very odd; she thought everyone knew about her father. We interred him a-Tuesday, she said. My father has passed on. . . . There was still a taint of native Scottish accent clinging about the words; but less welcome, more hurtful to Morris's ears, was the fact that she said *passed on* as the smugly self-conscious say it— People whose religion forbids them to fear death, and bids them rather to rejoice in it; yet who fear death nevertheless, with internal groans and writhings, with actual transports of terror—fear it as they must fear any riddle supposedly explained and yet acutely baffling to their credulous little souls— The same people who trill: *Well, we must not speak ill of The Dead—* (And why not, pray, when so many of The Dead worked avidly to earn condemnation, and are said to be existing still as entities?)— People who attach the utmost significance to as universal a phenomenon as an individual's extinction, a surviving individual's bereavement; and make claim to importance because an experience common to all mankind has now befallen them—

She said, *Passsssed onnnnn*, in a musty whisper and it offended the young man to hear her intone the words. He stood aware that this hard-faced woman despised every moment of her own poverty, and also despised every person who was not afflicted with the same ailment; and he knew also that she was miserable before her father's vanishment, and would be more miserable now—that if she loved her father she loved him as a duty taught and performed, and never in her years had she asked him to describe a nightingale; and there were no nightingales in Scotland or in Indiana; and God might pity the unfortunate who did not wonder about them!

Uncle Dave Foster allowed Morris to purchase three rumpled newspapers emanating respectively from Cleveland, Indianapolis, New York City. The most recent was eight days old, but one and all were replete with accounts concerning Mr. Barnum and the anticipated visit of Mademoiselle Lind. It seemed that all over the country people talked of almost nothing else. Morris went home by way of Wild Cat Creek. Two or three miles upstream he sat in sycamore shade and twisted his face, squeezed down his brows, poked with his finger, seeking to spell out as many details as possible. Often the words were foreign words, they made no sense to him; he felt thwarted, almost enraged.

. . . In Germany, whither she had gone to study the language, in 1844 she essayed the role of Vielka in the Feldlager in Schlesien *by Meyerbeer. We are further reliably informed that this role was written especially for her.*

. . . She will sing this concert at the new Jenny Lind Hall, now being erected by Mr. Tripler.

. . . En route to American shores, accompanied by Mademoiselle Ahmansen, chosen by the Northern Nightingale as her intimate companion throughout so many successful appearances on the Continent; together with Herr Max Hjortzberg, her secretary; and of course M. Benedict, Signor Belletti, and others.

. . . Furthermore predicted that Mr. Barnum may suffer a mortal wounding in the pecuniary region, for it is their strict belief that not even this popular and unrivaled songstress could draw money for the projected one hundred and fifty nights out of a single year!

. . . One of our exchanges makes mention of a Jenny Lind Tea Kettle which, being filled with water and placed on the fire, commences to sing in a few minutes.

. . . An opera dancer named Mlle. Lundberg first observed the child and took note of her gifts, when Jenny Lind was but nine years of age; and through the discernment and influence of this actress, the talented little songstress was admitted into the Stockholm Conservatory at an age when most sweet young things are being taught needlework via the sampler.

. . . Expected to sail from Liverpool during the middle of August, and may be conveyed here aboard the fine new American steamer, the Atlantic.

This was a matter of dust and echo coming down through cracks of a structure with which Morris Markham was in no way familiar nor would be. Disliking towns, scowling at the notion of a City he had never seen, he was not tricked into awe by the reiterated pressure of foreign names, foreign culture, monies, theatrical gossip. The important thing was that she was a nightingale, and a nightingale was a bird which sang like no other, and a bird song was the one melody which might prevail. Away with organs and flutes, away with the common Glees! The song must be wrapped in feathers, must be shrilled through an open beak. . . .

Morris rose from the log where he had sat for so long, and smoothed the newspapers, folding them carefully to be passed on to neighbors who would welcome them (but not through such growing addiction as his own). He thought, They'd never dare call her a nightingale if she didn't sing like one. So she must.

Who sang now?

Almost no one. Twas close to August.

But take that cardinal, cutting into the thicket yonder, flashing like a red missile among the trees. (Morris called it not a cardinal but a Redbird; and so was the towhee a Ground Robin, the dickcissel a Little Meadow Lark, the scarlet tanager a Firebird, the myrtle warbler a Yellow Rump. A bunting became a Blue Canary, a vireo was a Preacher Bird.) Take that Redbird. When he was a boy, Morris had thought it fun to ascribe words to the woodland chants, the piping exhortations delivered in incredible volume with the spring. It was amusing to think that the Redbird cried to his mate in a rapid whicker: Pretty-pretty-pretty-pretty– Or that he declaimed from tallest tree peaks: What? What? What? What? Cheer! Cheer! Cheer!– Or it was chilling to consider that the Cat Owl, engaged in dismembering his living prey while the victim screamed in agony, could chortle with fiendish delight: Oh, ho, ho, ho, ho, ho!– Or you'd hear the Jay screeching his own name a hundred times, in a brazen brag. Or you'd know that the Lazy Bird (some called it cowbird) was burbling of wells and moss and cool wetness as he said: Pump water, pump water, pump water– Or you'd be aggravated by the incessant plaint of the Preacher Bird: Here I am, here I am! Don't you see me? Don't you see me? Here I am! . . . But as an adult Morris grew to believe that he was visiting an indignity upon the birds by trying to distort their speech into human utterance; and perhaps he was detracting from his own dignity as well.

In soul he lived closer to animals, woodpeckers, and turtles, than he did to his own race. He did not bear for them that treacly all-enraptured love of the self-styled Lover of Nature; he was too near to them for that. All his life he'd seen the shrike (he reckoned it to be the Butcher Bird) impaling his kill on a thorn, the better to rend it; he'd seen a shrike butcher a baby garter snake, a fine golden-winged grasshopper, a melodious lark sparrow (he called this the Quailhead). Liddy Howe laughed lightheartedly and said in her cozy little voice, Oh, Morris, I wish you'd a-been here. There was a saucy red squirrel up that tree where the robins got their nest, and they was just *scolding* at him—and he scolding at them, in the meanest way— I like to died a-laughing! Morris smiled, but he knew the truth which Lydia did not know: that red squirrel had visited the robins' nest in order to lunch off pale blue eggs or tender warm-blooded baby robins. The fox ate the mouse, the barn owl gobbled the mole, the lynx galloped off with the young woodchuck in her jaws, the hoot owl swept silently upon a lizard . . . the dreaming pale green moth, a cotton-bodied silent beauty with long curved streamers depending from its wings . . . it idled in rising moonlight among fresh-leaved oak boughs; and there was suddenly a brindled rush and a vanishment, and flakes of debris floating down . . . the whippoorwill had it. Silver coasting minnows swept and played in brown shallows, seeming to delight in their own bright flashes as the sun came to sparkle them—then ensued a splash and roiling, and many shiners racing away, and a handsome bass was lingering to swallow down the ones he'd caught.

All nature slew all nature.

Morris had come across trite doggerel, one time or another, in which the vocation of gunner or trapper was blasted, at least by inference. Preachers and poets would have him believe, then, that all tribes of underbrush and waters were a roving contented family, dwelling as kin, harmonious, belonging generously to God and to each other, and never frighted until man approached with his powder and shot and traps, with his nets and birdlime and fishing gear? Morris Markham knew these folks better than that: they fared forth, preying with a resolution the most ardent human hunter could never achieve— Their paltry brains were full of plot and trickery, and all primed for a single purpose: their crops and bellies were full of each other.

During his one visit to southern Indiana he'd come across a fish and a moccasin snake, cemented together, flopping and wriggling desperately on the ground beside a bayou. The fish had sought to swallow the snake's head, and that head was still fastened inside the scaly jaws, even though the snake had blundered back to terrestrial safety. With a stick Morris struck the pair apart, and in another instant the situation was reversed: the snake had whipped across to the flapping enemy as it spatted desperately toward the water, the snake had seized one side of the fish's mouth with its own jaws. Nailed together in reciprocal lust for the kill, the two tumbled into the pool; Morris saw them no more, he did not know who became the victor and dined with voracity as a result. He recognized only that in wild places and among the true wild inhabitants, there was no truce requested or given, unless all fled together from enemies more terrible than any they might rear up among themselves—the elements, the floods and fires—and always the onslaught of Him Who Bore the Man-Smell.

So these inhabitants among whom he'd spent his young years were killers, all except a few prim vegetarians among them (and those killed green beauty for the sake of their appetites). But it was not fitting to put English words or any other kind of words into their mouths; actually the Redbird did not say: What? Cheer!— He spoke in clean piping accents which defied translation. It was an insult to this vigorous personage, with his smart crest and family loyalty and cleanly habits, to attempt the translation. No more did Morris fancy a dancing bear with a soldier's cap strapped upon his flat head, or a fox in a cage, or a scraggly wolf with collar and chain. He'd seen all such and found no amusement in the spectacle. Even domestic pets should be allowed to retain their natural decorum. A man halted a gaily painted wagon on a vacant corner lot in Indianapolis, and he set up a wooden plaftorm at the rear of the wagon; and here were also a canopy and coal-oil torches. People thronged round in twilight to see the show, Morris stood with them. The bearded proprietor had a hoarse ceaseless flow of language, and many boxes filled with bottles of Pinkley's Gold Medal Tonic & Revivifier, which he would sell three-for-a-dollar. He owned also a troupe of nervous panting dogs with matted white hair and uptwisted tails. These dogs had been taught to leap, barking, from stool to stool, and even through flaming hoops; they wore beribboned bonnets and little ruffs around their middles. The man called them his girls, and spoke of them as Aunt Althea, Aunt Betty, Aunt Sophronia, and so on. Morris was so annoyed by the whole business that he lay awake at his tavern for a long time that night, very nearly persuading himself to visit the itinerant pitchman and release those canine aunts from bondage, even if he had to employ force to do so. But what use?— He understood dogs, and was positive that the whole yapping gang would come scuttling back to the only home and master they knew.

You weakened a critter by making it walk in the habit and posture of man, making it speak as with the tongues of men—

But—Angels?

The Reverend Mr. Allardice, immediately before he was wafted into his especial Presbyterian heaven— He'd said that a nightingale spoke with the voice of an angel.

And though I have the gift of prophecy, and understand all mysteries, and all knowledge. . . .

Morris made no pretense to a gift of prophecy. He took pleasure sometimes in prophesying, but only to himself, and only concerning matters in which he held long experience: the position of the horns of the moon, frogs croaking in the daytime, slack ropes tightening, flies biting hard, sundogs flaring. He pretended to understand no thick mysteries. In fact he found sedate pleasure in unsolved mysteries, was glad that the mysteries of nature were many; he would have been provoked at having everything revealed.

Morris went home and stood in front of The Picture, looking at The Picture. Twas the only one in the house, it had been freighted from Ohio along with the furniture. Morris supposed that it had been painted by a friend of his Aunt Eunice, since always she referred to the artist as Friend Hicks. Across the bottom the title was spread in letters: *Peaceable Kingdom.* Aunt Eunice informed young Morris, when often he stood gazing and speculating, that there had been a poem which accompanied the painting but the poem was long since lost. She tried to quote it, beating time with ladle or knitting needle or spoon or whatever she happened to be holding . . . something about, *The wolf with the harmless kid laid down, and not one savage beast was seen to frown.* Morris loved The Picture because it was replete with animals, and he set deadfalls for all of them in his imagination. Some were reclining, some seemed merely wandering idly with their tails in the air; there was a bearded lion who looked very much like a neighbor of the Markhams (the boy always called this lion Mr. Jerusha Tuttle, to himself) and a wildcat who looked as if he were just about to burst into tears. There mingled also goats and lambs, foxes and squirrels and calves, together with an extensive spotted critter which Aunt Eunice called a lee-oh-pard. (Uncle Melly said that there were no lee-oh-pards to be encountered in Ohio or Indiana, though a traveler had told him that sometimes they were taken, out in the Texas country. Morris hoped secretly that Uncle Melly was mistaken in this, and that some day he might meet a lee-oh-pard face to face—decorative spots, pale belly, snaky tail, sharp-pointed ears, and all.) Appearing on terms of the utmost intimacy with this aggregation was a fat-faced fat-armed child—sometimes Morris decided that it was a little boy, sometimes a girl.

Sposed to be the Christ child. Think that's what Friend Hicks had in mind.

Reckon not, Aunt Eunice.

Now why?

Cause he hain't got no big shiny ring around his head. I seen some pretty pictures of the Christ child. Over't the Regan place. Every last picture's got a big shiny ring.

Now, you hear me, Morris: that's cause the Regans is *Catholics.*

What's that?

They don't worship like most folks. They worship *the Pope.*

What's that?

Mean old man that *don't even live in the United States.*

Why not?

Cause he hain't got *sense* enough, I reckon. Now you fetch me some more kindling. And haste to finish skinning out them squirrels, else we won't have no stew by the time Unk gets home. . . .

Nowadays, as a solitary adult, Morris regarded The Picture as still representing a mystery which he did not wish interpreted fully. If Friend Hicks had meant to convey the preachment that a Little Child should (solely by radiated goodness, and with a wave of his sausage-shaped arm) lead a gang of warring critters into harmony and bliss, that was all very well with Morris. He'd mastered the art of tolerance, did not desire to quarrel in theory with this message. But he was confident that in actuality the wildcat would make one leap and seize a toothsome lamb, the fox would grasp yonder snake in his jaws, the lion would maul the lugubrious ox. Nor would the Little Child escape unscathed from such fanged and snarling riot. But if Friend Hicks thought otherwise, Morris was determined not to shatter his quaint belief: he hoped merely that Friend Hicks would stay out of the woods for the safety of his own bacon. But what other ideas might be limned here? The notion that an eccentric mite had left the houses of Humanity and preferred to dwell amongst ewes and polecats? That was much more to Morris Markham's taste.

Or—once again—had the animals taken command of the world? Could be.

Here was a knot of folks gathered under trees across the river. Very tiny they were, and seen at a great distance. There were a few white men in odd hats, a few Indians. Seemed to be arguing about something. Maybe saying, How soon are the animals going to start bossing us? Maybe saying, Well, they got that Little Child over there; and are they going to gobble the Child first, and then cross the river and finish us off? Or are the animals more liable to come swarming after us, make a meal of us, and keep the Child for a tasty dish later on?

Had the animals eaten up all the birds?

Couldn't be. There was still a wingèd creature (yes, looked to be some kind of pigeon) hovering right on top of the Child, kind of pecking at the little feller's hand.

Ah. *Had they eaten the nightingales?*

Better make up my mind, thought Morris. Fore they *do* eat up every nightingale on earth. Then I'd never get to hear my Swedish one a-singing. . . .

Even as he faced decision, a bird opened its beak and throat and heart somewhere beyond the apple trees which grew close against one side of the primitive house. Aunt Eunice had demanded that Uncle Melly acquire some fruit trees and set them out, moment the house was built; she said twould make the place seem more like home. So the trees were established in the soil for a matter of only eight years or thereabouts—they'd never amounted to much. Blossoms gave a great promise annually, but a scanty fruit crop which followed was knotted, scabby, stung by flies. Morris was no horticulturist. Why should he bother himself with such husbandry, when there were thorn apples and crab apples and wild grapes adorning the landscape —when dewberries puffed amid luxuriant vines for the picking? Those low scrubby apple trees had been colonized by light little bodies more active than his. Mating strains were trilled, grasses and hairs fetched, nests made; pure white paint speckled the fresh leaves.

Still it was no regular tenant who sang now, but a stranger, and one uttering a message . . . the Potato-bug bird, with rose spilling over his white breast as a rosy melody spilled from his pulsating soul? Never. Morris knew that song, he'd fed upon it since first memory. Catbird, thrasher? Never they. He'd been calmly drunk on their music a thousand times, could recognize the grace-notes, count himself lucky to hear them and know them.

No, this was a new song, and what singer had come straying to utter it? There it was again, unrestricted and bountiful. High, low, up, down, thin, flat, vibrant, dispirited, rolling, falling, shafted aloft . . . *they were at once pipe and flute and harp, as played by delicate fingers in the shadowed flowery places where they went a-soaring.*

O Reverent Allardice, now deep and wormy in your grave! Did you send this singer and this song to me? Come they by your order?

For you had heard the caroling of saints.

O Reverent Allardice!

(A pair of mockingbirds had flitted warily northward out of their normal reaches; the male knew himself as an adventurer more hardy than his brothers; thus he sang. But to Morris Markham the newcomer was now a nightingale, and would remain so in memory, for all vicissitude and heartbreak awaiting. The omen was complete, the sign arranged—a sign unseen, but heard in devotion by welcoming ears.)

Got to go.

XXXIII

After the Indians returned the brutalized Harriet Mead and Mrs. Taylor to their cabin, long prevailing icy winds had moderated. The Wahpekute headed northeast across treeless prairies, and struck the Inyaniake again in the southeast central portion of Clay County.

In this region, on a stretch where water moaned from north to south beneath a narrow pavement of ice, stood the homes of the Plouray brothers.

Claude Plouray had selected a claim on the east bank, Arnaud on the west. (The brothers cast their eyes at future commercial possibilities. They foresaw with luck the advent of a sawmill, a gristmill—a store and post office and, above all, a bridge which might guarantee dryshod traffic past their doors. There was no need for a bridge in this season. The river ice was thick enough to hold a herd of buffalo.) Through part of the winter a deep-trodden path ranged from Arnaud Plouray's cabin past armored trunks of box elders, curving around cold-split maples, and willows which seemed stunted by that same cold. The path had been marked across the stony river surface, past a square-cut hole where rarely fish came to breathe and to be clubbed. The path then rose into a low flat eastern valley where stood the bachelor abode of Claude Plouray and his dog Babine. The brothers might be flooded out in any normal spring season, but they had taken a chance. They'd looked at tufts of flotsam jammed dryly into tree forks, had seen that such wreckage was old and bleached; perhaps no other flood would rise for years to come. Both brothers had worked for the Dousmans at Prairie du Chien before they came west. They felt that a Little Sioux flood would be a picayune beside the Mississippi's wide brown eruptions; here was most certainly a small valley, a safe one. They were sick of the Big Water and its demands and menaces.

Inkpaduta smelled their smoke before he made camp. Younger members of the band had seen that same smoke marking the sky.

More *Washichun*, said Roaring-Cloud.

Tomorrow we go to their lodge, declared his father.

Perhaps cattle?

Aye, fresh tenderloin, cried many voices in expectant concert.

Makes-Fat-Bad assumed the role of *Eyanpaha,* or village crier. Among the Titonwanna there was no hunting of cattle, but forever a hunting of buffalo; and since he knew no chant for an order to a cattle hunt, he sang as he would have spoken for buffalo.

He sang: *The saddle bind. . . . Children dear, for half a day I will kill.*

. . . Harken to the Western One!

. . . He cannot wait for day. He would go now, and soon in darkness.

. . . Wouldst go by night, when no cattle can be seen?

. . . And in day we take sugar from whites!

. . . I have no caps to fit the strange gun which I steal before we take white women to our lodges!

. . . After a night with those two white women, you have no need for caps. You have need for a new *che.*

. . . I'm younger than thou, with thy bitten-off nose!

Inkpaduta announced in a manner to quell argument or discussion: Here are good trees and shelter. Wind passes above us from this hill. Women, make camp.

He added, as a kind of sop to the overly ardent and active, In day, if no storm comes, we go to lodge of the *Washichun.*

He washte kta. That will be good!

For the past five or six weeks Claude Plouray had been in residence with Arnaud and Arnaud's wife, Marie. As temperatures fell and storms persisted, it seemed a waste of firewood—and the energy needed to cut it—for fires to be maintained in two cabins. There was but one bed in Arnaud Plouray's home, and the crannied loft was untenable for a man sleeping alone. (Babine was a long-legged long-eared tawny creature—part hound and part greyhound, and an uncompromising burden to be lugged up the straight ladder.) So Claude slept on robes in front of the fireplace, with the dog snuggled against him for additional warmth. Nowadays the path to Claude's own cabin was deep in blown snow, the fish-hole in the ice had not been chopped open for a fortnight. The cabin on the west bank, with its three human tenants and the lone animal, huddled squatly under tall guarding cottonwoods, a scraggly cube of logs and frozen mud—it was gray and somber as an old skull already, though only eight months old. Thin blue smoke puffed or streaked or wandered from the charred chimney's crest, subservient to winds which twisted provokingly even in this sheltered gulley. Crusted drifts, caked to various thicknesses at various depths, sloped up to the window frames on north and west sides. Old Jo Harshman and Morris Markham had each stopped there for a night's lodging during milder periods of weather. The Plourays were excited by Harshman's tales of Fort Dodge, and deer and elk wandering heedlessly into the settlement, and Fort Dodge residents killing them there. Claude was hopeful of securing meat in this way, and he stepped out of the cabin every hour or two, trusting to find wild game at his mercy in the snow. In this singular program he was unsuccessful, but Babine insisted that some creature was housed in a rough cavern at the base of an upended basswood tree, only a short distance up the slope behind Arnaud's thatch-and-grass stable (he owned four oxen and a cow; the critters were getting through the winter poorly). Investigation proved the tenant to be a male black bear. Claude slew the bear at close range with twin blasts of his old double-barreled shotgun . . . the creature's flesh proved excellent, taken even in hibernation. This was the only fresh meat the Plourays tasted all winter until they were forced to slaughter an ox; they lived mostly on mush and fish; but, by the middle of February, Arnaud felt compelled to take up some puncheons and open the potato hole he'd dug for seed-potato storage beneath the floor. They still had a layer or two of salt pork at the bottom of their barrel, but were grown exasperated with this fare, and tasted it seldom. They had put by two kegs of wild grape wine the previous year; it was all gone by December. Claude brought a demijohn of rum over to the west cabin when he moved in with his brother and sister-in-law. . . . Seventeen-year-old Marie, who had been taught her letters and numbers by a priest at Prairie du Chien, constructed a calendar on which she checked off dates meticulously; and she did her best to observe the more important Saints' Days. . . . The most difficult periods for Claude (aside from his perpetual disappointment at not being able to secure deermeat with a club) were those hours of darkness when he lay cuddled with the snoring Babine, and pretended to be sound asleep; and thus, in pretense, could not take obvious note of the squirmings and gaspings made by Arnaud and Marie in their bed. . . . They had no book except a shabby old breviary, and a Harper's stereotype edition of *The History of Poland; from the Earliest Period to the Present Time*, by James Fletcher, Esq. Both Plourays could read English, but haltingly. The history had been found by Arnaud one sunny afternoon in September, when he visited a camp site vacated by two wagonloads of movers the previous morning. If and when the movers missed the possessions they'd carelessly left behind them on a log, they did not wish to make a return trip for purposes of salvage. They had neglected to take with them a small red willow basket containing the history book, two table knives, a pewter saltcellar, a Dubuque newspaper, and a chunk of hard yellow cheese sewn into a cloth. Marie was delighted with the basket, and used it for gathering haws; also the cheese was very good when melted. Polish names offered an insurmountable difficulty to any reading for entertainment, however, during the cruel winter—names like Mieczylas, Radzieiowski, and Leszczynski. Also there were words, not names, to baffle erudition:

metempsychosis was one, on Page Sixty-nine, and sometimes through vague disorderly dreams one of the brothers found himself in furious combat with an angry metempsychosis more deadly than rattlesnakes. By February, Claude had made his toilsome way chonologically to Page Ninety-nine, and there he halted. *Only joy of my soul,* read the sentence, *charming and beloved Mariette! I have passed a very bad night here.* So he had indeed. The intimate presence of the puffy-lipped Marie (or Mariette, as he now called her sometimes in his mind) was not calculated to moderate the yearnings of a lonely and womanless man, kept from gratification by a wilderness and by family morals, religion, and ethics. . . . It was a wilderness which tied and blanketed them, a savage unfriendly season seeming integral to the whole realm. It was as if summer and succulence had never existed hereabouts, never could exist. Wolves (fugitives from the even more desperately stricken regions farther north) came prowling, sniffing for food—they came every night, sometimes they dared to approach even by day. Babine's greyhound blood stood him in good stead: he came through the snow with enormous striding bounds when fleeing from wolves. The enemies had been unable to catch him; but for all that he did not stray far from the house. Marie was reluctant to go outside for almost any purpose, especially from dusk to dawn. If her husband or brother-in-law were in the house when she needed to Go Out she would make them turn their backs while she used the slop pail . . . between storms the soot-ridden snowbanks nearest the cabin were traced in stippled yellow by the men's urine. These people might only grovel sadly, and pray for a relief from freezing Furies. Never had they or any other settlers been led to believe that an Iowa winter could be like this. They'd never seen the like in Prairie du Chien. There was more snow this year than they remembered in their Canadian boyhood. The coarse stinging dust of it blinded their eyes if they ventured onto the prairie. . . . Marie was the first to pray for leniency, for a suggestion of springtime thaws in the congealed gloom claiming them; but by this season of late February both the brothers prayed also, audibly. They would have felt no shame, no matter what profane watcher sneered at such childishness as they clasped their rosaries. They had been far removed from religious profession for a long time. Arnaud never went to Mass on those occasions when a Mass was celebrated at Prairie du Chien; Claude went but seldom. Now they would have risen cheerfully in gauntest blackness of early morning, and wallowed their way to a chapel, ignoring wolves as they went . . . there was no chapel, no candles but their own bent dirty ones (they kept the diminishing store of candles in an old tin teabox, to cheat the ravening mice), no *Introibo ad altare Dei. . . .* Many people supposed that the Plouray brothers were twins because of their close resemblance each to the other, but in fact Claude was two years older than Arnaud. They were thick of wrist and ankle, swarthy of complexion, their large blue-gray eyes looked faded and whitish, shining out from such dark faces. They were congenitally hirsute; they had been the sort of boys who show the faint suggestion of dusky delicate mustache growing on their upper lips at the age of ten or twelve. Had they been girls they would have menstruated early. They were slow of speech, equally slow of thought, they seemed to ponder a great deal about nothing in particular. At home in Quebec when they were tiny boys, and later in the woodlands of Ontario, they were subject to the brutalities of a sadistic father who lashed his children nearly into unconsciousness for the most trivial infractions of fiercely imposed discipline; and both exhibited that underlying sadness which is engendered by early cruelties. When their father died from being squeezed between logs of a tumbling boom, they sat dutifully during the Recitation, and walked politely behind a hastily banged-together coffin; but they had only hate in their hearts, did not wish to forgive, would never forgive, there seemed no good reason why they should forgive. Arnaud owned a savage temper; he was not aroused easily into wrath, but when once enraged his fury clung to him like smoldering phosphorus. If Claude's vindictiveness equaled his brother's he kept it better controlled. . . . Claude would probably have been married some years before Arnaud was wedded to Marie Caquelin (her mother was a laundress, and did washing for the rich Dousman fur-trading family; Marie lugged the wash back and forth; this was how she met Arnaud) but the girl, Alice Quimper, was afflicted with consumption even before she caught Claude's eye, and she died within a few months. Here in wastes of Iowa it happened that Claude had seen another female who reminded him of his lost Alice. Her name was Emma Mead and she was only a child, but Claude liked to look at her. It meant a tramp of between fifteen and twenty miles across prairies when he visited the Mead home (farther, if he followed the river valley in order to avoid plaguing winds) but he went to the Meads' now and then just the same. Traveling between storms, he had visited the down-river settlement in early February, and carried a present of turnips; of course the turnips were frozen when he got there. Claude returned home two days later than anticipated. Arnaud and Marie feared him frozen to death in a drift, and all three drank rum that night to celebrate the safe return. . . . When they dwelt in Wisconsin, the brothers had worked for Hercules Dousman only long enough to save sufficient money to buy Western land. They hated the lumber business, hated the fur business, feared the large river. Their mother's people had been farmers and village shopkeepers in Canada, and in Brittany before that. Claude and Arnaud thought that nothing could be so fine as to have a village enterprise of their own; and they dreamed of establishing a new town where they might rule commercially in time, as Dousman ruled at Prairie du Chien. Each considered that he was enough of a gambler, in a small way, to be happy in the hazard of facing an uncertain but conceivably rewarding future. . . . Just now they had no dread of years to come, if the weather would turn normal and thus decent. But they were alarmed about a possible protraction of gale and hard-biting frost beyond the usual expectancy of winter; that was why they prayed. Might not the sun have been agitated in its position, might not stars have bumped? Possibly the Earth planet itself was disengaged from its regular station in the firmament? Such disaster seemed horrifyingly plausible.

They prayed again in this late February dawn, pressing their knees against the rough cold floor as they addressed a large crucifix hung on the logs. They prayed for spring, when they bent their heads in Grace above plates of fried potatoes and a pot of scalding but very weak tea (their tea was almost gone, everything was almost gone).

Babine had been restless for several minutes. He skulked back and forth from door to fireplace, growling, and finally began an extended whine as if perplexed. The Plourays thought that wolves came near. Claude took his shotgun from its brackets, cocked and capped the gun, and unbarred the door.

Oh, yes, said his brother. Twas bitterly cold during the night. Wolves, without a doubt—

Claude opened the door and slid quickly into the gray morbid world. If I can knock one over, we'll have wolf soup! It was a jest, one of the small and heavy and obvious jokes the young man was apt to make sometimes, but even this humor was beyond Marie, she could not keep up with it. Her shocked cry rang after him: Claude, I don't know how to *make* wolf soup—

He saw no wolves, he scouted only as far as the end of the cleared space which led to the woodpile. Wood was as near exhaustion as was provender. (They planned that as soon as this wood was used up, the three would move across the river to Claude's house. His supply of wood had been untouched for nearly two months: it would be sufficient for their needs, even if snows descended for another unbelievable six weeks.)

Claude came back into the cabin and uncapped his gun. Babine, you hush, sir!

No wolves? asked Arnaud. He carried his stool to the table.

They've been here. Tracks all over—

I don't know how to *make* wolf soup, repeated Marie accusingly.

Claude tossed his blanket-coat to the bed, took off his cap of musk-rat fur (Morris Markham had shot a few rats in the fall, and he gave pelts in gratitude for favors of hospitality; Marie sewed caps for both brothers), and fetched his own stool. Babine coiled underneath the table, still moaning about enemies outside. Claude prodded the dog into silence, tapping his boot against Babine's head. Forget the wolves, he ordered.

But they were not wolves. The trio had worshiped briefly at Grace, praying again for warm weather as so frequently they prayed; they'd half finished their fried potatoes, when there sounded muffled hasty steps in the snow. The door was flung open, wide to the cold, and three Indian men stepped roughly into the room, stamping snow from their legs. These men were Bursts-Frog-Open, His-Curly-Sacred, and the grim-faced old Titonwan, Makes-Fat-Bad-Smelling-Wind. They moved in high spirits, for prospects of tenderloin lay ahead.

While Claude Plouray scouted beyond the front door, the outlaws had been examining a stable which stood sheltered in a depression behind the house. Hungry wolves kept a trail trodden deep into congealed drifts around the structure. It was easy for the Indians to approach without much effort and put their eyes at cracks between the poles—places where weedy insulation had been ripped out. The gaps were not wide, could not have been left wide, predatory beasts would then have wriggled through. But enough light pierced the various gaps to reveal a cow and the three surviving oxen. . . . Marie would have wept, Arnaud would have made his own doom promptly with his fists, could they have seen what was in the intruders' minds. . . . Those critters had been guarded so jealously during hard months! Hours of repair work on stable walls and door— Almost daily repairs were needed. The watering, the shoveling of dung, the dragging of prairie hay from stacks nearby— Now only half a stack was left. Warning gunshots at night, when wolves grew overly insistent . . . many times, when it was light enough to see, Arnaud or Claude tried to shoot wolves. With his rifle Arnaud killed or wounded wolves on three occasions. The Plourays shuddered at hearing cannibals fall promptly to their screaming chore of destruction. . . . If Innocence the cow could be made to survive until the weather broke, then movers might come through the country again, and surely one party of them would have a bull. If not, there was a bull fifteen miles down the river, and there was said to be another bull at the Irish colony over east. Innocence could be freshened up again, she'd have a calf, they'd all have milk . . . thus they'd planned. Wholesale slaughter of their precious critters was inconceivable.

At the Wahpekute camp that morning excitement ruled when panther tracks were discovered close by. In Inkpaduta's family the heart of a panther was considered the best possible medicine for craft in the hunt. If the panther were a male, his testicles should be dried, and then pounded to a powder which made an aphrodisiac without peer. It was this latter consideration, chiefly, which drew Inkpaduta to a panther hunt. He had not felt inclined to approach Corn-Sucker since snows began to fall; he had been sentenced by age to stand by, and watch the young men enjoying themselves with the white woman and girl whom they'd carried to their camp. Panther testicles were desirable. Of course the beast would probably turn out to be a female. After careful examination of the tracks Inkpaduta feared as much. He could have been more certain, tracking in mud or dust. But still— There was a chance! To anyone acquainted with the sexual activities of those huge thin cats, there was presented a challenge and a stimulation. . . . One male cat in a given range; four—or even five or six—females; each woman-cat had her own lair, they did not dwell amicably in a lodge with the male; but the fierce male had visited each woman in her turn; spitting kits in the nests were proof of this. . . . *Hunhunhe!* A human being should have been born with such treasures in his scrotum. He, Inkpaduta, should have been born with them!

It followed that Roaring-Cloud, Fire-Cloud and Rattle-Strike were ardent for trailing as well. The tracks were very fresh, the panther had come by at dawn or shortly before, bickering dogs sniffed at deep wide prints in the snow; they snarled, their hair went up. There was something very peculiar about the tracks. Recurrently there appeared two five-toed prints but only one four-toed print, and often a dragging mark. Did this panther have but three feet?

Most of the other men elected also to postpone any possible acquisition of beef. They did not hunger. While settlers farther down the Little Sioux had been on short commons, the groceries stolen from various Kirchners, Watermans, Frinkes, and Meads had formed a handsome aggregate. Ox meat and chickens made up as generous a larder as the Wahpekute wished to carry along with them; the sleds were loaded with this plunder. The Meads' dog had been a huge white hound with black ears, and this frozen dainty was cut up and dumped into stewpots as soon as the Indians made camp the previous evening. Inkpaduta saved the head for himself; there were few things which he enjoyed more than boiled dog brains, and he ordered Corn-Sucker to fish out the head before the brains were cooked loose. He carried this steaming skull with him when he strode for official examination of the panther trail, and he sucked delightedly at the apertures while conversing about a hunt to follow. Nay, no one in the band was hungry this day, nor had hungered the day before, nor would be hungry for many days to come! If the two young Leaf-Shooters exiled from that easternmost Wahpekute village— If these youths (the former My-Soldier and the former River-Boy) chose to go gallivanting after tenderloins instead of pursuing an erotic prize, it was quite agreeable to Inkpaduta. He made no attempt to enforce demands upon his unkempt associates unless, in considered opinion, it served a purpose worth the risk. They all existed in some degree of fear of him; but he took good care to cater to their unbridled essential lawlessness; he would have no band about him, no village to command, were it not for the fact that these madmen had been disowned by their kin.

As for Bursts-Frog-Open and His-Curly-Sacred, they felt no need of any therapy supposedly afforded by panther testicles. They were young, could grow erect in any desirable minute, they felt themselves immortal. Age was a perplexity which might befall others . . . not them, not them!

Makes-Fat-Bad had dreamed of buffalo during the night, he felt now that Fate should produce fresh beef for him. Beef was not buffalo, but it was the only passable substitute. There were almost no buffalo in these regions (the week after he joined the outlawed Wahpekute, they had glimpsed a herd of five; but their horses were feeble, they'd managed to kill a single heifer; and she was of no great size, scarcely larger than a calf). Often Makes-Fat-Bad dreamed of raw buffalo tripe, liver, tongue, other particularly toothsome portions, as any exiled Titonwan would be bound to do. Often his heart was bitter as a gashed spleen, the venom had poured over meat of his soul from this ruptured milt, the meat of his soul was spoiled. He did not dream only of buffalo, he dreamt also of war. He saw, in such fancies, his native Lakota village preparing for a raid. He danced with the others, went riding with shield and buffalo horns. He killed two Ree. *Ihlatan!* he cried, displaying scalps. (He did not say *Ihdatan* as these coarser-spoken Easterners did.)

. . . His wife had given him offense, he beat his young wife to death, he was banished. He drifted through the land of the Ihanktonwanna. The Ihanktonwanna would not have him, they propelled him ever eastward. In this nasty repository—with these people, and only with these people—had he found a home.

Still often he dreamed of buffalo.

Good! We kill now, he'd said as he and his two young companions peeked at the Plouray cattle.

At first His-Curly-Sacred was all for slaughter. But the astute Bursts-Frog-Open stood ready to counsel sagely and sanely, as he had done more than a year and a half before when he bore another name, when Jim Dickirson felled him with the grindstone fragment near Clear Lake.

We kill, he scoffed, and the people in the house hear sounds of our slaughter! Bullets fly from the house—the *Waschichun* have shelter, we have none, we are exposed. Instead let us go begging, say that we are friends. Then later, when the whites accept us—and we have taken their guns—when women have pulled down our lodges, and we are ready to travel—then do we kill cattle! We drive them out ahead of us, we drive them on a warmer day, when there is sun and no wind and no more snow about to fall. We kill cattle as we go, we cut out the tenderloins. No one shoots at us because we have taken their guns, they cannot shoot!

Aye, cried His-Curly-Sacred, impressed by the soundness of this reasoning. And are there women in this nearby lodge? We do not know. There may be women. I find a white girl—a virgin, as that last one is a virgin— I make her squeal long, it is good that I make her squeal. *Nakash!*

I dream of buffalo, said Makes-Fat-Bad stubbornly.

You have your *hanhanna wotapi* this day, you have breakfast. You eat chicken and dog. Your belly is full!

We go into lodge of whites! His-Curly-Sacred was now determined to abide by his friend's advice.

But I dream—

We go, we go!—and Makes-Fat-Bad was made to follow his youthful companions, since he could not conveniently go slaughtering beef alone. By the time they'd reached the cabin he was disposed to regard the whole matter rationally. No beef today. . . . There would be fresh beef the next day, or the next.

All three Plourays leaped to their feet in fright and amazement when the Indians burst in on them. Marie screamed, Babine roared—but retreating as he did so. Neither Claude nor Arnaud had dreamt that any Indians were near, they'd not seen a red face since December; then they'd welcomed only two women who came begging and were sent on their way with sugar and a chunk of pork. The outlaws did not pillage those settlements farther down the Little Sioux until ten days after Claude last visited the Mead home.

The Plouray brothers would have snatched their guns, but the intruders stood between them and the weapons. The Indians were driving their hands about strange businesses: pointing up two joined-together fingers, moving those fingers on high; compressing their hands before their faces; cupping their hands, dragging them down below their chins. They were signing for Friend and Eat and Drink, but the Plourays stared frightened and uncomprehending.

Hay-wo, said the deep coarse voice of Bursts-Frog-Open.

This seemed a reassuring overture, no matter how unceremonious the entrance, and Claude felt relief. He was not rapid enough of wit to feel disquietude at observing the visitors' attire (only after the vagabonds had left the house did he and Arnaud begin to wonder aloud about costumes of these Indians, and to become uneasy in the reckoning). The Dakota were draped in blankets when they came in. But, as they slid the folds from their shoulders, it could be seen that Makes-Fat-Bad wore a jacket of jeans material and His-Curly-Sacred rejoiced in a stone-marten cape. This cape had once been the property of Mrs. Waterman's aunt, and was bequeathed to Mrs. Waterman when the aunt died. It was heirloom and treasure though pitifully shabby, with patches of fur worn down to the skin . . . the plump old aunt would have turned over in her grave had she been aware that her cape could eventually honor the muscular body of a thieving young Indian. . . . Bursts-Frog-Open was clad in a coat stolen from the Kirchner family—a coat of German tailoring, with green velveteen collar and lapels, and ornate wooden buttons carved to resemble chestnuts. In contrast to such civilized garments the creased breech-clouts and filthy leggings and filthier hides seemed incredibly heathenish.

The two younger men were grinning, making gestures to indicate the act of drinking.

Whiss-kee?

We have no whiskey, said Arnaud in English. He repeated the same words in French. At the sound of this tongue the Titonwan remained sullenly impassive as before, but Bursts-Frog-Open and His-Curly-Sacred were pleasantly affected. They'd had some slight contact with French traders in southern Minnesota. Promptly they cried: Ah, aye, these people are French!—and His-Curly-Sacred applied also the Winnebago word for French, *Waqopinina.* The Plourays understood neither Dakota nor Winnebago.

To the Wahpekute a thought of Frenchmen and a thought of liquor were synonymous. They went snorting around the little room, searching for a jug. However, the rum demijohn was out of sight, kept down in the potato cellar underneath the floor because of its bulk. The Plourays had few possessions, but the tiny house was crowded with what they did have. The intruders looked under the bed, they pulled open drawers in a chest, took the lid off the flour barrel. There were two or three inches of wheat flour still remaining in the bottom of the barrel. His-Curly-Sacred leaned over the edge, reached down with his long arms, and straightened up with two handfuls of flour. Simultaneously he flung flour at Arnaud and Claude. Not much of the flour reached the brothers because the tall Dakota was at least eight feet away from them, but white powder flew like gun-smoke.

Marie shrieked an inarticulate rebuke.

Twould be better to laugh, said her brother-in-law.

Pretty mess they're making of my house!

Makes-Fat-Bad, relaxing in warmth of the cabin, lived up to his name, noisily. Ah, the dirty wicked *thing!* cried Marie.

Claude exclaimed suddenly, Put down my gun! Makes-Fat-Bad had lifted the weapon from its bracket and was examining it in scorn. *Agi,* he mumbled. One hammer loose—

We take not guns now, His-Curly-Sacred warned. One man looks angry. He would fight.

Both men angry! replied Makes-Fat-Bad. *Ho!* But we are three. We kill beef now?

Nay, wait.

Kill men, take woman?

That Old One says no kill.

But That One is very old! He is not my father! He is father of the Twin Ones!

You fight That Old One? asked His-Curly-Sacred witheringly.

Makes-Fat-Bad made the sign of contempt, but said nothing more about killing. Meanwhile Bursts-Frog-Open had occupied himself with staring intently at Marie Plouray. His nostrils dilated visibly as if he were drinking in the smell of her. He had taken no part in flour-throwing or gun-handling, and did not even turn his head to observe Makes-Fat-Bad as the flat-faced Titonwan thrust the shotgun back into its place. He addressed his fellow Wahpekute instead.

This woman for me!

She is fat, fat almost as the wife of Rattle-Strike, fat as that daughter of Inkpaduta is fat. I desire a woman who is thin! That young white woman we take from cabin where child cries loudly, and where we whip child—

But this woman. Her face is soft, she is all soft. *Washte!*

Remember you the Yellow Hair, at that lodge long ago where you break the stone-that-turns? I think of her.

Nay. Too thin, too young. She has no hair on her *shan.*

That is long ago, as I say. Now she has hair. If ever her I find, her I fuck!

Nay. For me, this woman here.

It was Bursts-Frog-Open who had snapped the ribbon from little Emma Mead's neck and appropriated her single treasure of jewelry: a shining marble. The marble had been given to the child by a youthful admirer who regarded the carnelian as his favorite and luckiest, and held it to be a gift of price. He'd gone to great pains to drill a hole and attach a loop of gilt wire by which the orb might be suspended. Bursts-Frog-Open was much taken with his stolen trinket; he knotted the ribbon together and wore the thing constantly, hung around his neck as it had hung around the little girl's. He considered that it might have some properties as medicine, but just what they might be he did not know. Never removing his gaze from Marie's face, he now slowly slid the ribbon over his head. He said, *Hinni.* Thou wearest. He pushed up against the table and held the marble across to Marie as she cowered by her husband.

Ah, cried Marie, I don't want that pesky *thing!*

Take it, urged Arnaud. He is trying to be friendly.

But I don't want that dirty old *thing.* He's been wearing it right next his dirty old *skin.*

Take it, take it! the Plouray brothers insisted, and at last Marie allowed the marble to be pressed into her reluctant hand.

Bursts-Frog-Open said, to Marie: I go. I go now. I return!

The young wife had no idea what he was saying but she gave an exclamation of disgust.

There is rifle here in this house? asked Makes-Fat-Bad. I see it not. We seek now?

He could have found the gun with ease (it hung in its accustomed place, but Marie had carelessly flung her flannel nightgown over it when she dressed at dawn, while the menfolks were attending to the stock).

We come again, said His-Curly-Sacred. It is good that Bursts-Frog-Open gives the stone-shining-red-and-white to this woman. They think not that we take their guns, but we come soon, take guns.

Echahe! Kill beef too! *Children dear, for half a day I will kill—*

We go!

Go! Return! *Hdichu!* said Bursts-Frog-Open. He reached suddenly across the table, trying to touch Marie. She yelled: Husband, make him *stop!*

Arnaud Plouray's savage temper still lay quiescent. The only crime committed by Indians within his observation and experience was the act of thievery. It seemed to him rather as if these rude visitors were worshiping his wife honestly—that possibly they regarded her as a white goddess of one kind or another—

Did not, perhaps, the ruffian endow his marble with magic? Indians were apt to beg for things or even to take things without permission; but when they offered gifts, themselves, importance should be ascribed to the deed. Various treaties (at Fort Atkinson, Fort Crawford, Fort Snelling, or in adjacent areas) had been signalized by an exchange of gifts. Arnaud had heard this told in reminiscence by fur traders who'd been present at the ceremonies.

Well, then!

His store of sugar was puny, but Brother Claude owned more sugar in the house across the river. Arnaud brought out the sugar pail. He poured rations of misshapen lumps into three big broken-nailed hands extended to him. Marie berated him, but he knew that he was wiser than she, he let her protests fall on deaf ears. The Indians bundled themselves up in their blankets and filed out. Claude held the door open . . . one fellow cried, Hay-wo! as they went. The shorter older Dakota halted by the woodpile for a moment and stood gazing toward the stable. He was the one who carried a revolving rifle (seldom did you see an Indian armed with such a weapon. Arnaud Plouray had never before seen one in possession of a revolving rifle. Before long Arnaud had a notion that the Dakota recently were up to worse mischief than they had just demonstrated). Then the man went on, following his younger companions down rippled river ice among protruding boulders and tumbled tree branches.

The Plourays watched from their window until all the robe-wrapped figures had gone out of sight behind willow banks.

There must be more of them, said Claude.

You mean squaws and children?

Perhaps more men, too.

Claude put on his coat and fur cap. I'm going over to my house, he said. They may have been there, and broken in and stolen things. . . .

He took his shotgun, and went out to wade in fresh drifts. It had been at least a week since Claude had occasion to visit his cabin. Soon the relatives heard distant sounds of hammering. But Claude returned within the hour to report that there were as yet no signs of depredation on the east bank of the river, there were not even tracks to be seen in the vicinity. Not knowing how else to secure the door efficiently, he had barred it on the inside, removed the frame of the single window, wriggled back through; and then nailed some scraps of heavy planking on the outside. He doubted that any Indians could wrench off the boards with their hands. Commonly Indians owned no hammers or chisels.

The panther, an old male, was hunted down and killed by the Wahpekute that day. As demonstrated by their laziness and reluctance to hunt during autumn, these men were not avid for the chase. They'd preferred to wait for possible Agency bounty rather than to lay in the supply of meat which might have been secured by a more enterprising and frugal colony. But Inkpaduta, driven eager by thought of reward, spurred them in pursuit of the big cat. He told stories of men who had been rejuvenated, or had their sexual prowess intensified, by acquisition of panthers' testicles. He did not invent tales for the occasion; the invention of a story was beyond him: he'd heard a recitation of such incidents many times, and believed the stories wholeheartedly. The panther was discovered in a basswood tree several miles below camp, and fire from rifles and muskets brought the thin tawny thing flopping to the ground. For a bare moment the creature appeared to have been killed outright, and dogs swarmed upon him. But the *inmutanka* slew two dogs and wounded more before finally he was shot to death. Inkpaduta'd observed that the beast was a male when he was still in the tree, Inkpaduta's wet red-rimmed eyes were glaring. *Ho,* he said. *Itonpeya, itonpeya!* Carefully, shoot carefully! Do not destroy the testicles! . . . In immediate examination of the cat a mystery was solved. Though the Wahpekute did not know it—though Claude Plouray did not know it, and never would—Claude was responsible for the success of this hunt. Early in the winter he'd fired his shotgun at a vague shape prowling around his cabin by night. In the morning there were blood-marks to be seen, but Babine refused to follow the trail.

Claude supposed that he might have wounded a wolf on this occasion. Actually several buckshot had struck a panther in its right hind foot. Infection distended the paw and made it almost useless; this explained the peculiar dragging marks seen amid the snow. In a winter wherein even unwounded beasts perished of starvation, the crippled predator subsisted on short rations—he was skin and bone—the injured foot stank even in the cold. But male organs were intact: genitals did not shrink even when flesh fell in against the ribs. Inkpaduta wrapped the testicles carefully in a piece of bloody skin and stowed the parcel against his belly. . . . In time of famine the entire carcass would have been butchered eagerly; on this day only the heart, liver, and tongue were removed. Also the penis was cut out to be preserved as ceremonial medicine.

The Wahpekute bludgeoned two mutilated dogs still whining in the snow, and tied the bodies to their horses. They carried off as well the carcasses of those dogs ripped open by the panther in its death struggle. Already wolves were drifting like spooks behind nearer thickets . . . soon they would feed on *inmutanka's* remains. The hunters turned back to the northeast, taking a short course across the prairie; and here was wind, with dry blowing snow building a golden haze beneath the stark sun.

In such weather the *Heyoka* might be parched and perspiring . . . Inkpaduta consulted with the *Heyoka* greedily in theory. They were gods to be implored to, when one thought of panther testicles and prowess which might be imparted by such a charm. *Heyoka* were concerned especially with libidinous activities. But with these gods everything went by the opposite: in dragging summer days when heat baked a plain to brown, and cut dry mud of the sloughs into irregular curling cakes, the *Heyoka* shivered like aspen leaves, their teeth chattered like shot or stones in a gourd, they were miserably cold. True icy blasts, such as ruled throughout this unforgettable winter, sent the gods into a lather of sweat; just now, for instance, they must have erected themselves some shading screens of weeds, far out on the pale drifted prairie, and there they sat sweltering even in the nude. For they could assume the shapes of men readily. Inkpaduta considered them usually to be occupying the shapes of men. Ah, they laughed when they were sorrowing, screamed with glee when pain was inflicted upon them; they groaned dismally when they felt a pleasure! The *Heyoka* were contrariants; chagrined by the killing of the lame panther, they must be rolling in laughter at this moment; and if, on the other hand, they were enraptured at observing the animal's death, they must be dripping with tears, just as they dripped with oil which oozed from their hides in the cold.

As a delinquent from early youth, Inkpaduta knew that he held an especial kinship with perverse fellows . . . in his mind's eye he saw himself walking as that one of the *Heyoka* who bore a drum. *Echahe!* —he carried also his bow and deer-hoof rattle, and they were spurting with that same fire which streaked against the earth when Thunder-Birds were active! But in his right hand the god (and Inkpaduta also, through imaginings of identification) managed a drumstick. And that stick was in the shape of the *Wakinyan,* the Thunder-God himself! He held the poor bird by the tail, he slapped him in cadence against the membrane of his electric drum.

Inkpaduta had not the nature of a song maker, but a weird song ascended from darkest most brutal recesses within him. He could not shape the song, could never whittle the emotion into words. Had he been able to sing, he might have uttered such a poem as: Heyoka, *the panther we have killed.* Heyoka, *the panther we have killed.* Heyoka, *the panther we have killed. Now I eat powder of his testicles, and may thou make stiff my* che!

Roaring-Cloud rode close. *Ate,* my father, you have magic balls of the panther?

Aye.

What portion give you to me?

Thou'rt young. I need, you need not.

You told us all, that thus we trail and kill panther! For this purpose!

Fire-Cloud heard the discussion, and moved hastily to demand also a share. Rattle-Strike, One-Staggering, and the rest pushed their ponies forward, until the mass of riders grew around him, and Inkpaduta was forced to halt. Those who'd been riding in the rear of the file now learned the nature of the contention. Promptly their voices rose in reiterated demand.

Panther testicles! they cried.

Alone you cannot trail and kill panther!

This we do for you, we do with you!

All get!

Aye, all!

A single mutineer—or two, or three—he might have frightened away with black looks, by exertion of the awful legend grown up about him. But a mass rebellion was more than Inkpaduta dared face. Also his twin sons and his son-in-law were as insistent as the rest; his original tribute to the efficacy of this medicine was returned to haunt him. Eight dissident voices sounded like the vehemence of a whole tribe. There was no Society of Soldiers among these reprobates, but here could be felt the exertion of soldiers.

Vaguely, fleetingly, he had memory of that night among the Ihanktonwanna when he was restrained, accused, upbraided, scorned, ordered away. And all so unjustly—only because he had kicked and beaten the woman Half-Face, his wife, and she had yelled loudly.

It was highly unfair, but there remained nothing which he could do about it.

And now these demands.

You tell that barest bit of the powder causeth one man to do the fucking of five! cried Rattle-Strike. I would fuck five!

I have no wife to lie with me, One-Staggering declared. I need a woman.

Bahata cried shrilly, I wish no woman, but I would have more power for *iwichahu.* Who wishes not more power?

. . . Need many women—

. . . White women—

. . . Young white girls—

Highly unfair, as with the Ihanktonwanna!

. . . We hunt panther. Panther we kill. Panther is man panther—

. . . It is That Old One who says we hunt, That Old One who says we take testicles, That Old One who says—

. . . All for That Old One we do this thing?

. . . *Hinte!*

. . . *Eze! Iyeshnicha!* Fie upon thee!

. . . Refuse all!

. . . We refuse!

Again, there remained nothing which he could do about it.

He spoke steadily, gruffly. The eldest man present besides Inkpaduta was He-Has-Done-Walking, who had seen perhaps three tens of winters, perhaps three-tens-more-four. The youngest was On-Oldish-Man who had seen two tens of winters. The absent Bursts-Frog-Open and His-Curly-Sacred were slightly younger than that, but still they were absent; and Makes-Fat-Bad was older than anyone else except the leader, but neither was he present. Here was age speaking to youth, and even youth in revolt would listen. Gradually the hubbub lessened, the men straightened from slouching warily on their horses. Their black eyes peered less murderously out of their cowling.

He said: You not know what it means to be old! I am old, you are young. When one is old the *che* falls limp. In some times it is like a strip of fat, it has no bone inside. Desire you *che* with no bone? If you live long, as I live long, someday you have *che* with no bone! Then will you wish for the balls of a panther. These must be scorched until they are hard and black. Then a woman is made to grind and pound them . . . they must be smoked in the heat, smoked continuously, long smoked. It is this powder, mixed with grease, which a man eats. *Kamdupi.*

He said, You demand, I give.

It is good that you give! The mutter of assent and acceptance rose from several throats; most of the men said nothing, but their silence was in the manner of agreement. Inkpaduta pushed past them and led on across the tableland.

In this area the prairie was never swelling and rolling, it was flat as if it had been leveled by tools. Wind streaked in rough gusts, gently now, rougher again, it burned past the ears. Manes of the puzzled stolen horses blew sharp, and stung the faces or hands against which they were whipped . . . always winter, always cold, this was a world of cold. The *Witehi*, the Hard Moon, had been a hard moon indeed; this was the end of the Raccoon Moon, and not a raccoon could be found; the Sore-Eye Moon approached (or perhaps was come already; people always argued about Moons) and all eyes, not only the rheumy eyes of Inkpaduta, would be sore with cold.

On reaching the camp, Inkpaduta discovered that Corn-Sucker was gone to gather wood with two other drudges. Woman-Shakes built a tiny fire in the lodge according to her father's direction. Then an odor came to his sensitive nose, and in fury he expelled the woman from his presence; she was *ishnati* and had not confessed to the fact. She must go and dwell in a separate lodge with another woman who suffered the same condition. Inkpaduta cried to Rattle-Strike that his wife should be beaten, and Rattle-Strike said, Aye, that he would do!—but by nature he was indolent, not easily made wrathful, and practiced cruelty only when aroused sufficiently in a fight. Rattle-Strike went into the lodge of the sequestered women, ripped out a staff which held the tipi lining, laid this lightly across the shoulders of his wife a few times. She howled as if she were half-killed, and all the while Black-Young-Woman, wife of Has-Intercourse, forgot to mourn longer for her dead child and sat laughing. Rattle-Strike himself began to laugh, he could not help laughing, the whole matter was comical. But his father-in-law, hearing yells, was satisfied: he growled that it was good that his daughter had been whipped. He hoped only that she had not affected the panther testicles deleteriously by her presence.

Inkpaduta himself did a woman's work and tended the fire. He felt that he should have done this all along. It was a wee fire, the size of his hand; the larger fire in the center of the tipi was blazing to supply heat and was impractical for his purpose. In the tiny flame he burned tobacco, a few whiskers cut from the panther's face, and some hair off his own head. Could he have managed to ejaculate semen he would have burned some drops of this as well. He did think to prick his finger and squeeze out globules of blood which sizzled to his satisfaction. He was no mystery man, he was a man of deeds and violence, but he thought that the *Heyoka* or any other gods concerned might now be propitiated by sacrifice of male hair, male whiskers, male blood. As an afterthought he burned one of the stolen banknotes. He was enormously puzzled by this riddle of white people's money. Gold and silver he understood, he had owned gold and silver coins, had spent them.

But . . . paper? Still, this scrap of paper bore cabalistic marks, and also the picture of a white man. It was not truly money. Yet he knew that the Wood brothers at Springfield would give him powder, caps, sugar—would give a variety of desirable commodities—in exchange for the bit of paper; hence the thing became *wakan* and fit to be consigned to the flame with ceremony.

He had barely concluded his ritual when the door was blocked by the thick bent figure of Corn-Sucker. She came creeping in to deposit a great bundle of firewood.

Go, said Inkpaduta, without looking at her again.

I am cold.

Go, d'ye hear?

My husband, we have large fire. Why build you small—?

He did not allow her to finish her query. He sucked in his breath with an explosive sound. *Hunktiya!* he roared, reaching about for something to throw. Corn-Sucker wailed softly and ran limping out of the door—limping indeed!—she had strained her ankle in slipping on the ice. A broken billet of wood sailed through the lodge door after her and missed the woman's head by inches. Corn-Sucker ran to a lodge across the way, the tipi of the dark-faced He-Wears-Anything. His wife, Mahpiwinna or Cloud-Woman, had been one of Corn-Sucker's companions during the icy hours of wood gathering.

Why weep you? asked Cloud-Woman.

I weep not.

Ah, you weep, said the astute Cloud-Woman. You weep but with no tears! Sit by fire, she added kindly. The women, with one obvious exception, had grown fond of Corn-Sucker and often demonstrated to her a kindness which they did not offer commonly to each other, and which some of them did not even award to their own children. Corn-Sucker was so docile, so willing to toil, she did more than her share at every communal task, she did not screech at the others or fight with them, she never stole. (The decent Wahpekute folk did not steal, among themselves—they stole only from whites, as any respectable Wahpekute should—but it was common practice in this camp of the Damned and Debased to thieve away bits of food or firewood. Sometimes one woman would spy another in the act; then she might fly scratching and spitting and kicking at the robber. A great battle would ensue, the men would watch and grunt in rare amusement.)

Corn-Sucker had not yet learned that a male panther was killed, but now she heard. She received the news also that her husband sought to pre-empt the trophies for his own use, but had been warned by the men that he must share.

A quiver of excitement shook Corn-Sucker's spirit at the thought of magic testicles, and wonders which they were said to impart to him who employed such medicine. It was long since Inkpaduta had ordered her to his robe, or had thrown himself down on hers. The last such act of excitement occurred on an unseasonably warm day before storms set in, when the Wahpekute were still encamped in the land of the *Minisota.* Corn-Sucker found a tree where tiny apples flourished, falling off in such profusion that they reddened the bare ground among the leaves. These apples were shriveling but still sweet . . . Corn-Sucker thought of them as *mamua* but heard the Dakota speak of them as *taspan* . . . they had soft yellow meat inside, large seeds, many worms. But she was gathering them just the same, rejecting those with wormholes: and she treated herself to bites of the fruit while working so, and her mouth was filled with their spicy richness. She sang a song, she thought of her lost home and people of that-other-life-once-lived-and-it-was-not-a-bad-life-as-this-is-bad. Sun and shimmering water combined to build a bluish haze through open glades; there came the jarring cry of squirrels, and twice the sound of guns somewhere near the lodges of whites not too far away. Then Corn-Sucker heard a step, turned her head, saw her husband. Inkpaduta put aside his weapons and sprang upon the woman as she tried to rise, hurling her back upon the ground with such force that her vision was blotted out for a moment. He held her arms in iron grip, he squeezed and gnawed and gasped and chewed and whined as he labored at her body. In the months she'd known him, the Hidatsa woman had learned that by a certain responding and quivering motion of her loins (if his weight and violence might let her practice it) she could experience a climax repeatedly while her partner was achieving his single culmination . . . he demanded her rarely enough. This was the solitary joy which existence afforded. Again she thought of rearing stallions and whimpering mares . . . this was the reason she'd been drawn into *kidahe*. . . .

Panther testicles? To form medicine? But he would not know how to do this thing. He was no conjurer.

The gossip said: Inkpaduta sends his daughter from the lodge, and Rattle-Strike does beat her.

Why sends he Woman-Shakes-With-Cold from lodge? asked Corn-Sucker timidly.

She is *ishnati.* It is not good she makes fire for panther—

The gossip continued, but Corn-Sucker heard little of it. She had her clue now; it was substantial, and indicated much. Soon she arose quietly and slipped across trodden snow and frozen filth to her own tipi. There she crouched outside, summoning courage. Finally she nerved herself to the ordeal of peeping into the lodge. Inkpaduta glowered across a heap of burning coals. He had impaled the testicles on a steel ramrod and held them high above the glow.

I know why you have wrath, Corn-Sucker murmured. *Woshihda.* This I know.

Begone!

Nay, my husband. I help thee.

How help?

It is the man-balls of the panther. These you would cook?

Aye, he muttered. But not cook. Smoke, dry.

This I understand. Did I not make for you good tobacco, best tobacco?

He regarded her balefully. She knew why—it was because she was a woman. But she was glad in this moment that she was a woman: because surely Inkpaduta would consume some of the panther testes, even though compelled to share with other men. Should the medicine be as strong as reputed, then would she profit. Because she was a woman and the wife of Inkpaduta.

You are *ishnati?* he demanded rudely.

Nay, nay, Corn-Sucker told him, almost laughing as she spoke. She took his resulting silence for permission to enter the lodge, and so now she did enter.

She approached the tiny fire, and rejoiced when he did not threaten her.

This I understand, she said, indicating fire and objects toasting there.

You are not a man. You never kill *inmutanka!*

That is true. But my second father, Gray-Other-Goose, kills panther, many panther, when he is young. The testicles suffice him until he is old: when he is old he takes my mother for a wife, he takes three wives, he lies with all. And he has many more winters than thou, when he does this thing with three wives!

Inkpaduta considered this intelligence for a long while. In so doing he drifted into reverie and considered cunning. How might he find a way of circumventing the demands of the men in his band, of circumventing the desires of his own sons? It would take trickery of the keenest sort. Never for one moment had he intended to live up to his promise to share, if by some means he could keep the treasure for himself. Sitting now before the coals he saw them turning to white, then to ash. He motioned for Corn-Sucker to feed the fire. She accomplished this chore with despatch, chopped off slivers from a log, kept the fire going efficiently.

Inkpaduta believed every word which his wife had told him about Gray-Other-Goose (believed, in almost demented embracing, as men adhere with passion to fables which reflect their desires). He might thrash his sinless wife horridly—might bruise her, rape her, ignore her, starve her, fling her from him. He knew that always she would be cringing willingly before him once more, no matter what torture or indignity he slashed her with. He had a vital appreciation of her virtues nevertheless. He observed her as a dedicated slave, he gobbled her cookery; it was merely that he gave her no reward—the thought of rewarding Corn-Sucker never entered his mind. He had no notion of equability, would have considered himself weakened by demonstrations of charity or affection. But he had never known this woman to tell a lie. Forever she uttered truth, when indeed she spoke. She did not prattle idly like most women.

So the old Hidatsa, Gray-Other-Goose, demonstrated a power to be derived from this medicine; and he had actively possessed three wives when he was older than Inkpaduta? *He washte!*

He addressed her gruffly. Woman.

Aye?

You take, he said, and passed the ramrod into her hand.

He went to the lodge of Roaring-Cloud and found there three of the men smoking. It was good that they had taken much tobacco from the whites recently. When the men were not gorging themselves on butchered beef and dog meat, on the last of the stolen chickens, they were smoking.

They sat long, and told tales, all boasting. More men joined them, the boasts grew higher and more colorful. They had no spirit water . . . ah, they wished for spirit water! But they could smoke, and tell stories of war and pony-stealing.

Meanwhile Corn-Sucker never wavered in her devotion to the strange little orbs, the scorched and smelling fruit. She erected a tripod and the ramrod hung point downward from this, precious lumps turning lazily above the blaze. She worked them back and forth upon the skewer as necessary, to equalize exposure to heat and smoke. She tended the fire in the same manner in which she would have tended an ailing baby, did she have an ailing baby (but she felt now that never would she know motherhood).

A song waxed within her, as always her songs must grow, because she was a singer and possessed of these poems, and no abusive force could put them down.

O great itupa, itupa *with the long tail!*

You had many wives, you were strong and hard with all your wives.

Now it is that the wives must lament, the kittens will spit in lamentation after they are born.

Why scream the cats in sadness and in rage?

It is because the adutsua, *the seed of their father, now dries above this blaze.*

Burn steadily, O fire! Curl thickly, O smoke! One day the strength of a panther may be found within the testicles of my husband even though he is old.

As for Inkpaduta, a chance reference to dog meat by one of his sons crystallized an intent which he had held all along. It named for him the direction in which he should proceed.

With still an hour or two of daylight remaining, he left the lodge to its choking smoke and the men to their stories; he said that he was going to search for more panther tracks—no, he would go alone!—in a dream it had been shown him that he should do this thing! He took a course downstream on the ice, then swung along a narrow gulley where snowdrifts gave proof that no wood gatherers had ventured, and where he might detect the approach of an intruder advancing from any direction. There, under roots of an upended willow, he built a private fire; and succeeded in charring a dog's bone into stinking burnt blackness before the raw sun had slipped behind the prairie's rim. This hot bone he concealed under his blanket and smuggled it back to the camp—returning in stark dusk, with wolves howling behind him. In a later and extremely secret session he scraped the burnt relic into coarse brown powder, working earnestly with the point of his sharp knife until no one would ever have known the origin of the stuff. Mirth possessed him, in contemplation of his own deviltry. Nay—this material no longer resembled bone, twas only powder, a substance referred to as *kamdupi.* Had it been possible to use dog testicles he would have employed them. But living dogs had devoured much of the offal of the dead dogs, and their privates along with the rest of the grisly garbage; furthermore there would have been no opportunity for an extended process of smoking and drying out the dog seeds. Thus a bone must serve.

He inquired of Corn-Sucker: With what mix you the panther balls, when you pound them small at last?

My second father, Gray-Other-Goose, did use fat of a buffalo bull.

We have no such fat, woman. We kill no buffalo.

Aye, but beef—

We have beef-bull fat?

After some reflection, Corn-Sucker produced a certain parfleche and opened it and smelled of the contents. Then she tasted, nibbling just a bit of the whitish tallow. Aye, husband! Well I know this fat. It is fat of the brown beef-bull—the *kedapi*—which you kill, in that same lodge-of-white-people-where-scatter-feathers.

(Bahata had enjoyed his sport with mattresses and pillows at the Frinke house, ripping them open and reveling in whirlwinds of feathers.)

Inkpaduta said, This you use for panther testicles.

Aye, my husband.

And some I eat now. Give!

He took a generous handful of the suet and went away munching; then, once gone from Corn-Sucker's observation, he hid a wad of it. In clandestine session he kneaded the fat together with powder of scraped charred dog bone. Dirt and sweat of his hands were also worked into the paste . . . old blood of the slain with which his hands were painted, fresh unshed blood which did not adorn his hands as yet but would stain them soon . . . selfishness and bitterness, the bile of hate feeding out through his pores from that rancid reservoir snuggled hot amid the big man's entrails . . . all the crazed ugliness, the lie, the wound, the torturing, the jeer, the laziness, the embattled contempt . . . he exuded these oils and acids from his flesh. So the paste became vile venom, it tasted so.

The next day Corn-Sucker awarded him the product of her dedicated chemistry (she'd risen at frequent disciplined intervals, all night long, to guard the small fire and those bits which shriveled over it). Then ensued a long application of the pestle, the pound of stone on stone . . . grinding until fragments were reduced to grain, the grain to salt, the salt to clay so light it could be puffed away with the mouth. And then the mixing with the suet. . . .

I give you, she whispered in humility, and offered a folded membrane with its greasy wealth.

He said, Good!—and ordered her out of the lodge, and saw that the door was secured.

Tradition had never told whether the magic should be swallowed down at a single meal, or doled out to oneself from time to time, as needed. Inkpaduta rather inclined to the latter belief. He ate a portion of the stuff at once—it was most appealing to his palate—and then wrapped the rest of it away in his medicine bundle. A man's medicine bundle was *wakan*, twas his own, no one dared open Inkpaduta's bundle but himself, until he was dead. Enemies might open it, if he fell in war, but he did not expect so to die.

Into the original membrane he now stored his wad of false bone-powder-and-beef-fat. It looked very much the same as the other, but made a larger mound. No one except Corn-Sucker might know the difference and she would never see it again; for now there should be nothing but male appreciation and dreams of male hardihood.

The word that Corn-Sucker's work was finished had gone through the camp. Most of the men were waiting in the lodge of Roaring-Cloud when Inkpaduta stalked there, and the others came at once. Everyone was soon assembled except for Bursts-Frog-Open, and no one knew exactly what had become of him.

His fellow Easterner, His-Curly-Sacred, said: Without doubt he goes to the near lodge of whites again. There is a woman—

Also cattle!—cried Makes-Fat-Bad excitedly.

Is this woman good for us?

Not for me, replied His-Curly-Sacred. She is fat.

Fat is good.

For me, I have thin white woman!

For all of us, said Inkpaduta, we have fat. The fat of a bull, into which is put the crushed medicine of panther testicles. We are nine who go to hunt the panther. *Napchinwankana.* Only nine! Is this not true?

He wichaka! That's the truth! There was a concerted rising of voices and repeated affirmations of this fact. Suspicious glances were cast toward the two men who had not gone hunting panther. It was feared that they might have the effrontery to demand shares. But His-Curly-Sacred, in the pride of extreme youth, made a gesture of contempt at the mere thought of such medicine being needed or even desirable in his case. Makes-Fat-Bad was more concerned with future tenderloins than with aphrodisiacs; so these two soon left the lodge amicably, pausing only for a few ceremonial puffs of tobacco smoke to show their fellowship.

Eight pairs of eyes watched Inkpaduta's knife as the leader cut and apportioned. There was some disagreement, some challenge, some measuring and reassorting—a bit was taken from this pile, added to that. At last the portions were held to be divided fairly. Immediately several people wished to gamble, to wager each his allotment against the others' . . . there lifted also the clamor of certain voices, the voices of young men bragging of what they might do when once the prowess of the panther had entered into their own organs.

Inkpaduta rose and went away through snow and frozen slime. He was falling progressively into a more sullen frame of mind. At first he had been delighted with his prank; but now, for some vague reason not understandable, it seemed that in tricking the others he might also have tricked himself. Just how this could be he did not know, but the feeling was there. He felt thwarted, and why? He felt a savagery which must necessarily find expression in violence. When Corn-Sucker offered him dog stew he threw the bowl at her. Actually he was very fond of dog stew. Now he hated himself for wasting it.

On the previous day, after the three Indians departed, the Plouray brothers had gone seeking fish. It was the one possible way in which they might endow their larder; and they'd waited for a day wherein they might not run the risk of freezing their faces the moment they stepped out-of-doors. Winds were creasing prairie drifts anew, but there could be felt a degree of shelter in this river valley. Nervous busy gray-and-white birds with tilted tails were flicking through the brush, trying to feed, as also were the squat birds with bluish backs, which went quacking up and down tree trunks, seeming to search for insects amid curls of bark. (True to their peasant natures, and like most settlers of the region, the Plourays did not know the names of these birds. Scarcely did they know the names of any birds.)

The brothers had ordered Marie to secure the door when they left, and as they walked they began to voice fears deriving from the white people's garments worn by their visitors at breakfast time. They wondered about weapons carried by at least two of the Dakota. . . . Such exhibits of evidence had been there all along, but the Plourays did not respond quickly to fresh evidence and fresh influences: it took a while for new notions to penetrate. They held the traditional *habitants'* reluctance to adjust themselves to novelty.

Twas a revolver he carried, a revolving rifle!

I thought it like the one belonging to old Mr. Cunningham. When he used to come to Prairie du Chien?

Yes, that's right. Twas what they call a Cochran.

I thought that tallest Indian had a Model Forty-one . . . Army rifle, looked like to me. Such as soldiers carry.

Claude, where would an Indian get a coat like that other was wearing? Like a foreign jacket—

One wore a fur cloak. Like a woman's—

I think they're robbers!

Might even have killed someone, somewhere!

(They'd not voiced their compounding alarm to Marie, they'd only bade her to keep the door barred.)

Stray winds washed loose dry snow from peaks of the drifts, and the sun held a suggestion of warmth as it touched the rigid snow-stuffed timberland. A mile or two up the river lay a spring feeding from under a bank, with colored deposits of minerals making stratification beneath the surface. It was what might be called a hot spring, though the flow was by no means hot; the Plourays noted, however, that this was the last point to freeze. With their own fish-hole locked solidly for these several weeks past, and with ice thickened to impenetrable plating, they felt that the spring area was one place where they might be able to cut through.

Arnaud carried an axe, Claude fetched his shotgun. . . . They had agreed that they must not venture up and down the river in solitary journeyings. In December, after the stream was newly frozen over, Claude had walked into a region of gummy ice. It kept bending and sinking under his weight, and strangely the first that he knew of peril was when he saw willow branches on the shore solemnly rising higher and higher before his vision. Claude tried to run, slippery elastic ice would not let him flee, he fell to his knees, kept sliding, scraped wildly for support. Then the yielding surface collapsed with a horrid sound, and he was in the water. But his feet touched bottom; he could stand and breathe, and was in no immediate danger of drowning. He had a fearful time bursting loose those wide ragged slabs, all the way to the shore; at last he clambered out, shuddering, and scrambled to the house in rapidly stiffening clothes. He caught a very bad cold, the cough slid down into his chest, he was feverish for two nights. And suppose the accident had occurred at a different place, suppose he had fallen into one of the deeper portions of the Little Sioux! He might have gone under the ice, and that would have been the end of Claude. His brother became impressively grave about the matter. Never, never should either of them venture to any distance upon the ice when alone! At the crossing between the cabins—yes, that was all very well— If one fell through he could cry for help, the other would rush to the rescue. But nowhere else! Thus the brothers traveled together.

They spent nearly the entire day in chopping a hole and in poising above the opening, fresh-cut willow clubs in hand.

A few wolves sneaked within sight from time to time—within sight, but well out of shotgun range. No other wild animals could be seen: not a single emaciated deer . . . snows were too deep, surviving deer must be yarded up in timbered swampland somewhere beyond their ken. The men made a usual fair division of labor: Arnaud cut the clubs while Claude hacked at the ice, Claude built a warming fire while Arnaud was chopping (Arnaud had an affinity for edged tools, he was skillful at handling and sharpening them). Fire melted down the surrounding crusts, and soon it sizzled in the middle of a steaming pool. Water would have extinguished the blaze were it not for a plethora of dry broken fuel sticking up above the drifts. Limbs, stumps, whole dead trees of small size—these could be dragged across the blaze with a minimum of effort. Flames snapped up through the tangles, high above a hot darkening pond. Claude tried to roast several potatoes which he had brought along. But two were burnt up completely; the rest, reposing long in hot water at the fire's base, emerged soggy and scalding but still nearly raw. The Plourays ate them nevertheless, they felt weak and starved.

Fish began to appear gliding in leisurely swarms under dark water of the new-cut hole. You could see them stacked as they swam, sometimes very near the surface—could even see details of the quivering tinted fins and tails, the wide coarse pattern of rounded scales on the heads. It was exasperating, maddening. Why had the Plourays been such dolts as to forget the necessity for fish spears when they removed to Iowa?

Fish spears indeed. Who'd ever envisioned a polar winter like this?

Every few minutes the fish would march deliberately, emerging from mysterious caverns beneath the ice, shimmering in layers, one troop above another troop. Every few minutes the clubs came down, together or singly, making a great splash, fetching up spasms of icy water to freeze promptly in the eyebrows and on the beards and over the ragged clothing of both men. Stubbornly they lifted clubs above their heads and slammed them into the hole, praying that by mere persistence they might somehow win through . . . at last Arnaud cut a longer club, and held it before him with his two hands, in the pose of a railroader managing a tamping bar. He jabbed down against the next swarm of fish drifting under him—jabbed with all his might—and was rewarded by the sight of a fat pale creature turning over and over, breaking the water's surface as the splash subsided. Claude flung himself down and seized the thing before it was lost beneath the ice. He hauled it out. The brothers bent, freezing even as they gloated, to examine their prize. Arnaud rapped the fish with his axe. Pinkness purled amid trampled mud around the hole.

The men went up to their fire to warm themselves once more, to make an attempt at drying.

Well, a trifle of luck at last! Is that what you call a sucker, Claude?

White sucker, I think. Twould go maybe five or six pounds?

Oh, no, I'd say at least eight. But I can't understand it. You took quite a number of fish from that hole in front of the house, earlier in the winter—

That's just the point: earlier. The fish are swimming deeper down now. We can't reach them by striking with clubs. Colder it gets up here in the winter, the thicker the ice, the deeper the fish swim to try to keep warm.

Well, I got this fellow.

Yes, yes! So we must try the straight downward thrust, as you did.

Success came in the shape of two more white suckers, and three fish which Claude thought were of the type called buffalo. The largest was the one first taken by Arnaud, the smallest might have weighed two pounds. Both men were confident that they had stunned a great many fish with their thrusting or jabbing tactics, but the creatures were lost under the ice. . . . Waning daylight began to diffuse the trampled sooty river's edge . . . gush of the fire shone brighter against gathering dusk. It was time for the Plourays to be gone. They hastened away down the stream, frozen booty swung over their shoulders, new icicles forming fangs in the hair around their mouths. They'd had some fortune, but what a miserable exhausting way in which to secure food! They were sniffling and hungry; their backs ached; scarcely could they feel a hard surface beneath the clods which their feet had become. Bare stiff trees lining the narrow river stood like remote but threatening ranks of witches . . . trees hinted of more dangerous enemies lurking around the next bend . . . trees said, Ah, we're spectral . . . so are you . . . but wait. Hush . . . just wait. There's something *worse*. . . . Boots of the two men went thud and slide, their fingers stiffened, the rigid slabs of dead fish thudded against their buttocks and backs.

(This was in the same hour when Inkpaduta came pacing up the river toward the outlaws' camp, some distance downstream, with the hot bone against his belly, and deceit in his soul, and wolves accompanying him.)

As the Plourays floundered up a slippery path toward the house, Claude was certain that he saw a wolf crouched beside a tree, waiting to spring. Later his brother would declare that there was no animal threatening them, that Claude suffered a distortion of vision and fancy; but Claude insisted always that the wolf was there. He dropped his fish, and fired the shotgun into shadows. The blast brought an answering shriek from Marie inside the cabin.

What is it? Arnaud called back.

Wolf!

Where?

Claude could not reload; the ammunition carried in his pockets was soaked and frozen; he deemed it worthless until thawed out and dried carefully. He peered into frigid gloom but now could see no sign of a wolf living or dead. Then, responding to an imperative yell from the house, he gathered up his three fish and the empty shotgun and hurried on.

In the crowded disordered shack the demoralized young wife had managed to keep a fire going, and its warmth was a godsend.

Marie clung wailing against her husband.

Marie, the brother-in-law gasped. What's the matter?

Indians! said Arnaud.

Indians? Again? Is she hurt?

I see no blood. . . . Arnaud shook the hysterical girl. Marie! Answer me! Are you wounded? Did the Indians—?

Claude tossed his burdens aside and rushed to fasten the door.

But the door's not broken down! We told you to keep it barred. We told you—

The first intelligible words which Marie might speak were: Did you see Babine? The dog . . . did you see him?

No. Where is he?

He is out by the woodpile. Dead. The Indians killed him.

Sometime in the middle of the afternoon Marie had become increasingly annoyed by stench of the chamber pot. This had been used during the night, used again by herself several times during the day, its reek was solid in the small room. The young wife looked out carefully: sun was still fairly high, the day bright if clouded, she saw no sign of wolf or Indian. Babine had been fussing and whining, Marie admitted later, but she thought nothing of the dog's carryings-on—he always acted that way when his master was gone. It seemed safe for her to go out-of-doors. Marie wrapped herself in shawls and carried the offensive receptacle out to a drift beyond the low woodpile . . . drifts, old and solid underneath, new and sugary on top, formed a barricade around an area before the door, an area which had been shoveled comparatively clear. Marie thought that Babine came bounding out beside her, but she paid little attention to the beast—she was too occupied in emptying the pot and rubbing it out with snow. She heard a rush and snarl, then a pained yelping. A single gunshot stung her ears. Marie cried out loudly, dropped the pot, ran back toward the door. The long-legged mongrel was quivering in death throes—she saw blood, saw froth on the dying animal's mouth— Grinning on the doorstep was an Indian who had visited the Plouray house that morning, the young one wearing gray-and-green jacket of foreign cut. Another Indian stood near the corner of the house—he must have been the one who'd shot Babine; curiously he examined the mechanism of that strange gun he carried.

I yelled and said, I'll get my husband!

What'd they do then?

They were jabbering back and forth! I— I ran on in here and tried to get your gun. Your rifle, husband. I didn't know how to load it, but I thought perhaps twas already loaded, and I could shoot the Indians if they tried to hurt me. But that tall one twisted the gun right away from me, and kind of threw me back toward the bed. Then the other one came into the house. They shut the door and I nearly died: I think I did faint away for a minute or two. But most of the time I watched them, and listened . . . I'd quit yelling. I was fearful they'd kill me outright if I kept on hollering. They were having some sort of argument—

Arnaud gasped, Marie! I must know!—and he kept shaking the plump body in his grasp. Did they perform the violation?

No, she sobbed weakly. No.

Thanks be to God!

But they frightened me so— And he pretended, he made motions—

Which one?

Young one.

Didn't the man with the fur come too?

I—didn't see him. Twas that same older crosspatch one, and big stout young one. Arnaud, they carried off your gun—

God damn, I'll hunt them down!—

They—made another mess of the house. Knocked things off the shelves. They—hunted—found your shot and powder— Yours too, she said to Claude. They carried off all the ammunition. They looked under the bed again and—I think they were searching for Claude's shotgun—

It seemed that Marie would never stop talking, she babbled protractedly even as she huddled with averted face while the men put on dry clothing. Yes, just the two Indians returned, she did not again see the man with the fur! These two seemed arguing about something. The older man kept pointing toward the stable, the younger one pointed at herself, at Marie. Ah, they shut her up in her own house! They jammed a stick through the wooden door handle so that she might not open the door from the inside; windows were too small for her, she could not scramble through a window. The Indians went to the stable. Marie poked some chinking from between logs at the rear, she watched the ruffians at the stable, she was certain they were going to take the oxen; but they did not lead out or kill an ox or the cow. They'd carried Arnaud's rifle off with them. Later they returned, still in a discussion which seemed at times to approach anger; they withdrew the stick of wood and re-entered the house. She thought her doom was come.

Why indeed had she not barred the door?

Ah, they'd carried the bar outside!

Again they hunted for the missing weapon. They pawed through drawers of the chest. One climbed up and looked into the loft. No, he did not actually creep *into* the loft—twas mainly a barren place, there were only a few walnuts there, and heaps of old hay where Markham and Harshman had slept— The broken spinning wheel, a few items like that— And downstairs again, the sullen older man stole Marie's looking glass, the hand mirror with rosebuds painted on the back, her pride and joy. Mrs. Jane Dousman herself had given Marie that mirror, at Prairie du Chien, and there was only one little chip out of the edge. But the Indian took it away with him, he seemed to like it, he kept looking at himself in the mirror. For the first time he actually smiled.

Powder, shot, caps. They'd taken the flask and pouch and boxes, the old polished horn. And the butcher knife—

The very crucifix on the logs. . . . Almost she'd prayed that the interlopers would try to remove it, and the good God might have smitten them dead.

They didn't try to take it?

No, they poked it with their dirty old fingers! I think the older one might have snatched it loose. But the young one—that awful one that gave me the marble—he kept pointing at me, and then at the Holy Cross, and he kept repeating the same word, over and over. *Waw-kahn,* he'd say. I shan't forget it to my dying day! *Waw-kahn,* that's what he said!

And then?—

Twas awful! I can't tell you, husband.

By God, Marie, you tell me—

But I can't, husband! Not with Claude here—

You yourself said that there was no violation!

Thank Heaven, that is the truth. But he—he—

You whisper to me, tell me—

Claude said, I'll go outside for wood.

He went out into stark evil night, and stood and brooded briefly above the blotch which had been his friend Babine. Claude had heard that commonly Indians ate dogs, and he could not understand why the killers had not carried off the body. (It happened that neither of them had ever seen a beast with greyhound's conformation before; they believed Babine to be sickly—probably the flesh was unfit for food, perhaps poisonous.) Claude thought, Oh, tis a pity. I can't bury you, poor dog. Couldn't possibly dig a grave. And I daren't fetch you inside, for Marie would scream and retch, and your unfortunate body might begin to smell and— So the wolves shall have you. Poor dog! Then he loaded his arms with logs and went back into the looted house.

Later, when Marie was sleeping or seeming to sleep, and Arnaud nibbling at hot fish in front of the fire, Claude asked his brother what the Indian had done.

Made signs, made motions. I'll kill him, does he return. I think he was trying to make her understand that he intended to ravish her. Not then. Later. . . .

Motions?

Thus. Arnaud twisted and wriggled his hips. He extended his left fist with the thumb erect, encased the thumb loosely with his right hand, moved the right hand rapidly up and down.

Oh.

So I shall kill him.

They've stolen your rifle, we have no proper ammunition for the shotgun—

Have you forgotten my pistol? They didn't find that. I went to look, while you were outside. No, thank God, I had it well concealed!

(Arnaud's pistol was actually a revolving pistol, frequently called a revolver by this time; it had been acquired by him neither through purchase nor as a gift. Nor had he stolen it, he was not a thief, was proud that he was not a thief. There were so many of the latter along the Big Water. And truly, perhaps the man who put the pistol into his possession had stolen it somewhere. . . . One night, some years previously, when Arnaud was superintending the preparation of a cargo to be sent to St. Louis from the warehouse at Prairie du Chien, he looked up suddenly in lantern light to see a young man standing beside him. Here was a blondish fellow, rather roughly dressed, his clothes smeared with soot flakes—but many people who traveled the Mississippi were covered with soot perforce. And somehow this stranger had the stamp of the military about him. . . . *Comment ca va?* the young man greeted Arnaud; and Arnaud Plouray replied politely if abstractedly in French; but soon he found that his visitor could speak or understand no French beyond a manner of greeting; so the remainder of the conversation was carried on in English. . . . Is the Agent anywhere about? . . . No, no. Tis late; he's long abed. . . . Could you go waken him? . . . Certainly not! That's Mr. Hercules Dousman, and he's asleep at his house, and he'd give me the mischief if I went routing him out for anything short of a fire! . . . The young man seemed to grow more nervous by the minute. Indeed, he said. Well— And then, more or less irrelevantly: I must get to the *Royal Arch* at the landing. She's going down-river in an hour. . . . Very well, sir.

Whyn't you go? Please excuse me—I must check these bales. . . . Arnaud had caught a strong odor of whiskey, and he was impatient at being delayed in his work by some wanderer who possibly was in a drunken condition. . . . The young man looked around, saw that other workers were at the opposite end of the shed. Look here! He addressed Arnaud Plouray in a rapid coarse whisper. I have something, I must leave it somewhere, it's too valuable to throw away, but I don't want to carry it with me tonight. Are you a foreman? . . . I am indeed, said the puzzled Arnaud. Foreman of the night gang at this time. . . . The stranger cried: Ah, that's good. And you have the look of an honest man. Are you indeed— An honest man? . . . Of course I'm honest!—was the more than indignant reply. . . . Good, good. Then please to keep this for me—and a moment later Arnaud felt a heavy weight in the side pocket of his coat, and the young blond man was striding rapidly away through shadows. Arnaud called: Hi, wait! Hold on a minute!—but the stranger kept hurrying toward the wide door of the warehouse. Plouray put his hand into the sagging pocket and drew out, to his amazement, a revolver which gleamed as if it were almost new. Arnaud did not own a revolver, knew little about such weapons, had handled them in curiosity only a few times. At the door the man halted, turned, called clearly: About the first of the month. I'll be back about the first of the month!—and then vanished into the night. . . . Of all the damned things in the world! One minute Arnaud had been examining the stenciled address on a canvas-covered bale, the next he was standing there holding the pistol of some stranger, and wondering what on earth had happened. He ran to the door, but the young fellow was out of sight, gone on past sheds somewhere. Had a murder been committed? Why had the man been so eager to dispense with his gun, at least for the night, and until the first of next month? . . . Well, Arnaud dared not go in search of him; there was the shipment to be checked, and no one else of responsibility or in authority anywhere about. He put the revolver on a high shelf, covered it with his cap, and went on working. Half an hour later he got hold of a youth, an intelligent Hoosier lately come to the fur company there, and sent him questing down to the *Royal Arch* before the boat should steam off in its belated departure. But the boy returned and said that the boat was crowded, people were sleeping around on the decks, he could find no one who resembled the man described by Plouray. Soon they heard the deep frog-voice of the *Royal Arch*'s whistle, so that was that. . . . Arnaud took the weapon home with him—he saw that it was fully loaded, and was proportionately nervous—and put it in his budget-bag. It seemed to have no trigger; in short, the revolving pistol itself was as mysterious as the circumstances surrounding its deposit with him. He waited apprehensively for news of a slaying, news of a body found with holes of small-caliber pistol bullets in it. But nothing of that sort occurred. . . . So came the first of the month, so came the last of the next month and the first of another month. No blond young man with squarely held shoulders and whiskey breath, no information or explanation of any sort whatsoever. A whole year passed, and more than that: no word, no solution. . . . In a later season, when Arnaud and Claude were planning to leave for the West and worked at getting an outfit together, the younger brother carried the mysterious weapon down to the local gunsmith for examination. A very dandy arm! exclaimed the gunsmith. This is a Colt's Baby Paterson, thirty-one caliber. Why, here's rust showing. When did you last fire this arm? . . . Arnaud confessed that he had never pulled the trigger of the weapon—thought it had no trigger, in fact. . . . Oho, Plouray! That's just the point. See here, the trigger is recessed underneath. Bring the hammer to full cock—so—and the trigger springs out, ready to fire. . . . The artisan conducted Arnaud into the yard behind his shop, where a heap of sandbags did duty as a backstop for his primitive range. There the two of them fired many rounds. Mr. Doty, the gunsmith, instructed the young man in the intricacies of the pistol. Arnaud flinched dreadfully at the first few firings but soon brought himself into control; the same eye and hand which managed knife and hatchet might also manage a pistol, he was led to believe. He exclaimed with satisfaction when, at some ten paces, he burst a whiskey bottle into fragments—and on only his second try, too! Mr. Doty rubbed off the rust, cleaned the revolver, and sold to Arnaud a small store of appropriate ammunition. He taught him how to operate the loading lever. He dispensed to him also a holster—it was a bit too roomy for the gun, but it had a buckle on the flap, the revolver could not fall out and be lost. Arnaud carried the holster on his belt throughout the entire journey westward to the Little Sioux, but never had occasion to fire the gun once—all the game moved at too great a distance. He used a rifle instead. He killed one deer and one raccoon, and thought that he had wounded several other deer; but, however badly wounded, they fled away and were lost.)

Between the lowermost drawer of the chest and the solid bottom of the chest structure was a space several inches deep. Here the Baby Paterson was kept, holster and all; but the charges had been drawn out, according to Mr. Doty's advice, and the gun was wrapped in an oily cloth within the holster.

Well enough, Arnaud. But what of caps and—?

Right here, over't this end. Doty said to keep the ammunition away from oil or twould be spoilt. So I put it here, at the other end. The Indians didn't get it, may the good God damn their souls! Observe—here's the little boxes of foil cartridges. And caps.

Claude came to help his brother slide the heavy drawer back into place after revolver and ammunition were removed. Arnaud drew a stool up to the table, and asked Claude to hold a candle behind him while he loaded the gun.

Not too close. Some powder might have spilled—

So you really intend to kill him.

My God, but yes! What if it had been your wife who—? Suppose Alice hadn't died. Suppose you'd married her. And had moved out here, and an Indian appeared, and—?

I can't suppose anything about it, Claude told him quietly. Alice is dead. You know that. Claude made the sign of the cross, put down his candle, and went to attend the fire.

But suppose she'd lived, instead, and you'd married her, and—?

My dear brother, please don't speak of Alice. I try not to think of her.

Very well, I shan't mention her again. But *you* would shoot—just as you shot at that wolf. Or the shadow you *thought* to be a wolf.

I suppose so. Arnaud, what if they come back—tonight? Indians sometimes go warring at night. Remember Father Galtier's story about the massacre when—?

But the door is barred tightly.

They might smash a window.

Too small—they'd not manage to crawl through. And if they tried, I've my axe. And now the Baby pistol here, all loaded—

But, Arnaud. They might *fire the house.*

Ominous events, and the apprehension following, had sharpened the brothers' imagination. They passed the next few hours beset by various formless frights. Claude displayed his fears and gave voice to them more than his brother, for Arnaud's wrath had a single instigation, single core, single purpose and outlet waiting ahead. Both men were bone-tired but they did not become drowsy until late. Arnaud sat on a stool close to the fire and stared at the low blaze as if he were stuffed to rigidity by a taxidermist, and had glass eyes, and the eyes were fixed. Claude leaned close against the door from time to time, listening to the empty outer world and wondering numbly what shapes might be moving with stealth. Then wolves came and discovered Babine. They snarled and fought over this prize, while the bereaved master joined Arnaud at the fire and tried to cover his ears. Marie moaned in her sleep and, since she had a slight cold, snored as no young woman should ever snore.

Wind was rising. There came not much fresh snow, but the more recently fallen dry snow fled before the wind, driving like salt or finest shot, lashing the cabin's windows, strumming with the sound of sand. Once Claude opened the door a crack, to peer outside. Wind fairly tore the heavy door from his hand and whirled in with an explosion of snow. Claude had to heave his body against the door to shove it into place.

No Indians abroad now! said Arnaud, as he brushed resulting sparks and ashes from his clothing.

Claude wondered aloud about it, for the first time. . . . Where do they live, in weather like this?

Must have a camp. Must have wigwams.

Where?

I don't know: in the timber somewhere. They come, they go, they seem to have no reason for coming and going. Remember? Some of them came by, early in the winter. Then we saw no Indians until they rushed in upon us yesterday morning.

This morning.

No, I looked at my watch. Tis the new day. After midnight.

We should sleep.

I'm not drowsy, Claude.

But you told how weary you were, when we'd finished at the fish-hole up by the spring. You were weary at dusk—

That was before I knew the Indian had been here again. Before Marie told us what happened. Claude, I must kill him.

Well, you've your pistol loaded—

Yes. *Yes!*

Bursts-Frog-Open said to His-Curly-Sacred, long after full daylight had come: I think of her *chowohe,* I think of her belly.

Of what belly?

Belly of the white woman.

His-Curly-Sacred said in scorn that he believed the white woman to be entirely too fat.

But in night I dream. My *che* is strong in night! I need no medicine from panther.

Nor I!

These two dwelt, along with One-Staggering and the Titonwan, in a small lodge which served as a kind of bachelors' hall. When first they joined the band, the two eastern Wahpekute youths had been invited or even urged to live in the lodge of He-Has-Done-Walking; and they tried this domestic arrangement for a time. They were welcomed by the wife of He-Has-Done-Walking, an ugly and profligate creature whose husband would lie with her only when he was drunk. She was the monster who'd been saved by Corn-Sucker when she lay drugged and freezing in the winter's first storm; and she was the thief who seized Black-Young-Woman's silver disk. Mashtinchahankashi, or Female-Cousin-Rabbit, had considered that the advent of two lusty and lusting young men in her life would be of signal importance. (Women referred to her as Man's-Female-Cousin-Rabbit, since a woman's female cousin bore a designation different from a man's.) Her husband did not care who lay with her, though he had a fondness for watching such activity, and would indulge himself in this undignified vice whenever it was possible to do so. The two youths soon tired of paying their board-and-room, as it were, by means of such disagreeable cuckolding. Female-Cousin-Rabbit was lewd, verminous; she talked incessantly; furthermore her snarling children were undesirable as tipi-mates to say the least. Accordingly the newcomers approached One-Staggering and Makes-Fat-Bad with appropriate gifts and were accepted as brothers, and changed to their lodge. Through continual bickering and bargaining with the rejected Female-Cousin-Rabbit and Cloud-Woman, the wife of He-Wears-Anything, they managed to have their tipi set up along with the others—managed to have fires built, and food cooked for them. This was easy enough in times of plenty, such as the present, but very difficult to manage when the band lived on a starvation diet. The woman demanded exorbitant pay for services rendered, and never let the four bachelors (two of them actually were widowers) forget they lived continually in debt. Female-Cousin-Rabbit yearned for the marble which Bursts-Frog-Open had taken from little Emma Mead, and she was enraged when the gossips told her that he had given the marble to a white woman instead of to herself. Also she fancied the stolen hand mirror—the glass taken from Marie Plouray by Makes-Fat-Bad—and made the Titonwan deliver this prize over to her, the moment he displayed it in camp.

Makes-Fat-Bad was still sulking about it some fifteen hours later. Also he was aggrieved because he'd permitted the burly young Wahpekute to dissuade him from killing the Plourays' cow or one of their oxen.

We kill cow, we eat *napcho*. Tenderloin! We kill no cow, we eat no beef, we have no *napcho*.

Tomorrow you kill cow, O brother!

Makes-Fat-Bad declared with acrimony that Bursts-Frog-Open had said the same thing the day before. . . . You say I wait to kill beef, you take white woman! This is true, what I say. But you do not take white woman—

Thus he continued, absorbed in complaint. He felt sincerely that he had been robbed of a fair opportunity to revel in the red cutlets which he craved.

Bursts-Frog-Open sought to explain the situation, both to the thwarted Titonwan and to his other companions. As usual he spoke tellingly, and the others listened with a certain interest; even Makes-Fat-Bad was willing to listen again.

. . . So what had happened? The woman was there in the lodge of the white French, and she was alone when they found her. White men were not present to offer resistance. But only one gun had been discovered, to be carried off for safety's sake. Where was the other gun? Yes, yes, it was a mere shotgun, and old and rusty—they'd seen it the morning before—but it was still a gun, and a man could be killed with it. So what if Bursts-Frog-Open actually had taken the woman, either there in the white lodge, or after dragging her to the *wanitipi,* the camp? Then might white men appear with their gun—or perhaps they might lie in wait beside the river. In this way the white men might kill Bursts-Frog-Open, or one of the others— Even Makes-Fat-Bad: conceivably he could be the victim who'd be slain before he had any opportunity for defense, any time in which to overpower the white men and take their gun away from them!

Down river, declared the stubborn Makes-Fat-Bad. We kill beef. We kill beef at the lodge-of-the-old-man-you-wear-his-strange-coat. We kill beef at the lodge-of-the-crying-girl-child-whipped-with-stick. We kill beef at the lodge-where-Bahata-scatter-feathers. Do white man shoot us? Nay!

For this reason: we take guns, they cannot shoot! . . . In satisfaction at having stated a logic quite incontrovertible, Bursts-Frog-Open licked the last of his breakfast off his mouth and picked his way between drifts toward the river. Always there was some sort of clean-swept highway on the ice if winds had blown. Bursts-Frog-Open decided that he should take the white woman in her own quarters rather than undergo the ordeal of kidnaping her and bearing her off to camp.

It was simple enough to accomplish this latter feat when many men were concerned, and only two or three women, as had occurred previously.

But in the present situation no other men seemed interested in the fat-young-woman-of-the-French-whites.

If he were to fetch her to his lodge he would need to take his pony. Unshod ponies traveled perilously on ice.

(Oh, twas a great thing to see the Two-Legged-Ones-from-the-East with their *mazakaga,* and metal shoes made by the *mazakaga,* the man-forms-metal, and nailed upon horses' hoofs! This he had seen before he was grown tall, when he did not have so many winters, when his name was My-Soldier, when he lived with his parents and people of their village, when they all traipsed to Fort Clarke to stare, to beg, to wonder at soldiers. . . . With the soldiers was a *mazakaga.* His fire was small, but hot and glowing . . . it made a bar of metal turn red as a haw. *Whuff, whuff* said the bellows in a strong gasping voice. What a song was sung by hot spirits living in the intense blaze, what a sound was made by the hammer, how the small spirits went flying high and out like stars when the hammer swung down! The young My-Soldier had crept close, and was burned by one of those same spirits. . . . Here it was, still visible on the back of his hand, the mark left by that hot spirit! And the big man with the hammer had laughed to hear him, My-Soldier, cry out in pain and fright. Ah, a very great *mazakaga!* But the Wahpekute had no blacksmith. Were there blacksmiths among the Dakota people, among the Chippeway, the Winnebago? If such there lived, no one told of them. . . . After he was burned, My-Soldier waited quietly—at a safe distance, this time—until a horn blew loudly, and the blacksmith went to eat food. So did most of the soldiers go away to eat food—all but one soldier with a gun, who remained near the forge, pacing back and forth. Surely it was food that the soldiers had gone to eat, because a strong smell of cooked meat and other good things issued from that log-lodge into which they went; and some of the Wahpekute women, the mother of My-Soldier among them, huddled outside that building to beg. But they were given nothing, and finally a white soldier with a long knife fastened on the end of his gun— This man appeared and shouted loudly at the women, and pretended that he might cut them with the long knife; so the women were frightened, and they went away; but the mother of My-Soldier said later that she did not think that the man really would have cut them with his gun-knife, it was only that he pretended he might cut them. And while all this occurred, My-Soldier lingered near the forge, and when the soldier's back was turned, he stole four nails. They were bright and flat and sharp on the end; it was a fine thing to have such nails. He kept them long, he carried them with him when he was exiled from his father's lodge and from the village of his people. But, during this current winter, a day came when Female-Cousin-Rabbit declared that she would prepare no more food for Bursts-Frog-Open if he did not give her gifts. She said that he had given her no gifts for a very long time. She was weary, and busy with her own lodge and family; and so also she would not set up the lodge for Bursts-Frog-Open and his companions, because none of them had given her gifts in many days; nor would she fetch them more firewood. So each man gave to her a gift; and the gift which Bursts-Frog-Open gave to her was the four-nails-of-the-white-*mazakaga*-now-tied-together-with-a-small-piece-of-wire. So he no longer owned the nails, but Female-Cousin-Rabbit owned them. She wore them around her neck; and sometimes she would lift the nails in her hand, and shake them at the former owner, and she would make her face more ugly than it was, and she would taunt him, and he did not like this.)

Aye, the Wahpekute had ridden successfully on a panther hunt, but only through the best of fortune had they missed losing a horse or two.

If a horse suffered a broken leg it was then that you shot him and ate him.

Horse-beef was good and it was sweet.

But twas better to have a horse to ride, when snowdrifts were not too deep.

A horse wallowed and failed and fell into exhaustion, in thick snows where a dismounted man might progress steadily.

. . . Pony, I ride thee not! . . .

The remains of Babine the dog had been pulled apart by wolves, and most of the portions eaten. The frozen skull and a few bits of bone and hide did not offend eye and heart—that loose wild snow of early morning had covered them. More snow impended. Frost on windows of the Plouray house congealed in a thickening floral growth. Most of the windowpanes were cracked, or had been damaged even more severely; a stuffing of rags substituted for the missing fragments; but areas still intact might be blown upon and rubbed with the hand, and thus a watch toward the south could be maintained. In west and northwest the sky darkened perceptibly. By early afternoon winds were striking again mercilessly if sporadically, and dry gusts were taking breath away from the Plouray brothers when they went outside for firewood.

I wish he'd come, said Arnaud.

Where is the revolving pistol?

Here, inside my shirt. Inside my outer shirt.

With that shawl hanging round you, one can't see the bulge. He'd never know you were armed, would he?

I think not.

Arnaud, where will you shoot him?

Through the heart, if I can manage it.

But— Whereabouts?

Arnaud hesitated. Not in the cabin, not before the eyes of Marie. Doubtless she'd faint and—

Twould be bad for her to witness such a thing.

Yes, twould. Oh, I've a good notion. There's the rum. . . .

Arnaud explained rapidly with something of a boy's enthusiasm. Ordinarily his dull wits did not qualify him as a schemer, but in this exigency he brought forth a plan, examined it, found it substantial and was proud of the novelty. . . . They would have some rum handy, but keep the jug hidden. They would offer the Indian a drink of rum and make him understand, by signs and pointing, that more rum was hidden in a *cache* down by the stable. They would take the Indian to find this rum. Then, out of sight of Marie, Arnaud would cock his revolver and pull the exposed trigger, perhaps while the Indian's back was turned. There were five rounds in the cylinder, and these could be fired as rapidly as Arnaud's fingers might cock and pull, cock and pull.

What if you should miss with all five?

I tell you I shan't miss! If he had approached *your* wife and—

Never mind. Let's get back inside ere we freeze.

Bursts-Frog-Open hung about the place for several hours before finally he made bold to show himself. Initially he took up a vantage point behind a screen of stark grapevine coils and clinging brown oak leaves; it was as if he were on a hunt (but a hunt for a woman instead of a hunt for meat; and his pulse pounded steadily within his cold body as he remembered how he had watched and waited for other women . . . first, the Winnebago child . . . next, his cousin Little-Fire-Woman . . . next, a white girl who strayed afield from her parents' wagon to gather strawberries . . . next, a woman of the Blue Earth Wahpekute; so he dared not visit that village again).

In making a circle about the premises, though keeping slyly behind trees and drifts, he found no trail left by departing men, no trail in any direction. Not necessarily did this indicate that the white men were in the cabin, but it might mean that. The main path leading down to the river was banked in spots with blown siftings of the night, and not one fresh print of boot or moccasin could be seen. There were old tracks in plenty, but all were filled up with new white dust.

Could it be, however, that men of the household, gone away on yesterday, had not returned as yet?

Then was the woman still alone?

Nakash! If so, Bursts-Frog-Open might take her there in her own lodge, he would not need to drag her to the lodge-of-the-cattle.

These reflections, however, were dispelled when he observed first one man, then the other, visiting the woodpile. Later the two came out together. Stealthily the Dakota withdrew to the vicinity of the stable and there saw that the whites had visited the shack at an earlier hour, probably to attend to cow and oxen. Unobserved from that blank wall of the house which faced the stable, Bursts-Frog-Open made bold to enter and warm himself in proximity to the beasts.

. . . The whites still had the old shotgun.

. . . He was one and they were two, and they would most likely fight if he attempted to carry the woman away; he was larger and stronger than either of the white men, but the two of them might be a match for him.

. . . When raiding those settlements down the river, Inkpaduta had cautioned the Wahpekute repeatedly against killing. Inkpaduta did not wish for soldiers to come: he had been a prisoner of white soldiers some years earlier, and did not desire to repeat the experience.

. . . If he, Bursts-Frog-Open, killed one or both of the white men, Inkpaduta would become angry and might kill him while he slept, or persuade someone else to kill him.

. . . It was better to wait.

. . . He would watch again on the next day, he would watch long until he saw that the woman was left alone. Without doubt she would have the door barred, but he could break down the door. Then would he take her.

. . . Two white men, armed with one ancient shotgun, would scarcely attack the Indians' camp.

. . . If they went to seek soldiers they would have to go all the way to Fort Ridgely—or were there still soldiers at Fort Dodge? In either case the Indians would be departed when soldiers came.

. . . Skies threatened, there would be snowstorms walking the prairie toward this place. So—no white woman today. Perhaps . . . the white woman . . . tomorrow?

. . . Now he would go to lodge of the whites, would demand food. Those men had offered no resistance except by voice when he and Makes-Fat-Bad and His-Curly-Sacred first pushed their way into the lodge and performed their mild ransacking. The men had not fought when His-Curly-Sacred threw flour upon them.

. . . He thought that they would give him food!

Boldly he walked up the path from the stable, went round to the front of the cabin, pushed against the door. *Nakash,* the door was secured as he had believed that it might be! Bursts-Frog-Open struck and kicked against the door with hands and feet, he banged the door with the butt of his gun. The door opened.

The settlers seemed paler than ever, their pallor was the color of fish, twas like pale paint above their beards. The fat young woman cried out, and backed away into a corner behind the men. Oh, she was very fat, comfortably fat! He thought of her belly, thought of her lubberly *aze,* the breasts ready for chewing, he thought of the soft moist *shan* which must be hers. These thoughts stood brightly in his intent gaze as he looked upon her and (knowing that she could not understand what he said, but wishing to say it nevertheless) he declared to her: I have you! I have you when men are not here. I have you tomorrow. Your *shan* will be good!

Husband, squealed Marie, what's he *say*ing?

Arnaud's tongue slid out under the curly beard and ran along his dry cracked lips. Who knows?

Asking for food, I think, muttered Claude.

Yes. But where is the rum?

Here, in this gourd.

Yes . . . I poured it . . . Arnaud's hands were trembling. Hastily he put his hands behind him so that the Indian would not see how they were shaking. . . . Claude, and his voice was a squeak. Offer rum . . . to him. . . .

Bursts-Frog-Open saw the shotgun in the corner. He went there deliberately, picked up the weapon, saw that it was not capped. This I take! You cannot shoot if I take gun!—and his wide dirty brown face showed the glee which spouted within him. How tractable these white men appeared!

The elder of the two was holding forward a gourd. Then he drew back the vessel, tilted it against his mouth, pretended to swallow, but he did not drink. Again his hand came forward, offering the drink to Bursts-Frog-Open.

Why did not the white man drink?

Perhaps the drink was bad!

Bursts-Frog-Open was holding his right hand flat and with fingers extended, swinging it rapidly in front of his body, twisting his wrist as the hand swung. It was an emphatic gesture of refusal which could be misunderstood only by an idiot. He growled: You do not drink, white man.

He's frighted of it, said Arnaud weakly.

But they *do* drink. All Indians do. They asked for whiskey the other day—

Bursts-Frog-Open summoned up his scraps of English from a past wherein Abbie Gardner and Jim Dickirson were commingled. You—man—jib—whiss-kee?

Yes, yes! Claude nodded violently.

Not whiss-kee, his brother cried. Tell him—rum!

This—*rum*. Indian, this—rum! Good!

Cautiously the Wahpekute bent his head and put his nostrils close so that he might smell. He looked up delightedly. Ah, this is spirit water, he affirmed in recognition.

He likes it—I think—

Look ye here: I'll drink! Arnaud pushed forward, wrenched the gourd-cup from Claude's hand, and shook some of the raw stuff down his own throat. He coughed, rolled his eyes, liquor ran from the corners of his mouth. He shoved the gourd toward Bursts-Frog-Open. Good, Indian! Good, good!

Joooood! droned Bursts-Frog-Open. He needed no further inducement. He tipped the receptacle and drank all the rest of the rum, swallowing it down in coarse strangling gulps. He gave an inarticulate cry; the gourd fell from his hand. He stood marking with fingers the course of the drink as it moved down into his stomach, then slapped his hand excitedly against his middle. Jooood! he yelled again.

He began his death march, never dreaming that this was the last stroll he would take. The white men had pointed to the gourd, then pointed toward the northwest corner of the room, then they made repeated signs of drinking. They had beckoned Bursts-Frog-Open out of the door, preceded him past the corner of the lodge, and there halted and pointed directly toward the stable. They made more drinking signs. *Washte, washte!* Good, good! These French whites were *tawachin washte,* they were good-natured, and this was a marvel in itself. He had taken their guns, Makes-Fat-Bad had killed their dog. His-Curly-Sacred had thrown flour at them. All three Indians had blundered into the house and pawed the people's belongings about; two Indians had frisked there again. He himself had told the woman by word and sign that he would take her. And on this day Bursts-Frog-Open bullied the whites once more. . . . What were the results? Sugar first, spirit water now.

Whites were docile, they were weaker than women, they were like female whelps whose eyes were not open as yet, whelps who must be fed by their mother's milk. *Ho,* he would drink spirit water, drink much. He would amuse himself with these men who were not men truly, but only blind mewling cubs. He would cry, I shoot thee!—and point his gun at them; or he might load the shotgun which now he had stolen, and point that, and cry: I shoot thee!—again and again, and see them blanch. *Ho!*

Seldom had he envisioned himself as lying dead, he was too young to consider death for himself. Vaguely he'd supposed that he might die sometime in war or in a brawl, or might be slain treacherously by Inkpaduta, or shot—perhaps from cunning ambush—by some man who considered himself wronged by Bursts-Frog-Open, or by the relative of some woman he had taken to lie with. But the notion of death was vague, he held no haunt of it, never saw himself rendered bloody and mute. There was a song he'd heard sung in his native village when Healthy-Gray-Bear led the men out to make war. This song was said to rise from a dream which came to the leader. Four black spirits appeared to the leader . . . he saw enemies rendered inoffensive as these French whites who now moved in the path between solid old snowdrifts. The enemies went like buffalo cows being driven where a proud hunter willed, and the proud hunter wore a buffalo mask to make it possible for him to creep or scamper close; the cows were docile, he herded them in the safety of his disguise.

I make my way with my face covered. I make my way with my face covered. The people are buffalo. I make my way with my face covered. . . . Night now passes along.

They all stepped up over the drifts, they were in the region behind the stable. The only tracks to be seen were tracks made by Bursts-Frog-Open in his recent prowlings, and marks left by the whites when they fetched hay to the cattle. Here stood what was left of the haystack, a sodden mound of tough prairie grasses, and toward this mound Claude Plouray led the way. Arnaud had fallen a few paces behind the Wahpekute. Claude bent down and began to dig into snowy hay with his hands; even as he did so he heard the solid mechanical click of the revolver's being cocked. Bursts-Frog-Open heard it as well, and whirled, wondering. Arnaud's hand was shaking flimsily as he fired the first shot. The bullet missed its intended target and went deep into the hay mound beside Claude, striking dangerously close to the brother. The young Wahpekute was so astonished that he did not even lift one of the guns as a defensive club. He was still carrying the Plourays' shotgun as well as his own Hall carbine (stolen some weeks before); his arms were full of guns. Arnaud could not remember later whether the Indian actually sprang upon him, or even attempted to spring, while Arnaud was clawing back the Baby Paterson's hammer for a second shot. Not more than two or three seconds elapsed between the first shot and the second.

The people are buffalo. I make my way with my face covered.

The war song had not yet been driven out of the mind of Bursts-Frog-Open—it thudded within, for all the amazement which paralyzed his body before the bullet penetrated. Arnaud's second shot found lodgment in the young Indian's abdomen. Guns fell from the victim's grasp, he threw one hand against his middle as he staggered forward. Arnaud cocked and fired again; he missed completely and the lead sang off into the woods; he cocked and fired again. This fourth bullet fulfilled his prediction and hope that he might shoot Bursts-Frog-Open through the heart. He did shoot him through the heart. The man pitched against a drift, rolled half over, tried to lift one hand, the hand dropped loosely. A shoots-six!—was the only thought which possessed the Wahpekute in his dying moment. This French white has a shoots-six! What—? Where—?

He lay motionless, with black eyes still open and bewildered. His blanket was fallen down to his knees, and folded loosely around his sturdy legging-clad legs. The wound made by the first bullet oozed its blood down the slope of the dark bare belly, ran into the depression of his wadded navel, then trickled off to one side. There was a hole also above the heart, in the gray-and-green German jacket, but no blood soaked up through the thick woolen cloth.

You got him, Arnaud! Claude Plouray heard his own voice shaking out the words, trying to be casual, but somehow sounding merely disapproving.

It was not a shoots-six, it was a shoots-five. One round remained still in the cylinder. Arnaud stepped forward unsteadily, tried to cock the weapon again, his thumb slid ineffectually off the hammer, his thumb was all ice, the pistol hammer was all ice (he thought that it was, though truly it was warm from firing and from his clutch). Not . . . dead . . . yet . . . maybe. He croaked the words, and tried again to cock the pistol; this time he succeeded. He held the muzzle close above the Indian's scarred forehead near the hairline (over the wound given by Jim Dickirson when he struck with his grindstone fragment) and he pressed the out-sprung trigger. A slight spray flew up from flesh as the bullet went in. Now appeared the round burnt hole in the skin—so prettily and perfectly round, the hole, as if it had been tooled by a craftsman.

There, said Arnaud in a whisper. There.

Climate and other circumstances contrived to preserve the body of the dead man. In an ordinary night wolves would have banqueted and thus dispersed the corpse over a wide area, but no ordinary night ensued. The temperature sank fast, wind ruled; by the hour of darkness it might have been twenty degrees below zero—the Plourays did not know, they owned no thermometer. Then, as freezing air warmed reluctantly, a new snowstorm came drilling across the prairie and smashed into timberland along the Little Sioux. The body of Bursts-Frog-Open lay where it had fallen, but smothered from sight, bereft of odor by merciful snow. Also wolves inhabiting this range were drawn out to the south and west by a wallowing starving horse (stolen from the Wilcoxes more than a week before, but abandoned by the thieves when they saw that the horse was sick. They left it to its fate before they encamped below the Plouray cabins). Sickly and weak the animal was in truth, but very stubborn about dying. It had lurched hopelessly on the homeward path, and wolves banded in pursuit. Even while Bursts-Frog-Open lay stiffening solidly in his thickened entombment, the shaggy gray starvelings were hooting around the horse's fresh carcass five miles away.

The brothers returned to Arnaud's house to find a blubbering Marie who crouched, rosary in hand, before the crucifix on the wall. She had heard the shots, she feared that the Indian had killed the menfolks. Then, even as she gave Arnaud a hysterical welcome, she swore that other Indians would advance upon them and exact revenge.

You shouldn't have shot him. No, no, no!

By God. He stole our guns. See here—I've got the shotgun back. He planned the violation! You! He planned to rape you, Marie! He made signs!

No, no, no, no. Now they'll catch us, a swarm of them. The tall one, the older one with the cruel face— Others! They'll all come, they'll *burn us at the stake!*

While she lay wailing on the bed, chanting prayers between her sobs, Claude and Arnaud began to confess a disquietude. Could the shots have been heard in the encampment of the Indians? How far away, indeed, was the encampment? Those shots had been very loud, they had struck like thunderclaps against the ears. It was remarkable: how could a small weapon like the Colt's Baby Paterson make such a great noise? It was like the booming of a drum. Suppose the Indians had heard—

Tis storming again. Worse than ever. They'll never come in this. But— After the storm, Arnaud? After—?

We've got weapons now. And ammunition. See, I've loaded the revolver again. You load the shotgun—

But suppose there's an entire tribe. There could well be.

We'll have to fight.

But they'll set the house on fire. I remember tales I've heard. I remember tales told by Father Galtier in Prairie du Chien—

God damn Father Galtier! Arnaud shrieked in frenzy. God damn Prairie du Chien! May the good God damn all priests and— And Indians— God damn *us!*

This mouthing served only to increase Marie's woes and to intensify her wailing. Before long, Claude hauled the table aside, took up loose puncheons from the floor. He lifted the demijohn from its concealment, and in the next hour or two the brothers finished off all the rum which was left. Already exhausted by physical exertion of the day before, the almost sleepless night following, the day of waiting, watching, the impact of the slaying (Arnaud had never killed a man before— He'd knifed a man when he was much younger, but the fellow recovered and lived to be knifed fatally by another French Canadian later on)— Already impoverished in spirit, bodies a-twitter, stomachs seeking to reject the liquor even as the brothers swallowed more— They dwelt soon in stupor, Arnaud clung in sickly fashion to the bed beside his wife, and the wife screamed with nightmare— She'd dreamt that Claude and some Indians, working together with despicable harmony, were carrying her off to some lonely place behind icebergs.

Before dawn the brothers, retching and disconsolate, decided that they must leave at once. Should Indians surround this cabin the occupants would never have a chance. There was the possibility of freezing to death somewhere along their line of flight, but it was a chance which must be taken. No, no, never—they could not remain safely in the house! Oxen must work in pairs, under yoke—they had no ready way for harnessing the three surviving oxen. And a single yoke could never drag an unwieldy cart through mounds of snow. And in any event oxen were too slow—their cattle were too weak from thin diet. They'd have to go away on foot, trusting to reach a haven among friends before they perished of hunger, before they lay icy as the dead Indian was now lying. Fort Dodge? The Irish colony over east? They did not know where to go, but they must leave in the first hour of daylight—run before Indians found them. Snow had ceased falling, but the wind still eddied and whirled. At least marks of their flight would be filled in and covered over almost as soon as they were made. . . . Ah, try to be sane, try to be wise, try to make a plan!

Marie, for the love of Heaven, fasten that bundle more tightly!

Arnaud, shall you carry your rifle?

No, I must take an axe instead. If we are caught by night we'll need to seek a grove, we'll need a fire, else we'll die of cold. An axe is essential—

Then I'll carry the Indian's carbine. Twill be more useful than the shotgun, if we're pursued—

Marie, did you put in the fish?

I've got those chunks I fried whilst—

Marie, Marie, you must put on more stockings, woman! The snow is deep—

Let us all carry dry stockings in our pockets. Then we'll have a change. Pity we can't carry extra boots—

But I've only the one pair of boots and—

Leave this, leave that, leave the broken spinning wheel, leave the skillets and kettle, leave the figured delaine dress; leave the molasses, leave the strychnine; leave the heavy crucifix, the red willow basket, the flour barrel, the sugar bucket; leave behind *The History of Poland; from the Earliest Period to the Present Time;* the empty demijohn—leave that, leave everything; the plates, the feather beds, the tubs, the yokes for oxen and yoke for human necks; the residue of medicines, the candle molds, the candles; the old shotgun—ah, let it stand in the corner; the bureau, it stands beside the gun—ah, twill be burnt when the house is burnt; and pillows, the broadcloth coat for dress-up, the grater, the pitchers, the vase, the churn—all must be left, must be abandoned to be burnt up; oh, the salt—oh, the ladles, the nightgown, the gaiters; the one-legged bed, the rugs made from rags, the washtub, the big iron kettle; leave them all; leave the snuff, the rest of the potatoes, the hazel-switch broom, the summer sunbonnet, the pigs of lead, leave the combs, leave the flute on which you used to play in days more carefree, Arnaud Plouray! Leave the grubbing hoe, leave this, leave that, leave all—

They decided, in this last frantic moment of retreat, that they should strike southwest across open prairie toward the settlements on the lower river. Claude advocated this course naturally, since the Meads were his friends. Indians must be encamped somewhere immediately south of the Plouray house—that was where they'd come from, that was the direction in which they'd departed—

No use in going north. Indians—always hanging about the lakes up there— And so few people at Spirit Lake—

Tis thirty or forty miles—

There's more settlers down on the Coon River—

Yes! And we could swing back, south and east from the Meads', if we must escape all the way to Fort Dodge or that other town—

Newcastle or Webster City, they call it—

Marie, that shawl's not warm enough. Wrap yourself in a blanket! Draw the shawl over your head—twill help to shut out the wind—

Here, here's a blanket—

Where's the bundle of food?

Here, here! Have you your flint and steel?—

Oh, my good God, the ammunition—

My tinderbox—

Poor Innocence the cow! They'll butcher her—

Yes, yes. Hurry—let us go now!—

They tumbled along the path toward the stable. Arnaud was ahead. Marie trotted after him, Claude brought up the rear. Arnaud ran to open the stable door, he caught up a stick and thrust it into the wide crack between crude-cobbled door and crude-cobbled post and thatched walls—thrust it tightly into the crack so that the door might not be blown shut—

Oh, poor Innocence! And our miserable oxen—

They might survive, might nibble twigs and bits of bark! At least they can wander out and forage for themselves—

If the Indians don't butcher them first.

They might survive. God knows, God alone knows—

Arnaud called sharply: Claude, not that north side of the stable! Here—this side—on the south—

Promptly his brother understood. The body of the Indian lay beyond the northwest corner near the residue of haystack, and Arnaud did not wish Marie to see that body: she was a-tremble now, she might be unnerved completely should she see the corpse of the dead enemy. They waded through deep soft snow, still swirling and wind-marked, along the south side of the stable. There was a path of sorts leading up through the woods to a lip of prairie beyond, but it would be drifted badly . . . and all that keen wind striking down through rigid trees . . . if Marie collapsed they'd be forced to carry her, and in so doing they would never reach the Mead house by nightfall . . . battering through so much snow. . . .

They turned uphill, west, once they were beyond the stable. Arnaud halted, and motioned for the others to pass him by. Marie, he called, when they were past. Go ahead—up the hill—don't look back— Understand? *Don't turn around.*

Claude watched him as he approached the mound, sharp-edged by knifing breezes along its summit, where the body was concealed. Only one moccasined foot could be seen, thrusting out from the pile. Arnaud used his axe as a shovel or broom, brushing snow back and forth in a rapid sweeping motion until the upper portions of the figure were exposed. Then Arnaud lifted the axe and chopped fiercely, several strokes. Some pale reddened chips seemed to fly upward as the blade drove home and through, and into the solid pulp of frost beneath the body. Claude turned quickly to look at the toiling figure of Marie beyond them, and then he approached his brother.

Arnaud! What are you—doing—? What—have you—? Then he could only stand in disgust and horror, staring down.

D'ye see? I cut it off.

The head— Oh, it's— My God, Arnaud, why? Why?

A thought came to me, d'ye see? The Indians— If they find him they'll think that some other Indians killed him. Perhaps enemy Indians from another tribe? Of course that's what they'll think— They may not burn our house after all!

But you're white, Arnaud! You're civilized. White people don't go around cutting off people's heads—

Ah, that's what I mean. White people don't—but I did. Ah, *le cochon!*

He gave the body a kick, and then jumped at the pain in his toes, for the body was frozen solid.

My God, Arnaud—don't linger— Come on! We've got to help Marie. She's fallen down—

They went struggling uphill through barricades of drifts and logs and windy thickets. Breezes danced in from all sides, burning hard against the fugitives' faces, flapping their clothing and blankets, hurling loose snow like salt to conceal the indentations made by plunging frantic feet. In another half-hour no eyes could have discerned that anyone had gone that way.

By midday it was decided that all the Wahpekute should rove in search of the missing Bursts-Frog-Open who was *awanka,* who'd spent the night lying out somewhere or other. He was not loved . . . few in that band knew the taste of love or had the capability for such sensation—except for Corn-Sucker and gentler souls among the witch-haired women. Even His-Curly-Sacred did not truly love his brother-of-an-Eastern-village; but their companionship was habitual. Therefore it irked the tall young man to be deprived of his crony. The two of them had participated in mutual villainies since they were boys. Neither would have objected to slaying the other if inducement were sufficient; but they stood together for long as a vigorous unit, and His-Curly-Sacred was plagued by the thought of standing alone. Also there was the matter of curiosity. Most of the men were interested in learning whether or not Bursts-Frog-Open had actually taken the white woman of his choice. They wondered what he had done with her.

In the beginning it occurred to no one, not even to Inkpaduta, that the missing Wahpekute might have been cut down by whites. Inkpaduta believed that such a thing was impossible. Inkpaduta and his people might steal from whites, might take their ponies and food and women; but they had killed no whites. They did not expect whites to kill them or even to resist. Only a youth might think so.

Since Bursts-Frog-Open was believed to have returned to the Plourays' the previous day, the searchers went there first, with His-Curly-

Sacred and Makes-Fat-Bad leading the way. They were pleased at seeing wan smoke still rising from the chimney, and they thronged into the house exulting in prospects of sugar.

A few minutes later they bent or squatted around the beheaded body back of the stable. All except Makes-Fat-Bad: he had little interest in the dead man. Cattle occupied his attention and enthusiasm. He was engaged in driving the beasts out of the stable and shooting them. *Napcho!* he yelled repeatedly. Tenderloin, good tenderloin. *Napcho!* He began to sing the song of the buffalo hunters even as he lifted the Cochran rifle to fire again.

The saddle bind! Children dear, for half a day–

The rest paid no attention to Makes-Fat-Bad, though they would demand meat later, would never allot him all the tenderloins merely because he was killing cattle.

Suddenly Inkpaduta arose grinning out of the circle. All knew what this smile meant. His sons knew it only too well. They could recall how he had smiled like that when he was beating them when they were small. What he had discovered here was affront and challenge.

How many whites say you?

His-Curly-Sacred said: Two men, one woman. They are French whites. They speak the words of French.

Roaring-Cloud cried: No one can trail! Snow blows! It is thick, becoming thicker–

Aye, Inkpaduta agreed. We trail them not. But there are others of the *Washichun*. What of those by lakes to the north, what of those *Washichun* at Okoboji?

Inkpaduta called in a loud voice: We bite them in two. This is war! –and wind took the words away from his mouth, and set starved crows in the woods to echoing them. *Zuya!* the crows were calling. Make war! *Zuya!*

XXXIV

As he and Joe Thatcher worked on the loading platform of the Waterloo mill, hoisting meal and flour barrels aboard the sled, two big hands slid from behind Harvey Luce to aid in his lifting. A grinning red face, guiltless of beard, was thrust close. Harvey cried out: Brother Bob!—and Joe Thatcher stood amused to observe two stout men engaged in bear-hugging. The plump ruddy youth was introduced as Robert Clark, and there ensued much talk of Ohio. Clark, although barely twenty-one, boasted a religious passion nearly as severe as that of Harvey Luce. He had lived on a farm beside the railroad right-of-way when Harvey toiled in Rowland Gardner's grading crew. The Clarks' deep well furnished countless gallons of drinking water to thirsty workers. Robert, then in his teens, described vividly a life of debauchery which he led prior to conversion. There was no mire of sin in which he had not floundered!—actually he'd committed adultery with a neighbor's wife at the age of fourteen; he'd gambled away money received for a relative's colt sold at the fair; on numerous occasions he'd swilled down an entire bottle of brandy. But an itinerant evangelist came to trumpet warnings in a tent near the Clark home; and young Brother Bob, who attended sessions with a gang of idle clowns for the purpose of jeering, instead yielded his soul to the Master. After that he carried a Bible in his right coat pocket and hymn book in his left; tirelessly he chanted his delight at standing among the Redeemed. . . . Resident now in Waterloo, he led Luce and Thatcher to the new house of his beaming parents. There ensued a feast in which an entire roast of pork and a peck of sausages were consumed, mostly by the visitors. Joe thrashed in the baffling comfort of a spare bed while Brother Bob and the elder Clarks escorted Harvey Luce to prayer meeting, where Harvey testified impressively.

Before the next noon Robert Clark announced his intention of accompanying the Okoboji pair on their return journey.

Joe ran his eye over the big young man. You reckon to take up land there, soon as the weather breaks?

Divine Wisdom'll aid me in all decisions!

Yes, I spose so.

In time, said Harvey, Brother Bob plans to be one who'll carry the Word.

Well, an extry pair of hands and a hefty body like his won't come amiss when we travel with a load like ourn. But I'll tell you again—Harvey's likely told you already—twill be a mean journey. Dangerous, too.

You mean—Indians—?

Aw, these Indians in Ioway ain't nothing but a gang of beggars. I could take my goad, and handle any ten that *I* ever see. But it turned mighty warm today, and if the weather stays like this, ice is bound to break up. Maybe we'll be in spring afore we know it. We got I don't know how many rivers to cross, and some might be in flood.

But the children of Israel walked upon dry land.

True, true, Brother Bob! *And the waters were a wall unto them on their right hand.*

We could get upset and drownded just the same, Joe insisted stubbornly. If all the snow should melt on the way, how'd we manage with our runners? Could only hope to borry or buy a wagon somewhere or other.

Robert's father said: We been here several years, Mr. Thatcher. Winter hain't never broke up this early before, so I doubt you got much to fear along that line. I'm willing for Son Robert to go—think it's a very good idee, in fact. Let him make a claim if he will. He's now at man's estate; and Providence alone knows—he may decide on a secular career stead of being a preacher. I've never regretted our move to Ioway for a minute. What with my gristmill and sawmill and farm land into the bargain— I've prospered and am prospering. So if Son wants to go further west, I'll never discourage him.

I didn't mean to be discouraging him, sir. Just a-warning. Gad, enough settlers come to Okoboji, I can open up a smithy.

Thee we adore, Eternal name,
And humbly own to thee,
How feeble is our mortal frame,
What dying worms are we.

Thatcher shook his head often as they plowed back through renewed cold, over long dun rolls of prairie into Franklin County. He could not understand why men as stanchly built as Harvey and young Brother Bob might describe themselves as feeble. Why did they refer to themselves as languishing vermin, when they were hale in the physical vigor of manhood?

At Hampton the travelers found a loaded sled and three recruits standing ready to accompany them. Jonathan Howe had been instigator of this project: and Asa Burtch and Enoch Ryan joined in. Jonathan yearned for spring and for matrimony with almost equal intensity. It seemed that he might accelerate both season and event by hastening to the lakes for a preliminary survey.

Joe blinked at his brother-in-law. You calculate to settle alongside us too, Asa?

Well, I'd been thinking it over ever since you went on to Cedar Falls. Course, a bad winter is a bad winter, in any condition. But I like the sound of your country out there. So does Elviry . . . lakes and all. Enoch Ryan feels the same way: this here Franklin County's too bare. We all growed up amongst trees, and we like 'em. If you want to stock your region with Howe in-laws and connections, we don't mind being some of the cattle.

First customers for my new forge, I'll be bound!

How's that?

Folks keep moving to join us, we'll have a fair little settlement fore you can say scat. That means I'll set up shop, once I can scrape together enough *tin* to freight in an anvil and all. . . .

However, the return trip was in some ways infinitely more difficult than the eastbound journey had been. On these drift-strewn plains, prevailing winds sliced from the northwest, and stung men's faces and watered their eyes. When toiling toward Hampton and Waterloo, it had seemed to Luce and Thatcher that they were being cuffed, but still shoved along by the wind. Now every gush of air was an entity and an enemy in one, seeking forcibly to restrain them. There was little except hay in the single sled when going east. Now their own sled and the one from Hampton were burdened solidly. Joe Thatcher's critters (rather than Harvey's cattle, these had been chosen for the journey because they were in better condition) were into the fourth week of misery: they staggered under yoke. Twas a question of how long they'd be able to stand on their feet, let alone heave the necessary weight.

A few advantages accrued. Those fresher oxen, yoked to the Hampton sled, could proceed in advance and break the trail when necessary. And portions of the old trail were still visible in many places . . . often the wandering sluiceway would be filled with fresh-blown snow, although no enormous precipitation had occurred during recent weeks. It was easier for six men to push two sleds than for two men to push one sled, when the going grew rough. The going was rough most of the time. Joe and Harvey worked in trance; they said little to the others; soon the greenhorns seemed also to have lost their power of speech. Hours passed with only a few remarks exchanged curtly, under shadow and weight of all space, all weed-studded emptiness on an unfriendly planet that lived without life.

Enoch Ryan was thick-chested, swarthy-faced, big-nosed. (He looked more Jewish, in ignorant but popular conception, than most Jews.) His father's people exchanged the Arra Mountains of northwest Tipperary for the Iron Mountains of southwest Virginia, soon after the American Revolution. Enoch, called Een more frequently, was born in Wythe County. There bubbled a yeasty uncertainty, a frothing for nebulous improvement, throughout blood and brains of these Ryans. Perpetually they made changes, generation after generation of them. (A different lord; another cottage—not better, perhaps, but different; a different county or even country; new hills, new streams to live beside, or flatter land to walk.) Seldom were they able to count a profit beyond the cherished treasure of altered horizons, strange air to breathe, stranger tales to tell. Een went along with his parents from Virginia into Kentucky when he was but fourteen; and when he was sixteen he took his widowed mother to Illinois. There he married, but the frail little wife died in 1854 after losing her baby. Een's mother died the same year. Een became haunted and generally embittered. Illinois had abused him, he felt. He went west to build a sod house on a fork of the Cedar River, in Iowa, a few months before the Howe clan arrived from Indiana. After his marriage to Elvira Howe, Enoch chafed still; he envied the in-laws who'd penetrated the lake-watered timberland of the northwest. He joined ardently with Jonathan Howe and Asa Burtch in opinion that there was no point in waiting for springtime—sloughs would be brimming then, prairies too soft; best get along to Okoboji while there was footing for the teams. Once thaws ensued, the men could put up their cabins; then, when the landscape had dried out sufficiently, they'd return to the Hampton neighborhood and escort wives and children—and Jonathan's bride—to Okoboji with comparative ease. No housebuilding; the houses would be up already, so the settlers could devote full attention to planting and cultivation.

An illusion of future benefits to be obtained kept Een Ryan going, just as had the knowledge that they were saving their families served to sustain Harvey Luce and Joe Thatcher in the struggle of that eastbound expedition.

Ryan endured one misery which did not twist in hurtful harness around the others. That was his fear of ice. Before he left Virginia he had acquired this dread, all in a short hour. He had seen a wreckage perfected by ice (more awful than the injury which came upon Carl Granger beside his Okoboji cabin, yet stemming from the same pale unyielding inscrutable force). Others might chop the stuff, Enoch Ryan would not lift his axe against it. He ignored ice, he blanched as if in sudden sweat (so a dog behaves often enough, after he has chased rattling wagons gaily, and then, in quick shock, has been pinched and lamed by the turning of a wheel. It may be that this dog will never look at wagons again. He twists his head away when they go by, he does not look, he does not dare to look . . . says to himself, There are no wagons).

Mountains of memory and of his childhood stayed with Een Ryan even on the prairie. They were of that lean Virginia portion, ridges like tines of a collection of rusty forks dumped down upon a table top. You could stand on any of the higher mounds and see more enviable and substantial hills toward the west; then you would start honing for the Bluegrass far beyond.

First fitful warmth of spring might come mincing on a day in late January. Might be pockets of snow surviving on northern slopes, and rounded steps of ice would be curving over boulders . . . seepage had not gone into the ground, but had frozen; and then other seepage had frozen atop it, and then icicles had formed from the straighter portions of declivities. So the icicles were little pillars and organ-pipes. You could tap them, if you were straying that way, and make a sound with your tapping. Last discordant tragedy would occur when you tapped too firmly, and the icicle broke into fragments on its dying tone.

But spring crawled and whispered. Grasses said: Yea, we are verdant underneath. There is all this dank brown atop. Watch the freshness come turning up. See? Even as you looked the hint was there, the glance of greenery! So our sheep have found it, studded one above the other on the heights. . . .

Twas a steep rough staircase the sheep made as they fed. You imagined that you could go climbing up a mountain, stepping upon sheep, stepping from wet woolly back to wet woolly back, and the smell of their wet wool would be in your skin and stay with you. It was not a bad smell, though strong and pungent. There was spring in that smell, too; and all other smells were in the spring. Pines and similar cone-bearers were scattered through grayer heavier forests, and all the streams, running under their last shells of ice, were talking of the trout soon to come flirting. Chickens went foraging farther in the thin warming sun than they had gone to feed when snow was there. They found seeds and such edible relics, dried for them through the winter, still good to eat. Chickens croaked this news back and forth in blurting tones. . . . Yes, Mr., if you traveled with your rifle to the Gap, across the nearby line into Grayson County on south, twas said that the lower richer hills were turned pea-green even in January.

Clouds came to meet you at noonday, if you walked nearby through a gorge of musical icicles. The brittle formations were thicker here, more tempting, more tubular; they played a grander tone when you struck them with a stick. A neighbor lass named Vixy Vanting went that way with Een Ryan when he was first in his teens. Actually Vixy had been given the name of Esther; but she had a towering temper, even as a baby; once, in a rage, she struck and ripped at her father, and he laughed and said that she was a little vixen. So they started calling her Vixen. The name stuck, and was made into Vixy round the neighborhood. The girl still had her temper, and would demonstrate it barbarously if any boy said that she might be unable to do the things that he could do. Her fierce blue eyes and thin mouth and high cheekbones went along with the temper and seemed to make it fit. And her hair was always blowing loose, no matter how tightly her mother made her bind it.

Now Vixy had a stick in her hand, she was using it to play tunes with. She claimed that she could play *Pop Goes the Weasel* on icicles —had done so. Een challenged her to do it again.

Down came the ice, first a spadeful and then a cartload, then it seemed like a whole houseful, and it nigh to knocked the two young folks clean across Grayson County and into Carolina.

Enoch was hurled off the shelf where they had been standing in foolish dangerous play. Vixy was under the ice, her left arm broken. Smaller chunks of ice, baby-size, had knocked her flat; then fell the man-sized chunks, smashing down a second later, unable to hold such weight aloft when adjacent props were removed. Een Ryan rolled the splintered boulders of ice off the girl and cut his hand in doing it: the heavy white stuff was sharp as glass. He dragged and mumbled. The wits were knocked fairly out of Vixy Vanting. She was not conscious of any pain for a time, nor could she speak.

Oh, Vixy, he wailed, when at last he had her in a walking position, and was pulling her down the path, urging the tottering limbs into motion, trying to hold torn shawl around torn body. Oh, Vixy, that bone of your arm's a-sticking out, clean out through your frock!

She said, Yes, in a voice squeezed and tender. Twas a gentle sound she made, not at all the wiry boyish utterance to which she was addicted.

But Vixy, you know? Can you hear me? You got your wits?

Again she uttered that mysterious sweet-tempered, Yes, though she walked with eyes polished and glossy as the two-whorled marbles which Een's mother had bought with her egg money, and gifted to him at Christmastide.

These scrawny persons strolled in a new intimacy confirmed by experience of blood and whitish-tissued bone. Bits of ice and snow and yellow clay clung to Vixy's gray shawl as the boy pressed it around her; there were dark places, almost black, where blood oozed through. The sun appeared and proclaimed the spots to be reddish and thus wicked.

Een moved with a pace as congealed as the girl's. (Oh, she'd never sought hurt and mutilation deliberately, she'd only wanted to go playing a tune, to show off to him while playing a tune.) Now he despised the false January springtime wetting the mountains. He had been deluded by drip of fresh-born water under rippled cakes. This region bred him; he should have known its tricks as surely as he knew that he had been nourished on persimmons and chinquapins. Winter still dwelt like a witch amidst gaps and forest crannies. Ice was still here to wreck you! A doctor would have to be fetched from somewhere or other, a doctor with a knife; Een had heard of such people, although he had never seen one. The doctor would take his knife and cut off Vixy's arm at the shoulder. Maybe he would use a bucksaw; for no granny-woman could ever heal an arm like that.

New ice would be assembled, there'd be more storms. . . . Twould be May and June before true spring frolicked, with creamy waxy glories appearing amid slabs of shiny leaves which rolled through the thickets. Enoch's grand-uncle, who had taught both school and singing school in his time, said that the true name was rhododendron, but that was a hard word to say; many called them catawbas, and Een's mother always spoke of them as rhody flowers.

Go tell Aunt Rhody her old gray goose is dead.

Twas not a good song to think of now; but Enoch could not help thinking of it, because the notion of rhododendron flowers had occurred.

The girl collapsed as he tried to lead her through the run below the Vanting house. This stream was no longer frozen: there was ice only among larger rocks on shore, and the water talked freely, blackly. Here were stepping stones to be employed when the stream was at ordinary depth, but there could be no thought of using these now. Een took the girl with him into the shallows, and felt cold rushing around his legs, as it must be washing around hers; then she wilted. The old tune played along with his distress. *She died in the mill-pond, she died in the mill-pond, she died in the mill-pond, standing on her head.* Vixy fell against him, pressing the wounded arm into his side. She gave a snarl through teeth from which the lips were drawn back, her face looked like a fox's. Een Ryan managed to get his arms around her, one arm behind her back, one under her limbs. He hoisted Vixy (he was small for his age in those years). Somehow the boy progressed through the stream with his grotesque burden. Stones bit against his submerged shins as he staggered. Rocks chewed the hide from his legs; he feared that he would fall, and both he and Vixy would die in the water like Aunt Rhody's Old Gray Goose. Later it was told that Een called for help, as he went tripping drunkenly. He could not recall having yelled, but he must have done so. A man-grown cousin of the Vantings, who happened to have ridden by for a visit, came running to take the injured girl in his arms.

That same man-grown cousin rode his mule to the home of Doc Kerry, many slippery miles away, and Doc Kerry returned with him through the night, carrying knives and saw in his saddlebags. Early the next morning the doctor cut off Vixy Vanting's arm, while a horde of relatives stood soberly in the yard, not saying anything to each other about it. In the house there were two granny-women helping out, and one of these opened up a poke and produced a puffball which she had saved along with berries and simples in the loft of her cabin. They insisted on thrusting the small portion which remained of Vixy's arm, thrusting it into the powdery puffball. This was after Doctor Kerry had performed an occult function which he called ligation and which the grannies greeted with resentful headshaking, just as Doc Kerry looked upon their ministrations with disgust. Vixy did not die, though when folks heard her screaming during the operation they were certain that she would die. You could hear her, clean up to the Ryan place. Vixy lived, to sit hard of eye and shrunken of face, to sit and turn her face away from Een Ryan when he came shuffling to the stoop in a spring which followed. She kept a portion of her shawl across her shoulders always (would keep a shawl around her forever. And she would never catch a husband. Everyone knew that. She'd have to be a maiden aunt, living with brothers' or sisters' folks, after the parents were dead and gone; and everyone could understand that, too). She kept the folds pulled more tightly against her unbulging left side—no bulge, because the bulk of the arm was gone.

Howdy, Vixy.

Howdy.

Ah . . . how you doing?

Well enough.

Ah . . . I kilt a polecat yesterday.

Sure enough?

Yep. Shot him down by the run. Pa's gun.

Oh.

You . . . want the pelt?

No.

Right pretty spots on it.

I don't want no polecat pelt.

Ah . . . we're going crost.

Crost where?

Crost the mountains. Kentucky.

Oh.

I come to say Goodbye.

Goodbye, Een Ryan.

Goodbye, Vixy.

He looked back from the edge of the stream (that same gushing ford with the Old Gray Goose rocks in it) and saw her sitting motionless, a skimpy twist of colorless gown and shawl settled against the rubbed post of the stoop. She wasn't weeping, just sitting there. So he would see her indefinitely in recollection.

Enoch Ryan did not like ice. He was afraid of ice, he gritted his teeth when touching ice or walking on it.

Thou, whom my soul admires above
All earthly joys, all earthly love,
Tell me, my Shepherd, let me know.
Where do thy sweetest pastures grow?
Where do thy sweetest pastures grow?

It seemed to Een Ryan and Jonathan Howe that Brother Bob Clark, supported most ably by Harvey Luce, sang all the way from Shippey's Point to Okoboji. Yet that could not have been true; the zealots sang only some of the time, sang only when slashing winds relented and gave them breath and opportunity.

During the afternoon of Friday, March sixth, three households of the Okoboji neighborhood were gladdened by the advent of bewhiskered red-eyed wanderers who came lurching from southeasterly prairies, weighted with packs of provisions.

Explanations were offered quickly.

Lizzie Thatcher's heart went down into her shoes.

But did Jody *have* to stay at Shippey's?

He sets great store by your oxen, Liz, and wished to save 'em. We fetched up at Shippey's bout noon Wednesday, and three oxen had gone down that morning. Took the strength of all six of us men to get the poor critters back on their feet. They couldn't have hauled those sleds an extry twenty rod; we was right lucky to be close. So Joe and Asa are staying with sleds and cattle, and won't try to drive 'em out for a week at least.

Lizzie blinked rapidly, and Lydia Noble came to hug her. Now, Liz, you wouldn't want Jody to lose his critters? And loads of groceries and stuff?

Course not. It's just been so long, that's all.

Jonathan Howe feared that the toes of his right foot were frozen, he wished to push on to his parents' cabin at once. Accordingly Een Ryan remained at the Noble-Thatcher place (more room there than at the Howes'); and the rest went ahead, with Brother Bob and Harvey Luce assisting the handicapped Jonathan by turns.

That evening Morris Markham received tidings from Ryan which gave him satisfaction. Morris owned but a single yoke of oxen. He'd bought them in Franklin County the previous year, along with a two-wheeled cart in which his possessions—traps, guns, and ammunition, mainly—could be freighted to the lakes. The team, named Free and Mont at the whim of a previous owner, had strayed away during the late warmth of November. The initial storm of winter covered their tracks before Morris could go searching. He held to the belief that they had frozen or starved somewhere on the prairie; but now he pricked up his ears when Enoch described two beasts which the travelers discovered, lean but living, in a grove as they trailed on foot from Shippey's.

You say they're both kind of tawny?

Yes, but one's darker than tother.

That could be Mont. Happen to notice any brands?

They wasn't too skittish and we got a good look. We wondered how they happened to be there. They was branded on the left flank, both of them.

Morris explained: Feller I bought them from was a Free-Soiler who got drove out of Kansas. He raised his oxen in the Kansas country, and most everybody brands there. His name was Underwood. So he made his mark to be a straight bar with a U right below it.

That's what we seen.

Be danged.

Alvin Noble said, Well, you got your critters raised up from the dead, Morris. When you going to seek them?

Tomorrow, if tain't storming.

. . . Don't get lost, Morris, they said to him brightly in the dawn.

He had to go burdened, twas tempting Fate to go afield unless you carried the few needfuls: rifle, knife at the belt, small axe at the belt, blanket-pack, and sack of victuals. Flint-and-steel. The few needfuls. But weighty. Oh, yes, weighty.

Like a soldier, so burdened. Kind of.

Don't get lost, Morris.

Now, I just won't.

Hope the wolves hain't et your critters fore you get there!

Ain't no wolves about.

Hope the Indians hain't stole them.

Ain't no Indians about.

Bright the air, hard the prairie crust, long the fresh chill shadows, glaring that risen sun. Might warm up a trifle, this very day. And tomorrow too. Couldn't go on being such mean weather forever. Man couldn't trap in the springtime, course. But there never was such a winter before—what everybody's still a-saying—and probably never will be again.

Farewell, Een Ryan, lean-to mate and bedfellow of a single night. Farewell, frail Lizzie. And goodbye to you also, O Liddy with the light laugh, the sweet small eyes, the fruity mouth.

I never had a spat with Liddy in my life.

Course not. Nobody could.

Farewell, Baby Dora, waiting for the Pa who couldn't come, who had to rest his oxen; and Uncle Asa had to stay there too, down to Shippey's Point.

But you ain't going that fur, Morris. Only going fur as the grove of timber which Een marked out for you with a stub of lead pencil in the firelight.

Goodbye to you as well, owlish J. Q. A. Noble who's now reformed, who's a big boy now and doesn't pee-pee when he's quilted up aloft.

Farewell, mild-spoken Alvin with long-calloused hands and solemn poet's gaze. . . . Can't even shoot a squirrel? You'll never make a hunter.

Might warm up a trifle. And tomorrow too. . . .

Ain't no Indians about.

Morris, don't you get lost.

I won't.

XXXV

Shortly after Luce and Thatcher first departed for the settlements, the wandering hunter Jo Harshman had moved in with the Red Wing Company. Harshman was not well acquainted with any of the Okoboji dwellers except Morris Markham, who had encountered the old man many times during previous months. But he was liked by Gardners, Mattocks, and Howes, having taken a meal or spent a night at each of their cabins previously (impelled by his fondness for children). There was more room for him at the Red Wingers' house. The bunk of William Granger, above that of Carl, stood ready to receive a guest. (While constructing the cabin, the Grangers suggested building a series of bunks, such as they'd seen on shipboard. Bert Snyder agreed that it would be a space-saver if they did this, though he wrestled Harry for the privilege of a choice when it came to their own corner. Harry won that particular encounter; he demanded the lower bunk; he feared to fall out of bed in his sleep, and also disliked clambering up and down. Bert insisted that Harry had attained nothing: the air was infinitely better upstairs!— What would happen to the man downstairs if the man upstairs should wet the bed, or become nauseated in the night? Ah, Bertell would have chosen the upper bunk if he had won the fall!)

Harshman appeared one day during the first week of February with a rawhide string wrapped around the base of an index finger. Pretty nigh off, he said in an unimpressed tone. Blame axe slipped when I was chopping. If I'd been too fur away I'd of finished the job then and there, but I figured I could make your place by today noon. Reckon you can sew her on for me, Doctor? . . . He had traveled from Okabena Lake, up in the Minnesota country. He owned snowshoes and could flap along at high speed. He had not thought of going to Springfield; he said mildly that he didn't like Doctor E. B. N. Strong—couldn't abide the man no way.

Isaac Harriott examined the wounded member, and shook his head. No good. You've kept this thing tied up too tightly and too long. Look: the effused blood is putrefied.

Hate to lose a finger.

Say part of a finger. We'll try one joint, the top one—distal phalanx.

But see these shattered fragments! And I don't like the smell of this colored serum oozing out.

It don't smell too pretty, that's a fact.

My preference would be to take off both the first and second joints—distal and middle—and leave you merely a stump: the proximal. But if you don't mind experiencing a second operation—and you may have to, I warn you now—we'll try one joint only. Maybe we can save enough skin to make a satisfactory flap, maybe not.

Glad it's the left hand. Tain't my trigger finger.

Harshman drank a cup of brandy and the work proceeded at once. Bert acted as surgical assistant. He announced afterward that this was the first amputation to occur in the Harriott Free Public Hospital of Spirit Lake City. There appeared to be insufficient tissue left to close the raw area properly. But to Harry's satisfaction the smell of effused liquid became less offensive daily, and there seemed to be no absorption of poisonous fluids into the patient's circulation.

When relating his triumph to Alice he recalled previous conversations. The mention of phenol entered significantly into his report.

. . . Wasn't that what you said all along? Twas your thee-o-ry.

. . . A theory isn't a proven fact, woman. This isn't a proven fact yet, not by any means; though granulation's progressing at a favorable rate. But who knows what other factors are involved? I should need to employ the same procedure in many other cases before I proved anything.

. . . Reckon you will. Harry—

. . . What?

. . . Keep a-whispering, so's no one can hear, there in the cabin. But— Am I *showing* anything as yet?

. . . To my practiced eye, yes. Probably just because I know! To the gaze of others, no. You're a biggish woman, dear Allie. Little women show it more.

. . . How soon do you think the weather'll break? So's we can go and get married.

. . . Harshman says it's going to be meaner and meaner. Says twill be the latest spring ever; and he's been in this Iowa country for nearly thirty years, and knows Indian signs and portents. Don't you worry, More-Precious-Than-Rubies! Tis an old saying, and known well in my profession: the *first* baby can come any time. The rest take nine months.

. . . Reckon Mr. Harvey Luce will be upset.

. . . Too bad *he* isn't eligible to marry us. But he's not here now, anyway. How do you think your parents will—react?

. . . Oh, Pap'll cuss and rare around. Mam'll tell him to shut up, and claim she knew it all the while.

. . . Would Big Jim get out his shotgun?

. . . Not less you jilted me.

. . . I have every intention of doing just that. What are the chances of a kiss or two, before we go shivering back inside?

. . . Chances are right good.

In any but bitterest and most blinding storms, Harshman would rather have been among trees than forted up against the cold. He was old, no one knew his age, never did he volunteer the information, perhaps he did not know his own age for a certainty. A quaint lilting, almost deceiving, smile lived forever on lips hiding under the tobacco-painted beard. Jo Harshman chewed tobacco except when trapping or stalking. He explained that the necessary expectoration would leave a deposit and odor to affright the animals.

Following surgery performed on his shattered finger, Jo had been welcomed as a fellow winter-prisoner along with the younger men.

There bean't naught to trap or hunt in the wood now. (This was Carl's opinion.)

Said Harry: Why not stay till winter breaks? We've plenty of room.

Said Bert: If you are to stay with us, we receive more of the entertainment than appears in a Reading. To speak most frankly, I am sick unto the death of this Hiawatha! He is silly.

Better not let Mr. Gardner hear you say that, Bert. He's devoted to Hiawatha.

But, Harry, Hiawatha is too much of a perfection. Never does he do anything wrong! With the mittens of magic: he takes rocks and grinds them into powder. He has also the moccasins of magic; he walks a whole mile at each step he takes. He finds the roebuck, and kills him dead instantly with his very first arrow. I will now venture the assertion that the roebuck is a European deer of the genus *Capreolus,* and is not to be found in North America. Only by Hiawatha is the roebuck discovered here! Does Morris Markham find him? *Mais non!*

Jo Harshman asked: What kind of critter's that? You say a deer?

Bert tried to explain about the roebuck, Hiawatha and all; he recited Longfellow's version of the porcupine's quill-shooting proclivities. The hunter snorted. Don't have much chance for the reading of books, he said. He added slowly: Ruther than the opportunity to read, I'm glad the Lord give me a keen pair of eyes. I've used 'em, and used whatever little brain was in my skull as well. I like to go around watching things happen, watching what critters do by themselves and with one another, and then thinking about it afterwards.

He said: Thankee for the invite, gentlemen. I'll move in. Ain't bite nor profit in the timber just now.

Jo was gone away before any of the young men stirred, the next morning. It must have been dead dark when he left, but twas a clear night with stars. No one worried about him during the day except Harry, who growled that the old man would probably bruise his mutilated finger, and the whole job would have to be done over again, with Harshman now losing the second joint. At dusk they heard a rapid click and crunching of snowshoes, and Lee galloped to head a welcoming committee. Harshman never told them where he had been; he must have traveled all day long (he snored heavily that night, which most times he did not do). He'd fetched, as his contribution to the larder, a bag of solid pemmican weighing all of twenty-five pounds, and the skinned carcass of a lynx, both frozen solid. This critter, he said, ain't no ordinary bobcat. Tis what they call a lucivee up Pembina way. I been there too, but long ago. . . . He was amused when they told him about Markham's Okoboji veal and the mystery surrounding that meat. . . . Wildcats in this region ain't too good eating. But up yonder, and all through the Red River country and beyond, folks set great store by the lucivees—white folks as well as Injans. Don't get many of them big gray fellers down here, cept in a real bad winter like this. They go a-prowling long distances, hunting for a meal. I was lucky to shoot this one.

Where had he hidden the pemmican and lynx carcass, how had he secured them against the thievery of hungry animals?

I got my ways.

He'd been named John to begin with, but neighbors called him Jo when he was small—kind of a joke, he guessed it was—so the name stuck and he used it. In some ways he reminded Harry of Doctor Maws—mostly because of his flow of picturesque reminiscence. But in body and physiognomy he might have served as a symbol of the ancient capable woodsman. He stood nearly as tall as Bert, but now his shoulders had bent and drawn into twin peaks, his neck was twisted slightly, he carried his head bent forward as if searching for some treasured object which he had but recently lost and was confident that he could rediscover. Harshman's snapping brown eyes held the same delightful coals which scintillated in Liddy Noble's gaze. Children felt that he was going to chuck them under the chin when he approached, and usually they were not disappointed. Yet no one ever called him Uncle Jo—he seemed too undomesticated for that, too much a dried-out springy tenant of the thickets. . . . If Sardis Howe had felt inclined to draw a rotund traditional Giver of Gifts, she would have sketched promptly the common conception of St. Nicholas or Father Christmas—beaming, round-bellied, red-robed. Had she been asked to sketch a solitary elderly rifleman who'd spent fifty years in sliding quietly through woodland gullies, a passable portrait of Jo Harshman would have been traced by her pencil. His kinky beard and mustache were wide at the top, the beard went to a pointed tuft below his throat. That throat was browner than long-used leather, and seemed to possess an unusual endowment of visible cords and a remarkably protuberant larynx. Jo wore charms around his neck on greasy strings, or carried deep in mysterious pockets. . . . When Harry cut away at Harshman's finger he said nothing (like any good surgeon he did not speak, except to direct or request, when in the process of operation) but he was amazed at the toughness of the integument, the ligaments and muscles: the most resistant to the blade which he'd ever seen. In intimacy of their dwelling the three young men saw portions of Harshman's body exposed; his body was that of an athlete who might have been staked out and weathered, warped this way and that by sun and moisture, but toughened immeasurably in the very process of drying. Most times he did not move quickly, but you thought that he sped like a weasel when he was twenty. There were bleached wads of scar tissue gnarling out of his hide here and there; he did not speak of these scars, did not try to explain them except in the most casual manner when telling a tale (you wondered which scar was the one he meant in that particular reference). The little toe on each foot was gone, frozen years since; he'd cut them off himself when gangrene began its rot. No wonder that he made light of his most recent amputation. Jo Harshman had been subject to the usual variety of perils bound to beset anyone who'd go for a soldier with a riffraff gang of Tennesseans while still a boy—who'd accept his native bottomlands as playground and workshop (but later march in a northwesterly direction to choose other thornier patches where not many people moved, where snakes and ague were the order of the day). In Jo's own opinion, the most dangerous moment was when his canoe tipped over in a flood, and, drenched and palsied, he clung long to a bending loosened tree with an Illinois river boiling and crawling closer every minute. Tall young feller rode a log down to take off Jo Harshman and the friend who shivered with him. Twas a mean cold day, with water brown as glue. The tall young feller who plucked them off had a rope attached to his log; people on the bank heaved hard, and hauled the three of them to safety. Jo thought he minded still the tall young feller's name: they called him Abe. He wondered what had ever become of him. Abe Lincoln, or something like that.

The return of Harshman to Okoboji meant much to the Gardners, for he fetched news of Eliza. He had lingered briefly at Springfield only a fortnight before, and could report the girl as appearing in good health and spirits. No, he'd not been to the Strong place (he twisted his face whenever he mentioned Doctor Strong). But Henry Tretz had escorted Eliza to the home of Harshman's cousin, one Sunday afternoon, to see if the visiting hunter might have news of her family.

We talked quite a spell. Seems like young Tretz is squiring her, these days.

Pa and Ma hain't never seen him, cried Abbie breathlessly. But I seen him at Clear Lake. I used to tease Liza bout him.

Reckon you can still tease her, then, child, for he seems to be a devoted swain.

Frances Gardner was kneading her apron with her hands. And you'd consider him a real respectable young man, sir?

Pears respectable as they come. He's a regular Dutchy, course—square-headed and all. But sturdy and polite.

And Mrs. Strong had her baby all right?

Yes, doing fairly well, I hear. Mother and child both. But she's the puny sort. Don't help her none being married to that blow-hard.

Never was Harshman the uncommunicative hermit of legend. He loved to talk, and often his speech had the cadence of verse—almost as if he practiced the lilt and flow of words when he roved alone. To Bert Snyder he seemed a living storybook, a scroll of articulate rationality and observation. With his advent as a fellow resident in the hard-run community, the Readings soon changed their character. Jo Harshman could read but he much preferred the art of the spoken anecdote.

He loved to share human company, twas another of the amiable puzzles in his nature. Harry and Bert discussed the fact.

But it is a drollery! If he desires to be among people, why with deliberation did he choose the forest for his existence?

Maybe he didn't like people so well when he was young.

So, in dwelling constantly in the wilderness, he came to appreciate humanity?

Couldn't that be true? Morris Markham: take him. He's peculiar but he has— Serenity. Maybe old Jo acquired serenity only after he'd been a hermit for a long time. Then he discovered that he liked folks after all; but twas too late for him to change his way of life.

I enjoy to hear his tales of the Black Hawk Purchase, and of the Honey War!

When the folks in Iowa Territory marched out to fight the Missourians?

Très bon! And something else: there is not much food in our region now, until the sleds make their return; but there is much worry—

Nobody's fallen sick, Bert. Not yet, praise the Powers That Be.

But when *l'ancien raconteur* speaks, worries are instantly forgotten! They listen in rapture.

Ever see anything like the way that stump of his is healing up?

It is because you are the great doctor.

Ah, hush. You and Allie—you spoil me with praise.

Harry noticed that Bert fell silent, immediately on the mention of Alice Mattock's name. It seemed that Bert had done this a number of times of late, and it gave discomfort to Harry. Was it possible that Bert had, in some fashion unperceived, discovered the fact of Alice's pregnancy? And that he disapproved so severely, and felt that Harry was so much of a sinner, that he could not bear the slightest reference to the young woman? Very un-Bert-like! That couldn't be it; but, if not, what was the matter?

Might Bert also have fallen in love with Alice?

That was a wretched thought. Best not entertain it, not for one second. Fret about the absent Luce and Thatcher instead, start fussing about what might ensue if the two men were lost and stiff upon the prairies. More sense to such apprehensions, they had a sounder basis. Twas wise to start considering what the families *would* do if that supply sled failed to arrive.

Harry heard the two thin horses whickering hungrily in their trampled pen beside the stable. He went to drag their meal of prairie hay from a dwindling stack.

Bout ten twelve year past when I was dwelling in the Red Rock country, we had a man there by the name of Henry Lott. Some folks spelt his name with one *t* and some with two—them as could spell at all—but I don't know how he spelt it, nor if he cared. He might of been a direct descendant of the Lot in Genesis, for he was a wretched sort clean through. And so was the Lot in the Bible bad: slept with his own daughters, you'll recall; though maybe twasn't his fault truly, since the daughters got him blind drunk in the first place, and probably he didn't know just who he was sleeping with, or if he was a-sleeping. I mean the Bible Lot, not Henry. But Henry he was bad in other ways. I run a line nigh to his place and so I kept an eye on him. I didn't want to lose no fur, and didn't care for Henry's looks. He claimed he was a horse dealer, but if you substituted still another word for dealer—one that rhymes with it—you'd be closer to the truth. Often two, four, six horses hid off in the brush alongside his house; and then they'd vanish in the nighttime, taken off somewheres or other; and come another week there'd be some different horses. With his rat face and shady acts, for all of that he had the nicest little wife I ever see. Brown-haired woman with soft eyes, and gentlest manner with her children. Well-spoken, too. You looked at her and you thought: There's a lady. However, you would wonder, did a gentlewoman get herself hitched up to any sneak like Lott? Oh, the ways of love are stranger than men can conclude! You know, I've always held a liking for these pretty bugs, the flying kind. Butterflies and such. I've set in forests by the hour, also, watching beetles push a little wad of dung, or watching ants go hustling with their provender. . . . One time I come acrost a beauty, a night-butterfly (what some men call moths, though I think moths are only millers). It had just crept from its cocoon, the little wings all wet, and bright and lovely with their soft dressed buckskin color; and little lace of pink out towards the edge . . . lopsided circle like an eye of blue on lower wings. I set and watched that little lady for so long. She pumped and pumped her tiny wings, they grew and grew. See, they tote blood or juices or whatever, right inside their bodies when they come a-busting from the damp cocoons. They beat and buzz their wings faster than you can see, and wings grow large and fair, right there before your eyes. Not many folks know this, I reckon. It's like they were a-pumping all that liquor, forcing it into hollowness of their wings; and so they do; and in maybe a quarter-of-an-hour-like those pinions they have growed from just the size of your thumbnail to where they're maybe five six inches clean acrost. You watch a thing like that and you'd never doubt the story of Our Lord when he come forth from His tomb, for tis a Resurrection every time a bug like this gets born. Anyway, I took the pretty critter long with me, for she weren't dry and ready for to fly no way—not yet, not till evening. Twas a She all right, her body was just a-puffing out with eggs. Come night I unfastened the hat I'd carried her in, drew out the thorn with which I'd pinned the brim together, and I tied that little lady around her body with a soft string of yarn. Not so's to hurt her—not too tight—just firm enough to restrain her, so's she couldn't fly away. Once she was mated I'd unloose the yarn, and let her go about her business of a-laying eggs on all the leaves of willows or the maples. Anyway, I set up to watch the romancing, and if that weren't a sight! I had some scraps of old mosquito bar within my pack, for skeeters they was awful bad that June, and nights I had to tent the stuff above my face to get some sleep. So I kept my Miss Night-Butterfly all jailed, and couldn't a single male get at her, long as she was in that sack of skeeter bar. She didn't lack for suitors—no, not she. If there was one I reckon there was fifty. And all her kind—the same tan shades, with winking eye-marks on the wings—for bugs don't breed acrost the way some people think they do. She sends her strong fierce odor down the wind; she tells them that she's there and live and ready, she says This Is the Strength of Life I'm spraying out to you, she says Oh Come and Share That Life With Me, and Make My Eggs To Hatch When Once I've Got Them Laid! You seen these big bugs breed, perhaps?—they do it bottom end to bottom end, and clinging eye to eye so long; and when you see their eyes in torchlight glow or firelight, it's like their eyes were gems or coals of fire too. I said that there was fifty? Maybe more—I couldn't scarcely guess. They hovered round that sack of skeeter bar where I had hung it on a bush, and they were saying, Let Me At You, Darling, Let Me At You. Oh, Look At Me—I'm Prettiest—No, no, he ain't— Just look at *me!* A cloud of flipping silky wings they were, their feelers standing out like antlers; for in this kind the males have antlers that would put an elk to shame: look just like a branch of pine. I joyed those dancing males for long; I couldn't sleep and didn't want to. Just so charmed at watching all the silent whisper of their wings, the rustle of the mass of them. Then finally says I to myself,

Jo Harshman, you're the meanest of the mean! Now don't you interfere with Nature any more, no matter how you like to watch them hover and to whirl! So then I let her out, and tremulous she crept amongst the leaves. And who did she select? You'd never guess. Here were these scores of huge fine fellers, perfect as to wind and limb, with all the pollen flying from their bodies as they whipped their wings, and saying, Lady, look at me! Oh, look at *me!* A dozen, certain, that you'd think were ath-a-letes or chieftains in their strange dark world of night, and vaunting all their hardihood. And to which one did she say: I love you. Marry me! . . . I liked to spank that lovely thing, I was so peeved. A measly little squirt—one feeler broke half off, and half the colored powder knocked from off his wings. I reckon he was lame as well, and couldn't fly but only at half speed. Here was the cream of all the forest hovering, and *that's* the one she took and tied to. Ways of women, they are strange. So be it. Come the morning, there she was, still tied upon the bush, but Husband he had left; and when I come he rose up from the place where he was resting, and winged away lopsided in the dawn. You flea-bit little pup!—I says. Just like in life of folks: you've planted all your aimless weak-kneed seed within the body of a splendid girl, and future generations bear the cost. So then I cut the yarn from off the Mrs. and I let her go to laying.

You'd wonder why I tolt you this, about the bugs? Well, that's the story of the Henry Lotts as well. When Mrs. Lott was young I'll warrant you that any man with ginger in him would of wanted her. (I met another such a one—oh, years before—in Davenport. She'd run off with her father's coachman; and he was fat and ugly, quarrelsome too; he couldn't hold a job of work, because of kissing Betty all the while; and she was scrubbing in a tavern, making beds and emptying the pots, to feed a man like that! Again I say: the ways of womenfolk are queer.)

I went there first—the place where Henry Lott was living—to ask the lend of needle and of thread. I'd broke the only needle that I owned. Being kindly like, she did the sewing for me: I had tore my clothing bad. I'm kind of one to play with kids, and so I played with her'n, and tolt them stories . . . give my favored one (his name was Milt, and he was maybe eight years old) a handful of some basswood buds I'd picked, and showed him how they was so good to chew. Old Lott, he weren't to home, but course I come acrost him later on. You looked at him and you said Rat right off, or maybe you said Skunk or something worse. And later on, his wife she tolt me she was kin of some old governor back East . . . I mind the name, twas Huntington. Well, here's a lady gently born, and she's a slave to some rapscallion in a shanty nigh to the Des Moines— Dirt floor, by gad, that's all they had! Though I have seen him gay and treating, putting out hard coins and buying liquor for some soaks, to maybe separate them from their horses later on.

Sallow and slim and dark he was. You didn't hate him specially because of sallowness, like he was suffering from yellow janders all the while— Nor for his cold and angry eye— You hated him because he was the breath of evil. Like a wind from out a thicket where an animal is laying dead, and laying dead too long, you got the taint of him if you had half a nose. I used to pass their dooryard frequent, cause I had some deadfalls long the valley which began beyond; and oftentimes I'd see that woman with a blackened eye or with her face all bruised, or see the children cowering from Pa.

In '46 the neighbors paid a call on Henry Lott. They fetched their guns along. They said, You're moving, Mr.

Where? says Lott.

Oh, anywheres, they says, but *here*. Cause if you ever come again to Marion, there's one direction you'll be moving further, and that's *up*.

They showed him that they had a coil of fresh new half-inch hemp. They says, You're gone as of a Sunday! So he had to be.

He loaded all his truck and family. I've heard folks tell, that seen them go, how Mrs. Lott was crying . . . like she'd never see Red Rock again; and so she never did. Oh, there was places wide and emptier far up the river, with nosey neighbors not a-bothering; so that's where Henry went. Right up through Polk and Boone, and into Yell and Risley, as they called them counties later; or Webster, as they call it now; although I hear they're fixing for to change again.

He built himself a place right next the corner of Yell County. I passed nigh there in '48, and hung around in brush, just like an Injan on the warpath, laying low until I seen him leave the place. I wished to say Hello to her and to the kids, soon as he was safely out the way, and so I done. He weren't a giant man, and I weren't scairt of him account his size. But always he was mean and quarrelsome, and I didn't want to have to shoot him, with his family upon the scene. So after he'd took off, I went and yelped. Did my heart good to be welcomed, specially by Milton. The boy had growed a bit, and he was maybe ten or so, but sadly peakèd, like he didn't get enough to eat. Or maybe he was so beat down by Henry Lott he couldn't prosper any way. As for the Mrs., she went into tears to see a friendly face again. It was so lonely for her and the younguns, dwelling off there in that wilderness the way they did. So why had Lott a-settled there? Twas plain to see: I smelt his whiskey over all the place—or what might pass for whiskey, if a feller had no scruples. And there was bales of fur hung up, but well I knowed that Henry had no trapline. He'd got those furs from Injans for his whiskey, like enough, and course that was again the law. . . . Also plenty horse-sign, out in nearby timber: hoof marks and manure, and some of that was mighty fresh. As I come up the Des Moines River, I heard some tales of horses that was missing. So Lott he'd run them off, one, two't a time, from settlements like Boonesboro and like Pea's Point and such. The Injans wouldn't bought no horses off of him: they'd have stole them, too, if they got half a chance. His wife she said that Lott was gone sometimes for weeks on end, which meant one thing to me. He was herding stolen horses direct across the country, past Boone River and the Skunk, to settlements along the middle Cedar or the Ioway.

There was various bands a-drifting nigh: Sauks, Pottawatomies, and one mixed herd as well. This gang was headed by an old feller what I used to know. His name was Chem-iss-nay or that was how it sounded. But white folks called him Johnny Green, and he was really a good-natured soul, and friendly as a kit to any whites, whenever they'd half let him be. Mind one time I seen a funny thing: a younger whom I knew, right next to Fort Des Moines, he had a little sled, and he was out a-sliding on it. Old Johnny Green come by wrapped up in blanket, fish-spear in one hand and string of fish in tother He watched this kid a-playing with his sleigh. Maybe he'd never seen the like afore, although I've witnessed Injan children managing with sleds made out of buffalo—the ribs, you know. The old chief watched and watched, and I was watching, too, and it was downright comical. Finally the old feller put down his spear and fish, and come to where the little boy was standing side his sleigh—and shaking in his boots, no doubt. If twere a stranger Injan, now, I'd riz right up from out the bushes, for the good Lord only knows: he might have meant some mischief. But I didn't think that Johnny Green had one mean bone within his body; so it proved. He made signs unto that kid, and next thing that I knew, the younger had forgot his shakes, and was a-setting down on his own sled, and Johnny Green was pulling him, and laughing as he done it. It was so simple but still quite a sight: the little pale-haired kid with his yarn tippet and his mittens, setting solemn on that sled, with the old Injan chief a-hauling him. But still it didn't long continue, for old Johnny figured Turn About was fair enough. He halted then, and made signs for the little boy to get from off the sled. Old Johnny set thereon himself; just got right down upon that sleigh, right on his haunches, wrapped his blanket gravely, and he signaled for the kid to pull. Twas quite a load, but surface of the crust was icy, and the sled slid fair. Back and forth then did that kid go laboring, hauling the old Injan chief, and how I laughed to see it. So might anyone.

But tweren't just friendly souls like Johnny Green who stood to enter Henry's life where he was dwelling. For he was up again the Neutral Strip. It run a good share all the way crost Ioway, though people argued bout the boundaries. The Government had fixed it in a treaty with the chiefs, and twas again the law for any white to dwell therein; twas sacred to the Injans and their hunting solely. I asked of poor pale Mrs. Lott, if any Sioux had been around. You know, these ones that call themselves Dakota. No, she says, she reckoned not, but never would have known the difference. I didn't comment much on that. I figured that she'd know the difference soon enough, if any Sioux appeared. I didn't wish to fright her any more than she was panicked to begin with.

I kissed the little girls and give them all the raspberries I had within my pouch, and then I went away. But it was sad to think the Sioux might come.

And so they did, when winter fell again. Tweren't outlaws, nor no beggars like this gang you see around the lakes sometimes, that bunch that trails with Inkpaduta (though they're mean enough—especially if they get to stealing spirit water). Twas Sisitonwans. Well I knowed the Head Man that they had: we called him Red-All-Over, for that was how his people named him—Sintomniduta. Still, he had another name, and better known, for he had blowed some fingers off his hand one time, when he mishandled firearms, and so Two-Fingers was his newest name. Napenomana.

He run me out one time. Most ordinarily they don't give much heed to one lone hunter; but somehow they'd got their dander up on this occasion. Could be that it was thought of Lott that had them peeved! I'd camped within a deep ravine which I called Boneyard Holler, for it was thickly loaded with the bones of buffalo. Cliffs was sharp above, and Injans used to drive the buffalo across the prairie, whooping and a-raising Cain until they had the buffalo so muddled that the dumb beasts never knew just where they was a-heading. Then off them sudden little jagged cliffs they'd go, and meet their doom beneath! Tis wasteful and tis mean, but lots of Injans do it; they don't care—just so they get the liver, tenderloins, and tripe.

Well, there I was, knelt down and cooking bass for breakfast, and old Two-Fingers—Red-All-Over, call him what you will—come up like he had risen from the earth. Previous I'd never heard a sound. He had a dozen more longside him, and they all was cross as sticks. The big old feller pointed south, and he said in his deep voice: Harshman, go! For well he knowed my name. But what he really said was, Hazamani go!—for that was what they called me: Walking-Berry. They can't make the sound of *r* no way. . . . I'd hunted, up that river, scores of times, and no one ever bothered me before. But he meant business, and the young men with him looked right evil. Some of them was scarcely more than boys, and ordinarily them are the worst: they got to kick or cut or shoot to show they hate the whites, and prove that they are men. I tolt Sintomniduta that I was a brother to them all, and offered him a looking-glass—one like the traders sell, you know—the little kind. I often carried such for gifts, and sometimes it done good, and sometimes not. But Red-All-Over, he was feeling mean, as I was saying, and he took that mirror and he smashed it gainst a rock. When that occurred, I didn't long delay. I said, It's good enough. I'm scatted, and I'll go!—and gathered up the dunnage I had spread. I was packing this same rifle that I'm packing now, but in that year it was brand-fire new, and I concluded it was lost to me, when one of them mean young ones picked it up. I tolt myself, You better go while you still got your hair, if you *ain't* got your gun. They all was jabbering. I turned my back and lifted up my pack and started off, and never looked around. But then the old chief hollered: Hazamani! So once more did I turn, and he was holding out my gun, and I went back and got it. I figured I was mighty fortunate, because he had such decency within him, and didn't set me out adrift without a gun.

But never did I walk that Neutral Strip again, until—

I weren't the only one they sent a-scooting out of there. There was surveyors once who crossed the river, with their instruments and chains. I don't know if they was from the Government or not; I reckon so; and maybe they was privileged to come in. They'd drove a line of stakes, the way them fellers do, and they was squinting down their little telescopes and such, when up rode old Two-Fingers and a passel of his men. Less time than what it takes to tell it: them surveyors come a-kiting back acrost the river fast. Their stakes was busted, and their queer machineries . . . I reckon they was glad to move alive.

Well, back unto the tale of Henry Lott. Twas winter, as I said, and desperate cold. Lott wasn't home the moment that the Sioux appeared. He'd rode off with his eldest son, somewhere or other—could be that he was teaching sonny how to steal. I never liked that tallest boy, he was the shifty kind. But she was home—the gentle little mother, with her girls and Master Milton, pick of all the litter. The Injans pounced upon them. Twasn't drunken deviltry or just to be a-having fun; twas serious business with them, for Lott had built that cabin where he had no right to be. Them Sioux, they didn't desecrate the woman—twasn't war; they might have, in a war. But this was just to tell the Lotts to go, and make sure that they did. They pushed her out into the snow, with all her children; then they smashed the furniture apart, and broke the dishes, caved in barrelheads. They carried off the store of furs and any valuables Lott had assembled. Only thing that frail poor lady could have done, she did: which was to sob and wring her hands. But little Milton, he was mighty brave. He whispered to his Ma: The moment that them Injans turn their backs, I'll go for help! And so he did, swift off, a-running through the woods in snow. Pears like he had it in his mind to go for distant neighbors on the river, many miles below: the Crooks and Peas and more. And that old friendly chieftain Johnny Green, together with his band, was camping close, and gol knows that they hated all the Sioux. Young Milton might have made it, if it hadn't been so fur; but he was thinly clad. His Ma said that he hadn't nothing on him but a shirt and breeches, cause the Injans had snatched off all their shawls. Tis sad to think of now: that little figger, plodding in the brush and down the icy stream, a-trying to be brave and go for help the way a grown man would. And all the time the cold around him, getting colder, colder, and no hand to help. So, thinks the poor lad, now I got to rest awhile! And so he did. He found a hollow basswood, crawled inside, and there he rested long. The longest rest of all, which each of us must take some time. But he was young to slumber into his.

Poor Mrs. Lott was raving when her husband finally come—and burning up with fever, so the girls did say, and stricken in her mind as well. But none of them was frozen, for the fire of the burning furniture had kept them warm. Twas night before the husband sallied back, and course the Sioux long since was gone. Next dawn Lott started out to track his son. It hadn't snowed no more, the trail was plain; and so he come at last to that same basswood log where little Milt was resting. I trust he shed a tear or two, though he was only partly human. Wait until you hear! . . . And Henry rolled some rocks and closed the open end of that big log: twould keep Milt from the wolves. We give a decent burial when spring had come—I know, for I was there and helped. But Milton's mother: she weren't there, because she died as well as he. She found her burial on that same hilltop where the cabin stood. One time I went there afterward and set a grapevine on her grave. I'm glad to say it's doing fine; it's clumb clear into nearby trees by now. Some other neighbors took the daughters home, to raise just like their own. They knew that Henry Lott was never fit to be a father to those girls. And so he disappeared, and took the one remaining son along with him. Don't know just where he spent the years that followed. But it was like he went to school, you see, and Satan was the master with the switch.

The Sioux they up and sold their lands in Ioway unto the Government, and that was pleasing to a man like Henry Lott. It meant that he was free to enter these new northern counties. Far far up the long east fork of the Des Moines, was where he went, and course his son accompanied. He sold his whiskey right and left, to Injans and to whites alike. There wasn't anyone to stay him. With the boy growed up at last to help, the man grew bolder by the minute. Now there was movers going through, all headed for the Boyer River or the Little Sioux or even spots beyond. They lost a sight of horses, it is told. And, being greenhorns, most of them concluded it was Injans that had run their horses off. Near at hand most people wouldn't trade with Henry Lott, or buy a horse from him. They knew that such were stolen. So further east was where he found his customers, just as before. Tweren't the same as in his Red Rock days: this was an empty country where he dwelt; there weren't no neighbors close at hand to run him out. Just bands of Injans hunting now and then, and buying whiskey Lott had freighted in from distant settlements. Till there come a settler and his family, a mile or so away, and twas Sintomniduta who had come.

The old man was right elderly by then, and didn't lead his band no longer. He had his mother with him, too, and maybe she was fourteen years his elder: a little squirrel of a woman, nearly bald, and with a wrinkled face, and talking every minute, the way old critters of her kind will do. But the wife he had along with him was young and strong, and they had four fine children. There was other kids as well: the orphans of a friend or relative, a boy and girl. The family had built themselves a cabin out of poles and sod, the way the Injans do up Minnesota way, and they was living peaceful on their fish and prairie hens. Old Red-All-Over's sight was getting bad; but still he knew me, when I happened past. He called me by my name; the women fetched me out some prairie chicken stew; and all was friendly as could be.

I thanked Sintomniduta for the kindness he had done me, giving back my gun some years before. I give him a good ration of tobacco too, and then I went my way again. Twas in the autumn, three year back. Well, then—

In January, in a right mild spell of weather, here come Henry Lott arriving with that precious son of his.

We seen some elk, he says.

And Red-All-Over asked just where.

Why, up the valley, just a little ways!

I reckoned the old Injan didn't know to whom he spoke, for Henry Lott had shaved off all the beard he used to wear. It was the orphan boy, named Josh, who told this story later on, and he related that the Injans all believed the Lotts was strangers.

Why, goodness! says the old chief, or some words to that effect. I'd like to drop an elk, for I've grown old and can't hunt much, and we ain't tasted critter-meat within a month of Sundays.

And so with trembling and delighted hands, he loaded up his gun. The women had to help him mount his pony, for he had come to be afflicted by the rheumatiz. So off they rode in snow and sunshine . . . Henry Lott was telling stories of those wondrous elk, and old Two-Fingers-Red-All-Over traveled anxious for the hunt to come.

They let him live until they'd gotten out of sight and sound, and then they shot him in the back, and left him laying there.

They waited till the night had come, before they kilt the rest. Lott and his son, they painted up their faces, and whooped and hollered, wild as anything, to make their Injan victims think the Sauks had come. They busted in the cabin door and went to stabbing, clubbing. Twas just about the bravest thing two men might ever do. I don't know which thing was the most heroic: to bust the head of that old Injan granny, or to club the brains from out the youngest baby boy. They thought they'd kilt them all, you see; but there was voices left to speak. The little orphan girl was far too quick for them: she crawled in shadows, through the first dread minutes when the whites attacked, and then she scooted out the door and to some bushes where she squatted down. The orphan boy—the one named Josh—was mute and bloody, so they reckoned they had finished him. They doubtless didn't know how many children dwelt there, nor that another one was hiding in the brush.

After they'd done their work and gone, the little girl crept out and tended to her brother. For ten long days them children dwelt among the corpses and the ruins. They chewed on willow bark like animals, but stayed alive. So white folks finally found them. I don't know what befell the little girl, but learnt last year that Josh was living over here in Palo Alto with some folks named Carter.

Henry Lott and son had fled into the south, avoiding all the settlements they could. When they met up with people—lonely places here and there—they'd tell of how they seen a gang of Sauks with war-paint on. Down south of Homer, they attempted to dispose of things they'd stole from the old chief, and out his cabin; but people were suspicious, and they wouldn't buy. When folks got word of what had happened up on Bloody Run (that's what they call the crick where it occurred: they named it so) men took their guns and started trailing. But twas too late, for Lott had managed his escape; and out in western Ioway, he and his boy, they joined some movers who was headed on to Californi-ay. Word got back in time: he died out there, the Regulators shot him. So we folks in Ioway were cheated of the justice that we longed to give.

A wonder that the Injans don't arise and slay us all!—that's what I've heard repeated scores of times. I've even heard that Inkpaduta is a brother of Sintomniduta. Likely it's the *duta* on both names that makes for such imaginings. It's stuff and nonsense, for one is Wahpekute and the other was a Sisitonwan, but that's how stories get around.

I've watched these children round here playing Injan games from time to time—the Mattock kids and little Rowly Gardner and his nephew Bert. I hear them say: I'll be a white! You be an Injan! No, I want to be a white!—cause whites is good, and Injans all is bad—

Two wrongs don't make a right, the wise men say, and fifty wrongs won't make a thing but fifty wrongs. I'd like to drawed my bead-sight fine on Henry Lott before he got away.

During February, Isaac Harriott kept a diary (somewhat sporadic in its entries) to busy himself. He had few patients and hence few professional records to maintain. When he'd performed his share of wood-carrying, horse-tending, ox-tending, and cooking, washing, cleaning—there were still many unoccupied hours. If he'd been able to spend this time with Alice nothing could have pleased him more, but she had many duties of her own, and Harry did not wish to put an obvious strain on his relationship with the Mattocks by being too much in evidence at their cabin. Thus he began a series of entries in his ledger, and planned to copy these bits of information, duly edited, for inclusion in letters to Illinois and St. Paul, the next time mail could be dispatched.

. . . Mon. Feb. 9. Wind from NW strong and steady, barometer steady, temperature 7 a.m. 2 above. Luce and Thatcher gone almost one week, I wonder how they fare. Carl still complaining of headaches and I worry about this; could be a cranial fracture which no amount of exploration can reveal, but I doubted any fracture in the first incidence, and believed Concussion only. Nevertheless he has good appetite, no apparent spells of dizziness, and gets about almost as well as is normal. J. Harshman gone hunting—fruitlessly, I fear. A bad patient, impossible to keep him quiet. But he is mending well. Bert and I tried to cut a new fishing hole where our old one was, but gave up in disgust and right chilled too. Allie heard us chopping and came down all bundled up to tell us J. Mattock had decided to butcher another ox—or cow, I forget which—and he & Robby then engaged in butchering. Gave us an invite, which we passed on later to Carl, and to Harshman on his return. All went to Mattocks at sunset and enjoyed fresh beef, a real Godsend. Tomorrow Bert will convey some to Howes & Noble place, whilst I take to Gardners, as the others will be occupied with final details of butchering. J. Mattock said loudly that he had piles, and feared nobody could cure him. I volunteered but he only cussed and laughed about it. Seems to me his *hemorrhoidal* difficulties are mainly imaginary? Somewhat chillier tonight, merc. down to 3° below. Wish Allie & I were married and in our own place.

. . . Sat. Feb. 14. Not much wind. Temp at sunrise 11 above. Some snow has fallen in last couple of days. Scraping the meal barrel in earnest these days. J. Thatcher and H. Luce gone nigh two weeks. Bert says the latter must be preaching to unregenerate soldiers at Fort Dodge, and thus has forgotten his errand! But I should think it would have taken them this long anyway, and possibly they had to continue on to Web. City. Simply amazing the way J. Harshman's stump is behaving. Couldn't make much of flap, so there are sizeable areas of granulation, but all so firm and solid. Sensitive of course, but excess fluid long since gone. He is a sturdy old buck of a man, and highly delightful as a companion. Calls me Isaac, which few do. Went to Mattocks at noon to prescribe for my patient. Have not been trying internal remedy until this day, but used external glycerine & tannin compound, worked into several oz. tallow. Has given him considerable relief, but thought I should try to *speed the parting guests* (piles) with internal therapy as well. Employed the tried & true which I used for Mrs. Rusk last year: cream of tartar, pulverized jalap, senna, & flowers of sulphur 1 oz. each, with nitrate of potash ½ oz. and golden seal 1 oz. Am trying one tsp. 3 times per day. He is really amusing if you get so you can tolerate his eternal cursing & obscenities; and I think actually a good man at heart. Else he could not have fathered my dear Allie! By the by, she tried her hair after a new fashion, all braided & wound. One Dr. I. Harriott spoke firmly about this and bid her put it back in that great curl which she did in prompt obedience. I started one letter to Pa & Ma, one to Dr. Taney. Don't know when I can send, but just to be writing to them did me good. In honor of what Bert calls Feast of St. Valentine we had squirrel stew for supper, but pretty poor meat, and few *veg-it-tables.* Carl G. almost as loquacious as J. Harshman this night, and telling us about Harvest customs in England. Made us all hungry. Still warmer, merc. nearly 20° as I retire.

. . . Sun. Feb. 15. Awakened late, nigh to freezing, with fire nigh out; all had neglected, since we *yarned* late. On proceeding to exterior regions to get wood (my turn, and overdue, I fear) was greeted with appalling temperature drop to 12 below. And our house buffeted by winds. What trees have not snapped & split in protracted cold are now busily snapping & splitting, you can hear them off in the timber. Bert in dreadful mood. (Same old thing.) Even geniality of J. Harshman cannot cheer. Leave him alone, I say, and he'll come home etc. C. Granger says that when they began harvest in Brit. Isles they blew a tin horn to call the men together, soon as it was light. Then everybody had a drink of old beer, specially brewed for the occasion. He said he and Wm. were so poor when young they scarcely tasted beer other times; and beer-drinking is all the rage in Brit. He says the horn also was blown at breakfast time, at 11 in the morning, for midday or mid-afternoon dinner, and at four in afternoon. Then they ate a special cake called Fourses Cake, thick with raisins. Ah, I wish we had some now. They poured beer over the crumbled cake often, which I do not think I would prefer. Made my way to Mattocks late in day, and found Patient fairly blooming. Much soreness departed, he says, and also the costive condition lessening (I had told him this was essential, and prescribed accordingly). He says not many Drs. could have done this well by him, and that he now thinks I am best G—— d—— doctor in the f——— world. My beloved Allie pays him little heed, just goes on serenely with whatever she is doing. Little Jackson Mattock showed fever symptoms, I treated accordingly. Stayed to supper (stew again, with corncake to *sop* with) and then A. and self took brief constitutional if so it could be called; but too bitter, and still bad wind, and we fled back to house. On way down to Narrows, coming homeward, a great limb crashed not more than a rod behind me. A real fright indeed! Temp. at 9 p.m. approximately 5° but somehow seems colder. Found B. Snyder reading his favorite long-treasured magazine, *Blackwood's,* by fire; and consider this to be a good sign that he is out of his *dumpish* condition or will emerge soon. Lee hurt paw, possibly on ice or in crevice; I soaked & poulticed for him; promptly he tore off the bandage, and I gave him a slight *licking,* & repoulticed; and now he lies lugubriously at my feet, but with poultice *intact,* as I write these lines. At 10 Bert still reading, squinting close through firelight, but grinned at me a while ago; so he is *saved* again! Both others long asleep, C. Granger snoring wickedly. When will Spring arrive? She will be welcome.

. . . Sun. Feb. 22. Bitterly cold for past two days, and angry winds. Can read temperatures no longer, for a tragedy ensued: the case containing thermom. & barom. was blown from its nail sometime during Mon. night, and both instruments broken. Too bad, had thought it anchored securely enough to withstand any ordinary gale; but this was not an ordinary one, and also there was solid ice where it landed. I doubt there has ever been a winter like this before on Earth. On this day 125 years agone was born the Father of Our Country, one G. Washington. Hope his mother enjoyed an easy delivery, and that the weather was kinder than this. Have been thinking about my phenolic treatments. (Thought of them in turn brings recollection of hydrochloric acid & my patient Mr. Flandrau whom I treated in St. Paul. Wonder how he is making out with his Indians up yonder. Think it should be a rather nervous business, sole alone in the middle of a whole wild tribe; western Minnesota Indians said to be very wild indeed. These local fellows, as observed early in the winter & before, are debased, ignorant & pathetic. All they want is food and maybe ornaments. Must remember to bargain with them for a few *Injun* odds & ends, for Ma and also Mrs. Maws might like some beads or quillwork of the Sioux. Or Mrs. Rusk? I doubt it. If indeed they do ever pass this way again.) Laz and Glad looking very sorry. The oxen worse, and that is partly my fault, and maybe Bert's. We both cheat on the hay ration for the oxen, and give more to our horses. Begin to wonder when we must shoot another ox. We are asked to Gardner-Luce abode for a Reading this night, but twould be silly to attempt the journey unless wind abates. It is now 6 p.m. and am just back from Mat. house, and got blown off my feet on the way going, couple of hours ago. So indeed no Reading tonight. Allie serene & beautiful as always, no amount of hardship or miseries ever gets her *dumpish.* I am pleased by J. Mattock's condition—no *piles of trouble* any longer. At least he complains of none. Odd to think that he will be grandfather to my child. I am now fully as eager as Allie for the winter to break up. Ever since December we had planned to go to Springfield, or Des Moines City as some call it, where there was said to be a *parson* in residence—a distance of only eighteen miles or so. But recently J. Harshman informs me that the preacher lingered there but briefly, and went on someplace else; so we shall journey to Fort Dodge soon as weather permits. Frankly I do not think Lazarus could stand the trip, not until he receives proper feed. The man Shippey s.e. from here owns horses, and perhaps can supply them for us. (It may be necessary for me to borrow from Bert if financial demands are excessive; I hope not; *I do not like to be in his debt monetarily speaking, nor in anybody's.*) For reasons which I shall not herein set down, some people might think it unwise for A. to make such a journey; but I say *Bosh.* Her state of health is superb. And I feel superb merely in the thinking of her.

. . . Tues. Feb. 24. Almost warm today, for a wonder, and melting a trifle in sunny places. Have given much thought to a treatment by application of C_6H_5OH, the solid rather than the fluid variety. Trouble is, different samples of the liquid form differ much in energy of action; such has been my experience. Also have observed that the fluid is sold in various degrees of purity. Now, tis almost absolutely insoluble in water but dissolves readily, as I know, in any of the common fixed oils (i.e., olive). But the glacial form melts readily by placing the vessel containing it in warm water for a few minutes. Would that I had some of this crystalline substance in my kit; then would have the effrontery to employ it in my next *case.* Might it be procured in Fort Dodge, whither we shall wend our way for marital rites & honeymoon? If one of the merchants had a respectable stock of drugs, such might be the case. Must make up a list so as not to be unduly harried at the last minute. Bound for a Reading tonight. Bert rode to Howes late yesterday when the breeze let up, in order that horses might rest before today's trip to Gardner mansion (almost said Luce *manse.* Ho, ho). Also plenty of extra feed for them at Noble-Thatcher abode, only one mile beyond. C. Granger has another bad headache. This worries me, as do not like to administer too many pain-killers. Found Mother Mouse and whole family of young in my budget bag: they had made a cozy nest in part of an old sock & the remains of a 5 dollar banknote. I could ill afford to lose the latter, and entertained thoughts of murder. However we are all so amused by the tiny critters that we have decided to keep them as pets, and J. Harshman & I constructed a small cage for our *menagerie* out of splinters & scraps. Bert will laugh with glee when he sees them. But C. Granger said lugubriously, Aye, six more mouths to feed. But later he shared his food with the mother, so that was just talk.

. . . Wed. Feb. 25. Still pleasant. But Harshman shakes his head and says Just Wait. Last night at the Reading he told a most exciting tale (as it has grown the custom for him to do, in place of his taking his turn with a book). Twas in the town of Bellevue, Eastern Iowa Territory, in the long ago. They were trying thirteen robbers & murderers, members of a gang once to be feared; and everyone put a bean in a box. Two sorts of beans were furnished, red & white: the reds to signify a vote for whipping & exile only, the white beans for hanging. There were eighty citizens in all, casting these peculiar little ballots. By a margin of only Three Beans (imagine!) the people voting for whipping won out, and lives of the culprits were spared. J. H. said blandly that he voted for hanging, thought they deserved it. The rascals were then placed in boats, given three days rations, and shoved out into the Mississippi River with a warning that they must never return. J. H. said that he reckoned they never did, either; but didn't know, as he went Southwest soon after. There was much more to the lurid tale than this bit, but I was interested in the trial, and manner of judgment. Bert is in a fine state of dudgeon, he is wholly furious with himself. And why? It began last evening, when we reached the Luce-Gardner house and discovered how mortally depressed the families were at protracted absence of Harvey Luce & J. Thatcher. What can have befallen them, and where are they? Well, we have all been wondering about that; in fact, privately, I consider that they may have perished in this miserable weather, quite unknown to fellow men and relations. But Bert was stricken by thought that *he alone* could have prevented this hazard. If only he'd had sense enough to think of it et cetera et cetera &c. His plan was this, arrived at belatedly: We would have gone on a diet of flesh and bone, like the Esquimaux. There would have been no need for Thatcher and Luce to freeze on distant open plains, no need for their risking death by freezing and starvation. No meal or flour necessary: this was a delusion to which all succumbed in idiocy. Observe the Esquimaux! Do they have grains, cereals, vegetables? Not a morsel. Yet they flourish in more frigid zones than this. *We should have killed the cattle in the community, as needed; all could have thrived on their meat.* Then he, Bertell Snyder, would have footed the bill for new oxen for the entire neighborhood, come springtime. He was wholly serious about this. I must confess that such a notion never occurred to me, but admit it to be sound. He is wealthy, and could so afford to pamper his neighbors (if that is the word). Only a man with his warm heart and eager affection for folks in general might have considered such a course, however tardily. Tis not his usual sulks which plague him at the moment: it is the knowledge that he possessed the means and willingness to do this thing; and did not think of it; nor did any other person, insofar as we are aware. He was close to weeping (indeed had tears starting in his eyes) as he asked me if the little ones, like Baby Mandy and others, could have gotten through on broth, meat, marrow &c. I am confident that they should suffer no disaffection (except possibly a tendency towards loose stools until adjusted) from such fare. Also J. Harshman knows what buds, barks & the like are edible and even beneficial, and has lived on them *he says.* Ox & willow stews? Beef & basswood? Happy to say that the generous Bert did not communicate his misery to all; solely to Allie, Miss S. Howe and myself, once we were departed. I wondered at his silence and unresponse during the evening, then we learned the reason. Today I am torn between amusement, sympathy & regrets, and observe Bertell Snyder to be inconsolable. This is the longest entry in my Journal which I have made (attempted to brighten things up by including the White-Beans-for-Hanging episode) but made a botch of it, I fear. Two baby mice have died, and underwent *cremation* in the fire. Wood getting short. Regard our dwindling supply with alarm. For it means that we must soon go a-chopping, whatever the weather.

. . . Thurs. Mar. 5. This very morning (it is now 7 p.m.) B. Snyder, C. Granger & Self achieved the impossible and took *eleven fish* through the ice, most of them fine big specimens. Ice had grown more porous because of recent milder temperatures, and we were able to open a large hole. We employed lines with heavy weights, going deep near bottom; and for some reason these strange monsters took bait willingly. Yesterday J. H. shot a very starved looking otter, and we baited with its innards: to our satisfaction much appreciated by the fish. We shared with Mattocks, Gardners, Howes et al: and apparently Bert has lingered at the latter residence to spend the night. When visiting the Gardners with our bounty, I found with disquietude that R. Gardner used up all his seed-corn to feed family this past month. They ground it in their coffee mill. He talks seriously of going to Fort Dodge to replace the seed supply, as prairies might be impassable when everything melts. I try to dissuade him, but he is obstinate. I said his folks needed him and so forth. Very well, he declared, he would wait for the return of Mr. Luce; *then* he would go to Fort Dodge. But I wonder if Luce actually will return??? Poor fellow—he and J. Thatcher both. Carl has bad ear ache tonight, doubtless from exposure standing out on the ice. Put in oil &c.

. . . Fri. Mar. 6. Last of mice now dead, and the mother missing. Twould seem that she did not wish to feed them in captivity and *snuck* out and ran away. So endeth our menagerie. Allie says, however, that they boast huge rodent population in the Mattock region, and she will be glad to supply new specimens for our cage if they can be *ketched*. (Her own word for it. She is a perpetual joy to me.) Not much fresh snow has fallen of late. For this reason Robby M. says he will accompany R. Gardner if Gardner goes to the Fort: dark old drifts do not hurt Robby's eyes. When he had his last attack of snow-blindness I dosed him with the tried & true India Prescription which I got from Doctor Taney. Sulphate of zinc 2 grs.; tinct. of opium (laudanum) 1 dr.; rose water 2 ozs. Extremely favorable reaction on the part of this patient, and immediate also. He paid me in currency of which he has a small store. Wish I knew more about ophthalmia and indeed all ophthalmics. But am more interested actually in surgery, and have always been so: surgery and general internal medicine. If Bert builds the hospital I shall use my phenol approach without a quiver. At least in desperate cases. I consider this to be wholly ethical, though some might doubt. And I employed it in the case of J. Harshman. His tough old finger-stump is sound as a nut. Both ears of C. Granger now affected, though perhaps unrelated to his recent traumatic injury. He is quite deaf, and suffers some pain. He is disheartened. Carl said a most peculiar thing today, and I think I can set it down precisely: Come Saint Mark's Eve, I wonder if they'll see *me* going into the church; and will they see me coming out again? I do not know what was meant, nor did he seem eager to explain. Have heard of St. Bartholomew's Eve (from B. Snyder) but never of St. Mark's. Must remember to ask Bert if he knows. But it is midday (at this writing) and he is not yet returned. Doubtless he'll be along during the afternoon, or by dusk.

. . . Sat. Mar. 7. Momentous tidings from Bert. He did indeed reappear yesterday, and bursting with news. Harvey Luce returned, together with the Howe son John, who'd come from the town of Hampton. Also some friend of Luce, name of Clark I think, and another person who remained at the Thatcher place. But J. Thatcher himself remained at Shippey's Point, with his brother-in-law Burtch, and the *two* sleds the party had driven from the settlements. Beasts utterly collapsed, and must rest before they can be induced to complete the journey. So two sleighloads of provender are So Near And Yet So Far. The men who footed it in brought what meal et cetera they were able to pack upon their backs. Great is the rejoicing to know that all are safe. We had practically given up on them, or perhaps twas only myself. Today is a fair day with sun. Later: my especial chum Daniel McElroy Mattock came across the straits to fetch us some bacon—the first we have seen in many weeks, and how delectable the taste! We fried some immediately, and discussed this *viand* with appreciation. Twas brought over to the Mattocks this a.m. by the man who remained at the Noble-Thatcher house last night: another relative of the Howes name of Ryan. Our little community is bulging with newcomers. He brought also the gossip that M. Markham departed at sunrise to pick up his long-vanished oxen, which were discovered *wintering* in a grove at some distance from these lakes. Even C. Granger perked up when he smelt the bacon, ear aches and all. Today and tomorrow I will try new medication—a packing which may bring some relief. But the most remarkable circumstance has befallen our beloved B. Snyder, and will result in a marked change in his existence. I fear it is too complex a matter for my feeble pen to describe in this Journal, but I have never seen him so beaming.

During snowbound weeks Bertell Snyder had written two letters to the parents of his dead friend Eric Pakington, and he longed for the opportunity to post them. He felt that strong inclination to embrace a remembered emotional past which imbues a man in a season when his current life seems running too plainly and without expression. Yet a thought occurred: was this ice which suppressed a stream for but the moment? Come thaw, would there live foam and spraying, a gushing not to be contained?

Already memories of his comrade had grown exaggerated in some proportions and lineaments—too grotesque here, too enriched there, too heroic over all. Bert observed that the lens of time was not the most accurate microscope with which the past might be examined, no matter how firmly his life and Eric's were interlaced before a final riddling volley sounded.

He owned but one inanimate souvenir of Eric. This was a copy of *Blackwood's Edinburgh Magazine* which had been sent by Eric's bookseller along with a bundle of other copies, and, long delayed in uncertainty of delivery, came into Bert Snyder's hands only after his friend lay dead. He selected one issue to save—he might not keep them all for practical reasons. He took the magazine for December, 1848 (twas Volume 64, No. 398)

He said to himself: Eric survives in these pages, although Eric held no great concern for the *Miseries of Ireland, and their Remedies* (he would have cared deeply, had he known Ireland). But he would have read, impatiently and resentfully, the paper entitled *Republican First-Fruits!* Twas written by a pen dipped into a jaundiced inkwell. Will forever the self-appointed pundits report cynically, sneeringly, concerning any form of life which they have neither the courage nor the masculinity to face on its own open terms; and possess neither the inclination nor the audacity to participate in? Aye, forever!—and in the future, as now, there will be magazines sacred to their weakling boredom. *The great serio-comic drama enacting in France since February last* . . . ha-ha, Eric, how laughable was that bullet which found you out? The eager sweaty illusion of Liberty, Equality, and Fraternity is kicked about through *Blackwood's* pages like a poppet abused by an ill-mannered child. *Today a tribe of Sioux paid us a neighborly visit,* M. Louis Reybaud is quoted as having written. *We invited them to join our brotherhood. They scalped two of our brethren. Father, this concerns us greatly. Two scalped and the others not. Where is the equality? They should have scalped us all.* Very well: Reybaud has earned the right to say what he pleases; but the mincing little minxes who find satisfaction in nothing but sneers have earned no right to go tossing their heads and shrugging their nervous shoulders and making deprecating gestures with their hands! . . . What say you, good hardy Eric? . . . Send them to the flower stall, and let them sniff and recoil from all perfume? . . . Ah, they'll never go. They'll perpetuate their own supercilious kind, one way or another; and so the pages of certain future magazines will smell as sour as *Blackwood's*. . . .

But there were lines from Mrs. Hemans included in this copy. When Bert Snyder read them first they struck a somber symphonic echo which affected him for days. He could not remove their private significance from his mind nor did he wish to. It was almost as if his friend, now perished, had stretched a hand from the grave, turned the page for him, and said: Observe. Does this remind you of anything?

The magazine underwent fraying vicissitudes until, in Quebec, Bert found an old couple who worked gentle miracles in tooled leather: they were bookbinders by trade. They fabricated a silk-lined case in which the battered *Blackwood's* might be preserved. This flat pouch occupied the same place in the affection and importance of Bertell Snyder which a medicine bag filled among the Dakota. He had not produced it at Readings during this fierce winter, had declared that he owned no books to offer; all his books were left behind at Red Wing. Frankly he could not imagine any of the neighbors waxing enthusiastic over *Sigismund Fatello* or *Eastlake's Literature of the Fine Arts*. But Bert recalled that his magazine contained a peculiar little sea story. He fetched *Blackwood's* along when he carried fish to the Howe and Thatcher-Noble houses on the fifth of March. He should not force the weakened Gladiateur into a return journey on the same day; but knew that he would be invited to sleep in front of the Howes' fireplace, as he'd done a few times during recent weeks.

Sardis brightened at his coming. It seemed that she usually did, to Bert's own observation. He was not inordinately impressed by the reception she awarded him: he'd never made romantic gestures toward her. He thought simply that if he were a young woman in a lonely situation he should be glad if almost any visitor appeared.

When the fish had been accepted with some excitement, Sardis declared her intention of accompanying Bert on to the Nobles' for a glimpse of her sister Lydia. Accordingly she was invited to ride the outward mile and the return mile, while Bert walked beside the horse. By three o'clock in the afternoon they were nearing the Howe place again, and Sardis, boldly examining the bulge in Bert's saddlebag, discovered the British magazine.

I think you're mean. All this time you had a magazine, and never fetched it along to a Reading!

Twas of the sort I did not believe would interest all. It is too— What is the word I seek? In French it is *ésotérique*.

Guess I don't know that one.

It means— Ah. Sacred perhaps to a few? To a circle of inner minds? Specialized?

What's this magazine about?

Literature, art, contemporary history—

But I like *those.* Just wish I knew more about them.

For that reason I have now brought the magazine. To read with you—not with the Gardners and all—

Oh, dear, it's just useless, trying to have a decent Reading here at home! Liddy and Alvin and Morris came over one night, and we tried. Twas hopeless.

But why—?

Count of my young brothers, drat them. You see, they're too old to sleep through it, way the children do over't the Gardner place. And they're still too young to enjoy it by taking part. Oh, Alfred and Jacob are big enough now—they're round Abbie's age somewhere—and might be all right if it weren't for the younger ones. But Philetus and Levi just put them off. They get to snickering and poking and making noises, and snorting through their noses; just plain acting the fool. Then Pa grows distressed, and vows he'll take a switch to the lot of them, if they don't behave— So how's a body to have a Reading with all such gibber-jabber going on? That night we made out to study all the gods and goddesses in Crabb's *Encyclopaedia;* cause we didn't have anything else to read except an old Dubuque newspaper we'd read to death already—and course the Bible too—but we have that every morning— And emigrant guidebooks that we were sick to death of. Well! I read about Neptune, and we argued about his trident, and whether it was truly like a pitchfork— And then was Lydia's turn, and she tried to read about Pan, and those Limbs of Satan which are my brothers just spoilt everything. It says: *He is represented as a monster, with horns on his head, and the legs and feet of a goat—* That was just pie for those boys. They started in straightway to pretend that they had horns, and back in the shadows they were pretending to be goats, and saying *Baa;* and then Pa had to threaten them with gad and— There's no fit Reading on *our* premises!

I have been thinking. We should have a fire of our own.

Where on earth?

On the outside. In that thicket nearest your house? Suppose I build for us a camp of the half-face. What Morris Markham calls a cat-faced shed?

Kind of like a wigwam?

It is a small shelter with a leaning roof, and is constructed out of boughs. Ah I have built them often when in Canada. See, we have much sunlight left to us. There is time!

Can I help? demanded Sardis.

Fetch an axe and a sharp knife. I shall take some of the thickness of that cedar. And employ the big fallen oak for part—

To the immense interest of the Howe clan, Bert had built his little leaning shack before sunset; also he dragged up a supply of firewood. The boys were ruled away, whatever their pleadings and protestations of good conduct. Sardis declared flatly that there wasn't room for them. After fried fish had been devoured down to the last scrap of greasy skin, Sardis and her mother hastened to do up the plates while Bert got his fire going. Then the young pair, together with the parent Howes, gathered in shelter of the new-cut brush. The fire raged high, was too hot and too close immediately . . . Bert hauled the whole thing further back through steaming snow. At length the party made themselves comfortable, between blaze and blankets, and Bertell Snyder began on *The Green Hand.* No one of the listeners had ever smelled salt water, but this tale was a new one; and they followed it dutifully at first. *In his blue jacket, white canvas trousers edged with blue, and glazed hat, coming forward to the galley to light his pipe, after serving the captain's tea of an evening, Old Jack looked out over the bulwarks, sniffed the sharp sea-air, and stood with his shirt-sleeve fluttering as he put his finger in his pipe, the very embodiment of the scene.* Old Joel and Mrs. Millie were asleep before a half hour had passed.

The natural flair for the dramatic evidenced by Sardis was a source of amusement to Bert. When it came her turn, she adopted the hoarse tomboyish voice of the born young lady amateur determined on an utterly masculine presentation. Had she been able to walk about while reading, she would have stamped and swaggered. *If a fellow was green as China rice, cuss me if the reefers' mess wouldn't take it all out on him in a dozen watches.* Bert laughed without restraint, but still silently and in sympathy, in concealment of his beard. Here was this shining slim creature, intrinsically feminine in every curve of her body and twist of her voice, attempting to transcend the boundaries of sex by a simulated gruffness! Had she garbed herself in men's clothing, pasted on a false mustache, and thrust a quid of tobacco into her cheek, she would still have been no more convincing than a daffodil. *There's some'at queer i' the wind! I thought he gave rather a weather-look aloft, comin' on deck i' the morning! I'll bet a week's grog the chap's desarted from the king's flag, mates?* He kept studying Sardis, and for the first time tried to imagine how she must have looked when she was a little girl. (He did not realize, in whatever sophistication he owned, that when one grows to love fellow human beings, one often imagines what they were like when they were small.) He had played the clown to her in a kind of deliberate relaxation, just as he did to others at the lakes. Suddenly he felt no longer any desire to do so. Why, he thought, this is an earnest joy which never have I admitted to myself before. She is woman and child all together: woman and child in harmony, she does not lose the stature of one state by reverting to manifestations of the other! . . .

When the end of this short story was attained, Bert applauded in a manner which brought the elder Howes into wakefulness and, quickly, retreat.

Don't set up too long, daughter.

Why not?

Cause tomorrow's another day.

I'll set up, said Sardis determinedly, just as long as Bert is willing to keep on with the Reading. I'm sorry you folks fell asleep. Couldn't understand half of what I was reading, or what he was reading before, but twas thrilling about the press gangs—

Bert Snyder, you aim to sleep here?

Why not? You have been generous with robes, and there's plenty of wood—

But if you fall fast asleep, fire'll go out, and you might freeze? Better come inside, when Sardis comes, and spread them same blankets by our fire?

Very well. For I can build up your fire anew when I come.

A mighty and a mingled throng,
Were gathered in one spot . . .

*

None spoke—none moved—none smiled.

*

Your voice to whispers would have died
For the deep quiet's sake;
Your tread the softest moss have sought,
Such stillness not to break.

What held the countless multitude
Bound in that spell of peace?
How could the ever-sounding life
Amid so many cease?

Was it some pageant of the air,
Some glory high above?

*

Or did some burdening passion's weight
Hang on their indrawn breath?
Awe—the pale awe that freezes words?
Fear—the strong fear of death?

So this magazine became a lodestone to draw out compelling memory. Bert saw but one thing when he spoke the lines: Gigouzac, and herds upon the cavern's walls.

Ardently, and months earlier, he introduced Harry to these lines; he'd been appalled at the lack of response.

. . . It is as if Mrs. Hemans had entered the hill, and also observed what I discovered there.

. . . Yes, some of the lines, Bert. But there's too much that wouldn't apply. *The soldier and his chief were there, the mother and her child.* What on earth has that got to do with all the wild animals portrayed by prehistoric artists?

. . . Can you not understand? It is not in the entirety of the verses that I find what I would seek, what I would entertain. It is only in portions thereof—

. . . Well—

. . . But you are stupid!

. . . I'm not stupid in the least. It's just that I think there's so much which doesn't apply—

Bert was more deeply hurt than the triviality of his sulking would indicate. Harry had been disposed to regard the whole matter lightly; he thought that Bert was attributing undue significance to a few poetic scraps! He did not realize that Bert repeated the lines to himself in his mind, often, when he was going to sleep. They were as a prayer which should be treated tenderly, evoked when necessary, depended on, fondled, taken out of a mystic chest and arrayed lovingly. *What held the countless multitude bound in that spell of peace? How could the ever-sounding life amid so many cease?* The very question, the fact that no answer could be offered: these were sufficient to enforce a religion which was pointless yet none the less compulsive.

Copious extracts from Mrs. Hemans' verse were included in a leading article—a critical (perhaps chiefly laudatory) evaluation of her work. Only a person blessed with phenomenal eyesight would have been able to read the tiny type in which the lines were set forth, beside this jumping blaze; the light was too uncertain. But Bert Snyder had memorized the poem when first he discovered it. Now he sprawled upon the tattered bedclothing, journal held open at the proper page; he'd spread the pages ritualistically, not through necessity. His soul was in his recitation. (By this time he prided himself that he could render the lines with almost no trace of surviving accent.) When he finished, he put down the magazine gently upon its leather case, and turned to seek his companion.

She sat staring into weakening flames with her white hair turned ruddy. Unfortunately her first remark gave to Bert Snyder annoyance and a spasm of disgust.

She said: We need more wood on the fire.

Yes, yes, he exclaimed, outraged. You must forgive me for letting it die down!

How could he have been so witless as to consider that this young peasant might be properly affected by verses which were a weird holiness to him? He climbed to his feet and approached the careless woodpile which he'd assembled between old snowbanks. He lifted a dead dry sapling, he snapped the thing into four logs by violent blows against the nearest tree trunk. Still incensed with the innocent Sardis (and himself as well) he heaved the fuel. Sparks showered widely, Sardis brushed sparks from her shawl and skirts.

The man was able to discipline himself into some form of apology. . . . I am sorry to be so careless. Are you burned?

The girl shook her head. Then, to Snyder's surprise, she spoke his name softly— She uttered it just once: both syllables, the full *Bertell* which few people used. She made the name into gentle music as she spoke.

There were both tribute and query in her utterance.

Yes? he asked, still rude and uncompromising.

That is beautiful.

You mean the flying embers? Shall I make more for you?

You must know what I mean: the poem. I couldn't discuss it for a minute. All I could do was just sit and wonder. Bertell, will you please to say the poem again?

He cleared his eyes of the vexed tears which had sprung into existence so suddenly. If you wish, Miss Sardis. The verses are very important to me. I should not wish to have them regarded as frivolous.

He could not bring himself to rejoin her for the moment; he stood aloof and unsheltered beside the fire, moving slightly to avoid a drift of smoke, not looking down into shadows where the young woman sat huddled beneath the crazy lean-to. Bert spoke the title: *The Silent Multitude,* and then began once more.

A mighty and a mingled throng,
Were gathered in one spot;
The dwellers of a thousand homes—
Yet midst them, voice was not.

He gained tenderness and confidence as he went on with this second reading; yet he was startled at discovering that he felt a strong desire to reach down and gather Sardis into his arms. When he'd met her first in the warm autumn, her vivacious energies and naïveté had amused him at first, then engendered a certain boredom. He thought idly that he might be able to seduce this girl if he wished to; then in hasty remorse he branded himself as a worthless wretch for even entertaining the notion. Here was a girl who should be properly wedded to some stalwart farmer or woodsman . . . her warm outgiving little spirit would be torn if he, Bert, were to play any flippant games with her. He'd thought it wise to demonstrate no attitude which could be construed however remotely as flirtatious.

What did he need most of all?—for what did he hunger? For pity—and the appreciation of his fairest reveries. In England while still distressingly young he had persisted in reciting the Hemans poem to a most unappreciative audience consisting of the fair-haired governess with whom he'd formed an erotic attachment. She was untouched, she passed the whole thing off with a nod. On other occasions—in Quebec and again in New York—he had drunk himself to a point of sentimental saturation, and then insisted irrationally on trying to share *The Silent Multitude* with partners whose favorable response could be imagined only by a drunken numbskull like himself. Thus he grew to consider this particular personal loveliness as an orphan thing—bruised, outcast, and not to be produced readily for the common gaze or hearing. Even the faithful Isaac Harriott had failed him, although only perhaps because he chanced to be in a literal-minded mood . . . Harry's reaction seemed a slight and a grievance nevertheless.

At last, in this absurd little rustic kennel, he was detecting a long-sought sympathy so vital to his need.

Only flames talked with their myriad light voices, after Bert had finished with the second reading. He waited eagerly, long . . . the girl said nothing. At length he knelt beside her in order to examine her face. She was almost rigid, gazing past him, past the fire, but her eyes were swollen with excitement.

Her lips moved slightly, she seemed about to speak. Yes, yes . . . she was speaking . . . in a profound wonder next to anguish. . . .

The words came gently from her lips, she shivered at uttering them, Bert shivered at hearing her. *Your voice to whispers would have died for the deep quiet's sake; your tread the softest moss have sought, such stillness not to break.*

It took a moment for him to regain the power of speech. You have read my poem before!—he cried.

Bertell, is it yours?

No, no, no, it is of Felicia Hemans! I could not make up a poem, I have tried. My poems are an abomination! But you must have read it—

Never. Just heard you speak it tonight.

And already you are able to quote those lines with such exactness and—and—?

It's cause I wanted to keep them, just to have. Seems like I've always been able to do that, especially if I love something.

He cried, And do you love more than the words— More than the mere music of sounds— Do you love something else that lies behind?

Tis all a great big mystery. . . . Still her face showed that she was dreaming of it. . . . She said: Tis a very quiet place. . . .

Could you tell me what you see, when you walk softly in this quiet place?

Her eyes were closed. She whispered, Like the name of the poem. The Silent Multitude: they're all waiting.

Bert Snyder's voice was breaking. A Thing Called Waiting. Do you feel that?

Oh, yes, yes—I reckon there must be A Thing Called Waiting somewhere—

Where? Miss Sardis, tell me where? *Please tell me—*

Her answer came very slowly: I don't know exactly. A dark place. Then—seems like someone brings a light, and you can see them—

See who? See who? Tell me—

The silent multitude—

Who are they, who makes this multitude?

Still her eyes were closed. Seems like it could be—all sorts of critters. . . .

. . . At last he took her hand, not fondling it; he held her hand with ease in a manner of reverence.

Must you go into the house and to sleep?

No, she exclaimed. Not yet, I don't want to!

Then I will tell you the story of a cavern.

In this new telling he found tranquility he had never known before.

Throughout most of the following day Bert was content to linger at the Howe cabin. He followed the suddenly priceless Sardis with his eyes, waited raptly for her to speak; he was positive that he found invigoration in each word she uttered. But he earned his keep: helped Old Joel and the boys in caring for the critters, and later worked with Alfred and Jacob at improving the half-faced camp and enlarging its proportions. The boys were delighted with the shaggy lean-to, they planned to sleep there immediately. With gravity Bert deeded the structure over to them, with the sole stipulation that the camp would be available to the elders on any evening when they chose to have a Reading there. When he could think of nothing else to do, he chopped wood. Then the lame but beaming Jonathan appeared, along with Luce and Clark, and Bert withdrew to let the Howes welcome their tall son adequately, and treat his frozen foot. A packet of rice was made up for the Red Wing Company, and Bertell Snyder rode Gladiateur through the dusk, still entranced. He experienced, in somber emptiness of the woods, that proud cool detachment which becomes the apparel and habit of a prospector who has at last discovered the lode which he knew must be waiting all along (it wanted only the scratch of a miraculous pick to expose it!). News of the wandering neighbors was gratifying; so was the knowledge that two wagon-sleds filled with provisions stood near at hand . . . ah, these awarenesses became a joy for the entire community, and rightly so. But in selfish titillation of his own personal thanksgiving, Bert could scarcely admit to proper appreciation. Sardis accompanied him in illusion, she rode beside him into the years ahead. She would be his physician and minister, his guardian, his witch, the foil for his own humors. . . .

He began to sing as he crossed the Narrows, and sang so loudly and compellingly that even Carl Granger heard him through medicated lint with which his ears were stuffed.

Harry, seems like I hears summat. Be it wolves?

Au clair de la lune,
Mon ami Pierrot,
Prête-moi ta plume,
Pour ecrire un mot—

It's Bert, Harry shouted to his deafened comrade. He's in good fettle, too. He only bellows that song when he's feeling so.

Harry pulled on his coat and ran to accompany Bert in the stabling of Gladiateur. He explained that Harshman had been absent, hunting, since the previous day. (Jo had stated no intention of remaining in the woods overnight, and Isaac Harriott was concerned about this. Harshman declared that where there was one otter there might be two beaver; he expatiated on the tasty qualities of cooked beaver-tail. This was the tag end of the mating season, but the beasts might still be moving about; he should be able to get in a shot if he were patient. In fact Harshman did appear later that same evening; he had taken only one beaver. They all thought the rich tail to be savory, but there were not many bites per man.)

Bert was in such a transport that he refused to be concerned about Harshman's absence, Carl Granger's sore ears, or any other problem or misfortune. He stood confident that all his own dark emotional puzzles were near to resolution—so, if such good fortune befell him, then good fortune should attend all his friends promptly. Bad ears would heal up, wandering hunters return laden with game; incoming sleighs would glide creaking to the Okobojis with celerity; the entire neighborhood must soon feast, and bask in the smile of Providence.

Ma chandelle est morte,
Je n'ai plus de feu.
Ouvre-moi ta porte,
Pour l'amour de Dieu.

If you keep howling that wretched foreign song, how can we ever talk?

Talk, talk? Wait until I talk to *you!*

By gol, you act demented. What on earth has happened?

Everything—everything has happened!

Everything good, I take it?

Harry, do you wish to have any riddles of existence solved? You have but to request me, my friend: I will solve them for you! Come, it is not too cold. Glad has his food and water, Lazarus is happy to see him; all is well. The presence of horses keeps us warm. We sit upon this heap of hay. I must speak to you, *immédiatement.* Have you your pipe in the pocket of your jacket? Let us smoke— Here—I pass my pouch to you, and I shall strike one of these sulphur matches brought today from the settlements by *Jonathan Howe.* Ah—you have heard me correctly! The sled is returning, and with more people—two sleds, in fact. They are at Shippey's. I tell you of these facts first. You must know that Mr. Harvey Luce and Joe Thatcher have not frozen to the death.

. . . Soon we go into the house to inform Carl.

. . . But first, while we remain here alone, I must tell you much more. A miracle has befallen.

. . . Harry, do you remember the verses which I love so dearly and which are so important to me, in *Blackwood's Magazine? The Silent Multitude*—?

. . . Her understanding, Harry! It is itself beyond understanding. When she began delicately to repeat: *Your voice to whispers would have died for the deep quiet's sake*— I thought: Ah, I have heard of situations like this, have read of them. But never did I think such a marvel would befall me. Twice I recited, Harry—only twice. Already her memory had caught the words and held them!

. . . I told her all, as many months in the past I told to you the story on the prairie. Would you know what she said, when I related how Doctor Pelacoy ordered: Leave them be, let them be locked in the cave? What were his words? *Let the beasts stay put . . . let them keep a little while longer.* She made an interruption in her clear tone (actually it is the voice of a goddess, and why was I so deaf as never to detect it before?)— She said, Yes, but one day you must go back and open up their jail. They should not be imprisoned forever. Twas that your father and grandfather had no right to claim them, and surely they would have done so! . . . *Mon Dieu,* imagine this if you will! Not imagine— *Believe* you must. This prairie girl, a daughter of Indiana farms, who has never seen a city—whose whole young life has been subject to the limitations of the poverty-stricken and untutored— She knows what is in my heart and in my soul. So the beasts of the twenty thousand years agone come herding into her own heart as well, and she stands mutely to accept their lesson. As if she were a nun, Harry, standing in warm gold of Heaven's shrine, and waiting for her *canonisation.*

. . . I ask for so little and yet so much: I ask for complete understanding. She offers it to me, she is capable of offering it, and more. Ah, her little speeches come pouring like water from a spring artesian, erupting into air. As in those tales recounted by trappers who have been among the mountains at the Far West. There is steam and heat in them– Whence come they, Harry?–from what deep source rise these boiling fountains of hers? I shall tell you. From that vast powerful lake of her understanding and appreciation, buried in all its force within her soul. Why, I have worn a blindfold over my eyes, have had muffs tied upon my ears! Until last night I possessed no appreciation of the gifts of this fabulous creature–I was as a petulant child. Harry, I say this now to you in sincerity: I grew so selfish, so resentful, that I could not bear to consider the happiness which you find with your Alice. I was jealous– Believe me, my friend, I must now admit this to you, even though you will be amazed! I did not demonstrate my jealousy–this I know–but nevertheless I owned it. You had discovered treasure. I had found none. I thought I was as worthy of joy as were you; why was it that I was selected by Fate to remain empty-handed? Harry, think of the exaltation I now feel! I shall be empty-handed no longer.

. . . I am no fool, I am positive that she will have me when I offer myself. We are attuned–it is so apparent. I can give her more than any of a thousand men–than any of a hundred thousand. This you know, and this I know; and this she will recognize as well; she is bound to recognize it. Thank the good God I am strong and still young, I am but a few short years the elder of herself. Can you imagine the pleasures which await me, in escorting this responsive and talented young woman out into wider existence? You should have heard her reading the tale of the sailors–she was trying to *be* a sailor as she read–but never one sailor has she seen! Can you imagine how those eyes will enlarge themselves with excitement as she gazes for the first time upon waves of the ocean? Woodlands of masts which grow in a harbor, the blue wonder beyond? Ah, true, you have never seen them yourself; but you own the imagination, you can believe how it will be. Think of the delight I shall have in seeing her dressed with taste, in style and color! How all other men will turn to regard her– High-piled snowy hair of her head– Think of the gay bonnets she will soon be wearing! So she too will be rich, and what a satisfaction to her soul! For she has every daintiness of nature, every born generosity within her dear heart. Do you remember when we went to our *pique-nique* at the bee tree? The very first day I knew her; and she spoke of things she would enjoy for humanity– Harry, I was limited and insensate then, I am no longer so! She said that when she was small she wished that she might go through the world seeking out ragged children whom she should feed and clothe; and she would remove them from their squalor, and have them washed and dressed, have their hair combed; she would put them into clean beds for their rest, and sing to them: *You are my own small angels.* Do you remember:–she sang then the small song she had made, about her angels! We were as fools, Harry—you and your Alice, and I above all— For we laughed. Not in cruelty—perhaps in some appreciation— Still, we laughed. But in truth she shall have her angels— There are so many children in the world who would benefit from that love she is prepared to give— Her only sadness will come in the knowledge that she cannot feed and possess them all!

. . . The world will be better because in it there is a Sardis. I will be the better because I possess her. For possess her I must; this is essential.

. . . No, not with all the busy family, the throng of young brothers about. This day I said nothing.

. . . Tomorrow? *Mais non,* I shall not go tomorrow. There is no indication for this. Her brother Jonathan has but arrived. Six months and more they have been apart from him. Tomorrow is no time for me to perform the intrusion.

. . . Sunday. That is when I go. It is appropriate to the day of God. I shall go in the afternoon, and that night we sit alone by our dear fire— Where first she knew The Silent Multitude and received them, where she perceived gigantic wonder of them, and so communicated to me. Sunday begins my happiness. Sunday I walk thankfully into an enlarged world.

XXXVI

Undiscerned by any neighbors, the Wahpekute set up their lodges in a glade surrounded with thick brush, midway between the Gardner house and the Mattock house, late Saturday afternoon. *Unktehi* came to Inkpaduta that same night. The creature erupted from its den at the bottom of West Okoboji and emerged through ice. The lake split for many fathoms in each direction as the enormous beast came through. Inkpaduta thought that he had risen in his lodge where he slept in the principal position (beyond the fire, opposite the door) and had circled the fire and other sleepers; and that he had gone, walking high above the snow, not in it— He'd gone out of the camp, past the last stockade of tree trunks with old crusts and meltings making armor on their northwest surfaces— Thin hard wind had knifed at his battered ears and the dangling lousy hair around them; and he thought that a kind of soldier society of naked *Heyoka* trotted beside him to escort, to show the way.

O Thou Old One, cried the *Heyoka,* we suffer!

Why suffer?

The heat kills. Ho-ho! We laugh as we suffer; because this cold is so intense, and causes us to perspire freely.

Where go we, O *Heyoka*?

Go we to Okoboji.

Why go we?

Unktehi comes.

Tis not a true thing which you say! The nearest of such gods dwelleth far up the big river beyond the fort where are the white soldiers, far past the city of the whites, far under the water-curling-on-end which we call *ha-ha.*

Nay.

Then where dwelleth he?

In this place, said the *Heyoka,* and they went dancing away with their bows and deer-hoof rattles, laughter rising stark as they hurried and were boiled by the cold.

Inkpaduta stood alone, but not for long was he alone. Before him stretched the thick sickle of the western Okoboji lake (and all that happened was happening still by night, but the great sweep of white and pearl was suffused with light of its own, he could see clearly even with his sore eyes). Came the sound of a mouse: *squeak,* said Mouse. Came the sound of a blackbird in summer: *ka-ting!* said Blackbird. Came then the sound of a gunshot, came then the sound of a large deep drum, came then the sound of a cannon such as was fired by white soldiers, the very-great-gun-drawn-between-wheels, the *mazakan tanka:* came finally the heaped and exploding sounds of many cannon. Ice of West Okoboji quaked. Gaps were widening, raw jagged chunks of ice rose and teetered. A horn came piercing up and out. It was the color of the horns worn by white men's cattle, but it was longer than is tall the greatest oak. Then came the other horn; beyond doubt these were the horns of the *Unktehi.* Inkpaduta had heard of these horns through all his years, yet even so he was stricken by their mightiness. Then came the head of *Unktehi,* and that head was larger than a hill, the eyes were larger than ponds of water, the nostrils were deeper and darker than caves; and rivers of steam as thick as the width of a lodge were drifting up into the night.

The *Unktehi* stood on all four legs with broken slabs of ice as large as white men's houses tumbling, grinding, smashing off his back as he arose.

O *Unktehi!*

O Thou Old One!

Wouldst eat me?

Nay.

Wouldst trample me?

Not I! (The voice, gigantic bull voice bellowing up to strike sky, and fall to earth, and quiver forests as it fell.)

Nahon waun. I am hearing.

Then hear ye well. Pay heed.

I am hearing.

Ye would slay the whites, Inkpaduta?

Echahe! With my people, I plan to slay whites. We steal, we take cattle and horses and dogs. Many things also we take: guns, clothing, money, food, blankets, many things. We have the white women in our camp. But we have not killed. Now we kill, and take their hair, and dance.

I would have *woshna.* Would have sacrifice!

But I am no *woshnakaga,* I am no priest.

You make sacrifice, all of your people make.

This we do. What sacrifice demand you?

You take no scalps.

How can we dance, after we kill, if we take no scalps?

You may dance, but you take no scalps.

No scalps?

No hair of the whites!

(Inkpaduta thought that he and the god repeated this dialogue, the pleading question and the abrupt answer, for a long time.)

The *Unktehi* named all who were with Inkpaduta, beginning with the twins. Roaring-Cloud must take no hair. Fire-Cloud must take no hair. Rattle-Strike must take no hair. On-Oldish-Man must take no hair. His-Curly-Sacred-Penis— Makes-Fat-Bad— All were named, and Inkpaduta was informed repeatedly that no hair should be removed from heads of the dead white people.

This is the sacrifice demanded of us?

Woshna. This I demand.

Then this we do.

You tell your people?

Aye, I tell them this is the *woshna* which we give, for you are the great *Unktehi,* the god of waters, and your name does signify the most vital energy, and your power is in your tail and in your horns, and you, This One *Unktehi,* are a male, your male orbs are bigger than bull-boats, your *che* is longer than a lodge-pole and thicker than the body of a fat man; and if you were a female you would come from the earth, and I would call you Grandmother; but you are a male and come from water, and so I address you as Grandfather!

. . . O My Grandfather? *Tunkanshidan*—

What wish thou?

What penalty befalls, do we not make the sacrifice of take-no-hair, as you demand?

Unktehi's voice roared, telling him: Evil would come into thy mouth, and the mouths of all thy men. Thus the teeth would come loose, and come out in thy food and in their food. So never again could you eat meat, could they eat meat.

Unktehi said further: Evil would come into thy throat, the throats of all thy men: thus never again could you drink, could they drink spirit water. The good hot spirit water would bulge in the mouth unswallowed, and would be spit out and drooled out, and thus wasted because of evil which closed the throat against it.

Grandfather, is that all?

Is that not enough?

Nay. . . .

Then this I say to you now, and this is true what I say: thy *che* and the *che* of each of thy men would become useless. Twould become as limp and soft as the lips of a woman's *shan.* No amount of the ground-up panther testicles would suffice! You eat bowls filled with the powder-mixed-with-fat, the pulverized balls of the *inmutanka,* as some men eat corn you eat this quantity— But nay, but nay, but nay! The *che* becomes soft as string; and in time it is filled with *wichahunwin,* with putrefaction. And so it rots away. And you have nothing but a hole where once did grow the man-thing—as stares a hole in the face of That One of thy people whose nose is bitten off!

Thus, said the great dangerous god, you make the sacrifice of take-no-hair.

O *Tunkanshidan,* this we make.

The *Unktehi* went back to its lair. With tumult, ragged blocks of ice reassembled themselves above the den of this departing deity (they had skipped and teetered aside as *Unktehi* pressed down among them) and there was the sight of huge head and ears withdrawing, the tall curved horns going down the last of all; and then there burst the sound of cannon firing as the cakes fell into their places, and then the single impact of a hand upon a drum; then a gunshot sound, and the wiry snip of Blackbird's voice and the squeak of Mouse . . . broken masses had pressed smoothly together, cracks tightened and disappeared, mounds of blown rippled snow were in place, boulders frozen at the marge stood undisturbed. The western Okoboji lake lay extensive, congealed without a scar.

The *Heyoka* returned to him, sweating. They leaped in exhausted rhythm beside Inkpaduta, they dashed perspiration from their eyes.

. . . His left hand, the side of the left palm of Inkpaduta, gave him sudden pain.

So be it! cried the nude *Heyoka.* We laugh, for this is such a hurting matter; and some would weep; but we are *Heyoka* and thus we scream with joy. *Unktehi* has stabbed thee with his horn!

The god did cut my hand?

Aye, as he departed. You see it not, you feel it not? The sharp horn of the *tatankatanka*—the greatest ox of all—has jabbed thee!

Inkpaduta found himself propelled through space as an arrow goes. In one manner or another *Unktehi* must have re-emerged quietly, unseen, from beneath the icy fastness. He'd clamped the feet of Inkpaduta against his bowstring (no other god was stout enough to do it . . . but there were many gods . . . still the oversized ox with fierce forces stored in horns and tail: this god was largest). *Unktehi* had kept the tough dark body of the outlaw stiff as an arrow, and had gripped the bow with his left hoof, and drawn the string with his right hoof, and pulled until the bow sang softly in its bending, and the string whipped with heroic power against the feet— It did seem as if Inkpaduta felt the pressure of that bowstring creasing his hard foot-flesh, between both heels and sets of toes—even now (when he sat wakened and living). It did seem that the back of his aching head had been bumped by the straightening bow as he whistled on his course—

Away he went, arching high, making a bird-rush in the dark chill air as any well-scraped arrow makes its bird-rush and its slither—Away and high and far, and curving in great speed toward earth, and ripping through the lodge-cloth, and landing with a tremble amid his robes—

Corn-Sucker, lying near, said softly: My husband. Why speak you?

He sat up, blinking.

My husband? she asked again.

Some other sleeper in the lodge cried out petulantly from his slumbers.

Inkpaduta grunted: I talk not with you. I am with *Unktehi.*

. . . Aye, his left hand did give pain, the blood did run. The fierce god's horn had gored him! It was a sign for all to see.

(While sleeping, the mad old Wahpekute had flung out his arm, and his hand struck down with force. Among trivial loot carried away from the Plouray house was an empty bottle; the bottle bore the embossed shape of a woman in its rippling texture, and one time it had been filled with brandy, but only a trifle of the brandy smell remained, scarcely worth sniffing at. Carelessly the bottle was tossed to Woman-Shakes-With-Cold by her husband, and just as carelessly she had let two little boys make off with it. They squabbled over ownership of the flask, they slammed and scratched in their fighting, the bottle was broken by contact against a cooking pot. It was one of these jagged chunks of glass which Inkpaduta's hand encountered when, sleeping and provoked by dreams, he struck wildly with his open hand. There was the usual untidy rubble within this lodge, however freshly established—mud from melting earth, fresh-sucked bones, other debris less identifiable—and the wicked glass fragment lay unseen, undetected, never to be glimpsed in faint firelight, to be pushed into obscurity by a moccasined foot before morning.)

Wonderingly the man moved close to the fire, and held his gross hand near a rising flame, that he might see. He was very glad that the *Unktehi* had not struck harder with its horn-tip. Then his very hand might have been torn away!

Soon after daylight all women were ordered from the tipi. Men gathered there to smoke and to hear Inkpaduta tell of his interview with the god. Even younger men (who doubted most of all) felt a twitching of awe within them as they examined That Old One's left hand. Blood had ceased to flow copiously, but the horn-wound was gashed raw and oozing amid old blood which dried.

His-Curly-Sacred, recalling uncomfortably dire prophecies concerning himself which had been made in his native village (not too far from this very region, now), would actually have joked about the occurrence, and sneered at the tale as representing a mere dream without weight or portent. This he would have done, were it not for fear of Inkpaduta.

Does not the *Unktehi* mean that only That Old One takes no scalp? This he says to me! He does say: All thy people!

Does not the *Unktehi* mean only thy own sons?

All in these lodges are my people! Who is Head Man? Is that one called He-Wears-Anything-That-Makes-Him-Look-Frightful a Head Man?

Inkpaduta's right hand slid to his holster. He was the only one armed with a shoots-six, and now he was drawing out the weapon.

Itoyetonka spoke nervously. I am not Head Man!

Is Has-Intercourse-With-Vagina now Head Man? Inkpaduta drew back the hammer of his shoots-six.

Nay! cried Hushan. I am not Head Man.

Is—?

Fire-Cloud addressed his father: *Ate.* Thou art Head Man.

That is true which you do say! I say this now: I am old, but do not wish that my *che* becomes soft, that my *che* rots away. Who wishes this for himself?

(Certainly no one did. There sounded a muffled chorus of Nays and Not I's.)

Then this also is true: who takes hair, him I kill! With my eyes I see the *Unktehi* burst ice of lake apart. With my ears I hear his voice, and these words he speaks. He demands *woshna,* the sacrifice of take-no-scalp. This every man does make with me, this *woshna,* or I kill! What man does say he takes the hair of these whites?

No one spoke. Inkpaduta growled unintelligibly. Slowly he released the hammer of his revolver from its cocked position, and slid the weapon back into the holster. He did not secure the flap, but kept the holster-flap open and held his hand near it. He brooded in indignation at any thought of rebellion on the part of the rest, as long as they remained within that lodge.

Several of the men waded northwest through drifted woods, proceeding with caution—partly because of the condition of the forest with its concealed logs and stiffened thickets and ice-bound nooses of grapevine—but chiefly because they were timid about approaching a region inhabited by the *Unktehi.* As in the case of their leader, most of them had believed heretofore that many *Unktehi* dwelt in broader lakes far to the north and east; that the nearest one lived in a box of iron directly beneath the Falls of St. Anthony. Inkpaduta's experience (attested so believably by the horn-mark on his left hand—oh, twas fortunate for him that he could still use his hand, and open and close the fingers—) had convinced everyone that the most innocent body of water might jeopardize them by housing gods not readily propitiated.

All had sinned against various gods from time to time. They had abused custom and dictum, had ignored the pattern of conduct laid down by Head Men or soldiers. But as a result they carried guilt with them forever—little parfleches of guilt which soaked an indelible stain through strong skins and into the vitals of these men. Guilt makes for vulnerability . . . their hearts were impure, the strength of each man was not as of the strength of ten or even two. Beneath their crude brawling challenging exteriors they felt weaker than women. They would need to make many deaths, exert themselves sexually with captives— Would need to cut down domestic animals, rip open feather beds, kick and maul without stint— Need to perform a variety of such acts before again they might esteem themselves, and dare to question or offend the gods whom they'd first learned about in childhood.

Aye, they had been told that they'd forfeited all right to red dish and red spoon in the future world; and this would not be a glad thing which befell, if true; they felt exceedingly uncomfortable about it; it would not be pleasant to eat through eternity with one's pleading fingers, and lose all the juices, when other people who'd tramped the Way of the Souls were gourmandizing happily—red bowls filled steaming and tasty, red spoons operating busily! The gods were many but none was wholly benevolent. Calmer-tempered gods were apt to grow irascible if even slightly provoked; and the majority were demons who dealt in treachery. Each man knew this; he had been told, early in life; the recollection persisted through all offenses. Consider the *Unktehi's* choice enemies: those Thunder-Gods or Thunder-Birds—*Wakinyanpi.* Far at the western end of the world was their mountainous lodge with its four doors and four guarding sentinels: deer at the north door, beaver at the south, butterfly at the east, bear at the west. And such soft and beautiful coats were worn by these four sentries—delicate down of the female swan, dyed to scarlet! (The down so fancied by Bahata.) But there was nothing soft and beautiful in practices of the Thunder-Gods and their retainers. Always they made war, there was no limit to the murders; you'd think them sated with killing for many generations past, but they could not be sated. . . . And what of *Takushkanshkan*—the Moving-God, the God-of-Motion? He controlled the thoughts and feelings of all Dakota. He could put a man's brain into a beast, and the beast's brain into a man . . . the hunter would go stammering in circles, bereft of the wit to use his weapons; and deer or buffalo or bear, or even raccoon or skunk, could chortle at eluding him. Ah, when a man was in any sort of trouble, then did the God-of-Motion rejoice! . . . *Takushkanshkan* dwelt in boulders (but so did the *Tunkan,* the Stone-God), and was he in this stone or that stone or the stone yonder?—and he was very uneven of temper, and often offended by a man even when the man had tried desperately to offer no offense—and all sly or filthy or rotten-flesh-grabbing creatures were in his clan, and served the Moving-God: the raven, the carrion crow, the buzzard, fox, and wolf.

Wood-Gods, Gods-of-Gluttony, and always the shivering or perspiring *Heyoka.* . . . So many forces to pursue you, trick you, cheat you, torture you, slay you in the end. Earth and waters, the very sky overhead, reeked of their capriciousness, their ire and malice.

The Wahpekute peered out at solid expanse of that lake which forced its long notched spearhead into the north. Were there cracks still remaining, as relics of the *Unktehi's* emergence? Inkpaduta had related that the ice closed down tightly, abruptly, above the descending god's head and horns. But still there might be fissures which had not grown back together. . . . One man pointed, said, *Toko!* Behold! . . . Near at hand, curving over toward the northern shore, was a rough new crack in the ice; all could see it clearly, the fresh-risen sun made a flashing ornament of the edges.

Each outlaw issued some puny prayer within himself. They did not speak, they went back through the woods to rejoin Inkpaduta. They were sullen—suspicious and resentful, each of the other. They suffered the discomfort of young men who are irked by the knowledge (recognized in inner secrecy and reluctance, but still recognized) that forces which they cannot control are manipulating them—to no apparent purpose; and that derision is being spoken; and that somewhere someone is laughing at them.

XXXVII

What do you offer us, Day?

Everything, says Day.

Husband, you got to rise so soon?

Got to. You heard what Harvey said, and Clark. Road's not too bad, all the way down past the Irish colony. If Robby and I start early we'll make record time. Think maybe I planned right—you can feel the air. Warming fast.

Abbie declared softly that she wanted to rise, and help Pa. There sounded a stirring in the Luces' bed. We might as well all get up, Harvey murmured. Twill help set them on their way at an early hour.

Evening gray, Abbie chanted, *and morning red, sets the traveler on his head.*

Frances Gardner gave a light chuckle. You behave, daughter. This is a morning gray. *Sets the traveler on his way.*

Harvey would not be left behind in the business of quotations, but preferred his own brand. *They shall run, and not be weary; and they shall walk, and not faint.*

Robert Clark had already roused from quilts on the floor. Is that Ezekiel, Brother Harvey?

Isaiah. Forty, thirty-one.

In polite tribute to a visitor, Brother Bob was asked to perform the Scriptural reading on this morning. He and Luce had backed in a quantity of meal, flour, and bacon, and saleratus and salt as well; together with sugar and coffee to gladden all hearts. In contemplation of fresh biscuits, prattle of the small boys was reduced to a minimum.

Clark turned to St. John's version of another memorable meal.

There is a lad here, which hath five barley loaves, and two small fishes: but what are they among so many?

And Jesus said, Make the men sit down. Now there was much grass in the place. So the men sat down, in number about five thousand.

Usually in that household Bible reading followed upon breakfast, did not precede it. Harvey and Bob, in excess of thankfulness at homecoming and at the possession of adequate loaves and fishes, had seen fit to reverse the procedure. The rest could not say them nay, though their mouths were watering even as they listened.

This was the moment chosen by His-Curly-Sacred to push open the house door.

The tall young Wahpekute had scorned joining in any expedition to *Unktehi's* quarters. He'd tried to tell himself that he did not believe in the existence of *Unktehi,* or in the validity of a warning delivered by Inkpaduta, although he'd felt moments of squeamishness during the recital of the encounter. He wished that Bursts-Frog-Open might be living still; he needed some sustaining force in his attitude. His-Curly-Sacred affirmed repeatedly: I do not fear *Unktehi!*—and tried to turn away from any consideration of wide-spread horns, treelike legs, rocklike hoofs.

Inkpaduta said, First we do not kill. First we beg. . . . This had been the pattern followed during the ascent of the Little Sioux (although no killing had come about). And they should take guns of whites, if possible: it was good to kill, it was not good to be killed. The most southwesterly lodge of the *Washichun,* the outside house of this little settlement, must be visited initially: any sanity of tactics suggested nothing else. The rest of the band would come herding in at any moment, but he who appeared first was likely to be the best served. Tawachehawakan did not know who lived in this cabin, did not know that Abbie dwelt here. Now, on observing her, he was confident that he remembered her from the Clear Lake day, the piece-of-grindstone day . . . that was long before. Lightning of excitement ripped his body.

He stared, he called her Yellow-Hair. He said, *Hinzi!*

The family had been happily unaware that there were any Indians in the neighborhood, and groaned at their coming. Abbie regarded the young wild man with utter loathing. His-Curly-Sacred made signs for Give and Eat. He did not say Peeeeez, he only swaggered silently, after the one word of recognition. He only made the signs.

Husband, we got to feed him? We haven't et.

Reckon we got to. They all expect something to eat, every time they come.

Mary Luce cried in fury, I vow, it's fairly taking the victuals out of the children's mouths!

Her husband pushed gently past her and took down one remaining stool which hung in the corner above their bed. We got to feed the hungry and clothe the poor. Least, much as we're able. That's what it says—

In the Scriptures, I spose! cried the annoyed wife. Well, I wish it didn't.

Mary!

Brother Bob closed the Bible, the meal was begun. The children did not eat at second table in this home: Mary held the baby on her lap, and the little boys alternated between roosting on their fathers' knees or standing to munch at the tableside; or sitting, when there was sit-down room enough for all. The boys had withdrawn to the end of the table farthest removed from the visitor, and regarded him with round eyes. His-Curly-Sacred snatched with both hands. He gobbled and grunted, he pushed slab upon slab of fried mush into his broad mouth.

He shan't get the whole of that bacon, Frances Gardner exclaimed. Nor the pork, neither. First we've seen in weeks! She rose in annoyance to lift a big tin plate and bear it to the other end of the table. His-Curly-Sacred sprawled in her direction, trying to reach, but she eluded him.

Sweat was standing on Rowland Gardner's forehead. Don't wherrit him. In a low voice. Don't wherrit him, Frances, I beg you.

Big pig! cried Abbie.

Daughter, you take care. He might make trouble.

He's making trouble enough already. Just look at our breakfast—

But don't—

The door banged open again, and was held wide as the Wahpekute shouldered into the house. Many began to speak, even before they'd crossed the doorstep. Peeeeez . . . jib, jib, jib . . . whisk . . . eeeeet? Deep-throated words came forth like lines of verse sung by children in a Round. Immediately the smell was a visible thing, like loam or silt, it stuffed the room as grain within a bin, you could have ladled it with a peck measure, could have shoveled the smell. Women herded in as well; demands emanating immediately from Female-Cousin-Rabbit rose shriller than cries of the rest. Her sullen filthy children wormed their way up to the table's edge. The little girl clawed for a small pitcher—treasured flask of syrup which had been saved for festivity such as this. Her brother struggled to wrench the prize away; syrup flew into the air; the children growled and fought amid splatters of syrup.

Some accompanying laughter came from the Indians.

Oh, cried Frances Gardner, on the verge of tears. What'll we do, what'll we do? They're just taking everything. There goes the last of the meat—

Tell you this, said her husband. I'm not going to Fort Dodge—not today—not with a gang of wild men around.

To say nothing of wild children, cried his eldest daughter. I never *seen* such behavior!

Son Harvey. Gardner's voice rose in agitation. . . . Do you and Brother Bob get over there in front of our guns . . . gainst the wall. . . . Yes, over there. I can't move. They got me fairly pinned in this corner.

Harvey said, Mr. Gardner, I don't think they mean no harm.

They got me upset. I ain't going to Fort Dodge.

. . . Shakily he thought: Why, it's been like this my whole life long. Seems like I try to do my best and work hard, seems like we all do our best, and work real hard; but just when I think I've got matters happily laid out, long comes something to spoil it.

(These thoughts came to him in a crammed staring flash, crowded, superimposed one upon the other; yet equally readable, equally to be discerned.)

Half an hour ago, all was well. Warmest day we've had: nigh like spring. And Harvey'd come back safe and sound, and the sleds would be along with provisions most any day now. And I was bound for Fort Dodge to get the seed corn, and other little things: things the women-folks were wanting. Like a new tin thimble for Abbie, cause the little boys had played with Abbie's thimble, and lost it down a crack or knothole somewheres. And all that list which Wife wrote out for me. Even books and newspapers—oh, yes, new books!—we could afford a couple, surely. And papers— Just to think! And seed corn. There's something so golden in the idea of seed corn: the whole idea, not just the color of the corn itself, but what it promises. I didn't think I'd enjoy the trip too well, with only Robby Matheson for company; but he's a steady lad, at that; we wouldn't have no trouble.

And now, and now—

Oh, I was right excited at the thought of returning to Fort Dodge once more, for the winter's been so long, so very long and hard. And all that seed a-needing to be fetched; and buying a light wagon on shares with Matheson and maybe Mattock as well. It's like that dream I used to have, clean back when we were headed for the Shell Rock River, just fugitives who didn't really need to run away. And then I had that dream I'd had at other times: bout wild men coming through our window, in a kind of lattice-kind-of-house, and all the awful things they did to us, and how they were a-laughing while they did the things. It seems I'm not relieved from any dreams—the nightmare ones at least. I've been so worried all along, so awful worried. . . .

Husband, look you here. I opened up the flour barrel, and they—

Ma, don't you give them one more thing. Not one more *thing!*

But, Mary, your Pa says that we mustn't anger them.

. . . Inkpaduta had pushed his huge shape into the cabin last of all, he stood back from the riot at the table. Inkpaduta did not beg.

Ate, said Roaring-Cloud. All our men are here.

Makes-Fat-Bad-Smelling-Wind is in his lodge. He sharpens knives to cut out *napcho.*

We need not Makes-Fat-Bad.

Here are three men, and all look strong. They would fight. We must take ammunition, take guns.

How ask you of whites for ammunition? I know not the name.

I know the name, cried His-Curly-Sacred. I give name. I ask for ammunition.

He tried to shove closer to Rowland Gardner. He lifted up his rifle, pushed it out across the disordered table, patted the lock with his hand. Pow-duh, he said. You–white–man–jib– Pow-duh. *Mazakan.* Jun! Jun! Jib–pow–duh–

Harvey Luce said, Mr. Gardner. I don't think we ought to let them have no powder. Seems to be what the poor feller wants, but– Might put ideas in their heads.

Tawachehawakan displayed the cap which lay beneath the hammer of his rifle. Kapp, he repeated. Kapp!

Gardner said, Way it always is with them. You got to give, when they come asking. Everybody says the same. That's how to keep out of trouble, whether we like it or not.

Other men were taking up the demand, now that the syllables had been uttered. They kept repeating them insistently to the best of their ability. Kapp! Pow-duh. Jib–jib. Kapp! Baby Mandy added her complaint to the turmoil. She was affrighted by this commotion, the smell and noise.

My cap box–over there above the fireplace–

Rowly tried to grasp at his father's pant-leg as the man worked his way through the press. S'all right, little boy, Gardner croaked. S'all right. Ain't nothing to–to fuss about– S'all right, bubby. Once more his mind went back to dread imaginings which had affected him in slumber. . . . Twasn't like this. No, those wild men in his illusion had been murderers. And these were only beggars, but–but– So many of them! Dang it all, he couldn't go to the Fort. How long would the Indians keep a-camping here? Because they must be camping somewhere hereabouts. And how long would he have to stay at home, count of that? He wouldn't dare to leave the family alone–not even with Harvey and– He wouldn't dare.

He prayed quickly unto his own dear Lord: O Lord, it seems as if I'm sore afflicted. Please to lift the burden from my shoulders.

His hand closed on the cap box, twas flat and circular. He tried to remove the lid with care, it came off with a snap, the box jerked in his hand, several caps flew wide. He'd give them out, divide them fairly. He'd say, Two for you, and two for you, and two for– The noseless face of One-Staggering loomed before him, the hand flew, the fingers bent, the little box was whipped from Gardner's grasp. Gardner reached out, trying to retrieve the caps; the Indian laughed and whirled away.

A coarse rumble of approving voices rose once more: they stuffed the low-ceiled room with noise. *Washte!* He takes caps from white man. Good! The cabin was a-quaver with their stench and ugliness. Would they never go, would they never *leave?* A big dark hand, a hand with yellow horny nails, brushed fairly in the face of Harvey Luce, and tried to reach beyond his shoulder. Luce jerked back his head. His powder horn was hanging just behind, and the hand was reaching for the strap. Oh no you don't, Brother, said Harvey Luce. You don't! His own hand came up, he caught the brown wrist, exerted all the strength of his right arm. He turned the wrist away. It was Roaring-Cloud who'd tried to steal the powder horn, and a low cry rose behind him. Many voices were trying to speak both anger and disbelief, and all in a single united indrawn breath. *Washichun* resisting? What now, what next? Roaring-Cloud tried to train his gun on this square-built antagonist who had risen so astoundingly to confront him. He was carrying a smoothbore with an exceptionally long barrel, he had to step backward. The disorganized herd was close and all around; Roaring-Cloud backed fairly over a child of Female-Cousin-Rabbit. His mighty moccasin crushed hard upon the frail foot of the little girl, her shriek jolted the room. There was space now, the weapon's muzzle swung against Harvey Luce's chest.

No you don't, came Harvey's whine again. He was breathing heavily, astonished at his own temerity, his quickness to act. His doubled clutch cemented tight around the gun barrel. He felt, rather than thought, I'm stouter by far than this tall Indan. I work and chop and dig and drive and push. Just think how Joe Thatcher and me, we had to push that sled; and so I got a strength, and God Almighty says, Servant, I'm aiding you. . . .

Roaring-Cloud was big; but he had never toiled like Harvey Luce, did not contain such force within his shoulders and his arms. Down, down the muzzle turned, until it grated on the floor at Harvey's feet. Roaring-Cloud stood with feet apart, still trying to resist the pressure, all sharp black hatred shining in his cross-eyed gaze.

Now we kill!

Inkpaduta glowered from the doorway. We go.

Why go we now? You say that we make war, you say we kill.

Witkotkoka! Fool! the father said. Two more white men come.

A mumble rose round him as others swung their glances through the open doorway. . . . *Echahe!* Two white men. . . . They come from forest. . . . Aye, they come. . . . And both have guns. . . . Both!

With five white men to fight us, we try to make war? Inkpaduta sneered. Some die! It might be *thee* who dies, My Son.

Go we now, Thou Old One?

Aye, go. All go.

His-Curly-Sacred vowed: When we return, we take the Yellow-Hair. We kill her not. I take!

They trooped into the dooryard, the whole blanketed bristling column, they carried much of their stench with them, much remained behind.

Bert Snyder and Isaac Harriott had been awakened early by activity of old Jo Harshman. He prepared a meal at the fire while the world was still dead dark.

Where you bound? Harry asked sleepily.

Hunting, Isaac, hunting. I think twill be the warmest day we've had. But don't delude yourself: spring hain't come by any means.

You're after beaver?

They're moving about these days. Depends what fortune I have in getting a fair shot.

Where do you hunt them, Jo?

Pond I know, said Harshman shortly, and in another five minutes he was gone.

Never will he tell you! Bert chuckled in his upper bunk. He says always that he goes somewhere, he has his ways, he tells nothing more. He is like a child who has stolen plums and hidden them away; he will relate nothing.

I've observed that most hunters and fishermen are like that. Did you finish your letters, Bert?

Snyder's letters were in order, folded and addressed. He had written two, both very brief: one to the Pakingtons, one to Colonel Fardeau. He had not written to the Pakingtons for a year at least, had not written to Fardeau since he left Red Wing. Harry, relying on copious extracts from his journal, had prepared fat missives for his parents, for Mrs. Rusk, and for both doctors dear to him.

Harry, at what hour does Mr. Gardner depart?

He said they hoped to get an early start.

Then we should take the letters across the straits to Robby at once.

Robby, fiddlesticks! He'd be apt to feed them to the cattle, or leave them behind, up in his loft. No siree. I'm rising at once, I'll take the mail to the Gardner place myself. We'll thus feel more secure.

I shall accompany you. Have you forgotten?—this is Sunday, the day of God, the day of supreme importance to me. This is the day I walk into a wider world! The letters are as much my responsibility as your own. I shall go with you, and we'll take our rifles. Who knows? —we might be the ones to find the beaver.

They breakfasted hastily on warmed-up rice, they appreciated those fruity colors which brightened increasingly, low in the eastern sky. Harry had a notion that the sun would rise in unusual merriment on this morning. For a moment he thought that Harshman must be mistaken: spring was at hand, surely. The young men shouldered their guns, left Lee jailed in the cabin with his sleeping master, and crossed the icy Narrows. There was a route through woods by which a traveler might proceed directly toward the Gardner-Luce cabin without deviation in the direction of the Mattocks'. It joined the main pathway at the edge of a small clearing (where children gathered berries in a pleasanter season). A few minutes later, Bert and Harry were halted in surprise at the junction, gazing into the Wahpekute camp.

By gar. They have returned.

Wonder if it's the same ones who were around here when the snows began?

One is never to know, they are so nomadic. But all are harmless in this region. Come, let us go a-calling. Bert added in mischief: You are proud at being able to speak their language?

I remember it, too. Harry repeated: *Ateunyanpi mahpiya ekta nanke chin.*

Again, what is the meaning?

Means, Our Father which art in Heaven.

I suggest that you employ that as a salutation....

Gingerly they moved into the ring of tattered lodges. Dogs were circling, active and vociferous. Makes-Fat-Bad had witnessed the two whites in their approach. He looked to the loading of his Cochran rifle, for suddenly he felt very much alone: the only man left in the village. Inkpaduta had said that there must be no killing until the whites were convinced that the Wahpekute band had come but to beg. So the Titonwan had no wish to go soliciting with the rest—his time would come later, when there was *napcho* to be cut. He withdrew into dark recesses of the bachelors' lodge and scowled unseen. There were but three women remaining in camp: Corn-Sucker, who as usual had not accompanied the expedition; the wife of Fire-Cloud, who nursed her sick child resentfully; and Woman-Shakes-With-Cold. She was still sequestered, still in the *ishnati* condition (as she had been for many days. Bad spirits were in her body, and her body was weak, and there was no mystery man in this village, and the plants from which she might have made a tea to aid her were not available in winter, and no one knew quite what to do, and most of the other women did not care, and her husband hated her. . . . Could Isaac Harriott been made to understand her state, and had he been carrying his satchel, he would have offered assistance promptly, in the shape of his favorite emenagogue pills: precipitated carbonate of iron; and gum myrrh, aloes, oil of savin, tincture of Spanish flies. One pill at each dosage, from one to three times daily. He would not have considered this unfortunate to be merely a filthy savage, he would have thought of her as being a female patient in desperate need of his aid. He would have felt a pity and a pride).

Corn-Sucker was assailed by fright and sadness at seeing these young white men approach. She had been preparing to boil beef for a stew. This was beef chopped out from the slaughtered Plouray cattle, it had been drawn along on a sled with other provender. Twas frozen, twould need to boil long. She would add meal and beans to the beef. The beans also should be long boiled: they were very hard. She thought of beans which she had raised and eaten in the past: the red, the spotted, the shield-figured. But best of all was the *amaca shipisha,* the black bean. Always they yielded more on each vine. Corn-Sucker thought of herself as first treading the vines, trampling the heap again and again so that little beans would not fly and lose themselves in space beyond the outspread skins—the threshing floor—when they were flailed. And this should be on a dry day in autumn, with wind coming steadily to help at the winnowing.

A friendly wind blew across the brown river, and blew away broken pods and dust; so beans fell at my feet.

I gave my thanks to thee, O wind.

Then did I prepare black beans boiled in the great kettle of my mother, boiled with buffalo fat or bone grease. All ate, and all said, These beans are good.

This was long ago.

From her lodge door she peered out nervously. All people in the band knew that Inkpaduta planned to make war; but these white men did not know. Corn-Sucker slid the corner of her robe across her mutilated face. She wished that these whites had not come, she did not wish to see them killed before her eyes. She had never seen a man killed. But she had seen people die, had seen her father dying after the French whites shot him. These were not pleasant matters to witness, and she did fear to turn her eyes upon a sudden death. *Tsakak!* Many whites were wicked and were cruel. It was whites who cut off the head of Bursts-Frog-Open. All in the village said this thing, though she herself had shrunk from peeking at the body. Female-Cousin-Rabbit had seen, and so she told of it loudly. But some whites were kind. People in the nearby lodge of the great-white-man-who-had-eaten-much-meat: they had not set the dog on her, they had given her corn mush and other food. And they made a great noise, and they smelt strong and strangely; but still they laughed. They had not beaten her. She'd made a song for them. . . .

Harry and Bert halted before the lodge and spoke reassuringly to the little Hidatsa woman. They bent down and peered boldly into the smoky tipi, trying to adjust their eyes to the gloom.

Only the lady of the house is at home. Good day to you, Lady of the House!

You do not speak the Dakota language which you know, my dear Harry.

Don't see any sense in calling *her* Our Father which art in Heaven.

Ah, try it by all means. It may be that she is a Christian, and will respond.

In amusement Harry yielded to the urging, he repeated the line taught him by the half-breed Renville. He was confident that he spoke the syllables correctly, Renville had said that he had a good ear. (Because he knew a little Latin and Greek, words gained in medical studies?) The woman giggled tremulously, and held the robe closer before her face, and shrank back.

Bert cautioned, Say nothing about your *chay*.

Hush. She may know the word.

Indeed Corn-Sucker did know it, but she could not imagine that these whites were using a word of the Dakota language. She thought only, How odd for a friendly-sounding white voice to speak a syllable known to me! Language of the whites is strange. . . .

Harry led the way into the lodge, he hoped to acquire some small items of Indian manufacture. Surely, thought Corn-Sucker, you do not come for food. Whites do not come to lodge of Dakota to seek food. She tried to put down her timidity by reflecting how she had visited the house of the *Mashi* without invitation. Yet her pulse was throbbing. The shorter of the two whites, the man with yellow hair, smiled at her. She thought that she should grin in return.

Harry's first birthday gift from Atta Rusk had been in the form of cambric handkerchiefs she'd sewn for him. He had one of these with him now; twas folded in his coat pocket, though the goods had not known pressure of a flatiron since Harry left St. Paul. Once white-and-blue, the kerchief was now of gray-and-blue; but this shred of flimsy cloth shone to Corn-Sucker as a thing of beauty. The dew-cloth was canopied behind her (most of these slovens did not bother with a tipi lining but Corn-Sucker tried always to erect one). From a pole sustaining the dew-cloth hung a blanket band. It had been manufactured by one of Corn-Sucker's aunts or big sisters: the array of sewn porcupine quills was still beautiful, even if broken and raveling. Toward this band the young white man directed her attention. She turned, following his pointed finger, and then with her eyes she followed his finger as it came back to indicate himself. Slowly he waved the handkerchief before her . . . once again he was pointing, at Corn-Sucker, at the blanket band, at himself, at the handkerchief. It was difficult for her to believe that he was in earnest. He wished to possess her shabby stained blanket band, and to offer in exchange that magnificent piece of colored cloth for which her soul already hungered? Might she not manage with only the one blanket band then remaining to her? Surely. Many people in the camp had no blanket bands at all; they used straps stolen from the whites, or hide thongs.

You–give–strap. Me–give–*handkerchief*. His words were incomprehensible, his gestures charged with meaning. This was not a blanket strap belonging to Inkpaduta or to any other member of the household. It was her own, she'd brought it from her village! She uttered a trill of delight, and reached swiftly to take down the band

and press it upon Harry. In return the soft blue-and-gray marvel came into her hands.

Harry, have you ever thought of becoming a trader among the Indians? You can grow very rich in that way. But what will be said by Madame Rusk when she learns that you parted so readily with one of her beautiful handkerchiefs?

I've still two left; but this was wearing out anyway.

Then you have cheated the unfortunate squaw.

Not at all. See how she sits fondling it. Dang it, maybe I could have gotten two straps, stead of the one.

Lo, the poor Indian! Poor Lo is cheated forever!

Once more, hush! See that big bag over yonder? It's a beautiful thing, with all those do-dads, even if torn and dirty—

What would you trade her for it?

Haven't got a thing. But we're lingering; let's get along to the Gardners; or he'll be gone without our letters.

. . . Once Harriott and Snyder were returned to their own cabin, the doctor prepared a substantial addition to the letter he had written his parents. Later, if there was time, he would copy this postscript and append it to the other letters as well. Having chipped away the sealing wax with his knife point, Harry spread out the document, reread the final portion hastily, and then began a new sheet emblazoned with an ornate *P.S.*

. . . Sun. Mar. 8th. It now appears that the posting of this missive will be delayed at least for a day or two. R. Gardner is not making the trip to Fort Dodge on this day; and we stopped briefly at the Mattock place on our way home to apprise Robby Matheson of the fact. (He was not ready to depart by any means, had been a slug-a-bed.) The Indians who hang about the lakes from time to time, have returned, and are encamped on the path leading from Mattocks' to Gardners'. B. Snyder and I stopped at their wigwams and did a little trading with the savages, who do not appear truly savage—just dirty and forlorn. But when we reached the Gardner place, found the folks acting like all possessed. They had been terrified by a begging party from the camp. Indians have no manners according to our notion, have never been taught any. So Gardners and Luces were truly upset. Bert and I tried to reassure them, but I fear to little avail. After all, *we had been in the middle of the camp,* and found the few denizens disposed in friendly fashion. But at Gardners' a party of others snatched hungrily for food & tried to secure that which they prize above all else: ammunition for their weapons. Well, they possess no gunsmith's shop or hardware store at which such commodities may be purchased!! So I think their eagerness should be excused. Of course they were talking in a strange tongue, frightening the children by their chatter and filthy appearance, and generally making nuisances of themselves.

Harvey Luce had some sort of scuffle with one. I didn't receive the gist of it, as Gardners and Luces all were talking at once, including children. Truly nothing to occasion desperate alarm (if people would only keep their senses and not go into hysterics!). Tis difficult to retain a sane outlook when women, and the small fry too, are all in a fit. On our arrival at home, C. Granger informed us that Indians had appeared at our place as well. He gave them something, though not much could be spared, not until the sleds come in this week, as all feel confident that they will do. Carl's ears improved. After examination, I should say swelling also diminished, and thus congestion at a lower ebb. Have repacked, using a slightly different medicament, and now my long-suffering patient is deaf as a post, stuffed tight. Bert and I revisited the Indian camp briefly on our way back from Gardners'. I had no cash by me, and had already traded the bit of liquid assets I owned, i.e.: one cambric handkerchief. But Bert had in pocket a gold dollar, and this he loaned to me. (N.B. Repaid him once we were across our threshold. I favor discharging my debts *promptly.*) For the coin I was able to secure a superb bag, and shall one day come a-fetching it, packed perhaps with a portion of my own possessions; but more likely with gifts for you, dear Ma and Pa. Tis a beautiful thing, made of buck or doeskin, or maybe buffalo, and replete with ornamentals & paintings of the most curious sort: quills, beads, etc. Must have required many toilsome weeks to fabricate this, and I am amazed at getting same for one dollar. Granger says he has seen them before, among Indians on the River, and they call such a portmanteau a-bag-for-every-possible-thing. Tis now nearly the middle of the afternoon, and we have dined. The last of our new rice and the last—oh, woe!—of our bacon. Now J. Harshman has just come in, lugging two big beaver, seeming well pleased with himself, as indeed he has the right to be. What will boiled beaver be like? I have tasted only the *caudal appendage* heretofore. Shall close now, as the house is full of talk: Bert and Harshman engrossed in imperative argument, and asking me to step in. Your Humble Servant, Wilderness Doctor & Devoted son. . . .

If they'd only been here when the wild men came, Gardner cried, over and over. If they'd only seen what happened!

Carrying loaded guns, he and Clark and Luce withdrew to the stable for a conference.

At least the Mattocks had been informed of the situation, when the Red-Wingers stopped by to tell Robby that the Fort Dodge excursion was postponed.

. . . But they'll belittle it, Gardner declared. Just see if they don't.

. . . Folks up on East Okoboji should be informed, right off.

. . . But we ourselves ought to go to the Mattocks', and tell them just how bad it was.

. . . And stop at the Red Wing cabin, too, and try once more to make them understand.

. . . I swear, Son Harvey, we all might be scalped while we slept!

When I cry unto thee, Harvey quoted, *mine enemies turn back.* You stay with the folks, Mr. Gardner, Brother Bob and I are younger and spryer. We'll carry the tidings.

. . . No, no, the others were tired from their long journey—they'd reached the lakes only two days before—he himself should go on the mission of warning. The question was debated lengthily, but finally the juniors won their point. They armed themselves, said Goodbye to children and womenfolks.

Mary clung tightly to her husband before he departed. I'm scairt clean through, she whispered.

I will not be afraid what man can do unto me. Them's good words, Mary.

Hope so. Oh, I hope so. . . .

As they started east, they thought they saw shapes dodging in and out among the trees. Both men observed the motion: animals, birds? They could not be certain. They stopped, irresolute.

Somebody up ahead. . . .

I think so too, Brother Bob.

I don't know much bout Indians. . . .

Me neither, Brother Bob.

But you snapped your hand fast, when that one tried to put his gun on you!

The Lord was a-helping.

Aye, that's right! With the Lord's help, and trusting on Him, we should win through!

If our Faith does not falter. . . .

Harvey added cautiously: But I don't reckon it's smart for us to just plain stand here. Should them Indans really wish to shoot us—them benighted souls!—and agonizing in the clutch of Satan— They could do it easy. Seems like maybe twould be best if we went a long way round—

He drew Brother Bob along, turning aside from the open path, and leading circuitously where old snow was shallowest. He explained as they traveled: Indians were encamped about halfway between the Mattocks and the Gardner-Luce cabin. Well, then: if the two messengers proceeded first to the Mattock place or the home of the Red Wing people, Indians were certain to observe them. Did the Indians plan to pile mischief upon mischief, they might waylay Harvey and Brother Bob—might capture them, restrain them, bind them—and thus prevent a warning being carried to other homes—

Might even kill us!

My defence is of God, which saveth the upright in heart.

True, true, Brother Harvey! *God judgeth the righteous, and God is angry with the wicked every day.*

Tain't their fault. They just ain't had the Word, that's all.

You mean to go to the furthest houses first?

Harvey thought that such a course might prove wisest, and would serve to bemuse the savages. It was now his intention to proceed directly north across the ice of West Okoboji, although not angling toward the Red Wingers' place opposite the Narrows. If Indians observed that they were headed, not toward any other cabin, but into untenanted woods beyond the Okobojis, doubtless they'd lose all interest in the two travelers.

Course, there *is* the Marbles', in the direction we're a-going now. But it's a fur piece.

How fur?

Must be six-seven mile as the crow flies. But I don't reckon them Indans even have knowledge that the Marbles are located there, for they settled long after us folks did. I don't guess them Indans know anything about it! Then, once we're acrost, over in that timber, we can circle back towards the east and reach the Noble-Thatcher place, first.

That's the house where Een Ryan's a-staying?

Yes, where we left Een day-before-yesterday. Mrs. Noble's his sister-in-law—

Then we'll go there first, then make our way back towards the other houses; and probably the Indians won't know what we're up to?

Though an host should encamp against me, my heart shall not fear.

True, Brother Harvey! *And now shall mine head be lifted up above mine enemies round about me.*

They crossed the open ice boldly, filled with sudden confidence, glorying in sunshine which fell almost warmly on their shoulders. Both were enduringly thankful to God for this suggestion of spring. Harvey Luce said that the winter was past; Robert Clark declared that the flowers would soon appear on earth, and that the time of the singing of the birds would soon be at hand; and both spoke feelingly of the voice of the turtle. From a shadowed vantage point among old snowdrifts as gray and sodden as coffin pillows, several ruthless persons saw them receding across the damp ice.

They go not to lodge of other whites!

They go not there.

We kill? asked the eager Roaring-Cloud.

His father ignored him. He muttered: *Waziyatakiya!* They go northward.

Now they go too far, we cannot kill!

Inkpaduta snarled: We kill when I say kill! We do not kill until I say! But northward are soldiers—

Do they seek soldiers?

After a moment's consideration, Inkpaduta directed: You follow, My Two Sons. When whites are far from lodges of other whites, then do you kill. Do not kill so near lodges that guns are heard! Remember the words of *Unktehi*— You take not hair.

Aye, Thou Old One. We take not hair.

Or—I kill thee.

Echahe. Or we are killed by thee.

The twins trailed after Clark and Luce, over damp-drifted forested uplands north of the Narrows, over three erratic miles as the Sabbath afternoon came melting between oaks and hickories. A few surviving chickadees were released from starvation amid sheltered tree-crotches; they busied themselves importantly along with juncos, feeding on the first minute insects which crept the bark in response to this gentle thawing. Thus there were sounds in timberland all around —sounds ahead, and sounds back yonder where the two white men had printed their tracks. The Wahpekute could have been noisily careless—and often were— Loosened insulations of snow, disturbed by the men's passage, fell from branches or grapevines. They made a certain thud and rattling as solid strips broke apart. The myth of the utterly silent Indian was disproved steadily; even the birds remarked upon it. But Brother Harvey and Brother Bob gave no heed, had no further fears. They felt safe, far removed from any menace of truculent beggars, and were singing as they went.

Yet a few years, or days, perhaps,
Or moments pass, in silent lapse,
And time, to me, shall be no more.

So ran the ancient selection known as Quincy, designated as an L. P. M. Major in young Robert Clark's lone treasured hymn book. He did not know what this designation really meant (he had learned the hymn from his mother, and felt that it should be sung as she sang it). Sometimes he wondered vaguely what those mystic L. P. M. symbols might indicate. . . . Unlike his friend, Clark had been dragooned into no oath excluding him from the ministry. He wished decidedly to become a preacher, and thought that he should be one in time. To him, at twenty-one, a precious future lifted like promising unsurmounted hills ahead.

No more the sun these eyes shall view;
Earth o'er these limbs her dust shall strew,
And life's delusive dream be o'er.

In common with Harvey, in common with the entire robed marching multitude of addicted believers so ubiquitous in their world,

Robert Clark cried that he was but a worm or a worthless lump of mortal clay. He entertained in simultaneous glee the assured notion of his own immortality.

Harvey Luce was never so gratified as in this hour of extinction. He had pushed his stumpy body across torturing ridges all the way from Cylinder Creek; had been faced with threat and new responsibilities immediately upon arrival; had felt amid his loved ones the increased strain of want, deprivation; knew that he was thwarted in fetching in the load of foodstuffs (would everyone starve before food could be brought? It was an exalted misery to be contemplated). He saw that Rowland Gardner was delayed in his own journey to Fort Dodge, saw that the heathen were circulating and raging. Now another exhausting path must be stamped over ice and around the borders of retarding drifts; feet must be bruised, hands chilled, the heart leadened so that, in turn, it would be able to bounce through a miracle of sacrifice and abnegation. There was even an additional burden in the sacred music chanted by Brother Bob, for Harvey did not recognize the words and could but guess at the tune.

His hoarse breaking voice followed pluckily, in dedicated attempt to share every grimness of the suggested doom.

Earth o'er these limbs her dust shall strew,
And life's delusive dream be o'er.

Near the east shore outlet of East Okoboji, a mighty thudding blow was directed against his back, and was delivered; and it sent him sprawling forward into the snow with outstretched hands, and earnest amazement in his open eyes. Brother Bob lay beside him, knocked down by an equally well-aimed blast of buckshot, and also completely uncomprehending. The shots were fired at some distance from the Noble-Thatcher house, so no one therein recognized the little volley for what it was. (Morris Markham might have risen in alarm, but he had gone away.) There was not time for Harvey's brain, in its last seconds of nourished activity, to frame and hold a vision of home, Mary, Bertie, Mandy, or even of Jesus. He died fast, could not feel the manually delivered bludgeoning which came later, could feel no cutting, have no realization of martyrdom. Those bodies, once they had been hacked by the jeering twins, would not be revealed to any other human eyes until an unvexed June. This was in itself a new foiling, and highly unfair. One should not labor through one's young years with the bright trophy of immolation hung like a sausage on a stick ahead, and never be able to obtain it consciously.

Harshman said, Gardner and Luce are right. To be affrighted.

What under the sun—?

Mean just what I say. I asked Bert if he seen a big old Injan with like smallpox marks all over his face. He says he seen him, a-leaving the Gardners'. Tis Inkpaduta. His crowd is meaner'n sin.

Bert cried, My dear Jo, on many occasions we have discussed the Indians. Always you say to give them food, offer presents, treat mildly with them—

Don't recall us ever discussing Inkpaduta. He's an outlaw and murderer: got slung out of his own tribe, count of it. I mind mentioning him when I was telling about Sintomniduta, but you never asked me no questions. He's here, and might be in evil mood. We got to take steps. Ain't you disquieted about your young Miss Alice, Isaac?

I haven't thought there was the slightest cause for alarm. Bert and I stopped at their camp, and we traded—

Bert says you didn't see none of the menfolks to home. Twas men that frighted the Gardners, wasn't it? Might be whipping themselves into a rage. Recommend that we hustle right over to the Mattock place, get the whole family, fetch them back here. If it come to a fight, this house would make a better fort than the Mattocks'. Ain't no cliff the Injans could hide behind. Mattocks are right up against the brush, but you fellers have got open ground on three sides—you could see enemies approaching. More'n that, this place is a sight smaller. Snugger, tighter, not so rambly: we'd have six grown men amongst us to watch every side. I think we could hold out, here. Not over there.

Jo, are you serious?

Never was more serious in my life. I'm telling you what I think. I been in this country a good while.

Bert sighed. Then I tender my apologies. I had laughed at your reaction when first I told you— But now I know you are sincere.

I know Jo's sincere, too, Bert. But it's a tempest in a teapot—

Harry, make no more remonstrance. Do as Jo says. Take your gun.

Harshman warned, Shot flasks and powder and all such! Might need them. What about Granger?

Isaac Harriott drew a deep breath. Now it was he who struggled to control his temper. He was thinking: Of all the nonsensical things in the world! Entire community going into alarm because of a few beggarly drifting Indians! Indian wars are a thing of the past, except perhaps in the Far West. Everyone says so. This is not the Oregon country, nor yet Florida. Tis the *Iowa* country, and—

Sulkily he slid a strap over his shoulder, he took up his Sharps breechloader. His voice was angry and high as he gave a summation to Granger. . . . Jo thinks we might expect some sort of trouble from these Indians, Carl. I don't wish you going outdoors at all, not with fresh dressings in your ear. You remain at home whilst we go to fetch the Mattock family. Can you hear?

Aye.

Understand?

Aye. I have no fear of they savages. Gave un sugar and—

Harshman said, Tell Granger to bar the door, soon as we're outside. Hear that? Bar the door.

That I'll do. But I have no fears.

As they crossed the ice there was for the first time an ooze of water underfoot. Melting! cried Harry.

Harshman did not turn. Don't get your hopes too high. Spring ain't here yet.

. . . Ah, it might be many days before the lake achieved its independence again. Long-drawn cruelty of weather still gagged the region, strangled its voices, robbed the lakes of their ability to speak and shimmer. A stifling of ice had been forced into Okoboji's mouth. The areas dared not twinkle in their free charm, cold dissuaded them, cold ruled yet. How often, Isaac Harriott thought, good lakes, when you were younger and freer (as also I was then younger by months) did I walk close to touch and taste you. Twas a pointless occupation, as are so many amiable things which human beings do without purpose or profit! But I liked to be beside you, lakes. Here I first stood near my Love and heard her voice calling across the strait. Forever I shall name this region as an area sacred to her and to me. No matter what changes ensue, Okoboji can belong to no one else.

Promptly he hid his thought (as sentient people conceal their best beauties, not because they are ashamed, but because so few men can share their secret elations with them).

Bert Snyder produced a lugubrious fancy. Harry. . . .

Bert, know what this is? Youth against Age. Gardner's middle-aged, Harshman's an old man. Look at him, striding in advance. You see: Age has seen too many perils, felt too many doubts. So the tendency of elders is to inflict their own uncertainties on the young. Weight us down with them, depress us—

I have some doubts of my own. I wonder suddenly if it is possible—The *fraises* may well be gone.

What in tarnation—?

The *fraises de bois*. Wild strawberries. I had such fondness for them when I was a boy. Each year I observed the flowers, and watched as the first fruit formed, and awaited hungrily the day when they would be red enough to pluck. Once they occupied all my thought through springtime—this dream of the *fraises de bois*—and then it happened that I became ill, and lay sick. When at last I could walk abroad once more, I went with frail steps into the forest beyond our walls. The *fraises*, they were gone. The season was departed, and berries with it. How I wept!—but the pure small strawberries I could not bring again. And now— I have been so laggardly, so without discernment! Might not my *fraises* be vanished when I go to claim them?

Stuff and nonsense, Bert.

But once more I have long been ill, my dear Harry— Sick with the sickness of stupidity!

You're permitting old folks' apprehensions to give you the pip. There comes Daniel McElroy Mattock, rushing out to greet us. . . .

Jim Mattock offered his opinion of all Indians, ancient or contemporary, as the men came in. Bastards stopped here a while ago, and started carrying off my hay. God damn lazy sons-a-bitches! I says, If you want hay, why in hell don't you cut it in warm weather, way we do? Two of those pricks, by God—and a couple of squaws trailing after— Twas the damn squaws that was pulling hay from the stack, by the armload. I give one a good slap on the rump, and she yelled like all possessed; then they dropped the hay and scooted. One of the menfolks started to turn his gun in my direction, and I grabbed the gun away from him, and kicked his ass halfway down to them trees— Then Robby come out with an axe, so both the men made tracks—

Did you give the gun back to the Injan? Harshman wanted to know.

Throwed it up on top the God damn stack. But when I remembered, and went to fetch it, fucking gun was gone!

Mr. Mattock. You'll be better off over at our place. Get your folks together, and come long. Yep, *now.*

. . . From concealment in gray melting woods, nine Indians had watched as the Red-Wingers went by. Kill? inquired a muttered chorus.

Inkpaduta said, Perhaps more *Washichun* come. Then we kill all.

He was influenced in this decision by the cunning accumulated in adult years dedicated to a pursuit of treachery. He did not know that the whites would soon re-emerge, accompanied by the Mattock household; he only felt that they might do so. With resource and caution he ordered his companions to crawl to designated places. Hushan was told to lie behind that pocked hummock where currant bushes maintained a drift; Rattle-Strike and He-Wears-Anything were stationed at a fallen basswood; others flattened elsewhere amid bluish shade and crusty peaks. The woods were marked with the striped shadows of afternoon. As the Wahpekute slid into them, a few birds had been speaking, but now chickadees and downy woodpeckers were vanished. The immediate timberland held a pervasive calm which would have been ominous if noted. Had Jo Harshman walked alone, he of all might have observed the silence with suspicion; but his canniness was blunted by presence of the rest, by excited voices of children.

Bert Snyder and Jo Harshman led the migration. Mary Mattock shepherded Agnes and the boys; but Jackson and Jacob broke free and scampered ahead, desiring to march with the leaders; they idolized the Frenchman and the ancient hunter, as Danny idolized

Isaac Harriott. The boys and their father made a great deal of noise. Jim Mattock waddled, still fulminating against hay thieves. Robby Matheson handled his shotgun timidly. (He was too dull to be susceptible to most common fears but actually he was terrified by firearms. On the very first hunting trip of his life he had seen a defective weapon burst at the breech, and maim the man who held it.) Danny Mattock was not with the changing shuttling maundering little troupe, but no one realized that he was not there. Harry and Alice brought up the rear, with Robby immediately ahead.

I am warming reluctantly for you, said Sunlight.

One day there will be a tardy spring, and a congealed residue of winter will drain away.

Not yet, not yet.

Now Harry welcomed the notion of forting-up in his own quarters along with Alice. He suspected still that Jo had been dramatizing his experience in order to impress the rest (the admitted perquisite of any veteran). How would they sleep, if Harshman insisted that the Mattock tribe must remain overnight? Well, the three females would occupy bunks, of course; maybe the two littlest boys should take the fourth bunk. The men must rest necessarily on the floor. But he'd whisper to Alice to take the low bunk in the far corner—his own. Thus he could arrange to lie on the floor beside her, and reach up and hold her hand through lingering darkness (as at the Gardner house, one memorable night). He felt grateful because the letters had not been sent off. He should be able soon to append a vivid postscript describing this incident. . . .

Inkpaduta held ready his shoots-six. Two of the others had repeating rifles, the rest were armed with single-shots. Inkpaduta had said, All shoot when I say. Men have guns. Shoot men first.

Shoot we not women?

Shoot men first. We wish not to die.

It is not good that we be killed, Itoyetonka murmured sagely.

As the talkative migrants straggled into close range beside the frozen Narrows, the heart of Inkpaduta puffed within his chest, twould burst soon. It would be a taut bladder exploding, swollen to unbearable dimensions by his whole-souled rejoicing. He had never slain a white before, he had longed to slay whites. For decades he had been gnawed with desire to do the deed he was now about to perform. *Kill all! All!* Soldiers were far away, so were villages of other whites, there was no chance for reprisal. If all were slain there would be no one left to carry the news. It might be summer before bones were found.

He selected Jim Mattock as his own first target: as the largest target of all, Mattock belonged to the Head Man. Inkpaduta prayed that no portion of the volley be wasted on children. Children could be knocked on the head. They would scatter, screaming, but they could be caught.

He dreamed not only of *Unktehi.* He had owned other delightful dreams in which he slammed white children to the death.

He yelled, Make war! with all the force of his breath.

He had rested the barrel of his revolver in a crevice of branches, sighting as one sights a rifle. Mattock walked only a few fathoms distant. With leaping pleasure he saw the fat man throw his hands against his chest, and let his eyes start when the first bullet went into him. The rest of the Wahpekute fired raggedly. One gun missed fire—it was the revolving Cochran in the hands of Makes-Fat-Bad. Several times the gun had missed fire when its owner was trying to kill cattle, but he clung to the weapon stubbornly.

Bert Snyder waved his arms on high and made himself appear much taller than he was, as he fell. A load of buckshot tore through Jo Harshman's seasoned face and out through the top of his skull. He witnessed nothing except a crash of white light. Robby Matheson died in unwarranted agony, for shots directed against him went into his stomach and bowels: he kicked and cried in old snow. A bullet intended for Isaac Harriott missed him by a yard, and went through the darling breast of Alice Mattock instead. She was aware of surprise, surprise, she endured no pain. She had walked at Harriott's right hand; the attack came from the forest at his left. Harry sprang in that direction, the screech and blast drew him. Never did he know that Alice had fallen. . . . So Jo Harshman was right after all! Well, I'll be damned! I'll be *damned!* . . . Enormity of the thing flared in his brain. This is monstrous, monstrous!—and must be put down! There must be an immediate avenging and punishing!

(Since the stealing of the first Old Jupe and that spiritual tussle which followed, Harry had thought of himself as best qualified to serve mankind within the structure of his own art. Gradually, through association with Maws, Taney, and subsequent human contacts, he became aware that man must be so purposed or he will shuffle in futility. Charles Flandrau felt the same in his addiction to the law.) Never before had Harry desired to effect a wholesale wounding, wholesale persecution and extinction. Now he was consumed with such ambition. Like the monster in that sainted room at Mercuès, described vividly by Bertell Snyder (the Alain de Solminihac room of Bert's boyhood, with beast trampled, stabbed by a spear) these rascals represented veriest evil, they'd best be done away with. His decision flared with the first gunshot and cry. He dared not look behind him, his enemies leaped in front, they flew like dancers in a reel. *Dear Allie,* he thought, *Allie back yonder, you are mine to protect.* He had half a wild worry because his Sharps was not a revolving rifle, one of the newfangled kind—and half a wild joy because he did hold a

Sharps, and it was loaded, capped. He looked through a stained-glass window with a figure on it; the figure was that of the Aged Pioneer who sat at his doorstep of an evening, talking to grandchildren, telling them. Through and beyond this form upon the pane, in brutal afternoon the foe rioted toward him and he brawled to meet them. There was not time for him to lift the gun to his shoulder, he directed the barrel, picked the nearest Indian, twas Inkpaduta, Harry did not know who it was, he'd never put eyes on Inkpaduta until this day, and had seen him only when the Wahpekute withdrew from the Gardner house. His thumb forced back the hammer as he swiveled the weapon, his index finger squeezed hastily, too hastily. He missed. The explosion kicked the gun into his ribs. Harry was struck on the other side, his left side, he thought someone had thrown a club. It was a bullet which hit him, he'd never been struck by a bullet before, he had no time to consider the sensation or feel more than the single impact. *More-Precious-Than-Rubies, I protect thee!* The empty Sharps twirled in his hands, he had it reversed, his right hand was still in the area of the gunlock, his left hand wrapped the barrel. He jabbed the butt up and out and around, he thought someone fell, he couldn't be sure. Someone must have fallen . . . he'd caught a glimpse of a vast hummock made by Jim Mattock . . . must have seen, couldn't remember . . . Mattock shot down when the volley came? *Dear Allie back yonder, shan't let them get you.* Indians scooted directly at and past him, flounder and flapping of loose garments, shreds and feathers, brandished weapons, slabbed faces, flying braids. Mattock down, Harry had seen; Harshman dead, Harry didn't know; Alice dead, Harry didn't know; Bert Snyder down, Harry didn't know that; Robby Matheson a-squirming, Harry didn't know. Behind him the Wahpekute thrust their knives into Mary Mattock, ran down the squalling Agnes, ran down the bunny-darting boys. Harry didn't know . . . he had the grinding notion that if he possessed a Swift's drug mill he would pulverize enemies with the pestle. Enemies? He'd never owned an enemy before! *Never had one* . . . the words tried to blow between his sagging lips. He was among trees, had mauled and twisted his way there. Yells were high and low and coarse and growling and coyote-barking all around. Again he swung his empty weapon through and among them, and felt once more a body sprawl away. Slam 'em, he thought. Heal later, if indeed they must be healed! There came a blow, a blow, again someone had hit him hard, there was winking light but he could see a face through it. Salt stung his nostrils, he breathed nothing but salt; twas not the salt of snow, twas hot salt and searing. Face which he saw was a dragon's face, and dark, it had no nose. I thought all dragons owned noses; this one doesn't. Get it! His hands arched together around the barrel, as when he'd been a boy at play: another boy tossed a ball, and so he'd have a stick in his hands, and so he'd swing the stick and try to hit the ball in flight. He swung, put every force and yearning into the scope. That noseless countenance was swept away, but with only part of his blow, only part: a hurt jabbed through hands, into wrists, up arms, rocked his body with the jar. The gun-butt had struck a tree, it flew away. The word *Broke* started out of Harry's mouth but did not issue forth. *Oh, most silver pinwheel!* He was down at last, and they clustered round him, screaming as carrion birds had never screamed. He had an errand, he rushed urgently into space.

Daniel Mattock was paralyzed. Such terror'd never overwhelmed him before in the nearly-thirteen-years of his life—not when he was chased by a bull, not when he fell into an Indiana well, not when he saw a fast team of horses run away with old Mr. and Mrs. Dingman in Delaware County, and smash their wagon against an elm. Twas the concentrated fright engendered by hobgoblins never clearly imagined or discerned, and thus made miserably credible (because their horns or feathers were formed in the vapor of fancy, of nightmare . . . worse menace than the Alderney bull with spotted shape and speed).

Once an ornery older boy adjured him, Danny, don't you dast go in that root cellar.

Why not?

Not down in that potato hole, even if your Ma sends you!

Whwhwhy not?

Cause there's *Ghosts and Things.*

This was all the boy had said but it was enough. With whines Daniel refused to perform a mission to which he was ordered. He felt the punishment of his mother's hand against his backside, heard her cry: Don't you sass me and say No, Daniel McElroy Mattock! I tolt you to fetch me them parsnips, and I mean it, else I'll go cut a big switch!

So he'd descended into dank smelly darkness and felt his way among shrouded lumps of vegetables; he'd scented decay, breathed mildew, slid his feet through rotting substances. He'd heard rats scatter away, peeping like so many impure chickens as he proceeded whimpering. His torture was not composed solely of evil existing odors or blackness or rats: it was made of imaginings distilled from mere suggestion. . . . Did It have claws? He might not know. Were the Ghosts and Things male or female, were they armed, did they have faces like those skulls dug up in Farmer Fielding's gravel pit, did they wear fur or did they dress in tatters? He could not construct the answer to any of these questions, did not have the strength or aptness. All that he knew was that he believed he was beset, or at least watched, by Frights who populated the place. The jest of their wavering shapelessness was the worst thing about them.

So it stood with the Wahpekute: long they had been limping as pitiable clowns. You had to guffaw, as the Mattock family guffawed—all except Alice—when that Indian woman came a-begging months earlier: the squaw who went out to skate and stagger upon ice while they watched her ludicrous arm-wavings. The aborigines stank, they wore rags or absurd fragments of white people's garb; the most grotesque parade of Antiques and Horribles (some folks called them the Dreadfuls, some called them Calathumpians) on Fourth of July, with bell-ringing and horn-blowing and cat-calling, could not have come up to this assortment of grunting dark-faced men. Christ, my hogs are a hell of a lot more human than that gang! Danny's father roared. My cattle have got the better of them when it comes to brains, by God! . . . Here, in the first suggestion of retreating winter, clowns were turned into panthers. Suddenly they had changed—without reason, with no apparent instigation, without remorse or excuse. Their villainy held no logic and thus became an incredibly more termagant villainy than might have been managed by professional footpads or pirates, from whom viciousness was expected. The foolish dog, grown inexplicably rabid, seemed a demon worse than a wolf.

Things were loosed from a root cellar at last, and they had caught up with Daniel Mattock. There was but one place to go, he went there: under the bed.

Ordinarily that region was occupied by a trundle bed, but Jacob and Jackson had been playing at Mover that morning (a game they managed frequently indoors: they would attach a rope to the trundle bed, and take turns at being oxen or passengers traveling somewhere). So the trundle bed was not in its place, there was room for Danny. In dimness he pushed himself against the bottom log and felt blades of cool air arising between the puncheons. At first he was too terrified to make any noise, so no one in the family knew that he was hidden. Everyone left the house in a mixed-up rush. Daniel did not realize that all were gone until too late.

Why did not parents and dear Doctor Harriott return, where were they? He began to sob—not in entire hopelessness, but with that vague desperation of the weeper who half believes that mournful monotony of his plaint may in some manner relieve a pain. He cried steadily, damp dull sounds building nearly to the strength of syllables in his throat and in echoing space behind his nose. *Uh-huh-huh-huh-huh-huh-huh.* He cried on, sickened by the dreary noise, powerless to stop it. . . . Get up and run? Run where? He couldn't run, couldn't move his legs, didn't want to move his legs. Oh, there was shooting, he could hear guns, a lot of guns! There rang pliant screams—and all interspersed and tied together with imagined hooting of timber wolves and owls and other beasts and birds. And then one more shot, a single shot—no more wailing, no more hullooing, just the wolf and owl noises, or were those stranger dogs a-barking?—*uh-huh-huh-huh-huh-huh-huh!*—did the Indians have dogs along with them?—he had seen no dogs. (Once he'd run away from gypsies when he was little; he and Agnes and Big Sister Alice were coming from school—Jacob wasn't big enough to go to school, Jackson wasn't born—and they stood at the head of the hill by the Haas place and saw wagons coming—yes, those were gypsies, the wagons were brightly painted, and led horses followed behind; and seated in the first wagon was a huge man in a pale blue shirt with a dirty colored scarf tied around his head. So the children ran, away, away, running hard, gasping under their breath: Gypsies! *Gypsies!*) It was like that now, but a more passionate hysteria because he lay aimless beneath the bed; and one of those Indians had worn a shirt as blue as the shirt worn by a gypsy, and maybe that Indian was a gypsy, maybe all Indians were gypsies, and gypsies Indians, and *uh-huh-huh-huh-huh-huh-huh!*—where oh where were his folks?

. . . The medicated lint, with which Isaac Harriott had stuffed the ears of his patient, prevented Carl Granger's hearing those rapid rounds of fire which sounded only a few minutes earlier. Carl had barred the door dutifully when the others departed, and only vaguely did he sense a thudding delivered against the door itself— He saw rather than heard pounding, for the big wooden bar was moving back and forth in its sockets under pressure. Behavior of the dog Lee, however, was unmistakable; Lee was snarling *Indians,* and quivering his body and wrinkling his mouth above the teeth. Carl arose groggily from the bunk where he'd been lying, and slid the bar loose . . . aye, if there were any of the ragged beggars outside, and attempting to enter thus unceremoniously, he'd fling them into the nearest snow-drift, he would. They shouldn't come a-bothering of him, when already that morning he'd doled out sugar to a smartish few. He selected a moment to open the door when Hushan and He-Wears-Anything had stepped to either side of the entrance, and Bahata raised his gun to blast at the door itself. Instead there was presented the target of Carl Granger. Bahata blew a hole through Carl's chest. Even while he still folded and tottered, swaying bewildered on dying feet, He-Wears-Anything struck with a broadaxe which he'd picked up from the woodpile. The wide sharp blade bit halfway into Carl's head through his right cheek and aching right ear, and impact swung his strong body flopping into the trampled yard. For a scant moment he saw merry-dancers more colorful, more sweepingly impassioned, than those fateful streamers witnessed years before in Aldington. *Aye, see un.* . . . Lee plunged to grasp Bahata by the calf of his leg; He-Wears-Anything, though amused by this spectacle and by the aggrieved Bahata's attempts to club the bulldog loose from his hold, obliged by withdrawing the bloody axe from Carl Granger's head. He lifted it on high for one quick downward stroke which cleft Lee's spine in two.

. . . Across the Narrows, the miserable One-Staggering crouched at the timber's edge, resting his cracked head in his hands; but Inkpaduta and four other men frolicked among scattered bodies. All wished that they might take hair—even the leader wished this—but the shadow of *Unktehi* disciplined them and they refrained.

I kill, I kill, I kill! *Tapi!* They die!

They sang sometimes in cadence, sometimes singly.

He-Has-Done-Walking stammered jubilantly, Also I kill! I am one who kills, I use a knife, I stick it into this old woman as she tries to run away. See!— *Wanyaka,* here is the hole made by my knife. Now again I stick my knife into her. Again! I kill!

Wimachashta! I am a man, announced Rattle-Strike. I kill.

I boast!

Inkpaduta declared, I kill! I kill a man, I kill part of another man, I kill a boy-child of whites. But where is other boy?

What boy name you? Both are here.

There is another, he is taller than these small ones. He stands outside his lodge when first the three men come. But he is not here.

This is true, the thing told by That Old One! said Rattle-Strike with conviction. Him also I see beside the lodge. His hair is red.

Inkpaduta roared, His hair is red, and Red-End am I named. I claim the boy with hair of red!

Where is he? Does he flee among the trees?

Nay, he is not with his people as they come.

He taku hogan ka? asked Inkpaduta loudly. What kind of fish is that? What kind of fish is that, which lives when I am fishing for him?

He led in the race toward the Mattock house. Rattle-Strike and others were younger, they pressed on the heels of the leader; and his son-in-law was ardent in desire to beat Inkpaduta to the managing of this one remaining death (if not engaged in war, Rattle-Strike would have thought twice before offending his wife's father; but this was indeed war, all men went mad in war). Older than the rest or not, Inkpaduta was first in at the cabin door. He'd had the head start.

Danny Mattock thought that his parents, or perhaps Alice and the doctor, were returned to save him. He yelled with inarticulate relief as the door was flung open. His squawk of supposed recognition was sufficient to disclose Danny's whereabouts. Inkpaduta bent heavily and fastened a huge blood-smeared hand around the skinny ankle. Some splinters from raw puncheons (forever unstepped on, there under the bed, never polished by grease and usage) drove through the boy's shirt into his back as he was dragged across the floor (he did not feel them). Inkpaduta caught the other kicking leg in his free hand—

he had discarded his gun at the door when he heard Danny cry out. He pulled the gangling shape against himself as he arose, holding the boy upside down. In this moment Daniel McElroy Mattock thought of his mother. He considered in blinding rapid recollection the smell and feeling of her, thought that he heard her laughing somewhere, perhaps chiding him . . . there flashed the time when she had given him a gooseberry tart hot from the oven, so hot that he could scarcely eat it . . . he called for her. The intruders were in uproar at finding him thus belatedly. Mary Mattock could never have heard his appeal had she been there and alive.

Three times Inkpaduta, holding the boy by his ankles, drove the round head hard against the floor. The little house echoed with each hollow blow of hollow head against a hollowness of split logs. Then, with Danny silent as the dead, and seeing that his eyes seemed set and dead, and that blood issued copiously from nose and ears and sagging mouth, Inkpaduta tumbled the body upon a corner bed. He proclaimed, So you see! Again I kill! *Idatahn!*

Rattle-Strike stepped back to give his father-in-law room for dancing if he willed to dance; but Inkpaduta did not dance at this time. Rattle-Strike stumbled across the trundle bed where Jacob and Jackson had played at Movers. (They had heard of Kansas, or at least Jacob had; hence they played that they were movers going out to Kansas. You got your gun, Mr.? Yep. I got mine too. Hey, there's a deer over there, great big deer. You shoot him, Mr.! Boom! All right, Mr., I got him all shot! Now we better get down and make camp for the night.) He nearly fell in his stumbling. With rage he bent, gathered up the trundle bed with its wadded covers, and hurled the whole mass into the fireplace. Flames puffed, frying oily blanket wool, clotting tightly around the dry wood. Makes-Fat-Bad called approvingly: We make more fire, we do women's work, we make fire!—and broke into recognizable laughter at his own humor. He picked up stools, tossed them upon the welter, he heaved the table over the pile of flame. This wreckage, together with other objects which other men tossed, extended well out into the room. The floor accepted its initial searing while the ruffians plundered and mauled things about, while they still lingered in the cabin. But neither flames nor smoke burst from the door as Inkpaduta led down triumphantly to the Narrows again. In due time the blaze would advance until it embraced the entire cabin.

Daniel McElroy Mattock, who would have been thirteen if there had been another June for him, became stimulated eventually into dazed half-consciousness. His skull was fractured but he was not killed as yet, only half-killed. Presently he became aware of a high-pitched sound running through chaos. He thought languidly that this cry came from one of the pigs (once he had a father, once there were hogs in existence . . . once, once some people . . . bad people, good people? The vague faraway reedy sound was surely a cry, an audible inescapable prolongation of distress).

It had taken the blaze more than two hours to creep along boundaries of the fireplace junkpile and—charring, gnawing with smoldering persistence—to ignite the floor and finally the walls of the Mattock house. It was dark outside when the clearing began to blossom richly with a fair light which threw its paint in every crackling direction, and even dressed the abandoned dead, the farthest ones on dreary ice, with coloration. Darkness or flamelight, it made little difference to Danny Mattock. He could not move, could not reckon, could value no more, guess no more. The Wahpekute had gone away and made more deaths before the house-fire began its final chortling, and some of the Wahpekute had come back with members of their families: both male and female ears listened to the gargle of that fire, and to an elusive scream which wound aloft like a snake, or banner waving—stifled in time, broken into yips and coughs, a scream crippled in its termination. Danny was not completely paralyzed, he could feel even if he could not direct his limbs into withdrawal. The blaze approached steadily from northern and eastern portions of the room; and the bed whereon his body lay was in the northwest corner; so the end of it all was as protracted as any gush of fire might permit. Danny's feet were fat and black before the roof fell in. Even his murderers halted in a kind of inquiring silence when they heard the elfin song he sang. The Mattocks could never have been called a religious family—not they. But in grip of one civilization or another, Danny had been exposed to brief sessions of Sabbath school, especially when a picnic or Christmas celebration seemed imminent (with free fare to be distributed). Thus he had heard of Hell, had heard Hell described. He thought even before he died that he was in Hell; and he was.

Warning glow of Danny's pyre was observed neither by Howes nor by anyone at the Noble-Thatcher place. Beside cozy more delicate more domestic fires, the inhabitants along East Okoboji had been talking, over their evening meals. Gratefully they discussed an imminent arrival of sleighs filled with provisions, they spoke of those new folks who would come out from Hampton in the spring. They did not step out of their houses to observe that hollow-blooming rose of light near the Narrows.

But brilliant flame did reveal bodies scattered along a path and onto ice at the scene, and paid especial flickering tribute to that long sprawl once known as Bert Snyder (years earlier known as Robert Didier). His subtraction from life, his ultimate withdrawal, had been accomplished almost painlessly. Yet there'd been time for the herds of his youth to come storming over him.

A mighty and a mingled throng
Were gathered in one spot. . . .

He thought that they were detached from the cavern where for so long they had been tranced and suspended, and swarmed heedlessly to smite him with their hoofs, to assail him with claws and horns. Why, I have done nothing to deserve this!—was the thought which rose sluggishly, and then stopped beneath the surface of consciousness, a hollow bubble of thought, but not yet bursting in murk. He summoned every strength, for he felt that he must publish immediately an explanation of long-kept mystery . . . about Silence and A Thing Called Waiting. Ox and ibex, cave wolf and woolly rhinoceros, and— *Zut!*—the *equidae*, the Chinese horses— Every last one of them is elemental, voices counseled him. They have been here since the beginning, and they began before there was a beginning, and the elemental matters will persist until the end and beyond that end; for there will be no end to such matters. You may die, and She may die, and He may die; and the antler-marked murals may die, and the paints may corrode; the fur-clad protoplasts who painted them also died, and the animals which they painted also died! But ochre, or the torchlight, or rotting-bone smell or rotting-flesh smell—these revive as a fume, and in time that fume becomes explosive; so it will bang and burst, and form new forces and new dusts, all spinning countlessly through space; and as they spin with hard increased acceleration, they squeeze a fresh yeast from dry dusty fissures by the very speed and power of their vortex; and some of the stenches will become a moisture and a heat; that moisture and that heat will fan and nourish life, twill grow, twill spread, twill take form and become flesh again; and glimmerings of a spirit will arise within those skins, and thus novice souls will be activated, only themselves to go to sleep in time, as the cells surrounding them sleep and change. And then once more— Fumes arising!—and the chemicals and energies extending into wondering brightness, worshiping brightness, a fervency of air and space more compulsive than sight of any painted throngs. And why was I here?—and why were You?—and what did We do? We did nothing, performed no proper rite; but on and on the alchemy is consummated through other caves and in ultimate projections of gases and sunlight. We did nothing. But in the resounding future We will. O dear God and O dear Silence and O dear All— We *will.*

XXXVIII

Throughout the day, on through the afternoon and into baleful sunset season, Rowland Gardner spoke a disjointed prayer to his Lord. Please don't let nothing bad happen to Thy servant, Harvey Luce! He's got to come back safe to his wife and little ones. He's just got to! Numerous times, O Lord, Thou knowest, I've been out of patience with Harvey, count of his excessively religious ways and manners; but Thou knowest he's diligent and good-hearted, and tries to do his best by Mary and the children. Please don't let nothing awful happen to him, don't let nothing happen to *us*. Leave me never have another nightmare like the ones I've had before: such as big tall wild men climbing up the walls and forcing in through windows, and tearing us apart. Wish I hadn't heard all those Indian tales that Cousin Philo used to tell, when I was little, back at the East. And then one time I read Captain Church's book about Indian wars of olden times, and it was plumb full of accounts of dangers and slaughter. . . . *A doleful, great, naked, dirty beast he looked like. Captain Church then said, that forasmuch as he had caused many an Englishman's body to be unburied, and so to rot above ground, that not one of his bones should be buried. And calling his old Indian executioner, bid him behead and quarter him.* And more like that, it's all mixed up, but all was terrifying. If these Indians come back, I'll give them every smidge of ammunition in the place—I promise that, O Lord!—so's they'll be pleased, and go away, and not harm a hair of anybody's head. They would do that, if I was kind to them, and generous, wouldn't they, Lord? Oh, I'm confident they would. Thou knowest, Lord, Thou knowest! Please make them to not come back; and if they come back, make them go away without hurting us. Maybe sometimes in the past I have faltered at serving Thee, dear God in Heaven, dear Jesus and All, and—dear Holy Ghost. (I've been confused about you Folks, for I could never quite understand about the Holy Trinity, and just where the Ghost came in. I reckon maybe other Christians have felt the same way at times.) Thou knowest I have faltered at properly serving and keeping my family; and if I had served and kept them properly, I wouldn't have brought them into any dangers such as this. But I didn't expect to, surely. Thus perhaps also I have not been the laborer in Thy vineyard which I should have been. But if Thou art enraged, please, oh please, do not turn Thy face away; and do not punish the rest of the family for my sins of omission or commission. I know I oughtn't to have felt so lustful when I lay with Frances, because tis bad to entertain a lust, and I did entertain it . . . yes I did, so many times, and thus I made myself unworthy of Thy love. Please keep us in Thy care; please keep us safe. . . .

Behind southwesterly trees the sun was building a fierce glow, the sun was making itself into a private fire around which witches might be circulating. The popping of faraway gunshots rebounded from the sounding board of Okoboji ice, an hour or two before; and after that more shots tapped out sporadically, their echoes came a-rapping into the glade.

What's that noise, Pa? asked Rowly, and the other smaller children turned their faces up.

Just folks a-hunting in the woods, said Rowland Gardner's palsied mouth. S'all right, bubby. Just folks gone hunting.

What you suppose they're hunting, Pa?

Oh, deer, I reckon.

Why, there ain't no deer around! You said so, Pa, and that was why we couldn't have no meat!

Oh, well, just folks a-hunting something.

. . . The twins were long since returned from East Okoboji. At sunset they skulked, together with their father and six others of the Wahpekute, in brush beside the path leading to the Mattock site. Makes-Fat-Bad and One-Staggering were not with them. The Titonwan was still engaged in hunting down the last of the Mattock oxen, in munching hot raw ox-liver, in drinking up the steaming red sauce. *That is good sauce; it is the best sauce.* Women were put to work at cutting out tenderloins and other choice portions. Isaac Harriott's last blow with his clubbed rifle had been a partial success. The butt of the gun encountered One-Staggering's head, in that same instant when it was broken against a hickory tree. Had it not been for the tree, Harry's desperate swing would have shattered the upper half of Tachanachekahota's skull. But there was that interference, that glancing; thus the victim lived still. He was suffering. Two men aided the injured Dakota back to camp; but once there they lost interest in him, and left him to the mercies of the women, if any mercies would be meted out. They ran to join others in pillaging the Red Wing cabin, in voicing cries of wonder at the medicines in Harry's kit. (They thought that these white men kept a store, and had bottled goods to sell; but they were frightened by queer smells, they did not wish to taste. They were more than delighted at finding even a limited quantity of brandy.) One-Staggering lay groaning on a matted hide in his lodge, and hemorrhage mingled with mucus which drained from his nose-hole. His face would not be blackened on this night, he was in too much pain for that. Faces of the other men would be painted with charcoal; this blackening was not to be removed until they were finished with their war. Violent tradition demanded that they should so mourn for the dead they'd made. Everyone knew that if you killed an enemy, you then put on mourning for him, and you sang your song.

Something I've killed, and I lift up my voice. The Eastern Two-Legged-One I've killed, and I lift up my voice.

It was sad to think that *Unktehi* had demanded the sacrifice which he did, but there was no help for it. Fresh damp-stained hair could not grow from their belts or be waved aloft. . . .

Ate. Why wait we here?

I would know whether this man shoots.

Ate, there is but one man left in that house.

Aye, one man.

He shoots not more than once, then we break down his door!

It may be that the door opens, it may be that we need not break it down. But it may be that he has more than one gun, and so he shoots twice. Wish you to be shot by this white man?

Fire-Cloud cried, If the white man can kill me, so will I let him kill me!

There came a chorus of approval from the others, a restlessness amid the bushes. Inkpaduta saw that there was no halting them any longer, although in his opinion they were taking an unnecessary risk. There must be some way in which the white man could be coaxed into emptying his weapons, before the actual assault was made. . . ?

Inkpaduta kept the lids of his sore eyes fluttering, trying to clear the rheum away as he stared toward the house. Rowland Gardner stepped outside to reconnoiter. The old Dakota lifted his rifle. No, the distance was too far; he might miss.

We go! snapped Inkpaduta. We go to beg, then we kill.

There was a garbled chorus: *Washte, washte!* They stepped from the timber, rising up from low hard drifts in hazel and gooseberry thickets.

Gardner saw them emerging, and the beat of his heart filled his entire body, pulsated in his extremities, banged at his ears. He stepped back into the house. *Nine!* He tore the single word free, it sounded extremely shrill and nasal.

Both the Luce children began to whinny before the outlaws were halfway across open ground. Nine Indians were coming: that was enough to set the children off. Yielding to the persuasion of example, Rowly Gardner added his louder blubbering to theirs. The Wahpekute pressed with determination into the cabin and fetched back their smell; this time there was the odor of fresh blood as well—their moccasins were wet with it, the rest of their garb was touched by red. They went into the house, and the door stood open; they went into the house, and there was only the dull dark oblong of the doorway to be seen; they went into the house, and they signed that they wanted flour, and there was a little flour left, and Gardner turned toward the flour barrel. A single gunshot knocked its reverberation out into the trees. That was when the women's screams came up. Roaring-Cloud had shot Rowland Gardner through the heart as soon as his back was turned.

For only a moment the yells increased in volume. Then a wet waving scarecrow with streaming stringy hair and a mass of raw color for a face— This object was propelled across the doorstep; this object had been Mary Luce, twas Mary Luce no longer, twas but an object, it dove headlong against a congealed drift along the woodpile. Two or three big shapes came waltzing in pursuit, they had their guns on high, they tamped the butts down, they made a paste of the object's skull. Nor had they intended to destroy Mary Luce: she was young, they meant to keep her and use her. But Frances Gardner tried to snatch the gun, even as Roaring-Cloud fired it: that sufficed. All were enraged by any resistance, and now must batter and cut. Frances twisted as a core in the spinning fruit of encounter, her clothing was ripped as hands came seeking and snatching, her hair was plastered against her belabored head. The first blow was all she felt; then gun-butts muted her. Some of the raiders had the happy furious notion that they were working out a spite against *Unktehi. Unktehi* had ordered that no scalps be taken; therefore was it not good to ruin the scalps?—then no one should feel a regret at not being able to strip them off! *Zuya, zuya!* they growled, striking down, muddying their weapons in Frances Gardner's blood and brains.

Abbie had been holding Baby Mandy in her arms. She sat in Mary's little Boston rocker as the door was opened . . . Bertie and Rowly fled to squeeze themselves against her knees. *Ahhhhh—ahhhhh—* Abbie, Abbie!

Seven-year-old Rowly was wrenched away. Kechonmani cried: I cut off the head of this child, as did whites cut off the head of Bursts-Frog-Open!

Inkpaduta dragged all that was left of the elder woman and hurled her tousled wreckage beyond the step and into snow. Do not cut off the head of white child! he cried gleefully over his shoulder. That is not the way! A better way I use: I kill three children of the Sauk, long ago. All three I kill in this way—

What is the best way to kill white child? came a cry in unison.

Bring out of lodge, bring to this oak tree. Bring white children, take them by the heels. . . . Ah, here is white child! Now take white child—like this! Like this—

Less play Statue!

Less!

Oh swing me, swing me. . . .

So now you are swung, small children, now you are whirled and wheeled, you'll see the chilly dusky world go spinning: it is a world you never really knew, and one which you can claim no longer.

What did you own, what owned you, what was your resounding bliss, O bigger boy? The chunk of bread and 'lasses; the slippery elm; the bird you chased and couldn't catch; the bear you never got a chance to tempt with salt; the game you played, the Punch-and-Beckon with your elder sisters, and you tried to guess who gave the punch, and tried to free the prisoner by beckoning, but you were small, you couldn't play the game so well; the home-knit Christmas mittens; hickory nuts; the crabs you wished to eat, but they were hard and sour. . . . What was your fear and grief? You never grew quite tall enough to have abundant fears! . . . The wrastle-wrastle with that other little boy; the admonition and the slap; the being quilted up on high, and listening to droning voices of grown folks who read. Ah, wish upon a star, the way they've taught you! *Twinkle, twinkle, little star, how I wonder what you are. . . .* Hear the stories of the Indians your grandsires met in Eastern woods; and hear as well the Bible tales which Brother Harvey tries painstakingly to teach you: Jesus when He was a little boy, Joseph, and Baby Moses in his woven boat. . . . Eat once more the heel of hot corn-loaf with good rich grease upon it; or feel the cut of limber willow-switch when you are punished, when you jig and howl. Enjoy once more the bag-swing that your father made for you: grain-sack stuffed with prairie hay, depending from a rope; and sport to run and dive and fling yourself in air, and snap your hands around the rope and feel the good strong impact of the bag between your legs. So you set it into motion, so you're swinging past the ridge.

You are swinging, swinging. . . .

Perform your tiny chores, O other boy!—and scrap with Rowly; poke your finger at the baby, pretend you're going to bite her, hear her glee, she ducks her face away from yours, she knows that you won't bite. And still you'd also like to tame a bear some day, you hope that one will come around: a jolly shaggy bear, so you can teach him tricks. And say your prayers; ah, Bertie, never miss your prayers before you go to sleep. For Pa is sad on any night you've missed your prayers. And be allowed to climb in bed sometimes with Ma and Pa, and snuggle down between them, and they make their jokes with you. Pa has a trick, he hasn't many tricks, but he has this: he takes your nose between his thumb and finger, squeezes, squeezes, then he says abruptly: Now I've *got* it!—and you look to see, and sure enough he seems to have a piece of your own nose, stuck right there in his hand, and then you keep a-feeling of your nose again, to see how much of it is gone, and everybody laughs. Oh, it is warm in bed with Ma and Pa; not time to go a-swinging then, no chance for it; but some time . . . swinging, swinging. Say farewell to gingerbread: so long since you have eaten any, yet you recollect the taste of it. Remember how those punkin-heads were smelling when the candles scorched against the lids? Remember how the sharp triangled eyes were glowing, how the teeth were laughing in the mouth? And Granny cooked the taffy for you all; you pulled and pulled, you greased your hands and pulled and pulled, and made a rope and got it stuck upon your hands; and part way through, they worked the nutmeats in; and then, when it was stiff, came Granny's shears, a-snipping, snipping, and the little cornered pieces flew. Oh, it was good to chew, and how it lasted, lasted!—and you and Rowly heard ghost stories which the rest were telling, and they said that this was Halloween, and so you'd have ghost stories; but you grew afraid, and whimpered, and you sought your mother's lap; then you were safe and trusting. Let your eyes grow round and staring, as your father tells of Daniel . . . and the lions wouldn't bite him, not at all; and those three Hebrew boys—Shadrach, Meshach, Abednego—they went right in that fiery furnace, stood among the flames; but God was with them and they never even got a scorch. Now say the Grace that you were taught . . . Pa says, Now let our Bertie ask the Blessing; so you ask it in a mumble, like you're scairt; but only scairt because in that one moment you are rather close to God yourself.

And now you're even closer, closer to Him, as you swing.

Oh, see the baby as she goes upon her final whirl! For when you see a baby, baby girl, you're looking at a ball of clover-bloom, pink clover-bloom; and sweet the taste of milk upon her fat pink mouth—the mother's milk she's sucked for long. But now she's large, and talking, she is eating grown-up things, and yelling with a grown-up cry when she is frightened . . . she is frightened now, and listen to her yell as she goes swinging, swinging. A baby girl is phoebe song and flower pollen, she is curly feather of the smallest birds, and she elects to trot, trot, trot, and jump when there is never reason for a jump. She is a sacred pebble picked up on the shore; she has a treacle-taste, a smell of wild rose from a warmer day; she has her dirty dolly and she loves to cuddle it, though all the rags are coming out; she has her baby-talk, and everybody laughs to hear it (when there's time for them to listen to her talk). The baby girl is thistle-top and kitten-fur; she is as gentle as the cattails when they're ripening (sometimes she screams like any fiend). Tender little hands go long exploring, touching all the things they shouldn't touch. No, no, Baby, say the monitoring voices, that's a Mustn't Touch! You let go at once, or I'll just give you . . . spanking . . . yes, she knows the word, she knows it well, one of the first she ever learned. She laughs and runs away, her hands are laden with sweet dough or batter that she's thieved away. Skin as soft as any ribbons, perfume of the fat creased neck; fragile hairs which grow on dandelion stems, and so you have them on your neck, O baby girl; and you're too young to go fast swinging in an orbit, through the last cramped space of This Your World You'll Never Know; but you go, and whirled as both the boys were whirled.

What will be your dream, soft children? Lambs and puppies, sugar of the dawn? Or but a velvet silence over all?

His-Curly-Sacred had been the first to put his hands upon Abbie, to hold her mewing and squirming in his arms, and claim her.

The rest played in a random riot: kicking furniture about, indoors and out; tearing pages from books; rummaging for spirit water, finding it not; but emitting shrill chicken-cries of triumph each time a dish was hurled, each time a garment was torn in twain. Bahata jigged about the dooryard, holding the body of Baby Mandy aloft, lowering it against the ground, waving it on high again, making a song as he danced. *I kill smallest child of all! This is a girl-child of the whites, and her I kill, her I kill. This is the smallest person to be killed. Her I kill!* He toyed with the notion of bearing the tiny corpse back to camp; but it was a long way to carry the thing, and there were other bodies in that direction which could be mutilated—they awaited whatever attention anyone might choose to bestow.

Hda! Go home! he ordered, when at last they were circling away through growing dark. Go home, white child! He threw the baby into the cabin.

His dance and deed went unwitnessed by Abbie, who was mauled away up the path by Tawachehawakan. The Mattock cabin blazed merrily beyond the woods. A death song was being sung by Daniel Mattock; but His-Curly-Sacred would not hasten there to witness the spectacle or to revel among the dead. He had a live thing with him, it was a live thing on which he'd set his heart. He hauled the girl into the bachelors' lodge, where the wounded One-Staggering sniffed and mourned in neglect. His-Curly-Sacred wrestled Abbie to his own heap of robes.

She saw his wide dirty smeared face diffusing, expanding, contracting, scrolling itself before her: there was enough light in the lodge for that. She saw the face beyond, and then coming closer, and then she was on her back and the face was above her. Oh, Ma! Ma! *Ma!* (Twas a senseless appeal: Frances Gardner lay growing steadily icier before her door.) *Ma!* . . . Ah, you're hurting me, you're . . . *hurting me! Maaaaah!*

Inkpaduta sat gazing at the fire, sat longer than anyone else; every man and woman of the band was asleep at last—even the unhappy Corn-Sucker—yet he sat with pipe grown cold and held stiffly. The fire gave to Inkpaduta a memory of certain fires which had burned long ago. How many fires had he seen? He wondered about this, knowing vaguely that in so wondering he was again demonstrating his uncommon age. Not too many Wahpekute survived past five tens of winters. He knew no companion of his youth who had lived as long as he had lived.

Once he lay sick beside a small river far to the south and east (in this season the sun rose in the direction where that river lay)— It was a river which his people named Shungidansan: the River of the White Fox. There, in boyhood, he had chafed miserably on his robe. Horrific spirits gathered round him, he saw their leering faces, cried in his heart because these blank-faced spirits (the color of bits-of-flat-slate-stone-found-in-gravel, their faces were) had been strong enough and warlike enough to infest the lodge. At that time Inkpaduta had lived possibly ten winters.

One of the spirits began to shrink: it was a medicine the spirit owned, he could make himself smaller and smaller without even moving from his squat. When the spirit started out he was taller than any man in that Wahpekute gens: but soon he made himself no taller than a big-black-bear-walking-on-all-four-legs; then he made himself no taller than a wolf, then no taller than a fox, then no taller than a hare, then no taller than a mouse, then no taller than a bright-green-beetle-who-pushes-dung-balls-about-and-smells-bad. In this size the spirit approached closer to Inkpaduta, walked up his chest, climbed the thin pillar of the boyish neck, forced a way into his mouth, forced a way down into his throat. There the spirit remained —but swelling himself meanwhile until he was gaseous and bouncy as a floating drowned animal in a summer flood. In this bloated condition the spirit could shut off the boy's breath. He persisted in doing so. Inkpaduta could not draw in the air he needed, nor expel air already contained in his hot body, so now he must strangle to death.

Through filmed gaze he saw father and mother and many other people gathered near him. He wished to scream out at them, wished to say, Oh, take the bad spirit out of my throat, he chokes me! And drive all these other spirits from the lodge; beat them with sticks, drive them off!— But he could say nothing, he might utter only a petulant squeak like the sound of a coarse wind harping through dead branches.

This boy dies, spoke Wamdisapa with sadness. (It was a sadness which would not prevent his beating Inkpaduta often and brutally in the future, whenever Wamdisapa had traded for much spirit water with the Frenchman who had rum to sell; and no other fathers beat their sons—no, not one father!—no one except Wamdisapa.) This boy dies.

The boy does not die, said Iwashtedanmani. (He was called He-Walks-Slowly because he was born with a clubbed foot.)

Then you make better medicine!

Ah, the boy does not die!

He-Walks-Slowly began once more to agitate the rattle in his left hand. It was a rattle made from the skull of a domestic cat which had wandered away from that same French trader who sold spirit water. Every scrap of the cat had been used by He-Walks-Slowly. It was common knowledge that he had some of the brains still, dried and salted. And these brains were very strong medicine indeed (and fearfully expensive); but they were for use only in treating a patient wounded in war, or one who had fallen from a high place, as a cat might fall if shot while climbing. (That was the way this cat had died.) He-Walks-Slowly wore the skin of the cat often when summoned to the sick; he had it on, now, as a head-dress—with the patterned cat's head all dried and tufted above his own forehead, and the tail dangling down his back. . . . The skull which formed the rattle had all its holes stopped with clay tightly baked. Inside were two buckshot which He-Walks-Slowly claimed to have removed from the body of a Chippeway whom he'd killed—though many people scoffed at this statement, and asserted privately that He-Walks-Slowly had never in fact slain a Chippeway or any other enemy. However no one ever made such a detracting statement within the hearing of He-Walks-Slowly, because all were afraid of this mystery man.

Does not die, does not die. . . .

Ah, my son dieth! Inkpaduta's mother began to wail, but in exasperation Wamdisapa thrust her out of the lodge.

He does not die, cried He-Walks-Slowly, rattling away until his warped hand was a blur. Moisture began to show on his face. . . . He does not die, does not die, does not die! I see him now as I see many moons to come. He lives for many many moons, he is very old when he dies. He has close to *kektopawinge*— He approaches a thousand moons in age when he dies! He lives for seven tens or eight tens of winters! He grows very very old. The cat tells me this. Now I sing a song with the tongue of the cat, so no one except the cat and I understand!

He sang in the language of white men's cats, and all relatives in the lodge were greatly impressed to hear him do this; although but two of them had ever seen white men's cats. Yet they did not doubt that He-Walks-Slowly had knowledge of that language.

Thus the bad bloated spirit diminished in size, and rolled himself into a ball no bigger than a hickory nut; and in this form he came leaping out of Inkpaduta's gasping open mouth; he had made himself into a substance clabbered and yellowish and bad-smelling. The sister of Inkpaduta's mother, who also was a wife of Wamdisapa, took up the bad spirit on a stick and looked at the spirit curiously. Everyone gathered round to see the thing and smell it; and after that several more bad spirits (little brothers of the first and largest one) came also leaping like wet yellow frogs of smallest size, came jumping out like limp insects which swim in a pond or buzz amid marshland reeds; and all of them flew with ugly cries from the open mouth of the sick boy; all were equally evil and smelt equally bad. These spirits were examined also, though some were too small and soft to be taken up with a stick, so it was necessary to gather them up with a bone squash-knife. It was decided that they should be burnt; so all were burnt, even the largest first-master-spirit-of-them-all. They made wild cries when they were put into the fire, they sputtered and cried in pain, they sang songs of death with great pain and also with a new if small bad smell. He-Walks-Slowly sat close to shake his rattle, this time cupped in two hands, until his two hands were but a blur as the one hand had been before. So the spirits were burnt, so they died.

And that was another of the many fires, that fire on the little River of the White Fox— The many fires which Inkpaduta had known.

He had lived a long time.

Now he had lived, he thought, for five tens of winters and for perhaps five winters more.

He was very old.

He was strong, still.

He could kill, still.

He had killed.

He sat quietly, reviewing the recent deaths he made. They were good deaths, with much blood. People had screamed in dying!

He thought of He-Walks-Slowly again (tied atop a rack, long ago, and with bones at last falling loose through rents in the decayed robe. When they trotted past the place one day, Inkpaduta had said to the twins: I show bones of He-Walks-Slowly, for one time he drives bad spirits from my throat. And also, besides his rattle made from cat's skull, That One keeps cat's brains in his pouch; but it costs a pony if That One uses cat's brains in his mysteries; and so a poor man with no pony to give, might die. But That One would make mysteries for a rich man who gave him a pony; or also if a rich man had mercy, and offered a pony which the poor man could not give!).

Brains of white children on the texture of oak . . . he thought of those brains, but they were not dried and salted as had been cat brains hoarded by He-Walks-Slowly.

Many, many fires.

Ten thousands of fires? It could be. He did not know.

He thought of another fire. . . .

It was as if he could see this other fire before him. Not close before him (as Inkpaduta now sat, with fire near) but at a distance. It was on a prairie; and it seemed that many figures crept stealthily toward the fire, which burned wide and bright; and these were the figures of men, not of spirits. But the men were small men.

The men were boys!

Who were these boys?

And when burned this ample fire?

And why burned such a fire?

Women constructed the fire so they might make ash cake. Women built the fire in a time of harvest, after all corn had been shelled from cobs, and after all the cobs had been placed in a great pile. Each family had its own pile; and boys from one family were forbidden to raid against their own family's fire; but they made raids against the fires of other families; and if they were caught they were whipped vigorously; and if they were not caught they went bounding off across the plain—to reassemble from scattering in the end, and brag about their exploits—once they'd reached some place of safety where neighbor women could not pursue them.

Echahe—yes, twas believed that boys of a family should not come creeping to disturb their own family's fire; but usually several fires burned at the same time; and with many boys prowling about, and in darkness lit only by separate crimson patches where the cobs burned, one might never be certain which fire one was approaching, or which boy was caught. For it was like men going to war. The boys had painted their faces with mud.

Aye, it was indeed like war (a very small war between boys and women). No one was ever killed in this small war; but it was possible to be hurt by being burned; and it was true that a cousin of Inkpaduta, a boy named Wichotahenhiyeya or Many-Persons-Are-There, had lost an eye as a result of such encounter . . . from that time forth he had but one eye left to him: his name was changed.

Ho!

In that season Wamdisapa, the father of Inkpaduta, had fought in a great battle against the Sauk; and though he killed several Sauk, he was pierced by two arrows and cut by a knife. He lay long in the lodge. A pony was paid to the mystery man for the use of his cat's brains; but by this time the brains may have been very old and weak, for they did not drive out the evil spirits which had entered Wamdisapa's body through holes made by arrows and knife—not for many moons.

So Wamdisapa's brothers believed that He-Walks-Slowly should give back the pony to Wamdisapa; but He-Walks-Slowly did not do this thing.

. . . Bad spirits kept living inside Wamdisapa, and they talked often within his body, making a great outcry as they talked; and one of them thrust out his tongue through the hole . . . it was a long tongue, rather soft and wet, and people could see this soft pink tongue of the spirit; it was only after more moons had passed that the spirit's tongue grew dry, and at last it fell off; the spirit could talk no longer because the tongue had fallen off and had been destroyed in the fire, and had had tobacco and yarn burned with it, and also some hairs from the scrotum of the first wolf ever killed by Wamdisapa; and these hairs were a portion of Wamdisapa's medicine, and were kept rolled in a thin heart-skin in his medicine bag; but it was good to burn them now, in thanks, because the bad spirit's tongue fell off . . . and this last hole in the man's body was closed, and no more bad spirits could crawl inside his body.

But that year the people did not hunt muskrats in the spring, because of the father's illness. They remained in the forest until the Planting Moon; then they moved to their prairie village, and women planted corn by the river. Buffalo came near, men rode out and hunted, women remained in the village . . . many buffalo were killed, so there was much meat and many skins. These were the thin springtime skins for making fine robes; the thicker skins for tipi covers were taken in the fall. Wamdisapa grew stronger in time; and all were happy because of this, or said that they were; except perhaps Inkpaduta, the eldest son, for he knew that once his father was grown strong enough he would beat Inkpaduta as he had beaten him before. And first came much rain, and then much heat, and there came rain and heat together, and then more sun. Corn grew as it had never grown before.

And when all the corn had been shelled there were great piles of cobs. And these cobs were put into baskets, and all the women waited until there should come a quiet night when no winds blew across the prairie, and smoke would rise as straight as a lodge pole; for only on such a night could ash cake be formed. The dry bare cobs were guarded as a treasure: no horse might come to chew at them or kick them about, no dog was permitted to run across them (for the dog might squirt water on the cobs); and smallest children wished very much to play with the cobs (for the cobs smelt like corn and bran and smoke and flowers, and when you touched them they were soft, but hard underneath, and it was good for children to fondle them); but this the children were not allowed to do when ash cake waited to be made.

For ash cake was the best, the very best flavoring of all; it was better than spring salt; and sometimes it was called the cake of ashes and sometimes the crust of ashes, and sometimes it was called by other names. No matter how much ash crust was made, it was always gone before winter came. And it was a great present for one woman to give to another. She would say, You are my sister, and I would be good to you, and give to you a gift; and this present which now I give you is ash crust! And the other woman would exclaim, *Inah! Inama!*—to let her sister know how astonished and delighted she was.

And all the cobs must be pure and untouched and untrampled.

But the boys—

Ah, the boys—!

For when weather was calm, with the plain moon-lit or star-lit and motionless with no winds riding or walking— Then did women march to a high dry lonely place beyond the village, then did women bear their baskets of cobs; and these they would heap, each in her own family's pile, and at a distance apart. Then the piles of dry cobs would be fired; and the weather must be right, with all breezes dying at sunset, prevailing into vanishment, leaving the night smooth and silent so that heaps of smoldering cobs might not be touched by the slightest vapor stout enough to disturb ashes. For over the smoldering falling dying fires a crust would be formed. There would be red underneath, red glowing for a long time, red glowing until daylight while the women stood on guard; but over the color would be congealed a solid thickness of unblemished ash. And this would solidify, it would harden like a delicate membrane; and of this coating the ash cake might be compressed and squeezed into balls by the hands of women and girls. But only when it was cool enough, and still clinging and damp, with the smolder of glaring cobs far underneath. And sometimes a woman might gather as much as to build four or five balls, from the crust over a fire where the heap of cobs had been piled to the height of a child—to more than the height of a child: almost to the height of the woman herself. Four or five balls of the delicious ash crust she might gather; but seldom more than that many.

But the boys— *Yun!*

As darkness came down and settled like a bird with wide wings coming slow to the ground, so there would rise a truancy and uncertainty among boys of the village. These were boys who owned ten winters, or maybe ten again two winters, or ten again four winters—boys whose legs and arms were stretching—the boy who had his first hair around his *che* or who had not yet grown his first hair around his *che*, but soon would do so; the youth who had not yet gone alone to a hill to pray and sing, but would go to a hill to pray and sing and dance (quite by himself; and dancing night and day without ceasing) before many more winters had passed.

There would ensue a scampering and gliding and a crawling; and soon all boys would be missing from the village; but willows and weeds along the river might have new tenants. Out on the prairie, guarding their precious cob fires, the women would grip their sticks tighter, and say to each other: Let the lookout be sharp and close! The boys will be here soon! If a boy comes, you must make haste to strike him.

(For if the boys reached the fires, and disturbed them, there could be no ash crust or ash cake or ash balls for flavoring, because the small-hot-quiet-spirits-who-live-in-cob-fires would not permit the crust to form if they were disturbed.)

Down where mud was thick and pasty and sticky, each boy would have smeared his face. Each boy would have cut willow switches for himself—strong limber strands of the green willow, thick enough to hold a weight on the end of the switch, but limber enough to bend with quick sharp ease. And they would make balls of the firm damp mud. And on an end of the willow strand the mud ball would be fastened, sticky and tight. And each boy would make more than one switch-with-a-mud-ball-on-the-end-of-it, he would make as many as he could carry with him when prowling the dark.

And this was like a war; but a very small war between women or girls, and boys who were not yet men.

And when the boys had crawled close to the firelight, and were ready to attack, they would rise suddenly with yells, and throw themselves forward. And then all the women would yell as well, and rush at the boys with the small clubs which women carried to drive away boys such as these.

If boys upset the fires, there might be no ash crust for flavoring! *Yun!*

But first they would have to reach the fires, and always the women built their fires as far from the stream as they could; because that made it most difficult for boys to raid them, because it would be farther for the boys to creep with their mud-ball weapons, and many of the mud balls might fall loose from switches and be smashed or lost, before the boys came close.

If there were one chief among the boys (usually a taller youth with hair already around his *che;* and one to whom the others would pay much heed) this boy might say: Brothers, we go very cautiously, we make no noise as we crawl, we hide behind each bush or tuft of grass, we fasten weeds to our heads, and lie instantly quiet if the women look our way; and so they think that we are but weeds or tufts of grass! We must attack all the fires at the same time, for only that way can we surprise the women! You, End-Red, shall take your band and raid my family's fire. You, Many-Persons-Are-There, shall take your band and raid End-Red's family's fire. I, named All-Bulls-Feeding, shall take my band and raid the fire of the family of Many-Persons-Are-There!

(In this way an attack would be planned. But only if there were among the boys a Head Man who was believed to be a Head Man; and sometimes there was no admitted leader; and sometimes also the women had a leader, and she sent scouts to circle and watch for signs of the enemies' approach. But the women and girls might walk about, and at last they would meet and say: *Hiwo!* No boys have come, there are none to be seen! . . . Then they might become no longer vigilant, and would fall to talking and laughing; because that is the way women are, they fall to gossiping, they do not well know how to make war.)

All over the prairie a multitude of grasses would be moving, and lying silent for a while, and then moving on in silence through darkness; and it was all good because the night was still and had no winds blowing, and up beyond the village the prairie wolves sang far and loudly on ridges. And in earliest nighttime (at the beginning) there were night birds who threw themselves like knives on wings against the insects—swooping far aloft, and riding wisely until they sensed that insects were near below them, and then hurling themselves down with cries and open mouths. But there came no threat of Thunder-Birds far to the west across prairies (because the women would not build cob fires on a night of thunder; because no rain must come to spoil the ash, nor must winds blow). And it was good, because of smell of smoke—it made you think of hunger, but only hunger when there was food to eat; not hunger when there was no food, for that was bad! And it was good because of light of fires stealing wide and wild and tinted bright against the far blue and far black of the prairie; and also the boys' bare bodies gliding over the ground like silent snakes, and the notion of war inside them, and love of war in their hearts; and all were ready for the attack, and each gripped his weapons tightly, and they made no sound among them (except for very smallest boys, who sometimes laughed, or tried to talk; and thus they made a sound); and again the small wolf off beyond in talking darkness, and again the big frogs of the prairie slough—the last big frogs to talk before frost had found them; and in all this grumble of animal and frog and low burning of the fires going down to ash so wide and darkly red, there lifted the fierce cool smelling of the smoke; and in some ways the black cool wide smelling of the night was blue, and in some ways it was black and envious and promising; and this was no night of frost, but a night before frost; but the thought of frost was there with the thought of war; and the breath of smoke was there as if tobacco burned; and silent silent silent came the boys to make their raid.

Zuya!

Takpe! They would rise, burst forward in a charge.

. . . As when the lodge of ants upon the prairie is left untouched, and so you see no ants; and then you mash the ant-lodge with a stick or with your horse's hoof, and so the ants gush forth in racing tribes. . . . As when you see a grove beneath the dawn, and all is silent, motionless, with trees well weighted down. And then there snaps the sound of just one shot!—and then the pigeons rise a-swarming.

So was it when boys attacked the fires. With yells, with howls . . . the women's figures flying in their gowns, the boys (with no gowns) circling and their bodies shining rosy in the light, and war-stripes or hand-marks of black mud like paint upon their bodies. Then came fierce showers of the spark, each place a spray, a mad explosion of the sparks where willow wands were striking, and their balls of mud were like the down-sweep of a stone or club.

For it was for this reason that the boys descended on the blaze!

They loved to wield their mud balls, with fire fastened on the mud. Each boy—if he could only dodge those women and approach the glaring blaze!—slammed hard his willow stick, and forced the ball into the flames and coals, and drew it quickly forth again. And now he held a sparkled ball of colored sputtered sparks; and now his willow switch was like a bow, the ball was like an arrow (but still round and glowing); and with this limber switch to be his bow, he'd send the bright ball streaking on its course; and he might have more balls to throw, if he could only safely reach the blaze again and put them in.

Chichute! every boy might scream. I shoot thee!

. . . And up and down, and wild and fast, and in and out, and meeting in the air, and crossing in the night, the balls went flying, each hissing with its trail of sparks, and popping, flaring when it hit the ground. And women also sometimes found the balls upon them, bursting in their very hair (but even so you scorned to aim at women, you aimed at other boys; but so not always was the aim of boys unerring) and fresh cries came forth; and many boys also were captured by the women and the girls (but usually the smaller boys) and so their howls arose as they were struck with sticks and slapped with hands and pushed and dragged to further punishment.

So was it of this fire mashing, spurting in the night, that Inkpaduta thought, while sitting lonely by a low hot fire in the snow. With all the others now asleep (except the one white girl who moaned) he smoked and he remembered.

Next morning he would rise to kill again.

But now he thought, he saw with old-man's-eye-remembering, he heard with old-man's-ear-remembering. Therefore. . . .

Twas good. Because the prairie was a thing alive and warm with traceries; the bright balls streaking, and the yells (and that was how the cousin lost his eye, with mud ball striking, and the coals upon it; so no longer was he spoken of as Many-Persons-Are-There, but he was called His-Bad-Eye-Cannot-See; and so when he was grown he could not see the Chippeway who came, and so they killed him).

Next morning Inkpaduta would rise to kill again. *Chichute!* he would cry in heart, the while his face said nothing nor did laugh; and he would hit and batter, he would make more deaths because he hated, and he wanted war. *Eesh!*

XXXIX

A sack of meal which Jonathan had fetched in with him from the cargo left at Shippey's— This was used up by Monday morning, and Old Joel Howe decided to go to the neighbors again. Knowing that two loads of supplies would arrive soon at the lakes, he did not feel apologetic about borrowing as he had felt earlier. Howe thought, as he slouched along through fresh cold of a clouded day, with empty bag over his shoulder— He thought that the various families here along the Okobojis had achieved an intimacy and mutual trust never demonstrated back East. Twas because of the privations endured together. He knew through family chronicles that much the same situation prevailed in Kentucky during early days. But on the Kentucky frontier there were atrocious dangers, and here in the Spirit Lake country, except for the possibility of freezing or starving, there were no threats. There weren't any Shawnee Indians around. Just groups of beggars rarely. It must have been right scairy, to dwell as his ancestors had dwelt, considering a recurrent peril of painted invaders who might rush to tomahawk you at any given moment. The word *pioneers* came into Old Joel's mind . . . he thought of ancient tales, considered buckskin chronicles of Simon Kenton . . . must have been hard days back yonder, harder than modern times.

Pretty weak feed, these past two months. But spring couldn't be far distant now. The previous day had been almost balmy, though now a raw wind blew miserably and loose snow whirled before it.

This was March, ninth day of March. Take a month hence: twould be the ninth of April. April meant spring. Couldn't mean anything else.

Soon as weather permitted, and soon as Jonathan's swollen foot permitted, they'd go to examine the acreage marked off for Jonathan and see whether it suited. If he didn't cotton to it, they could step off another claim in a different direction.

Twas good to have your eldest son under your own roof again. Old Joel regretted, however, seeing the young man in pain. That foot of his had gotten more than a tinge of frost; twas really frosted bad. But they'd rubbed and soaked, and after three nights in the cabin Jonathan could now hobble around with a stick for a crutch.

He was a good boy.

They were all good children.

Mr. Howe considered, in tranquility, the other children who had died nearly twenty-five years before. Just think—they'd all be long growed, had they survived. And would have lots of children of their own.

This enlarging colony might become very nearly a Howe project; at least Howes, with all their kin moving here, would be in the majority. Liddy and her folks; and now Enoch Ryan coming in, and Elvira to be escorted there in the spring. Same time, Asa Burtch would go back for *his* wife, and Jonathan go to marry *his*. Cabin after cabin there'd be, all tenanted by some Howe relatives or connections.

Even with vile winter and thin fare, twas more promising than Howard County, Indiana, had ever been.

And Sardis. One of these days she'd marry; doubtless she'd dwell close at hand also. And then, when the younger boys got growed. . . .

Old Joel had been reading from the Forty-sixth chapter of Jeremiah after breakfast. Sardis asked for Jeremiah especially; she often did; she announced boldly that twas because of the poetry contained therein. Old Joel liked the Proverbs better, but— He wondered whether it was quite decently religious for his youngest daughter to profess such excitement over the Bible's poetry. Was the Bible *supposed* to be poetical? Harvey Luce would probably shake his head and say No. But Harvey always seemed so kind of gloomy about the Scriptures anyway—almost like he was pleasured at being gloomy.

Properly or not, the majesty of Jeremiah still chased and resounded in Old Joel's brain. He thought it a valuable thing; if you had the Bible in your mind, constantly, then you should come to no harm. Activity of the Bible within your memory and your soul could keep you in the approved path. *Order ye the buckler and shield, and draw near to battle?* Sardis liked that, her big eyes gleamed as her father read. *Harness the horses; and get up, ye horsemen, and stand forth with your helmets?* Twas strange for an eighteen-year-old female to become so excited at hearing such words . . . sometimes she'd interrupt in peremptory fashion and cry, Pa, read that again! But she was a strange critter, with her songs and verses. *Egypt is like a very fair heifer, but destruction cometh?*

Old Joel Howe trod along the south shore of East Okoboji . . . he did not know whether he'd call on the Mattocks or on the Red Wingers. There wasn't much choice, when it came to distance, but he seemed to recall that at last information the Mattocks had been completely destitute of both flour and meal. Better chance, probably, over across the straits at that cabin of the young men.

Before him stretched, pocked and rippled, the surface of an indentation, a flat bay forming the southwest corner of East Okoboji.

Twould be much shorter if he went down to the ice and cut across. Though he disliked walking on ice; twas tricky; he didn't hanker after the notion of falling flat on his back, not at his age.

Yes, yes. He was getting on. All of fifty-two, now.

Age was something you couldn't avoid, not in any case. *Let not the swift flee away, nor the mighty man escape?*

Once established in his course across the ice, Joel Howe was amazed at hearing a confusion amid trees along the lake shore at his left hand. He turned and halted, saw ponies moving along uneven ground, dipping out of sight momentarily, coming up into view once more. The first thought was that Doctor Harriott and Bertell Snyder approached; but that couldn't be—there were too many horses. More than two, indeed. Now they were emerged from sheltering dark underbrush: three, four, five— He stood and counted.

Sakes. Indians.

Now, that did beat all! Hadn't been any Indians around since December; and they *would* pick a time like this to come a-begging. He thought, Why couldn't the poor hungry things wait until the sleds got here? Then we'd have something to give them. And usually they come afoot before, and now they're all a-riding.

Well, folks at the cabin would just have to make them Indians understand that no food could be spared. Tell them to come round again next week, and they'd get a few fixins. Or let them return to the Mattock place (from which direction they seemed to have come) and probably they'd receive some pumpkin rings from Mrs. Mattock. Everybody at the lakes was deathly sick of the pumpkin taste by now.

But horses were urged down to the lake's margin; the dark and dirty paupers were coming toward him instead of progressing on to the cabin. He thought first: They seen my sack, and think I got something in it, something good to eat— Then he remembered: the sack was empty. . . . Or maybe they were wishing to plead for a gift of money? Certainly he had no coins to spare. He wished that he could speak these people's language, or that he knew a series of signs. Then he might inform them: first, that they'd have to wait for their donation until the loaded sleds arrived; and, second, that they oughtn't to go bothering around the Noble-Thatcher place, cause Joe Thatcher wasn't to home, and—

The Indians dismounted, they left their horses, they came on toward Joel Howe. Six, seven of them . . . all men. Seeing them thus advance in a tattered windy mob, with horses behind them, and some horses whickering, and icy breeze snapping at their manes and tails . . . horses of Jeremiah, as described in that Biblical chapter freshly read . . . Joel remembered the verse, and suddenly he was intensely glad that these black-faced mendicants were not Shawnees.

For Shawnees, as described forty-five years earlier by Uncle Benny, bedaubed themselves with stripes when they went to war. But why were these folks approaching him so smeared with plain charcoal? Twasn't paint . . . no . . . when Indians went on the warpath they painted up, and twould be dreadful to see them thus, and know that they were coming after you. *Come up, ye horses; and rage, ye chariots; and let the mighty men come forth; the Ethiopians and the Libyans, that handle the shield; and the Lydians, that handle and bend the bow?* For the first time in his existence, Joel Howe wondered consciously what the Ethiopians and Libyans and Lydians had looked like. Indistinctly he'd considered them as wearing long robes, something like the Disciples and other Israelites displayed in engravings. . . . Bows and arrows. Mightn't the Lydians, at least, have looked something like Sioux Indians? Never occurred to him before. *Let the mighty men come forth?* Most of these fellers were right big.

They came to him. A huge man with a pitted face was grinning. Twas nice to have them friendly. They swept around, huddling close, almost shoving him; he smelled them even in the rushing breeze and its pebbled starch swept from drifts. No, Old Joel thought, I wouldn't never of made a real pioneer, like my daddy Uncle Benny. I'd of been too blame scairt of them Shawnees. There in Kentucky and all.

Come up . . . and rage . . . and let the mighty men. . . .

Even Simon Kenton must have been scairt, times.

Now I got to make them understand when I say: I hain't got nothing to give?

Hot metal stabbed the skull of Old Joel Howe. Silver-white light was all he saw, he felt nothing. This was no season in which to be surprised; he could not claim such a season, it did not exist for him; but for a moment it seemed that something had been left unsaid and unexplained. His kindly scrub-whiskered face smashed against the ice, and there rose peals of delight which neither he nor any other white person might hear, and there ensued mayhem which he might never feel. He was a dead pioneer. Previously he had never realized that he was a live one.

The Wahpekute left Old Joel Howe stretched on the ice with coarse snow lashing round him. They scampered to their horses and charged rapidly upon the Howe cabin. Within four minutes from the time they crashed in at the door, every member of the family, except one, lay dead. They would not have killed Sardis—nay, *Hiya!*—had they known her age. But her back was turned as the first man came in at the door with gun held ready, and he saw only the white hair. . . . Old Mrs. Millie Howe was at the fireplace, heating a fresh flatiron for

Sardis, who was pressing clothes. With that flatiron Millie Howe's head was crushed. Of Jonathan the slayers said, *Echahe!*—the young white man was brave! He fights even when he has no weapons, and we all have weapons, so him we kill. But he is firm of heart. *Chantesuta!* As a brave man Jonathan deserved to lose much blood. They let him lose it, slashing him repeatedly up and down the face and chest. . . . Thirteen-year-old Jacob was the only person left alive, though they thought that he was dead when they went away. He'd run out into the yard; but there His-Curly-Sacred caught up with him.

The Dakota held brief jollification amid Howe furniture, dishes, other belongings. There was much here to steal, many things to play with; some of the men danced as they ravaged, and some sang; but there was more slaughter to be performed. They knew that another house of the *Washichun* waited only a short distance beyond. The outlaws covered that mile rapidly. Inkpaduta believed that they should begin by begging; the whites might have heard distant shots and so be on their guard. Thus the Wahpekute approached cautiously, but there was no need, these people had not heard. Alvin Noble's great gray eyes stared in solemn disapproval when they shot him; and of course the women were shrilling, they could not hear Alvin plainly as he spoke. But his wife must have harkened with a secret ear; it seemed to her, later, that she perceived his voice speaking in surprise. Saying: Liddy, I am shot! She remembered his taking several steps toward the door before he went forward on his face. . . .

Inkpaduta cautioned the rest: These women are young. Do not kill!

Aye, we take, we do not kill.

Kill children. . . .

Aye, children!

They carried J. Q. A. Noble and Baby Dora into the dooryard. They took them to a tree which grew there, and yelled proudly after each swing. Both the young white women had fainted. So they were carried out and hung across a horse.

Enoch Ryan was the only person who fought. Like Jonathan he fought with his bare hands; but bare hands are not good in a fight against guns and knives. After the mortal shot, Een Ryan lived long enough to hold a single thought in his mind. It sat like a bright stone fastened within the cold lava of eternal darkness. Een did not think, strangely enough, of the mother he had loved or of the pitiful little wife who died, or of his lost child. He saw momentarily a pinched and hardened face, he thought of Vixie Vanting, the girl he'd known in Virginia mountains.

Bahata took the bodies of the men by their feet and pulled them through the open door, heads bumping as they struck the wide puncheon step, and again, with a different sound, as they hit the ground. One after the other Bahata dragged them to the blank side of the cabin. Let others bang children, let others cope with women! He had mutilation to perform (mutilation of a most intimate sort) and he did not wish to be disturbed, he would absorb himself in this task. And then (he'd seen pillows and feather ticks) he would wallow in gossamer glory . . . hurl out his arms and grunt delightedly as feathers drifted against his face. Desiring tools which he did not possess, Bahata went in search of them. He found Alvin Noble's carpentry chest . . . strange knives and clubs were in this box. He planned to employ a chisel—he called it a knife-with-a-very-small-edge—in carving at the white men's bodies. He would strike with this narrow knife, strike hard. Like this!—and he stuck it into a feather mattress, he ripped with the blade, feathers began to puff. O down, the softness! . . . He would not waste time in carving at dead men—not now—he might come back to do so later. Again feathers were enchanting him. So the bodies went untorn; Alvin Noble lay flat on his back with bruised face chilling, his poet's gaze congealed—facing the sky, looking up through blowing snow and seeking something. Enoch Ryan (who hated and feared ice) was left with face turned down. His open mouth pressed lovingly against a sheet of ice as if he were gaining nourishment from it. Bahata ran demented with ticks and pillows until they were nothing but empty bags. Open breadth of prairie next to the house was soon laced and weaving with a softer snowstorm than that put down by the weather.

We go, we go! the others called to him repeatedly.

But he paid no heed; he thought of himself as emancipated from even the slight degree of bondage and obedience demanded by the elder reprobate. On-Oldish-Man sang and spun in feathers, sometimes he threw himself down and rolled in feathers, and then he came up to dance and wave again.

Ate, complained Fire-Cloud, I have no horse. For we have tied both women across my horse.

One is waking now. She utters cries!

She is tied securely, she cannot fall.

Take you the horse of On-Oldish-Man, Inkpaduta directed him. This gave immense amusement to the rest. They shouted their agreement. It would teach Bahata a lesson: he should learn that he could not conduct his silly pastimes and keep the rest waiting.

Are there other whites?

There are no more, for we have killed them all.

Unyaksapi! We bite in two!

Thus they were charmed as they rode, leaving On-Oldish-Man behind with his feathers. He would have to trudge on foot like a woman or a slave. . . . But he hurried, he skipped, he overtook the band at the Howe place. They'd stopped there: the boy Jacob was sitting up in the yard, although unable to speak; it was necessary to make sure of this youth's death before they left. They took good care that he should die this time. The Indians had made an error in removing their captives from the horse, so there were the white women to be held back—one especially was trying to aid the boy— The Wahpekute had to haul her about roughly to keep her out of the way. She yelled in the tongue of the whites, she yelled long: Jacob, Jacob! Brother Jacob!—and with grins they tried to imitate her cries.

Bahata came circling and stamping to join them. He sang many songs, and all together; sometimes even his companions did not know what he sang, and then again they could hear him and could understand.

White children, he sang, *white children. O girl-child, O larger boy-child! I said to you,* Hda. *Go home. But you do not go. So now you travel on a journey. White children, I have you, and you journey with me. Your bodies!* Nitanchanpi!

Surely enough they traveled with him. The baby girl was swung by one hand, the boy was caught up under the other arm.

Witkotkoka, cried the rest.

They discussed him among themselves.

. . . Is he not a fool?

. . . Aye, he is a fool!

. . . Consider the strange deeds which he performs: never does he lie with a woman, he wishes to lie with a man.

. . . No one dances with feathers as he does dance. Ah, a fool indeed!

. . . We laugh!

. . . Now comes he with two dead children of the whites, and he has carried them far.

. . . Why does he carry them?

. . . Because he is a fool!

Bahata sang: *White children, small white children, with me you journey; but now you come to the end of your journey.* He carried both the little oozing shapes up to the house, stamping in his polka as he went, and while the mothers shrieked as if they were being pulled apart.

Bahata changed his song. *White women, white women,* he called as he jounced to the door. *Your children come to the end of their journey.* First the body of Baby Dora, and then the body of John Quincy Adams Noble, was tossed through the door and into the heap of other refuse tangled there, where the white hair of Sardis gleamed prettily in dim light of this day.

Corn-Sucker was grieved when she learned that children had been killed, and more than grieved to know that, of these children, some were mere babies. She understood that in a war women and children were killed as well as men. It had been very wrong of the whites, she considered, to slay Bursts-Frog-Open and then separate his head from his body. In natural compassion she was grateful for the fact that she'd seen no one killed. This was war: deaths had been made, captives taken. These white girls were dragged to the camp, and Corn-Sucker, along with Woman-Shakes, had been ordered to braid their hair as a symbol that they now belonged to the Wahpekute. The captives were there for men to lie upon whenever they willed; in other capacities they would serve as slaves and beasts of burden. Such matters and deeds were a natural by-product of the circumstance of war itself—Corn-Sucker remembered hearing her own grandmother tell of it. When the grandmother had but twelve winters, she was carried off by a band of raiding Ree who swooped up from the lower Missouri. More than one Arickaree did lie with the grandmother, even though she was so young. Later she became the substantiated property of the man who first captured her by flinging a robe over her head, bundling her up in the robe, and lugging her away over his shoulder. (The girl-grandmother had been rendered hysterical during this awful event, and said that for many years thereafter she used to wake herself up, grunting about it. She thought that she was screaming; in her dreams she was screaming, but actually she was but making a gutteral sound which caused her to wake.) She bore this man two children, but both died when they were very young. Grandmother's name was Daughter-of-New-Moon, although when she was among the *Adakadaho* they called her by another name. Daughter-of-New-Moon was rescued one fine day, after some years of captivity, when a band of Hidatsa fell upon their southern neighbors in retaliation for various wrongs; thus she became restored to her own people on the Knife River. She was very sad about this at first, for she had been long with the Arickaree, and the man she called her husband was now slain. But after a time, and with a new husband, she was glad to be with her own people once more. She gave birth to four more children, and all these lived to be grown. This was the grandmother who gave comfort and refuge to the naughty Corn-Sucker when she was tiny and frightened by imaginary avenging owls.

Corn-Sucker could not make herself believe that modern white women would ever be happy among the people of Inkpaduta's band, for she herself was not happy, and she was the wife of the Head Man. The pale young things seemed frail, and one of them could walk only with the greatest pain, and another limped also. Corn-Sucker thought that probably they would die of hardships which compounded before them, or else they would be killed by the men. It was not pleasant to contemplate such a fate, even in the case of white enemies; but it had been long since Corn-Sucker found anything pleasant to contemplate.

She sorrowed over the killing of the babies. If only Inkpaduta, instead of killing babies, or allowing them to be killed, had fetched a couple of them to Corn-Sucker, she would have been so happy!—though doubtless the babies would die also—as the child of Black-Young-Woman had died, and as several other children, she was told, had died before she came to the band. It was not a good life for small children, or even for men and women: this she knew. Still she said to herself stubbornly: I wish that they had brought me one baby or two. For now I fear that I will never bear a child, and long have I wished for a child of my own! Had I a white child, here to adopt, I would treat it gently, gently. It should not starve. Had I any food, I would give it to the child, rather than eat food myself. . . .

She thought of the *Makadishtati,* the House-of-the-Infants. This was a legendary cavern not far from the Knife River; and there, in that cave, dwelt mysterious small children. Indeed, many people thought that all children dwelt, for at least a space of time, in the House-of-the-Infants (before they were put in the bodies of Hidatsa women, to be born eventually). In fact there were so many babies in the House that they jostled and pushed one another about. Sometimes they even bruised and hurt one another!—there was corporeal evidence to this effect, and some people doubted, but most did not doubt. Corn-Sucker had seen children who showed the effects of the thronged and tumbled conditions in their previous abode. Sometimes a child was born with a head badly bruised, sometimes there were scars or spots on its little face or elsewhere on its body. These were not injuries incurred following birth (as when Corn-Sucker had been hurt); the children bore such marks as they issued into the world. Since the mystic cavern was so crowded, without doubt they received their wounds in the fashion stated.

Corn-Sucker had never visited the House-of-the-Infants; but she'd heard of women who did so, especially in the past. These were women who were childless and who wished very much to become mothers. Childless husbands could go there as well; but they must fast long, before they crouched outside the cave. Then a man, weakened and in spiritual condition following his fast, could take up a position behind a boulder within sight of the cavern (this must be on the leeward side of the cavern, with no wind blowing from him to give warning of his presence). Should he have a vision of infants, then he went away in full confidence that he would become a father within the year.

Women who visited the House-of-the-Infants must follow a different procedure. Twas necessary for a woman to carry with her some tiny toys: a ball, and a little bow and arrow. These she should place, at sundown, in front of the cave's mouth, and then occupy herself in night-long vigil. In the morning she should approach the entrance once more, and learn whether any of the toys had been removed. If the ball were taken, then the eager woman knew that she would bear a daughter within the year. If bow and arrow were gone, that meant that she would give birth to a son.

The tribes of babies emerged from the *Makadishtati* only at night, and they were extremely wary. But their infant leader had been in the House for a long time, and thus he was wise; the others followed him and obeyed his commands implicitly. His nose was good, and he could detect a human being's presence in the slightest taint of any breeze; and the *Makadishtati* was a huge place—it went far into the earth, though the entrance was but a span in width. So out they'd all come trooping, by night and through the narrow entrance. If the leader smelled no person lurking about, then would the infants have much joy at being released temporarily from their jammed quarters. They would romp and bound in glee, flinging their small naked bodies into the air . . . it was told that people who watched by moonlight had seen them dancing so. No herd of antelopes, the *uhi,* or other horned beasts might go leaping with as much joy as the naked babies displayed! Veterans of visits to the House said that the songs these children sang in their sport were both plaintive and majestic. Then— Let their Head Infant but catch the mildest scent of man in his sensitive nostrils, and he was sped back into the cavern in a flash, taking all the other children with him. There, in fine silted dust which paved the ground, would be found tracks to mark what had occurred. Little footprints were in the dust, they had been seen. . . .

Were I returned to the land of my own people, and did I dwell in a happier lodge than lodge-in-which-I-dwell-now, I would go to the Makadishtati. *I would take the ball and the bow and arrow, and seek knowledge of a daughter or of a son to come to me.*

But I am far from the House-of-the-Infants. I may not approach. I will never have a child.

Ah, Little White Babies Who Were Killed, I am sad because you were not put into my arms instead of being slain!

If one of you were a girl, then would I name her Mouse-Sits-Up-Tomorrow, because that was the name of the ikupa *whom I loved. But most times I would call her* Itahu; *this is the Hidatsa word for mouse. I would not use the Dakota word, which is* Kitunkadan.

If one of you were a boy, I do not know what I should name him; but I would give him a good name.

Far in the dusty House-of-the-Infants near the Knife River, there may be a baby waiting to be claimed by me. But that baby will wait in vain.

Within me is a small wounded animal.

Always.

XL

Morris Markham recognized that he could consider the Present cannily, but less and less did he prefer to concern himself with thoughts of the Future. He went back into the Past sometimes: usually he was strengthened or at least encouraged by such reflections. But during winter's blight, its hardship and disappointment, he found himself opposed increasingly to a long view ahead. He'd explore about as far as next season, that was the farthest he cared to venture.

. . . Traps ought to go out early.

. . . Best to alter my notions. Forget that myth about first-snow-you-can-track-a-bobcat-through.

. . . But not set any traps until tis truly cold. Then bait and set.

. . . Unsprung unset deadfall never hurt anybody. Scrape away the crusted ice, and set the blame thing when it comes time! Same way with steel traps.

Thus, disposing of the Future, he paraded out secret memories and reviewed them when such diversion was needed. A man would have a bad time of it, at a solitary fire in a windswept grove, had he never planted those seeds which could grow into memories. Morris thought about women only when he wished to do so deliberately. Never did women come billowing around him in an uninvited tantalizing bevy. He could order them away, marshal them into a remote pen reserved for such fair prisoners. Could say, Stay put until I want you.

(All except one woman. She never mingled with the rest, nor needed to; she had ethereal breeding, she was blessèd and removed. Sometimes he spoke her name, but in a whisper; and only when some beauty became attendant in his life; then he thought she'd given him this treasure, and she shone at her distance, approving, lifting up her voice.)

. . . Two or three years after the boy Morris left school he had begun to have the dreams which possess developing youths. He was horrified with himself, after each event of such nature, and lay convinced of his own eternal damnation. In these sexual illusions he was concerned commonly with some female member of the numerous Radley clan who lived on their adjacent farm; in later midnight sessions he also shared imagined sexual activity with some of the Howe girls. Quite naturally Morris considered that such experiences were peculiar to himself—an eccentricity never practiced by any other fellow. (He had no inclination to confess his depravity to Uncle Melly, who likely enough would have been a poor advisor in any event.) But since the boy could not honestly identify his conscious behavior as abnormal during daytimes, he grew inured to his own supposed transgressions. He shrugged them off, buried the recollection, tolerated himself as a divergent sinner who really meant no harm. If his life had not been so secluded he would have been less mortified. For eventually it came about that, in sharing summer farm-work with other lads, he encountered mutterings, gigglings, smutty allusions which taught him that he but shared a weakness common to all young males.

One gingery autumn day, when he was going on eighteen, Morris returned from his bird hunting to find a wagon halted near the corner of the Markham estate, and a tent pitched. The mover said that he hailed from western Virginia, and was bound for Illinois; he'd set up camp at the foot of Morris's own lane in order to accommodate a favorite mare which was about to foal. The man—his name was Tyburn—had wife and daughter with him. The dark-red-haired daughter, called Carrie, was a year or two the senior of Morris in age. Morris was immensely excited by Carrie's hair; and he longed to put his hands in it, or perhaps even bury his face amid rich mink-colored locks. But still with no conscious ulterior motive, and truly only because he was generous by nature and by habit, he offered to share his birds with these people. So Morris was invited to supper, and listened to a harangue on the bleak unproductive hills which Mr. Tyburn swore he had left behind him forever. Carrie helped her mother in preparing the meal, and Morris had ample opportunity to enjoy the glow of firelight upon her tresses. Following a banquet of roasted quail and doves, the mover produced a jug, and professed to be offended when Morris declined to join Mr. and Mrs. Tyburn in a small libation. The libation, however, extended itself into a debauch on Monongahela whiskey which left the parents snoring beside the fire, and Morris sitting tongue-tied but still able to worship the dark-bronzed beauty.

She said, Wasn't the moon pretty?—and Morris agreed that it was. The young woman put her hand around his, and drew him to his feet. Still gripped and touching in this fashion, the pair wandered to view the moon, perhaps from a better vantage point (indeed the moon did seem closer), but certainly in more privacy. A grove adjacent to the Markham house lay dry and shadowy, carpeted with patches of seeming blue or silver. There was a mystic unreality about the whole evening, and Morris, in exciting proximity, began to feel that he had had many drinks from that scorned jug. Carrie must have divined his emotions, for promptly she tickled the palm of his hand with her fingernails. The untutored Morris was not familiar with any signal thus conveyed. But he began to respond wholeheartedly, after Miss Carrie had taken the initiative and flung her arms around him and pushed her face close to his own. Soon she emphasized her desires and determination further, lifting up her skirts to reveal the slim naked body underneath. The palsied youth, not wishing to confess himself as virginal, could only mutter: That's my house over yonder. I got a bed. . . . Many weird experiences befell him. He had never heard of a nymphomaniac, and did not know that such creatures existed. Carrie Tyburn drained her victim of his hardihood through three successive nights. He began to feel that if this activity continued, he should never be able to hunt or trap again. On the fourth night he bolted the door.

In a late hour Carrie lurked outside, treading lightly on her bare feet, and whining, Morris, please let me in. Please! We're going on in the morning, and I just want to say Goodbye. Morris declared feebly that they could say Goodbye through the locked door. Carrie began to snarl and pound. Eventually he nerved himself to the task, and admitted her to his house and, soon, to the bed again.

What if your Pa should find us? Morris asked for the tenth time. She only replied, as always: Oh, they probably know where I'm at!—and then snorted at the notion of parental disapproval. . . . She gave him a lock of her hair to remember her by. The next day, after the Tyburns' departure, Morris burned the lock in the kitchen stove, and felt some relief when it was consumed. He considered that it took him at least a fortnight to regain his normal strength, posture, and energy. Sometimes he thought that he should never regain them.

Later he became more assured about his powers. While going the round of a farthermost trap line one wintry day, Morris heedlessly left his mittens behind him after performing a skinning job in the field. He spied an isolated farmhouse and stopped there to warm the stiffness out of his hands. In this way he encountered a plump woman, Mrs. Floss Ritenour, recently widowed, whose natural benevolence of spirit was equaled only by the generosity of her proportions and her inclinations. Mrs. Ritenour had two children; Morris made much of this little pair, and visited the home frequently until spring. In April the lady's father appeared, to escort her back to Michigan; Morris's second and most comfortable liaison was terminated. He wondered sometimes if he had fathered a child for the widow. He wondered, too, if he had fathered a child for Carrie Tyburn, but suspected that he hadn't.

The last year or two of his teens saw him with a love here, a love there, but he made no attempt to dispense an affectionate intimacy in his immediate neighborhood. He counted the local young ladies as purest examples of Christian womanhood, and would have died before putting a hand on one. He became that most equable of individuals: the man who can embrace a body available, but who does not feel himself destructively bereft if no frolic offers for months on end.

Fortune conspired against Morris Markham in his ox-finding expedition. With little difficulty he discovered the oxen, but on examining their condition he concluded that it would be senseless to attempt driving the critters home. He had no immediate need of them; they'd made out thus far; shrunken as they were, what was the advantage in herding them to Okoboji?

At sunrise on Monday his weather sense told him that a severe storm might ensue. Let the cattle be caught by angry new snows, away from sheltering thickets which had preserved them, and they'd go down.

. . . Lot smarter to leave 'em here.

. . . Wait till it warms for certain, and the drifts are gone. Then fetch over another yoke hitched to one of them Red River carts, with a good load of hay. Feed the critters up, and drive them back.

. . . Glad I'm not a farmer, fooling with oxen all the while.

. . . Plague take the critters.

. . . Air feels like something's brewing. Best get along.

In the first hour after leaving the timber, one of Morris's snowshoes split apart. The shoes had been his pride and joy; he'd made them of white ash, under Jo Harshman's direction. Alvin Noble understood the process of steaming wood, and that helped; Morris himself buried a deerskin rolled up with hardwood ashes, buried it in a mudhole and left it for a week until the hide could be softened and scraped and trimmed for lacings. No one else at the lakes had thought it necessary to provide himself with snowshoes. Some of the rest even laughed at the hunters for anticipating such necessity. Jim Mattock said that if he'd thought he was coming to any damn country where he'd have to lash any sons-a-bitching snowshoes to his feet, he wouldn't of come, by God!

Morris tried to effect repairs by binding the frame— No use, twouldn't hold. Wind began to blow the grating salt into his eyes even while he knelt. Couldn't travel on one shoe, twas worse than having none. There was a wall of stunted crab-apple trees along the side of a dark drift: Morris hung the snowshoes there, he hoped he'd find them again. He headed for the Okoboji country. Before mid-afternoon fresh snow was wrapping as he wallowed through shallow valleys and out into the drive and bluster again. He came to a ridge where persistent planing winds had left the raw ground exposed, and here were a few glacial boulders protruding. He knew this spot, he'd named it Sparkle Rocks, in his own mind; often he'd set his course for home by the position of these big rocks. So he could set a course in this mean storm . . . and lose it half an hour later, as the wind went shifting. Only Morris Markham's best skill kept him from trudging in a fatal circle. Night came blanketing, snow was alum in his mouth, lips were cracked and frozen; but twould be death to camp here fireless, he had to reach the timber. He struggled on, wondering what time it was . . . seemed like half the night had gone, but doubtless twas only ten or eleven or so. Must have traveled thirty mile since morning, and thank the Lord he hadn't tried to drive them oxen home! At last trees began to loom; whine of breezes was muted, disorganized by the thickening forest. Morris could draw a decent breath, and try to figure out just where he was. It took him another half hour to reach a conclusion at first unbelievable: he'd missed the knotted twist of lakes completely. That was a familiar creek down ahead . . . here he stood, maybe a mile below the Gardner house, a good five miles to the south and west of his own home. Twasn't any joke what a storm could do to a man's judgment, when she came stickery and mean.

He stumbled into a track which twisted toward the north. This was the route first worn into identity by wheels and teams when Rowland Gardner and Harvey Luce went out to cut their prairie hay. There were impediments in the shape of icy old drifts lying across the way, but a man on foot could circle these easily, even a man walking upon bruised benumbed feet. On either side the barren trees offered no promise, no kindness, but they restrained the wind. Snow squalls might have worked a fitful mischief in the open regions, but hereabouts there was scarcely any fresh fall.

Reluctantly trees drifted away, they widened and spread. Morris recognized in exhausted laggardly fashion that he'd come round the last bend of the trace. The Gardner house waited on a slight rise of ground among its oaks.

He sniffed for a welcoming odor of wood smoke. Twasn't there. The Gardners must have let their fire go down, and here it was only the middle of the night, by all sane reckoning. Interlaced meaningless patterns of paths, tracks old and new, rubbed there by the householders' feet, the feet of children . . . tangled in a skein across the clearing. From the solid blot of house structure not a single sparkle emerged. Oh, often he'd approached that house before by night; and always the tiny orange eyes, the streaks and pencils of light had come forth to strike him, saying Howdy.

. . . Fine way to say Hello to a feller! With a dead fire!

His stiff face twitched in an attempt at smiling.

Where could everyone be?

Maybe it had something to do with Harvey's return; probably that was it. They'd all had a Doings somewhere: kind of a celebration festival.

At the Howes', maybe? Jonathan's arrival, and the coming of Ryan, might have been excuse enough for a Doings.

. . . Kind of a play party where everybody took the children? And then they decided to stay all night?

Funny, he thought, they didn't say anything to me about it, fore I left. Must have got it all up on the spur of the moment.

. . . But I don't care too much about merrymakings anyway.

He came up through gloom toward the door, and then was bumped nigh to sprawling: he'd tripped over a rocking chair which lay upended. One of the rockers was broken off, and the place where it was broken was splintery and jagged, and it had scratched right through Morris Markham's heavy garb into the flesh of his leg. Mary Luce's Boston rocker, the only one in that house: a treasured chair fetched all the way from Norwalk in Ohio. Morris minded how Mary was proud of telling that the rocker was of very ancient make, and had been given to her as a wedding present by the housekeeper of Harvey Luce's uncle.

. . . The children, the little boys. How ever could they have been so unruly and so mean? They'd dragged that chair outside the house, and ruined it?

Morris shifted his rifle to his left hand and rubbed the sore place on his leg. Good thing I was wearing these leggings, he thought. Like to tore my leg half off. He lifted the broken chair and saw that its attached stuffed cushions were frozen solid, hanging in chunks. Then it had been there quite a while. His next thought was . . . *robbers!*

He took several cautious steps toward the door, and saw that it was open . . . yawning blackness meaner, more dangerous. His foot touched a queer shell. The wooden sugar bucket, with bottom busted out.

Robbers, he thought in increasing horror, and even sought to shape the word with creased cold lips. Mounds of tumbled clothing here and there, littering the immediate dooryard. Jo Harshman had spoken of a gang of outlaws, down below Fort Dodge somewhere; people all were feared of them, because of the lootings and beatings they meted out. One man had been shot and—

But such a fur piece for them to come. So very fur to come! They wouldn't be a-plundering clean up to Okoboji.

What about . . . the folks?

Hello. Hello the house!

But not too loudly, couldn't make it loud, his throat could barely build the sounds.

Gardner? Luce? Hey, folks.

It's me, it's Morris. Where be ye all?

Staring silence of the cold and open house ignored his salutation and his fussings, took the words, assorted them in rapping echoes, threw the words back in his face.

Oh, he'd sat with the Red Wing Company one night when old Jo Harshman told of Henry Lott. And here and now the thought of Lott returned. Maybe that villain wasn't killed in California after all. Maybe he'd come back to the Iowa country to do some further wickedness—against the whites, this time!

Other pictures flickering, the voices in his frozen brain. Tales he'd heard when he was young—Mingo stories, Delaware stories.

Couldn't be twas Indians. We hain't got that sort around. Just the beggar kind.

As if he drove against a visible tangible barrier, Morris forced his way through the door. Hello . . . didn't sound like his own voice: a spectral gasp, voice of a ghost, he heard the single word return echoing. *Hello . . . hello . . .* voicelessness with which unpopulated silence rewards a timid greeting.

I got to make a light. I got to see.

Morris leaned his rifle inside the door. His foot touched some sprawling object, his toe slid fairly beneath it. Laboriously he bent down and explored with his fingers, after he'd pulled off his mittens. He felt the body of a huge doll.

. . . Even gone and took the children's dolls, and strewn them all about. Ain't even dolls are safe from this kind of burglars.

He felt panic starting in his feet, he wished to whirl and snatch his rifle, blunder into the dark and run away. But no, he mustn't run, he couldn't run, he had to see. Breeze came from outside and made a rustling sound . . . papers, scraps of paper blowing. He felt and heard them skipping lightly on the floor. Morris unbuckled the wallet hanging at his belt, his fingers sought out flint and steel, a pinch of tinder. He struck, he struck again; ah, sparks were scattering, they wouldn't catch. Gol dang, they wouldn't catch . . . the flame began. Crumpled paper put itself against his leg, he grabbed it up and set the paper into blaze. He twisted it, caught up another piece, he made a little torch.

No order in this place. Just wreckage, refuse. Everywhere, thought Morris. End to end, from hell to breakfast, everywhere. Window busted out, and paper leaves and paper leaves . . . why, leaves from out a book! And here's the book with pages all torn out.

He took some more, to twist them for his torch, to make a larger torch.

Let's have a Reading.

Ain't had a Reading in quite a while.

By the shore of Gitche Gumee,
By the shining Big-Sea-Water,
At the doorway of his wigwam,
In the pleasant Summer morning,
Hiawatha stood and waited.
All the air was full of freshness
All the earth was bright and joyous. . . .

He saw half-a-candle, snatched it up and lit it from his glaring torch, and dripped the drops upon a bench which still stood upright; and he placed the candle there. With one more torch he tried to stalk around the place . . . so upset twas hard to walk! Oh, dishes shattered, and here were shreds of clothing, here a pair of pants—just ripped in two, torn leg from leg. He came back toward the open door, and halted, looking down, and seeing there the doll.

Doll.

I said—a *doll.*

Great big horrid-colored teacup busted half in two. And that's her head.

Aw, I don't want to touch that little thing! Poor little thing . . . but . . . touch her . . . no, I can't. I felt the dolly once, but can't touch it ever more.

He started for the door, he couldn't gain the door, he strewed his vomit on the way.

Another candle . . . walk outside and take a look. Oh, yes, I thought twas heaps of rags and clothes before, and now I see what's in the heaps. Oh, yes, they're dead and frozen stiff. All dead, all dead and stiff.

Poor Mr. Gardner, who could hate you so?

And children . . . who could hate you all?

And here's the Mrs. Same old pink calico she wears so frequently.

I guess—I guess that this is Mary Luce.

And—both the boys.

Yes, little boys.

But—Abbie. Where is—?

She and Luce and that new feller must be laying round somewheres.

With candle shielded by his hand, he squatted down amid dark-frozen blood, and looked around. It's best to look around, because you'll learn a thing or two. There ain't a boot-track anywhere about; here's only moccasins, just moccasins. And me and Bertell Snyder are the only ones in our whole colony who ever put on moccasins. And even there, right smack inside the door someone had stepped in blood, and wearing moccasins, and then it froze.

Just couldn't be. Just couldn't be.

Can't be.

And yet it is.

Ain't no Indians about.

I got to go clean back inside . . . forget that doll, forget that doll, and never *look* . . . and get my other candle.

On the doorstep he was horribly possessed again: the retching gulping emptiness. He'd thrown up everything he had, but still the spasms tore him. Get a-holt, he thought. Oh, Mr., get a-holt yourself.

Mattocks. They're the closest. Got to go and tell them, got to break the news.

He put the butts of candle in his wallet, he folded in a few torn pages of the book as well: twould help to make a light, in case he needed light again.

I wish that God had saved you all, he cried within his sundered heart. I wish that you'd been spared. But no, He couldn't spare you, didn't even want to. Who's the God who lets a thing like this occur? Tain't the same one that we worship, same one that we pray to!

Maybe the Indians are right, and there's more gods than one.

He took his rifle, went away from that vile house and its unspeaking dummies near the door. He started for the Mattock place, as fast as he could drive his legs. He tried to run at times, when ways were open, then he slowed again; his legs were mighty tired: thirty miles at least that day, and then—

Morris Markham blundered halfway up against the lodges of the Wahpekute, before he ever realized just where he stood. A dog barked; then he saw the dull light coming from the fires, heard a mutter there. *They've set their camp across the path.* The tired feet of Morris rooted down, they grew through hummocks of the trampled frozen slush, seemed to go so deeply into ground. He was a wintry tree a-growing there along with other wintry trees. Why did not the blow descend, the blade or bullet find him? He waited for a thud, for scabrous hands to close around his neck.

Again the dog was barking, and a human murmur followed on. Why speak you, dog? a voice said in Dakota. There are no more whites, for we have killed them all! Close tight your mouth, O dog!

The ears of Morris heard the words, his brain was powerless to fathom them, he had no knowledge of the meaning of those run-together sounds; but still the last two syllables, the *shunka* clung to him. As if they'd been expounded in his head, and so he heard them echoing, the way he'd listened to that last Hello. *Shunka* . . . *shunka* . . . took a slow step backward; then another step. The dog had ceased its barking but it growled with steady sounding current. In cold stench of this midnight Morris lingered, immobile. Can't I move? he prayed. Oh, Lord Almighty, let me move! He was poisoned by their dragging fire-smoke, the putrid knowledge of their scattered defecation. And brooding heavier than that, and over all, there was a bane within his mouth: the oily taste of death and deviltry cooked there by devils whom he'd thought were only hopeless wanderers before.

Step back, he counseled in his soul. He talked to Lord Almighty once again: Please let me step. Please let me go . . . and backward, *backward*. Feet came loose, he lifted them. Back up, back up!—there ain't a chance to warn the rest, unless I get away!

Reflected glow of fires in the lodges inched from him, and soon no longer could he hear the dog. With shrill relief the man could wish to scream aloud: They never budged. They never knew! I walked right up on them, but still they never turned a hair! The fires faded, faded, smoke was falling loose, the underbrush arose and blotted out the camp. Morris turned with stealth, and something flicked against his foot. He bent and groped, and then he held the object, lifted it before his eyes. He felt the thing all over. So it was: a wooden bear.

Tis Bertie Luce's wooden bear. I've seen him playing with it often. Don't need no further proof than this.

Morris picked his way among the trunks, avoiding noisy thickets where his tread would make a snapping sound. He bumped the trees sometimes, and tears were stinging in his eyes, and so he thought himself as blinded now and then; but still he groped and felt and clawed. . . . Now, head ye south—oh, widely, widely. . . . That's enough. And now I'm headed back northeasterly again . . . more easterly, or think I am. Yes, I know that big dead walnut tree, a kind of landmark: pale, with all the bark stripped off by weathers, and its talons turned against the sky.

Here is the path, I'll take it east, and tell the Howes.

Reckon the Mattocks are all dead as well; too close, just like the Gardners, just as close. They're bound to be destroyed.

. . . Three miles at least from where I struck the trail.

. . . *And tell the Howes, and tell the Howes.*

. . . No light, no light! I'm coming here, this is their place, I've passed the stumps where they cut down their trees; still I can't see ary light!

. . . Lord, give me one pinpoint of that light I need to see, to prove they're here and living.

. . . There ain't needle-prick nor color, smell of smoke or anything like that.

He went up like a wraith across the yard. (It was too dark, he didn't see young Jacob's body lying near.)

They been here, too. I guess they kilt them all.

The door was closed, it wasn't barred, but things were lying everywhere around outside: the broken things, the affirmation of the fact. He pushed against the door, it swung an inch or two. And he'd go in, if he could stop his shaking; make a light again. So he put down his rifle, tried elusive flint, it took a while. He held the blazing tinder wad against the paper edge, and watched a flame creep loose and wide; he lit his candle once again. Breathing hoarsely, Morris swung the door until his candlelight could show what lay beyond. . . . *All in a pile.* He heard the words resound so flatly. *All in a pile.* There ain't no use to count or wonder! Candle-flame picked out a pretty silver glimmer from the hair of Sardis Howe. . . . Blood should stay bright, Morris thought. Should stay real bright, in this chill weather; but it don't, looks kind of darkish now. Looks kind of old brown, yet looks fresher than the Gardner place. . . . So, if they got the Howes, they must have got my folks. They knew the house was there. They must have got them all. . . . He had no memory of walking from the Howes', of closing up that door and turning toward the east again and toward the north. Can't remember . . . heard his own voice saying loudly, once in woods between. Can't remember leaving there. Must have done so, cause I'm nearly back to home again. Home, dear home. And then he heard the family a-singing, Sardis leading off as usual: *Mid pleas-ures and pal-aces though-oh we may roam.*

Before he reached the Noble-Thatcher door, he waded deep in feathers, then he slipped on fur. He picked it up—the thing he'd stepped on—always picking something up. It was a lynx hide, one of his; but, like the trousers which he'd found, a lynx hide torn in two. He made his little light again, and looked for bodies. Couldn't see a one; only feathers, and the broken furniture and dishes scattered round.

No baby dolls? He'd thought to find them readily.

He didn't look behind the cabin, thus he didn't find the bodies there. He peered into his lean-to . . . nothing much . . . his bedclothing, his chained and hanging traps, his robes: they all were gone.

I couldn't stay, he said. I couldn't possibly. Fireplace or no. I'm freezing, and I need the heat or else I'll die; but—gad, I can't stay here. For I'd go mad. He had a sudden vision of himself gone mad, gyrating, waving arms about, whooping through the night; floundering to toss the snow against his head and face; and getting up again to run in circles. . . . Got to get some warmth.

And here was Liddy's sewing box. Alvin had made it for her as a gift, on Christmas or her birthday—Morris couldn't remember which. Twas cherrywood— Or maybe cedar?—and it had a kind of pattern inlaid on the lid. Here was the box, but it was crushed: someone had chopped the smooth-grained stuff. Twas practically reduced to splinters, but these shreds would start a fire burning well. Morris filled the crazy crate with other kindlings . . . in the woods, down in that next ravine . . . Indians would never see the glow, if they came back a-prowling.

He made his fire, roosted by it till the darkness paled; he didn't dare to sleep, but kept himself from freezing. He went back to the Noble-Thatcher place to read a record made more legible by dawn. There might be food the Indians had overlooked? . . . No, no, they hadn't missed a thing. But surely no smashed baby dolls were here. They might have took them captive, Morris thought. Seems like I've heard of Indians a-capturing white children, long ago. And then they raise them as their own. . . . The notion made him feel a little better.

He went out behind the house. Alvin Noble and Een Ryan waited on his finding. Morris didn't vomit any more, he only cried a while.

Across the silent lake, and to the south, there was a point where you could see the smokes from both the cabins at the Narrows: Mattocks', and the Red Wing place. Morris went, he looked until the day was well established; he could see the distant shoreline, fuzz of trees. No smokes, except from where the Indians were camped below the Mattock house.

. . . That means they got them all. Got everyone cept me.

. . . I got to head away from Okoboji. Head for Springfield. Maybe I can get there soon enough to warn the Springfield folks, and so they'll stand a chance.

. . . My folks, they never had a chance.

. . . And Okoboji means a Place of Rest.

. . . Rest well, dear ones, rest well. Rest well, O baby doll.

Morris Markham coughed, he wiped his eyes, he swung away and started north and east.

Late that afternoon he had found shelter, and lay collapsed in a bachelor's cabin built at a bend of the Des Moines River. He wanted to go on, the man wouldn't let him move. Look at your limbs, Mr. Or feel 'em! They're puffing up like all possessed. Bet you couldn't walk safely another forty rod. Which reminds me— The man exhibited a jug, and poured out a cup of the contents for Morris. This *is* Forty-Rod, the best kind, and you got to drink this down, fore I give you even a bite to eat.

Morris's host was a settler named George Granger who had moved in, the previous year (no relation whatsoever to Carl Granger, though they had all met and stared suspiciously at one another, when William was still resident at Okoboji). With amusement he was called George-on-the-Line, because one side of his claim extended into Iowa, the other into Minnesota Territory. He received Morris Markham and his horrid tidings with the mere remark: That's bad. But he tended the exhausted trapper gently, and promised that he would go on to Springfield with him as soon as Markham was able to travel.

More'n fifty miles, back and forth, up and down, in all this weather—? On the go since Monday morning, you claim—? Just lay tight. You hain't going no place right now, murders or no murders.

Unaccustomed to drinking Forty-Rod or anything resembling it,

Morris lay in wretchedness of heart and body, loose shapes thronging near, loose voices whispering. The black misery of Okoboji was ruled away. No brain dared for long to retain the memory.

. . . Or it would leave me mad.

. . . Yea, leave you mad.

. . . Who said that?

. . . Don't know. Who said what?

. . . You having bad dreams, Mr.?

. . . You are having bad dreams.

. . . Leave him mad.

. . . Quite pleasantly warm in here.

. . . Folks had said there was a nightingale.

. . . Miz Howe, please ma'am, I'm Morris Markham. Could I have leave from you and the Mr. to trap on your land?

. . . Said the nightingale was mad.

. . . And this is trivial, this Present here or somewhere else, and the Past is mighty small punkins, too. But you can't help remembering even little things.

. . . How long? Nigh onto seven years.

. . . And hate New York, and hate all cities.

. . . But she will take you up to that high place, and she. . . .

. . . And she. . . .

Kom kiyra, kom kiyra, kom kiyra,
Hoah! hoah! hoah! hoah!

At Detroit, in 1850, Morris had purchased an elaborate ticket, paying a total of eight dollars and fifty cents: the fare from Detroit to New York. At Buffalo, more money was demanded. But here's my ticket, mister— Sorry, that hain't a ticket good for all the way— (It had more printing, more decorations than a piece of paper currency. Canal boats, lake steamers, and railway trains were displayed.) They tolt me at that office in Detroit— Look here, sir, pay heed! We don't care what they *tolt* you in Detroit— The man said this ticket was complete—Detroit to New York— But your fare's marked Paid solely to Buffalo. You got to shell out more— The man said—

Aw, cried the ticket collector carelessly, you must have got yourself in the hands of a runner. They're always trying that on greenies.

Morris was compelled to pay an additional five dollars and fifty cents for the tariff from Buffalo to New York City. And in Albany they contended, when he tried to board the river boat, that his ticket was valid only from Buffalo to Albany; an additional fifty cents, Albany to New York, was extorted.

He'd been one hour in New York, and was breakfasting on crackers, cider, and hard-boiled eggs in a tavern on the waterfront, when he was approached by a bland gentleman wearing a silk hat. This fellow gave the name of Mr. Schuyler Baird and declared that he was a State employee, he'd seen Morris boarding the river steamer in Albany. He gave an effusive welcome to the stranger. Morris knew that he must appear as an outlander, an unforgivable rustic. At home he would have been considered remarkably dressed up; people might have asked him if he were bound for church. But here his was the attire of a clown. He wore his best boots; but they were thick, scuffed, soaked with oil, rippled by long wearing, and he had tucked his pants of coarse jeans cloth into them. These New Yorkers did not wear their pants tucked into their boots, and their pants were not of jeans. His shirt was made of pale blue flannel. Store-bought goods; and the shirt had been stitched by Farmer Mast's mother-in-law, who did neighborhood sewing. He wore a treasured black jacket which had belonged to Uncle Melly but was worn seldom by the old man. Uncle Melly had not been Morris Markham's match in size, but his arms were fully as long as Morris's, and their excessive length had given Uncle Melly a rather apelike appearance. So the sleeves fitted handsomely, but the coat was too short and too meager, it could not be buttoned across the front. To top this all off, Morris was wearing a hat made of straw. These other people wore hats of silk or brushed beaver, or of some hard stiff cloth.

On his first day in New York City, Morris expended between fifty and sixty dollars, and with very slight value accruing. Mr. Baird suggested and received a fee of five dollars for services rendered as scout, carriage-seeker, companion, and hotel room-securer. Baird whispered to the Indiana visitor that unquestionably he would be refused accommodations at the Irving House unless a satisfactory gratuity—five dollars, again—was awarded to the hotel clerk. This functionary, a pomaded fatty named Chadsey, grew affable on the receipt of the offering; but that did not prevent him from inflicting a double rate for the ornate room finally made available to Morris. Mr. Baird had expressed a willingness to head a sightseeing tour, but met with refusal; finally he took a ceremonious leave. Two hours after his departure, Morris produced a twenty-dollar bill which he had changed for Mr. Baird (now being himself in need of smaller change for carriage fare and the like). Chadsey the clerk, without grace or patience, informed the newcomer that the bill was one of the crudest attempts at counterfeiting which he had ever seen. He also declared that he had never laid eyes on Mr. Schuyler Baird before. By this time Morris was not certain whether every inhabitant of New York City would cheat him roundly, if given the opportunity, but he rather supposed that they would. Nevertheless he considered it essential that he cast off the uniform of greenhornery. He knew no advice to seek except that of Mr. Chadsey. Recognizing the universal sin of bribery and corruption as practiced in these parts, Morris visited a neighboring tobacconist and purchased a paper bundle of Havana segars. Artlessly he presented his offering to Mr. Chadsey; but the clerk did not take offense, he instructed Morris about his wardrobe. There was only one place to go, he said, and that was to H. & D. H. Brooks & Co. Next morning Morris repaired to the corner of Cherry and Catherine Streets, and found the Brooks brothers established in a huddle of cobbled-together buildings with a wooden canopy covering the sidewalk. The clerks all appeared to be English gentlemen of an extremely old school. The customer was taken in charge by a senior of the lot, whom Morris assumed to be a retired earl. Eventually Morris appeared in trousers of somber plaid, a tan waistcoat piped with blue, and was the owner of two coats: a lightweight cassimere for warm weather and daytime wear, a black frock coat for evening. His stock was of blue tartan (the whalebone stiffeners gave him perpetual agony). He purchased boots at a Fulton Street shoe emporium, and Mrs. Beman of the Astor House prepared shirts for him on an advertised twelve hours' notice. Brooks provided his hat, also tan, of brushed beaver. Before the end of the week Morris was fully tricked out in these new gauds. He regarded himself distrustfully in a deep pier-glass at the head of the Irving House stairway. But, once brushed and generally barbered, no one turned to look at him in the street again, except perhaps with envy for the ease of his stride.

On Sunday, the first of September, Morris lingered for hours on a wharf among more people than ever he had seen in all his life. They were so many that he thought of himself as sole alone. (He could not have rested solitary if there had been five people near, or twenty, or even a hundred; here were human beings in such profusion that they could not affect him, no matter how they whistled and pressed.) He remembered a day when he wandered through swamps of Jasper County, almost to the Illinois line, and halted near Beaver Lake as a flight of pigeons came across. First he thought they were smoke arising—wet woods were afire and burning brown!—then he heard the howl of their wings and knew them for the mass they were. They clouded up from the south, they forced their steady beating way, pushed the terrain flat below them, thudding it down to insignificance by pure majesty of numbers. They came not by dozens as the coots and geese, not by hundreds as he'd seen the blackbirds move, nor yet by thousands. They shot steadily in a column at least a mile in width, a river of birds flowing in across the southern horizon and flowing up over the zenith, and down into the north, and out of sight, and flowing and flowing, a muscular drifting waving torrent of pigeons. How many millions rode that air? He did not know about a million, had to stop and estimate . . . let's see: a thousand thousand were a million. And what was next? A billion? He did not know what a billion was: a hundred million, a thousand million, a million million? He thought that the pigeons flew in billions. He could not recognize them as birds, there were too many, they were but an immensity. Beaver Lake was struck by hail, water splashed and roiled as far as he could see, twas the droppings of those birds, crazy hordes which made a sound tornadic in their passing. They filled his nostrils with their smell. Even that night when he was camping, the smell was solid around him, an acrid musty odor of pigeons and the storm of dung which they'd put down.

Two mourning doves upon a limb? A band of warblers speaking earnestly, with little lightning squeaks and dashings, through the brush? These he recognized and knew. But not a magnitude.

I stand alone, he said.

He must have spoken aloud; vaguely he was aware that faces turned to look at him. He did not mind their staring. He knew, for the first time in his remote and steady-treading life— He knew the loneliness of one within a crowd. He knew now what a crowd might be, he'd never known before.

Morris roosted on a packing case so cumbrous that the carters could not move it, they'd left it on the pier a-Saturday. Mr. Chadsey said, That's where she'll come. Canal Street pier. So Morris walked before the dawn from Chambers Street and Broadway, looking seriously at an unfolded map, halting at corner after corner to examine his map in the growing light. Going on, picking his difficult way through this bricky jungle, hunting for street signs, finding them sometimes, sometimes going astray and then retracing his steps to the proper street. Prostitutes drifted up to importune; he didn't answer, looked away, kept going on. These were leftovers from night, tired slovens of the alleyways, so filthy in their dress they might have lured a lunatic, they could not lure a man. Once some thieves followed him, he heard them coming lightly, big sly threatening figures, one was limping. Morris turned swiftly and drew out the pocket pistol which he'd acquired a few days before. The men edged away into shadows, then he heard them scooting off down a narrow space between two buildings. He thought: And city people say they're feared of *woods!*

During the long morning, foggy and sunlit by turns, more and more people began to assemble upon that pier. Mostly they were men, but there was a scattering of ladies who accompanied important-looking gentlemen with ribbons fastened diagonally across their chests. Workmen tested the guy-wires and foundations sustaining two triumphal arches. These edifices suggested Christmas to Morris (he thought of Sardis Howe bursting into song: *Deck the halls with boughs of holly*) for they dripped with evergreen branches as well as flowers. The lettering on the first span was difficult to read, he was so close to it, he had to stretch his neck and twist his head. W-e-l-c-o-m-e-

J-e-n-n-y-L-i-n-d. The second arch was nearer the gates, he could see that easily. J-e-n-n-y-L-i-n-d-W-e-l-c-o-m-e-t-o-A-m-e-r-i-c-a. Now and again, above odors of tar and smoke and vegetable decay, through the acridity of brackish water smell, he could scent the evergreens, imagined that he could smell the flowers. He was grateful for the reassurance brought to him by his nostrils. He'd tried to think of nightingales; this seemed no fit place in which to consider them. But the stray woodsy perfumes said to him, Somewhere there are still timberlands and birds winging through. *They were united to one another in love, they had communion in each other's gifts and graces.*

Through noon and earliest afternoon the mass of watchers thickened. Markham had looked at adjacent ships swaying against hawsers, wedded to other wharves by those same cables—had gazed down the long thin groves of masts and spars, and seen folks gathering in the flat open glades. He'd supposed that they were passengers but recently come upon deck. Then nearer at hand he saw queues inching up the gangplanks, saw wide unruly street throngs narrowing down as they were squeezed through gateways, as they paid admission fees. The moored ships were galleries for the accommodation of those who'd come, drawn by a fascination never felt before, a revering wonder they might not admit.

Morris composed a letter to the Howes, and was regretful that he would never set it down on paper and send it by mail. But in telling loved ones of the experiences which befell he would also be confessing the addiction which had drawn him to this place. That he could never bring himself to do. No one at home must know why he'd come, no one must ever know.

Mr. & Mrs. Howe & All the Family. Respected Friends: Allow me to inform you of the scene when the *Atlantic* finally arrived at Canal Street. I never saw people like that before. Maybe few other folks ever did. I heard some of the policemen a-talking: they said there were thirty or forty thousand people there, all looking out of windows, or standing on the roofs of buildings. Or crowded on the decks of other ships drawn up alongside. Or on the edges of the wharves; and some of them fell right into the water when they got shoved. From my place on that big box I had a close look at everything, and especially at the Nightingale. She was setting with some other ladies and a lot of gentlemen, up on a high place on the ship; folks was a-screaming, Look up there, that's her! On the wheelhouse! Twasn't long after the ship stopped when she come down. She had hold of the captain's arm. Policemen pushed and made a wall ahead of her, because the crowds stood solid. Then other people, special people of this city, they come and give her flowers, and there was lots of bowing and talk, and all kinds of welcoming. Then the police would press against the crowds again, and make more room so's she could move. They were trying to get her to a carriage but twas a mighty hard thing to do. I looked at her and I felt sad at first. I thought, Can this be her? For I'd expected she'd be beautiful; but her form was kind of chunky, and her face was chunky too. I thought of a picture Liddy likes to look at—all in colors: Liddy tolt me that the young girls in the picture, they were peasants from some foreign place. She said that they were dairymaids, and going to milk cows. That was how I thought of Jenny Lind at first. And then I thought: It couldn't be that she's a peasant and a dairymaid, for she's a Nightingale. So I felt better, even though her nose was thick and broad as anything. Soon she donned a veil, and so you couldn't see her face any more; and then the captain put her in his carriage, and they drove away.

I guess there must have been ten thousand people all around the corner where the Irving House is built, the rest of Sunday afternoon. I stood there watching too—although I had a room inside, but didn't wish to linger in the room. Preferred to stand, and watch for her. She come up to her open window—on the Broadway side— Oh, three-four times. She'd smile, and wave, and then the crowds would give another yell. Twas rather frightening to see so many people, all a-looking in their wonderment—and kind of greediness— A-looking at one solitary woman. And a stranger, whom they'd never heard a-singing. They'd just heard tell.

That night a big procession come a-sweeping in. Folks said that there was twenty companies of firemen a-standing guard. And every fireman he had a torch in hand. And all the glow and waving of the flames; and every now and then some flames would fall from off a torch, or maybe they would drop one, and then there'd be the whooping of the crowds, and it was kind of frightening again. They said that there was full two hundred musicians standing there to play the serenade for Jenny Lind. I thought I counted more than that. And all the shine of fire on their dazzled horns and such. Then once again the Nightingale, she come up to her window, and you ought to heard those people and the noise they made. Then the band it started in to play. They played *My Country, Tis of Thee* and *Yankee Doodle* and some more, and Jenny Lind she liked them. I could see her clap her hands each time.

I've tried to see her often, since, but it is hard to do. Count of that veil she wears when she goes out, tis hard to see her face. And all those folks around her all the time, just every time she moves. But when she left the Irving House and moved to the New York Hotel, I followed on. I had to give the man ten dollars, gold, to get a room. But I was willing, and I give it eagerly. My money isn't going to last forever, at this rate. But I hain't been robbed; just cheated; swindled now and then. I guess you might bug out your eyes at my new clothes, but you hain't never going to see them. I went down to that ticket auction that they had, in Castle Garden. Cost a shilling to get in; I heard it told that there was most four thousand folks—and mostly men, they were—at the auction. You want to know how much the first ticket cost? Seemed like half those people wanted to have the honor of buying the first ticket. I even tried to bid, myself, but there was too much yelling; and I couldn't understand how they were managing; and the price went soaring high, so I give over. Man named Genin was winner of the right to buy the first. He spent a fortune: two hundred twenty-five dollars he paid. And that was just to be the first. I bought my ticket later on. It said in the newspapers that prices averaged out at six or seven dollars, but I paid a sight more than that—so much that I won't even tell you, in this letter that I'll never write.

God keep you all, beloved friends. I feel so far away from everything. I walk and stare, I don't belong, I'm getting thinner than a rail, I don't half relish anything I eat. I keep a-thinking of the Wednesday night to come: eleventh of September, that's the night. Then I'll get to hear the Nightingale. I've tolt myself I'll hear her once, and then I'll go. I've parted with a sight of cash—more than you or anyone in all the world will ever know. Sometimes I feel right mean about it: thinking how my friends are poor, and you are poor, and why couldn't I have give these sums to you instead? And then the notion of the Nightingale, and how the song may sound, it rises up, and fair to breaks my heart. God keep you, friends. I pray that all is well with you. You'll never get this missive that is in my heart. I wouldn't dare tell anyone that it was in my heart. You don't know what a city's like and so I trust you never come to learn. And nobody will ever know that I was here. You'll say, and all the neighbor-folks as well: *Well, Morris, where you been? Oh, places,* I'll reply. *Just up and down, and back and forth, and all around.* You'll never know that once I heard the Nightingale. Twill be on Wednesday night. I wonder how I'll live till then. God keep you, friends.

Kom kiyra, kom kiyra, kom kiyra,
Hoah! hoah! hoah! hoah!

He knew not what she was telling in those peculiar words of her Swedish Echo Song, he knew not any story inherent in her recitation; but for Morris there existed a clarity unperceived previously in his lonely muddled woodsy life. In taking the Eastern plunge he had ventured into a thronged elder realm, and promptly discovered a horde of venal humans, petty, grasping to excess. He'd feared lest the illusion of his nightingale be discolored, wrenched away from him.

But the blonde woman carried him into Mallorcan mountains and moonlight melting there. He listened, as if along with the sainted Reverend Mr. Allardice, and heard a glory of God extolled. Not as a parson might do it—no sepulchral intonation, no discourse on creed or sectarian attitude—but with that same appreciative reverence in which secretly the toughest man might push his seeking nose into lilacs.

The very notes themselves, thought Morris, speak her name.

Jenny Lind, Jenny Lind.

It had been an unruly assemblage before whom she first lifted up her voice. Now Morris observed that people were tamed. The crowd had descended upon this hall like a plague, rude and tussling. Men tore the sleeves of one another's jackets, stamped upon one another's hats; women screamed at finding themselves caught in the press; soberly bewhiskered individuals knocked out the window-lights with their walking sticks, seeking in final desperation to secure an entrance by this means. Innocent folk had tempted fate with a careless display of their tickets, and found the tickets snatched from their grasp. The place reeked of contention, of positive diabolical furies; but at last there ruled a solid hush, for Jenny Lind was singing.

Jenny Lind, said her voice, *Jenny Lind.*

Who cared for the words she uttered, or dared to spend himself in seeking out their meaning? She sang the high refinement of a legend long sought but little used. She sang the tender slip of evergreen, sang marsh and mountain, sang in reaches hitherto beyond the attainment of migrant flocks who flew. Immortal, she cried, immortal! I am immortal. I shall sing forever, and in these heights. Would you be immortal, too? If you would, you have only to listen. Put your ear to my tender throat and hear the robin-notes swelling.

There is indeed a purity which defies the pollution of mankind.

Come to the hill with me. Grass is green and comforting. If you are an old person, and ailing, I will nurse you there. Nurse you with my cool hands. If you are younger than that, but hungry, then I will feed you—feed you with my hands.

What shall I feed you?

Spice cakes!

The cakes, then, and tasty cheese to go with them!—and draughts of milk to wash your dinner down.

Come with me to my hill pasture. I have a house there, and comfort waiting you.

I have a house built of sun and grass.

A bird began its carol in twilight, and persisted all night long. The morning came; twas bright and pink, and I looked out and saw the bird and heard her singing still.

Come with me to the fair smooth place. If you're a child, I shall snatch up my gown and run beside you. I'll teach you little plays, cool games in clover on the heights.

And I shall teach you prayers to say.

If you're a baby, I shall wash you, dress you, improvise some tunes upon your toes and fingers. And you shall live forever there with me. You'll be my baby always.

If you're a young man, you shall love me there. Oh, I have everything to offer you!

Oh, love me, *love* me, darling!

If you're dying, then you shall never die. There is no death. You heard me sing it from the peaks. No death, no specter gray to come a-riding.

My hill, my hill: the mound of fresh and blowing herbs. You'll need to meet me there, for I shall be all things to you.

Yes, I'll be.

Kom kiyra, kom kiyra, kom kiyra,
Hoah! hoah! hoah! hoah!

Morris put this woman into the sky, along with every tender singer who'd ever brushed the blue with her wings. He cared not if his nightingale had become lark or dove, or one of those mysterious singers among the apple trees at home. At last he'd heard her voice, and it made a new world for him, and might for all.

Later he was impressed with her gracious charities, but in the long run they meant nothing: one did not expect an angel to be anything other than angelic. Never again could the heavily populated world seem as sordid as Morris's own recent experience proclaimed it to be (with a shiver, he wondered if this was something which had happened to him before . . . he'd heard of the process of reincarnation, although he did not remember hearing it so named. He wondered if in another Age, with himself contained within another rough bearded tanned shape, he had not stood with companions upon a chilly midnight pasture, to watch more than one Jenny Lind fly down through unearthly light to sing).

The worshipful fact was that her song, and her song alone, had brought her so much of the world's wealth, the world's acclaim. Music made by others was forgotten already—the sixty-piece orchestra, Benedict, Belletti, who were they? Ah, there'd been a trio for voice and flutes; but it served only to demonstrate the rough uncertainty of any instrument made by human hands, unfashioned with soft mystery as God had fashioned Jenny Lind.

Or perhaps Mr. Barnum thought that he had fashioned her, with his gesturing showman's hands?

Never did, thought Morris, with as much grimness as was left to him. Barnum never did. God's done it, God and Heaven's done the whole thing. And—and maybe all the other angels too—the ones besides Jenny, the ones Paul the Apostle said that he might speak with the tongues of. . . .

Hours afterward, staring at the high dark ceiling of his hotel room, Morris felt compelled to admit justly that he was in Mr. Barnum's debt. He would not have heard the nightingale, she would not have ennobled his existence and now become a part of it, had it not been for P. T. Barnum. He could still hear the showman's voice, as the dignitary stood upon the platform at the concert's conclusion: I feel compelled to disregard the fact that Mademoiselle Lind herself begged me not to mention on this evening one of her own noble and spontaneous deeds of beneficence. Her share of the proceeds of this concert will, I believe, be close upon ten thousand dollars, every cent of which she has declared her intention of devoting to charitable purposes. I shall now mention the manner in which she wishes this large sum to be applied.

Barnum read from the paper in his hand.

Morris endeared her with the thought: I see you again in sky-blue gown, with roses in your hair and at your bodice. What wonders will you never cease performing, upon that high Eden meadow where you would take us?

To the Fire Department Fund, three thousand dollars. Spose that's just because firemen marched to the Irving House with them torches, first night she was here? Couldn't be.

To the Musical Fund Society, two thousand dollars. Course I don't know nothing about such matters, but could it be they take care of musicians who are old and friendless? Might be. Imagine Jenny Lind grown old and friendless! She'll never be, not in that immortal life which her tongue and throat have promised us, and which she's building for us all afresh. Couldn't nobody ever turn that fair stranger from their door. . . .

Home for the Friendless, five hundred dollars. Society for the Relief of Indigent Females, five hundred dollars. She says just like Jesus Christ said it: we all got to be friends to each other—Do Unto Others and so on. So there won't be any friendless any more. And I'm not certain that I know what indigent means; sounds like they might be kind of mad or cross; but maybe they grew that way because they were poor and tired, like the Widow Campsie, daughter of Reverent Allardice. . . . *Oh, Reverent Allardice! For I had heard the caroling of saints. . . .*

Phineas T. Barnum, reading on and on. *Dramatic Fund Association, five hundred dollars. Home for Colored and Agèd Persons, five hundred dollars.*

I was almost asleep for a while, laying here and remembering Barnum's voice and all the charities, and whilst I lay like that—almost asleep, or even quite asleep for one brief moment—I had a little dream. Dreamt that it was some time following the Resurrection, and Jesus walked through some pretty woods—maybe like on the south end of the Howe place, over across the crick. Twas May, and there was scarce another thing in all that timber cept sweet williams. Thick and scattered wide and palest purple, they were growing there. And then Christ come a-walking through, and He had a whole procession with Him, just an endless parade. Like twas all sorts of animals, and birds a-flying overhead, and agèd folks a-hobbling with their canes, and some on crutches, too; but kind of smiling as they went, as if they knew that He would heal them by and by. And colored people, too: old worn-out nigger people that had worked so hard and got so little, and still they loved the Lord and hadn't lost their hope. Then so quickly Jenny Lind was up above them, way high up amongst the trees, and she was singing. Twas like that Jesus knew it all the time, and He'd expected her to sing; the other folks, they looked surprised; but Jesus kind of nodded, and He smiled as if He knew it all along.

She sang not only midst the trees, but in the open sun and moonglow too.

Colored and Orphan Asylum, five hundred dollars. Lying-in Asylum for Destitute Females, five hundred dollars. New York Orphan Asylum, five hundred dollars. Protestant Half Orphan Asylum, five hundred dollars.

I don't quite make that out about those half-an-orphans. Must mean just the ma or pa is dead. I'm a full-fledged orphan, and I've been for long.

Roman Catholic Half Orphan Asylum, five hundred dollars. Old Ladies' Asylum, five hundred dollars. So the Catholics have got half orphans too? Funny thing; don't quite understand it, like I said.

So that's the sum of it, that's the ten thousand.

Tain't just that she gave away all that money tonight—though precious few people could ever afford to, and fewer would want to if they could afford it! Tain't just the good that a gift can do, for all unfortunates and for the sick, and poor old lady ones, and poor old colored ones, and orphans and half orphans too. What counts is the fact that she wanted to do it, and she did do it; and she's done it before, and she'll do it again. It shows that we can trust her.

So forever we can trust the richest music that we hear. . . .

He'd fretted for the sight of her, and after that he'd fretted for the sound; and so he'd earned both privileges, by patience and by cunning, and by waiting and observing. He'd come a-trailing and a-seeking. Here at last he held the prize he sought: he held her in his hands and in his heart, would always keep the bird-thing safe.

The trouble was: he'd visioned up all beauty and all goodness and all melody, and wrapped them in the body and the voice of Jenny Lind, and now he couldn't shake her off. He'd seen her first upon that crowded pier, with troops of men in shiny hats, and ladies with their gems and thick-fringed shawls and fancy bonnets clustering around; and all the bowing and the flower-offering; and then the passing neath the shadow of those arches set to honor her. He'd seen the peasant face, and named her as a dairymaid, although he didn't know whether he'd seen a dairymaid before (perhaps the Howe girls and the Radleys—they were dairymaids at times?). But not for long might he discount the legend and the thought of how twould be to hear her sing! And then the march of firemen, the herds of police, the other riffraff herds; the drunken fools; the screech that went aloft when she came with Barnum to the window. . . . Then remembering how he'd hung about the halls and waited for the spectacle of her upon the stair. And so he'd seen her, coming down or going up, and mounting to her carriage, and being handed out.

. . . Here now in the New York Hotel, Morris lay suffering and twisted on his bed. He had misplaced his spiritual mittens, and there was no friendly fire toward which he might stretch his fingers. He sought to warm himself closely before a star, there blazed many exalted flames within the star. The star was all afire, but how could he reach it? There were too many millions of miles in between. So let him dry up as an ancient dries? Or let him explode as a stripling explodes, wet within his bed? Or let him become permanently deranged at thinking of it, thinking of it and her? He grew sick in reckoning the walls and floors, the space of chambers which held him away from her. Might it not be wiser if he changed hotels once more—immediately—in the middle of this night?

There was something else which he might do.

He arose, dressed, smoothed his hair, and went down the stairs. Thousands of people had followed Jenny Lind home from the Castle Garden that evening, and they roared in the street until she stepped to her little balcony and acknowledged the tribute of their presence. Members of the Musical Fund Society attempted to demonstrate gratitude in an impromptu serenade, but were drowned out by the crowd's hullabaloo. A few of the society's members lingered on the premises, celebrating in public and private parlors. So men were still drinking here, and hospitably two different groups invited Morris to join them; he muttered his thanks, and declined. He filled a pipe and sat alone in the shadows, removed from lamps. The pipe's smoke grew very hot, it seemed burning his mouth, twas close to strangling him. He emptied out the ashes and dropped the hot pipe into his pocket. He stood up, smoothing the nap of his beaver hat with his sleeve, as he had seen other men do. He walked outside in rigid purpose. The cobblestones and sidewalks were littered with rubble left by crowds: torn newspapers, cigar butts, apple cores—some woman had even lost a shoe, and it lay in the gutter squashed and trodden flat by other feet. Now, with throngs departed, there was room for the row of carriages which usually waited at night near the entrance, drivers and horses dozing. A single-seater was first in line, and Morris climbed into it. The driver jerked out of his slumber and turned to blink at him.

Where to, squire?

You should know, Morris replied.

Is it cards or women you're after wanting at this unseemly hour, sir?

A woman. One woman.

They drove to Madam Bright's, just off Houston Street. Only three girls were available at this hour, according to the madam; all the others had prior commitments for the night. The trio came swaying in for his appraisal, and the embarrassed Morris crooked his finger at a pink-faced roly-poly lass who said that her name was Madge. Promptly Madge pleaded thirst and hunger. The two of them occupied a private chamber while Madge, in talkative exuberance, discussed cold chicken and white wine and biscuits, though her patron could barely taste or swallow. There was an ornate lamp with a peach-and-blue shade, there were paintings of sylphs and bulls upon the wall; statuettes of demure maidens; and a bed with a betasseled pink spread waiting beyond.

But less than half an hour after the first wine had been poured and the first pullet sliced, Morris arose abruptly, saying to Madge and to the world, Nope. Can't do it. He threw a heavy gold coin on the table—more than enough to equalize the tariff and leave an acceptable gift for the girl—and walked quickly to the street.

Got to go.

The next morning he bought a secondhand carpetbag and stowed his old Indiana clothing in that. At the pier he was told that the next boat for Albany was filled; no space available; but again . . . bribery. . . . In Buffalo he sought out a minister and measured him with his eye. You ain't tall enough for these, Morris said. But maybe you know somebody taller who needs clothes. I want to give these new duds away . . . no, I ain't crazy. Just want to give them away. . . . He finished the homeward journey wearing his jeans breeches and Uncle Melly's jacket; and he walked the last leg of the journey by night, and no one saw him arrive.

Morris, where on earth you been?

Oh, here and there.

XLI

. . . Screaming won't do no good.

. . . We screamed . . . we all screamed. But it didn't do any good.

. . . Nothing does any good.

. . . My Jody, please come find me!

. . . I got no Alvin to come find me.

. . . I got nobody to come find me. For Pa is dead, and I know they got Harvey and Brother Bob Clark as well. For when we crossed on West Okoboji ice and started north, menfolks mongst the Indans were jabbering away, and laughing, and pointing towards the east, like over towards the Thatcher place somewheres. And then one of the mean tall ones—he kind of patted his gun, and kept holding up two fingers, and looking at me and laughing, and then he'd hold up two fingers again. So that means that Harvey and Brother Bob are dead as well; and there can't no one ever come to find me, cause I haven't got no one to come.

. . . John Quincy Adams Noble, if you dast pee-pee *one more* time whilst you're quilted up—

. . . Why, Jody, don't you mind how she always fusses like that, when she wakes up wet and hungry?

. . . Abbie, swing me, swing me!

. . . Oh, Lizzie, honey, guess what? They're going to have a taffy-pull, over at the Masts', come Saturday evening. And Alvin Noble, he wants to scort me! And now comes the very best part: that big Joe Thatcher wants to come along and scort *you.*

. . . Liddy, wouldn't it be wonderful? Honest to goodness, I really think it might be true this time, cause it's been ten days, or maybe eleven. I should of started a week ago last Sunday, and I never have been late before. . . . Oh, I got to hush now. Can't tell you any more, cause here come the menfolks in the door this minute—

. . . *Liza's mad, and I am glad, and I know what will please her. A bottle of wine to make her shine—*

. . . Land knows, it's simple enough to make pickles that way, cause you don't have to cook them a-tall. But the only trouble with that receipt is that it takes so blame much sugar! And sugar's costly these days. But what I was going to say was: if you have got plenty of sugar, and don't mind the expense, then, after you've soaked the sliced gherkins at least overnight in strong brine, and washed all the brine off of them, then you just put in quantities of sugar—great big double handfuls of it—and then pour the vinegar over the top. Course, you've got to keep it in a nice cool place whilst they're soaking. Last time I put 'em in a big wooden bucket—yes, that one over there—and then I let it hang down in the well just about two whole days and nights. And then I'd corned that last leg of beef we had, and when I cooked that corned beef, and had some boiled potatoes, and give Alvin leave to try the new pickles— Well, you ought to seen the way he rolled up his eyes! He said: These pickles are just plain *heavenly!*

. . . Jody, I'm worried about that cough of yourn. Now, I'm going to get right up—yes, I *am*— I'm going to get right up out of bed, and you stay here; and all I want to do is heat a little turpentine and lard together; then I'm going to rub it on your chest; and I'm going to cook up a big dose of honey and butter and vinegar, and—yes, you *are*— You're going to take it! Don't you tell me how to deal with you, Mr. Smart! How'd you like to catch the pu-*monia*?

. . . And not a one of these little fairy tablecloths was here when we passed late yesterday afternoon! Do you member? But *now* just look at 'em: all over the grass. . . . So that means just one thing, Rowly: means that the fairies have been having a party, and having tea.

. . . *Give us this day our daily bread, and forgive us our trespasses as we forgive those who trespass against us.*

. . . O Jesus Christ, O Heavenly Father! My God, my God, my *God!* My little boy, my— *Alvin!* And— My *baby boy—!*

. . . *Aaaaahh!* Dory, Dory—

You have been put down into that dark cold shaft or well kind-of-place. All of you have been put there. It's a place that's got something squirming in it; and even deeper deeper in the shaft voices are coming back to haunt you, to make some sort of sport with their narration.

Why, yes indeed, they're reading Indian stories, reading from books. Or else people are telling the stories.

You don't know which, you don't care.

. . . *We were kept bound all that night. The Indians kept waking . . . made strange noises, as of wolves and owls, and other wild beasts. . . . Being satisfied with this sort of mirth, they proceeded in another manner: taking the burning coals, and sticks flaming with fire at the ends, holding them to my face, head, hands, and feet, and at the same time threatening to burn me entirely if I cried out. . . . On the 8th of July, five Indians, a little before night, fell on an outhouse in Reading, where they surprized a woman with eight children;*

the former with the three youngest were instantly dispatched, and the other they carried captive; but one of the children unable to travel, they knocked on the head, and left in the swamp. . . . They made their way toward Susquehanna, and passing near another house . . . they immediately scalped the mother and her children before the old man's eyes. Inhuman and horrid as this was, it did not satisfy them; for when they had murdered the poor woman, they acted with her in such a brutal manner as decency will not permit me to mention. . . . Two of the Indians took one of the dead bodies, which they chose as being the fattest, cut off the head, and divided the whole into five parts, one of which was put into each of five kettles. . . .

You heard the stories, and it happened to other folks in the long ago; but now it has happened to you, and you didn't think it would be like this.

There was that faraway night when all your throats were worn raw with shrieking. Tears ran no more. Ah, yes, you'd tried to shriek, because of all the things they were doing to you. You'd tried to shriek, but all you could manage was a growling noise.

And that was distant, distant, upon the Okoboji shore; and then you walked and walked; they made you walk, they made you carry things. That was Doctor Harriott's horse up ahead. And that was Bert Snyder's horse, too. What were their names? . . . Laz and Glad. And they were kind of whinnying; but no one let you ride them, or ride on any other pony. They made you walk, they made you carry things, and go a-staggering. And sometimes they would point their guns at you and make as if to shoot. You hoped they'd shoot; but no, they didn't shoot—just pointed guns and made an awful laugh, and said gruff words, and then they laughed again. You went a-walking and a-limping on; and then that crust would break, it kept a-breaking and it cut your skirts to pieces, and it cut your limbs as well.

. . . And then that next night (never quite so distant), and the things they did to you again. But by this time you'd faint and never know . . . and never know, and never know . . . just feel the bruises and the rawness afterward. And then the last night . . . twas in a kind of grove . . . and in the morning, all the men were standing on the edge of camp, and pointing. There was smoke: they saw it. Smoke down in those trees, and where was that? It might be Spirit Lake, way yonder over there; so that smoke, it might be from the Marble place. You didn't know, you didn't know, you didn't care so much. But there was said to be a Mrs. Marble, so you ought to care, and still you couldn't. You saw the menfolks taking snow and rubbing all that black stuff off their faces, and you thought maybe they'd take some paints, just like the Indians you'd heard about, and paint their faces. But they didn't: they just rubbed off all the black, and then they took their guns, and they went toward the smoke, and you were left behind with just the womenfolks.

The men went toward the smoke, and found the Marble place. They watched their chance, they made their chance; and then they shot William Marble in the back; and in one second he was dead. He didn't know what had happened. But his young wife– She knew.

Fire-Cloud said that he would write of this deed, and of other deeds done recently. He said with pride: When more *Washichun* come, they see what I write!

His father grunted in disparagement. I read your writing, so I know. Whites cannot read your writing.

The pictures. They know that the pictures are made by Mahpiyapeta! They see pictures! said the stubborn Fire-Cloud.

The Wahpekute had concealed their ponies in a nearby grove. Already the tall and unmistakable figure of His-Curly-Sacred moved at a considerable distance among those trees, as he took Peggy Ann Marble away with him. She had writhed and wrestled at first, and His-Curly-Sacred had been compelled to whack her over the head two or three times, to demonstrate that no resistance would be tolerated. The little battle had caused amusement among those who still crouched around the body of William Marble, searching the dead man's pockets, and pulling at his clothes, to see if anything of importance was concealed underneath (besides the money belt which Inkpaduta had snatched off while the body was still warm).

The men had pointed to the struggling pair, and cried: He wishes to be first to take white woman!

(They considered this a typical attitude on the part of His-Curly-Sacred. They did not quarrel with him about this. All who wished had already enjoyed themselves with white women, and soon would take their turns with this new one.)

Perhaps he has her in the forest?

Nay, he likes not to lie with her in snow!

Tawachehawakan waits until he has her in the lodge upon his robe!

Indefatigable whiskey hunters were turning the interior of the Marble house topsy-turvy in their effort to discover spirit water. Fire-Cloud joined them there; but he was hunting only for an axe, and soon discovered the implement. With axe in hand he returned to the dooryard and selected an ash tree near the edge of the bluff. From experience he knew that marks put upon the smooth inner wood of the *psehtin* would be legible for a long time to come. He barked out a section of the tree and then went to cut a few sticks to be toasted in the house fire. By the time he was ready to begin his artistry, a gallery was assembled. (Since the rest had already secured what loot they fancied . . . actually there were not many articles removed. Most of the men were sated with plundering these small cabins, and collecting meager articles contained in them. Inkpaduta had declared an intention to pillage the Wood brothers' store at Springfield; everyone looked forward to that. The women especially chattered about wonderful bolts of goods to be seen in that store. And they would find spirit water at Springfield if not in this lonely place.)

Fire-Cloud set to work with his sticks. He scratched deeply upon the tender frosty inner surface which his knife had smoothed. He drew a picture of water, to show that he was telling of victims in the Okoboji and Spirit Lake regions. He drew the lakes. Six cabins had been visited locally, and he put them all in.

There was some objection.

But one lodge was burnt!

Aye. One lodge.

It was the lodge where That Old One slays white-boy-with-hair-all-red. That was in flames!

I make flames, said Fire-Cloud, and he drew them—uncolored—as he thought, rather cleverly. He began to put in the bodies of dead whites: men, women, and children. But soon there was a squabble: people thought that he had not put the bodies in the right places, or near the proper cabins; and there were not enough of them. The artist said that there was not room enough to put in all the dead whites, it would take too long. Also he needed to include at least some of the Wahpekute. Though he enjoyed writing by pictures and leaving indefinite messages on trees, he was growing rather weary of the task before him. It was too complicated; he would rather go along with the rest to kill oxen and enjoy fresh blood and heart-meat.

He designated himself by making a fire cloud above one figure; but this brought surly objection from his father.

Thou art Head Man, my son?

Ate, I am not Head Man, thou knowest. But I cannot make End-Red for you. I have no red.

Sometime you write how many I kill!

I say now, father, that I do this thing. There is red paint in the trading store to which we go?

Eyakesh. We go there, take red paint. You build pictures for me.

I build them!

The others had joined Makes-Fat-Bad in slaughter of the cattle. Soon they were all squatted happily among steaming lacerated carcasses of the Marbles' beasts . . . the hot blood was good. They drank much of it, and also they ate the last of the contents of Peggy Ann Marble's sugar-bucket. They felt it unfortunate that the hair of the dead man could not be taken; but angrily Inkpaduta assured all that the restriction was still in force.

But we kill again! We take woman again. We find gold money and also fresh beef. Do we not dance this night?

Dance, dance! cried several eager voices.

Wachipi. There is dancing this night, said Inkpaduta.

Makes-Fat-Bad sang loudly as they returned to their camp. He knew that it would be futile to plead with Inkpaduta for a lifting of the scalp-ban; but nothing had been said about not singing a scalp-song. He croaked out words which he had learned among the Lakota a generation in the past, long before he first rode to make war. Most of the Wahpekute had never heard this song before, and even Inkpaduta listened with interest (he also was reminded of his youth).

The men with tangled hair!

It is they who kill enemies in morning.

Some of the party began to intone a response.

Because they get up early in morning, without waiting to comb their hair. . . .

Ho!

That is why they kill enemies. They wait not to comb!

Hoah! Ho!

You sing more, ordered Inkpaduta. So Makes-Fat-Bad did sing again. *The men with tangled hair—*

XLII

The people of the Des Moines City were to Morris Markham an assortment of unruly shapes who wavered before his eyes and refused to stand still long enough to be ticketed. Some of them he thought he'd known before, it seemed as if he didn't know them now. The Wood brothers, George and William . . . he'd done some trading with them in the autumn. He heard their flat tones deriding him by implication, even though the actual words they uttered were noncommittal.

But I tell you, Mr. Wood, everybody's dead, down there to Okoboji. Kilt by the Indians.

That's what you say.

I seen them laying dead.

Hah. When you say all this happened?

Some time between last Saturday morning, when I left to go hunt oxen, and late Monday night, when I come back.

We hain't seen any hostile Indians around here. Didn't have none when we lived up to Mankato, neither.

Kilt everybody at the Gardners', everybody at the Howes', everybody at . . . my place. There wasn't any smoke rising from the Mattocks' nor the Red Wing fellers': that means they must be dead as well. Indians was camped there. I nigh to walked into their camp.

Hah.

Listen, Mr. Wood—and you, too, damn it— Brother over there. Mean to say you don't believe me?"

Ain't saying we do and ain't saying we don't.

(Tiny pale unyielding eyes behind the smudged spectacles; small ears turned out, standing out too round and tight against the sides of the terse smooth-shaven faces; the squeezed compressed lips, signaling their stubbornness in the very power of compression. The manner which says mutually: I'd like to get something out of you, but I ain't going to let you get nothing out of me! Buy, buy—you'll have to persuade me to buy . . . I'll buy as cheaply as I can. And then I'll sell to someone else, and I'll build up the price to whatever height the tariff can bear. And then, after I've sold, I'll have regret only that I couldn't get the price a mite higher. I shan't believe the thing that's told me, for I am born to lie; and so I demand that the belief be embraced that all other men are liars as well. But I will lie prudently, I'll try not to get caught at it. . . . Buy, sell . . . sell never at a loss! My soul is murdered if I lose! And the man with means shall be toadied to, and the man without means shall be scorned, unless perhaps I can take away even that which he hath not; then he shall be emptied out and cast aside. Would you offer the opinion that my shop and holdings are in danger? Perhaps you're telling me that because you want to buy them cheaply, want them for your own profit! You shan't have your profit, but I'll have mine! Offer me no threat of disaster, or I'll have the law on you! I will! Yea, I break the fairest moral laws, I break all laws of benevolence, all laws of simple humanity, because I do not believe in them. They do not exist for me, they are not laws. But the man-made laws, the statute-laid-down laws, these I touch with chary hands. Never will I break one of those laws unless completely confident that I cannot be caught. I will cheat only the man who is too careless, too weak or baffled, too lacking in shrewdness, to cheat back. I'll support the church in my niggardly fashion, because that is the accepted thing to do; and when a church actually is built and becomes a fixture here, I shall in turn become an officer of that church. If they make me treasurer because I am a successful businessman, and reputed to be wealthy, and reputed thus to know a great deal about money and its care—then I shall accept, meekly, and with sanctimonious utterance, and shall seek to find the means whereby some of God's money may cling to my fingers. Never fear—I assured you that I'd not be caught.)

I'm just telling you folks what happened down there. I thought you'd—want to be warned—

What you *say* happened! Mr. Markham, we know these Sioux Indians right well—traded with them for a long time. There's even several families and villages of 'em dwelling not far from here, and they come to the store frequent. Hain't never harmed a soul.

Morris said, Seen my friends a-laying butchered.

Could be. And butchered by *white* rascals, like as not.

William Wood said, Indians are our best customers, else why would we be here, and doing business? They may be poor, and they may be dirty, but I trust 'em.

Hain't so poor, said Morris bitterly, but that you expect them to buy from you.

George Wood cried with spunk: Mr. Markham, you know as well as I do that there's gangs of robbers and horse thieves, here and there, down in the Ioway country—

Wasn't none at Okoboji.

Could be white claim-jumpers, couldn't it? How many of those folks you claim was killed, had proved up on their land, or bought it fair and square? Maybe somebody come to run them out, legally, and they resisted. Happens all the time—even in Minnesota Territory.

Morris Markham turned before he left the door. Go to hell, he said. Both of you.

The Woods kept the only store in the region; but other families of the Springfield community were scattered for miles along the river or out east, past hills, on the upper prairie. A mile and a half beyond the Wood brothers' place stood the log double house of one J. B. Thomas, who was a Justice of the Peace. Morris had never met Mr. Thomas, but George Granger knew the man well, and lingered long enough to make Morris acquainted with these people, before he himself hastened back down the river toward his own cabin. (Granger planned to take to the woods if the Indians came near.) Thomas had no great love for the grasping Wood brothers, nor did he have any reason to respect their opinions in this matter. As a Justice, he'd needed to take many depositions with regard to debatable facts or intricate circumstances not understood by most; and he fancied that by this time he could identify a truthful man, and recognize him when he spoke. Thus Mr. Thomas felt his heart fluttering and his throat grown dry as he listened to the trapper's recitation. He was convinced that this lean stranger was telling the truth.

We'll have the other neighbors in at once, was all he said. He sent his two elder sons speeding to fetch them.

That night, for a third time, Morris gave his tale. He found no one to doubt him, not even Doctor Edwin Benjamin Nodworth Strong. Noddy Strong turned into a waxy jelly at the mere thought of savage depredations. His voice rose above all others in demanding that soldiers should be sent for. Immediately!

Ridgely's closest, said Morris. Want me to go?

Mr. Thomas told him: You look to be about used up, as tis, tramping through this snow the way you been doing. All we'll ask of you is that you give affidavit—an utterance, in full legality—sworn before me as Justice of the Peace. Then the soldiers'll know they're not coming on a wild-goose chase.

Thomas said, after further consideration: I think twould be wisest to have word sent to the Lower Agency, even though the Fort's a mite closer. Major Flandrau is acquainted with some of us. He wouldn't be so apt to discount this story, as might some of the officers at the Fort. . . .

Morris, duly sworn, deposed to a boiled-down summary of the facts; meanwhile others of the community signed a formal request for the assistance of troops. The sturdiest two of the young men were selected as messengers. Both were unmarried. Their names were Joseph Cheffins and Henry Tretz.

Morris fell asleep with his head on the table, while the others still planned at measures for defense. He'd said slowly through his exhaustion: I don't want to have to be the one to tell the Gardner girl. But I'll go, if you think best, to wherever she's a-living, and tell her. Ruther not.

It's your own house where she's living, Doctor Strong. . . .

Ah . . . yes.

Ain't doctors customed to the delivering of tragic tidings?

Strong sighed, rolled up his eyes. He said, I shall inform the little creature. (What he actually meant was that he would tell his wife, and then the shaking sickly woman would be called upon to do a deed which the doctor had not the courage to perform.)

Morris was bent with his cheek pushed against the hard board. Once in a while he muttered; more often he snored lightly; but sometimes he was awake to hear voices coming through to reach his open sleepy ear. . . . No, there wasn't room for everybody to fort up at the Thomas house. Twas the largest, and convenient because of two big rooms and a dog-trot between. But the Wheeler house was strongly built; twould do for some of them to stay there. . . . If anybody wants to try and persuade George and William Wood to join us, they're welcome to go! I don't believe our friend Markham would care to try again . . . there was some strained laughter. Voices mingled, drew away, left Morris considering a variety of new shapes which walked without voices. Man named Bradshaw, another named Smith, another named Carver. . . . No, he guessed Smith wasn't there, he just heard them talking about him. . . . Doctor Strong, and the Thomases, and a man named Adam Shiegley, and another named Stewart. What did they say? Could he remember? Man named Skinner . . . must be women to go with many of these names. Morris thought of women as he dozed; thought of captive women, saw them being led off with thongs around their necks, heard them blubber at him. Through drugged dozings he managed to reiterate a thankfulness that Fate had not sentenced him to tell his story to Eliza Gardner, and see her cry. He'd done enough mourning already. Like many who have been compelled to stare at a ghastliness, he felt that he'd stand callous in the mist of other people's tears.

Eliza Gardner was possessed by blind adoration for Henry Tretz, she stood ready to offer him the whole sum of her devotion. She considered abject intimate domestic slaveries which she might perform—scraping mud off his boots, trimming his glinting hair and beard, preparing favorite foods, warming his bed before he crept into it at night, doctoring him when he was ill. Again she would be gone into fantasies wherein she put Henry into an immense gilded throne-chair, garbed him in robes of plush, circled his head with a crown, and then knelt before him, alternately to pray and to profess loyalty. Eliza would have been appalled to hear (indeed would never have believed) that another human being could surpass her in awarding an affection focused upon this same masculine object.

Such idolatry was exuded by eight-year-old Willie Thomas. Willie lived only for the sight and presence and feeling of Henry Tretz. He introduced Henry's name into his Now-I-Lay-Me chant, promptly on their first meeting. When he performed his small but numerous family chores, he liked to imagine that Henry was there, helping him to do chores. When Willie broke a wheel of the pushcart which he used in his play, he did not weep as his mother expected him to do: he but smiled with assurance and said, Henry'll fix it. When very small, Willie had owned a battered plaster dog which he used to fetch to table with him; the family sat amused, when not too occupied with their own food or conversation, at seeing Willie wave his stubby spoon, offering morsels to the glass-eyed dog before he put them into his own mouth. Willie was too shy nowadays to indulge in a token feeding of Henry Tretz, but at least he did it within the limits of his mind. He would select a particularly toothsome bit of fried pork, push it to the side of his plate, mentally reserve it for Henry. With regret Willie would eat this piece the last of all. In so doing it seemed that he had not achieved an identity with, but rather had lost a clutch upon, the target of his affections.

The previous autumn, Tretz had come from his home to help Mr. Thomas in chopping the winter's wood. For three memorable nights Henry slumbered on a pallet in front of the fire, and Willie was allowed to sleep with him.

Willie wished to rename the family dog, who was called Benny, as Henry. He became lugubrious when his parents scouted the idea.

His mother said, If we don't get to the end of this Henry business, I don't know what we'll do.

A mallard was gathered in from the river, it had a broken wing, it could not fly. For a time Willie Thomas kept the duck as a pet, and named it Henry. He cried quarts when the bird died at last; he held a private funeral, and put a flat stone over the grave with Henry Duck's name inscribed thereon in red chalk letters. Rains washed the word away, but Willie renewed it. When at last snow covered the sacred spot of interment and the grave could no longer be visited, Willie used to look out across mountainous drifts and still see, with his mind's eye, the gravestone far underneath.

Several times during the winter, in visiting the center of Springfield, storms prevented Henry Tretz from returning to his own home. Those occasions became Christmas, Thanksgiving, and Fourth of July commingled. The naturally affable and child-loving Tretz was moved by the mere contemplation of Willie Thomas . . . the child was wispy and frail, with eyes too big for his little face . . . strangers took him to be five years old, rather than eight. To make matters even more sad, he had an impediment in his speech. To him the mighty Henry was captain, mentor, bear-killer, teacher, guard. Henry could muster and command a regiment of stalwarts, and perhaps had done so in Germany, for all Willie knew. He could hoist logs which even the strapping Mr. Thomas might not manage; and best of all, he told wonderful stories. Some were fairy tales, many were anecdotes of his own childhood. His English had improved during recent months. As I was a boy in Bavaria, said Henry, my uncle gives to me a *pfennig*. So I am rich. Where do I go? I go to the lady of the bakeshop. Frau Müller is her name, and she gives to me for my *pfennig* a fine cake. I go down the street eating a bite of my cake, and find there a horse. It seems to me he is saying, Little boy, give to me some of your cake! So then to the horse I give some cake, *ja*. He says that it is good for me to do this. I eat more cake, and then it is that I give more to the horse, and then I eat more, and give to the horse, until all the cake is gone. Then what does that horse do, to thank me for my kind giving of the cake? He bites me! *Ja*, you have heard. On my hand he bites me, and very nearly does he take off one finger. See?—the scar is here, and all from the unkind horse, so long ago.

Also Henry had been a bad boy, and had stolen pears and been soundly whipped in consequence, *ja*. . . . And one time a neighbor child—her name was Kätchen—fell into an abandoned cistern, and the entire village rushed in an attempt at rescue, but it was too late, poor Kätchen was drowned. . . . And one night in cold weather there was a fire at the house of the *Bürgermeister* and the roof was burned off entirely, and in this blaze the *Bürgermeister's* aunt lost her life. . . . A barracks stood not far away, and often did soldiers march through the street with fife and drum. This was the way the fife sounded. . . .

Should Willie like a new story, or did he prefer one which had been told before? *Ach*, the Town Musicians? Very well. Once on a time in Germany was a poor donkey; he was so old no longer could he carry sacks to the mill. He heard his master say, The old donkey now I sell to the glue factory, for them to boil him into glue, he is no good to me. So far away runs the donkey. And then he meets beside the road one dog. He says, Why is so sad? Then Dog tells him he is so old he was no longer any good to hunt, to be one watchdog. And so his master says, Him now I kill! . . . Come with me, Dog, says Donkey, so on together they journey. Then it is that they meet one cat, *ja*. The cat is crying. I am sad, says Cat, because I can no longer catch the mice and rats, and my mistress says—

Henry Tretz carried with him this assortment of delights. Also Willie worshiped the power of Henry's arms and legs, the reddish hair which grew from his tough clean skin, shining dampness of pleasant blue eyes.

Often at night the little boy looked up at a remote moon, and the moon beamed steadily back at him; and to himself Willie Thomas named the moon Henry.

When Tretz and Cheffins went north for help, Willie believed that they might be back in a day or two. He did not understand about icy distances involved. When a week elapsed without return of the messengers, Willie was gone deeply into brooding at his loss. He did not eat well, his pale face grew thinner, his eyes looked more hollow than before. It was difficult for anyone to sleep profitably or deeply by night, crowded into the double house as they were. Babies fretted, missing their home surroundings; tempers grew taut. Half-grown children quarreled senselessly about nothing, and regularly Willie Thomas was possessed by nightmares concerning Him who'd gone away. (On rare occasion his hysterical imaginings permitted the appearance of a colorful pageant: soldiers did come to the rescue, with Henry marching at their head, and fifes and drums sounding.) Mostly there loomed a fierce extensive forest from which smoky faces peered with threat, and out of which emerged howls that set the child to waking and wailing.

Friday, March 26th, dawned warm and welcoming. Men said it was a fit time to increase their wood supply . . . they joked a little about how long the war with the Indians might last. (They jested on this subject only when Morris Markham was well out of hearing.) The cruel knowledge ruled them: settlers *had* been killed at Spirit Lake and the Okobojis, that was certain. Now they'd been warned: what had happened further south could happen at the Des Moines City. Weather fair, woods abundant, axes sharp, they clicked steadily. Womenfolks and children peered from the Thomases' door, and talked of strolling in nearer timberland— Surely twould be safe, if they stayed within sight and call of the house? The eldest Thomas boy ran to the woodcutters at noon, to tell them that a meal was ready, but the men shook their heads. . . . Only another hour or so: then they'd have enough logs assembled to last them through any siege . . . better wait awhile for victuals. About two o'clock the axemen began to emerge from brush, driving their ox-teams, the chained loads of fresh logs creaking and checking as they moved.

Willie Thomas, wandering in the dooryard, loaded his two-wheeled pushcart with chips and pretended that he was a grown woodcutter fetching in fuel. He envisioned himself as dressed in a red flannel shirt like that worn by Henry Tretz. Henry had bought his shirt goods at the Woods' store; the brothers had a large stock of this scarlet material. And of course Eliza Gardner stitched the garment for him, after he hinted bashfully. Red flannel thus became the uniform of royalty, emblematic of the virtues and hardihood of Henry Tretz. In happier dreams Willie'd seen Tretz returning (sometimes commanding the soldiers, sometimes not) always red-clad and exuding joy, yielding the bright assurance of his ruddy person.

The Thomas house was too far removed from the river itself, and from the Woods' store, for any of the house-dwellers to hear rapturous yells with which Inkpaduta's people raided that store, or for them to hear the crackling of the brush fire which consumed the body of the trusting William Wood; or for them to hear shots which put an end to his brother George.

. . . Bahata had not discovered any treasure of crimson swansdown, but at least he found the excitement of crimson itself. Gleefully he ripped at a stolen bolt, unfurling brilliant yardage. *Duta!* he cried. Observe! I have scarlet. *Duta!* . . . It mantled and folded and bulked around him; he was alive with color, reveling and flaming, and winging himself with red. He alone was left to circulate madly, far down the road, as Inkpaduta and the twins and the rest snaked up out of a ravine adjacent to the Thomas house. There was no one except Willie in the yard; the woodcutters were gone inside to eat; they'd promised themselves that they would unload the logs after dinner.

Thou Old One, said Rattle-Strike to Inkpaduta. On-Oldish-Man dances in the road—

It is good that he dances.

Why good that he dances?

The *Washichun* see him dance, they come out to watch—

The Wahpekute spread through ragged timber, taking careful shelter behind trees and solid shrunken drifts, much as they had done when they lay in wait at the Okoboji Narrows. They'd gathered up the Woods' stock of rifles and revolvers; few of the men had ever fired a shoots-six, most had them now, they were eager to try. They wormed into position, spreading effectively, dangerously, until all portions of the Thomas yard and the door itself, were commanded.

Down the sloping road, fleeting like a huge turkey with spread red wings, appeared the flannel-draped Bahata. Henry! was all Willie Thomas could think, in his wan little mind . . . his thin limbs did not fly as fast as he would have liked—he wanted to speed with these Good Tidings of Great Joy. It seemed that he could barely crawl but actually he ran like a marten.

Henry! he screamed, bursting in through the doorway and then out again in the same jump. Henry's coming up the road!

The surprised pack began to swarm from the dog-trot's entrance, children danced this way and that, children got in the way, a bulk of women's garments blocked the way, men came pushing behind. . . . Henry? Where is he? . . . Must be him down there, David Carver exclaimed. I see something red!

Ate? whispered Roaring-Cloud. We shoot now?

Few come out. . . . *Wanna, wanna!* Now, now!—and Inkpaduta led the firing.

The huddle of whites rioted back into the house, spraying blood as they went. Willie Thomas's father had been hit in the wrist, an artery was spurting. David Carver had buckshot in his lung, Drusilla Swanger was struck in the shoulder. The heavy door banged shut and was barred. In the yard beyond, Willie Thomas cooed like a dove on its nest. A revolver bullet had gone through his head; but he lived, he was making sounds.

His mother fought against the women who restrained her, fought her husband as he tried to embrace her with his unwounded arm. That's my boy! she screamed. That's my Willie! I got to go to him!

Mrs. Thomas, you can't go, you dasn't go.

He's shot down! That's my Willie! I got to get to him! Let me go, let me go!

Mrs. Thomas, you can't.

Outside, the pigeon cries grew weaker steadily, became lower in tone, more of a mumble, then they ceased altogether. Willie died in profound confusion. He died in the belief that Henry Tretz had done something cruel to him, and Willie couldn't understand why.

The citizens of this Des Moines City had been nourished on distorted accounts of forays in the Ohio valley, along the Wabash, across Kentucky meadows, and in ancient woodlands back East. They believed that Indians invariably fought to the death. Vaguely they mingled illusions of Tecumseh, Pontiac, King Philip, Black Hawk, and other heroic redskins. They had no way of knowing that the despised offscourings of the Wahpekute would go squeaking in flight if they thought that any resistance imperiled their bodies. It took only a scattering of stubborn shots from the Thomas house to send them kiting. Of all the riffraff pack, only two had ever acquitted themselves in stand-up battles where armed men fought armed men, and knew whom they were fighting, and cast away their common human fears in the speed and drama of conflict. (Inkpaduta had fought only in that manly way long before worms of avarice, laziness, and brutality putrefied his spirit.) Rifle balls now beat the air too close to the ears of Roaring-Cloud and Fire-Cloud for their satisfaction. Hushan displayed himself above a stump, and then fell back as a blast sent dust of rotten wood into his eyes. There was an enraged young woman in the house named Louisa Church. Her husband had traveled down to Webster City on an urgent errand, and she was quite alone in the responsibility of defending her babies. Her sister, Drusilla Swanger, was wounded when the first volley came into that unsuspecting group outside the door. Drusilla could not assist in the resistance, except through a murmured prayer. Keep praying, said Louisa Church, and she poked a gun out through the splinters of a broken windowpane. Bahata slid his big body past the trunk of an oak tree, and Mrs. Church closed her eyes and jerked the gun's trigger. Her lucky shot ripped through Bahata's clothing and licked his side. She was not confident that she had killed him when she heard him howl, but Eliza Gardner was.

We stay here and we die, Bahata told Inkpaduta, palpitating.

The Head Man had been thinking very much the same thing.

There are other lodges of whites. . . .

We go to other lodges!

The cabin of the Stewart family was much more to their taste, with nobody forted there except the Stewarts and their children. At this residence the outlaws soon considered contentedly that they had met with complete success; but a boy named Johnny eluded them, and hid in underbrush behind the house while the visitors riddled his father, and pounded his mother and little sisters into berry-stained pulps. In early evening Johnny Stewart crept to the Thomas home, where he was very nearly shot for a crawling enemy. He was taken in through the window. . . . Folks tried to give him food; he wouldn't eat it; they tried to talk to him reassuringly; he wasn't hearing. He'd only sit huddled against Miss Swanger as she bent her unwounded arm around him. He chewed the nails of his dirty fingers; he made little sounds now and then, mouse sounds.

But people at the Thomases' did not know that the attackers had withdrawn to wet themselves in easier blood—to fire a few shots through the door of the Wheeler house (there was no Mr. Wheeler present, he was far away, and Henry Tretz had been in charge of the premises); to shoot cattle, steal every horse they could find, go rampaging through the Woods' store once more in search of treasures which might have been overlooked the first time; and so at last to head for distant *Mdehoka*—the Heron Lake where they were now ensconced, women and captives and all.

They sang new songs improvised among themselves, since Bahata had recovered sufficiently from his fright to pulverize with bliss the Stewart baby, and since Makes-Fat-Bad had acquired much *napcho.*

They sang: *New deaths we make. We make death of white men, of white woman, of white children. These we make, and those Two-Legged-Ones know that we have been there.*

Ho! Ho!

We take ponies, and on these ponies we fasten bundles of red cloth.

Ho!

We have much beef, and it is good beef, and fresh. Our ponies are loaded with many things.

Ho!

We make deaths!

. . . We dasn't stay here.

. . . We dasn't.

. . . They'll be back.

. . . You mean you think they're gone?

. . . Might be hiding all around outside.

. . . Ain't heard no shots in quite a while—not since dark.

(Even then a company of soldiers was punching through snowdrifts in the direction of Springfield. But these people believed that Henry Tretz and Joseph Cheffins must have perished, or soldiers would have appeared long before this. They had no way of knowing that the two young men had lurched at last to Flandrau's quarters at the Lower Agency, half-crazed by their exposure and exertions, nearly snow-blind into the bargain. Tretz and Cheffins might have been frozen into permanent immobility: no one would have been the wiser. . . . Twould be suicide to remain in the house any longer; but if they could flee quietly, without any Indian discerning them. . . .)

. . . Spose they killed the oxen?

. . . Don't know.

. . . If there's oxen left, we can travel.

. . . I'll go see, said Morris Markham.

. . . All night they floundered out across drifted ridges. They were going too far to the east, dawn showed them their error, they tacked painfully toward the west again. Snarls of the children clawed incessantly against their ears, until finally their hearing was made torpid; no longer might they heed the children, or worry because they were hungry and shuddering with cold. Wounds had been stoppered with rags, Thomas's half-shot-off hand was dangling. The women worked fumblingly but successfully to improvise a sling for his arm, a sling which would hold up the awful weight of that hand. They made it out of one of Mrs. Thomas's petticoats, and blood came through again at all this motion and straining; then it froze.

How far to Fort Dodge, how far to Webster City?

The three men who could walk, and Thomas's elder sons, were on foot ahead of the sleigh or alongside the oxen. Unwounded women and children came slouching behind in the path broken by team and sled. Plates of sharp broken snow-crust lay at absurd angles, tilting this way and that, reaching up to knife the skirts and toiling legs. Men's pantaloons were gashed away and fringed; rags hung around their scratched raw calves like sodden poultry feathers. Mrs. Strong had no milk in her breasts for her baby . . . within shawl-wrappings the child tugged wearily against her empty flesh. Anxiety and terror bottled up the milk, kept it from exuding. Mrs. Strong's husband had gone to the Wheeler house on the previous morning, to dress wounds of two patients who were among those gathered in that smaller fortification. Strong was fascinated by the stumps he'd made; he had taken off both legs of a Mr. Henderson, and one leg of a Mr. Smith. He thought that those amputations were done neatly, beautifully.

(A man like Silvanus Waggoner could deal with frozen hands and feet, even in an isolated shack—could work with them, save them, keep them attached to a living body. But Silvanus Waggoner needed to do such a thing because he was no surgeon and did not know how to cut. Doctor Strong knew the use of knife and saw, knew all about the ligatures which must follow, knew the single flap, the double flap methods . . . he grew tense with a stiff delight in contemplating such activity. Henderson and Smith had stayed out in storms on the prairie too long. So their legs were frozen, so they must suffer. Twas their penalty and their trial when they looked up through sweat to see and hear E. B. N. Strong saying: Tut, tut, poor fellow! But I fear that your limb—or maybe both—will have to come off. . . . They were his patients, he was the doctor, they must yield to his verdict. He felt the doughtiness of a gladiator in his nerves and muscles as he worked, slicing other people's nerves and muscles.)

So, when the forlorn hungry band cheered weakly at encountering another troop of fugitives, Mrs. Strong believed that she would find her husband among them. He was not there.

The man named Skinner said: We must have lit out about the same time you folks did—maybe afore. Damn Dakotas put some bullets through our door. That was all, though they come close to killing a couple of us.

John Bradshaw's eyes swept the huddled group. Where's Henderson?

Left behind. Had to leave him—two legs cut off! Rob Smith tried to walk, hopping along on his one limb; but that was no good, so he give up and went back to the house. We're just hoping the devils don't come back.

Probably back, long before this, said Bradshaw. Reckon them poor fellers are dead right now.

Where's Doctor Strong? asked Jareb Palmer. Don't see him.

He took off.

Took off?

Skinner kept his cracked voice low; he didn't wish Mrs. Strong to hear; but her great plaintive eyes stared out from her wrappings.

He run away. Just cut and run.

Where to?

Lord knows. Wouldn't listen to reason, wouldn't stay.

Maybe he tried to come over to the Thomas place, said Bradshaw. To see after the Mrs. and the babies? And then maybe the Indians got him on the way?

Tain't likely. He knew you were all dead, for a fact! He says, They're all dead, over there to the Thomases'! I won't stay, I tell you! I won't stay! You can't keep me no longer!

. . . Nor could the crushed Eliza Gardner understand why Doctor Strong was not with the party from Wheeler's. Mrs. Strong, she whispered drearily. Mrs. . . .

Don't talk to me, Liza. Just . . . don't talk to me.

The ragged new recruits paced beside the sled. There were only a few bites of food left in any bag or pocket, and now these were brought out and offered to the wounded, but they refused to eat. Bits of meat rind and frozen cornbread and porridge were given to the children. Mrs. Strong took a morsel of mush and reduced it to pap in her mouth, and tried to feed the baby, mouth to mouth. Twas a hopeless procedure: the baby gagged, stuff dribbled down its chin.

. . . They gazed ahead and saw what seemed to be the tossing figure of a man bounding like a nervous fly in pale distances, careening elusively into shallows and over comparative heights of land, bound with determination to flee, to elude them. . . . A fly shape to begin with, it turned in time to a man. And if a human soul were prancing in retreat within that same gnat body, the soul would have typified the refugees as Dakota. Their swaddlings were coarse and blowing, their rags might have been feathers, they carried arms: that much could be seen. *Indians!* the striving runaway fragment seemed to yell . . . grotesque fleeting of his remote body spread itself into renewed chaotic endeavor. But he tricked himself: the fugitives with their sledge, however starved and snowbitten, progressed in a reasonably direct course on higher ground. And the ungoverned tiny man who went springing ahead was defeating his own purpose, dashing heedlessly down one flat valley and up the next, miring himself in an old drift, and then bursting loose into alteration of a path which could but lead him back to the direct avenue of flight. As he progressed in these widespread meanderings, distance between the scrambling man and his supposed pursuers lessened perceptibly.

Spose he thinks we're the enemy? asked Morris Markham.

Jareb Palmer observed, He's stopped now. Pulling off his boots. Reckon he thinks he can make better time that way, but he's bound to freeze his feet. . . . Look at that! There he goes again.

Morris squinted across the drifts which strung between. He had met the man only once, but felt that he could make an identification. Ain't that Doctor Strong? he asked, and his question was followed by prevailing silence.

Then Mrs. Strong spoke from the rear of the sled. No longer was she a slave . . . her tone was steeped in hatred and contempt. Doctor Weak, she said.

That night, even while people from Springfield cowered starved and doleful, there lay in bivouac not far away a throng of one hundred and twenty-five dedicated men. Most of these had the wire of youth stringing through their bodies, a few were older, the commander was downright elderly. All were imbued with a single purpose. They had pressed northward through soggy or icy hillocks for nearly a week, and were low on rations; but they were driven by pointed thought of folks in the Spirit Lake country, so they kept going. Their leader was an ex-army sutler named William Williams, sixty years of age, whose ardent courage was still high, but whose military experience was not profound. For years he had worn comfortably the title of major. He had gained this during service with the Pennsylvania militia, and it protracted as a kind of humorous courtesy; but now he felt that he must earn it in fact. For days his voice had rung sharply. He'd stride back and forth along the straggling column, pleading, directing, exhorting. By night he went from group to group, where boys clung together for warmth behind sleety wagon covers, or under the wagons themselves, or in nests of prairie weeds. He inspired the cringing rustic lad who was already feeling homesick and bereft. He massaged the strained shoulder of a bearded giant . . . advised the one who had grown worried about his family at home, and wondered whether he should turn back . . . yes, yes, Williams agreed, he must turn back, by all means! To the devoted swarm who chose to continue north, he had nothing except inspiration and magnanimity to give. . . . He'd permitted them to depart, prepared only as they might have been prepared for a quick trip to the house of a neighbor. Furies of weather and circumstance jumped destructively around Major Williams and insisted that he was wrong. In his sad heart he knew that he was very wrong.

Two trappers, haltingly briefly at that cabin beside the Des Moines River, learned from George Granger of the tragedy. They trotted south as fast as their legs would carry them, and labored into Fort Dodge with the appalling news. Like Morris Markham in the Wood brothers' store, they were not believed. A few days afterward several young men of unquestionable integrity and prominence came gasping into the village with an identical report. Couriers then rode out to spread the information to adjacent villages. A company of earnest volunteers came trudging from Webster City, twenty miles distant, the very next day. His sutler's experience had given Williams an affection for military organization. Instantly three companies came into being. A, B, and C: the two former organizations from the Fort Dodge area, the latter comprising the Webster City contingent. Each was complete with a staff of officers, commissioned and noncommissioned; there was even a surgeon, for a certain bold Doctor Bissell had joined the ranks, but he had almost nothing in the way of medical supplies to work with. For armament the boys lugged a miscellaneous assortment of flintlock muskets, shotguns, dragoon pistols. There was a Brown Bess which had drawn English blood in the Revolution, and a modern Paterson breechloader. The first night, when they camped on the road, it was discovered that they owned an average of but one blanket or comforter per man. No one knew for a certainty the amount of rations freighted along in various vehicles, horse-drawn and ox-drawn alike—least of all the commissary officer. The table of organization as set down in William Williams' correctly legible script was impressive. In fact there teetered up out of those southern counties a zealous but bungling mob.

On Sunday, March 29th, they believed that signs of the Sioux had been discovered close at hand. The commander told off a party of ten men to scout in advance of the main body. A young Minnesota resident was named to head this squad. His selection might have been termed an act of sheer genius: the man was hardy, intelligent, a veteran of the Mexican War. He was glad to be separated from the tumbling procession, and to march in advance with his own men. He was in front, that's where he'd wanted to be since an evil rumor first came down the river. He'd been on his way to the Minnesota border, hauling supplies for family and friends, when word of the massacre was muttered. He thought of his wife and his tiny boys and his sister-in-law . . . he couldn't sleep, he walked up and down all night. Folks told him, there at McKnight's Point in Humboldt County, to wait: a makeshift regiment was coming from Fort Dodge; he'd better wait and join it, he could do nothing alone. Now he was rewarded for his exercise of self-discipline: he strode in the van, and so he was the nearest of all to his wife and children, and that was what mattered.

Slowly, bending to left or right as necessity showed the way, the ten scouts went tramping. They were a mile or two ahead of shoving shoveling comrades who toiled at aiding teams and wagons through the winter's accumulation. The prairie was made of old frozen dough; and it was not stuffed with any plums or raisins, there was nothing to eat in the prairie or on it, nothing to taste. The boys' faces were wind-burned and snow-burned, their cheeks were sore, their eyes watering.

Far in a vacant glaring north the scouts saw a speck. They thought that perhaps it was a lone cottonwood stub, blackened by fire. Or it might be a sod hut from around which all drifts had been blown away; or the shape of a dark-skinned cow, abandoned in death, unshrouded by snow.

Is it moving?

Tain't moving.

Yes, it is.

Tain't.

The veteran drew out his ramrod. This is the way to tell, he said. He rested the ramrod across a boy's shoulder and bade him hold as still as possible. He put the tip of the rod upon the darkened faraway dot, held the thin metal stick rigidly, squinted along it. Bit by bit he saw the speck creep to one side.

Indians?

Could be. We'll deploy as skirmishers.

He spread his handful of troops through the only cover available: a straggle of stunted brush along the border of a frozen slough. The men looked like barbarians themselves as they crouched, wrapped in torn blankets and shawls, with bits of home-knit comforters hanging . . . burdened with pouches and powder horns, and some of these young men wore their hair long, in frontier fashion.

The speck fell apart, turned grayer, began to own a few other pale shades in its content. Now you could see the spotted tan of oxen.

Can't be Indians. Indians don't have oxen.

Indians could have stolen oxen.

We'll give 'em a good dose, soon as they come within range. . . .

The captain said, Hold your fire until I give the order!

Ought to take them by surprise, Mr.

I'm in command, young man! You'll obey orders!

Aw. . . .

(Professional soldiers might take very well to being ordered around; these boys didn't like it, they weren't soldiers. They wished to let everyone know that they were not soldiers, and didn't want to be.)

I said, Hold your fire. Do you understand?

Oh, all right.

A minute took a long time. A minute was an old bone being dragged across the plain by a crippled dog . . . assorted shapes came forward no longer, but clung together close to the sled and the oxen. One small figure moved forward: a wild figure, flapping in blankets and carrying more than one gun. He seemed to be carrying an armload.

Be damned! said the veteran. They're putting out an advance guard, kind of a picket. Never heard of savages doing that. When I give the command *Forward*, everybody get up and move ahead! Don't fire until I give the word.

How'll you give the word?

I'll issue the command *Fire*. Plain enough to suit?

Oh, all right.

They crawled up the slope, held their gaze hard against the cluster of blanketed shapes and shawl-wrapped shapes; water was in their eyes, the glare and stare of sun-on-snow impaled them.

The voice of their captain, William L. Church, racked their ears. *Hold fire!*—and then he was running ahead. His yell came back to sting their ears. *My God! There's my wife and babies. . . .*

Howdy, Morris.

Howdy, Asa.

Here's—Jody—

Howdy, Jody.

Uh . . . howdy.

We never—thought to find you with these Springfield folks, Morris.

Never thought I'd be with 'em. Ah—where'd you drop from?

Well, you see, we was there at Shippey's when we heard about it. We started out on our own—left all the oxen and stuff at Shippey's. Then we heard this expedition was a-coming, so we figured maybe we could do more good if we waited for them. So when they come by, we joined up. . . . You going to join?

I'll join.

Morris, you was—up there? Up home?

Yep.

Things was really—pretty bad?

Yep.

You didn't see—Lizzie—?

Didn't see her anywhere around. The house was all ruint. They took everything out—you know, made a mess. Plundering, I'd guess you'd call it.

Ah . . . Morris, you didn't find . . . Dora?

Didn't see her around.

Nor . . . her body?

Nope.

What about . . . Alvin?

He was there. At the house.

Whereabouts?

Out behind. He, and that feller Ryan.

Was they scalped?

No, wasn't nobody scalped. Can't understand why, but they wasn't. Jody, I want to say one thing: I didn't go in at the Howes'. There was—just a big pile in there. I looked at it, and then backed out. Could be they was all there, the rest of them. I mean—Lizzie and Liddy and both the little ones. I don't know. Or could be they was taken prisoner.

That's what I don't like to think about. . . .

(Yea, you know it isn't good to think about it, and you wish you didn't have to think about it; but you think about it all the time, because that's all there is to think about. Sometimes you do sleep, out of sheer trembling exhaustion; but every now and then you make a hoarse sound, and wake yourself up, and then you lie there. And you do eat—oh yes, indeed! You know you're eating because there was food upon that plate, and you had a fork, and you sat there and—Pretty soon you looked down at the plate, and saw that the food was gone. So you must have eaten it, but you couldn't recall having eaten it—and didn't remember any flavor, didn't remember biting and chewing. Nobody could have stolen the food off your plate, because there wasn't anybody else around. You wouldn't let there be anybody else around. You didn't even want to eat with Asa and Morris. You just wanted to be by yourself. There was always a log or a wagon-tail or a stump or some little patchy place off by itself, where you could sit and turn your back on the others and not look at them, because you didn't want to look at them. You had to move among them, you had to be with them; but you didn't want to look at them. Somehow, however, you were aware that they looked at you; and they whispered together, drew close, whispered; then they looked again. You knew what they were saying. . . . That's that fellow Thatcher. He comes from the Spirit Lake country, up there at Okoboji. . . . They say the Indians kilt all his family? . . . That's what they say. . . . Pshaw, is that so? . . . That's what they say. . . . Or maybe carried off his wife? . . . Pshaw, is that true? . . . Which one is he, again? . . . Big thick-set young fellow. Great big arms on him. . . . Kind of freckled? . . . The one that sets over there all by himself. He doesn't want to set and eat with the rest. Just keeps to himself. . . . Pshaw.)

The name of W. L. Church was removed from the rolls, and he took charge of his wife and tiny boys. There were other men whose health or nerves were failing; they, too, were sent back to the south along with the refugees. The main command followed a track broken by the Springfield sled and oxen, by scratched feet and legs of the fugitives. There were bloodstains along the way. Men thought of that Valley Forge they'd read about in their school books. . . . They went up to Granger's Point, and there they heard for a fact that soldiers were already in the Springfield area, but the Sioux had fled to the west. There was nothing more which the expedition might do now, except to inter the Okoboji dead.

Major Williams said that he was calling for volunteers.

Something's out there.

What is it?

Don't know. Something. . . .

Whereabouts?

West. Looky there . . . can't you see?

Oh, yes. Think it's a bird?

Awful cold weather for birds!

Think it's an animal? Deer, maybe? Maybe a catamount?

No, it's something too big for a deer or a catamount, too big for a single person. Still, it kind of seems to have wings. . . .

Great big eagle, maybe?

Well, they do have eagles in this country; you see them when the weather is warmer; but I don't think that's an eagle right now. Maybe it's just a bunch of people with pickaxes, a-digging, cutting up the clods.

What for?

They've got to make a place to bury folks, and the ground is hard.

Why they going to bury them?

Because the folks are dead.

Did they expect to die?

No more than most men and women expect to die. Reckon we'll all die sometime. . . .

But why did these folks die?

Cause they had a notion, and they was a-following it. The notion took them way over yonder. So now other men are digging their graves.

And then the men'll all go home?

They'll try to, but they'll have a hard time doing it.

What's to stop them from going home?

Oh . . . weather.

Heck, the winter's over. It's April, it's spring now.

That's what *you* think! Going to have some of the worst tempests of the year, right in the next week: fierce winds, lots more snow. And cold. Oh, very very cold!

Well, I'm sorry to hear about that.

Reckon they'll be sorry when it happens.

You mean—twill kill 'em?

Some of them. Did you ever try to sleep out in the open when twas twenty below, and your clothes was wet, and you had nothing to cover you but a single blanket, and nothing to keep you warm cept the man laying next to you?

They ought to have figured that out when they was coming. Ought to have had better sense!

Sure they should, Mr. But Americans don't always have better sense.

Why not?

Count of their hearts.

What's the matter with their hearts? Sickly?

Nope. Their hearts ain't very wise sometimes. Just—big.

How big?

Big enough to carry a lot of things in them.

Ah, I kind of see now. Think Americans will always act that way?

Day they don't, there won't be no more America.

If that's how it is, and they're burying the dead now, don't you think we ought to utter some kind of prayer?

You hold the book. Somehow I can't see to read.

Thou knowest, Lord, the secrets of our hearts. . . .

XLIII

Sometimes One-Staggering had his wits about him, more often he did not. Since his youth he had always been heavy of body, wearing the wide face which commonly accompanies such a build. Now his disfigured dark countenance had gone limp and loose, as if the bones were removed from within. He received almost no nourishment; generally he refused to accept food if indeed anyone thought to offer it. Rarely his tent-mates, Makes-Fat-Bad and His-Curly-Sacred, having gorged themselves on tidbits of beef, raw or cooked, were moved to put some chunks before him; but an inordinately devilish spirit occupied the jaws of the wounded man, and would not let him move those jaws without great pain. Voices chattered constantly within his swollen left ear, distended in its dry blood; voices talked on up into the ringing skull.

He thought that one voice was that of his father-in-law.

. . . Are you not glad that I bite off your nose? You should not have fought me, after drinking spirit water! *Toko!* Behold! I did bite off your nose; but that was after you lay in hiding, and leaped out, and struck me down with a club. That was after also you struck down my daughter who was your wife, and before you fled from the village where all of us lived. Bitten-Off-Nose, Bitten-Off-Nose, are you not glad that I do this thing to you?

Thin red fluid no longer dribbled from the cavity in the middle of his face; but on that very day when the outcasts left Heron Lake, One-Staggering became subject to convulsive gasps and retchings. Wadded strings of evil-smelling spirits issued both from the nose-hole and from his mouth. He lay back upon robes and could not move when the women took down the lodge, he could not climb upon the sled. Others were compelled to lift him.

Corn-Sucker thought it sad that anyone should die in neglect, starved and untended. At night when they encamped, she worked long after the others were fed, making a soup of beef. She carried the hot stew to One-Staggering; timidly she offered it, and even put the spoon in his hand. He looked up at her through firelight with hopeless clouded gaze. And he did try to eat of the soup, and two or three times he swallowed some broth down; but it was too hot, it burnt him, he wailed. Then when it had cooled he did wish to put a piece of tender meat between his teeth, and so he tried to do this thing; but then he wailed once more, and the meat fell from his jaw; and again, when he tried to drink of the soup, it ran out of the sides of his wide mouth. He pushed the bowl from him, upsetting it when he did so. . . . On the next morning, the little woman attempted repeatedly to feed him; twas useless. He could not or would not eat, and so he closed his dull eyes, and lay back once more. Again people lifted him upon the loaded sledge when it was ready.

The wanderers had gone not much farther on their march when a lightning of alarm quivered through the lodges. Men snatched up their guns and concealed themselves hastily amid nearby willows. The women were made to smother the fires immediately. Captives were hustled off into another barren grove of small trees down the stream, they were made to lie flat. The Wahpekute women worked in frenzy to take down the lodges and pour water on fire-coals; and the ailing One-Staggering and a sick child were taken into shelter with the captives. Kechonmani was posted as sentinel. Every now and then he would point to the east, and then point to his gun, and then indicate the white women individually, demonstrating the manner in which he would kill them when it became necessary. But his wife, Female-Cousin-Rabbit, was there also, with her knife. She showed how she'd put this knife into the bodies of white girls. . . . Rattle-Strike crept to a lone cottonwood standing at a distance, and made his way up into lower branches. After a long while he came down; and when he had returned to tell his father-in-law what he'd seen, those nearest Inkpaduta heard the news. There was much laughter. They have turned back!—men said. *Nakash!* They turn back, they are women!

But even if unidentified pursuers were indeed women it was not good to remain longer in this place. The outlaws traveled at once, traveled long, nor did they stop for night. They went ahead in darkness; and all were exhausted when finally they did halt at a great distance.

It was on the next night that One-Staggering went to walk the Way of the Souls.

Tawachehawakan came to the lodge of Inkpaduta when the night was black and said: That one dies.

A man dies?

Kachanachekahota dies. He makes strange sounds, then blood and water run from his mouth. He sleeps. His flesh is cold, cold for long, his limbs are stiffening. He is dead.

It is good that he dies, said Inkpaduta.

He is Dakota. Why is it good that Dakota dies, and dies because he was struck by white man?

So, struck by white man, he is no good to us. But we take great care! Half-Face, awaken my sons.

. . . They were on their way to the bachelors' lodge when a strange sound hit the dark air. It was the voice of Makes-Fat-Bad, for he thought that ritual demanded a Song for the Dead; and this departure of a soul, occurring only a fathom or two away from him, gave reminder of a time when his brother succumbed to wounds received in war, in another lodge far to the west.

My brother, is your face covered? Your face shall be covered. My brother, you did not wish to walk the Way of the Souls, but now you travel there. My brother—

The burly doubled-up shape of Inkpaduta burst like a bear through the lodge door. He threatened Makes-Fat-Bad with the Titonwan's own gun.

But, Thou Old One, he dies! A lament must be heard.

Thou wouldst tell white women that this man dies? And wounded by a white man, and so he dies?

The captive women do not know what I speak.

They know if you sing for dead man. Sing no more! No one sings!

The body of One-Staggering was bound in the oldest muddiest most-torn blankets which the lodge afforded, though many blankets and robes in that lodge were in bad condition. The twins and the two surviving inmates of the bachelors' tipi took turns in carrying the corpse far down the ice of a narrow meandering stream where they had squatted for the night. Pale snow and paleness of the midnight sky lighted their way.

Inkpaduta mused privately, considering that a scaffold should be erected. But no axe was at hand; it would be difficult to cut the necessary poles by night, and with knives. Therefore, when they came to a tree of sufficient size, the twins ascended the split twisted trunk, and the body of One-Staggering was passed up to them. They bound it in the branches, out of reach of wolves. All believed that a ghost of this man might be privileged to come back to annoy and terrify them, if they allowed his body to become the prey of animals. . . . Once the disposition had been made, they returned to camp, and at first the men who had wives refused to discuss the matter with them. But later they did tell.

Most of the band considered in final reckoning that it was well for the noseless man to perish: he had been a pest, groaning and drooling about the premises. No longer would they have to lift him on top of bundles in a sleigh! The white captives might wonder what had happened to the injured man; but their mere wondering would harm no one. All in the band were relieved to think that no other of their number had been beaten down in the recent raids. Bahata especially was glad (for that charge of lead fired by Mrs. Church from the

Thomas house had skinned his side). He had stood too close to death, he did not desire to be tied up in a willow on a desolate watercourse.

Inkpaduta's infinitesimal conscience was not entirely clear in the matter. Appropriate recollections came stalking from the past to exasperate him. He thought of the time-honored keening which he had sworn must not ensue, thought of the food which would not be put out, the medicine bag unhonored. He was plagued by a notion that one or another of One-Staggering's souls might come a-vexing. . . . He tried to sleep, could not sleep, tried to smoke: a stray spark flew up and burnt his eyeball. He could not help feeling that One-Staggering had something to do with that occurrence. Before morning Inkpaduta brayed that camp must be struck immediately. He cuffed Corn-Sucker along to the business of giving orders to the rest.

Bleak sunrise found them once more on the westward track. Many more days found them on that same westward track . . . and for a while struggling through copious snows which came whipping out of season, and through a last merciless cold . . . and on into a reluctant spring ruling the drab land wherein they moved.

. . . Stolen sleds long since were left behind. Now ponies were loaded with heavy packs; the women were loaded as well—not merely the captives, but all women. Quantities of goods stolen from the Springfield settlement were dumped out amid pasty snow. The captives staggered through a meaningless blur of daylight hours. Then there'd be camp once more, with dogs snarling through dimness . . . yap of children . . . scraps of food tossed to the whites. The protracted raping of earlier episodes was repeated seldom; the men were tired too, and already weary of the daily-less-attractive bodies of these girls. Each woman descended to the mode and habit of a beast; she was but a starved ox or donkey, she carried things upon her back. She bent her head, looked at the ground, accepted blows and shoving without lifting her voice to complain. She had been shunted from the Earth she knew, she walked upon the surface of a planet where no other life was stirring. The bruised face of Peggy Ann Marble was blued and bloated. Abbie's features seemed to have been hacked out by a rough saw. The agony of Lizzie Thatcher puffed anew: her leg was swollen to the waist. Lydia Noble tried to keep as close to her beloved Elizabeth as she might; but often she was jerked away and told to go ahead: she could move more rapidly than Lizzie, even in her native lameness. Wamdenichawin, or Orphan-Woman, the wife of Roaring-Cloud, removed a heavy cradle-board from her own shoulders and added this *iyokapa* to the mighty burden which already Abbie Gardner was carrying. Abbie could not see the infant as it hung against her; but she'd seen it other times, and knew that it was abominable; and she recognized the stench of it. Twas swaddled in a mass of feathers taken from some bed in Springfield, and these polluted wads of makeshift diapers had not been changed. Leaving out the matter of extra weight (as if one might) the cradle-board became an object intolerable. Abbie by degrees managed to work one hand loose from a supporting strap at which she strained; and, reaching rearward, slyly, with tortured wrist and elbow pushed to the limit of their bending, she found that her fingernails could reach the baby's face. Thus she'd pinch or scratch the child, or in some way assault it, every time she saw that the eyes of others were turned away and no one might observe her. There'd be that second's gap before the yowl burst forth—time enough for her to twist her hand away and seize upon the innocent strap once more. Time and again the mother came scurrying to upbraid the child, to shake it, try to stop its screams . . . succeeding, she would march again. . . . Once more, the proper opportunity, and Abbie could scratch. This dread activity extended for half a day, until Wamdenichawin, unable to tolerate the screeching, decided that her baby did not like the white girl and did not wish to be carried by her. Perhaps it was the white odor which sent the baby into frets? All knew that *Washichun* smelt different! Then it would follow that the child should not be carried by a white! Orphan-Woman made the best of it, swung the cradle-board from her own shoulders, stamped ahead.

. . . Liddy, where you spose they're taking us?

. . . Some far land.

. . . They ain't done It to us for a while. Do you spose that could mean that we shan't have to suffer It again?

. . . I prayed.

. . . I've prayed a thousand times. God don't hear our prayers.

. . . Reckon maybe He hears them. For we were taught that God always hears. Maybe God's just a-waiting, cause He's got His reasons.

. . . What reasons could He have?

. . . Tain't for us to ask.

. . . But I keep asking.

. . . Now, honey, try to get some sleep. Them womenfolks will kick us out of this here robe, first moment it gets light.

. . . Oh, Lid, my whole leg's like it was on fire.

. . . Now try to . . . sleep.

They went down toward a river; twas called the Big Sioux by the comparatively few whites who knew it, and the Indians called it Chankasnasnata; but a designation would have meant nothing to Elizabeth Thatcher, no more than the proper designation of a hundred other streams of varying sizes which she had crossed. She held to the fierce notion that Baby Dory might be waiting somewhere in brown foamy tangles ahead. She thought, Shouldn't tell no one about this! For the notion of Dory was absurd—she knew that the infant was long since dead, had seen her swung by one leg with a dark hand closed crushingly upon frail twisted foot and lower limb, she'd heard the sound as that small head popped open on the oak. But . . . Baby Dory? Might she not be peeking up and out of water and brushwood in this valley which loomed closer with each jarring shivering step? Elizabeth looked to see the child, and could not see her, could not see her.

A thousand trees were gathered here. The trees had become tired of upright existence and so lay down to encamp tangled in the wet. Force of melting snow shot heavily against them. Two bare trees hung sidewise with their roots still anchored, another dozen of assorted sizes had swept with the flood to scrape and bob against the rooted fallen trunks; and thick the sodden boughs, and thick the carpet of weeds and leaves and grassy rubbish which made a scum across upstream areas. Tis like a bridge, Liz Thatcher thought, and we can walk across. They'll make us do it. There was another such barricade far down the river, and tiny figures moved upon it—the stronger faster people who'd gone stronger faster, and so they had preferred that bridge to this one, and were crawling there; and at shore some of the women were unloading ponies, readying the ponies for the swim across.

Jo. Jo— Woo-man—

Voice of the tall one known as Tawachehawakan— The white women spoke of him as Tawa-all-them-other-words. . . . He was more to be feared, they reckoned, than almost any other Indian—except Roaring-Cloud, who used them so badly— And Inkpaduta himself, with all his gasping coarse attempts, his spitting in your face because he couldn't do the thing he'd set himself to do.

Tall and youthful Wahpekute—this one, this Tawa thing—had been the first to long abuse poor Abbie; and probably he'd be the last to do it, too, when they were all worn down and dying. Die they must. Oh, die they surely would.

Jo!

Yes, said Elizabeth Thatcher, and began her stumbling dragging pilgrimage out toward the tangled bridge of trees. Her fat and blackened limb— She'd swing it from the hip, lift the toothache weight of it, push out the mauled sore wad of foot, and press it down, and lift her weight upon the bruised and puffy thing, and put the other foot, the better foot, ahead. She moved with body nearly doubled, eyes turned squarely down; the pack of lead and tipi cover which she carried kept her body bent that way. But it was bad . . . the gown all sticking once again . . . thin-stained and triple-stained, the faded ragged cloth across her breast, that left breast which had swollen up and caked and darkened; it had finally burst; there was the sticky crooked crack where flesh was split, and other rawer pinker flesh was oozing from the crack; so it exuded, stuck its juice against the cloth which pressed; and so it dried, and then again it tore and hurt, a-pulling loose; and there were all those paints of pink and yellow on the rag with which she'd tried to bind her breast.

Dory, Dory. Lips to close around, the greedy mouth to tug, the tiny fists to knot and squeeze, the while a greedy throat is swallowing; the while a greedy baby throat is making feeding sounds. The greedy baby nose is breathing fast.

Now, was that Dory out ahead?

A small thing flapping, beckoning—?

A brownish thing.

But why was Baby Dory brown?

. . . A bird, a bird! the Wahpekute voices cried, and someone shot. The bird escaped, it lifted, flapped, and flew.

Not Dory. No.

. . . A bird! *Zitka, zitka!*

Well, Dory somewhere out in all those barks and trunks and trees and drifted stuff a-tangling; and folks could travel over, and hear the yellow waters piercing flat and fast beneath, and boiling out the lower side; for other figures were floundering on that downstream barricade, and ponies were a-swimming. Sky was damp and gray with spring, but sometime there would come the summer, and a bee again . . . fluff-headed dandelion on the grass, and Dory rolling, catching at it . . . sometimes there would shine a buttercup. And smell of new green peas a-boiling. Sometime Jody saying: Got our supper ready, Liz? I'm fair to starve.

Put one distended mass of skin and stinking toes within the loose-bound moccasin (split twice upon the hem because the foot was twice the size of any other living foot . . . had lost its shape, twas just a lump)— Once Ma said, Liz, your tooth is *ul-sur-ate-ed.* Now I got to prick it for you, and we'll get this needle red and hot just so no horrid humors can come in.

Put bad foot out. . . .

No, press it on that solid root. And there's a place to step beyond, and put the other foot. . . .

That Old One says this woman is no good to us!

That Old One knows. *E!* So know I. She cannot walk.

She is no good to walk, she is no good to lie upon!

Eyakesh! There is now bad smell about her.

Her *shan* is nothing. Also does she weep.

We go too slowly.

Eyakesh! We have more white women still. We have three other women.

Does That Old One say we kill? . . .

And hear a wide brown angled twisting river (twas a dozen rivers big and little, coursing down or eddied back, or curdled in the bayous and nameless overflows beyond, among the drifted fallen forest)— Hear the river saying: Lave and purl . . . we're water sounds and water witches. . . . What's in the pot for supper, Liz? Oh, new green peas!

She felt a hand upon the great slave's weight she'd borne, she felt the pack a-lifting, felt her hurt back straightening. And she looked up in wonder to behold the very tall young Tawa-man. He'd lifted off her pack, was loosening the raw and greasy bands which cut her flesh and mauled the might of all the world against her.

She saw Abbie Gardner creeping close at hand, a vague face with the burns of wind upon the cheeks and nose, the peeling patches showing; both the oily braids were glowing in their dirty yellowness. And, ah, that small face drawn and pointed— Why, tis like a hickory nut! thought Lizzie Thatcher. That poor child! Her little face is like a hickory nut.

Abbie. Say to Mr. Thatcher—

What? Why, he ain't here.

Liz hoped to say: No, but you're very young. Younger'n me; I'm nineteen. Could be you'd live it out. Could be you'd live for *long*. Because— You see— We're at this river. And he took my pack. And tweren't just kindness. Never has a one of them seen fit to do a thing like that afore.

She hoped to say these things. But she could only mumble: Tell 'im that I—wanted—wished to see.

Oh, Mrs. Thatcher, tell him what?

On out the strong big hands are forcing. Past that pointed tree-bough spread and angling with the current hard against it, and lifting all that hundred tons of fatness which I call my bad foot. And trying now to shove the better foot ahead. . . .

And oh, I've slipped, I'm falling far. . . !

But tweren't a limb I fell across. . . !

Why, what a *mean*. . . !

He *tripped* me. . . !

So he had. Indeed the young man (former River-Boy and now His-Curly-Sacred-Penis) had thrust his sturdy foot and long hard leg behind her aching swollen one, and twisted his entire body; so he sent her far. Out and whirling . . . ho, ho . . . laugh to see the sky beneath, and water up above, and all those barks and twigs and trunks of trees extended.

What a splash! . . . the only thing that she could think. *Oh, what a splash I made.* And dark down here. And kind of cold, but I can't breathe, although it's better for my bad limb, probably, to have it in the water, like a poultice kind of . . . got to see my Jody man. That's what I call him, times, in fun. My Jody man. I reckon he is up above.

And with that desperate hauling of her arms she broke from out the surface, fresh and startled. Current had her, whirling her, and— Who was that a-screaming? Abbie Gardner, child, she thought most sternly. Don't you make a noise like that!

And here's the current twitching me this way and that, but I know how to swim—oh yes, I do—for all of us, we used to go in that big hole on Wild Cat Creek, back home, and Sis would tell me: Now, you kick your feet like anything, and just keep clawing with both hands, and you'll stay up.

Dog-fashion, that was what my sister called it. She was bigger, and her name was— Name was— Name—

Why, here's the bank, and all these roots a-hanging down, and I'll grab onto them because I've got to see my—husband—once again—

The stick came hard against her head. It was a splintered limb, torn off from some tall tree, a long thin limb, and there were faces of the Indians above.

She looked up wildly through the spray and saw those clubs come striking, seeking.

See this woman! To the shore she comes. . . .

Did she show speed like this when walking?

They were laughing.

Never!

Tohinni? When did she go fast, as goes she now?

When? *Tohinni?*

They were laughing.

Oh, strike her hand! Reach down thy stick, and break her hand from off that root.

She clings hard, she is strong as any man!

Echahe! In water she is strong!

This was sport, and they were laughing as they played their game.

Club smiting on her hand and club upon the other hand, and long pole gouging at her throat and turning back her head. Oh, mean, she thought, how very mean some folks can be! Then bobbing, ducking, feeling strong limp fingers reaching up to pull her into darkened coolness—

But I don't like it down in here. The water gets up in my nose and I can't breathe, and where was it like this before? . . . Why, Wild Cat Creek again! Twas when the Reverent Mr. Moore he put me down, he held a kerchief folded right across my eyes, and I was glad but shuddering as well, and fearful of the water. All I'd think was: Soon I'll be a full-fledged Campbellite, just like my folks. A true Disciple, that I'll be! And then, says Reverent Moore, do you accept? Do you accept? Do you *accept?* The bell-warm voice a-ringing closer. Yes, I says, I do, I do! Then I Baptize you in the name of the Father, and the Son, and of the Holy Spirit . . . down and deep and black, and water coming up my nose.

Again she burst the surface. Once more her eyes were reaching out and saying, Don't you hit, oh please don't throw them clubs at me again! And so she drifted on and on, and sometimes it was dark, and sometimes it was brighter. Once again she took the air and breathed it in, but soon was breathing water in as well. She did not hear the shot (upon that other bridge of tumbled trees was Peggy Ann; she thought the Indian was shooting at an otter, but he turned and laughed and said, White woman), did not hear the gun's explosion, did not feel the lead go in, she thought someone had thrown another but a larger club. Then gracefully she sank, and lower comfortable and warmer, saw the baby laughing rolling beckoning. Why, you were here, you funny little midge, and all the time! And what did you, you naughty Dory, think you was a-doing? Playing Hide-and-Seek? Yes, playing Hide-and-Seek! Oh, Jody, hain't that child the *limit?* Doll-sized hands a-gripping at her, jolly gurgle coming forth.

XLIV

During that spring Morris Markham roved uncertainly through border communities. He camped in woods along the Des Moines River, the Boone, along White Fox Creek and Lizard Creek. Fish were the mainstay of his diet. He purchased or traded for a little cornmeal, now and then, at some cabin. Sometimes he thought of his sorry oxen– Perhaps they were still alive and languishing in their distant grove? He considered his collection of steel traps, borne away by the Indians, probably to be tossed out later on. Perhaps some of the traps might have been pried or broken apart, in order to form utensils or even ornaments. He could not imagine any wandering Indians as possessed of enough purpose and discipline to operate a trap line. Furthermore the cold weather was fled.

After wintering in Franklin County, and after buying his oxen and equipment in 1856, Morris still had more than two hundred dollars left as a personal fortune. Ordinarily he kept a few dollars by him, in his wallet; might come in handy when, on some unexpected occasion, he visited a settlement. The rest of the money, all in coin, he'd buried in a lonely place—not on the Noble or Thatcher claims. He'd thought originally, Who can tell? I might be gone on a hunting trip. Long gone—maybe off in Minnesota—and then somebody would offer Alvin and Jody a good price for their land, and they'd get out, and then what about the money? Well, twas far in the woods, reposing in a broken pot of aboriginal manufacture which he'd discovered when he was digging up a fox's den. Morris wondered when he'd ever go back for his money. Didn't seem to be much purpose in going. He couldn't lug a lot of heavy coins around with him wherever he went, and he was deeply distrustful of paper currency. Lots of counterfeit and wildcat scrip along the edge of this new country. . . .

He halted at both Fort Dodge and Webster City, asking after members of the relief expedition whom he'd known, wondering how they fared and how they'd got back. Two men, he learned, never returned: Johnson and Burkholder. They were long lost up there on the prairie somewhere (eleven years would go by; and then a man'd be stringing fence around his acres, and he'd find scattered bones, and buckles, and the crusted remains of a powder flask, and guns; and all the farmers, with excited wives and children, would gather in hot summer sunshine to speculate about this discovery; and then someone would remember to take off his hat). Burkholder was from Company A . . . Morris didn't know him; he'd gone with Company C, himself. But he remembered Johnny Johnson, captain of Company C: big fellow from Pennsylvania, quiet and handsome; everybody seemed to trust him. The good die young, Morris quoted. But that wasn't quite true: Old Joel Howe was old, and Jo Harshman even older, and they had died, and they were good. Perhaps crushed doll-babies were the best of all, because they were the youngest? . . . The sprawling tragedy of Okoboji made no better sense to Morris now than it had made in the first place. At Webster City he saw Tom Bonebright and John Maxwell: they'd both been with Company C; Maxwell was designated as first lieutenant. Several other fellows, Markham was told, had died of pneumonia or some similar ailment shortly after they returned from Dickinson County. A protraction of the waste and senselessness . . . those people hadn't done any good; they'd wanted to help, sought to do good, some had died in the seeking. They were willing, they were brave, they owned the holiest of intentions; but they were badly led. Great wonder that more of them hadn't died as it was! Any men, young or old, should have known better than to go out on the open prairie at that time of year, dressed as they were dressed, equipped as they were equipped, provisioned as they were provisioned—or rather, *un*provisioned.

Leastways, they did manage to bury the dead.

Leastways, many as they could find. . . .

Vividly came the remembrance of Jody Thatcher, sitting off by himself with his face turned away, while the rest were warming at a fire, and cooking and eating. That was one picture Morris would never be able to strike out of his mind. He'd eradicated some other pictures already: refused to lift them, unshroud them. . . . Like chalk on the school slate I use to have, back in Ohio. Rubbed out. Funny: those are the words Jo Harshman always used for folks who were slaughtered by Indians. Rubbed out, he'd say. . . . Sounded odd. A death wielded by Indians was in no way a sponging: twas more of a smash than that.

Folks were friendly in these parts, and especially inclined to hospitality when they learned that Morris was from the lakes. Shortly after the massacre there'd been a widespread scare down here. Couple of men were out a-scouting, looking for Indian signs. Everybody was still mighty nervous, all through northwestern and central Iowa; and some other scouts saw those horsemen at a distance, and mistook them for Sioux. That was how it started, it rolled like a snowball. People kept rushing from their homes and boiling south, alarming neighbors as they went—so that they, the neighbors, might hitch up and flee.

Some hustled all the way to Boonesboro, some even to Des Moines. Some, folks guessed, were still running, and might never return, even though they'd left clothes a-hanging on their pegs and supper on their tables. Morris supposed that you couldn't blame the settlers very much, or even laugh at them; not when you realized they'd heard vivid descriptions of what occurred up in the Spirit Lake country. But plenty of people hadn't run away, or else hadn't run far, and were now returned. Many begged Morris Markham to spend a day or two with them. Sometimes he stayed, because he was lonely and heartsick, and appreciated the mere business of sitting down to eat hominy again, or the matter of playing with children. He always worked for his share of the keep: chopped wood, fed stock, even did a little ploughing. But a night or two of cabin life sufficed; then he was irked, and gone soon.

He left warming weather and started north once more into a cooler delayed spring. Yea, he promised to return in the summer; he'd hoe corn, cut hay, fell trees, do anything they wanted done. Still he was numbed by his bereavement, he made pathetic substitutions. There'd always been a home where he might be saluted as an intimate, from the first time when he met the Howes. Now he had no place to squat, except beside his own withdrawn riverside blaze.

He pitied himself, he pitied the dead more.

Morris lay down to rest in a midday when springtime light was thin but enviably yellow . . . it held a pacifying warmth when sun lay upon your hand. He had been hungry, had eaten heavily, now he wanted to doze. His bed was of violets in full bloom. Their twisted purple faces kissed his own face where he was pillowed. Heart-shaped leaves and springy long stems made an enviable cushion under his body and around it. Many birds were trilling as he dozed, and all spoke with the voice of Her who'd promised immortality.

. . . Can't be immortal now.

. . . Can't believe it no longer.

. . . All dead. Got kilt by the Indians.

Ink of destitution flowed out of his soul and into his throat, and left him breathless but still managing to weep.

Jenny Lind, he sobbed unspeakingly. You promised much, but still you didn't know, you didn't know. . . . Bird notes were rolling in the willow trees.

In middle May the wanderer had drifted up to the Minnesota River; after some hesitation he stopped at the Lower Agency and spoke to Agent Flandrau. With surprise Morris found himself receiving a cordial invitation to supper, and to pass the night.

Didn't think the name Markham would be known to you, Mr. I been as far as this river only once. Then I was at Ridgely.

Have you forgotten an affidavit to which you put your name, Mr.

Markham? Cheffins and young Tretz had it with them when they arrived here.

I had forgot about that.

Also you subscribed to the petition for relief, carried by those same messengers. I don't have it in my files now: twas directed to the commanding officer at the Fort, and I turned it over to him, naturally. But your own deposition is still in my possession. Allow me to search it out—

I don't really need—

Have it for you in a jiffy!

Within a few minutes Flandrau produced the document. Twas written on thin blue-lined paper, and dated erroneously *March 9th, 1857*. Charles Flandrau pointed this fact out to Morris. . . . Obviously Mr. Thomas was acting in haste, somewhat alarmed and confused! That same date is incorporated in the body of the text. But the request for troops is dated March fourteenth, and I assume that your deposition should have borne the same date.

Guess it must have been the fourteenth at least, when Granger and I finally got to Springfield. . . . *This is to certify that I, Morris Markham, on the 9th day of March, 1857, went to Spirit Lake and found there a quantity of Indians . . . I think the most of the inhabitants put to death. . . .*

Morris passed the paper back to Flandrau. I was just looking at what Mr. Thomas wrote, sir. *Sworn to and subscribed before me, J. B. Thomas, J.P.* Could have been one of the last things he ever set down on paper.

He wasn't killed?

Nope. Shot through the wrist, when the Indians attacked his house later on. When we got down into Ioway, and run up against them volunteers, Mr. Thomas's hand was just a-dangling by the cords. Course it had to be cut off.

Right hand?

Left. But I noticed that he wrote left-handedly.

Charles Flandrau was more disturbed by Morris's unexpected visit than he dared demonstrate. The hunter's very appearance at the Agency was mute affirmation of that tragedy which had taken place nearby. Flandrau told himself that he had been powerless to prevent its occurrence; but he felt discomfort in recognizing that, if he had given money to Inkpaduta in November when the outlaw came to Redwood, doubtless those Spirit Lake people would be living still. *Doubtless?*—he thought, during supper. Tis a word used carelessly, and I have used it so in my mind. *Beyond any doubt:* that's what it means. And Inkpaduta is poison mean, an admitted killer, wholly unpredictable. Might not Inkpaduta have chosen to bathe in blood, whatever his fortune in hand, however long his pocket? He might indeed! Pray be more sparing in your employment of the word *Doubtless,* sir.

Morris found satisfaction in hens' eggs which were fried along with meat for supper. The first civilized fare he'd eaten, he informed his host shyly, since leaving the Iowa towns.

You spend most of your time in the wilderness, then?

That's right.

Yet you were a member of the colony at Spirit Lake?

Okoboji. I lived with the Nobles and Thatchers, when I was to home. Had a lean-to, end of the house.

Relatives of yours?

Friends and neighbors, in Indiana.

Ah. Were all of them slain?

Not Jody Thatcher; he was with his oxen down at Shippey's. He went back to the lakes with the volunteers, when they—buried folks. They didn't find neither of the young women. Reckon they were carried off.

We've heard persistent rumors here, Mr. Markham—filtering, as it were, through local Christianized families. Some say that Inkpaduta took four women captives, some say three.

Had a thought to try to follow them, myself. Out across the Big Sioux, or wherever they've gone to. But then I knew twas foolish. Couldn't do nothing by myself.

No, no, twould be a serious mistake! You might only succeed in bringing death to the captives, if indeed they still survive! Colonel Alexander and I have been working on a plan for a rescuing party to be sent in that direction, but are confronted by the identical problem: tis the habit of hostile Dakota to kill captives, rather than give them up. There must be some wiser plan, such as paying a liberal ransom. But how to find Inkpaduta? He's wily, fugitive in his habits. The other Wahpekute and neighboring tribes avoid contact with him whenever possible. . . .

Charley Flandrau produced whiskey, following the meal; Morris accepted a glass, but only as a courtesy; he touched the liquor to his lips, set it down. Flandrau drank enough to loosen his tongue but not enough to dull his wits (he wielded stern discipline against himself in this regard). He said that, of the murdered citizens, he'd known only Doctor Harriott personally. He called to mind their one meeting in St. Paul; he displayed the very bottle into which Harriott had poured prescribed hydrochloric acid. Twas all gone, long since . . . yes, yes, he was keeping the flask as a memento of a splendid young man.

If he'd lived, Mr. Markham, he might have gone far in his profession. Very far indeed!

Might. I've kind of quit thinking about the dead ones. Doesn't do any good. . . . Morris added, terminating a long silence: I think more about the young ladies who was carried off. The soldiers followed them, or so I've been told. And then the soldiers—just turned back.

Flandrau arose suddenly and struck his hands together. Mr. Markham, I'm going to show you something. Perhaps it's not wholly ethical in me to do so, but— You've been associated intimately with those unhappy settlers, associated intimately with the entire series of events. You've as much right to read what I shall set before you, as anyone. It may explain the situation more completely.

He took a spare candle and went away to rummage; he came back in a few minutes, drew the lamp closer to Markham, put a roll of foolscap into his hand. Tis a copy of a report written by Captain Barnard E. Bee, commanding Company D, and addressed to First Lieutenant H. E. Maynadier, Adjutant of the Tenth Infantry. Read away, sir. Do let me know when you've concluded. I'll go to my desk, I've a few accounts to cast up before retiring.

Sir. On the morning of the 19th of March last I received from the Head Quarters of this Post an order to proceed with the effective force of my Company to Spirit Lake on the Southern border of Minnesota, where it was reported certain houses had been plundered, and citizens killed, by a Band or Bands of Sioux Indians. The Call for assistance came from Des Moines City on the Des Moines river some fifteen Miles North of Spirit Lake. At 12½ P.M. my Company numbering forty eight rank & file was en route to its destination taking by advice of experienced guides a long and circuitous route down the Valley of the Minnesota as far as South Bend for the purpose of following as long as possible a beaten track. The season was unpropitious for Military operations, the snow lay in heavy masses on the track which I was following, but those masses were thawing and could not bear the weight of the men, much less that of the heavy sleds with which I was compelled to travel. The narrative of a single day's March is the history of the whole—wading through deep drifts, cutting through them with the Spade and Shovel, extricating mules and sleighs from sloughs, or dragging the latter up steep hills or over bare spaces of prairie, the men wet from morning till night and sleeping on the snow. Such were the obstacles I encountered while still on the beaten track, the terminus of which was at a farm belonging to a man by the name of Slocum. From this point to the Des Moines was an unbroken waste of snow. An attempt had been made to carry provisions through, but had failed.— Mr. Flandreau the agent for the Sioux and Mr. Prescott an experienced guide and interpreter started with me from the Fort, and pushed on as far as Slocums, to try and discover the truth or falsity of the report, upon which my march was ordered— On their return, they stated that nothing definite could be learned, that the roads were almost if not quite impassible, and that as I must necessarily be absent several weeks it behooved them to return. I proceeded to South Bend on the Minnesota river where I purchased additional rations and moved on to Slocums. On arriving there I learned that the sleighs which had attempted to cross over to the Des Moines were still on the prairie at an immense drift some seven Miles off. I therefore sent my guide Joseph La Framboise to examine this drift, and report as to the practicability of my turning or crossing it. He returned and reported that it could not be passed without work. This determined me to remain at Slocums the next day, while a working party should clear the road; by so doing I obtained time to send for a couple of beeves in the vicinity. On the morning of the 26th of March I left Slocums and commenced the most arduous part of my journey—but before my Camp was struck, two settlers from the Des Moines came in ostensibly after provisions and reported that the Indians (some thirty lodges) were encamped at a grove some eight miles above the settlement, where a half breed by the name of Coursoll or "Caboo" as he is known among the Sioux had located a claim. This report determined me at once to strike for this grove, and I so directed my guide. To make any headway with my sleighs, I was compelled to break the road with the head of my Column marching the men by fours and relieving each at every fifteen minutes whenever the Bugler whom I left with the rear guard sounded the halt the Company would ground arms and fall back to the assistance of the sleighs. I encamped that night on the Owotowon some fifteen miles from Slocums. The ensuing day brought me the same difficulties but in the Evening when I made my camp on Cedar Lake I was compelled to drill my men tired and wet as they were, as skirmishers, for some were recruits and had no instruction in that branch— This day we must have made some eighteen Miles. The following day March 28th, about four Oclock in the afternoon, after a most laborious march of about twenty miles I found myself near the grove in which I was confident that the Indians were encamped I halted, loaded my Rifles, told my men that when I gave the word attention their Knapsacks must be thrown off (to be taken up by the rear guards, which I ordered to halt with the train at that point) and that not a whisper must be heard. I also notified them of my object, to surround the lodges with bayonets fixed, but to offer no violence unless they were attacked or unless they should receive Orders from Lieut. Murry or myself. As soon as I was sufficiently near I gave the word, Off went the Knapsacks and scarfs and gloves; up came the broken down and sick who had been with the sleighs, and with as light a step, as though the days march had been an afternoons drill, the company moved quickly to the grove— The nest was there but not warm— the lodges had been struck several days— I scoured the whole grove without success, but finally met Caboo who informed me, that Inkapah dutah's band had "wiped out" the settlement and gone to Heron Lake, some twenty five miles off, in the direction of the Yankton Country, that he was confident the Indians were there although their determination was to join the Yanktons who were fighting the troops on the Missouri. Weary from my long march I made my Camp and after reflection concluded that I would still leave the settlement unvisited until I made an endeavor to overtake this band of Sioux. At Retreat I called for volunteers for pursuit– The Company as one man moved to the front. I then made a detail of an Officer two non Commissioned Officers and twenty privates to take three days rations, directed the remainder of my Company to take one day's rations, ordered the teamsters (all of whom had also volunteered to pursue) to select all the mules which could possibly be ridden and to be ready to lead them in the morning and sent the men to their tents without sound of bugle– In the Morning I had them waked up by the voice fearing that the bugle note would give Notice of my presence and soon started on my march to Heron Lake. I directed my guides (for Caboo had joined me) to intercept the trail of the Indians if possible so as to shorten the distance, which they did effectively as I only had to march some fourteen or fifteen Miles. I had some difficulty in crossing the Des Moines which was rising and breaking up, but by throwing hay on the ice succeeded in crossing my mules. When we neared the grove about one Oclock P.M. I selected certain men to ride the mules, and directed Lt. Murry in case the Indians ran from the timber as they were likely to do, to mount at once follow as rapidly as possible and bring them to action, sending the mules back in order that more men might be hurried forward. The approach to the Lake was somewhat concealed, every thing was still and quiet the guide went ahead, a shot was fired and he turned back: in an instant my men were deployed as skirmishers and advancing a little quicker on the flanks encircled the grove but again were we doomed to disappointment. The Camp was there with all its traces of plunder and rapine books scissors Articles of female apparel furs and traps were scattered on the ground, the marks of some six or seven Tepis (lodges) were there but they had been struck Friday night or Saturday morning. This was Sunday afternoon–there remained a single chance, some four Miles distant was another Lake and Grove towards which led the trail of the Indians I directed Lt Murry to mount at once and dash for this grove, but if the signs which he might find there were as old as those before me, to lose no time in unavailing pursuit, but to return. This last he soon did with the report that a stop had been made there but that the guide reported the signs two days old. From Caboo's statement and the marks in the Camp, the Indians had twenty three or four horses, they had fully two days start of me; as the settlers had reported *thirty* tepis I thought it possible that there were other bands about the settlement; I was in a country destitute of provisions behind me and separating me from the few supplies I had was the Des Moines river rising rapidly, these considerations joined to the fact that my men were jaded and foot sore from a march of one hundred and forty miles, the difficulties of which I have but feebly portrayed— that I had no saddles for my mules, and that only thirteen of them could be ridden; all these things induced me to return, mortified and disappointed to my Camp. I will endeavor to make the remainder of this report more concise and instead of copying from my journal the daily record of my movements, will state the facts of this outrage as I gathered them from Caboo and friendly Indians and as I saw them with my own eyes. Before doing so however I must state that on the morning following my march to Heron Lake I despatched Lt Murry with a command to Spirit Lake to scout for Indians, gather facts and bury the dead should any such be found while I took a party down to the settlement with similar objects in view. I now present the following as the facts Some six weeks or two months since Inkapah dutahs band mustering some twelve or thirteen warriors were hunting in Iowa on the Inyan Yankey or Little Sioux river— A dog belonging to one of the Settlers attacked an Indian and was killed by him. The Owner punished the Indian and other Citizens probably fearing the consequences took the guns away from the whole band, leaving them no means of providing their daily subsistence. These Indians bore no great love to the whites at best, two of the Chiefs daughters had married Sioux of the Yankton nation both of whom were with the party. They determined on revenge returned to the place where their guns had been stored, found it unguarded got possession of their arms, and swept the valley of the Little Sioux up to Spirit Lake. On this Lake were several houses scattered at wide intervals through the grove all of these they plundered Killing the inhabitants and probably bearing off with them some women. A man by the name of Markham had been absent from Spirit Lake; on his return he went to the house where he boarded or was employed and found its inhabitants lifeless on the floor; he ran to another house and found Indian lodges pitched before its door, he then made his way to the small settlement called Springfield or Des Moines City, and gave the alarm, the Inhabitants collected in two houses on the east bank of the river, on the west was a single house belonging to a man by the name of Wood who carried on a large traffic with the Indians many of whom resort to the Des Moines during the winter and Spring for the purpose of hunting. While the settlers on the East bank sent to Fort Ridgely for assistance this man Wood with his brother remained on the west bank, ridiculed their fears and when Ink. a pah dutah's band came in from Spirit Lake traded with its members until a few days before the troops arrived, and then told them they had better Keep out of the way, for soldiers were coming. This brought affairs to a crisis the Indians crossed the river, plundered the vacant houses, found one house unfortunately occupied, its owner Josiah Stewart having left the house where the Settlers had congregated and returned to his own homestead with his wife and three children— Here the Savages revelled in blood. When I visited the Spot, the Father lay dead on his threshold, the Mother with one Arm encircling her murdered infant, lay outside the door, and by her side was stretched the lifeless body of a little girl of three Summers;— the eldest a boy of ten escaped.— Attacks where then made on the two houses of which I have spoken. In one, no damage was done; in the other, a man by the name of Thomas had his arm broken, his son some ten years of age was Killed and a young woman was slightly wounded. The Indians then crossed the river, Killed probably both of the Woods, although I only succeeded in finding the body of one of them, plundered the trading house, and hurried off with an abundance of guns, powder, lead and provisions to ascend the Des Moines and join the Yanktons. This was Thursday Evening. I arrived Saturday Evening, being too late by two days. I found on Monday Morning when I reached the settlement, that the inhabitants had fled, and I learned from a man by the name of Henderson who had been abandoned, he being a helpless cripple, that they had started down the river Friday morning. Several Settlers had returned with me and after me from Slocums I sent one of them after those who had fled to bring them back, telling him that I would leave a sufficient guard to protect the settlement, and that I was satisfied no other Indians were engaged in the affair than Ink a pah dutah's band, and that they had certainly fled. On the strength of this, some returned and reported that all would return if the guard was to be permanent. I could give them no information on that head but stated that I would take the responsibility of leaving an Officer, Two Non Commissioned Officers and twenty Privates but that further action must come from my Military Superiors. I then returned to this post taking a route directly across the Country as led by my invaluable guide—La Fromboise— Four marching days brought me to the Fort. In conclusion I feel it my duty to recommend the establishment of a post on the Des Moines River. A great check has been given to settlement and civilization by this massacre. Settlers and pioneers would be most unwise to risk their lives, and those of their families in a region which from its facilities for hunting and fishing, and (should the settlement extend) for plunder and violence may be termed the Indians paradise— A sure retreat is offered to any band of savages which may be tempted to become hostile; the Missouri offers a refuge; the vast country lying between the Minnesota and the Missouri with its numerous lakes and groves affords countless places of concealment; and although Fort Ridgely lies within a few days march, yet as is shown by my expedition, an outrage may occur at a season of the year which would render it impossible for troops to reach the scene of distress under several days. Immediately about the Des Moines Settlement the timbered land is claimed, but the country has not been surveyed, and I doubt not an eligible point for a post could be easily found. Supplies probably would have to be furnished from South Bend.

While expressing my regret and disappointment that the object of my Expedition was not attained, viz: the punishment of the Indians I would be doing injustice to the Officers and men of my Company were I not to bring to the notice of the Commanding Officer the cheerfulness and patience with which they encountered the fatigues of no ordinary a march; and perhaps I would be doing injustice to myself did I not assert that I used the best energies of my nature to carry out the instructions which I received. It was one of the saddest moments of my life when I saw the Stewart family dead by their cold Hearth stone, but then and there my conscience told me that they had met their fate by no fault of Mine.

I enclose for the consideration of the Commanding Officer a Copy of the Order I published at Camp Alexander and also of the instructions I left with Lieut. Murry.

And am Very Respectfully

Your Obdt. Servt. . . .

Morris said, I wasn't employed by Noble and Thatcher. Never had been. We were just friends back in Howard County. And I didn't go there first: tried to, but got lost in the snow and dark, and fetched up at the Gardner place.

That's all nonessential to the body of the report. You'll be the first to admit that.

Course.

But perhaps you understand more readily now, what difficulties were encountered by the soldiers. No snowshoes!—you should be aware of that! Leather shoes instead—and all their back-loads, and accompanied by a ponderous Army wagon on wheels, drawn by six mules—about as fit for such a march as an elephant is for a ballroom, sir!

Yep. But there's something else. . . .

I am so thoroughly convinced of the imbecility of a military administration, Mr. Markham, which clothes and equips its troops in exactly the same manner, for duty in the tropical climate of Florida and the frigid region of Minnesota— Damn it all! In time I hope to enlighten that non-progressive institution! The Government hasn't yet requested me to investigate and report the facts in this case, but I have a notion that before long I *shall* be asked to do so. I shall take advantage of the invitation, if ever tis forthcoming. Pray have no doubt as to that!

There's something else. . . . He says they started towards the grove, with the guide ahead; then somebody fired a shot, and the guide turned back. What shot, Mr.? Who fired it?

Ah. Captain Bee doesn't say, does he?

Nope. I know this feller he calls Caboo. Down the Des Moines City way they call him Joe Gaboo.

I know him myself, Mr. Markham—am well acquainted. He's really named Joseph Coursolle.

You trust him?

See no reason not to!

I wouldn't trust one of them half-breeds further than I could boot an ox.

Those are strong words, Mr. Markham.

Can't help it. Could be he said the tracks and signs at the camp were twenty-four hours old, when actually they was fresh. That Army captain, he wouldn't have known the difference. Maybe he's soldiered in Florida and Mexico and such places; reckon he hain't soldiered much in the snow. Nor gainst the Dakotas. And what's all this here about, *I would be doing an injustice to myself did I not assert that I used the best energies of my nature to carry out the instructions—?* And this here about, *My conscience told me that they had met their fate through no fault of mine—*

Ah. Then thee thinks that the gentleman doth protest too much?

Beg pardon?

So do I, Mr. Markham, so do I!

I don't quite get your meaning.

Perhaps I don't, myself. Was merely yammering something in the nature of a quotation, and a purely gratuitous comment of my own. . . . Gad, I'm sleepy. May I suggest that we retire?

Suits me, said Morris. But he lay long awake.

XLV

Abbie held a tight perpetual thought of the ague. . . . During the Shell Rock period of her family's existence, and again at Clear Lake, she had suffered this ailment. (It seemed all must know it—all who would seek a home in a moist new country with its native effluvia.) Her poor spleen had turned to stone: she'd felt a rankling core within a body otherwise pliable and quivering.

She believed that the squeeze of illness was returned to rattle her tenderest organs again, and permanently. Long ago in innocence she had embraced gentility and mirth—light desirable traits and substances, which her family held must rule the world (or would prevail eventually through God's benevolence and the example of Jesus). Now they were wiped out of her life; nor did they exist in any other life around her. That spleen had been forged as a lump of iron within. The pattern of earlier years, once thought to be firmly established, was bashed to bits. It had never lived; there'd been no Mrs. Hubbard, no kindly old painting displaying mystic charm of a countryside in faded English oils. There'd been no gumdrops to dissolve blissfully in the red mouth of a child, their taste and texture had never ruled. . . . What little-girl-wraith appeared before a fire, to sit and warm her hands? Nay, she'd never come, and the fire burned not. Tag ends of recollection blew like leaves or rags from the past; but the past was a stern empty chamber; and how had such rubbish ever settled there in the first place? Abbie wondered at the mechanical insistence of her own physical entity which kept her breathing and walking. Why should she wish to breathe and walk?

Dainty memories swelled themselves into gargoyle shapes. They were bloated, bejowled.

There had never been the frail colored wildness of a flower called a lupine, replete with calyx and corolla. There had never been Hide-and-Seek, never children scampering.

> A bushel of wheat and a bushel of clover.
> All 'at ain't ready
> Can't hide over!

A bushel of wheat and a bushel of rye.
All 'at ain't ready
Holler, Aye!

*Com*ing!

Nor had there been the nutshell which she carved to share with Eliza, nor the teasing about Henry Tretz . . . never Abbie's Bad Dream.

Abbie observed a semblance of her mother frequently in her mind; but her mother was not in natural state, working or admonishing or doing affectionate little deeds. She saw Frances Gardner instead as she'd last seen her living: twisting in combined clutch of greasy hands, and all the material of blankets and trade calico and feathers and miscellaneous shreds of white men's attire streaking round her as the woman whirled helplessly, spinning in the middle of an inhuman wheel of bodies. Abbie could not rise from her chair, she had Baby Mandy in her arms, the two boys cowered against her, meshed in her skirts. She saw the bright red-painted butt of one gun swung on high again, and wondered dully why that Indian had painted his gun so recently, so stickily; and then again she knew what paint it really was. *Zuya! Zuya!* Coarse chorus of muddled voices cried the syllables. They abused her ears in spectral loneliness of cold spring nights on these plains. *Zuya!* She'd learned a few words of the Dakota language by this time; but she heard no one repeat those angry insistent sounds, and did not know what they meant.

Humped beneath her pack, she exerted through hours and rains and days, in this slow-moving vagrant herd.

Ain't nothing but this. Ain't nothing.

She thought that once she had attended a picnic, she suffered vague recollection of smooth sweet pinkish meat fastened to curving chop-bones . . . something about a salad made from potatoes and onions, a salad in a brown crock, and the cloth being lifted? Then fingers of forgetfulness touched her lightly, charitably; they smoothed her brain, she remembered nothing more. There'd been no picnic, no meat and salad.

. . . Came a week when the Wahpekute band had no meat, and no one seemed to hunt successfully, though some of the men went out and tried. The few streams which they crossed were too roily, too filled with silt: no fish could be taken by any means. Orphan-Woman and Black-Young-Woman bade Abbie to accompany them in their own form of hunting. They searched out the burrows of small animals and tried by various means to compel the critters to emerge from their dens. Abbie was stationed with a club, on guard beside one hole, while the two women cut slim wands of willow and thrust them repeatedly into other entrances which led, apparently, to the main burrow. In this way two ground squirrels were taken, though only when

Abbie was demoted to the post of pusher-with-the-willow-stick. She herself did not club the ground squirrels, nor was she allowed any taste of them, except the opportunity to crush a few leftover bones, with bits of fat and gristle clinging. Later, once more promoted to the rank of woman-hits-with-club, she brought her weapon down upon the back of a sickly skunk which had crawled forth. The animal managed to spray her before he died: Abbie took a dose of oil all over her rags and blanket-scraps. The Wahpekute uttered cries and made signs of disgust, and ordered her to stand away from them, to stand down wind. Abbie had always considered that she might be nauseated by a concentration of skunk musk, but this misfortune did not prevail. The stuff smelt better than the other smells amidst which she lived. It had the odor of something burnt, oily and burnt, black or brown; but twas a clean intense odor with dark purity about it.

. . . Again she was ordered on a skunk hunt by Female-Cousin-Rabbit: she must go, or accept a beating. But Female-Cousin-Rabbit, routing out one of the shaggy beasts and pursuing it with flailing club, had the bad luck to snap her bludgeon in two. The skunk went safely to earth. Twas a good quarter-mile to any timber where a new weapon might be secured; the witch left Abbie on guard at the den's mouth, she demonstrated that the animal must be driven back if he attempted to emerge. Soon Abbie saw a dark snout and bright beady eye; she did not know how still a mouse might keep (all the mice she'd ever seen were anything but quiet) but she remained frozen in her tracks while the skunk reconnoitered and then fled away up the nearest stream-bed. Back came Female-Cousin-Rabbit, and inquired, *Manka?* Abbie signed that the animal was departed, she showed where he had gone. Female-Cousin-Rabbit was so overwhelmed with rage that she could not even strike at Abbie with her fresh-cut club. Fool, fool, fool!—she whooped, stamping in a witless circle. Thou hast let the *manka* escape! *Niktepi kta!* Thou shall be killed! If less hysterical she might have done harm to the white girl; but sheer fury drove her into a state of abject idiocy—she did not even know the way back to camp, Abbie had to guide her.

. . . One day they were encamped in a flat valley where not a tree grew, not a bush, where not a sliver of wood could be found. Abbie was sent to gather fuel; this was an errand on which she was permitted to depart alone. Inkpaduta had no fear that she might hide or in some other manner elude the band. They could run her down at any moment—there was no place for her to go, no food or shelter, no one to aid her; she was as safe for their purposes as if she'd remained in camp. In this case the assembling of fuel meant gathering dried saucers of buffalo dung which appeared in wasted grass. Ah, the growth looked lifeless . . . but here was a mysterious blush of tan which sometimes approached green on southern slopes. Abbie was given a ramrod from an abandoned musket, she was instructed by signs as to how she must proceed. This was mere iteration of what she'd been taught before: she should impale the buffalo chips upon the ramrod, one after another, as fast as they were discovered. Of course the platters of manure were dried by weather, dried by age—never fresh, or the Wahpekute would have rushed for a hunt. Old dung cakes they were, better than wood for slow fires. But only a few buffalo had passed that way, and one had to search and search. In her wanderings Abbie came to a hilltop where ambitious puss-bloomies were seeking to expand. She knelt and looked at the budding flowers as long as she dared. Almost had they escaped detection, hidden in hard grasses there, but her sharp eye caught the fuzzy gray-purple of buds: twas a purple like a shadow. Only one flower was opened enough for her to see the golden fringe of secrets inside, and she observed that a few tiny flies were skipping there already. Another week, maybe, and this whole hill would be colored with them. Had ever she picked huge short-stemmed bouquets of these pretties, wound them with grass to hold them together? It seemed likely. She thought for a moment that she could hear the conversation of bees.

. . . Ma didn't call 'em puss-bloomies at all: she called 'em easter-flowers. And Pa said that lots of folks called 'em wind-flowers. . . .

Ma, Pa, who were they? What—? Who was that other girl she'd gone with, gathering such pale lilac-sweet things with the dandelion-gold in their centers? Could she remember?

Nay, it had never befallen. There were no previous easter-flowers, or whatever you wanted to call them. They had never grown. Nor had Abbie grown; she'd just been here all the time, been with these wild men. So she would continue with them into eternity.

Suddenly she reached down, her right hand closed on the open flower, her fingers bent and tightened. She compressed, crushed and crushed— She exerted mountainous strength in her hand: the strength of boulders, solid weight of a falling log which might pin a man to the ground. She opened her hand and looked at the mangled rag. She let it fall through her fingers, and stood up to go gathering more cakes of dung, more *tachesdi.*

. . . Abbie awakened from sleep, awakened herself with a snarl. She sat in stinking chill, her hand pressed against her mouth, dreading the cuffing she'd receive if her thin wail had roused up the wrong people. But no one else had awakened, she was safe. She'd shrieked because she'd witnessed again those messy outflung baby dolls beneath an oak tree in the Gardner dooryard. She'd seen spongy relics, stuff contained within their skulls, when children's heads were driven against the solidity of that tree . . . stuff still clinging to the hard-ridged bark.

Looks like scrambled-up eggs.

Yes, so it does: scrambled-up eggs in a skillet.

You've taken the bulk of the eggs up, but these few scraps remain.

Eggs.

Wearily the kind fingers of forgetfulness began their swabbing. Rowly, Bertie, Baby Mandy were expunged, they'd never been. Abbie sat rigid in dimness of the lodge, licking the back of her hand.

. . . His-Curly-Sacred (the monstrous tall thing known to Abbie as Tawa-all-them-other-words) met a party of far-straying Sisiton-wanna while he was hunting; they had with them a canteen of spirit water, and His-Curly-Sacred made a trade for this whiskey. He gave the other hunters a signet ring (to secure this, he'd chopped off a finger of Bertell Snyder). When His-Curly-Sacred reached the Wahpekute camp he managed to hide his treasure until it was half-consumed; then, in the act of drinking, he was discovered by Female-Cousin-Rabbit. She levied upon him immediately for long-overdue wages . . . she would perform no more domestic duties, she cried, unless he gave her the rest of the whiskey, canteen and all. But he had drunk enough spirit water to make him feel enormously virile, and he met a cringing Abbie Gardner when she came in with a load of cottonwood sticks. The tipi which His-Curly-Sacred shared with other men was conveniently vacant—the rest were gone to the lodge of He-Wears-Anything, where they gambled with stolen gold coins. Tawachehawakan yanked Abbie into the vacant tipi and threw himself upon her. Yellow Hair, I fuck you until you yell for mercy; and I show no mercy!—nor did he display any. Abbie had long since given up screaming for her mother when such abuse was effected; she was able to murmur only: No, no, no . . . no . . . when she sobbed, during the ordeal and afterward, no tears flowed. Once His-Curly-Sacred had expended his passion he rolled off Abbie's body and, numbed by the unaccustomed spirit water, fell snoringly asleep. His knife had slid from securement while the young Wahpekute delighted himself, and the knife lay upon a robe within reach of the girl's hand. So easy, she thought. Twould be just as easy as scat. Her tired dirty little hand went out and touched the rust-flecked blade. She traced the blade's edge, went on and explored the hilt . . . the young man grunted amid his snores. Where might she strike? One quick thrust and . . . where was the heart? Left side. Course it was . . . but how far down the left side? Beneath that hard hairy nipple, that might be the place? He was deep in sleep. If she struck forcefully he would never waken, there'd not be time for wakening. . . . Somewhere there was a Bible being held open, a Bible being read from. Her father's voice? Who was her father? Rowland Gardner? He loved to read aloud. Quickly (but faintly and distantly) he might have said that he'd read from the Fourth Chapter of Judges . . . Harvey would approve of that. Harvey Luce? What indeed had become of Harvey Luce? Perhaps he lay unmoving in the tent of Jael . . . *took an hammer in her hand, and went softly unto him, and smote the nail into his temples, and fastened it into the ground: for he was fast asleep and weary.* Then another voice said flatly, *Thou shalt not kill.* Abbie's hand dragged away from the knife, and her face began to wad itself until it was inhuman. Pa. Pa-ha . . . she blubbered out the word, her distorted mouth shaking, she added many ha-ha's to the name. Pa-ha-ha-ha-ha—

She felt a sense of someone's departing from the lodge and leaving her alone with the critter who'd mauled her. She thought someone walked off with slow gigantic strides, and bore all her past away with him as if it were stored in a pack he carried.

XLVI

While riding on a hunt, Makes-Fat-Bad and His-Curly-Sacred met up with a party of Wahpetonwanna. They chased a young buffalo cow squarely into the path of these strangers. They'd made their kill and were eating the fresh heart, when the other Dakota approached and sat their horses, watching. A few words were exchanged which could scarcely be called amenities: the Titonwan's speech served to identify him (it was known throughout the Isantie that there was a Far-Westerner among Inkpaduta's men). The arrogant His-Curly-Sacred, nerved by contempt for these docile Easterners, settled the matter insofar as they were concerned. He bragged that his people had killed whites at Okoboji, and were even now encamped at the Big-Woods-All-Together, along with three surviving women captives.

The other hunters were Christian Indians from the Yellow Medicine. Several of them knew Charles Flandrau personally, and all had come under the spell of the impassioned missionaries Riggs and Williamson.

They discussed their afternoon's encounter that evening while they cooked meat, before they said Grace, during and after the meal, before they chanted evening prayers. Two brothers, sons of a pillar of the church named Spirit-Walker, were imbued with the idea that one or perhaps even all of the captive girls might be rescued.

Said the elder, Sihahota or Gray-Foot: All know that That Wicked One is ever anxious to gain ammunition. We have with us much ammunition. Enough powder to fill a small keg. . . .

Aye, someone objected, but That Wicked One would demand more.

If Major were here, what would Major say?

The younger brother's name was the same as one of the twins —Mahpiyahoton—but among his white friends he was known as Sounding-Heavens rather than as Roaring-Cloud. He was occupied seriously in reckoning not only what Charles Flandrau and the missionaries would do or would wish to have done, but also in considering what his own father's reaction might be.

He said, They are white women. Captives. We rescue them if we can.

. . . We dare not attack Inkpaduta's village. White soldiers are needed!

. . . Soldiers are too far away!

. . . We dare not attack—!

Sounding-Heavens and his elder brother explained that they had no wish or plan to attack. Should they attack, the girls would be killed to prevent their being rescued.

This I propose, said Gray-Foot. I propose that each man give to us whatever he can spare. We have with us more blankets than we use; all can give blankets. We have one gun more than is needed. It belongs to my brother, who has two guns, and can spare one. We take with us this gun. We have among us many ornaments. Some are silver.

But, rang the unhappy chorus of disapproval, all men treasure their ornaments!

. . . I have a gold coin, and this I value.

. . . I have the medal that the British give to my father. Must I lose my medal?

. . . *Echahe,* I have arm-bands. But I wish not to lose arm-bands.

Gray-Foot asked firmly, Forget you all the story of the Prodigal Son, as told by our Fathers Riggs and Williamson?

We forget not. But—

Shina iyotan washte kin hė aupo, ka inkiyapo. Bring-thee-that-most-good-blanket-and-ye-put-it-on-him! Is this not in the story of the Prodigal Son? I say now that the white women in the village of That Wicked One are Prodigal Daughters.

Aye. But—

Ka mazanapchupe wan nape kin en iyekiyapo. And-finger-ring-on-the-hand-put-ye! Is it not the same as doing the bidding of the father in the tale, if we employ blankets and ornaments and other valuable things, to bring all or one of these women to their own people?

Sounding-Heavens voiced the most compelling argument. Major will not see us lose our treasures for all time! He writes letter, and when again come payments for annuity, come also new ornaments and blankets and ammunition, to take the place of those things we now give up!

There was a feeling of agreement in the camp—reluctant assent, perhaps, but still a willingness to comply.

The hunters recited the Lord's Prayer in unison, as they had been taught, and then lay down to sleep. One or another remained on vigil through the night. The knowledge that Inkpaduta was resident at that lake of the Big-Woods-All-Together was enough to induce nervousness; each man was willing—nay, eager—to rise from his robe when he was awakened to stand a turn of sentry duty.

Morning came up with wistful springtime delicacy of color. After devotions, and after meat had been toasted and eaten, the hunters assembled the goods to be offered.

There is wealth here.

Aye, wealth!

Carry this treasure not directly into Inkpaduta's camp!

Nay, we hide it first. Then, if agreement is made, we bring the wealth.

Inkpaduta may slay both of thee!

Gray-Foot and Sounding-Heavens were apprehensive. But they said: There is danger; still we expect not to be slain. That Wicked One knows that all people west of the Yellow Medicine would follow him, to slay him in turn.

O brothers, we fear for thy lives!

The missionaries would wish us to go.

But men say that Inkpaduta is *wachinhnuni,* he is insane!

Major Flandrau would wish that we fetch white women, if we can do this thing.

But he may be *witko!*

True, brother. He may be drunk.

All were reluctant to part with the two bold sons of Spirit-Walker. . . . We fear!

Aye. Gray-Foot began to quote: Though through the valley where is death-shadow walk I, no evil fear I. . . .

His brother joined in the Psalm's recitation. One by one the rest added their voices, until there rose a reassuring general murmur on the last words: In lodge of the Lord forever dwell I! Farewells were exchanged. It was agreed that if any captives were rescued they should be conveyed at once to a village farther north, on the east bank of the Big Sioux, where other Christianized Dakota were assembling as they came in from the hunt.

. . . Hour after hour the brothers rode to the west. Both had hunted through this country annually or sometimes twice a year, since they had ten-again-four or ten-again-five winters. They knew that they would reach another smaller lake before they reached the lake of the *Chanptayatanka,* the Big-Woods-All-Together. Then they could decide about concealing ransom materials. Of these the new gun, still unfired by Sounding-Heavens and thus unblooded (except by its previous owner) was clearly an item outstanding. Sounding-Heavens had received this weapon as a gift when he proved himself heroic in the previous autumn, near the Upper Agency. A group of white strangers had come up the Minnesota to look over the land; after being welcomed and entertained by the agent, they went out on the river to fish. One of the visitors selected a light canoe which he managed to upset; he could not swim. Sounding-Heavens was hunting in timberland nearby, and ran to the river on hearing cries. He was a capable if clumsy swimmer, and performed the rescue with despatch. Mr. Mitchell presented him with a favorite gun on the spot; also later he sent groceries to the young man's family from the trade store. The rescuer named his weapon after the donor: Mish-ell, since laboriously he had been taught to pronounce the letter *l* by the Williamsons. The gun was a Plains rifle with handsome inlays of German silver, and boasted a beaded case manufactured especially for this weapon by the Winnebago. (So Mr. Mitchell informed his rescuer through interpreters, though Mahpiyahoton himself had never seen a live Winnebago; theretofore he had believed that such people existed only in legends repeated by elders.)

A led pony, used by the brothers on this hunt but actually the property of the father-in-law of one, an old man named Flies-Twice, carried the goods. Six blankets; a green hide which bore a few whitish spots; some eight pounds of gunpowder packed carefully into parfleches; a bag in which donated items of jewelry and personal apparel were stored; and the Plains rifle. The Christians did not know how many captives might be bought with these materials; they hoped that the disgraced and disgraceful Wahpekute might yield up all three young women, but they doubted it.

. . . Gradually a fringe formed on the western horizon beneath idling foamy clouds. The fringe fell apart into an identity of straggling trees which bordered the first lake on the route.

Brother, we are near the Big-Woods-All-Together. Here we hide horse and the things he carries?

There are not enough trees, not enough forest in which to hide horse and other valuables.

But if we go on with them, we come soon to the village of Inkpaduta's people!

The brothers dismounted and prowled about, searching for signs of the Wahpekute. . . . The wanderers had passed that way, but the trail was old.

They decided to take a risk: to continue on to a larger lake, thicker woodland. They went warily, Gray-Foot scouting ahead, Sounding-Heavens leading the burdened pony; and taking advantage of every curve of landscape.

The sun was behind ominous clouds when at last they reached their goal, and a hasty hiding took place. Powder, rifle, smaller articles were wrapped with care and jammed into a hole beneath a broken cottonwood. The pony was tethered. The path of the raiders could be discerned: they'd moved north along the western shore. The Wahpetonwanna rode on this course. They had crossed only one tiny creek and were picking their way through adjacent trees when a voice shouted angrily. Gray-Foot and Sounding-Heavens halted, they did not lift their weapons. They sat their horses in silence while four of the Wahpekute took form amid brush and came toward them. All the threatening strangers had revolvers belted on (the Wood brothers never considered that their stock-in-trade would be distributed so far to the west!) and two—He-Wears-Anything and His-Curly-Sacred—had drawn their weapons.

Wahpetonwanna, you come far from your people!

We ride far. We wish to see That Old One. We wish to talk.

Why wish you to see That Old One? . . . The Wahpekute was understandably suspicious. He'd left these men with their band thirty-odd miles distant, only the day before, and now two were come riding. . . .

We would see him. We would trade.

What would you trade? It may be that Inkpaduta does not wish to trade.

We would buy white women.

His-Curly-Sacred taunted: Men do not buy white women! Men take white women without paying. Men kill white men and then take white women. This we do! We are men!

We would see That Old One, Gray-Foot repeated obstinately.

His-Curly-Sacred was inclined to expostulate, but Rattle-Strike stepped forward and asserted his prerogative as son-in-law. It may be that That Old One wishes to trade, he said. I know not. I have a wife who is daughter of That Old One. But I know not. He may trade, he may sell white women. He may not trade, may not sell white women. O brothers, you come!—and he led in escorting them into a wretched community where soon they sat as guests, shocked by filthiness and disorder apparent, and by evil behavior of children who ran at large.

With some trepidation Rattle-Strike went to inform Inkpaduta of the visitors' arrival. He would not have been surprised if his father-in-law had threatened him, merely because he permitted the Wahpetonwanna to approach. On the other hand, if done out of an opportunity for profitable exchange, the old marauder might have reacted with fury. One could never be confident of anything about Inkpaduta, except his essential unpredictable qualities.

The Head Man did not assail his son-in-law. He growled an edict: all three white women should be put in a separate lodge, and no one was to approach them until Inkpaduta gave permission. Also another tipi should be set up to house the callers; he wished them kept to themselves. . . . For some time Inkpaduta had been toying with the idea of selling his prisoners. He thought this might be done at a good price at one of the Missouri River forts where there were soldiers. He knew that the Yanktonai did not prefer to have him pass through their country, especially on such an errand. But it was unlikely that they would object with violence: they would only tell the Wahpekute to be gone, they would hustle them on and on.

He asked if these visitors had come laden with goods. . . .

Most of the band welcomed the coming of the brothers, since it gave them an opportunity for a social evening of smoke and boasting.

Their own bragging, among themselves, about murders managed in Iowa and Minnesota Territory had chafed and re-echoed until each was heartily sick of the other's stories. Christianized visitors might have no killings to boast about; but at least they formed a new audience, and this in itself was stimulation. It quickened appetites. The men ate meat for long. They had no spirit water, but they owned their recollections; and memories heated their blood after they had eaten, and made them determined to impress the strangers, to horrify them if possible.

Idatahn!—said Fire-Cloud, rising and speaking robustly, to draw attention of all. I was first to kill!

His twin brother heckled him. I was first, along with you. The first to kill. I boast!

So we kill first, the two of us, Fire-Cloud was forced to agree. We kill together! We kill two white men, and both have guns, and they do not see us or hear us before we shoot. We are more quiet than wood-mice in the snow, and so they hear not, nor know when we come upon them. We take no hair, because of words of *Unktehi*. . . . I boast!

Hushan yelled in his turn: I am second to kill white child! I kill smaller of two boys at that same house. But I am very strong. I hold him by one foot only. So I put his head against the tree! Only twice I do this, because I am very strong! Twice—then his head is broken. One not as strong as I would hold both feet; but I hold one!

This went on for some time, with several men clamoring to be heard. Inkpaduta rose at last and began a recital of the deaths he had made. The rest had heard his narration many times. The twins knew it by heart. It included family murders; killings within the band where first he dwelt; Sauk (and Sauk children); Chippeway also; the two Pawnee. Sounding-Heavens and Gray-Foot had never believed that such a bloody account could be cried aloud. They sat shuddering, and praying. They knew Inkpaduta's reputation, they recognized that these stories must be true. They wondered why any of the white women had been left. Why had not all been killed?

For hours the Wahpekute cried their accomplishments, until voices were weak and husky, throats dried out.

Inkpaduta leered at his sickened visitors. You boast not, Wahpetonwanna. You know not how to kill?

Nay, Thou Old One. We know how to kill; but we kill not. Not as you.

You are women.

We are not women. Our God tells us that is wrong to do things which thou hast done.

Your god is god of *Washichun!*

He is God of all. Listen to His words?

Listen not!

Gray-Foot had been considering the story of Daniel. He thought that these outlaws were lions. But he believed so intensely in the Lord that he thought the bandits would not dare to harm him . . . perhaps would not even wish to.

He said: My heart is sad when I hear these things. I know that the heart of my brother is sad, *nakun.* You cannot do these things, Thou Old One, and escape punishment. These are wicked deeds! You pay for them—in this world, or in the world to come.

Inkpaduta roared that he would pay for nothing. He would take what he wanted, had always done so, would continue to do so!

Someday you pay, said Gray-Foot.

Not I. I will not pay! Inkpaduta made the same sign of contempt which he had made many times before.

(In contrary fashion, he was not enraged or even excessively indignant because these Christians had not applauded the boasting. He was even pleased that he had been censured for wrong-doing. It gave him a renewed sense of his own resistant invulnerability.)

Belatedly the strangers were permitted to bed themselves in the lodge prepared for them. They had many misgivings about retiring at all, and agreed that one should keep watch while the other slept. One or the other lay motionless through the rest of the night, cocked rifle trained on the lodge's doorway, and alert also to the slightest scratching of any lifted lodge-cover behind him. In thankfulness they repeated an early morning prayer together, and requested that the Lord lend assistance to their efforts.

. . . Haggling began . . . it was as if much spirit water had been drunk the night before. People came to the conference yawning, and Inkpaduta himself let it be known that he favored postponing further discussion until evening.

Gray-Foot told him calmly, That cannot be. We go this day.

Why go you today?

Later I tell you. I cannot tell now, said Gray-Foot mysteriously. But he added as bait: We have articles of great value.

You are wealthy? *Wizicha?*

We have pony. He is young and stalwart, and has a white face. This pony has hunted buffalo. He is very fast.

We have ponies.

You have no such pony as this! Nor have we, among our people, any like him.

I would see this pony. What else offer you?

We wish to buy the three young white women whom you hold. We offer powder.

How much powder?

As much as will fill a small keg. We offer blankets.

New blankets?

They are but little used. They are heavy trade blankets of the best cloth—the blankets of many points. You may see for yourself the many points marked upon the blankets.

Inkpaduta asked churlishly, Where have you these things concealed? Is the pony inside your shirt? Have you powder and blankets fastened to your belts? I see them not!

We have put them very near. We bring them forth if you say you sell white women.

Inkpaduta smoked and studied for a while, then asked more equably: What else have you?

We offer a fine rifle, and it has a pouch to cover it, a pouch with beads. The rifle's name is Mish-ell. There is silver upon this gun. It is better than any gun we have—better than any gun among your people.

Sanpa? More?

More we offer for the captives. We offer ornaments—silver, brass, other sorts—

I would see these things.

Gray-Foot looked at his brother, and both the young Christians arose out of the circle where they had been sitting. We go, and we bring these things.

Some of my people go with you.

We go alone.

Inkpaduta declared in wily fashion: Tonight we have council. *Eze!* I say if I sell.

We are gone before this night.

Why go you?

Because, said the amiable spokesman, if we return not by the time we have told our people, then our people come. It is not even one sleep for them to come, for they are men who ride fast. All our people ride fast!

Whatever notions Inkpaduta might have had about seizing the proffered trade goods, and then relinquishing not even a single prisoner, were thus squelched.

He thought: At least I sell but one.

He signed for his own men to remain seated.... They waited, smoking, dozing, eating bits of buffalo fat, until at last the Christians came into camp, leading the white-faced horse.... Goods were spread out and examined. Sounding-Heavens made much of the spotted hide which was included in the goods and had not been mentioned before. All knew, he said, the medicinal properties of a spotted hide in peace and in war.

The pony was appraised, the rifle hoisted and sighted. Blankets were spread out, the array of trinkets displayed. Inkpaduta and his followers went through a lengthy process of devaluing the goods. Just as inflexibly Gray-Foot and Sounding-Heavens persisted in exaggerating the worth of each article.

In midafternoon Inkpaduta said: I sell one woman. If, in addition, you give me two more ponies.

These things have the worth of three women! cried the exhausted brothers.

The value of one.

Why give we two more ponies?

Because I say.

Then would we walk.

You walk.

It is not good that we leave these things with you. We take them back!

Echaesh. You take, said Inkpaduta airily. He composed himself as if for slumber.

The Wahpetonwanna went outside to confer in private. Brother, said the younger, I feared this thing. Now must we give up our own ponies.

I, too, feared this thing. But if he will not sell all, then we must take one woman. And we walk!

Nitokichonze kin u kte. Thy kingdom come! We take one woman. . . .

They went back into the lodge, and asked Inkpaduta which girl he would sell. He told them with a shrug that he did not care: they might take any one of the three.

Roaring-Cloud (who to his surprise had been permitted to seize upon the spotted robe as his share of the treasure) escorted the visitors to that tipi where the three whites were kept. With fast-beating hearts the two Easterners conducted their own private examination and appraisal. Neither could speak a word of English, except to mutter a form of greeting. Their Biblical lore, their conversion, had been gained through offices of the Reverend Mr. Stephen Riggs, who was fully conversant with the Dakota language, and taught them in Dakota.

The youngest, with yellow hair?

Brother, because she is youngest, we take her not.

Why take we not youngest?

Because also I think she is strongest.

They say that already they kill one woman. They put her into a river.

But I think they kill an older woman next time, before they kill a younger! Perhaps she lives, and someone can buy her on another day when more goods have been brought. I think this is what Major would say and wish us to do.

What you say is good, brother. Then which of the others do we take?

Dechadan, said Gray-Foot. He indicated Lydia Noble. She is weak and she is very sad. Her perhaps they would kill first! He beckoned and grunted at Liddy, he motioned for her to come to the door of the lodge.

Liddy turned her face away and hung her head.

That one!—cried Roaring-Cloud behind them. She should be killed!

She does not come when she is told to come. I beat her for this before. I beat her again!

We take other, said Sounding-Heavens sadly.

They motioned to Peggy Ann.

Often, with increasingly iron determination, Margaret Ann Marble told herself that she would do everything asked of her: she would perform any work, yield to any agony or persuasion. It was the only way in which she might keep alive, and she wanted to remain alive. She had no William, no home, no life worth clinging to; yet she clung. . . . If in this moment there lurked the wet grain of a child inside her, that child was the child of one of these brutes. Why should she wish to live? Yet she wished to live. She rose quickly, and came out of the tipi.

Eesh, said the brothers approvingly. It is good that you come.

Aptly the mother of the two young men had been named Gentle-Woman. That was forty years earlier, long before missionaries came into the land with fervor and essential sweetness. Had she been born in another realm and with skin of different hue, the wife of the good Wahpetonwan, Spirit-Walker, would have been accorded that admitted supremacy which is nigh to saintliness. (She would have been the first to drop her work and go trotting to a home struck by tragedy. If a friendless and impoverished girl, fleeing the wrath of bullying parents, had wandered into her village in a pregnant condition, she would have given the girl shelter, nursed her tenderly, and searched out an agreeable foster father and foster mother after the baby was born. She would have been the one of her neighborhood who cooked up strengthening stock for the sick . . . she would have marched boldly to defy the drunken man who beat his wife and children, and to lead him to justice—by the ear! She would have been the first to toil at a church supper, the last to leave after dishes were washed . . . she would have polished the dishes with her towel until they shone.)

Peggy Ann was comatose when fetched into the tipi of Gentle-Woman and Spirit-Walker. She and the brothers suffered a sorry trip: neither ransomed nor ransomers had much to eat before they reached that temporary village on the Big Sioux. Also they were compelled to cross an area where spring fires had raced during a dry week previously: the entire plain was ashy, a waste of thin blowing charcoal dust, and spiked heavily by cooked weed-roots which bit and tore against the treading moccasins. Peggy Ann's feet, and the tougher feet of the brothers as well, were bruised, aching, swollen. . . . Peggy Ann was so accustomed to male attack, that she could not imagine at first why these two men did not fling themselves upon her. She had thought that they would do so; all Indians must. But when they prayed, and smiled, and pointed serenely at the sky, almost grudgingly she realized that these were creatures of a different stripe. And, for Indians, very cleanly. . . . But she discounted their prayers, as she had come to discount the existence of any personal God who practiced unceasing benevolence. God perished in the instant when William Marble was riddled; and He had been buried, buried deep, with every successive encounter—when her wrists were vised, her face defiled by spittle, her throbbing legs braced apart. She did not deserve the sum of villainies, nor the smallest part thereof, any more than William in his honesty and simple ambition, in laboring persistent resource and abiding decency, had deserved extinction. The God whose praises she'd been taught to sing would never have sanctioned such acts. Therefore He did not exist. People had been wrong all the while, and probably would be compelled to admit to their delusion eventually.

> And long shall timorous Fancy see
> The painted chief, and pointed spear,
> And Reason's self shall bow the knee
> To shadows and delusions here.

Someone had instructed these primitives in mumblings which were in fact an outrageous falsehood, and special missionaries should now be told off for the purpose of awakening their grim intelligence about the matter, just as her own bitterness scouted the notion of Heaven and compelled her to sneer at the very stars. . . . So they were conveying her to the East; and what should she find there? It appeared that in time she would move among white people again. And every man would become a walking breathing rough-voiced reminder of that nobility held out to her and then snatched away. Twas an outrage to preach a lie, to persuade mankind to accept a demonstrated falsehood! Yet she supposed cynically that most preachers would not be punished for so doing. Only doe-eyed dolts like herself and William (and other women captives, and the relatives they'd lost, and the babies—ah, the babies!) would be punished. That had been demonstrated, tattooed across the very skin and face of Nature. . . . In the lodge at Lac qui Parle, with its figured dew-cloths and furry robes and pleasant meaty odors, the mother of Gray-Foot and Sounding-Heavens put first one foot and then the other of Peggy Ann's into a jar of lukewarm water in which peculiar brown leaves had been steeped until they were soft and pungent. She soothed the tormented feet with her wrinkled hands, and Peggy Ann looked curiously at the top of the woman's head, as that head bent before her . . . saw hair unfouled by vermin, and adorning a brain-case which must harbor only the most generous thoughts. She considered frankly: I should jeer at you for your very simplicity; but I shall not. . . . I am too tired. . . . If this act gives to you a satisfaction I shall let you indulge yourself. . . . Your good-natured skull could be caved in with the utmost ease! A reeking hard rod could come jabbing into that secret sluice which helped to give life to your children—that wistful emptiness which you guarded as a girl, and for the possession of which all should cherish and treasure and respect you. I am by far younger than you in years, but infinitely more elderly in an awful wisdom implanted by cruelties drilled in, pounded in! Like your barbarous childish self, I once took pride in the simple matters, the woman matters. I prepared pike, and the menfolks praised my cookery, and some of them said they wished their wives could cook like that. And, like you, my face was broiled in my exertions; and, like you, I was informed of a Golden Rule (villainous and shabby fakery!) and thought that life cross-stitched upon the pattern of such a sampler should be a pure and dainty enterprise. As you have done, I ground the corn, and stirred and enriched the meal, and built a blaze to toast it. Both, both!—we made a home, we hoarded sugar, brewed the sweet drink . . . each said to her man: Come, now, it's ready. . . . We fabricated beds, and closed the door against the cold, and when the man was weary from the work he did, we petted him and tried to make him feel a better man. . . . You have your children, I have none. But had I owned them, they would be putrescent fragments now . . . ah, long decayed. You think your world is not corrupt? Twill rot. Wait and see. . . .

Riggs and Williamson, the missionaries, came to fetch her to the Upper Agency on the Yellow Medicine. The fatherly Reverend Mr. Riggs sat beside her in the lodge of Gentle-Woman and Spirit-Walker, and held Peggy Ann's hand. (Her hands were healing nicely; there had been cuts, abraded places, but the cuts had scabbed at last . . . a few scars left in permanence upon her hands, only two small ones on her face.)

I'm sorry that we were so late, daughter. They delayed in bringing the word of your arrival.

It don't matter.

She had been seeking for a stencil which she might cut, a stencil of words to use. She'd found it.

You have been in good hands, daughter. These people are Believers, staunch and tried. . . . Riggs chuckled in honest delight at her being rescued, at her being alive.

She said to herself, I shall not be delighted. . . .

I'd thought to find you in rags, daughter. I'm pleased to see that Gentle-Woman has tricked you out nicely in Indian attire. . . .

(Peggy Ann's moccasins and leggings and her fringed hide gown all were of the best materials, prettily ornamented with quills, soft and pliant, more flattering to the body than the dress of many white women.)

Of course, once I have delivered you safely into the hands of Mrs. Riggs—and Mrs. Williamson, too—they can prepare for you more civilized attire. Twould be in better taste.

She said, It don't matter.

My dear, how many are now left behind? How many still in the hands of Inkpaduta?

Two. Least, there were two when I left . . . might have killed them both by now.

I trust that such a brutal happenstance has not occurred!

It happened before, when twas still rather cold weather. Mrs. Thatcher . . . I was crossing on the other trees, down below. Twas at a good-sized river, and there were trees all tumbled down. We had to walk across on them. They made us do it; and I was walking on the other pile of trees, downstream, so I didn't see it happen; but Abbie Gardner saw. She said an Indian just shoved the poor thing in . . . they were hitting Mrs. Thatcher with clubs each time she tried to catch hold of the bank. And then . . . another Indian . . . he was standing right beside me . . . he shot at something in the water. I knew the word for *otter* by that time—they'd hunted out two or three, and we had 'em.

She thought about it for a minute or two.

Boiled. Twasn't good. . . . So I says to him, *Ptan*? And he says, No, twas a white woman that he'd shot.

The clutch of the Reverend Mr. Riggs' hand was firm but lenient. He tried to do kindly little things to her hand with his own. He was a good man, blessed with gallantry and tenderness.

She thought, He's trying to be nice. Everybody's trying to be nice. It don't matter.

Mrs. Marble, pray don't dwell upon the miseries which you have been enduring. I trust that the merciful hand of a just and powerful God will wipe away these horrors from your recollection.

It don't matter.

We do need to know: who are those two still in the hands of the red men?

Mrs. Lydia Noble. And Abbie Gardner—she's but a girl.

Poor little soul. Oh, poor little soul! However, I'm glad to be able to report that Mr. Flandrau, and Colonel Alexander at the Fort, are devising some scheme for the rescue of your fellow unfortunates.

She wished to tell him that this didn't matter either. But for some reason she could only sit dumbly, looking at his lined patient face, wondering how many missionaries of a contrary kind it would take to undo the harm which his sincere belief had already effected by a misrepresentation of facts. She thought (as if looking at herself when removed to a great distance, as if looking through a telescope): You've grown extremely knowledgeable, Mrs. Marble.

Will you excuse me now, daughter? I have business with the Indians. Reverend Williamson will come to take my place and bear you company. God bless you, my dear.

It—said Peggy Ann. It—

Then she thought: Cat's got my tongue. I'll say nothing. Nothing at all.

Gray-Foot and Sounding-Heavens discussed the matter of remuneration with their father, and with Gray-Foot's father-in-law, Flies-Twice. They sat in a council which grew to include both missionaries before it ended. Others in the band of Wahpetonwan hunters must be reimbursed for their outlay in powder, ornaments, robes and the like; but all were honest people (of course they were honest—they were Christians) and it was felt that they would not demand any profit—only articles of value to equal those they'd sacrificed. Jewelry, blankets, and powder could be purchased from the traders; and the brothers knew exactly what had been donated, and were confident that, money in hand, they might be able to make a restoration of objects identical, or at the worst, a reasonable facsimile. The gun had been their own, the three ponies their families' own. . . .

The Reverend Mr. Stephen Return Riggs prepared a document which was delivered to Flandrau on that same morning when Peggy Ann was put into his charge.

Hon. C. E. Flandrau—Father: In our spring hunt, when encamped at the north end of the Big Wood on the Big Sioux River, we learned from some Indians who came to us, that we were not far from Red End's camp. Of our own accord, and contrary to the advice of all about us, we concluded to visit them, thinking that possibly we might be able to obtain one or more of the white women held by them as prisoners. We found them encamped at the *Chanptayatanka,* a lake about thirty miles to the west of our own camp. We were met at some distance from their lodges, by four men armed with revolvers, who demanded of us our business. After satisfying them that we were not spies, and had no evil intentions in regard to them, we were taken into Red End's lodge.

The night was spent in reciting their massacres, &c. It was not until the next morning that we ventured to ask for one of the women. Much time was spent in talking, and not until the middle of the afternoon, did we obtain their consent to our proposition. We paid for her all we had. We brought her to our mother's tent, clothed her as we were able, and fed her bountifully with the best we had, ducks and corn. We brought her to Lac qui Parle, and now, Father, after having her with us fifteen days, we place her in your hands.

It was perilous business, which we think should be liberally rewarded. We claim for our services $500 each. We do not want it in horses, they would be killed by jealous young men. We do not wish it in ammunition and goods, these we should be obliged to divide with others. The laborer is worthy of his own reward. We want it in money, which we can make more serviceable to ourselves than it could be in any other form. This is what we have to say.

Mahpiyahoton.
Sihahota.

In the above statement and demand we, the undersigned, father of the above young men, and father-in-law of one of them, concur.

Wakanmani.
Nonpakinyan.

May 21, 1857.

Men will say they're daft, said Stuart Garvie.

Flandrau whistled at the idea. This man won't, I can assure you! Let us for a moment review our own experience, Garvie. It can't be told that we entered the camp of Inkpaduta without trepidation, can it? When the situation is duly examined and understood, I am confident that the sum requested will not be deemed extortionate.

But have you got the thousand dollars to pay them?

Not I, I've barely five hundred. But I'll get it from one source or another—never fear. . . . Ha, I have a very good solution, just occurred to me: we'll float a Territorial bond for the remaining five hundred dollars, by Jove! And I'll stake my life that it shall be paid when due. Those two chaps risked their lives to save that hapless woman, and they must not find the whites deficient in sympathy or appreciation. . . . Pray ring the bell, Garvie: over there beside you on the table. We'll have them in and tell them that their wishes shall be complied with. . . .

When first Charles Flandrau met Peggy Ann, she was dressed as Gentle-Woman garbed her; but when next he saw her, the pretty barbaric attire had been ruled away. She stood smothered in folds and bunches of drab calico (sewn together in distressed speed by appalled wives of the two missionaries).

Grief, Garvie! Tis a most depressing situation.

Whit wey?

Did you see our fair captive?

Aye. They've made an old rullion out of her.

Are you familiar with Moore? No, of course not—just Robert Burns. But Moore has some lines which I now recall. I should say I'm driven to recall them! *The heretic girl of my soul shall I fly, to seek somewhere else a more orthodox kiss? No; perish the hearts and the laws that would try truth, valor or love by a standard like this.* Well, well. Old rullion or no, I must prepare to take her to St. Paul and turn her over to the Governor. Then she'll be off my hands, and I can devote my wits to something more to my natural taste: planning a punitive expedition, along with Colonel Alexander. . . .

In St. Paul, once installed at the Fuller House, he put Margaret Ann Marble into the chaperonage of the proprietor's wife.

Mrs. Long, I scarcely know what to say. But this is a matter for your prudence and control. Just look at that poor girl—

She does look a sight, said Mrs. Long with candor.

Get hold of a seamstress, and do what you can with her. I'll scrape up the funds somewhere. Certainly I don't want Governor Medary to see her looking like a scarecrow.

She's a widow, ain't she? asked the woman. I think black would be fitting.

Black let it be. Anything but that dowdy gray coffin-lining the missionaries have draped her in!

. . . Mrs. Long made Peggy Ann into a pillar of black, a stitched-in mass of skirts, shawl, veil, and bonnet. She chattered in triumph as the last fold was adjusted, the last pin slid into place.

Now, do take a look at yourself in the glass, dearie, and tell me if that ain't more becoming.

Peggy Ann said, It don't matter.

Heavens to Betsy, is that all you can say? cried the bewildered chaperone.

Peggy Ann whirled on her, and for a moment the woman lifted her hands in defense. She thought that this Fury would come scratching and striking.

Would you say anything better, if you stood in my shoes, Mrs.? Anything smarter than what I got to say? No, you wouldn't. You wouldn't know how. Nor neither would anybody else. They fetch me to Minnesota and up here to St. Paul, and tell me I'm a heroine. The agent says he's paid those Indians a thousand dollars, just for bringing me. And now I hear they've raised up a purse of money for me—for me, myself!—and they're going to give me another thousand dollars. How much good'll that do? Will it bring back my husband? Not so's you could notice it. Will it make up for all the feel and smell of slimy Indians a-crawling over me? It won't. Will it make up for anything? No—not the Indians' thousand dollars, or the thousand dollars they're giving me, or any other thousand dollars, or any other— I—I— If they want a heroine, that's what I'll be. I don't care whether I'm dressed in calico, or widow's weeds, or what. I'm going round and show myself—that's what I'm going to do. Just like I was a freak, like one of Mr. Barnum's freaks. That's what I'll do. Do you want to see a captive of the Indians? Well, look at me, look at me, *look at me!*—and her voice penetrated the walls.

Mrs. Long sat down on the sofa, threw her hands over her face, burst into tears.

Several people came to cluster, whispering outside the closed door. They knocked circumspectly.

XLVII

The Ihanktonwanna were coming in from their spring hunting. Inkpaduta's people met up with band after band as they moved northwest. Most of the plains residents would have nothing to do with the nomads, they received them coldly if indeed they were even allowed to enter the camps. About a fortnight after leaving the lake of the Big-Woods-All-Together, however, a party of Wazikute were encountered. These were a branch of the Ihanktonwanna known as Pine-Shooters (why, no one might ever know; no more than the Wahpekute knew why they themselves were called Leaf-Shooters) and a man of substance was prominent among them. His right leg had been amputated above the knee; he preferred to spend most of his time in a special saddle he'd had made. Often he even ate his meals while mounted. When it was necessary for him to dismount, he must needs hobble with a rude crutch.

This man's name was Wamdushkaihanke—Snake-Comes-To-Its-End. Many people knew his story, and he was regarded with some degree of awe because of his mutilation as well as his wealth. No one knew of any other Dakota who had but one leg.

It was in this way that Snake lost his leg:

As a boy of ten-again-four winters, he had been wandering far from his parents' lodge one day, accompanied by a slightly younger sister. Her name was My-Second-Child—Mihapan—and she was thought to be very pretty, and all in her family were proud of her beauty. But she was an energetic girl who enjoyed very much doing things which were done by men and boys; hunting was a man's business, but My-Second-Child loved to hunt. Her brother enjoyed having her with him. Most women did not handle a bow with skill, or had never even tried, or did not wish to try; but My-Second-Child could shoot well. Her mother and aunts and big sisters tried to dissuade her from unwomanly pursuits, with small success. At the first opportunity she would neglect her domestic chores, and glide out into the distance with her adored Snake-Comes-To-Its-End. On this day the two young people observed a novel spectacle: they saw a column of black smoke which moved steadily down the prairie. They thought at first that it was a fire in the grass. But there was not much grass to burn—it could not be grass, the smoke was too high and thick, it strolled from the north into the south! It was as if the smoke were *wakan*. And Mihapan said to her brother, It is moving on the great river—the Upshizawakpa, the River of Mud. He said to his sister, Let us go and see this thing!—for both young folks were bold by nature. So together they crept forward. At last they lay behind some driftwood, and before their eyes was an overwhelming spectacle. A huge canoe, larger than any *chanwata* or bull-boat ever seen by man, drifted in the river. The canoe was on fire, it had a tall mouth as big as a tree trunk, and from that mouth came fire sounds and sparks swirling. There were circular blades which thrashed noisily into the water; and in the vast boat were many white men. Then, with much new noise, and with shouting of the whites, the fiery boat halted at the bank near at hand. Men with axes went ashore, and they began to chop wood. And other men carrying guns also went ashore, as if they were come to hunt. For a while Snake and his sister observed the scene with fascination, but at last Snake said, My sister, we go! The white men with axes are cutting ever closer to us; and they would kill us were they to find us here. This is true, what I speak! So they withdrew with caution, and crawled up the valley of a creek, until they thought that surely they were safe, and far from sight of whites. But then there sounded cries, there came a rush of men. Some of the hunters had separated from the main party, and even now stepped out of that same creek valley. There was no direction in which the frightened pair might flee; they could not escape. The two Wazikute did run, but several bullets sang near them. Snake feared that his sister would be shot; if they were not killed at this moment there might come an opportunity for escape in a later hour. He gasped, We run no longer!—and quickly the howling white men raced up to the young people, and seized them, and dragged them to the river. There they were placed aboard the fire-boat. There sounded roaring laughter. The white men pawed My-Second-Child, and began to rip her garments from her body, and several of them struck other men with their fists. Snake burst from those who held him, he snatched a knife from one man's belt, and with this knife he tried to fight, to take his sister from those with whom she struggled; he cut two men; but he was struck over the head with a pistol butt; he slept, slept long, slept in pain. When he awoke he lay in a sticky pool of his own blood. The noise of the boat's fire was great, and noise of those knives which chopped at the water was great. Night had come. The pretty sister had been placed upon a robe at the other end of the vessel, and there the white men lay with her. Snake sought to go to her, but a huge white man struck him with his fist, and so he fell to the deck; when again he awakened he was tied with cords which cut his wrists. He could hear the moaning of My-Second-Child as men lay upon her. Many of them had been drinking spirit water; they sought to go back to lie upon My-Second-Child again and again; and some fought among themselves, until a Head Man came and fired a pistol into the air, and talked fiercely; so the white men did not fight longer. But still they lay upon the girl, turn after turn– There were many who lay upon her that night! In the morning she slept, and moaned constantly while she slept; and there was blood upon the robe. Then there rose up one of the men, and he went unsteadily and tried to hoist himself upon Mihapan again; but he was *witko*, he was very drunk, and quickly Snake's sister twisted away from him. She ran to the front of the long canoe, and the man tottered after her; and the girl scrambled off the front of the boat and went down into muddy water, and the boat passed over her. All the white men talked loudly as this occurred. One flew at the drunken man who had been pursuing My-Second-Child, and he did beat the drunken man over the head with a stick of wood until he fell and did not move. And others sped to the back end of the boat and pointed at the whirling blades beating into water; they talked long, and gazed at the river; but there was no further sign of My-Second-Child. . . . Next day Snake was put to woman's work. A rope made of iron-mingled-together was fastened around his leg, and the portion of this rope which made the fastening was *wakan:* Snake might not loosen it no matter how he tugged. A knife was put into his hand, and a fat bearded white who wore no clothing above his waist– This man showed Snake how he must remove the skins from peculiar round roots, by using the knife. (Within the skins those roots were snowy; they were much like the *tipsinna,* or wild prairie turnip, but larger.) Snake thought that he should use the knife to kill the white man when he came close; or perhaps he should use the knife to slay himself. But if he killed the man who did the cooking (aye, each day and nearly all day the bearded-white-man-with-no-clothing-above-his-waist was doing woman's work) then others of the *Washichun* would beat him until he was dead. Twould not be good to die in such a manner; and actually Snake did not wish to slay himself, because he thought that if he lived it might be possible for him to escape. So he did what was demanded of him: he sliced skins from those roots. He ground corn in a mill as he was taught to do, he ground brown berries in the mill; these *Washichun* did like to drink a soup which was made from the powder resulting. Many days later, because he appeared docile, the rope of iron-mingled-together was removed from Snake's leg, and he could walk about; and some of the whites would amuse themselves by striking the youth, or lifting him up by his hair or his ears; but some did not strike him—some smiled—there was one man who gave him tobacco and a small pipe-of-the-whites; thus he could find satisfaction in smoke. Often he prayed when he smoked. . . . One day they halted at a fort made of logs. Another day they halted at another such fort; and finally they came to frequent villages where there were both whites and *Ikchewichashta.* One Indian came close to the fire-boat and spoke to Snake-Comes-To-Its-End. He said that he was Omaha, but had been a prisoner of the Dakota when he was a boy, and could still speak in that tongue. Where take me these whites? asked Snake. They have killed my sister, or caused her to die— But they do not slay me. Where take they me? The Omaha said, To a big village, where there are many lodges built of stones and wood, and many also are built of square pink stones; and there are many wonders. The Omaha told Snake the name of that huge village, but Snake could not learn to say the words; he could say only Sayn-Woo-Eee; and some of the whites used often to laugh, and they would persuade Snake to speak the words again. They would bribe him with sugar or tobacco, and so once more he would utter the words: Sayn-Woo-Eee. After many sleeps the fire-boat came to Sayn-Woo-Eee. It was all that the Omaha had said, with rows on rows of enormous lodges, and many boats; and a number of these also were fire-boats. Their own fire-boat came slowly up to the bank— The very banks were built of stones and wood! A man tossed the end of a rope to Snake, and motioned for him to leap ashore with the rope and fasten it tightly as he had been taught to do while coming down the muddy river. So he leaped, but he was not accustomed to landing on a shore built as this shore was built— His feet slipped when he struck the shore, he fell, he rolled into space at the river's edge, the boat loomed above him, the lower portion of the boat came tightly against the shore, but the right leg of Snake was caught between; he heard a grinding sound, he felt the demolishing of his leg, heard his own howling. He slept. He awakened to find himself singing songs; he was on a wooden table, strong hands held him there, held him fast, and spirit water was being poured into his mouth— It burned, he tried to gulp to keep himself from drowning in spirit water— It did burn as he swallowed! He coughed and strangled. A man whose hands and wrists were red with blood was sawing at Snake's leg, and cutting him with knives. Snake strangled long, he went into a black place, there were evil spirits there. They danced round him. . . . Then once more he could see, and could feel an agony. He slid down his hand to explore, but his leg was not complete, it ended immediately above the knee. A white man with a tender voice was offering soup to Snake, he kept putting a spoon to Snake's lips. This white man had a face as pink as a rose, his face was *gitkatka,* and he did not dress like other whites, he dressed as a woman might dress, he wore a long gown fastened with a rope around the waist. Snake lay, not aboard the vessel which had fetched him to Sayn-Woo-Eee, but in a lodge of whites. (He found later that it was built of square pink stones.) On the wall hung a *wakan* object; often the *Washichun* made gestures in front of this thing. It showed how a man was put to torture—his arms were spread wide, he was pierced by skewers, blood could be seen. So it was true that sometimes whites did torture whites; not only did they torment the Indians who fell into their hands! But in this lodge there was no cruelty, except that displayed upon the wall. When the *hupaksa,* the stump of Snake's leg, was no longer so sore, and when juices oozed no longer from stitched folds of flesh, then did the pink-faced man in the long gown give to Snake a crutch. He taught him how it must be employed. This good man was both a holy man and a mystery man, and among the whites he was known as a Peest. In fact there were several other Peests or *manka* dwelling in this lodge, but the pink-faced Peest was Head Man and his name was Budda Tummas. All through the winter Snake-Comes-To-Its-End lived there, with Budda Tummas and Budda Teem and Budda Jun and the rest; but the winter was neither as long nor as severe as in the land of the Dakota. Snake did woman's work each day—he cut skin from roots, he was given other tasks to do. He learned to use the crutch which they had awarded him, though frequently he tumbled down at first. But when he was not doing woman's work, he sat alone. His heart was empty of anything except bad spirits. Often they crawled out of his heart and into his belly; then he was truly sick. He thought of his sister, and thought in the night that he heard her moaning. The Peests tried to teach him the tongue of white men, but he did not wish to learn; only a few of the words did he learn (and promptly he forgot those, once he was gone. They did teach him that most of them were not actually priests, but were monks; and soon he was able to call them monks instead of *manka*—which are small black-and-white animals with a ferocious smell). There were Indians in the great village of Sayn-Woo-Eee occasionally, but no Dakota among them; they were of other nations. Once a party of Sauk wandered past the lodge of the Peests, and scowled at Snake as he peered out through the barred gate. They made threatening gestures, but they were without weapons, they could not harm him. Budda Tummas attempted to persuade Snake to make motions in front of the *wakan* image on the wall. He talked long and patiently to Snake, but the boy did not even attempt to understand what was said, he did not wish to understand; he made signs of refusal, and he was weeping within. It might have been in the *Magaokada-wi,* the Moon in Which the Geese Lay Eggs, when one day Snake was made to gather together the possessions which had been given him—the *wakan* book, the *wakan* beads (but these he refused to employ), the extra shirt, his soap and towel . . . a few more things, a few other articles of white men's attire. He was bidden to take his crutch and go thumping down the road beside the plump Budda Jun. Budda Jun had with him two big bags. Some other Peests and *manka* and a few people who were not such, accompanied them. Down to the river they went, and there lay a fireboat with smoke pouring. Snake was terrified understandably when he glimpsed the boat, but still an excited hope shivered within him. Farewells were exchanged, and Budda Jun and Snake traveled up the river in this new fire-boat. A few days later some white hunters put out from shore in a canoe, they waved violently, the larger vessel was slowed, and finally one of the white hunters was pulled aboard, pack and rifle and all. He was a rough-skinned man whose shirt was of Indian manufacture, and he chewed tobacco and spat, chewed and spat. That evening Snake realized that this hunter was regarding him with curiosity, and soon the man came over to talk to Budda Jun. Then he moved to where Snake sat gazing at the river, and squatted on the deck beside him. In the tongue of the Dakota—the language of Snake's own people, the Ihanktonwanna!—he inquired, You are Dakota? These were the first truly intelligible words which the boy had heard since he spoke to the Omaha in the previous autumn. The man talked with Snake, then to Budda Jun, then to Snake again. Snake did tell this white man of how he and his sister were taken captive, and how his sister met her death . . . the hunter shook his head. The *Washichun wakan,* he said. The Holy White Man tells that you are unhappy in lodge of whites. . . . *Echahe!* I am sad. . . . You are sad because your leg is cut off. . . . Not only am I sad for that reason. Also I am sad because I do not wish to dwell in lodge of whites. . . . Then let your heart be filled with joy, for you journey to your own country! Holy Man goes far up the Muddy River to fetch to Indians a story of the white man's god. . . . *Echahe!* My heart shall now be filled with joy! So it came about: one day the fire-boat was made to stop, and Snake-Comes-To-Its-End was put ashore with his crutch—he was put down beside a camp of the Ihanktonwanna. They were not of the Wazikute, but one of them did know the Head Man of Snake's father's village; and so the boy was mounted on a borrowed horse, and two young men of this band escorted him to his father's lodge. It was only one sleep distant, and part of another day. The father of Snake gave presents to the helpful young men, who were of the Pabakse band, the Cut-Heads. Then all mourned deeply for the lost My-Second-Child; the mother especially mourned with a loud voice.

. . . Snake-Comes-To-Its-End began to prepare a home for himself on horseback, but he could not go racing on a hunt. It would have been ludicrous had he painted, and prayed for fortune with a war party . . . how could he make war? Nor could he dance, nor do many other things which delight the hearts of young men. He participated in none of the ceremonies incident to an initiation into maturity, except that he prayed and fasted and sat long on a lonely hill, and entertained visions.

By the Wazikute he became recognized as a man because of his epochal journey, and his dwelling in lodge-of-white-Holy-Men; and because no other person had but one leg. He considered seriously a career as a mystery man. But often as a boy he had been more disgusted than frightened by the antics of those individuals who cowered, writhed, shook rattles, tasted excrement, wore ludicrous garb, and generally made themselves obnoxious. He would not devote his life to such monstrous behavior. He'd had an illusion (while he spent foodless days on a bleak ridge, with no one around except coyotes). He'd dreamt that Budda Tummas stood before him and lifted his robe, and drew forth a small snake. This was important to Wamdushkaihanke because his name was Snake-Comes-To-Its-End: there must be especial significance in a vision like this. Buddas Tummas said: If you give me but half a snake, I give you this whole snake! So in his dream Snake went hunting for reptiles; he found a rattler, and cut it into two pieces with his knife. The tail of this snake he gave to Budda Tummas when he returned, and he accepted from the Peest the whole snake originally offered to him. Budda Tummas then said: If you give me two pieces of this snake, I give you two whole snakes. So once more there was a cutting, and now Snake owned two reptiles intact. They kept up this exchange for some time, until the youth had a veritable nest of the active twisting creatures tied up in a large robe. Give nothing away, warned the Peest. Then he departed. Naturally the imaginary nest of snakes vanished as well.

But the youth thought that he had learned a lesson from this, and would profit from it. If you gave but half of something, and got a whole something in exchange, it was good; if you gave two somethings and got back four somethings, also it was good. . . . Snake could hunt no longer, so he traded off his arrows; but he traded the arrows for an old gun which would not shoot. Then did Snake toil lengthily over the rusty gun, he worked upon it with grease, he pounded the bent hammer into shape. He was patient, and his hands were very busy; so he made the gun to shoot. And then he traded the gun for powder, and he kept the powder dry, and put it away with care . . . he saved the powder, for he could not use it, he could not hunt. Men of the village went hunting buffalo, and they expended all their powder, and they wished to hunt more; but they had no powder, nor was there any trader coming through the land. (Sometimes French traders came that way, but not frequently.) Then the men approached Snake and said: We need powder, for we wish to hunt more. But we have no powder, and you have powder; so let us have some. . . . Snake sold to them the powder, he received robes in exchange. He traded those robes for two colts. . . .

He became a rich man, but he wished that he might have even more wealth. He possessed two wives, three sons, a number of daughters, a herd of horses. When a young man wanted one of his daughters for a wife, he had to bring many gifts before Snake would permit the marriage to take place; and thus those of his daughters who were married were wedded to rich men. Snake had a slave: a young Assiniboin who had been captured when he was a child, and was brought up among the Ihanktonwanna. Snake paid two ponies, a shoots-six, and a fine tipi cover for the Assiniboin. Accompanying his master, the *wowidake* rode every place where Snake wished to ride. That was far . . . to other villages . . . to the haunts of antelope hunters, or men who took skins of the tall cranes. The slave led other ponies also, to carry back goods acquired; the ponies were apt to return heavily laden. The Assiniboin was strong, and by this year Snake was bent and shrunken in body; so the slave lifted him off his horse or put him upon the horse as needed. Head Men and prominent soldiers alike treated Snake with respect, and some of them were in his debt. He had power, although he was not a Head Man himself.

. . . When Inkpaduta fell in with the Wazikute, a Head Man said to Snake: We like not this man—this End-Red. He kills many; his own father does he kill; all know this to be true! Also he is a thief. We like not thieves. And he does not speak the truth: he speaks from both sides of his mouth, he speaks like a white man. His people go to the north, and we go to the north, but we do not wish to travel with him. So we shall not travel with him!

But Snake had seen the two white girls; and immediately on meeting with the Wahpekute he had heard about the selling of one white woman and the death of another. Especially had he listened eagerly to the story of the sale. He told his friend, Then go to the north as you will, on a separate path; but I stay with Inkpaduta for a while, and travel with him.

Why should he do this?

Because he thought to buy the two young white women!

Once he owned them, he might take them to a fort on the Missouri River, and there he could sell them to white soldiers for an inflated price. He did plan to give but half a snake, and to receive a whole snake in exchange!

So the other Wazikute went as they chose; but Snake, with his slave and with a few members of his family, remained with the Wahpekute and journeyed along with them. Snake was not pleased with these ruffians and their ways and the dirt they spread around themselves; but if he owned the white women he would receive riches in exchange for them. Snake would do almost anything in order to secure riches.

Some people find it difficult to speak with Ihanktonwanna; but Inkpaduta did not find it difficult, because he had spoken with many, and constantly Snake wished to speak with him.

. . . You smoke, Thou Elder One?

. . . I smoke.

. . . I have here the best tobacco, and I give you some of this best tobacco.

. . . *Echahe. Kin washte.* It is good.

. . . It is bought from white traders at a fort on the Big Muddy River.

. . . Go you to such a fort?

. . . I go. I am at such a fort in the Planting Moon and again in the Deer-Rutting Moon. I go. You cannot go.

. . . I cannot go. Soldiers would kill me.

. . . Aye, you would be killed! But I can go. I could take white women there. You cannot take white women there. . . .

In this vein they continued. Snake inquired of Inkpaduta as to the price received for the one white woman who had been sold. In his account, the outlaw exaggerated immensely the payment. He said that he had received five ponies, five guns—yes, five guns!—and much ammunition, and much jewelry. But Snake only smiled within himself and said nothing, because he had heard from others of the Wahpekute just how much was paid. He knew that Inkpaduta would take much less than the amount described.

Wamdushkaihanke said that he would like to buy the white women. Inkpaduta said that he would not sell them. Snake repeated that he was willing to buy, and thus it went for a long while, until Inkpaduta asked Snake what he would pay.

I would pay one *shuktanka* for each of the white women—two *shuktanka* in all.

Oh, I am not a child, but you think I am a child; but I am not!

However, a bargain was struck very soon thereafter. Snake, in securing possession of the captives, paid nothing but ponies. He paid six *shuktanka,* but he owned many, and he was confident that he would receive more than the value of six ponies when finally he disposed of his property. Inkpaduta accompanied him to look at the herd, and was allowed to select three of the horses (he chose the best) and Snake himself selected three (the poorest). Then the two men smoked once more. The reason that Inkpaduta sold his prisoners was this: he was afraid, as time went on, that white soldiers might find him. White soldiers had not come close to him, after he left the Okoboji country, except one time; and that one time the soldiers had come close, but then they turned away. If soldiers came again, he would kill the captives before letting the soldiers have them. They were his captives; he did not wish the soldiers to take them! Thus he would receive nothing in exchange: the captives would be dead, and he would have nothing of value. But if he sold them now, he would have six ponies; he needed ponies, for many of those stolen from the whites had died. . . . Also, he could not lie upon the young white women with any success; he had tried, he had tried all, before one was killed and another sold. (Many weeks previously he had eaten the last of the *inmutanka* powder in its beef-bull fat; but he might as well have been eating clay.) He could not do what he wished to do with them, even though they were young . . . he had thought that in this way he might partake of their youth. But young men could lie upon them, and did. The heart of Inkpaduta was gloomy as a result of this contrast: the contrast between the young men who could do the thing, and himself, who could not. . . . So it was well for him to sell the captives: thus constantly he would not be reminded of his old age, because when he heard the white women crying—and in a certain fashion—in one lodge or another, he knew that the twins or Tawachehawakan or some other youngish man, or men, dallied with them; and he felt old and he felt weak, and did not like to feel that way. . . . He was glad to part with the white women. But he'd pretended to Snake that he was not too glad to do so, and that six ponies were a paltry price.

His son Roaring-Cloud said to himself: I like best to lie with the woman who is slightly lame, the woman with small eyes, and whose child I kill. I like to lie with her because she makes such a strange noise with her mouth, and tries to twist her head, no matter how tightly I clutch her hair with one hand. She tries to crawl away from me, and it makes me very glad when she does these things . . . I am able to do much, much to her! So That Old One, my father, sells her to the Wazikute? I care not. I shall lie with her still, and whenever I wish to do so. I do not lie with her today; but perhaps I lie with her tomorrow.

Liddy Noble and Abbie toiled at a task to which they were set: they were pounding dried buffalo scraps to a powder which might be put into pemmican. It was a hard thing to do: the buffalo scraps were tough, they had to be beaten and mashed with a wooden club; each piece was stabbed and crushed with the round end of the club a hundred times, before the strings would come apart. So their hands and arms were aching, their bodies jarred by the incessant pounding. Corn-Sucker had shown them how to do this work. She thought that if she were a white captive she would be glad for someone to show her how to pound meat; for, if one was pounding meat, one would not be put to other more difficult and more demanding tasks. It was easier, Corn-Sucker thought, to pound meat—for at least one was sitting down! —easier than laboring along with a great load of wood upon one's back. Still, the white women were weak, and it took them long to make the dried meat small. . . . They were working in the lodge of Corn-Sucker, and if Roaring-Cloud wished to take the white woman he could not take her in the lodge of Corn-Sucker; but must drag her away to his own lodge or into the bachelors' quarters.

Mrs. Noble, what's that awful old man with one leg going to do?

I don't know, Abbie.

He come in and he put his hand on you, and he made a lot of funny motions. Then he put his hand on me, and—

I don't know, Abbie.

Seems like I recollect one time seeing Indans do that before. Mrs. Noble, do you think he's *bought* us?

I don't know, Abbie.

Mrs. Noble, you oughtn't to quit pounding. . . .

My hands get so tired.

Mine too. But if we don't get this meat all mashed up, somebody's liable to thrash us.

I don't care. . . .

Abbie began to cry. It just breaks my heart, Mrs. Noble, to see you look so—

I don't care about nothing. You want to know why?—and her voice rose a little. Abbie, you're a young girl, and— But even so, by now you know bout such things. Abbie, I'm in the family way.

Oh, Mrs. Noble!

Wonder you ain't too; but maybe it's cause you're younger and never had any children, and— I don't care, Abbie. I just don't care any more. Alvin's gone, and—J.Q.A.'s gone. And the Indians done it, and now— They've done this to me, and—

Roaring-Cloud lifted the flap and came crouching into the lodge. He reached down, caught hold of one of Liddy Noble's long greasy braids, and jerked her face so that it might turn up to his.

He said, Come!—in Dakota, and pointed toward the door.

Liddy's eyes were closed. She did not whimper as the pressure tightened, as her braid was pulled. Harder, harder—

Abbie said, He wants you to go with him—

She kept her eyes closed. I ain't a-going.

Mrs. Noble, I reckon you better go!

Roaring-Cloud yelled, *Hidu ka ish nita!* You come, or you die!

Mrs. Noble, I don't know what he's saying; but you'd better go, or he'll kill you!

I don't care if he kills me, said Liddy softly.

Roaring-Cloud fell upon her, hauled her up, she was a yarn poppet in his grasp. He whirled Lydia through the lodge door, he snatched up a billet of firewood and rushed out after her. She lay motionless, as she had been flung. She had given nothing but affection, and a housewife's and a mother's and a friend's small interest to the world . . . and a wife's. Ah, yes, a wife's. It seemed unfair that she should be rewarded with this terminating violence, but she had not found the world to be fair. Abjectly she waited for the blow. It came.

Snake was sitting on his horse in front of the bachelors' lodge when the attack occurred (this was the most remote tipi in the encampment). Thus Snake was not close enough to interfere, even had he been sufficiently vigorous to resist Roaring-Cloud and save the life of the girl. He had been bargaining with His-Curly-Sacred for possession of a watch—(Bert Snyder's watch, with a bullet dent in the case). He heard the bellowing of Roaring-Cloud: I strike thee, I strike thee, Bad Woman, I strike thee! There mingled also the sound of the flailing, the yells of children who jumped about at witnessing this spectacle. Snake pushed his horse to the scene and sat staring in horror at the motionless figure, the bleeding head, while Roaring-Cloud stood wiping his hands on his robe.

The woman dies? he cried.

Roaring-Cloud said, She groans still, but she will die. I strike hard. She will die.

But she is mine, she is not yours to kill!

I kill!

Why kill my white woman?

She is bad, her heart is bad. I tell her to come with me and she comes not.

Why goes white woman with you?

She is mine, Roaring-Cloud said scornfully. I lie with her many times; but now I lie with her no longer, because she dies.

Roaring-Cloud stalked into the lodge of Corn-Sucker and his father, where the two captives had been quartered even after their purchase by the new master. He did not look at the collapsed and wailing Abbie Gardner, but flung himself down, muttering.

Outside, Snake-Comes-To-Its-End still shook in futile rage upon his horse. I take other white girl into my lodge with my wife and my slave, he screamed. Her you kill not!

Take her, said Roaring-Cloud.

Nor could Snake win any satisfaction from Inkpaduta, when the Head Man rode back into camp. Inkpaduta had been hunting, more for sport than from necessity. He was in a comparatively affable mood, for he had not missed, he had shot three ducks which came down on a small pond. He enjoyed fresh duck-meat, and thought to have Corn-Sucker prepare these dainties at once. . . .

I have joy, he told Snake honestly. My son does not kill this woman while still she belongs to me. He waits until you have paid me three ponies. Then he kills.

Now your son gives to me three ponies, because he has killed my white woman!

He owns no three ponies to give.

I must be paid!

Never will he pay you.

. . . Liddy Noble had made peculiar long-drawn *m* sounds for perhaps half an hour after she was struck, then she lay silent. Abbie was not permitted to go to her, nor did anyone else attend her. Once Abbie screamed at the top of her lungs: Won't somebody please do *something* for her? *Please*! But no one knew what she was asking, nor would have responded had they known.

The body lay through the night, very close to the lodge door, with legs bent and knees drawn up under the dirty hide skirt.

Corn-Sucker said plaintively, It is not good that the dead white woman lies so.

Let her lie, Half-Face, d'ye hear? We go tomorrow.

By the next morning a number of children had overcome their fear of the corpse. They brought their little bows and arrows and began to shoot. None could shoot well; but after repeated tries, a few arrows did find lodgment in the body. The older children told smaller ones that the white woman's ghost would follow them if they tried to remove the arrows, and at this the little children were frightened and did not try to remove the arrows. But later some older ones did pull them out, and so they kept the arrows.

Children shoot dead white woman, said Makes-Fat-Bad tolerantly.

His-Curly-Sacred told him, But they shoot not well. We show them how men shoot!

Accordingly, when the last lodge had been pulled down and the last bundle was ready to be carried, these two stood at a distance, and each shot several arrows, and two arrows shot by Makes-Fat-Bad went into the body, and one arrow shot by His-Curly-Sacred. So Makes-Fat-Bad told everyone that he could shoot the best.

But Bahata said: I shoot best of all!—and so he went off to an even greater distance, and so he shot, and his first arrow went into the body.

The son of Female-Cousin-Rabbit now saw that indeed there was nothing to be feared from this white woman; so when his mother was busy doing other things, he took his mother's knife and went to the body and knelt beside it and sawed away at both the thick braids of hair.

People said, The boy takes hair. What will *Unktehi* say and do?

He does not truly take hair. Not unless the scalp is pulled off.

Wichaka. That is true.

The boy sawed until the braids were cut off, and then he tied them to a stick; so he had a whip which was really two-whips-together. He found great sport with his two-whips-together, whipping first his sister until she howled and ran from him, and then whipping other but smaller boys. While they traveled that day, he made an even greater sport by walking close to Abbie Gardner, and occasionally lashing out with the braids and striking her across the face. And when the surviving captive bent her head and pulled away and made faces, and when she wept, it gave joy to the child. His mother laughed to see him do this thing, and a few other people were amused as well. Corn-Sucker did not laugh, she thought the deed vicious. She thought it wrong of the Wahpekute to leave the body lying as they left it.

O young white woman, woman who walked lamely, was it one of your babies who was killed? I have heard that this is true.

If they had not killed your baby, but had killed you instead and had brought the baby to me, then would I rear the child as my own.

But they killed the child, they did not bring it to me.

Now they kill you as well! It is the son of my husband who kills you. But he did not really need to kill.

If you walk long on the Way of the Souls, it may be that you find your child there.

But never can I find a child, not even in That Place. I have no child to seek.

XLVIII

Stuart Garvie asked, How many men are you sending, Charley?

Flandrau chuckled. Volunteers have not been lacking! Not since they've heard how those two Wahpetonwanna are to be rewarded—the boys who brought in Mrs. Marble. It's still a case of pick and choose, and I've selected three of the best: good Christian souls—deacons and elders, so to speak. Right away I put my finger on Paul Mazakutemani.

Aye, he's a good one, and sober as a judge.

Garvie, I've seen judges in my time who were not exactly sober. But, in my own good season I do hope to become a judge, and sober into the bargain! Ha—let's see. Next I thought of John Other-Day. You know—Antetutokecha. Then I thought that Iron-Hawk should be the third. Chetanmaza.

The Scotsman nodded, applauding his friend's choice. But he asked, Have ye no had a bit trouble in getting an outfit together? And trade goods, to offer yon Indians?

By gum, I merely ran my credit with the traders! Here's the list.

Flandrau, with a pardonable flourish, spread the paper before Garvie's gaze.

Wagon and double harness	$110.00
Four horses	600.00
Twelve three-point blankets, four blue and eight white	56.00
Twenty-two yards of blue squaw cloth	44.00
Thirty-seven and a half yards of calico	5.37
Twenty pounds of tobacco	10.00
One sack of shot	4.00
One dozen shirts	13.00
Ribbon	4.75
Fifty pounds of powder	25.00
Corn	4.00
Flour	10.00
Coffee	1.50
Sugar	1.50

When first arriving in this Territory I fear that I couldn't have stretched my credit to the extent of a Shanghai hen. But now that I'm a man of at least implied substance, and holding a certain dignity of position— Read the list, Garvie, read the list. Commercial credit can supply a better stake than you and I might have won together in shooting wolves!

. . . Shoots-Metal-Walking said, Brothers, we go now to Agency office. We say farewell to Major before we depart.

John Other-Day told him, We cannot say farewell to Major, because he is not there.

Where goes he?

He goes to Fort, he talks to Head Man at Fort. It is told that many soldiers will be sent . . . they go to the West: four or five companies of soldiers. Then will they surround the camp of End-Red. But this will not be until after we have bought the other two white women, so that they may not be killed by the wicked ones!

(The gossip was correct. Such a plan had been mapped by Flandrau and Colonel Alexander in collaboration. But it was not to be carried out. Only a few days after the wagon with its teams left the Agency, and while Charles Flandrau was escorting the ill-clad Peggy Ann Marble to St. Paul, a despatch was received at Fort Ridgely which promptly negated the punitive expedition. Colonel Alexander was ordered to proceed down the river by steamboat at once, with his entire command, to join eventually in Albert Sidney Johnston's demonstration against the Mormons in Utah Territory. There could thus be no march into the Dakota country, no surrounding of the Big-Woods-All-Together.)

The Christians wore their ordinary rough garb in which they farmed or hunted commonly. But in the loaded wagon they had placed some bags which were held in immense esteem. The bags contained Go-to-Meeting clothes. Each man was provided with a dark suit and a white shirt with stiff front. Their wives had learned painstakingly to starch the shirts, and they would put them on before they drove into the lair of the wild Indians. They felt that not even their heathen cousins could fail to be impressed by snowy boiled shirts, by the solid black hats which they would put on.

At the *Chanptayatanka* they found garbage marking the Wahpekute campsite; the trail was fairly old and led into the northwest. They would follow it—they could go very fast with their high-wheeled wagon and powerful team; they might be able to cover in one day a distance which it would take Inkpaduta's band three sleeps to accomplish. . . . Weary of jolting in the rig, they were glad to be on foot again . . . idly they strolled amid the refuse of the camp, carefully avoiding numerous curls and wads of drying excrement; stepping among bones, shreds of cloth, broken ironstone plates, a tin cup trodden flat; and examining with repugnance the relic of that stone-marten cape which had served its usefulness for Tawachehawakan and was thus thrown away.

Other-Day saw something silvery, he picked it up. *Maza,* he said. The others came to see. Twas a strange tool, twisted into a half-circle; but it did not seem to have been manufactured in that shape. (Hushan had tried to use it as a prying implement in some minor gunsmithing; it had bent, and so was discarded. This was Isaac Harriott's scalpel: the same with which he'd opened Bert Snyder's shin, on that first night so long ago . . . the scalpel with which he'd destroyed the union of so much other flesh in order to promote a better healing underneath.) The Christians were puzzled by this thing, and at last put it in with their hub-wrench and other wagon tools. They thought that Major Flandrau might be table to tell them what it was. . . .

They bumped for hours on the northwest route. Abandoned campsites were strung on this course like flat ugly beads.

Birds, said Iron-Hawk, pointing ahead. He had the best sight of all, and so could witness the cloud of birds first; but soon the others saw.

No one of these is the bird which bears thy name, O brother!

Nay, these are carrion birds.

There was an odor coming to meet them, so they drove warily into the area of the camp where Lydia Noble had been struck down. Dark-plumaged birds talked raucously about this interruption, and went flapping away. The men left their wagon and protesting horses . . . one had to go back and hold the team . . . but the other two came on; and finally, with hands over their faces, they stood looking down.

This was once white woman, said John Different-Day (actually that was his Dakota name, but the whites called him John Other-Day; so when he spoke his name in English, which he could do, he said John Other-Day as well).

When she threw back her head to laugh, it went always to one side, turning on her long graceful neck. . . . Her breasts must be things of beauty—her bosom was so round, her waist so slim. . . .

So now there is but one white woman left!

The other white woman at the Agency said that one was young and one was older. Which can this be? The young one?

Brother, I cannot tell.

Nor can I tell.

We should cut poles, said Iron-Hawk. But here there are no trees—not even small trees.

It would not be good that we cut poles. She is a white woman. So she goes into the ground.

Echahe. Into ground.

It was decided that a trade blanket should be sacrificed to serve as winding-sheet.

We have blankets of blue and blankets of white, said Shoots-Metal-Walking. In which wrap we her?

White is color of purity, and we say now that the heart of this woman, young or older, was *echedan.*

Aye, a pure heart. . . .

Put her body into white blankets. . . .

Will not one blanket suffice?

Let us give her two, said John in generosity. White is emblem of the innocent, as told us by our earthly Fathers.

They had a spade, they had an axe: such implements were necessary when journeying by wagon through a region without roads. After wrapping what remained of the corpse, they carried their bundle to a cleaner place on a mound beyond assorted rubbish which marked the camp's circle. They chopped deeply into hard earth, pried out the clods. They worked until the sun was low in the sky, and then their hole was deep enough. They buried the body, and stood in doleful ceremony around the lumpy little mound.

Mahpiya ekta token nitawachin echonpi kin, maka akan hechen echonpi nunwe. Heaven is how thy will is done the, Earth upon so done may it be. . . .

Now must we fetch stones to put upon this grave!

So wolves of the prairie may not dig.

If we cover this woman's couch with many stones, then indeed wolves displace them not.

Can we find enough stones? There are not many.

We shall seek stones. . . .

They hunted long through tightening dusk, they discovered enough rocks, and brought them one by one, and covered the grave with them.

And pray once more, said Iron-Hawk.

Wokichonze kin, wowashake kin, wowitan kin, henakiya owihanke wanin nitawa nunwe. Kingdom the, strength the, glory the, all these end none thine may be. . . . Amen.

Shortly after Snake-Comes-To-Its-End, traveling still with the Wahpekute, entered the chief village of his own people he considered himself very illy used.

Soldiers of the Old Dogs Society, they take my white girl!

No harm is done you, brother. We take not your property without payment.

But I buy these women for a profit, and now I have none. No women, no profit!

For the two women, O brother, you say you give six ponies. That is true, which you speak?

Eesh! Yun!

Then to you we give six ponies. What lose you?

I lose profit I would make if I were to sell this girl at a fort!

The Head Man explained again patiently. He went over the whole matter, and in some ways he was almost amused at the single-minded obstinacy of the cripple. But he pretended that he was not amused—only saddened, as one must so often be in speaking words of justice. He said that the Ihanktonwanna wished to run no risk of having troops come to attack.

. . . Had not This One of their people gone deliberately to travel with the outlaw Red-End and his people?

. . . That he had done. But—

. . . Had he not lived with Red-End's people, put his lodge beside theirs?

. . . He had. But—

. . . And he had bought two white women; but one he had not protected. He had not been able to protect her, and so she was slain! Who wanted soldiers to come against them, perhaps with cannon?

We take young white woman, said Angry-Running-Calf, the Head Man, finally and firmly. To you we give six horses.

I lose nothing. But—

We, and we alone, shall determine in council! There are those here who would buy this girl.

Aye, I did see them come, and they wear clothing-of-the-whites. They wear shirts of white iron. This I see long ago in Sayn-Woo-Eee!

But few others of the Wazikute had witnessed such attire, and they thronged to gaze. They talked shyly with Iron-Hawk and Shoots-Metal and John Other-Day. They assembled, as did their women gather to examine Abbie Gardner. . . .

The Wahpekute were still present, but they had been made to pitch their camp to one side of the village, in what might have been called a remote suburban area. There were but five lodges of Inkpaduta's people now to be put up. Most of the ponies had died . . . several had been eaten. Gladiateur had died; but Lazarus still stood. He whinnied piteously sometimes when Abbie Gardner came near. She thought that the horse seemed to know her, she could not be certain. Oh, she thought, he's thin! Seems as if I knew him once when he was . . . in better flesh than this. . . .

At the council, Abbie was held to be worth two horses, seven blankets, fifty pounds of powder, twenty pounds of tobacco, twenty-two yards of blue squaw cloth, thirty-seven and one-half yards of calico, a parti-colored heap of ribbon spools, and the bulk of the eatables fetched along by the Christians.

Inkpaduta sat in his own lodge, in a rising rage. Twas a warm day. The tipi cover had been hoisted, and from afar the big Wahpekute could be seen as he sat smoking. You could not have told just who he was, because his head was hidden by the rolled-up cover. He sat in shadow, but with air playing across him, a breeze for comfort. You could have seen him and said: There sits a monster without a head! Perhaps his head has been cut off, we do not know! . . . But it cannot be cut off, for there is smoke issuing. So he is smoking. . . .

He said to Corn-Sucker in rare confidence: My heart is dark.

She appreciated this revelation. Usually his heart was dark, but usually he did not speak of it so.

Why is dark your heart?

Men say that I am a fool.

Why are you a fool?

You call me fool?—and his ugly red-rimmed eyes sneered up at her.

Nay, she said fearfully. I do not call you fool. You call yourself fool—

Inkpaduta struck at Corn-Sucker, but she faded from him, the blow missed. . . . His untoward utterance had made him appear weak! He did not wish to appear weak—he wished only to appear strong, to seem dangerous, to be dangerous. He thought that he was an idiot because he had sold the two white women for only six ponies. If he had waited until the Isantie came to trade, he would have demanded much more than the Yanktonai demanded. He would have exacted many ponies, many guns, and especially much trade goods! He would have asked for better ornaments than those received for Margaret Ann Marble; he would have claimed and probably received a whole wagon-load of cloth and blankets and boxes of tobacco, kegs of powder! He had been a fool; and now he knew it, and surely other people would think him a fool. There was no end to the sordid consideration of his own stupidity. It went around him like a dance. Almost he thought the very shapes of himself and of Snake-Comes-To-Its-End, conjured up in recollection, were stamping and posturing. . . .

Might he not sit quietly removed while the Christians concluded their trade, and started to the East; and then might he not follow with the twins or with others, and kill the Christians—lie in wait for them in order to incur no risk to himself, and then kill them when they had no expectation that an enemy was about? Thus he had lain in wait before, thus he had effected previous deaths! Might he not do the same now?

Every puff of bitter tobacco told him that the answer was negative. He dared not kill these visitors. If he did, he in turn would be killed by the Ihanktonwanna; they were many in the region. Here in this very village were ten-again-nine tens of lodges: more tipis than were owned by the entire Wahpekute family from which he had been expelled. All bands of Wahpekute put together could not set up that many lodges! And these were not only the Wazikute people of the Ihanktonwanna, but there were others as well: the Hunkpatidanna, the Pabakse, the Kiyuksa.

He dared not kill, and steal back the white woman, because in turn he would be killed. He felt miserable about this. Vast injustice had been done to him; and mainly by himself; the realization did not make him feel any happier.

A group of women were examining Abbie Gardner's skin. They would make signs for her to draw up her sleeve. When she demurred, they put their hands on her and dragged the sleeve up, tearing it as they did so; for she wore old scraps of rotten calico which did not fit . . . they were hand-me-downs, little pieces she had saved along the way from discarded attire of unknown white women . . . once she recognized a torn waist which had belonged to her mother . . . the memory fled away from her again. She did not recognize the waist.

. . . Where the sun has not burned it, her skin is very white!

. . . I did not know that there was such white skin!

. . . Nay, I knew not that any woman had such skin.

. . . I have heard that there are many white women with white skins among the Eastern Two-Legged Ones.

. . . But this I never see before!

. . . Her hide is paler than the pale dog which my husband doth keep tied for fattening!

. . . Aye, she is paler than the milk which comes from a buffalo cow.

. . . What of her breasts, are they pale too?

They opened Abbie's clothing and looked at her breasts while she tried to shrink away.

. . . Her breasts are very pale!

No longer did Female-Cousin-Rabbit have any claim upon Abbie—that share which might accrue to any member of the band which had stolen her. But the woman was a bully as well as a sneak. She found pleasure in frightening the girl, or in thinking that she had frightened her. She stood rashly among women of the other family, and whenever she could catch Abbie's attention she would say aloud: Strange Indians come to buy you; but why think you that they wish to buy? They wish to kill you! Like this!—and she'd make a gesture.

Or again she would say: *Chichute!* I shoot thee!—and would pretend that she had a gun, or that she was going to fetch a gun from somewhere or other, and shoot Abbie with it. Or she would show her how the captive's head would be pounded with a stone, her face smashed flat. . . .

The Ihanktonwanna were disgusted. You speak not truth to young white woman!

She understands not what I say; but when I make signs, then does she understand.

But this is *woitonshni* which you speak, it is a lie. Those men with shirts of white iron, they buy her, but they do not kill!

Corn-Sucker heard the wrangling as she went out with a jar for water. It was wicked of Female-Cousin-Rabbit to say such things; but she knew that everything which Female-Cousin-Rabbit did was sinful.

She made a song for Abbie as she went down to a brownish stream which flowed narrowly deeply into the James River at this point. She dipped up water while she built the song.

Young white woman, strangers take you in their wagon, they carry you far. You return to land of your own people.

But your people are dead.

What do you there, young woman? Will you have a baby?

Hao, *you are young! If you have a husband, then also a baby you will have. You will not need to go to the House-of-the-Infants.*

I could not own one of the white babies, for they were killed. . . .

I pluck for you now this wild rose, and I give you this as a sign that you go to your own land. But I will never go to my own land again.

Within me no longer is a small wounded animal. Within me is a small white child; but the child has died.

Girl, to you I give a rose.

There was a tangle of thorny plants near the edge of the creek. Some of the blossoms had fallen away, one was still in the perfection of its wide pale blooming . . . golden fuzz shone out in the center of the pinkness, and there was a pleasant smell when you held the thing near your nose. Corn-Sucker carried this rose tenderly in her free hand so that she might not squeeze it. When she came to where the women were still grouped around Abbie, she put the rose in Abbie's hand. The girl crushed the flower spasmodically and threw it from her.

In St. Paul, at the Fuller House, Mrs. Long had a much easier time of it with Abbie than she had had with Margaret Ann Marble. This girl was younger, and should necessarily be more tractable. She had not been married, was not a widow, and though all her family but one were said to be dead, it would not be appropriate to dress her in raven weeds like the previously rescued captive. Mrs. Long told herself that she had provided a proper costume for the girl—with a bit of color in it—but still modest. To her pleasure Flandrau seemed to think the same thing.

On the day before the steamboat was to leave for Dubuque, Mrs. Long came to Abbie where the silent girl sat as usual: on a stiff sofa, staring blankly. Her pale eyes shone from a face so heavily tanned that the eyes seemed mismated to the face, they did not belong. (Mrs. Long had been once in the south of Scotland, and there she met gypsies with tawny hair—although tousled and dirty gypsies—who looked something like Abbie . . . blue eyes shining out of bony brown faces, and with an angered wildness about them.)

Abbie, child.

The girl broke from her trance. What?

There's a gentleman to see you.

Nother. . . ?

This one's most insistent.

Who is he?

He says his name's Mr. Elbridge. I don't know him, but he seems a gentleman.

. . . The hotel proprietor's wife was curious as to what Mr. Elbridge might have to say. She escorted him into the little parlor, and he paid fulsome respect to the erstwhile captive. He was a thin man with a long narrow nose which clung against his face as if reluctant to leave it. He wore sparsely trimmed whiskers, and carried a pair of eyeglasses in his nervous hand. His wide cruel mouth twisted up in a forced smile, and his brown eyes bore that varnished appearance which seems to stem from perpetual tears of sympathy.

Little lady, he said, dear little lady! You have suffered much. I had hoped to be here for the ceremonies of welcome; but unfortunately was delayed by a mechanical failure of our steamboat. I have come far to see you, little lady. I should like to have a private conversation, if you do not object—

What about?

You have lived through strange and exciting experiences! And the world should know of them. I do believe this most sincerely! I tell it to you now with the utmost sincerity! You understand, dear little lady? I think that if this story can be told— Let us say, put into book form, as it well deserves to be—

Abbie was off in a dark lodge . . . hands reaching for her, and there was heavy breathing, and she heard herself whining in terror and hurt. She heard herself hooting as Lizzie Thatcher was tripped . . . heard the thud as Roaring-Cloud swung the wood against Mrs. Noble . . . heard. . . .

She told Mr. Elbridge: I got some money. They give me a purse of gold. Captain Bee did, and his soldiers raised it mongst themselves. There was four dollars gold in there, and I don't know how much change. And then, when I got here, they'd raised more money for me. And Governor Medary, he give me the money. And they put a feather bonnet on my head: twas an Indian bonnet, what they call a war-bonnet. But I didn't see none of the Indians wearing bonnets like that when—when—

I guess, she said, that money's a pretty good thing to have. I never had none before. But course then I had folks and—I don't remember—

She began to cry.

Dear little lady, poor distraught little lady, let me offer my tenderest sympathy to you! Let me say this: It would be well to have your story told.

Abbie said, I couldn't write no book. Wouldn't know how.

Ah, but there are ways of overcoming that difficulty! I myself am a journalist of some reputation and skill. Now, I propose that you allow *me* to tell your story, just as you would have it told. Insofar as the public is concerned, it shall be *you* who tells your story. Do you follow me? There is, I believe, a great deal of money to be made from such a book. . . .

There came racking out of her that essential viciousness which dwells in all human beings; it had been whetted and directed by her experience and was now let loose. Her girlish voice was suddenly contorted, sharpened into the tone of a virago. How much? she snarled.

XLIX

Once he'd seen and smelled salt water as he stood at the Battery. But Morris Markham had never seen the open sea, nor had he felt desire to go skirmishing in search of it. He could read and listen; therefore he knew that men had come down from mountains, or crawling up out of caves, sniffing for that brine into which they had never before put their hands or feet or faces, yet amid which eventually they would stow their bones. Morris was lured by no imagined storms, captivated by no mermaids, nor yet excited by wet blowing ballads of piracy, water spouts, Trafalgars. He thought that the ocean was a place where man must sensibly go voyaging if born to seek its spray—just as he himself had trotted originally into Ohio woods when he felt need for refuge.

Above all he yearned for that comfort which people, lonely by nature, find only in solitude furnished them by nature.

He understood, when nowadays he walked along dull creases which movers' wagons had put into prairie grass, why many folks were ardent for the sea even when its spray had never blown above their cradles. Because, once out of sight of land and other craft, the waters must be unchanging through the centuries. There would never be debris or globule which had not gone swelling and surging before. If monsters rocked their chilly greasy bodies below the waves, or came bursting up to blow and flap, they were critters who had been there since first they were formed. They were not the product of sudden ingenuity or the acquisitive canniness of merchant and municipal planner. If one looked at the ocean, even when elderly (an ocean over which he had journeyed and in which he had fished and delved through his life), he would not feel the shock of the land-dweller who recognizes a bundle of trees and roofs and spires towering where only weeds waved in his first recollection. He would not experience the bitterness of him who was once familiar with a slough where the redwings were ornate, and went back in after years to be stricken by sight of a factory. Always you could plow your large fields of water and never leave a furrow; but the lowliest prairie, because it was land, accepted each track and indentation.

And said: People ride and walk here! Wherever they have penetrated and marred, more will come flocking.

So Morris felt an envy for the distant sailor whose bell-bottom trousers he had never pulled on, whose pea jacket he had never put around his shoulders. Where one tough array of wheels went slicing, there would appear eventually the imprint of a thousand more. In time the early morning which charmed a lone man now, would buzz with briskness of determined little people bound to establish a mart and go to buying or selling something. No ocean would ever accept such antics because of the ocean's very depth, danger, timelessness; but the prairie was vulnerable to human approach and seizure.

I'd better leave this Ioway country, already so scratched and squatted upon, and take to the woods.

But just as surely the woods cannot contain me forever, or retain their original sanctity and credit.

Some feller will come and chop a piece out of the woods, and build a store, and put up a sign!

Timberlands around the lakes were purple-hazed and mysterious again, they smelled of smoke and ripened things. Morris Markham roamed up the Des Moines River, and cut across to East Okoboji. He did not walk in the vicinity of his former home, nor close to any of the other cabins he had known. He'd heard that a doctor named Prescott was the new proprietor hereabouts. This man was supposed to have paid Eliza Gardner cash money for the Gardner and Luce properties, and to have bought the Howe place as well; gossip at Fort Dodge reported that the same fellow had jumped the Red Wingers' claims. So he wants to own the whole Okoboji country, thought Morris. Let him. Who cares? Not me. I never took up land, and have no intention of doing so before I'm elderly.

(Morris considered that Doctor Prescott might get into trouble with the Government if he tried to enforce his title to more than the one claim allowed him by law.)

Doesn't matter.

They're all dead, cept Jody and me and Abbie and Mrs. M.

Maybe after Abbie's growed, she might want to come back here.

Not me.

(He planned to scout some promising beaver country, and get out his traps—unset, naturally—before cold weather clutched. He didn't intend to be caught napping by quick onrush of storms, not ever again. He'd heard attractive stories about beaver farther north.)

Might go all the way up to the Red River country.

Stop in and call on Major Flandrau on the way.

But not go prowling around any other of these here Okoboji cabins.

Don't get lost, Morris.

Ain't no Indians about.

He spent the night encamped on a belt of land which dammed between Spirit Lake and East Okoboji; then he made a wide westerly circle, avoiding the Marble area, and struck out north once more. Strangely it seemed that Morris was more able to consider the small entangled lives which had been lived beside these lakes, once he was away from the waters, plodding on Minnesota prairies. He thought of himself as representing the crudest but most persistent vitality. He was not the wise and jaunty critter which a Snyder or a Harriott had been— Oh, never would he be so ardent, so tingling. No, he was a lichen, he was of the moss, he continued in minor growth across elemental stones, he tufted with other miniature fungi on toothpicked stumps where winds had snapped the trees apart. He was of a low and simple order; but the cold did not kill him; nor might he readily be burnt or drowned away.

Morris fired his rifle to secure a delayed breakfast. He heard that single shot go echoing, echoing while he cooked his kill and picked the flesh from bird-bones. Always he had been struck by the essential finality of a gun's report: a sound which could be neither excused, overlooked, nor apologized for. Also he had notion that explosions of the future might bloom with wickeder death than could be contained within the barrel of a Sharps or a Maynard. People talked of new rifled cannon, breech-loaders no less, a-building in England or Germany or some such place; twas recounted in the newspapers. Well, in this year of 1857 you—or the Wahpekute—could burn down a Mattock cabin and roast the body of a boy, and it was grievous. But if folks constructed breech-loading rifled cannon, they'd fling shells for miles, and thus spread a blight over half-a-dozen village houses by the mere twitch of a single lanyard.

All the bears and wildcats would be killed.

Too many weapons, weapons too immense. At Fort Dodge recently Morris had witnessed whole wagonloads of pigeons. Extra boards were nailed high around the wagons' boxes to hold the mass—but weather was too hot, the pigeons were spoiling. Men said that they planned to use the cargo as fertilizer for their fields.

The pigeons would vanish.

Thunder and flash: deer gone, people gone, woods knocked down.

But later, lichens renewing.

He was indeed a fungus, or a scrap of such filmy rudiment. And lichens could grow again even where stones were fire-charred.

As he traveled north that forenoon Morris met up with a party of movers. They were an aggregation: five loaded wagons—large wagons, requiring four stout yokes to move each—together with men and boys on horseback, and a young woman mounted on a high-strung spotted colt. There was a herd of cows as well, and one sedate bull calf. They'd come all the way from Pennsylvania, the travelers said, and Morris thought that they must be Pennsylvania Dutch: some of the elders seemed incapable of speaking English, and even the younger people talked with pronounced accents. They were headed for the Thorny Wood River country, they announced, and wished to know if Morris had ever been there. No, he hadn't.

He suffered an eerie idea. Wasn't that big bald man almost as fat as James Mattock? And there was one with hair and beard much like Rowland Gardner's . . . that might have been Sardis Howe on the skittish young horse, if only the girl's hair had been paler.

Gone, gone, gone, to smite the sun.

Back in Pennsylvania there was one who came inquiring at a door, and found strangers only; and he was told, No, they're all gone, Mr. Gone to some new Western place.

Morris's throat was dry. He croaked: There's quite a scad of you. Planning to found a town, maybe?

They beamed all over their faces, they told him that was what they hoped to do. They'd lived not far from Harrisburg, Pennsylvania, and so they planned to name their new town in honor of Harrisburg!

A tiny boy came climbing down perilously over a wagon wheel. He was just about the size of J. Q. A. Noble, and his hair was the same color; from the back, as witnessed when he clambered, he could have passed for J. Q. A.'s twin brother.

Can I pick him up?

They wondered at this, they grinned, but permitted him to lift the child; the child was willing as well. Morris played a game with the little boy. It was the same ritual he'd gone through with the departed Noble child. Twas pointless, didn't make much sense; but Morris could remember someone doing that with himself when he was small. You put your finger on the eye of the child and said: Eye winker! Then you put your finger on the child's nose and said: Nose knocker! Then you pinched the soft cheek and said: Cheek cherry! That was the way the play went. Children always laughed at it.

Suddenly Morris set the child down. Got to be on my way, he said.

The Pennsylvanians journeyed to the west, the woodsman cut their trail and started north again. He thought it likely that there were babies in those wagons, babies whom he hadn't seen. Perhaps one of the babies was even now complaining because of wetness (certainly not for hunger's sake—the tribe were all too well fed for that)—as Baby Dora had wailed occasionally in the Noble-Thatcher house, as Morris had heard her through the logs. True, Baby Dora wept seldom; better to think of her as laughing . . . she'd squealed so engagingly, with that loose all-encompassing chuckle of infants who seem to know much more than they may tell. Morris reached a little summit of prairie which fell away toward a slough beyond; he must go eastward to avoid the slough. In that moment his heart opened out to the movers afresh. He turned and stood waving at them steadily, waving them on their explorative course, praying that no nasty fate should overtake the child whom he'd held briefly.

There was another, very similar, play in which he used to indulge when he held J. Q. A. Knock at the door, he'd say, rapping his knuckle lightly against the child's fair forehead. Peek in!—and he would pretend to raise an eyelid of the little boy, and peer into the depth of his eye. Lift up the latch, Morris would say, applying slight pressure under J. Q. A.'s nose. And finally: Walk in!—and this called for the boy to open his mouth and let Morris's finger pretend to be a visitor entering the house.

Knock at the door,
Peek in. . . .
Lift up the latch,
Walk in. . . .

He observed an answering flutter, a flashing of aprons or kerchiefs perhaps, from the vicinity of the wagons. He could not be sure. Maybe the Sardis-Howe-kind-of-young-lady on the frisky horse had waved in return.

. . . Blackbirds by the cloud: redwings and yellowheads alike. He roved past the borders of the slough. Tall reeds concealed each water-pool as if it were a secret treasure, they guarded jealously, the birds also were guards, they cried at you when you came nigh. Birds bustled busy in the air, came down to sway again, to make their *chink* and shining wire sound. Brown wives soared and gossiped along with the menfolks.

Would ever people come to breed and cry in numbers like to these?

Twas possible, twould happen if a city rose. Morris thought of New York: that angry darkening of humanity upon the tops of buildings and of wharves when Jenny Lind approached the shore.

In time there might be cities on this very prairie; but he rather thought that he'd not live to watch them grow.

When he reached the next long fold beyond the marsh, and mounted it, he perceived that his movers were but a crawling smudge in the southwest.

Something waiting, way out there ahead.

What is it? What can it be?

Don't know. Something.

Morris said: They'll keep a-coming. Nothing on this earth can stop them. Twould take the power of Heaven to halt them in their tracks, and Heaven ain't a-going to do it. Heaven established them upon this earth, one way or another, and put that in their breasts which causes them to wish to move. So they'll always be a-moving. Maybe sometime folks'll cover up the whole entire sphere, if people keep on a-having babies; and then in some future age there won't be no place left for them to move to, here on earth. So they'll need to move to other whirling places in the sky.

30 June, 1956
24 May, 1961

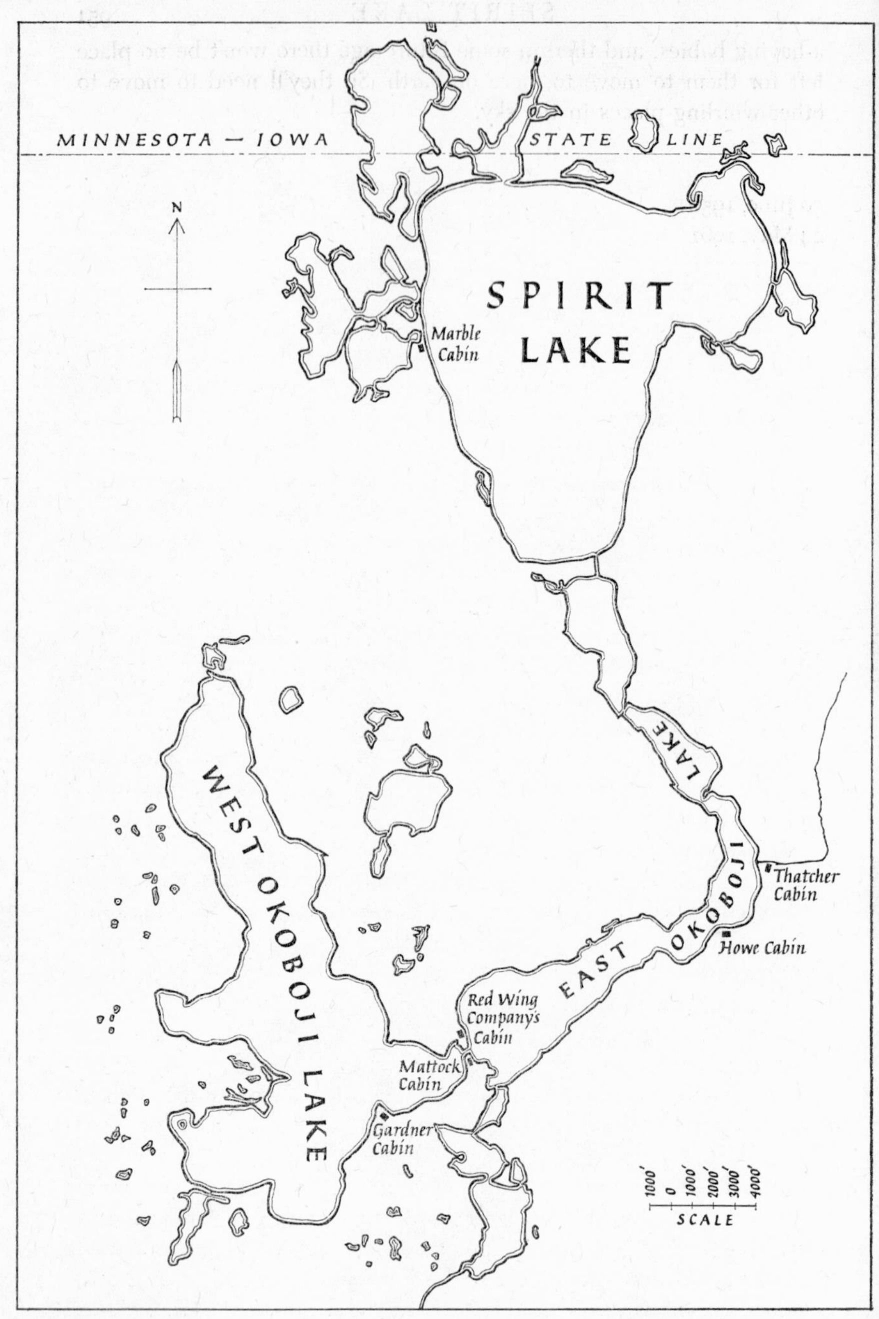

THE LAKE REGION: THE SCENE OF THE SPIRIT LAKE MASSACRE

NOTES AND BIBLIOGRAPHY

Individual traits and personalities attributed to the majority of characters in this novel are mainly fictitious. In some cases sufficient data could be obtained to suggest at least a founding on fact; but generally the history of individuals and family groups is invented. The first white inhabitants of the Okoboji region were people of obscure origins, their lives undocumented.

It is regretted by the author that he relied on the statement by Thomas Teakle (*The Spirit Lake Massacre,* page 60) that Asa Burtch was a brother of Mrs. Joseph Thatcher. Information acquired recently suggests that this is erroneous, and that Joseph Thatcher was married to one Elizabeth Blake. The author can take refuge only in shelter of the above paragraph.

The Plouray episode is fictitious.

Particulars of the massacre, with certain preceding and subsequent events, are offered as sound fact, with historical details accompanying, wherever sufficient evidence could be found to identify the actuality.

In describing the raid along the Little Sioux River, the author placed some reliance on a diary written by Jane Bicknell (Kirchner) which has been offered in at least two published accounts: in *The Palimpsest,* October, 1928, in an article by Bessie L. Lyon, entitled "Hungry Indians"; and in *The Iowan,* issue of February-March, 1956, in an article by Curt Harnack, entitled "Prelude to Massacre."

Obviously the only portion of the historical sequence which could be documented soundly in original sources is the Relief Expedition itself. But for reasons of narrative exigency, the details of this Expedition (occurring some weeks following the massacre) have not been presented at any length.

It would be impossible to exaggerate the debt owed by the author to the State Historical Society of Iowa, for lucid and all-encompassing publications. Particularly, great dependence was placed upon numerous articles which have appeared in *The Palimpsest,* monthly magazine of this group, through the past forty-one years. Also values were achieved from a study of the *Iowa Journal of History* (formerly *The Iowa Journal of History and Politics*), published by the Society along with *The Palimpsest,* at Iowa City; and from old files of the *Annals of Iowa,* formerly published under auspices of the Historical Department of Iowa, at Des Moines.

Voluminous collections of the Minnesota Historical Society, published at St. Paul in annual volumes, must be singled out for especial mention.

Despite his statement in the second paragraph of these notes, the author wishes to acknowledge that Thomas Teakle (*The Spirit Lake Massacre*, published at Iowa City, Iowa, in 1918, by the State Historical Society of Iowa) wrote an exhaustive and impressive work. It contains a few annoying contradictions, but so do many histories. No one attempting to describe this moment of Iowa's past, in any form, could do so without having recourse to Thomas Teakle's book.

A volume entitled *The Midwest Pioneer: His Ills, Cures & Doctors*, by Madge E. Pickard and R. Carlyle Buley (New York. Henry Schuman. 1946) would be invaluable to any writer wishing to describe the professional life of a young physician and surgeon of the period. The presentation of Doctor Isaac Harriott was aided greatly by reference to this work.

Dr. William J. Petersen, Superintendent of the State Historical Society of Iowa, and his wife, Bessie R. Petersen, gave generously of their energy and talents, and the author is indebted deeply to them.

An adequate presentation of the Dakota attitude, culture, and speech would have been impossible of attainment had it not been for the patient counsel of the Reverend Father John F. Bryde, S.J., Superintendent of Holy Rosary Mission at the Pine Ridge, South Dakota, Indian Reservation.

Through the process of advice, consultation, introduction or actual involved research, the following persons have contributed to the completion of this novel, and the author is glad to list them by name:

Dr. Roy P. Basler, of the Library of Congress; Mr. Edward W. Beattie, Jr.; Miss Christine Coffey; Sister M. Cuthbert, O.S.F.; Mrs. Mabel Dahlberg; Miss Mabel E. Deutrich, of the National Archives and Records Service; Mr. Clifford Dowdey; Mr. Henry J. Dubester, of the Library of Congress; Miss Frances Edwards, of the Norwalk (Ohio) Public Library; Mrs. Vilma Florsheim; Mr. Jerome Fried; Dr. Thomas C. Garrett; Mlle. Thérèse Genies; Mrs. Phyllis G. Gossling; Miss Ernestine Grafton; Mr. Edward S. Hall, of the Goodhue County (Minnesota) Historical Society; Mr. Phil Hamilton, of the Kokomo (Indiana) Public Library; Dr. Claude W. Hibbard, of the University of Michigan; Dr. D. A. Hooijer, of the Rijksmuseum van Natuurlijke Historie, Leiden, Netherlands; Mrs. Irene Layne Kantor; Mr. Tim Kantor; Mr. Carl Leiter; Miss Jean McKechnie; Mr. Wilbur H. McVay; Mr. Ralph Newman; Miss Willa Rankin (Miss Rankin was formerly a secretary to the author, and assisted in early research in the 1930's); Mr. Eldon G. Roswurm; Dr. George Gaylord Simpson, of Harvard

University; Dr. Sigmund Spaeth; Mr. Alexander Summers, of the Illinois State Historical Society; Mr. William Targ; the Rev. Mr. A. W. M. Watson; Dr. Waldo R. Wedel, of the Smithsonian Institution; the late Mr. George Warner Young of Des Moines, and his son, Dr. George Gerber Young.

Books consulted by the author, and not mentioned above, are included in the following list:

Agriculture of the Hidatsa Indians. Gilbert Livingstone Wilson. Minneapolis. University of Minnesota. 1917.

A History of Dickinson County, Iowa. R. A. Smith. Des Moines. Kenyon Printing & Mfg. Co. 1892.

A History of Travel in America. Seymour Dunbar. New York. Tudor Publishing Company. 1937.

An Hour-Glass On The Run. Allan Jobson. London. Michael Joseph. 1959.

The Battle Field Reviewed. Rev. Landon Taylor. Chicago. n.p. 1881.

Dakota Grammar, Texts, and Ethnography. Stephen Return Riggs. Washington, D.C. (Department of the Interior) Government Printing Office. 1893.

Daniel Boone. John Bakeless. New York. William Morrow & Co. 1939.

Ethnography and Philology of the Hidatsa Indians. Washington Matthews. Washington, D.C. (Dept. of the Interior, Miscellaneous Publications—No. 7) Government Printing Office. 1877.

Father Taylor: A Story of Missionary Beginnings. Harvey Ingham. Des Moines. Privately printed. n.d.

Forty Years a Fur Trader. Charles Larpenteur. Chicago. The Lakeside Press. 1933.

Galland's Iowa Emigrant. Dr. Isaac Galland. Chillicothe, Ohio. Printed by Wm. C. Jones. 1840. (Reprinted by Carroll Coleman At The Prairie Press in Iowa City, for the State Historical Society of Iowa, Iowa City. n.d.)

Goodbird the Indian: His Story. Told by himself to Gilbert L. Wilson. New York. Fleming H. Revell Company. 1914.

Grammar and Dictionary of the Dakota Language. Edited by Rev. S. R. Riggs. Washington, D.C. The Smithsonian Institution, 1851.

History of Clay County, Iowa. Samuel Gillespie and James E. Steele. Chicago. S. J. Clarke Publishing Co. 1909.

The History of Clay County, Iowa, W. C. Gilbraith, n.p. 1893?

History of Cerro Gordo County, Iowa. J. H. Wheeler. Chicago. The Lewis Publishing Company. 1910.

The History of Delaware County, Iowa. n.a. Chicago. Western Historical Co. 1878.

History of Emmet County and Dickinson County, Iowa. n.a. Chicago. The Pioneer Publishing Co. 1917.

History of Franklin & Cerro Gordo Counties, Iowa. n.a. Springfield, Ill. Union Publishing Company. 1883.

History of Franklin County, Iowa. I. L. Stuart. Chicago. The S. J. Clarke Publishing Company. 1914.

History of Hamilton County, Iowa. J. W. Lee. Chicago. S. J. Clarke Publishing Company. 1912.

History of Hancock County, Iowa. n.a. Chicago. The Pioneer Publishing Company. 1917.

History of Iowa. Benjamin F. Gue. New York. The Century History Company. 1903.

The History of Minnesota. Rev. Edward Duffield Neill. Minneapolis. Minnesota Historical Company. 1882.

The History of Minnesota and Tales of the Frontier. Judge Charles E. Flandrau. St. Paul. E. W. Porter. 1900.

The History of Philip's War. Thomas Church, Esq. J. & B. Williams. Exeter, N.H. 1829.

History of the Spirit Lake Massacre. Abbie Gardner-Sharp. Des Moines. Mills & Co., Printers. 1885.

The History of the Wars of New-England With the Eastern Indians. Samuel Penhallow, Esqr. Printed by T. Fleet. Boston. 1726. (Reprinted in Cincinnati. 1859.)

Illustrated Historical Atlas of State of Iowa. (Compiled by ?) A. T. Andreas. Chicago. Andreas Atlas Co. 1875.

The Indian Sign Language. W. P. Clark. Philadelphia. L. R. Hamersly & Co. 1885.

Indian Wars of the United States. William V. Moore. Philadelphia. Jas. L. Gihon. 1854.

Jenny Lind in America. C. G. Rosenberg. New York. Stringer & Townsend. 1851.

John Brown Among the Quakers, and Other Sketches. Irving B. Richman. Des Moines. The Historical Department of Iowa. 1894.

Medical Classics. Vol. 2, No. 1. Compiled by Emerson Crosby Kelly. Baltimore. The Williams & Wilkins Company. September, 1937.

Memoirs of a Surrey Labourer. George Bourne. London. Duckworth. 1930.

Minnesota in Three Centuries. Lucius F. Hubbard and Return I. Holcombe. The Publishing Society of Minnesota. 1908.

Myths and Legends of the Sioux. Marie L. McLaughlin. Bismarck, North Dakota. Bismarck Tribune Company. 1916.

North American Indians of the Plains. Clark Wissler. New York. The American Museum of Natural History. 1912.

The Northern Border Brigade: A Story of Military Beginnings. Harvey Ingham. Des Moines. Privately printed. n.d.

Once Their Home. Frances Chamberlain Holley. Chicago. Donohue & Henneberry. 1892.

Personal Recollections of Minnesota and Its People. John H. Stevens. Minneapolis. n.p. 1890.

Prairie du Chien. Peter Lawrence Scanlan. Menasha, Wis. Privately printed. 1937.

Reminiscences of Newcastle, Iowa. Harriet Bonebright-Closz. Des Moines. Historical Department of Iowa. 1921.

Roster and Record of Iowa Soldiers. Vol. VI. Miscellaneous. Des Moines. Published by authority of the General Assembly. 1911.

Sketches of Iowa and Wisconsin. John Plumbe, Jr. St. Louis. Chambers, Harris & Knapp. 1839. (Republished in facsimile by the State Historical Society of Iowa at Iowa City. 1948.)

Sketches of Iowa, or the Emigrant's Guide. John B. Newhall. New York. J. H. Colton. 1841. (Republished in facsimile by the State Historical Society of Iowa at Iowa City. 1957.)

The States and Territories of the Great West. Jacob Ferris. New York and Auburn. Miller, Orton and Mulligan. 1856.

Tah-Koo Wah-Kan; or, The Gospel Among the Dakotas. Stephen R. Riggs. Boston. Congregational Sabbath-School and Publishing Society. 1869.

True Stories of New England Captives. C. Alice Baker, n.p. Cambridge, Mass. 1897.

Western Scenes and Reminiscences. n.a. Derby, Orton & Mulligan. Buffalo, N.Y. 1853.

The Western Tourist and Emigrant's Guide. New York. J. H. Colton and Company. 1854.

With Pen and Pencil on The Frontier in 1851. Frank Blackwell Mayer. Saint Paul. The Minnesota Historical Society. 1932.

ABOUT THE AUTHOR

MacKinlay Kantor was born in Webster City, Iowa, February 4, 1904. His parents were separated before his birth, divorced soon afterward. The future novelist spent a chaotic childhood and youth in Iowa and in Chicago—years marked by poverty, hard work, and occasional moments of comparative luxury. He started to write seriously at sixteen, became a newspaper reporter at seventeen, and an author devoted exclusively to fiction at the age of twenty-three. Mr. Kantor's first novel was published in 1928. Since then thirty-four of his books in all have been appreciated by readers in America and abroad: novels, verse, collections of short stories and novelettes, juvenile books, and histories. His novel of the American Civil War, *Andersonville,* won the Pulitzer Prize for fiction in 1956. He has come to be regarded as a foremost interpreter of the essentially American flavor and scene. He has lived actively, intensely in that scene. MacKinlay Kantor's accomplishments vary from the Hollywood motion-picture complex (he wrote the original story for the world-famous "The Best Years Of Our Lives," which won many Academy Awards) to a year and a half spent living the life of a patrolman in the New York City Police Department. He has achieved combat experience in two wars and was personally decorated by the commander of the United States Air Force. Mr. Kantor was married in 1926 to Irene Layne, an artist. Their daughter, Layne Shroder, published her first novel in 1957. Their son, Tim, a former Air Force flyer, is now a photo-journalist in New York. The Kantors divide their time between their home in Sarasota, Florida, and Europe.

THIS BOOK WAS SET IN

CALEDONIA AND JANSON TYPES BY

HARRY SWEETMAN TYPESETTING CORPORATION.

IT WAS PRINTED AND BOUND AT THE PRESS OF

THE WORLD PUBLISHING COMPANY.

DESIGN IS BY ABE LERNER AND LARRY KAMP